mary Randa

ABOUT THE AUTHOR

Mary Stewart's career as a novelist began in 1954 with the publication of *Madam, Will You Talk?* Since then she has published ten other highly successful romantic suspense novels. In 1968 she was elected a Fellow of the Royal Society of Arts. In 1971 the Scottish chapter of the International PEN Association awarded her the Frederick Niven prize for *The Crystal Cave*, the first book in her acclaimed trilogy of novels about the Arthurian legend that also includes *The Hollow Hills* and *The Last Enchantment*. Born and educated in England, Mary Stewart now lives in Edinburgh with her husband.

MARY STEWART

FOUR COMPLETE NOVELS

MARY STEWART

FOUR COMPLETE NOVELS

Touch Not the Cat

The Gabriel Hounds

This Rough Magic

My Brother Michael

AVENEL BOOKS · NEW YORK

This Omnibus edition was previously published in separate volumes
under the titles:

My Brother Michael Copyright © MCMLIX, MCMLX by Mary Stewart
This Rough Magic Copyright © MCMLXIV by Mary Stewart
The Gabriel Hounds Copyright © MCMLXVII by Mary Stewart
Touch Not the Cat Copyright © MCMLXXVI by Mary Stewart

This 1983 edition is published by Avenel Books,
distributed by Crown Publishers, Inc., by arrangement with
William Morrow & Company, Inc.

Manufactured in the United States of America

Library of Congress Cataloging in Publication Data

Stewart, Mary, 1916–
  Mary Stewart—four complete novels.

  Contents: Touch not the cat—The Gabriel
hounds—This rough magic—[etc.]
  I. Title.
PR6069.T46A6   1983   823'.914   83-3720
ISBN: 0-517-412969

h g f e d c b a

CONTENTS

Touch Not the Cat

For my uncle George Rainbow

And some win peace who spend
The skill of words to sweeten despair
Of finding consolation where
Life has but one dark end.

from "The Riddlers," by
Walter de la Mare

1

It is my soul that calls upon my name.

—SHAKESPEARE: *Romeo and Juliet*
(Act II, Sc. ii)

MY LOVER came to me on the last night in April, with a message and a warning that sent me home to him.

Put like that, it sounds strange, though it is exactly what happened. When I try to explain it will no doubt sound stranger still. Let me put it all down in order.

I was working in Funchal, Madeira. Funchal is the main town of that lovely Atlantic island, and, in spite of its having been a port of call for almost every ship that has crossed the ocean since sometime in the fourteenth century, the town is still small and charming, its steep alleys tumbling down the lava slopes of the island's mountain spine, its streets full of flowers and trees, its very pavements made of patterned mosaic which glistens in the sun. I was working as receptionist and tourist guide at one of the new hotels east of the town. This sounds an easy job, but isn't; in tourist time, which in Madeira is almost the whole year, it is hard indeed; but what had led me to apply for the job was that very few qualifications seemed to be needed by a "Young lady of good appearance, willing to work long hours." Both these qualifications were mine; appearance was just about all I'd got, and I would have worked any hours to make some money. Whether I was the best for the job I don't know, but it happened that the people who owned the hotel had known my father, so I was hired. The old-boy network they call it. Well, it works, as often as not. You may not get the brightest and the best, but you do get someone who talks your own language, and who is usually someone you can get back at the way it will hurt, if they let you down.

It's barely a year since the things happened that I am writing about, but I find that I am already thinking of my father as if he were long gone, part of the past. As he is now; but on that warm April night in Madeira when my love told me to go and see him, Daddy was alive, just.

I didn't sleep in the hotel. The friends who owned it had a quinta, a country estate a few kilometers out of Funchal, where the pine woods slope down the mountains toward the sea. You reached the place by a lane which led off the Machico road, a steep gray ribbon of lava setts, bordered in summer with blue and white agapanthus standing cool against the pine woods, their stems vibrating in the draft of the running water in the levada at the road's edge. The house was big and rather ornate in the Portuguese style, standing in wide grounds full of flowers and carefully watered grass and every imaginable exotic shrub and flowering tree, dramatically set against the cool background of mountain pines. The owners lived there all winter, but at the beginning of April, most years, went back to England to their house in Herefordshire which lay just across the Malvern Hills from ours. They were in England now, and the quinta was shuttered, but I lived in what they called the garden house. This was a plain, single-story building at the foot of the garden. Its walls were pink-washed like those of the big house, and inside it was simple and bare—scrubbed floors and big echoing gray-walled rooms slatted all day against the sun, beautifully quiet and airy, and smelling of sunburned pines and lemon blossom. My bedroom window opened on one of the camellia avenues which led downhill toward the lily pools where frogs croaked and splashed all night. By the end of April the camellias are just about over, the browned blossoms swept away, almost as they drop, by the immaculate Portuguese gardeners; but the Judas trees are in flower, and the angel's-trumpets, and the wisteria, all fighting their way up through a dreamer's mixture of cloudy blossom where every season's flowers flourish (it seems) all year. And the roses are out. Not roses such as we have at home; roses need their cold winter's rest, and here, forced as they are into perpetual flower by the climate, they grow pale and slack-petalled, on thin, over-supple stems. There were roses on the wall of the garden house, moonbursts of some white, loose-globed flower which showered half across my bedroom window. The breeze that blew the rain clouds from time to time across the moonlight tossed the shadows of the roses over wall and ceiling again and again, each time the same and yet each time different, as the roses moved and the petals loosened to the breeze.

I was still awake when he came. He had not been to me for so long that at first I hardly recognized what was happening. It was just my name, softly, moving and fading through the empty room as the rose shadows moved and faded.

Bryony. Bryony. Bryony Ashley.

"Yes?" I found I had said it aloud, as if words were needed. Then I came fully awake, and knew where I was and who was talking to me. I turned over on my back, staring up at the high ceiling of that empty room where the moonlit shadows, in a still pause, hung motionless and insubstantial. As insubstantial as the lover who filled the nighttime room with his presence, and my mind with his voice.

Bryony. At last. Listen. . . . Are you listening?

This is not how it came through, of course. That is hard to describe, if not downright impossible. It comes through neither in words nor in pictures, but—I can't put it any better—in sudden blocks of intelligence that are thrust into one's mind and slotted and locked there, the way a printer locks the lines into place, and there is the page with all its meanings for you to read. With these thought-patterns the whole page comes through at once; I suppose it may be like block-reading, though I have never tried that. They say it comes with practice. Well, he and I had had all our lives to practice; I had known him all my twenty-two years, and he (this much I could tell about him) was not much older.

I suppose that when we were children we must both have stumbled and made mistakes, as normal children do with reading, but I cannot remember a time when we couldn't confront each other, mind to mind, with ease. To begin with it seemed like sharing dreams, or having (as I believe is common among children) an imaginary companion who shared everything with me, and who was more real even than the cousins who lived near us, or than my friends at school. But, unlike most children, I never spoke about him. I don't think this was through fear of ridicule or disbelief; the experience was something I took very much for granted; but somehow, imposed over those thought-patterns, there was a censor which wouldn't allow me to share him with anyone else, even my parents. And the same censor must have worked with him. Never by the smallest sign or faltering of the patterns did he let me know who he was, though, from the shared memories that we had, I knew he must be someone close to me, and it was a safe bet that he was one of my Ashley cousins, who had played with me at Ashley Court daily when I was a child, and who had later on shared almost every holiday. It's a gift that goes in families, and there were records that it ran in ours: ever since the Elizabeth Ashley who was burned at the stake in 1623, there had been a record, necessarily secret, of strange "seeings" and thought-transference between members of the family. By the same token my lover knew me, since I was the only Ashley girl, and for the last year or so had addressed me flatly as "Bryony." There again, I only use the name for convenience; you might almost say he called me "You," but in a manner which identified me fully. In return I called him "Ashley," in an attempt to make him identify himself. He never did, but accepted the name as he had accepted "Boy" and sometimes, in unwary moments, "Love," with the same guarded and gentle amusement with which he parried every attempt I had lately made to force him to identify himself. All I could get from him was the assurance that when the time was right we would know each other openly; but until that time we must be close only in thought.

I know I haven't explained this well, but then it is a thing I have known all my life, and that I gather very few people know at all. When I was old enough to see the gift as something unique and secret, I tried to read about it, but all that could be found under headings like "Telepathy" or "Thought-transference" never seemed quite to tally with this easy private line of communication that we owned. In the end I gave up trying to analyze the experience, and went back to accepting it as I had done when a child. Though I gathered from my reading that gifts like this could be uncomfortable, and had been in times past downright dangerous, it had never worried me to possess it. Indeed, I could hardly imagine life without it. I don't even know when he became a lover as well as a companion; a change in the thought-patterns, I suppose, as unmistakable as the changes in one's body. And if it seems absurd that one should need and offer love without knowing the body one offers it to, I suppose that unconsciously the body dictates a need which the mind supplies. With us the minds translated our need into vivid and holding patterns which were exchanged and accepted without question, and—since bodily responses were not involved—rather comfortably.

It was probable that when we met and knew one another physically it would be less simple, but at the moment there seemed to be no prospect of this. You can't, out of the blue, ask a second cousin who has given no hint of it: "Are you the Ashley who talks to me privately?" I did once try to probe. I asked Francis, the youngest of my three cousins, if he ever had dreams of people so vivid that he confused them with reality. He shook his head, apparently without interest, and changed the subject. So I summoned up my courage to ask the twins, who were my seniors by almost four years. When I spoke to James, the younger of the two, he gave me a strange look, but said no, and he must have told Emory, his twin, because Emory started probing at me in his turn. Full of questions he was, and rather excited, but somehow in the wrong way, the way the psychical research people were when Rob Granger, the farmer's son at home, said he'd seen a ghostly priest walking through the walls of Ashley church, and everyone thought it might be Cardinal Wolsey who was there as a young man; but it turned out to be the Vicar going down in his dressing gown to pick up the spectacles he'd left behind in the vestry.

My lover says—and he said it in clear only yesterday—that I have got so used to communicating in thought-blocks that I am not good with words any more. I never get to the point, he tells me, and if I did I couldn't stick there. But I shall have to try, if I am to write down the full story of the strange things that happened at Ashley Court a year ago. Write it I must, for reasons which will be made plain later, and to do that I suppose I ought to start by saying something about the family. What I have written so far makes us sound like something from a dubious old melodrama—which would not be far wrong, because the family is as old as Noah, and I suppose you could say it's as rotten as a waterlogged Ark. Not a bad simile, because Ashley Court, our home, is a moated manor that was built piecemeal by a series of owners from the Saxons on, none of whom had heard of damp courses; but it is very beautiful, and brings in something over two thousand a year, not counting outgoings, from the twenty-five-penny tourists, God bless them.

The family goes back further even than the oldest bits of the house. There was an Ashley—tradition says he was called Almeric of the Spears, which in Anglo-Saxon is pronounced something like "Asher"—who fled in front of the Danes when they came raiding up the Severn in the tenth century, and established his family in the densely forested land near the foot of the Malvern Hills. There had been settlers there before; it was said that when the British, earlier still, had fled in front of the Saxons, they had lived on like ghosts in the fragments of a Roman house built where a curve of the river let the sunlight in. Of this early settlement there was no trace except the remains of some tile kilns half a mile from the house. The Saxons dug a moat and led the river into it, and holed up safely until the Conquest. The Saxon Ashley was killed in the fighting, and the incoming Norman took his widow and the land, built a stone keep on the island and a drawbridge to serve it, then took the name as well, and settled down to rear Ashley children who were all, probably to his fury, fair and pale-skinned and tall, and Saxon to the bone. The Ashleys have always had a talent for retaining just what they wanted to retain, while adapting immediately and without effort to the winning side. The Vicar of Bray must have been a close relation. We were Catholics right up to Henry VIII, then when the Great Whore got him we built a priest's hole and kept it tenanted until we saw which side the wafer was buttered, and then somehow there we were under Elizabeth, staunch Protestants and bricking up the priest's hole, and learning the Thirty-nine Articles off by heart, probably aloud. None of us got chopped, right through Bloody Mary, but that's the Ashleys for you. Opportunists. Rotten turncoats. We bend with the wind of change—and we stay at Ashley. Even in the nineteen-seventies, with no coat left to turn, and with everything loaded against us, we stayed. The only difference was, we lived in the cottage instead of the Court.

Nothing is left now of the formal gardens, which had once been beautiful, but which I had never known as other than neglected, with the wild, tanglewood charm of a Sleeping Beauty backdrop. The lovely, crumbling old house on its moated island, and the wilderness surrounding, were all that was left of an estate which had once been half a county wide, but which by my father's time had shrunk to a strip of land along the river, the gardens themselves, the buildings of what had once been a prosperous home farm, and a churchyard. I think the church officially belonged as well, but Jonathan Ashley—my father—didn't insist on this. The church stood in its green graveyard just beside our main drive gates, and when I was a little girl I used to believe that the bells were ringing right in the tops of our lime trees. To this day the scent of lime blossom brings back to me the church bells ringing, and the sight of the rooks going up into the air like smuts blown from a bonfire.

This was all that was left of the grounds laid out by the Cavalier Ashley. He, incidentally, must have been the only Cavalier throughout England who did not melt the family silver down for Charles I. He wouldn't, of course. I suspect that the only reason his family didn't officially turn Roundhead was because of the clothes and the haircut. Anyway, they saved the Court twice over, because my father sent most of the silver to Christie's in 1950, and we lived on it, and kept the place up after a fashion until I was seven or eight years old. Then we moved into one wing of the house, and opened the rest up to the public. A few years later, after my mother died, Daddy and I moved out altogether, to live in the gardener's cottage, a pretty little place at the edge of the apple orchard, with a tiny garden fronting on the lake that drained the moat. Our wing of the Court was put in the hands of our lawyer to let if he could. We had been lucky in this, and our most recent lessee was an American businessman who, with his family, had been in residence for the past half year. We had not met the Underhills ourselves, because, eight months before the April night when my story starts, my father, who had a rheumatic heart, contracted a bad bronchitis, and after he recovered from this, his doctor urged him to go away for a spell in a drier climate. I was working in an antique shop in Ashbury at the time. We sold a bit more of the silver, shut the cottage up, and went to Bad Tölz, a little spa town in Bavaria, pleasantly situated on the River Isar. My father had often been there as a young man, visiting a friend of his, one Walther Gothard, who now had a considerable reputation as a *Kur-Doktor*, and had turned his house into a sanatorium. Daddy went there simply to rest, and to be cared for by Herr Gothard, who, for old times' sake, took him cheaply. I stayed for a month, but he mended so rapidly in the air that it was impossible to worry any more, so, when the Madeira job was suggested, I was easily persuaded to go. Even my lover, when I asked him, said there was nothing to go home for. I only half liked this kind of reassurance, but it was true that none of my cousins was at Ashley, and the cottage in winter and the damps of early spring looked lonely and uninviting; so in the end I took the job, and went off happily enough to the sun and flowers of Funchal, with no idea in the world that I would never see my father alive again.

Bryony?

Yes. I'm awake. What is it? But the trouble was there already, in the room. It settled over me in a formless way, like fog; no color, neither dark nor light, no smell, no sound; just a clenching tension of pain and the fear of death. The sweat sprang hot on my skin, and the sheet scraped under my nails. I sat up.

*I've got it, I think. It's Daddy. . . . He must have been taken ill again.
Yes. There's something wrong. I can't tell more than that, but you ought to go.*
I didn't stop then to wonder how he knew. There was only room for just the
one thing, the distress and urgency, soon to be transmuted into action; the
telephone, the airfield, the ghastly slow journey to be faced. . . . It only
crossed my mind fleetingly then to wonder if my father himself had the Ashley
gift; he had never given me a hint of it, but then neither had I told him about
myself. Had he been "read" by my lover, or even been in touch with
him . . . ? But there was denial stamped on the dark. With the denial came
over a kind of uncertainty, puzzlement with an element of extra doubt running
through it, like a thread of the wrong color through a piece of weaving.

But it didn't matter how, and through whom, it had got to him. It had reached
him, and now it had reached me.

Can you read me, Bryony? You're a long way off.

Yes. I can read you. I'll go . . . I'll go straight away, tomorrow—today?
There was a flight at eight; they would surely take me. . . . Then urgently,
projecting it with everything I had: *Love?*

It was fading. *Yes?*

Will you be there?

Again denial printed on the dark; denial, regret, fading . . .

Oh, God, I said soundlessly. *When?*

Something else came through then, strongly through the fading death cloud,
shouldering it aside; comfort and love, as old-fashioned as potpourri and as sweet
and sane and haunting. It was as if the rose shadows on the ceiling were
showering their scent down into the empty room. Then there was nothing left but
the shadows. I was alone.

I threw the sheet off and knotted a robe round me, and ran for the telephone.
As I put a hand on it, it began to ring.

Ashley, 1835

He stood at the window, looking out into the darkness. Would she
come tonight? Perhaps, if she had heard the news, she would think he
could not be here, waiting for her; and indeed, for very decency, he
surely ought not to have come. . . .

He scowled, chewing his lip. What, after all, was a little more
scandal? And this was their last time—the last time it would be like this.
Tomorrow was for the world, the angry voices, the laughter, the cold
wind. Tonight was still their own.

He glanced across in the direction of the Court. The upper stories
showed, above the hedges, as a featureless bulk of shadow against a
windy sky. No lights. No lights showing anywhere. His eye lingered on
the south wing, where the old man lay behind a darkened window.

Something like a shudder shook him. He tugged at his neckcloth, and
found his hand shaking. She must come. Dear God, she had to come. He
could not face the night without her. His longing, stronger even than
desire, possessed him. He could almost feel the call going out, to bring
her to him through the dark.

2

Find them out whose names are written here!

—Romeo and Juliet, I, ii

MADEIRA TO Madrid, Madrid to Munich, from Munich the express out to Bad Tölz in the Isar Valley; it was twenty-seven hours after the telephone call came from Walther Gothard before the taxi slid up to the sanatorium doors and Herr Gothard himself came down the steps to meet me.

Twenty-seven hours is a long time for a man to hold on to life when he is rising sixty with a dicky heart and has been knocked clean off the road by a passing car and left there till the next passerby should find him. Which had not happened for about four hours.

Jon Ashley had not held on for twenty-seven hours. He was dead when I got to Bad Tölz. He had come round long enough to speak to Walther, then he had slept; and sleeping, died.

I knew, of course. It had happened while I was on the plane between Funchal and Madrid. And then it was over, and I blotted it out and watched the clouds without seeing them, and waited in a curious kind of limbo of relaxation while the Caravelle took me nearer and uselessly nearer his dead body; and waited, too, for my lover to come with what comfort he could offer. But he did not come.

Walther and his wife were divinely kind. They had done everything that had to be done. They had arranged for the cremation, and had telephoned the news to the family lawyers in Worcester. Mr. Emerson, the partner who dealt with the Ashley affairs, would by now have been in touch with Cousin Howard, the father of the twins and of Francis. And of course Walther and Elsa Gothard had been closeted, hour after hour, with the police.

The police were still asking questions, and with most of the questions as yet unanswered. The accident had taken place on the road up from the town, just at dusk. This was the way my taxi had brought me. The Wackersberger Strasse climbs out of the newish quarter of the town beyond the river bridge. Once past the last of the houses the road reverts abruptly to its country status and winds, narrow and in places fairly steep, through the climbing woods. My father, who had been so much better (said Walther) that he had been talking of going home for the summer, had gone down to the town to buy some things he needed, including a bottle of Walther's favorite brandy as a gift, and had apparently started to walk back. No doubt he would have taken the bus when it caught him up. But when the bus climbed that way there was no sign of him. A car, going fast, and clinging to the edge of a bend, had apparently struck him a hard, glancing blow which flung him clear off the road and down the slope into the edge of the wood. He hit his head on a tree trunk, and was knocked unconscious, hidden from the road by the bushes into which he had been flung. The car drove off, leaving him lying there, barely visible in the dusk, until some four hours later when a cyclist, pushing his machine uphill at the edge of the road, ran a tire over a jag of the broken brandy bottle. When he wheeled the crippled cycle to lean it against a tree trunk, he saw my father lying among the bushes. The man took him at first for a drunkard; the brandy still reeked in his clothes. But drunk or no, the wound on his head was black and crusty with blood, so the cyclist wobbled off down the road on his front rim until another car overtook him, and he stopped it.

It was Walther Gothard's. He, growing anxious after two buses had come and gone with no sign of his friend, had telephoned various places where he thought the latter might be, intending to drive down himself and bring him home. Finally, failing to locate him, he set out to look for him. He took the unconscious man straight up to the sanatorium, and telephoned the police, who, having examined the scene of the accident, confirmed the doctor's guess at what must have happened. But four hours' start is four hours' start, and the guilty driver had not been traced.

Herr Gothard told me about it, sitting in his big consulting room with the picture window framing the prospect of rolling pastures, smooth as brushed velvet, and looking as if they had been shaved out of the thick forests that hung like thatch eaves above them. A bowl of blue hyacinths on the desk filled the room with scent. Beside it lay the small pile of objects which had come from Daddy's pockets: keys, a notecase I had given him with the initials *J. A.* stamped in gilt; a silver ballpoint pen with the same initials; a penknife, nail clippers, a handkerchief newly laundered and folded; the letter I had written to him a week ago. I looked away from this at Herr Gothard, who sat quietly, watching me, the gold-rimmed bifocals winking on his broad pale face. No longer Daddy's friend, with a shoulder I could cry on if I needed it; now he was just a doctor, who had heard and seen it all before, and the room itself had held so much of pain and emotion and courage that it was colored by none of them. I sat calmly, while he told me what had happened.

"He came round toward morning and talked a little, a very little. Not about the accident, though; we questioned him as much as we dared, but he seemed to have forgotten about it. He had other things on his mind."

"Yes?"

"You, mainly. I couldn't get it clear, I'm afraid. He said, *'Bryony, tell Bryony,'* once or twice, then seemed not to be able to put it into words, whatever it was. I thought at first he was anxious in case you had not been told about the accident, so I reassured him, and said I had talked to you on the telephone, and that you were on your way. But he still worried at it. We got a few snatches, no more, none of which made much sense, then in the end he got something more out. It was *'Bryony—my little Bryony—in danger.'* I asked what danger, and he could not answer me. He died at about ten o'clock."

I nodded. Between Funchal and Madrid; I knew the exact moment. Walther talked on, professionally smooth and calm; I think he was telling me about Daddy's stay in Wackersberg, and what they had done and talked of together. I have no recollection of anything he said, but to this day I can remember every petal on the blue hyacinths in the bowl on the desk between us.

"And that was all?"

"All?" Herr Gothard, interrupted in midsentence, changed direction without a tremor. "All that Jon said, you mean?"

"Yes. I'm sorry. I wasn't really taking in—"

"Please." He showed a hand, pale and smooth with scrubbing. "I did not imagine you were. You ask me what else Jon said at the end. I have it here."

He slid the hand into a drawer of the desk, and brought out a paper.

I don't know why I was so surprised. I just stared, without moving to take the paper. "You wrote it down?"

"The police left a man to sit by his bed," explained Walther gently, "in case he managed to say anything about the accident which might help them to trace the culprit. It always happens, you know."

"Yes, of course. I knew that. One never quite thinks of oneself in those contexts, I suppose."

"The officer spoke very good English, and he took down everything Jon said, whether it seemed to him to make sense or not. Do you read shorthand?"

"Yes."

"It's all here, every word that was intelligible. I was with Jon myself most of the time. There was another emergency that morning, so I had to leave him for a while, but as soon as he showed signs of coming round they sent for me, and I stayed with him after that until he died. This is all that he said. I am sorry it does not make more sense, but perhaps it does, for you."

He handed me the paper. The pothooks straggled a little wildly across the page, as if written too hurriedly, on a pad balanced on someone's knee. Walther slid another sheet of paper across the desk toward me. "I made a transcript of it, just in case. You can compare them later, if you like."

The transcript was typed, with no attempt at making sense. Just a string of words and phrases, punctuated seemingly at random.

> Bryony. Tell Bryony. Tell her. Howard. James. Would have told. The paper, it's in William's brook. In the library. Emerson, the keys. The cat, it's the cat on the pavement. The map. The letter. In the brook.

It broke off there, and started again on a fresh line:

> Tell Bryony. My little Bryony be careful. Danger. This thing I can feel. Should have told you, but one must be sure. I did tell Bryony's [word indistinguishable]. Perhaps the boy knows. Tell the boy. Trust. Depend. Do what's right. Blessing.

I read it aloud slowly, then looked up at Walther. My face must have been blank. He nodded, answering the unspoken question.

"I'm sorry. That really is all, exactly as we heard him. You see where he found it too much for him, and stopped for a while. He was still conscious, and worrying at it, so we let him speak. The last word, I'm not sure about that. I thought it might have been 'bless him,' but the officer was sure it was 'blessing.' Does it make any sense to you at all?"

"No. Scraps here and there, but no. Nothing important enough to be so much on his mind then. I'd have thought—I mean, if he knew how ill he was, I'd have thought . . . you know, just messages."

"Yes, well, it may mean more later, when you have had time to study it."

"There's this about a letter. It might all be there. Did he leave a letter?" I knew the answer already. If there had been a letter for me, Walther would have given it to me straight away.

"I'm afraid not," he said, "and there was nothing mailed from here within the last day or so. I checked. But it is possible that he took something down with him to mail from Bad Tölz yesterday. In which case it will be on its way to Madeira. No doubt they will forward it straight away to your home."

The last sentence came with perceptible hesitation. There is something strange, I suppose, in the idea of a letter arriving from the dead. I didn't find it so. It was a break in the clouds of that dark day. Something of the sort must have shown in my face, because Walther added, gently: "It's only a guess, Bryony. The word itself was a guess. If there is anything, it may not even be for you."

"I'll find out once I get home."

I would of course have to go home to England now, and it had already been arranged that I would take my father's ashes back to the Court, as he had wished.

Walther nodded. "And after that? Do you intend to stay there?"

"I'll have to, I think, until things are settled."

"It may take a long time."

"It's sure to. It'll be beastly complicated, I gather, but Mr. Emerson will do all the fixing. I suppose Daddy told you that the estate doesn't go to me, but is entailed to the nearest male heir? That's my father's cousin, Howard Ashley, who lives in Spain."

Walther nodded. "Your lawyer said something about it when we spoke over the telephone. He had not been able to get in touch directly with Mr. Howard Ashley, he said. It seems that he is ill."

"Yes. Daddy told me so last time he wrote. It's a virus pneumonia, and I gather that Cousin Howard's been pretty bad. I don't suppose he'll be able to attend to any business for a long time. Emory and James will have to see to things."

"So I imagine. It seems that this was one of the things your father had on his mind. Emory—a strange name, surely?"

"I suppose it is. It's an old Saxon name that crops up in the family from time to time. I think it's the same as Almeric."

"Ah, then I have also heard it in Germany. They are twins, are they not, this James and Emory?"

"Yes, identical twins. When they were boys, no one could tell them apart, except the family—and sometimes, when they were trying it on deliberately, not even the family. It's not so hard now, but I still wouldn't bet on it if they really tried to fool you. They're twenty-seven. Emory's the elder, half an hour's difference, something like that."

"A big difference when it comes to inheriting an estate," said Walther drily.

I said, just as drily: "A crumbling old house that never quite got over the flood ten years back, and a few acres of garden gone wild, and a ruined farm? Some legacy."

"As bad as that? Jon loved it."

"So do I."

"And your cousins?"

"I don't know. I don't see why they should. They were brought up there, the same as me; Cousin Howard had a house less than a mile away. But whether they want a beautiful old millstone round their necks I've no idea. Beautiful old millstones take money."

"I understood they had plenty of that."

"I suppose they have." Whether they would want to spend it on Ashley was another matter which I didn't pursue. I did not know a great deal about the wine shipper's business which Howard Ashley had started some years back, except that it had always seemed to prosper. In the early days, when it was relatively small, it had been based in Bristol, and the family had lived near us in Worcestershire. Then when the twins were about thirteen, and Francis eleven, the boys' mother died, and after that the three of them seemed more or less to live with us at the Court. Certainly they spent their school holidays with us; their father was in Bristol during the week, and his housekeeping arrangements were so erratic that my mother finally intervened and took my three cousins in. There would have been ample room, in those days, for Howard as well, but, though there had never been anything approaching coolness between him and my parents, they could not have happily settled to share a house. The three boys were dispatched home to their father most weekends, until, some five years after his wife's death, Cousin Howard went off to Mexico City to negotiate a deal of some kind, and met a Spanish-Mexican girl and married her. Her family was wealthy, and also connected with the wine trade. Howard's deal had been with the girl's father, Miguel Pereira, who owned a share of a prosperous business in Jerez. Howard took his new wife off to Europe, and they eventually settled in Spain. Emory took over the Bristol offices, and James more or less commuted between the two.

"Would your cousin Howard want to come back to live at Ashley?" asked Walther.

"I've no idea. I don't honestly know him so very well. I was only fourteen when he left, and I was away at school most of the time. I doubt if his wife would want to live there, though. She's years younger than Cousin Howard, and she'd hardly want to settle in a remote little place like Ashley. But I suppose one of the boys might."

"The boys . . ." Walther said it half to himself, and I realized that he was thinking of the paper I still held in my hand. But he only said: "I understand the two elder ones are in their father's business. What about the youngest?"

"Francis? Oh, he is, too. Rather reluctantly, I think. He doesn't have his family's head for business—he's more like our side. But he's with his father now in Jerez. I think he went into it almost absentmindedly, while he marked time and thought out what he really wanted to do. He has to earn a living some way, and I suppose Spain is as pleasant a place as any. He's a poet."

"Oh." Walther smiled. "A good one?"

"How would I know? I never got much beyond Yeats and Walter de la Mare. Didn't want to, considering the sort of things that get printed now. I can't understand a word Francis writes, but I like Francis, so let's say he is a good one."

The sun twinkled on the gold-rimmed glasses. "He's not married, is he?"

"No." I met his eyes. "And nor are the twins, Dr. Gothard. At least, they weren't when I last saw them. We're not wildly good correspondents, my cousins and I." (Except for you, Ashley my lover. Emory? James? Francis?) I raised my brows at Walther. "You've been listening to Daddy, haven't you? That was his plan, too. Get me back to Ashley somehow. . . . But Francis would be no good, obviously. It would have to be the eldest, and that's Emory."

He smiled. "Something of the sort was in my mind, I confess. It is such an obvious solution. You stay at Ashley, and so do your children. I am sure your father had some sort of hope that it might happen. I think he saw you staying on there."

"He didn't say who with?" I was looking down at the paper in my hand. *"This thing I can feel. . . . Perhaps the boy knows."* And then, *"I did tell Bryony's"*—Bryony's what? Bryony's lover? I wondered sharply, but with a kind of certainty about it, whether my father had known, or guessed, enough about my secret love to bank, entail or no, on my lifelong connection with Ashley Court.

"No," said Walther. "He didn't." My thoughts had gone on from my own question with such speed that for a moment I couldn't make out what he was referring to. He saw this; he was very quick, was Herr Doktor Gothard. He nodded to the paper in my hands. "You were studying that. Have you worked some of it out?"

"Not really. It sounds as if there's some paper, perhaps the letter he speaks of, where he's written something important to me, and perhaps to Cousin Howard."

"And James."

"Yes, I suppose so. But why James? I mean if Daddy *had* told Howard, then Howard could have told the boys, whatever it was. It sounds as if it was a family matter. So why just James?" (Like a treasure hunt, I was thinking, the mystification of papers and letters and maps. It wasn't like him. Jon Ashley was sane and direct. So what did it mean? And why James?) I added, aloud: "This paper or map or whatever, he says it's 'in William's brook.' Well, that simply does not make sense."

"I know. A brook's another word for a stream, is it not? I thought it was, and I looked it up to make sure. It cannot mean anything else. I thought you might know what he meant."

"No idea. You said you were sure the words were right."

"Those, yes. To begin with he was pretty clear. I thought there might be a stream at Ashley, something with a local name, perhaps."

"Not that I know of. There was a William Ashley, certainly, early last century. 'Scholar Ashley' they called him; he was a bit of a Shakespeare scholar, in a strictly private and amateur way. He was a poet, too. But the only brook in the place, apart from the river, is the overflow channel that helps to control the level of the moat. It's never been called anything but the Overflow." I stopped, struck by an idea. "It might have been made by William, I suppose. There's a maze at Ashley, and he built a pavilion in the middle, where he used to retire to write. The stream runs past the maze."

"'The map'?" suggested Walther. "A map of the maze?"

"Perhaps. I don't see why it should matter. I've known the way in all my life, and so have my cousins." I shrugged. "In any case, it's nonsense. How could a paper—a map, whatever you like—how could it be in a stream?"

"I agree. But the next bit is surely more sensible. This paper could be in the library, of which perhaps Mr. Emerson had the keys? Does he keep keys to the Court?"

"I suppose he must have a set. One complete set was handed over to the tenants. They live in the south wing, and normally all the rest of the house is locked up, except for cleaning, and when the place is open to the public, but the Underhills have to have the keys to the locked rooms, because of fire regulations."

He merely nodded, and I didn't elaborate. I assumed that Daddy had told him about our latest tenants. The Underhills were wealthy Americans with permanent homes in Los Angeles and New York, and temporary ones, one gathered, here and there all over the world. Jeffrey Underhill was President of Sacco International, a heavy construction firm which carried out government contracts in every part of the globe. The family had been living in Los Angeles while the daughter, Cathy, was at school there, but now they had come to England for a year's stay, to be near Mrs. Underhill's sister, whose husband was stationed at the USAF base near Bristol. As far as Mr. Underhill was concerned, it didn't seem to matter where he was based; I gathered he managed to struggle home most weekends, but spent his weeks shuttling between Paris, London, Mexico, and Teheran, where the company's current major operations were. He had told Mr. Emerson that it didn't make a bit of difference where he was actually domiciled as long as he got "back home" to Houston, Texas, for Board Meetings, and that his wife was keen to live for a while in a "real old English home," and that it would do Cathy a world of good to have a taste of country peace and quiet. Myself, I wondered about that; I had never been to Los Angeles, but one could imagine that Ashley, in contrast, might possibly not have much to offer to an eighteen-year-old girl with all the money in the world to burn. But they had stayed, and liked it, and I gathered that Cathy was still there with them.

"The bit about the cat," I said. "Do you think the car might have swerved to avoid a cat, or something, and was going too fast at the bend, and mounted the pavement and hit him?"

"It is possible. That's the way the police see it. There actually is no pavement on that section of the road, but there is a kind of footway worn in the verge of the wood, and, heaven knows, Jon might have been speaking loosely when he talks of a 'pavement.' That was where he had to stop talking and rest for a while."

"But this last bit, Dr. Gothard. He wasn't speaking loosely there. He says I have to be careful, and there's some danger."

"Indeed." His eyes were troubled. "When he speaks of 'this thing I can feel,' he seems to mean danger of some kind. It could hardly be pain; he was under sedation."

"He wouldn't mean that." I took a breath and met the kind pale eyes above the glinting half-moons of glass. "You're a doctor, so I don't expect you to believe me, but some of us—the Ashleys, I mean—have a sort of . . . I can only call it a kind of telepathy. Empathy, perhaps? Er, do you have that word?"

"Certainly. We say *'mit fühlen.'* The power of entering imaginatively into someone else's feelings or experience."

"Yes, except that in our case it's not just imaginative, it's real. I've only known it work between members of the family, and it's kind of spasmodic, but if someone you love is hurt, you know."

"Why should I not believe you?" he asked calmly. "It's reasonably common."

"I know, but you'd be surprised—or perhaps you wouldn't—what people don't believe, or don't want to believe. The Ashleys have had this thing in one degree or another as far back as about the sixteen hundreds when the Jacobean Ashley married a gorgeous girl called Bess Smith, who was half gypsy. She was burned for witchcraft in the end. After that it seems to have cropped up every so often, but we kept quiet about it. Anyway, it isn't the kind of thing you tell people. Nobody likes being laughed at."

"You really think this is what your father meant?"

"It might be. I've sometimes wondered. We never spoke about it, but I'm pretty sure he had it to some extent. I know once when I was at school and fell out of a tree and broke my leg, he telephoned about ten minutes later to ask if I was all right. And last night in Madeira . . . Well, I felt something, and I think some of it came from him. And on the way here in the plane this morning, at ten o'clock, I knew."

He said nothing for a while. An early bee zoomed in through the open window, circled droning in the sunlight, then homed in on the hyacinths and crawled up them, its wings quiet. Walther stirred. "I see. But at the end, as you see, he states that he 'told' someone, presumably meaning that he told him about this important paper, and about this danger to you. If it is so very important, no doubt 'he' will tell you. And if 'the boy knows,' then perhaps 'the boy' may tell you, too?"

I watched the bee. I wasn't prepared to meet those kind, clever eyes. I still had this one to think about, myself. *"I did tell Bryony's . . . Perhaps the boy knows."* Bryony's lover? It would take a bit of adjustment to come to terms with the fact that my father had known. And if he had told my lover something that mattered urgently to me, then my lover could tell me, and the mystery was no mystery.

The bee, abandoning the hyacinths, shot straight for the window like a bullet, achieved the open pane by a beewing's breadth, and was gone.

Walther straightened in the big chair. "Well, we shall leave it, I think. Yes? You must try to forget it for the moment. When you have rested, and when the next few days are over, then you may find your mind fresher, and you will see. It is very possible that Mr. Emerson may have the answers already, or whoever of your family comes over on Friday. One of them surely will, and will take you home? It may be 'Bryony's cousin,' the one who knows it all."

"So it may. Dr. Gothard, will you tell me something truly?"

"If I can."

I knew from his eyes that from a doctor that meant "If I may," but that was fair enough. I said: "If the driver of that car had brought Daddy straight up to you here, could you have saved him?"

I saw the wariness relax into relief. That meant he would tell me the truth. "No. If he had been brought straight in he might have lived a little longer, but I could not have saved him."

"Not even till I got here?"

"I think not. It was a matter of hours only."

I drew a breath. He looked at me curiously. I shook my head. "No, I wasn't thinking of anything as dramatic and useless as revenge. That's a kind of self-defeat, I always feel. But if you had said 'Yes' I'd never have slept until the police found the driver who did it. As it is, he ran away out of fear and stupidity, and maybe he's being punished enough already. If the police ever do find him—" I paused.

"Yes?" he prompted.

I said flatly: "I don't want to know. I mean, I don't want to be told who it is. I won't burden myself with a useless hate. Daddy's gone, and I'm here, with a life to live. Those are the facts."

I didn't add what I was thinking: that he might not be quite gone, not from me, not from such as me. I would go back to Ashley, and there, perhaps . . . But I wasn't sure where that path would lead, and anyway that was another secret that was not for daylight. Walther said something about its being a sensible attitude, and something more about my being very like my father, and then we talked about the arrangements for the cremation on Friday, and for the day after that, when nothing more would remain for me but to take my father's ashes home.

Ashley, 1835

The wind moved in the boughs outside. Creepers shifted and tapped against the walls of the pavilion. Since the old man had been ill, the place had been neglected—mercifully, he thought, with a wryness that made the young mouth look soured and wary.

He strained his eyes against the darkness. Still no movement, no sign. He pushed the casement open a fraction, listened. Nothing, except the rush of the overflow conduit past the maze, and the wind in the beeches. Sudden gusts combed the crests of the yew hedges toward him, as if something were flying past, invisible. A soul on its way home, he thought, and the shudder took him again.

At least let us have some light. He shut the window, and the night sounds died. He pulled the shutters close, and fastened them, then drew the heavy curtains across.

A candle stood on the writing table. He found a lucifer and lit it. At once the room flowered with light; golden curtains, rose-wreathed carpet, the bed's rich covering, the glittering sconces on the walls.

If he ever came here again, he would light those, too.

3

Good King of Cats, nothing but one of your nine lives. . . .
                                        —*Romeo and Juliet*, III, i

I DIDN'T go straight home when I got to England. The first priority was a visit to Mr. Emerson, our solicitor, to find out if he had had a letter from my father, and if he could throw any light on the jumble of words on Walther's paper.

No one had come to the cremation. Emory had telephoned from England, not to me but to Walther, to say that Cousin Howard was still very ill, and that since Francis was away on leave, James was tied to the Jerez office. Emory himself could not be free on Friday, but would come to Ashley as soon as possible. He had no idea where Francis was; walking somewhere, he thought, in the Peak District. Presumably the news had not got to him yet. No doubt he would call me as soon as he came back. Meanwhile, said Emory, love to Bryony . . .

So much for Bryony's cousin who would tell me what Daddy had meant, and take me home. And so much for Bryony's lover, who said nothing, either by day or night.

When I arrived in London I took the train straight to Worcester and booked in at a small hotel where no one knew me. Next morning I telephoned Mr. Emerson, and went to see him.

He was a youngish man, somewhere (I guessed) in his upper thirties, of medium height and running a bit to flesh, with a round, good-tempered face and hair cut fashionably long. He had a small shrewd mouth, and small shrewd brown eyes camouflaged behind modishly huge, tinted spectacles, like a television spy's. Otherwise he was correctly dressed and almost over-conventionally mannered; but I had seen him fishing the Wye in stained old tweeds and a snagged sweater, up to the crotch in the river and swearing in the far-from-legal sense of the word as he slipped and splashed over the boulders, trying to land a big salmon single-handed. I liked him, and Daddy, I knew, had trusted him completely.

It was almost a week now since my father's death, but Mr. Emerson did not make the mistake of being too kind. We got the first civilities over, then he cleared his throat, shifted a paper or two, and said: "Well now, Miss Ashley, you do know that you may call on me to help you in any way. . . . It will take a fair amount of time to sort out your father's affairs, as you know. None of that need trouble you, as long as you find yourself quite clear about the way the house and property are left."

I nodded. I had practically been brought up with the terms of the Ashley Trust, as it was called, which had been designed by an ancestor of mine, one James Christian Ashley, who had inherited the property in 1850. He was a farsighted man, who had seen, even in the spacious days of Victoria, that there might come a time when the incumbent of a place like Ashley might find it hard to protect what he, James Christian, thought of as a national treasure, and might even seek to disperse it. This, James Christian was determined to prevent. He created a trust whereby, though the Court itself must go outright to the nearest male heir, no part of the "said messuages" might be sold or disposed of unless with the consent in writing of all adult Ashley descendants existing at the time of the proposed disposal. My grandfather James Emory had managed, with the connivance of his brothers and one distant cousin, to sell a couple of outlying farms which edged the main road, and to make a tidy sum out of some meadowland earnestly desired by the Midland Railway, and the proceeds had kept the place in good heart until the cold winds sharpened to the killing frosts of the Second World War. Since then, apart from the family silver, which had been sold with his cousin's consent, all the articles my father had sold had been things bought since 1850 or brought in by marriage, and consequently uncontrolled by the trust. If my cousins had been in need of funds they would, I knew, have found themselves fairly well down to the scrapings.

Mr. Emerson was going on. "There's no immediate hurry over that. We can perhaps have another meeting when you are less, er, pressed." I knew that Walther had told him what my first business was at the Court. He shied delicately away from that, and went on: "Then there is your father's Will. He told me you have seen a copy, and know all about its contents. It covers everything not included in the entail, or embraced by the trust. The most important item is of course the cottage which is now your home. This, with the orchard and garden, and the strip of land running along the lake as far as the main road, was purchased after the creation of the trust, and comes, in consequence, outside its terms. It is left to you in its entirety. The Will is quite straightforward. There may be things that you wish to discuss at a later stage, but for the moment, would you like me just to take everything over for you? Settle what bills there are, and sort your father's correspondence? Or perhaps you would rather go through his letters yourself?"

"The personal ones, yes, I think so, please. I'd be glad if you'd deal with any business. Mr. Emerson—"

"Yes?"

"Has Daddy written to you recently? I mean, in the last few days?"

"No." He looked down at his fingernails for a moment, then back at me. "I was talking to Dr. Gothard on the telephone yesterday, as a matter of fact."

"Oh. Did he ask you about a letter, too?"

"Yes."

"And tell you about the paper?"

"Paper?"

"The notes he took about what Daddy said before he died."

"Ah, yes. Of course he did not tell me what had been said. This"—with a sudden, dry primness—"was on the telephone."

"I wanted to ask you about that, too. Most of it Herr Gothard and I couldn't make out at all, but there is one reference to you, which we thought you'd be able to clear up for us. I made a copy for you. Here."

He took the paper and read it swiftly, glanced briefly up at me, went through it again slowly, and then a third time. Finally he laid it on the desk. He leaned back in his chair, with his hands flat on the blotter.

"Well. Yes. I see."

"It's nonsense to you as well?"

"Pretty much, I'm afraid. But I think I can explain the reference to me. The tenants of the Court have a set of keys, but not a complete one. Certain keys were detached from that set, and are in my keeping. I have, for instance, the strong-room key, and the one to the old muniment chest in the Great Hall, and—yes, the small wall safe in the master bedroom, and also the key that opens the locked cases in the library."

"*Have* you?" Here, at last, was a fragment that might make sense, though I was still far from knowing what sort. The locked cases in the library at Ashley housed William Ashley's collection of Shakespeariana, and his own mercifully slim volume of verses, along with the distinctly curious (in the book-trade sense of the word) collection made by William's son, the scapegrace Nick Ashley. The grilles had been fixed after my father had found Emory and James, at the age of twelve, happily conning one of Nick's tomes called *Erotica Curiosa,* fortunately in Latin, but with illustrations. Within a few days it was behind bars, along with the rest of Nick's additions to the library, and those of William Ashley's Shakespeare books that we imagined might be valuable, and a few other odd volumes, mostly in Latin. I remember how Emory worked at his Latin for a whole term, till he found he would never get near the keys anyway, so he went back to normal.

"The wall safe's empty, I know that," I said. "Do you know what's in the strong-room nowadays?"

"There's very little. Only what's left of the eighteenth-century silver, and one or two small things. I believe there are some pieces of your mother's which are to be yours."

"Those, yes, I know about them. Nothing else? No papers, letters, maps?"

"Not that I recollect. No, I'm sure there aren't. All the Ashley papers are lodged with us. That goes for the muniment chest, too. There's nothing there now but spare blankets and the old stable books and various other oddments. Oh, and a dozen or so volumes of Emma Ashley's diaries." He added, drily: "A voluble lady. She was James Christian's mother, wasn't she?"

"She was. Is that where the diaries are? They used to be in the locked section of the library, along with the other family books, but heaven knows *they* never needed to be locked away from anyone. She was a very good woman, and a fearful bore. I think she spent her whole life trying to expiate poor Wicked Nick's sins." I thought for a moment. All the rest of the family books were presumably still in the locked cases, and by the terms of the trust they would go with the house. Most of the valuable books that did not come under those terms had already been sold. Perhaps it would not be such a formidable job after all. "Do I need Cousin Howard's permission to look around in there?"

"No."

"Then—" I stopped and sat up. "I've just remembered something."

"What is it?"

I said slowly, thinking back, "I think Daddy was going through the books in that section not long before we went to Bavaria. I remember seeing a stack of leather-bound books on one of the library tables. He'd been dressing the bindings. He'd done that with other valuable books from time to time, so I thought nothing of it. He took one or two of them home, too, to the cottage. Perhaps he found something about the family, or even about the trust, that he thought we ought to know."

"It sounds reasonable. It could be checked, but it'll be a big job. Books always take the devil of a time to look through. You can hardly tackle that library on your own."

"I could look, though, couldn't I? The shelves are pretty empty now, apart from the family tomes, and they'll all still be there." I smiled. "I might for decency's sake have to hand some of Nick Ashley's lot over to my cousins to go through. If they don't want to be bothered, I've a friend who would help, Leslie Oker, who has the secondhand bookshop in Ashbury. I suppose that, in any case, everything will have to be valued?"

"I'm afraid so. Well, I think you're right to take this very seriously." He laid the paper down on the desk in front of him. "Anything that was so much on your father's mind at such a time . . ." He let it hang. His eyes went to the paper again, and he read for a minute, frowning. Then, with a quick movement like a dismissal, he opened a drawer and slipped the paper into it. "You're going to Ashley today?"

"Yes. This afternoon. Mr. Emerson, what's the position about the Court? Am I still allowed access to everything?"

"Certainly. Nothing may be removed or sold, naturally, but it is still your home until your father's Will is proved and the estate is wound up. That will take quite some time." His eyes twinkled. "The mills of God work like lightning, compared with the law."

"So they say. What about the tycoons?"

"The what?"

"Sorry. It slipped out. It's what Daddy and I used to call the Underhills."

He laughed. "It figures. They have a year's lease, which will be up in November. Mr. Underhill spoke to me on the telephone and offered to move out straight away if it would help you, but I told him that I imagined you and your cousins would wish him to stay put, at any rate for the time being. Things won't be settled for months, and at the least it means the Court will have a caretaker. Do you approve?"

"That's the kind of thing I leave to you. It sounds fine to me."

"Good. Your cousin Emory agreed, too. He was speaking for his father. You knew Mr. Howard Ashley was ill? Yes, of course . . ." He cleared his throat again. "Look, I know you want to go back to Ashley as soon as you can, but do you really want to stay there on your own? My wife and I would be delighted if you'd come to us for a few days. . . . And it was her suggestion that I should ask you, so I'm not putting my head on the domestic chopping block, I promise you."

"Well, thank you very much. It's terribly good of you both, but honestly, you don't have to worry. I'll be all right, really I will." I didn't add that I would not be quite alone. I never was. I thanked him again, moved by the kindness of these people who had known my father well, but me hardly at all.

He waved my thanks aside. "Still, I'll give you our number—not the office, which you have, but my home number. I think you're going to find the next few weeks very difficult ones, and I want to insist to you that though we—my firm— will be acting for Ashley as before, which will in future mean on Mr. Howard Ashley's behalf, we'll do all that we can to help you. I know it goes without saying, but still one says it."

"You're very kind."

"And have I made it clear I don't only mean legal help? For instance, how do you propose to get out to Ashley this afternoon? Have you a car?"

"No, I came up by train. I'll take the bus to Ashley Village. There's a good one that stops at the road end beyond the church."

"And on your way back?"

"I've got a Lambretta. It's stabled at the farm."

"What about your luggage? If you're going to move back into your cottage tomorrow—"

"I haven't much; most of it's still in Madeira. But Rob Granger can come in for that. He has a car."

He nodded, and we talked for a while longer. He still seemed worried about my decision to stay alone in the cottage, and I spent some time in reassuring him. He also cast out feelers, very delicately, to find out what I proposed to do with my future, when Ashley was no longer mine. Would I, he asked, go back to Madeira when everything was, er, settled?

"I don't think so. They'll have replaced me by now, anyway; you just can't do without a receptionist for an indefinite period. In any case, I'd thought of that job as strictly temporary, just till Daddy was well enough to come home. I don't suppose my old job in Ashbury's still open, but I expect I'll find something."

"What's the money situation? I can advance you something, you know, out of what your father has left you."

"I'm all right for a bit, but thanks." I got to my feet. "You said you had a lunch appointment, and it's nearly half past twelve. I'd better go." I held out my hand. "And thank you for everything, Mr. Emerson. You've been terribly kind. Believe me, I'll come running to you the moment I need help of any kind."

"I hope you will."

We shook hands, and he moved to open the door for me. I paused in the doorway. "I almost forgot . . . I wonder, would it be all right for you to let me have the keys to the Court? I don't want to go to the house today, but I might go in tomorrow, and I'd rather not trouble the Underhills yet."

He looked surprised. "Of course. But surely, you can use your father's keys? The master set has them all."

"I haven't got them. I thought you must have. Do you mean you only have the ones you mentioned?"

"Yes, only the four. I gather they were detached from the ring Mr. Underhill has. The other set, the complete master set, was certainly in your father's possession. Didn't Dr. Gothard give you his things?"

"Yes. He did have keys on him, but only the ones for the cottage, and for the side door to the Court—the kitchen door, really, at the East Bridge." I hesitated, obscurely troubled. "If you haven't got them, who could he have left them with? One of my cousins?"

"I don't see why," said Mr. Emerson, slowly. "How very strange." He frowned over it for a few moments, then the professional mask was smoothly back in place. He went to a drawer, unlocked it, and took out a small ring of keys, which he gave to me. "You must certainly have these. I'll get in touch with your cousin Emory and see if he knows anything about it. It may even be that both sets were left with the Underhills, or with someone else at Ashley. Whoever has them will probably give them to you as soon as it's known you're home. Otherwise, I'm afraid you will have to approach the Underhills."

"So it seems," I said. "But it is all right for me to go in?"

"Certainly."

"And if I get the keys, to keep them for the time being?"

"Yes, indeed." He opened the door for me. The brown eyes behind the trendy spectacles were anxious and kind. "Miss Ashley, let me insist to you that the Court is still yours until the Will is proved, and the estate duly handed over."

"Yes. Thank you."

"As for the keys, no doubt there will be some perfectly rational explanation," he said, as he showed me out. I got the impression that he was talking to reassure himself as well as me, and that in reality he disliked and distrusted mystery as much as I did myself.

"No doubt," I agreed, and went downstairs and out into the street.

Just outside the offices of Meyer, Meyer, and Hardy there is a pedestrian crossing. The light was at red, *Don't Walk*. Just under it, on the very edge of the pavement, a black cat was sitting, waiting apparently for the light to change to green. As I paused beside him he glanced up. I said to him, "Can't you reach? Allow me," and pressed the button. I have a theory that the button never has the least effect on the lights, which are totally unaffected by pedestrians' needs, but at that exact moment the light switched to green. *Walk*. The cat got straight up and walked across the zebra-striped way, tail in air. He was black as coal. "I may need you yet," I told him, and followed him onto the crossing.

There was a shriek of brakes. I jumped half out of my skin, and stepped back to the pavement. The cat bolted clear across and vanished into a shop doorway. A white E-type Jaguar clenched its big groundhog tires to the road, and stopped dead half a foot from the crossing. The girl who was driving glanced neither at me nor at the fleeing cat. She sat watching the red light with impatience, one hand tapping the wheel, the other pushing back the long, dark-blond hair. I had a glimpse of dark eyes shadowed under an inch or so of mink eyelash, a sallow, small-featured face, with that Pekinese look which is for some reason typically

American, and a wide unpainted mouth. When I had gained the other pavement in the black cat's wake, the lights changed behind me, and the E-type snarled off into the traffic of the crowded street, cut competently between two buses, and vanished. Something made me glance back. On the other pavement Mr. Emerson had emerged from his office, complete with bowler and rolled umbrella, presumably on the way to his lunch date. He, too, had paused, and was watching the E-type out of sight. Then he noticed me, and mouthed something across the roaring flood of traffic pouring between us. I thought he said, "The cat," but he was pointing after the vanished Jaguar. I nodded, waved, and smiled, and walked back to my hotel.

Ashley, 1835

On the writing table, beside the candle, lay his father's books and papers, held down by a glass weight shaped like a peeled orange. The waxlight glimmered in the curved segments, and a dozen tiny images mocked him; the fair young man, a slight figure in frilled shirt and pantaloons, standing there, somehow incongruous and lonely against the richly elegant background of his mother's room.

He moved abruptly, striding over to the table, scattering the papers that lay there. He pulled open a drawer. From inside it, his mother's picture smiled up at him. Always, when he had used the pavilion, he had hidden her; or hidden from her. Now he lifted the portrait, and stood for a long time looking at it. Then, smiling, he set it back in its place on the writing table, facing the room.

Facing the bed.

His father's papers, those dry, exquisitely penned little verses, lay unheeded on the floor.

4

Come, he hath hid himself among these trees . . .
Blind is his love, and best befits the dark.

—Romeo and Juliet, II i

THE BIG gates at Ashley Court stood, as always, open. I went in, soft-footed on the mossed surface of the avenue, and walked up under the lime trees toward the bend from which one could see the house.

Evening, and the last of the rich, slanting sunlight threw the lovely tracery of the gates long-drawn across the uncut verges. Windflowers and pale blue speedwell sprinkled the grass, hazing the green as delicately as a breath misting glass. Fetlock deep in wild flowers, the lime boles shone bronze through their feathering of sorrel-colored buds. The young leaves overhead, just unfurling, showed as transparent as stained glass against the light.

I reached the bend in the drive. From here one could see the house, its walls of rosy Tudor brick reflected richly in the still glass of the moat. No one was about; no movement anywhere. I stood in the shadow, looking at Howard Ashley's home.

For anything so old it was curiously serene. It stood foursquare on its island, an oddly harmonious hotchpotch of the centuries' building. The Norman keep still stood, altered and added to when the main gate with its battlements was built in the twelfth century. The original drawbridge had long ago been replaced by the single span of stone, just wide enough for a car, which now leads into the small, square courtyard. The Great Door lies opposite the main gateway, and is Tudor, giving straight onto the big hall with its vast fireplace and blackened beams. The rooms to the right of the courtyard are Tudor, too; the parlor with the priest's hole (reopened in 1880) and the small dark Council Chamber with its coffered ceiling and coats of arms. To the east of the main gate stands the banqueting hall, a fourteenth-century structure with the medieval timbering still intact. I had never known this used, except to show; it had been damaged in 1962, when money had been too tight for too long, and the big storm of mid-September brought the river down in flood and broke the High Sluice which controls the flow to the moat. Before the lower sluice could be opened to relieve the Overflow, and let the water safely into the lake, the cellars and the low-lying floors of banqueting hall and kitchens were flooded. My father repaired the High Sluice and made good the kitchen premises, then dried out the banqueting hall and left it alone. The only good thing, he had remarked, about the Court's precarious situation between river and lake was that fire insurance premiums were almost nil. . . .

"Lake" was rather too grand a name for the sheet of water which lay below the banked-up moat. I forget when the artificial pool was first dug; to begin with it had been a stewpond for keeping fish, then later it had been enlarged and planted with lilies, with a willow or two and a monstrous grove of gunneras. It was still called Mistress Nancy's Pool, which sounded better than The Stew, as it was labeled on the maps. Between moat and Pool was a grassed bank which Rob, the gardener, kept cut after a fashion with the Flymo, just as he kept the beech walk and the main avenue clear and neat-looking. He kept some sort of order, too, in the walled garden with its two remaining glasshouses. We sold most of the produce, and this paid Rob's wage and that of the village boy who helped him. Beyond that there was little that could be done. The rose garden with its moldering statues was an impenetrable Sleeping Beauty affair, and the woods beyond the Pool had long since engulfed the orchards, with the exception of one stand of apple trees beside the water, where the cottage stood that was now my home.

It was dusk already. As I stood there the sun, imperceptibly, withdrew, and the light cooled to blue and then to shadow. Still nothing had stirred except the two swans, serene on the moat, and the whisper of a rising breeze in the branches. No light showed in the house. I went quickly up the drive for another fifty yards or so to where, on the right, between banks of rhododendrons, the Court's private pathway led to the churchyard.

This had originally been the only way to the church. The lych-gate stood there, and beyond it a tunnel of ancient yews. The lych-gate cast a thick blanket of shadow as I went through, and suddenly, it seemed, day had gone and the evening was here. From overhead came that twilight sound, the rooks settling on their nests, their muttering broken from time to time by the sudden flap of a wing, or a throaty yell as some bird flung upward, startled, from its perch. Ahead of me the church showed only as a looming shadow against the furred and shifting shadows of the trees. The yews flowed upward in the breeze like smoke.

I didn't mind the dark. I had trodden every centimeter of this path since I could remember. Someone had mowed the graveyard grass recently, and there was the smell of the sweet cuttings in the air; some of the swaths had fallen and dried on the pathway. I could not hear my own footsteps until I trod on the stone of the church porch and, shifting the crematorium's casket carefully into my left hand, groped for the big iron ring of the south door.

It opened readily. Ashley (it seemed) was still secure from the contagion of the world's slow stain; we had never locked our doors; and please heaven we might never need to. Inside the church it was almost dark. The smells, familiar as childhood, met me as I went in and shut the door behind me; old dusty hassocks, wood gently warping in the scent of the beeswax and turpentine still used by Miss Marget the church cleaner, like her mother and her mother's mother before her. The smell of leftover Easter lilies rather past their best. The smell of hymnbooks and dead candles.

I didn't touch the light switches. I walked slowly up the center aisle toward the faint glimmer of the east window.

I had come tonight with the casket, instead of in the morning when the Vicar expected me, because there was a kind of vigil I wanted to keep first. I would leave the casket overnight in the church where all the Ashleys had been baptized and married and buried, and where my father's memorial stone would stand with the rest; then in the morning—early, early, when there was no one to see—I would come and scatter his dust. So much I had decided for myself, and it seemed right.

But now that I was here, alone in the dark church, there was no more self-deception possible. I had not come just to keep vigil. I had come for something of my own. I wanted, with a queer uncomfortable mixture of longing and guilty hope, to try with all the strange power that I knew I had in me, to see if here, in the place where the Ashleys came from and returned to, I could open my mind to whatever message Jonathan Ashley's maimed brain had tried to send me. *"Tell Bryony. Tell her. . . . My little Bryony be careful. Danger."*

When I was halfway up the chancel, I paused. There were ways and ways of trying to talk with the souls of the dead, and here, I knew suddenly, darkness was wrong, smacking of things which a church should not be asked to house. I would light the sanctuary lights. Feeling somehow absolved of what I meant to do, I took the casket up to the altar steps and laid it there. Some faint residue of light from the east window showed the great jar of lilies, ghosts full of fading scent. These, I knew, would have come from the Court. Rob and the Vicar, between them, grew them each year for Easter. . . . Again, familiar as the cot blanket of childhood, the place wrapped itself about me. I stepped back, rehooked the cord across the chancel rail, and went to the vestry where the switches were.

This door, too, was unlocked. I pushed it open, fumbled on the wall beside it, found the switch and pressed. Nothing. I flicked it again. Nothing. Tried the other three on the board, and with each one, nothing.

All this took only a few seconds, but I suppose my mind was preoccupied, so I took in, but failed to register, that the vestry was as airy and as full of tree sounds and rookery sounds as the churchyard itself. Also, that the papers on the Vicar's table were lifting in the light breeze. Even as I noticed them, one or two drifted to the floor. Simultaneously another movement caught my eye, sending the blood out of my heart with a contraction as painful as a blow. The outer door of the vestry stood open, and against the darkness beyond it, another darkness moved. A tall figure, robed. Then the door shut with a click of the Yale lock. The papers subsided with a rustle to the floor. The only sound was the tick of old wood settling in the night, and the chime of the clock in the church tower telling the three-quarters. Only the papers on the floor, barely seen in the dimness, affirmed the truth of what I had seen. The open door, the vanishing figure, seemed no more than the negative of some dream still printed on the retina as one opens one's eyes from sleep.

I swallowed hard, and willed my heartbeats to slow down again. A robed figure in a darkened church? Absurd. They had a word for the silly penny-dreadful, didn't they? Gothic, that was it. Robed nuns and ancient houses and secret passages, the paraphernalia of melodrama that Jane Austen had laughed at in *Northanger Abbey*, and that we had all laughed at when the psychical research people had investigated Rob Granger's specter in this very church. My specter would, of course, be the same as his; any robed figure leaving a church vestry and locking it after him was reasonably likely to be the Vicar. And the dead switchboard? No doubt Mr. Bryanston thought it safer to turn off the mains at night. And probably, I thought, as I reached for the main switch bar, which was certainly up, he would come back when he saw the lights go on.

I had left all the switches on, vestry, chancel, altar floods, organ steps. When I pressed the bar down, the whole east end of the church leaped into light. I stood for a moment, listening, but could hear no sound of returning steps. I picked the papers up from the floor, and took a quick look around the vestry. No sign of any other disturbance. I laid the papers on the table, beside a neat pile of books that looked like parish registers, and weighted them with an ink bottle. They were accounts, I noticed; no doubt parish accounts left here for the next council meeting. I waited for a little longer, listening, but there was no sound. I switched out all the lights except the altar floods, then made my way back into the dimness at the west end of the nave, and sat down. The lights bloomed softly on blue carpet and bistered lilies and the gilded heads of the angels that held the hammer-beams. Slowly, the silence settled back like dust.

There are parts of one's life that are, and ought to remain, private. What passed then between me and whatever else was to be spoken with in the dark of All Hallows' Church is my affair. I believe I had had some idea that trying to open my mind's powers here would sanction the act, but the Hallows themselves apparently didn't see it like that. In the way I had known it before, in the way I wanted it now, nothing came; nothing but silence.

Till, just as I got to my feet and started for the vestry to put out the light, the vestry door opened and a robed figure entered the church.

The Vicar. As I had thought, the Vicar, a prosaic figure in his cassock, with his spectacles glinting in the light. It didn't stop me jumping half out of my skin before I registered who it was and went sheepishly to meet him.

"My dear child! It's you! I understood you were coming over in the morning. I saw the light just now when I went into my study, and came across to see who it was. Did I frighten you?"

"You did give me a start. I'm sorry I dragged you out again, Mr. Bryanston. I hope you don't mind my coming here this evening? I'm coming back in the morning, as I told you, but I—I wanted to leave the casket here overnight. I was going to call and tell you, before I went back to Worcester. Do you mind?"

"Of course not. Come whenever you like, the church is never locked."

He took his spectacles off and began absently to polish them on his cassock sleeve. He was a man comfortably into his middle sixties, with curly gray hair thinning back from a high forehead, a rounded face with the fresh skin of a child, a long upper lip and a habit of looking over his spectacles down the arch of his nose. He had longsighted gray eyes distorted by the thick lenses of his gold-rimmed glasses. He had been at Ashley as long as I could remember. He was a widower and, it was hinted, lived a good deal more peacefully since the departure to a better world of his ambitious and lively wife. Mrs. Bryanston had seen Ashley merely as a stepping-stone to preferment and a town living or a place in the Close, and thither, with the relentless efficiency of an earthmover, she would have transferred her gentle husband, who asked nothing better from life than what he found at Ashley and his other parishes of One Ash and Hangman's End. But fifteen years ago he had buried her in the churchyard, and now he would no doubt be a peaceful permanency, plodding happily from church to garden and back again, gently delivering Sunday after Sunday an address from notes on suspiciously yellowed pages, and keeping the whole parish supplied with seedlings grown in the Court gardens, of which he had the run. He and my father had got on very well together; they seldom discussed anything more spiritual than chess, but I had heard Daddy say that Mr. Bryanston's faith was the kind of rock on which any Church could be built. At any rate, the Vicar suited Ashley as well as Ashley suited him.

He was talking now to me, with an ease quite unlike Mr. Emerson's hesitant kindness, about my father's death. Comfort, you might say, was his profession, but he had a way of offering it, not as if it were his daily stock-in-trade, but as if he really cared, not only about my father, which I knew, but about me. To me—as indeed it had been to Daddy—churchgoing had always been so much a part of country life that it was something one never even thought about, as much a part of Sunday's order of the day as the ritual sherry before lunch (which also invariably included the Vicar); the Church's feast days and holy days were ways to chalk the year off on the calendar, so that Michaelmas was the time of bonfire smoke and purple flowers and getting one's woollies out again, and Easter was lilies and spring cleaning, and Lady Day was high time to prune the roses. But now, coming with trouble in my hands, I saw a little of what was behind the sober yearly ritual. There were things one grew away from and, I knew, would never again see one's way to believing, but I listened and felt the better for knowing that the Vicar believed as literally as might be in the resurrection of the dead.

"You said you were going back into Worcester for the night?" he asked finally.

"Yes, but I'll be here again in the morning. I'll come first thing, so that I won't get in anyone's way."

"You won't do that, my dear. Come as early as you wish; you'll want the world to yourself, I have no doubt." He fished a thin old half hunter out of a pocket and peered at it. "Dear me, you've just missed a bus. I shouldn't have kept you so long . . . the next one doesn't go for an hour and a half. Perhaps you'd like to come across to the Vicarage? I don't know what Mrs. Henderson has left for my supper, but no doubt we could stretch it a little."

"That's awfully good of you, but no, thank you, Vicar. I wasn't planning to catch the bus anyway; my Lambretta's at the farm, and I'm going across to get it now. They've got it stored for me in the barn there."

"Ah. Well, take care. The roads get busier every day, and it's dark already. Dear me, and it will soon be summer, will it not? If you see Rob will you tell him that I'll be down in the old orchard tomorrow, not in the greenhouse? I must finish the spraying before it's too late."

"Of course. Well, thank you for everything, Vicar. I'll go out by the south door. If you want to put the main switch off again, don't wait for me. I can see quite well."

"Main switch?" He looked about him vaguely, as if the thing should be to hand. "What do you mean? Why should I put if off?"

"I thought you had, just before I got here. You mean it wasn't you who was in the church when I arrived?"

"Certainly not. I haven't been over here since about three o'clock. When was this?"

"About an hour ago, I suppose. I came in the south door and went up to the vestry to put on the altar lights. The main switch was off, and there was someone just leaving. I didn't see who it was, but I thought it must be you."

He was looking puzzled. "No. It might have been one of the churchwardens, I suppose, but why should he turn the mains off? How very extraordinary. I suppose you're quite sure the main *was* off?"

"Certain. And there's another thing I'm sure of: if it wasn't you in the vestry, then whoever was there didn't want to be seen. I've a feeling he threw the switch when he heard me at the door, to give himself time to get out and away without being recognized. I thought it was you because you're the most likely person, and besides, I think he was wearing something long, like a cassock. You haven't suddenly acquired a curate, have you?"

"No, alas. I suppose it might have been one of the choir men, coming back to pick up something he'd forgotten after service yesterday. . . . But why should he be wearing his cassock, and why turn out the light? It would hardly have mattered if either you or I had seen him."

"I may have been wrong about the robe. It really was only an impression; it was pretty dark. Perhaps it was just one of the churchwardens. He was carrying something—I'm quite sure of that."

"What sort of thing?"

"It's hard to say. A box, perhaps, or it could have been a book, about the size of those registers on the table."

"I can't see any reason why one of the wardens should come for them. They're not the Ashley registers. I only brought them over from One Ash after Evensong yesterday. I promised to do a search for a Canadian who wrote to me about his forebears, but I have not had time to look at them yet. . . . And there again, the main switch, I really cannot see why . . . Dear me, it's beginning to look like a real mystery, isn't it?"

He was looking so worried that I tried quickly to reassure him. "I don't suppose it's anything at all, really. I may easily have been mistaken."

"Let us hope so, my dear, let us hope so. All the same"—turning decisively back to the vestry—"I'd better take a look to see if anything has been touched. The church safe . . . perhaps it could be a temptation. But surely, no one at Ashley . . ."

He paused in the doorway of the vestry and looked carefully about him.

"I had a look round when I put the light on." I spoke from behind him, looking over his shoulder. "It all looked tidy except for those papers, and some of them were on the floor. But that was the draft from the door. I put them back, but you'll probably find them out of order."

"No matter, no matter." He went to the table and glanced through them. "All here. And the registers, too . . . eleven, was it, or twelve? There were some from Hangman's End, as well. I shall have to check them. But really, there is nothing there of interest to anyone. And nothing else even disturbed. The cupboard . . . yes, that's all right. And there was nothing in this drawer but pencils and so on, and there is my spare cassock still hanging by the door, so that was not what you saw. . . ."

He turned finally, with reluctance, to look at the safe. "Well, let us hope not. . . ."

But when he stooped over the big clumsy metal cupboard the look of anxiety deepened. I saw him fingering some scratches near the lock. "These, would you say they look new? It's so hard to tell. Unless something happens like this to make you look closely, you don't notice the marks that your own keys make every day. I'm afraid we had better look inside." He reached into his cassock pocket and pulled out a ring of keys.

"I suppose you keep the Communion plate in the safe," I said. "Anything else?"

"Nothing that anyone might want to steal. Only our own registers. And the Communion plate itself is of very little value—though value, as always, is relative. The plate we use now is quite modern, as you probably know; it was your father who suggested that we lodge the old plate in a safer place than this, when the prices went up so steeply, though I doubt if anyone else would have realized how very valuable the old church silver was. Did you know that the chalice and paten were Elizabethan, by John Pikenynge, and the alms dish even rarer? 1534, I believe, with the marker's mark of a basket. The ones we use now, though pleasant enough, are not—Ah," as the safe door swung open, "thank God."

He said it as if he meant it. I was looking over his shoulder. It certainly looked as if nothing had been touched. The back of the safe was stacked with registers, and some baize-wrapped shapes stood in line in front of these. "Exactly as I always put them," said the Vicar, counting. "Yes, yes, all present and correct. He didn't try the safe at all, or else he found the lock too much for him. I prefer to think—I do think—that his visit was an innocent one. Yes, indeed, that is almost certainly so. We live in sad times when one can entertain suspicions on such slender grounds." He shut the safe, locked it, and got to his feet. "However, this is a lesson to me. I cannot bring myself to lock the church, but perhaps I will— yes, I think I must—lock the vestry. And I shall do so straight away. There. Perhaps you'll come out this way after all. . . . Dear me, it's really quite dark now, isn't it? Can you see your way to the farm?"

"Yes, thank you. And don't worry about it, Vicar, I'm sure you'll find it was one of the wardens, or someone quite harmless like that. May I come and see you in the morning? If you're in the apple orchard, I'll see you anyway, when I go to the cottage. I'm moving in tomorrow. I'll give Rob your message."

"Thank you, my dear. God bless you. Good night."

Ashley, 1835

Seeming a long way off, the church clock chimed the three-quarters. He glanced at the gilt carriage clock on the bed table. It was fast. Five minutes.

He fidgeted about the room, fretting like a spurred horse. His foot struck one of his father's books, lying with the papers, where it had fallen. He stooped, and began mechanically to collect the scattered things together. The book, lying spine uppermost, showed the name *Juliet*, glinting in gold. He slapped it shut, and, straightening, stuffed book and papers together in the table drawer, and shut it.

The sound was sharp, final. The old man was dead. His father was dead. He was Ashley now, Nicholas Ashley, Esquire, of the Court. Now, he thought, it will soon be over and done with. If each of us, in our own ways, can find the courage.

But habit made him twitch the curtains closer over the shuttered windows, to hide even a glimpse of the candlelight.

5

O Lord! I could have stay'd here all the night
To hear good counsel. . . .

—*Romeo and Juliet*, III, iii

THE BUILDINGS of what had once been a fine home farm lay about a hundred and fifty yards beyond the churchyard. The quickest way to get there from the church was by the lych-gate, and through a corner of the Court gardens. I made my way carefully along the pitch-dark tunnel of the yew walk. I was conscious of my empty hands. The black yews smelled unbearably sad, sharp and smoky; frankincense and myrrh, memory and grief.

I would not think that way. I would not.

The Yew alone burns lamps of peace
For them that lie forlorn.

That was the way to think of them. Peace I had had offered to me, and loss was not yet. This was still my home, and it still held what I had come here to find.

I went slowly down the muffled path toward the gate. The shadows of home reached out for me, comforting me, closing me round.

So, at the same moment, in the same shadows, did my lover. He was here. He was here in the cool night, stronger and closer than at any time since I had left Ashley. Every shade of feeling came, direct as if spoken, strong as the scent of the breeze sieving the yew trees. There was welcome, pleasure, and with it all a kind of apprehension. I paused to identify this, and unbelievingly registered it as guilt, or shame. . . .

I had just reached the lych-gate. The darkness here, cast by the roof, was palpable. I paused, groping before me for the latch of the gate. Guilt or shame? From him? From me he must have been getting a mixture almost as confusing: surprise, questioning, reassurance making it clear that whatever it was, I was with him, and part of it. . . .

My hand, groping in the dark, touched cloth. For one wild, heart-stopping moment I thought he was here, and that I had touched his sleeve. Then through the loose folds I felt the wood of the gate. Some garment or rug had been left there, draped over the top bar. My brain identified it even before my fingers had felt the ribbed silky surface, the weight of the cloth. A cassock. The robe I had seen him wearing, flung down here as he left the churchyard . . . Guilt and shame indeed. The kind of thing he might be feeling if he had recently been in the vestry, trying locks he should not have tried, carrying away things he did not want anyone to see?

What is it? Was it you in the church? I asked the question sharply, but got no reply. The patterns were fading. He was moving away.

At the same moment I heard, close at hand, steps going fast through the graveyard grass, away from me. He must have been standing all this while, motionless, on the other side of the wall of yew.

Lover? Lover!

He ignored me. The steps quickened. I heard the faint *ping* and thrill of the wire that crossed a gap in the broken wall between the churchyard and the Court gardens. Beyond the gap was the tangle of a neglected shrubbery, and a door into the old, high-walled garden where the glasshouses were. And now, faintly behind the black of the trees, I saw the light slacken into silver. The moon was rising. In a moment she would be above the trees, and there would be light enough to see.

Near me was a gap between the yews. I thrust through it, and ran across the grave-humped grass. I knew every tombstone, and its name, as well as I knew the books in the schoolroom shelves. The dead would not mind my step; we had known each other a long time. I reached the gap in the wall just as the moon showed enough to send a gleam along the wire. I laid a hand to it; it was humming still. I clambered through into the whippy undergrowth of the shrubbery. Elderberry and ash saplings, raspberry canes gone wild, ivy trailing snares along the ground, and somewhere the peppery sweetness of lad's-love. Nettles, too, knee high. I swore under my breath, and plunged forward onto the trodden twist of moss that was the path to the walled garden. The gate in the high wall stood ajar, and there was moonlight on the apple trees beyond. I ran through, and paused at the head of the shallow, slippery steps.

Across the center of the garden, from east gate to west, ran a wide avenue of apple trees, espaliered with stretched arms like stiff ranks holding hands. The moon, sailing as swiftly as a galleon with a fair breeze, cleared a beech tree to light the ranked blossoms, and between them the empty pathway hatched with their shadows. Nothing moved, except the boughs of the high trees beyond the wall, shifting in the light wind and sending dark and glitter flying across the glasshouse roofs.

Then I saw him, for the second time that night, still no more than a tall shadow melting into the other shadows. He, too, had paused. He was standing in the shelter of the far gate. Beyond him lay the old rose garden, and then the maze, and the apple orchard where my cottage stood, and the water meadows beyond the Pool, where the field path led to the village.

I hesitated. He must know who was pursuing him. If he wanted me, he had only to wait for me. In fact—I realized it now—he *had* waited for me. I had been a long time in the church. He could not have failed to catch my response to him, back there at the lych-gate, and now, standing as I was full in the moonlight, he must see me and know I had followed him.

He was looking, I was certain of it. I heard the creak of the gate opening in the far wall, and then the pause. I stood getting my breath and trying to open my mind to reach him again. But nothing came except that muddled mixture of exhilaration and amazement and guilt. I wondered again, but this time wholly without blame, what he had been doing in the church. Whatever it was, I was with him; I had to be. I sent him all I had of love, and need and longing, and got the answer, more clearly even than the wind across the trees. *Not yet. Trust me. Not yet.* There was another creak as the garden gate shut fast. The latch dropped. I was alone in the garden.

I trudged back the way I had come, and, regaining the churchyard, went by the normal route to the farm.

The darkness hid the dilapidation of the big farmyard. Barns and sheds lay on the left, and on the other side the chimney stacks of the farmhouse stood up into the moonlight. The house had been empty ever since the farmlands, which were not part of the trust, were sold. The farmer who had bought the land had not found it worth his while to repair the house, which had stood empty now for years; it was used as a storehouse and even, occasionally, to house young stock. The hens roosted there, and pigeons nested in the attics. Adjoining it, and in heartening contrast, were the two farm cottages, which still belonged to Ashley. These showed whitewashed walls reflecting the moonlight, and brightly lit windows with gay curtains.

In the cottage nearest to the farmhouse the Hendersons lived; Mr. Henderson, a man well into his sixties, was sexton and gravedigger to Ashley and One Ash; his wife "did for" the Vicar, and obliged at the Court when asked. She also cleaned and mended for Rob Granger, who lived in the other cottage. When I was a child the Grangers had lived at the big farmhouse, but a couple of years after Mr. Granger's death, when the farm was sold, Rob and his mother moved into the cottage. Mrs. Granger herself had died not long after, and now Rob lived alone.

As I crossed the yard the door of his cottage opened, and he peered out, silhouetted against the light.

"That you, Miss Bryony?"

"Oh, Rob, hullo! How nice to see you again. Yes, it's me. How did you guess?"

"Well, I reckoned you'd be coming across for the bike. I knew you were here. I saw you come out of the church. You went after him, did you?"

I stopped dead. "You were there? Do you mean to tell me you saw him?"

"I did. Quick as a hare out of the vestry door and behind the yew walk. He stood there the best part of an hour."

"You actually *watched* him?"

"Aye, I did."

"And you didn't ask him what he was doing?"

"I didn't rightly like to, seeing who it was."

There was a pause of seconds. At the moment when it would have been remarkable, I asked: "Well, who was it?"

He looked surprised. "You didn't talk to him, then? I made sure he was waiting for you."

"Apparently not. Who was it?"

Something, in spite of me, must have come through my voice. He said quickly: "You've no call to worry. It was only your cousin. One of them, that is. I couldn't tell for sure, not in that light, or lack of it. But an Ashley; I couldn't mistake that."

"Then why did you stay to watch him?"

"I don't rightly know." He showed no resentment at the rather sharp question. "The way he came running out of the vestry . . . I didn't recognize him at first, so I went up, careful, under the bushes by the wall, where I could see. I saw the church lights go on then, for a minute, and saw it was one of the Ashleys. I guessed that it might be you in the church. Then the main lights went off again, but you didn't come out."

"No," I said. "I—I wanted the dark."

"I guessed that. And I think he did, too. He stayed there, waiting for you."

I said nothing. I was fighting back disappointment so acute that I was afraid he would notice it. I stood looking down, uncertain what to say next. I had quite forgotten my errand to the farm.

"Won't you come in?" said Rob. "No sense in standing out in the yard. Come in now, do."

He stood back in the doorway to let me through. I went into the kitchen where, it was obvious, he had just been about to cook his supper. There was a place set for one at the table, and beside the stove were a pack of sausages and some tomatoes, with a packet of peas defrosting in the warmth.

I checked. "I'm afraid I've come at a bad time."

He went past me and threw a couple of billets of wood on the fire, then hooked a foot round the leg of a chair and hitched it forward.

"You haven't at all. I've got your bike here for you; it's not in the barn; I brought it into the scullery. And I got a can of petrol for it. It'll not take a minute to fill up and get it ready. But look, why don't you stay a bit first? I was just making a bite of supper, and you're welcome to have some. There's plenty. It's only sausages, dead easy if it suits you."

Since I had obviously interrupted his cooking, and just as obviously he wanted his meal before he started getting the bike ready for me, I accepted. "I'd love that. Look, I'll cook while you set for me, shall I?"

"O.K. Want some chips with it?"

"Yes, please."

Mrs. Henderson had left her apron hanging behind the door. I put it on, and busied myself at the stove. I got the grill going, and laid the sausages and tomatoes to cook while Rob took things from drawers and cupboards, and, neat-handed as a sailor for all his size, laid the extra place and sliced some bread and tipped another helping of frozen chips into the frying basket. There was no question of looking out the best china for Miss Bryony; I had been an intimate of the Granger household all my life, and had taken things just as they came. Fish and chips straight from the newspaper, and yellow shop cakes with marshmallow cream, had been the "tea at Mrs. Granger's" treat of my childhood. I watched Rob set the knife and fork and find an extra plate to heat, and I felt the blackness of the yew walk, the loss and disappointment, recede from sight. Here, with the bright fire and the tick of the cheap alarm clock, the hiss of frying chips and the smell of sausages, was yet another welcome that Ashley was holding out to me. This, too, was home.

Rob glanced up and caught the tail end of the look, but gave no sign that he understood it. He was a tall young man, big-boned, with big hands and feet and the deceptively slow movements of the countryman. He was very dark, brown as a gypsy, with black hair, and eyes so dark that it was hard to tell iris from pupil, and harder still to read the expression in them. His speech, too, was slow, but the soft country voice and his habit of silent pauses masked a fair intelligence which should have had a better chance to develop. His mother had been the village schoolteacher, a gentle, lonely girl who had fallen for good looks and what she thought of as simple ways, and had married Matt Granger, a handsome lout who first of all neglected, and then frankly ill-used her and her child. I myself as a child had never realized why little Robbie, as he was called then, had sometimes stayed off school, or sometimes come with bruises as if he had been fighting. But when Matt Granger tumbled drunk into the Overflow one night and was drowned, Rob took on his father's job of running the home farm with no emotion apparent other than deep satisfaction and relief; and though she said nothing at all, Mrs. Granger, quiet as ever, seemed happier. She died some two years later of a neglected cancer, soon after Rob, for all his struggles, had had to admit defeat over the farm, which his father had run into the ground and deep into debt. My father, having sold the land, invited Rob to stay on as caretaker and man-of-all-work around the Court. It was something of a surprise to everyone when Rob, who understandably enough had never been devoted to Ashley, and who might have done better for himself elsewhere, accepted and stayed.

He came to my elbow, watching as I turned the sausages under the grill. "Shall I do those now?"

"It's all right. Nearly done."

"I'm sorry about your dad."

"Thank you. I brought his ashes home, did you know? That's why I came tonight. I wanted to put them in the church. Did the Vicar tell you?"

"No."

"I'm coming back in the morning to—well, to scatter them."

He had lifted the pan of peas off the stove, and was busy draining them. He added a knob of margarine and shook them to dry in the hot pan. He said nothing.

"Rob—"

"Mm?"

"You're sure you couldn't even make a guess?"

He must after all have sensed my trouble, back there in the yard. He didn't ask me what I was referring to, nor did he lift his eyes from the peas. He shook the pan thoughtfully. "If I had to, I'd have said it was one of the twins, but you know yourself they're bad enough to tell apart in daylight, let alone a black evening like this."

"Could it have been Francis?"

"Might have been, I suppose. But I'd have thought he was a mite too tall for Francis."

"But it could have been?"

He did look up at that. "I suppose so. Why, were you expecting Francis?"

"No. But if it wasn't Francis, it would have to be Emory, and—"

I stopped. I had never taken it further, even to myself, and I certainly could not do so to Rob. It could not be Emory, the secret friend with whom I had shared my thoughts since childhood. It could not. If it had to be one of those two, it must surely be Francis . . . Francis, who was nearer my own age, and of whom— where one could touch that elusive and self-contained personality—I was unequivocally fond. Emory, the eldest of the three, was, as they say, something else again. I had never had any illusions about Emory. As a child, of course, I had adored my tall cousin, so easily dominating the rest of us, but generous about allowing a small girl to tag along where he led the Ashley gang. He had grown into a tough-minded man, determined, and quietly self-sufficient. James, his twin, had a touch of the same ruthlessness, but tempered with something less aggressive. Francis, as tough in his own way and very much quieter about it, had opted out of most of our ploys and gone doggedly on with his own affairs. A loner, my cousin Francis. But then, I supposed, that was what writers had to be. And surely, if it were he, I would have had a hint of it from him . . . ?

Francis or Emory . . . But, in spite of the knowledge, I found myself thinking about James as I had last seen him.

An Ashley to the fine bone; tall, with fair hair which had darkened slightly—to his relief—as he grew older. The long gray eyes of all the portraits, straight nose, hands and feet too small-boned but well shaped. Pleasant voice. A way of doing what he wanted, and doing it so charmingly that you overlooked the self-interest and thought he was doing you a favor. Clever, yes; shrewd, yes; not perhaps over-imaginative about other people's needs, but kind, and capable of great generosity. About his attitude to women, or his relationships with them, I knew nothing.

I had my mother to thank that I was able to be so objective about my father's family. She had been a highly intelligent, incisive woman, who had written a couple of novels that had dropped dead on the market, but that had contained a good deal of quiet but acid observation of the people around her. It was she who had taught me to stand back sometimes from life and look at it, even to stand back from those I loved.

Certainly from those I thought I might love. Which brought me back to my troubled thoughts, and the cottage kitchen, and Rob saying: "Why should it?"

"Why should it what?"

"Be Emory?"

I must have looked quite blank. He said patiently: "In the churchyard."

"Oh. Because James is in Spain, and Emory's over here. He rang up from England on Wednesday, when I was in Bavaria. Look, Rob, the chips are done, can you strain them?"

"Sure." He lifted the pan over to the draining board. "Well, then, say it was Emory. Seems funny he didn't want to see you."

"Maybe. Rob, you said you saw him coming out of the vestry. Did you see when he went in?"

"No. I was down shutting up the greenhouses, you see, and when I came back

I heard the dogs barking, so I took a look around, and I saw the vestry door was standing open. I didn't think it could be the Vicar—for one thing the dogs wouldn't bark for him; then I saw whoever it was was using a flashlight, so I waited to see him. I thought it might be some of the village boys out for a lark. Then I saw you going into the porch." He grinned. "Say this for you, Bryony, you don't make more noise than a bitch fox. Remember when I used to take you poaching? I never heard you till you came right up to the church door."

"Then?"

"I'd half a mind to follow you in, in case there was something wrong, but then the flashlight went out and I saw this chap coming out of the vestry, sharpish, and bolting away across the graveyard. I'd have followed him, only I saw it was one of the Ashleys. And he didn't run far; stopped right by the yew trees, and waited. I reckoned he was waiting for you. He was out of sight of me there, but I'd have seen him if he'd moved. I hung around and watched, just in case. . . . Then the Vicar came down, and went into the vestry, but the chap didn't budge. Did he see you, do you suppose?"

"I think so. If not then, he must have seen me later in the kitchen garden. The moon was quite bright."

I spoke flatly, with my back to him, but I felt him pause. Then he said: "Well, when he bolted across the wire I came home. It was no business of mine, and he didn't mean you harm, that was obvious. What was he at in the vestry, do you think? It seems funny, bolting away like that when he must have known it was only you."

"Yes, doesn't it?"

"There's another queer thing, he had a long coat on or something. Does Emory wear a cloak? Someone told me they were all the fashion now in London."

"I don't think so." I hesitated. "Actually, Rob, he'd taken a cassock from the church. It must have been one of the choir men's—the Vicar's spare one was still there. He must have snatched it up when he heard me. Don't ask me why, I've no idea. He left it under the lych-gate."

"Funny thing to do."

"You're telling me. Did you see what he was carrying?"

"No," he said. "Look, those sausages are done."

"So they are. Can you eat four? Not too many chips for me, thanks. Oh, before I forget, the Vicar told me to tell you he won't be in the greenhouses tomorrow, he's going down to the old orchard. What are you doing down there?"

"Spraying the trees, and tidying up a bit. Things that should have got done this winter past, but there wasn't time, with all Mr. Underhill wanted doing about the house. But now, with you coming back . . . are you coming to the cottage?"

"I think I might, for a bit anyway."

"Moving in tomorrow?"

"Yes. I thought I might see Mrs. Henderson and ask her to get things aired for me."

"You don't need to bother. It's done." He grinned at my look. "We thought you'd be back soon, and when the Vicar told us you were coming over tomorrow we got the cottage opened up. So you can settle straight in anytime you like."

For some absurd reason I felt the tears sting suddenly behind my eyes. He could not have seen, because I had my back turned to him still, but he said, just behind me: "You've given me too many sausages. Divide them properly. The kettle's boiling; will you have tea or coffee?"

"Coffee, please. I only want two sausages, honestly. Are they from Roper's? Their sausages were always the best."

"Aye." He spooned Nescafé from the jar and made two cups. "Remember the sausage rolls we used to get at Goode's stall on a Saturday?"

"Do I not! Here, then, let's start."

Over the meal we talked easily, he of the Court and the Underhills, and of his girl who belonged to Ashley and whom he meant to marry before the year was out; I of Madeira and Bavaria and then, irresistibly unloading it all, of the accident, and the puzzle of my father's final message.

"Rob, does the phrase 'William's brook' mean anything to you?"

"William's what?"

"I think it was 'William's brook.'"

He shook his head. "Uh-uh. Never heard of it that I can remember."

"Could it be the Overflow?"

"I never heard it called anything else but that, did you?"

"No. I only asked because I'd wondered if Daddy meant you when he said, 'Perhaps the boy knows.'" I sighed a little and pushed my plate away. "That was fine. Thanks very much, Rob."

"You're welcome." He got up and began stacking the plates. "Shall I fix your bike for you now?"

"If you would. I'll wash up while you do it."

"O.K." Then, easily: "Where are you putting your dad's ashes? In the enclosure?"

He might have been saying something about the washing up. I found it oddly comforting. Family talk; as familiar as with my own cousins, and without the constraints that I had, for obvious reasons, felt there sometimes.

"No, he didn't want that. Too much like putting fences round him, he said." The enclosure was the Ashley grave plot, where, within the iron railings, the family had lain since the Giles Ashley who had died in 1647. "He said he'd had enough of that when he was a prisoner of war; he wanted the open air. So I'll be coming back in the morning, very early, before there's anyone about."

"I'll be about, very likely, but I'll not disturb you. If you want breakfast when you've done, I'll be frying up at about seven o'clock. You can go down to the cottage after. I'll take your things along. Suit you?"

"Suits me."

He disappeared whistling towards the scullery, and I began to carry the dishes over to the sink.

Ashley, 1835

Surely she was not often as late as this?

The sane part of him insisted that she was. There had been nights when she had been prevented from coming at all, and he had waited all night long in this fret and torment, raw with longing, only to rant and curse at her when, the next night, braving who knew what rough perils from her family and the village see-alls, she came again.

He spared a thought for her, hurrying to him through the windy dark, wrapped in her old cloak, the maze key clutched in her hand. "The key to heaven," she had called it, and he had not laughed at her for the phrase as he might have done, my God, yes, even a month ago. He had had to bite his lips to stop himself saying, "The key to my heart."

That had been when he first knew for sure. She was the one. Of all of them, she was the one.

6

With tears augmenting the fresh morning's dew. . . .

            —*Romeo and Juliet,* I, i

FIVE O'CLOCK in the morning. England in May. The time they always used to sing about. And well they might, I thought, buzzing along the country roads on the Lambretta with the early sun brilliant on the wet hedgerows, and the meadow grasses furred with dew as thick as hoarfrost. Heaven knew when last I had been out so early; I had forgotten the light, the sweetness of the air, the newly washed smell of everything, the fat lambs' calling, the thrushes going wild in the hawthorns. Forgotten the hawthorns themselves, frothing with maybloom along the road, with cowslips and cuckooflowers almost hiding the hedge bottoms. Forgotten the cuckoo, shouting in the echoing distance. Forgotten, even, the other preoccupation that went with me.

But here he was, crowding me. *Hullo,* I said, but gaily, without anxiety. *Shall I see you today? Shall I see you today?*

I wouldn't be surprised, said he, and the doors slowly closed between us like a cloud drawing over the sun.

There was no sign of life from the Court. Curtains hung close over the windows. On the moat the swans sailed with their six gray young, and a blue heron fished busily for roach. The air was pure and very still.

I took an hour, alone in the great neglected gardens. The swans cruised unheeding, the heron fished on. The rabbits in the orchard sat bolt upright to watch me, their fur outlined with light and their pricked ears as transparent as shells. The beautiful old house dreamed above its reflection, rose-red brick and glittering windows mirrored in the still moat, and moving faintly in the wake of the swans. Not mine, I thought; never mine again. All that had vanished, blown away on the sweet morning air with Jon Ashley's dust. *Hic manet.* Here lies he where he longed to be. And where shall I lie? Shall I be brought back here one day, to become, however insubstantially, part of this garden and this glimmering air? And who will bring me?

I walked for an hour, but nothing spoke and no one came.

There were bacon and eggs for breakfast, and fresh bread baked by Mrs. Henderson. Sunshine poured into the cottage kitchen. Last night's fire had been cleaned out and relaid, and the room was neat as a ship's galley.

"You do yourself well," I told Rob Granger. "She'll be lucky. Do I know her, by the way?"

"I doubt it. She's a kind of cousin; used to live near Ashley Village, but her folks moved away. She'll be back soon, then we'll be making plans."

"Well," I said, "tell her from me that she's on to a good thing."

He grinned, and said, "Oh, she knows," and cut a couple of slices off the loaf. "Honey?"

"Thanks." And not just with the cooking, I thought, as I spread honey on the lovely, crusty bread. There was something solidly dependable about him, a kind of inbuilt strength; the sense that day-to-day frets would pass him by like the rain driving against a tree. Not a man to hurry; he looked, and was (as I remembered from childhood squabbles), as obstinate as a mule, and apparently as set in his ways as a plough horse that knows no other job. His ease of manner with me came from long acquaintance, but it came also from a self-confidence that was part of him; not the kind of confidence that was bred into my elegant Ashley cousins, but something hacked out of a hard life, as a fluid line of sculpture is in time hacked out of hardstone. Yes, she would be lucky; it was to be hoped, for my cousins' sake, that she would be content to stay at Ashley, and not persuade Rob to leave.

I said something of the sort, but he merely made a noncommittal sound through a mouthful of bread and honey, then said, as soon as he could: "It'll be strange, with Mr. Howard here. I can't imagine it, somehow. Will you stay, yourself?"

"I don't know. I suppose I shall, for the time being. I really haven't got round to deciding anything yet."

"Mm. I dare say there's no hurry. These things always take a long time to settle, and the way the Court's tied up, it could take years."

"Is that supposed to be comforting?"

"It comforts me," said Rob. "Give everyone time to get used to the idea. It won't seem the same without Mr. Ashley . . . and without you."

He spoke so simply that I took it straight, as a fact and not a compliment. "It comforts me, too. I somehow can't take it all in. Not quite yet."

"Well," he said, "don't try. There's plenty of time. And maybe Mr. Howard won't want to come here at all." He grinned. "Mind you, everyone in the village is wild to see his wife. I don't know what they think a Mexican is like, but I know Miss Marget was talking about totem poles, and Mrs. Henderson told me that Mrs. Gray—you know, the head of the Mothers' Union—made a speech last week about race relations and the color bar. Very broad-minded, she was, I believe."

I laughed. "Actually, she's pure Spanish, and from her photos, rather gorgeous. But I must admit I can't quite see her—either of them—settling here."

"Then it'll be Emory's? Seems funny, doesn't it," said Rob slowly, "that James loses all that by about twenty or thirty minutes? Must be queer to be a twin."

"Very, I should think. But I don't know if James counts it as 'losing.' There's no money here, Rob. The place is lovely, but very soon now there'll be a time when no one can keep it."

"So I reckon. But wouldn't you have thought the National Trust, or someone like that, would have taken it on? I mean, a place like this, that historians and such go wild about . . . ?"

"The National Trust won't take any property over unless it's endowed, and how would we manage that? I know Daddy tried everything and everybody. I think in the long run that someone—some body like the Pilgrim Trust, or even the Department of the Environment—would step in to preserve the house, but I doubt if they'd ever bother with the gardens and the land. That's bound to go, history or no history."

"Well," he said, "don't get me wrong, but it looks to me as if you'll be thankful yet that it's not your headache."

"I'm sure you're right. To start with, it'll be Mr. Emerson's, poor man. He'll have to sort out all the legal tangles—what he calls the dead man's hand."

"Dead man's hand?" Rob looked faintly shocked, and I paused in surprise, then realized that he must think the lawyer was referring to my father.

"I only meant the trust. . . . You seemed to know how the place was tied up? He meant my umpteenth great-grandfather, the one who created the trust, reaching from the grave to make things awkward for all of us."

"Oh, aye, I get it. Your dad did talk about it once. You all have to consent before you can sell anything, isn't that it?" He pondered it for a minute. "Could be awkward, yes, but he meant well, and it seems to me he's maybe made things a mite safer for you, the way it's turned out. I mean, they can't sell your cottage over your head, even if they want to."

"They couldn't anyway," I told him. "All the bit they call the 'cottage strip'—the old orchard, and the strip of land along the Pool as far as the One Ash road—none of that's included in the trust. It was all Daddy could leave me, but it's mine."

He was looking very thoughtful. "If they did want to break the trust, and sell the rest up, would you consent to it?"

"That would depend. We might have to sell the land, to endow the house. I know that Daddy had that on his mind. But I'm not quite sure what it would mean to you, for instance, and to the Hendersons. We didn't get as far as discussing that." I looked at him. "If the trust were broken, Rob, what would happen to you? Would you be able to buy this house for yourself?"

"I don't think so, but then I mightn't want to stay. You don't need to bother yourself about that. You've enough to think about for yourself." He straightened in his chair. "Anyway, this isn't just the morning to talk about the future. I shouldn't have asked you about your plans; I'm sorry. But, you know, once all this, your dad and everything—once it's gone a bit into the background, and once you've found out what he wanted you to find out, it'll all settle itself. It'll work out, believe me it will. Only, you've got to let it take its time."

I nodded, and finished my tea, soothed by his country common-sense. Time; there was always time in the country. Leave things to themselves, and they grew, and ripened, and were cut down, all in the right seasons. Now, it seemed, was the fallow time. "Well," I said, "we'll give it a chance to work out. I'm certainly in no fit state of mind to make decisions. I've got to get all the complicated legal stuff settled first, and by the time the mills of God have ground all the facts to a powder I'll have sorted myself out, too—or perhaps it'll be decided for me. But there is something I can do straight away. I can have a look for the paper my father spoke of, and try to find out what he meant; if there's something he wants me to do. I'll have to get into the Court to do that. I've got my own key to the east door, but I expect all the rooms are locked on the public side, aren't they? I don't want to explain myself to the Underhills yet. I suppose you've no idea who has the main house keys?"

"Yes," said Rob. "I have."

As easy as that. *"You* have?"

He nodded. "Your dad gave them to me before he went to Germany. Didn't you know? Mr. Underhill's got the other set, all the public rooms as well as their own; they have to have them because of fire, and because of the quarter-pounders"—this was our private name for the tourists who paid twenty-five pence each—"but your dad told me he'd given the private keys off that set to Mr. Emerson. He left his own lot with me."

"Well!" I said with relief. "There's an end to *that* mystery! You've no idea what mayhem Mr. Emerson and I were picturing! I've a feeling he suspected they'd been stolen from Daddy when he was knocked down. Apparently I'm allowed to keep them, officially, till all the legal business is settled."

"You'd better have them now." While I had been speaking he had pulled open a drawer in the dresser, and fished out from somewhere a bunch of keys which I recognized. "Here you are, then. Do you know which is which? They go in order, from here. That's the main door, then the Priest's Parlor, the Council Chamber . . ." He clicked the keys round on the massive ring, like beads on a rosary. "They're in order for the tour. Was there any room you wanted specially?"

"Yes, the library."

He selected a key. "That's it. No, leave those things. Mrs. Henderson will do them. Would you like me to go in with you this morning?"

"No, I don't think so, thanks. I've been thinking, Rob; there'll be quarter-pounders going round today, won't there? If I go in on my own, with keys, someone's sure to see me, and ask questions. I'll leave the keys with you for now, and I'll go round with the tour myself, and just take a look in general, then later on I'll introduce myself to the Underhills, and ask them if I can come and go in the house as I want. What time's the first tour?"

"Half past ten." He dropped the keys back in the drawer, and shut it. No question or comment. "Stay here till then if you like. Or do you want to go down to the cottage this morning?"

"Yes, I'll do that."

"That'll be Mrs. Henderson at the back door now. She'll want a word with you, I dare say. See you later." He smiled and went out.

Mrs. Henderson was small, brisk, and sixtyish, with graying hair "done" each week as unyieldingly and unvaryingly as a metal helmet by "our Eileen" who was the village hairdresser. She had vivid blue eyes and a high patch of color on each cheek, and was as efficient, as quick, and about as silent as a computer in full schedule.

"Well, now, Miss Bryony, it's nice to see you back again, though I'm sorry about your poor dad, I was just saying to the Vicar last week, for all Mr. Ashley's had to go off to that hospital in Germany he didn't look all that ill to me and mark my words, I said, he'll be back here with us sooner than he thinks, but believe you me, Miss Bryony, I never thought my words would come to pass this way, nor that when I saw you back with us it would be just to pass on yourself. And when I say pass on, you know I don't mean what it might look as if I mean, I just mean that everyone knows now that the Court will have to go to Mr. Howard, though folk are wondering, and I know you'll not take it amiss, Miss Bryony, whether Mr. Howard's wife will take to it here, I mean, I'm the last person to have any prejudices at all, and nowadays you daren't even talk about nigger brown any more, dare you, but colored is colored, and she'll have been brought up different to us as like as not, not to mention religion, and that's another thing, coming from where she does she'll be a Catholic, I dare say, and whether Mr. Howard's turned or not, the children will, won't they, and what's the Vicar to do with the church and the living and all, and very funny it would look, wouldn't it, if the next Ashleys had to go all the way to the Catholic church at Hangman's End?''

While she was talking she had taken her apron down and put it on, helped me finish clearing the breakfast things, stacked them, run hot water into the sink, and started to wash up. I found the tea towel and wiped, letting the monologue run over me as I had let it run over me every time I met Mrs. Henderson, even after an absence of less than twenty-four hours. Sooner or later she ran down and stopped for breath, and then from long practice I was adept at picking out the one topic which I might want to pursue; or rather, at ignoring the dozen or so topics I wanted to avoid. I spared a thought for the Vicar and Rob Granger; how, each day, did they cope with this? Then I realized I had seen the answer: the Vicar went down to the greenhouses, and Rob, when she arrived, smiled sweetly and left by the other door.

"Mr. Howard's wife is not colored," I said, "she's Spanish. And if you remember the portrait on the stairs, we've had a Spanish lady here before, and it seemed to work. I'm told Mrs. Howard's very beautiful, and she probably is an R.C., but I doubt very much if they'll come to Ashley. Have you seen my cousin Emory lately? Or Francis?''

But Mrs. Henderson was just as good as I was at fixing on the topics she wanted. "Now you come to mention it, of course I knew about the Spanish lady. There was that song about her, wasn't there? But that was in the days when everybody was Catholics, anyway, so it didn't matter. The Vicar told me. And now I come to think about it it wouldn't be her children that came to Ashley Court, it's Mr. Howard's own. And when I say 'own,' of course I mean—''

"Yes, of course. The twins and Francis. Have any of them been here recently?''

"And of course if Mr. Howard doesn't come back," said Mrs. Henderson, with obvious regret for a rich source of gossip slipping from her grasp, "then it'll be Mr. Emory and his wife, and a very nice girl she is, and everyone says the same, though a bit young for it—''

"What wife?''

"Not for marriage, I don't mean, because nowadays they're ready and willing for anything before they're turned fifteen, though I can't see myself that marriage and a family brings you much except a load of housework and cooking, but they will do it, and I suppose it's nature's way—''

"What wife?''

"What's that, Miss Bryony?''

"I said what wife? You said Mr. Emory and his wife. Is he married?''

She had certainly captured all my attention at last. She shot me a glance of triumph, turned on the hot tap, and held a jug under it to rinse, taking her time. "Well, not yet, but take it from me, it's only a matter of time. It's that Miss Underhill, Cathy her name is. Didn't Rob say?''

"No.''

"If that isn't just like a man. They never take a blind bit of notice of anything that goes on under their noses, more interested in the football pools and the tomatoes down in those greenhouses than in what's happening right here in our village. Now, that's the dishes done. Don't you bother any more, I'll put them away. You don't know where they go.''

"Of course I do. I'll do them. So my cousin Emory's been going out with the Underhill girl? Are they actually engaged?"

She wrung out her dishcloth and draped it over the edge of the draining board, then fished below the sink, brought up a red plastic bucket, and began to fill it with hot water. "I don't know about engaged, they don't call it that now, do they? They go with someone, or they have a steady, or they have a thing going, or they have it off with someone, if I've got that right—"

"I don't think you have, quite, but never mind, I know what you mean. How long has this been going on, and do you really think it's serious?"

"Knowing Mr. Emory, I'd say it was." She turned off the taps and for the first time stopped working and stood looking at me, the bright blue eyes shrewd and quite serious. "You know him, he was always one that knew his own mind and went straight for what he wanted, and pity help anything that stood in his way. Nice about it, oh, yes, of course, being an Ashley, but he gets what he wants."

The smiler with the knife under the cloak. Yes, we could do you down and smile at you with great charm while we did it. It was a useful talent, I supposed. At any rate it had got the Ashleys where they were, and kept them there for a few hundred years. I said: "Is she pretty? Tell me all about her."

She told me, but I wasn't listening. I would meet Cathy Underhill soon enough. I was thinking about my cousin Emory, that determined and clever man. Whatever he wanted to do, he would succeed in. Now, it appeared, he wanted the Underhill girl. If he had picked her and was serious about her, he must count her fortune just as a bonus; he had plenty himself, even though the business in Bristol (which had been very much Emory's pigeon for years) hardly put him in the Underhill bracket. "Never marry money, but go where money is." It was like Emory's hard good sense—the steel-hard Ashley wish for continuity—to marry an asset; and if he was fond of her it was the affection, and not the fortune, that was the bonus.

I was also thinking about my lover. Where did this leave us? And why, for heaven's sake why, could he not be as open with me as I was with him? I was rapidly, I thought, having more than enough of mystery.

Trust me. It came suddenly, clear and close.

Oh, you were reading me, were you? Well, you'll know what I think about you. Where are you?

Not far. It was fading. *Not far.*

Where, though? Here at Ashley?

The faintest quiver of amusement came through, mischief, but with a touch of comfort, like a pat on the shoulder which tells you to relax and it will be all right soon . . .

". . . Going down to the cottage this morning?" Mrs. Henderson was asking.

"Yes. Rob tells me you've opened it up for me already. It's marvelous of you, Mrs. Henderson. Do you mean I can move straight in?"

"Yes, indeed you can. It's all aired and clean, and if it's a matter of stores, groceries and such, I put what I thought you'd need for a start, and there's a list on the kitchen table, and you can pay me when you feel like it. And when I pop down to the village this morning, as I shall have to do, the Vicar being out of butter and self-raising, I'll call at the farm and tell the milk to come, and if I let

Miss Marget at the Post Office know, then you'll be settled in in no time, and very nice it'll be. And the meat comes Tuesdays and Fridays, you'll remember that. I can take any orders you want up at the Vicarage, and pop them down to you—"

I left eventually, overwhelmed with kindness and offers of every sort of help under the sun, and made my way down to the cottage.

The Vicar was in the orchard, spraying the apple trees with fervor and a lavish hand. I could hear him talking busily, but then I saw Rob's dark head some distance off on the far side of a hedge, and realized that the latter could not hear a word. Nor was he meant to. The Vicar was talking to the apple trees. Rob's dog lay near him, head cocked and deeply interested, but when he saw me he got up and came over, tail waving. Neither the Vicar nor Rob seemed to notice me as I crossed the orchard and pushed open the wicket which gave on the cottage garden.

The first thing that struck me was the tidiness. If I had thought about it at all I would have expected the cottage garden to match the outlying parts of the Court gardens for enforced neglect, but this garden was a small marvel of neatness. The two plum trees were pruned and well shaped and budding fatly; the Fribourg rose around the window had been carefully trimmed, and the clematis was a cloud of blossom as high as the roof; the rows of raspberries were as regular as guardsmen, the strawberries were already strawed, and the plots to either side of the path were hoed and raked and planted within an inch of their lives. The path where I stood was clear of weeds, and thickly edged with chives and parsley. The brimming rain barrel below the gutter was painted the same new green as the door, and had a fresh metal ring. The step was clean, and the door open.

Inside was the same; Mrs. Henderson had put all to rights, and it was charming and neat, with a pot of pink geraniums in the window, and the fresh smell of polish everywhere. The box of groceries stood on the kitchen table. Upstairs, I knew, all would be ready for me. I had only to pay my bill at the Hog and Oak, get my things brought over here, and walk in.

Which was no reason why, leaning my elbows on the sill of the dormer window that looked from the bedroom eaves out over the apple trees, I should find myself, for the first time since my father's death, crying helplessly as if there was neither love nor hope left in the world.

Ashley, 1835

My God, he thought. I've forgotten the list. My father was right to rave at me for a vicious libertine. It had seemed amusing, once, to keep a list of them, like the stable books; physical marks, breeding, performance, staying power . . .

And her name on it, too.

I'll burn the list. Not even read it again. I'll burn the books, too, all of them. No more light-o'-loves. She is the last, I promise it. Only let her come tonight.

But something in him, remembering, cast a lingering backward look at the time past, and he felt heavy and full of dread, as if he were signaling in vain across a waste of blowing darkness.

I'll go along, no such sight to be shown,
But to rejoice in splendour of mine own.

—*Romeo and Juliet,* I, ii

TWO BUSLOADS of quarter-pounders were already lining up when I got to the gate. There was a trestle table set up the other side of the bridge, inside the gatehouse, and here a young woman sat taking the money. I had never seen her before, and she obviously did not recognize me. She didn't even give me a glance as I took my ticket, declined to buy a colored brochure on Ashley Court, and wandered out into the sunshine of the courtyard to join the group waiting outside the main door.

The girl from the gatehouse escorted us round. She had read what there was to read, and did her best to make the place come to life.

"This is the Great Hall. It's from Henry the Eighth's time, but there's no record that the King was ever here. You see that little winding stair over there . . . ? It leads to the gallery. When Cardinal Wolsey was a young priest he lived here for a time; he was the family chaplain and had to read aloud to them during meals. I suppose he got his food afterward. . . . Notice the carving on the gallery rail. It's original. But the shield in the center with the crest was added later, in the nineteenth century, when the family took the motto 'Touch Not the Cat but a Glove' from their Scottish connection. You can see the motto again carved on the stone shield above the fireplace. It was William Ashley the author who had the old Tudor chimney-breast taken out and this Gothic one put in. It was much admired. Thomas Lovell Beddoes mentions this room in one of his poems. You'll find it quoted in the brochure. This way, please."

We straggled along after her. It was a comprehensive tour, good value for money. We saw it all. The Tudor parlor where the priest's hole stood open to view, the Council Chamber with the carved ceiling and the coats of arms and the paneling polished like silk; the dining room with the Queen Anne ceiling where the water-light from the moat rocked and rippled as the swans floated by below; the long drawing room with its terrace of narrow lawn and rose-hung parapet edging the drop straight to the moat. We saw the pantries and the stillroom, the cellars, the kitchens with the spits and the vast chimney (we ourselves had done our cooking in one of the pantries); then upstairs to the bedrooms and the gallery, and, at last, the library.

This ran the full length of the north wing of the house. It was a tall room with a heavily corniced ceiling, and pillared Corinthian openings for doors and windows. The walls were completely clothed with shelves, and at intervals shelves stood out from the walls to create bays, each bay a self-contained room in itself, with table and heavy chairs of Spanish leather. Here and there stood glass-topped display tables for more valuable volumes; and in earlier days there had been, one to either side of the fireplace, a pair of ancient celestial and terrestrial globes. The fireplace was in keeping with the room, being a wide affair with a carved marble mantelpiece, the top slab upheld by Atlas-like gentlemen with suffering expressions, and the crosspiece decorated with carefree and rather charming putti. The huge metal basket below, which had been designed for logs, was empty, and in front of it, inside the leather-seated high fender, stood the unlovely device which was heater and humidifier all in one. The library had once been my favorite of all the rooms at Ashley; I could remember the firelight on the mellow leather of the books, and the warmth of the big rug before the blaze, and being allowed to turn one of the big globes while my father told me about the countries which passed by so quickly under my childish hands.

Now its only beauty was one of proportion; it was a sad ghost of a room, with the cool north light showing the empty shelves, or, sadder still, the shelves where two or three worthless and abandoned volumes took the space of twenty, and lay fallen in their places. Under the glass of the display tables the faded velvet showed darker patches where treasures had once lain. The globes had gone long since under the hammer. In the farthest bay were the locked sections, three sets of shelves behind gilded grilles. The section which had held valuable books was, like the display tables, empty of them; the other two were still filled with the books that Emory had striven in vain to be allowed to read—the private collections of Scholar William, and of Nicholas Ashley, his son.

The guide was saying something about Nick Ashley now, and people were smiling. One or two of them drifted over to look at the titles behind the grille, and I went with them.

The topmost shelves in William's section were filled with a miscellaneous assortment of volumes: a herbal, a few bird books, a county history or two, and a book of county maps, books on hunting and game preserving, a history of the Clan Chattan, and one or two thin reprints about local affairs. There were also a few stray volumes from the *Journal* of Emma Ashley. But on the more accessible shelves, Shakespeare predominated. The *Complete Works,* in a massive, illustrated edition, comprised ten of the volumes, and I could see at least three other editions, flanked by commentaries and essays, and a few separate copies of some of the plays. Notably, there were three different copies of *Romeo and Juliet,* and beside them the volume which explained this interest, a book entitled *A New Romeo to His Juliet,* which contained, I knew, William Ashley's poems to his wife, Julia McCombie, whose badge he had scattered so lavishly through the house. It was a marvel, I thought, that he had not removed the Italian putti and put Julia's badge there instead: it appeared in every other room; it was scrolled over the front gate, carved in the panels of the staircase, even in two of the misericords of the church choir. It was also carved—a country job this—in the pavilion which stood at the center of the maze. Even looked at down the centuries, such devotion was a trifle overpowering; and to William's contemporaries, and possibly even to Julia herself, it must have been formidable, not to say stifling. After her death at twenty-six her widower, distracted with grief, had shut himself away with his books and his writing, and had had little, if anything, to do with the son who was too like the dead wife.

Our guide was telling the story now, under the portrait of Nicholas, aged eighteen, which hung over the chimneypiece.

". . . He was only seven when she died, and he was more or less left alone, one gathers, except for a series of tutors, none of whom lasted very long. He grew up wild, and he got wilder. I suppose it all sounds very corny and over-dramatic now, because it's been overdone as a story line, but of course this story's true, and it did have a really dramatic ending."

It was certainly dramatic, and it was probably most of it true. What we knew about Wicked Nick's life and death came mainly from the journal of his successor's wife, a lady almost as wordy as Queen Victoria, and every bit as virtuous. Poor Nicholas suffered a good deal in the telling, and the girl—the last of his girls—had been allowed to sink into oblivion. But the main facts were there in Emma Ashley's diaries, and were, indeed, the only interesting part of them.

Nicholas, who had adored his gentle mother, found himself, at her death, almost completely ignored by his father, and in turn bullied, deferred to, or encouraged in his growing wilfulness by a quickly changing series of tutors. What must have started as normal, healthy high spirits changed with this mishandling into wildness; and (one could read between Emma Ashley's disapproving lines) an affectionate nature, starved and repulsed, became sullen and intractable. Spoiled in the truest sense of the word, Nick Ashley had early succumbed to what his Aunt Emma called "corruption," though, from the veiled hints in the diaries, it was hard to gather whether this had been vice on the Gilles de Rais scale, or merely the sexual experimenting normal for a young gentleman of his time.

Nicholas' father fell ill when the young man was a few months short of twenty-two years old. William Ashley, who was sixty-one, was thought to be dying, but was sufficiently in command of his senses to worry about who should succeed him. A marriage contract was hastily drawn up between Nicholas and the Lady Helen Colwall, younger daughter of the family then living at Ledworth Castle. It is not known what the betrothed couple thought of one another, but the very drawing up of the contract must have been a miracle of diplomacy, because—*vide* the virtuous Emma Ashley-Nicholas, with his father safely bedridden, was indulging himself with nightly "orgies" of illicit love.

"There's a tradition," our guide was saying, "that he used to meet them in the pavilion in the center of the maze. How they found the way in I don't know; his valet is supposed to have led them in, like girls being brought to the Grand Turk. His father must have known something about it, and there are stories of terrible quarrels, because William kept the pavilion sacred to Julia's memory, and most of his poems were written there. Well, Nicholas took it over. There are engravings showing it made over as a love nest, with a huge bed, and a big mirror let into the ceiling above it, and lots of silk curtains and shaded lamps, but I should think that was just a myth; it doesn't seem likely that Nick could have had the pavilion done up like that while William was still alive. . . . Anyway, just a month before Nicholas was due to be married to Lady Helen, William Ashley died. Nick had been keeping company with a girl from a nearby village, and this time he'd been a bit rash, because one of the girl's brothers was the Court gamekeeper, and on this particular night—the night after William died—the man was out after a poacher, and his brother was with him for company, when they saw their sister coming out of the maze. Well, they knew what that meant. They waited outside till Nick Ashley came out. Nobody knows what happened, whether they quarreled with him, or just lay in wait and shot him down, but Nick Ashley was shot dead. The brothers weren't ever caught. They took a ship from Bristol, and got clear away. The Ashley estate went to Nick's uncle—his father's brother. That was the Charles Ashley whose wife wrote the diaries." She smiled. "And that's the only story I've got for you. It's certainly the only tragedy recorded at the Court. For a place as old as this, it's got a strange reputation for peacefulness. There isn't even the breath of a ghost."

"Not even at the pavilion?" asked someone.

"Not that we know of. But they say that no one except the family—and of course gardeners and so on—has been there since. So perhaps the sad ghost of Wicked Nick haunts the maze to this day, but nobody meets him, and the family keep him dark."

Did we? I never remembered feeling anything but sympathy for poor Nick Ashley, bracketed, so to speak, between the melancholy William, and the pharisaically virtuous uncle and aunt who had inherited the place on his death. The young face in the picture showed weakness, rather than wickedness, and along with it a good deal of charm. And already, at eighteen, the painter had caught, in the expression of the long gray eyes, a look of settled unhappiness. The story made the legends of the maze and its "orgies," the tilted love mirror, and the collection of pornography later locked in the Court library, appear in an altogether kindlier light.

"The portrait is by Stevens," the guide was saying, "but it was sold, and that's a copy. Now, the clock underneath it . . ."

Nick Ashley was dismissed, and everyone looked obediently at the French ormolu clock which stood below the portrait, its gently swinging internal organs winking through the glass. I noticed in passing that it was still ten minutes or so lag of the truth, but then my attention fixed itself with a click about eighteen inches to the right of the clock. When I had last been in this room there had been a small T'ang horse there, which, though it was damaged, was worth five or six hundred pounds in any market.

But it was not going to market, not again. It was not there.

There was nowhere else for it to stand in the library, except perhaps in the safety of one of the display tables. I looked with a flicker of worry at the space where it had been. If the Underhills had taken a fancy to it and moved it across into one of the rooms they rented, it was their responsibility, and perhaps they had no idea of its value.

The party was beginning to leave the library. As I followed them, I lingered to look inside the display tables; it was just possible that some careful hand had removed the little horse to the safety of velvet and glass. But no. And, now that I looked with attention, there were fresh shapes showing in unfaded velvet among the remaining objects of virtu. Here, too, things were missing. A little oval—that had surely been a miniature? And that irregular bit of dark green had held a Chinese jade seal carved with a lion dog.

"Please?" said the guide. I looked up with a start. She was standing by the open door, waiting for me. All the others had gone. I could hear them making their way, chattering like a crowd let out of school, down the staircase. "I have to lock up," said the girl.

"I'm so sorry," I said, "keeping you waiting. I was interested . . . You do it very well, the place comes alive. I've enjoyed it such a lot. Er, did you say 'lock up'? You mean you lock the rooms behind you each time as you go?"

"Oh yes. It's such a big, rambling place, and there are still a lot of valuable things here. We have to be very careful. All the rooms are locked except the ones that are being lived in. We open and shut them as we go through."

"The keys you use; who keeps them as a rule?"

She looked faintly surprised, but answered me readily enough. "I have to give them back to the people who live here. They're tenants; the family's abroad just now."

"Oh. Well, thanks very much," I said, and went thoughtfully out in the wake of the others.

Ashley, 1835

She was here at last.

The light step on the verandah, the hand on the door, the slight figure in the shabby cloak slipping quickly into the room, then shutting the door carefully behind her so that no faint sliver showed. The cloak, thrown aside, falling across the writing table where, year after year, his father had sat alone, writing those sterile verses to his love.

"My love."

Her hair, loosened from the hood, fell like rain, straight and dark, but full of rainbow lights from the candle. Her dress slipped to her knees. She stepped from it, and her hands went to the laces at her breast.

Outside, as if at a signal, a nightingale began to sing.

His thoughts spiraled. The light, the night, the nightingale. *O, she doth teach the torches to burn bright!* Her breasts were bare now, her waist. Her petticoat followed her dress to the floor.

The room echoed with the nightingale's singing. That damned keeper, he remembered, had threatened to shoot the bird . . . Damned keeper, indeed. Her brother. My brother's keeper . . . He was getting light-headed.

"What are you laughing at, then, love?"

"I'll tell you afterward. Here, my sweetest girl, come here to me."

8

. . . the wild-goose chase . . .

—*Romeo and Juliet,* II, iv

"AREN'T YOU Miss Ashley?"

The voice, a woman's, and American, brought me out of my thoughts with a thump, and back to the sunlight of the courtyard, where I now saw a big American car parked in the shade on the other side of the yard. A man was just vanishing through the side door, carrying a suitcase; from his tailoring I guessed it was Mr. Underhill. I turned to greet the woman who had spoken. "Yes, I am. And you must be Mrs. Underhill?"

She was a woman in her middle forties, groomed to a high gloss with that combination American women have of know-how and sheer hard work and skilled use of materials. She was shortish, and without the hard work she might have been dumpy, but instead she was dainty, in a creaseless cream suit that might as well have borne its Fifth Avenue tag on the outside. A high-necked silk sweater hid her neck, and her face had the paled-off sunburn which afflicts Californians when they have been too long in sadder climates. Her skin was dry, with fine lines showing at eyes and mouth, and showed evidence of ceaseless care. The dark-brown lashes were a giveaway for the blond hair.

"I'm so glad to meet you." She put out a hand. "But Jeff and I feel awful that it had to be for this reason. It was terrible news about your father; I'm so sorry. We've both been so distressed for you. Everybody says what a very fine person he was."

She talked on for a little while about Daddy, asked where I was staying, and seemed pleased when I said I planned to live for a while in the cottage by the lake. She had a gentle voice and manner that went with her Dresden-china appearance, and seemed to feel a genuine regret about my father, and a real concern for me.

"How did you know me?" I asked her. "Did Mr. Emerson tell you I was coming?"

"No, he didn't. I knew you from the picture in our bedroom."

My parents' room, of course. I said: "Is it so like? It isn't a very good one, and it was painted years ago."

She laughed. "Well, I can see you're not seventeen any more, but you're not that much older, are you?"

"I feel it. I'm twenty-two."

"Look, what are we standing out here for? Come right in, Jeff's dying to meet you, I know. He's just flown in from Houston, and he'll be home for a few days. Isn't that marvelous? It seems kind of strange inviting you into your own home, but come right on in."

Like us, the Underhills used a side door. We went in together. I said: "I didn't actually come over just to call. I was planning to do that this afternoon. I've been down at the cottage seeing what was needed, and then I came up here, and—" I laughed rather apologetically. "Actually I went round with the guided tour. It seems silly, but I was rather curious to see how they did it."

"Did you really? Well, fancy!" Her eyes danced. "So I needn't feel so bad at inviting you into your own home, when you've had to pay twenty-five cents to go the rounds. . . . And I have to tell you, Cathy and I have been around a couple of times ourselves. It was a good way to learn all the history, and boy, have you had some history! Kind of uncomfortable, some of it, but very interesting, and seeing everything right here in its own place beats the schoolbooks hollow." She paused at a corner. "We're in what they call the small drawing room; I don't have to tell you the way. You'll stay to lunch with us, won't you? Now"—as I made the ritual protest—"I won't take no for an answer. We have a light lunch, salad and such, and it couldn't be easier. In any case, we're having a guest already, so it's easy to stretch it." She smiled like someone with a secret that she knew would delight me. "Guess who it is? Your own cousin."

Any delight I felt was certainly tempered with questions and uneasy memories of last night in the churchyard, and, too, with some speculation about the gossip Mrs. Henderson had passed on to me. I said: "You mean Emory? How lovely!" with what was meant to sound like unmixed pleasure, but as Mrs. Underhill

opened the drawing-room door and gestured me past her, I saw her eyeing me
with her own brand of speculation, a slightly wary look, which, under the
circumstances, was natural. One up to Mrs. Henderson and the village gossip, I
thought: it was just such a look as might be given to the about-to-be-dispossessed
Miss Ashley, whose privilege ticket back to the Court had been picked up by
Miss Underhill.

"Yes," she said, "Emory."

"Well, isn't that nice!" I said cheerfully. "I haven't seen him for ages. And of
course I'd love to meet your daughter. Thank you, I'd like to stay, very much."

The "small drawing room" opened from the longer drawing room, from
which it could be divided by a pair of tall doors. These were shut now, making a
room about thirty feet by eighteen, with three long windows looking out on the
strip of lawn and rose beds which was the terrace above the moat. The water-light
moved prettily on the ceiling. They had hardly rearranged the room at all, I saw,
and there were bowls of tulips and bluebells, and stands of cherry blossom which
lighted the alcoves to beauty, and which must have been arranged by Mrs.
Underhill herself.

"Let's sit down, shall we?" she said.

There was a fire of logs in the hearth. She motioned me to a seat near it in the
corner of the big chesterfield, and took the other corner herself.

"I gather," I said, "that you know my cousin quite well?"

"Yes. He and Cathy—Cathy's my daughter—met a while back, and after they
got acquainted they found there was this connection, that she was staying at
Ashley Court. A real coincidence, you might say. Well, of course she asked him
over, and he's visited here a few times. He's a real charmer, don't you think?"

"I've always thought so," I agreed, "and so's his twin. You've met James?
And Francis, the youngest brother? No, well, he's been abroad a lot in the last
few months. They used to live here with us, most of the time, when we were
children; I expect Emory will have told you all about that." I hesitated
fractionally, then hit the ball into the open field. "You know, I suppose, that the
Court will belong to Emory's family now?"

She looked embarrassed, and made quite a little business of picking up a
cigarette box, offering me one, then taking one herself and lighting it. "He did
tell us something about the way things were left, but of course it was all
seemingly in the future then. Your father was still a young man, as things go, and
nobody ever thought of a tragedy like this." She seemed to be going to say more,
then let it go. "It seems you had some ancestor who tied everything up so that it
had to be inherited by a man. I can think of some ladies I know who'd be hell-
bent on doing something about that right now . . ." She smiled, leaned across
to tap ash off her cigarette, then looked up at me frankly. "I must say, Miss
Ashley, it seems kind of tough to me. Isn't there anything that can be done?"

She sounded as if she meant it. Some tension that I hardly knew I had been
feeling slackened in me.

"I doubt it. Certainly there's nothing to be done about the 'heirs male'
inheritance; that's been built in ever since the place started. The really awkward
'tying up' that the old man did was the trust that stops even the heir from selling
any of the unentailed property without the consent of the whole family. Luckily,
so far, we haven't fought much over it." I smiled. "And I don't see why we
should start now. I expect Emory will do all right; he usually does."

"You don't sound as if you minded one bit."

"I don't believe I do. People like the Ashleys had a very good run for their money, after all."

She got up then to shift one of the logs in the fireplace, and I turned the subject with some compliment about the flowers, and the talk went off at a comfortable tangent to the garden, and the contrast between California and the cool temperate climate that we in Britain use as a daily basis for grumbling, but that produces the loveliest gardens in the world. . . . I listened with only half an ear; I was looking round the room, trying not to do it too obviously, to see if the T'ang horse was there, or the seal, or anything else which should have been in the locked part of the house. I saw none of them, but I knew that soon, and the sooner the better for her own sake as well as mine, I would have to tell her about the missing objects. I wondered a little desperately how in the world one broached such a subject. For a lunch guest, however much a part of the furnishings, to ask her hostess suddenly where the valuables were and who kept the keys to the rooms they had been removed from was one of those things that even Aunt Edna of the Problem Page would have found tricky. Well, I thought, it wasn't something that would improve with keeping. If you have to ask something, then ask.

"Mrs. Underhill, there's something I've been wondering about. Perhaps you can help me. The guide who took the party round told me that the rooms on the public side of the house—the ones you don't use—are always locked, and that she gives the keys back to you and your husband for safekeeping. What happens if you're out, or away from home?"

"They're left with that nice Rob Granger. He has the other set, and he always keeps an eye on things if we're not here. He's hardly ever away, but if he is, he leaves keys at the Vicarage. Why do you ask? Don't you have keys yourself?"

"It's not that; I can get Rob's if I need them. It's just . . . Mrs. Underhill, I noticed something this morning that worried me—maybe I should say puzzled me, because I'm quite sure there'll be a simple reason for it." I hesitated, then plunged. "One or two small things that used to be in the library aren't there any more. I wondered if you knew where they'd been moved to."

She looked startled, and her cigarette froze still, halfway up to her mouth. "Miss Ashley, there's nothing been moved that I know of. What sort of things?"

"Small things, ornaments. I wondered if perhaps they'd been put in the strong-room for safekeeping."

She shook her head. I noticed how sharply the lipstick outlined her mouth, standing out blue-red against the creamy colorless skin. "Do you mean really valuable things?"

"Well, there's a little Chinese horse, in unglazed earthenware, a sort of biscuit color, with a mended leg. It doesn't look much, but—"

"A Chinese horse? Unglazed biscuit? For heaven's sake, not a T'ang horse?" She looked so horrified that I realized that, coming from America's West Coast, she probably knew far more about the value of Oriental ceramics than I did.

I said hastily: "Yes, but not a very good one; it was small, and it was damaged. Please don't look so worried! I just noticed that it had gone from the mantelpiece in the library, and there was a miniature gone from one of the showcases, just a little Victorian thing, and a piece of jade, a seal with a lion dog on it. You haven't seen them anywhere else, have you?"

"No, I have not. They're not in this part of the house, that's for sure. Miss Ashley, this is just awful!"

I saw with remorse that she had lost the remains of what color she had. Her lips, under the paint, had puckered into fine, dry lines. I began to feel a bit like an executioner. "Look, please don't worry so, I only asked. The odds are that Mr. Emerson's put them away in the strong-room. He may have decided they were too easily portable, with loads of people going through the rooms every day. I can ring him up and ask him. I should have done that before I bothered you. Please forgive me."

"Well, of course, but—oh, here's Jeff. He might know something about it . . . Jeff, this is Miss Ashley. She's coming back to stay for a piece, and she'll be living in the cottage by the lake. Isn't that wonderful? But right now she's staying to lunch with us. Miss Ashley, this is Jeff, my husband."

We said how do you do and shook hands, and, like her, he said the right things about my father with that enviable American warmth and ease of manner. He was a big man, broad in body, and of heavy build, with the same look as his wife of physical health worked for and maintained at concert pitch. He had dark hair graying, and a broad face with slightly flattened features, oddly familiar, though for the moment I could not place them. The cheekbones were wide, with a slightly Slavic look, and the eyes were dark and very shrewd. The long mouth gave nothing away. He looked just what he was: a rich, clever man, a killer in business hours, and kindness itself in his time off.

Before I could stop her his wife had told him about the missing objects, and I was able to witness the Jekyll-into-Hyde transformation I had just guessed at. The pleasant smile vanished, the black brows snapped together, and hard dark eyes looked straight through my brain to scrape the back of my skull. Or that was what it felt like. "Tycoon" had not just been a joke word. In the business jungle of America, Jeffrey Underhill was one of the larger carnivores.

He didn't waste time on apologies or worry; he asked two or three questions, so smoothly that you hardly noticed they came barbed, and then said: "The first thing is to call the lawyer. I'll do that now. It seems to me very likely that he's taken some of the small things into safekeeping." He glanced at the clock on the mantel. "Cathy went to pick Emory up, didn't she? They're not back yet?"

"No," said his wife. "He called up to say he had to get the later train."

He nodded, and made for the door, but paused there with his back to the room, his head bent, as if thinking. Then he turned back to me. He still had that gloss of calm which politicians and high-ranking businessmen affect, but the next question came out that little bit too abruptly. "You only noticed things missing from the library, that's right?"

"That's right. Though until I'd seen the T'ang horse was gone, I didn't really look. But, Mr. Underhill, please—I didn't mean to start a thing like this. This is making me feel terrible. There's probably a perfectly simple explanation, and—"

"Sure there is. But the sooner we have it the better. I'll call this lawyer right away, even if it does spoil his lunch hour for him. But the point I was going to make was, would you like to go look around again on your own, and make a check? You might find the things somewhere else, or you might find more things missing. Either way, the sooner we get them tagged the better. It's barely a quarter of twelve. I doubt if my daughter and your cousin will be here much before one o'clock. What do you say?"

"Yes, I'd like to. Thank you."

"Fine. Now, Stephanie says you went around with the guided tour; that means you've no keys of your own. Right?" He crossed to a bureau which stood between two of the windows, took a small key from his vest pocket and unlocked it, pulled open a drawer and took out the big bunch of house keys. No, I could acquit Mr. Underhill of carelessness. He handed me the keys, said, "Fix me a martini, for God's sake," to his wife, and went out. One got the impression that the dust began to settle as soon as the door shut behind him.

My search, which was fruitless, finished at length in the big schoolroom of the nursery wing.

I don't quite know why I went there; I certainly never expected to find any clue to the missing objects, and I have no recollection of climbing the noisy lino-covered stairs to the third floor. It may be that I was still a little breathless at the Underhills' swift reaction to my inquiries; possibly it was just Jeffrey Underhill's normal way, but I felt as if I had started a full-scale criminal investigation almost before I was sure that anything was really missing. Before I faced them again, I wanted time to think. I glanced at my watch. Still something short of twelve-thirty. I shut the schoolroom door behind me, crossed to the wide window seat, and sat down, looking down at the tops of the big beeches that edged the Pool.

The sun poured into the shabby room. Dust motes swarmed like a gauze filter, making a soft-focus dream-world out of reality. The sun was bright as the suns one always remembers from childhood. The dusty, slightly stuffy smell of the unused schoolroom was the same as it had been ten, twelve, fourteen years ago. Beside me on the faded cushions of the window seat sat three old friends, grubby and gray with much loving: the Hippo family, Hippo, Pot, and Amos, whose names Francis had chosen, and which, as children, we had found excruciatingly funny. The old dappled rocking horse stood gathering dust; I had christened it Dawn, which my cousins thought sickeningly girlish, refusing to call it anything but Rocky. There were the desks, with their dried and crusted inkwells, where James and Emory, and later Francis and I, had sat learning to read and write and cipher before we went to school. A white-painted shelf still held the beloved storybooks, the Andrew Langs and the Arthur Ransomes and the C. S. Lewises, their battered covers containing each its bright autonomous world, those magical kingdoms one is made free of as a child, and thereafter owns all one's life.

Below the shelves was the cupboard to which, prompted by Leslie Oker, my bookseller friend from Ashbury, I had, before going abroad, transferred some of our nursery treasures from the open shelves. There was a steadily growing interest, he had told me, in the work of illustrators like Arthur Rackham and Edmund Dulac and Kay Neilson; and I myself, looking through Christie's catalogues, had seen prices ranging into the hundreds for the scarcer volumes. So I had locked the books out of sight, and hidden the key. Small beer, perhaps, compared with T'ang horses and jade, but there was love to be reckoned with as well.

T'ang horses and jade. Valuable books? Not dreaming at all now, but right back on the spot with my problem, I crossed to the cupboard and tried the door. It was not locked. With a jerk of sudden apprehension, I pulled the door open.

The books were all there, just as I had left them.

As I relaxed, I realized how falsely keyed up I had been: to be as valuable as the ones I had seen in Christie's catalogue, they would have had to be the "deluxe" editions, signed by the artist and limited to a few hundred copies; not the nursery editions we had had, read and re-read until the pages showed the handling, and the covers were dented and soiled. These were not objects of value, but only of love.

I pulled out the nearest. It was *Grimm's Fairy Tales,* and the drawings were so familiar that my own imaginary concept of the stories was little more than an extension of these pictures. There was the Goosegirl with poor Falada, over whom I had wept as a child; Hansel and Grethel with the dreadful old witch; the Princess dreaming on the rock among the yesty waves, with the Dragon's long head on her lap . . .

"The Princess and the Dragon." I swung round as if that underhung jaw had bitten me, and stared up at the schoolroom wall, where, dark on the faded wallpaper, two empty oblongs showed. Two pictures had once hung there, original illustrations by Rackham, one from Lamb's *Tales,* and the other this very drawing from Grimm, "The Princess and the Dragon." A great-aunt of mine had bought them for a few pounds when they were first exhibited, and given them to me when I was a child. I had taken them down from the walls and locked them with the books, away from dust and damage. Now, both cupboard and wall were bare of them. And this time I had not miscalculated. They were the real thing, irreplaceable, and worth the kind of money that few people could afford to lose. Certainly not me.

I still remember the rush of anger I felt. I slammed the cupboard door shut, got to my feet, and went back to the window. I pushed it open and leaned out. As I did so I thought I heard a car turn into the driveway. That would be Emory and Cathy, I supposed, but I made no move to go downstairs. I needed a little longer to myself before I faced the company and heard what Mr. Underhill had to tell me. I knew as well as if he had already said it, that Mr. Emerson would know nothing about the missing treasures.

The sun was blazing full from the south. I shut my eyes. The scent of the garden came floating, sweet and calming as sunlight on water. I opened them again, and watched the water itself below me. The bullrushes were still, inseparable from their reflections; the willows trailed their hair in the water; the irises were budding. The pen swan slept on her nest, head under wing, the cygnets beside her. The cob floated near with all wing set, in full beauty.

Lover?

I'm here. What is it?

I hardly knew that I had called to him, until the response came, quickly and warmly, like a hand clasping another that reaches out blindly for comfort. Call and reply, as clear and easy as if they had been formulated in words—clearer, for words confuse as often as they explain. Between long-familiar lovers the language of the body needs no speech; with us, our minds had for so long dwelt familiarly the one with the other that the exchange of thought was as telling and as swift as a glance between intimates across a crowded room.

But to describe it, words must serve.

What is it?

Things have disappeared. The horse has gone from the library.

The what? For once it came with a catch of puzzlement. *I thought you said the horse had gone from the library.*

I did. I sent him as clear an image as I could, and felt him accept it.

Oh, that one. Yes. It's gone?

That, and other things as well. And now I've found some pictures gone from the schoolroom, valuable ones . . .

He had already picked it up, before I even knew I had formulated it. *And you think they were stolen. Is he phoning the lawyer?*

You knew that? How?

Oh, from you. You're as open as daylight when you're upset.

Am I? Then why didn't you come when I was in the cottage?

Because it was time you cried it all out, and that's a thing one wants to do by oneself. I left you alone. But you should have known I was there.

Yes. It was resigned, almost flat. *I should have known. But I'd have liked you closer.*

Bryony—

Yes?

Sweet Bryony. The patterns came through delicate and warm, like gentle hands touching my cheeks.

Oh, God. It went out with all the longing of loneliness. *I want you so.*

The touch changed, no less gentle, but now electric, thrilling as live wire. There was a quick burst of something as strong and deafening as static, which grew in intensity like pain growing, like sound increasing up to the very limit of tolerance.

Then it shut off abruptly, and the door opened, and my cousin stood on the threshold.

Ashley, 1835

"I was afraid you'd missed the way."

"Oh, no, it's easy, now I've got the key."

"I thought you might have said, 'I'd always find the way to you, my lover.'"

"So I would, so I would. I didn't have to use the key tonight. I remembered every turning, just as you drew it for me on the map."

"There you go again. Well, I shall say it for you. If you were hidden at the center of the darkest and most tangled forest in the world, I'd find you."

"Like the prince in the fairy tale?"

"Or like the lover in the play. 'There is my north, and thither my needle points.'"

"Eh, now you're laughing at me. That would be dirty meant, surely?"

"It would. Do you mind?"

"Why would I? There's neither dirty nor clean between thee and me, just what's true, and what could be wrong wi' that?"

"Nothing. Nothing ever was, and now, why, now . . ."

9

Why, how now, kinsman!

—Romeo and Juliet, I, v

"HULLO, BRYONY."

"Why, Emory, how lovely!" To my own surprise, my voice sounded quite normal as I greeted him. "I could hardly believe it when they said you were coming to lunch today! And to meet you here, of all places, just like this, out of the blue . . . . Doesn't it seem ages?"

"If you knew how guilty we all feel about 'here,'" said my cousin. He smiled at me. "You're looking wonderful. I was talking to Bill Emerson, and he said you'd taken it all marvelously. How are you really?"

"Oh, I'm fine. Everyone's been sweet to me, and it's been easier than I ever thought it could be. You mustn't any of you talk about 'guilt'! That's just silly. We've known all along just what would happen, and—"

I broke off. He had come into the room and was approaching me, threading his way along the row of desks. They looked very small beside his height; his fingertips barely brushed them. It put time in remembrance. He caught the look, and paused. "What is it?"

I said, uncertainly: "James? It *is* James, isn't it?"

I faltered to a stop, meeting the amusement in his eyes. Thrown off guard by the recent exchange with my lover, and by the mental dramatics preceding my cousin's entrance, I felt myself color as I stared up at him, absurdly at a loss.

The only thing certain about this man was that he was one of my cousins. He was a tall man, fine-boned, with the pale skin that tanned (even in the Spanish sun) no more than sallow; fair straight hair, thin-bridged nose, gray eyes. His shirt and tie were in complementing shades of gray that, either by accident or design—and with him I knew it would be design—exactly matched his eyes. But any impression of the over-trendy or the effete was wiped out as soon as you looked into those eyes and saw the set of the mouth. His mouth was the only feature that was not Ashley; a close mouth, long-lipped, folded at the corners as if it liked to keep secrets, or keep control. It gave him a withdrawn and wary look, rather at variance with the Ashley part of him. I remembered his mother; a child's view of her was all I had had, but I could still vividly recall a clever domineering woman who kept her own counsel, and secured her ambitions in her own way. If she had passed that driving side of herself to her sons, it might augur well for Ashley Court. There was more character, I thought, in this clever and wary man than there had been in my own gentle father. Maybe, by that token, these Ashleys would do better here than we had done.

His smile put time in remembrance, too. It held a very familiar sparkle of mischief. "Don't tell me you're slipping, Bryony darling! We never could put one over you. No, it's Emory. Aren't I the one you wanted?"

"Yes, of course, but—"

"Didn't they tell you I was coming over from Worcester with Cathy?"

"Yes, they told me, but . . . Oh, all right, so I'm slipping." I returned the smile. "Well, whichever you are, it's up to me to say welcome to Ashley Court.

And of course I mean welcome. This 'guilt' thing is nonsense, and Daddy would have been the first to say so. Don't let's hear about it any more, please.''

I uncurled from the window seat, got to my feet, and held out both hands for his. He took a couple of quick steps forward, and his hands closed round mine. He drew me into his arms and kissed me, a cousin's kiss, on the cheek.

I pulled away sharply, an instinctive movement that he tried to stop, then he let me go. He was laughing. I drew breath to speak, but before I could say anything, he put his hands up in a gesture of surrender.

"All right, don't say it. I admit it. I should have known we still couldn't fool you."

"Then why did you try?" For some reason I didn't stop to analyze, I was angry.

"For fun," he said lightly, and waited, as if challenging me to say more. I was silent. It was not just the moment to start explaining that, even had I found it easy to confuse James with Emory, I could not confuse a touch, much less a kiss. The moment he had taken my hands, I had known who it was. The hazy sunlight drifted between us, dazzling. Through it I saw his eyes, still smiling, and—I was sure—aware.

But he began to talk about my father. I listened, and thanked him, and made some sort of reply, as well as I could for the crowding thoughts that just then were overriding all else. I found suddenly that I couldn't meet his eyes, and turned away to sit down on the window seat again.

The cool, pleasant voice paused. When he spoke again it had changed, subtly. "Bryony. Try not to be too sad. We'll look after you." He hesitated, then added, as if he were answering something and dismissing it, as indeed I supposed he was: "It's not time to talk yet, but don't worry, we'll work something out."

The words were gently spoken, but to me they seemed to go ringing on and on. I said something, I'm not sure what, and then asked quickly: "How's Cousin Howard?"

He half sat down on one of the desks. He seemed completely relaxed. "He's a little better; at any rate, he's out of danger, they say, but he's still very ill. He'll have to retire, did you know? Things have been a bit difficult all round . . . I'm afraid there'll be no question of his coming over for a long time. When did you think of having the memorial service for Cousin Jon?''

"I haven't talked to the Vicar yet. It could wait, I imagine, till Cousin Howard's mobile. That would be better, wouldn't it?"

"I know he'd like to be there."

"I suppose Emory's over with him in Jerez," I asked, "since you're here?"

"He did go over a couple of times, to see Father, but he's been here most of the time—in Bristol, that is, or London. Father's retirement has been putting the pressure on a bit."

"And you? When did you come over?"

"The last week in April. Miguel coped for us in Jerez, so I could help out here with Twin. We felt pretty bad about not getting over for the cremation, but it simply couldn't be done. I'm sorry about that."

"It's all right, I understand. Have you heard from Francis yet?"

"Not a word," he said. "I gather you haven't, either? He must still be incommunicado in Derbyshire. Who's he with, do you know?"

"No idea. I thought, knowing Francis, that he'd be on his own."

He lifted a shoulder. "Probably. Well, no doubt he'll turn up soon."

"James—"

"Yes?"

"James, was that you in the vestry last night?"

He straightened, startled. I saw the pupils narrow in the wide gray irises, then his eyes went momentarily blank, as if he were making some lightning calculation. Then he said: "Vestry?" as blankly.

"Yes, vestry. It wasn't?"

"It was not. Why the hell should I have been in the vestry?"

"I've no idea. I went to the church late last night, and I saw someone in the vestry. He was leaving just as I went in. He went out across the churchyard wall and into the walled garden. He saw me, but he didn't stay to talk."

"Sounds crazy. Why should you have imagined I'd run away, from you of all people?"

"I don't know. Could it have been Emory?"

"Well, the same applies, I would have thought." He looked at me. "What makes you think it was one of us?"

"I got that impression. Only vaguely—but I thought it was one of you."

"Well, didn't you try speaking to whoever it was?"

He waited for my reply, his eyes wide now, and guileless. I knew that look. It was the "I was never even near the orchard" look, with the apples literally tumbling out of his trouser-pocket. I smiled to myself, and let him see the smile, and watched the flicker in his eyes, and was certain. I turned away toward the window, picked up Pot, and set him on my knee. "No. Oh, well, never mind. What would you be doing there anyway? I just thought it must be one of you, and I got the impression it was you. And talking of Emory, what's all this about him and Cathy Underhill? Have they really got a thing going?"

"Yes. They met, quite by chance, at some do in town, and when they got talking they found the connection with Ashley. Then one thing led to another, and—yes, you might say they had something going."

"Serious?"

"I'm not sure. That is, I'm not sure from Twin's side of it."

"Then you are sure from Cathy's?" I asked.

"As far as one can judge, yes again."

"You and Emory used not to have secrets from one another."

"We're big boys now."

"Not too big, apparently," I said, rather sharply, "to go in still for all that 'Twin' stuff that used to annoy everyone."

"It's convenient," he said, with a slant of the eyebrows that he didn't attempt to explain. Didn't have to. I knew just when it had been "convenient"; when he and Emory were standing in for one another, either for fun and confusion's sake, or even for pay. One twin, who had pressing business elsewhere, or who was avoiding trouble, would cajole, blackmail, or just plain pay the other to substitute for him. It was significant that as often as not James was the one who was blackmailed into ringing for Emory. The maddening way they had had of calling each other "Twin" had made it desperately hard to catch them out when they wanted to confuse the issue. It was also typical that the habit had been deliberately cultivated. Even as boys, my cousins were to be reckoned with.

"Do you mean," I said slowly, "that you haven't just come here today with

Emory and Cathy? That you brought Cathy yourself, and that *she* thinks you are Emory?"

He gave me a sideways glance, half amused, half wary. "You sound very fierce."

"Well, damn it, it could matter. Why did you do it, James?"

"Oh, nothing deadly. Just that he'd had to stand her up once before, and didn't care to do it again. Besides, I wanted to see you."

"Surely you could have come anyway?" I asked. A pause. "Who told you I was here?"

The fair brows lifted a fraction. "Why, Emerson, of course. How else would I have known?"

I glanced up, but he was looking out of the window over my head. "Have you stood in for Emory before—with Cathy, that is?"

"Only once."

"And now here, today, in front of her parents. Do you really expect me to back you up?"

"You always did."

"This could be different. I haven't met her, but it sounds like the sort of situation one ought not to play about with. If she is serious about him, she might get hurt."

"Why should she get hurt if she doesn't know? She'd be hurt if she knew she'd been stood up again."

"Oh, all right," I said resignedly. "Damn you, James, you've no right to put me in this kind of position. We're not children any more. It's a bit late to tell the truth now, so I'll try not to give you away."

"That's my girl." There was nothing in his tone but the offhand approval that there had always been when I helped him. I smiled, and pulled Pot's ears, and thought how little he'd changed, and how much.

"Penny for them," said my cousin.

"I was just thinking that we might never have been parted at all."

"Meaning?"

I sidestepped the question. "Oh, only that it seems like yesterday, you and Emory playing your games. James, I meant what I said. Don't ask me to do it again, because I won't."

But he wasn't listening. He was looking out of the window over my head, and I saw his gaze sharpen.

"Did you know one of the beeches had gone?"

"Yes. Rob told me it had to come down after a storm in February. It's an awful pity, making a gap like that."

"Yes, but have you noticed what you can see through the gap?"

I turned. "No. What?"

He nodded downward. "You can see the pavilion now, and almost all the layout of the maze. You could never see any of that from the house before— Bryony!"

"What is it? You made me jump."

"I've seen it for the first time. Why didn't we ever think of it? It's the coat of arms!"

"What is? What are you talking about?"

"Look," he said impatiently. "The design. The layout of the maze. I know it's overgrown and all blurred in places, but it's the pattern—you know that queer geometric pattern carved on the fireplaces, round the 'Touch Not the Cat' crest? That's it, surely?"

I stared down at the intersecting lines of the maze. Overgrown though it was, the sun picked out the pattern in shadows sufficiently clear to prove him right. "Good heavens, so it is! Well . . . after all, the maze was very much William Ashley's fine and private place, wasn't it? I always wondered why he put that odd square design behind Julia's badge. He even uses it for a bookplate in his own books, I remember that. And talking of books—" I looked up at him. "James, some things from the library seem to have disappeared."

He seemed hardly to be listening, still intent on the sunlit maze below. "Ah, yes." He said it absently. "The horse and the lion dog seal. Did you find anything else gone?"

I didn't answer. Not aloud, that is. *So you knew, did you, Ashley?*

He seemed to come to himself with a start, and turned. "It's very odd, that maze. It makes one wonder . . . I'm sorry, you were saying? Something about the T'ang horse and the jade seal going missing."

"I didn't mention them. That was you."

He nodded. "The Underhills told me. They said you were looking round to see if anything else was gone. Have you checked?"

"As well as I can, without an inventory. I haven't found the things from the library, but then Mr. Emerson may have put them away somewhere."

"No. Underhill had just telephoned Emerson when we got here. He knew nothing about the things. It's certainly very odd. Did you find anything else missing?"

"The pictures Great-Aunt Sophie gave me. The ones from there." I pointed to the wall.

He frowned. "Those? Damn it, who on earth would have wanted a couple of nursery pictures?"

"Those 'nursery pictures,' as you call them, are originals, and they're really pretty valuable now, though they'd be hard to sell. I mean, they couldn't very well be advertised; they're unique. James, what on earth can have happened to them?"

"God knows. Are you quite sure they're gone? They may have been put away somewhere. Take it from me, you'll find them in a cupboard or something."

"I put them away myself, in that cupboard, and it was locked. It's not locked now, and they're gone. It's the obvious conclusion that they've gone the same way as the T'ang horse and the seal."

The frown deepened. "You may be right." He hesitated. "Look, Bryony, I can see this is rather worrying, on top of everything else, but do try not to fret yourself over it. Can't you just leave it to Twin and me, and Emerson? We'll follow it up. There'll be some harmless explanation, I'm sure. Who'd take this sort of thing, anyway? The schoolroom isn't even on the public side."

"That's the point, isn't it?"

He stopped, arrested. His brows shot up. "You can't mean the Underhills?"

"No, of course I don't. I know nothing about them, except that I like them, and surely to goodness they were vetted when they took the house. But the point is, what earthly reason could people like that have for wanting to steal anything like this—or anything at all, for that matter?"

"Well, leave it, honey." He hesitated. "Don't take me up wrongly, but you really don't have to worry yourself about it. That's our job." He paused, then slanted a gentle look down at me. "Do you mind?"

"Give me time. I don't know." I began to uncurl from the window seat. "Did they send you to take me down to lunch? We'd better go, I suppose."

"Bryony." His arm fell lightly across my shoulders. I sat very still. "I've got to talk to you. When can we talk? They said something about your moving into the cottage. Is that true?"

"Yes. I was down there this morning. Rob and Mrs. Henderson have got it ready, so I think I'll move in today. I—I'd like to talk to you, James. There's a lot to say . . . after lunch, perhaps? Or would 'Emory' have to take Cathy somewhere?"

"No. But after lunch he's got to have a chat with Jeff Underhill about the lease of the Court. After that I might be able to come down. You're going to stay the night there?"

"Yes."

"Then I'll see you. Now I think we'd better go downstairs. It's all right, there's no hurry. Stephanie said to take our time; she knew we'd have a lot to say."

"What's been decided about the lease?"

"Officially speaking, they should be allowed to stay till it runs out. That'll be in November. Neither Emory nor I see any reason why they shouldn't. Do you?"

"Does that matter?" I asked.

The arm moved a little on my shoulders. "So you do mind."

"I tell you, I don't know." I got up abruptly from under the arm and moved to the door. "Let's go down."

"Taking your old bedmate down with you?"

"Taking my *what?*" Then I realized that I was still clutching Pot. I dumped him back on the window seat, said, "Damn you, James," but not aloud this time, and made once more for the door.

He followed me. "When you were in the library, did you notice if all the books in the locked sections were still there?"

"There again, I wouldn't know without the catalogue. I didn't notice any gaps."

We clattered down the schoolroom stairs. "Perhaps you'd better leave that job for us, anyway," he suggested.

"Like hell I will. I'm of age, and in any case probably all the worst ones have gone. Don't forget Emma Ashley burned a few of them."

"Grandmamma Savonarola. So she did. Pity," he said cheerfully. "Well, you're more than welcome to William Ashley's collection. All his dear little verses to his Julia, and his Roman studies, and his own personal editions of the simpler Shakespeare plays."

"Are any of them simple?"

"I would have thought that *Romeo and Juliet* and *Julius Caesar* posed fewer problems than, say, *Measure for Measure* or *Timon.*"

"Would you? You might be right." I said it absently. I was wondering whether to tell him now about my father's last words to me, and my interest in William Ashley's books. But we were already halfway down the great staircase. A portrait hung there, a dark girl, painted rather stiffly, but with beauty showing even through the stylized familiar features of the minor "society" portraits of the time. She was standing beside the sundial in the old rose garden, one arm resting on the pillar, the other holding a basket of roses. She looked stiff and faintly ill at ease in the gray satin and starched lace of the seventeenth century. Bess Ashley, the gypsy girl who had talked to a lover no one could see, and who went to the stake for it. Behind her, almost obscured in the yellowing canvas, was a black cat, familiar of witches.

I stopped. "James, do you ever have dreams?"

"Dreams? Of course I do. Everyone does. What sort especially?"

"Oh, about the future. People you're going to meet, and then you do meet them. That kind of thing."

"Precognition, you mean?"

I hesitated, then was deliberately vague. "I wouldn't say—no, not really that. Just something that's a bit more than coincidence . . . You dream about someone, and—and talk to them, someone you don't really know, and then you seem to see them or hear from them almost straight away. Next day, even."

There was a little pause. He seemed all at once to notice that we were standing in front of Bess Ashley's portrait. He shot me a look, hesitated, and opened his mouth to reply, but at that moment Mrs. Underhill came out of the drawing room to the foot of the stairs and spoke, and the moment passed. I ran down with an apology forming, but Stephanie Underhill brushed it aside and began to say something in an undertone which sounded like, "Do you mind, I wanted to ask you, don't say anything—" Then she stopped short, with a smile which didn't do anything for the anxiety in her eyes, as a girl emerged from a door at the other side of the hall and ran across to take James's hand in hers and say:

"Emory! You've been an age! Where were you both, for heaven's sake? In the middle of the maze?"

It was the girl from the E-type Jaguar. I recognized her straight away, the look of her father somehow translated into long, dark-blond hair and mink lashes, and the wide, unpainted mouth that had been sulky then, but now was full of laughter and charm. She was taller than her mother, but not by much, and slim to swooning point in a tight pair of blue jeans with big stitched pockets, and a loose sweater reaching like a tunic to the hips. The sweater should have been white, but wasn't, and I saw that the edge of one sleeve was beginning to unravel. But the cult disorder didn't seem to go deeper than the clothes; she was glowing with happiness and well-being, and the glow, it was very obvious, began and ended with my cousin. Her fingers twined in James's and clung, and the look she sent him would have melted bedrock.

"Cathy—" began her mother, but James was already disentangling his fingers from hers, and saying:

"You haven't met my cousin yet. This is Bryony. Bryony, Cat Underhill."

"Hi, Bryony. Nice to meet you. I'd have known you anywhere."

She held out a hand, and I took it. "That's what your mother said. That portrait must be better than we thought."

"Oh, it's not just that picture. When you've lived here for a bit you certainly get to know the Ashley face." She sent a glancing look up at James again, then added, seriously, to me: "I'm sorry. I guess I should have said right away, I'm really sorry about your father. It was awful."

"Thank you. Didn't I see you in Worcester yesterday? You stopped at a crossing to let me and a black cat over."

"Gosh, sure, I remember that. At least I remember the cat; I'm afraid I didn't notice you. He had his nerve, didn't he? I nearly ran him down. And a black cat, too, just when I can do with all the luck I can get."

"Oh? Why, specially?"

She took me by the arm as her mother began to shepherd us toward the drawing room. "Nothing special. Just that I always seem to need more luck than I can get. Who doesn't? Come along in and get a drink. Pop's still away telephoning somebody. What'll you have? Emory will pour it. Did you and the cat both get away all right?"

"He was even quicker than I was. And I solved a problem, meeting you like this."

She widened her eyes at me over her martini. They were dark like her father's. The mink eyelashes made them look enormous, Bambi-type. "A problem?"

"Yes. I'd just left the lawyer's office. It's beside that crossing, you probably know that? I saw him watching you, too; he pointed you out to me, and I thought he said 'Cat,' and I couldn't think why. I mean, if he'd meant the black cat, I could see that myself. . . . Now I know. We'd been talking about the Court, and your family, and now I've just heard my cousin call you Cat. He must have been meaning you. Well, that's one of the mysteries on the way out."

"'One of the mysteries'?" she asked. "Are there some more?"

"I certainly hope so," said Mrs. Underhill warmly. I glanced at her in surprise, but she hurried on: "All this time in a moated grange straight out of Tennyson, and not even the sniff of a ghost or a secret passage or any of the things you might expect! Miss Ashley, Cathy and I have been just longing for you to come and tell us the secrets about the Court that aren't in the books. The guides seem pretty strong on history, but they can't know all there is."

So she didn't want to talk about the missing objects in front of her daughter. Fair enough. I laughed. "I'm sorry if it hasn't come up to expectation. There isn't much, but there is a secret stair, as a matter of fact; it's a very tame affair, but it may have been useful in its day. In a way it's a sort of secret inside a secret—it goes down from the priest's hole into the wine cellars."

While I had been speaking, Mr. Underhill had come back into the room. He had his tycoon look again; he must have finished his call to Mr. Emerson before James came up to the schoolroom, so perhaps he had been telephoning to business associates all this time. But he shed it, and said, genially: "I knew all those stories about priests were true."

"Would you show us this stairway, Bryony?" Cathy sounded eager, genuinely so, I thought, in spite of the slightly over-anxious touch which meant either that she was nervous of the "real" Ashley who had owned all this once, or that she was trying to placate the girl she was hoping to supplant. "Right away after lunch?"

"Of course, if you want me to."

"Honey," her mother intervened, "maybe Miss Ashley doesn't feel like doing that just now."

"Oh, for goodness' sake, I'm *sorry* . . ." The contrition, like the eagerness, was a little too emphatic. "I guess I just forgot. What must you think of me?"

"It's all right," I said. "It's sweet of you, but don't worry about me. I'll be delighted to show you the stair after lunch."

"And talking of lunch," said Jeffrey Underhill, "where is it?"

So for the moment mysteries were shelved, and we went in.

Ashley, 1835

He lay on his back, staring up at the dark square of the ceiling mirror. Beside him she slept deeply, like a child.

They had made love first, as always, with the candle still alight. He remembered how at first she had protested, and he had insisted. She had given way, as she always gave way. Everything, everything that he wanted, he had to have.

Strange that this, which had been almost the rule of these affairs, had come so differently, granted by her. Strange that this acquiescence, subservience, even, should have taught him, not, as with others, boredom and then disgust, but gratitude and, finally, love.

The candle had burned low. Soon, when it was not too strenuous a task to stretch his arm for the candlestick, he would blow it out. The room smelled of burning wax, and the lavender water she made each summer, and used to rinse her hair. He would open the window to let the dawn in, but not yet. Dawn always came too soon.

10

. . . If ye should lead her in a fool's paradise, as they say, it were a very gross kind of behaviour, as they say: for the gentlewoman is young; and, therefore, if you should deal double with her, truly, it were an ill thing. . . .

—*Romeo and Juliet*, II, iv

LUNCH WAS a very American affair, plates of salad with cold chicken, cheese, and fruit all served together, with crisp rolls, and coffee poured for a starter. Apart from the coffee, which I persist in wanting later, it was delicious, and perfect for the middle of a fine warm day. Also, the water was iced, a luxury for Ashley. Contemplating the amount of ice in the crystal jug, I wondered if, in the interests of American sanity, the Underhills had installed a freezer of their own. Our old refrigerator had never made more than twelve smallish cubes at a time in all its long, long life.

During lunch conversation was general, and I thought I could feel Mr. and Mrs. Underhill working to keep it so. But afterward, back in the drawing room over more coffee, Cathy came straight back to the subject they obviously wanted to avoid.

"When you talked about mysteries, Bryony, what did you mean? Not the old stair, I guess; that would never be a mystery to you."

Jeffrey Underhill's head turned, and his wife bit her lip, but I had had time to think. I said smoothly: "Why, no, it was something that my cousin and I found in the schoolroom."

Cathy looked at James, then, quickly, at me. "In the schoolroom?"
"Yes. Have you ever been in there?"

"No, I have not! The only parts of the house I've been in outside our own apartments are the rooms they keep for show. Why would I go in the schoolroom? What's up there?"

"A few reminders of time past, that's all," said James. "A family of hippopotami in gray velveteen, and four battered school desks, with empty inkwells. Highly symbolic, but—"

"I suppose so," said Cathy, impatiently. "But what's the mystery?"

"What hippopotamuses?" asked her mother. "What on earth are you all talking about?"

I laughed. "Nothing that's in the schoolroom, anyway. Something outside. We found a new view from the window, a view of the maze."

"Oh, the maze!" Cathy, her eyes bright, came forward, looking excited. "If you knew how I'd wondered about that maze! And the elegant little roof you can see . . . a sort of summerhouse, isn't it? I've walked all around the outside of those darned hedges to find the way in, and I even went in at two of the entrances, but I simply couldn't get through all that stuff, and anyway, I knew if I did, I'd never get out again. Gosh, I suppose you know the way in? Do you mean you can just walk right in as far as that summerhouse and out again, without getting lost?"

"Oh, yes. So can my cousin, unless he's forgotten. Have you, Twin?"

I caught the glint in James's eye. He knew quite well that I found it impossible to address him directly as "Emory." I always had; so I had learned to use, when necessary, the irritating expedient the boys had invented.

"I don't know," he said. "I'd hate to try, without you there to guide me. But that's what you were going to tell them, wasn't it? We've got a map now."

"A map?" asked Cathy. The excitement she was showing, genuine or not, generated a sort of extra emphasis, so that the word "map" set up an echo in my mind. *"The cat, it's the cat on the pavement. The map. The letter. In the brook."* I pushed it aside for the moment. James was explaining.

"Yes, a map. That was the mystery we solved just now in the schoolroom. When we were up there we noticed that one of the old trees on the edge of the lake had come down, and we could see clear through the gap to the maze. And from that height on the third story the layout can be seen almost completely. A bit blurred where it's overgrown, and not altogether easy to follow if you drew a plan from what you saw, but what it did tell us was that there are plans everywhere in the house."

He paused for effect. The two women looked amazed, but Jeffrey Underhill's brows came frowning together for no more than three seconds, then he said: "The coat of arms. I've wondered about that."

"Good God, you're quick," said my cousin admiringly. "Yes, it does seem an unlikely design, now one knows, doesn't it?" He nodded toward the carved fireplace. "There, Cat, you see it? That uninspiring pattern surrounding our enigmatic motto. That's a map of the maze."

"Well, for heaven's sake!" Cathy jumped out of her chair and ran to examine it more closely.

"Do you mean to tell me," demanded Mrs. Underhill, "that you didn't know this, either of you, till this very morning?"

"We'd no idea," I said. "There's never been anywhere from which you could see the maze from above, unless perhaps you'd climbed out on the pavilion roof, and that's not really been safe for years. And of course from the garden you can't see the pattern at all."

"An aerial photograph?" suggested Mr. Underhill. "That could be interesting, if half what I hear about the history of this district is true. Has it never been mapped?"

Though his voice sounded interested, I got the distinct impression that he spoke with only half his mind on what he was saying. He was absorbed, a long way away from us, in some frowning abstraction. So, I imagined, must the tycoon's reaction always be to small talk; smooth from long practice, and clever because he couldn't help it, but with the burning-glass of his full attention focused a light-year or so away from this pretty room, and the trivialities we were talking about the maze.

"I suppose the Ordnance Survey must have taken pictures," James was saying. "They certainly mapped the district. We've got their maps, but they don't show the actual design of the maze, and I've never seen a photograph."

"In any case," I said, "it's all terribly overgrown now, with the hedges leaning together in places. From the air, I think it would just look like a huge thicket. What you really need is a plain geometric map like the one on the coat of arms, and then a machete. Mr. Underhill, there was something—"

He looked up from his coffee cup. I had been wrong. His attention, all of it, was right here in this room. It met me, palpably, and stopped me short.

"Yes, Miss Ashley?"

"There was something I wanted to ask you. Would I be in anyone's way if I spent a bit of time in the library? I want to go through the family books in the locked sections. They ought to be sorted out fairly soon . . . if that's all right?"

"Well, of course," said Jeffrey Underhill. "The house is yours, you know that. You don't need my permission to use your own part of it. Or this part, for that matter. Did Emory tell you that he and I are going to talk later on about the extent of our lease?"

"Yes."

"Well, meantime, please do your best to forget we're in the house at all. Go where you like. Now, what about keys? Do you want to keep my set?"

"No, thank you." I fished them out of my handbag. "I can get Rob's."

"Good. Then there'll be no difficulty about the tours." He took the keys from me, and laid them on the coffee table in front of him. "Stephanie, will you let the guide have these back this afternoon, please?"

"You leave that to me, dear," she promised, and began once more to tell me how welcome I was to anything and everything the Court could still offer me. She was interrupted by Cathy, who was over at the fireplace, busily tracing out the design of the maze in the stone.

" 'Touch Not the Cat . . .' It's a queer motto, isn't it? Emory said it was enigmatic. I say it's just plain arrogant. What does it mean? What is this cat they put in the middle of the maze? It looks more like a tiger!''

"It's getting on that way," said James. "It's a Scottish wildcat. There are lots of stories about them, but one thing's for sure, they can't be tamed, even if you take them from their mother while they're still blind and sucking. You'd not touch one of those lightly, glove or no glove."

"Goodness!" exclaimed Mrs. Underhill.

"A bit out of place here, perhaps?" commented her husband. "One gathers that the gloves they use in these parts have been velvet for rather a long time."

"Yes," said Cathy. "How does a Scotch wildcat get down here, right in the middle of England? And what does 'but a glove' mean?"

"Without a glove," I said. "It comes from an old word, 'butan.' The motto belonged—still does, I believe—to the Scottish Clan Chattan. One of the Ashleys married a girl called Julia McCombie who belonged to the Clan. She was a beautiful girl, and he was wild about her. He altered the whole place for her, did the house up specially, and built the pavilion in the maze. . . . The maze itself was here already; there's an engraving somewhere that shows it newly planted sometime in the eighteenth century, with a pretty little classical folly in the middle, a sort of imitation Roman temple. William Ashley pulled that down and built the pavilion that's there now. It must have been lovely when it was new. He built it as a sort of summerhouse for Julia; he raised it so that she could sit there and have a view right across the hedges of the maze."

"I suppose that's why he put the Scotch cat in the middle of the maze on the coat of arms," said Cathy.

"And he took her family motto as well?" said Mrs. Underhill. "How very romantic. But didn't the rest of the family mind? Surely they must have had a motto already?"

"Oh, they did. But the odd thing is that it was almost the same. It was 'Touch Me Who Dares,' and the crest was a creature like a leopard, so I suppose it seemed natural to poor William to use the coincidence, and put Julia's crest everywhere instead."

"Why 'poor William'?" asked Cathy. "What happened?"

"They didn't have much time," I said. "She died not long after he'd got the pavilion finished. He went peculiar then, used to shut himself up in the pavilion, and blocked some of the paths in the maze, and devoted himself to his writing and his studies. He wrote verses to her, too. There's a little book of them in the closed section of the library, called *A New Romeo to His Juliet*. He had her painted as Juliet. She's the one on the main landing, with a view of the maze behind her."

"Why, that's really romantic!" Mrs. Underhill said in her gentle voice. "And that's my favorite of the portraits, too. This will make it very interesting indeed to see that pavilion, if you're really sure you can find the way—"

"Oh, yes!" cried Cathy. "Do say you'll take us in, please, Bryony!"

"Of course. We'll go now if you like. But if we're going through that maze, Cathy, you ought to put on something you don't care about. Whatever you wear will probably end up in tatters."

She grinned. "You English are the politest folks. As if I didn't know just what you think about this sweater. Don't pretend you don't know these are my very smartest rags. Patches special extras by Bonwit Teller."

"You will do us all a favor," said her father crisply, getting to his feet, "if you get that sweater torn to pieces, so that even Cathy refuses to wear it."

"I'll do my best," I said, and Cathy laughed, and turned to my cousin. "Emory, you're coming, aren't you?"

"Some other time," said my cousin. "Your father and I have some talking to do."

"Okay. I'll just go change my shoes, Bryony." She ran from the room.

Mrs. Underhill saw me eyeing her cream linen suit, and shook her head. "Some other time I'd love to. But not right now, if you don't mind. I've things to do."

"If the things to do include the washing up, then let me help you do it before we go."

"No, you certainly will not. What's the machine for? And look how many dishes there are. It will take one minute and a half, and not a second longer. Now you just go off with Cat, and forget about it. And don't leave without calling in again, will you? It's been a real pleasure. Get Cat to bring you in for tea."

She went, with James pushing the trolley for her. Jeffrey Underhill, with a word to me, went after them. I waited for Cathy to come back, watching the flicker of the log fire which looked pale in the sunlight, and thinking about the echo of Herr Gothard's voice, and the "William's brook" which might or might not be "William's book," and the cat which might or might not be Cathy Underhill.

To have a view now from the pavilion, it would have to be built on stilts like a water tower. The yew walls of the maze were eight feet high, and hadn't been clipped for some half-dozen years, so leaned over, top-heavy, to make the path in places into a black-green tunnel. Underfoot the weeds had seeded and reseeded into a long pale pash of sun-starved grass and groundsel, all too generously sown with nettles. In summer, what with the weeds underfoot and the dust harbored by the choked evergreens, the labyrinth would be impassable, but the main hazard now seemed to be the roosting birds. The hedges were full of them, and as we pushed our way past they exploded angrily in every direction. The smell of the yews as we disturbed them was as thick as smoke. Here and there a thin patch let a probe of sunlight through to gild the tiny green cones that clung along the feathery branches. Lamps of peace. Or was that the fruit? Must I wait for autumn and the lovely green-and-rosy acorns to glow along the dark boughs?

Lover? Lover, are you with me?

The only reply was Cathy, bravely treading behind me like Wenceslas' page. "Why did they ever make mazes? Just for fun?"

"When this one was planted it would be for fun. It was the fashion then to have follies, like mazes and grottoes and Grecian temples, in your garden. But the idea was ancient, wasn't it? There was the Labyrinth in

Crete. I don't know if that was the first one. The legend said that Daedalus invented it for King Minos to hide the Minotaur in."

"Oh, yeah, I knew about that. I just read that fabulous book by Mary Renault . . . it was really a sort of storehouse, wasn't it? Do you suppose," asked the tycoon's daughter, "that it was a sort of primitive safe? You know, the treasure right in the middle, and even if thieves got in, they starved to death looking for a way out?"

I laughed. "It's an idea. But you were more likely to find a tomb in the middle than a treasure. I read somewhere that a maze was supposed to be the path the dead follow on the way to the world of spirits. Once at the heart of the maze, and nothing could touch you again; you'd reached a place outside the world, a place without bearings."

"In other words, you'd died?"

"Yes. Like the ships that went astray in the magic mists, and ended up in the Wondrous Isles. They say compasses won't work in a maze."

"For goodness' sake! Have you ever tried?"

"I can't say I have."

"And you really have been to the middle and out again?"

"Lots of times."

"Then I'll risk it," said Cathy buoyantly. "Oh, look, there's a gate. Where does that go?"

Here and there in the thick hedges was a tall, narrow gate, more than head high. I tried one; it was locked. A wren flew out of somewhere to perch on it, chattering angrily. "They were really put in to make it possible for the gardeners," I said, "but they've been used when people got stuck, and couldn't find the way out."

"Are they all locked?"

"Oh, yes, and the keys have been lost for years."

"Are you *sure* you remember the way?" she asked, a shade uncertainly.

I laughed at her. "Fairly sure. We could always climb on the pavilion roof and scream."

"If we ever get there."

"If we ever get there," I agreed. "No, here, it's this way."

"But we're heading right back for the house! I can see the chimneys!"

"I know, but it's right, it is really. You can trace it out tonight on the fireplace."

"If I ever see the fireplace again. Okay, I have to trust you, don't I? It's like something in *Alice*, you just turn your back on the pavilion and find yourself walking right up its front steps. . . . Oh!"

This as, just in front of us, under the last bending frame of black evergreens, a bright patch of sunlight struck green from flowery grass, and, rising from the flowers, were the elegant steps of William Ashley's pavilion.

The pavilion was as overgrown with weeds and lichens, and as dilapidated as the maze itself, but it was still charming. It was built of wood, with a steeply pitched roof of shingles gone silver with time. The roof-ridge was scalloped with carved shells, and at the corners curly dolphins waited to spit rain down into the gutters. The gutters themselves were warped and gaping, and held a remarkable selection of flowering weeds. A verandah, edged by a balustrade, and sheltered by the overhang of the roof, surrounded the pavilion on all four sides. The front door had carved panels and a charming knocker of a leopard's head with a ring in his mouth. To either side of the door stood tall windows with slatted louvers fastened over them. Honeysuckle and clematis and a host of other climbers had ramped up the wooden pillars and along the balustrading, and were reaching to seal doors and windows. We pushed them aside and mounted the steps.

"Touch not the cat," said Cathy, and reached past my shoulder for the ring of the knocker. She rapped sharply at the door.

There are few sounds so dead and hollow as the knocking on the door of an empty house. I felt a kind of goose-feather of superstition brushing my skin, and must have made an instinctive movement of protest. Cathy, unmoved, sent me a smile.

"Just to wake Wicked Ashley up," she said. "What's the matter?"

"Nothing. You made me jump. Anyway, one's always better not waking things up that are sleeping."

"I thought you said there weren't any ghosts."

"I've never met one," I said. "But if there are any at Ashley, this is where they'll be."

"Well, whether he's awake or not, he's not answering," said Cathy. "Anything against me trying the door?"

"Nothing at all, but you'll find it's locked."

"You're right. Oh, dear, can't we get in after all?"

"There's a way in through one of the side windows. Round here."

There was a way of opening the window shutters at the south side of the pavilion, and we were soon inside and pushing the creaking leaves open to let in the light and air.

The pavilion was larger than such places usually are. It had once, of course, been elegantly furnished, but now all the furnishings had gone except for some relatively recent garden stuff, a table and a daybed and a couple of cane chairs.

"Well, here you are," I said. "I'm afraid it's rather a dusty end to the romance."

"Is that the table where he wrote his poems?"

"I doubt it. That's late Victorian. I'm afraid all the original stuff has gone."

Cathy's eye fixed itself on the one impressive feature which remained. This was the ceiling, which was made of one huge looking glass framed in gilt and mounted within the elaborately molded cornice. Its smeared and flyblown surface was slightly angled, its frame of dirty gilt scrollwork supported, apparently, by birds and ribbons and swags of roses. The glass caught the sunshine from the open window, and laid a rhomboid of gritty light across the foot of the daybed and along the floor.

"Surely that's part of the original building?" she asked. "What a pretty idea, to have a mirror ceiling. If those brackets in the walls held sconces, the place must have seemed just full of candlelight. Is this in any of the old pictures?"

"Yes, I'm afraid it is."

" 'Afraid'?"

"There's a set of rather randy engravings," I told her. "I'm afraid the mirror's not a bit romantic, really. Oh, yes, it's certainly old, but I think it was put in by your Wicked Ashley, William and Julia's son. It rather gives one ideas about all the wild parties he had, and the ladyloves he brought here, till the brother of the last one shot him. The engravings are rather imaginative about it, anyway, and the mirror certainly shows in those, right over where the bed was."

"Oh, for goodness' sake, is that what it was for? You know," said Cathy, pivoting on her heel and watching herself in the tilted mirror, "I cannot imagine it would be any fun at all watching oneself having sex. Can you?"

"Distinctly off-putting, I'd have thought."

She turned again, slowly, on her heel, and her look round the grubby, echoing room was sad. "It surely is a dusty answer," she said.

"I'm sorry."

"Oh, don't be. I don't know why the past is always sadder if there's something a bit beautiful about it. And this place must have been beautiful."

"Keats says that about melancholy." I quoted it for her:

> "She dwells with Beauty—Beauty that must die;
> And Joy, whose hand is ever at his lips
> Bidding adieu. . . ."

"Yeah, I remember that. He was right, too." Cathy's look dwelt on me for a moment, with something in it that I couldn't understand. Then she looked past me. "Oh, look, there's a little bit of Julia left here, after all."

Above the daybed, on the wall against which presumably Nick Ashley's big bed had once stood, was a molding in plaster, a sort of bedhead applied to the wall itself. At its apex was the familiar coat of arms, thickly grimed and gray, with its motto and its rampant wildcat. This looked as if it had been molded from one of the carvings in the house; it showed the grainy texture of the stone, and even a chip or two. There were still traces of paint, but time had done badly by it; it was rubbed and flaking, and in places barely distinguishable.

Cathy leaned across the daybed to look at it. "Well," she said, "what do you know, here's the map again. Just to make sure you could get out of the place, even if you'd forgotten how you got in." She licked a finger and rubbed the grimy plaster. "Did you notice? I think someone's marked the way. Yes, there's the bit just before we got here, when we were heading straight back towards the house."

I followed her, kneeling on the daybed and peering up at the dirty molding. "I believe you're right. I'd never noticed."

She rubbed harder. "They're not done like that in the house, because I was looking." She laughed. "I expect Nick Ashley drew it in so that his girl friends could slink off home to their husbands, and leave him still peacefully sleeping it off. Hey, this plaster's crumbling a bit, I'd better leave it alone." She straightened, rubbing her hand down the patched jeans. "This place really could do with a paint job, couldn't it? I only hope that mirror's safe. It certainly doesn't look it. You know, with a good cleanup and a rug and some furnishing, this could be quite a place, still, wouldn't you say? It would make a guest cottage if you put a bed back in, and a few other things."

"For people you didn't like? Show them the guest cottage and forget to tell them the way out?"

She laughed. "Well, it's an idea. Anyway, what would you want a guest cottage for, with a place the size of the Court? No, it's fascinating just as it is."

I wondered if the gaze she sent around the pavilion was more than just idle. My next question came straight out of the speculation, but it sounded casual enough. "How long have you known Emory?"

"Not long. We only met last month, but it seems longer. I mean, he's easy to know, wouldn't you say?"

"I can imagine. And James?"

"I met him soon after, but I've only seen him a couple of times. My, but they're alike, aren't they?"

"Tweedledum and Tweedledee," I agreed. "Could you ever get them mixed up, do you think?"

She laughed. "I hope not. Could you?"

"I don't think so. I never did as a little girl, but that's a long time ago, and we don't meet so often now. I admit that when I saw him today at the Court I wasn't quite sure which it was till he told me."

We had gone outside while we were talking, and I pulled the long windows shut and fastened the louvers across. We went down the steps. The honeysuckle let its arras down behind us, and the pavilion was shut in once more with its dust and its silence.

"I guess," said Cathy, ingenuously, "I could still get them mixed up if they tried to fool me, but they're too nice to do that. Besides, Emory—" She stopped. "Say, what's that perfume? I don't see any flowers except daisies and those yellow things."

"Lilies of the valley. They've gone wild there under the hedge in the shade. You can't see the flowers—those stiff green leaves, see? Let's pick some for your mother, shall we?" I stopped and pushed the leaves aside, hunting for the waxy bells. She kneeled beside me, and did the same. I said: "You were saying. Emory?"

"Oh, nothing."

I let it wait for a minute. "Emory's special, isn't he?"

"Special? Why, of course! Bryony, I'm just crazy about him!" She laughed up at me, her eyes brilliant. She meant, it was obvious, every word; but it came a thought too easily, as if she had said it before, and would say it again. Paradoxically, I found the over-emphasis soothing; it gave her confession the flavor of powder-room gossip, the easy euphoria of the evening out. "Don't *you* think he's just fabulous? I'd do just *anything* for him!"

She stopped, seeming to catch some echo in her own voice that embarrassed her. She bit her lip, and colored up, turning quickly away from me, her hands searching busily among the green spathes. The long hair swung down to hide her face.

"Bryony, about Emory. Do you mind?"

"Mind?" Taken by surprise, I sat back on my heels, regarding her averted head. Then I answered as she had spoken, directly and without guile. "No, I don't. Of course I don't. There's no reason why I should."

She, too, sat back at that, turning to face me once more. The flush had subsided; she gave me a clouded, smiling look, where some obscure hint of trouble showed still. She started to speak, broke off, considering something else, then rejected that, too. Kneeling there among the flowery grass, with the rhinoceros-folds of the enormous sweater dwarfing her body, and her hair falling anyhow over brow and shoulders, she looked far younger even than eighteen.

I said, easily: "I don't wonder you've fallen for him: when I was your age I was wild about him. But then, I was wild about the others, too." I smiled at her. "Tell me, where's the difference when it comes to being 'special'? Why not James?"

"Well, for one thing, I haven't seen all that much of him, and for another—"

"Yes?"

The fabulous mink lashes dropped suddenly to shadow her cheeks. She bent to the flowers again. "He has a girl already."

"How do you know that?"

I hadn't meant the question to come out quite so sharply, but she appeared to have noticed nothing. "Because he said so," she said simply.

"Oh." I bent to add another flower to the spray in my hand. "Have you met her? Did he say who it was?"

"No. There." She straightened. "Mom'll be wild about these. Shall we go back?"

"Sure. Let's go back by the path along the Overflow."

We came out of the maze into full sunlight, and crossed the little bridge. Primulas were out along the stream, nodding in the draft made by the running water.

"Why do you call it the Overflow?" she asked as we followed the mossy path along the edge.

"Because it's just that. It controls the level of the moat. There are the two sluices, the High Sluice, on the other side of the house, that lets the water from the river into the moat, and this one here that lets it out into the Pool. The Overflow wasn't much more, originally, than just a ditch to carry floodwater away, but a few years ago the High Sluice broke in a storm, and the lower sluice couldn't cope with the flooding, so parts of the house were damaged. They put a new High Sluice in, and dug this channel deeper as a safety precaution."

"Gee, I'd never thought that living with a moat around you could be dangerous."

"It's not really. And if the sluice had been kept properly it never would have been. Actually"—I laughed—"the moat is pretty useful. Its main use being that it reduces the fire insurance premiums."

"Well, and that's another dusty answer," said Cathy. "Here I was thinking that a moated grange was the most romantic thing ever— Oh!"

"What is it?" I asked.

She had stopped, and was pointing. I had been walking behind her. I came up to her shoulder and looked.

Between the moat and the lake below it, cutting down through a corner of the grassed bank, was one of the prettiest monuments in the Court gardens, a cascade with a fishing cat. At the head of the bank was the heavy sluice gate, which was normally kept shut, and to either side of this the normal outflow from the moat was channeled to lapse, fall by fall, toward the Pool. The water stair, a natural-looking cascade of rock, thickly set with ferns and trailing plants, led the fall into a corner of the Pool from which, through bigger rocks green with the moss of many years, the water ran down into the deeply cut channel of the Overflow. On one of these rocks, just where the water slid toward the first rush of the Overflow, was a stone cat, its outstretched paw reaching into the flow, gracefully curved as if to hook a fish.

Or rather, the cat had been there. Now there was nothing but the gate with the water cascading down the rocks beside it, and on the stone where the cat had been, the ugly iron staples stuck out, rotten with rust and twisted crooked with the fall of the statue. The cat itself was lying in the basin under the water, with the fish tranquilly shuttling to and fro across it, under the broken paw.

Ashley, 1835

A sound from the door dragged him from the shallows of sleep. Someone was there, on the verandah.

He was alert, instantly up on one elbow. Perhaps Fletcher had come: something was wrong? His uncle had arrived before he was expected? This little world of peace and love had been broken before its time; the too short night was over.

But all was silence. He relaxed again, to see her eyes, darkly shining, watching him.

"What is it, love?"

"Nothing. Something waked me. Look, the moon's almost down. A little while, and it will be getting light. No, don't go yet. I have something to tell you, but it will wait. It will wait a little longer."

11

Nor what is mine shall never do thee good:
Trust to 't. . . .

—Romeo and Juliet, III, v

As I had promised, I went back to tea with Cathy and her mother, then took myself off to my cottage, to see if Rob had brought my baggage in from Worcester.

He had, and had even carried it upstairs for me and dumped it on the tiny landing.

Before I unpacked I went to the telephone and dialed the number of the secondhand bookshop in Ashbury.

"Is Mr. Oker there, please? Oh, Leslie, it's you. This is Bryony, Bryony Ashley. Yes, I came back a couple of days ago; I'm back at the cottage. . . . How are you? Good. How's everything going . . . ?"

Talking to Leslie had about it something (I imagined) of the ritual of Eastern bargaining; you had to go through the routine of question and answer first, the answer being the shorter exercise of the two. Mr. Oker loved talking, and there was no hurrying him; one got to business eventually, but by way of health, the weather, trade prospects, the latest news, and any extra juicy items of local gossip that were worth passing on. The routine, I suppose, had originally been evolved as part of a softening-up process, the patter before the hard dealing. In sober fact, Leslie gave very little away, but the impression he fostered, of a genial and impulsive gossip, stood him in very good stead: strangers who were deceived by his effusive and rather camp manner into hoping for an easy bargain would come suddenly, and to their disadvantage, up against a very knowledgeable and wily operator. Leslie Oker was about as impulsive as a two-toed sloth, and rather less effeminate than a tomcat. The kindness, though, was real.

Thanks to it, the preliminaries today were short. After only three minutes, at least two of which were devoted to my welfare, and to praise of my father, Leslie paused, and then said, directly: "But you didn't ring me up just to tell me you were home, dear. What can I do for you?"

"Well, something's come up, and I wonder if you could help me, please. Just a quick query. You remember showing me that limited edition of *Rip Van Winkle* last year, the one illustrated by Arthur Rackham? I wondered what sort of price his work was fetching now? I don't mean the books, I mean the original illustrations?"

"Well, it's not exactly my line, as you know, but I'd say you'd be lucky if you came across one at all. Is this some particular drawing you want to buy?"

I laughed. "You know me better than that. I don't want to sell one, either. I just want to know the sort of value, if you wouldn't mind. Just an idea."

"The last one I saw listed in a catalogue," said Leslie, crisply, "was a watercolor drawing from *Comus,* and it was priced at eight hundred pounds."

"Oh. I see. Thank you. Leslie—"

"Yes?"

"If you should by any chance come across some mention of Rackham drawings for sale, would you not say anything about this, but just phone me straight away?"

"Of course. But how very intriguing." The light voice showed little but a gentle and sympathetic interest. "I gather one is not allowed to ask why?"

"For now, no. But I'll come in as soon as I can, and tell you all about it."

"This *is* exciting," said Leslie comfortably. "Of course, Bryony dear. Count on me. And perhaps I could give the grapevine just a teeny, teeny shake? But tell me soon, won't you, before I *die* with curiosity?"

"That'll be the day," I said, and he laughed, and rang off.

James came down after supper, just as I was finishing the washing up. He hoisted the empty cases into the roof space for me, accepted a cup of coffee, then followed me outside to the seat under the lilac tree facing the Pool. Dusk was falling, and the air was very still. The surface of the Pool lay quiet and shining, ringing into ripples here and there as fish rose for the evening hatch. There was a heron still fishing among the reeds at the far side. The rooks were settling for the night, and making a great to-do about it. Like clouds behind the cottage roof, the orchard trees showed pale and frothy with blossom, and tallest of all, the pear tree, like a central fountain in a water garden, held up its plumes of springtime snow. A thrush was singing in it, alone, as freshly and as passionately as if this was the first song in the world. From somewhere in the middle distance, toward the Court, came the sound of someone hammering.

"Rob puts in long hours," said my cousin.

"I wonder if he's mending the fishing cat."

"Fishing cat?"

"The one at the sluice where the Overflow leaves the moat. It's broken. I saw it this afternoon when Cathy and I were coming back from the maze."

"Oh? That's a pity. It was a pretty thing. Did you ask him to fix it?"

"No, I've not seen him this evening."

"Well," said James, "why should he trouble? More likely he's propping up one of the gates, or mending a roof, or even chopping some bushes down.

Wasting his time, whatever he's doing. The whole place is falling to bits, and it would take more than Rob Granger to stop it."

He spoke without bitterness, and quite without intent to hurt, but with some special seriousness in his voice that made me look searchingly at him. He met my look gravely, then took my empty cup from me and set it with his own on the flagstones under the seat. Then, as before in the schoolroom, his arm came gently round my shoulders, drawing me close. I could feel his heartbeat, perhaps a shade too fast.

"Bryony, love, it's time we had a talk, you and I."

I waited, feeling my own heartbeat quicken imperceptibly to match his. I was very conscious of the beauty of the evening, the scent of the lilac and the song of the thrush and the lovely long planes of light on the lake in front of us.

My cousin cleared his throat. "You may be angry, and as a matter of fact I think you're bound to be angry, but if you've any sense you'll hear me out, and in the end, I hope you'll help me." His fingers, cupping my shoulder, tightened a fraction. "You have to be on my side. You know that. You have to be. It's the way things are."

The thrush stopped singing, as suddenly as a turned-off tap. The heron, too, had decided to give up for the night. He must have done well, I thought; he was having trouble with his lift-off. I watched him in silence as he lumbered into the air, and flapped away.

"Bryony?"

"Yes, I'm listening. Go on."

There was a short pause, while I felt him looking at me. I heard him take breath. "I'll start at the beginning. And I may as well start by confessing the brutal truth. My father—we, the lot of us, are in a jam. A real jam. We're desperate for ready cash and we have to find it some way, and find it fast."

This was in no way what I had been expecting. I was startled, and showed it. "But surely? I thought Cousin Howard—your family's always seemed to be doing so well. I mean—compared with us . . . And I thought you were riding really high now, with the Jerez office doing so well, and with the Pereira backing. I know Daddy thought the same. What's happened?"

"The trouble is, everything's happened, and all at once." He stirred. "My God, that's the truest proverb in the language: 'troubles never come singly.' All the demands that we could have met if they'd come separately, and at the right time, well, they all seemed to come at once. . . . I told you that my father will probably have to retire. If he does, there's not much guarantee that Pereiras will go on backing us. Why should they? And the Bristol offices are hardly an asset; they're mortgaged. If we had time— But the point is, we haven't. This illness of Father's has put a gun to our heads."

And now, I was thinking, this has happened. Because of my father's death, this huge liability, Ashley Court, has fallen on them, too.

"But I thought Juanita had quite a lot of money of her own. Wouldn't she help tide you over with a temporary loan, and give you the time you need?"

"Ironically enough," and his voice held no irony, but only a rather flat distaste at having to talk about the matter at all, "the main part of her money is tied up in a trust, and can't be touched. These trusts," said James, and left it at that.

I said nothing. The evening was silent and empty. The light had gone from the lake. The lilac's scent had evaporated with the cooling air.

"So," said my cousin, "my father applied to yours to see if he could help us."

This time I really was startled. I sat up. "James, you can't be serious! You must have known we were run into the ground."

"Oh, yes, we knew that. But you had Ashley."

"*Ashley?* But what on earth use is Ashley, when it comes to meeting a mortgage? It's the biggest liability this side of the National Debt!"

"As it stands, yes. It just pays for its upkeep and nothing to spare, we know that." His voice went flat. "What I'm talking about is the Ashley Trust."

"I see. You mean that's what you 'applied' to Daddy for? To break the trust?"

"Yes."

"When was this?"

"The first time was in November of last year," he said. "I never saw his answer to my father's letter, but it must have given room for maneuver, since Father still seemed to have hopes he would consent."

"The first time? He asked him more than once?"

He nodded. "He wrote again recently, and he had a couple of telephone talks with your father. This was when Cousin Jonathan was in Bad Tölz, of course. My father didn't want to press it, because he knew Cousin Jon ought to rest, but— well, things were getting desperate. The last time, though, Cousin Jon said he couldn't even consider it." He was silent for a moment, his head bent. "I've been thinking about the reason for his change of heart, and I can't really understand it. As you know, things have been sold in the past, and no one's ever argued much about it. I think he must have been feeling so much better that he was planning to come back here, so he decided that as long as he could keep the place in some sort of order, he'd do just that. After all, it was your home."

"And his. He loved it. You're not just talking about 'things' this time, James? I take it you're talking about the place itself. The land."

"Yes." He gave me a gentle look. "Didn't you know anything about this?"

"Nothing. Of course if there'd been any question of breaking the trust he'd have had to bring me in as well. I'd have to consent, too, you know that." I thought for a moment. "It didn't occur to anyone to try and break Juanita's trust rather than ours? After all, she's Cousin Howard's wife."

"Well, of course it did. But that trust can't be touched at any price. It goes to her children, or, if there aren't any, it can be broken when she's forty."

"Which is quite some time away."

"Too long by half. If it was only six months, it would still be too long for us."

"So," I said, "now Daddy's dead, you come to me, and ask me to break ours."

He was silent.

"That's what you've been leading up to, isn't it? Isn't that what you want?"

"That is what we want," he said.

A pause. I said abruptly: "Did Daddy give any reason for being so dead set against it?"

"No. He would hardly even discuss it. He really never mentioned it to you at all, even indirectly?"

Even as I shook my head, I realized, in a sudden moment of enlightenment, that he had. *"Trust. Depend. Do what's right."* This was one of the things that had been weighing on his mind. Until I knew the rest, I could take no action.

I took refuge in a half-truth. "I can't say that he did. He may have thought that your money troubles were your own affair, and shouldn't be broadcast, even to me. But of course he spoke about the trust generally, once or twice. I do remember his saying that Cousin Howard seemed to have put down roots in Spain, and didn't seem to have the kind of feeling for Ashley that might bring him back to look after it. He didn't say it as a criticism, why should he? He said it 'wasn't to be expected, but it was a pity.' That kind of thing. But I know he hoped that Emory or you might feel differently. You'd lived here, after all, with us. Do you?"

"Are you asking me to speak for Emory?"

"If you can. I know you said you couldn't speak for him when I asked if he was serious about Cathy Underhill, but you must know how he feels about Ashley." I gave him an inquiring look. "And I would have thought the two might almost be the same. I mean, if he was thinking along the lines of marrying Cathy—"

"He'd be able to afford to keep Ashley as it should be kept? I suppose so," said James, "but the plain fact is, he doesn't want to keep it at all."

From beyond the lime trees the church clock tolled the half hour. It sounded remote and serene. The distant hooting of an early owl spoke of mystery and the coming night.

"And you?" I asked him. "No, James, it's all right. I do understand. But I've got to know the truth. You said I had to be on your side, and that's true. I am; you know that. We're not talking about family now, or people, just about bricks and mortar and trees, which might mean a lot to one person, but don't have to to another. So tell me. Do you want Ashley yourself, or even a part of it?"

He took his time. When he spoke at length his voice was quiet, but I could feel the tension in the arm that encircled me. "I think you know the answer, don't you? When we were talking awhile ago about the fishing cat, I said the place was rotten, and that's true. You know it is. It's been falling to pieces, bit by bit, for years. It's a burden to the living, even if you count keeping it going as homage to the dead. That's not the way to live now, when the dead can no longer supply the living with the means to keep their memorials going." He took a breath like a sigh. "I'm sorry, love, this is the wrong time to talk to you like this, but you asked me. I doubt if you've had the time to think about it yet, since Cousin Jon died, but you can't seriously expect either of us, Emory or me, to go on running this—this National Trust reject, even if we did have the money to do it with? There are other things to do with money, Bryony. For us, anyway."

"I suppose so."

"All right, so Cousin Jon might have thought we should want to. But you're a different generation, you know the score. These are the seventies, and the world's wider than Ashley Park. If there aren't the means to save it, then it'll have to go. We've got to face that."

"James, I'm facing it."

His arm tightened, and he held me close. His cheek touched my hair, but he didn't attempt a caress. "Well, I've said what I promised to say, and I'll leave it. But you will think about it, won't you?"

"Of course I will. But Daddy only died a week ago, remember, and until I know what he wanted, and why—"

"I know, love, I know. I'm sorry. This is a hell of a time to talk to you about breaking trusts and leaving Ashley, but when we started this we weren't to know what would happen to your father. And now my own father's ill, and worried half out of his mind, and things are pressing, and—well, hell, there it is."

Another of those silences. The hammering had stopped. I thought of the fishing cat lying broken under the water, and, for some reason, of the pavilion with its riot of honeysuckle and the sagging walls of yew and Cathy's voice asking: "Is that the table where he wrote his poems?"

"Francis," I said suddenly. "How does Francis feel about all this? I thought he loved Ashley."

"He does," said James. "He's a throwback, is Francis. Anyway, he wouldn't notice if the place fell to pieces round him, as long as he could sit in the maze like William Ashley, making verses. What on earth did I say? You jumped."

"Nothing, really. Only you were reading my thoughts. Do you often do that?"

A pause, as long as four quickened heartbeats. Then he said, easily: "Twin and I do it as a matter of course. Shades of Bess Ashley, the gypsy, didn't you know?"

"It must save a lot of telephone calls," I said lightly.

He laughed. "Oh, it does. But you were saying about Francis. I doubt if he would refuse to help break the trust. The point is, even if we did break it, we wouldn't have any designs on the house itself. That's unsaleable, so one might as well make a virtue of necessity, and leave it alone as a corner of ancient England on its own tight little island. It's the land that would have to go."

"For what?"

"For whatever would bring the most money."

"Building land brings the most."

He answered what I had not said. "Well, and why not? People have to have houses. And when they drive the new motorway across Penny's Flats, we'll be in Birmingham commuter country." He must have felt something in my silence, because he added, rather edgily: "Look, Bryony, you said you'd be realistic. Just because we played here as kids doesn't mean our kids will ever have the chance, or, my God, *want* the chance."

"I wasn't. I was thinking about the other people involved. That must be what was making Daddy think twice. There's the Vicar, for instance. What happens to the Vicarage? I suppose that would be safe enough, though I can hardly see Mr. Bryanston hemmed in with housing projects, and without the garden. But there are the Hendersons, and Rob Granger. Would you sell their houses?"

"Why not? They'd have first option to buy them themselves."

"The Hendersons might, but I'm sure Rob can't afford to."

"Then he ought to. He had the farm, after all. If he didn't manage to make a go of that, there's no reason why we should be responsible—"

"Be fair. His father drank every penny they ever made, and knocked Rob and his mother around on Saturdays for good measure. He left them in debt up to their necks, and if Rob hasn't managed to save the price of a house since the old brute died you can hardly blame him. What's more, if it weren't for Rob this place would have dropped to bits a darned sight sooner."

"O.K., O.K.," he said, half laughing. "What have I said? Sorry, I didn't mean it like that. I've always liked Rob, and I know what he's done for you and your father. And now I've made you angry when I want you to listen."

"I'm not angry. It's not that I'm not on your side, James. I am. And I was listening. You were talking about commuter country. Well, all right, all being equal, that's the way things might have to go. But had you thought? Ashley hasn't an outlet to Penny's Flats."

His head turned, sharply. He stared. His eyes, in the close dusk, looked dark, gypsy Ashley eyes. I felt a queer little tingling thrill at the base of the spine, and looked away. He said, sharply: "Of course it has. That's its whole value. This strip along the Pool runs right through the apple orchard to the road."

"Yes, but that's not Ashley Trust. It's mine."

"Oh, I see." He sounded amused. "Holding out, are you?"

"For the present, yes. I've got to have a home, and I'm planning to stay here till . . ."

"Till?"

"Well, for a bit," I said, evading it. "James, let's leave it for now, may we?"

"Of course, if you say so. But—"

"Yes? But?"

"There was something else. As a matter of fact," he said, rather abruptly, "I haven't even got to the hard bit yet. Look, would you like—shall I get some more coffee?"

"No, don't bother, for me. Go right on. What is the hard bit?"

"Well, I was saying. After your father had refused to consider the trust any further, my father asked Emory and me to do what we could, as quickly as possible. Emory and I talked it over, and we agreed to go to Bavaria and talk to your father. He must obviously have had reasons for his decision, which he didn't want to talk about by telephone, and which might be too complicated to write. But before that it seemed only sense to—well, to take a look at Ashley itself."

"So then?"

"I meant, take a look at it with the idea of a sale in mind." He cleared his throat. "Obviously, we wanted to get into the Court and find out, as a basis for discussion with your father, what there was in the way of quickly disposable assets. We didn't approach your father about this because . . . well, damn it, it was a little difficult under the circumstances. He was ill, and he'd have thought we were being a bit previous. A foot in his grave, as it were. I'm sorry."

I said nothing.

I could feel tension running through his arm. He said abruptly: "We didn't get in touch with the Underhills either, because there was no need. I told you about that. By pure chance—it really was pure chance—Emory met Cathy at a party, and she asked him down."

"Convenient."

I felt his look. "You sound a bit abrasive. Don't you like her?"

"From what I've seen of her, I like her very much. I'm just not sure that I like her being used by Emory."

"Did I say he was using her?"

"Isn't he?"

"I wouldn't put it like that." But I thought he sounded uncomfortable.

"That had better be true, you know. Jeff Underhill is what they call a tough cookie, and at a guess he adores his daughter. If she's fallen for Emory, and I think she has, and hard, then Emory had better reckon it as serious."

"I imagine he does. I only said that he didn't plan to live at Ashley on her money." He sounded thoroughly edgy now. "Damn it, do you have to assume he's going to damage her in some way? If a girl like that falls for you, you've got to be a bloody plaster saint not to take a second look, at least."

"So you have."

Somehow, almost unnoticeably, his hand had lifted from my shoulder, and his arm now lay harmlessly along the back of the seat. "It's the James-Emory thing that gets you, isn't it? You'll have to take my word for it that nothing's happened that Cathy would mind remembering, even if she ever found out we'd played that game with her. Which she won't." He glanced at me again, but I made no comment. "Actually, I don't like it any more than you do. . . . There are things I'd rather be doing than escorting an eighteen-year-old who's in love with someone else. I don't think Emory ever would have started it, but in a way Cathy herself forced it on us."

"How on earth?"

"Oh, there was one date they had made, and Emory couldn't keep it. When he phoned, she was so mad that he thought she'd call the whole thing off, and this was just at the time when we very much wanted to get down to the Court, and if there had been a quarrel with Cathy we could hardly have come down, even through Emerson. So Emory soothed her down and got me to go instead. It never crossed her mind. It was a harmless sort of date—she and Twin hadn't known each other more than a few days, so I didn't have any soft lights and hot music to face. . . . And today it was a case of coming down to see Jeff Underhill, rather than of making love to Cat. Believe me, I've no idea how far Twin's pushed the boat out, nor do I want to. I wouldn't bet on not giving myself away to Cat, and God help us all if that happened." I caught the gleam of a sideways, smiling look, and one finger came away from the seat back and touched my shoulder blade, a feather touch. "If you like, love, I'll promise you here and now not to do it again."

"That's up to you." The words were indifferent, but I felt myself relaxing, and the arm came round me again. "Go on," I said, "did you check the 'disposable assets' between you after all? Great jumping beans!" I sat up again, my hand to my mouth, regarding him wide-eyed in the dusk. "The T'ang horse? The jade?"

"I'm afraid so." He was speaking quietly, straight to the almost invisible flagstones at his feet. "Bryony, they were ours. I promise you we only took them after your father's death. This last week. I promise you. We badly needed a bit of ready cash, and Emory knew of a market, so . . ."

I listened to the tone, rather than to the words. I knew it well. James, led into something by Emory, loyal to his twin but knowing all the time that whatever they had done was, to say the least of it, dubious. Emory, I knew, was more than capable of playing rough, and James, playing with him, had sometimes suffered for it. But Twin had always been right.

I was aware of silence. He had run out of words. I heard myself asking, in a hard voice quite unlike my own: "Did you have to take the pictures from the schoolroom? You might argue that the other things were going to belong to your family anyway, but the pictures were my own, and I loved them."

"I know. I'm sorry. I—it was a mistake. They were taken by mistake. They haven't been sold. As a matter of fact, we planned to put them back, but there hasn't been a chance today."

"Today?"

"Yes, today. They were only taken yesterday. As soon as I found out, I said they must go back, but by that time you were at the Court, and you'd seen the T'ang horse was missing, and you had started asking about keys. It . . . well, it was awkward."

"I suppose it was." I felt a little dazed. "Just a minute, James. You said, 'They were only taken yesterday.' Who took them, then? Emory wasn't here, was he?"

"No. Cat took them for us."

"What?" A whirling pause, while I tried to assess it. " 'For us'? You mean 'for Emory.' "

"If you like."

"I do like." My voice was sharp. "It makes a difference."

"Well, then, for Emory. Look, don't worry, you'll get them back. It was just—"

"I'm not worrying about jade or pictures or anything else. I'm thinking about Cathy Underhill. You got that girl to steal for you."

"That's a hard word."

"It's a hard fact."

"Aren't you making a bit too much of this? The things were ours."

"Perhaps I am. But not nearly as much as her parents would make of it, I'm sure of that. I thought at the time they seemed almost too upset for what had happened. It made me wonder."

"Her parents? For God's sake, you're not going to make a thing out of it, are you? Bryony—"

"Wait a minute, James. This takes some getting used to. Let me alone for a bit."

I got up abruptly and walked away from him, across the newly cut strip of lawn to the lakeside. There was a low wall there, a length of ancient stonework that had been left to edge the garden; its fissures were planted with wallflowers and toadflax and some trailing glaucous fern that looked silver in the dusk. I stood there with my back to my cousin, staring out over the dimming Pool, but without seeing that or anything. It was wrong, so wrong. . . . Yet because it was James, I couldn't give way to my first instinctive reaction; because it was James I must make myself stop and think. . . . Be civilized, I told myself, this sort of shocked recoil isn't even instinctive, it's a conditioned reaction to what you've been taught to call theft.

Well, all right, think. *Was* it theft? As soon as the legal formalities allowed, all these things would belong to Howard, and by the same token to his sons. James had said with perfect justice that the day was gone when the dead could help the living to watch over the property they had amassed and handed down in designs too vast for today to cope with. And it was my cousins who would have to cope, not I. The fact that Jon Ashley was now one of the dead ought to make no difference. My reaction was an emotional one, nothing more. James knew that; he had tried to spare me; but I had forced his hand by my actions at the Court today, so he had had to tell me now, raw though I still was from my father's death.

I thought again, briefly, about Rob and the fishing cat. . . . Yes, James was right here, too: the place, and the life it had represented, was falling to pieces. Even this cottage, the idyllic little cottage with the view of the lake, with its fruit trees, and the honeysuckle and the Fribourg rose, had woodworm and rising damp which I could not afford to combat. If I sold some of my mother's Worcester porcelain to pay for it, that would be ethical. Why should not my cousins, the owners of Ashley, sell the pieces that were theirs? And why, if they were driven for time, should they not have done it this way?

It came back to the one answer: Cathy. And here I had even less right to judge. I had no idea of the strength of Emory's feeling for her; nor had I stopped to question the circumstances under which she had "stolen" the missing articles for my cousins. For Emory, that is. My father had long ago said that Howard would never take on Ashley or any part of its responsibility; it was squarely on Emory's shoulders, and if Emory had chosen to jump the legal gun . . . Yes, it was to be laid at Emory's door; I still did not believe that James was, in this, anything other than a follower, loyal as ever to whatever course his twin suggested.

I sat down on the wall, still facing the lake, forcing myself to calmness. I owed my cousins something better than this shocked recoil. I thought again of the quiet nights filled with my lover's presence, of his support and warmth and love, of the strength he had given me. I thought, too, of the recent strange hesitancy, the impression of guilt and insecurity which, now, I thought I could understand. It had only showed itself since I had come back to England; it had begun last night, when I had seen James in the church vestry. Doing what? That, too, I had begun to guess. The object he had been carrying was large and flat, like a book, or a portfolio. He must just have picked up the Rackham pictures from some hiding place; not the vestry itself—that would have been asking for discovery. But, except on church-cleaning days, there were a hundred places—under the seats in the side aisles, under the pulpit, behind the stacked hassocks near the font—any of these places would have made a cache, safe and dry, where Cathy could have hidden the objects she had abstracted from the Court.

So James had snatched a cassock from the choir men's pegs, had fled up the nave in front of me, switched off the mains, and, while I was approaching up the church, fumbled with and opened the catch of the vestry door. Whoever came into the church would only see the vanishing cassocked figure, and would come to the same conclusion as I had done. . . .

Well, now I knew. And I understood my lover's refusal to come into the open. It was because the affairs of daylight must be settled first. Before anything could be complete between us, we had to settle with the realities of a difficult situation, the hard economics of how and where to live, of Ashley Court and Daddy's Will and the theft of the jade and pictures. What I had called to myself the facts of the daylight world. And the other world, the starlight one, where love was easy because it ran like poetry from mind to mind, that would have to wait. I knew now what he meant by his repeated *Not yet, not yet;* I had to come to terms with what he really was; the outer man, not just that other half of me whom I knew as well as I knew myself. We had reversed the norm, he and I. It had always seemed to me that the love we had, being fuller, must be easier than most; now I saw that it was harder. Nor was the outcome certain. It would depend on my handling of this uneasy and tangled affair, on my finding out what my father had meant and what he had wanted. I must do my job as Jon Ashley's deputy, and then, when Ashley was accounted for, my lover and I could come to terms. This was what he had seen already. He knew me, and he knew that there were things about him which I might find it hard to accept. He could not be sure of me until I had seen the whole truth about him, and accepted it with love and understanding.

I do not think that at that moment I had any doubts about his identity. I stared at the water and opened my mind to him, the query forming in the dimming air. *This is why we have to wait?*

He came in. *This is why.*

But I understand now, and I accept it all. Won't that do? You know I love you, you know that. I have to. That's the point, isn't it? Whatever you may have done. Whoever you are.

A flurry of love, as real as petals falling, and the little catch of amusement that I knew so well. *I'll hold you to that.*

There really were petals falling. A spray of clematis, caught in the breeze of evening, shed its fading petals on the dim grass. I looked at my cousin at last, across the dusk-filled space. He was watching me steadily, saying nothing, just watching, patient and intent. Then he smiled, and something twisted inside me, like a cord stretched between us that had felt a sudden tug. Blood thicker than water, whatever that might mean; or creatures inhabiting the same pool, over whom the same wave breaks. There seemed no need to speak. There were the Ashley eyes, shadowed in the growing dusk, the fair hair, the casual pose that masked tension. The picture of the real man was blurring, almost as if the imagined picture of my lover was beginning to superimpose itself over the reality of the cousin who sat under the lilac tree and watched me. The outlines wouldn't quite fit. Not yet. Not, I suppose, until I had accepted him whole, starlight and dreams and the harsh light of tomorrow.

A shadow moved along the lakeside. Something flew up from the reeds with a squawk and a splashing of water. Rob's collie, hunting along the water's edge, had disturbed a moorhen from her nest. As if it had broken a spell, I spoke aloud.

"It's all right, James. Please don't worry about this any more. You've a perfect right to do what you think best about the stuff in the house. . . . It's yours, after all, and if you need it now instead of later, well, that's your affair, too. I suppose we'll have to think what to say to the Underhills, but let's leave it for tonight, shall we?"

"I wasn't worrying," he said, "not really. Blood's thicker than water, whatever that may mean."

I heard the smile in his voice. His easy assumption of my complicity (why did that hard word occur to me?) took me off balance again. I said nothing.

The flash of the smile then, and he got to his feet. He must after all have misinterpreted my silence. Almost before I knew he had moved, he had crossed the grass as silently as a cat, and putting out his hands, pulled me to my feet and into his arms. His mouth found mine, gently at first, then with quickly growing excitement.

"Bryony. Bryony. It's been so long."

A thrush broke out of the lilac boughs and went skimming across the orchard wall with a cry of alarm. I put my hands against my cousin's breast and held myself away from him. "James. But I thought—"

He kissed me again, stifling what I was trying to say. He said, against my mouth: "You've always known it was me, haven't you?"

"I—yes. I wasn't sure. It used to seem so easy once, but—no, wait, please."

"Why?" He pulled me close again, and when I moved my head away he began to kiss my hair, my cheekbones, my throat.

"No, please, don't make it any harder. I've just begun to understand. We've got to get all this business over first."

He persisted for a little while, but, meeting with no response, finally let me go, and laid a gentle hand to my cheek. "All right, all right. This isn't the time. But don't let's be too long about it. I'm so afraid you'll get away from me again."

"I won't do that. Let's go in, shall we, James? Do you mind bringing the cups?" He stooped and picked them up, then followed me back into the cottage. "Are you staying at the Court tonight?" I asked him.

"No. I'll go back to Bristol." That heart-twisting smile again. "I may as well, since you're turning me down."

"For heaven's sake!" I tried for a light tone, but it came out edged. "Did you really expect me to ask you to stay here?"

"Well, perhaps that would have been pushing it a bit. I'm a patient man." No overtone to suggest that there had been any other sort of conversation between us. "I'll telephone Herr Gothard tonight, I think, to see if there's any news. Have you got his number handy?"

"Yes. I'll write it down for you, shall I?"

I went to the bureau, and swtiched the lamp on. I found a pen and a used envelope, scribbled down the number, and handed it to him.

He glanced at it, and pocketed it. "Thanks. Oh, where did you find my pen? I dropped it somewhere, and I've been looking for it all over the place."

"Yours? Are you sure?"

"Sure I'm sure. It's mine all right. Look at the initials. Where on earth did you find it?"

"In—in the churchyard. Beside the path."

I thought he must have noticed my hesitation, but apparently he did not. "Oh. Yes. Well, thank you." He pocketed it, kissed me again, and went. I stood for a long time beside the lamp, thinking of nothing, my mind closed, a gate slammed shut in sudden panic to keep him out.

Because I knew something, now, that I dared not let him guess at. He and Emory had done more than know my father was ill when they had come to Ashley to check the "disposable assets." They had known he was dead.

The pen I had picked up, from among the small clutter of objects in the bureau, was the silver ballpoint pen with the initials *J. A.* It had been lying there, along with my father's other effects that Herr Gothard had handed to me. I had not recognized it as Daddy's, but there had seemed no doubt that it was his. It had been found, Herr Gothard had told me, beside his body, on that lonely country road in Bavaria.

I don't know how long I stood there, staring, but without seeing it, at the lamp and the big gray moth which had blundered in through the open door behind me and was crazily beating itself to death against the light. My mind, like the moth, beat and fluttered against a truth so alien and so destructive that I could not, would not, believe it on the evidence of the facts.

Heaven knew I did not want to draw the conclusions that followed from it, but they had to be drawn. The first, which seemed now hardly to matter, and which followed from his easy acceptance of my lie about finding the pen in the courtyard, was that James had in fact been the prowler in the vestry. The second was one that mattered very much indeed. James must have been there, beside my father's body. And he had neither helped the injured man, nor made his presence known.

I could see only one further conclusion to come to. James had driven the hit-and-run car that had knocked Daddy down. James had killed my father.

That night, lying wakeful in the quiet little bedroom, I watched the moonlight moving slowly across the floor and, with every ounce of effort I could summon, kept the doors slammed against my lover. So strongly insistent was his presence at times that, as on that night in Madeira, I could have sworn I saw his very shadow move across the floor. In my grief and loneliness I must have faltered, because I caught it, as clear as a whisper; just my name, insistent and appealing.

Then I turned away and shut him out again, and listened, for the rest of the night, to the church clock chiming in the tower.

Ashley, 1835

The candle guttered in a pool of wax. Beside him she stirred, and murmured something, then sank back into sleep. Light, cast by the mirror, slid over her bare shoulder and the curve of a breast. Light o' love, he thought. It's a beautiful phrase. She is my light of love.
He reached a hand and doused the small, fluttering flame.

12

. . . a divine, a ghostly confessor,
A sin-absolver, and my friend profess'd. . . .

—Romeo and Juliet, III, iii

NEXT MORNING, as soon as I could, I went to see the Vicar.
He was on his knees in the biggest of the ruinous greenhoues, contentedly rummaging about among the young tomato plants. The hothouse stood against the twelve-foot wall of the old kitchen garden, and many of its panes were broken, and had been replaced by odd pieces of plywood or polythene sheeting. The heating system, of course, had long been out of use. The original staging, too, had long since rotted; Rob Granger had dragged it out and burned it, and rigged benches from old trestles and some planks from one of the derelict farm buildings. The sun was pouring in, reflecting warmly back from the whitewashed wall, and the place smelled pleasantly of newly watered soil steaming in the warmth, and the musky scent of tomato leaves.
"Hullo, my dear. Were you comfortable in the cottage last night?"
"Very, thank you. What are you doing?"
"Tying up the tomatoes. Rob strung all these canes last week, and now the plants are big enough to train. Excellent young plants, aren't they? I don't know what's so fascinating about tomatoes, but they really are delightful to work with. So easy, and such a big return for such a small investment."
I laughed. "That's too worldly by half, Vicar. You should be drawing morals about it; tall oaks from little acorns grow, and something something fountains flow."
"So I should, so I should. Well, there's a moral in it somewhere, I'm sure. . . . Dear me, now I sound like the Duchess in *Alice in Wonderland.* Did you want me for anything special?"
"I wondered if I might talk to you," I said. "Sometime when it's convenient. There's no rush."
His hands, holding the furred leaves gently, paused. His eyes, distorted so

grotesquely behind the thick glasses, searched my face. "It's always convenient." He let go the plant, and began to get to his feet. "Here and now, or shall we go up to the Vicarage and make a cup of coffee?"

"Here and now, if that's all right. No, don't leave the tomatoes. Can't I help you with them? I know how to do it."

He made no demur, knowing, I suppose, how much easier it is to talk when one's hands are occupied. He started work again, and I moved to the other side of the row from him, and followed suit. Above us the robin, who was always on the watch for whoever was gardening, flew in through a broken pane, saw there was nothing doing, scolded for a moment, then flew away. Silence, except for the rustling of the tomato leaves, the snip of scissors cutting twine, and the drip of a tap into the tank.

"Mr. Bryanston, do you believe in telepathy?"

" 'Believe in'? I don't query its existence; I don't think one reasonably can. There have been too many instances of it, thoroughly documented; and now I think it is being seriously researched. Can you be more specific? I take it you mean thought-transference, but this takes a variety of forms."

"I think I mean it in its most straightforward sense, communication between mind and mind, straight across without even any bodily presence."

"Yes, I see. Well, my answer stands. One can't query the existence of such a phenomenon. I think I may say that I am bound by the history of my own Church to accept that such things have happened. Elisha, for instance, was telepathic—or else an uncommonly good guesser."

"Perhaps he was just a pretty good judge of human nature?" I suggested. "Gehazi had cheated him before, hadn't he? I suppose you are talking about the time Gehazi took pay from Naaman, then hid the cash and told Elisha he'd never been near him?"

The Vicar's eyes twinkled. "That was a very good education you had in Sunday school, my dear."

"Yes, wasn't it? Was that what you were thinking about? Elisha knew all about it all the time, didn't he?"

"He did. 'Went not mine heart with thee, when the man turned again from his chariot to meet thee?' A bad moment for the liar Gehazi. Perhaps, as you say, Elisha just knew his man; but the text does not preclude knowledge of what had happened at a distance, and out of sight."

We worked for a few moments in silence. Then I said: "When I said, 'believe in,' I think I meant have you had any experience of it?"

"Experience at first hand, no. At second hand, I am told so. Like everyone else, I had an aunt who had premonitions, at least thirty percent of which were correct. And we have all met people who claim to have foreseen things, some of them probably truthfully. No, I'm not joking; I can see that this matters to you. In any event, such cases as I have come across myself have mainly concerned the kind of instinctive prevision which used to be called divination, and was legislated against as far back as, dear me, Deuteronomy. Along with witches and familiar spirits it was an abomination unto the Lord." The fine eyes were gently merry behind the distorting lenses. "And that, I am certain, you are not, my dear child, and could never be. Am I to take it that you yourself have had firsthand experience of this 'communication between mind and mind'?"

"Yes, I have. Not just premonitions, either. Messages, conversations even, coming clearly from another mind straight into mine. What I would call telepathy."

"Well," said the Vicar, "you are an Ashley, are you not?"

My hands checked, the fingertips tightening on a shoot so that it broke. "Sorry," I said mechanically, then looked up at him. "You *knew?*"

"I know the history of your house. And I have read all the family papers that were kept in the library, including some of the otherwise lamentable stuff in the locked shelves. There are records of the kind of thing you talk about, and some of them have an authentic ring. And I know that in your family there's a history—a record, I should say, since some of it is undoubtedly spurious—of unusual mental powers which appear from time to time in members of the family. Elizabeth Ashley, the 'witch,' seems to have done little to deserve that title except to be heard talking to someone who couldn't be seen, and on two occasions conveying information which she claimed had come from her 'secret friend,' and which knowledge could not otherwise be accounted for. If she had escaped burning, her husband would almost certainly have repudiated her. Apart from the fear of witchcraft, he suspected her of taking lovers. But you know all this."

"Yes."

The kind eyes regarded me for a moment, before returning to the work in hand. "It's never easy to be different. But I gather you know that only too well? You too have a secret friend?"

"Yes."

He was silent, not looking at me this time. I said, and heard pleading in my voice: "Vicar, please believe me."

"My dear, I do believe you. I am afraid for you."

"My mind is *not* abnormal, not in any other way, that is. But as far back as I can remember, I've been able to talk to this—this person."

"Only one person?"

"Yes."

"A real person?"

His voice was mild and inquiring, but the question shocked me. I straightened, staring. This had never occurred to me. "Well, of course. It—it never entered my head . . . Do you mean it might be someone . . . Oh, no, Vicar, he *is* real. It's one of my cousins."

"I see." His look of trouble deepened. "Yes, I see."

"But what are you suggesting?" I demanded. "That it could be some fantasy thing I made up as a child, and now can't get rid of? I mean, I know that children do invent imaginary friends, but for heaven's sake, they grow out of that, and it isn't that, or anything like it! It's a real relationship, Vicar, I promise you!"

"I have conceded that already." His voice was sharp, for him. "My dear child, what have I said to put you in such a state? If this is true at all, and I have said that I believe you, then I prefer to believe that you are in touch with another real and living mind. I gather that you don't know yet just who it is?"

"No, not yet. But it must be another Ashley, and he's here somewhere, and we can talk—communicate—about what's going on. We can stay in touch at quite a distance, too. When I was in Madeira he told me about Daddy's accident."

And I thought I knew, now, how he had known. James had been in Bavaria. The message, made faint and difficult by sheer distance, must have come straight to me from the scene of the accident.

Something the Vicar was saying got through to me. "You're sure the news didn't come to you from your father himself?"

"It couldn't have. We didn't have that sort of communication, just a—well, a feeling for trouble. I knew he was ill, or hurt, but he himself could hardly have—" I stopped, swallowed, stared. "You mean you *knew* about this? You knew all along? And that my father had it, too?"

"To some extent."

I was silent, thinking again about the message that Herr Gothard had written down for me: *"My little Bryony be careful. Danger. This thing I can feel. . . ."*

"Did he know about my 'secret friend'?" I was grateful that the Vicar had given me this name for my lover. "Lover" was not a title I was prepared yet to use aloud.

"He never mentioned it, nor, indeed, did he give any hint that he knew you possessed this gift. His own was, I gathered, much slighter; he occasionally had moments of premonition, or perhaps extra clear-sightedness. They were all, as far as I know, connected with you. He seemed to be sure, rather beyond guesswork, when you were in trouble, or needing help."

"Yes," I said, "I knew that."

The Vicar carefully snipped off several lengths of twine, threaded them through a buttonhole, then shifted his kneeling pad, and addressed himself to the next row of plants. "You said your friend was an Ashley. That must surely narrow the field considerably?"

"Yes." Even to myself the syllable sounded harassed and dejected, hardly the tone used by a friend or a lover. Another of the shoots bent in my hands, almost breaking. I apologized, and, abandoning the tomatoes, went to perch on a rickety stool beside the water tank. The Vicar never paused in his work, but moved on steadily down the row, half turned from me. I leaned back against the warm wall. The robin flew in again, scolding, and I saw that he had a nest high in the roof, in the tangle of passionflower which flourished in a corner. He swayed on a bending stem, cocked his head to regard us with bright eyes, stopped scolding abruptly, and vanished into the leaves. The peace, the sunlight, the warmth, the steady rhythm of the work with the plants, slid down like calm over troubled waters. Without any conscious decision I found myself telling the Vicar all about my lover. Not about James; nothing about last evening; only the long communication between mind and mind until last night's slamming of the doors.

When I had finished there was another of those pauses. Then he said, with his gentle, unsurprised calm: "Well, thank you for telling me. You make it very clear. Now, I take it, something has happened which has worried you and driven you away from him, to me?"

"Yes. I came because I think I know who he is, and I think he's done something very wrong indeed, and I want to know what to do. Normally speaking, I think I'd be able to tell right from wrong myself, but this is different. It's knowing him the way I do—being sure, after all these years, that we are more to one another even than normal lovers, that we are part of one another whether we like it or not. . . . Do you see? Betraying him, even if he's very wrong, would be like betraying myself, or even somehow worse."

He straightened up from his task, but did not look at me. He knelt there for so long, looking down at the tomato plants, that I thought he had forgotten my presence and my question. Finally he sighed. "My dear, I'm no help to you. Perhaps if I took time to think . . . Yes, I must do that. And pray, too . . . This is quite outside my experience, and outside my book of rules.

There was a time when I would have said that right was right and wrong was wrong however one found out about it, but time changes one's mind about that. In a way one might say that an intimacy of the kind you've described is like the intimacy of husband and wife; and the law recognizes that; it would be intolerable if the one were allowed to betray the other. I think—yes, I think that if you do indeed hold the key to someone's inner thoughts, you must not betray them."

"I see," I said. "Yes, that's what I thought. At least, I didn't think, I felt it. Thank you."

"If he has done something so very wrong, then it will surely come to light without you. But I think that if you see him about to hurt others, or to do more harm, then you must use this unique relationship that you have, to dissuade him. In fact, if this bond between you does make you two sides of the same medal, then the decision for right in you could counteract his drive toward wrongdoing. Yes, perhaps that is the answer. Since you have this, er, privileged communication, you must pay for it in this way. In other words," said the Vicar, kneeling there in his old patched jacket, with the scissors in his hand, and looking like the law and the prophets rolled into one, "in other words it is your duty to act as the voice of his conscience, if he has not a sufficiently powerful one of his own."

"'Stern Daughter of the Voice of God,'" I said, a little dismally.

"Exactly. Not an attractive lady, Duty. One of Wordsworth's more inspired descriptions, I feel. Does this sound so very daunting, child?"

"A bit. But just at the moment it does seem to be about the only thing I can do—if I dared communicate with him at all. I can't betray him out loud. Not to anyone else, I mean."

He had finished the row of plants while he was speaking, and now, getting stiffly to his feet, he crossed to a potting bench for a new ball of twine. Looking away from me, he spoke again. "Bryony."

"Yes?"

"This is not a safe road that you are treading."

"I've realized that. That's one of the reasons why I had to talk to you. Up till now, you see, it's been marvelous, and so familiar . . . I've known it so long . . . being able to talk to him about everything, exchange everything, just as if he was part of me and I of him. There was nothing but happiness, I was never alone, always someone I could turn to. . . . And it seemed to me that there was nothing but joy in the future, that when we actually, physically, found one another, it would just be a continuing of what's been going on all our lives. It was so serene." I looked down at my hands. "After Daddy died I thought all I had to do was to come home to Ashley, and I would be able to find him, my 'secret friend.' But he said no, it wasn't time yet, we must wait. And now I think this was because he didn't dare let me near him, knowing what he had done. I felt so much alone. . . . Then, just as I thought I'd found him, I discovered that he'd done something terrible, really terrible, so bad that all this time he's managed to keep it secret, even from me. I only found out by accident. That's why I came to you, to ask what to do."

"You found out 'by accident'? You mean that you read a thought he didn't want you to read?"

"No. You can't do that. I told you, you can close your mind. For instance, he can't know what I'm telling you now. No, this was a—a daylight thing. I saw something he didn't realize would give him away."

"Then you are not betraying your secret life if you do something about that. There's part of your answer, I believe." He looked at me, then gave a nod. "But that's not the whole answer, is it? You cannot think of betraying him, whatever he does, yet you cannot live with what he is doing?"

"Yes. Yes, that's it exactly."

"Then, my dear," he said gravely, "you must live without it."

It was the answer I had come to myself, but still it came like a knell. Like a full stop. Like the gate slamming.

"Without *him?*" I said.

"Yes. Without this private life that you have come to depend on. You cannot keep as part of you something that is alien to what you believe, something you know to be wrong. The ancients used to call it 'possession.' It was a good word, for ownership by something alien; the turning aside of oneself from one's own straight track."

"I know. I know. I've already cut him off. I knew I had to, and not only because I was afraid of his finding out what I knew about him. This is what made me wonder if the whole thing, this 'gift,' as I used to think of it, is evil? I can't believe it is. I've lived with it all my life, since I was tiny. It was comfortable and happy and good, and later, when it became more serious, it still seemed to be good. Believe me, Vicar, I know it was. I know he was, too." My hands had gripped together in my lap. "And the awful thing is that I can't bear to be without him. I feel worse than being alone, I feel mutilated, like losing half oneself, or not being able to breathe properly, or something like that. If it was so wrong, why is it worse without him?"

"That I can't tell you. I can only say that it is a grave mistake to commit oneself to anyone or anything that may get beyond one's control. I don't for a moment suggest that this gift of yours is fantasy, but it might be said, perhaps, to share the same qualities and defects. There's the same danger that, as reality approaches, there will be a falling off."

I had thought about this, too. "You mean like those people who spend all their time reading stories about ideal lovers and ideal relationships, so that a real ordinary man or woman never can measure up?"

"Something like that. Any imaginary world has its dangers. The edges between light and half-light are indistinct, and tend to blur more and more the longer one looks at them. You know, Bryony, you've given me almost too much to think about. Will you give me a little more time, and come and talk to me again? I'd like to clear my mind. I'm sorry I haven't been more help."

"Oh, you have, you have. You believed me, and that's almost enough in itself. Thank you for that."

"My dear child," he said, then, smiling: "You've relieved my mind, too. I said you were treading a dangerous road; I doubt if I need have worried about you. You have a clear head, for so young a woman, and you are not afraid to think things through. That's not as easy as it sounds, and not common at all. Was there anything else you wanted to talk about? I see Rob Granger on the other side of the garden, and he seems to be coming this way."

I turned to look out through the glass. Rob was standing between the rows of vegetables, pointing something out to the boy, Jim Makepeace, who helped him sometimes. Jim nodded and picked up his spade, and Rob headed toward the greenhouse. I turned back to the Vicar, and asked quickly: "Did you ever find out what the prowler was doing in the vestry?"

"Yes, indeed. What a very strange thing that was! I am glad to say that I was right in thinking that no one from these parishes would have attempted to open the safe. It had not been touched."

"No? Do you mean that nothing was missing after all?"

"Nothing of value—that is, none of the 'valuables,' but something worth much more in its own way, and quite irreplaceable. One of the registers."

"One of the *registers?* A parish register?" The ones at Ashley, I knew, went back without a break to the sixteenth century. It was a serious loss, but for the moment I could not get far beyond a sort of blank amazement and reassessment of what I knew. What in the world could James have wanted with one of the parish registers? Anything less like a "disposable asset" I couldn't imagine. "But I thought you said no one had opened the safe?"

"Oh, not one of the Ashley registers. One of those which were on the vestry table, from One Ash. Unhappily, it is one of the earlier ones which is missing, the second volume, 1780 to 1837. . . . The latter, as no doubt you know, was the date on which the full procedure of registration was instituted as we know it today. Before that it was a question of signatures, or indeed marks, from the parties concerned. In the registers before 1754, when the Hardwick Act was passed, there is merely an entry of the fact of marriage; nothing else was required. . . ."

"But surely—" I was thinking hard. If James had laid the pictures down on the vestry table in the dark, while he fumbled for the main switch, he might just possibly have picked the register up in error, and carried it away. It seemed unlikely, but I made a mental note to telephone him as soon as I could. It was obvious that the Vicar was very worried; the thing must be put back without delay. "But surely, it won't have been stolen, Vicar. Who would want it? It'll turn up soon, you'll see."

"Quite, quite. I comfort myself with the thought. I am not seriously worried," said the Vicar, looking very worried indeed. "It seems clear that someone must have wanted to consult it, and seeing it here, has simply borrowed it. It will be returned in time, surely. The fault is mine, and only mine. When I left the volumes in the vestry, it never entered my head that anyone besides myself would be interested enough to abstract one of them. Indeed, I still may be mistaken; I shall be going to One Ash tomorrow afternoon, and will make sure. . . . Ah, Rob, good morning. Were you looking for me?"

"Good morning, Vicar. Mrs. Henderson said to tell you that a young couple called from Hangman's End about a license."

"Oh, dear," said the Vicar, "and I did want to get the plants finished this morning."

"I'll do them," I said. "That is, if you'll trust me after breaking that shoot."

"Of course, but you must have plenty to do."

"I'd like to finish them," I said. "Good morning, Rob."

"Good morning."

"Are the Underhills at home today?" I asked him.

"They're going out later. But Mrs. Underhill said if I saw you to say you were welcome at the house anytime. She tried to phone you this morning, but you'd gone out."

"Oh, thanks. I'm going to take a look in the library, Vicar. I thought I'd look through the family section."

"Oh, yes. Well, anytime you want me, you know where to find me. Rob, what have you done to your hand?"

"Nothing. Hit it with a hammer, that's all."

"Was that you mending the fishing cat last night?" I asked him.

"Fishing cat?"

"The cat statue at the Overflow. It's broken off. Had you seen it?"

"Oh, that, yes. The metal's rotten. I left it be. It's not much use wasting time on that kind of thing." It was an echo of what my cousin had said last night, but without the bitterness; Rob spoke with an indifference verging on the surly. He was already making for the door. "I was wedging the sluice gates shut, that's what you heard. Looked as if they'd been tampered with, but then the whole thing's rotten anyway."

"Is it safe?"

"Safe enough. The High Sluice can take care of anything the river likes to send down, and the Overflow's there to keep the moat level steady."

He was at the door, opening it. I got quickly to my feet. "I'm going over to the Court again. May I have your keys now, please, Rob?"

"You know where they're kept. Help yourself." The greenhouse door shut behind him.

"His hand must be hurting him more than he'll admit," said the Vicar. "He's not usually rude. I hope it's nothing serious. Well, I must go, I suppose. If you really will finish the tomatoes for me—?"

"Of course I will."

Alone in the greenhouse I went back to the plants. The silence of the glasshouse, the stillness of the air, and the monotony of the task were somehow soothing. God knows I had plenty to think about, but I thought about none of it, not then. I shut myself off from it as the glass shut me from the air outside, content to let my mind stay closed and blank, and to work automatically along the rows of plants.

What slipped it into my mind I do not know, but it was suddenly there, clear as if spoken . . . no, not as if spoken; as clear as if it were written up between me and the garden, scrawled on the steamed glass.

William Ashley, 1774–1835.

It might be pure chance that a parish record of William Ashley's time had vanished, but also it might not. And anything to do with William Ashley was of interest to me, at least until I had managed to interpret my father's cryptic words.

I was on the last row of tomato plants. I finished the job as quickly as I could, then let myself out into the air, and hurried toward the Court.

Ashley, 1835

"You have the key safely?"

"Aye. See? But I'll not need it."

"Never be too sure. You know what they say about a maze?"

"No. What, then?"

"That a compass won't work there. While we're here, we're in a world without bearings and directions. Even if you could see the weathervane, it would be no help. We're outside the world."

"Sounds like we're dead, surely?"

"Hush, oh, hush. It just means that once we're here, at the center, no one can touch us."

"Till we go out again."
"Even then. Nothing can touch us now."

13

And what obscured in this fair volume lies
Find written . . .

—Romeo and Juliet, I, iii

No GHOST had ever walked in the Ashley library, but now, as I let myself quietly into the still, spacious room, it seemed haunted, probably only by the frail parchment ghosts of the books that had vanished from the shelves. It was so empty that it echoed. Somehow, I thought, a library looked worse than an ordinary room that had been stripped of its furniture. The books had been the brain of the room, its soul, its *raison d'être*. I shut the door quietly behind me, as if afraid of disturbing those pale ghosts, then, ashamed of the impulse even as I gave way to it, turned the key. Quietly as a ghost myself, I walked the length of the room to the locked cases which housed William Ashley's books, and Nicholas' sad little collection, pushed the library ladder up close, then climbed up and unlocked the grille.

"William's book . . ."? I might as well start with Scholar Ashley's own verses. I took out *A New Romeo to His Juliet,* sat down on the top step of the ladder, and opened the book.

There was the bookplate with the maze and the rampant wildcat with its grim motto—how touchable had Julia Ashley been? I wondered briefly—and opposite this the dedicatory letter with its extravagances which, for once, and how pathetically, sounded no more than true.

"To the peerless and beautiful Mistress Julia Ashley, my wife . . ."

I read it through. It was much the usual letter, fulsome to our ears and circumlocutory, but through it came very clearly the idolatry he had felt for her. The touch at the end was pure pathos.

May we never reach that end, but if we do, let it be together,
that we may never from our palace of dim night depart again.

YOUR ROMEO.

I turned the pages slowly. The work was privately printed and very prettily produced; it was doubtful if William Ashley could ever have found more than a local immortality, but to me, another Ashley, the book was fascinating. A great many of the verses were about the Court. One or two of the shorter ones I knew already; they had been printed elsewhere, and we had been set to learn them as children. Each poem had, as head- and tailpiece, some small and rather pretty engraving, and these I found enthralling. There was a picture of the main bridge, more or less exactly as it was today; a distant view of the Court minus the Victorian gables and a chimney or two; a view of the orchard beautifully kept and improbably heavy with fruit; one of the maze, trim and neat and little more than shoulder high, with a detailed drawing of a pavilion perched for the artist's convenience on a high platform that had certainly never been there.

The poem below this picture was called "The Maze":

> In this fantastickal and Cretan maze
> No Theseus to find the centre strays;
> This gentler Monster lurked within these Groves
> What time the Romans trod their secret ways.
>
> No Cretan Bull guards the abode of love,
> But where the gentle waters, straying, move,
> See! Dionysus' creature here enskied
> To greet our 'raptured gaze . . .

And so on. It was bad verse; so bad and so meaningless that, conversely, I thought there must be meaning there. William Ashley's poems were usually transparent as glass, his conceits more than simple, only lamely imitating the stately periods he admired. "Secret ways," I thought. It was surely only the usual conceit about a maze, the Greek myth of Theseus and the clue. Then why "Romans"? Well, it probably hardly mattered. But the maze was William Ashley's private refuge, and the pavilion was built for his Juliet. And past the maze went the Overflow. I read on.

Time passed slowly. Somehow the silence of the library, which should have helped me to concentrate, oppressed and distracted me. The clear north light showing up the half-empty shelves, the stuffy smell of a locked room, the waiting echo of emptiness, seemed to symbolize the vacuum inside my mind, the shut gate, the lack of presence. . . . Try as I would, the parable of the swept and garnished house kept coming back to me. "Possession," in any context, was a forceful, not to say frightening, word.

The thought came between me and the book, so persistently that I knew I could not go on reading here. I decided to take the books back to the cottage, make myself some lunch, then telephone Herr Gothard and find what James had said to him last night. After that I would settle down once more to my reading. I carried the *New Romeo* down the steps and laid it on a table, then climbed back to lock the grille.

A title in one of the Shakespeare shelves caught my eye, and the name *Juliet* in gilt on tooled tan leather. The real thing. Any comparison with Scholar Ashley's transports would be unfair in the extreme, but some impulse, sparked off perhaps by the thought of the star-crossed lovers and my own divided house, made me take the small volume out. Then I locked the grille, let myself out of the library, and locked that, too, behind me.

There was very little delay on the line.

Herr Gothard was at home. Yes, Herr Gothard would speak with me. . . .

"Bryony? How are you?"

"I'm fine, thank you, Herr Gothard. Can you hear me all right?"

"Perfectly. Now, how can I help you?"

"I'm awfully sorry to trouble you again," I said, "but there were one or two things I wanted to ask you. I, er, I understand that my cousin James was to telephone you last night?"

"That is so. He did telephone me. He has not been in touch with you about this?"

"I've been out all day. I wondered what news you had had for him."

"Ah." He sounded faintly surprised that I should have telephoned Germany rather than Bristol, but he went on with his usual calm courtesy. "I'm afraid there has not been much progress here. There is no sign as yet of the car which did the damage, but the police are still making inquiries."

"Yes, I see. Thank you. Did he—did my cousin ask you anything else?"

"No, only questions about the accident—had they found the car, were there any more clues to who had done it, all the same questions. I am sorry I have nothing more to tell you. And yourself? You are well?"

"Oh, yes, perfectly, thanks. There was one thing I wanted to ask you, though. Do you remember, among Daddy's things that you gave me, a silver ballpoint pen?"

"Ye-es . . . ach, yes, of course I do! It had his initials on it, yes?"

"That's the one. Where was it found, do you know?"

"Beside him on the road."

"That's definite, is it? It wasn't found in his pocket?"

"No. I remember that. It was found later, when the police went back to search the place."

"Herr Gothard," I asked, "do you ever remember seeing him use it?"

There was a pause while he thought. "No. I cannot say that I do. Why? Is it important?"

"I'm not sure," I said. "Look, Herr Gothard, something has turned up here. . . . If I send you a photograph, would you please show it to the police and ask if anyone in Wackensberg or Bad Tölz remembers seeing such a man? And surely they could find out if he hired a car, and all that sort of thing?"

"Certainly." I heard the sudden interest, and perhaps even enlightenment, quicken his voice. He had guessed, had Walther, why I had rung him in Germany rather than James in Bristol. "Why is this, Bryony? Does this mean that you have found some evidence yourself which points to someone? How definite is it?"

"I don't know. Something happened yesterday, and it made me wonder. . . . I can't say any more now. But, Herr Gothard—"

"Yes?"

"Please don't say anything about this to anybody but the police, will you? I mean, if anyone else should telephone from England—"

"I understand." And now I was sure that he did. His voice across the wire sounded troubled, even grim. "You can trust me. I shall say nothing until it is time."

"Thank you. I'll send the photograph straight away."

"Please do. I shall do all I can."

"Thank you," I said. "Good-bye."

I cradled the receiver, then came round sharply in my chair at the sound of a step on the flagged path outside.

"Hi, Bryony," said my cousin Emory.

I felt myself go white. He stopped short, and said contritely: "I'm sorry. Did I frighten you? I thought you must have heard me coming."

"Not a sound." I forced a smile. "Well, hullo. It's lovely to see you."

"Is it? You looked as if you were seeing a ghost, one of the nastier sort."

"Oh, dear, did I?" I got to my feet with a gesture of welcome. "Come in, Emory, do."

He bent his head under the lintel and came into the little room, and took my hands and kissed me, just as James had done in the schoolroom at the Court.

"You know, it is a bit like seeing a ghost." I said it apologetically. "I guess I must have stopped being used to you and James. And for heaven's sake, he was wearing that same shirt and tie when he was ringing for you yesterday, I'll swear he was. Don't tell me you wear the same clothes now? That really is taking it a bit far!"

I was talking perhaps a shade too fast, all the time casting back in my mind for what I had been saying on the telephone as he approached the cottage door. How much could he have heard? What might he have made of it? Certainly he seemed quite easy and natural, the old charming Emory I remembered, and none the worse for what the romantic novelists would have called a hint of steel under it all, but which I, who had known him too well since boyhood, had occasionally described as "bloody overweening Twinmanship."

He laughed. "Yes, and you had him taped in two seconds flat, I gather. Not that he was trying to ring the changes with you; it never worked, and neither Twin nor I have ever wasted time on things that don't work. . . . Well, it's lovely to see you again. I wish it could have been a happier homecoming for you."

I ushered him into one of the chairs by the hearth, and sat down myself where I had been before, beside the round table where William Ashley's books were lying. Emory leaned back in the armchair, took out cigarettes and offered them. I shook my head. He lit one for himself, and blew out a cloud of smoke.

"James rang Herr Gothard last night."

"Yes, he said he would." I made it sound as noncommittal as I could. He had of course seen me telephoning as he approached the cottage door. I knew I had used Walther's name toward the end of the conversation. How near had Emory been then? And when I referred to the photograph? If he had heard me, he would think it strange that I didn't tell him straight away that I had called Walther myself. Stalling for time, I asked him: "Would you like some coffee? Or tea, perhaps?"

"No, thanks." His voice gave nothing away, either of surprise or suspicion. "He would have told you about it himself, but the call came through rather late, so he didn't try to get you till morning. You must have been out?"

"Yes, I had to go out fairly early." I tried a safe tack. "Had Herr Gothard anything special to tell him?"

"Nothing, I'm afraid," said Emory. "That is, he said there hadn't been any progress, and followed it up with all the usual bromides—the police are still on the job, and so on."

"Yes, well, I would think that a hit-and-run accident is about the most difficult thing there is to trace, wouldn't you? And in a tourist area, in the tourist season, just about impossible."

He nodded. A pause, while he drew on his cigarette, inhaling deeply. I found myself beginning to relax. I was sure that he had heard nothing. He looked perfectly normal, calm, and unbent, with just the right hint of trouble showing in his face. My cousin Emory, the *alter ego* of my secret friend, who, whatever James had done, must know all about it, too.

He was saying gently: "You do realize, Bryony, that we may never know?"

My gaze met his, with, I hoped, exactly the same gentle concern and lack of guile. It felt strange to be deceiving my cousin, even though only by omission. What made it strange was, I knew, that he was so like James. . . . "Of course. To tell you the truth, I can't find it in me to agonize much about that." I turned, abruptly, to the real truth. "All that matters is that my father's dead, and, since I can't imagine that anyone would have wanted to kill him deliberately, I don't see that it helps much to run yapping after the fool who caused an accident." I looked straight at him. "Do *you* think it could have been anything but an accident?"

"I? No, of course it couldn't."

"Then you'd agree with me?"

"What about?"

"I mean, do you feel you can't relax or try to forget it until the police in Bavaria find out every last detail of what happened?"

He blew a smoke ring, and leaned his head back to watch it rise. With this new dreadful suspicion sharpening its rat's-teeth on the edges of my mind, I wondered if he couldn't meet my eye. He spoke to the ceiling. "It may sound an awful thing to say, but if it's going to take a long time, and cost a lot of money, no." He met my eyes then. "That may not sound pretty, but I'm paying you the compliment of the truth."

That it was indeed the truth, no more and no less, I knew very well. I waited, saying nothing, keeping a calm steady gaze on him; the old interviewer's trick by which you hope to stampede the victim into saying rather more than he meant. But Emory was not easy to stampede. He smiled at me as he leaned forward to tap ash from his cigarette. "That goes for the inquiry, too. What has happened to us as a family can't be changed by apportioning whatever guilt there is. That's a matter for the police, and they're the ones it will satisfy. It can't do anything for us, except keep a wound open. Both James and I feel that it's better forgotten."

"I'm sure you do." I said it flatly and pleasantly, but I saw his gaze flick toward me. I looked away, and began to arrange William Ashley's books neatly side by side on the table in front of me. "Well, I suppose the police will go on probing away until they do find something, or else have to close the case. There's no point in our doing anything more. When I'm next in touch with Herr Gothard, or with Mr. Emerson, I'll tell them so."

There was no telling whether Emory was relieved or not. He merely nodded, and drew on his cigarette. I looked away, afraid that my gaze was too intent and too inquiring. It was shocking how quickly I had been able to adapt myself to suspicion. Only two short days ago it would have been unthinkable. And now . . . It was shocking, too, how easily I had adapted to deception. I smiled, and peeled off smoothly into talk about my homecoming, and Madeira and Bad Tölz, and Emory followed my lead with the same smooth ease. I wondered if there were still things he wanted to know. For me it was simple; I stayed off the doubtful ground and waited to see if he would tread on it.

He did, but not straight away. He spoke of the Underhills, and I found myself hoping that he would keep off the subject of his relationship with Cathy; I had had enough of that for the moment, and there were things I was more concerned with. I need not have worried. James would certainly have told Emory of my reactions to the "theft" of the Court treasures, and for the present Emory preferred to let that lie. He did, when he was talking about the Underhills, make a sidelong and innocuous reference to Cathy as "a sweet girl and very easy to be fond of," but when I declined the bait he went on to talk about Jeff Underhill's business, and the family's eventual departure from the Court.

"And what are you going to do, Bryony? James seemed to think you wouldn't stay here—in the cottage, that is."

"How could he?" I said, more sharply than I meant to. "As far as I remember, I didn't tell him what I intended to do."

"And here am I," said Emory, with a smile that was as disarming in him as in his brother, "hammering at you within twenty-four hours about your future. And you know why, don't you? Cousin Bryony, dear sweet Cousin Bryony, have you had time yet to think any further about breaking that thrice-damned trust and letting your poor and dishonest relations have a pound or two to fiddle with before they're due to it?"

I had to laugh. "Well, if you put it like that—"

"I do put it like that. Cards on the table, cousin dear. An Ashley could always be relied on to look after his Ashley self with the greatest possible devotion."

"Which," I said smoothly, "is exactly what I'm doing."

The faintest line between his brows. "And what exactly does that mean?"

"It means no. I will not break the trust."

He flung his cigarette into the hearth. "For God's sweet sake, Bryony—"

"Not even for that. No. Not yet."

"But have you thought—" he began.

"Give me time."

I'm not sure what showed in my voice and face, but he bit back what he was going to say, and sat back in his chair. He gave me a long look. It was a shrewd look, and one I didn't relish under the circumstances. I said, rather quickly: "Emory, will you and James please do me a favor?"

"Such as?" He sounded understandably wary.

"Don't take me up wrong, but would you both just not hound me for a day or two? Just, in fact, keep away from Ashley till I've had time to get my bearings? I'm not saying that I refuse utterly and for ever to break the trust. I don't see that you should have the Court, just as it stands now, tied round your neck like a millstone for ever, but surely there can't be all that urgency about it? Good heavens, you haven't even let me talk to Mr. Emerson! I've got to, surely you can see that? Another week—only a week would give me time to think it all out . . . ." I paused, and finished drily: "And surely you can live for a week on what you got for the T'ang horse and the jade Fo-dog seal?"

He looked startled, then he burst out laughing. "No police, Cousin Bryony?"

"No police. But leave it alone, Cousin Emory, or I might surprise you yet. And leave Cathy Underhill out of it, or I *will* surprise you, and that's a promise." I got up. "Now I'm going to make some tea. Will you stay and have some?"

I half expected him to refuse, but I had underestimated him. He leaned back in his chair, still smiling. "I'd love some. Thank you." He was obviously enjoying the situation. Yes, I thought, as I went through to the kitchen, that was my cousin Emory; not the shadow of regret or guilt for anything he might do. That was the Ashley self-sufficiency—and just where, one might ask, did it part company with the criminal mentality? A look back through the family records might make one wonder; and these were days as wild and violent in many ways as the days of the Norman marauders with their rule of strength, or the days of their "civilized" counterparts the elegant duellists and the Mohocks of the eighteenth century. It threw the memory of James and his gilt-ridden contrition into very sharp relief. I had been right, I thought, I had been right. Whatever wrong had been done to Cathy, or even more to my father, it must have been Emory who had acted. It would not, could not, be James. Surely, the most that James had done had been to hear of it afterward, and feel himself bound to stand by his twin's actions.

And the silver pen with the initials *J. A.*? There must be an answer even for that. Emory might have borrowed his brother's pen, and left it on the Wackersberg road. It was even possible that James had not missed it, and genuinely thought he might have dropped it in the churchyard.

When I went back into the sitting room with the tray, my cousin was standing by the table, with one of William Ashley's books in his hand.

"What's this?"

"I've been checking through the locked section," I said. "No, not the porn, so you can put it back. Its only Shakespeare. I thought it might be interesting to read *Romeo and Juliet* again, alongside William Ashley's attempt to play Romeo."

"Heavens, why?"

"Just a thought. Do you still take three sugars?"

"Yes, please." He turned the volume over and looked at the spine. *"The Tragicall History of Romeus and Juliet*. Hm. It's a poem, not a play. I thought you said it was Shakespeare? Listen to this:

"This barefoot friar girt with cord his grayish weed,
For he of Francis' order was, a friar, as I rede.
Not as the most was he, a gross unlearned fool,
But doctor of divinity proceeded he in school.
The secrets eke he knew in Nature's work that lurk;
By magic's art most men supposed that he could wonders work.

My God," said Emory, "they made their money easily in those days, didn't they? I could do better myself."

"What on earth? Let me see."

He ignored me. "It can't be a prologue or something, can it? No, I thought as much. It isn't the play at all. . . . Wait a minute, it isn't even 'Romeo.' It's 'Romeus.' *Romeus and Juliet,* and not Shakespeare at all. It's by a chap called Brooke."

"Brooke?"

It came out in a kind of yelp. He looked up, surprised. "Yes. Why? Do you know it?"

But I had myself in hand. "No. Sorry, I spilled some hot water on myself. It's nothing. Have a biscuit. You were saying?"

"This isn't the Shakespeare play. It's a poem called *Romeus and Juliet,* by Arthur Brooke, and it seems to be—hey, it's dated 1562!" He sounded excited.

"I say, I wonder if this could possibly be Shakespeare's source for his play, or something like that. I don't know the dates, but surely 1562—hell, yes, that's long before he was writing, isn't it? When did Elizabeth come to the throne?"

That was the kind of thing we knew at Ashley. "1558," I said, reluctantly. "It might be, I suppose, but I can't see . . . Look, Emory, leave the books, will you? I haven't had a chance to look at them yet, and I really think we should go through them pretty carefully, and get someone who's an expert. They might be valuable. Wait till I've checked them; we don't want to risk marking them—"

"'Might be valuable,' indeed! Anything first printed in 1562 stands a damned good chance of being valuable, I'd say."

"Well, don't start counting chickens till we know a bit more about it. I'll tell you what, Emory, I'll write, first thing in the morning. I think someone at Hatchards, or even perhaps the British Museum—"

"Why don't you just telephone someone now, this minute? This is your line of country. Isn't there someone local who might at least have a rough idea? What about what's-his-name, Leslie Oker, over at Ashbury? He'd have some idea, surely?"

"I don't really think—" I began, unwillingly, but he ignored me.

"At least he'd have some way of looking it up. Do you know his number?"

He already had the directory in his hand, so there was not much point in stalling further. I gave him the number. He pulled the telephone toward him and began to dial. His movements were quick, incisive, excited. At least, I thought, as I sat across from him sipping my tea, I would be able to read the thing before I had to send it away. Emory could hardly insist on taking it from me. From the length of the poem, and the apparent tedium of the verses, it wasn't a task I particularly looked forward to, but I would do it, even if I had to stay up all night. For that this, at last, was "William's Brooke," I was quite sure.

Emory was talking rapidly into the telephone. "Yes, Arthur Brooke, *'The Tragicall History of Romeus and Juliet,* written first in Italian by Bandello and nowe in Englishe by Arthur Brooke.' It's dated 1562. There's a piece at the bottom of the title page which says, *'In aedibus Richardi Tottelli Cum Privilegio.'* Yes. Yes, quite small . . . about four by eight . . . tan leather with a brown edge to the paper. No, no inscription, except the owner's bookplate, and that's reasonably historic, too. Put in by William Ashley, his own bookplate. He died in, let me see—?"

He raised a brow at me, and I supplied it. "1835."

"1835," said Emory into the telephone. "Yes, well, I don't know about such things, but I'd say it was in pretty good shape. No, no crest or anything on the cover. Oh, the title page is a bit yellow, with some of that brown spotting."

"Foxed," I said, behind him.

"My cousin says you call it foxed. Not badly, no, but I've only just glanced at it. . . . Yes?"

Silence from Emory, while the telephone talked. It was a loud telephone, and, even with the receiver held tightly to my cousin's ear, I could catch something of what Leslie was saying. But even without that, I could have caught the gist of it from my cousin's face, where growing excitement fought with worry and slight apprehension. Eventually, after a few more brief queries, and expressions of thanks, he rang off, and turned back to me.

"He knows the book." He spoke very quietly, with a calm belied by the gleam in his eyes. "That is, he knows of it; he's never seen a copy in his life. And for a very good reason. There are only three copies of this particular edition known. One of them isn't perfect; it's at Cambridge. A second is at Oxford, in Duke Humphrey, and I'm not sure about the third. If this is a fourth . . ." A short laugh, which betrayed his excitement. "He says he has no idea how valuable it might be, but there's only one thing certain, that it is very valuable indeed. There's a snag, of course, there'd have to be. It may have been re-bound. He couldn't tell, from my description. If it has, of course, its value will be diminished—but it would still fetch a lot of money . . . enough, anyway, to see us through. What's the matter, Bryony? You look as if you hardly cared."

I could not tell him that I was conscious of only one overmastering wish, to have him go and leave me alone with the book and let me read it. I picked it up and began to turn the pages. "Why, of course I'm pleased! It's marvelous, Emory! And I see no reason at all why you shouldn't sell it. The only thing we mustn't do is rush it, and even if we do send it to Christie's to sell, you know they might take ages. They wait for the right book sale, and that mightn't be for months."

"Yes, I understand that. But they could give us some idea, surely, of what it might bring? One can borrow on expectation, you know."

"Fair enough," I said. "I think the best thing to do is to send the book up to an expert, and let him have a look at it. No, Emory, please—" This as his hand reached for it again. "You'll have to leave this to me. I promise you I'll see about it tomorrow, but I want to ask Mr. Bryanston about it first."

"Mr. Bryanston? What does he know about it?"

"Quite a bit, you'd be surprised. And then I'm going to ring up Mr. Emerson, and see just where we stand."

His brows drew down quickly. "He can't have any objection, surely?"

"I didn't mean about this. I meant about the trust."

It was blackmail of a kind, and it worked. He hesitated, then smiled and nodded, and to my great relief, at last got to his feet and took his leave. He was going back to Bristol this evening, he told me, and yes, he would keep his promise and stop badgering me about the trust.

"But for heaven's sake, you will see about this book straight away, won't you? And if you can get into the Court and look at what else is there—?"

"Yes. As soon as I can."

"And let me know?"

"Of course," I said. "Or James?"

"Of course." The echo held an inflection of surprise, as if it went without saying. As, I reflected, it did. I had been right. And that left me—and my lover—where?

"Emory?"

He was in the doorway. He turned. "Yes?"

"Where's Francis? Have you any idea?"

"Not the least. I dare say he'll turn up when he feels like it. It's obvious he can't have heard the news yet. Why, do you need him for something?"

"It would be nice," I said carefully, "if he were here, don't you think?"

"Well, of course," said his brother, then kissed me again and went away.

I watched him right out of sight past the orchard and beyond the maze and the Overflow, then I went upstairs and began to hunt for a photograph which Walther could show to the police in Bad Tölz.

He turned his head on the pillow, searching with his cheek for the hollow where her head had lain. The linen was cold now, but still smelled faintly of lavender.

"Eh—" he said it aloud, in her phrase "—eh, but I love thee."

The moon had set, but faint shadows moved with the breeze, as the creepers fretted at the walls. The shutter masking the south window moved, creaking, as if some ghostly hand had pushed it. For a half-dreaming moment he thought he saw her again, kilting her skirts to climb the low sill, then standing tiptoe, laughing, watching herself in the glass.

"What is it?"

Then the shutter went back with a slam, jarring him full awake. The room was empty.

14

. . . Comfort me, counsel me.

—*Romeo and Juliet,* III, v

IT WAS a good photograph, taken the last time the twins had been at Ashley Court together, showing them both with Rob Granger on the banks of the Pool. They had been fishing for eels, and the picture showed Rob just tipping the bucketful of wriggling creatures out on the grass, while the twins stood over him. James was laughing, while Emory, looking away into the middle distance, was sober. Both were good likenesses, even though the photograph was four years old. If either of the two had been seen at Bad Tölz, there would be very little difficulty in identifying him.

I wrapped the picture up and found an envelope to fit it. A very commonplace action, but it felt like burning a whole fleet of boats, and crossing a delta of Rubicons. Then I sat down and resolutely addressed the envelope to Walther. I had only the haziest idea as to how much it should cost air mail to Bad Tölz, but finished by putting enough stamps on to carry it well east of Suez. That done, I locked William's books away in a drawer, and, without giving myself time for further thought, set straight out to post the letter.

The pillar-box was nearly half a mile away, where the side road from One Ash, winding past the church, met the main road. I took the shortcut across the farmyard.

In the old days of the farm's prosperity this had been the stackyard, with the row of stacks spaced beyond the big Dutch barn crammed full to the roof with straw. The cool caverns of the old cart sheds had housed the farm machinery, and whole families of cheerful hens that perched, crooning, on mudguards and shafts, and laid enormous clutches of eggs in various secret places which took,

Mrs. Granger used to say, an expert egg-diviner to discover. Now the afternoon sun beat down through the gaps in the perished roof of the barn, striking a rusty harrow left there to rot, and the raw green paint of Rob's cultivator, a stack of oil drums and a pile of chain. An old wagon with a broken shaft stood like an exhibit from some badly kept museum. Two of the sheds had been fenced across with hurdles, and pigs slept there in the slatted sunshine. In another stood Rob's battered fifth-hand Ford Cortina, and the fourth opening was filled with a stack of firewood. The hens remained, diminished in numbers but not in stately cheer; they clucked and strutted and raked among the fallen straw, ignoring Rob's collie which lay curled asleep on the mat outside his cottage door. As I crossed the yard the collie woke and smiled with lolling tongue and tail beating the ground, but he didn't move. I caught a glimpse of Mrs. Henderson at Rob's window, then the door opened and she appeared in the doorway, wiping her hands on her apron.

"Miss Bryony! Won't you come along in and take a cup of tea? The kettle's just on the boil for Rob, and I've made a batch of scones."

My first impulse, with the package for Walther weighing heavily in my hand, was to make some excuse and go on my way, but something made me hesitate. The smell of the freshly baked scones came meltingly out on the air, along with the scent of woodsmoke and polish and the smell of ironing. I could see the laundered clothes hanging on the kitchen pulley. Details hardly noticed, but adding together to something deep out of the past that answered, like an echo to a bell, the distress in me that I had hardly recognized as yet, and had barely yet begun to suffer: James and my dead father, and the evidence of the silver pen; my rejection of my secret friend, and now, in this envelope in my hand, something that might be his betrayal. Before I even knew I had spoken, I said, "Thank you, I'd love to," and headed for the door.

"Come along in then, dearie," said Mrs. Henderson, "and I'll make the tea. Rob's just got in."

She vanished into the doorway. I followed her.

Rob was there at the sink, in his shirt sleeves, washing his hands. I saw he had taken the bandage off his left hand, and had been carefully cleaning the injured thumb. He greeted me rather shortly, as he had done that morning, then his eyes fixed on my face and he straightened, speaking in quite a changed voice.

"Is something wrong, then?"

I opened my mouth automatically to deny that anything could be wrong, but somehow no words came. Instead of the brittle, conventional denial of "Nothing at all. What should be wrong?" I found myself saying with all the force of unhappiness, "Oh, Rob, it's all so awful," and I put a hand to my eyes.

His hand, still damp, took me very gently by the elbow and steered me to a place at the table. "What you need's a cup of tea. It's making now. So come your ways and sit down."

I don't remember that I ate anything, but I drank the strong, scalding tea, and watched Rob and Mrs. Henderson eating scones and bramble jelly, and listened to the two of them talking over the commonplaces of the day—the shirt she would take home to mend, the pie she had made for him to heat at suppertime, the mousehole that she had found when she swept the back bedroom. The two of them addressed remarks in my direction from time to time, but never anything I had to answer; the talk went around and over me with the instinctive tact of long-standing affection. They were hedging me about with kindness, and I knew why the sunlight in the stackyard, the cottage smells, the sound of Rob's warm country voice, had suddenly and unaccountably broken me down. I had been here before. As a little girl I had come often to the Grangers' house, sometimes for comfort and refuge from the boys' games, sometimes just for a "visit" with Mrs. Granger on the days when Rob's father was safely distant at market or down at the Bull. It had been the farm kitchen then, not the cottage, but it was the same: the faded rug, the old dresser with the green and blue plates, the brown teapot, the smells of baking and freshly ironed clothes, and the warmth and welcome that all these things added up to. I had loved these visits, tea with "bought cakes" (which as a child I had thought so much better than anything we had at home) and sardines on toast and tinned fruit and condensed milk, while Mrs. Granger listened to Rob and me boasting about what we had done and dared that day at school in the village. I had never understood her faded edginess and her air of always listening for an unwelcome footstep; nor did I guess why, if Mr. Granger came back while I was still there, I was expected to get up and go straight home. Nor had Rob's sullenness meant anything except "Robbie's sulks." What happened when Matt Granger came home at night was a well-kept secret, and had never touched little Miss Bryony. Well, that was over now, and the familiar warmth lapped me round, and from somewhere came comfort and calmness.

When tea was done I helped Mrs. Henderson clear and wash the dishes, while Rob pushed the cloth back from his end of the table, and spread his account book and papers out and got on with his figuring. He was surprisingly quick and neat. The sums looked complicated, but long before I had dried and stacked the dishes he had shut the book and put the papers aside and picked up a sheaf of what looked like highly colored catalogues or holiday brochures. He read them intently, paying no attention to the two women moving around him. He might have been alone in the room. It was curiously soothing.

Mrs. Henderson took her apron off and hung it behind the door. "Well, that's it for today. I'll let you have the shirt by the weekend, Rob. Shall I feed the hens for you?"

"Thanks, yes, I'd be obliged."

She took her leave of me then, and I thanked her for the tea. She had obviously assumed my distress to be caused by my father's death, and by the loneliness of my first night back at Ashley. She had too much natural delicacy to say anything directly, but she came as near to it as she could. "Are you all right at the cottage, Miss Bryony? Is there anything else you want?"

"Nothing at all, thank you, Mrs. Henderson. Everything's fine. You got it lovely." She went then, leaving me with Rob.

He laid the papers down and pushed them aside. "Now what's to do? Can't you tell me? Seems like it might be bad trouble, to upset you like that."

"It might." I sat down at the other side of the table from him. He watched me, saying nothing.

It was very different from the recent tête-à-tête with Emory; no tensions, no careful reticences, no attempts to see past an apparent meaning to a real one. And different, too, from talking with my cousin James; there, as well, had been the sprung overtones of emotion, of a difficult affection, of a personal distress. And in both interviews I had felt the impact, doubled because united, of a strong personality and a calculated desire to drive me into action over the Court and the trust.

Here there was none of that. The dark eyes that watched me steadily were not

Ashley eyes, those wary, clever eyes with their cool self-sufficiency and their self-absorption. Rob could have no axe to grind, nothing to gain, nothing he wanted from me. He was not even, like the Vicar, bound by a set of rules which could force me to an alien action like the betrayal I was contemplating. He was just an old friend, someone belonging to the Court, who had known it and me and Jon Ashley all his life; a real person, kind, uncomplicated, who would listen without judgment unless I asked for it, and would answer me then with plain and disinterested common-sense. I supposed he loved the Court; I didn't know; but he knew it, and he knew me. Neither fear nor favor . . . He had never feared anything, Rob Granger, except perhaps, when he was a child, his brutal father. And he had no reason to show favor, now that my father was gone, to any of us above the others; only to Ashley itself. Or so I thought.

"Rob," I said, "it's something awful, and I oughtn't to tell you, but I've got to tell someone, and there's no one else."

Vaguely to my surprise he didn't say, "What about your family?" or even, "What about the Vicar?" He merely gave a little nod, as if that was reasonable, and waited again.

I swallowed. "I think it was James who knocked Daddy down. I think he was there, in Bad Tölz. They picked up a silver pen with the initials *J. A.* just where the accident happened. When they gave me his things I assumed the pen had been his, though I'd never seen it before. And yesterday—yesterday James saw me using it, and said it was his own. He didn't know where he'd dropped it, he said, but it was his . . ."

He had listened without moving. Now he stirred, and asked, sharply for him: "Did you tell him where it came from?"

"No. Oh, no. I told him I'd found it in the churchyard the night before last."

"Did he accept that?"

"Yes. He didn't even seem surprised."

"Meaning that it was him in the vestry—or at any rate in the churchyard—that night."

"You could say so," I said. "Oh, he denied it when I asked him before, but I know James, and I was sure then that he was lying, and he knew I thought so. He took it as a joke. Last night he didn't even trouble to go on pretending. I know what he was doing there, too—though I don't really understand all about it. It doesn't matter anyway, not compared with this."

"What does matter," said Rob bluntly, "is that he shouldn't know you've any call to suspect him of being in Bad Tölz."

"I'm sure he doesn't. It was all quite casual. He just pocketed the pen and went out."

"Wait a minute." Rob was frowning. "What was the date your dad was knocked down? The thirtieth of April, wasn't it? Well, James was here then, or thenabouts."

I sat up abruptly. "Are you sure?"

"Sure enough. I saw him. He called here to pick up the Underhill girl."

"Rob, are you sure it wasn't Emory?"

"Well, no, I suppose it might have been. I didn't speak to him—I was busy working along the drive when he drove out with the girl. But the Underhills said afterward that it was James. I remember that, because of course I thought it was Emory with her; you'll know they're sweet on each other, of course?"

"Yes." I added, thoughtfully: "So he wasn't ringing for his twin that day? I wonder why?"

I had spoken softly, to myself, but Rob had not only heard, he had gone there with almost electronic speed. "So they've been doing that, have they? Can I take it that that wasn't Emory here yesterday, then?"

"No, it was James. It was Emory today, though." I looked at him across the table. "Rob, don't you see? It probably was Emory here that day with Cathy. Which means it was James in Bad Tölz."

"Would it matter which of them it was in Bad Tölz," said Rob forcefully, "if he was driving that car?"

I didn't answer. I was looking down at my hands, which were pressed flat on the table in front of me, covering the letter as if to hide it. Then I looked up at him. I knew that all the strain and uncertainty, yes, and the longing, too, must be there, naked to view, in my face and eyes. I didn't care. I saw him take it all in in one swift, summing look, then he said, in a voice carefully empty of sympathy: "Yes, I can see it would. But it doesn't help to take on about it, not till you know a bit more."

It braced me, as it was meant to. I sat back in my chair, and let my hands fall into my lap. "I'm sorry. Throwing it all at you like this. It's your own fault, you know, for being so easy to talk to."

"Maybe because I'm just part of the fittings. I belong in the garden, sort of, along with the trees." There was no edge to the words. He was smiling. "It's all right, you know. You can tell me anything—it's likely enough I'd know it anyway, with my ear to the ground most days."

"Like telling the bees?"

"I reckon," he said, comfortably. He stretched, then got to his feet and leaned his shoulders back against the mantelpiece. His look was solemn again, a little heavy. "Well, you've told me. Never mind why, but you don't want it to be James. But you can't leave it at that, you know. You'll have to find out. Whichever of them it was, even if you don't want to know the answer, you've got to go on and find out. That's true, isn't it?"

"I suppose so. But—"

"And there's something else you'll have to face." He hesitated, then finished abruptly. "As far back as I remember, Bryony, whatever one of them was in, the other was in just as deep."

"Not James." It was meaningless and purely defensive, but he answered the implication rather than the words.

"Maybe not. But he was always there after the fact, as they say. Anyway, we have to find out, don't we? Are you up to facing that?"

Somehow I wasn't up to facing him. I looked down at my hands. "I have to, haven't I? You just said so."

"Yes." It was abrupt and uncompromising. As unswerving a judgment, I thought with vague surprise, as the Vicar's. I still couldn't look at him, but I turned my head to the window, where the curtains swelled and swayed in a sudden breeze. There was a pot of pink geraniums on the sill, the twin of the one at my cottage. The breeze brushed a fading head of flowers, and a scatter of petals floated down into the room. One of them, drifting to the floor beside me, stirred a memory; the petal floating from the clematis last night. Last night; before I had known what I knew now. When all I had had to worry me was the "theft" of a few things from the Court. It seemed a lifetime ago.

Bryony. Bryony, love.

I must have jumped in my chair. I felt my nerves tighten like a net pulled in by a fisherman. Somehow, in that unguarded moment of memory, he had managed to reach me. It came with the breeze, sweet as the summer air; it was round me like the falling petals; comfort, love, longing as strong as anguish. So strong that for one awful, choking moment I thought he would be able to see through my mind into the contents of the envelope that lay beside me on the table.

Get out! Do you hear me? Leave me alone. You know why.

Yes, I know why. Bryony . . .

All right. Did you do it?

No reply. Just that longing and love, hopeless and receding.

Did you do it? Were you there when he died?

No answer. He was gone. Above me Rob's voice was saying, with that careful lack of warmth: "You don't have to look like that, Bryony. Whoever was driving that car, you surely can't think it was anything but an accident, so—"

"Well, of course it was an accident! But why keep it quiet? Why not stay and—and help him? He wasn't dead."

"Would it have saved his life if they had?"

"No. No, Herr Gothard said not. But it might have prolonged it. He might have lived till I got there . . ." I choked on that one, and then managed to add, more steadily: "That's not true, no. Herr Gothard said it made no difference. But one can't help feeling—"

"No, you can't," said Rob, "but you can think as well, and that'll help. Come on, think about it. Say it was one of your cousins knocked your dad down. O.K. What was he doing in Bad Tölz in the first place?"

"I—I suppose he must have gone there to see Daddy."

"Right. Must have. Well then, what about?"

There was only one answer to that, too. "About the Court, breaking the trust. They need money. James says they need it very badly."

"Who doesn't?" said Rob drily. "I suppose the difference is, what do you do to get hold of it? Yes, I know, but there's no need to look like that, love"—the country endearment came out as "luv," as natural and meaningless as when the local shopkeepers or bus conductors used it—"because we're taking it as an accident, aren't we? All right, go on thinking. Your cousin—we'll call him Emory if it makes you feel better; and he could easily have had a loan of his brother's pen, and never missed it when he dropped it—Emory goes to see your dad to talk him into something; it doesn't matter what, but it was urgent, or he wouldn't have gone to that trouble. Now, since your doctor pal never saw him, Emory must have been on his way up to the hospital when he overtook your dad on the road. Didn't recognize him in the dark, we'll say—"

"*Of course* he didn't recognize him! You couldn't ever think—"

"Hey, calm down, I said we were taking it as accident. Well, he knocked him down in the dark. And after that he panicked and drove off and never said a word. It happens. It's human. It's the reason for all the hit-and-run jobs there are."

"I'd like to accept that. But it doesn't fit, does it? He must have recognized him *after* the accident. Don't forget that whichever of them ran Daddy down must have got out of the car to look at him, and if Ja—Emory leaned over him long enough to let that pen drop from his pocket, he must have recognized who it was. The car's lights would be on, too."

Rob nodded. "He ran away *because* he recognized who it was. Don't you see?

Your cousin went there to talk your dad into something. He went because he was desperate for money, and his own dad hadn't managed to get yours to part with anything, or agree to break this trust. Then by accident he knocks your dad down on the road and hurts him badly; he must have known how badly. Anyway, he knew about his heart. . . . Well, put yourself in his place. How's it going to look if he, of all people, is involved in an accident like that, and then your dad dies? The people who stand to gain are him and his family. They're the only people in the world who might want your dad dead. No—" quickly, to forestall me, "I'm not saying they did. I'm saying that's what the police would have said once they ferreted the story out."

"Yes. Yes, I see. But even if they didn't dare pick him up and get help for him, surely they—Emory—could have telephoned from somewhere and *told* someone where he was, and to go and help him?"

"What sort of German do they speak?"

"Oh, yes, that would have given them away. Of course. But, Rob, just to leave him lying like that—"

"I know, it takes a bit of swallowing. But I've known your cousins as long as you have, remember, and I'd say they were realists. You told me yourself it wouldn't have helped your dad if they'd stayed by him." He left the fireplace and sat down where he had been before, resting his folded arms on the table and leaning forward on them. "That's it, you see. I dare say you'll find that they were only planning to look after their own interests. But it went wrong, and now you've found out, and the very thing's happened that they'd have given their eyeteeth to avoid; you've been set against them."

I said nothing. It fitted, all too well. Whichever twin had been beside my father and dropped the pen, the other would no doubt have been ready to create an alibi by confusion, either in Bristol or in Spain. This was why neither man had come to the cremation, or showed up at Bad Tölz to see me home. I would have recognized him, and if there had been questions later, this might have destroyed whatever alibi they had concocted between them. It could have been either of them telephoning from England; Walther was not familiar with their voices, and it was perhaps significant that the caller had not asked to speak to me. I began to wonder, but with the dullness of emotional exhaustion, if Cousin Howard was involved as well. If neither twin had been in Spain at the time of the accident, would their father say so? Was he, even, well enough to know? But, with England, Spain, and Bavaria only hours apart by air, heaven knew it would have been easy enough for the twins to create their own kind of alibi.

And Francis . . . The thought came suddenly, unbidden and unwelcome. He could not be mistaken for his brothers by anyone who knew them, but at a frontier, with a passport belonging to one of the twins . . .

I slammed the door on that one. I would not even think it. I sat slumped in my chair, staring at the envelope, while my thoughts trailed off into weary confusion.

"How long have you been sweet on him?"

My eyes came up to Rob's with a jerk, but somehow, I wasn't startled. It seemed natural to be asked. The strange thing was that now I found myself hesitating. The old, direct country phrase didn't fit what I was feeling; the half-guilt; the two-way pull of the affection I felt for my cousin, contrasted with the total abandonment to the possession of my secret friend. "I—It's hard to say. Of the three of them, I suppose it was always James. But in the last few years . . . And now, since I got back home . . . In love with him? I just don't know."

No one could have claimed this for a coherent answer, but he nodded, his rather somber look lightening as he smiled. "Well, you've got yourself into a rare muddle and no mistake, love; and I doubt it hardly helps to have the pair of them taking turns to sit on your doorstep and pressure you to do things you don't want to do." The smile deepened at my look. "I told you I was just part of the landscape. You'd be surprised the things I know. It was obvious, anyway. It'll take months to prove your dad's Will and get everything sorted out, but if you'd agree to break the trust now and let the land go, they could borrow on that promise straight away." A pause of silence, broken by the uneven ticking of the clock. "Bryony, how much do you really care about this place? Would you want to stay on here?"

I said, rather wearily: "Everyone keeps asking me that, and I keep saying I don't know yet. How do I know what I want to do with the rest of my life? And how do I know—I mean, are you talking about James?"

"No, I wasn't. We've gone through all that. Whether you're sweet on him or not, you'll have to find out what really happened, or you'll never be able to get along with either of them, will you? No, I was talking about your cottage. What the Vicar calls Naboth's Vineyard."

"Calls it *what?*"

"Naboth's Vineyard. I asked him what he meant, and he said something about the Polish Corridor. Talks very sideways, sometimes, Mr. Bryanston."

"I know what he meant, I think," I said. "The cottage and the orchard are the only outlet from the Court to Penny's Flats. The gardens wouldn't be much use to a building contractor without access to the main road."

"Aye, that's it." It was apparent that Rob, too, knew exactly what Mr. Bryanston had meant. "So you see how much it matters to them to keep on the sweet side of you. And you see why it matters not to let them make a guess at where you really found that silver pen."

I must have been staring. I suppose I knew quite well what he was saying, but something in me could not accept it.

"All right," he said, with a return to the old, uncompromising manner, "I'll spell it out. You won't like it, mind, but I've got to say it. I've had it on my mind ever since you told me what your dad said. You've got to give a thought to its maybe not being an accident at all."

"But it must have been! You can't honestly think that James—or even Emory—"

"I'm thinking nothing. I'm telling you that you've got to be ready to believe anything of anybody. Your dad talked of danger, didn't he, and told you to be careful? There's no magic about an Ashley that says they couldn't kill a man, is there?"

"No. My God, plenty of them have. . . . But nowadays, one of my cousins kill my father for gain? No."

"Well, I agree with you. I'm only saying it could happen. We none of us know what a chap's capable of, or even what we might be capable of ourselves. I'd have thought the last few years would have taught anyone that." He reached a hand across the table and touched mine, gently. "All I'm asking is that you do what your dad said, and be careful. Keep it in mind that even your cousins might get nasty, even with you. There's a lot here we don't understand, and till we do . . ."

He let it hang.

In the silence that followed, without looking at him, I turned the envelope over and showed him the address.

"I see." His voice held satisfaction, and something else I couldn't put a name to. "You mean I've been wasting my breath? You've made your own decision all along?"

"In a way. But you haven't wasted your breath, Rob. I'm not quite sure if I ever would have mailed it, but I will now."

"What's in it?"

"A photograph. Do you remember the one of the twins and you that day you caught all those eels? When you tipped them out beside the lake?"

"Aye, and the half of them went straight back in." He laughed. "And Emory called me a—Emory was pretty mad."

"There's no need to be coy. I remember quite well what Emory called you. He had a right to be mad. They'd spent hours catching them, and they needed the money."

They always needed the money. Neither of us said it aloud, but amusement died abruptly. He put out a hand.

"Will you let me take that to the post for you?"

"Thanks very much, but don't bother. I was going anyway."

"I'd rather you let me take it."

"Don't you trust me to post it?"

"Don't be daft," said Rob. He got to his feet and stretched, then gave me that disarming smile of his again. "Well, maybe you'll let me walk you along to the corner, and we can watch each other post it? Come on."

The collie got up to follow him, and so did I.

Ashley, 1835

Memories stung him, banishing sleep.

"Nick?"

"My love?"

"He won't speak? You're sure he won't tell on us?"

"Certain. He knows where his duty lies, or, better still, where his meat and drink come from."

"But your father? Oh, Nick—"

"My father be damned."

He had meant it, too. He shut his eyes.

15

This night I hold an old accustom'd feast,
Whereto I have invited many a guest,
Such as I love; and you among the store,
One more, most welcome, makes my number more.

—*Romeo and Juliet*, I, ii

WHEN I got back to the cottage there was someone sitting on the seat in the shadow of the lilac tree. My heart jerked painfully, once, then settled back to its even beat as Jeffrey Underhill got to his feet and came out into the mellow sunshine of the lawn.

We greeted one another. The tycoon manner was as much in evidence as before, but somehow scaled down by the setting of lake and sky and the huge trees beyond the orchard. Perhaps a man like Jeffrey Underhill needed rooms and company, the setting of his own kind of jungle. Then I saw that I was wrong. This was still the same high-octane personality, but the mask of power was being held, as it were, deliberately in front of a very ordinary, anxious father. His manner was as smooth, as pleasant, as incisive as before, and with never a hint of worry showing, but the Ashley seventh sense, prompted by what I knew, saw it as the manner of the Chairman of Directors preparing to present an adverse report to his board. *Cathy*, I thought, with my heart accelerating ever so slightly, *he wants to talk to me about Cathy.* I found myself looking away from him, as if it was I who had been at fault rather than my cousins and this man's daughter. As I led Mr. Underhill into the cottage I reflected, with a twist of wry amusement, that this Chairman of Directors had a very good technique indeed. In this case it had even been unconscious; I thought I could acquit him of using it deliberately on me.

He settled himself in one of the armchairs as if he had all the time—and the quietest mind—in the world, refused the offer of tea, waved aside my apologies for not having any gin, and opened the meeting without delay.

"I had to come and talk to you, Miss Ashley. Something my daughter Cathy has told me has disturbed me very much."

I made some kind of assenting sound, and waited, with what was meant to look like mild inquiry, but the clever dark eyes probed mine for a millisecond, then the brows twitched down, as Mr. Underhill registered that I already knew what he was about to tell me.

He told me, all the same. It was Cathy's version of the story I had heard from James. Emory—and James passing for Emory—had persuaded the girl that the contents of the Court were legally theirs, and that "Cousin Bryony," when she knew, would not mind a few small objects being abstracted and used straight away, rather than wait for the long processes of law. Cathy had obviously had no idea that the estate must by law be left intact for valuation; and the twins had told her that I, Bryony, was, if not firmly engaged to James, at any rate his for the asking, and therefore an interested party. So she had taken the T'ang horse and the other small objects from the library, and then—this time on her own initiative—the Rackham pictures from the schoolroom. The church, always left unlocked, had been used as a cache and a pickup point.

Mr. Underhill told me the whole story, straight and without excuse, just as he would have put a report across. Facts and only facts. The rest I could supply for myself. He still obviously had no idea that the twins had been playing tricks with identity; he referred all the time to "Emory," with no apparent suspicion that sometimes the man had been James. I looked away from him, kept my thoughts to myself, and worked it out as he talked.

He had got to my own return from Bavaria. The night when I had inadvertently seen "Emory" in the church, said Jeff Underhill, he had been picking up the pictures which Cathy had taken. They had been hidden in the old ambry which was now blocked from casual sight by the choir men's wardrobe. Next day had come my discovery of the theft, and my questions.

"My wife and I guessed right away that Cathy might have something to do with it, but naturally we had to talk to Cathy first, before we could say anything to you."

"Of course." I must have looked surprised. "But why should you have guessed that? Had she said anything?"

He was leaning back in his chair, his eyes on the prospect of leaves and sky beyond the cottage window. He might have been studying the weather, to judge the fishing prospects for the morrow. But then he turned his head, and the eyes that met mine were those of a deeply troubled man.

"I have to be honest with you, Miss Ashley. We guessed it might be our daughter because we have had this kind of problem before."

I felt my eyes widen. Though something in me—perhaps that Ashley seventh sense again—had almost seen it coming, I couldn't think what to say. But he did not wait. If it had to be said, he would say it and have done.

"It started when she was in high school. We lived in California then, just outside Los Angeles, and—well, it's not perhaps the easiest city for a young boy or girl to grow up in, and Cathy soon got problems. She is—" a pause, so brief that one hardly registered the effort it hid "—a very loving and warmhearted girl, and she follows her impulses without always seeing where they will take her, or what they will cost. She takes," added Jeffrey Underhill, quite unnecessarily, "more after her dear mother than after me."

I said something that was meant to sound both soothing and noncommittal, and was rewarded by the flash of sudden humor in his face, as he said, with a return to his old manner: "I am neither generous nor impulsive, Miss Ashley. Nor am I easily guided. But my wife and daughter are altogether better folks than I can ever be. So when my little Cat got into bad company, the next thing we knew she was right there in the middle of a full-scale classic teen-age problem, and believe me, she could have finished anywhere. She was in with a real wild bunch. They used to steal things—things that didn't matter, but it was stealing for all that—and wreck things, and drive cars away—having fun, they called it, getting kicks. There was this boy she was crazy about, and while that lasted . . . Well, I'll spare you the rest. She got herself out of it in the end. It took a long time, but, being basically sweet and good like most of these silly kids if they get the chance, she got herself out of it, with God's help and with ours."

He spoke with devastating simplicity. Once again, I could think of nothing to say. But he didn't seem to expect an answer. He was going on.

"That was one of the reasons we decided to live away from home for a few years. You'll understand, it doesn't much matter to me where I'm domiciled, as long as I'm within commuting distance of Houston, Texas, and of New York." The gleam of a smile again. "Well, I can't rightly say that Ashley Court is commuter country for New York and my other current ports of call, but as you know, the girls—my wife and Cathy—took a real fancy to it, and things seemed to be working out just fine. Then, as you know, this happened. When you told us there were valuable things missing, we were terribly afraid it was beginning again. When Cat and her set had stolen things before it was a kind of wild thing, not a real sickness; but now we were afraid she was really sick. This kleptomania is a mental thing, you know that, not just a teen-age problem that can be gotten through. So Stephanie and I talked it over most of last night, and again this morning, and then we asked Cathy about it. She told us everything. She'd had it on her mind ever since you came here, and she—I think she was glad to tell us."

My mind was twisting and turning like some trapped thing trying to find the light. It was worse, far worse than I had thought. Even this minor affair of the "disposable assets" had in it the possible springs of tragedy. Yet one more thing for Twin to answer for . . . I hardly noticed that this time I hadn't specified which twin.

"But, Mr. Underhill, this is awful!"

He misunderstood me. "Miss Ashley, I know that it's as bad as it can be, and it might look a real hanging matter from where you're sitting right this minute, but I have to tell you that when Cathy went into all this legal routine about trusts and disposable assets that Emory really owned, and all that stuff, we were so relieved that our daughter must almost have gotten the impression that what she'd done was quite O.K. Which," he added, with uncompromising dryness, "it was not."

"Mr. Underhill—"

He lifted a hand about an inch from the arm of the chair, and I stopped. "No, let me say it first. I'm not often stuck for words, but I find this very, very hard. We owe you an apology, that goes without saying, and Miss Ashley, you have it. I must say this as well: if there is anything we can do to put this thing right for you, you have only to ask. That is the least I can say. I'll get those items back, and into their places, just as if this had never happened, if it takes all I've got."

Coming from someone like Jeffrey Underhill, it was quite an offer, but somehow it didn't seem in the least absurd. And he meant every word of it. As for the apology, there was no point in my disclaiming, since for once my honest opinion was probably the exact one that it would comfort him to hear. But before I could speak he said, with another of those probing looks that seemed to get right past the eyes and into the mind: "You don't seem very surprised by what I have been telling you. You knew how the things were taken."

"Yes. My cousin told me last night."

"And it troubles you a whole lot, I can see that."

"Not really. Other things trouble me, but not that. Honestly. I'll tell you exactly how I feel about it, Mr. Underhill. When my cousin told me, I was shocked. It was wrong, though perhaps it wasn't quite as dishonest as it seemed. But what I was really angry about was the fact that they'd used Cathy. I don't have to go into the reasons for you—and I certainly didn't know what you've just told me about her trouble, or I'd have been angrier still—but it seemed to me a terrible thing to do, and I said as much. My cousin would pass that on to his brother. As for the horse and the other things, please forget them. No, I mean it. Officially they will belong in the end to Emory's family, and if we start looking for them now to buy them back, all this might have to come to light, and that wouldn't help anybody. It might even put us on the wrong side of the law." I remembered something. "Mr. Underhill, did Cathy say anything about a church register?"

"A what?" He sounded blank.

"One of the parish registers they keep in the church. It's gone missing."

"She certainly said nothing about that. I'll ask her. But why should anyone want to take a thing like that? Is it valuable?"

"Not intrinsically. It is very old, and I suppose it's interesting, but only to local people, one would think."

"Maybe someone borrowed it for research, and forgot to bring it back."

"Probably. I only asked because when I saw—er, my cousin that night in the church, I thought he was carrying something like a big book, but it was probably the Rackham pictures."

"Yes, now, those pictures. They're a different matter from the other stuff, surely? Aren't they your own?"

I nodded. "And they're unique, and recognizable, I'm afraid. If you could get those back for me, Mr. Underhill, I'd be terribly grateful. There won't be any trouble, either, I promise you; I'll say I sent them for sale myself, but I thought better of it. That should put us all in the clear."

"You're very generous."

Here I did disclaim, but he insisted on thanking me, and then, as I had half expected, went on to tell me that he and his wife had decided to cut short their tenancy of Ashley Court. They had, he assured me, been considering going well before November, because of my father's death and the legal business which would ensue. Now they had decided to move immediately to London, staying there for just as long as it took Mr. Underhill's agents to find him a house to rent in Paris. They were going, he said, with a quick look at me, tomorrow. He had talked with Mr. Emerson, and all was settled. The rent of the Court was paid till the full term . . . and so on and so forth. Everything but the real reason for the sudden departure.

He finished. Then, because this was Jeffrey Underhill, and because I respected him, I came straight out into the open with what, in delicacy, he had not said.

"You're taking Cathy away from Emory."

This time a pause that could be felt. Then he said, flatly: "Yes, I am. I think it best. I'm sorry."

"You needn't be." I said it equally flatly. "I respect your reasons, and what's more, I think you're perfectly right. But what will Cathy say?"

"That I can't tell." He spoke a trifle heavily. "She's been in and out of love, the way these kids understand it now, ever since she was fourteen years old, so we'll hope this is no more serious. Right at this moment the only thought she seems to have in her head is that we're going to live in Paris, France. I told you that it makes no difference to me where we live, and it will certainly be more convenient to live in Paris than in the village of Ashley. I've given that as the reason, and I'm just hoping that Nature will do the rest."

I laughed. "You're a clever man, Mr. Underhill, and she's a lucky girl. I doubt if even Emory can compete for long with Paris, France."

He got to his feet, and I followed suit. He stood there on the hearthrug, seeming to dwarf the little room. He looked down at me. "I find it a great pity that we should leave the Court just when you come home, Miss Ashley. You are a very lovely girl, and I'm proud to have met you. I reckon you know how hard this has been, and it's good of you to understand. May I hope that you will come and visit with us in Paris? I know the girls would appreciate that very much."

I didn't point out that I wasn't quite in the bracket that makes weekend visits to Paris. I just thanked him, and saw him to the door, and down the flagged path toward the wicket gate.

"Shall I be able to say good-bye to Mrs. Underhill? I expect she'll be far too busy packing and so on, but perhaps I could telephone her in the morning?"

"She's certainly hoping to see you soon. I'm not sure how she's fixed tomorrow, but she'd like to have you call her, I know. She had some plan that she wanted to put to you, and I was hoping that Cathy—" He paused with a hand to the gate, and turned his head. His face changed subtly, and he cleared his throat. "Why, here's Cathy coming now. I kind of thought she would."

Cathy was coming down through the orchard. She had a frock on this time, of some pale summery stuff that gave a floating movement to her walk as she came slowly through the dusk of the old gray trees. The effect was romantic and ethereal, like those soft-focus films they use for television advertisements, but when she saw us at the cottage gate and waved, the halfhearted quality of the gesture gave her away. She was taking her time, and being self-conscious about it, because she was nervous. In other words, she was coming down to apologize.

As I waved back and called out a cheerful greeting, I realized that Jeffrey Underhill had left me. He had melted from my side as quietly as a real jungle cat, and was standing over by the ruined wall, looking out at the sunset light on the water, and making quite a ceremony of lighting a cigar. He was just nicely out of earshot. Yes, a smooth performer, Mr. Underhill. I liked him very much.

. . . "Had to come to tell you I was sorry." Cathy hurried it out in a small, breathless voice, like a child who wants to get it over, and is not sure of her reception.

She had stopped on the other side of the wicket gate, and was gripping the top with both hands. I dropped mine over them. I was almost four years older than Cathy, and just at that moment felt about four hundred. "It's all right," I said quickly. "You don't have to say any more. Your father's been talking to me about it, but I knew already. I know you only did it because you were fond of Emory, and it's his fault and not yours. I mean it, really. I'm not just saying it to comfort you. . . . How could you be expected to know what's right or wrong in English law? And besides"—I smiled—"I know my cousins rather well. If I started to tell you now about the things they'd pressured me into doing that I knew I never should have done, we'd be here till midnight. So forget it, please."

"Oh gosh, I wish I could! You're just sweet, but honestly, you don't fully understand." The pretty Pekinese face was intently earnest. She hadn't put on the mink eyelashes, and her eyes looked oddly unprotected. I thought there were tears there. "Honestly, Bryony," she repeated, "I wouldn't have done such a thing to *you*, but I thought it was all on the level, and it was just a case of getting a few things out for the boys to use, to save all the fuss with those people who fix the tours. And then I found those pictures upstairs, in the cupboard along with the books, and when I found they were valuable, too, why, I just took them as well. . . ." She swallowed. "And then you came and started asking about the things, and I began to think it wasn't O.K. after all, and then I found the pictures were really yours, your very own, all along. . . . And honest, Bryony, I just feel so awful I could die. Will you ever forgive me?"

"I did, just as soon as they told me about it. Hey, Cathy, don't cry." I slid my hands up to her wrists and gave her a little shake. "I told you I never thought it was your fault. It's all over and done with, and there's no harm done, and your father's going to get the pictures back for me, so let's forget it, shall we?"

I talked on for some time, reassuring her, being careful not to throw too much of the blame on Emory, for fear of putting her on the defensive for him, though I thought that she was a little less than starry-eyed about him herself; in fact, I got the distinct impression that she would rather not have talked about him. So far, so good. The very fact that she had come to talk to me like this, when it would have been so easy for her to go tomorrow and never see me again, showed that Cathy Underhill must have a grain of her father's toughness in her after all. I didn't share her father's fear that she might revert to her teen-age "problem," but it was no thanks to Emory that she had not done so. I found myself feeling a little better about mailing that photograph to Bad Tölz. About James, I refused to think at all.

Cathy, however, had him on her mind. "You know, James didn't have anything to do with it. Truly he didn't. And I know that when he saw those pictures he would have wanted to come straight and make me put them back. James is very, very fond of you, and he wouldn't do a thing that would hurt you."

"I know."

One freak shaft of sunlight, molten red, shot through the horizon clouds and touched the highest tip of the pear tree. The thrush was there, sitting preening his breast feathers, ready for a song.

I looked back at Cathy, watching me with those vulnerable, anxious eyes. "And now," I said, smiling, "what's all this about Paris?"

Jeffrey Underhill's cigar was about half smoked through before Cathy, talking now about Paris, and her mother's plans, came gradually back to her sparkling norm.

"And we're going tomorrow, and there's this fabulous party, and we want you to come! Please say you will, Bryony! Mom particularly told me to ask you."

"Well," I was beginning doubtfully, when Mr. Underhill, catching the new tone of his daughter's voice, turned away from his scrutiny of the Pool, and came back to us across the grass.

"Cathy means to London, Miss Ashley. I left her to invite you herself, but I don't think she's explained. We're giving a party tomorrow night. It's been planned for quite a while; it's our anniversary, so we're having a few friends along to celebrate, and we'd be honored if you would join us. As I told you, we're settling down in London for a few days before we go on to Paris, so we thought we'd make this a good-bye party at the same time. Stephanie's been on the telephone all afternoon, and she's wild for you to be there, too. Say you will come."

"Please say you will!" urged Cathy.

"It's terribly kind of you, and thank you very much. I'd love to, of course, but—" I hesitated.

Cathy immediately looked anxious. "Bryony, we wouldn't want to pressure you into doing anything you didn't want. Maybe it's too soon after losing your father?"

"No, it's not that." I was thinking that if the party had been arranged some time back, then no doubt Emory and James would both be there. Unless, of course, Jeffrey Underhill had let Emory know that he would no longer be welcome? I thought him quite capable of it.

"Then please do come," urged Cathy. "It'll make me really feel as if you forgive me for the awful thing I did. When I *think* about it—"

Jeffrey Underhill, at my shoulder, intervened. "Perhaps Miss Ashley has too much to do here, Cat. Remember, she has only just got home." Then to me: "It would be wonderful if you could spare us the time, Miss Ashley, but you mustn't let Cathy pressure you. I know she and Stephanie would feel very honored if you could come, but please don't trouble to decide now. If you'd like to call us in the morning, when you've had time to think it over—?"

"Look," I said warmly, "I'd love to come, I really would. I can get the late afternoon train."

At this they both joined in, with such enthusiasm that you would have thought the party was being given solely for me. They would drive me there themselves in the morning; they would put me up—"hire a suite for you" was Jeffrey Underhill's way of putting it—at the Dorchester; they would bring me down again next day, or whenever it suited me. They would do anything, if only (they seemed to be saying) I would grace their party by being there. I could hardly tell them what was in my mind: that if my two cousins had indeed been invited earlier, and if Emory, who could be as impervious to snubs as he wished to be, took the trouble to come, and to lay on the charm . . . It was for Cathy's sake as much as anything else that, in the end, I accepted, thinking grimly that, even if I had to use blackmail again, I would see that my eldest cousin kept his distance from her, and gave her breathing space. Then, glancing at Jeff Underhill, I saw that he had read my thoughts. He gave a half nod, threw his cigar away toward the water, and said: "Don't you worry; I can take care of that."

"Take care of what?" demanded Cathy.

"I'm sure you can," I said.

She looked from one to the other of us. "What are you two talking about?"

Her father let himself out through the wicket, put an arm round her, and scooped her up toward his side. "Nothing to do with you. Now say good night, and we'll leave Miss Ashley in peace."

"Good night," I said.

They went together through the dusking apple trees, arms round one another, his head bent to listen, hers raised in excited talk. A child who had been let off punishment, and a man who could take care of anything. So that, I thought, was that. And now, back to my own problems.

The thrush, unnoticed, had been singing for some time. Soon the owls would be out, and after them the stars.

Rather drearily, I latched the wicket and went back into the cottage, fished William's Brooke out from its hiding place, and turned on the reading lamp.

Ashley, 1835

He threw back the coverlet and, still naked as he was, trod lightly across the carpet to the window. Beyond the open shutter the daylight showed an oblong of gray. He pushed the glass wide and leaned out. The hedges of the maze loomed dark, but with a faint shine on them of dew.

It was later than he had thought. Already a thin plume of smoke was rising from the kitchen chimney stack. No matter, though. No lights showed yet, and no one would be there to see him as he let himself in through the side door.

And she—she would be home by now, and they were safe.

16

My dreams presage some joyful news at hand . . .

                                   —*Romeo and Juliet,* V, i

I HAD had supper, and read for an hour, and I had still only reached line 357.

"What hap have I," quoth she, "to love my father's foe?
What, am I weary of my weal? What, do I wish my woe?"

So Arthur Brooke's Juliet . . . Sighing, I lowered the book and sat back, pushing my hand through my hair as if I would clear a quicker way through the shuffling press of words. It would have been dull reading anyway, but I found it hardly possible to take in any meaning, with my brain running ahead looking for something, no matter what, that might be the tenuous clue to this other Ashley maze. But look I must—even, if I had to, as far as line 3020 . . . I tried again.

But when she should have slept, as wont she was, in bed,
Not half a wink of quiet sleep could harbor in her head,
For lo, an hugy heap of divers thoughts arise,
That rest have banished from her heart, and slumber from her eyes.
And now from side to side she tosseth and she turns,
And now for fear she shivereth, and now for love she burns.

I soldiered on for perhaps twenty minutes more, then shut the book with a snap. It could surely wait. It was impossible to get right through it tonight, and if I was going to London tomorrow, I would take the book with me and hand it over to someone at Christie's who would know how to value it. It would have been civil to let Leslie Oker look at it first, but he would surely understand.

I put it to one side and picked up William Ashley's *New Romeo.* Here again, from the center of the maze on the bookplate, the wildcat snarled and clawed. "The map?" Certainly the map. But why? I turned a page and ran my finger down the list of contents.

The Catamountain.
The Maze.
Corydon's Farewell.
The Minotaur's Lament.
What Palace Then Was This?
The Lover Leaves His Mistress.
The Lover Returns.

And so on. Well, the poems could not be worse than Arthur Brooke's, and at least they had the merit of being short. I turned to the first one, "The Catamountain."

> What hunter is there who could think to meet
> In these low lands the leopard from the sun?
> Long hath he lain here, silent 'neath the feet
> Indifferent, which all unknowing tread
> Across the spotted catamountain's head.
> See! By his side the wine-god Bacchus runs,
> His basket brimming o'er with lusty grapes
> And in his train the lesser godlings go . . .

The Romans again, it seemed. Probably, I thought, only the usual classical conceit. But no, here was the cat I was looking for . . .

> And now in this late age he comes anew
> From Scotia's heights, the catamountain wild,
> Brought here by thee, my gentle lady mild.
> As Venus led him locked in flowery chain,
> So thou, my Julia, bring'st thy wildcat tame.

A shadow fell over the page. I looked up with a start, but it was only Rob, pausing outside the casement. The thrush hadn't even faltered in its song.

"I thought you were going to be careful. Sitting here with the window open, and so deep in a book that you never even heard me coming."

"Well, but it's early still. I never thought . . . that is, I thought you meant tonight."

"I did, mainly. I just came down to see you were all right, and properly locked up."

I shut the book and put it with the others, making rather a play of it, to hide a touch of embarrassed shame for my cousins' sake. "You're taking this very seriously, aren't you?"

"Aren't you?"

There was no answer to that one. I got up. "All right, I'll shut the window now. Are you coming in?"

"For a minute, then."

I shut the casement and drew the curtains. I heard his voice speaking to the collie, then a vigorous scrubbing of shoes on the doormat, and he came in rather gingerly.

"Sorry about the shoes, but I think they're dry now. I came across the orchard after I'd shut up the greenhouses."

"Would you like a cup of Nescafé?"

"I wouldn't mind." As I went into the little kitchen he picked up *Romeus and Juliet.* "What's this?"

"I forgot to tell you. That's what Daddy must have meant by *'William's brook.'* See it? William Ashley's copy of something by a chap called Brooke. It's awfully rare, apparently. Daddy must have found out how valuable it was."

"Hm." He turned the small volume over, weighing it in his hand as if that would somehow give a clue to its worth. "Maybe so, but I wouldn't have thought he'd be troubling himself about that; not then. What else was it he said? Something about a paper or letter in it?"

"There's nothing. I looked. I was reading it to see if there was something in the text that would give me a clue, but it's next to unreadable."

"Looks it." He put it down, and picked up the *New Romeo.* "Is this valuable, too?"

"Oh, no. That's just William Ashley's own poems. They're not much better than poor Brooke, but I like the pictures."

" 'What palace then was this?' " read Rob, and puzzled his way through a few more lines. Somehow, I thought, the artificially stilted verses sounded even worse in Rob's voice with the soft country vowels. Worse than hothouse, somehow; distorted, wrong.

He put the book down and followed me into the kitchen. He leaned against the jamb and settled down companionably to help me watch the kettle boil. "Is that stuff supposed to be good? It sounded terrible to me, but then I'm no judge."

"I'm not, either. I don't think it's anything great."

"What was all that about, anyway?"

"Heaven knows," I said. "I haven't read that one yet. I got bogged down over Ariadne's clue in 'The Maze.' "

"Harry Who's clue?"

I laughed. It was the first real laugh since I had come home. "Oh, Rob! A girl called Ariadne. She gave Theseus the clue to follow into the maze. Greek myths, you know. William's writing about the maze, and getting a bit precious with his Greeks and Romans."

"How should I know? We can't all do Greek and Roman at school, can we?" said Rob, unworried.

The kettle boiled and I made the Nescafé. "Don't come the ignorant peasant over me, Rob Granger. You did Greek myths at Ashley School along with me. I remember it perfectly well. Here."

He took his mug from me and followed me back into the sitting room. "Don't be daft. I never did Greek in my life."

"Well, heavens, neither did I. I meant we did the stories in English. Don't you remember that book with the pictures? Icarus with those gorgeous big wings, and the Gorgons with snakes in their hair, and the Minotaur? That was the monster who lived in the middle of a maze, and Ariadne got this ball of wool or whatever, and gave it to Theseus, and he went in and fought him."

"Yes, I remember that." He sat down in the armchair, stretched his long legs in front of him, and stirred his coffee. It was the chair Jeffrey Underhill had sat in, and I could not help a flash of comparison. Rob did not, as the American had done, dominate the room, but somehow his quality of relaxation, of looking at home wherever he happened to be, made itself quite as strongly felt as the other man's powerful composure. "He had a bull's head. A black Dexter, by the look of him. Tricky-tempered beasts."

"Don't you remember, we used to play it here in the maze? I had the ball of wool, and you were the Minotaur, and I had to show Theseus the way in."

"And got lost," he said, grinning. "I remember sitting there in the middle and hearing you hollering for help, and wondering if I'd ever get out myself. Then James came in and killed me."

"I told you you knew the story."

"Aye, I remember it now. I never was much of a hand at stories, was I, but I was good at sums. I had the better of you there, every time. You used to copy from my book."

"I did not!"

"You did. And who was it told the teacher that a polygon was a dead parrot?"

"Isn't it? Oh, Rob, you've made me feel better! Another cup?"

"No, thanks."

He set his empty mug down on the hearth beside him. "Did I see Mr. Underhill going up through the orchard with Cathy? Had they been here? I suppose they came to tell you they'd be leaving tomorrow?"

"You knew?"

"Well, yes. I'm the caretaker, remember? She told me when I went up to the house. Must have been while he was with you."

"That wasn't all he came for," I said. I gave him the gist of what had passed, and he thought it over for a few moments, then looked up.

"Are you really going to this party?"

"I think so. Cathy was very upset, and I think she'd feel that everything was all right if I did go. Besides, I'd like a chance to put things straight with Mrs. Underhill."

"Will your cousins be there?"

"I didn't like to ask, but the party was arranged some time ago, so I imagine they will be, unless Mr. Underhill tells them they're not welcome any more. I wouldn't put it past him."

"Then I'll take you to the train."

"Well, thank you, but I can use the Lambretta, and leave it in the station yard."

"And carry your party frock?"

"I've done it before." I smiled at him. "But it was nice of you to think about it."

"I wasn't," said Rob uncompromisingly. "I was thinking that I didn't want James or Emory to drive you."

I was silent for a moment. "Rob, you can't, you really can't think that this 'danger' thing could involve Emory or James deliberately harming me."

"I don't know." He made a restless little movement, rather unlike him. "We've had all this. Which of us knows what he'd do when pushed? And they are being pushed. Let's not leave it to chance."

"That's pure melodrama."

"Maybe." The stubborn line was very pronounced round his mouth. "But to see that they don't is pure common sense." A glimmer. "We peasants have a lot of that."

"But they don't know about the silver pen and the photograph."

"No, but they know you're no fool, and they want something badly enough to make them do what they've already done."

"Yes, I see. Once we admit that the thing's been done at all, it doesn't matter about the motives. I'll be careful. Well, all right, thanks. And the Underhills asked me to stay the night, so you don't have to meet the milk train . . . Rob?"

He looked an inquiry.

I asked: "Have you heard anything yet about Francis?"

"Not a thing, but then you know Francis. He never did write letters, or listen to the radio, or behave like anyone else. I remember him saying once that he had his own means of communication, and that was good enough for him."

I looked up. "Did he? What do you suppose he meant?"

He moved an indifferent shoulder. "His poetry, I suppose. Is it any better than that stuff there?"

"What? Oh, yes—that is, I don't know. I don't understand a word of it." I picked up my own empty mug, and crossed to pick up Rob's from the hearth. "I wish he'd show up, that's all. I just get a queer feeling that it might solve a thing or two."

He got to his feet. "Well, I'd better be going. Thanks for the coffee."

"You're welcome. At least you won't worry about me tonight if the twins are both away in Bristol."

"No. But I'll still take a look, if I may, to see if the door has a decent bolt. That's something I never checked. Would you like me to leave Bran with you?"

"Oh, no. He'd whine all night. I promise I'll lock the doors and windows, and I've got a telephone."

And time was, I thought, as Rob went to look at the back door, that I'd have had a private line if I needed it. But not any more. Not one I can use . . .

He finished his inspection and came in. "Seems O.K. You should be safe. Well, I'll go now. Good night, Bryony."

"Good night. And Rob—"

"Yes?"

"Thanks for everything."

He smiled. "For nothing. 'Night."

When he had gone, with Bran like a shadow as usual at his heels, I locked and bolted the door behind him, feeling a fool as I did so. For all that had happened, for all he had said, this was still my old familiar place, and the men we had been talking about were my own cousins. One of them, in spite of all seeming, might still be my own dear friend.

But I bolted the back door and checked the window catches for myself, and when I went up the narrow stair, I took the Brooke with me, and went to sleep with it under my pillow.

I woke with the feeling that I had just come out of a lovely and familiar dream. There had been a beach, a long, long shore of golden sand which stretched as far as the eye could reach. Farther. Ninety miles . . . Why did I think it was ninety miles long? There were dunes behind it, pale sand with long reeds blowing in the wind. The ocean poured and poured eternally in from the west. Tall grasses with feathered tops nodded and blew. The sky was huge and clean and the sand felt hot and the wind full of the sea's salt. Lonely, beautiful, quiet and safe.

Safe, safe, safe . . . The word went on echoing in Rob's voice round the dim walls of my bedroom. I remembered it all, then, the book under my pillow, the locked doors and windows, my cousins away in Bristol, the telephone by my bed if I should need reassurance.

The moon was bright. I slipped out of bed and went to the window. The striped print curtains hardly kept the moonlight out. The lattice was open. Feeling half silly for doing so, I kept carefully behind one of the curtains and looked out.

The window faced on the orchard. The moon was full on the blossoming trees. At the near corner, tallest of them all, the old pear tree lifted its graceful boughs, etched as black and symmetrical as the leads across a white window where moonlight poured. The bloom was like a cloud, piled shapes of light, and shadow that wasn't shadow, but just a dimmer moonwhite. It was a tree in a dream.

A shadow moved under it, intercepting the moon. Someone was standing there.

No, I was wrong. The pear tree's clouded shade was still again, and empty. It had been a trick of the moonlight, nothing more, something conjured up by moon and blossom, and a silence that should surely have been filled with nightingales. Lovers' time; Juliet at her window; Romeo under the orchard trees in the moonlight:

> Lady, by yonder blessèd moon I swear,
> That tips with silver all these fruit-tree tops . . .

But it was not. It was an ordinary, empty night, where I dared not even summon what I had been used to of comfort. No lover to lure back like a bird on a silken thread. If I were to play Juliet at all, it would be Brooke's Juliet, with her hugy heap of very prosaic fears and her hithering-thithering torments of indecisive love.

I went back to bed. But not to sleep. The hugy heap was as oppressive as a heavy quilt. I lay and watched the ceiling and thought about James, and all the uneasy tangled skein of what had happened.

I could not believe, even with the evidence, that he was guilty. But Rob had said—and it was true—that we none of us know what we are capable of. . . . And if he was guilty, what then? Was I to deny this powerful tie between us? Was I to believe it was only an accident of blood, of family, rather than a natural—God-given?—indication that we were sides of the same complete human being, that we had to be mates? Was it both arrogant and foolish to pretend that I was any better than, or indeed any different from, him? We are all capable, Rob had said. Not of killing my father, no, that I would never believe. But if it had been an accident, and the rest the result of natural panic afterward . . . I had said that I would forgive. And if I could extend that charity to strangers, how much more to my cousin?

I sat up, hugging my knees. I put my forehead down on them, pressing it hard against them as if that would clear my thoughts. Was I, like so many of my generation, so afraid to condemn, so fearful of "priggishness," that I was in danger of letting the good things slide, and accepting the far-from-best, till it became the norm, and excellence was forgotten? Society kept him and protected him. Was it priggish in me to want him to obey its law?

I lifted my head again. No, it was simpler than that. Panic after an accident was forgivable; to use it for profit was not.

But there was nothing I could do until the answer came back from Herr Gothard. I was still on my own. And I must stay that way until the mystery, such as it was, was solved.

It sounded easier than it was. I lay down again in my quiet airy bedroom, and watched the moonflung shadow of the pear tree move imperceptibly across the ceiling, and so strong was his insistence at that darkened door that I could have sworn that I saw his very shadow move with it, more substantial than the image of the blossoming boughs.

For one weak second I took my hand from the bars, and felt him close beside me, so close that . . .

Close beside me. I sat up like a pulled puppet. It had been so near, so insistent, so powerful and instinct with protection, that I knew he was here in the flesh as well. And I knew where. In the same moment's flash my opened mind had received another pattern: the pear tree's blossoming boughs, between my eyes and the moon.

He was in the orchard, under the pear tree. And whatever he had done, whoever he was, he meant me no harm.

I flung back the bedclothes and reached a coat down from behind the door. It was a soft light fur fabric, with a high collar and a tie belt. I fastened it round me, then, barefooted as I was, ran lightly down the stairs and out into the orchard.

The collie met me before I had gone two steps past the gate. I stopped dead. Rob came out from under the pear tree into the moonlight.

I managed to speak, but it came out like a croaking whisper. "What are you doing here? It must be two o'clock."

I thought he hesitated, but his voice sounded quite normal. "I said I'd keep an eye on you, remember? Are you all right?"

"Yes, thank you. But—do you mean to stay here all night? I'm sure there's no need."

"It's a nice night. I was thinking."

"What—what about?"

"As a matter of fact I was thinking about New Zealand."

"New Zealand?" It was so improbable that I found my voice. "Oh, I remember—those brochures in the cottage kitchen."

"Aye." He hadn't moved. He seemed to be waiting. The collie was jumping up at me. I fended it off absently, and went slowly toward him over the wet grass.

"What about New Zealand, Rob?"

"I was thinking that's where I'd like to go when I leave here. Up to the North. I was thinking about the Ninety Mile Beach."

I said shakily: "So was I."

I took another step toward him. He moved as fast as the collie had, and took hold of me, pulling me tightly against him. As he began to kiss me, the hugy heap of trouble melted like snow, and above us in the pear tree a nightingale began to sing.

If the laden arches of pear blossom had suddenly sprung to life like a fountain, tossing a plume of bright water as far as the moon, it would hardly have seemed surprising, so great was the release, the flood of joy that swept through me. Through him, too. I felt light and happiness pouring through his mind into mine, and back again, like a tide race meeting the outflow of a river, clashing and doubling and throwing up drowning waves of pleasure. We were both perhaps a little mad. We clung and kissed and clung again, wordless. I doubt if either of us could have spoken. Everything had already been said, everything shared. This was the end of the courtship, and not the beginning. Even my body seemed already to know his. This was how I had thought it would be, this complete knowing, this spontaneous melting and meeting. This was why, when James had made love to me, and I had found myself shrinking from him, I had been puzzled and afraid, no longer trusting the bond between myself and my secret friend.

Now it was I who held fast, and murmured: "It's been so long, so long. No, don't let me go."

"I'll never do that. Not ever, not now." His voice was muffled and husky, the country accent sounding stronger than usual. I was shaken yet again by a wave of love so powerful that it seemed to tear me apart to take him in.

"Rob, oh, Rob." I ran my fingers into his hair, tilting his head back so that the moonlight, intercepted faintly by the blossoming boughs, lit his face. "How on earth I didn't guess it was you . . . All the time, all the time I'd been thinking it had to be James or Francis, and yet it never seemed right. And all the time it's been you: it was you I ran to when I wanted help or comfort; it was your house that was home. And then this last few days, it was always you. . . ."

"Bryony." It came out on a long breath, fierce with relief and the pent frustration of years. "Bryony . . ."

It wasn't returning sanity, but the chill of the soaking grass on my bare feet, that made me draw away eventually and say: "Rob, let's go in now."

"Go in?" He repeated it as if he had hardly heard me, then shook his head like someone surfacing from deep water, and said it again, understanding. "Go in?"

"Yes. The grass is wet, and my feet are like ice."

"The more fool you for not putting your shoes on." His hold on me was relaxed now, affectionate. His voice was his own again, and he was smiling. "All right, you'd better go in. High time you did, if you ask me. Come along." He picked me up as easily as if I were a sack of meal, and began to carry me back across the grass to the cottage.

"Actually," I said, "I meant both of us. Won't you stay?"

There was a pause of seconds, then he shook his head. "No. I've waited all my life for you, and I reckon I can wait a bit longer. We'll leave all that for its right place."

"Which is?"

"After we're married." Then, as I took a breath: "Tomorrow night."

"Oh, Rob, be your age. You need a license, and a special costs twenty-five pounds, and where do you think we can raise that? And if *you* start on at me about breaking the damned trust for a bit of ready money—"

Rob said something rather rustic about the trust, and stopped to kiss me again. I pulled my mouth away. "It can't be tomorrow night. It can't be for ages."

"Why not?"

"Well, even if you could get a license tomorrow, the Vicar probably wouldn't consent to marry us on the spur of the moment."

"Spur of the moment nothing. I told you I've waited all my life, and so have you. Anyway, I've talked to the Vicar. He thinks it's a good thing."

"Does he? But he didn't know that I—"

"Oh, yes, he did. He's known for a long time how I felt about you, and then after you'd talked to him yesterday I reckon he saw the whole thing. He never told me anything you'd said to him, but he did let on to me that your dad had said he'd sooner see you wedded to me than to anyone else he knew."

"Daddy did?"

"So the Vicar told me. Better ask him yourself. But I don't think he'll worry much if we ask him to marry us straight away."

"N-no. Perhaps not. I did tell him about—well, about what we had together. And if Daddy really said that, and if the Vicar knew all the time that it was you—"

"Seems so," said Rob. "Well, I'll see him first thing, shall I? All he can do is refuse, but I think he'll consent."

"But the license!"

"I've had a license burning a hole in my pocket for two weeks now. It cost six pounds," said my lover. "Farsighted and thrifty, us peasants. Do you think I'd spend twenty-five quid on getting a woman when I can get one for six?"

"You could have one for nothing right now."

"Marriage or naught," said Rob austerely, and set me down laughing on the cottage step.

Ashley, 1835

It was cold. Shivering, he dragged his clothes on, and flung the fur-lined cloak round himself. His hands were shaking again. Defiance ebbed. He tried to recall his earlier mood of courage, but the cold hour before daylight was not the time for bravery. This was the hour when men were executed; the hour when they were least resistant, cared less. He supposed there was some mercy in it; but for the condemned, as for lovers, dawn always came too soon.

17

Believe me, love, it was the nightingale.

—Romeo and Juliet, III, v

NEXT MORNING I was up early, so early that the dew was still thick on the fruit blossom, and the orchard grass shone and glittered as if newly hosed down.

I sang as I got my breakfast ready. When I opened the back door I found a milk bottle standing on the step, and propped against it a package wrapped in brown paper. I knew the neat, slightly over-careful writing. And I guessed what I would find in the package; the books about New Zealand. I carried them into the kitchen and propped them against the milk jug and read them with my breakfast.

It already seemed as if the idea of New Zealand had been in my mind for a very long time; I wondered if, all unknowing, I had been sharing Rob's thoughts about it. Certainly, as I turned the pages, I found here and there pictures which seemed familiar, and names which came like echoes of something already spoken. Already I had accepted the idea of going there; of leaving Ashley, perhaps not exactly without a backward look, but without any of the heart-tearing that until yesterday I would have thought inevitable. I suppose that I was so much a part and product of this old, old place that I had never really envisaged life outside it, but now it seemed as if this had always been a foregone conclusion. My feeling was one of release rather than of loss. If this escape from old ties was what my lover had in mind, then by definition so did I. . . . A shared mind— and how well I knew this—was a shared desire.

I could see clearly, now that I knew him, the reasons for his doubts and hesitations, and for his long-drawn-out refusal to reveal himself. Perhaps he would not, even now, have nerved himself to come into the open, had it not been for my father's death. That had left me homeless and alone; it had also left me, perhaps no worse off than I had been before, but without Ashley itself at my back. It had, so to speak, brought me into Rob's orbit.

So much became clear, and with it the whole pattern of my lover's actions. The night I had come home to Ashley church, it had been Rob, waiting and watching for me, whose thoughts had come to meet me; and the mixture of exhilaration and nervousness, which I had misconstrued as guilt, was now explained. Later, the curtness which I had ascribed to his hurt hand could well have been because he had been held a helpless witness to my scene with James. Rob could never have doubted "what we had together," but I could see that he might well have doubted the outcome. And what he had feared most of all—I could see it now— had been my first reaction to the discovery that my beloved secret friend was only Rob, the boy from the home farm.

But now it was done, and here we were, and this bright morning with its dew and day-song could not dispel one stranded cobweb of last night's spell. "Tomorrow," he had said, and now tomorrow was "today," and it did not feel a day too soon.

Rob, where are you?

The signals were perceptibly fainter, like batteries beginning to fade. I stepped the query up and got the answer. He was in the greenhouses.

As I approached I saw him through the glass. He was up on a tall stepladder, mending the hinge of one of the ventilators. He saw me coming, gave me a smile and a sideways lift of the head, and went unhurriedly on with the job. He looked just the same as ever, his movements as he fitted the screwdriver to the thread and began to turn it, quite deliberate and relaxed. If I had not been receiving from him a current of excitement something akin to a burst of a thousand volts or so, I would have thought him unmoved. Nor did I have to ask him what the Vicar had said; I had known, roughly since breakfast time, that this was really and truly my wedding day.

I sat down on the stool beside the water tank and watched him in silence. In silence? The air was fizzing like champagne. The sun-motes sifting down through the tangle of white jasmine stung like sparks along the skin. Rob hadn't even looked at me again. He laid the screwdriver down and reached in a pocket for a fresh screw. Then, still with those steady, unhurried movements, he tackled the other hinge. He might have been alone.

I thought it was time to calm things down into words. "Thank you for the picture books."

"Don't mention it. Like them?"

"Love them."

"So when do we start?"

"Any time you like. For our honeymoon, perhaps?"

He gave the screw a last twist. "I reckon our honeymoon will take care of itself."

"I reckon it will. Rob, how long have you had this New Zealand dream?"

"Years now. There was something on the telly a long time ago—color it was; I saw it down at the Bull. It got to me, I don't know why. It seemed right for me, somehow. Ever since then I've read about it, off and on. Happen you never knew, but some folks of mine went out there, years back, and they've done well farming up in the North Island. Jerseys, mainly. Mum used to keep up with them, writing at Christmas, you know how it is. Then after she died I wrote to New Zealand House in London, and asked about emigrating. It seems there's no problem for a farm worker. I wouldn't need a sponsor, either; the Makepeaces— my folks out there—laid a welcome on the mat for me."

"But you didn't go."

"How could I? I was waiting for you." He said it quite simply, moving the creaking hinge experimentally as he talked. "It's true, you know that. After Mum died there wasn't anything much to keep me here. I liked your dad, but if it hadn't been for you I'd have gone, all that time back."

"I wondered why you stayed here. There didn't seem much future for you. Rob—"

"Mm?"

"Would you have asked me, if my father had still been alive?"

The mended hinge seemed to satisfy him. He picked an oilcan up off the top step of the ladder and began to trickle a few drops through into the rusty joint. "I don't know. I've asked myself that. Maybe I'd have talked to him first. I don't know."

"If you had, he might have told you what he told the Vicar."

"He might," said Rob. "I still don't really understand that."

"Don't you?" I smiled to myself. He didn't look down, but he caught it, and a little current of affection ran between us, as settled and placid as if we had been married for years. The champagne sparkle had subsided slowly from the air; the place was a deep, still well of contentment. I laced my fingers round an upraised knee and tilted my head to him. "So you see you needn't have worried, after all."

"Maybe not. But I wasn't to know that. The way I saw it, it'd have been a queer enough thing anyway, a man like me and a girl like you, let alone having this link between us as well. . . . That would have taken some explaining, wouldn't it?"

"He'd have understood."

He gave a slow nod. "I think so, too. I used to tell myself that. It didn't help much. There was always the moment when I was going to have to say, 'Mr. Ashley, sir, I want to marry Miss Bryony.'"

"I meant I think he'd have understood because he had something of the same gift." He looked, not surprised, but inquiring. I nodded. "He never said so, but I think he did."

"How d'you make that out?"

"Oh, one or two things that happened. There was a time once when I was hurt at school, and he knew without being told. That kind of thing. And I think that when he was dying he tried to get to me, and couldn't, but he had enough of a link with Ashley to get here. And you were here, and you got the signal and sent it on to me."

"A sort of Telstar?"

"Sort of, I suppose. Yes. It worked, anyway. The news came from you, not from him."

"It was a bad night, that." He propped the ventilator open, pocketed his tools, then leaned his elbows on the top step of the ladder, chin on fist, looking away from me to the creepers that festooned the rafters. "I'd been asleep, and I came awake, all very sudden, as if someone had kicked me in the head. It ached like that, too, I remember. First of all I thought I must be sickening for something, then after a bit I got there. And I didn't like what I got. Then somehow, like I always did, I began to think of you, and I knew what I was telling you. I suppose if boiling water or something flows through a pipe, the pipe gets scalded. That's what it felt like."

"Poor Rob. But you helped. Oh, my God, you did. If he hadn't been able to get to you . . . And that's another thing. This—this gift we share. I'm sure now that neither Emory nor James has it. James did tell me once that they could 'read each other's thoughts,' but I'm certain that—if it was true—he was just talking about the sort of link a lot of twins have with each other, a kind of sixth sense—intuition, really. Not what we have."

"And ours is the seventh, maybe?"

"Well, isn't it?" I tilted my head to smile at him. "That's how I think of it, anyway. Special and magic . . . I'm certain the twins don't have anything of the same sort. If they had, this last few days would have been even more difficult than they have. It was so awful having to shut you out."

He reached out a hand and began absently to guide the jasmine tendrils to their curled grip on the wires. "I once saw a picture," he said reminiscently, "called 'Love Locked Out.' It struck me at the time he shouldn't have been drooping there propped against the doorpost. He should have been hammering the bloody door down."

"You didn't. Not quite, anyway."

"Not for lack of wanting to."

"I suppose it was just as hard for you as it was for me. Harder, really." A spray of jasmine, too sharply jerked, loosed a tiny flight of fading flowers. They drifted past me, some of them to float on the water of the tank. I reached an idle finger to rescue the nearest. "Rob, there's something I still can't understand. It's what's been setting me wrong all this time about you, even though I know I must really have *wanted* it to be you. I thought it had to be an Ashley. So I never looked beyond my cousins, though heaven knows, since I grew up, I've never really felt anything about them at all. Not this way. It's really had me coming and going. But in that case, where do you fit in?"

He smiled. "Didn't you know? Straight down the wrong side of the blanket ever since donkey's years back. Makepeace, she was called, Ellen Makepeace. That ought to tell you that my stock's just as bad as yours, Miss Bryony Ashley."

"Ellen Makepeace? That was the girl Nick Ashley was shot for, surely. Her brothers shot him."

"That's the one. And they got on the next ship to Australia, and ended up in New Zealand." He started down the ladder. "And as for Ellen, a nice decent village lad called Granger married her, and they had a baby nearly nine months later. She said it was a Granger baby, and so did he, and everyone took it that

way, it being easier. Our family certainly took it so. But now you and I know
better, don't we? It must have been Nick's baby, and the Ashley thing—this
mind-talking—came down with it, right to me." He stood over me, smiling.
"What is it? Why are you staring? Can't stomach the idea of me being part
Ashley, too?"

"I was wondering why I hadn't seen that, either. You've even got the looks.
Oh, not what they call the Ashley looks, but you've got Bess Ashley's hair and
eyes."

"The gypsy look. Aye." He laughed. "I could see it myself, once I knew
where to look."

"Well, but if you know, then all the Grangers must have known. . . . Your
father and mother—"

"No, why should they? It's only this mind-talking that made me even begin to
guess at it. Oh, everyone knew the story about Nick Ashley, of course they did,
but I never heard it told any other way except that the Granger boy made an
honest woman of Ellen, and it was his own baby. It's a long time ago; why should
anyone bother? But then this started, this between you and me. When I was a kid
I thought nothing about it, but since I've got older, and thought a bit more, that's
the only explanation I can see. I'm the only one who guessed it, because no one
else knew the way you and I can talk."

"Did you find it harder this morning?"

"Yes. And I reckon this might be why. . . ." His arms went round me, and
we closed again, mouth to mouth, body to body. Two creatures becoming one,
lost and oblivious, glassed in from the world in our own quiet well of content.
"As good as last night?" he asked at length.

"Better, except there's no nightingale."

"What do you mean?"

"The nightingale last night, singing in the pear tree. Didn't you hear it?"

"There was nothing in the pear tree."

"There was a bird singing. It must have been a nightingale. Heavens, Rob—"

"You were imagining it. If that's what kissing me does for you—"

"I was not imagining it, and if kissing *me* stops up all your faculties—"

"Not all. Some it starts going."

"About the wedding, Rob—"

"Yes?"

"The license was all right? It really is today?"

"Eleven this morning. It's all arranged."

"*It is?*" I got my breath. "Look, isn't that perhaps rushing it just a bit—?"

"Who was rushing it last night?"

"I didn't mean that way. I meant it's after half past nine now, and—"

"Great jumping beans, so it is, and I haven't fed the hens yet!" said the man
who hadn't heard the nightingale. He kissed me hurriedly again, for good
measure, then let me go and picked up the stepladder. On the way to the
greenhouse door he hesitated, and turned. I got it again, the love and the longing
and the uncertainty which, now, I understood. "Bryony, honey, am I rushing it? I
thought when you said last night—I thought you wanted—"

"You thought right." I went to him, and put the palm of my hand gently
against his still rough cheek. "Oddly enough, my darling Rob, you read my very
thoughts. . . . And now go and feed your hens, while I find something to wear
for my wedding. See you in church."

* * *

Mr. and Mrs. Henderson were the witnesses, and Mr. Bryanston, gently beaming, took the service. Rob even produced a ring, which fitted. The church was full of the smell of lilac, and the flowers massed by the chancel steps still had the dew on them. He must have picked them at first light. The church door stood open, and the churchyard scents came in, elder-flowers and dewy grasses and the violets that grew by the porch, along with a faint smoky spice from the avenue where the yew burned its lamps of peace. For me no longer. I would lie forlorn no more.

The Vicar flattened a hand on the pages of the register, and Rob signed it. Not "farmer" or "gardener," but "man of all work." I liked that. It sounded proud, somehow, coming from him. When he put the pen in my hand I signed against my own name, "unemployed." I saw him watching over my shoulder, and the corners of his mouth deepened in a smile that did something severely clinical to the base of my spine.

"By the way," said the Vicar, "I almost forgot to tell you. The missing register is back, and I think quite unharmed."

"Which goes without saying"—this, unexpectedly, from Mrs. Henderson—"seeing as where I found it."

"*You* brought it back?" asked the Vicar in surprise.

"I did. I'm sorry you've been worrying yourself, Vicar, because there was no call. It's been in my house since Sunday, safe and sound, and to tell you the truth I clean forgot about it."

"Well, I must say, I'm very glad to have it back." There was some restraint apparent in the Vicar's voice. "Though, my dear Mrs. Henderson, I wish you had told me. If you wanted to consult it—"

"Me consult it? Why, Vicar, what would I want with those old books?"

"Well, then—" began the Vicar, but I had seen Mrs. Henderson's sidelong look at me.

"Where did you find it, Mrs. H.?" I asked her.

"In your cottage, Miss Bryony. I found it when I tidied up ready for you to come home, and I took it home with me, meaning to take it straight to the Vicar, but then Martha Gray came up, wanting a bite of tea, and we got talking, and I clean forgot. I won't pretend I'm not at fault, because I am. When your dad left he asked me most particular to take it back for him, him having been too ill to see to everything, and there, if I didn't forget it again till this very morning!"

"Talking about our wedding she was, and it put her in mind." Mr. Henderson made his first and last contribution to the conversation. It was hard to tell whether the dry sound of his voice was the result of long disuse, or of some disillusion provoked by the memory of that earlier wedding.

As ever, he was ignored. The Vicar, indeed, began to say something, but Mrs. Henderson was still looking at me, and I raised my brows at her. "I'd no idea it was there. Just whereabouts did you find it?"

"In your dad's room, it was. I wouldn't be likely to have mentioned it to *you*, Miss Bryony, not wanting to remind you of things, and I thought nothing of it, seeing as I expected Mr. Ashley would have told the Vicar he had the book. If," said Mrs. Henderson, showing signs of taking umbrage, "the Vicar had seen fit to mention to Henderson or me that it was missing—"

"I should have, I should have. The fault was mine. Indeed, now I come to think of it, I believe Mr. Ashley did mention his interest. . . . Now, why did I not think of that? Of course no one blames you, Mrs. Henderson; indeed, we are most grateful to you for bringing the book back. And now perhaps, this morning, on this very happy occasion . . ."

As the Vicar, soothing with long practice, trotted competently into the breach, Rob moved quietly past me to the table, and began to leaf through the pages of *One Ash: 1780–1837* which lay there.

I looked over his shoulder. The pages were all numbered, in beautiful copperplate, and they were all there. But Rob turned each one, looking, I knew, for some other paper which might have been hidden between the leaves. The paper. The letter. My father must have been studying this register, along with the family books, just before he had succumbed to the last attack that had banished him to Bad Tölz.

"Nothing there," I said in an undertone.

"Seems not," said Rob. "It looks as if some of them signed it after the wedding breakfast instead of before, doesn't it? But then maybe their hands were shaking as much as mine was. Weddings," said my husband, his left arm sliding round my shoulders, "are strictly for the birds." He added, softly: "So far."

"You took a lot of care that this bird should have a pretty wedding, all the same. The flowers are lovely."

"Well," said the Vicar cheerfully, appearing at Rob's other side, "we must be very thankful that all has ended so well. I confess I was worried about our little mystery. But now all is clear, and no blame attaches to anyone. I am quite certain now that the fault was mine, and mine alone. I am sure that Jon must have told me he wanted to look at the old registers, and I have simply forgotten. Dear me. I shall lock it away now, with the others. Were you looking for something in particular, Rob?"

"Not really, Vicar. But look, here's something. A funny sort of coincidence, wouldn't you say?"

His finger pointed to an entry, the third from the top on page 17. It was dated May 12, 1835. The signatories were Robert Granger, Laborer, of Ashley Parish, and Ellen Makepeace, Spinster, of One Ash. "Signatories" is not quite the correct word, for whereas Ellen had signed her name in a writing that was tremulous but correct, against the name of Robert Granger, Laborer, of Ashley Parish, was his mark, a large X.

"See?" said Rob to me. "It's happened before. I'd better put the kiss in, too." He did so, while the Vicar, beaming, and tut-tutting over the coincidence, carried the register over to the safe to lock it away. Mrs. Henderson bustled forward to follow up Rob's kiss and take one for herself, and Mr. Henderson, seizing my hand, pumped it up and down silently, as if conceding that this wedding, at least, was a matter for congratulation.

"And now," said Mr. Bryanston, "you'll all come over to the Vicarage for a glass of sherry, I hope? Rob didn't give us very much notice, so I'm not at all sure what we can manage in the way of a wedding breakfast, but I imagine—?" This with a justifiably nervous glance at Mrs. Henderson, but that lady remained miraculously unperturbed, while Rob shook his head.

"No, thanks very much, Vicar. We'd like to come over for the sherry, but don't trouble yourself further than that. We've got an errand to do in Worcester, and then we'll find some lunch for ourselves."

"Ah, yes, excellent." The Vicar straightened from shutting the safe. "Well, that's that. Now I still have one duty to do, and it's one I never forget: to kiss the bride. Bryony, my dear . . ."

And then, the formalities completed, the wedding party trooped across the churchyard between the somber beautiful yews, to sherry at the Vicarage.

Since there was now no question of my going to London for Cathy's party, we had decided to take the copy of *Romeus and Juliet* straight to Leslie Oker for a first opinion. Leslie himself was not there when we called, so we left the package with his assistant, and then made our courtesy visit to the offices of Meyer, Meyer, and Hardy to tell Mr. Emerson what had happened. The interview with a surprised and—though he hid it well—slightly shocked Emerson was brief and to the point. Rob left the first part of it to me. Once the lawyer had got over his surprise he seemed to assess the marriage and find it good. At any rate it was a solution to my future, which had worried him. He said so, diplomatically, and added his wishes for our happiness. He knew Rob well, of course, and obviously liked him; but there were adjustments to make in considering him now as my husband. Mr. Emerson did it well, and with great tact. I saw the tiny smile at the corners of Rob's mouth again, and thought suddenly, "My God, I've married him. Rob Granger, the garden-boy." The mixture of strangeness, tenderness, and sheer sexual excitement took away the power of coherent thought and struck me silent. I saw from the flicker of his lashes that Rob had taken it in, then he, as smoothly as any practiced politician, took over the interview. He told Mr. Emerson about his plans for emigration, discussed some of the details, touched on the trust and the future of the Court, arranged another appointment in a few days' time, and got himself and me out of the office and back into the sunny street with a minimum of fuss.

He slid a hand under my arm. "And now we eat?"

"We certainly do. I'm starving."

"It takes me that way, too. Would you have liked to go to the Star, or the Olde Talbot, or some place like that?"

"Not unless you've thought better of that picnic basket I saw on the back seat of the car." I laughed. "So that's why Mrs. Henderson didn't fuss when the Vicar asked about lunch. Did she get it ready for us?"

"She did. Do you mind?"

"I do not. Lovely. I don't want other people yet, just you and me. Where are you taking me?"

"Mystery tour," said Rob, opening the car door. Then he got in beside me, and the car threaded its way out into the traffic, through crowded sunny streets, then turned over the river bridge and headed for the open country.

He took me to a place I had never visited before. A narrow lane crept downhill between high hedges, and there at the foot, where a humped bridge crossed the river, was a patch of grass verge just wide enough to park a car. "And not a square foot for anyone else," said Rob with satisfaction, as he set the brake and killed the engine, and the sound of running water took over the peaceful afternoon.

Beyond the bridge was a steep wooded bank, through which the lane curled up again and out of sight. On the nearer side, cut in a wide hollow, was a flat pasture as smooth as a lake, through which the river wound, deep and slow, between clay banks alive with nesting martins. Behind us the pasture rose in a steep green bank seamed with flowering hawthorn, and honeycombed by rabbit warrens. A few sheep moved slowly along the hillside. Rooks cawed by their nests in the trees along the river, and a woodpecker worked somewhere out of sight. In the distance the sound of a tractor emphasized, rather than disturbed, the peace.

Rob spread a rug in the sun on the river's bank. The big trees shifted and rustled overhead, casting toward us a light-leaved net of shadows. The breezes shifted and ran, cuckooflower and marsh orchis and cowslip faintly moving, with the grasses shining and darkening between them. The sheep watched us incuriously, and their lambs watched us not at all, being more than busy over some intricate game halfway up the rabbit-pitted hillside. No other creature was in sight except the birds that went past on the May breezes.

"The Garden of Eden," I said, surveying it with pleasure.

Rob dumped the basket beside the rug. "And not an apple tree in sight. Now, which comes first, love or food?"

"Rob, you've got to be joking! If anyone came down the lane—"

"I was joking. If you knew how hungry I was . . . I was up all night, remember? I think I got some breakfast, but it doesn't seem to have had much effect. What's she given us? Cold duck, is it? That'll do for starters, anyway. Come on, love, let's get this lot unpacked before I fall apart."

I started on the basket, while he unearthed the beer and put it in the edge of the river to cool, then we both got going enthusiastically on the food Mrs. Henderson had provided.

I suppose it was a very strange wedding breakfast. I can't remember now all that we talked about. It may even be that we didn't talk to begin with, but that our thoughts moved out and mingled as they had done before. We knew each other so well already that all the important things had been said. If we talked at all it was about the food, the day, the reactions of people to what Rob persisted in calling, with amusement, our "mixed marriage."

"It's plain old-fashioned you are, Rob Granger," I told him.

"Maybe. But it's only your sort that keep saying that class doesn't exist or doesn't matter. Let them go down on the wrong side of the blanket like me, and see how much it doesn't matter."

"You mean Ellen Makepeace's slipup with Nick Ashley? That's a long time ago."

"No, I didn't. I meant the cottage and castle thing."

"Oh, is that all? Well, my cottage is a good bit smaller than yours now."

"So it is."

"And we're sharing the same blanket."

"So we are." He handed me his plate, then stretched his length contentedly along the rug, leaning up on one elbow. He reached for a stalk of grass and began absently to chew it. A lock of dark hair had fallen forward, half hiding his face; the sun, splashing light through the moving leaves, sent sparks of color through the black. His shirt was open, and I could see the glint of a gold chain against the hairs of his chest, and the pulse beating strongly in the hollow of his throat. There was a faint moist shine on his skin, from the heat, or from the beer. I shut my mind to him before he read me, and stolidly began to pack the debris back into the basket. Once again, irresistibly, I was remembering the patterns of his love that had come to me in the past, the love mixed with doubt, and with something that at times had been hopeless longing. That lover was gone for ever. I could forget the starlight, where love had been easy because it was in the mind, like poetry. This was the real, the daylight man. This was the man I would lie with tonight, and live with for the rest of my life.

"If you chew grass you get liver flukes," I said.

"Then I'll be crawling with 'em by this time," he said equably, but he threw the chewed stalk away. He pushed the hair back from his face. "Anyway, what you were saying about class, that wasn't the point."

"I know. And I don't say it doesn't exist, but I think it's nothing to do with money or family, or the old-fashioned things that went to make it up. I think it's habits of mind and ways of thinking."

"Well, yes, but that takes you right back to family, doesn't it? You're always more comfortable with people who were brought up the same way as yourself."

"Till something else overrides it."

He smiled. "Like now? Aye, but if ways of thinking count, then you and I aren't far apart."

"That's what I keep trying to tell you. Anyway, as long as neither of us minds, it doesn't matter."

"Why should I mind? I'm getting the best end of the bargain. And you're useful around the garden, which will be something when we're trying to scrape a living for ourselves out of the bush."

"And you're pretty good about the house, which ditto."

"So," he said, picking another grass stalk and beginning to chew that, "if we both make out in bed—"

"Well, for heaven's sake, don't you know how you make out in bed? I thought country boys spent all their time smooching in haystacks."

"Haystacks are overrated," said Rob. His voice had an odd expression, and looking up I saw the faintest of tinges under the brown in his cheeks. I thought at first, not really believing it, that he was embarrassed; then, with a stab of surprise that was curiously poignant and even nervous: Great heavens, I do believe he doesn't know any more than I do. . . .

His eyes came up to mine, and I knew he had read me. I went scarlet in my turn, and then suddenly we were both laughing, and in each other's arms.

"Oh, Rob, I just thought you were conventional."

"What's conventional except right? I didn't want it last night because if it was worth waiting for, it was worth waiting till now; and I don't want it now because I don't want it out here in a field with thistles. I want it at home, in bed, and for keeps, on a dark night with no one interrupting. And now you know why."

"Oh, Rob. Darling Rob . . . I suppose we'll manage somehow. People have."

"Well, there's evidence. At least between you and me there'll be no questions to ask."

"At any rate you can't pretend you've never kissed a girl before."

"I didn't tell you that, did I?"

"No. No . . . In fact, I'd say at a guess that you've had rather a lot of practice."

"Practice was what it was, then. Come to think of it, why should I go into haystacks—old-fashioned you are, aren't you, it's the back seat of a car these days—with girls, when I've had my own girl lined up since I was knee high to a grasshopper? I don't deny I've let a bit of steam off now and again, but I reckoned the real thing'd keep for you."

"Rob, love, you're out of the Ark."

"And a proper old sex-ship that was, come to think of it. Well, all right, you tell me: would you have gone with anyone else?"

"No."

"Because you were waiting for me."

It was a statement, not a question, but I answered it. "Of course. Rob, if you had been with another girl, do you suppose I'd have known?"

"Probably not, if I'd taken care to keep you out. But you'd have found out afterward, I guess." He gave me a look that was only half amused. "I knew when you were kissing James the other night. I was about ready to strangle the pair of you, except that I knew the muddle you were in."

"So you were. And there was I thinking I'd found him—you—at last, and wondering why I didn't even like it."

"I didn't get it all that clearly." He lay back on the rug, thinking. "Somehow, this one thing, sex, I mean—it's the only thing you and I don't seem to know about each other, right down to the last thought." He rolled over on his back, put his hands behind his head, and narrowed his eyes against the sky. "Maybe because it's something we've got to share physically. The one seems to switch the other off, somehow. I don't know. . . . Anyway, somehow, I don't think it'll be all that difficult." He was silent for a little, relaxing in the sun. "What would you like to do now?"

"Do?"

"What I mean is, how are we going to put the rest of the day in till it's decent time to go to bed?"

"Oh. Well, there's always television."

"Aye." The syllable sounded sleepy, and it occurred to me suddenly that the "man of all work" who had watched outside my cottage most of the night had probably been up again at five o'clock, going about his jobs.

I touched his hair. "Why don't we just stay here till we feel like going home, and get a cup of tea somewhere on the way?"

"Fine, if that's what you'd like. I think this day'll hold up till then. But we'll get storm before night."

"Oh, no! Are you sure?"

"Pretty sure. There's been rain in the hills, and I think it's coming this way. But not yet, don't worry. . . ." The dark lashes shut. Time passed. He lay so quietly that I thought he slept, but then he said, without stirring: "Day's beginning to drag a bit, wouldn't you say?"

" 'Gallop apace, you fiery-footed steeds.' "

"What's that?"

"Something Juliet said when she was waiting for Romeo."

"Them again."

"Yes." I did not say what I was thinking, that it had occurred to me, thinking about the play yesterday, that in some ways our secret love was much like theirs, a starlit descant to the family feuding and matchmaking of daylight. As long as the lovers could hold their private world inviolate, all was well, but when the warring factions crowded in . . .

"Forget it," said my lover. His eyes were open, and he was watching my face. "Whatever it is, we'll work it out together. And right this moment, today's our own, and after we've got your cousins' affair sorted out, so's the rest of our lives. Forget it. This is us."

He stretched an arm across and I slid onto it, with my head in the curve of his shoulder. The sun was hot. Overhead, the lacing of boughs slid a light and moving shadow over us, tempering the sun. A heron flapped ponderously upriver. The lambs slept on the warm hillside. Even the rooks were quiet.

I think we talked awhile longer. Our thoughts moved and mingled, but without the same clarity and force as before. No need now, I thought sleepily, with our bodies touching; with his hand cupped warm and gentle under my breast, and my hair under his cheek. No need. Here is my rest. We slept.

Ashley, 1835

At the door he paused, and looked back at the room. The faint light showed it clearly enough to his sharpened senses, but he could have shut his eyes and traced, accurately, every flower on the carpet, every line of the plaster maze on the wall, every fern on the frame that held the ceiling glass.

Fletcher would come later and straighten the bed, and put all to rights.

Never again, he thought. It would never be the same again. They had had their time outside the world, at the still center, in the Wondrous Isles. Now they must submit to the drag of the polar world outside. That they might change one happiness for another did not occur to him. Happiness was not the air he breathed.

He shut the door gently behind him, and trod down the slippery steps into the maze.

18

How cam'st thou hither, tell me, and wherefore?

—Romeo and Juliet, II, ii

WE HAD arranged to go back to my cottage rather than to Rob's, because the latter, so near to the Hendersons', gave less privacy. When we got there we found that Mrs. Henderson, though respecting our desire to be alone, had nevertheless, contrived that we should be welcomed. On the sitting-room table was a note which wished us well in the most substantial way possible. "Supper in oven," it said, and we found an excellent casserole gently bubbling there, with jacket potatoes hot and soft beside it on the shelf. The table was laid, and held, besides, an apple pie, a bowl of cream, and a generous wedge of cheese. We had brought a bottle of champagne in with us, and we drank this with supper, then washed the dishes together, while the dusk drew slowly over the shining lake outside, and the thrush sang its heart out in the pear tree.

"Make the most of it, mate," said Rob. "It's going to be a rough night." He caught my look, and grinned. "I was talking to the thrush. I warned you we'd get a storm, didn't I?"

"You did. Is it really going to rain? It's been such a lovely day."

He cocked his head to one side as he picked up the last dish and started to dry it. "Listen."

I listened. I heard it then, behind the thrush's song. Volleys of wind sifting the orchard trees; blowing and ebbing, then blowing again in gusts suddenly strong enough to keen in the telephone wires. The lake water darkened and gleamed under the racing cat's-paws.

"This'll fetch down a deal of the apple-blow," said Rob. "Here, I don't know where it goes." He handed me the dish, and I saw him glance at the clock, but I was wrong about the reason. He was reaching for his jacket, which he had hung over the back of a chair. "Bryony . . ." His apologetic look, which in someone I didn't love I'd have called hangdog, spoke for itself.

"I know," I said, "don't say it. you've got to go and feed the hens."

I found I had been watching for just that smile. Eleven short hours, and already a half-glance from him, amused and tender, could do this to me. We forge our own chains.

"They'll be in bed long since. Mrs. H. did them for me. But I'm afraid I will have to go up to the Court and take a look around. I always do a night-watchman round on the public side, and tonight, with the family gone up to London—"

I clapped a hand to my mouth. "Oh, Rob, I quite forgot! I never rang Cathy up to say I couldn't go to the party! I did try this morning, but no one answered, and I meant to try again from Worcester, but I forgot all about it. How awful!"

"Couldn't you ring up now? It's barely ten. Happen they'll forgive you when you tell them what made you forget. Will you tell them?"

"Will I not! They'll be delighted, I know. They think the world of you. But I can't telephone them now, I don't even know where the party was to be held. I was to go to their flat and have dinner with them, and then go with them to the party. They'll have gone by now. . . . Oh, how awful of me."

"I shouldn't worry. They'll think you missed the train or something. They may ring up here to find out what happened."

"I hope so. I could try the flat again, I suppose."

He still hesitated. "Do you mind my leaving you? I'll be about an hour, I expect. If you like, I'll wait till you've phoned, and you can come with me?"

I shook my head. "No, go ahead. And don't hurry yourself; after I've done the phoning I'm going to have a bath, and I've got a lot of tidying up to do. Heavens, what on earth will I say to them . . . ? It'll sound a bit funny as an explanation, coming out of the blue. Would you call yourself an accident, or an act of God, or what, Rob?"

He grinned. "I'll leave that to you. Maybe you'll be clearer about it, come the morning." He had been checking doors and windows as we talked. He came back to me. "Now, as your husband, Bryony Granger, do I rate a latchkey?"

I went to the bureau where my father's things still lay in a little pile, and took his key. I held it out on the palm of my hand.

Yours now, Ashley. The familiar name-pattern slid through.

Mine now.

Our eyes met, and the signals faded abruptly. He took the key delicately, as if he dared not touch me, hesitated briefly, then smiled and went. The door latched shut behind him, and seconds later the garden wicket swung and clashed. I heard a pause in the thrush's song, then it began again.

As I dialed the Underhills' flat, and then sat listening to the vain threshing of the bell, I reflected that I could very well do with the hour on my own. It was a little disconcerting to have to stage-manage one's own honeymoon at such short notice.

No reply. I put the receiver back, then ran upstairs to find that Mrs. Henderson, bless her, had been there, too. She had put fresh sheets on the double bed and turned it down ready. There were clean towels in the bathroom; she had even brought Rob's things across for him, and laid out the razor, with pajamas and dressing gown and a clean shirt for the morning. The room had been newly cleaned, and smelled of polish and the sweet scent of cowslips jam-packed tight in a bowl on the windowsill.

After all, there was plenty of time. I had a bath, hunted out a pretty nightdress I had bought in Funchal, then sat down to brush my hair. It was barely half an hour since Rob had gone, but already it was full dark, and without, tonight, even the light of moon and stars. Clouds had come piling up, seemingly from nowhere, into a black sky, and the fitful wind drove a loose bough of the Fribourg rose knocking against the glass. Even as I paused to listen, hairbrush in hand, the force of the spasmodic gusts increased. I could hear the growing fret and rush of wind in the orchard branches, and the slapping of water on the shingle at the Pool's edge. Rob had been weather-wise; it would be a rough night.

On the thought, I heard him come in, the soft click of the spring lock almost drowned by a sudden rattle of rain flung against the casement. A current of fresh damp air came with him.

I half turned toward the door, but he did not approach the stairs. He trod lightly into the sitting room, and paused.

No further sound. He seemed to be standing still, listening. I could picture him, head aslant, wondering, perhaps, what his cue would be to come upstairs.

My bedroom door opened straight on the small landing, from which an open stairway descended into the sitting room. I pulled on my housecoat, went to the head of the stairs, and leaned over the banister. The room below was in the shadows. I could see him standing near the door, with a hand up to the light switch.

"Rob? You've been quick. D'you know, Mrs. H. even got the bedroom ready and laid your things out—?" I stopped dead. He had turned quickly at the sound of my voice, and looked up. It was not Rob. It was my cousin James.

We stood staring at one another for a few stretched seconds of silence. Juliet with a difference, I thought, with a wry flicker that had nothing to do with amusement. Then, forcibly, damn and damn and damn. We were to have had tonight, at least, before the world broke in.

Perhaps after all I could save it. It would be twenty minutes or so before he got back from the Court; if I could get this over, explain what had happened, and get rid of James before Rob had to come back and face him . . .

"James—" I began, and started down the stairway.

Stopped again. The cottage door opened a second time, and Emory came in. He took out the bunch of keys which James had left in the lock, dropped it into his pocket, and shut the door carefully behind him. As he turned, he saw me. I couldn't see his face, but he stopped still as if he had been struck.

"Bryony! I thought you were in London!"

"Well, as you can see, I'm not." I said it slowly, looking from one to the other. "I forgot the party. Silly of me, wasn't it? But here I am. What do you want?"

"You forgot the party?" James's voice sounded strange, quite unlike his usual assured manner. "What do you mean?"

"What I say. You seem to have forgotten it, too."

"Well, not exactly." Emory's ease of manner was a little too good to be true. "Our invitations were canceled. I suppose we have you to thank for that."

"It's possible. So what brings you here?"

Dark as it was, I saw the glance that went between them, vivid as an electric spark. "I saw your light go on," said James, as if that explained everything.

"So?" I said coldly. "That still doesn't explain why you let yourself into my house like this, and how you happen to have a key. Or why you came here, thinking—hoping?—I'd be away. Well?"

"The fact is—" began James, but Emory cut across him.

"We thought you'd be in town, so we borrowed Mrs. Henderson's key."

The word "borrowed" held no touch of irony, but I knew that, had they spoken with Mrs. Henderson, she would be bound to have told them about Rob's and my marriage, and that we would be home tonight. I could translate well enough. She kept the cottage keys hanging on a nail inside her back door, which, like most doors in the country, was rarely locked. My cousins must have watched their chance to abstract the keys from their nail, then come down here.

Emory flashed me a smile, which, however, did not color his voice; this was the voice of an man thinking quickly; of a man in a hurry. "It's a diabolical liberty, I know, but time pressed. Since you're here, that makes it easier."

"Makes what easier?"

"There was something we wanted rather urgently."

"I see." And I thought I did. I pulled the housecoat closer round me, belted it, and began slowly to descend the stairs. I was remembering, with a quick slam of the blood in my heart, the mysteries that had yet to be solved. And I remembered, as clearly as if it were my lover telling me again, that these two could be dangerous if they were driven to it. Perhaps, I thought suddenly, they had put two and two together about the silver pen, and that was why they had come here. . . . But no, they had thought I was in London; this visit had nothing to do with that mystery.

Resolutely I put the thought aside. I concentrated on the present, and on keeping my mind shut to Rob: if he had received the sudden jagged pattern of fear which had zigzagged across my brain a moment ago, he would come straight here at the run, and an awkward—surely no more than awkward?—scene could easily become nasty. There was still time enough, I thought, to grasp the nettle and tell them what had happened, and then get rid of them.

I reached the foot of the stairs. The light from the bedroom door, spilling out on the landing above, showed me James's face. It looked tense, and rather pale, and his eyes burned on mine with what looked like anger. I said, as easily as I could:

"It's late, and as you can see, I'm on my way to bed. What did you come to get? I suppose it was the books? Well, I'm sorry, but they'll have to wait till morning." I crossed to the window and began to draw the curtains. "Put the light on, Emory. That's better. The Brooke isn't here, anyway. I told you I was taking it to be valued. And I'd like to keep the other one for a couple of days longer, please. After that, you'll be welcome. And if you've anything more to discuss, that will have to wait, too. So, since there aren't any other objects of virtu to interest you, then I suggest—"

"Not even you, seemingly," said James.

"What?" I had been straightening the curtains. I swung round and looked at him. I saw Emory turn, too. A tiny chill stroked the skin along my bare arms, like a cat's fur brushing up.

"You were expecting Rob Granger," said James. Then, across me to his brother: "She thought I was Granger. She called down to tell him the bedroom was ready, and then came out. Like that."

"Rob Granger?" said Emory, then, drawling a little: "Well, well, well." Silence for two blood-beats, while the eyes of both cousins took me in from head to foot. Hair loose to my shoulders, the hairbrush still in my hand; slippers, the scent of the bath; my housecoat wrapping me to the ankles, but parting to show the nightdress underneath.

I crossed to the fireplace, sat down in one of the armchairs, and regarded them both calmly.

"Yes, Rob Granger. So now, if you don't mind, I'd rather you went. He'll be coming soon, and it would be embarrassing for everyone if you were still here."

James came slowly forward. He was looking sick. It came to me with surprise that perhaps he had really cared; the scene in the garden the other night had not just been part of the twins' play for the breaking of the trust.

"I'm sorry, James." I said it gently. "What can I say? Only that it took me as much by surprise as anyone. And it's for real. I know now that nothing else was. . . . You know how I felt about you when we were in our teens; well, it just didn't work out. I don't know why. It's the way things go. It turns out it was Rob, all along, but I hardly realized it till today. You might say it was just one of those things; you don't see them coming, but then they come out of nowhere like the Severn Bore, and everything gets swept away in the flood."

A sound from Emory, a muffled exclamation that sounded almost like a laugh. Then he said, impatiently: "Look, Bryony, what the hell's it matter if you're sleeping with Rob Granger? Leave it, Twin. Can't you see it makes it a whole lot easier?"

"Makes what easier?" I demanded. "And I'm not sleeping with Rob Granger, not in the sense you mean. I married him this morning. Now do you see why I forgot Cathy's party, and why I want to get rid of you both?"

It was a bombshell, of course, and I hadn't meant to drop it quite like this. But even so, it didn't explode in quite the way I had expected. Emory moved forward, and the two of them stood, one to either side of my chair, staring down at me. Though I was used to the resemblance, had played with them both since childhood, it was somehow uncanny, the two faces, so very alike, looking at me with the same still, rigid expressions.

But there were differences. James was as white as paper now, with that curiously sick look, as if something in his mind was cringing from reality. Emory wore a look I was unfamiliar with: a pale, hard expression, the gray eyes narrowed, with the lower lids lifted and the eyes themselves quite expressionless.

I said, steadily: "Yes, we're married. It really did happen just out of the blue. I'll tell you about it some other time, but we just found out quite suddenly how much we meant to one another. So there it is. . . . And here we are." I turned a palm upward in my lap. It was a sort of gesture of relegation; an "over to you."

The pause seemed to last for ever, then they both spoke at once. As Emory began, quickly: "So he'll be over here soon? How soon?" James found his voice. He seemed to speak with difficulty. "So you're going to stay at Ashley? Here?"

"This is a much nicer cottage," said Emory, "than the one he has in the farmyard."

I suppose I must have gaped up at the pair of them. The conversation seemed to be taking a turn toward sheer irrelevance. Or so one might have thought, if it had not been for those cool Ashley eyes meeting on me like searchlights concentrated on a target, and the impression I got of those quick Ashley brains reappraising some situation I hadn't yet grasped.

"No," I said, rather sharply, "not here. I've some other news for you. I'd have told you tomorrow, in any case. We plan to emigrate. Rob's been thinking of it for ages, and we spoke to Mr. Emerson today about it. I want to go, too. It's the best thing, you must see that." I looked at James, and tried a smile. "I told you before that all I wanted was time to let the future show itself, and now it has. So surely that's your problem solved, too?"

James didn't answer. Above my head the concentration had shifted. I looked up at Emory. They were consulting one another in silence across me, as if I wasn't there. It is always irritating to be ignored; this was more, it was curiously disturbing. So was Emory's next remark.

"You can stop worrying, then, Twin."

I raised my brows. "Doesn't it concern both of you? I meant that I am now prepared to break the trust. I told Mr. Emerson so today."

No answer. My over-sensitive mental antennae picked up some powerful and urgent message that couldn't be spoken. James's eyes were still fast on his brother. Emory nodded to him, then smiled down at me.

"You must forgive us for seeming so eager to lose you, but you know the situation. Of course that's wonderful news about the trust. So, since it's working out so well for everyone, it seems we can offer you our congratulations. And the bridegroom, too, of course."

Plain, ordinary words, kindly, even; but there was no kindness in his voice, only briskness, with a burnish of flippancy, that left nothing to respond to.

James saved me the need. He was pursuing something of his own, still with that disturbing urgency. "Then you'll sell the cottage strip."

"Well, yes," I said slowly. "I hadn't thought about it yet, but why not? This is one bet I don't feel like hedging. We shan't come back."

James's face went slack with relief, and I saw color come creeping back. I had some reappraisal to do there, myself, it seemed. Not only did he urgently want the property; he was eager to see me go. Emory pegged it home, saying, swiftly, and with an easiness that seemed worked for: "What splendid news. It really is reprieve, Twin."

"Reprieve?" I queried.

Emory moved away from me, to perch on the edge of the table. He seemed relaxed now, and totally at ease. "I think you should be told, cousin dear, that it really was becoming more than ever urgent that we should be able to sell the Court, and sell it quickly. We've got a big speculator interested now, but he won't look at the property without access to Penny's Flats. And we are being hurried. Our dear stepmother's father finds himself suddenly in need of funds, so he proposes to transfer back to Spain some of the capital he put into the Bristol business. Something to do with marriage trusts for the two other daughters; dowries, they call it still. Quaint, don't you think?"

"I see. And it's tied up, is that it?"

"You could put it that way if you like." Emory sounded amused. "It so happens that it's in use elsewhere. We've been repaying the interest so far in installments, but now they want the principal back. . . . And I'm afraid it isn't there."

The reappraisal was easy after all. "You mean you stole it," I said.

"You have such a way of putting things," said Emory.

Another silence. Then I got to my feet. "Well, there doesn't seem to be much more to say, does there? My husband and I"—the phrase was like a shield— "will see Mr. Emerson again as soon as we can, and let him get on with breaking the trust and transferring the cottage strip to you." I took a breath, trying to control my voice, but it came out edged. "I hope he'll be able to get its worth out of you, and in cash, because Rob and I are going to need it. But for the present the cottage is still ours, and I should like the keys back, please, and then I'd like you both to go."

Without a word Emory drew the keys from his pocket and dropped them on the table. They fell with a little jingle. He slid lazily from the table's edge and straightened up, still smiling. James cleared his throat again, but said nothing. I suppose we must have stood there for only a few seconds, but it seemed to stretch out like a year; three strangers, parting, in a cold room.

I felt curiously numb, I suppose with shock, though I should have been prepared, after the Bad Tölz affair, for the realization that Rob had been only too right about my Ashley cousins; they were more than just self-willed and ruthless men; they were criminals. There was no need, now, to hear from Walther about the photograph. I knew for certain, as if my father himself had told me, that it had been Emory there on the Wackersberg road, and Emory who had gone (in the person of James) straight to Jerez, while James had doubled for him here at home. As before, I crushed the thought aside, in case Rob should catch its echo and react to it. All I wanted now was to be rid of the twins and their dealing, and for ever. I was conscious of a dull kind of hope that, once the arrangements were made with Mr. Emerson, I need never see my cousins again.

But even so, when the keys fell from Emory's hand to the cottage table, the sound they made was a tiny knell to the past. Yet another knell. Ashley was gone from me, and with it, how much more.

I shook it off, and, turning abruptly, went to the door and opened it. The wind was higher than ever, tempestuous. The beech trees beyond the orchard roared and swayed against a fast-moving sky where the clouds, massing and countermassing, piling and breaking and streaming off in spindrift, left blinks and glimpses of the moonlit immensity beyond. The orchard, with its pale tents of blossom, reeled in and out of light and shadow, its torn flowers snowing down the gusts of wind. The rain had stopped.

To my relief the flying moonlight showed me the path still empty, and away beyond the roaring boughs a light still in the Court. But it showed me something else. The lawn in front of the cottage was under water as far as the lilac tree. The level of the Pool must have risen half a meter. And while I watched, a gust of the driving wind sent the water slapping across the flags almost to the doorstep.

"It's all right," said Emory, just behind me. "That's what we meant by 'reprieve.' We'll go across now and shut the High Sluice. So, dear cousin, lie easy in your marriage bed."

"Shut the High Sluice?" I whirled on him. I felt myself go as white as a sheet. "What do you mean?"

He took me by the shoulders. Behind me the door, caught in a gust of wind, slammed shut again. He shook me, quite gently. "I told you it's a reprieve. We haven't been quite honest with you, my dear. We didn't come all this way just to get the books. You were going to give those to us anyway, weren't you? We came to—well, to hasten your decision to sell the cottage strip."

No misunderstanding this time. I got the whole picture straight away. "You wanted to flood the place again? You mean you opened the High Sluice deliberately, and on a night like this?"

"We could hardly choose our night. We had to take the chance, with you and the Underhills away. The weather was just a bonus. It quickened things up a bit for James—he was the one at the Sluice. I was otherwise engaged."

"And you needn't tell me how. You made the alibis. It was your turn, wasn't it?"

The gray eyes narrowed. "What do you mean?"

I caught at my flying thoughts. I had been thinking about the Bad Tölz alibis, but I knew better now than to push my luck, not under those Ashley eyes. I said hoarsely: "I was thinking about Cathy."

"Oh, that. Yes, that was work wasted, but I've always been one to write off my losses. I don't bear you any grudge over that, Bryony, my dear; not the way things seem to be turning out now." A brief laugh as Cathy was dismissed. "Well, now you know the lot. We reckoned another bad flood would put paid to the cottage, and force your hand. Brutal of us, wasn't it, but needs must, they say, and the devil's certainly been driving for the last six months or more. . . . Believe me," said Emory, sounding sincere and very charming with it, "we'd have been sorry about the cottage, if you really liked it, but you should have more sense than to get sentimental about a gold mine."

The words set up an echo of some kind: James speaking with regret and genuine bitterness about the Court and the dereliction everywhere. And somewhere in the distance the sound of hammering.

"Luck all the way," said Emory. "Luck for you, too. Your being here tonight might have bitched the whole thing up, quite apart from the fact that Rob Granger usually goes home as soon as he's done his rounds at seven, or else away down to the Bull. As it is, I suppose he'll be coming along this way at any minute, and he'll be bound to notice the water level. Tell him there's no need to trouble; we'll go straight to the High Sluice now."

"But—" I began, then shut my teeth on it. I wasn't going to tell them that Rob was doing his rounds now, and would certainly, darkness or no darkness, have seen the level of the water. His reaction, I knew, would be to check straight away on the sluices. He must not run into my cousins tonight on the same errand. If I could get rid of them now, I could call him in my own way, and warn him off.

"You'd better hurry, then," I said quickly. "The way the Pool's risen it looks as if the Overflow can't carry it all away. It must be coming over the bank already. For pity's sake, Emory—"

"Calm down, calm down. We can get the Low Sluice open."

"You certainly can't! It's been wedged shut again. You should never have touched it, it's been unsafe for years! Just get the High Sluice closed before there's some real damage done. . . . You'd better get going."

But as I turned to open the door for them again, the telephone rang.

Ashley, 1835

A cock crowed from the direction of the farmyard. Night's singer was silent, and day's first chorus had died to desultory pipings. A rustle from somewhere near the edge of the maze made him pause and listen, head aslant. A badger on its way home, perhaps. Or a roe. If deer had been in the garden again he must tell the keeper to take the gun out after them today.

Today . . . Today was not just another day. Today he would have to face them. His father was dead, and he was Ashley. From somewhere he must find the courage to face them with what he had done. Then, afterward, she would be with him.

Something showed pale on the grass near the mouth of the maze. Stooping to peer, he recognized the kerchief he had given her: it was of silk, and, for fear it should be seen, she wore it always in her bosom. Wondering how she had come to drop it there, he picked it up, and, smiling, held it to his face. The gentle fragrance of lavender brought her near again, and with her the sweet days of summer.

Still smiling, he walked out of the maze.

19

The letter was not nice, but full of charge
Of dear import, and the neglecting it
May do much danger.

—*Romeo and Juliet*, V, ii

THE THREE of us stood as if struck still, while the harsh threshing of the bell drowned out even the wild sounds of the night. Then I made a move. Emory's hand shot out and gripped my wrist.

"We're not here, remember? And neither are you. Leave it."

"It might be Cathy."

"And if it is? She doesn't know you're back here. Leave it."

I was angry now. "It's my phone, Emory. I shan't tell anyone you're here, if you're afraid. But what is there to be afraid of now? Your crime's been called off, hasn't it?"

"There's a light in the Court." James spoke quickly, from the window. "Rob must have gone over. If he's seen the water level he may be telephoning here before he goes over to the High Sluice. She'd better answer, or he might think something's up."

"Could be," said Emory. Then, to me, swiftly: "Is he likely to call help in if he's seen the level?"

"I doubt it. He's quite capable of dealing with it himself. He's kept the Court going for long enough."

I did not trouble to keep the bite out of my voice, but Emory didn't seem to notice. "Well . . ." he said, and stood back.

Only as I picked up the telephone did the other possibility present itself. As late as this, the call must be urgent. It would certainly not be Rob, but it might well be Herr Gothard. He would not have received the photographs yet, but he might speak of my promise to send them; or he might even be ringing to tell me of some other progress made toward identification of the guilty driver. I had the receiver half back to its rest, but a voice was already talking quickly, and very audibly, through it. Not Herr Gothard; it was Leslie Oker, not even waiting for me to respond, but in full and joyous spate with his news.

"Bryony? My dear, I simply had to ring you. I know it's a dreadful hour of night, and I'm sorry if you were asleep, but I've been trying to get you off and on all day, and when you hear what I have to tell you I'm sure you'll think it was worth it. My dear, the book . . ."

It was a loud telephone, Leslie's obvious excitement carrying through almost as if he were in the room. Beside me, Emory made a sharp movement of interest. I started to speak, but Leslie wasn't listening. He swept on.

"I just had to tell you—I'm as certain as can be that the book's genuine. It's been re-bound, and that will take something off its value, but it's still very valuable indeed. I wouldn't like to guess at a figure, until I've found out a little more about it. . . . In any case, when you come to the real rarities, you can't put a figure on them until they go into the sale room. But it could be very valuable, very valuable indeed . . . museum stuff . . . provenance . . ."

He talked on about the book, half technical jargon that I hardly took in. I put a hand tightly over the mouthpiece, looked up at Emory, and spoke under my breath. "Well, there's your answer. Ready cash, or at any rate something to borrow on—collateral, do they call it? Now I hope you'll leave my home to me for as long as I need it?"

I doubt if Emory even heard the bitter little gibe. His eyes were gleaming, and he mouthed something; I thought it was "How much?" I shook my head as the telephone quacked what was obviously a question, and took my hand off the mouthpiece again.

"Sorry, Leslie, I didn't catch that. What did you say?"

"I said, when I lifted it, I found something that might be in its own way even more interesting. It's a bit long, but do you want to hear it now?"

"Hear what? Lifted what?" I asked unguardedly.

"The bookplate. That curious rectangular design with the crest in the middle and that weird motto of yours, 'Touch Not the Cat.'"

Something jarred me right back to the alert. "Oh yes, that," I said quickly. "Well, look, Leslie, I should have told you sooner, the book isn't officially mine any longer. Since Daddy's death all the family things belong to my cousin Emory. I'll tell him to get in touch with you, and—"

He didn't hear the rest, and for a very good reason. Emory's hand had come between my mouth and the telephone, covering the mouthpiece again. His other hand closed on the receiver, over mine, and lifted it away from me. Held in midair in front of me, the metallic voice quacked on, all too clear.

". . . Sorry to hear that, dear, because really, such a *find* . . . Of course, moving it won't militate against the value of the book at all, since the bookplate was put on so much later. After the rebinding, too, did I make that clear? In fact, it looked to me as if it had been lifted before, and pasted down again; recently, I'd say . . . so I felt quite justified in lifting it again, and indeed, I was right, because the original flyleaf was there. It puts the whole thing beyond the bounds of doubt. But this paper I was telling you about, that I found under the bookplate, well, that's of real family interest, I would think, because there's a note from one of your family, and the whole thing, love, looks like a *mystery* to me, too Gothic, really, but what fun. Listen."

We listened, all three of us. Whatever Leslie had found, I did not see now how I could stop Emory from finding out about it. All he had to do was ring Leslie back himself. It was his book, after all.

Leslie was explaining. "It looks like a page from a church register. It's numbered seventeen, and there are only three entries. They may all be interesting, I don't know, but the third one will just fascinate you. It's dated April fifteenth, 1835, and it records the marriage of Nicholas Ashley, Esquire, of Ashley Court, to an Ellen Makepeace, of One Ash."

Not for worlds would I have put the receiver back now. My mind meshed into gear like a racing engine. The consequences could wait; I had to know. *"The paper, it's in William's Brooke. In the library . . . The map. The letter. In the Brooke."*

"Yes," I said, "go on."

"Further down the page someone has written a note. It's signed 'Charles Ashley.' Do you know who he was?"

"He was Nick Ashley's uncle, William Ashley's brother. He succeeded to the Court after Nick Ashley was shot."

"Oh. Well, a note from him. It says—it's rather long, so I'll paraphrase the first bit—he says he bribed the clerk to recopy the page omitting the Ashley entry, and something about the incumbent—is that the Vicar, dear?—being a dependent. Does that make sense?"

"I think so. One Ash was one of the Ashley benefices. If there was a younger son or a poor relation they were given the benefice. I suppose Charles Ashley could put pressure on him to keep quiet about the wedding. Is that what he says?"

"Could be. He says—shall I read the rest to you?"

"Yes, please."

" 'It is said that the girl goes with child, and should she bear it before the nine months' term is up since my nephew's death, there will be those who, for their own base ends, will rumor it abroad that the child was already begotten on her by my nephew, before she married her husband. But it is neither right nor fitting that the fruit—if it be so—of so hasty and base a connexion should take the property from the hands of my own fair family who are sprung from alliance with the highest in the County, and who are of a fair age and disposition to administer the Estate. Moreover, and it is this which has driven me to act as I have done, the brothers of the said Ellen Makepeace did kill and murder my nephew Nicholas, so to my mind it were better that the child were born dead, than usurp this place with blood upon his head. So, God be my witness, it is not upon my conscience to do what I have done. The girl bears herself lowly, and has avowed publicly that the child is that of her own husband.' " A pause, during which I could even hear the rustle of the paper in Leslie's hands. He gave his little laugh. "She would, of course, poor creature. The dear Squire would probably have had the baby quietly put down otherwise. Well, well, poor things. Past history is always a good deal better in the past, isn't it, Bryony dear? Does all this mean anything to you?"

Emory lowered the receiver to me again. I didn't look at him. I cleared my throat, but even so my voice came out rather unfamiliar, borrowing, falsely, a little of Leslie's own over-exuberance:

"I think so. Yes, I think so. Leslie, I'm terribly grateful to you. It's all so exciting, isn't it, and I'm awfully glad you rang. May I come over tomorrow, perhaps, and hear all about the book, and look at this paper? We'll have time to talk about it then."

"Well, of course. This awful hour . . . But I knew you'd like to know straight away. Look, there's a chap in London who'd know more about the *Romeus* than I do. I'll give him a buzz in the morning, shall I, before you come?"

"Please do. Thank you, Leslie. But Leslie—"

"Yes?"

"This friend of yours—ask him about the book's value by all means, but would you please not tell him anything about the letter; not till we've had a look at it, and worked out what it means?"

"Well, of course not. It's safe with me, dear." No emphasis, but I knew it was. "Good night."

"Good night. Thank you for ringing."

The telephone went dead. Emory's hands relaxed, and he stood back from me. I put the receiver down half blindly, so that it fell with a clatter. James picked it up and replaced it, and I sat down rather heavily in the chair beside the table.

"That was sensible," said Emory. "Well, how many more surprises do you suppose this night will hold? This Ellen Makepeace . . . if she actually had that baby—"

I hadn't looked at either of them, but James, prompted perhaps by something in my expression, or by some stray instinct of the Ashley gift, or, what was more likely than either, by some residuum of jealousy, got there with frightening speed.

"She did. You can bet your bloody life she did. Makepeaces . . . One Ash is full of them, and the Grangers are connected." Then, savagely, to me: "That's it, isn't it? Rob Granger—that's who it is! You can bet your life he goes straight back to this stupid, so-called marriage. That's why you did it, isn't it? Why you married him? Because you knew he was an Ashley, and legit., at that. Why else would you marry a lout like that?"

"Shut up, Twin." This, sharply, from Emory. "That sort of thing gets us nowhere. Bryony, did you know about this?"

They would only have to look in the parish register, or even, country memories being what they were, ask any adult in One Ash, to find that Ellen was indeed Rob's ancestress "straight back." I nodded. "I knew he was an Ashley, but I didn't know about the marriage. Neither does he. He told me he was descended from Nick Ashley, but on the wrong side of the blanket. That was all."

"Oh, he knows that much? Then I suppose all his family know, too."

"Only the same story we've been hearing all our lives, that the brothers shot Nick for debauching Ellen, and that she married the Granger lad and had a baby son, but swore on the Bible it was her husband's, so people accepted it."

"And all the time," said Emory, with a twist to his voice, "she was telling the exact truth. Poor Charles. He must have fairly sweated it out until he saw she was going to be sensible."

I said nothing. I was thinking about Ellen Ashley. I felt consumed with pity for that girl, bereft and helpless, swearing on the Scriptures to protect her lover's child, and hugging to herself the comfort that all the time it was the truth. Poor Ellen. I wondered how Robert Granger had been with her, and how much he had known or guessed of the things she kept in her heart.

"Are you trying to pretend," demanded James, "that Rob never guessed?"

"That he was legitimate? Of course not, why should he? If there had ever been a hint, even that he was an Ashley by-blow, our family would have known, but I told you, it was accepted that the baby was Robert Granger's. His family may have talked about it among themselves, but nothing more than that. Have you ever even heard a rumor? I haven't."

"But you said he'd told you that himself."

"Yes. He knew because"—I looked from one to the other—"because he has the Ashley gift. You know about that. Well, so have I. That's why our marriage happened as it did, so suddenly. I'd meant to tell you about that, anyway; I felt I owed you that."

It seemed very strange that I should ever have felt I owed James anything. Now, if I owed an explanation to anyone, I owed it to Rob. So I told my cousins quickly, the merest sketch, and they listened, not arguing or even very surprised; they were Ashleys after all. They knew the history of the "gift," and had themselves claimed some kind of intuitive link.

"You'll tell him all about it now, I suppose?" asked James, when I had finished.

"Can you think of any reason why not?"

"Well, my God—" began my cousin, but Emory stopped him.

"Let her talk. Go on, Bryony."

"Well, why not? Do you think I can stay married to him all my life and not tell him something that might matter to him like this? He ought to know he's a true Ashley, and that his great-great-grandfather wasn't just a brat fathered on a light-minded girl. He ought to know that Nick Ashley loved Ellen enough to marry her."

"Or that he was scared silly of her brothers." That was James.

"That's stupid!" I spoke hotly, as if I were defending Rob himself. I knew, as well as if they had told me, why Nick and Ellen, just for those fatal few days, had kept their marriage secret. They were trying, like Rob and me, to keep something to themselves for a while before the world broke in. And with even less success.

I straightened wearily in my chair. "Look," I said, "why don't we call it a night and talk about it tomorrow? With Rob, if you like. As I see it, what we've found out will make no difference, one way or another, to what happens here at Ashley. But if you two don't get on your way now, and do something about the High Sluice—"

"To hell with the High Sluice." It was odd how James seemed to have taken over the scene. "Are you seriously trying to tell us that if you tell Granger all this—this old-time Gothic trash, do you seriously tell us that he won't be tempted to make it public? Claim the Court and everything that goes with it? Stay here with you and play lord of the manor? Someone like that couldn't resist it."

"Rob knows even better than you do what it would mean to have this place unloaded on him," I said hotly. "I know he doesn't want to stay here, and neither do I. Do I have to keep telling you? This won't make any difference to us at all."

"Except that you'd have some money to emigrate with," said James. "Rather more than the cottage strip will net for you."

"If we claimed it, and if the claim was upheld."

"Are you trying to say that he wouldn't even try to claim it?"

"How many more times do I have to say it?" I regarded him with weary dislike. "Even if we wanted the Court—or wanted the money the sale would bring—can you see a claim like this standing up in a court of law? It wouldn't even be worth trying."

"Your father must have thought it would," said James obstinately. "This is why he refused to break the trust the second time we asked him. He must just have found out about Rob Granger."

"Yes." I spoke with sudden, complete illumination. (*"I did tell Bryanston that she and Rob should marry. Perhaps the boy knows already that he's an Ashley. Tell the boy who he is. This trust; it's his concern now. You can depend on him to do what's right. You have—both of you—my blessing."*) I sat up straight, speaking earnestly. "And he was going to do the right thing, as I am, and tell Rob all the truth, and leave it to him. He has to know. That's all, James. Further than that it's up to him, and I've told you what I think he'll do: cut his losses, as I'm doing, and go."

Emory stirred. "Leslie Oker saw the paper, and you can't tell me he'd keep quiet about a juicy item like that."

"He will if I ask him to. In any case," I said impatiently, "what does it matter who knows about it, if we don't press anything? Mr. Emerson will do as Rob asks him—and, for pity's sake, can you *imagine* a claim like that being made today, in the nineteen-seventies? Gothic trash isn't in it. Can you imagine a courtful of lawyers arguing over an 1837 parish register, and whether or not Bess Ashley really did hand telepathy down the family?"

"All right," said Emory, "so imagine it. Whether you want it or not, let Oker once start talking, and there'll be questions asked about our claim to the place and our right to sell it. And there simply is not time to let the lawyers make a meal of it, and spend ten happy years arguing the pros and the cons of the Ashley gift, while in the meantime Pereira sues us for twenty thousand pounds in no time at all."

"We could destroy the paper, and square Leslie Oker." This from James. They were at it again, talking across me. I believe I said something more, but they ignored me.

"Even if he can be squared," said Emory, "he's probably talked already."

"Well, but without proof—"

"Any inquiry would mean the kind of delay we can't afford."

"That's true," said James.

"Too bad, isn't it?" said Emory.

"Well, what are you going to do?"

"It shouldn't be too difficult," said Emory, "to fix things."

I saw it then, through the weariness and worry, and I knew, against all belief, that Rob had been right. Cousins or no, these men were dangerous, even to me and mine. Quick thinking, violent men, who knew how to profit from accidents . . .

I don't think I moved, but James, still on that odd telepathic wavelength, took a swift step and got between me and the telephone. I had made no move to touch it. I shut my eyes and reached for Rob.

But across the first groping signal I heard James say, urgently: "It's true, you know, Twin, she can talk to him. Look at her." Then, in sudden, unbelieving revulsion: "Emory! No!"

Something hit me hard behind the ear, and I went out like a smashed lamp.

Ashley, 1835

His limbs were stiff, and heavy as if bound with iron. The pain in his chest exploded through his whole body, then to a slow, unmerciful aching. He moaned, but could hear no sound.

He was lying on cold, soaking grass. He must, he thought dimly, have fainted. He remembered—surely he remembered?—going out of the maze; the drenched grasses, and the yew trees glimmering, heavy with shining, under the faint morning stars. There had been shadows moving at the mouth of the maze, a rough whisper, a hand grabbing at him, then the skin-prickling sound of a cocked fowling piece . . .

The memory faded, and with it, slowing into a drowsy warmth, the pain died. His head felt light and empty, and he had the strangest fancy that he was floating above his own body, drawn upward from its chilling weight as if the air sucked him away, leaf-light. Then it, too, faded.

20

And the place death, considering who thou art,
If any of my kinsmen find thee here.

—*Romeo and Juliet*, II, ii

I HAD a headache, and it was dark. At first I thought the noises were in my head, but, as I slowly swam up into the headache and the chilly air, I realized that the creakings and the splashes, and the keening gusts of wind, were realities, as was the slam of wood on wood that had finally wakened me.

It took me a little time to come fully to myself, and discover where I was. At first, groping for my bearings through painfully returning consciousness, I thought I must be somewhere out in the open; I was lying on what seemed to be hard ground strewn with twigs and dead leaves and broken shards, with the smells of wet earth and growing things and rotting wood blown round me strongly on the gusty drafts. But then, slowly, walls and a kind of roof built themselves out of the near-darkness round me, and I saw that I was in an enclosed space perhaps the size of the cottage sitting room, but with a ceiling so low—a meter or so above me—that I could hardly sit up without striking my head. I could only see this much because the walls, though surely solid enough, showed here and there a crack or a knothole through which filtered a gray and fitful light.

I dragged myself shakily to hands and knees, and crawled to one of these to peer through.

I saw a thick, ragged hedge, blocking a square of windy sky; grasses whipping in the wind; nearer at hand the dim tangles of some thick creeper swinging and beating like waves against the balustrade of a rustic stairway which cut diagonally across my vision. Everywhere was the sound of trees and water, and the reeling gray light of a moon behind wind-driven cloud.

I had it then. This was the pavilion, at the center of the maze. The slamming noise was the broken shutter which had worked loose and was swinging to and fro in the wind, and the stairs beside me were those leading up to the verandah and the pavilion's door.

They led upward, past me. I was under the pavilion, in the space below the floor, with the access door beneath the verandah slammed shut and—as I groped dazedly to discover—securely jammed from outside.

A gust of wind, carrying a scatter of small debris, struck the pavilion, and a draft whipped through the crack where I crouched, blowing my hair stinging into my eyes. I came fully awake then, with all that had happened vididly back in mind, slotted neatly into place like items on a computerized account; and with it, all that was due to happen, which I suppose I had seen in that one brief flash of illumination, so brutally cut off by Emory's blow.

Some dim memory I still retained, of quick incisive instructions from Emory to James, and of protests overruled. I must have surfaced into consciousness from time to time, enough to catch snatches of the argument that ensued. I knew now why James had looked so strained and sick; he had after all cared enough— or been frightened enough—not to want to see me harmed.

"I tell you, Twin, she'll be perfectly safe." That was Emory, impatience held hard on the curb. "I'll put her in the pavilion and lock her in. She'll be above water level there, and she'll be out of action long enough. . . . No one to hear if she shouts, and by that time we can be on the other side of the county."

"But she's seen us here, and for God's sake, Emory, if anything happens to Rob Granger, you can't expect her to sit mute. Our alibis are blown before we start."

"Very well, then." Quick and smooth. "She goes. You agree?"

"No! Are you crazy? Look, we've got to think of something else—"

"Such as? You can't have it both ways."

A pause, then from James, slowly: "I think we can. I'm willing to bet she'd say nothing, whatever she might think she knows about an accident to Rob. . . . Yes, all right, so she's married him; all that crap she gave us about it, if you can believe it . . . never last out the honeymoon, even, a lout like that . . . Look, Twin, I mean it. She's never said a word about her father's death, has she? About its being one of us . . . And she knows. She cottoned on to that pen of mine that you dropped, I'm certain she did; but she's never said a word, and it's my bet she never will, just as she held her tongue about that stuff Cathy stole."

"Well, but Cousin Jon's death was an accident. She'll know this won't be."

"All the same . . ."

So much came back to me, more or less clearly. The outcome, however arrived at, was clearer still. Whether James had, in the end, agreed with Emory's plan to dispose of me, or whether he had simply turned a blind eye to whatever his twin might do, I did not know. But I would have taken any bet that it was Emory who had carried me into the maze, and Emory whose hand had shut the trap on me.

Even so, I was far from acquitting James. So far he was clean of anything other than minor villainy, but the very fact that I was here proved that, as always, he would go along with whatever Emory suggested. It was easy to guess what that was. They would use the almost aborted plan for flooding the cottage strip, and improvise with it an "accident" that would take care of Rob. As for me, I could not escape, nor, however hard I shouted, could I be heard, even without the torrent of noise outside in the stormy night. The twins would leave the High Sluice open, letting the swollen river pour into the moat, and soon, when the moat brimmed its banks and finally burst them, and the Pool flooded clear down through orchard and maze, I would certainly drown. No doubt the access door of my trap was cleverly wedged to look as if some floating spars or boughs had been jammed there by the flood's force after my body had been washed under the pavilion. And Rob? They would lie in wait for him and kill him, and in the morning his body, battered by the flood, would be found where apparently he had run to rescue me. The two of us, star-crossed lovers, drowned on our wedding night as the flood swept through the cottage; and all the while the twins, securely alibied, miles away . . .

There was no flood yet. Straining my ears I could hear the ripple and rush of the Overflow as it skirted the maze; full, but not yet too full. I might still be in time. Emory must have meant to hit me harder, and keep me out for as long as was needed. Perhaps James had interfered as his brother struck me; or perhaps Emory had not reckoned on the streams of chill, reviving air that poured through the trap where he had lodged me. By the time he had carried me here and wedged the door, then struggled back again through the dark maze, the gap in my consciousness might not have been too long.

Rob. Rob.

I put the call out with all the strength I could muster. It was more difficult than it had ever been. I could sense how faint the patterns were, reaching out through the blowing dark. Without quite realizing I had done it, I switched the signal, using the old pattern that I had been used to—and which now, ironically enough, was real.

Ashley, Ashley, Ashley . . .

Yes? It was faint, the faintest of responses, but the wave of relief, that melted me back against the wall like wet paper collapsing, showed me the strength of the fear I had had for Rob. He was still alive, and, from the serenity of his response, unsuspecting and unmolested.

Bryony? Serene no longer. He had got the fear pattern. *What is it? What's happened?*

I lay back against the wooden wall, staring inward, away from the garden, at the descending weight of darkness that was the pavilion's floor, so close above my head.

Danger for you. It was all I could do to send the warning patterns, without giving him some inkling of my own imminent peril. Some of my fear must have got through in spite of me, because his response was violent, a blast of static that rocked and splintered the thoughtwaves, and sent me back to simple messages of reassurance that took every ounce of control I had: *No. No. I'm all right. I'm safe. Wait . . .*

I found I was shaking and sweating, in spite of the cold. I made my mind blank, and rested for as many seconds as I dared. At least he was warned. I shut my mind momentarily, straining to shut out the image of the dark cage that trapped me, and to conjure up instead a picture of the pavilion above, with the moonlight wheeling and backing through the swinging shutter, sending light and shadow shimmering across the mirror overhead. Whatever happened he must have no whisper of the danger in which I lay, or he might do just as my cousins wished, and come running back toward me, past wherever they lay in wait for him. Forewarned might be forearmed, but there were two of them, and they had surprise and darkness on their side.

I opened to him again, and began painfully to send those patterns out. My cousins opening the High Sluice; the river racing through to fill the moat; the Overflow still taking it, but not quite, and somewhere the banks of the moat crumbling to let the great weight of water down into the brimming Pool. The slow flood lipping the cottage garden, reaching through the apple orchard for the low-lying floor of the maze . . .

The image of the lower sluice slid across the pictures, like a quick shiver of alarm. He knew, even better than I, what would happen if too great a weight of water piled against those rotten gates; or worse, what would happen if anyone tried to move them. He came back at me then, light-edged with relief: *The pavilion: that's where you are?*

I had got it to him, then: he thought I had taken refuge there, and was safe, perched above the encroaching water. *Yes.* I sent it urgently. *Yes, I'm safe. But you, Ashley, danger for you. Take care, love, take care.*

I knew he must have got from me the image of the two dark figures lurking in wait somewhere, watching for him. There was a brief flash of a reply, which came slightly distorted, zigzag, as if with interference, or as words would come if one was breathless: *I've got it. I'm on my way. Stay where you are . . .*

It was fading. If he had got my fear at all he must have thought it was only for him. As I believe it was. If he was to save himself, and perhaps me, too, he must not be weighed down by fear for me.

My little Bryony be careful. It sprang out of the night and faded, blown down the wind. A pattern coming strangely, not with the smooth familiarity of Rob's patterns, but as if straight out of the night, and as if spoken.

Then a sound, sharp and distinct, like a shot. From somewhere near the Overflow, at the entrance to the maze.

I hurled myself back at the wall of my prison, my hands straining flat against the wood as if nailed there, my face to that windy crack. *Rob? Rob?*

They could not have shot him, they could not. It was to have been an accident. Surely I could not have guessed wrongly about that?

A sound came, breaking through the very thought, shattering it. A cracking, creaking noise, like a big door strained to breaking point. The noise was drowned by a lashing gust of wind, then in the lull behind the wind it came again.

Ashley? He had gone, as completely as if a line had fused. I think I was still calling him, on a silent, jagged pattern of terror, when, drowning out all the other storm sounds of the night, the lower sluice smashed under the weight of wind and water, and the flood came.

It came in a tidal wave, that smashed through the ancient walls of the maze and broke, filthy and swirling with the weight of the whole moat behind it, against the pavilion. The old structure seemed to shake and groan as if it would tear from its moorings in the grass, and buck away down the flood like a ship dragging her anchor. Then the water found its way in. There was a choking, fighting eternity, in which every second seemed like an hour, when the water pounded the gaping walls, spurting through with terrifying power. The jets shot in from every side, splashing and swirling together to join in a whirlpool which started, as rapidly as a sink filling under the taps, to rise from ankle to crouching thigh, to waist, to breasts. . . . And with it rose the debris of years, whirling and battering its way round the trap, so that even the imminence of drowning seemed less fearful than the blows from floating spars and fragments of planking with rusty nails still in them, and the weedlike nets of twigs loaded with the slime of mud and clods and trailing grass. I thrust myself upward against the ceiling as hard as I could, holding both arms bent in front of my face to protect mouth and nostrils from the swirling filth. If the pavilion floor were only as solid as it had seemed, it might trap even an inch of air for me to breathe, until the flood poured past, as it surely would in minutes, then spread through maze and orchard and cottage garden, and went down . . .

The pavilion floor was not solid. As I pressed up hard against it, it lifted slightly, like magic, into clear air. There was a crash as a section of planking upended itself, and fell aside. I straightened up, breast-high in the pouring floodwater, then pulled myself clear, and up on to the pavilion floor.

Almost before I was clear, the flood was at the brim of the trap. I slammed the square of planking back again, grabbed the end of the daybed, and yanked it across the floor till a leg stood squarely on the trap, then jumped on the bed and craned to look out through the broken window shutter.

What I saw was a worldful of moonlight, with neither bound nor horizon, just a glimmering, shadow-tossing expanse of water and sky merged into one, with clouds, and the shadows of clouds, driving and melting across the moon and the image of the moon. Trees billowed black against the sky, or flung down nets of branches to trap their own wild reflections. There was no maze, no orchard, no avenue of beeches between me and the Court; only this shining otherworld of moonlight, of trees like shadows, and shadows like clouds.

Something went past on the flood; an arm, a stiff hand clutching at air, a black shape slowly turning. Even as the terror took breath in me to cry out, I saw it for what it was, a dead branch borne along to lodge against the pavilion steps.

I shut my eyes, squeezing them tightly together, but inside the lids, against the fizzing darkness, there were still those images of death. I opened them again, straining through the chaos of emptiness and dying wind, to find my love.

There, as before, was the waste of moonlit water, broken with black shapes of trees and bushes, and, visible from moment to moment as ripples and wind swayed the intervening boughs aside, the smashed remains of the lower sluice where the loosened water of the moat plunged down to swell the flooded garden. No light glimmered now, where I knew the black bulk of the Court to be.

I stretched higher, straining to see. And I saw Rob.

He was bent half double, seemingly oblivious of danger, wrestling with the wheel of the sluice. For a numbed and speechless moment I looked to see my cousins jump out of the darkness at him, but nothing happened, and then I saw that where he stood the ground was dry, and willows grew there, and the monstrous shapes of gunneras, and I recognized, with no flicker of disbelief, or even surprise, the High Sluice, a full third of a mile away from me, and on the far side of the Court.

Whether I really did see anything, or whether—as happens with childhood memories—I have added his story to the shadowy and nightmare impressions that I, on the edge of the tragedy, received, I do not know. But it seems to me now as if, across the nearer scene, the other, now clear, now dislimning and fading like an image stamped on gauze, or an old film twice exposed, came and went, as real and vivid to me as the window frame under my hands. It was something that had never happened before, nor has it again. I can only explain it by suggesting that in that time of near-death we were so close that there was more than communication between us, there was identity. I saw with his eyes, but at the same time I saw with my own.

The twins, intending to go back to the High Sluice, had left the wheel still in place. Rob wrenched at it, and it turned, smoothly in its oil, and the heavy gates surged slowly shut till, with a final suck and swish of water, their flanges met and gripped, held by the weight of the incoming river. He made sure of them, then tugged the wheel off its hub, picked up the flashlight which he had propped on the gate to light the job, and ran back the way he had come.

The path was still sodden along the moatside, but the level was dropping fast, as the bulk of the water poured through the broken sluice gate and the gaps it had torn in the bank of the moat. He sloshed and slithered past the end of the East Bridge, then paused to pitch the sluice wheel down among the roots of the nearest lime tree. Then he switched off the flashlight, and, more cautiously, began to make his way down the path that led to the Overflow.

The water was still coming over here, pouring through the lip of the moat where it had torn its way. In places it rushed down with frightening power, carrying a dangerous freight of branches and stones and pieces of timber. The moon spun out from a bank of driving cloud to show the swans, wings set like sails and the six cygnets safely aboard, paddling past on the flood with ruffled dignity. The rooks were up in the high night, complaining. The farm dog barked, but no light showed there, nor any through the Vicarage trees.

He floundered down toward the maze. Under the beeches it was black dark and he went cautiously, straining his eyes for any movement that might be a man. Beyond the beech trunks, and the islanded bushes of the shrubbery, the maze showed only as a moving flood laced with driftwood and the tracery of hedge tops. But the pavilion stood foursquare, with water no higher than the doorsill.

He paused, getting his breath, backing in against a beech bole in deep shadow. He held the heavy flashlight clubbed ready in his hand.

Safe, love? he asked me.

Safe.

At that moment, clearly audible above the noise of wind and flood, came another crack like an echo of the first, and with the crack a cry. It came from the lower sluice.

Rob ran forward. The water was almost to his waist. He struggled through the bushes, slipping and stumbling on mud, till he could see the sluice gate. Here, through the smashed gate, the water still poured in a white torrent, but the banks immediately to either side of the sluice were heavily reinforced with stone, and had held undamaged. Over them, where the double water stair had fed the Overflow, loud slopes of smooth water slid to swell the flood below.

Then he saw James. The latter was kneeling by the sluice, half in the rushing water, one arm hooked for support across what remained of the smashed gate. In his other hand was an axe.

Ashley!

The warning burst in my head, and I saw Rob check momentarily. They were both clear to me now: James, the wet leather of his jacket gleaming like an otter's, the axe poised and ready; Rob armed only with the flashlight, fighting for a foothold on the slimy stones as he scrambled up through the sliding slab of the cascade. But my cousin made no move to attack him; he seemed, indeed, not to have noticed Rob's approach. He was stooping low over the smashed rubble of timber wedged below the sluice. Still holding with his left hand, he bent forward and began to hack with what force he could at a spar which, wedged clear across the channel, held down a mass of wreckage.

Then Rob shouted something, thrust the flashlight into his pocket, ran forward to the edge of the channel, and dropped to his knees.

He had seen what lay below the spar, and so had I.

Emory was alive. His head and arms were clear of the rushing water, his hands gripping painfully at the rough stones of the wall, but his shoulders were pinned down by the wedged spar, and his body held submerged by the tangled mat of weeds and branches, invisible in the pouring flood.

Rob threw himself flat, and reached downward to grip one of Emory's wrists.

James, with his back to him, had apparently neither seen him, nor heard him shout. As Rob leaned down, reaching for Emory, my other cousin looked sharply round. He abandoned the spar he was attacking, turned quickly and got to his feet, axe in hand.

Neither Rob nor I was ever quite clear about what James had meant to do. He was yelling something, and the axe swung high. Then his foot shot from under him on the slimy wood. He lost his footing, and fell hard across the spar. The axe flew from his grip. He scrabbled there for a moment, his body down across his brother's, then the water swept him away and down, out of sight past the trunks of the flooded trees. At the same moment the spar, loosened no doubt by James's fall, cracked again, swung in the current, then spun loose and away. The clutching hands were torn from the stones, breaking Rob's grip, and suddenly Rob was alone at the sluice, with the water roaring past his feet, and the moon sailing out high and white to light the waste of moving water where there had once been a fair garden.

Ashley, 1835

He moved a hand. It met the familiar, soft folds of a coverlet. He was lying, warm and naked, in his bed in the pavilion. His limbs felt heavy still, but with the aftermath of loving. The linen under his cheek was wet with a forgotten grief.

Linen? It was silk, and smelled of lavender. He opened his eyes. Her hair, soft and silky and alive, was spread under his cheek on the pillow. As he raised himself, suddenly light and wide awake, she smiled up at him.

"What is it, love? What ails thee?"

He ran a lock of her hair through his fingers. "I had such a dream, Nell. I dreamed I was dead, lying out there in the grass, and my ghost came drifting back to look for you, as they say ghosts drift back to whatever anchors them to earth. But you had gone, and all I could do was wait here, lonely, while the years passed, and were empty; only the other ghosts came and went. And while I waited here, watching for you, the trees grew, and the ways tangled, as if the place still shut its doors against you, and I thought you could never find your way to me again."

"But I came."

His head went down to hers. His tears dried against her cheek. "You came. And they can never part us now, Nell, never again. This is ours, for ever, love. It was death that was the dream."

21

JULIET: It is not yet near day:
           It was the nightingale, and not the lark . . .
ROMEO: It was the lark, the herald of the moon,
           No nightingale . . .

—Romeo and Juliet, III, v

So MUCH I believe I saw, then there was nothing but the sheen of water and the moon out over it, and a rack of cloud blown away down a dying wind. The trees still roared. The water still poured past the pavilion. It had flooded the steps, and crept in under the door, and was meandering across the wooden floor. Pool joined pool and runnel, runnel. But before the shining skin had joined and flooded the boards, the water's impetus seemed spent. Movement ceased. The shallow pool lay, reaching from the threshold to the center of the floor, but going no farther, the last ripple of the flood that had drowned the garden, islanding the pavilion like a ship floating.

What brought me back to myself was the sound, distant yet unmistakable, of Emory's car starting. I stiffened, turning my head to listen, guessing the direction. Yes, it was his, and parked by the sound of it on the curved sweep outside the church gate, near the road. I heard the driver—James, surely?—gun the engine hard, twice, and then the wheels gained the surface of the road, and the sound faded rapidly westward. My cousins—both presumably, for neither would have left the place alone—had gone. Let them go, let them go. Whatever the reckoning had to be, that was for tomorrow.

There is a gap after that, while I tried to reach Rob again, but shock, or exhaustion, or cold must have so numbed me that I simply sat there on the bed waiting for him to come. It didn't even occur to me that he had never known his way into the maze, and that I was penned here at the center, as inaccessible as any Sleeping Beauty.

I suppose I could have guided him through, if I had been able to hold my mind clear. Left and next right . . . straight . . . right and next left . . . straight . . . U-turn sharp left and repeat the lot in reverse . . . the first gate should now be beside you on your left-hand side . . .

But I didn't, and he never asked. I felt something move out of the dark like a

caress, and knew he was sensing my exhaustion. I got it faintly, very faintly:
Hold up, love, I'm almost with you.
I didn't know how. He was coming. I thought about nothing else. I waited.

Either he had found James's axe, or he had been up to the farm for another. I
could hear the steady, hacking sounds, and the splashes, coming gradually nearer
as he approached me through the maze. Slowly, but straight. He was cutting his
way through. The hedges, overgrown and already sparse through neglect, had
been further damaged by the weight of the flood and the debris it carried. I could
hear the ancient stems parting, and the swish and splashing as he forced his way
through. The yews that some long-dead Ashley had planted, and that had taken
two hundred years or so to grow and thicken into those lovely head-high walls;
and now Rob was slicing his way straight through, to me.
Rob Ashley. No one had a better right.
The crashing stopped. I heard the surging splash as he thrust through the last
hedge, then he waded across the moonlit water of the clearing, and ran up the
steps to the door.
Love?
Here. The south window, Rob.
The shutter went back with a slam, and his shadow blacked out the moonlight
in the window. It wasn't James's axe he was holding, it was a heavy woodsman's
axe from the farmyard; he had even thought to bring a dry blanket, which he
wore wrapped like a burnous round his head and shoulders. He clambered
through, and landed with a thud and a squelch on the flooded boards. Then he
was beside me on the bed, holding me tightly and kissing me, and I was kissing
him, and somehow, at some point, our soaked clothes came off and we were
together under the warm rug, while the accumulated terrors and tensions of the
night swelled and broke in a fierce explosion of love, and, with no more thought
or reservation than two wild creatures mating in the woods, we took each other
and then lay together, clasped and quiet, and outside, I swear it, the nightingale
began to sing.

If anyone told me now that I could have slept like that, in all the damp and
discomfort of the flooded pavilion, I would not have believed them. But,
between love and exhaustion and deep happiness, sleep I did, and so did Rob,
wrapped tightly together under the rug, and neither of us stirred until the early
sun, reaching the window, threw such a dazzle of light from the water outside
onto the ceiling mirror that it beat against our eyelids and woke us.
"It's still singing," I said sleepily.
"What is?"
"The nightingale. I told you—"
"That's a lark."
"Oh? So it is." I came awake then, to the blaze of sunlight and the morning
birds and the warmth of Rob's body along mine. He was lying half on his back,
eyes wide and wakeful, but with every muscle and line of his body relaxed,
warm and still, into the morning's contentment. "Have you been awake long?"
"It doesn't seem like it. I suppose I woke at my usual time. Always do, even
on holiday. First time I ever woke like this, though." His arm tightened, and I
moved my cheek deeper into the hollow of his shoulder. "Bryony—"

"Mm?"

"What did they put the mirror on the ceiling for?"

I gave a little snort of laughter, deep into his shoulder. "I forgot all about that. It was supposed to be put up there by some loose-screw—your ancestor Wicked Nick gets the blame—so he could watch himself in bed with his lady friends. Good thing it was dark last night. Just think how off-putting if one suddenly saw oneself—"

"That's the point. One couldn't."

"But one can," I protested. "And very cozy we look, all bundled up like this."

"Aye. But then the bed isn't where it ought to be. You can see where that was by the molding on the wall over there. The way that mirror's angled, if you were lying on the bed all you'd see was a piece of the floor hereabouts." He tilted his head back, examining it. "Is it meant to be like that, do you think? Or have the supports gone from one side? If so, maybe we should get out from under."

"It's always been like that. Well," I said, "poor Nick's been libeled about the mirror as he has about a few other things. Ellen Makepeace, for instance."

He misunderstood me. "Oh, it was true enough about her. Funny, isn't it, to think it all started here, him and her and the garden in the moonlight, and maybe even your nightingale . . . If he cared for her, that is."

"Oh, he did. He cared very much."

I heard the smile in his voice. "You might just be prejudiced."

"Maybe I am. But he did. I know he did."

I said no more. There would be time later to tell him what I had found out about Nick and Ellen Ashley, and what had happened in the cottage last night. Time to tell him about my narrow escape from the trap under this very floor. Time to find out what had happened to my cousins, and where they had gone. Time for all the things that the immediate future must hold; and after that, time for the real future, ours, Rob Ashley's and mine. But for the moment, let it go, let it go. Let us keep, while we could, our own island world of joy. *It is not yet near day. It was the nightingale, and not the lark.*

"What's the time, Rob?"

"Don't know. I forgot to wind my watch, I can't think why. . . . Not much more'n half past five, I'd guess."

I gave a little sigh, and relaxed again. "Lots of time, then, before anyone comes this way and sees the water and starts looking for us . . . What is it, love?" This as Rob sat up and began to unwind himself from me and the blanket. It felt cold without him. "Where are you going?"

"Nowhere. But I'm going to move this bed back to its proper place."

"I told you, the mirror's quite safe."

"I dare say," he said, laying hold of the bed, and running it back with a powerful screech of wood against the wall. "But I'd sooner be out of range."

"Why?"

"This is why," he said, getting back on the bed, and pulling the blanket once more over the pair of us.

When I woke again Rob was not beside me, but as I turned over I saw him, fully dressed and kneeling on the floor near the foot of the bed.

The sun had moved appreciably higher, and now the mirror's light fell, like a spotlight or a burning glass, straight to the boards between the window and the foot of the bed, where the trapdoor lay. Where the water had washed over it last night was an irregular patch of damp, already beginning to steam dry in the warmth. The flood had scoured the dust of years from this section of the floor, and now, quite distinct in the clean floorboards, could be seen the sawn edges of the trap, with, midway along one edge, what looked like a knothole in the wood. In this Rob had inserted a finger. As I sat up to watch, he gave a heave, and the trapdoor came up from its bed. He carried it to the wall and propped it there. Then he dropped to his knees at the trap's edge, peering downward.

I opened my mouth to tell him about my experience of last night, when something about his expression stopped me. The light, reflected upward from whatever water still lay below the pavilion, lit him sharply, and showed his eyes, narrowed against the dazzle, intent on something below. Without looking up he made a beckoning gesture, and nodded downward. "Bryony. Look here."

His voice held discovery, and a kind of awe. I swallowed what I had been going to say, and instead twisted round on the bed till I could lie prone, peering down over the foot of it, into my prison.

The force of last night's flood had swept through and then subsided, leaving the debris piled up against the walls and supports where the whirlpool had flung it, and scouring the center clean. Water still lay there, a sheet of clear glass a few inches deep, lighted fiercely from above, where the angled mirror threw the sunlight down.

It lit a picture, or rather, part of a larger picture; the head of a leopard, snarling, with one paw upraised, the claws out and ready. The eyes were huge and brilliant, done in some lustrous shell-like stone which caught and threw back the light; the teeth gleamed white and sharp, and the yellow fur with the black spots, washed clean by the rush of the flood, shone as brightly as on the day the mosaic was laid and hammered down to make the floor of some Roman's home.

We looked at it for some time in silence. A stray draft of air moved the water, and the upraised paw stirred. The eyes glared, and the yellow fur ruffled; a young leopard, rousing, as vivid and alive as when, all those wild centuries ago, some Roman took and built over this quiet corner between river and hill, and brought his artisans from Italy to make this marvelous thing.

"That's mosaic work, isn't it?" asked Rob. "Looks like part of a floor or something; a big one, too. It must be pretty old to have been buried clear under the maze."

"I wouldn't really know, but I'd have said it was Roman."

"Roman? As old as that?"

"I think so. There were Romans here, a long time ago, and there was a tile kiln not far off."

"Yeah, I know. At Tiler's Hatch, where the flooded pits are. Do you suppose there's more of it?"

"I wouldn't be surprised. Perhaps when William Ashley cleared the ground for his pavilion he found this, and so—"

" 'The cat, it's the cat on the pavement,' " quoted Rob, very softly.

I sat back abruptly. I could feel my eyes dilated with the fierce, reflected light, as the last piece of the puzzle fell into place. "Of course! *Of course!*" I looked up at the wall above the bedhead, where the wildcat ramped in the center of the plaster maze. "That's it, isn't it? The old crest was the leopard, but through time people forgot why. Then poor doting William borrowed Julia's wildcat and her motto, and then, when he found this, he drew the maze round them for a coat of arms. But how do you suppose my father found out about the mosaic?"

"Well, you said he'd been studying the books. It was all in the poetry, wasn't it? I reckon," said Rob comfortably, "that if you'd taken enough time over them, you'd have found it out for yourself. 'What palace then was this?' Remember?"

"Of course," I said again. I drew a long breath. He was right, it had all been there, carefully riddled down in the little verses for anyone who knew; the spotted catamountain, the leopard from the sun, even the glass mirroring another flood: "But where the gentle waters, straying, move, See! Dionysus' creature here enskied. . . ." I lay down again, peering at the exposed mosaic. "No sign of Bacchus and the lesser godlings. They must have covered them up again, and just kept the Cat. No wonder the Survey never traced the Roman site. What d'you bet, Rob, that if we cleared the maze away, we'd find the rest of the villa?"

"You might say I made a start at it last night. I wasn't thinking about much, except getting through to you. But I doubt if the maze could ever have been put right again even if you wanted to." He added, slowly: "I suppose that you couldn't put a value on a thing like this?"

"Not really." I knew what he was thinking; that here was something which could save Ashley—the part of it that I loved—from the bulldozers of the contractors, and make it worth someone's while to clear the gardens and expose this magnificent find for people to see. There were societies and trusts and generous individuals who would join the local Archaeological Society to work on the site and preserve what was found there. Whatever the future might bring, it was certain that no builders would be allowed to touch this part of Ashley.

I bent again over the trap. The leopard flexed his claws, and his eyes glimmered. I had certainly been too close to him, last night, down there in his secret lair. It was easy to imagine that the scratches on my body were not just from the flotsam of the storm, but from those cruel claws. "Touch Me Who Dares." Yes, the Cat had been here before the Ashleys ever came, and he would outstay them.

Rob got to his feet, and pulled me into his arms, blanket and all. "Time we got out of here, I'm afraid. And time you put your things on. You're getting cold. Here they are, they're dry now." As I obeyed him, he carried the trapdoor over and began lowering it carefully into place. "Well, and so what do we do about it? Keep quiet, like William?"

I laughed, belting my housecoat around me. Neither it, nor the pretty nightdress from Funchal, would ever be the same again. "Old Scrooge that he was, he seems never to have told a soul. He doesn't even seem to have told Nick, just hugged it all to himself, and put it down in those little poems. No wonder he died of a heart seizure when he heard that Nick was using the place as a love nest."

"And then Nick got the blame for the mirror, too. Eh, well . . ." The trapdoor was firmly in place. He straightened. "Well, that's it. And now, the day's got to start. It won't be a good one, that's for sure, but at least we can face it together, and the mystery's almost over."

"'Almost'?"

"I meant we've just about found out all your dad was trying to tell you. All but the last bit."

"I know that, too," I said.

"Well, then?" asked Rob.

I shook my head. "Not now. I'll tell you the whole thing later . . . after breakfast."

"Breakfast!" He stretched luxuriously, giving me that wide, warm smile of his. "You're dead right; that comes first! Your kitchen'll be flooded, but we might find some bacon and eggs in mine. Coming?"

We went out onto the pavilion steps. Now we could see how far the water had gone down; below us in the clearing it was not much more than seven or eight inches deep. In the windless morning air it lay still as glass, and under it, like a garden set in crystal, the grass and flowers stood straight, held by the lucid water as perfectly as if it were the air. Inside the gentle mirror the turf stood green and springy, with above it the buttercups floating, wide open to the sun, each petal supporting and supported by the weight of clear water. A shoal of heartsease stared up with violet faces, like underwater creatures watching the light. Even the pale speedwell was held in its frail perfection, not a petal torn. The lilies of the valley stood motionless, wax and ivory, flowers in a Clichy paperweight. A small rudd, lost from the moat, flicked by through the daisies with red fins winking.

We held hands and walked down the wooden steps into the lovely shallow glass of the maze. I led Rob through, and up past the wreck of the lower sluice, where the fishing cat, tumbled in the mud at the foot of the water stair, bore witness to the rashness of the men who had meddled there.

There was debris everywhere, but the moat was back in its borders, and the swans guddled happily in the Pool, with their gray flotilla alongside. The old house dreamed above its reflection, with nothing but a tidemark to show how high the water had risen last night. On the mud of the drive, under the lime trees, stood a rusty-looking Volkswagen. And on the main bridge, gazing around him, was my cousin Francis.

The other Ashley. Fair hair and gray eyes and elegant bones, and the same sweet line to his mouth that my father had had. My gentle cousin, the poet. He was surveying the wrecked garden, the mud lying on the bridge, the waterlogged avenue, with a contemplative expression that held no more than a suggestion of dismay.

He looked up and saw us approaching him. If he noticed anything strange about Rob's crumpled clothes, or my nightdress and bedraggled housecoat and bare feet, his expression gave no hint of it.

"Bryony!" he said, his face lighting. "Rob, nice to see you! What on earth's going on here? It must have been some storm last night, to leave a mess like this. I would have thought the High Sluice would stand even a cloudburst."

"It would, if it hadn't been meddled with," said Rob, flatly. Then, as my cousin's eyes widened: "Aye, it's more of a mess than you think, Francis. We've a lot to tell you, and it's not good hearing, but I'm afraid it won't wait."

My cousin glanced from one to the other of us, and for the first time seemed to notice something odd about our appearance. "All right, then. Tell me."

Rob looked at me, and nodded. "It's your story, love. Go ahead."

So I told it, right from the beginning on that steep Bavarian road, leaving out nothing but the parts of it that were Rob's and my own. I said nothing, either, of the secret of William's Brooke; that was something I would have to tell Rob when we were alone. When I got to last night's scene in my cottage with Emory and James I hesitated, wondering how to gloss over Leslie Oker's telephone call, and the reason for Emory's sudden, murderous decision. But I need not have worried. Rob's growing anger at the scene I was describing was blinding him to everything but his own fury. To this day I am not sure whether his explosion of rage over Emory's attack on me was in words, or whether it burst straight from his mind into mine with the force of an armor-piercing shell. By the time he had got hold of himself, the tricky part was past, and the tale was told.

After I had finished there was silence. Rob sat down on the parapet of the bridge beside me, slid an arm round me, and drew me to him. I could still feel the ebbing shock wave of anger and protective love. Outside and beyond it, like something barely relevant, I was conscious of the tremor running through his arm. He kept silent.

The sun was really warm now, and the light skimmed glancing off the water below us. I half shut my eyes and leaned back against Rob's arm. Francis stood with his back to us. At some point in the story he had turned away to take a couple of paces across the bridge, and he stood there by the other parapet, looking down at the water.

We had been lucky, I thought, that the first herald, so to speak, of the daylight world had been the one man who could share its burdens with us. I knew that Rob, running parallel with my drifting thoughts, was, like me, thinking ahead, trying to come to terms with that world and what the night's work would mean, not only to Ashley and my family, but to our own future.

Some of it could be guessed at. Even if Emory eventually recovered (which, from Rob's account of his apparent injuries, seemed unlikely), the twins would never come back to Ashley, either to make a claim or to fight one. With Rob's claim hanging over it, the land was unsaleable, and therefore profitless to them. And any threat to Rob or to myself had been voided by last night's action; once Mr. Emerson and the police knew the whole story, Emory and James might count themselves lucky if they could keep clear of us. I would make sure of it, I thought. I would write down the story of the last few days, fact for fact, and lodge it, with photostats of the relevant papers, as surety for the future. Further than that, out of mercy for the twins' sick father, and for Francis himself, we surely need not go? Under English law, unless Rob and I chose to press charges, there were none that could be made. The hit-and-run accident in Bavaria was another matter; however relieved I was to know that it had indeed been an accident, I could not forgive Emory's subsequent act of brutal self-interest; but I was still not prepared to add to his father's troubles by giving information to the Bavarian police. I would telephone Herr Gothard as soon as I could, and ask him to send the photograph back for my files. As for the debts the twins had incurred, William's Brooke, as well as endowing the Court, would take care of those, and set their father's mind at rest. Then, presumably, the twins—or James, the survivor—would settle in whatever haven was left to them. South America? Mexico? Wherever it was, they would have to start again from nothing, and James, if left to his own devices, would fare no better than he deserved. . . . I could not find it in me to care, one way or the other, so long as I never saw them again. All I would ever grieve over would be, not the evil man and the weak man who had been here last night, but the two charming and wilful boys who had lived here with us, so long ago.

Francis turned and came back to us. He was grave, and rather pale, but otherwise gave no sign of emotion. It was like him that, when he began to speak, it was about my bereavement (which had been news to him), and my unexpected marriage, and not about last night's near-tragedy.

He was interrupted. Somewhere down the avenue, beyond the trees, a car door slammed. There was the sound of voices. Three men, two of them in police uniform, appeared round the bend of the avenue, and after them, hurrying to join them, the Vicar. They paused when they saw us on the bridge, and Mr. Bryanston raised a hand in a gesture conveying both relief and greeting. Even at that distance it had something about it, too, of a blessing.

". . . If we could just tell them the bare outline now, and let Emerson handle the rest?" It was Francis speaking again, rapidly, an eye on the approaching men. "He'll have to know it all, of course, then he can advise us. What I'm most immediately concerned with is what I'm to tell my father."

"It seems to me"—Rob, his anger gone, sounded his old calm, practical self—"that there'll be no need to add to your dad's troubles by telling him what your brothers were after last night. We'll think up some story for him, just as soon as we know where we stand with the law. The truth can wait till he's well enough to hear it . . . if he has to hear it at all."

He paused, glancing at me. I don't know what he read there, but he nodded as if answered, and spoke again, quickly, to Francis. "Something else I'd better say. I don't think, saving your presence, that your brothers will be in any hurry to come back, so it looks as if this lot's going to land on you. Now, we'd had plans, Bryony and me, to emigrate. That will have to wait a bit. We couldn't walk out and leave you in a mess like this, so if you want us to, we'll stay around, and help you get things straight. I don't know much about the sort of discovery we made this morning, but Bryony thinks that, given a push in the right direction, the place might even start to pay its way. So we'll help you push it, mate, and then it's all yours." He slanted another look down at me. "Eh, love?"

"Yes, Rob." I looked around me at the shining water, at the grassy banks sloping straight into their own intense and clear reflections, at the tops of the orchard trees beyond, where the thrush's song, no doubt, still echoed in the blossoming bell tower of the pear tree. Then I looked again at the heir to all this, with all that it owed to the past, and the load of questions that was its future.

If he chose to stay here, to push the Court back onto the map in whatever guise—National Trust monument, market garden, farmstead, building site—I would help him do it. If he chose to claim it for himself, and stay here for the rest of our lives, I would do that, too. But if he chose in the end to leave the care of the place to Francis, who loved it . . .

Yes, that would be it. When I had told him everything, I knew that he would still say with that tranquil expression, and the dark eyes fixed on his own, our own, far horizon:

"Francis Ashley mate, it's all yours."

The Gabriel Hounds

For Helen King

AUTHOR'S NOTE

This story is freely based on the accounts of the life of the Lady Hester Stanhope. I have tried to shorten my references as much as possible, but for those who are interested, the list of books on page 219 will act as a guide and also an acknowledgment of my main sources. My debt to Doughty's *Travels in Arabia Deserta*, and also to Robin Fedden's marvelous *Syria and Lebanon* (John Murray) will be more than obvious.

One other word may perhaps be necessary. In a story of this sort it is inevitable that officials are mentioned by office, if not by name. Any references to Government bodies, Cabinet Ministers, frontier officials, etc., are made purely for the purposes of this story, and do not refer to any actual holders of these offices, living or dead. Moreover, though the Adonis Valley certainly exists, the Nahr el-Sal'q—with the village and the palace of Dar Ibrahim—does not.

I should also like to thank all those friends, from Edinburgh to Damascus, who have given me so much generous help.

M. S.

1

No vain discourse shalt thou hear therein:
Therein shall be a gushing fountain;
Therein shall be raised couches,
And goblets ready placed,
And cushions laid in order,
And carpets spread forth.

—THE KORAN: *Sura* LXXXVII

I MET him in the street called Straight.

I had come out of the dark shop doorway into the dazzle of the Damascus sun, my arms full of silks. I didn't see anything at first, because the sun was right in my eyes and he was in shadow, just where the Straight Street becomes a dim tunnel under its high corrugated iron roof.

The souk was crowded. Someone stopped in front of me to take a photograph. A crowd of youths went by, eyeing me and calling comments in Arabic, punctuated by "Miss" and "'Allo" and "Good-bye." A small gray donkey pattered past under a load of vegetables three times its own width. A taxi shaved me so near that I took a half step back into the shop doorway and the shopkeeper, at my elbow, put out a protective hand for his rolls of silk. The taxi swerved, horn blaring, past the donkey, parted a tight group of ragged children the way a ship parts water, and aimed without any slackening of speed at the bottleneck where the street narrowed sharply between jutting rows of stalls.

It was then that I saw him. He had been standing, head bent, in front of a jeweler's stall, turning over some small gilt trinket in his hand. At the blast of the taxi's horn he glanced up, and stepped quickly out of the way. The step took him from black shadow full into the sun's glare, and, with a queer jerk of the heart, I saw who it was. I had known he was in this part of the world, and I suppose it was no odder to meet him in the middle of Damascus than anywhere else, but I stood there in the sunlight gazing, I suppose rather blankly, at the averted profile, four years strange to me, yet so immediately familiar, and somehow so inevitably here.

The taxi vanished into the black tunnel of the main souk with a jarring of gears and another yell of its horn. Between us the dirty hot street was empty. One of the rolls of silk slipped from my hands, and I grabbed for it, to catch it in a cascade of crimson just before it reached the filthy ground. The movement and the blinding color must have caught his attention, for he turned, and our eyes met. I saw them widen, then he dropped the gilt object back on the jeweler's stall, and, ignoring the stream of bad American which the man was shouting after him, crossed the street toward me. The years rolled back more swiftly even than the crimson silk as he said, with exactly the same intonation with which a small boy had daily greeted his even smaller worshiper:

"Oh, hullo! It's you!"

I wasn't a small girl anymore, I was twenty-two, and this was only my cousin Charles, whom of course I didn't worship anymore. For some reason it seemed important to make this clear. I tried to echo his tone, but only managed to achieve a sort of idiotic deadpan calm. "Hullo. How nice to see you. How you've grown!"

"Haven't I just, and I shave nearly every week now." He grinned at me, and suddenly it wasn't the small boy anymore. "Christy love, thank goodness I've found you! What in the world are you doing here?"

"Didn't you know I was in Damascus?"

"I knew you were coming, but I couldn't find out when. I meant, what are you doing on your own? I thought you were here with a package tour."

"Oh, I am," I said, "I just got kind of detached. Did Mummy tell you about it?"

"She told my mother, who passed it on to me, but nobody seemed very clear what you were doing or just when you'd be here, or even where you'd be staying. You might have known I'd want to catch up with you. Don't you ever give anyone your address?"

"I thought I had."

"You did tell your mother a hotel, but it was the wrong one. When I rang them up they told me your group had gone to Jerusalem, and when I telephoned there they referred me back to Damascus. You cover your tracks well, young Christy."

"I'm sorry," I said, "if I'd known there was a chance of meeting you before Beirut . . . Our itinerary was changed, that's all, something to do with the flight bookings, so we're doing the tour back to front, and they had to alter the Damascus hotel. Oh, blast, and we leave for Beirut tomorrow! We've been here three days now. Have you been here all the time?"

"Only since yesterday. The man I have to see in Damascus isn't coming home till Saturday, but when I was told you'd be about due to arrive here, I came straight up. As you say, blast. Look, perhaps it's a good thing they've turned your tour arsy-versy—you needn't go tomorrow, surely? I've got to wait here till the weekend, myself, so why don't you cut loose from your group and we'll do Damascus together and then go on to Beirut? You're not bound to stay with them, are you?" He looked down at me, raising his brows. "What on earth are you doing in a package tour, anyway? I wouldn't have thought it was exactly your thing."

"I suppose not, but I got a sudden yen to see this part of the world, and I didn't know a thing about it, and they make it so easy—they do everything about bookings and things, and there's a courier who speaks Arabic and knows the score. I couldn't very well come on my own, could I?"

"I don't see why not. And don't look at me with those great big helpless eyes, either. If any female was ever entirely capable of looking after herself, it's you."

"Oh, sure, Black Belt of the *n*th degree, that's me." I regarded him with pleasure. "Oh, Charles, believe it or not, it's marvelous to see you! Thank goodness your mother caught up with you and told you I'd be here! It'd have been lovely to have some time here with you, but it can't be helped. I'd planned to wait around in Beirut after the rest of my group goes home on Saturday, so I'll stick to that, I think. Have you had a good trip? A sort of Grand Tour, wasn't it, with Robbie?"

"Sort of. Seeing the world and brushing up my Arabic before doing some real work in Beirut. Oh, it all went like a bomb . . . We drove down through France and shipped the car to Tangier and then ambled along through North Africa. Robbie had to go home from Cairo, so I came on alone. It was in Cairo I got Mother's letter saying you were coming on this trip of yours, so I came straight up, hoping we'd coincide."

"Did you say you had to see someone here? Business?"

"Partly. Look, what are we standing here for? This place smells, and any minute now we'll be mown down by one of these donkeys. Come and have some tea."

"Love to, but where do you propose to find tea in the middle of Damascus?"

"In my little pad, which is the nearest thing to the Azem Palace you ever saw." He grinned. "I'm not at a hotel, I'm staying with a man I knew at Oxford, Ben Sifara, I don't know whether you ever heard your father mention the name? Ben's father's a bit of a V.I.P. in Damascus—knows everyone and owns a bit of everything, has a brother banking in Beirut and a brother-in-law in the Cabinet— Minister of the Interior, no less. The family's what they call a 'good family' over here, which in Syria just means stinking rich."

"Nice going. At that rate we'd be well up in the stud book."

"Well, aren't we?" My cousin was crisply ironic. I knew what he meant. My own family of merchant bankers had been stinking rich for three generations, and it was surprising how many people were willing to overlook the very mixed, not to say plain bastard blood that pumped through the Mansel veins.

I laughed. "I suppose he's a business contact of Daddy and Uncle Chas?"

"Yes. Ben made me promise to look him up if ever I was in Syria, and Father was keen for me to make contact, so here I am."

"Big deal. Well, I'd love to come. Just wait a moment till I get my silk." I considered the brilliant mass in my arms. "The only thing is, which?"

"I'm not wild keen on either, if you want the truth." My cousin lifted a fold, felt it, frowned at it, and let it fall. "Nice texture, but the red's rather fierce, isn't it? People'd post letters in you. And the blue . . . ? Not, but not, for you, my love. It doesn't suit me, and I like my girls to tone."

I regarded him coldly. "And just for that I'll buy them both and have them made up in stripes. Horizontal. No, I do rather see what you mean. They looked all right in the shop."

"Since they keep it pitch dark in there, they would."

"Well, fair enough, I wanted it for a dressing gown. Perhaps in a dim light . . . ? I mean, the pattern's rather nice and Eastern . . . ?"

"No."

"The sickening thing about you," I said tartly, "is that you're sometimes right. What were you buying for yourself along Woolworth Alley, if it comes to that? A ring for Emily?"

"A jewel for my love, certainly. A blue bead for my car."

"A blue bead for your—? A *blue bead* for your car? Now this I really do not believe!"

He laughed. "Didn't you know? Blue beads ward off the Evil Eye. All the camels and donkeys wear them, so why not the car? They sometimes have rather fetching turquoise ones. Never mind now, I can get one any time. Do you really want some silk? Have a heart, anything you get at home will be just as good, and you won't have the trouble of carrying it."

The shopkeeper, who was just behind me, and whose presence we had both completely forgotten, here said with justifiable bitterness: "We do all right till you come. The lady had very good taste."

"I'm sure she had," said my cousin, "but you can't expect me to stand for a dressing gown in pillar-box red or budgie blue. If you've anything else more suitable perhaps you'll show it to us."

The man's expression lightened to pleased comprehension, and, as he took in my cousin's obviously expensive clothes, anticipation. "I understand. Forgive, sir. You are the lady's husband."

"Not yet," said Charles. "Come on, Christy, let's go in and buy it, and then get out of this and go where we can talk. My car's in the square at the end of the street. Where is your party, by the way?"

"I don't know, I lost them. We'd been through the Great Mosque, and then we were all trailing in a sort of croc through the souks and I stopped to look at the stalls, and then they'd sort of gone."

"And you let them go? Won't they start combing the souks with bloodhounds when they find you're missing?"

"Probably." I gathered up the silks and turned to the shop doorway. "Charles, if there was some really luscious off-white—"

"Seriously, hadn't you better telephone the hotel?"

I shrugged. "I doubt if they'll even miss me before dinner. They're used to me wandering off by now."

"Still the same spoiled little madam I love?"

"I just don't like crowds. Anyway, look who's talking! Daddy always said you were spoiled rotten yourself, and it's true, so help me."

"But yes. Dear Uncle Chris," said my cousin placidly, following me into the black cave of the shop.

In the end I did buy white, some lovely heavy off-white brocade which, not much to my surprise, Charles seemed to conjure from some dim shelf which the shopkeeper hadn't previously shown me. Moreover, it was cheaper than anything I had yet seen. Nor did it come as much of a surprise to hear Charles talking to the shopkeeper and his assistant in a slowish but what seemed to be passably fluent Arabic. He might (as my parents had often told one another in my hearing) be 'spoiled rotten,' but nobody had ever denied that he had considerable intelligence when he chose to use it—which was (as they insisted) about once a month, and then entirely in his own interests.

When we had reached the square, followed by the shop boy carrying the silk, Charles's car was instantly recognizable—not by its make or color, neither of which could be seen, but by the six-deep crowd of small boys who stood round it. On investigation it proved to be a white Porsche 911 S. And because I loved my cousin and knew my stuff, I promptly gave him his cue.

"What a little beauty! How do you like her?"

He told me. He opened the bonnet and showed me. He almost stripped her down to demonstrate to me. The small boys loved it. They crowded in, twelve deep now, open-mouthed and staring, and probably taking in rather more than I did of the MacPherson struts and lower wishbones, compression ratios and torques and telescopic dampers . . . I let the loverlike phrases roll over me and watched my cousin's face and hands and remembered all the other times—the electric train set, the kestrel's egg, the first wristwatch, the bicycle . . .

He straightened up, hauled a couple of boys backward out of the engine and shut the bonnet, paid off the two biggest who had presumably been on guard for him, and gave the shop boy a tip that startled him into fervent speech. We drove off.

"What's he saying?"

"Just 'thank you'. In other words, 'The blessing of Allah be upon you, your children, and your children's children.' " The car threaded its competent way out of the packed square, and turned down a narrow rutted street with every telescopic damper working overtime. "This means you, more or less. I hope we're still engaged?"

"Faute de mieux, I suppose we are. But I seem to remember that you broke it off yourself, and in writing, when you met that blonde female—what was her name, the model? The one that looked like a Belsen case."

"Samantha? She was very chic."

"Oh, sure. They have to look that anyway, don't they, so that they can wear all that far-out clobber standing up to their knees in the sea, or stable straw, or empty Coke bottles or something. What happened to Samantha?"

"Probably met her just fate, but not with me."

"Well, that was ages ago—just after the last time we met. No one else in my way? You can't tell me you've been going straight for four years?"

"Are you joking?" He changed down, turned sharp left and accelerated down another filthy little alley with a total width of about a yard and a half. "But actually, yes. Virtually, if you get me."

"I get you. What happened to Emily?"

"Who the devil's Emily?"

"Wasn't it Emily? Last year. I'm sure Mummy said Emily—or was it Myrtle? The names you pick."

"I can't see that any of them are worse than Christabel."

I laughed. "You have a point there."

"As far as I'm concerned," said my cousin, "we're still pledged as from the cradle. The lovely lolly is still in the family, and Great-Great-Grandfather Rosenbaum, on whom be peace, can stop whirling in his whited sepulchre as from now, so—"

"Mind that puppy!"

"It's all right, I saw it—at least, the Porsche did. So that's settled. *Also gut!"*

"You take a lot for granted, don't you? Just because I stayed faithful all my teens, even when you had spots."

"A fat lot of chance you had to be anything else," said my cousin. "You were as fat as a seal puppy yourself. I must say you've improved." A sideways look, summarily brotherly, with rather less sexual appraisement than a dog-show judge. "In fact, you're rather gorgeous, coz, and I like that dress. Well, blight my hopes if you must. Is there someone?"

I grinned. "Watch it, love, or you'll find it's for real, and you'll be selling your car to buy a diamond."

"Suits me," he said lightly. "And here we are."

The Porsche slowed down and turned at right angles out of the street into a small unappetizing courtyard, where the sun struck blindly down into the dust, and two cats slept on a stack of battered petrol cans. In one corner was a wedge of indigo shade, and into this, with an elegant economy of effort, he drove the car and parked it.

"Front entrance, Damascus style. Looks like nothing on earth, doesn't it? Come in."

It didn't look at first as if the courtyard could be the entrance to anything. It was boxed, stiflingly, by its high, blind walls, and smelt of hens and stale urine. But at one side a big archway was forbiddingly blocked by a door whose warped timbers still held, in the massive wrought handle and hinges, a hint of some ancient splendor. Charles opened the door on a black passageway, which gave at the other end on an arch of light. We went through.

The light came from a second courtyard, this time an oblong about the size of a tennis court, with pointed Moorish arches on three sides holding a shady cloister, and on the fourth, at the end of the court, a raised platform or dais behind a triple arch, which made a kind of stage or small inner room. The back and sides of this dais were furnished with wide bench seats set against the wall, and I recognized the 'divan' or place where men of the East meet and talk. Even in modern Eastern houses today the sitting rooms are often arranged like this, traditionally, with chairs and sofas backed against the wall on three sides of the room. Low tables stood in front of the couches. In the middle of the court a fountain played; the floor was tiled with blue and white, and the miniature colonnade was jeweled and glittering with mosaics in blue and green and gilt. A turtle dove crooned somewhere, orange trees stood here and there in tubs, and where the fountain splashed I caught the gleam of a gold fin. The court was very cool, and smelt of orange blossom.

"Come into the divan," said Charles. "Yes, it's rather lovely, isn't it? There's something very satisfying about Arab building, I always think—all poetry and passion and romance, but elegant with it. Like their literature, if it comes to that. But you ought to see the furniture; my bedroom's done up with the rejects from Bluebeard's chamber."

"I know what you mean, I saw some choice pieces in those homey little rooms in the Azem Palace—all inlaid with mother-of-pearl like smallpox, or else pure Victorian and made of arthritic bamboos. But oh, Charles, the rugs! Look at those . . . and that blue one on the couch . . . am I really allowed to sit on it?"

"Go right ahead. I think Ben'll be in soon, but meanwhile as he keeps telling me, his house is mine, so what would you like? Tea?"

"I think I'd rather have coffee. What do you do, clap your hands and summon the eunuchs?"

"More or less." On the quite hideous inlaid table in front of me, there was a little brass bell. He picked this up and rang it, then prowled restlessly—he had always been restless—down the steps of the divan as far as the fountain, waiting. I sat down on the beautiful blue rug, leaned against the cushions, and watched him.

No, he hadn't changed. As children, we were always supposed to be very much alike, Charles and I; in fact when we were small, people had taken us for twins. This had always infuriated Charles, who in those days had been aggressively masculine, but to me, dumbly worshiping my clever cousin as only a small girl can, it had been a delight. As we grew up the resemblance had, of course, faded. There were still the basic similarities, the dark hair, high Slav cheekbones, slightly aquiline nose, gray eyes and spare build. Now he was some inches taller than I, and he had broadened, but had seemingly reacted from the aggressive masculinity of adolescence toward a sort of carefully casual elegance which somehow suited him, and oddly enough was no less male. He had on his North African travels acquired a fine tan, and this made his eyes look lighter than my own, though this may only have been in contrast to the black lashes which were (in Nature's unfair way) longer and thicker than mine. Be that as it may, Charles's eyes were beautiful, dark gray and thickly fringed. Occasionally still, I thought, the resemblance between us must be striking; a turn of the head, a trick of the voice, a movement. What we certainly had in common was the 'spoiled' quality that we were so quick to recognize in one another; a flippant cleverness that could become waspish, an arrogance that did not spring from any pride of achievement but was, I am afraid, the result of having too much too young; a fiercely self-conscious rejecting of any personal ties (including those of our families) which we called independence, but which was really an almost morbid fear of possessiveness; and something we called sensitivity, which probably only meant that our skins were too thin for our own comfort.

Perhaps I should explain here that the relationship between Charles and myself was at once closer and more distant than that between ordinary cousins. For one thing, we were not first, but second cousins, with nothing nearer than a great-grandfather in common; for the other, we had been brought up together almost from birth, certainly from the time when memory starts. I couldn't remember a time when I had not shared everything with my cousin Charles.

His father, Henry Mansel, had been the senior member of our—the English—branch of the family, the other male members being his cousins, the twin brothers Charles and Christopher. Christopher, the junior twin, was my father. Charles had no children, so when Henry Mansel and his wife met with a fatal sailing accident only a few months after the birth of their son Charles, my uncle took the baby to bring up as his own. Remembering no others, young Charles and I had of course always regarded his adoptive parents as his own, and I believe it came as a considerable shock to my cousin to be reminded on approaching his majority that he would eventually take precedence of his 'father' in the family's private corridors of power. A marked family likeness helped to close the ranks. Henry Mansel had strongly resembled his cousins, and they—our 'fathers', as we thought of them—were identical twins who had been, almost up to the time they were married, both inseparable and indistinguishable. They had, in fact, married on the same day, having chosen girls who bore no relation to one another, but who—as one could see still—had been of much the same physical type. Happily, the two Mrs. Mansels liked one another immensely—happily because, when Henry's death left vacant the family house in Kent and Charles took it over, his brother built one for himself within a mile of it. So Charles's adopted son and Christopher's daughter had been brought up together until four years ago, when Christopher had exported his family—Mummy and myself—to Los Angeles, from which earthly paradise we had occasionally escaped to stay at Charles's home, our own house being let for the duration. But my visits there had never coincided with my cousin's. In the intervals of Oxford he had spent his time abroad, enjoying himself doing what he called 'looking around,' and indulging the flair for languages which was part of our heritage from a mongrel ancestry, and which young Charles intended to turn to account when he went into one of the family's Continental banks. I had not flown so high. I had brought nothing home from Los Angeles except an American flair for dressing, an accent which I lost as soon as I reasonably could, and three years' experience of the frenetic world of American commercial television, where I had served a wild apprenticeship as producer's assistant in a small company calling itself Sunshine Television Incorporated—this apparently in blissful ignorance of the fact that like most companies it was normally referred to by its initials, *S.T.Inc*.

Now here we were again, my cousin and I, and back without effort on the same terms. It was not that we had been, like our fathers, inseparable—that wasn't possible. What had held us so easily together was, paradoxically enough, a sort of mutual rejection. We had each recognized in the other a refusal to be claimed, and respected this. This had made tolerable—and even funny— the thin-worn family joke about our engagement, and the 'convenient marriage' which would weld Charles back into place without legal awkwardness, and keep the cash in hand in the best dynastic tradition. We never knew—were never allowed to know—whether the idea of the match was anything more than a joke. I had heard my father insisting that the family characteristics were bad enough singly, but squared they would be lethal, whereupon Uncle Charles would retort that since my mother was partly Irish, and Charles's had been half-Austrian, half-Russian, and his paternal grandmother French, the stock would be strong enough to stand a match a good deal closer than that between second cousins. We also had a Polish Jew, a Dane and a German among our assorted great-grandparents, and counted ourselves English, which was fair enough.

To Charles and myself, familiar from early childhood with this light-hearted, dynastic match-making, the subject had little interest. It had occurred to neither of us, in actual fact, that we could be the object of one another's sexual stirrings. Reckoning ourselves as much proof against each other as brother and sister, we had watched with equal amusement and derision each other's first romantic adventures.

The affairs were brief, and inevitable. Sooner or later the girl would start assuming a claim on Charles, and be dropped without trace. Or, somehow, my own pinup would lose his gloss, Charles would say something less than forgivable about him, I would retort furiously, then laugh and agree, and life would be whole once more.

And our respective parents bore with us lovingly through it all, took off the leading strings, gave us the money, listened to what mattered and forgot the rest, possibly because they wanted freedom from us as urgently as we thought we wanted freedom from them. The result was that we went back to them at intervals like homing bees, and we were happy. Perhaps they saw more clearly than could Charles and I, the basic security in our lives which made his restlessness and my indecisiveness nothing more than the taking of soundings outside the harbor. Perhaps they could even see, through it all, the end that would come.

But here we were at the beginning. A young Arab in white had brought in a tray holding an elaborately chased copper urn and two small blue cups which he set on the table in front of me. He said something to Charles, and went out. My cousin came quickly up the steps of the divan and sat down beside me.

"He says Ben won't be in just yet, not till evening. Go on, you pour."

"Is his mother away, too?"

"His mother's dead. His father's sister runs the place for them, but she lives retired, as they say. No, *not* a harem, so don't look so curious and hopeful; she merely has a long siesta and won't come out till dinner time. Smoke?"

"Not now. I don't much, as a matter of fact, only now and again for effect, rather silly. Good heavens, what are those? Hashish or something?"

"No, absolutely harmless, Egyptian. They do look awful, don't they? Well now, tell me what you've been doing."

He accepted the cup of strong black coffee from me and curled back on the silk-covered seat, waiting expectantly.

Four years of gossip is a lot to catch up on, and we had never been letter writers. I suppose more than an hour had gone by, and the sun had moved over to leave half the court in shadow before my cousin stretched, stubbed out another Egyptian cigarette and said: "Look, what's all this about sticking with your group? Won't you change your mind and cut loose now? Stay till Sunday, and I'll drive you up—the Barada Valley's lovely, and there's a good road."

"Thanks all the same, but I'd better stay with them. We're doing that run by car in any case, and having a look at Baalbek on the way."

"I'd take you there."

"It would be smashing, but it's all fixed, and as a matter of fact I've packed, and you know there's all that silly business with visas here. Mine's dated tomorrow, and there's this business of a group passport, and there was such a hooha anyway about my staying behind after the group leaves for England on Saturday that I can't face it all over again. I think I'll just go."

"All right, then, I'll see you in Beirut. Where are you staying?"

"I thought I'd move to the Phoenicia once I'm on my own."

"I'll join you there. Book in for me, will you? I'll telephone you before I leave Damascus. What had you planned to do with the extra time, apart—I suppose—from going up to Dar Ibrahim?"

"Dar Ibrahim?" I repeated blankly.

"Great-Aunt Harriet's place. That's its name, surely you knew? It's on the Nahr Ibrahim, the Adonis River."

"I—yes, I suppose I knew, but I'd forgotten. Goodness, Great-Aunt Harriet . . . I never thought . . . Is it near Beirut, then?"

"About thirty miles away, along the coast road to Byblos and then inland into the mountains, up toward the source of the Adonis. The road runs up the ridge on the north side of the valley, and somewhere between Tourzaya and Qartaba there's a tributary river called the Nahr el-Sal'q that goes tumbling down to meet the Adonis. Dar Ibrahim's in the middle of the valley, where the rivers meet."

"Have you ever been there?"

"No, but I'm planning to. D'you really mean you hadn't thought about it?"

"Not a flicker of a thought. I'd certainly intended to go up the Adonis Valley and see the source where the cascade is, and the temple of Whoever-it-is, and the place where Venus and Adonis met—in fact I was thinking of hiring a car for the trip on Sunday, after the group go . . . But to be honest I'd forgotten all about Aunt H. I hardly even remember her, you know; we were in Los Angeles when she was home last, and before that it was—heavens, it must be all of fifteen years! And Mummy never said a thing about this place of hers—Dar Ibrahim, was that the name?—but that's probably only because her geography's about on a par with mine and she'd never realized Beirut was so near." I put down my cup. "Right in the Adonis Valley? Well, I might go with you, at that, if only to see the place and tell Daddy what it was like. I'm sure he'd think there was hope for me yet if I told him I'd trekked up there to put some flowers on the old dear's grave."

"She'd probably kick you in the teeth if you tried," said Charles. "She's very much alive. You really are a teeny bit out of touch, aren't you?"

I stared. "Alive? Aunt H? Now who's out of touch? She died just after New Year."

He laughed. "Not she. If you're thinking about the Last Will and Testament, that's nothing to go by, in the last few years she's sent them round about once every six months. Didn't Uncle Chris get the famous letter renouncing her British nationality and finally cutting everyone off with sixpence? Everyone except me, that is." He grinned. "And I was to have the Gabriel Hounds and her copy of the Koran because I showed signs of taking a 'reasonable interest in the real civilizations of the world.' That was because I was learning Arabic. In some ways," added my cousin thoughtfully, "she must still be very innocent if she thinks Mansel and Mansel takes an interest in anything whatever except for the basest of all possible reasons."

"Look, come off it, you're kidding me."

"About the Wills and so on? Indeed I'm not. She renounced us in beautiful round early-Victorian terms—her letters were period pieces, you know—the family, Britain, God, the lot. Well, perhaps not God exactly, but she was going to turn Mohammedan, and would we please send out a reliable English stonemason to build a private cemetery where she could rest forever in the peace of Allah among her beloved dogs, and would we also inform the Editor of *The Times* that the paper of the overseas edition was too thin to allow her to do the crossword puzzle properly, and she would like it changed."

"You can't be serious."

"As an owl," said my cousin. "I swear to every word."

"And what in the world are the Gabriel Hounds?"

"Don't you remember them? I suppose you don't."

"I seem to remember the phrase, that's all. Wasn't it something in a story?"

"A legend in that book we had called 'North-Country Tales,' or some such title. The Gabriel Hounds are supposed to be a pack of hounds that run with Death, and when someone's going to die you hear them howling over the house at night. I've an idea myself that the idea must have come from the wild geese— have you heard them? They sound like a pack of hounds in full cry overhead, and the old name for them used to be 'gabble ratchet.' I've sometimes wondered if the 'Gabriel' doesn't come from 'gabble,' because after all Gabriel wasn't the angel of death . . ." He glanced across. "You shivered. Are you cold?"

"No. One of them gabbling over my grave, I expect. What have they to do with Great-Aunt Harriet?"

"Nothing, really, except that she had a pair of china dogs I lusted after, and I christened them the Gabriel Hounds because they were like the illustrations in the book."

"A pair of—oh, no, really, you must be out of your tiny mind. That's schizophrenia, or is it skitso? Nobody in this world can want to own a white Porsche with one hand and a pair of china dogs with the other! I don't believe it."

He laughed. "Real china, Christy love, Chinese china . . . They're Ming as ever was, and probably museum pieces. Heaven knows what they're worth now, but since I had the good taste to fall flat in love with them at the age of six, and Great-Aunt Harriet with even better taste fell flat in love with me at the same time, she promised them to me. And stark raving bonkers though she undoubtedly is now, she seems to have remembered." He made a restless movement. "Oh, don't you see, it doesn't really matter about the dogs, they make a good excuse, that's all."

"For going to see her?"

"Yes."

"Taking your family responsibilities on your head at last?" I said it derisively, but he didn't laugh or disclaim, as I had expected. He gave me an odd, slanting look from under the long lashes, but said merely: "I don't want to pass up the chance. It sounds such a damned intriguing setup."

"Well, of course I'll go with you, out of sheer roaring curiosity, and let's hope she does remember you, because I'm darned sure she won't remember me. She must be at least a hundred."

"Not a day over eighty, I swear, and active with it by all accounts. She's a local legend, goes galloping about the countryside on horseback with a gaggle of hounds and shoots whatever there is to shoot for her own dinner."

"Gabble, you mean. I remember that about her, who could forget? When she stayed with us that time she brought eight King Charles spaniels."

"It's Tibetan terriers now, and salukis—Persian greyhounds, the dogs the Arab princes used for hunting. Oh, she's gone the limit, I gather—turned Arab herself, male at that, dresses like an Emir, smokes a hubble-bubble, never sees anybody except at night, and lives in this dirty great palace—"

"Palace?" I said startled. "Who does she think she is? Lady Hester Stanhope?"

"Exactly that. Models herself on the story, one gathers. Even calls herself Lady Harriet, and, as you and I well know, we've had a lot of queer things in the family, but never a Lady." He stared, not flatteringly. "What do you know about Lady Hester Stanhope?"

"Didn't I tell you? When we spent last Christmas at your house they put me in your room, and I read some of your books. You've an awful lot about the Middle East. Have you really read all that Arabian poetry and stuff? And the Koran?"

"All through."

"Well, you might say it was your library that gave me the idea of seeing this part of the world in the first place. We always did go for the same things, didn't we—or maybe you'd say I tagged along where you went . . . ? I'd always had vaguely romantic ideas about Petra and Damascus and Palmyra, but never thought about really coming here; then I saw the advert for this package tour, so I thought I'd join up, find my way about, then stay on after they'd gone and take my time filling in a few extras. One of them was Djoun, Lady Hester Stanhope's place."

"It's a ruin now."

"I know, but I still thought I'd like to see it. She was quite a girl, wasn't she? I read everything you had about her, and nice snappy reading it was, compared with some of those tomes of yours. I had flu just after Christmas and was stuck indoors for a fortnight, and Mummy hadn't time to rake round the bookshops for something more my weight."

He grinned, undeceived. "Don't work so hard at not being clever. I'm not one of your muscle-bound blonds."

"Neither you are," I said.

Our eyes met. There was a tiny silence, in which the fountain sounded oddly loud. Then my cousin got up and reached a hand. "Come and see the water lilies now the sun's gone. They shut while you watch."

I followed him down into the now coolly shadowed court. The lilies were pale blue, held on stiff stems a few inches above the water, where their glossy leaves overlapped the still surface like tiles of jade. Gold fins winked here and there below them, and a gold bee sipped water at a leaf's edge. A powder-blue petal shut, and another, till one by one the lilies were turbaned up, stiff and quiet for the night. Another late bee, almost caught by a folding flower, wrestled his way angrily out of the petals, and shot off like a bullet.

I watched half absently, my mind still busy with the recent fragments of information Charles had flung at me, the intriguing picture of the eccentric old lady who had dropped so long ago out of family reality into family legend. The picture Charles had just given me of her blurred and blended in the imagination with the vivid mental pictures I had built up during that Christmas period of enforced reading. It was true that I had found some of Charles's books heavy going, but the accounts of the eccentric Lady Hester had been extremely readable, not to say racy.

She had gone out to the Middle East in the early eighteen hundreds, an Earl's daughter in the days when rank counted for almost everything, a masculine peremptory woman who, as Pitt's niece, was also accustomed to political consequence. After traveling round in considerable state with a retinue which included lover, slaves, and attendant physician, she had decided to settle in Syria (as it then was) and eventually purchased for herself a mountain-top fortress near Djoun, not far from Sidon. There she had lived in Eastern state, dressing as a Turkish Emir, and ruling her household of servants, Albanian guards, Negro slaves, companions, grooms, and personal doctor with a rod of iron and at times, literally, a whip. Her fortress, perched on a hot bare hilltop, was described by a contemporary as 'an enchanted palace,' and was a world in itself of courtyards, corridors as complex as a Chinese puzzle, walled gardens approached by winding stairs, secret exits cut in the rock where the Lady's spies came and went, the whole exotic with murmuring fountains and luxuriant gardens. It was a deliberate re-creation of an Arabian Nights' wonderland with all the fantastic properties of Eastern fairy tale solidly at hand. Roses and jasmine, mute black slaves and nightingales, camels and sacred cats and Arab horses, she had them all. Fearless, utterly selfish, arrogant and eccentric, and growing with the years beyond eccentricity into megalomania, she meddled in local politics, defied the local Emirs, and placed herself—with some success—above the law. She finally seems to have believed in her own mystical destiny as Queen of the East who would one day ride crowned into Jerusalem at the side of the new Messiah.

The end came as it comes to the determined *puissante et solitaire*—she died alone, old and destitute, her fortune spent, her fortress rotting around her, her servants robbing and neglecting her. But she left—along with her debts—a legend that persists to this day.

It was certainly intriguing to think that it might be persisting in one form in the person of my own Great-Aunt Harriet. From what I knew of the lady, I thought she would (apart from the rank) fit into the role quite well. She had wealth, considerable personality and some scholarship, and had traveled widely and with a retinue which, though not quite as impressive as Lady Hester Stanhope's in

1820, had created quite as much stir and trouble a hundred years later. She had married an archaeologist, Ernest Boyd, and thereafter accompanied him on all his working journeys, hanging over and (it must be confessed) superintending his 'digs' from Cambodia to the Euphrates Valley. After his death she gave up active work and returned to England, but continued to take a deep interest in the Middle East, and financed one or two expeditions that stirred her fancy. Two years of England's weather had been enough. She had said good-bye to the family (this was the last visit that I remembered) and gone off to the Lebanon, where she had bought her hilltop refuge and settled down (she told us) to write a book.

From this fastness she had made one sortie, four years ago, just after my side of the family had gone to Los Angeles. She had come, she said, to settle her affairs—which meant removing her considerable assets to the Lebanon—pick up a mate for her revolting (Charles said) Tibetan terrier Delilah, and shake the mud of England off her skirts for good. This was the last I had heard. Whether she had in fact written anything at all during her fifteen years' exile nobody had any idea, except for the occasional remakes of her Will, which the family read with pleasure and then disregarded. We could get along as well without Great-Aunt Harriet as it appeared she could without us. There was of course no resentment on either side; my great-aunt merely personified in herself the family's genius for detachment.

So I still regarded my cousin doubtfully. "You think she'll see you?"

"Oh, she'll see me," he said calmly. "My mother was always pretty sarcastic about Great-Aunt Harriet's penchant for young men, but I see no reason why we shouldn't trade on it. And if I tell her I've come to demand my rights, viz. the Gabriel Hounds, it'll appeal to her; she was always a tough egg who liked people who stuck out for their dues. If I can get to Beirut by Sunday evening, what do you say we make a date of it together for Monday?"

"I'm on. It sounds intriguing, if I thought one could believe a word of it."

"Sober truth—or as near sober truth as you'll ever get in this country," promised my cousin. "Don't you know what they say about it? That it's a country where anything can happen, a 'country of prodigies . . .'" He quoted softly: "'The men inhabiting this country of prodigies—those men of rocks and deserts—whose imagination is higher colored and yet more cloudy than the horizon of their sands and their seas, act according to the word of Mahomet and Lady Hester Stanhope. They require commerce with the stars, with prophecies, miracles and the second sight of genius.'"

"What's that?"

"Lamartine."

"Makes it sound as if even Great-Aunt Harriet might be normal. I can hardly wait. But I'll have to go now." I glanced at my watch. "Heavens, yes, it's dinner time."

"I'm sure Ben would want you to stay. He'll be in any minute. Can't you?"

"I'd like to, but we've an early start tomorrow, and I've things to do." I stooped to retrieve my handbag. "And you're going to drive me home, dear boy, and no mistake. I'm not venturing through the dark streets of Damascus for you or anybody—even if I could find the way which I probably can't. Unless you simply lend me the Porsche?"

"There are some risks I will take," said my cousin, "and some I won't. I'll drive you back. Come along."

We crossed the court quietly together. Someone—the Arab boy, probably—

must have brought a lamp in and set it in a niche near the door. It was an Aladdin lamp of some silvery metal which was probably in daylight hideous; but in the dusk, and holding the small orange buds of flame, it looked quite beautiful. The deep blue oblong of sky above the open court was pricking already with brilliant stars. No ugly diffusion of city lights spoiled the deep velvet of that sky; even hanging as it was above the glittering and crowded richness of the Damascus oasis, it spoke of the desert and the vast empty silences beyond the last palm tree. The courtyard itself was quiet. The far murmur of city traffic, no louder than the humming in a shell, made a background to this still quiet, where the only sound was the trickle of the fountain. The well in the desert. A fish moved below the surface, and the flick of gold, caught by the lamp, seemed to underscore the beauty of the living water. One could almost hear the fish moving. A bird settled itself crooningly to sleep above the arcade in a rustle of leaves.

"A turtle dove, do you hear it?" Charles's voice, quiet as it was, made me jump. "The poets say she calls all the time for her lover—'*Yusuf, Yusuf,*' till her voice breaks in a sob. I'll ring you Saturday evening then, at the Phoenicia, to tell you when I'm coming."

"I'll be waiting. I only hope that after all this we get our Arabian Nights' entertainment at Dar Ibrahim. Oh, *you* probably will, fascinating creature that you are, but is there the faintest reason why she should want to see me?"

"She'll be delighted to see you," said my cousin generously. "Damn it, I was even quite pleased to see you myself."

"You must be slipping, paying me compliments like that," I said, preceding him to the doorway.

2

Adonis
Who lives away in Lebanon,
In stony Lebanon, where blooms
His red anemone.

—JAMES ELROY FLECKER: *Santorin*

I SUPPOSE I had assumed Charles to be exaggerating the Dar Ibrahim 'legend,' but it seemed he was right. I found it quite easy to get news of my eccentric relative in Beirut. In fact, even had I never heard of her, she would have been brought to my notice.

It happened on Saturday, the day the group left for London, and I moved myself to the Phoenicia Hotel to plan my brief independence and wait for Charles. On what was left of the Saturday I wanted to get my hair done and do some shopping; then on Sunday I planned to hire a car and driver to take me exploring up into the Lebanon range to the source of the Adonis River.

It was when I approached the desk clerk in the hotel, to ask him to lay on a chauffeur-driven car for this trip, that I came across my great-aunt.

The clerk entered into my plans with enthusiasm, almost managing to conceal his private thoughts about the inexplicable whims of tourists. If a young woman was eager to incur the expense of a car and driver to go up and look at a few dirty villages and a waterfall, then of course he would help her . . and (I could see the expert assessment of my clothes, my room number, and my probable bill) the more expensive the car, the better.

"And I understand," I added, "that right up at the Adonis Source there's the ruins of an old Roman temple, and another smaller one not too far away, that I might visit."

"Yes?" said the clerk, then hurriedly changing his intonation. "Yes, of course, temples." He wrote something, passing the buck with some relief. "I will tell the driver to include them in the itinerary."

"Please do. What do we do about lunch?"

Now this, it seemed, was talking. He brightened immediately. There was the famous summer hotel—I had heard of it, no doubt?—where I could get an excellent meal, and with music. Oh, yes, there was music in every room, continuous music, taped round the clock, in case the mountain silence got you down. And a swimming pool. And tennis. "And then, of course, if you make a slight detour on your way back you'll be able to see Dar Ibrahim."

He misunderstood the surprise on my face, and explained quickly: "You have not heard of this? Oh, Dar Ibrahim's a palace where an English lady lives, a very old lady who used to be famous, and she bought this palace when it was falling into ruin and filled it with beautiful things and planted the gardens again, and in the old days famous people would go up to stay with her, and it was possible to see over some parts of the palace, just as today you can see Beit ed-Din and the Crusader Castles. But now, alas . . . she is old now, and they say a little—" he made an eloquent face and touched his forehead. "The place is shut up now, and she sees no one, and she never leaves the palace. But I have heard what a wonderful place it used to be, and I have myself seen her riding out with her servants . . . but that is all changed, she is old, and it is a long time since anyone has seen her."

"How long?"

He spread his hands. "Six months, a year, I cannot say."

"But she's still there?"

"Certainly. I believe I heard talk of a companion, but this may be rumor. I think there are still two or three servants with her, and once a month supplies are sent from Beirut up to Sal'q—that's the nearest village—and taken across by mule."

"Isn't there a road?"

"No. The road goes along the ridge above the valley, and to get to Dar Ibrahim from the village one must walk, or go by mule." He smiled. "I wasn't suggesting you should do this, because of course it's not worth it now, you can't get in. I was only recommending the view. It's very fine. In any case, Dar Ibrahim looks all the better from a distance."

I said, trying it out: "Actually, I had heard of the place. I think I know some relatives of hers in England, of the old lady's. I'd thought of trying to see her. I'd wondered if perhaps I might write her a note and ask if I could visit her." Something—I'm not quite sure what—forbade me to explain to the clerk my own relationship with his local legend.

He shook his head doubtfully, but with a gleam of curiosity in his eyes which told me that my reticence had probably been wise, "I suppose you could try, but when she would get it, or when you would get an answer . . . There is a porter at the gate—" he shrugged—"but they say he lets no one through at all. He takes in the supplies and pays for them, and if there are letters, or if she has written letters, they are handed over at that time. But for a long time now she has received no one—no one, that is, except the doctor."

"The doctor? Is she ill?"

"Oh, no, not now. I believe I did hear of something last year—about six months ago, in the autumn, and the doctor going up each day. But she recovered, and now is well enough."

She had certainly been well enough, I reflected, to draft another snappy Last Will and Testament at Christmas. "A doctor from Beirut, was this?"

"Yes, an English doctor."

"Do you know his name?" I added, rather apologetically: "If I can't see her, I might get news of her from him."

The clerk could not remember the doctor's name, but he promised to find out for me, and indeed the next time I passed the desk he had it ready, a Dr. Henry Grafton with an address somewhere near Martyrs' Square. I thanked him, and went back upstairs to my room, where I picked up the telephone directory and looked up Grafton, H. L.

The number was there. After a little trouble I managed to get it, and a man's voice answered in Arabic, but when we had sorted ourselves out through his excellent French into his even better English, he had to disappoint me. No, Dr. Grafton was not here, Dr. Grafton had left Beirut some time back. Yes, for good. If he could help me . . . ?

"I was just making some inquiries about a relation of mine," I said, "a Mrs. Boyd. I understand she was a patient of Dr. Grafton's a few months back when he was in Beirut. I wonder—is she perhaps now on your list? The thing is—"

"Mrs. Boyd?" The voice was puzzled. "We don't have anyone of that name, I'm afraid. What's the address?"

"She lives outside Beirut, at a place called Dar Ibrahim. I believe it's near a village called Sal'q."

"Dar Ibrahim?" The voice quickened. "Do you mean the Lady Harriet?"

"Why, yes, I—I suppose I do," I said, feeling rather foolish. "I—I'd forgotten . . . yes, of course, the Lady Harriet."

"As far as I know she's fine," said the voice, "but she's certainly not my patient. In the normal way I would have attended her after Grafton left, but she wrote to tell me she had made other arrangements." Some undercurrent, perhaps of amusement, in the smooth voice made me want to ask what these were, but this was hardly possible. Probably (I thought) a letter renouncing the world, the English, and the medical profession, or at least another Last Will and Testament. "May I know who is calling?" asked the voice.

"Lady Harriet's great-niece. My name is Christabel Mansel. I'm here in the Lebanon on holiday, and I—none of us has heard from my great-aunt for some time; in fact, I'd got the idea she was dead. But then I heard she was still alive, and someone at the hotel here—I'm staying at the Phoenicia—told me Dr. Grafton had attended her, so I thought I'd ring him up to find out anything I could. You say he's left Beirut. Is he still in the Lebanon? Would it be possible to get in touch with him?"

"I'm afraid not. He went back to London."

"I see. Well, thanks very much, I might try to look her up myself."

There was a slight pause at the other end. Then the voice said, carefully expressionless: "One gathers she lives very much retired."

"Yes," I said, "I understood so. But anyway, thank you for your help. Good-bye."

"Good-bye," said the voice.

I found myself grinning as I put the receiver down. What was implicit in the pleasant voice was, unmistakably, the Arabic equivalent for 'and the best of British luck.'

Charles rang up that evening to say that Ben's father had been delayed, so he himself couldn't get up before Sunday evening at the earliest, and might not manage even that. "But in the name of all the gods at once," he finished impressively, "I'll be with you on Monday, or perish in the attempt."

"Don't ask for it," I said, "at least not till you've bought your blue bead. You told me this was a country where anything could happen."

I didn't mention my own inquiries about Great-Aunt Harriet, or that I was beginning to develop quite a lively sense of curiosity about the eccentric recluse of Dar Ibrahim.

The desk clerk had certainly done his best to get me a nice expensive trip. The car was a vast American affair with fins, air-conditioning, blue beads to ward off the Evil Eye, and hanging in the window a text from the Koran which said: "Place your reliance on God."

It also had an altimeter. This I didn't quite believe in until the driver, a lively sharp-faced young man called Hamid, told me we would be going from sea level to about eight thousand feet in one fell swoop, since the Adonis Source was right up in the High Lebanon. I settled down beside him in the front of the car, and watched the altimeter with fascinated amusement as we turned away from the coast at Byblos, and began to climb.

Hamid had underestimated the number of fell swoops that were required. At first the road was reasonable, and bored its way upward through villages and terraced fields, where the carefully spaced apple trees stood knee-deep in growing crops, and dark-eyed children played among the hens in the dust. But after a while the road shook itself clear of the little green settlements to climb more steeply through the last belt of cultivation before the flocks claimed the stony earth. Here still in every sheltered corner a neat terraced wall dammed in some carefully banked soil, and fruit trees were in meager bloom. On the more exposed terraces the thin green blades of some grain were growing, almost smothered by the sheets of spring flowers that grew everywhere, at the roadside, in the terraced walls, in the very seams of the rocks. Hamid stopped the car with smiling good nature and let me explore them with rapture; orchids, pale cyclamens, a huge flax-blue geranium, the scarlet-petalled Persian tulip, and the red anemone that flowers for Adonis.

Presently we were out of the cultivation and running along switchback ridges where gray shrubs clung to the rock, and the only flower was the yellow broom. The air was crystal clear, and in wonderful contrast to the heavy air of the coast. Now and again we saw a flock of the Eastern-looking sheep, cream or honey-colored or spatchcocked with black, moving with drooping ears and heads carried low as if always looking for food. Glossy black goats grazed with them, and each flock bunched closely round its shepherd, a solitary figure standing wrapped in his burnous, arms crossed over his stick, watching gravely as we went by.

The road climbed. The altimeter needle moved steadily to the right. The air grew piercingly fresh. The yellow broom dropped below us, and at the verges of the narrow way tufts of gray thin leaves hunched among the stones. The car swerved terrifyingly round bends with rocks threatening to scrape the offside wing, and on the other side a sheer abyss where crows and ravens tilted and croaked below us.

Then suddenly there was space on both sides. We were running along the hogsback of a dizzyingly exposed ridge with, to the left, a prospect of white rock and blue distance and crest on crest of wooded mountain to the sea; and deep down on our right, ice-green, flashing and hiding and flashing again as it rushed and curled down its great forested gorge, ran the Nahr Ibrahim, the Adonis River.

And presently, dipping through rocky gorges which here and there trapped the sun and allowed thin apple trees to blossom with their feet deep in the red anemones, we came to the Adonis Source itself.

The source of the Adonis River has been magic, time out of mind. To the primitive people of a thirsty land, the sight of the white torrent bursting straight out of its roaring black cave half up a massive, sun-baked cliff, suggested God knows what gods and demons and power and terror. It certainly suggested fertility . . . the river carries life with it for thirty water-seamed mountain miles. And where the water bursts from the rock the corrie is suddenly green, and full of trees and flowering bushes, and the red anemone grows along the torrent side.

So here, treading on the ghostly heels of Isis and Ishtar and Astarte and the Great Mother herself who was Demeter and Dia and Cybele of the Towers, came Aphrodite to fall in love with the Syrian shepherd Adonis, and lie with him among the flowers. And here the wild boar killed him, and where his blood splashed, anemones grew, and to this day every spring the waters of the Adonis run red right down to the sea. Now the corrie is empty except for the black goats sleeping in the sun on the ruined floor of Aphrodite's temple, and against the roar of the torrent the drowsy stirrings of the goat bells come sharp and clear. The rags that flutter from the sacred tree are tied there as petitions to the last and latest Lady of the place, Mary.

Even without the legends, it would have been breathtaking. With them, the scene of white water and blazing rock, massive ruins, and bright flowers blowing in the wind from the fall, was something out of this world. And as we turned eventually out of the corrie onto the track—it could hardly have been called a road—that would take us home by a different route, the scene had its final touch of Eastern fantasy.

A little way beyond and out of sight of the Adonis corrie, a few Arab houses straggled along the water-side. A path, a white scratch on the rock, climbed out of this at an angle to the road. And up this path, going easily, went a chestnut Arab horse, the white burnous of its rider filled out by the motion like a sail, the scarlet and silver of the bridle winking in the sun. At the horse's heels cantered two beautiful dogs, fawn-colored greyhounds with long silky hair, the saluki hounds which were used by the princes of the East for hunting gazelle.

A curve of the road hid them, and all at once it was time for lunch.

We saw the rider again, on our way down the other side of the valley. We had spent more than an hour over lunch, and the horseman must have used paths which cut off a thousand difficult corners that a car had to take. As we picked our way between the potholes into some tiny settlement in a lost high valley where the snow lay not very far above us, I saw the rider below, walking his horse down a barely visible path that took him thigh-deep through a field of sunflowers. The dogs were invisible below the thick, heart-shaped leaves. Then they raced ahead of him out onto a lower curve of the road, the horse breaking into a canter behind them. So clear was the air that I could hear the jingling of bridle bells above the thud of hoofs in the dust.

The squat peeling houses of the village crowded in on the car and hid him from view.

We stopped in the village to buy oranges.

This was Hamid's idea. We could have bought them at one of the dozens of stalls on the way out of Beirut, but these, he said, would be something special, straight from the tree and warm with the sun and ripe, divinely ripe.

"And I shall buy them for you as a present," he said, drawing the car to a halt in the shade of a mulberry tree and coming round to open the door for me.

The village was poor, that was obvious; the houses were nothing more than shacks patched with mud brick, but they were screened with vines, and each one squatted among its laborious terraces of fruit and grain. Some of the Goddess's fertility had spilled over into the place, for all its height. It must be sheltered from the worst of the winds, and there would be no lack of moisture as the snow melted. The carefully trapped water stood deep-green in square cisterns under the bare silver poplars, and the village—just a handful of houses in a natural amphitheater sheltered from the wind—was full of fruit blossom, not only the enchanting glossy trees heavy with the waxy flowers and fruit of oranges and lemons, but the snow of pears and the sharp pink of almond, and everywhere the blush-pink of the apple, the staple fruit of the Lebanon.

The sun was hot. A small crowd of staring children had gathered round the car; they were very small and rather engaging, with their thick black hair and enormous dark eyes and thumb-sucking curiosity. The place seemed dead, with the afternoon deadness. No one was in the fields; if there was a café it was only some dark room in one of the cotages; and I saw no women. Apart from the children, the skinny hens scratching, and a miserable-looking donkey with rope sores, the only creature moving was an old man who sat in the sun smoking a pipe. He could, indeed, hardly be said to be moving. He seemed to be smoking almost in his sleep, and his eyes turned up slowly and half blind to Hamid as the latter greeted him and asked him a question in Arabic, presumably who would sell us the fruit that hung still on the lovely trees.

The old man waited a full half minute while the question wound its way through his brain, then he removed the pipe from his mouth, turned his head through a full three degrees, spat revoltingly into the dust, and mumbled something to himself. Then his eyes resumed their myopic staring at vacancy, and the pipe went back into his mouth.

Hamid grinned at me, shrugged, and said: "I won't be a moment," and vanished into a dark doorway.

I wandered across the street, the children following. At the edge of the road was a six-foot retaining wall holding up, it seemed, the entire plateau on which the village was built. Below this were the terraced fields where I had seen the rider on the chestnut horse. The sunflowers were too tall and too thickly planted to allow the lovely profusion of flowers that I had seen in the lower reaches of the hills, but there were wild irises at the foot of the wall, and a blue flower like a small lily, and like shining drops of blood among the sunflower roots I could see the red anemones.

I climbed down. The children climbed down, too. I helped them, bodily lifting down the last one, a half-naked atom of perhaps three, probably with scabies. I dusted my hands off on my slacks and hunted for flowers.

The children helped. A big-eyed boy in a grubby vest and nothing else yanked out a handful of pinks for me, and little Scabies came up with a dandelion or two. There was a great deal of conversation, Arabic and English and (from Scabies) stone-age grunts, and we all understood one another very well. The clearest thing about the business was that I was expected to hand over something substantial in return for the company and the flowers.

"A shilling," said Hamid from above me, sounding amused.

I looked up. He was standing at the edge of the road. "Are you sure? It seems very little. There's six of them."

"It's quite enough."

It seemed he was right. The children grabbed the coins, and melted up and over the wall faster than they had come down and with no assistance whatever, except for Scabies, who was heaved over the last lap by Hamid, dusted off, and sent on his way with a clap over the bare buttocks. Hamid turned back to me.

"Can you manage it? Some of the stones aren't too steady."

"I won't bother. I'll just walk down and meet you on the road as you drive down. Did you get the oranges?"

"Yes. All right, then, don't hurry, I'll wait for you below."

The path where I had seen the rider was a dry and well-worn right of way some eighteen inches wide, going down at a slant through the sunflowers and descending by three or four stony gaps in the terracing. The huge flowers, heavy-headed, were turned away from me, facing south, and the path was a narrow chasm between head-high plants. I saw now that they were planted a yard or so apart, and between them some other plant with glaucous green leaves and plumes of brownish flowers fought its way up with mallow and cornflowers and a dozen other things toward the light. Where the horse had brushed through, the leaves hung bruised and crumpled, and above the honey-smell of the sunflowers there was the clean, musky smell of deadnettle.

I made my way down toward the road. At the gap in the wall leading down to the last terrace the sunflowers gave way to a more familiar crop of corn, and standing sentinel where the crops divided was a fig tree, its buds just bursting into young green. Its silver boughs held the buds up against the bright sky with an enchanting grace, and against the rough-cast of its stem some wild vinelike plant clung, with flowers as red as the anemones. I stopped to pick one. The vine was tough, and a hank of it pulled away from the trunk, uncovering something that lay below. On the bleached silver of the exposed stem, scrawled in red, was the sketch of a running dog. The drawing was crude but lively; the thing was unmistakably a long-haired greyhound with a plumed tail. A saluki.

It is surely common experience that when once something has been brought to your attention it crops up again and again, often with an alarming appearance of coincidence or even fate. It certainly seemed as if, once Charles had mentioned them, the creatures were going to haunt me through the Lebanon, but there was after all nothing so very odd about it; one might say that in England it is possible to be haunted by poodles. I went down to the road.

Hamid was sitting on a low wall at the edge of the road beside the car, smoking. He got up quickly, but I waved him down. "Don't bother. Finish your cigarette, do."

"Would you like an orange?"

"I'd love one. Thanks. Oh, aren't they gorgeous? You're quite right, we don't get them like this at home . . . Hamid, why do they grow sunflowers?"

"For oil. They make a very good cooking oil, almost as good as olive oil, and now the Goverment has built a factory to make margarine with it also, and offers a good price for the crop. It's part of an official campaign to stop the growing of hemp."

"Hemp? That's hashish, isn't it?—marihuana? Good heavens! Does it grow up here?"

"Oh, yes. Have you never seen it? I believe you grow the same plant in England, to make rope, but only in hot countries does it bear the drug. In past time there has always been a lot of it grown up in these hills—it's the right climate for it, and there are still places where the inspectors don't go."

"Inspectors?"

He nodded. "Government officials. They're very anxious now to get the growing of these drugs under control. A certain amount is grown legally, you understand, for medical use, and for every stage of its growth and handling you must have a license and be subjected to strict controls, but it's always been easy enough for the peasants in these wild parts to grow more than they declare, or to harvest the crops before the inspectors come. Now the penalties have been made stricter than ever, but there are still some who try to get past the law." He lifted his shoulders. "What would you? It pays, and there are always men who will take the big risks for the big money." He dropped his cigarette into the road and trod the butt into the dust. "You saw the old man up there, the one I spoke to?"

"Yes."

"He was smoking it."

"But can he . . . ? I mean—"

"How can they stop him?"

I stared. "Do you mean it's grown right here?"

He smiled. "There was some growing beside his house, among the potatoes."

"I wouldn't know it if I saw it," I said. "What's it look like?"

"A tall plant, grayish color, not very pretty. The drug comes from the flowers. These are brownish, a spike like soft feathers."

I had been carefully depositing my orange peel out of sight behind the wall where we sat. Now I sat bolt upright. "There was something like that growing under the sunflowers!"

"So?" he said indifferently. "It will be gone before the inspectors get here. Shall we go?" He opened the car door for me.

All in all it had been a strange and heady sort of day. And things seemed to be going my way. It seemed the inevitable climax to it that as I got into the car I should say with decision:

"You said you'd show me Dar Ibrahim on the way home. If there's time, I think I'd like to call there today. Would you mind?"

* * *

At about four o'clock we slid round a steep bend and into the village of Sal'q. Hamid stopped the car beside a low wall beyond which the land dropped clear away to give another of those staggering views of the Adonis Valley.

"There," he said.

I looked where he pointed. Here the valley was wide, with the river, magnificent and flowing swiftly, cutting a way down for itself between dense banks of trees. From somewhere to our left, beyond the little village mosque, fell the tributary river to meet the Adonis in the valley at the bottom. Between the two streams a highish, wedge-shaped tongue of land thrust out like a high-prowed ship down the valley's center, and on its tip, like a crown on the crag above the meeting waters, sprawled the palace, a seemingly vast collection of buildings running back from the edge of the promontory to spread over a fair area of the plateau. Toward the rear of the building the ground fell away sharply in a small escarpment shelving down to the level of the plateau, and here the palace wall rose straight out of the rock. Near the top I could see windows, a row of ornate arches looking out toward the village, but apart from these, except for a few small openings that seemed to be little more than ventilators, the walls were windowless, blank and white in the sun. Toward the back of the palace the green of sizable trees showed inside the walls. Outside, stretching back toward the roots of the mountains that divided the gorges of the Adonis and its tributary, the plateau stretched open and stony and barren as the valley of dry bones.

There seemed to be no way to get there except down a rocky track along the side of the tributary stream.

This Hamid was explaining. "And you have to cross the water at the bottom," he said. "There is a ford with shallow water, but sometimes in the spring, you understand, when there has been rain, it can be very deep and fast, and floods over the stepping stones. But it will be all right today. You really wish to go? Then I will come with you to show you the way."

It did not seem to me that it would be very easy to miss the way. I could see the path as far as the bottom of the hill, and—I am very long-sighted—I could even see the ford from where I stood. There must have been a stone bridge there at one time, for the ruined piles were unmistakable. And no doubt beyond that the track up to the palace would be equally unmistakable.

I looked at Hamid in his immaculately pressed dark city trousers and equally immaculate shirt.

"That's very good of you, but there's no need for you to bother, you know. I can hardly miss the way. If you'd rather stay here with the car, and perhaps find something to drink in the village, some coffee, perhaps, if there's a café . . . ?" I looked round me at the singularly unpromising gaggle of huts which was the village of Sal'q.

He grinned. "There is, but with all gratitude, I shall not try it today. I will certainly come down with you. It's a long way for a lady to go alone, and besides, I believe that the porter there speaks nothing but Arabic. You would perhaps find it a little difficult to make yourself sufficiently understood?"

"Oh, lord, yes, I suppose so. Well, thanks very much, I'd be terribly grateful if you'd come. It looks a pretty tough walk, I must say. I wish we had wings."

He locked the car, and dropped the key into his pocket. "Along here."

The path led round the wall of the mosque, past the little graveyard with its curious Moslem stones; the slender pillars with their stone turbans which indicated the graves of men, the lotus-carved steles for the women. The whitewashed minaret stood prettily against the pale hot sky. Past the crumbling corner of the graveyard wall the track suddenly turned downhill in steep zigzags, treacherous with loose stones. The sun was heeling over from its zenith, but still beat fiercely on this side of the valley. Soon we had gone below the lowest of the village terraces, where the hillside was too steep and too stony for anything, even vines, to grow. Some bluff of hot rock hid the stream from us, so that no sound of it came to our ears. The silence was intense. The whole width of the valley seemed to be filled with the same hot, dry silence.

Round a steep turn in the path we disturbed a herd of goats, black and brown with long silky hair, flop ears, huge horns and sleepy, wicked yellow eyes. They had been grazing on heaven knows what on that barren slope, and now slept in the sun. There were about thirty of them, their narrow clever faces—watching us with calculation and without a hint of fear—giving the impression somehow not that this was a herd of animals owned by men, but that we were walking through a colony of creatures who lived here by right. When one of them got leisurely to its feet and strolled into the middle of the path, I didn't argue with it. I got off the path and walked round it. It didn't even turn its head.

I had been right about the old bridge. The tributary (Hamid told me it was called the Nahr el-Sal'q) was not wide compared to the Adonis, but at this time of year there was fully twenty feet of it to cross, swiftly sliding water, shallow in places over white pebbles, in others tumbling with foam over split boulders, or whirling deeper in a hard dark green in pools which must have been breast deep. At the far side the water was bounded by a low cliff, perhaps five feet high, from which the bridge had originally sprung. The foundations could be seen deep in the clear water. On the side where we stood there was little left but a pile of large squared stones, some of which had been removed and roughly arranged in the water to make stepping stones about a yard apart.

"There was an old bridge here once, a Roman bridge, they say," said Hamid. "These are still the old stones. Can you manage it?"

He took my hand to help me across, then led the way straight for the foot of the cliff, where I saw a path curling its way up through tangles of wild fig and yellow broom toward the head of the promontory.

It was a steep climb but not difficult, obviously practicable for mules or even horses. We saw no sign of life other than the lizards, and the kestrels which circled above the cliff. There was no sound except that of the water running below us, and the scrape of our steps, and our breathing.

As we came out eventually at the top of the crag and saw the eyeless walls of the palace in front of us, I had the oddest feeling that the building was completely dead and deserted, that this was almost a place outside life. It seemed impossible that anyone should live there, least of all anyone I had known. No one, surely, who had ever been a part of my own extraordinary but vital family could shut themselves away here in this bone-white graveyard of a place . . .

As I paused to get my breath, eyeing the scoured pale walls, the locked gate of bronze, I found myself remembering the last time I had seen Great-Aunt Harriet. It was a dim childhood's memory . . . The orchard at home, at windfall time, and one of those soft gusty September winds with the leaves swirling, and the apples thudding into the damp turf. The sky was full of afternoon clouds and the rooks wheeling to go home. I remembered Great-Aunt Harriet's voice cawing like a rook with laughter at something Charles had said . . .

"There used to be a bell beside the door. You tell me what you want me to say, and if the old chap isn't asleep, we might get him to take a message," said Hamid cheerfully, leading the way across the dusty rock toward the gate.

3

This batter'd Caravanserai . . .

—E. FITZGERALD: *The Rubáiyát of
Omar Khayyám of Náishápúr*

THE MAIN gate—double leaves of studded bronze under an elaborately carved arch—was at first sight vastly impressive, but as one approached it could be seen that the heavy knocker had vanished from its hinge and that the carving had been fretted almost to nothing by the wind. The walls, high and blind, showed here and there the remains of some colored decoration, ghostly patterns and mosaics and broken marble plastered over and painted a pale ocher color which had baked white with the strong sunlight. There was a bell pull to the right-hand side of the gate.

Hamid tugged the handle. Distinctly, in silence, we could hear the creak of the wires as they strained, foot by rusty foot, to pull the bell. Seconds later, with a squeak and jangle of springs, it clanged hollowly just inside the gate. As the echo ran humming down the bronze a dog barked somewhere. After that, again, there was silence.

Hamid had just raised his hand again to the bell when we heard footsteps. Hardly footsteps; just the whispering shuffle of slippers on a dusty floor, then the sound of hands fumbling at the other side of the gate. It was no surprise to hear the heavy sound of bolts being dragged back, or that, when the gate began to open, it creaked ominously.

I caught Hamid's eye, and saw in it the same bright anticipation as was no doubt in my own. After such a build-up, whoever opened the gate to us could hardly fail to be an anticlimax.

But he wasn't. He was better than all expectation. One tall leaf of bronze creaked slowly open on a passage that seemed, in contrast to the sunlight where we stood, to be quite dark. In the cautious crack that had opened we could see a thin bent figure robed in white. For one mad moment—such had been the Hitchcock lead-in to his appearance—I thought the man had no face; then I saw that he was dark, almost black, and against the blackness of the passage behind him only his white robes showed up.

He peered out into the light, an oldish man, stoop-shouldered, his skin wrinkled like a prune under the folds of the kaffiyeh, or Arab headdress. His eyes, red-rimmed and puckered against the light, had a grayish look about them which spoke of cataract. He blinked, mouthed something at Hamid which I took to be Arabic, and started to shut the gate.

"One moment. Wait." Hamid was past me into the gap with one quick stride, and had a tough young shoulder against the gate. He had already told me what he intended to say. The quick-fire Arabic sounded urgent. "This is no ordinary visitor, but one of your Lady's family, whom you cannot turn from the door. Listen."

The old man paused uncertainly, and Hamid went on. "My name is Hamid Khalil, from Beirut, and I have driven this young lady up to see your mistress. Now, we know your Lady receives no visitors, but this young lady is English, and she is the daughter of the Lady's brother's son. So you must go and see your Lady and tell her that Miss Christy Mansel has come from England to see her—Miss Christy Mansel, bearing greetings from all the Lady's relatives in England."

The porter was staring, stupidly, almost as if he had not heard. I began to wonder if he were deaf. Then I saw he was looking at me, and that in the opaque eyes a sort of curiosity was stirring. But he shook his head, and again from his lips came those strangled sounds which I realized now were the struggles of someone with a severe speech impediment.

Hamid shrugged at me, expressively. "They didn't tell us the half, did they? 'No communication with outside' is right—this man's all but dumb. However, I don't think he's deaf, so I dare say he has some way of taking messages. There's no need yet for despair."

"That wasn't quite what I was feeling."

He laughed and turned back to the old man, who, gobbling and muttering under his breath, had been making vague attempts to shut the door against the younger man's determined shoulder and (by now) foot. Hamid raised his voice and spoke again, sharply. Even without his subsequent translation to me, the gist of what he said was obvious.

"Look, stop playing about with the gate, we're not going away until you've taken the message to your mistress, or sent someone who can talk to us . . . That's better! Now, have you got it? Miss Christy Mansel, daughter of her brother's son, has come from England to see her, even just for a few moments. Is that clear? Now go and give the message."

There was no doubt that the old man could hear. Open curiosity showed now in the face that shot forward on its stringy neck to stare at me, but he still made no attempt to go, or to invite us in. He shook his head violently, mouthing at Hamid and holding on to the edge of the gate with what looked like a mixture of obstinacy and apprehension.

I intervened, half uneasy, half repelled: "Look, Hamid, perhaps we shouldn't . . . I mean, forcing our way in like this . . . He's obviously had his orders, and he looks scared to death at having to disobey them. Perhaps if I just write a note—"

"If we go away now you'll never get in. It's not your great-aunt he's scared of. As far as I can make out he's saying something about a doctor. 'The doctor says no one is to go in'."

"The *doctor?*"

"Don't worry," he said quickly, "I may be wrong, I can hardly make him out, but I thought that's what he said. Wait a minute . . ."

Another spate of Arabic, and again the horrible stammering syllables from the old man. Flakes of spittle had appeared at the corners of his mouth, and he shook his head violently, and even partially loosed his panic hold on the door to flap his hands at us like someone driving hens.

"Please—" I said.

Hamid silenced the old man with a snapped word and gesture. "Yes?"

"Hamid," I said decisively. "This settles it, I insist on getting in. If I can't see my great-aunt, I'll see the doctor, if he's here. If he isn't, then someone must write his name and address down for me, and I'll go and see him straight away. Tell him that. Tell him I insist. And if you like you can tell him that my family can make quite a bit of trouble if anything should happen to my great-aunt, and the family not be allowed to know about it." I added: "And for pity's sake if there's anyone at all in the place who *can* talk to us, we want to see them, and fast."

"I'll tell him."

How he did actually express my demands I have no idea, but after a further few minutes or so of wrangling, the porter, filmed eyes turned up hideously to heaven and palms thrown up to disclaim all responsibility, pulled open the door at last and let us through.

Hamid gave the ghost of a wink at me as he stood back to let me pass him. "I told him you were exhausted with the walk from Sal'q and refused to wait outside in the sun. If we'd once let him shut the door I doubt if we'd ever have heard from him again."

"I'm sure we wouldn't. For goodness' sake come with me, won't you? I mean, something tells me I may not be welcome."

"I wouldn't leave you for worlds," said Hamid comfortably, taking me by the elbow to steer me into the cool darkness. "I only hope that you find all is well with the Lady . . . and I may easily have been mistaken in what that old dervish was trying to say. Well, at least we are inside . . . That alone is something to tell my children's children."

Behind us the gate creaked shut, and there were the ominous sounds of the bolts being replaced. As my eyes adjusted themselves to the dimness I saw that we were not actually in a passage, but in a high barrel-roofed tunnel about fifteen feet long which ended in another heavy door. To either side of the tunnel was a smaller door. One of these was open, and in the dim light of a slit window in the inner wall I saw an ancient truckle-bed covered with tumbled blankets. The porter's lodge, no doubt; perhaps originally a guardroom. The door opposite this was shut and padlocked.

The old man opened the door at the tunnel's end, letting in a shaft of bright light. We followed him into a big courtyard.

This would be the outer court of the original palace, the *midan,* where the Emir's people would gather with gifts or petitions, and where his troops would show off their horsemanship with games and mock fights, or ride in to dismount after battle or the hunt. Under the archways on three sides were buildings which must have been stables and harness rooms and perhaps quarters for soldiers; on the fourth, to our left as we entered, was a high wall beyond which I saw a glimpse of green. In its heyday, with the bustle of servants and the tramp of horses and rattle of arms, it would have been an impressive place. Now it was quiet and empty, but the scuffed dust showed recent evidence of beasts, and the place smelled of horses.

The porter did not pause here, but led us right-handed across the *midan* and in under the arcade, through another door which gave on a darkened passage. Through this his white robes shuffled dimly ahead. Vaguely I glimpsed passages going off to left and right, and doors, some of them open on rooms where it was too dark to see anything; but in one of these some kind of skylight shed a glimmer on sacks and boxes and a stack of broken chairs. The passage took three right-angled turns through this labyrinth before it led us out into another courtyard, this time small, and little more than a light-well lined with arched grilles, and one blind wall against which was piled a stack of timber. As we passed I saw out of the corner of my eye a streak of movement which, when I looked sharply that way, had ceased. Nothing. But I knew it had been a rat.

Another corridor; more doors, some of them open and giving on dilapidated and dirty rooms. The whole place had the air of something deserted long since, and lived in only by rats and mice and spiders. Not a floor but was filthy, with gaps in the ornamental tiling; the wall mosaics were dim and battered, the window grilles broken, the lintels cracked. A heavy, dusty silence slept over everything like a gray blanket. I remember that as we passed some crumbling wall a rusty nail fell from its socket with a clink that made me jump, and the rustle of plaster falling after it sounded like a puff of wind in dry leaves.

It was a far cry from the 'enchanted palace' that imagination—more powerful than reason—had led me to expect. I began to wonder with tightening nerves what I should find at the end of this quest. 'Stark raving bonkers' had been Charles's verdict, and had seemed, as he delivered it, no more than faintly comic; but here, following the shuffling guide along yet another corridor with its dim and dwindling prospect of warped and gaping doors, its uneven floorings, its smell of years-old decay, I began, quite fervently, to wish I had not come. The thought of coming face to face with the combination of the helplessness, senility, and perhaps sickness, which must live at the center of all this decay like a spider in the middle of an old dusty cobweb, could fill me with nothing but dismay.

Suddenly we were out into another courtyard. I had completely lost my bearings by this time, but from the fact that beyond the roofs on the far side I could see crests of feathery green, I guessed we were somewhere toward the back of the palace.

This court was about fifty feet square, and at one time must have been as ornamental as the one where Charles and I had talked in Damascus; but now, like all else, it had fallen into disrepair. In its better days it had been floored with marble, with blue tiled arcades and pretty pillars and a pool at the center. At the foot of each pillar stood a carved marble trough for flowering plants. These were still full of soil, but now held only grass and some tightly clenched, grayish-looking buds. There was one spindly tamarisk hanging over the broken coping of the pool. Somewhere, a cicada purred gently. Gray thistles grew in the gaps of the pavement, and the pool was dry.

Under the arcade to one side was the usual deep alcove in the shadow where, up a single step, was the dais with seats on three sides. I would have distrusted any cushion that this place might produce, but I need not have worried; the seats were of unpadded marble. Here the porter indicated that we should sit, then, with another grotesque bout of yammering directed at Hamid, he turned and went. Silence came back, broken only by the churring of the cicada.

"Smoke?" asked Hamid, producing cigarettes. He lit mine for me and then wandered back into the sunlight of the courtyard, where he squatted down with his back against a pillar, absently narrowing his eyes against the brilliant sky where the trees beyond the wall waved their green feathers.

"If she does not receive you, what will you do?"

"Go away, I suppose, once I've seen the doctor."

He turned his head. "I am sorry. You are distressed."

I hesitated. "Not really. I hardly know her, and I'm pretty sure she won't remember me. She spent most of her time out East till her husband died, and after that she only lived in England for about two years—that was when I was very small. She left fifteen years ago, for good, when I was seven. I haven't seen her since the time she came to say good-bye. I'd hardly be surprised if she just sent a message back now to say she can't even remember my name. That is, if the dervish gets it right . . . I wonder if he can give a message at all? As a noncommunicator he just about wins, wouldn't you say? He ought to be at the Royal Court."

"But surely your Queen would not—? Ah, here he is," said Hamid, rising, "and praise be to Allah, he has brought someone with him."

The 'someone' was a young man, a European, tall and thin and carelessly dressed, with light hair bleached to fair by the sun, and gray eyes. He had the slightly confused air of someone startled awake from sleep, and I suddenly remembered Great-Aunt Harriet's alleged nocturnal habits. Perhaps the staff slept during daylight? He paused for a moment in the shadow before dismissing the porter with a gesture, then came forward into the sun. I saw him wince as if its fierce light worried him, as he approached slowly and with apparent reluctance over the broken pavement. He looked about twenty-four.

His voice was friendly enough, and what was more, English.

"Good afternoon. I'm afraid I didn't get your name. I gather from Jassim that you have an urgent message for Lady Harriet? Perhaps you could give your message to me?"

"You're English? Oh, good." I stood up. "It's not exactly a message. My name's Mansel, Christy Mansel, and Mrs. Boyd—'Lady Harriet'—is my great-aunt. I'm in Beirut on holiday, and someone told me that my great-aunt was still living up here at Dar Ibrahim, so I came up to see her. I'm sure my people at home will be very glad to have news of her, so if she'll spare me even a few minutes, I'd be very pleased."

He looked surprised, and, I thought, guarded. "A great-niece? Christy, did you say? She never mentioned anyone of that name to me."

"Should she have?" My voice was perhaps a little tart. "And you, Mr.— er . . . ? I take it you live here?"

"Yes. My name's Lethman, John Lethman. I—you might say I look after your great-aunt."

"You mean you're the doctor?"

I must have sounded abrupt and surprised, because he looked rather taken aback. "I beg your pardon?"

"I'm sorry, it was only because I suppose you look—I mean, I expected somebody older. The porter told my driver that 'the doctor' wouldn't allow anyone to see my great-aunt, that's how I knew you were here. If he did mean you, that is?"

"I suppose he did . . ." He pressed the heel of his hand to his brow, shook his head sharply as if to wake himself up, and gave me the flash of an embarrassed smile. His eyes still looked blurred and unfocussed. They were gray, with wide, myopic-looking pupils. "I'm sorry, I'm still a bit stupid, I was asleep."

"Oh, goodness, I do apologize. When one's madly sight-seeing all day one tends to forget the siesta habit . . . *I'm* sorry, Mr. Lethman. It was just that when the porter said 'the doctor' was here I began to think my great-aunt must be ill. I mean—if you have to live here . . . ?"

"Look," he said, "we'd better clear this up. I'm not a doctor really, unless you like to count half a course in psychological medicine—" A quick look. "And don't let that worry you, either, because I'm certainly not here in *that* capacity! Your great-aunt's pretty fit, and all I actually do is keep an eye on the Arab servants and see to things generally, and provide her with a bit of company and conversation. I don't 'have' to live here at all in the sense you mean. All that happened was that I came here—to the Lebanon—to do some research for a paper I wanted to write, and I was marooned up here one day, driven to ground by one of the flash storms they have occasionally, and your great-aunt took me in, and somehow one thing led to another, and I stayed." His smile had something tentative about it, but oddly disarming, so that I thought I could supply the missing bits of the story quite easily. He added: "If you can think of a better place to write in, just tell me."

I could think of a million better places to write in, among them almost any room almost anywhere within daily reach of people, but I didn't say so. I asked: "How long have you been here?"

"Nearly a year. I came last July."

"I see. Well, it's a relief to know she's all right. So I'll be able to see her?"

He hesitated, apparently on the brink of saying something, then gave that odd little shake of the head again, and ran his hand back over his brow, almost as if he were smoothing away some physical discomfort like a headache. I saw Hamid watching him curiously.

"Look," I said, "if you've something to tell me, go ahead. But let's sit down, shall we?"

He followed me into the shade of the divan, and we sat down. I laced my fingers round one knee and turned to regard him. He still looked uncomfortable, though not in the physical sense; his long body looked relaxed enough, and his hands were slack on his knees. But there was a tight knot of worry between his brows.

"How long since you heard from your great-aunt?" he asked at length.

"If you mean how long since I myself did, I never have. In fact I only remember seeing her about three times in my life, and the last time was when I was about seven, but my family hears from her now and again. There was a letter last year some time—just before Christmas, I think it was. She certainly wrote as if she were fairly fit and in her right—that is, fairly fit. But it didn't bother much with news."

I got the idea that he knew what I meant, but he didn't smile. He was frowning down at his hands. "I only asked because—" A pause, then he looked up suddenly. "Miss Mansel, how much do you and your family know about the way she lives here?"

"I suppose we know very little, except the obvious things, that she's perhaps getting a bit more eccentric as she gets older, and that she's made her life out here for so long that it isn't very likely she'll ever want to move and come home again. You'll have gathered that our family's never been very strong on family ties and all that, and of course lately Great-Aunt Harriet's had this thing about cutting all her ties with England home and beauty—that's almost all her letters have been about, when she wrote at all. Don't think the family minded, they didn't. What she does is her own affair. But since I came out here I've heard a bit more about her, and I gather that now it's a pretty far-out kind of eccentricity . . . I mean, all this Lady Hester Stanhope imitation. Is it really true? Does she really live like that? Mr. Lethman, she isn't really bats, is she?"

"No, oh no," he said quickly. He was looking immensely relieved. "I wondered if you knew about that. It wouldn't be very easy to start explaining from scratch, but if you know the Stanhope story it makes it relatively simple. I won't say your great-aunt deliberately set out to be a modern 'Lady of the Lebanon,' but when she first settled here at Dar Ibrahim she did keep a bit of state, and various people made the comparison to her, and then she discovered that the old Stanhope legend was still very much alive among the country Arabs, and she herself got a good deal of benefit from it in the way of service and influence and—you know, the various by-products of celebrity. It was the locals who started calling her 'Lady Harriet,' and it simply stuck. Your great-aunt was amused at first, I gather, and then she discovered it suited her to be a 'character,' and in the way these things have, it gradually grew beyond the point where it could be stopped, and certainly beyond the point where she could treat it as a joke, even to herself. I don't know if you can understand this?"

"I think so," I said. "She couldn't detach herself anymore, so she simply went with it."

"That's it. Nor did she want to detach herself. She'd lived out here for so long, and in a way she'd made it her country, and in a curious way I believe she feels she has a kind of right to the legend." He smiled, the first smile of genuine amusement. "If you want the truth I think she has a fair amount in common with her original. Well, she simply settled down to enjoy it, and got a great deal of pleasure from the more picturesque details—riding out with the hounds and hawks, for instance, letting Dar Ibrahim be used again as a halt for caravans on their way from High Lebanon and Antilebanon to the sea, and receiving the occasional 'distinguished traveler'—mostly archaeologists, I believe, who'd known her husband and his work. She even meddled a bit with politics, and for sometime now she's been threatening—though I think it's only window dressing myself—to turn Muslim." He paused. "And then of course when I turned up out of the blue she was delighted. I was to be the 'resident physician' who has such a large part in the Stanhope story . . . you know that Lady Hester Stanhope kept her own doctor with her at Djoun? Well, when our 'Lady Harriet' took me in, and found I'd been halfway to a medical degree, it suited her down to the ground. So I get a courtesy title which impresses the Arab servants, and what I actually do is provide your great-aunt with company and conversation. I need hardly add that if she did need medical attention I'd get it from Beirut."

"Who does she have now that Dr. Grafton's gone?"

"Dr. Grafton?" He sounded quite blank, and I looked at him in surprise.

"Yes, don't you know him? Surely, if he attended her six months ago you must have been here."

"Oh, yes, I was, I was only wondering how you knew the name."

"Someone at the hotel who told me about Dar Ibrahim said my aunt had been ill last autumn, so I got them to find out who her doctor was, and rang him up to ask about her. I was told then that he'd left Beirut. Who does she have now?"

"She hasn't needed anyone since then, I'm glad to say. She's got a bit of a thing now about the Beirut doctors, but I've no doubt that if it's necessary I'll make her see the light." He smiled. "Don't worry . . . I really do look after her quite well, you know, and I run the place for her as far as one can. And if you're thinking about the general four-star-hotel atmosphere you've seen up to now, let me tell you that there are five courtyards, two gardens, three Turkish baths, a mosque, stabling for fifty horses and twelve camels, several miles of corridors including a secret passage or two, and as for mere rooms, I've never managed to count them. I use radar to get from the Prince's Court to the Seraglio."

I laughed: "I'm sorry, was I looking at the dust on the floor? Don't you have slaves to go with the décor?"

"Only myself and three others—Jassim the porter, a girl called Halide, and Halide's brother Nasirulla, who lives in the village and comes over during the day. Actually we manage quite well, because the old lady herself lives very simply now. I may tell you that her part of the palace is a bit better kept than this. Halide's a good girl, and looks after your aunt pretty well. You really have no need to worry about her."

"Did I say I was worrying? I didn't mean to throw you on the defensive like this. What have I said? I'm sure Aunt Harriet's having a whale of a time being Lady of the Lebanon, and I'm glad you're here to look after her. All I want is to see her for five minutes so's I can tell my people all about it."

Another of those pauses. Here we were, I thought; back to Square One.

He shifted on the hard seat, and glanced sideways at me.

"Yes, well, that's rather it, don't you see? The point is, we've standing orders to stall everybody off, and—" his gaze dropped again to his hands—"anything she's ever said to me about her family didn't lead me to think she'd make an exception there."

I grinned. "Fair enough, I'm not blaming you, or her either. But can't we let her decide for herself? I take it she doesn't know I'm here yet? Or will Jassim have got that across to her?"

"He hasn't seen her yet, he came straight to me. As a matter of fact, he gets more across than you'd think, but he didn't get your name. I wasn't sure who you were myself, till I spoke to you. I admit he isn't so hot as a messenger—you might call him one of your aunt's charities, like me—but he's pretty useful as a staller-off at the gate, and we can't get anyone much to stay here nowadays. There isn't much money, you know."

There was something about the way he said this, looking at me steadily with those curiously unfocussed eyes. I noticed that the whites were bloodshot, and he looked as if he didn't get enough sleep, but he seemed relaxed enough now, his long spare frame slack on the marble seat as if this were thick with silk cushions and Persian rugs. He was dressed in gray light-weight trousers and a blue beach shirt, neither of them expensive, but he wore on his wrist a really magnificent gold watch, bought no doubt in Beirut. I found myself remembering what Charles had said about Great-Aunt Harriet's penchant for young men, and some other corner of my mind came up with the phrase 'undue influence'. But this I ignored; it was after all irrelevant. If Aunt H could get a young man to run her ramshackle palace for her and give her the kind of company she liked, so much the better. Especially if it was true that there was very little money left. I wondered just how true this was, and if Mr. Lethman looked on the sudden irruption of a relative as a threat to his own position vis-à-vis the 'Lady Harriet.' In which case my good-looking cousin Charles might be even less welcome than I. I decided not to mention Charles till I saw Aunt H herself.

John Lethman was saying: "Jassim wouldn't have been able to see your aunt yet, in any case. She usually sleeps a good deal during the day. She's a nightbird, you know, like her original. So if you could wait a little longer, then I can go and ask her about it? Halide usually goes in to wake her at about six."

"Of course I'll wait," I said. "That is, if you don't mind, Hamid?"

"Not at all," said Hamid without moving.

There was a slight pause. Lethman glanced from Hamid to me and back, then consulted his watch. "Well, that's fine, it won't be long now, and we'll see." Another pause. He cleared his throat. "I suppose I ought to warn you . . . Of course I'll do all I can, but I can't guarantee anything. She's old, and sometimes forgetful, and—well, let's call it 'difficult.' And some days are worse than others."

"And today's been a bad one?"

He made a rueful mouth. "Not too good."

"Well, if she really doesn't feel up to seeing me, then that's that, isn't it? But tell her I'll come back any time she says, when she's feeling better. I'm in Beirut till at least mid-week, and I could stay on. I was going to ring up soon to tell my people what I was planning, and it'd be rather nice if I could give them news of her. In fact, Daddy might just be ringing up himself this evening."

" 'This evening'? Hadn't you understood? I meant it literally when I said she was a nightbird. She usually seems to wake up and be at her best at something between ten and midnight, and after that she's quite often up all night. If she receives anyone at all, that's when she sees them."

"Good heavens, she does play it for real, doesn't she? Do you mean that if I'm to see her, I've got to stay here all night?"

"Until pretty late, at all events. Could you?"

"I could, but I can hardly keep my driver here until the early hours of the morning. Could you put me up? Have you a room?" I meant 'a room that's fit to sleep in,' so the question wasn't as absurd as it might have sounded. Mr. Lethman seemed to be considering the question on its merits. There was a short pause, then he said, agreeably enough:

"We could certainly find you one."

I looked across at Hamid. "Do you mind? We can see what my great-aunt has to say, and if I do have to wait and see her later on, would you go back without me? You could call at the hotel and tell them I'm having to stay up here for the night, and—are you free tomorrow?"

"For you, yes."

"You're very good," I said gratefully, "thank you. In that case, could you come for me again in the morning? Wait in the village, don't bother to come right across as far as the gate."

"I will certainly come to the gate," said Hamid. "Don't you worry about that. But I don't much like going away now and leaving you here."

"I'll be all right. And I simply must see my great-aunt."

"Of course you must, this I understand. I am sorry, I know it's none of my affair, but surely it could be arranged that she could see you for a few minutes now, and then I could take you back to your hotel."

Beside me, Mr. Lethman straightened suddenly. His voice held a weariness and exasperation that was quite obviously genuine. "Look, I'm sorry about all this. I'm not making this difficult just for fun, you know, in fact I'm hating the position I seem to have got myself into, having to stall you off when you must think I've no standing in the matter at all—"

"I wasn't exactly thinking that," I said, "and you have got standing, haven't you? I mean, this is her home, and if she's asked you to live here, there it is, and no arguments. Even if you're not officially her doctor, I suppose you could call yourself her steward or something."

"Malvolio in person, yellow stockings, cross garters, and all." A flick of feeling in his voice that I didn't like, gone as soon as heard. He followed it with another of those disarming smiles. "But you see the situation's hardly normal in any way at all. I suppose I've got used to it, and in any case this is a damned queer country where one learns to accept almost anything, but I realize this place must seem pretty weird to anyone like yourself coming into it for the first time. It did to me when she first received me. She uses what were the Emir's rooms—the Prince's Court, we call it—and an old State Divan is her bedroom. It's kept pitch dark most of the time. The Stanhope woman did the same out of vanity. I don't know what your great-aunt's motive is, certainly not that, possibly just imitation; but I remember when I was taken along there at midnight the first time I wondered what sort of loony-bin I'd landed into. And lately she's taken to—" He stopped, and seemed to be examining the tip of one shoe with great attention. "How well do you remember your great-aunt?"

"Not really at all. My impression is that she was tall and dark and had piercing black eyes and wore black, things that flew round her like the White Queen's shawl. She did have a shawl, and she used to pin it with a diamond pin. I remember Mummy saying that her diamonds were filthy. That struck me as funny, I don't know why."

"Diamonds? I'm afraid they must have gone long since. I never saw any." He sounded regretful, I thought. "Actually she's not so very tall, though I suppose she'd seem so to a child. And as for her clothes now, they're part of the legend, too."

"Oh, I know, she dresses like an Eastern male. Well, why not?" I unclasped my hands from my knees and straightened a trousered leg. "I dress like a European one, after all."

"I wasn't fooled," said Mr. Lethman, with the first really human glimmer he had shown. The worried look had lightened a little. He got to his feet. "Well, I'll go and see what the score is. I'll certainly try to persuade her to see you straight away. It's possible she may, and welcome you with open arms, but if she won't, we can make arrangements for you to stay the night. All right?"

"All right."

"That's fine, then. I'll let you know the worst."

He smiled perfunctorily and left us.

I went over to the pool and sat down on the coping beside Hamid.

"Did you hear all that?"

"Most of it," said Hamid. "What you might call a funny setup, eh? Smoke?"

"Not just now, thanks. I don't very often, actually."

"He does."

"How d'you mean?"

"Hashish."

I stared. "No? Does he? How do you know?"

He lifted his shoulders. "His eyes, didn't you notice? And other signs—one gets to know them. He'd been smoking when we came."

"Then that's why he was so sleepy and other-worldly! He said he'd been asleep, and let me think it was just a siesta. I thought he'd probably been up part of the night with my great-aunt. Smoking! No wonder he resented being interrupted!"

"I don't suppose he was resenting you. The smoke can make you relaxed and easy-going, and not know what you're doing. He was finding it hard to think. I smoke it myself sometimes; everybody does in the Lebanon."

"*Do* you?"

He smiled. "Not when I'm driving, don't worry. And not much, me; I've too much sense, and it's dangerous. It affects different people different ways, and by the time you've found what it does to you, sometimes it is too late. Did you hear him say he was writing a book? If he stays here and smokes *marjoun,* he will never write it. He will think for years that he has only to start tomorrow, and it will be the best book ever written . . . but he will never start. This is what the *marjoun* does; it gives you visions and takes away the will to translate them. He will end up like that old man, coughing in the sun and dreaming dreams . . . . What will you do if he comes back to say the old lady won't see you at all?"

"I don't quite know."

"I'll tell you what I should do. If he says she will not see you, tell him that you wish to hear this from the old lady herself. If he will not allow this, then tell him that you can only accept such an order from a real doctor, and that you wish a doctor from Beirut to see her straight away. Oh, you can do this very pleasantly. Ask him which doctor he recommends, and what time tomorrow will be convenient. Then you tell me, and I bring you."

There wasn't much expression in his voice, but I stared at him. "What are you suggesting?"

"Nothing." He shrugged again. "Seems to me that things must go very much as he orders them here, and we only have his word for it that there is no money left. She was—I repeat was—a very rich old lady."

"But the family don't care about—" I stopped. It was patently no use explaining to Hamid that nobody wanted Great-Aunt Harriet to do anything with her own money except have a good time on her own terms. Anyway, there were other considerations here than money. I said, slowly: "If it's true that she's perfectly fit, I'd say she can probably take care of herself, and I'm also pretty sure she wouldn't thank me for interfering. All I want is to know that she is still 'hale and hearty,' and that being so she can dispose of her filthy old diamonds any way she pleases. He's probably right that she's done it already."

"Very likely." I didn't know whether Hamid's dry tone meant that he was thinking of the economies obviously practiced in the place, or of John Lethman's gold wristwatch. He added: "I do not suggest anything, me, but I have a very unpleasant nature."

"So have I. And if he really is smoking marihuana—hashish, that is—" I took a breath. "That settles it, I shall insist, whatever he says. I'm terribly sorry to have kept you hanging about like this, you've been very patient."

"You are paying for my car for the day, and for my time. How I spend the time is no matter, and it saves petrol to sit in the sun and smoke."

I laughed. "You've got something there. And you're right, I must see her. If necessary I shall play hell and insist."

"There's no need."

I jumped. I hadn't heard Mr. Lethman come back, but he was there, with Jassim behind him, coming quickly along the shaded side of the arcade, and looking as if he'd been hurrying. Or, I thought, as if he'd had a slightly dicey interview. At least he looked wide awake now, even brisk.

"She'll see me?"

"Yes, she'll see you, but I'm afraid it'll have to be later tonight." He made an apologetic gesture. "I'm sorry, I did try to persuade her, but I told you, it's not a good day, so I didn't like to press it. She's had a touch of bronchial asthma lately, nothing to worry about, but it sometimes prevents her from sleeping. She won't hear of calling the doctor, and since we still had the prescription from last autumn—it was the same trouble then—I didn't overrule her. In a way it's the remedy that's the trouble, rather than the disease. She find it depressive. To tell you the truth, the idea of a visit from you cheered her up a good deal."

"That's wonderful. I promise not to tire her."

"Have you made arrangements with your driver? I'll fix you up with a room now, before I go back to your great-aunt."

"It's all settled. Hamid's coming back for me tomorrow."

"Fine," he said, as if he meant it. "Well, if you'll come with me, Jassim will show your driver the way back to the gate."

As I said good-bye to Hamid, I thought I saw Jassim looking at me rather longingly, as if he would have liked to throw me out, too. But he eventually shuffled off into the shadows, and Hamid, with a final cheerful wave to me, went after him.

Mr. Lethman led me the other way, toward the rear of the buildings.

"So she didn't take much persuading after all?" I said.

"None at all," he admitted, "once she'd grasped who you were. To be honest she couldn't remember much about you, but she's very keen to see you now."

"I had a feeling she might be. Sheer roaring curiosity, I suppose."

He glanced down with what looked like surprise. "Well . . . yes, you could say so. Don't you mind?"

"Why should I? The motive doesn't matter as long as the result's all right. She's seeing me, isn't she? Anyway, it's only fair. What d'you imagine *my* main motive is for visiting Dar Ibrahim?"

"I—yes, of course." He sounded disconcerted.

"What's the matter? For goodness' sake, does that shock you?"

"No. But . . . you're a very unusual girl, aren't you?"

"Because I insist on my own way, or because I don't think relations are obliged to be fond of one another whether they like it or not? It's not unusual, it's only that most people won't admit it." I laughed. "Oh yes, I like to go my own way, but I recognize other people's right to do the same thing. It's about the only thing in my favor."

"What if their way isn't the same as yours?"

"Oh, if I feel really strongly about anything, it's full steam ahead and damn the torpedoes, but I'm open to argument. Where are you going to put me?"

"In the Seraglio."

"Well, that's putting me in my place, isn't it? Under lock and key?"

"Just about. At least, all the windows are barred." He smiled down at me, suddenly charming. "It's only because it's the best end of the palace, I assure you . . . We may be grudging hosts, but once we've had to give in, we do the thing properly. First-class accommodation, to make up for lack of welcome. Did you know that the Lady Hester Stanhope graded her guests according to status? I believe the third class used to get a pretty rough night."

"She would. It's nice of you to top-grade me when I'm giving you all this trouble."

"Heavens, it's no trouble. Actually I'm delighted you're staying—your great-aunt isn't the only one who likes company . . . I'm simply relieved she took it this way and I didn't have to quarrel with you. I'm certain your visit will do her a world of good—in fact, I can't help thinking it would be nice if she took a sudden shine to you and pressed you to stay for a few weeks, then *you* can sit and read the Koran to her at three in the morning, and give me a night off."

"Is that what you do?"

"It has been known. Shall I suggest it to her? How long can you spare?"

"I'll let you know in the morning."

He laughed, and pushed open a wooden gate that hung a bit crooked under a weed-grown arch.

"In here," he said, and ushered me past him.

4

And still a Garden by the Water blows . . .

—E. FITZGERALD: *The Rubáiyát of Omar Khayyám*

"OH!" I said, and stood still.

John Lethman shut the gate behind him, and came to my elbow. "Do you like it?"

"*Like* it!" I drew a breath. "What did it use to be?"

"Oh, just the Seraglio Garden. I'm afraid it's terribly neglected."

It was, of course, but this was a large part of its beauty. After the prospects of sun-baked stone and dusty ruin that had been assaulting my eyes all afternoon, the riot of green and flowers and the shimmer of cool water was wonderful.

It followed the now familiar pattern of the courtyards, a paved space decorated with flowers and bushes, with a pool at the center, surrounded by shaded arcades out of which opened the various rooms and offices. But this place was huge. Apparently the Seraglio rooms and garden filled the whole width of the palace, stretching well back over the flat surface of the plateau. On three sides of this vast space ran the arches of the long colonnades, throwing their pattern of sun and shadow over the doorways of what had been the women's apartments. On the fourth side—to the north—the colonnade marched with the outer wall where a row of delicate arches looked out across the Nahr el-Sal'q toward the village and the distant snows of the High Lebanon. High though these windows were, they were heavily barred with lattices so close that a hand could hardly have been thrust through them.

Within this frame of columns, long ago, some expert had laid out a big formal garden, and had somehow led water down from some high spring to feed the trees and flowers and fill the pool—no ornamental pond this time, but a wide stretch of water, almost a lake, which held at its center a small island crowned with a grove of trees. On this, at the heart of the green grove, I saw the glint of gilded tiles—the roof of a miniature building like an exotic summerhouse or folly; a Persian-style kiosk, with an onion dome, decorative pillars and latticed arches and shallow, broken steps.

There had once been a bridge across to the island, a slender, pretty affair; but now halfway over a broken gap yawned, some six feet wide. The lake itself was paved thickly with lily leaves, and 'at the edge the irises had spread into dense battalions of spears. All round the brink went a wide paved walk where ferns and briars thrust up the cracked marble slabs. From the shingled roofs of the arcades and down between the pillars jasmine and purple bougainvillea and roses hung festooned like cobwebs, and every cornice was white with birds' droppings and fully inhabited by doves calling *'Yusuf, Yusuf,'* like mad things. The contrast between the formal design of oblong lake, graceful arches and elegant kiosk, and the riotous natural growth that had invaded them, was excitingly attractive. It was like a formal Persian painting gone wild.

"Not a weed out of place," I said. "It's gorgeous! And to think I was always sorry for those poor women. Well, that settles it, Mr. Lethman, I'll move in tomorrow for a long, long stay. How long can you do with me?"

"Wait till you've seen your room before you commit yourself," he said, leading the way.

The room was midway along the south side of the garden. It was a plain square room, with a highish ceiling and checkered marble floor and patterned mosaic on the walls in panels of blue and gilt framing texts of Arabic writing. Unlike the other rooms I had seen so far, this one was clean, and well lighted by a triple window which looked straight out over the Adonis Gorge. The window was barred, but not so heavily as those which gave on the plateau. And for obvious reasons: the outer wall of the Seraglio apparently rose straight from the edge of the rock above the river.

"The bedroom's next door," said Mr. Lethman, "and the bathroom's the one after that. When I say 'bathroom,' of course, I mean the whole works, a hammam—steam rooms, cold rooms, massage rooms, the lot." He grinned. "But guess what, no steam."

"Any hot?"

"You can't be serious? But there is running water, straight off the snow, and it's all yours." The smile faded, and he looked at me a little doubtfully. "You know, it's terribly brave of you to stay. We're not geared for this kind of thing."

"I'm enjoying it," I said truthfully.

"I suppose whatever else it is, this end of the place must seem like a slice of real Eastern romance? Heaven knows I hope you can keep your illusions . . . I'm afraid the bedroom's not ready yet. I'll send Halide along to fix it up in a minute, and bring you some towels. Is there anything else you'll want?"

"Only a toothbrush, and I don't suppose the hammam runs to that. Don't look so worried, I was only joking. I'll do very well for one night, if supper could possibly include an apple? I hope Great-Aunt Harriet's régime does run to supper?"

He laughed. "Have a heart. What's more, you'll be glad to hear that Halide doesn't feed me on your great-aunt's diet! I'll have to leave you now, I'm afraid." He glanced at his watch. "You'd like a drink, I'm sure. I'll send one straight away. It'll soon be too dark for you to explore much, but go where you like—except for the Prince's rooms, of course, and either Halide or I will be there to fend you off if you lose your way."

"Thanks, but I'll just stay here. The garden's lovely."

"Then I'll be back to join you in about half an hour, and we'll eat."

When he had gone I sat down on the divan cushions, looking out over the gorge where the last of the light netted the tips of the trees with gold. Below, the shadows deepened through purple to black. It would soon be dark. I realized suddenly that I was tired, and hoped that when Halide came with the drink it wouldn't be the conventional Arab welcome of arak.

It wasn't, and it wasn't brought by Halide, but by a stocky young Arab who was presumably the brother, Nasirulla. He was dressed like Jassim in white robes, and came in silently with a tray which held a lighted lamp, two glasses, and a bottle of the golden wine of the Bk'aa. This is a lovely wine, light and dryish and about the best that Lebanon produces, and he couldn't have brought anything I'd sooner have had at that moment. I began to think kindly of Mr. John Lethman.

When I spoke to Nasirulla he eyed me sidelong, shook his head, and said something in Arabic. Then he set the lamp in a niche near the door, sketched a salaam, and went out.

With the coming of the lamp the darkness, as it always does, seemed to fall quickly. Only minutes after Nasirulla had left me the blue sky beyond the windows dimmed to blackness, and by seven o'clock it was quite dark.

I sat curled on the window seat, sipping the golden wine, and wondering what the night would bring.

It was very quiet. The night sky was like black velvet spangled with big stars, and, as if it had indeed been a velvet curtain, all sound seemed to be cut off, even the faintest murmuring of the river below my window. In the garden the doves had fallen silent and not even a breath of air stirred the feathery trees. Through the open door I could smell jasmine and roses, and some other strongly scented flowers, and below those exotic scents, as a sort of reminding undertone, the sweetish stagnant smell of the pool.

Mr. Lethman came back at about a quarter to eight, and with him Nasirulla with the supper tray. There was soup, scalding hot in a big thermos jug, and dish of *shawarma*—mutton flavored with vinegar, lemon, onion and cardamom seeds and grilled on a long spit. With this came a bowl of salad, a dish of pale butter and half a goats' milk cheese, a pile of unleavened bread and some apples and another bottle of wine. Nasirulla put this down on the low table, said something to Mr. Lethman, and then left us.

I said: "If you call this living simply, count me in."

He laughed. "I told you Halide fed me extra on the side. By the way, Nasirulla says she's on her way to do your room now."

"I'm giving you a lot of trouble. I mean, bringing the tray all this way for one thing. Where d'you usually eat?"

"Here, quite often." He added apologetically: "You'll probably find out, so I may as well tell you, these are my rooms. No, listen, please . . . I was going to sleep over the other side tonight anyway, so you're not to think you've put us to any trouble at all."

"Not put you to—? Mr. Lethman, I don't know what to say! Turning you out of your room!"

But he cut short my protestations by serving the soup and handing me mine in an eared round mug along with some Arab bread, then refilling my wineglass. It seemed almost as if he were bent on making amends for his earlier reluctance to let me in; or as if, once the Lady Harriet had accepted me, traditional Arab hospitality must have its way, and there was literally not enough that he and the Arab servants could do to make my stay a comfortable one. Any connection between my lively host and the harassed, sleep- or smoke-bemused young man of the afternoon seemed purely coincidental. He seemed to be laying himself out to entertain me, and we chatted pleasantly throughout the meal.

He knew a fair amount about the history of the place, and was very entertaining about what he called the Lady's 'cut-price court' of Dar Ibrahim, but I noticed that he said very little about Great-Aunt Harriet herself, and behind his reserve I thought I could sense respect and liking for her. Whatever else he mocked, and however much she might invite it, he did not mock his patroness, and I liked him the better for it. He was certainly interested in everything I could tell him about the family. The only thing I refrained deliberately from mentioning was Charles's presence in Syria, and the fact that he, too, was planning a visit. I intended to find a good moment to tell Great-Aunt Harriet myself that he wanted to see her, and so by-pass all the difficulties of persuasion at second-hand. Not that, if Charles was right, any persuasion would be needed. If she had agreed so readily to see me, whom she would hardly remember, then her favorite Charles was practically in already.

Halide brought coffee at nine o'clock, with the information that Nasirulla had gone back to the village, and that my room was ready.

She was not much like her brother in appearance, being younger and slimly built. She was a dark-skinned Arab, walnut rather than olive, with huge dark eyes, slim neck and delicate hands. Her dress was of bronze-green silk, a rich-looking material and a sophisticated color; her eyes were outlined with black in a way London would have recognized; and under the thin silk she wore, unless I was mistaken, a French—a very French—half-cup bra. Like a great many Arab women she wore her bank account on her wrists, which jingled with thin gold bracelets. No simple Arab maiden this one, and—if I was any judge—wasting no sweetness on the desert air. As she told Mr. Lethman (in English) about the room, she looked me over in her turn, and the message passed, clear from female to female in any language from Eskimo to Aborigine: "Not that he'd look at you, the mess you look in those trousers, but keep off my patch, will you, or I'll make you sorry."

Then, with the black eyes modestly lowered, she was saying to John Lethman, in her pretty, softly accented English: "When you have finished your coffee, the Lady would like to see you again."

She went out, leaving the door open. I watched her slim graceful figure vanish into the shadows of the arcade, beyond the small light cast by the lamp; but I thought she hadn't gone very far. In a moment or two I knew that I was right: where the waters of the lake reflected a faint grayness from the star-filled sky I saw a movement. She was waiting among the bushes by the water's edge, probably watching us through the open door.

John Lethman made no move to shut it. Since he was obviously anxious to finish his coffee and answer the summons, I hurried with mine, too.

Soon he got to his feet. "I'm afraid I'll have to leave you now, but I'll come back as soon as she lets me, and take you across. Now, are you sure you'll be all right here?"

"Why not? Don't worry about me, I'll be fine. I'll find a book."

"Of course, take anything you want. You can turn the lamp up quite easily if it's not bright enough; Halide'll show you how."

He turned his head sharply as a bell jangled somewhere deep in the buildings, sounding very loud in the hushed night. And from somewhere nearer, startled off by the violent and prolonged pealing of the bell, came the sudden furious baying of dogs. Big dogs, by the sound of them, inside the building, and quite near.

"What on earth's happened?" I demanded, startled.

"Just your great-aunt getting impatient. I'll have to go, I'm sorry. I'll be back to fetch you as soon as I can."

"But those dogs?"

"Oh, that's nothing, they always make that hellish noise when the bell goes. Don't worry about them, I'll shut them up before I come back for you."

"'Shut them up?' You mean they're loose about the place? They sound dangerous."

"Well, they're our watchdogs, they have to be. But they're only turned loose at night, and they can't get into the Seraglio if you keep the main door shut. You'll be quite safe." He flashed me a sudden smile. "Not to worry, it's not your night for being eaten alive—at least, not by the dogs."

He went. I heard the wooden gate shut behind him, and a few moments later his voice calling to the dogs. The baying stopped, and silence came back. In it I saw Halide, glimmering in the doorway in her green silk.

"If you will come this way, I will show you your room."

She had lit another lamp for me in the bedroom, and set it on a shelf near the bed.

This room was a twin of the other, but seemed bigger, as it contained no furniture but a narrow iron-framed bed, a flimsy-looking bamboo chair, and a hideous chest of drawers painted black, which held a rather beautiful lacquered looking glass and a battered old tin box with metal clasps labeled *S.S. Yangtse Maid*. The floor was bare and so were the window seats on the dais. The bed was made up with Irish linen, yellowish and not very well ironed, and the red honeycomb quilt covered what looked like the hardest and healthiest mattress in the world.

I didn't think somehow that this was Halide's patch; there would have to be a good deal more Eastern glamour about any affair of hers. Was that what John Lethman had meant by 'sleeping on the other side'?

However, it wasn't this thought which made me say: "I've turned Mr. Lethman out, haven't I? Where will he sleep?"

A shrug, not quite insolent. "There are plenty of rooms." When I didn't answer she glanced at me, perhaps a bit uneasily, and added with an attempt at civility dragged up with obvious difficulty: "He is with the Lady often at night. He'll maybe sleep in the morning."

"Oh, well, perhaps I haven't upset things as much as I thought." I smiled at her. "But I'm afraid it's giving you a lot of trouble, changing the rooms round twice."

She didn't make the usual disclaimer, but this may only have been because her English wasn't good enough for polite skirmishing.

"You have seen the bathroom?"

"Yes, thanks. Is the water drinkable?"

"Yes, but there was water on the supper tray. I will leave that. If there is nothing else—?"

"I don't think so, thank you. It all looks very nice, and I'm sure I shall be comfortable. Oh, would you show me how to turn the lamp higher, please? Mr. Lethman said I might look at his books while I was waiting."

Back in the other room she obliged, lifting the lamp down and setting it on the table among the books. I thanked her, and examined them while she began to stack the used dishes on the tray. She said nothing more, but I saw how she watched me, and it wasn't imagination to read a wary hostility into those quick sidelong glances. Irritated now, and wishing she would finish her job and go, I concentrated on selecting a book. As light reading for whiling away an hour or two they were hardly promising. An Arabic grammar, a few books on Syria and the Lebanon which I had already read during my convalescence in Charles's room, and a collection which might be said to represent John Lethman's homework—some volumes (also familiar to me) about the original Lady of the Lebanon: Joan Haslip and Roundell and Silk Buckingham and the three old volumes of Dr. Meryon's diary about his redoubtable patroness. I looked at the flyleaves. As I thought, they were Great-Aunt Harriet's own copies, presumably lent to her latter-day 'Dr. Meryon' for his close study . . . I skipped along the row. T. E. Lawrence's *Crusader Castles,* Guillaume's *Islam,* the Everyman *Koran,* Kinglake's *Eothen* . . . all Aunt Harriet's. No medical textbooks, which were presumably too bulky to carry on field work. The only things which carried his own name were—interestingly enough—Huxley's *The Mind Changers,* Frazer's *Golden Bough,* and a newish paperbound copy of Théophile Gautier's *Le Club des Hachachiens.* No novels except Dostoievsky's *The Brothers Karamazov* and Margery Allingham's *The Tiger in the Smoke.*

The last volume in the row was De Quincey. I turned the pages idly while Halide stacked the dishes rather loudly on the tray.

> The opium-eater loses none of his moral sensibilities, or aspirations: he wishes and longs, as earnestly as ever, to realise what he believes possible, and feels to be exacted by duty; but his intellectual apprehension of what is possible infinitely outruns his power, not of execution only, but even of power to attempt. He lies under the weight of incubus and nightmare . . .

Plus ça change, plus c'est la même chose. It was exactly what Hamid had said. I put the opium nightmare back as Halide lifted the tray and went with it to the door.

"I'll shut it for you," I said, moving to do so, but she paused in the doorway and turned.

"You are really the daughter of the Lady's brother's son?"

I worked it out while she stared at me across the dishes.

"Yes."

"Your father is also here in the Lebanon?"

"No."

"He is dead?"

"No," I said, surprised. "Why?"

"Then you travel alone?"

"Why not?"

She ignored this, too. She was intent on some line of her own which I couldn't follow, but which was obviously intensely important to her.

"You—you stay here long?"

Curiosity made me less than truthful. "As long as she'll let me," I said, watching her.

She said quickly: "She is not well. You will have to go in the morning."

I raised my brows. "That's for her to say, surely?" I added, with innocence concealing a flicker of malice: "But of course in a place this size I needn't be in her way. Mr. Lethman asked me to stay as long as I liked."

The black eyes flared, whether in alarm or anger it was impossible to say. "But that is not possible! He—"

Jangling, imperative, and sounding very bad-tempered, Great-Aunt Harriet's bell shattered the silence once more. Further away, but still obviously at large, the watchdogs bayed. The girl started, so violently that the things on the tray clashed and rattled.

"Saved by the bell," I said. "You were saying?"

"No. No. I must go!" Then, almost fiercely, as I made a move to follow and open the main gate for her: "Leave it! I can manage, I can manage!"

The gate shut behind her. I stared thoughtfully after her. Saved by the bell, indeed. I thought I could add the score. Whether or not John Lethman had a stake in Great-Aunt Harriet, I was sure that Halide had a stake in John Lethman. And I wasn't sure how that added up for Great-Aunt Harriet. I went back to the bookshelf.

It would be nice to be able to record that I was the kind of person who would pick up the Dostoievsky or the Huxley or even *The Golden Bough* and curl up with it for a glorious evening's read. But when eventually Mr. Lethman came for me as he had promised, he found me a few chapters into *The Tiger in the Smoke,* and half wishing I had chosen something less exciting for a night in the deserted wing of a ruined palace.

He was armed, not with an oil lamp, but with an enormous and very powerful electric torch.

"Ready?" he asked.

He led me back to the courtyard where Hamid and I had waited, but there we turned right, away from the main gate, the way I had seen him go to Great-Aunt Harriet. The place was vast, far bigger even than I had imagined. We seemed to walk forever up corridors, round corners, up steps, down steps, and across at least two more small courts, in the first of which a trickle of water showed that all the wells had not dried. As we traversed the second I heard, from behind a closed door, a scratching sound followed by a deep whining yelp that made me jump.

"It's all right, I told you I'd shut them up." He shone the torch momentarily toward the door, and in the gap at its foot I saw the gleam of a dog's damp nose snuffling at the air. "Sofi! Star! Quiet there! Watch your step, Miss Mansel, the threshold's broken here. This is the Prince's Garden."

I don't know quite what I had expected, something at least as grand as the Seraglio Garden, but in fact the Prince's Garden was very small. The air was heavy with the scent of jasmine, and I caught a glimpse in the torchlight of a low wall which might contain a pool, but the garden seemed to be little more than an oblong yard with one or two troughs of flowers and some small symmetrical trees in tubs. John Lethman shone the torch straight down on the cracked slabs of the footway, but he could have saved himself the trouble, for, from an open doorway about halfway along the side of the garden, light was spilling out between two small tubbed trees. It was only the dim orange light from a lamp like the one in my own room, but in the heavy darkness it seemed very bright.

He paused in the doorway to stand aside for me. His voice sounded different all at once, tight, wary, deferential.

"I've brought Miss Mansel, Lady Harriet."
I went past him into the room.

5

There came
A tongue of light, a fit of flame;
And Christabel saw the lady's eye,
And nothing else saw she thereby . . .

—S. T. COLERIDGE: *Christabel*

THE PRINCE'S divan was enormous, and in it prevailed what I can only call a luxurious squalor. The floor was of colored marble strewn here and there with Persian rugs, all very dirty; the walls were patterned with intricate mosaics, each panel framing in fretted stone a recess which must once have held a statue or lamp, but which was now empty except for an accumulation of rubbish—cartons, papers, books, medicine bottles, candle stubs. In the center of the floor the fountain had been roughly boarded over and now did duty as a table where stood a large tray of grayish silver holding a pile of plates and the remains of a recent meal. Beside this, on the floor, was an empty bowl labeled DOG. A chest of drawers in shiny mahogany, covered with more bottles and pillboxes, stood against the wall. One or two shabby kitchen chairs and a big thronelike affair in red Chinese lacquer completed the furniture of the lower end of the room. Dust lay everywhere.

A wide archway of delicately chiseled stone framing three shallow steps divided the lower from the upper section of the divan. Set right back in one corner of the upper room or dais was a huge bed, which at one time must have been a luxurious affair with legs shaped like dragons' claws, a high carved headboard, and hanging from the ceiling above it some sort of gilt device resembling a bird, which was supposed to have held bed drapes in its talons. Now one wing of the bird was broken, the gilt was flaked and dirty, and from the claws hung only a couple of rubbed velvet curtains which could have been any shade from dark red to black, and which sagged in big loops down on either side of the bedhead, almost concealing with their heavy swags of shadow the figure which reclined there in a welter of rugs and blankets.

The light which had flowed so generously out on the flagway of the garden hardly penetrated into the upper corners of the room. It came from an old-fashioned oil lamp standing among the supper dishes, and as I passed it, approaching the bed, my shadow seemed to leap monstrously ahead of me, then teeter up the steps of the dais to add another layer of darkness to the grotesque obscurity in the corner.

For grotesque it certainly was. I had expected to find Great-Aunt Harriet very different from a child's far-back recollections of her, but not quite so outlandish as this. As I had told John Lethman, I had retained merely a dim memory of a tallish hook-nosed woman with graying hair and snapping black eyes who argued fiercely with my father, bullied my mother over the garden, and had a habit of bestowing sudden and exotic gifts on me and Charles, in the intervals of ignoring us completely. Even had she been dressed as she was fifteen years before, I should not have known her. John Lethman had warned me that she would have shrunk, and this was so; and though I thought I would have recognized the jutting nose and black eyes which peered at me from the shadows of the bed curtains, nothing—not even Lethman's warnings—had prepared me for the sheer outlandishness of the figure which sat there like a Buddha cocooned in colored silks and gesturing with one large pale hand for me to come nearer.

If I had not known who it was, I should have taken her for some fantastically robed Eastern male. She was wearing some kind of bedgown of natural silk, and over this a loose coat in scarlet velvet with gold facings, and over this again an enormous cashmere shawl; but these draperies—in spite of the soft and even luxurious materials—had a distinctly masculine air. Her skin had a sallow pallor and her lips were bloodless and sunken, but the black eyes and well-marked brows gave life to the fullish, oval face, and showed none of the fading signs of old age. She had daubed powder lavishly and carelessly, and some of it had spilled over the scarlet velvet. Above this curiously epicene face she had twined a towering turban of white, which, slipping a little to one side, exposed what for a shocked moment I took to be a bald skull; then I realized that she must have shaved her head. This, if she habitually wore the thick turban, was only to be expected, but it was somehow the final touch of grotesqueness.

One thing I would have known her by; the ring on her left hand. This was unequivocally as big and as bright as I remembered from my childhood. I remembered, too, how impressed Charles and I had been by the way my mother and father spoke of the ring. It was a cabochon-cut Burma ruby, the size of a thumbnail, and had even in those days been immensely valuable. It had been the gift of some princeling in Baghdad, and she wore it always on her big, capable and rather mannish hands. The ruby flashed in the lamplight as, wheezing a little, she beckoned me closer.

I didn't know whether I would be expected to kiss her. The idea was somehow repellent, but another glitter from the ruby, indicating a stool near the foot of the bed, halted me thankfully.

"Hullo, Aunt Harriet, how are you?"

"Well, Christy?" The voice, little more than a whisper, had a strained, asthmatic breathiness, but the black eyes were live enough, and curious. "Sit down and let me look at you. H-m. Yes. You always were a pretty little thing. Quite a beauty now, aren't you? Not married yet?"

"No."

"Then it's high time you were."

"Have a heart, I'm only twenty-two!"

"Is that all? One forgets. John tells me I forget things all the time. I'd forgotten you, did he tell you that?"

"He said it was quite likely."

"He would. He's always trying to make out that I'm getting senile." She darted a look at John Lethman, who had followed me up the steps and was standing at the foot of the bed. He watched her steadily, and I thought uneasily. The sharp gaze came back to me. "And if I did forget you, it'd be hardly surprising. How long since I saw you?"

"Fifteen years."

"Hm. Yes. It must be. Well, now I come to look at you I suppose I would have known you. You've a look of your father. How is he?"

"Oh, he's fine, thank you."

"Sends his dear love, I suppose?"

The tone, still sharp, was wantonly provocative. I regarded her calmly.

"If he knew I was here, I'm sure he'd send his regards."

"Hm." She sat back abruptly in her corner against the pile of pillows, retreating into her cocoon of draperies with the little settling motions of a broody hen spreading herself down onto eggs. I thought the monosyllable was not unappreciative. "And the rest of 'em?"

"All well. They'll be terribly pleased when they hear I've managed to see you, and found you well."

"No doubt." No one could have called the dry whisper senile. "An attentive family the Mansels, wouldn't you say? Well?" And again, when I didn't speak: "Well, girl?"

I sat up straighter on my stool. It was very uncomfortable. "I don't know what you want me to say, Aunt Harriet. If you think we should have come to see you before, you could always have asked us, couldn't you? As it is, you know quite well you've been sending us all to the devil, solo and chorus, about twice a year for fifteen years. And if you'll forgive my saying so, I wasn't exactly welcomed with open arms today!" I added crisply: "In any case, you're a Mansel, too. You can't tell me my people don't write to you just as often as you write to them, even if it's only to thank you for the latest edition of your Will!"

The black eyes glittered. "My Will? Ha! So that's it! Come to collect, have you?"

"Well, I'd have a job, since you're still alive, wouldn't I?" I grinned at her. "And it's a heck of a long way to come for sixpence . . . But if you like you can give me my sixpence here and now, and I won't bother you again."

I couldn't see her expression, just the eyes, shadowed under brows and turban, watching me from the pillows. I caught a glance from John Lethman, half amused, I thought, and half apprehensive, as she stirred suddenly, plucking at the coverings. "I could have died out here for all they'd have cared. Any of them."

"Look—" I said, then stopped. Charles had implied that she liked to be outfaced, and certainly up to now I had had the impression that she was trying to needle me. But the Great-Aunt Harriet that I had remembered wouldn't have talked like that, not even to provoke a retort. Fifteen years seems a lifetime to the young: perhaps at the other end it's a lifetime, too. I ought to be feeling, not discomfort and irritation, but compassion.

I said quickly: "Aunt Harriet, look, please don't talk like that! You must know quite well that if there was anything you wanted—anything you needed—you've only got to let Daddy know, or Uncle Chas, or any of us! My family's been in America for four years, you know that, and I suppose we're a bit out of touch, but in any case it was always Uncle Chas you wrote to, and I understood from him—I mean, I thought you'd always made it so very clear that you wanted to stay out here, live on your own terms . . ." I made a vague, wide gesture that took in the neglected room and beyond it the dark confines of the sleeping palace. "You must surely know that if there was anything—if you were ill—if you really did want someone to come here, or needed help of some kind—"

Deep in its shadowed corner the bundle on the bed was so still that I faltered. The lamp had been burning low, but now some trick of the draft or unevenness of the wick sent up a tongue of light, and I saw the quick glitter of her eyes.

It wasn't pathos at all. The instinct that was forbidding me to feel compassion had been right.

"Aunt H!" I said roundly. "Are you sending me up? I mean, you're just teasing, aren't you? You must know you're talking nonsense!"

"Hm. Nonsense, is it? Meaning that I have got a devoted family?"

"Well, heavens, you know what families are! I don't suppose ours is any different from any other! You must know quite well you could cut us all off with sixpence till you're blue in the face, but we're still your family!"

"Hear that, John?"

He was looking, I thought, acutely uncomfortable. He opened his mouth to say something, but I cut across it:

"You know quite well what I mean! Just that if you needed anything, or anything happened to you—well, London to Beirut only takes six hours, and someone would be here and raising the place before you even knew you wanted them. Daddy always says that's what a family is, it's just collective insurance; as long as you're alive and well it just goes ticking along and takes no notice, but let anything go wrong, and the company moves in. I mean, look at my Uncle Chas when his cousin Henry died! Daddy says they never gave it a second thought, just took it for granted. Heavens, I do what I like, and nobody stops me going where I want to, but I know quite well that if I was in the least spot of trouble and got on the phone to Daddy, he'd be here in three seconds!" I looked up at John Lethman, hesitated, then added decisively: "And don't start teasing Mr. Lethman as well. It doesn't matter what you say to me, but I might as well make something else clear here and now, even if I may be speaking out of turn . . . Everybody'll be as pleased as Punch that he's here with you, so you'd better be nice to him, because the longer he stays the better! For goodness' sake, we're not neglecting you—we're just letting you get on with it the way you want to, and you seem to be making a pretty good job of it, if you ask me!"

She was laughing openly now, the cocoon heaving to the wheezing breaths. The big hand went up, and the ruby flashed. "All right, child, all right, I was teasing you! A fighter, aren't you? I always did like a fighter. No, I don't make it easy for people to get in to see me; I've had too much trouble that way, and say what you like, I'm getting old. You were very insistent, weren't you? If you're so full of this 'live and let live' of yours, why did you come?"

I grinned. "You'd be annoyed if I said it was family feeling. Call it curiosity."

"What had you heard to make you so curious?"

"What had I heard? You must be joking! I suppose you're so used to living in a place like this and hedging yourself with legends like a—well, like a—"

"Superannuated Sleeping Beauty?"

I laughed. "Bang on! I mean, yes, if you like to put it that way! But seriously, you're a celebrity, you know that! Everybody talks about you. You're one of the sights of the Lebanon. Even if I'd been no relation I'd have been told all about you and urged to come and look at Dar Ibrahim; so when I realized I had a copper-bottomed excuse to call to see you, and even bulldoze my way into the palace—well, boiling oil might have stopped me, but nothing much short of that."

"Make a note of that, John; boiling oil is what we need. Hm, you're a Mansel to your claw tips, aren't you? So everybody talks about me, do they? Who's 'everybody'?"

"Oh, this was just someone in the hotel in Beirut. I was planning a trip—"

"Hotel? Who were you chattering about me to in a hotel in Beirut?" She made it sound as if it were a brothel in Cairo.

"Not exactly chattering. It was the desk clerk, as it happens. I was planning a trip up to the Adonis Source at Afka, and he told me I'd be passing near Dar Ibrahim, and—"

"Which hotel?"

"The Phoenicia."

"It's new since you were in Beirut," put in John Lethman. It was the first time he had spoken. He still seemed ill at ease. "It's the big one I told you about, on the harbor."

"The what? Phoenicia? All right, go on, what were they saying about me in this hotel?"

"Nothing much, really," I said. "The desk clerk didn't know I was a relation of yours, he was just telling me this was an interesting place, and he said I might as well get my driver to come back by Sal'q and stop so that I could get a view of the palace. Then I told him I knew your family—I still didn't tell him who I was—and asked how you were and if he'd heard anything about you."

"And what did he tell you?"

"Only that as far as he knew you were perfectly all right, but that you hadn't been outside the palace for quite a time, and he told me you'd been ill a short while back, and had a doctor from Beirut—"

"He knew that?"

"Well, heavens, it was probably in all the papers! You're one of the local legends, after all! Didn't Mr. Lethman tell you, I rang the doctor's house up to try to get news of you—"

"Yes, yes, yes, he told me. A lot of use that would have been. The man was a fool. A good thing he's gone, a very good thing . . . Much better now, much better." The shawl had slipped; she pulled at it with a sort of flouncing irritation, suddenly pettish, and I heard her muttering to herself what sounded like "Ringing up about me," and "Chattering about me in hotels," in a whisper which was all at once not dry and sharp at all, but vague and blurred. Her head shook, so that the turban was dislodged even further, exposing a little more of that shaved scalp.

I looked away, repelled, and trying not to show it. But wherever I looked was a reminder of a slovenly eccentricity; even the clutter of medicine bottles on the chest was dusty, and dust gritted under my shoes as I shifted my feet on the floor. The room, big as it was, felt stuffy, and my skin prickled. I found myself suddenly longing to escape into fresh air.

"Christy . . . Christy . . ." The wheezing mutter jerked my attention back to her. "Stupid name for a girl. What's it short for?"

"Christabel. It was the nearest they could get to Christopher."

"Oh." She plucked at the covers again. I got the sharp impression that the eyes watching me from the shadows were by no means forgetful; that this was a game she played when it suited her. The impression wasn't pleasant. "What were we talking about?"

I pulled myself together. "The doctor. Dr. Grafton."

"I was not ill; the man was a fool. There's nothing wrong with my chest, nothing at all . . . In any case, he's left the Lebanon. Wasn't there some chatter about him, too, John? Some scandal? Didn't he go back to London?"

"I believe so," said Lethman.

I said: "They told me so when I rang up. They didn't say anything else about him."

"Hm," she said, and all the dry malice was back in her voice. "Probably put his plate up in Wimpole Street by now and making a fortune."

"I never heard any scandal, but it's true he's gone. They say his practice went to a very good man." John Lethman gave me a quick, speaking look, and then leaned forward. "Now don't you think you should have a rest, Lady Harriet? It's time for your tablets, so if you'll allow me, I'll ring for Halide, and see Miss Mansel back myself—"

"No," said Great-Aunt Harriet uncompromisingly.

"But, Lady Harriet—"

"I tell you, boy, stop fussing. I won't take the tablets yet, they make me sleepy. You know I don't like taking them. I'm not tired at all, and I'm enjoying the gel's visit. Stay where you are, child, and talk to me. Entertain me. Tell me where you've been and what you've been doing. How long have you been in Beirut?"

"Only since Friday evening. Actually, I came with a package tour . . ."

I started to tell her about the trip, making it as amusing as I could. I wouldn't be sorry when the interview was over, but the old lady seemed back on the beam now, and I had no intention of letting John Lethman, on whatever excuse, winkle me out of the presence chamber until I had, so to speak, introduced Charles. He wouldn't want to miss this bizarre setup, and he wouldn't be likely to be put off by what I had to tell him. I wondered in passing why she hadn't spoken of him herself, but I would soon discover that, and it was up to my cousin to fight his own way in past the opposition if he wished to.

So I kept clear of his name, and talked away about Petra and Palmyra and Jerash, while Great-Aunt Harriet listened and commented, apparently well entertained, and John Lethman waited in silence, fidgeting nervily with the bedcurtains, and with his head turning from one to the other of us like someone at a Wimbledon final.

I was in the middle of describing Palmyra when she startled me suddenly by reaching out a hand and yanking at a bellpull which hung among the curtains of the bed. The building echoed to the familiar clanging peal, and then to the noise of the baying hounds.

I stopped talking, but she said almost snappily: "Go on. At least you can talk. Did you visit the hillside tombs?"

"Heavens, yes, there was a conducted tour, we had to. I suppose that's not the right thing to say to an archaeologist, but one tomb looks very like another to me, I'm afraid."

"True enough. What happened to the party?"

"They went back to London on Saturday morning."

"So you're on your own now? Is that suitable?"

I laughed. "Why not? I can look after myself. And as a matter of fact—"

"Not much doubt of that. Where's that stupid girl?"

She snapped it suddenly at John Lethman, who jumped. "Halide? She can't be far away. If it's your pills, I can—"

"Not my pills. I told you I'll not take them yet. I want my pipe."

"But, Lady Harriet—"

"Ah, there you are! Where the devil were you?"

Halide came quickly across the lower part of the room. She could not have been far away when the bell rang, but she breathed fast and shallow as if she had been running. Her face was sallow, and she looked scared. She didn't spare me a glance as she crossed the floor and mounted the steps toward the bed.

"You rang?"

"Of course I rang," said Great-Aunt Harriet irritably. "I want my pipe."

Halide looked uncertainly from her to John Lethman and back again, and the old woman made one of those flouncing impatient movements in the bed and barked: "Well? Well?"

"Get it for her, please," said Lethman.

The girl threw another scared glance at the bed, and scurried down the steps to the dressing chest. I looked after her with a touch of surprise. Nothing so far had led me to think that she would be easily frightened, and it wasn't easy to see how my great-aunt could frighten her, short of the methods used by Lady Hester Stanhope, who kept a whip and club by her bed to use on her slaves, and who when service was poor had treated them all—her doctor included—to a purge she called the Black Draught, forcibly administered. I looked at the 'Lady Harriet.' She was sitting hunched like some peculiar Eastern jinnee in her welter of silks and blankets, and might, I thought, inspire nervousness, but not fear. But then something caught my eye on the wall above the bed. There were two sets of pegs in the wall, half hidden by the bed-curtains, and across one of these lay a stick, and across the other a rifle. I blinked at these in disbelief. There were surely, in the mid-twentieth century, limits to what could be done even here . . . ?

I really must get out of here soon. I must be more tired than I had thought. Or perhaps the strange food at supper . . . ? As I pulled myself together to go on with my story, I heard Great-Aunt Harriet saying, perfectly pleasantly: "Just a small pipe, my dear. And I'll have the amber mouthpiece."

The girl, hurrying with clumsy fingers, pulled open a drawer and took out a wooden box which appeared to hold tobacco and mouthpiece. These she brought to the bed, and fitted the mouthpiece to the tube of the apparatus that the Arabs called the nargileh, or hubble-bubble pipe. As she passed out of Great-Aunt Harriet's view behind the bedcurtains I saw her throw a quick inquiring glance at John Lethman, and receive a rather irritable nod. This, then, was the cause of her nervousness; she was in the familiar, awkward position of the servant being bidden by one master to do what she knew the other would disapprove.

Lethman said in my ear: "I can't offer you a cigarette, I'm afraid, she won't allow anyone else to smoke in here. In any case she only approves of herbal tobacco. I'm afraid it smells vile."

"It doesn't matter, I don't want one."

"What are you muttering about?" asked Great-Aunt Harriet sharply, peering. "All right, Halide, it's going very well." Then, to me: "Well, go on, entertain me. What did you do in Damascus? Tramped round the Great Mosque, I suppose, like a lot of gapeseeds."

"Exactly like gapeseeds, Aunt Harriet."

"Are you laughing at me, gel?"

"Well, it's such a gorgeous word. What are they?"

"God knows. Probably aren't any more. The world isn't what it used to be." She sucked at the pipe. "Did you like Damascus?"

"So-so. I didn't have enough time to myself. But something rather nice happened there, I ran into Charles."

"Charles?" Her voice was sharp, and I thought I saw Halide and John

Lethman look at one another again, quickly. "Here?" asked Great-Aunt Harriet. "What's this, a family convention? What the devil's my nephew Charles doing in Damascus?"

"Oh, not Uncle Chas," I said quickly, "I meant Charles, my cousin—my 'twin.' He's on holiday over here, too. He was to have come up with me to see you, but he probably won't be in Lebanon till tomorrow, and I'm afraid I stole a march on him. As a matter of fact it was he who sent me to see you in the first place; he's terribly keen to come himself, and I'd probably never have dared to barge in like this if he hadn't put me up to it."

There was silence. The pipe bubbled, rather sickeningly, and she blinked at me through the smoke. The air was acrid, and stuffier than ever, and I felt waves of heat coursing over my skin. I pulled myself upright on my stool.

"You—you do remember Charles, Aunt Harriet? You'll not have forgotten him even if you *had* forgotten me—he was always your favorite."

"Of course I haven't forgotten him. How could I? A handsome boy. I always liked handsome boys."

I smiled. "I used to be jealous, let me tell you! D'you remember that time— the last time I saw you—when you came to stay, and you brought the parrot and all the dogs, and you gave me an ivory fan, and you gave Charles the incense burner and the joss-sticks, and he set the summerhouse on fire, and Daddy was so furious he said he was going to send him home, only you said if he went you'd go too because the rest of the family were as dull as ditchwater, and anything Charles did shone like a bad deed in an insipid world? I only remember that because it's a sort of family quotation now."

"Yes, I remember. The way time goes. Sometimes fast, sometimes slow . . . and the things one remembers . . . and the things one forgets. A handsome boy . . . yes, yes." She smoked for a while in silence, nodding as if to herself, then relinquished the mouthpiece of the pipe to Halide without looking at her. The black eyes lifted again and fixed on me. "You're like him."

"I suppose I am. Not really anymore, now we're both grown up . . . though I suppose you remember him fairly recently. Something must persist. We've the same coloring."

"Very like him." It was as if she hadn't heard me. She was still nodding to herself, the black eyes veiled and absent, her hands unsteady with her shawl.

"Lady Harriet," said John Lethman, abruptly. "I really must insist you take your tablets now, and rest for a little. Miss Mansel—"

"Of course," I said, getting to my feet, "if Great-Aunt Harriet will tell me what I'm to say to Charles?"

"You may give him my regards." The whisper was harsh as the rustle of dry leaves.

"But—" I regarded her a little blankly. "Don't you want to see him? He'll be in Beirut at the Phoenicia with me, probably tomorrow. May he come up to see you? If it'd be less bother, he could come up tomorrow evening after dinner and wait till you're ready to receive him? He has his own car; he wouldn't need to stay, like me. I'd love to come with him myself and see you again, but if two people are too many—"

"No."

"You mean we can both come? Oh, that's marvelous! Then—"

"I mean I won't receive him. No. I have received you, and it's been a pleasure, but this is enough. You may take what news you have of me to my nephews Charles and Christopher, and be satisfied with that."

As I opened my mouth she lifted her hand and added, more kindly: "All this must be strange to you, but I'm an old woman and I have chosen my way of life, and it seems to me that the only good thing that age brings is the right to be as arbitrary as one wants, and to live as one wishes as long as one can afford it. However outlandish and uncomfortable you may think it is here, it suits me, and you can tell them at home that I'm perfectly well, and quite content with my way of life and the privacy I bought when I bought these high walls and that dumb fool at the gate and what service Halide chooses to offer. So we'll have no more protestations."

"But he'll be desperately disappointed! And what's more, he'll be furious with me because I've taken his turn with you, so to speak. You were rather his favorite relative, you know. And as a matter of fact, I think it was rather important for him to see you. I don't know whether you knew, but there's a plan under way for opening a branch of the bank in Beirut, and Charles'll probably work there—at least for a time—so while he's out here now I know he wants to make all the contacts—"

"No."

"Aunt Harriet—"

"I have spoken," she said, rather splendidly, with a flashing gesture of the ruby which was meant to obliterate me, and did.

I gave up. "All right, I'll tell him. He'll be glad I found you so well. Is there anything you'd like us to send you from England? Any books, for instance?"

"I can get all I want, thank you, child. Now I'm tired and you may go. Take my messages to your people, but don't think I want a spate of letters, because I don't. I shan't answer 'em. When I'm dead John will let you know. No, you needn't kiss me. You're a pretty child and I've enjoyed your visit, so now go."

"I've enjoyed it too. Thank you for letting me come. Good night, Aunt Harriet."

"Good night. John, you'll come straight back here when you've seen her to her room. Halide! Is that stupid girl going to take all night with those pills? Oh, there you are. Now don't forget what I've said, John, come straight back here."

"Of course," agreed Mr. Lethman, sounding relieved. He already had me halfway toward the door.

For a final parting, it had the strange note of casualness which seemed exactly right. I paused for a moment in the doorway and glanced back. Halide was once more at the dressing chest, shaking something from a small bottle into her hand. Beyond her, behind the orange glow of the lamp, the bed was a towering obscurity. As she turned to mount the steps once more, something moved in the black shadows at the foot of the bed, something small and gray and quick moving. For one flesh-creeping moment I thought there were rats even in the bedroom, but then I saw the creature leap on the bed, and the large pale hand came from behnd the curtain and stroked it. A half-grown cat.

Half wild as well. As Halide sat down on the edge of the bed the cat leaped aside and vanished. The girl, shimmering in her green silk, leaned foward toward the hidden figure of the old woman. She was offering her water in a tall, chased goblet. The scene looked like something remote and improbable, on a badly lighted stage. It could have nothing to do with me and Charles and daylight.

I turned and hurried out in the wake of John Lethman's torch.

The beam flicked upward for a moment to light my face. "What is it? Are you cold?"

"No. It's nothing." I took a deep breath. "It's wonderful to get out into the air. You were right about that tobacco, it's a bit much."

"Was that all it was? I got the impression that the interview upset you."

"In a way, I suppose," I admitted. "I must say I found it all a bit odd, and she wasn't exactly easy to talk to."

"In what way?"

"Well, heavens—! Oh, but I suppose you're used to it . . . ! I meant inconsistent, and forgetful, and the way she tried to needle me at the beginning. And—well, she *looks* so outlandish, and then that pipe . . . ! I'm afraid I was a bit tactless once or twice, but I'd always heard she hadn't much time for yes-men, and I thought it was probably best to tell the truth, flat out. I thought I'd upset her, the time she started muttering at me, but I hadn't, had I?"

"It takes more than that. Take it from me, she meant it when she said she was enjoying the conversation."

He was, I thought, a bit curt. But any sour reflections I might have had about this were shaken as he went on: "I wish you'd told me earlier about this cousin Charles. I might have managed to persuade her."

"Yes, it was silly of me. I think I'd some idea of finding out first how the land lay. Is she likely to change her mind?"

"Heaven knows. Frankly, I've no idea. Once she's made a decision it's pretty hard to shift her. I sometimes feel she's obstinate just for the hell of it, if you know what I mean. I don't know why she suddenly stuck her toes in like that."

"Neither do I. She adored him, you know—he was the only one of us she'd any use for." I added, ruefully: "Well, he's going to be furious with me for queering his pitch, which is what I seem to have done, goodness knows how! He's really pretty keen to see her—and not just out of curiosity like me. I don't know what he'll say. She must have talked of him to you, surely?"

"Oh, yes. If I'd only known he was here . . . Look out, mind that step. How long's he going to be in the Lebanon?"

"I've no idea."

"Well, if he has time to spare, tell him to leave it for a few days, will you, at least till after mid-week. I'll do what I can, and get in touch with you at the Phoenicia."

It seemed there wasn't much else I could do except trust to his good offices.

"Thank you," I said, "I'll tell him. When she's had time to think it over, I'm sure she'll change her mind."

"Stranger things have happened," said John Lethman, rather shortly.

6

Thy promises are like Adonis' gardens,
That one day bloom'd and fruitful were the next.

—SHAKESPEARE: *1 Henry VI*

IN THE night it rained.

I had got back to my room at some time between half-past one and two in the morning. The night had been dry then, very black and perfectly still, with nothing to suggest a storm to follow. Mr. Lethman saw me as far as my bedroom door, where I had left the oil lamp lit, said good night, and withdrew. I carried my lamp along to the hammam, washed as well as I could in a trickle of cold water, and then went back to my room again. There was no key, but I saw a heavy wooden bar on the inside of the door. I dropped this carefully into its sockets. Then I took off my outer clothing, turned my lamp down rather inexpertly and blew out the wicks, and climbed into bed.

Even though the hour was late, and I was tired, I lay awake for some little time turning the recent scene over and over in my head. I imagined myself telling Charles, telling my mother and father, and somehow none of the words seemed to fit or be right. "She seemed odd, she seemed ill, she's getting old, she's going to town a bit on this recluse thing—" none of these phrases seemed to fit the decidedly off-beat tone of the interview. And if she really was going to refuse to see Charles . . .

Well, that was Charles's problem, not mine. I slept.

I'm not sure whether it was the flash of lightning or the almost simultaneous crack of thunder that woke me, but as I stirred in bed and opened my eyes the sound of rain seemed to obliterate all else. I have never heard such rain. There was no wind with it, only the cracking of thunder and the vivid white rents in the black sky. I sat up in bed to watch. The window arches flickered dramatically against the storm outside, and the portcullis squares of the grille stamped themselves on the room over and over again with their violently angled perspectives of black and white. Through the window that I had opened the scents of flowers came almost storming in, vividly wakened by the rain. With the scents came, more palpably, a good deal of the rain itself, hitting the sill and splashing on the floor in great hammering drops.

Reluctantly, I got out of bed and padded in my bare feet across the chilly floor to shut the casement. Even while I groped in momentary darkness for the catch, my arm was soaked almost to the shoulder by the slashing downpour. I slammed the casement shut, and while I fought to fix the stiff and squeaking catch I heard, from the direction of the main gate, the sudden keening howl of a big dog.

It is one of the weirdest of all sounds, bringing with it, I suppose, race memories of wolves and jackals and such, overlaid by countless legends of death and grief. The first hound's voice rose in a throbbing wail, to be joined by the long tremolo of the other. The watchdogs, of course, upset by the storm; but I felt my hand instinctively clench stiff on the soaked iron of the window catch, while I listened with cold prickles running over my skin. Then I jammed the thing shut and reached for my towel to rub my arm dry.

No wonder a howling dog was supposed to foretell a death . . . As I scrubbed at my wet arm and shoulder I thought of the legend Charles had reminded me of, 'gabble ratchet,' the Gabriel Hounds, Death's pack hunting through the sky . . . Certainly all hell seemed to be loose up there tonight, full cry. In the old days anyone in the palace might well have believed the hounds of the storm to be crying death.

In the old days. And you'd have been superstitious then, and believed in that kind of thing. Whereas now . . . oh, nonsense, there was nothing wrong . . .

I flung the towel down and padded back to bed.

About five seconds later I discovered something a good deal more disturbing than any Gabriel Hounds. The roof was leaking. Moreover, it was leaking in the corner right above my bed.

I discovered this—it being dark, in the simplest possible way, by getting back into bed straight into the middle of a soaking patch, and by receiving at the same moment a large gout of water squarely on the back of my neck. It was followed almost immediately by another, and another . . .

I hurled myself back onto the cold marble, and started a frantic hunt for my shoes. Perversely, the lightning had stopped almost as suddenly as it had begun, and it was now quite dark. I found one shoe eventually, and stumbled about looking for the other, but couldn't find it. I would have to light the lamp. This, of course, meant finding my handbag, and the matches I hoped I was carrying—and by the time I had done this another pint or so of water would have emptied itself into my bed. I suppose it would have been sensible to drag the bed straight away from the danger point before starting the hunt for my effects, but from what I had seen of the palace appointments, I wasn't prepared to manhandle any of their furniture about the floors in the dark. So I hopped about, blasphemously groping, until I had found my matches, and then it took me another five minutes or so to manage the lighting of the oil lamp.

Once the room was lit it was the work of moments to find my other shoe and throw something on over my near-nakedness. Then I recklessly dragged the bed away from the wall. It came across the cracked marble with a dot-and-carry-one screech of broken castors. With it out of the way, the water dripped steadily onto the floor. It was only after some moments that I realized how loud the dripping was. The rain had stopped.

I went back to the window. As suddenly as if a tap had been turned off the rain had ceased. Already I could see stars. I pulled open the casement to find that in the wake of the storm had come a small erratic breeze, which was clearing the clouds and whispering among the trees of the gorge. After the chill of the soaking storm the breeze was warm, so I left the casement wide. Then I turned back to deal with my problem.

Most of the bedcovers were still dry, having been pushed back out of the way when I got out of bed myself. I heaved these off the bed, put them gingerly on the dry part of the window seat, then, more gingerly still, turned the mattress. It was of thick horsehair, with a fresh cover of unbleached cotton, and I could only hope that it would last me the rest of the night before the wet soaked up through it. I discarded the sodden sheet, piled the dry bedcovers back on, put out the lamp and lay down, clothes and all, to pass what remained of the night.

But not yet in sleep. The steady dripping just beside me on the marble floor seemed as loud as a drum beat. I stood it for perhaps ten minutes, then realized I would get no sleep until I stopped it. So once more I rolled out of bed, groped for and found the crumpled and soaking sheet, and put it down under the drips. In the blessed quiet that followed, another sound from outside caught my ear, and I straightened up and stood listening.

No hounds of Death now; they were quiet. This was a bird singing in the garden, full and loud and echoing from the water and the enclosing walls. Another joined it. And then a third, waterfalls of song rinsing the clear air.

I unbarred the door and padded out across the arcade.

The surface of the lake was faintly shining, lighter than the dim starlight it reflected. Spatters of rain shook intermittently from the bushes as the breeze wandered. The nightingales' song filled the garden, welling out of the tangle of soaked and glittering creepers.

A pair of white pigeons rocketed out from their roost in the western arcade and vanished with a clap of wings over my head. Something—someone—moved in the darkness beneath the arches. A man, walking along under the arcade. He was moving very softly, and above the noise of the birds and the rustle of the leaves I couldn't hear him, but this was no white-robed Arab. It must be John Lethman. Probably he'd come along to see how I'd made out in the storm.

I waited a few moments longer, but he didn't come, and I saw nothing more. The garden, but for the song of the nightingales, was quiet and still.

I shivered suddenly. Five minutes' *Nachtmusik* was more than enough. I padded back into my room, crossly shut my door against the nightingales, and rolled back onto the bed.

I woke to blazing sunlight and a tapping on the door.

It was Halide with my breakfast, a plate of thin unleavened bread, some cream cheese, the inevitable apricot jam, and a big pot of coffee. The girl looked tired, and still eyed me sideways with that sulky glance, but made no comment on the disorder of the room, the sodden sheet on the floor, or even the bed shifted four feet out from the wall. When I thanked her for the tray and said something about the wild night, she only nodded sullenly and went out.

But everything else was cheerful this morning, even the hammam, with sunlight pouring down through the blue and amber glass bells in the ceiling, and lighting the alabaster basins and pale marble walls in a swimming subaqueous light. The water trickled—colder than ever—out of a dolphin's mouth into a silver shell. I rinsed my face and hands, went back to my room and dressed, then carried the tray out into the blazing sunshine at the edge of the pool.

The golden heat, the high blue sky, made it difficult to remember last night's storm of pouring rain, but here and there on the path where the flagstones had sunk, or in the wells dug round the tree roots to catch the rain, the water still stood glittering, inches deep. The weeds between the stones looked already half as long again, the flowers brighter, the bushes glossy and refreshed. Even the water of the pool looked clearer, and beside it a peacock stood studying his reflection, with his tail fully spread, looking entirely artificial, like something from a picture book, or a jeweled bird by Fabergé. Some other bird, small and golden, flirted over a rose laurel. The little kiosk on the island, freshly washed, showed a gilded dome and a glimpse of bright blue tiling. One of the nightingales was doing overtime in the roses.

I wondered how John Lethman had got in and out last night, and why.

He came some half hour later. Whatever excursions he had undertaken during the night, they didn't seem to have affected him. He looked alert and wide awake, the blurred look gone from his eyes, which were clear gray, and very bright. He moved with energetic precision, and greeted me almost gaily. "Good morning."

"Oh, hullo. Nice timing." I emerged from my door with my luggage—a handbag—packed and ready. "I was just coming to look for you and hoping the dogs had been shut up."

"Always by day. Did they wake you last night? It was a bit rough, I'm afraid. Did you sleep through it?" Here his eyes went past me to the disorder of the room. "I say, rough was the right word, wasn't it? What happened? Don't tell me—the roof leaked?"

"It certainly did," I laughed. "Did you decide to rate me third class after all? No, I'm only joking, I shifted the bed and managed quite a bit of sleep in the end. But I'm afraid you'll find the mattress pretty wet."

"That doesn't matter, it'll dry in five minutes once it's put outside. I'm terribly sorry, the roof gutter must be blocked again. Nasirulla swore he'd cleaned it. Did you really sleep?"

"Fine, thanks, in the end. Don't worry, just think it's an ill wind that blows no good."

"Meaning?"

"If I hadn't come turning the household upside down, you'd have been the one under the waterspout."

"You've got something there. But believe me, you're no ill wind. Your aunt was quite set up last night after your visit."

"Was she really? I didn't tire her?"

"Not a bit. She kept me talking quite a time after you'd gone."

"No change about Charles, I suppose?"

"Not yet, I'm afraid, but give her time. You're ready, are you? Shall we go?" We moved toward the gate.

"Did she keep you very late?" I asked. "It seems hard, the way you burn the torch at both ends."

"Not very, no. I'd gone to bed before the storm broke."

"It woke you, I suppose?"

"Not a flicker." He laughed. "And don't think I'm neglecting my duty, will you? Your great-aunt thrives on disturbances like last night's. She tells me she enjoyed it. She'd have made a wonderful Katisha."

"'But to him who's scientific There's nothing that's terrific In the falling of a flight of thunderbolts?'" I quoted, and heard him laugh again, softly, to himself. "Well, she's got a point, I rather enjoyed it myself. At least, I enjoyed the aftermath. The garden looked wonderful."

I caught a quick sideways glance. "You went out?"

"Only for a moment; I went out to listen to the nightingales. Oh, look at the flowers! Is that because of the storm? More good from the ill wind, would you say?"

We were crossing the small courtyard where Hamid and I had waited yesterday. Here, too, the rain had washed the place clean, and the marble pillars dazzled white in the sun. At their feet the carved troughs were a blaze of red anemones, wide open and shiny as fresh blood in the long grass.

"My Adonis Gardens," said Mr. Lethman.

"Your what?"

"Adonis Gardens. I suppose you know the Adonis myth?"

"I know Aphrodite met him in the Lebanon and he died there, and that every spring his blood stains the river and it runs red to the sea. What is it, iron in the water?"

"Yes. It's one of the spring resurrection stories, like Persephone, or the Osiris myth. Adonis was a corn-god, a fertility god, and he dies to rise again. The 'Adonis Gardens' are—you might call them little personal symbols of death and resurrection; and they're sympathetic magic as well, because the people who planted them and forced the seeds and flowers to grow as quickly as they could, thought they were helping the year's harvest. The flowers and herbs sprang up and withered and died all in a few days, and then the 'gardens' with the images of the god were taken, with the women wailing and mad with grief, down to the sea and thrown in. See? It was all mixed up, here, with the Dionysiac cult, and Osiris, and the rites of Attis, and it still persists—only in nice, pure forms!—all over the world, believe it or not." He checked, with a glance at me. "Sorry, rather a lecture."

"I'm interested, no, go on. Why did you plant the gardens here?"

"No reason, except that this is the right time of the year, and it's quite interesting to see how quickly they do spring up and die, here in Adonis' own valley. Wouldn't you say so?"

"*I* would, sure. It's the kind of romantic notion that appeals to me like anything. But why to you? I mean, what have Adonis and Co. got to do with psychological medicine? Or is this Aunt Harriet's idea?"

"With—? Oh, didn't I tell you I was writing a paper? I was interested in the psychology of religious possession, and I'm touching on some aspects of the ecstatic religions of the near East—the Orphic myth and Dionysius and the Adonis story in its various forms. That's all. I've got some quite interesting stuff locally." He grinned, perhaps a little shamefacedly. "I haven't really let it slide, you know. Whenever I'm let off the chain I ride out and up into the hill villages. If you stay hereabouts for long you may—"

"Ride?"

We were in the *midan* now, the big entrance court. He nodded across it. "There's still a horse here. You know your great-aunt used to ride until only a couple of years ago? She really is remarkable—Hullo! The door's still shut. Nasirulla's not come over yet." He glanced at his watch. "He's late. Half a minute while I open it and give Kasha some air."

He pulled open the upper half-door, and latched it back to the wall with a rotten-looking wooden peg. In the dim interior a horse stood dozing, head down and ears relaxed. A chestnut Arab.

"Do you wear Arab dress when you ride?" I asked.

He looked surprised. "Usually, yes. It's cooler. Why? Wait a minute—didn't you say you'd gone to the Adonis Source yesterday? Did you see me up there?"

"Yes, at some village beyond the fall. I recognized the horse. You had the dogs with you." I smiled. "You looked terribly romantic, especially with the salukis. I may tell you, you made my day."

"And now I've spoiled the picture? Not an Arab Emir after all with his hawk and his hounds after gazelle, just a drifter who's found a lazy billet in the sun and will probably never have the *nous* to pull out of it."

I didn't answer, for the simple reason that I couldn't think how to. The words were bitter, but were spoken without a bitter tinge; and even if I had wanted to, there was no comforting reply to make. John Lethman must know as well as I did that his job, such as it was, would expire with Great-Aunt Harriet. Or would it? Was he actually playing for Dar Ibrahim itself, and a 'lazy billet in the sun' here eventually on his own? He had said it was a 'wonderful place to write in,' and however I might disagree with him, I could think of worse places for an unambitious man to settle in, for a dilettante life in a delightful climate, and with a houri thrown in . . . It might be that the dilapidation of the place was due, not to lack of money, but to age and indifference. John Lethman might well be aware—none better—what means there would eventually be, not only to run part of the place comfortably, but to escape from it at need. Not a bad billet at all.

We were at the gate. There was no sign of Jassim, so Mr. Lethman pulled back the heavy bolts and opened the bronze door. Outside, the sun blazed down white on the stony plateau. There was no one there.

"Your driver isn't here yet," he said. "If you'd rather come back in and wait—"

"Thanks very much, but I think I'll just walk down to meet him. And thank you for all you've done, Mr. Lethman." I held out my hand and he took it, but when I would have gone on he protested very pleasantly that both he and Great-Aunt Harriet had enjoyed the visit very much.

"And I really will do what I can about your cousin, but if I can't—" he hesitated, and the light eyes met mine and slid away—"I hope you won't feel too badly about it."

"I? It's none of my business. How she lives is her own affair, and if Charles is really set on seeing her it's up to him to find a way. Good-bye then, and thanks again. And I hope the paper goes well."

"Good-bye."

The big door shut. The palace had sealed itself off once more behind me, silent walls of baked stone throwing back the glare from the white rock underfoot. In front of me the valley stretched in all the hard brilliance of morning.

The sun was behind me, and the cliff path was in shadow. Here, too, the effect of last night's rain was immediately apparent. Even the rock smelled fresher, and the dust had caked into mud which was drying rapidly into a million cracks. I could have sworn that on some of the fig trees that clung to the face of the rock there were fresh green buds. I wondered if, when I got down to the foot of the cliff, I would see Hamid crossing to meet me.

But there was no sign of him, and when I reached the Nahr el-Sal'q I saw why. The river was in spate.

The ill wind had been at work here, too, and this time to no good that I could see at all. There must have been, high up in the catchment area, as heavy a fall as, if not heavier, than that which we had had in the valley. It may even have combined with melting snow on the high tops to come pouring down now into the valley, for the Nahr el-Sal'q seemed to have risen at least two feet, and to be coming down very fast indeed. Where yesterday afternoon the pile of stone that had flanked the old Roman bridge had stood at least a foot clear of water, now there was nothing to be seen but the angry white of broken water as the river, streaked with red mud, cascaded down to meet the Adonis.

There is something in all of us which cannot quite accept so sudden a reversal of circumstance. It did not seem possible that I could really be cut off on the wrong side of the river. It should be still as it was yesterday, swift but clear, and easily to be crossed if one could find the place. I stood there on the rocky edge which, this morning, seemed barely to clear the rushing level of the water, and stared about me rather helplessly. This must be why Nasirulla hadn't turned up for work this morning. Even if Hamid did come for me—and there was as yet no sign of him—he couldn't cross the river any more than I could. I was nicely imprisoned here between the roaring stream of the Nahr el-Sal'q and the still bigger torrent of the Adonis. Unless I could make my way up the valley between the two, and cross somewhere where the stream was a good deal narrower, I was certainly marooned. I suppose that, once the spate began to subside, it would fall as quickly as it had risen, but I had no means of knowing how soon this might be.

Meanwhile Hamid would certainly come to seek me from the village, so there was nothing much to do but sit beside the stream and wait for his appearance. Behind me the palace, standing back from the head of the cliff, was invisible, but ahead I had a clear view of the village strung high along the valley's edge. I looked about me, found a flat boulder washed beautifully clean by the night's rain, and sat down to wait.

It was then that I saw the boy.

There had been no movement; that I could swear. One moment, it seemed to me, I had been gazing idly at the torrential water and beyond it a stony bank full in the sun and ornamented with a few harsh green shrubs. The next moment I found myself looking straight at a boy, sturdy and ragged in his rustic kaftan, who could have been anything from twelve to fifteen years old. He was barefooted, and unlike most of the Arab boys that one saw, his head also was bare, covered with a shock of wild dark hair. His skin was dark brown. He was standing stock-still beside a bush, leaning on a thick stick.

He seemed to be staring straight at me. After a moment's hesitation I got off my boulder and picked my way back to the river's edge. The boy didn't move.

"Hullo there! Do you speak English?" My voice whirled away and was drowned in the roar of the water between us, and I raised it and tried again. "Can you hear me?"

He nodded. It was a curiously dignified nod, the sort of gesture one might have expected from an actor, not from a herd-boy. That this is what he was I now saw; one or two of the goats that we had seen yesterday were moving slowly and at random down the slope behind him, cropping at the thin flowers as they came. Then with a movement that was all small boy, and not dignified at all, he thrust his stick into the stony earth, and pole-vaulted down toward his side of the stream. Now we were barely twenty feet apart, but with all the roaring of the Nahr el-Sal'q between us.

I tried again. "Where can I cross the water?"

This time he shook his head. "Tomorrow."

"I didn't say *when,* I said *where!*" But he had, in fact, answered my question. The implication was clear. The crossing place, probably the only crossing place, was here, and the river would take twenty-four hours to go down.

My dismay must have been obvious. He waved with the stick upstream toward the towering cliffs that barred the head of the valley, and then down to where the two rivers rushed together in a wrangle of white foam stained with red. "Bad," he shouted, "all bad! You stay there!" A sudden smile, very boyish, showing two gaps in the even white teeth. "You stay with the Lady, huh? Your father's father's sister?"

"My . . . ?" I worked it out yet again. He was right. And it was Nasirulla, of course, everyone in the village would know all about it by now. "Yes. You live in the village?"

A gesture, not to the village, but to the barren landscape and the goats. "I live here."

"Can you get a mule? A donkey?" I had thought of John Lethman's horse, but somehow that would be a last resort. "I would pay well!" I shouted.

That shake of the head again. "No mule. Donkey, too small. You all drown. This is a bad river." After some thought he added in explanation: "There was rain in the night."

"You must be kidding."

He got the meaning, even though he couldn't have heard me. The gap-toothed grin flashed again, and then he pointed toward the village. I hadn't seen him look that way, but when I looked myself I saw Hamid, a slim figure in dark blue trousers and steel-blue shirt, detach himself from the dense shadow under the retaining wall that held the village to the cliff top, and start on his way down the path.

I turned back to the boy.

The goats were there, still grazing; the river roared; the distant village wavered on the cliff top in the heat; but down here on the rocky bank there was no sign of any boy. Only the liquid rocks shimmering up in the heat, and where he had been standing, a shaggy black goat, staring at me with those cold yellow eyes.

A country where anything could happen.

"By all the gods at once," I said aloud, "I could do with your keeping that promise, cousin dear, here and now, and no kidding."

Some ten seconds later I realized that the small figure in the distance was not Hamid at all, but Charles himself, coming fast down the slope toward me.

7

While smooth Adonis from his native rock
Ran purple to the sea . . .

—MILTON: *Paradise Lost*

CERTAINLY A country where anything could happen. After my disturbed night among the storybook paraphernalia of the palace—peacocks, mute servants, harem gardens—no touch of magic would have surprised me. What did faintly surprise me was that I should so immediately have distinguished Charles at such a distance from Hamid, whom I had been expecting. So immediately—and with such a calm uprush of pleasure.

I sat still on my boulder in the sun, watching him.

When he was still some way off, he raised a hand to greet me, then something seemed to catch his attention, for he paused and turned, apparently to address a patch of shade under a dusty bush. As I watched, the patch of shade resolved into a black goat, and squatting down cross-legged beside it the herd-boy, his stick lying at his feet in the dust. The conversation lasted a minute or two, then the boy got to his feet, and the two of them came down together toward the river bank.

I walked down again to my side, and we stood surveying one another across the twenty feet of turbid, red-streaked water.

"Hi!" said Charles.

"Hi!" I shouted. Then, not very brilliantly: "We're stuck. It's in spate."

"So it seems. Serve you right. Stealing a march. How's Great-Aunt H?"

"Fine. You're early. How did you manage?"

"Made it this morning. Hotel told me. Saw your driver this morning, told him I'd fetch you."

"You did? Fine, you go right ahead and fetch me! . . . Oh, Charles, the boy says it'll be in spate till tomorrow. What are we going to do?"

"I'll come over," said my cousin.

"You can't! It's hellish deep. Did you get rain last night in Beirut?"

"Did I get what?"

"Rain?" I gestured to a flawless sky. "Rain?"

"I can't think why we're standing twenty feet apart talking about the weather," said Charles, starting to undo his shirt buttons.

I yelled in alarm: "Charles, you can't! And it wouldn't help if you did—"

"You can watch or not as you please," said my cousin. "Remember the good old days when we used to be dumped in the bath together? Don't worry, I'll manage this lot."

"I can hardly wait to watch you drown," I said tartly. "But if you'd only *listen—!*"

He stopped unbuttoning and turned a look of inquiry. "Yes?"

I threw a quick glance over my shoulder. It seemed all wrong to be standing yelling about our private affairs in the middle of the valley, but all I could see was the tangle of bushes and trees on the cliff behind me. The palace was out of sight, and nothing moved on the path.

I shouted: "It won't do you any good if you do get across. She says she won't see you."

"Won't see me?"

I nodded.

"Why not?"

I made a gesture. "Can't tell you here. But she won't."

"Well, then, when?"

"Never—she meant not at all. She won't see anyone at all. Charles, I'm sorry—"

"She actually told you that?"

"Yes, and she seemed a bit—" Here my throat, sore with yelling, made me stop and cough.

I saw Charles make a movement of intense irritation, then he turned to the boy who was standing just behind him, closely attended by the black goat. I had forgotten all about him. I somehow hadn't counted him as an audience to our conversation, any more than the goats, or the rocks and stones into which he could apparently melt at will.

From the boy's gestures, aided by his pointing stick, it seemed clear what

Charles was asking him. And presently Charles turned back to me and raised his voice again.

"He says I can cross further up."

"He told me there wasn't anywhere."

"Still one or two things I can do that you can't," he retorted. "Anyway . . . hopeless . . . can't stand here yelling intimacies about Aunt H across twenty feet of flood water." A gesture indicated the palace, invisible above me at the cliff top. "Right underneath . . . hellish row . . . And I've got to talk to you. Ahmad says there's a place upstream. Can you make it your side?"

"I'll try."

I turned and began to make my way up my side of the stream. There was no path, and here the water ran close under the cliff, so the going was rough, and complicated by a fairly thick growth of scrubby bushes and small trees. Soon I lost sight of Charles and his guide as I battled my way among bushes and rocks, intent on nothing but keeping my feet.

The Nahr el-Sal'q seemed to flow for most of this part of its length in a gully fairly thickly grown with trees. These, and the broken terrain, made it impossible to stay always within sight of the water. I caught one or two more glimpses of Charles and the boy, then they vanished, apparently following some winding goat track up into the thickets.

I clambered on along my side of the gully for some half mile, to find the stream then curving and its bed shelving steeply up into a narrower gorge where the water dropped from pool to pool in a series of rapids, running deep and fast. Charles and the boy reappeared here, their path apparently clinging close above the torrent, but though the stream was narrow here, and everywhere full of rocks, there was still no place where it seemed safe to cross. And the narrower the gully the faster and louder grew the water, so that any kind of communication, other than by gesture, was impossible.

The boy kept pointing upstream in an Excelsior kind of way. Charles spread his hands to me and jerked an encouraging thumb. We toiled on, separated by the loud white rush of water.

It must have been after a full mile of painful going that the stream bed took a sudden and final lift and curve, and ran, in a manner of speaking, right up against the cliff.

In fact, of course, the stream came straight out of the cliff. The spring which fed the Nahr el-Sal'q was almost a miniature of the Adonis Source, leaping suddenly into the sunlight from a gash in the dry rock face that blocked the upper end of the gully. It was much smaller, less dramatic, and much less haunted. The spring, a spout of ice-green water, jetted out of the cliff with a roar that the echoes magnified, tossed itself into a churning pool, then went tearing off down among the white boulders of the gully. A few hanging bushes, soaked and ragged with the spray, waved in the breeze of the fall. The sun drove against the cliff where the water gushed, lighting the cascade into glittering brilliance, but below, where we stood, the place was in shadow and the wind off the water struck chilly.

I stared about me with dismay. If communication had been difficult down at the ford, and worse in the gully, here it was impossible. The roar of the water, magnified a dozen times by its echoes, bellowed round from rock to rock so that, though Charles and I were here barely eight or nine feet apart, we could not have heard a word the other spoke. Moreover, I could still see no way across. To cross the torrent here would have been suicide, and above the cascade towered a seamed and sunlit crag as high as a cathedral.

It was at this that the boy was pointing, and presently, to my alarm, I saw Charles approaching it. My yell of protest, of perhaps my wild gesture, reached him, for he stopped, nodded his head at me, jerked a thumbs-up gesture, then with apparent confidence approached the cliff. Only then did I remember that rock-climbing had been another of the ploys with which (*vide* my father) my cousin had been wont to waste his time all over Europe. I relaxed. All I could do was hope that Charles had, as he usually did (*vide* my mother), wasted his time to good effect.

It seemed he had. I have no idea whether it was in fact an easy climb, or whether he simply made it seem so, but there was very little to it. He went carefully, because in places the rock was wet or loose, but it was not long before he had gained my side of the Nahr el-Sal'q. He came down the last pitch at no more than a scramble, to land safely beside me.

"Hullo, Aphrodite."

"Adonis, I presume? Nice to see you, but if you've any idea of guiding my tottering steps back across the north wall of the Eiger with you, you can have another think. It's not on."

"I wouldn't risk my own precious neck trying. No, I'm afraid you're stuck, sweet coz. It's beastly cold down here, isn't it, and there's still a hellish noise . . . Shall we get up into the sun where we can talk?"

"For goodness' sake, yes, let's. I must say it seems a lot of trouble to go to, just to have a little conversation."

"Ah, not with you," said my cousin. "Wait a moment, I'll tell the boy—where is he? Did you see him go?"

"Haven't you guessed? That's not a boy, that's a faun. He's invisible at will."

"Very likely," agreed Charles calmly. "Well, he'll turn up when he wants his tip."

I followed him out of the gully, and we soon emerged on a small stony plateau where the sun struck hotly.

Here, too, the resemblance to the Adonis Source was underlined, for on the plateau stood the tumbled ruins of some ancient temple. Nothing remained now but the steep steps of the portico, a stretch of broken floor, and two standing pillars. It must only have been a small place originally, perhaps a subordinate shrine of the greater Gods of Afka, built at the tributary source, and it was weedy, forgotten, and undramatic. Tufts of some yellow flower grew between the stones, and halfway up one pillar where the masonry had fallen into a crumbling hole, a hawk had made an untidy nest liberally streaked with white droppings; but somehow the squared masculine-looking Roman stones, the honey-colored pillars, the pitted steps where the thistles grew, fitted with a kind of beauty into that wild landscape.

The steps provided a seat for us in the shade of one of the pillars. The roar of the cascade was cut off by the sides of the gorge, and the silence was intense.

Charles got out cigarettes and offered one to me.

"No, thanks. Oh, Charles, I'm awfully glad you came! What am I going to do? I can't climb across that awful rock, and the faun told me the water wouldn't go down till tomorrow."

"So I gather. Actually there is another way. He tells me there's some kind of track going up into the heights near Afka, but it's a hell of a way, and if I was to take the car up by road to meet you, you'd have to go on your own, and you'd never find it. I suppose the boy might manage to cross and act as guide for you, but we'd still probably never manage an RV in a million years. The place is seamed with tracks.''

"And probably creeping with wild boars and yelling tribes of Midian or whatever. Nothing," I said flatly, "will get me clambering up into the High Lebanon, boy or no boy."

"How I agree." My cousin leaned back lazily against the pillar and blew smoke at the sun. "If the water doesn't go down again before night there's only one thing to do, go back to the palace." He slanted a look at me, eyebrows raised. "That's certainly what I was hoping to do. What's all this about her not letting me in?"

"Just that she said she wouldn't, and as a matter of fact I'm not wild keen to go back there myself. I'll tell you about that in a minute ·. . . But look, I couldn't make out just what you were yelling at me down by the ford—you did say you'd seen Hamid, didn't you, my driver? He was to have come for me this morning."

"Yes, I saw him, and it's all right, I came instead. You knew Ben's father was delayed and couldn't get home till Sunday—yesterday? Well, he telephoned again last night to say he couldn't make it, had to go on to Aleppo and possibly Homs, and wasn't sure when he'd get home, so I told Ben I'd go back there later, but I wanted to come straight up to Beirut while you were here. I didn't try telephoning you last night because it was pretty late when he called, and I left first thing this morning—and I mean first thing, literally crack of dawn. There wasn't a thing on the road, and I came up the Barada Valley at the speed of sound, and the frontier post let me through in twenty minutes, which must be an all-time record for them. I got to Beirut about eight o'clock. Your driver was in the hotel lobby when I checked in and asked about you, and he told me you were staying the night here and he'd promised to come and fetch you. So I told him not to bother, I'd come straight up myself."

"As long as he hasn't lost another contract by giving me the day."

"Not to worry, I paid him," said Charles. "I'm darned sure he'll get another contract anyway, the Phoenicia's always full of streams of people wanting cars. He seemed pretty pleased."

"That's all right, then. He's a very nice chap, as a matter of fact. I had a lovely day yesterday."

Charles tapped ash off into a clump of weeds. "That's what I've come to hear about. After all the trouble we've gone to to have a little conversation, it'd better be good. What the devil do you mean by stealing a march on me, young Christy? Was Aunt H so disgusted with you that she refused to see anybody else?"

"Probably." I sat up. "Oh, my dear, there's masses to tell you! Actually, I'd no real intention of calling at the palace, but when we got to the village Hamid stopped the car, and it looked so near, sort of weird and romantic, and of course it never occurred to me really that she'd refuse to see either of us. Look, away down there, see? You can actually see it from here, too. It looks rather gorgeous, doesn't it? I must say distance lends enchantment! Close to it's just about dropping to bits."

You could indeed, from this high eyrie, see the end of the promontory on which the palace stood. As the eagle flew, it cannot have been much more than three-quarters of a mile distant, and in that clean and brilliant air even the branches of the feathery trees were clearly visible.

We were looking down on the back of the palace. I could see the high blank wall and inside it the flower-roofed arches enclosing the glint of the lake. Beyond the Seraglio sprawled the jumble of roofs and courtyards whose geography, even now, I couldn't guess at. From the distance the place looked completely deserted, like a ruin open to the sun.

"See the green courtyard and the lake?" I said. "That's the Seraglio where I slept."

"How appropriate," said Charles. "And Aunt H?"

"She has the Prince's Court."

"She would. Well, tell me all about it. Hamid told me you rather took them by surprise, but you got in in the end."

"'In the end' is right, and I didn't get to Aunt H till about midnight."

I told him my story then, omitting nothing that I could remember.

He heard me out to the end without much interruption. Then he stirred, dropped the stub of his cigarette carefully beside his foot on the stone, and crushed it out. He regarded me frowningly.

"Quite a story, eh? Well, we expected a queer situation, didn't we? But it's queerer even than you think."

"Meaning?"

He asked flatly; "Did she strike you as sane?"

I have often read about moments of 'revelation.' These seemed to be sudden—blinding lights on the Damascus road, scales dropping from eyes, and so forth. I hadn't ever thought about it much, except to class it vaguely as a 'miracle,' a thing that happened in the Bible or some other lofty context, and not normally—not in real life—at all. But in a minor and very personal way, I had a revelation now.

There was my cousin, the same boy I had known for twenty-two years, looking at me and asking a question. I had known him ever since I could remember. I had shared the bath with him. I had seen him smacked. I had jeered at him when he fell off the orchard wall and cried. I had discussed sex with him at the age when we had no physical secrets from one another. Later, when we had, I had regarded him with a tolerant and familiar indifference. Meeting him the other day in Straight Street I had been pleased, but not bowled over with delight.

And now, here, suddenly, he turned his head and looked at me and asked a question, and I saw, as if I had never seen them before, the gray long-lashed eyes, the well-cut dark hair growing thick and smooth, the faint hollow under the cheek bones, the slightly arrogant and wholly exciting cut of nostril and upper lip, the whole vivid intelligence and humor and force of the man's face.

"What's the matter?" he asked, irritably.

"Nothing. What did you say?"

"I asked you if Aunt H struck you as sane."

"Oh." I pulled myself together. "Yes, of course she did! I told you she was odd and woolly and said she forgot things, and she was really quite sharp and nasty in a way, but . . ." I hesitated. "I can't quite explain what I mean, but I do know she *looked* sane. However peculiar she was, and the way she was dressed and everything . . . Charles, her eyes were sane."

He nodded. "That's what I mean. No, wait, you haven't heard my side of it yet."

"Your side of it? You mean you've heard something more since we last met?"

"Indeed and indeed. I rang my people up on Friday evening to tell them I was leaving Damascus soon for Beirut. I told them I'd met you, and that we were going to spend two or three days together and we were coming up to see Great-Aunt H. I wondered if they had any messages to send, or anything like that. Well, my mother said they'd had a letter from her."

I looked at him, startled. "A letter? Do you mean another Will or something?"

"No, a letter. It came about three weeks ago, while I was in North Africa. Must have been just after you left. My mother had actually written to tell me about it, and when I phoned she told me her letter would be waiting for me care of Cook's in Beirut. What's more, she'd forwarded Aunt H's letter to me there." His hand went to his inside pocket.

"You've got it?"

"I picked it up this morning. Wait till you've read it and then tell me if it makes sense to you."

He handed me the letter. It was written on coarse-looking paper which could have been some sort of torn-off wrapping, and the handwriting was spidery and spluttery as though it had been written with a quill pen; which in fact it probably had. But it was perfectly legible.

MY DEAR NEPHEW,

Last month I recd a letter from my dear Husband's friend and colleague Humphrey Ford who you will remember was with us in Resada in 1949 and again in '53 and '54. He tells me that he recently recd the news from a Friend that Henry's boy, Charles, yr son by adoption, is at present studying the languages of the East with a view (he thinks) to adopting my dear Husband's profession. Poor Humphrey cd not be clear over this as he is getting sadly absent, but he informed me that young Chas will be traveling this yr in Syria. If he wishes to call on me, I shld make a point of receiving him. As you know I do not approve of the freedom with wch young people are brought up nowadays, and yr son is what my dear Mother wd have called a Scapegrace, but a clever boy, and wd be amused to receive him. There is much to interest him here in the study of Eastern Life and Manners.

I do well enough here with my small Staff who are v. attentive and a man from the village who looks after the dogs. Samson cannot abide the Dr. Young Chas will remember him.

Regards to yr Wife also to my other Nephew and Wife—the little girl must be well grown by now, a strange little thing, but like enough the Boy to be called Handsome.

YR. AFFEC AUNT,
HARRIET BOYD.

Post Scriptum—The Times continues flimsy so that I cannot believe Yr. Representations were sufficiently decided.

Post Post Scriptum. I have purchased an excellent Tombstone locally.

I read through the letter once, then clean through again, more slowly, and I think my mouth must have been wide open all the time. Then I gaped up at my cousin. He was leaning back against the pillar, head back, eyes narrowed under the long lashes, watching me.

"Well?"

"But Charles . . . when did she—is it dated? There's a squiggle at the top but I can't read it."

"Arabic," he said shortly. "Written in February. From the postmark it looks as if she didn't get it mailed straight off, and she didn't send it Air Mail, so it took nearly three weeks on the way. But that's not the point. It was certainly written after Christmas's Last Will and Testament. Would you or would you not say that was an open invitation?"

"I certainly would. Two months ago? Well, obviously something's happened to make her change her mind."

"John Lethman?"

"D'you think that's possible?" I asked.

"Not having seen the ménage, I wouldn't know. What's he like?"

"Tallish and rather thin, and slouches a bit. Light eyes—"

"My dear girl, I'm reasonably indifferent to him physically. Would you say he was honest?"

"How do I know?"

" 'No art to find the mind's construction in the face?' Well, I agree, of course, but what was your impression?"

"Not a bad one. I told you he was a bit off-putting at first, but if Hamid's right he wasn't back on the beam properly, and in any case it's obvious he was only doing what Aunt H had told him to. After he'd seen her he was all right. She probably told him he'd nothing to fear from that strange little thing, however much she resembled the handsome boy."

He didn't smile. "Then you did think he might be feathering his nest?"

"The thought had crossed my mind," I admitted, "once Hamid put it there. We both agreed we had unpleasant natures. Does it matter?"

"Hardly, as long as it's her idea as well as his."

"I don't think you need worry about that. I got the impression that she did exactly as she liked about a hundred percent of the time. I doubt if he could stop her doing anything she'd set her heart on."

"So long as that's true . . ."

"I swear it. You know, there's no sense in trying to build up something out of nothing. She simply changed her mind since she wrote that letter. It's perfectly possible she really had forgotten how devastating you were. People do."

"You must tell me about it sometime." He stirred. "Oh, God, I don't care what she's up to or how her mind's working, as long as things are going the way she wants them. It's just that she's as old as the seven hills, and alone except for this chap we know nothing about, and what you said about the hashish-smoking didn't sound too cheerful to me. He may be all right now, but he's on the road to nowhere, you must know that." He moved again, restlessly. "No doubt if she's lived here all this time she knows how many beans make five, and you say you got the impression she could deal with him—"

"Six of him."

"Yes. I'd have liked to see for myself, that's all. You have to admit that last night doesn't exactly chime in with this letter of hers."

"Would you expect it to? I wouldn't have thought consistency was her middle name."

"No, but—she gave no reason whatever for her embargo on me?"

"None whatever. I honestly did just get the impression that, having seen me, she'd satisfied her own curiosity, and now she wanted to get back to her own life, whatever it is. I told you, she seemed perfectly normal for long periods, then she'd suddenly look as if she were miles away and say the queerest things. I've never met anyone who was cuckoo before, so I wouldn't know how to tell, but I'd have said nothing worse than old and absent-minded. All I can tell you is, I quite like John Lethman, and Aunt H did seem perfectly happy and contented and not ill, apart from wheezing a bit. But as for knowing what she was thinking about, don't forget I hardly know her at all, and in any case at the time I wasn't feeling too good myself, what with that ghastly tobacco, and the stuffy room, and that rather revolting bubbling noise she made with her pipe. Oh, and Charles, I forgot completely—there was a cat in the room, and I didn't know it. It must have been behind the bed-curtains. I was feeling as queer as all-get-out, and thought it was just the stuffy room or something, but that must have been what it was."

"*Cat?*" His head jerked away from the pillar. His turn to stare. "Sweet Christ, was there?"

I was rather flattered than otherwise at the blasphemy. So Charles hadn't forgotten the thing I had about cats, or the real horror it was for me.

Now, a phobia can't be explained. And cat phobia—the genuine article—is something so grotesque as to be not quite believable. I admire cats; I love their looks; pictures of them give me pleasure. But I cannot be in the same room with them, and on the rare occasions when I have tried to kill my fear and touch a cat, it has almost made me ill. Cats are my nightmare. When I was a child at school my dear little friends found out about this, and shut me into a room with the school kitten. I was rescued, a screaming jelly of hysteria, twenty minutes later. It is the one vulnerable thing about me that Charles, even at his most horrible stage as a boy, never tortured me with. He doesn't share the phobia, but he is close enough to me to understand it.

I smiled at him. "No, I haven't got over it, I don't know if one ever does. I saw it just as I was leaving the room. It sneaked out from behind the curtains and jumped on the bed beside her, and she started stroking it. It can't have been there all the time, or I'd have felt rotten earlier, and I'd have guessed. It occurred to me there must be another door into the room that I didn't notice. Stands to reason there would be, in a room that size."

He said nothing. I went back to studying the letter in my hand. "Who's Humphrey Ford?"

"Who? Oh, the letter, yes. He's Oriental Studies, Professor Emeritus. He's as old as the hills—was a friend of my grandfather's, my real grandfather, that is, not yours. 'Sadly absent' is the *mot juste,* I may say. He had the reputation of giving the first lecture of term, then sloping quietly off to Saudi Arabia for a sort of perpetual Sabbatical. Before my time, praise be to Allah, but he was still around the place, and had me to breakfast once or twice, and even occasionally recognized me in the street. A nice old chap."

"Why hadn't you told her yourself you were coming?"

"I wasn't sure when I'd get here, and I thought it might be better to play it by ear once I was in Beirut."

"And Samson? Is it Samson, there's a blot? The cat?"

"Dog. Tibetan terrier. She got him when she was home last—he used to belong to one of the Boyd cousins who died, and she scooped him up and brought him back here as a mate for Delilah. He was originally called Wu or Pooh or something equally Tibetan, but she changed it to Samson, guess why."

"Too subtle for me." I handed the letter back. "I never saw the dogs, they were shut up except at night. John Lethman said they were dangerous."

"If Samson had taken a dislike to him, he was probably protecting himself, not you." He folded the letter and put it back in his pocket. I got the impression that he was talking slightly at random. "He was a savage little brute, as I remember, except with the family. You'd have been all right: don't they say there's some sort of family voice or smell or something that they recognize even if they've never seen you before?"

"Do they?" I laced my fingers round a knee and leaned back with my face lifted to the sun. "You know, Charles, that letter might work both ways . . . if she'd forgotten what she'd written in that letter when she saw me, she's probably forgotten now what she said about your not coming. See what I mean? In any case, I told you, John Lethman said he'd talk to her, and if his *bona fides* are okay, he will. Even if they're not—or is it 'it's'? . . . Even if it's not, he'll not dare just ignore you. It sounded as if he wasn't planning to; he talked about getting in touch with you. In that case you can produce Aunt H's letter and make him let you in."

"I suppose so." But his voice was absent, and he was making rather a business of lighting another cigarette.

"Or look, for goodness' sake, why don't you just come back with me here and now, because I am genuinely stuck here and *have* to go back? We can show John Lethman the letter now, and see if you can't bulldoze your way in to see Aunt Harriet tonight. He can hardly stop you if you're on the very doorstep . . . Charles, are you *listening?*"

I don't think he was. He was looking away from me, down the bright distance of the valley toward the palace.

"Look over there."

At first I could see nothing except the crumbling ruin sleeping in the heat, the fixed dazzling pattern of the rock seamed with violent shadows, the green of distant trees grayed by the heat haze. There were no clouds to move, or wind to move them. No sound.

Then I saw what he was watching. Some way from the palace, among the rocks and tangled bushes that marked the lip of the Adonis gorge, there was a movement which presently resolved itself into a man in Arab dress making his way slowly on foot toward the palace. He was almost indistinguishable from the countryside, for his dress was dust-colored, and his headcloth brown, and if Charles and I had not both had abnormally long sight I doubt if we would have seen him at all. He moved very slowly, disappearing from time to time as his path took him behind rocky outcrops or through the thick overgrowth, but presently he emerged on the open rock of the plateau behind the palace. He carried a stick in one hand, and seemed to have some kind of bag over his shoulder.

"Looks like a pilgrim," I said. "Well, he's in for a disappointment if he's making for the palace, and I don't see where else he could be bound for. The faun must be right, there's a path there."

"There'd have to be, wouldn't there?" said my cousin. "Did it never occur to you to wonder how John Lethman got back to the palace before you did yesterday?"

"Silly of me, I never thought of it. Yes, and I remember now, there was something about the palace being on the old camel route down from the High Lebanon to the sea. In that case there must be a resonable track." I grinned at him. "But not, Charles my love, not for me."

"On the contrary," said my cousin, "I'm beginning to think—Just a minute, keep your eye on that man."

The 'pilgrim' had reached the back wall of the palace, but instead of turning north to skirt the Seraglio wall, he went the other way, making for the corner where the walls literally grew out of the cliffs of the Adonis gorge. There was a clump of trees marking the drop, and into these he vanished.

"But he can't get round that way!" I exclaimed. "That's the way my bedroom looked. It's a sheer drop into the river."

"He's got a rendezvous," said Charles.

I narrowed my eyes against the brightness. Then I saw them among the trees, the Arab, and another man with him, this one in European dress. They came out slowly between the trees, obviously deep in talk, and stood there, tiny fore-shortened figures at the edge of the dappled shade.

"John Lethman?" asked Charles.

"Must be. Look there's someone else, I'm sure I saw someone else move among those trees. In white, this time."

"Yes, another Arab. That'll be your doorman, Jassim, I suppose."

"Or Nasirulla—oh, no, I'd forgotten, he couldn't get over today. Then it must be Jassim." I knitted my brows. "I don't understand, have they been waiting out there for him all this time? I haven't been watching, particularly, but if they'd come round from the front gate, you'd think we'd have seen them."

"There is a way round?"

"Yes, round the north side below the Seraglio arcade. The path goes through the trees above the Nahr el-Sal'q and skirts the palace wall."

"If they'd come that way we'd certainly have seen them. No, it's obvious there must be a back door. Stands to reason there would be. It must be hidden somewhere among those trees."

"Tradesman's entrance?" I said. "I suppose you're right. Look, he's handed over his pack, whatever it is. He's going now. Will they see us if they look this way?"

"Not a hope. We're in the shadow of this pillar, and what's more, the sun will be in their eyes. I wish we had a pair of field glasses, I'd like to see your Mr. Lethman. Yes, he's going. Watch the others. My bet is we'll never see them disappear."

Made tiny by distance, the little scene had a silent, curiously dreamlike quality. One moment there seemed to be three men standing beside the trees below the wall, then the next moment the traveling Arab had turned and was making his slow way back among the rocks, and the other two had vanished under the shade of the trees.

We waited in silence. The Arab had gone, the other two did not come out from the grove. There must indeed be another way into the palace. The distance was clear, the colors bright, but it still looked a very long way away. I thought with weariness, and then with irritation, of the long trek back down the gorge of the Nahr el-Sal'q.

I said suddenly: "I quite honestly don't want to go back there. Can't we scrub it?"

"Decided you'd rather try pilgrims' way into the High Lebanon?"

"No, but couldn't you somehow convoy me across the Eiger after all? It looked terribly easy."

"Did it?" He grinned. No further comment.

"You couldn't?"

"No, love, I could not. What's more I wouldn't, even if I could. It's obviously the will of Allah that you should go back to Dar Ibrahim, and for once the will of Allah is perfectly timed. By which I mean that it coincides with mine. You're going back—and I'm coming with you."

"You are? You mean you're going to show John Lethman that letter now, and get him to let you in?"

"No. John Lethman has nothing to do with it. You're going to let me in yourself."

I sat up abruptly. "If you mean what I think you mean—"

"Probably. There's a back door, a postern."

"So?" I asked sharply.

"I've been thinking . . ." He spoke slowly, his eyes still on the distant sprawl of the palace. "The place where we met this morning, the ford . . . that was out of sight of the palace?"

"Yes. But Charles—"

"And you said that when you first saw me coming down the slope below the village, you thought I was your driver?"

"Yes, but Charles—"

"Now, they've seen your driver, but they've never seen me, and anyway they wouldn't be expecting me any more than you were. If they were looking out at all this morning, all they would see was you going down to the stream to meet your driver, who was walking down from the village. Fair enough?"

"Yes, but Charles, you can't! Are you really thinking—?"

"Of course I am. Now shut up and listen. I want to get into this place for myself and see exactly what's going on, and I want to get in now, not wait on Lethman's problematic goodwill. All right, it looks as if this flooding of the river has provided a heaven-sent chance; the will of Allah, plain and clear. Your part of it's perfectly simple and straightforward. You go back there now to the palace, ring for old Jassim again, and tell him what's more or less the truth. Tell him you couldn't cross the stream, and neither could your driver, but that you both went up the Nahr el-Sal'q as far as you could, to see if there was a place to cross. You got right up to the source, and there wasn't any place you could cross, even with the driver's help." He grinned. "Couldn't be truer so far. So you told your driver to go back to Beirut, and call for you again tomorrow when the stream had had a chance to go down. You also gave your driver a message for your cousin Charles, to say you were staying here another night, and that you'd join him tomorrow at the Phoenicia."

"But, Charles—"

"They can hardly refuse to take you in. In fact, it sounded to me as if your Mr. Lethman was quite glad of your company. Who could blame him? If you had to live in a place like that you'd welcome the Abominable Snowman."

"Thank you."

"You're welcome. So, you get back into the palace. You told me that you could explore anywhere you liked except the Prince's rooms. Well, do just that. You'll have hours of daylight this time. See if you can find this back door; you said it went from your end of the palace anyway."

"It must do. I told you about the man walking through the Seraglio Garden last night. Whoever it was, I'll swear he didn't come past my room to the main door, so he must have got in and out another way. But—you're serious? You're really planning to break in?"

"Why not? If you can find the door, see it's unlocked after dark tonight, and Mohammed will come to the mountain."

"And if I can't find it?"

"Then we'll have to think of some other way. No windows at all looking back on the plateau—no, I can see that from here; there aren't. Well, but you said there was an arcade of sorts on the north side facing the village, and a path underneath?"

"There is, but the windows are all barred. Don't forget it was a harem."

"You said the place was falling to bits; aren't any of the grilles broken? Or could they be broken?"

"Yes, I think so. But they're right up high in the wall, and—"

"Well, I can climb," said Charles. "If the wall's in bad repair there'll be plenty of footholds. I've always wanted to climb into a harem."

"I'll bet. But why not try the direct approach first? With me, I mean, at the main gate?"

"Because if it doesn't work you mightn't get in either, and then there'd be no chance even of a break-in. And I'd sooner by-pass Lethman in any case."

I started to asy why, saw my cousin's face, and decided to save time and energy. I know Charles. I asked instead: "Well, once you're in, what then? What if you're caught?"

"All that'll happen is a bit of a row, or at worst a turn-up with John Lethman, and I'll risk that. It won't worry me, and at least I'll get to see Aunt H, if only to have her tear a strip off me."

I regarded him. "This I just don't get. I mean, curiosity is one thing, but this sudden outburst of devotion . . . No, Charles, it simply isn't on. It's all very fine and large, but you just can't do this sort of thing."

"Can't I? Look at it this way. You've got to go back tonight. You don't want to. Wouldn't you rather I was there, too?"

"Under the circumstances," I said, "I'd be glad of the Abominable Snowman."

"Thank you. Well then, sweet Christabel—"

Of course I protested further, and of course he won in the end, as he always had. Besides, his last argument was the most cogent of the lot. However 'romantic' my last night at Dar Ibrahim had been, I had no desire to repeat it alone.

"Then that's settled." He got decisively to his feet. "I'll climb back across now, and in due course, if they're interested, they'll see me going back toward the village. Now, you said you'd finished supper by about ten, and Aunt H didn't send for you until about twelve. Just in case she decides to receive you again, we'd better say that I'll be at the back of the palace any time from ten-thirty on. If you can't get the postern unlocked, I'll give a couple of barks like a hill fox under the wall, and if it's all clear for me to climb up, hang a towel out, or something light colored that I can see. Soap-opera stuff, I know, but simple ideas usually work out best. In fact, if it's climbable, I'd prefer the window, if the hounds get the run of the place at night."

"Lord, yes, I'd forgotten that . . . I don't know if I could do anything about them. If he does take me to see Aunt H again, there's a chance he may shut them up, but otherwise—"

"Have to chance it, don't worry. It's a big place. Let's get back, shall we?"

"What about the faun?"

"I dare say I could buy his silence, wouldn't you say?"

"I'm darned sure you could," I said.

"And there's no one in the village going to be able to cross the Nahr el-Sal'q to report that a white Porsche has been standing in the village street all day. Incidentally, I'll wait for a bit till I've made sure they've let you back into the palace. If they don't, come down again to the ford, and we'll think again. But I'm certain they will."

"It's all very well for you. I don't want to have to spend another night without even a nightie."

"That's not my fault, that's the will of Allah. I'll bring you a toothbrush tonight, but I'm damned if I'll climb back across the cascade carrying a nightie. You could always borrow a djibbah from Great-Aunt Harriet."

And on this note of unfeeling comfort he led the way back toward the cascade and the gully.

8

But who shall teach thee what the night-comer is?

—THE KORAN: *Sura* LXXXVI

IT ALL went exactly as Charles would have wished. It seemed almost too easy. Jassim may have imagined it was Nasirulla who was ringing for entry, for he opened the gate immediately, and when he saw who it was, let me in with not much more than a bit of sulky muttering, and in a moment or two I was explaining the circumstances to John Lethman.

If he was put out he concealed it very well. "How stupid of me not to have expected this, especially when Nasirulla didn't turn up. It's happened before after heavy rain when the snows are still melting. Of course you must stay. Did you really go the whole way up the river to try and find a way across?"

"Yes, right up to the source, at least I suppose it's the source, it's a sort of cascade coming out of the cliff. The driver thought there might be a way over if he helped me, but it would have taken a rock climber, and I jolly well wasn't going to risk it. So we gave up, and I came back."

"He's gone back to Beirut?"

I nodded. "He said there'd be no chance of its going down before tomorrow. So I gave him a message for my cousin Charles not to come up here, because Great-Aunt Harriet wasn't well enough to see him." I added: "That's how I put it, anyway. I'll explain better when I see him myself. Are you going to tell her I've come back?"

He hesitated, then turned up a hand, smiling. "I'm not sure. Let's defer the decision until she wakes up, shall we?"

"You play by ear, do you?"

"Exactly that. Come back to your garden, Miss Mansel. You're just in time for lunch."

Whether Jassim had managed to convey the news to Halide, or whether she would normally have shared the meal with John Lethman herself, I had no way of telling. Only a few minutes after he had shown me back to the room in the Seraglio Court, the girl arrived with a tray set for two, which she thumped down with patent resentment on the table, and then stood smoldering at me and directing a rapid stream of Arabic at John Lethman which sounded like nothing more nor less than the spitting of an angry cat.

He took it calmly, only once interrupting with slight irritation, and finally, with a glance at his watch, making some statement that seemed to satisfy her. At any rate it silenced her and sent her away, with another look at me and a flouncing swirl of black skirts. No pretty silks this morning, I noticed, and no paint; just a working dress of rusty black, and none too clean at that. I thought with half-irritated amusement that if it was competition she was worrying about, she need hardly count me; I hadn't seen hot water or a hairbrush for more than twenty-four hours, and must look the worst for my long, hot trek up the Nahr el-Sal'q and back; but it wasn't exactly possible to explain that I wasn't entering the competition anyway.

Lethman was looking embarrassed. "I'm sorry about that. Have a drink."

He brought a glass of wine and handed it to me. As I took it our hands touched. His was reddish-brown, mine pale brown; but both what you would call white. Perhaps she had reason after all.

"Poor Halide," I said, and sipped wine. It was the same cool golden stuff of yesterday. I added quickly: "It isn't fair when she has so much to do. Would she be offended if I left her something? I didn't this morning because I wasn't quite sure."

"Offended?" There was the slightest edge on his voice. "You can't offend an Arab with money."

"How very sensible," I said, and helped myself from a dish of *kefta,* savory meat balls on a mound of rice. "This waterfall I saw at the top of the Nahr el-Sal'q, does it have any part in the Adonis cult you were telling me about?"

"Not really, though there's a minor site nearby which was supposed to be a subsidiary of the temple of Venus at Afka. You wouldn't see it unless you climbed up out of the gorge . . . no? Well, it's hardly worth a special trip . . ."

The rest of luncheon passed pleasantly, and it was easy enough to keep him on impersonal subjects. This much to my relief. I didn't want to strain my talent for deception too far, and my recent meeting with Charles was just a little too vivid in my mind. Any further discussion of family affairs was better avoided, and I wasn't anxious to press for another interview with Great-Aunt Harriet. And here it seemed probable that John Lethman's interests coincided with my own.

As soon as lunch was over he got to his feet. If I didn't mind . . . ? He had things he must see to . . . If I would excuse him now . . . ? I reassured him quickly, almost too eagerly. The garden was drowsy with the afternoon's heat, and I would sit there, I told him, and doze over a book. And if I might do a bit of exploring later on? Not the Prince's Court, of course, but elsewhere? So fascinating . . . a chance I might never have again . . . and of course I wouldn't dream of disturbing Great-Aunt Harriet . . . no earthly need for her even to *know* . . .

We parted on a mutual note of restrained relief. After he had gone, taking the tray with him, I collected some cushions off the window seat and took them out into the garden, where I settled myself at the edge of the pool in the shade of a tamarisk tree.

It was very quiet. The trees hung still, the water was a flat, flashing glass, the flowers drooped in the heat. Near me on the stone a lizard slept motionless, not even moving when a quail shuffled past to settle in the dust, wings outspread. On the broken bridge the peacock displayed half-heartedly to a mate who wasn't even watching. Somewhere among the blazing magenta flowers of the bougainvillea which covered the arcade a bird sang, and I recognized last night's king, the nightingale. Somehow, he didn't sound the same as he had with the trappings of storm and starlight. Some finches and a turtledove started up in opposition, and the nightingale, with a trill that sounded like a yawn, gave up. I didn't blame him. I slept.

It was about an hour later that I woke, and the sleepy heat seemed to have overtaken the whole place. Now, there was no sound at all. When I got up from my cushions the lizard flicked out of sight, but the quail never moved its head from under its wing. I set out to explore.

There is little point in describing here in detail my wanderings of that afternoon. It wasn't likely that any outer gate would open straight into the women's quarters, but the 'postern' had been at the back, and since the Seraglio Court, with its rooms and enormous garden, stretched the full width of the palace at the rear, my search had obviously to start there. Now, the postern had apparently been hidden in the trees at the southeastern corner. When I looked out of my bedroom window I could just see the tops of these trees where they projected beyond the corner. They were level with my windowsill. The Seraglio was, in fact, a story and a half above the level of the plateau. The postern must open on some corridor below it, or at the foot of a flight of steps.

A hunt along the eastern arcade and into the recesses of the hammam on the corner convinced me that there was no staircase there, nor a door that could lead to one, so after a while I abandoned the Seraglio, and set out to investigate the untidy sprawl of the palace buildings.

I am sure that the place was not as vast as I imagined it to be, but there were so many twisting stairs, narrow dark corridors, small rooms opening apparently at haphazard one out of the other—many of them in half darkness and all untidy with the clutter and decay of years—that I very soon lost all sense of direction, and simply wandered at random. Every time I came to a window I looked through it to get my bearings, but many of the rooms were lit only by skylights, or by narrow windows giving on corridors. Here and there a window would look over the countryside; one small court, indeed, had an open arcade giving straight out over the Adonis Gorge, with a magnificent view of snow-clad peaks beyond, and a sheer drop to the river below. One ground floor window, I remember, looked north from the end of a black corridor, toward the village; but this window was barred, and beside it were two heavy doors with grilles inset, giving on what I had no difficulty in recognizing as prison cells.

After wandering for nearly two hours, getting my hands grimy and my shoes gray with dust, I was no nearer finding any door that could be the postern, or any staircase that took me down to it. Certainly during my wanderings I had come across several locked doors. The most promising of these was on the east side of the *midan,* a high door with a barred ventilator. But when (the place being apparently deserted for the afternoon) I pulled myself up for a quick glance through, I could see nothing except a yard or two of roughly cobbled flooring leading into darkness, apparently on the level and in the wrong direction. No sign of stairs—and in any case the door was fast locked. There were, of course, stairways in plenty that led crazily and seemingly at random from one level to another, but I found nothing that could definitely be called a basement or lower story. The longest flight of steps counted only twelve, and led up to a gallery surrounding some echoing chamber big enough for a ballroom, where swallows nested in the roof, and the bougainvillea had come in through the unglazed window arches. These, running along the gallery at knee height, lighted the two long sides of the chamber, one row looking out to the south, the other inward over an otherwise unlighted corridor. Hot buttresses of sunlight thrust diagonally in through the outer arches; round them the magenta flowers hung limp and still; the sound of the water from the gorge below came as little more than a murmur.

Quarter to five. I moved to the shady inner side of the gallery and sat down rather wearily on a deep sill to rest. Either the 'postern' was a mirage after all, or it was irrevocably hidden from me by one of the locked doors. My search could not have been anything but perfunctory, but I dared not take it further. The chance simply hadn't come off. Charles would have to climb in after all. And (I thought irritably, brushing dust from my slacks) serve him right.

In one respect my luck had been in; I had met no one all afternoon, though under the complex of watching windows I had been careful to preserve the air of an innocent and random explorer. I did wonder several times if the hounds were loose, and if the fact that they had seen me in John Lethman's company would make them friendly; but I need not have worried, I saw nothing of them. If they were still shut in the small court, they made no sign. Doubtless they, too, slept in the heat of the afternoon.

I was roused by the sound of a door opening somewhere below me on the far side of the corridor. The siesta was over, the place was waking up. I had better get back to my room in case someone thought of bringing tea.

Light steps on stone, and the gleam of scarlet silk. Halide paused in the doorway, looking back to speak softly to someone still in the room, her slim brown hands languidly adjusting the gilded belt at her waist. She had discarded her working clothes; this time the dress was scarlet over pale green, and her gilt sandals had high heels and curved Persian toes. The bird had its plumage on again, and prettier than ever.

Mating plumage, at that. It was John Lethman's voice that answered her from the room, and a moment later he followed her to the door. He was wearing a long Arab robe of white silk, open to the waist, and his feet were bare. He looked as if he had just woken up.

It was too late to move now without being seen: I kept still.

The girl said something more, and laughed, and he pulled her toward him, still half sleepily, and made some reply against her hair.

I edged back from the window, hoping they were too absorbed to catch the movement and look up. But almost immediately a sound, familiar by now but almost shocking in the drowsy silence, froze me to my windowsill. The bell from the Prince's Divan. And after it, inevitably, the clamor of the hounds.

I don't know what I had expected to happen then—some reaction from Halide, perhaps, like the fear she had shown last night; certainly a rush to answer that arrogant summons. But no such thing happened. The two of them raised their heads, but stayed where they were, Halide (I thought) looking slightly startled, and throwing a question at John Lethman. He answered shortly, and then she laughed. A stream of Arabic from her, punctuated by laughter, then he was laughing too, and the hounds stopped their noise and fell quiet. Then the man pushed the girl away from him, with a gesture and a jerk of the head which obviously meant, "You'd better go," and, still laughing, she put a hand up to push the tumbled hair back from his brow, kissed him, and went, not hurrying.

I made no attempt to move. I stayed where I was, staring after her. And for the first time since Charles had made his fantastic proposal for tonight's break-in, I was whole-heartedly glad of it. I could hardly wait to tell him what I had seen.

Halide had been wearing Great-Aunt Harriet's ruby ring.

There was no mistake about it. As she had lifted her hand to John Lethman's hair, the light, falling from some source in the room behind him, had lit the jewel unmistakably. And she had laughed when the bell had rung, and gone, but not hurrying.

I stared after her, chewing my lip. I had a sudden picture of the lamplit room last night; the old woman wrapped up, huddled in the welter of wool and silk on her bed in the corner; Halide beside her, watching all the time with that wary look; and behind me John Lethman . . .

He went back into the room and shut the door.

I gave it three minutes, then went quietly downstairs from the gallery, and made my way back to the Seraglio Court.

At first I thought that Charles's alternative plan—the 'soap-opera' one—was also doomed to failure. In the last brief hour between daylight and darkness—between six and seven o'clock—I explored the arcade on the north side of the lake. Still carefully looking as if I was interested only in the view outside, I wandered from window to window examining the metal grilles and the state of the stone that held them. All were sound enough—too sound for me to be able to do anything about it, and the only one that wasn't barred had been boarded up with heavy shutters. Here and there, it is true, a bar was broken or bent, or the edge of the grille had rusted out of the rotten stone; but the grille was in heavy six-inch squares, and only a gap of half the window would have served to let a body through. There was no such gap, nothing that would have let anything in larger than a cat or a small and agile dog.

And if there had been, I thought bitterly, surprised at my own furious disappointment, it would have been blocked up somehow. Charles and I had been too sanguine. This was after all a lonely place, and Great-Aunt Harriet had had the reputation of being rich. It was only reasonable, whatever the interior of the building was like, that the guards on the only accessible windows should be kept in good repair.

I am ashamed to say that I had stood there for a full five minutes staring at the barred windows and wondering what in the world to do next, before the thought hit me with all the beautiful simplicity and force of the apple dropping on Newton's head. One of the windows *had* been blocked. The end one. By a shutter.

And a shutter that was put up from inside could presumably be taken down from inside.

I ran along the arcade and peered anxiously at it in the now fading light. At first sight it looked horribly permanent. Stout wooden shutters with nails as big as rivets were closed tightly over from either side like double doors, and across these a heavy bar, or rather plank, was nailed to hold them together. But when I examined this more closely, fingering the nails that held it in place, I found to my joy that they were not nails, but screws, two to each end, big-headed screws that I thought I might be able to manage. Surely among the assorted junk that I had seen lying around, there would be something that would do the job?

I didn't have far to look; most of the rooms were empty, some even open to the air with doors broken or left standing wide; but three doors down from the corner I remembered a room that—when I had literally pushed my way in to find a way to the postern—had looked like an abandoned junk shop.

It had been at some time a bedroom, but would have rated a poor fourth class in the tattiest hotel guide. The sagging bed, the broken table, every inch of the dusty floor was covered with a clutter of the most useless-looking objects. I picked my way over a camel saddle, an old sewing machine and a couple of swords, to a chest of drawers where I remembered seeing, beside a pile of dusty books, a paper knife.

It was good and heavy and should do the job admirably. I carried it to the door and blew the dust off, to find it was no paper knife after all, but a quite genuine dagger, an affair with an elaborately inlaid handle and a workmanlike steel blade. I ran back to the shuttered window.

The screw I tackled first was rusty and had bitten deeply into the wood, so after a few minutes' struggle I abandoned it and attacked the other one. This, though stiff at first, came out eventually. I went to the other end. The bar was lying on a slant, and I had to stand on tiptoe to deal with the other two screws, but after some difficulty got one of them out, and the other moving fairly easily. I left it there. There was no point in opening the shutters yet, before John Lethman had been and gone. I didn't bother with the rusted screw; if I freed one end of the bar I could pull it down using the rusted screw as a hinge, and leave it hanging there.

No one was likely to miss the dagger. I hit it under the cushions of the window seat in my room, went along to the hammam to wash, and regained my room just in time to meet Jassim carrying a lighted lamp, a bottle of arak, and a note from John Lethman to say that he himself had to dine with Great-Aunt Harriet, but food would be brought to me at nine and he would come along at ten to make sure I had everything I wanted for the night.

The note concluded: *"I didn't tell her you'd come back. It didn't seem quite the time. I'm sure you'll understand."*

I thought I understood very well. I put the note into my handbag, and regarded the bottle of arak with loathing. I'd have given an awful lot for a nice cup of tea.

He came as he had promised, staying chatting for half an hour, and went shortly after ten-thirty taking my supper tray with him. At something just after eleven I heard again the furious peal of Great-Aunt Harriet's bell, and somewhere in the palace the sound of a slamming door. Thereafter, silence. I turned out my lamp, sat for a little while to let my eyes get used to the darkness, then opened the door of my room and went out into the garden.

The night was warm and scented, the sky black, with that clear blackness that one imagines in outer space. Hanging in it, the clustered stars seemed as large as dog-daisies, and there was a crescent moon. Here and there its light struck a gleam from the surface of the lake. A couple of nightingales sang one against the other in a sort of wild angelic counterpoint, punctuated from the water with rude noises from the frogs. In the shadow of a pillar I nearly fell over a sleeping peahen, which went blundering off with loud expostulations between the pillars, disturbing a covey of rock partridges which exploded in their turn, grumbling, through the bushes. A few frogs dived with a noise like the popping of champagne corks.

Altogether it was a fairly public progress, and by the time I reached the shuttered window I was waiting, with every nerve jumping, for the hounds to add their warning to the rest. But they made no sign. I gave it a minute or two, then tackled the window.

The screw answered easily to the dagger, and I lowered the bar.

I had been afraid that the shutters might prove to be fixed in some way, but the right-hand one shifted when I pulled at it, and finally came open with a shriek of rusty hinges that seemed to fill the night. Recklessly I shoved it back to the wall and waited, straining my ears. Nothing, not even from the nightingales, which had apparently been shocked into silence.

So much the better. I pulled the other side open and leaned out.

And I could lean out. I had been right about the reason for the shutters. Except for a few inches of crumbling iron sticking out of the stone here and there, the grille had gone completely. I hung over the sill and strained my eyes to see.

The window was about thirty feet from the ground, and directly below it ran the path which skirted the north wall of the palace. Beyond the path the rocky ground fell away in a gentle bank covered with bushes, scrubby trees, and a few thin poplars which clung at the edge of the drop to the Nahr el-Sal'q. Off to the left I could see the sizable grove of sycamores which shaded the top of the cliff path down to the ford.

Nothing of any height grew near, except the thin unclimbable poplars, and there were no creepers on the walls; but Charles, I thought, might be right, and the decaying state of the palace be in his favor. I couldn't see much in the moonlight, but here and there below me something furred or broke the line of the masonry, indicating that ferns and plants had thrust the mortar from between the stones, and the rock below that, though sheer, looked rough enough to provide holds for a clever climber.

Well, that was up to my cousin. I strained my eyes to see if I could see any movement, or even possibly the brief flash of a torch, but saw nothing. Beyond the near shapes of the trees all was darkness, a wide still darkness where blacker shapes loomed, but nothing was clear to the eye except the strung lights of the village and the distant glint of snows under the young moon. He would have had to make the climb across the top of the Nahr el-Sal'q by moon or torchlight, and even that climb was probably simple compared with this sheer wall below me, where he wouldn't dare use his torch at all. It occurred to me suddenly to wonder if there were a rope in the junk room, or anywhere else in the court. If so, one of the projecting pieces of iron might be strong enough to hold it. I hung my white towel over the windowsill as a signal that the way was clear, and turned to hurry back along the arcade.

Something moved in the bushes near the end of the broken bridge. Not one of the peacocks; this was too big, and moved too purposefully. I stood still, my heart suddenly thumping. It forged through the crackling thicket, and a thousand scents came with it, as sharp as spice from the crushed leaves. Then it came slowly out onto the flagway in the moonlight, and stood staring at me. It was one of the hounds. Almost immediately I heard a splashing sound, followed by the swift scrabble of paws on stone, and the other came racing round the edge of the lake toward me.

I stayed where I was, frozen. I don't think it occurred to me straight away to be afraid of the dogs themselves; I assumed John Lethman to be with them, approaching through the garden. What was frightening me was the thought of the telltale window behind me, with my All Clear hanging in it inviting Charles to begin his climb . . .

The second dog had stopped beside the first, and the pair stood shoulder to shoulder, rigid, heads high and ears pricked. They looked very big, and very alert. They were between me and my bedroom. Charles or no Charles, I'd have given a lot at that moment to have heard John Lethman's tread and his voice calling them in.

But nothing moved—they must be patrolling on their own. I wondered fleetingly how they had got into the Seraglio; Lethman must have left the main door open when he went with my supper tray, and like a fool I hadn't checked. Of course, if they did give tongue, Charles would hear them and be warned. Or if they attacked me, and I screamed for John Lethman . . .

The only thing to do was to stand perfectly still and stare back at them. The moonlight caught their eyes, reflecting back brilliantly. Their ears were cocked high, their long narrow heads making them look predatory, like foxes.

"Good dogs," I said falsely, putting out a reluctant hand.

There was a horrible pause. Then one of them, the bigger of the two, gave a sudden little whine, and I saw the ears flatten. In a sort of dazed relief I realized that the plumed tail was stirring. The smaller hound seemed to take a cue from this. Her ears went back, her head down, and she crept forward toward me, wagging her tail.

Relief made me feel weak at the knees. I sat down on the edge of a stone tub containing tobacco flowers, and said, on a breathless gasp; "Good dog, oh good *dog!* Here, chaps, here—and keep quiet for pete's sake . . ." What the blazes were their names? Soupy? Soapy? Softy? Surely not . . . ! Sofi, that was it, and Star, "Star!" I said, "Sofi! Come on now—here—that's right . . . Keep quiet, you great dollops, you great soft idiots . . . Watchdogs my foot . . . ! Oh, you horrible dog, you're wet. . . ."

And the hounds were delighted. We made a rather confused, damp, and reasonably quiet fuss of one another, till I felt absolutely certain they were safe to handle, then I got to my feet, feeling for their collars, ready to put them out and clear the field for Charles.

"Come along now, chaps. You'd better get back on the job, you dangerous brutes, you. We've got a burglar coming any minute now, and I want you out of here."

At that precise moment, from directly below the north wall, I heard Charles's signal, the sharp double bark of a hill fox.

The salukis, naturally, heard it too. Their heads went up, and I felt the bigger one—the dog—stiffen. But it must have sounded to them a fairly unconvincing fox—and a foreign one at that—for when I grabbed for their collars again, murmuring soothingly, they allowed me to pull them away toward the gate.

They were so tall that I didn't even have to stoop, but hurried along the flagged path with a hand hooked in each collar. That is, I tried to hurry, but whatever sounds they were hearing from the far end of the garden so intrigued them that they hung heavily against their collars, looking back now and again with little whining nosies deep in their throats, so that I expected at any moment the outcry to begin. But there was no outcry, and at length I got them to the gate—to find it, against all expectation, firmly shut.

No time to stop and wonder how on earth they had found their way in; there were probably a dozen decaying holes in the walls that they knew perfectly well. I concentrated on getting them shut out. It was a bit of a struggle to hold both dogs and get the door undone at the same time, but eventually I managed, and with a final pat pushed both hounds outside, shut the gate firmly on them, and dropped the latch into place.

For a moment all was stillness again. The sounds from the end of the garden had stopped, though, straining my eyes, I thought I saw movement in the far shadows. A moment later I heard the soft footstep. He was in.

I had started to meet him, when to my horror I heard the dogs begin to whine and bark just outside the gate; the eager scrabbling of paws on wood as loud as a charge of galloping horses. They still sounded absurdly friendly—too damned friendly; it seemed that even the burglar from outside rated a noisy welcome on the mat. I could see him fairly clearly now, coming rapidly along in front of the pillars of the eastern arcade.

I ran to meet him. "I'm sorry, but it's the dogs, the blasted dogs! They got in somehow and they're making a ghastly noise, and I don't know what to do with them!"

I stopped abruptly. The shadowy figure had come up to me.

"I'm fearfully sorry," he said, "did they frighten you? That idiot Jassim left a door open and they got through."

The newcomer wasn't Charles at all. It was John Lethman.

9

Of my Base Metal may be filed a Key,
That shall unlock the Door . . .

—E. FITZGERALD: *The Rubáiyát of
Omar Khayyám*

IT WAS probably a very good thing that the dark was hiding my expression. There was a long, ghastly pause, while I could think of nothing whatever to say. I did a desperate mental recap of the way I had greeted him, decided it couldn't have given much away or he wouldn't have sounded so unsurprised, thanked Allah I hadn't actually called him 'Charles,' and settled on attack as the best form of defense.

"How in the world did you get in?"

I thought he hesitated for a moment. Then I saw the movement of his head. "There's a door over in the far corner. Hadn't you found it in your wanderings?"

"No. Was it open?"

"I'm afraid so. It's not a door we usually use at all, it only gives on a warren of empty rooms between here and the Prince's Court. Probably his suite and personal slaves were kept there once." He gave a short laugh. "It isn't even fit for the slaves now, nothing there but the rats. That's probably why the dogs went ramping through—they're not allowed near the Prince's rooms normally, but Jassim must have left a door open somewhere. Did they frighten you?"

He was speaking softly, as I suppose one does instinctively in a quiet night. I was only half attending to what he said. I was wondering if the sounds I had heard before had in fact been sounds of Charles's climb, or only of John Lethman's approach. If the latter, had Charles heard him too, and waited at the foot of the wall, or was he likely to erupt at any minute from the window?

I raised my own voice to normal pitch. "They did rather. Why in the world did you tell me they were savage? They're actually terribly friendly."

He laughed again, a bit too easily. "They can be sometimes. I see you managed to put them out, anyway."

"They probably recognized me as one of the family—or else they saw me with you yesterday, so they know I'm allowed in. Are there only the two? Didn't she have some small dogs—pets?"

"She used to have a pack of spaniels, then some terriers. The last of them died just last month. You mightn't have got away with it if he'd still been around." Again the abrupt laugh. " 'Pet' was hardly the word, really . . . Look, I really am terribly sorry about this. You weren't in bed, I take it?"

"No. I was just thinking of going. I'd just put the lamp out, and I came out to look at the garden. Can you smell the jasmine and tobacco flowers? And don't the roses ever go to sleep?" I moved determinedly toward the gate as I spoke, and he came with me. "If it comes to that, don't you? Were you doing the rounds, or just trying to find the dogs?"

"Both. I was wondering whether you'd been counting on seeing your great-aunt again."

"No. I wasn't staying up for that, honestly. I was just on my way to bed. Don't give it a thought, Mr. Lethman, I quite understand. Good night."

"Good night. And don't worry you'll be disturbed again, I've locked the other door, and I'll see this one's safe."

"I'll lock it myself," I promised.

The gate closed behind him. There were strangled yelps of welcome from the dogs, and then the sounds receded into the labyrinth of the palace. At least the disconcerting little interlude had given me a watertight excuse for locking the Seraglio gate on the inside. The key turned with a satisfying *clunk,* and I fled back toward the open window.

It was my night for shocks. I'd got two-thirds of the way back along the water-side when a soft "Christy" brought me up short, and a shadow detached itself from a dark doorway, and materialized as my cousin.

I gasped, and turned on him furiously, and quite unjustly. "You high-powered nit, you scared me silly! I thought—when did you get *in?*"

"Just before he did."

"Oh, you saw him then?"

"I'll say. Lethman?"

"Yes. He got in by a door in the far corner. The dogs must have—"

"Like hell he did. He came from the island," said Charles curtly.

"From the *island*? He couldn't have!"

"I tell you I saw him. I heard some queer noises when I was halfway up the wall, so I went pretty cautiously, and took a quiet little gander over the sill before I climbed in. I saw you and the dogs making off down the path. I let you get down to the far end, then I couldn't hang on much longer, so I heaved myself in through the window. Next thing was, I saw him coming across the bridge."

"But—you're sure?"

"Are you joking? He went past within feet of me. I'm permanently crippled through jack-knifing down too near a prickly pear. After he'd gone by I went back into one of the rooms and hid."

"But if he's been on the island all the time, he must have seen me open the window. Those shutters made the most awful noise. He must have guessed why I was opening them up, so why didn't he tackle me, or wait a bit longer to see what I was up to? Charles, I don't like it! It's all very well saying that even if you were caught there wouldn't be much trouble, but this is just the kind of place they'd loose off a shotgun at you or something, on spec. *And why didn't he wait*? What's he gone to do?"

"Dear girl, don't get so steamed up. If he had seen you at the window he'd obviously have asked what the blazes you thought you were doing, and whatever guess he made, he'd have stopped you. So obviously he didn't see you. *Quod erat.*"

"I suppose so . . ." I added quickly: "Now I come to think about it—yes, the dogs could have been on the island. I saw Star—that's the big one—by the bridge, and when Sofi came there was a lot of splashing, and she was wet. Perhaps John Lethman heard them over there and went across to get them . . . ? No, that won't do, because then he'd have seen me. But he'd have seen me too if he'd come by a door in the far corner. He'd have passed me when I was at the window. Oh, I give up! Charles, what on earth's it all about? Why should he lie?"

"I don't know. But when we know how we know why. Is there really a door in the corner?"

"I don't know, I didn't see one. But it's terribly overgrown and I didn't really search, because it wasn't the right place for the postern."

"Supposing we look, then? He got in somehow, didn't he, and not by the main door. And if he was on the island all the time, and didn't ask you what the blazes you were up to, I could bear to know why. Does the main door lock, by any chance?"

"I locked it."

"And bonny sweet Christy was all my joy. What the sweet hell's that?"

"A peacock. Do be careful, Charles, they're all asleep."

"With cat-like thump upon our way we steal. Can you see in the dark, love?"

"Just about, by this time," I said, "And incidentally, so can John Lethman. You'd think if he was doing his rounds in this boneyard of a place he'd show a torch, wouldn't you? I suppose it didn't enter your head to bring one?"

"You wrong me every way; you wrong me, Brutus. But we'll do without as long as we can."

"You're very high tonight, aren't you?"

"The intoxication of your presence. Besides, I'm enjoying myself."

"As a matter of fact, so am I, now you're here."

"Watch it," said my cousin, "there's a prickly pear on your near bumper." He pulled back a bough for me, and dropped a casual arm round my shoulders to steer me through. "There's your door, I think?"

"Where?"

He pointed. "Under the luxuriant herb, whatever it is."

"You ignorant peasant, that's jasmine. It's terribly dark here, could we use the torch? That's it . . . aha!"

"What d'you mean, aha?"

"Look," I said.

Charles looked. He could hardly avoid seeing what I had meant. There was certainly a door, and it was certainly decayed, but nothing—neither dogs nor man—had been through it for a very long time. The weeds grew a foot high in front of it, and the hinges looked like spindles of wool, so thickly were they cocooned with cobwebs.

"Aha, indeed," said my cousin. "And a beautiful web right across it, too, just in case we thought it might have been opened the other way. But how corny, no clichés spared . . . but then things only become clichés because they're the slickest way of saying something. No, this door hasn't been opened since the last time the old Emir tottered along to the harem in 1875. *Videlicet*—if that's the word I want, which seems doubtful—the spiders. So he didn't come in this way, our John Lethman. Well, I hardly thought so. Come back, come back, Horatius."

I said blankly: "But there *can't* be a way in from the island!"

"We can but look," said Charles reasonably. "Hullo!" The beam of the torch, narrow and bright and concentrated, speared down through the weeds at the foot of the wall, to light a tombstone, a small flat slab let into the masonry, and carrying a name deeply tooled: JAZID.

"A graveyard, no less," said Charles, and sent the torchlight skidding along a couple of feet. Another stone, another legend: OMAR.

"For goodness' sake, turn it up!" I exclaimed. "D'you mean it really is a graveyard? In here? But why on earth . . . ? And anyway, they're men's names. They can't be—"

I stopped. The light had caught another one: ERNIE.

"Charles—"

"So that's it. I remember Ernie quite well."

I said, exasperated: "Be serious, for goodness' sake! You know perfectly well that Great-Uncle Ernest—"

"No, no, the dog. He was one of the King Charles spaniels she had when she first came out here. Don't you remember Ernie? She always said he was called after Great-Uncle Ernest because he was absent over everything but meals." He sounded pretty absent himself, as if he was thinking hard, but not about what he was saying. The torchlight moved on. "It's the pets' graveyard, hadn't you guessed? NELL, MINETTE, JAMIE, still the spaniels . . . HAYDEE, LALOUK, those sound more Eastern . . . Ah, here she is. DELILAH . . . Alas, poor Delilah. That's the lot."

"They can't have got round to him yet."

"Who?"

"Samson. John Lethman says he died last month. Look, must we spend the whole night in a dogs' graveyard? What are you looking for?"

The torchlight drifted along the wall, met nothing but a tangle of creepers and the ghostly pale faces of flowers. "Nothing," said Charles.

"Then let's get out of here."

"I am coming, my own, my sweet." He snapped the light out, and swung back an armful of stems to let me through. "I suppose that's a nightingale singing its ducky little heart out up there? Damn these roses, my sweater must look like a yak's pelt by now."

"What does it take to make you romantic?"

"I'll tell you someday. Can you manage this?"

'This' was the bridge. The faint moonlight reflecting back from the water below made the broken gap clearly visible; it wasn't as far as I had thought, perhaps five feet. Charles jumped it first, light-footed, and more or less caught me as I jumped after him. And soon, with a hand in his, I was treading carefully off the bridge onto the rocky shore of the island.

This was very small, being nothing more than an artistically placed tumble of rocks, planted with bushes and shrubs long gone wild, but designed to lead the eye up to the grove of shade trees (of a kind I didn't recognize) which overhung the kiosk. This, as I have said, was a small summer pavilion, a circular building with slender pillars supporting a gilded dome. The door was an open archway, and to the sides, between the pillars, fretted lattices of stone made fantastic patterns where the moonlight fell. Wide shallow steps led up from the shore, and a tumble of creepers hung half across the doorway, darkening the interior. My cousin let go my hand, pulled some of the tangle aside, and flashed his torch on. With a clap and flurry of wings two pigeons hurtled out over his head, making him duck and swear, then he led the way in.

The interior was empty except for a small hexagonal basin in the center of the floor where there must once have been a fountain playing. A green fish, solid verdigris, gaped dry-mouthed over dead water which hardly reflected back the torchlight. On two sides the floor was bracketed with wide semi-circular couches, cushionless and filthy with twigs and birds' droppings. The wall opposite the doorway was solid, and painted all over. Charles shone the torch on this.

The painting was done in the Persian, rather than the Arab style, for I could see trees with fruit and flowers, and figures seated under them clad in rich blue and green robes, and something that might have been a hunting leopard leaping after a gazelle on a golden ground. I supposed that in daylight, like everything else in the place, it would be faded and dirty, but in the fleeting rich yellow of the torchlight it looked enchantingly pretty.

The scene was in three panels, a triptych divided by painted tree trunks, stiff and formal, following the line of the pillars that framed the section of wall. At one edge of the center panel, all down the side of the trunk, a dark line showed.

"Here we go," said Charles, approaching it.

"You mean it's a door?"

He made no reply. He was playing the light slowly over the picture, his hand following the probing beam, sliding and patting over the surface of the wall. Then he gave a grunt of satisfaction. From the middle of a painted orange tree a section of the leaves seemed to detach themselves into his hand; the ringbolt of a door. We turned it and pulled. The painted panel opened on quiet, accustomed hinges, showing a gap of blackness behind.

I found my heart beating faster. A secret door can't fail to be exciting, and in this setting . . . "Where can it possibly go?" Then, as he made a gesture of quiet, and jerked a thumb downwards, I said on a whisper that threatened to choke itself with sudden excitement: "You can't mean an underground passage?"

"What else? You notice this wall's flat, but if we looked round the back of this place, in the grove, we'd find the outer wall followed the curve of the rest, and the building was circular. There's room in the segment for the head of the shaft." He laughed at my expression. "Not so very surprising; these old palaces had as many doors and passages and secret exits as they had wormholes—all the go in the good old days when you slept with armed guards round the bed and ate with a couple of slaves tasting for poison." He added: "This is the harem. The Emir would have his private stairway, one would think."

"My God, it's all it needed! Now all we want's a magic carpet or a genie in a bottle."

He grinned. "Hope on, hope ever, we may get one yet." The light played over the door. "This must be how he got in, and the dogs. In that case it probably pushes open quite easily from the inside, but I don't trust it, and I don't want to be locked down there forever like the Mistletoe Bough. Let's find something to wedge it open with, shall we?"

"Down there?" I asked in alarm. "You're not going down?"

"Why not? Can you resist it?"

"Easily . . . No, actually, Charles dear, this is all very exciting, but we shouldn't. It feels all wrong."

"That's just the setting. If this was the back stairs at home you'd think nothing of it. It's all this Arabian Nights' stuff that's getting you."

"I suppose that's true. Can you see?" This as he shone the torchbeam into the gap and stepped over the sill.

"Perfectly. There's a steep flight of steps here, in good repair, and even reasonably clean."

"I don't believe it," I said, as I took his outstretched hand, and stepped carefully over the sill after him.

But it was true. From just inside the painted door the steps went steeply downward, spiraling round a central column. This seemed to be richly carved, and on the curved outer wall there were more paintings, similar to the one on the door. Dimly I could see the trunks of trees, and green interlacing boughs, and a pale flower-dotted ground where a racing camel, curiously elongated by the curve of the wall, carried a moustachioed warrior waving a saber, and a lady unconcernedly playing a zither. Fastened to this wall was a handrail of some blackened metal that could have been brass, held at intervals by elaborate lizards or small dragons which clung riveted to the stones. Certainly an important staircase, a royal staircase, the Prince's own way to the women's quarters. It would be his regular and by no means secret way; merely his private stair, as richly decorated and attractive as his own apartments. The pavilion was in fact the top story of a circular tower or stone shaft which was let down through the center of the lake into the solid rock on which the garden had been built.

"Coming?" said Charles.

"No—no, wait—" I hung back against his hand. "Haven't you realized—if this is the Seraglio stair from the Prince's rooms, that means Great-Aunt Harriet's, and she'll be wide awake, probably with John Lethman reading aloud to her out of the twenty-seventh Sura of the Koran."

He stopped. "You've got a point there. But it must go somewhere else as well."

"Must it?"

"The dogs came this way. I doubt if they're allowed to roam the old lady's bedroom at night, so they must have got through from elsewhere. And what's more, doesn't it occur to you that this might be a way to the postern?"

"Of course! It was on a lower level! But oughtn't we to wait a bit? If we met someone . . ."

"I must admit I'd sooner not," said Charles. "You're right, we'd better leave it for a bit." He followed me back into the pavilion, and behind him the painted door shut silently on a cushion of dead air. Back in the latticed moonlight it was comparatively easy to see the way. He switched off the torch. "What time does she settle down?"

"I've no idea," I said, "but John Lethman'll probably be around for a bit yet. Are you going to try and see her when he's gone?"

"I don't think so. Unless it were urgent, I wouldn't do it this way. It'd be enough to frighten an elderly person into fits, bursting in on her in the middle of the night. No, if I see her at all it'll be the legit way, daylight and front gate and one clear call for me. But you know, on what's happened up to now I'm damned if I'll clear quietly out without taking a good look round. Would you?"

"Probably not. Anyway, if I've got to spend the rest of the night here I'd rather you spent it with me than not."

"Such passion," said my cousin tranquilly. We were at the bridge now, and he paused and cocked his head to listen. Stillness held the place. No shadow moved. He started softly across the bridge, and I followed him.

"You're not going out of this court?" I whispered quickly. "The dogs'll make an awful row—"

"No. I'm not interested in the part of the palace they let you loose in, only the part they didn't. The gap looks wider from this side, doesn't it? Think you can jump it if I catch you?"

"I can try. Charles, you said 'they'? Are you making a bit of mystery out of all this? There's really no reason to suppose—"

"Probably not. I'm probably wrong anyway. Tell you later, alligator. Now jump." I jumped, slipped on landing, and was caught and held. Ridiculous that I hadn't realized until this minute how strong he was. We climbed down off the bridge and pushed our way through the rustling bushes.

He said over his shoulder: "Just in case we don't find the postern down there, we'll go now and take a look at my other line of retreat, shall we? I saw a rope in that room full of junk along here—at least I think I did. It would make life easier on the downward trail."

"I thought there might be one there. I was just on my way to look when the dogs caught me. Do you suppose John Lethman got in via the island last night, too?"

"You can bet your boots he did," said Charles shortly.

"But why not say so? Why lie? Did it matter?"

"Only if he wanted to stop you knowing there was a way under the lake."

"You mean he was afraid I'd by-pass him and go straight to Aunt H on my own?"

"Possibly. But it seems a lot of trouble to go to for something that wouldn't have mattered very much, wouldn't you say?"

"I suppose so. And after all, I might have found it by myself. He didn't stop me wandering around exploring in here."

We had gained the flagged pathway. After the darkness of the pavilion and the overhanging bushes, it seemed light here. Something shuffled rustling into the undergrowth, clucking to itself. I saw Charles slant a look at me. "Why didn't you go over to the island before? I'd have thought that'd be the first thing. It's dead romantic."

"I meant to, but when I got to the bridge . . ." I paused. "Yes, I see, you mean that's what he counted on? I probably could have got across the broken bridge by myself, but it didn't seem worth the bother."

"There you are. Unless you were wild keen, which you'd no particular reason to be, he could reckon you wouldn't be likely to bother. And even if you had jumped over you'd probably never have realized the painted wall was a doorway."

"But if it was all that important that I shouldn't find the staircase, why put me in this court at all? I know it's probably the only reasonable bedroom, but if it *mattered*—"

"Simply because it is the Seraglio, and was designed as a sort of five-star jail. There's probably a million ways in and out of every other corner of the palace, so he had to put you here and spin you the story about the savage dogs to keep you in. What's more," he added, not sounding worried about it all, "we'll almost certainly find there's another door at the foot of the spiral stairway—the one Jassim left open for the dogs—and it'll equally certainly be locked now."

I glanced at him, but he hadn't got the torch on, and I couldn't see his face. "And if we do?"

"Well . . ." said my cousin, and left it at that.

I asked sharply: "You don't mean that you could pick the lock?"

He laughed. "That's the first note of honest admiration I've heard from you since the time I blew the apple-loft door open with carbide. Christy, my sweet, you were born to be a banker's moll. Take it from me, lock picking is practically required study in Mansels."

"Well, naturally. But—" I paused, then went on slowly: "What this amounts to is that there really is something wrong going on . . . I haven't had time to tell you yet, but this afternoon I saw Halide wearing Great-Aunt Harriet's ruby ring—you remember the one?—and she and John Lethman are certainly having an affair, and not paying very much attention to Aunt H, either, from the look of things—which seemed odd, after last night, when they were so attentive in front of me."

I told him then, very quickly, about the little scene I had glimpsed this afternoon. He had stopped to listen, and against the moonlight I could see the attentive slant of his head, but when I had finished he made no comment, merely moving on along the arcade.

I followed. "And why did he lie to me?" I persisted. "There must be some reason for the lies about the way he got in, and the hounds, too . . . Oh, he passed it off tonight, but he really did make a lot of it before, how savage they were, and how unsafe it would be for me to wander about. He made rather a thing about their being loose at night."

"Probably wanted you contained in your own court while he carried on his affair with the girl."

"Come off it," I said curtly. "He was carrying that on with me wandering about the place all afternoon. Anyway, the palace is big enough, heaven knows. Charles, she really was wearing that ring, and if you ask me—"

"Hush a minute, I want to put the light on. Can you hear anything?"

"No."

"Then stay out here and keep your ears open while I go in and look for a rope."

He vanished through the doorway of the junk room.

I looked after him thoughtfully. I might not have seen him for four years, but I still knew every tone of his voice as well as I knew my own. For some reason he had suddenly clammed up on me. There was something he knew, or something he thought, that he didn't propose to share with me. He had been stalling very well, but still he had been stalling.

"Ah," he said, from inside the room.

"Found one?"

"Not so long as a cur's tail, nor so strong as a cobweb, but 'twill serve. Hold the torch while I test it, will you . . . ? Good grief, is's filthy . . . well, I wouldn't exactly climb the west face of the Dru with it, but it should help me down the wall if we don't find the back door."

He emerged from the room, wiping the dirt off his hands. "And now a wash, and a wait. We'll give it an hour, shall we? As long as I can get out of here and away by first light . . . It's even possible the Nahr el-Sal'q may have gone down dramatically by morning, and I can save myself a lot of trouble by cutting straight across it and away before anyone sees me."

"Where's your car this time?"

"I left it about half a mile below the village. There's a small quarry where I could get it off the road and pretty well out of sight. I did play with the idea of spending the rest of the night in the car and coming across for you myself in the morning, but there's always the risk that someone might see it standing there in the small hours and Nasirulla bring the news over before you're clear of the place. And if I ever do want to see Aunt H, I don't fancy having to talk my way out of that one . . . So I left a message for Hamid to come up for you at half past nine tomorrow, and I'll go down to Beirut and wait for you there. And now show me your bathroom, Christy mine, and we'll listen to the nightingales while I get my picklocks sorted out."

10

O softly tread, said Christabel.

—S. T. COLERIDGE: *Christabel*

BUT THEY weren't needed after all.

When we set out again the thin moon had drifted higher, clear of the island trees, and by her faint light we negotiated the bridge once more, and made our way up into the pavilion. The painted door swung out silently, and Charles wedged it open with a stone. Torchlight speared ahead of us into the black gap as we stepped delicately inside and started down the spiral stair.

The paintings slid past us, spectral in the moving light. Domes and minarets, cypresses like spearheads, gazelles, hawks, Arabian stallions, fruit trees and singing birds . . . and at the bottom a door.

Shut, of course. It looked massive and impassable in that frail light, but to my surprise, when Charles put a hand to it and pulled cautiously, it came easily, and with the same well-oiled silence as the one above. I saw then that the latch was gone, and where the original lock had been was a splintered panel of wood. Part of the place's history, no doubt, that smashed lock . . . The door had been secured again in more recent times—by a stout hasp and staple and a padlock— but a lock is only as strong as its moorings, and these, like the rest of the palace appointments, were rotten. The padlock was still in place, and locked, but on one side the hasp had been pulled away from the crumbling jamb, and hung there with one socket still holding the useless screw, the other empty.

This, then, was how the dogs had got through. It seemed probable that they had broken the lock themselves, and tonight, since otherwise it would surely have been mended again. And the damage was obviously recent, for splinters and sawdust showed on the floor, and when Charles shone the torch down I caught the gleam of the fallen screw.

"Luck," he said softly.

"Good for the Gabriel Hounds," I breathed.

He smiled, and beckoned. I soft-shoed after him through the door.

It was very dark, a great arched passage with ribbed and vaulted ceiling where the torchlight seemed little more than an impertinent gleam. We were at the end of a sort of underground T-junction, under a vault made by crossed arches. Our door closed one end of the top shaft of the T. A few yards along from us on the left, an open archway led off into blackness, some sort of passageway down which came a draught of air. Straight ahead, and closing the top bar of the T was another door. Like the main gate of the palace, this door was of bronze, its panels elaborately worked and its surface—in spite of age and damage—retaining the silky beauty of hand-hammered metal. To either side of it were ornate iron brackets which must once have held torches, and beneath these we saw recesses in the wall, man high like sentry boxes. The archway itself was carved, and held traces of peeling paint.

"Must be the Prince's Door," I whispered. "You were right, it's the low road to the Seraglio. See if it's locked."

But he shook his head and sent the light shifting from the door toward the passageway on the left.

"Line of retreat first," he said softly. "This way to the postern, what do you bet? Shall we go see?"

The tunnel was long and curved, not quite level, and very dark. Our progress was slow. As far as I could see the walls were of rough stone—no paintings here—and at intervals bore rusty iron brackets for lights. The floor was rough, too, big slabs of paving with a border of crude cobbles, all worn, filthy, and treacherous with holes. Once a scuffle in the blackness made me stop and clutch at Charles's arm, but the rat or whatever it was made off without my seeing it. The passage bent to the left, turned uphill a little, and met another at right angles.

We paused at the junction. Our passage was the main stem of another T, this time with a bigger passage crossing the head of it. Charles put the torch out, and we stood for a moment listening. The air was fresher here, and it was an easy guess that this corridor was open to the upper air. Then from somewhere away to the right I heard, fainty, the snuffle and whine of the hounds.

Charles flashed the light that way momentarily, to show the rough floor of the tunnel mounting in wide and very shallow steps. "That probably goes up to the gate you saw in the *midan,* which means, unless I'm wrong—" He turned the beam to the left, and almost immediately it seemed to focus on something lying in the middle of the sloping way. A scattered trail of droppings, horse or mule. "I'm not wrong," he said. "This way."

A minute or two later we were looking out through the grove of trees at the edge of the Adonis Gorge.

The postern gate was built into the solid rock, recessed deeply into it, and below the level of the plateau behind the palace. A steep ramp cut from the rock led down to it through the grove, and the roots of the sycamores, level with the lintel, reached bare and twisted like mangroves half across the top of the doorway. A buttress protected it on the landward side, and weeds and creepers grew profusely among the tree roots and overhung the cutting from above. Anyone approaching from the plateau would have seen merely a buttress jutting out into the grove, and beyond this the drop to the Adonis Gorge. The ramp was just wide enough for a laden beast, and the gate was a heavy studded affair in excellent repair, both locked and barred.

"You see?" said my cousin. "Just big enough to take a mule or horse—an emergency door—and then the long passage leading under the Seraglio and up to the *midan.* Well this'll save me a climb, praise be to Allah. Nice of them to leave the key in the lock, wasn't it? Come back in—no, don't shoot the bolts again, I think we'll leave it unlocked." Inside the shut gate again he glanced at his watch. "After two. They can't stay up all night, surely?"

"If anyone's still awake, it'll only be Aunt Harriet."

"Yes," said my cousin. "Well . . ."

He was looking at the ground, fiddling with the button of the flashlight. As it came on again, I caught his expression. This was abstracted, even bleak. He glanced up suddenly. "Shall we go back now?"

"Back? To the Prince's Door? That'll be locked, too, I expect." There must have been something in the ancient secrecies of the place that were making themselves felt; I found myself almost speaking with relief, and I saw him give me another quick glance.

"Possibly, though I doubt if they'd have the place sealed up internally, so to speak. Christy—"

"Yes?"

"Do you want to go on?"

"On?" We had reached the first T-fork and turned into the home run. "Back here, you mean? Where else can we go?"

"I mean on to the Prince's Door. Would you rather just go back to the Seraglio?"

"Would you?"

"No, not now. But if you'd rather get out from under and leave it to me—"

"Do me a favor, will you? I'm not afraid of John Lethman, even if you are."

He started to say something, apparently thought better of it, then grinned and said merely: *"En avant, mes braves."* We went on.

And the Prince's Door wasn't locked. It opened silently, and beyond it was a long, vaulted corridor, pitch black and very still and quite empty. Charles paused. The torchlight seemed almost to be lost in the blackness ahead of us. I thought he hesitated a moment, then he went forward. I followed.

The corridor, like the spiral stair, had once been richly decorated, but though it was swept and reasonably clean underfoot it was in bad repair, and the painted landscapes on the walls were faded and peeling, and even in the torchlight could be seen to be very dirty. The floor was of marble, overlaid with some drab and tattered matting, on which our footsteps made no sound. The air was still and dead and smelled of dust.

To either side, at intervals, were doorways of the kind familiar to me from my wanderings in the palace, most of them gaps of darkness where broken doors hung open on emptiness or confusion. Charles shone the light into the first of these, which seemed to contain nothing but large earthenware jars.

"Nothing there but forty thieves," he commented.

"What did you expect?"

"Heaven knows . . . And here's Aladdin's cave. Half a minute, let's look."

At first I couldn't see what had caught his attention. The room seemed to contain much the same jumble as the 'junk room' in the Seraglio; furniture, ornaments, cobwebs—the same dreary and neglected clutter of years. On a rickety chest of drawers was a pile of books, rather less dusty than the rest.

The torchlight probed along the pile, and after it went Charles's fastidious fingers. He turned the thickest volume spine upward. "I thought so."

"What is it?"

"Chambers's Dictionary."

It had fallen open in his hand. I peered at it in the torchlight. "So useful. Did you know what a cusk was? It says it's a torsk or a burbot. What d'you know? Crosswords, Charles."

"As you say." He shut the book on a puff of dust, and picked up another.

This was smaller than the dictionary, but had a more important look, with thick leather covers which, under their fine graying of dust, seemed to be elaborately tooled. He handled this gently, and when he blew the dust off I caught the gleam of gilding.

"What is it?"

"It's a copy of the Koran, and a rather gorgeous copy at that. Take a look."

The paper was thick and felt expensive, and the Arabic script, beautiful in itself, was enhanced by the ornate designs which headed the Suras, or chapters. It was certainly not the kind of book I would have imagined anyone would throw out into a dusty room to be forgotten.

He laid it down without comment, and the light was sent straying further over the debris. It halted suddenly.

"See what I see?"

At first, among the gray anonymous rubbish, all I could distinguish was the shape of a battered violin, something that might have been a pair of roller skates, and a tangle of leather thongs and buckles and tassels which resolved itself eventually into a couple of bridles. Behind these and half hidden by them were two dusty objects that looked like ornaments. China dogs.

Even so, I stared at them for a good five seconds, I suppose, before I got there.

"Charles! Not your Gabriel Hounds?"

"Indeed and indeed." He knelt down in the dust beside the tangle of leather. "Hold the torch, will you?"

I watched him as he carefully lifted the bridles aside and took one of the china ornaments in his hands. I noticed with some wonder how gently, reverently almost, he handled the thing. He took a handkerchief out of his pocket, and began to wipe the dust away.

Slowly, under the gentle ministrations of the handkerchief, the thing emerged. It was a creature which might have been a dog or lion, about six inches high, made in vivid yellow porcelain with a glowing glaze. It was sitting back on its haunches with one paw down, and the other poised delicately on a fretted ball. The head was turned over one shoulder, at gaze, ears back, wide mouth grinning as dogs grin. It had a thick, waving mane, and its plumed tail curled over its back. Its air was one of gay watchfulness, a kind of playful ferocity. Its mate on the floor, her bright coat fogged with dust, had a plume-tailed pup under her paw instead of a ball.

"Well, my God, who'd have thought it?" said Charles softly. "What do you think of them?"

"Heavens, don't ask me, I'm not up in these things. Are they really meant to be dogs?"

"They're what are known as Dogs of Fo, or Buddhist lions. Nobody seems sure exactly what kind of creatures they were."

"Who was Fo?"

"The Buddha himself. These are the only creatures in the Buddhist mythology that are allowed to kill, and then only in the Lord Buddha's defense. They're officially the guardians of his temple." He turned the glowing creatures over in his hands. The wrinkled pansy-face grinned like a Pekinese over the pretty ball.

"Do you know," I said, "I've a feeling I do remember them. But why do you suppose they've been shoved out here? I mean, I'd have thought—"

"Yes," said Charles. He set the dog down again on the floor, straightened up abruptly, and took the torch out of my hand. I got the impression he hadn't heard a word I'd said. "Shall we get on with the programme?"

Without waiting for an answer, and without another glance at the contents of the room, he led the way quickly back into the corridor.

Here was silence and darkness, and the still smell of unused, dusty air. The trees of the faded, painted landscape slid past, punctuated by the dark cave-mouths of empty rooms. Then ahead of us the corridor curved slightly to the left, and on the outside of the curve the torch picked out another doorway, the same arched shape as the rest, but very different. Here was no empty cave, no sagging and rotten timber. The arch was blocked with a door of oak, brand new and solid as a ship, and it was not only shut fast, but locked with a new brass padlock.

The light paused on this for a moment, then moved on to the next door. Here again a new lock winked.

I said under my breath: "The real treasure chambers, huh?"

My cousin didn't answer. The light slowly raked up the door to the barred ventilator above it, and down again, to fix on what stood beside it. He walked over to look, and I followed him.

Between the two doors, stacked against the wall, were a dozen or so cans, the size of small petrol cans, bright yellow with some sort of design on them. As the torchlight caught them I saw on the nearest, in bold black lettering: FINEST COOKING OIL. *Ideal for Frying, Mayonnaise, Salads*. And below this, something else. I stopped.

The light came back to me swiftly. "What is it?"

"On the tins," I said, blinking in the beam, which swept down from my face again to the pile by the door. "I just noticed—I can't remember where I saw it before. Oh, yes, now I've got it! It's nothing, Charles, only the design on the cans in red, the running dog."

"Yes? What about it?"

"Nothing, I suppose. It's not important. Just that I've seen it before."

"Where?" I looked at him in surprise. He sounded interested, even sharp.

"Sunday afternoon, up at the village Hamid took me to. I told you, didn't I? The sunflower field with the little sign on the tree trunk, the red dog that I thought looked like a saluki."

"This is the same?"

"I think so."

We stooped closer, and now under the drawing of the running dog I could see in smaller black lettering: *Hunting Dog Brand. Best quality, beware immitations.*

"Sal'q," said my cousin, half to himself. The torchlight was full on the tin. He looked absorbed.

"What?"

"That's what 'Hunting Dog' is, did you know? The word 'saluki' is the Arabic *seluqi* or *slughi* and means 'hound.' I imagine the Nahr el-Sal'q is some sort of corruption meaning 'Hound River.' Local produce, in other words. This is the same as you saw in the field?"

"Exactly the same." I straightened up. "Local produce it will be—sunflower oil, I suppose, and what I saw was a marker for the field. I think I read somewhere that the peasants use markers like that for their crops—I suppose it's sense, when a lot of them can't read. Heavens, this must be about ten years' supply! What on earth do you suppose they use it all for?"

He lifted one of the cans and put it down again. "Empty," he said shortly, and turned away.

I looked at him curiously. "Why so interested?"

"Not here," he said," not now. Let's finish this, shall we? And we'd better stop talking."

When we rounded the curve of the corridor, going warily, we saw some thirty yards ahead of us a stairway, a wide sweep leading up to a landing and another elaborate arch. The door was standing open, back to the wall, but in its place a heavy curtain hung across the arch. And at one edge of the curtain a line of light showed. We stopped still, listening. Even our own breathing sounded loud to me in the dead air. But nothing moved; no sound came from beyond the curtain.

Carefully shielding the torch with his fingers, so that only a rosy crack of light showed to dance like a glowworm toward the curtain, Charles mounted the stairs and inched his way forward across the landing to the doorway. He paused beside the curtain, with me at his elbow. The torch was out now, the only light the streak at the curtain's edge.

Still no sound. But now I could smell the curiously pungent scent of Great-Aunt Harriet's tobacco. This must be the Prince's Divan. She might be very near us. She must have been reading, I thought, and have fallen asleep over her book. I couldn't hear her breathing, but then the room was so vast, and if she had drawn the bed curtains before she slept . . .

My cousin put out a stealthy hand and drew the edge of the curtain back a couple of inches. He laid an eye to the crack, and I stooped to look.

It was certainly the Prince's bedchamber. And this was actually the curtain at the back of Great-Aunt Harriet's bed.

There was very little light in the room; the streak at the curtain's edge had only seemed bright in comparison with the outer darkness where we stood. The lamp stood on the table, its flame turned low, the smallest slug of light. But knowing the room, I could see fairly clearly. It was exactly as last night; the red lacquer chair, the unwashed dishes on the table, the hypochondriac clutter on the dressing chest, the dish on the floor with DOG now half-hidden with milk for the cat, and on the bed . . .

For one breathless moment I thought Great-Aunt Harriet was there too, within a yard of us, sitting where she had sat last night in her welter of shawls and silks; then I saw the room was empty. The dark corner at the bedhead held only the tumble of blankets, and the red of her discarded jacket and the fleecy pile of the shawl.

A moment later it hit me again, the cold wave of sickness and the shiver over the flesh, as the cat lifted its head and eyed us from the tumbled bed. Charles saw it at the same moment as I did, and as I backed sharply away he let the curtain fall and came with me. His arms went round me.

"Okay, okay, it's not coming."

"Sure?"

"Of course. You're all right, love, relax."

I was shivering, and the arms tightened. The top of my head came just to his cheekbone. "Give it a minute," he whispered, "then we'll go."

He held me like that for a while, till the shivering quietened, and I felt the cold leave my body. It was very dark and still. I knew from the sound of his breathing that he had turned his head away, and was watching and listening. He turned back, and I felt him draw breath to speak, then with an abrupt but stealthy movement his cheek came down against my hair.

"Christy—"

"Yes?"

A tiny pause. The breath went out like a light sigh, stirring my hair. "Nothing. All right now?"

"Yes."

"Come along then."

"You—you really didn't want to wait and see her? I don't think somehow—"

"No. Forget it, we'll go back."

"I'm sorry, Charles."

"So you should be." His whisper mocked me gently. "Brace up, love, it can't get you. Be a brave girl. Charles'll fight the nasty cat for you."

The terror receded. I laughed. "Big brave Charles," I said. "What if we meet the dogs? I'm fine now, thank you."

"Really? Then we'll call it a night, I think. Back to your harem, my girl."

The painted door was still wedged open, and the air outside in the pavilion was wonderfully fresh and sweet. We crossed the bridge to the gap, and I jumped it after him. He didn't let me go straight away.

"Christy . . ." He spoke softly, quickly. "There's something I've got to tell you."

"I knew it. I knew you were holding something back. Well?"

"Not quite that. I don't *know* anything. I've been making a few wild guesses, let's say. And I know that there's one thing very wrong, and it makes me smell a hell of a big rat. But—and I want you to take this if you will—I'm not going to tell you here and now."

"Why not?"

"For the simple reason that you've got to stay in this place until morning, and I haven't. No, listen, Christy . . . you've got to meet John Lethman and be civil and normal to him, and you never know, Great-Aunt Harriet may take it into her head to see you again, and—"

"'Civil and normal' to John Lethman? Then there *is* something wrong about John Lethman?"

"I told you I was only guessing. Most of it's only a guess. But you have got to stay here."

"So the less I know the better?" I said derisively. "Corny, Chas darling, corny! Blast you, I can *act* innocence, can't I? I'm doing it all the time. Don't be so maddening! If it comes to that, it's me that's in the middle of this, and not you! Come on, you've got to tell me! Is John Lethman Aunt Harriet's lover or something?"

"Heavens," said Charles, "if that were all . . ."

I argued, of course, but he wouldn't be moved. Eventually he let me go, and prepared to jump back across the gap. I said: "Why do you have to go back that way? Why don't you just shin down now from the window with the rope?"

He shook his head. "It's easier this way. Close the shutters now, will you, so there's nothing to catch the eye? Don't put the bar back yet, just in case. I'll go now. You get yourself to bed, I'll see you at the hotel in the morning." He seemed to hesitate. "You're not scared, are you?"

"Scared? Why on earth should I be scared?"

"Well, as long as you're not," said Charles, and left me.

11

So free from danger, free from fear,
They crossed the court: right glad they were.

—S. T. COLERIDGE: *Christabel*

I THOUGHT I wouldn't have slept well, but I went out like a light for the five hours or so until my breakfast came, and woke to a glorious morning, and the sunlit peace of the Seraglio garden with the ripple of water where a light breeze touched it, and the singing birds.

All the same, I remember that I came back to consciousness not of the romantic peace of the place, but of the incipience of something cloudy, the faintest shadow of apprehension coloring the day ahead. Even when I realized that this was probably only the result of Charles's hints about John Lethman, whom I would have to meet again this morning, and that the rest of the day would be shared with Charles himself, I still found that the Seraglio Court, the whole palace locked in its hot valley, afflicted me with a sort of claustrophobia, and I got up quickly and swallowed my coffee, restlessly eager now to get out of the place and back to the hotel and the life and color and vulgar bustle of Beirut. And to Charles.

Hamid had been told to come for me at half past nine, but it was barely half past eight when I finished the coffee that Nasirulla had brought me, lingered for a few minutes for a last look at the garden with the sun on the pavilion's golden dome, then let myself—by the orthodox route—out of the Seraglio.

My first apprehension had been removed by Nasirulla's appearance with my breakfast. If he was here, the river must be passable this morning. I decided to go immediately, and walk up to the village to meet Hamid there. I had tried to indicate to Nasirulla by signs that I wanted to leave early, and though he had merely stared at me in his unsmiling way without a hint of understanding, he must have told John Lethman, for I met the latter coming to meet me in the second courtyard, where the anemones of the Adonis Gardens had already, in the one day's heat, withered and died.

I thought he looked the worse for wear this morning, and wondered if the same could be said of me.

"You're up early," he said.

"I suppose I must have been worrying about the ford. I gather it's all right and I'll be able to get across?"

"Oh, yes. Did you sleep all right in the end after the alarums and excursions?"

"After the—? Oh, the dogs. Yes, thanks. Did you shut the poor things up? I admit I was a bit scared at first, but they were rather pets, and it's just another romantic episode to think about later on. But they're not like that with everybody, are they?"

"By no means. You must have something special." A smile that didn't reach his eyes. "I wouldn't say they're exactly savage, but they make good guard dogs, simply because they make a hell of a row if they hear anything out of the ordinary. I did shut them up, and it may have been a mistake."

I didn't want to ask him why, but he had paused as if he expected it, and it was certainly the natural question. At least the pause gave me time to get my face in order. I asked: "Why?"

"I should have left them on patrol. We found the side gate open. Anyone could have got in during the night."

"The side gate? Is there another gate, then?"

"There's one opening out on the plateau at the back. What with that, and letting the hounds into the Seraglio, Jassim seems to have had himself a ball yesterday."

I said, as casually as I could: "But would anyone break in? You don't mean you've found signs of something?"

"Oh, no. It's just that universal trust isn't a habit of mine, particularly since I came to live in this country. What time's your driver coming?"

"Nine," I said, lying, "but I thought I might as well take myself straight off, and walk over to meet him in the village. You've been terribly good to put up with me for so long. I know I said it all to you yesterday, but you can take it today that it's easily doubled."

"It's been a pleasure. Well, I'll see you out."

He didn't even try to sound, today, as if he meant it. Yesterday's calm had vanished, he seemed harassed and edgy. He hurried me through the smaller court with quick, nervous strides, a hand going to his face in that gesture I had noticed the first day, as if the skin was tender. He was sweating a little, and his eyes were inflamed. I noticed that he didn't look at me, but kept his face turned away, as if conscious or ashamed. I wondered if he were being hagridden by the need for a smoke, and looked away, embarrassed.

"Your Adonis Gardens are dying."

"Yes, well, they're meant to."

"Of course. She doesn't know I came back?"

"No."

"Well, I didn't expect you'd tell her, it's all right. I just wondered if she'd said anything more about my cousin."

"Not a word."

Short, sharp, and to the point. Well, he owed me nothing but my escape. And far from preventing that, he was as eager to get rid of me as I was to get out. He walked out of the main gate with me, and right to the edge of the plateau, and stood there to watch me start down the path. When I reached the ford I looked back, and saw him still there, watching as if to make sure I really went.

I turned my back on Dar Ibrahim for the second time, and trod carefully out over the stepping stones.

These were clear now, and already dry, but the water that swirled round them was higher than the last time I had crossed, and ran iron red, blood red for the dead Adonis. Twigs, leaves, scarlet flowers, had been rushed down the stream and strewed in debris on the banks. Two of the goats browsed desultorily among the jetsam, but I could see no sign of the boy. As I gained the far side of the stream and picked my way up the stony bank I saw Hamid—this time unmistakably Hamid—coming down the path toward me.

We met in the shade of a fig tree where three more of the goats were sleeping in a dusty heap. When our greetings were over I asked him the question that had been simmering on the surface of my mind ever since Nasirulla had brought me my coffee.

"Have you seen my cousin this morning?"

"No." He smiled. "He is very like you, that one, is he not? I should have thought brother and sister."

"He's actually a second cousin, but we used to be taken for twins. Family likeness runs pretty strong with the Mansels. You didn't meet a white sports car on your way up from Beirut? Or see one parked?"

"This morning? I saw nothing on the road at all except one car—a black one with an Arab driver—and a Land-Rover with three Maronite fathers." He eyed me curiously. "I know your cousin's car, I saw it yesterday. You mean he has also been for the night at the palace?"

I nodded. "This means he probably got away all right before he was seen. That's a relief . . . Hamid, you mustn't tell anyone, promise. Actually, my great-aunt doesn't even know he was there. She did see me on Sunday night—I'll tell you about it later—but she said she wouldn't receive my cousin Charles, and he needn't even bother to come up to Dar Ibrahim. Well, you know how he drove up yesterday morning from Damascus, and came up to meet me, but the stream was flooded, so I had to stay another night anyway. It was partly because of that, that my cousin hatched up a plan to get inside the palace and take a look round for himself." I went on to tell him rapidly the main facts: the meeting at the temple and the plans for the 'break-in.' "So I let him in and we explored a bit. We didn't see my great-aunt again, and my cousin didn't think it right to force himself on her like that, so I went back to bed and he went to let himself out by the back entrance. I was just hoping he'd got his car away before anyone saw it."

"I certainly didn't see it." Hamid, though obviously intrigued by my story, contented himself with reassuring me. "It's a Porsche, isn't it? I don't think you need worry. I know the quarry you mean, and I think I'd have noticed if the car was still there when I went by."

We had been climbing as we talked. Now I saw what I had been looking for, a patch of shadow under a tree thirty feet away, where half a dozen goats stood or lay, chewing and eyeing us with supercilious boredom. Among them the faun, shock-headed, grinning, squatted cross-legged in the dust and chewed a leaf with the same kind of disenchanted thoroughness as the goats.

"There you are!" I said.

"I am always here." It was said with a sort of cosmic simplicity that one could readily believe.

"It's all right," I said to Hamid, who had looked slightly startled. "It's only the goatherd."

"I never saw him." He regarded the boy doubtfully. "If he saw your cousin, Miss Mansel, the whole village will know by now that he spent the night at Dar Ibrahim."

"I don't think so. I've a feeling this boy isn't exactly an idle gossip . . . In any case if Nasirulla had known, you can bet Mr. Lethman would have had something to say this morning." I called to the faun. "Ahmad, did you see the Englishman leave Dar Ibrahim this morning?"

"Yes."

"At what time?"

"Just after daylight."

"About four o'clock, that would be," said Hamid.

"He must have stayed on for a bit after we parted, then. I wonder what for? However . . ." I turned back to the boy. "He went up this way to the village?"

"Yes. He went to get the white car which was in the quarry by the road."

Hamid's eyes met mine. I laughed, and he shrugged, turning down his mouth.

"You heard him go?" I asked, and the boy nodded briefly, and waved a hand toward Beirut.

I was surprised at my own feeling of relief. "Did he speak to you?"

"No. I was over there." A jerk of the head seemed to indicate some inaccessible tumble of rocks a quarter of a mile away. "He came from the gate at the back of the palace."

There was no curiosity in his voice, but he was watching me intently. I regarded him thoughtfully. "And this was very early? Before anyone else was about?"

A nod.

"No one else saw him?"

"No one, only me."

"And I am sure that you have already forgotten that you saw him, Ahmad? Or that there was a car?"

A brief flash of the white teeth, clenched on the chewed green leaf. "I have forgotten everything."

I fished some notes out of my handbag, but though the black eyes watched me unwaveringly, the boy made no move. I hesitated. I had no wish to offend his dignity. I laid the notes on the rock beside me, and put a stone on them to hold them down. "Thank you very much," I said. "May Allah be with you."

Before I had got more than two steps away there was a flash of brown limbs and a swirl of dust, and the notes had disappeared into the dirty kaftan. Dignity, it seemed, took second place to common sense. "The goats would eat it," explained the boy carefully, and then, in a rush of Arabic which Hamid laughingly translated for me as we moved off up the path: "And the blessing of Allah be upon you and your children and your children's children and upon your children's children's children and upon all the increase of your house . . ."

It was strange to find the hotel looking the same: I seemed to have been away forever, like Sleeping Beauty, in a storybook world. It was even the same desk clerk on duty, and he smiled and lifted a hand and said something, but I said, "Later, please," and went straight past him to the lift with only two thoughts in my mind, to get out of these clothes and into a gorgeous hot bath before I spoke to a single soul, or even thought once about Charles.

It was heaven to be back in my airy, modern, characterless and superbly comfortable room, throw my horrible clothes on the bathroom floor and climb into the bath. The telephone rang twice while I was there, and once there was a knock at the outer door of the lobby, but I ignored the calls without effort, broiled myself happily for a dangerously long time in a concentrated solution of bath oils, then climbed languidly out, dried myself, and dressed carefully in the coolest frock I had—white and yellow and about as far-out as a daisy—then rang down for coffee, and put a call through to my cousin.

But here at last the desk clerk caught up with me, slightly aggrieved and perhaps in consequence just a little pleased that he could disappoint me. Mr. Mansel was not there. Yes, he certainly had suite fifty, but he was not in the hotel. The clerk had tried to tell me; he had tried to give me Mr. Mansel's letter, but I hadn't waited . . . Then he had telephoned twice, but had not been answered. A letter? Yes, Mr. Mansel had left me a letter, he had left it this morning, to be delivered to me as soon as I arrived . . . Yes, of course, Miss Mansel, it had already been sent up to my room; when I had not answered the telephone, he himself had sent a page up with the letter. I hadn't answered the door, either, so the boy had pushed the letter underneath it . . .

It was lying out in the lobby, white on the blue carpet, startling as an alarm signal. I pounced on it and carried it back to the light.

I'm not sure what I had expected. Even after last night I couldn't see the situation vis-à-vis Great-Aunt Harriet as anything more than highly bizarre, but my disappointment at not seeing my cousin straight away was such that I tore open the envelope in a fury of irritation, and eyed the letter as if I expected it to be an anonymous obscenity, or at least a forgery.

But it was, unmistakably, my cousin's hand. And unequivocally ordinary, unexciting and infuriating. It said:

DEAR COZ,

I'm fearfully sorry about this, as there's nothing I'd have liked better than to forgather this morning once you'd got out of purdah, and hear all about it. Am particularly interested to know if J.L. let you see Aunt H again. Was nearly caught just after I left you. Aunt H came down the underground corridor with the girl, just as I was letting myself out at the foot of the spiral stair. I dodged back in time, but managed to get a glimpse of her. As you say, a weirdie nowadays, but she seemed active enough and was talking nineteen to the dozen to the girl. I was very tempted to pop out and have a word then and there, but it might have scared the daylights out of them, so I stayed where I was till they went in through the Prince's door, then I let myself out. No trouble. Picked up the car and got down here without seeing a soul. Didn't want to walk into the hotel at crack of dawn, so had breakfast at a café and rang Aleppo to see if I could catch Ben's father. Was told he'd left for Homs and is due home today.

This is where you're going to be blazing mad at me, especially after all my dark hints last night. I may have been wrong about that—something I heard her say to Halide explained quite a bit to me. Tell you when I see you. But there's still a bit of a problem, and the only person I can take it to usefully is Ben's father, and I gather he'll be leaving home again for Medina almost straight away. So I've gone down to Damascus to catch him. Sorry about this, I know you'll be mad at me, but bear up, I'll be back as soon as I can, tomorrow, possibly, or Thursday morning. Wait for me till then, and sharpen your claws. But don't, please don't, do anything else, there's a maiden—except extend your booking, and when I get back we'll have fun. And I think—if my idea works out—that I'll get to see Aunt H after all.

LOVE AND ONE KISS
C.

I read the letter twice, decided that my claws would do perfectly well as they were, and Charles was lucky he was halfway to Damascus right now, then poured out my coffee, and sat down and reached for the telephone. One was, of course, completely independent, and had run one's own affairs for years. One was twenty-two, and came of a family that declared itself indifferent. One certainly didn't need help or advice, and one didn't particularly like Great-Aunt Harriet . . .

But it would be very nice to tell Daddy all about it. Just for a laugh, of course. I put a call through to Christopher Mansel at Mansels of London, and then sat down to wait for it, drinking coffee and pretending to read Hachette's *Moyen-Orient* and watching the unchanging blue of the sky above the concrete skyscrapers of the changing East.

Daddy's advice was short and to the point. "Wait for Charles."

"But, Daddy—"

"Well, what did you want to do?"

"I don't know. It's not that, I suppose, it's just that I'm furious with him; he *might* have waited for me! It's so exactly like him to play it the selfish way."

"Certainly," said my father. "But if he was anxious to catch Ben's father he couldn't afford to wait for you, could he?"

"But why should he be? What's with Ben's father? I'd have thought if he wanted a useful contact he could get hold of some of our people in Beirut."

There was a short pause. "I've no doubt he has his reasons," said my father. "Do you know if he has actually made any contacts there yet?"

"Not unless he did some quick telephoning this morning. I suppose he could have talked to someone yesterday after his first trip up to see me, but he never mentioned it."

"I see."

"Shall I get in touch with our people?"

"If you want to . . . But I'd leave family matters to Charles for the moment, I think."

"Head of the family stuff? Big deal."

"It's as good a reason as any," said my father equably.

"Well, all right," I said. "For one thing, I haven't a clue why he's gone rushing off like this, specially if his 'dark hints' last night haven't come to anything."

"Did you tell me all he'd said in his letter?"

"Yes."

"Then I'd have said the sensible thing was to stop thinking about it. The boy seems to know what he's about, and he's certainly quite clear on one point."

"Meaning?"

"Meaning, my child, don't go doing anything fat-headed just because Charles is getting on your wick," said my parent frankly. "Forget him, and get on with your sight-seeing, and telephone him tonight to find out what he's up to. Don't dream of going up to the palace again without him . . .Christy?"

"I'm still here."

"Did you get that?"

I said: "I got it. Blast you, Daddy, men are all the same, you're still in the Stone Age. I can look after myself perfectly well and you know it. In any case, what's *wrong?* Why shouldn't I go up again if I want to?"

"Do you want to?"

"Well, no."

"Then try not to be more of an idiot than Nature made you," said my father crisply. "How are you for money?"

"Okay, thanks. But, Daddy, you don't really think—?"

The operator intervened, in that smooth mechanical voice. "Your time is up. Do you wish an extension?"

"Yes," I said promptly.

"No," said my father, across me. "Now go and enjoy yourself, my child, and wait for your cousin. Nothing's wrong as far as I can see, but I'd rather you were with Charles, that's all. He's got a lot of sense."

"I thought he was spoiled rotten and lived for nothing but pleasure."

"If that doesn't show sense I don't know what does."

"And don't I?"

"Lord, no, you take after your mother," said my father.

"Well, thank goodness for that," I said acidly, and he laughed and rang off.

For some absurd reason relieved and immensely cheered, I put my own receiver down and turned to the serious business of doing my face and hair and thinking about lunch.

I had planned originally to see Beirut at leisure and alone, and it was indeed idiotic to be annoyed that I had been left alone to do so. In any case there was nothing else to do with the afternoon. I went out to explore.

The Beirut souks are dirty and crowded and about as dramatic as Woolworths. Though my recent sojourn at Dar Ibrahim, and a lot that I had read about Beirut, had conditioned me to expect romance and excitement here, I have to report that nothing whatever happened except that I trod in a pile of rotten fish and ruined a sandal for good, and when I asked the name of some exotic blue powder in a sack, expecting it to be hashish or crude opium to say the least, I was told it was Omo. The Souk of the Goldsmiths was best, and I fell heavily for a necklace of huge turquoises, and almost decided to start a bank account like Halide's—so lovely, and so cheap, were the thin gold bracelets tinkling and glittering in their hundreds along the rods that spanned the windows. But I resisted them, and eventually found myself emerging from the souk into Martyrs' Square with nothing to show for the afternoon but a tube of hand cream and a gold-mounted turquoise bead that I had bought as a charm for Charles's Porsche before I remembered that I was furious with him and the sooner the Evil Eye got him the better I'd be pleased, and that if I never heard from him again it would not be a moment too soon.

It was dusk now, soon to be dark. Perhaps he had arrived in Damascus. Perhaps he had already telephoned . . . I got into one of the service taxis, and soon was set down within a few yards of my hotel.

The first person I saw was Hamid, leaning gracefully against the counter talking to the desk clerk. It was a different clerk this time, but Hamid smiled across the foyer at me and said something to the man, and before I had crossed to the desk the clerk had checked my pigeonhole and was shaking his head. No messages.

I suppose my face must have given me away, for Hamid asked quickly: "Were you expecting something important?"

"Only my cousin. I haven't seen him since last night."

"Oh? He wasn't here when we got back this morning?"

"He'd already left for Damascus," I said.

"For Damascus?"

I nodded. "There was a letter waiting for me when I checked back in this morning. He'd had to go early. I thought he might have been there by now, and phoned me . . . Yes?"

This to the clerk, who had been attending to some query from a sad-faced Arab gentleman in a red tarboosh, and who was now claiming my attention.

"I'm sorry, Miss Mansel, I heard what you were saying, and I wonder if perhaps there has been a mistake. There was a call from Damascus earlier. I understood it was for Mr. Mansel, but it might have been 'Miss Mansel.'" He spread his hands. "I am so sorry."

"Oh. Well, even if it was for me," I said reasonably, "I'd have missed it. I've only just come in. What time was this?"

"Not long ago, perhaps an hour. I had just come on duty."

"I see. Well, thanks very much, that may have been the one. Don't worry, it's not important—and if it is he'll call again. I suppose he didn't leave a number?"

"I don't think so, but I can check."

He reached a chit down from Charles's pigeonhole and handed it to me. It said merely that a call had been made from Damascus at 5:05. No name. No number.

I handed it back. "Well, I shan't be going out of the hotel again tonight, so if he does call again, you'll have me paged, won't you?"

"Of course. I'll tell the switchboard right away." He picked up the telephone and began to talk into it in Arabic.

"If you knew where he was staying," said Hamid, "you could ring him up yourself, now."

"That's just it, I'm afraid I don't. He's gone to see a friend, and it's only just occurred to me, I've forgotten the surname completely—can't even remember if I ever heard it, but I suppose I must have done. I've even visited the house, but haven't a clue what the address is." I laughed. "I could find out easily enough if I rang around a bit . . . they've connections in Beirut, and there's a brother-in-law who's something in the Cabinet—Minister of the Interior, whatever that may be."

"Among other things, the police," said Hamid cheerfully, "which should make him very easy to trace. Do you wish me to ask—?"

"No, no, don't bother, really. I'd much rather not disturb them. My cousin will ring again."

"Is he coming back to Beirut?"

"On Wednesday or Thursday, he wasn't sure."

"Miss Mansel." It was the clerk. "Here is some luck. The call came again while I was talking to the switchboard. It is for Mr. Mansel, but when the caller heard that he was not here, he asked for you. He is on the line now."

"Then it's not my cousin? All right, where do I take it?"

"In the booth just there, if you please."

The booth was one of those open stalls which are supposed to be soundproof if you lean far enough forward into them, but which in fact broadcast just about as well as the Whispering Gallery of St. Paul's. Just beside it, two Englishwomen were discussing the ruins of Byblos, a group of Americans were talking about food, and a French youth twiddled the knobs of a transistor, and in the booth next to mine the sad-faced Arab was apparently failing in sullen Arabic to get the connection he wanted. I put a hand over my free ear, and tried to get on with it.

It was Ben who was on the line, and in the general hubbub it was some time before we could sort ourselves out, and then he was decisive and a little surprised.

"Charles? Here? Not yet, at any rate. What time did he leave?"

"I've no idea, but early. He didn't telephone?"

"No. Not that it won't be very nice to see him again. He couldn't have waited and brought you along with him?"

"It would have been lovely, but I gather there was something fairly urgent he wanted to talk to your father about, and he wanted to be sure of catching him."

"That's what I was calling him about. My father's due home tomorrow from Homs. We expect him for dinner. I promised I'd let Charles know."

I said puzzled: "But he said, he definitely said . . . Oh, well, he must have got it wrong."

"What's that?"

"Nothing, I'm sorry, I'm in the foyer of the hotel, and there's a frightful row going on just behind me here. It's just that Charles seems to have got his days mixed—he thinks your father's due home today. Then he could have waited, after all, instead of walking out on me! Look, I wonder—I'm sorry to bother you, but could you please ask him to ring when he does arrive?"

"Of course I'll tell him. You're not worried, are you?"

"Not a bit," I said, "only mad as fire."

He laughed. "Well, look, I've had an idea. I've been longing to meet you myself, and I know my father would like to, so why don't you come down and join Charles here anyway—join the conference, whatever it is? Stay two or three days and I'll show you Damascus myself, and if Charles never does turn up, so much the better. How about that?"

"It sounds very tempting."

"Well, why not? Temptation's no use if it's resistible. Do come. Have you got a car?"

"I—no, I haven't. I've been using a hired one . . ." I hesitated. "Do you know," I added slowly, "I think I'd like to, very much. If you're sure . . . ?"

"Of course I'm sure." He certainly sounded it, he sounded warmly welcoming. "It would be lovely to have you. I was sorry I missed you before, and I know my father will be pleased. That's settled, then! We'll expect you. Did you get to see the Lady of the Lebanon?"

"The—? Oh, I forgot you knew about that. Yes, I did, but Charles didn't. To tell you the truth, he's a bit needled about it, and there are one or two complications and I gather that's what he wants to talk to your father about. He's making a bit of a mystery about it all. We had quite a turn-up there, Charles and I, but I'd better not tell you over the telephone."

"You intrigue me. I hope you don't mean there was trouble?"

"Oh, no, but he seemed to think there was something a bit off-key. He got all mysterious about it, and now he's belted off without telling me a word, and that's why I'm so mad with him."

He laughed. "I'll warn him."

"As if he'd care!"

"Well, we'll get it out of him between us. I'd certainly like to hear all about Dar Ibrahim! Then I'll see you tomorrow? Have you got the address?"

"Lord, no, I haven't! What must you think of me? Half a minute, I've got a pencil here, if you could spell it out . . . ? Mr. Who? Thank you . . . And the telephone number, just in case? Yes, I've got it. I'll read it back, shall I . . . ? Okay? Fine, my driver will find it. It's really marvelous of you, I shall love it. Does it matter what time I arrive?"

"Not a bit. We'll look forward to seeing you, and we'll show you the real Damascus this time."

The line—roaring and crackling and certainly bugged at the frontier—went dead. Behind me, the English ladies had switched to the ruins of Krak des Chevaliers, the Americans were still talking about food, and the Arab in the next booth, clinging to his receiver, regarded me with sour envy. I looked at him sympathetically, and emerged from my booth.

Hamid was still at the desk. The clerk looked up. "It was not the right call?"

"In a way it was. It was the people my cousin was going to see in Damascus. They say he isn't there yet. He may ring later when he does arrive."

"I'll have you called," he promised.

"Thank you." I turned to Hamid. "Are you booked for tomorrow?"

"Not yet. You want me?"

"Will you take me to Damascus, please? I'm going to see them myself. The name's Sifara, and there's the address. You'll be able to find it?"

"Certainly."

"I won't be coming back the same day, but of course I'll pay you for the return trip."

"You have already paid me for a lot I haven't done. No, don't trouble yourself.

I'll arrange to bring back another one-way fare from Damascus to Beirut. It's a perfectly normal arrangement and we do it every week. What hour shall I call for you in the morning?"

"Ten, please."

"And if the cousin rings?"

"Let him ring," I said. "We still go to Damascus."

But there was no telephone call from Charles that night.

12

But shall be overtaken unaware.

—E. FITZGERALD: *The Rubáiyát of Omar Khayyám*

AND NO telephone call in the morning.

Three times I picked up the paper where I had scribbled the number, and three times put a hand to the receiver. And three times dropped it. If he wanted to ring me, he would ring me. If he didn't, then I certainly wasn't going to bother him. The days of trailing after my cousin Charles were over, but definitely over.

Besides, I was going to Damascus anyway.

I left the silent telephone and went down to the foyer.

The morning was hot and cloudless. The familiar big car slid to the door at ten, and I slipped into the seat beside the driver, Hamid, immaculate as usual in his whiter-than-white shirt, gave me a cheerful greeting and swung the car away from the curb and up through the traffic of Bab-Edriss and the narrow streets behind the Great Mosque, to gain the long curve of the Route de Damas and climb away from the coast and through the summer gardens of the rich to the foothills of the Lebanon. Just beyond Bar Elias the road divides, north for Baalbek, and southeast for the junction whose left fork takes you to Wadi el Harrir and the pass between Mount Hermon and the Djebel of Sheikh Mandour where the frontier lies.

I had crossed this frontier before in the reverse direction, traveling from Damascus to Beirut with the group, so I was prepared for the long wait, the crawl from point to point, the four tedious halts and the frenzy of suspicion that the almost domestic frontiers of the Arab countries demand. We were fourth in line at the Lebanese side, but two hundred yards away, across no-man's-land, I could see quite a queue of north-bound vehicles, including a bus, waiting in the hot dust to be free of the Syrian border.

Hamid took the car's papers and my passport, and vanished into the concrete hutments which did duty as a frontier post. Time passed, crawling. The first car went through the barrier, stopped again for the car-check and the bribe to the gatekeeper, and crept across to repeat the performance on the other side. Fifteen minutes later the second car followed it. Only one in front of us now.

It was hot in the stationary car. I got out and climbed the roadside bank and found a boulder slightly less dusty than the rest, where I sat down. The hotel had provided a picnic, and I sat munching a sandwich, till I met the eyes of a thin dog which had crept to the edge of the road below me and was eyeing me wistfully, just out of stick distance. I held out the remains of the sandwich. He looked at it with his soul in his eyes, and came no nearer. I made to throw it down to him, but at the first movement of my hand he flinched violently away. I got up slowly, took two steps down to the road, leaned over and placed the bread and meat carefully in the dust, then retreated the few paces back toward the car. Watching me, the dog inched forward, every bone eloquent through his dirty skin, and took the food. The faintest movement of his tail thanked me.

"Was it nice?" I said gently, through my anger, and the dog's eyes rolled up whitely to me as the tail wagged again. It was so closely clamped to his body that only the tip of it moved, and I suspected it was the first time he had wagged it for years. The next sandwich, I saw, was chicken, a fresh roll full of luscious meat. I put it in the dust. He snatched it, more confidently this time, but even in the act of bolting it, turned and fled. I looked round. Hamid had left the frontier buildings and was approaching the car.

I had my door half open when I saw he was shaking his head. "I'm afraid there's something wrong. They say we cannot pass."

"Can't pass? Why on earth not?"

"Apparently your passport is not in order."

"But that's nonsense! Of course it's in order! What's supposed to be wrong with it?"

He was apologetic and unhappy. "There's no entry visa for the Lebanon . . . in fact he says that there isn't an exit from Syria, so you're not officially in the country at all, and he can't give you an exit now."

I stared. I hadn't quite taken it in yet. "Not officially in the—well, how the blazes does he think I got here? Tunneled?"

"I don't think he's worked that out. He realizes there's some mistake, of course, but he can't do much about it here and now."

I said angrily: "Well, isn't that nice? Have you got the passport there? May I see? Damn it, I came through this very frontier on Friday, there *must* be a stamp . . . Hamid, why do you have such a terrible alphabet? Have you looked through this yourself?"

"Yes, I did, and I'm afraid he's right, Miss Mansel. There isn't a stamp."

There weren't all that many stamps in my passport, so my hasty search didn't take long, and it did, indeed, seem as if he was right. I looked up, not prepared to admit even yet that the mistake, whatever it was, could actually prevent me from going to Damascus. "But I tell you, I came through here on Friday. They must have stamped it then, surely? If they didn't stamp it, it's their mistake. I certainly handed the passport over, and they let me through . . . Did you tell the man I'd been through here on Friday?"

"I told him you'd come from Damascus recently. I was not sure which day."

"I came with the group, five cars—twenty-two people and an English courier. It was Friday at about midday. If it's the same man on duty, he may remember passing us all through, and anyway, they'll have records, won't they? And the courier had a list; it would have my name on it. Would you please go back and tell him this?"

"Certainly I'll tell him. But you know, I think this may be the trouble; if you came through with a group your name was no doubt on the group passport—the 'list' your couriers showed. They do not always stamp the individual passports of these groups unless you ask them specially. You did not ask them for a stamp, no?"

"Of course I didn't, I never thought of it. I suppose our courier should have realized—he knew I was supposed to be staying on in Lebanon . . . But look, Hamid, this is nonsense! They surely must *know* I couldn't be here illegally! Surely they know you and your car? You must come this way often."

"Every week. Oh, yes, they know me . . . I can pass, and my car; our papers are in order. But not you, I'm afraid. The rules are very strict."

Another car, it seemed mockingly, revved up and moved off through the barrier. From the other side the bus arrived, shaking and roaring and churning up dust. I moved back out of the cloud to the road's edge. People were staring, but not much interested. This must happen every day. The rules, as Hamid had said, were very strict.

I said angrily: "It seems so stupid! It's like having this hooha between England and Scotland. It seems to me these days that the smaller the country the more silly fuss it makes . . . I'm sorry, Hamid, I didn't mean to be rude. It's just so *infuriating* . . . and it's beastly hot. I'm sorry."

"You're welcome," said Hamid, meaning it generously. His look was troubled and sympathetic. "But he will be coming back tomorrow, no?"

"Who will?"

"The cousin."

"I wasn't even thinking about the cousin," I snapped. But I was, of course, and Hamid had known I was before I did. I felt somehow vulnerable, a feeling which was new to me, and entirely unpleasant.

He was saying gently: "I know these frontiers are annoying to foreigners, but we have problems here, I'm afraid, big problems. Among other things a good deal of smuggling goes on . . . Do not mistake me, I do not say that anyone thinks you are taking part in this, but the rules have to be made and kept, and unhappily you have fallen wrong of them."

"Foul."

"Pardon?"

"I have fallen foul of them. Fallen wrong means something different. Smuggling? What sort of smuggling, for pity's sake? Do we look as if we were loaded down with guns or brandy or whatever?"

"Not brandy, no, not here. But you could easily be carrying drugs."

I raised my eyebrows. "Drugs? I suppose I could. I was forgetting where I was. One of my cousin's books called it 'the hashish run.' "

He laughed. "Is that the phrase? Yes, I'm afraid that Beirut has—shall we say it has certain reputations? And it isn't only hashish, I'm afraid—there's still opium grown in Turkey and Iran, and smuggled through to the sea. I told you the controls were tight now, and getting tighter. The National Assembly of the U.A.R. has been making representations to the governments, and the penalties are being made more severe, and as you see, things are a little fierce at the frontiers."

"I can see they have to be, I suppose. But surely they needn't bother tourists about this?"

"A few tourists have even been guilty. Quite recently two English students were arrested, and found guilty. Didn't you see it in the papers?"

I shook my head. "What happened to them? What's the penalty?"

"For them, imprisonment. They're still in Beirut. It used to be only about three years, but now it's a long term of hard labor. For a Lebanese national, besides the sentence, it would mean being deprived of his civil rights and registered in the police files as a trafficker—is that the word?—in drugs. And in other countries, much worse penalties. In Turkey, for instance, the penalty is death—and in Egypt now, and I think also in Iran. You see how seriously it is taken."

"But I thought you said the other day that it wasn't taken seriously in the Middle East? At least, you implied that nobody thought it very wrong to smoke hashish."

"Whenever a government takes anything seriously you will find that it is not a moral problem but an economic one," said Hamid cynically. "In Egypt, for instance, the problem is very serious—your addict is pretty useless as a worker, you know—and the Government has been getting badly worried about its illegal imports from the Lebanon, so it makes representations to the National Assembly, and unhappily at present we all have to take a lot of notice of what Egypt thinks and wants." He smiled. "So you see why things are difficult? They are also, I may say, difficult for the Customs men. Do you see the bus?"

This had, mercifully, switched off its engine, and was immobilized at the Lebanese barrier. The passengers had alighted, and were standing about while their papers were checked. They all had the fatalistic air of people prepared to wait about all day, and one could see why, for on top of the bus, piled up like a refugee's cart or a poor man's removal van, were what looked like the household goods of every person on board. There even seemed to be overstuffed armchairs and mattresses, along with rugs, bundles of clothing, filthy canvas bags which had once been labeled Air France or B.O.A.C., and a wicker cage full of unhappy-looking hens.

"They have to search all that," explained Hamid.

"For a few packets of powder?" I exclaimed. "Not really?"

He laughed. "But yes. Sometimes more than a few packets. And there are hundreds of ways in which the hashish can be disguised and carried. Only last week a man was stopped, a cobbler he called himself, and with his cobbler's kit there was a large suitcase full of leather soles for shoes. But these were hashish, powdered very finely, and then stamped into this shape. Sometimes it looks like gum, or jam, or sheeps' droppings."

"Well," I said, "I imagine that anyone caught carrying a suitcase full of sheeps' droppings through a frontier ought to be locked up anyway."

"That is very true," said Hamid gravely. "Well, if you like I will go and explain about the group passport. Will you wait here?"

"I'll come in with you if you don't mind, and talk to them myself. Does anyone speak English in there?"

"I doubt it, but I will translate for you."

The room inside the hut was small and stiflingly hot, and rather too full of stout olive-colored men all talking at once. The talk broke off as I went in with Hamid, and the uniformed man—stout and olive-colored—behind the office counter raised his eyes despairingly and shook his head. I explained, and Hamid translated, and the official listened as well as he could, while other cars piled up outside and the drivers shoved their way to the counter with their dog-eared papers, and the flies droned in the heat, and the smell of sweat and ink and Turkish tobacco was almost visible in the air.

But it was no use. The official was civil but firm. He nodded understandingly when I explained, he even commiserated with me, but that was as far as he would go. And the matter was clear. There was no entry stamp; how then could he affix an exit? He was sorry, but it was not possible; he had his orders. He was very sorry, but a rule was a rule.

It was obvious enough that he wasn't being obstructive, and he had been patiently civil in the face of considerable odds. I gave up at last, before my own temper frayed in the sticky heat, thanked him, and fought my way back out of the shed.

After the sweaty crowded room the hot air outside seemed almost fresh. I walked over to the car, wondering crossly what to do now. Go back, of course, that was obligatory; all I could do was salvage the day somehow and get Hamid to take me somewhere for a run. Baalbek, I supposed . . . I had seen Baalbek already, with the group, but it had been a crowded sort of day; perhaps if we went up the Bk'aa valley, taking it slowly, saw Baalbek again, then went back into Beirut by the road through the mountains . . . I could telephone Ben when I got back, there was no hurry for that, and tell him what had happened. It was disappointing, even infuriating, but it really didn't matter.

But by the pricking of my thumbs, it did.

I met Hamid's eye. I said suddenly, abruptly: "I know I'll probably be seeing him tomorrow, but I wanted to see him today, now, as soon as possible. Don't ask me why, I can't tell you, not in any words that make sense, but . . ." I lifted my shoulders, and spread my hands in a very un-English gesture, but one which must have been as familiar as every day to the Arab.

He said quickly: "You mean you think he is in trouble?"

"Oh, no, no, nothing like that. How could he be? I told you I couldn't explain. Well, if we can't get through, we can't get through, and there's not much point in staying here talking about it, is there? We'll just have to go back, and I'll ring up Damascus when I get to the hotel again. Thanks for being so patient with me, Hamid—it's terribly good of you to take such a lot of trouble for me. Oh Lord, wait a minute . . . I forgot! Did you fix up a return job in Damascus? What'll happen if you can't get there in time to pick them up?"

"It doesn't matter. I wasn't due to come back until tomorrow in any case. I can telephone, and someone else can do it." He opened the car door for me. "Don't give it a thought, today is yours. Where else can I take you? You've seen Baalbek?"

I hesitated. "I suppose it's too late in the day to start now for Homs?"

"Not really, but there's a frontier there, too."

"Hell's teeth, I suppose there is. We're nicely stuck, aren't we? Well, if you're sure it's all right about your Damascus job, I certainly wouldn't mind seeing Baalbek again on my own, with time to spare." But in the act of getting into the car another thought struck me, and I paused. "You know, I really think we'll have to call it a day and go back to Beirut. I've just thought—what's going to happen when I want to leave the country for London? Will I have to get a new visa, or go to the Consul and make inquiries about this wretched exit stamp, or something? If there are going to be difficulties, it might take time. I'd better do it straight away."

"I think you're right, but I don't think it will concern your Consul, I think we'll have to go and see the Chef de Sûreté in Beirut and get another visa. If you'll wait a moment longer I'll go back and ask the official here what we should do. And who knows, it may not take so very long. We might even be able to come back and get through to Damascus by nightfall."

Even I was not expecting the surge of pleasure and relief that this gave me. I smiled at him. "Oh, yes, that would be marvelous, and you could do your return job, too! Thanks a million, Hamid, you're very good!"

"For a smile like that," said Hamid, "I would be prepared to be very bad. The cousin is lucky."

And he disappeared into the buildings.

The car was like an oven, so I waited outside in the road. The bus—it was labeled Baalbek—had been unloaded, and the dirty baggage was lying in the dust and being prodded over by sweaty, sullen-looking men. People hung around, staring, smoking, spitting. One or two youths lounged nearer, eyeing me.

I glanced across at the office buildings. Through the open door I could see the shoving, vociferous crowd round the counter. Hamid might be some time. I left the car and climbed the bank again above the road.

This time I went higher, out of the dust and the petrol fumes, but still keeping the car in sight and directly below me. The road here was in a shallow cutting, and almost immediately as I climbed I found myself in cooler air and treading on grass and flowers.

There wasn't the profusion of flowers that I had seen along the Afka road, but the hillside was green enough, with sparse grass moving in the breeze, and the gray whorls of thistles, and drifts of some small white flowers that looked from the distance like frost. Over this in violent contrast, blinding over gray stone, went the blazing, cascading gold of the broom; and everywhere, thrusting up boldly from the hoar-frost veils of the white flowers, were hollyhocks—the simple familiar hollyhock of the English cottage garden, red and yellow and white, crowding wild among the rocks of a mountainside in Lebanon.

And a quarter of a mile away, where the same hollyhocks and the same broom flowered above the same rocks, that was Syria.

I had climbed, I suppose, about a hundred feet, and from this height I could see beyond the no-man's-land, beyond the Syrian frontier post, to where the road curved round underneath a rocky bluff and dropped down to cross the water at the bottom of the valley.

As always in this thirsty country, the green of the trees and cultivation followed the water, and the river wound its way south in a thick sash of trees and corn and vines which crowded along the valley bottom. Here and there, like green veins threading a dry leaf, the small tributary valleys ran down to join the main stream. I could see—perhaps a quarter of a mile beyond the Syrian frontier—one such tributary, curling down through the bare hillside with its ribbon of green, its few patches of growing corn, the bone-white stems of poplars with young leaves whitening in the breeze, and the dusty track where a donkey plodded with a woman beside it carrying a jar on her head. I was watching her idly, when I suddenly stiffened and stared, all attention now, at the point where that distant dusty track met the main road.

Just off the road was a small thicket of trees. And under those trees, something white, metallic. A car. A familiar car, parked there in the shade, nose to the south.

I think I have mentioned before that I am very longsighted. It did not take me more than a minute or two's staring to convince me that this was indeed Charles's Porsche. The screen of leaves prevented me from seeing if he was in the car, but soon I was almost sure I had caught a glimpse of movement beyond the bushes.

I turned and began to make my hasty way down to the road, arriving with a thump in the dust beside the car just as Hamid came out of the buildings.

He started without preliminary. "I think it will be all right. It is the Sûreté we must go to, so if we go back now—Is something the matter?"

Excitement and the sharp scramble had made me breathless. "I've just seen his car—Charles's—my cousin's! It's parked about a quarter of a mile past the other frontier. I went up there," pointing, "and you can see over that bluff down toward the river, and it's there, parked behind some trees. You don't suppose Ben's told him I'm coming, and he came to wait for me?"

"Perhaps, but it doesn't make much sense to me," said Hamid. "You're sure it's his car?"

"Pretty sure. At any rate it's a white Porsche, and they can't be all that common hereabouts. It must be his!"

"Which way is it facing?"

"South." Near us the barrier shut with a bang behind a south-bound car, and the Arab guarding it squatted down by the roadside and lit another cigarette. Beyond the further frontier the sun dazzled on the waiting windscreens. I frowned into the glare. "But you're right, it doesn't make sense. If he was all that eager to see me, he'd have waited for me yesterday, or else telephoned, not left it to a chancy pickup. But then what *is* he doing here? If he did get to Damascus last night, he'd hardly come straight up again before Mr. Sifara gets home, and Ben'll have told him I'm expected. Anyway, he was facing south."

Hamid said slowly: "I've been thinking . . . he may be going south from Homs. Did you not say that this friend, this Mr. Sifara, would be coming from Homs? It is possible that when your cousin telephoned Damascus he found this out, so he went to Homs instead."

"And spent last night there? I suppose so . . . but then why didn't he come back to Beirut this morning? You'd have thought, even if he still had business in Damascus, he'd have come for me, or at least telephoned."

"He probably did. If he rang up from Homs this morning and heard you had gone, he may have decided to drive down this way instead of the desert road, and catch you at the frontier. If they told him you hadn't yet passed here, then he would perhaps get himself through, and settle down to wait for you."

"I suppose so . . . or it may be pure chance, and he's just come this way to avoid the desert road. And now this happens!" I glared at the dusty road in an agony of frustration. "He may be gone at any moment, and I can't even get through to tell him!"

"No," said Hamid, "but I can." He smiled reassuringly. "Don't distress yourself, Miss Mansel, it's very simple. I will go through now and see your cousin."

"You? Would you?"

"Well, of course. I'll tell him you're here and can't get through the frontier. He may want to come back and take you to the Sûreté in Beirut himself, and if he does, I'll go straight on to Damascus and pick up my return job there. If not, I'll come back for you. You don't mind being left here?"

"Of course not. I'm terribly grateful. Yes, you're right, let's hurry in case he goes. I'll take the rest of my lunch packet up the hill and wait."

"And your handbag—and the jacket in case you need it—" He was already fishing for them in the car. "The coffee, yes? And fruit . . . so. If there is a crowd at the frontier, it may be a long wait."

"Please don't worry about me. In any case I'll be able to see from up there."

"Does he drive fast?"

"Sometimes," I said. "Why?"

"Only that if he doesn't know you're here, if it is just chance that he stopped there—he may be gone."

"Would you try to catch him?"

"If it seemed possible. Now, can you carry these yourself? I think I should go straight away."

"Of course I can. Don't wait for me, you go."

He got into his car and started the engine. "You said he was parked behind trees? Can I see him from the road, do you think? Exactly where?"

"A quarter of a mile past the other frontier, some trees on the right, and just beyond them a humped-back bridge. You can't miss it. There, the way's clear, you can get through. And thank you, Hamid, thank you—"

"Please . . . at your service . . ." A smile, a quick disclaiming wave of the hand, and he was off. I panted back to my perch above the road.

The Porsche was still there. I dumped my things among the flowers and shaded my eyes to watch. Since he had not already gone, my fear that this was just a brief 'comfort stop' must be unfounded. He must either have paused to eat, or in fact be waiting for me.

I peered down at the stretch of road immediately below me. The second Lebanese barrier was lifting to Hamid's bribe, and the big car sailed, windows flashing, through the stretch of no-man's-land. It checked at the Syrian barrier, and I saw Hamid jump out and hurry across to the buildings to show his papers. Since he was alone, and went this way frequently, they would surely let him go without more than a moment's checking.

I looked the other way at the Porsche.

Just in time to see the white car break out of the trees like a greyhound out of the slips, wheel right-handed in a swirl of dust, and shoot off down the road toward Damascus. Seconds later I heard the snarl of a racing change as he whipped over the bridge.

But by the time the sound reached me, the car was already out of sight.

13

As sure as heaven shall rescue me
I have no thought what men they be . . .

—S. T. COLERIDGE: *Christabel*

I DON'T know how long I must have stood there on the breezy hillside, staring at the empty stretch of road where the white car had been. It was as if I had been lifted up into the vacuum of its wake, and then dropped, dazed, into its dust.

I pulled myself together, and looked to see how far Hamid had got.

He was already at the second Syrian barrier, and showing papers—the car's papers presumably—at the car window. The man on duty took them, glanced, and gave them back. A bribe passed. A few moments later the barrier was pulled open, and the car was through and had gathered speed down the road till it disappeared from my view behind the bluff.

I suppose he cannot have missed the Porsche by much more than four minutes. In a matter of seconds he had reappeared on the stretch of road leading to the bridge, and I saw the dust mushroom up as he braked and brought the big car in to the verge by the clump of trees. He got out, must have seen straight away that the cover was not thick enough to hide the Porsche completely, and turned, hand to eyes, to stare south down the valley. He stood like that for only a second or two before he whipped back into the car, slammed the door, and was gone in his turn over the bridge and out of sight down the twisting road.

It was a safe guess that he had glimpsed the white car on the road ahead. And it was anybody's guess how long it would take for him to catch it. I reflected that a professional driver who must know the road like the palm of his hand might well be able to cancel out Charles's start, and even the difference in performance between the town car and the Porsche. Four minutes is a long time on the road, but if Charles had really been in a hurry he would hardly have spent so much time in the grove. The racing start could only have been due to high spirits; by now Charles was probably idling happily along admiring the wild hollyhocks on the slopes of the Djebel Ech Sheikh Mandour.

I sat down beside a patch of broom that smelled of wild honey, and ate my lunch. They had given me (besides the rolls stuffed with meat) a paper of black olives and some creamy white cheese and some little ravioli-like pastry envelopes filled with a kind of sausage mixed with herbs. By the time I had eaten as much as I wanted and started on a peach, the road below me was clear of traffic except for another bus—southbound this time—and the gatekeeper was obviously well away on his afternoon snooze. I glanced at my watch. Half past one. And the road still empty either of Hamid or the returning Charles.

And at two o'clock it was still empty. And at half past two.

Nor was there any question, even on the flowery hillside, of a peaceful siesta for me. Two of the Arab youths who had been lounging idly at the corner of the customs buildings had decided at length, after a grinning, nudging conference which I had pretended not to notice, to come up and talk to me. It was probably nothing more than curiosity which drove them, but they had only three or four words of American English, and I had no Arabic at all, so they hung around grinning and staring till my nerve broke and in sheer irritation I got to my feet and began to pick up my things.

I thought I knew what must have happened. Hamid, misled by my outburst of exasperation at the delay, had construed it as acute anxiety for Charles, and imagined trouble where I only saw annoyance. Either he was still determinedly pursuing the Porsche, or there had been some sort of mishap delaying whichever car was on its way back to me. And if I waited much longer and neither of them came, there would be no possibility of my getting to Beirut in time to visit the Sûreté office about a visa, and that would be that.

So when one of the Arab youths, leering, sat down a yard from me on a dusty boulder and said for the dozenth time, "New York? London? Miss?" and then made some remark in Arabic which sent his companion off into fits of mirth, and at the same moment a bus labeled Baalbek ground to a halt below me, I picked up the last of my things, said "Good-bye" politely and finally, and walked downhill to the road.

The thin dog was lying in the shadow of a parked car. He watched me with recognition, but (I thought) without much hope. I dropped the last of the meat rolls beside him as I passed, and saw him snatch it and bolt out of the way of the youths who were following me downhill. The crowd of passengers from the bus were standing about in the heat, apathetically watching as the customs men rifled the household goods of what looked like the entire Exodus. Someone was half-heartedly checking their papers. The gatekeeper let another car through, then relapsed into sleep. Nobody was bothering very much about anything. Even the two youths had abandoned the chase.

I went into the buildings, to be met by the slightly glazed and wholly unwelcoming stare of the olive-colored gentleman behind the counter. It took a few minutes before I could find someone in the crowd with sufficient English to pass on what I wanted to ask, but I managed eventually.

"The bus," I said, "what time does it get to Baalbek?"

"Half past three."

"Is there one that goes from here to Beirut?"

"Oh, yes."

"At what time?"

"Five." A shrug. "Perhaps a little later. It gets there at six."

I thought for a moment. Baalbek was well off the direct road home, but there would be a good chance of getting a car there, and taking the shorter route back to Beirut through the mountains. That way I should be there long before the problematic five o'clock bus. In any case I had no desire to sit here for another two hours or so. Even the bus would be preferable.

"Will there be a taxi to hire, or a self-drive car, in Baalbek?"

"Surely." But he qualified it with a shrug. "Well, you must understand, it is late in the day, but possibly . . ."

"Where do I find the taxis?"

"At the temples, or in the main street. Or ask at the Adonis Hotel, just where the bus stops."

I remembered the Adonis Hotel. It was where the group had gone for lunch on Friday, and the manager, I remembered, had spoken reasonably good English.

I asked, "Where is the Sûreté in Beirut?"

"In the Rue Badaro."

"What time does it close?"

But here we stuck. "One o'clock" was the first dismaying answer. Then, from someone else, "Five o'clock." Then again, "It opens again at five o'clock till eight." "No, no, till seven." Then, with shrugs all round, "Who knows?"

Since the last guess was obviously the most accurate of the lot, I abandoned the questions, to add my postscript. "If my driver, or anyone else, comes back asking about me, tell him I've gone back to the Sûreté office in the Rue Badaro in Beirut, and then to my hotel, the Phoenicia. I'll wait there. *Compris?*"

They admitted it was *compris,* so I left them to it, said a thank you all round, and went out.

The bus's engine was roaring, and a cloud of black smoke poured from the exhaust. There was no time to do more than look quickly up the road for a white Porsche or a black taxi and to get in. Six seconds later, with a horrible shaking roar and a smell of soot, we were heading for Bar Elias and the Bk'aa road to Baalbek.

It was a horrible journey, and it ended perforce where the bus finished its run, in some dirty hot street within shouting distance of the ruined temples, and just in front of the portals of the Adonis Hotel.

I got out of the bus, shaking the creases from my skirt with a strong feeling that I was dislodging fleas from it in clouds. The bus went off to turn, the other passengers dispersed, and the filthy black fumes slowly cleared from the air. The street was empty except for a big, sleek black car parked at the curb, and just beyond it, incongruously, a white camel with a ragged Arab holding the headrope.

He bore down on me now, with a shrill stream of Arabic interspersed with a few English words, from which I gathered that I was being offered a ride on his camel for the paltry sum of five English pounds or more. I beat him off with some difficulty, parried his offer to pose for a snapshot for only ten shillings, and ran up the steps into the hotel.

I was lucky to find the manager himself was still around, and not absent, as might have been expected, on siesta. I found him in the little graveled court that did duty as a restaurant garden, sitting with a companion at one of the small tables under the pines, drinking beer. He was a smallish round-faced Arab with a thin line of moustache and various chunks of Beiruti gold about his person. His companion, whom at first I barely noticed, looked English.

The manager rose and came hurrying to meet me. "Madame—mademoiselle? You are back again? But I thought your party had left the Lebanon?"

"Good heavens, you recognized me?" I exclaimed. He was bowing over my hand with every appearance of joy. You'd have thought I'd spent a month in the hotel's best suite with all found, not merely bought a drink to take with the group's packed lunch a few days ago. "What a memory you've got! I'd have thought you had so many tourists here that you wouldn't even see them any more!"

"How could I forget you, mademoiselle?" The bow, the gallant look, assured me without a hint of offense that he meant it. He added, frankly, "As to that, I have only been here since the beginning of this season. So far, I remember all my guests. Please—will you sit down? Will you join us, it will be a pleasure?"

But I hung back. "No, thank you very much—there was something I wanted to ask you. I'm here on my own today, and I wanted some help, so I thought I would come to you."

"Of course. Please tell me. Anything. Of course."

He obviously meant it, but to my dismay, as soon as I began to explain my difficulty and mentioned a car, he made a *moue* of doubt, and spread his hands.

"I will do all I can, naturally . . . but at this time of day most of the local cars are already hired and gone. It is possible you may find one at the temples—do you speak Arabic?"

"No."

"Then I will send someone with you to help you. There may be a car still there. If not—perhaps I can find one—perhaps one of my friends, even . . . It is urgent?"

"Well, I do rather want to get to Beirut as soon as possible."

"Then please do not worry, mademoiselle. Of course I will do for you whatever I can. I am glad that you felt you could come here for help. I would offer to telephone for you now, but as it happens I had to get a car only ten minutes ago for one of my guests, and I had difficulty. But in another twenty minutes, perhaps, or half an hour, it will be worth trying again."

"Forgive me." It was his companion who spoke. I had forgotten all about him, and turned in surprise as he set down his beer glass and rose. "I couldn't help overhearing. If you really are anxious to get to Beirut, and there's any difficulty at all, I'm going that way and would be delighted to offer you a lift."

"Why, thank you—" I was slightly taken aback, but the manager intervened quickly, sounding relieved and pleased.

"Of course, that would be excellent! An excellent idea! May I perhaps introduce you? This is Mr. Lovell, mademoiselle. I'm afraid I don't know your name."

"Mansel. Miss Mansel. How do you do, Mr. Lovell?"

"How do you do?" His voice was English and cultured. He was a man of rather less than middle height, somewhere in his forties, with a face made Arab-olive by the sun, and dark hair receding from a high forehead. He was well dressed in a light-weight gray suit and silk shirt, and wore heavy-rimmed dark glasses. Something about him was faintly familiar, and I thought I must have met him somewhere before.

Even as the thought crossed my mind he smiled and confirmed it. "As a matter of fact we've met before, though without an introduction, and I don't suppose you remember it."

"I'm afraid I don't, but I did have a feeling I'd met you. Where?"

"In Damascus, last week. Was it Wednesday—or perhaps Thursday? Yes, it was Thursday, in the morning in the Great Mosque. You were with a group then, weren't you? I'd been talking to your guide while you ladies were admiring the carpets, and then he had to intervene in some minor international incident, and we exchanged a word or two while it was going on. You wouldn't remember, why should you? But do tell me, did the stout lady allow herself to be parted from her shoes in the end?"

I laughed. "Oh, that's what you meant by an 'international incident'! Yes, she did, and even admitted she wouldn't have wanted all that crowd walking on *her* carpets in outdoor shoes. There was a bit of a scene, wasn't there? I thought I knew your voice. That's it, then."

"You're on your own today?"

"Yes. In fact, I won't make a story of it now, but that's the reason why I'm stranded here today looking for a car. Do you mean you're really going straight to Beirut?"

"Certainly." He moved one square, well-kept hand to indicate the car parked at the edge of the road below the garden wall. I saw now that it was a black Renault with an Arab impassive at the wheel in native dress and white kaffiyeh. "If I can be of any help to you, I'll be delighted. I was intending to leave within a few minutes anyway. Of course, if you want to stay and see the sights here first, then you might prefer to take a chance of getting a taxi later, and Mr. Najjar will probably be able to help you." He smiled. "Any other day I'd have been delighted to show you the place myself, but as it happens I have an engagement in the city that I daren't cry off, so I'm driving straight down now."

"It's terribly good of you, and I'd love to come with you," I said. "I've seen Baalbek before—I was here with the group on Friday—but in any case I'm anxious to get back to the city as soon as I can."

"Then shall we go?"

The manager came with us to the car, the Arab driver whipped round to open the rear door, and Mr. Lovell handed me in, spoke to the man in Arabic, and settled beside me. We said our good-byes to the manager, and the car moved off.

We threaded the narrow streets quickly and skillfully, then gathered speed along the road to Beirut. In a few minutes we had passed the last of the houses crouching among their gardens, and on our right the great sweep of hill and valley stretched brilliant in the afternoon sun. The air through the open window was fresh and cool. I leaned back gratefully.

"Oh, this is heaven after that bus! Have you ever been in one of the local buses?"

He laughed. "No, praise be to Allah, I have not."

"I should have warned you to keep right away from me until I've had a bath."

"I'll take the risk. Where are you staying in Beirut?"

"The Phoenicia. But don't you bother about that, I can get a taxi from anywhere it suits you to throw me out."

"It's no trouble, we'll be passing it."

"Thanks all the same, but as a matter of fact I've a call to make first, in the Rue Badaro. I don't know where it is, but perhaps you do?"

"Yes, of course. Well, that's even simpler, it's practically on the way. The Rue Badaro joins this one just before the *place* where the National Museum is. If we cut through the side streets when we get to the city we can go in that way, and I'll drop you."

"Thank you very much."

His voice betrayed no curiosity. He had given me a brief glance—unreadable because of the dark glasses—when I had mentioned the Rue Badaro, and I thought he must surely know that the Sûreté Générale was there, but he was either too indifferent or too well-bred to question me about my affairs. He asked merely; "What happened to your group?"

"Oh, I didn't break away from them today! I'm only stranded and thrown on your mercy because I hadn't a proper visa and my own car went on . . . that is, there were reasons why I had to send my driver on to Damascus, even if it meant my finding my own way home to Beirut. The group actually left on Saturday, and in a way, that's the cause of the trouble." I explained briefly what had happened about the visa.

"I see. But how extraordinarily awkward. I suppose you have to get a new visa? Then do I gather it's the Sûreté you want in the Rue Badaro?"

"Yes." In spite of myself I cast a worried glance at my watch. "Have you any idea what their hours are?"

He didn't answer immediately, but I saw him give a quick glance at his own wrist, then he leaned forward and said something in Arabic to the driver. The big car surged forward smoothly at an increased pace. Mr. Lovell smiled at me. "You should be all right. In any case, I might be able to help you. Stop worrying."

"You? You mean you know someone there?"

"You might say so. I can see how the mistake occurred, it's no one's fault, and I doubt if there will be any difficulty in getting you a new visa. You'll have to pay another half crown, I'm afraid, and wait while they fill in a form or two in triplicate, but that's all it will take. So relax now till we get there. I promise you it'll be all right. And if you like, I'll come in with you and see you through it."

"Oh—would you really? I mean—if you've time? It's terribly good of you!" I found myself stammering in a sort of confusion of relief.

"Think nothing of it," he said calmly. "Do you smoke?"

"No, well, sometimes I do. Thank you, I think I will. Oh, are they Turkish?"

"No, Latakia—it's the best Syrian tobacco. Go on, try it."

I took one, and he lit it for me. The driver, who all this time had said nothing, was smoking already. Mr. Lovell lit a cigarette for himself, and leaned back beside me. His lighter I saw, was a gold Flaminia, and the cigarette case had been gold, too. The cuff links in the silk cuffs were of heavy gold with a beautiful, deliberately 'roughed' surface. A man of substance, and certainly a man of easy self-assurance. Someone of importance, perhaps? He had that air. I began to wonder if quite by chance I had found the 'useful contact' in Beirut that I had talked of to Daddy. It certainly seemed as if I could stop worrying about the Sûreté and the visa.

He was silent, half turned away to look out of his window. We sat for a while smoking in silence, while the big car sped silently south and west, then took the High Lebanon pass in its stride and began to nose downhill toward the distant sprawl of Beirut. I was content to sit back in silence and stop thinking. This was an interval, a gap in time, a moment to free-wheel before the next effort. And the next effort would be eased for me by the pleasant and competent Mr. Lovell.

It was only then, as I found myself relaxing, brittle tension melting like toffee into a sweet goo of softened bone and nerve and sleepy muscle, that I realized how taut and tight-strung I must have been, how senselessly, uselessly keyed up to meet something which could have been no more than a challenge of my own imagination. Something I had let Hamid see and feel, and which, because he had over-interpreted me, I had been left to sort out on my own. Well, I seemed to be doing just that . . . and meanwhile the car sailed on at speed, and the sun beat warm and heavy through the window, and the breeze stirred the ash in gray dust from my cigarette and feathered the smoke away in veils of blue nylon, and I was content to lift a lazy hand to wave it away from my eyes, then drop the hand, palm up, into my lap while I leaned back, tranquil, without thought.

My companion, seemingly as relaxed as I, was turned away from me gazing out at the view on his side of the car. Here the steep hillside fell away from the road in an abrupt sweep of rock-strewn green to the dark sprawl of forest and the gleam of running water. Beyond the forested stream the land rose again through terraced fields of gold and green and dark-gold to more stony heights, and the gray seams of snow. The poplars along the road's edge flashed and winked past like telegraph posts, bare and lacy against the far snow and the hot blue sky.

"Good Lord!"

Mr. Lovell, who had been gazing out almost dreamily, now stiffened to attention, whipped off his dark glasses, craned his neck further, and shaded his eyes to stare down the mountainside.

"What is it?"

"Nothing, really—rather a pretty sight, that's all. And not quite so out of place here as one might think." He gave a short laugh. "It still goes on, of course, the high romance—Haroun Al Raschid and the perfumes of Arabia and blood on the roses. It's an Arab riding down there with a pair of Persian greyhounds, you know them?—salukis, beautiful things. How very dramatic."

I didn't for the moment take in what he was saying. I was fiddling with the ashtray in the back of the seat in front of me, trying to stub out my cigarette.

He added: "He ought to have a hawk on his wrist, probably has, but it's too far away for me to see."

I looked up quickly. "Did you say a rider with two salukis? *Here?*"

It must be pure coincidence, of course. We must be miles on the wrong side of Beirut, and Dar Ibrahim was a long way away. It couldn't be John Lethman and the salukis. But it was enough of a strange coincidence to make me sit up straighter and say: "Where? Can I see?"

I had to lean right across him to see down the hill. He sat back to let me do so, indicating a point well below us and some way off.

The car was sliding smoothly round the outside of a bend. The road was bounded by neither wall nor fence, its verge only a yard of dried clay where thistles grew between the poplars, and beyond this the steep mountain-side. I peered down.

"I can't see anything. What's the color of the horse?"

"Bright chestnut." He pointed again. "There, look, just going into the trees. Quick. The man's in white. See?"

I strained to see where his right hand pointed. As I leaned close across him his left arm came quietly round me and held me fast.

For a moment I thought he was supporting me against the swing of the car on the bend. Then—incredulously, as his arm tightened—that this was a heavy pass; and I stiffened against it and tried to pull away. He held me, the arm like iron, his hand now gripping my left arm and holding it helpless. With my body pressed to his my right arm was imprisoned against him.

"If you keep still you won't be hurt."

The voice, whispering now, was recognizable. The eyes, too, uncovered and staring into mine. The long nose, the olive face that would look pale in lamplight . . .

But it was mad. If it was mad to suppose John Lethman was riding out here forty miles from Dar Ibrahim it was still madder to suppose that my Great-Aunt Harriet, disguised as a man of forty-odd, was holding me with this ferocious strength with one hand, while the other came up holding something that gleamed . . .

I screamed. The Arab driver drove smoothly on without even turning his head. He took a hand off the wheel to tap ash into the tray under the fascia-board.

"What are you doing? Who are you?" Gasping and twisting in his grip, I fought as hard as I could, and the car rocked, swinging wide on the next bend. But there was nothing coming. There was nothing on the road.

The dizzy swoop of the car round the bends, cliff on one side, open sky on the other, like the flight of a fulmar through an empty bright afternoon; the flicking pulse of shadow as the poplars whipped by; the unheeding silence of the Arab driver . . . all these combined in some curiously merciful way to insulate me from the nightmare of what could not—could not possibly—be happening.

He was grinning. From a few inches away, his teeth looked obscene, like something in a horror film. Great-Aunt Harriet's eyes blinked and glittered as he fought to hold me.

"*Who are you?*" It was a last gasp on the edge of hysteria, and I saw him recognize the fact. His voice was smooth. He had me still now, boneless, dumb.

"You remember now, of course. I told you we'd met before, but we weren't introduced properly. Henry Lovell Grafton, if you want it in full . . . Mean anything to you? Yes, I thought it might. And now hold still, or I'll hurt you."

On the phrase his right hand flashed down at my bare arm. Something pricked, clung stinging, was withdrawn. He dropped the hypodermic into his pocket and smiled again, holding me tightly.

"Pentothal," he said. "Being a doctor has its uses. You have ten seconds, Miss Mansel."

14

. . . Nor do I know how long it is
(For I have lain entranced I wis.)

—S. T. COLERIDGE: *Christabel*

I WAS to find that Dr. Henry Grafton had a habit of overestimating. It took about seven seconds to put me under, and when I woke it was to near-darkness, the thick closeness of a shut and windowless room lit only by the faint light from a small barred opening high in the wall above the door.

At first, of course, the waking seemed normal. I opened blurred eyes on a dark wall where shadows moved slightly like rags in a draft. It was warm and very quiet, a heavy airless quiet that slowly conveyed to me the sense of being shut in. A small fluttering, like that of a moth against a pane, pattered into my consciousness through the layers of drugged sleep. It worried me. I must move and let the poor creature out. I must open the window and let in the air . . .

But not yet; I wouldn't move just yet. My body felt slack and heavy, my head was aching, and I was cold. This last had its own compensations, for when I put a hand to my throbbing forehead the hand was damply cool, and comforting. I was, I found, lying on blankets. I scruffled a couple of these over myself, and turned on my face, cold hands against cheeks and forehead. The heavy lassitude of the drug still possessed me, and in a vague way—nothing was other than vague—I was thankful for it. I had an idea that something large, dark, and terrifying loomed and gibbered just out of reach; but something in me refused to face it yet. I checked my groping mind, shut my eyes against the blankets, and thought of sleep . . .

I have no idea how long it was before I came back to consciousness the second time: I imagine it was no great while. This time the return was final, sharp, and altogether frightening. I was suddenly wide awake, and fully aware of all that had happened. I even knew where I was. I was back at Dar Ibrahim. The smell told me, seconds before my brain caught up with my senses—dead air and dust and lamp-oil, and the indefinable sharp smell of Great-Aunt Harriet's tobacco. I was in one of the storerooms under the Seraglio lake, behind one of those massively locked doors in the underground passage where Charles and I had gone exploring to find the Prince's Divan . . .

That was it. That was the gibbering thought that had lain in wait for my return from the dead; the thought I had been refusing to face.

The interview in the Prince's Divan. Great-Aunt Harriet. Henry Grafton . . . I could only think of one reason for Henry Grafton's grotesque masquerade to fob off my persistence, for the dusty abandonment of the Chinese treasures and the beloved books, even for the glimpse I had had of the ruby ring on Halide's hand. Something had happened to my Great-Aunt Harriet which this gang had been in pains to hide. Not just ill, or even crazy—they must have known they needn't fear her family when it came to Will-making, and wherever Lethman and Halide might stand, I didn't think this was Henry Grafton's concern. And surely the risks were too great for the rewards? Nor could she be a prisoner, like me; there had been no attempt to stop me wandering where I wished through the palace by daylight.

Well, then, she was dead. And for some reason the death had had to be concealed. At the moment, my skin crawling with cold in that warm airless dungeon, I could only think of one reason for that. But whatever it was that had necessitated the masquerade and the midnight prowling, and now the elaborate operation that had hauled me back into the net, I was soon going to find out—the hard way.

And Charles who had apparently, heaven knows how, suspected the truth—Charles was miles away, heading for Damascus with Hamid after him. Even if Hamid caught him up and persuaded him to come back for me, it would be some time before they would find my trail. No one would miss me at the Phoenicia; and Ben had said "Come when you can . . ."

Christy Mansel, sunk without a trace.

Like Great-Aunt Harriet and her little dog Samson. Or like the Gabriel Hounds, locked away in the dust of the rotting palace forever . . .

This was sheer crying stupidity, the drug reducing me when I could afford it least to a useless contraption of slack nerves and jellied bone. I slapped the nerves down hard, sat up, and tried to look about me.

Gradually, the place took shape. A few feet of dusty floor near the bed where the dim light fell, a low ceiling hung with webs, a stretch of rough stone wall where a tumble of leather and metal—harness, perhaps?—hung from a rusty hook. The tiny flickering sound came again from outside, the fluttering of a wick in an oil lamp. The weak light wavered through the tiny grating to drown within a yard or two in thick darkness where, faintly, could be seen stacked shapes of crates, boxes, tins like small petrol cans . . .

I had certainly been right about where I was. The ventilator must look out on lamplight in the underground corridor, and the door below it would be one of those massively barred affairs with the uncompromising locks that Charles and I had seen. There would be no questioning that door. And there was, of course, no window.

The silence was intense, thick and suffocating like the stillness one finds in caves, the silence of underground. I held myself still, listening. My body felt stiff and sore here and there, as if there were bruises, but the headache was gone, to be followed by an awareness which at that moment was worse and more painful, a feeling of quickness, a light aliveness and nerve-end vulnerability, like a snail that has been torn from its shell and wants nothing better than to creep back inside.

The silence was complete. There was no way of telling if anyone else was still about in the palace. You would think I had been buried alive.

The cliché slipped through my mind without thought, then struck home like a poisoned dart, as with it came the quick vision of the rock above me, the tons of rock and earth with the heavy sheet of water lying over it. Man-made; fallible; rotten, probably, as the rest of the place was rotten. The weight must be terrific. If there was the slightest flaw in the rock above me, the slightest movement of earth—

Then with the rush of cold prickling over my skin, I heard it through the dead silence, the tick of settling earth.

I was on my feet, rigid and sweating, before commonsense broke over me like a breath of sweet air. The ticking was merely my watch. I stretched up on tiptoe near the door, holding my wrist high toward the ventilator. I could just see it. The little familiar face was like a friend, the familiar tick brought sanity and the knowledge that it was a few minutes short of six o'clock. It had been just on four in the afternoon when I had accepted the lift from Henry Grafton. I had been unconscious for more than twelve hours.

I put a hand down to the door and, for what it was worth, tried it. The latch lifted silk-smooth, but the door never budged a millimeter. This was so much a foregone conclusion that I hardly registered it with any emotion at all. I was conscious all the time of the positive effort involved in keeping at bay the image of the tons of rock and water pressing down over my head.

The sound which a little while ago I had been dreading came now like the lifting of a nightmare. A key in the lock.

When the door opened smoothly, in that accustomed, well-oiled silence, I was sitting, I hoped composedly, on the bed, trying to conceal with a straight back and poker face that I couldn't have trusted my legs to let me stand. My lips were dry and my heart thumping. What I expected I have no idea. But I was afraid.

It was John Lethman, carrying a lamp, and behind him Halide, as ever with a tray. I smelled soup and coffee as soon as the door opened. If I had thought about it, I'd have expected to be ravenously hungry, but I wasn't. He put the lamp up in a wall niche, and the girl came past him to set the tray down on a packing case. She let her big kohl-rimmed eyes slide sideways to look at me, and I saw pleasure there. The smile reached the corners of her mouth in a malicious little curl. The silk of her dress shimmered, bordered with gold, and I was sharply reminded of what my own state must be, crumpled from the blankets and with my hair all anyhow. I ignored her stonily, and said abruptly to Lethman:

"What's happened to her?"

"To whom?"

"To Great-Aunt Harriet, of course. Don't try to keep the charade up, I know your beastly pal was masquerading. Where's my aunt?"

"She died."

"Died?" I said sharply. "Was murdered, do you mean?"

From the corner of my eye I saw Halide's silks shimmer as she started, and Lethman turned quickly to look down at me. His back was to the lamp, and I couldn't see him clearly, but his voice was edged with nerves. "Don't be melodramatic. Naturally I meant no such thing. She died of natural causes."

"Melodramatic! Look who's talking, what with your underground prisons and your sloe-eyed charmer there and your dear little pantomime dame upstairs with his White Slaver techniques. Natural causes my foot," I said angrily, "be precise. What did she die of and when?"

He said stiffly: "I'm not going to answer questions. Dr. Grafton was her doctor, he'll explain."

"By God he will," I said.

He had been moving toward the door, but my tone brought him round again to face me. The light was on him now. I saw in his face a sort of startled reappraisement, even a kind of alarm, and he opened his mouth to say something, then shut it again without speaking. I thought he looked as edgy as his voice, a down-drawn look, with pouched flesh under the eyes that betrayed lack of sleep, and lines which I had not noticed before and which had no business to be there. What had certainly not been there before was the swollen bruise at the corner of his mouth and a nasty-looking mark like a weal from the cheekbone to the ear. I was just taking this in when Halide said, quickly and venomously:

"Don't let her talk to you like that. You are the master here."

I laughed. "It looks like it, doesn't it? For a start, who's been knocking you about? And you think I'm the one who's in trouble? Well, you'll learn. And I do assure you it'll pay you to listen to me and get me out of here. I should like to go now. At once, please."

He drew a sharp little breath, either of anger or effort. His voice was deliberately braced. "I'm sure you would. But you'll stay here just the same. Dr. Grafton will see you later."

"He'll see me now. After I've had a wash. And what's more, I should like my handbag back."

"It's there by the bed. Now stop being stupid, you must see you've got to do as you're told. There's some food. We'll leave you now, and if you've got any sense you'll take it quietly. If you behave yourself you'll come to no harm. All right, Halide."

"I don't want the blasted food!" I said angrily. "Will you stop behaving like Oddjob and take me to the bathroom?"

"Later." Halide was going, sliding out past him with a final gleam at me which made me want to slap her face. John Lethman was going too, closing the door.

I stood up and said sharply: "Don't be such a clot, Mr. Lethman. I want to go to the loo. You know—the loo, the lavatory, W.C. . . . do I really have to spell it out?"

"Oh." He paused, and I saw with pleasure that he looked once more disconcerted. It seemed obvious that he had expected, possibly even braced himself for, a scene along set lines of outrage and perhaps fear, and that this intrusion of commonplace reality into his thriller-situation had thrown him completely. He said at length, lamely: "Oh, well, you'd better come along, I suppose. But don't try anything. And it won't do you any good—"

" 'And it won't do you any good to scream for help, because I have a hundred Nubian guards within call?' " I finished the threat with a derision that got him right between the eyes, and sent my own morale rocketing. "Come off it and take me to the lavatory, Commander of the Faithful."

He made no reply. I laughed again, and went out past him. My exit was spoiled by the fact that I stumbled in the dim light over a broken flagstone, and my head swam dizzily with the aftermath of the drug. He took my arm, and I controlled the impulse to shake him off. For one thing, I needed the help; for another, he was probably determined to hang on to me, and I might as well go on turning the tables by treating the gesture as one of solicitude. So I thanked him and allowed him to escort me from the room. I don't know whether Halide followed: I didn't glance her way.

I had been right. This was the corridor under the lake, and my door one of the locked storerooms. There was the pile of tins still outside it. John Lethman led me up the stairs toward Great-Aunt Harriet's room. As we reached the heavy curtain and he drew it aside to disclose the bed, I gave an exclamation of surprise.

"Don't pretend you didn't know the way," he said sourly.

"I'm not pretending anything," I said. This was the truth; what had amazed me was the light. It was not early morning, as I had expected, but golden afternoon, six o'clock of a blazing day. And it must be the same blazing day on which I had set out for Damascus or my watch would have stopped by now. The pentothal had laid me out for barely two hours.

John Lethman stepped carefully through onto the dais, and handed me after him. I added: "I'm just surprised it's daylight still. It feels like a month since I was out in the open air and in pleasant company. Tell me one thing, Mr. Lethman, how did you get me here? Don't tell me you carried me over from the village in broad daylight."

"The car didn't touch Beirut at all, or Sal'q. There's a road off past Zahle, and after that a quite negotiable track up behind the head of the valley. You only had to be brought down a couple of kilometers or so from the car."

"Down the path behind the palace? I suppose that's why I'm as stiff as a board. What did you bring me on, a mule?"

Absurd though it may seem, I think I was angrier at that moment than I had been almost through the whole affair, angry and ashamed. There was humiliation in the knowledge of how these men had manhandled my unconscious and helpless body. So far, the thought made me want to run away and hide; but perhaps later on the anger would help.

He said: "The bathroom's this way."

It was the next door opening off the Prince's Garden. I escaped into the labyrinth of the hammam like a rabbit scuttling down a safe burrow.

It had in its day been a grander hammam than the women's quarters had boasted. The walls were alabaster, and the light came from overhead in all the rooms from lozenges of stained glass which threw jewels of amber and jade and lapis onto the rosy floors. The sunshine, muted by this, glowed among the labyrinth of peach-colored columns like light through a transparent shell, and the murmur of water trickling through the shallow channels and dripping into marble basins echoed like the sea in the corridors of a cave.

The cool touch of the water, the light, the blinding glimpse of the little garden as I had crossed to the hammam, dispelled immediately the claustrophobic nightmare of my prison. I threaded my way through the complex of rooms to the center of the cool stone maze. Here water splashed and glittered into a blackened shell that had once been silver, and a stone faun leaned out with a cup of wafer-thin alabaster. I took it from him, filled it, and drank, then took off everything but pants and bra and washed deliciously in the cool water, drying myself on my slip. The sunlight swimming down in its shafts of amber and amethyst seemed to soak into my body like oil, smoothing away the stiffness of the bruises. I shook my frock out and put it on, did my face and hair, and last of all dried my feet and put my sandals on again. I dropped the soaked slip in a corner, took another drink of water, rinsed the cup for the faun, then went out to meet John Lethman.

He was sitting on the edge of the dry fountain. I had only previously seen this garden at night, and now I got no more than a brief impression of a maze of yellow roses and a tumble of honeysuckle over broken pillars. John Lethman got quickly to his feet and started to speak but I cut across it abruptly.

"You needn't think you're going to get me back into that foul little room again. If this Dr. Grafton wants to see me, he can see me here. What's more he can see me now, in daylight. He needn't pretend anymore that he likes staying up half the night, so he can leave his turban and his nightie off." I marched past him into Great-Aunt Harriet's bedroom, flinging over my shoulder: "And if you want me to eat anything you can make that girl bring it in here."

He hesitated, and I thought he was going to insist. But he said merely: "As long as you realize that this part of the palace is locked right away. If you do try to bolt you won't go far, and even if you hid, the dogs would find you."

I laughed. "And tear me limb from limb? Big deal!"

I crossed to the red lacquer chair, and sat down with as much of the grand manner as I could muster, while Lethman, with a look of acute dislike at me, mounted the dais to pull the bell.

The familiar jangling peal bounced and ricocheted through the stillness, and, inevitably, the clamor from the hounds tore the afternoon to shreds. Somehow, the noise was comforting; they were on my side, the 'Gabriel Hounds,' Aunt H's dogs who had known my voice and my cousin's step, and who (I saw it now as the thought lit my mind like a sudden flare) perhaps disliked 'the Dr.' as much as Samson had done, and so were kept shut away except when on guard at night to keep the nosy Miss Mansel within bounds.

Before the echoes of the bell had died the bed curtains were pulled violently back and Henry Grafton came through the private door like a genie erupting from the lamp, and said furiously: "What the hell's happened to that girl? The door's wide open, and if she gets as far as the main gate that idiot's probably forgotten his orders by now, and he'll see her on her way with an illuminated address."

"It's all right," said Lethman, "she's here."

Dr. Grafton came up short like someone running into a wire, and swung round on me where I sat in the high-backed chair. For a nasty moment I thought he was going to come and grab, but he seemed to hold himself in with an effort, and gave me instead a long summing-up look that I by no means liked.

"What's she doing here?" He spoke to John Lethman without taking his eyes off me.

"She asked for the bathroom."

"Oh." The simple demand of nature seemed to disconcert Henry Grafton as much as it had Lethman himself. He teetered there on the edge of the dais, seemingly at a loss, while I sat poker-spined on my chair, trying to look several degrees cooler than an ice cube, and preparing to fight every step of the way should they decide to force me back into my dungeon.

"You rang?" said Halide, at the garden door. At least I suppose that's what she said, it was in Arabic. She was wearing Great-Aunt Harriet's ring.

She was looking at Grafton, but I answered in English. "Yes, we rang. Not for you, but since you're here you might as well bring the tray in here for me. I don't want the soup, thank you, but I'll eat the bread and cheese, and I wouldn't mind a cup of coffee while I'm talking to him."

She spat something at me—no pretenses now—and whirled furiously on the men:

"You're not going to leave her out here? Why don't you put her back in the room and shut her up again? Why do you let her sit there like that and give orders? Who does she think she is? She is nobody, I tell you, nobody, and very soon she will know it! When we get her—"

"Look, Halide—" It was John Lethman, feebly, but she ignored him, blazing at Grafton.

"You are afraid of her too? Why? Dare you not leave her there? Then why not give her some more of the drug and put her in the other prison? Or tie her up? I would do it, me!"

"Oh, belt up," I said wearily. "Never mind about the tray, I can last out, just stop yelling and making me feel like an extra in *Kismet,* will you? And I'd still like the coffee. You can heat it up again before you bring it. I dislike lukewarm coffee."

The look she gave me this time was pure bastinados and boiling oil and I was glad to have deserved it. She swung back to Grafton, simmering like a kettle, but he cut her short. "Shut up and do as you're told. John, for God's sake can't you clout some sense into her? It won't be long now." He added something in Arabic to Halide, more conciliatory in tone, and there was a brief exchange which seemed to mollify her. After a while she went, scowling.

John Lethman gave a sigh, half of relief, half of exasperation. "Sorry about that. She's been like a snake with the jitters for days. She'll come to heel when the time comes." He dabbed at his face, winced, and dabbed again. "Shall I take the Mansel girl back?"

"Not for the moment. You can get on. I'll talk to her here. And afterwards—" he finished the sentence in Arabic, and John Lethman nodded. His reply was wordless and quite horrible. He merely drew the edge of his hand across his throat in a murderous little gesture, and Henry Grafton laughed.

"If you can," he said in English. "All right, *ruh.*"

Lethman went out. I wanted to keep what miserable initiative I could, so I spoke immediately. My voice came out harsh and high with nerves, and surprisingly formidable.

"Well, supposing you start, Dr. Grafton. You've got quite a bit of explaining to do, haven't you?"

15

So bury me by some sweet Garden-side.

—E. FITZGERALD: *The Rubáiyát of*
Omar Khayyám

HE DIDN'T answer for a moment. He stood there eyeing me under dropped lids, still with that appraising, almost clinical look. His eyes were dark and shiny as treacle, and in contrast the heavy lids looked thick and waxen. The skin all round the eyes was brownish, like overripe plums.

He smiled. "You're a fighter, aren't you? I admire you for it."

"You excite me beyond words. Sit down and get on with it." He stepped down from the dais and crossed the room to get a chair which stood against the wall. He had changed his neat businessman's suit for dark trousers and a high-necked Russian shirt in olive green which made him look sallower, and did nothing to flatter his thick build. He looked very strong, with strength in the back of his neck, like a bull. My rudeness didn't even ruffle him. His manner was perfectly civil, pleasant even, as he brought the chair over and sat himself opposite me.

"Cigarette?"

"No, thank you."

"It'll help compose your nerves."

"Who said they needed composing?"

"Oh, come, Miss Mansel, I thought you were a realist."

"I hope I am. All right. There, my hand's shaking. Please you?"

"Not at all." He lit my cigarette, and waved out the match. "I'm sorry I had to do what I did. Please be sure I don't mean you any harm. I just had to get you back here and talk to you."

"You had to—?" I opened my eyes at him. "Oh, come off it, Dr. Grafton! You could have talked to me in the car. Or you could have talked to me before I left Dar Ibrahim, if you were going to drop the disguise anyway." I leaned back, drawing on my cigarette. The gesture helped to give me the extra touch of confidence I needed, and I felt my nerves beginning to relax. "I must say, I liked you a lot better in that neat little number you were wearing the other night. I quite see why you only interviewed guests at midnight. You and the room looked a lot better in the dark."

As far as the room was concerned this was certainly true. What could have passed in the lamplight for romantic shabbiness was shown up by daylight as plain dirt and neglect. The bed hangings were tattered and filthy, and the table beside me was sordid in the extreme with used cups and plates and a saucer half-full of cigarette stubs. "Well, all right," I said, still aggressively, "let's have it. And start at the beginning, please. What happened to Aunt Harriet?"

He looked at me frankly and showed an apologetic hand. "Be sure I'm only too willing to tell you everything. I admit you've every ground for suspicion and anger, but believe me it's only on your own account, and I'll explain that in a moment. As far as your great-aunt is concerned there's nothing to worry you, nothing at all. She died quite peacefully. You know of course that I was her doctor: I was with her all the time, and so was John."

"When did she die?"

"A fortnight ago."

"What of?"

"Miss Mansel, she was over eighty."

"I dare say she was, but there has to be a cause. What was it, heart? This asthma of hers? Plain neglect?"

I saw him compress his lips slightly, but he answered with the same pleasant appearance of frankness. "The asthma was a fiction, Miss Mansel. The most difficult thing for me to disguise was my voice. When John told me how persistent you were, and we realized you might be impossible to fob off, we concocted a story that would allow me to speak in a whisper. And, as you must realize now, the picture I had to give you of a forgetful and very strange old lady was far from the truth. Your aunt was very fully in possession of her faculties right up to the time of her death."

"What was it, then?"

"Primarily her heart. She had a very slight coronary last autumn, and another in late February—after I had come to live with her here. Then, as you may know, she was difficult about food, and latterly had periodic sickness and stomach trouble which added to the strain. She had one of these gastric attacks three weeks ago, a bad one, and her heart wouldn't take it. That's the story, as simply as I can put it. She was, I repeat, over eighty. One would hardly have expected her to get through."

I said nothing for a moment, drawing on my cigarette and staring at him. Then I said abruptly: "Death certificates? Do you have them here?"

"Yes, I signed one, for the record. You can see it any time you wish."

"I wouldn't believe a word of it. You concealed her death, you and John Lethman and the girl. One might even say you went to pretty fair lengths to conceal it. Why?"

He turned up a hand. "Heaven knows I don't blame you, in the circumstances I wouldn't believe a word of it myself; but the plain fact is that, far from wanting your great-aunt out of the way, I'd have done a lot—in fact I did do a lot—to keep her alive. I don't ask you to believe me when I tell you that I liked her, but you may believe me when I tell you that her death was damned inconvenient, coming when it did, and could have cost me a fortune. So I had a base motive for keeping her alive as well." He tapped ash on the floor. "Hence the mystery and the masquerade, which I'll explain in a moment. It didn't suit me to have lawyers or family invading the place, so I didn't report her death, and we've allowed the local people to think she's still alive."

"And then my cousin and I turned up, just at the wrong moment. I see. But the wrong moment for what, Dr. Grafton? You really had better start from the beginning, hadn't you?"

He leaned back in the chair. "Very well. I was your great-aunt's doctor for about six years, and for the last three or four of them I came up here once a fortnight, sometimes oftener. She was very fit and active for her age, but she was something of a *malade imaginaire,* and besides, she was old, and I think, in spite of her fanatical independence, a bit lonely. And living alone as she did with the Arab servants I think she must have had some dread of illness or accident that would leave her completely at their—in their charge."

I thought he had been going to say "at their mercy." I thought of Halide wearing the big ruby, of Nasirulla thick-set and tough and sullen, of the idiotically mouthing Jassim. "Yes?" I said.

"So I paid her a regular call, and this set her mind at rest—and besides, she enjoyed the company of a countryman. I may say I enjoyed the visits, too. She could be very entertaining when she was on form."

"And John Lethman? He gave me a version of how he got taken on here, but I don't know if it was true."

"Ah, yes, one of the few occasions where John managed a bit of lightning thinking. You may have guessed that he knows about as much as you do yourself about psychological medicine. He's an archaeologist."

"I . . . see. Hence my great-aunt's interest. Yes. I remember feeling a bit surprised when he talked about a 'loony-bin' . . . They don't, if they know what they're talking about. But the Adonis Gardens?"

"They're genuine enough. You could say they were his premise. The paper he was workng on was on the Adonis cult, and I suppose that's what suggested the exercise in morbid psychology—the 'ecstatic religions' nonsense he gave you when he was cornered. Not bad, eh? Apart from that, I believe he told you the truth. He was traveling around doing research for his paper, and camping up near the little temple above the palace, and got caught by a storm one day—just as you were—and came to Dar Ibrahim. Your great-aunt took a fancy to him, and asked him to stay on while he did his work, and without anything much being said on either side he settled down and started looking after the place for her. I must say I was thankful when he decided to settle here. It made my job a lot easier." There was the ghost of a smile I didn't quite like. He tapped ash off his cigarette again, delicately. "A nice boy."

"And useful?"

"Oh, certainly. He made a great deal of difference here. The Lady thought the world of him."

"I'm sure. But I meant to you. Useful to you."

The heavy lids lifted. He gave a tiny shrug. "Oh, yes, to me. I find him an excellent partner in my—business."

"Yes, well, let's come to that now. Your business. You've been at Dar Ibrahim ever since you left Beirut? Yes, it figures. You were the 'resident physician,' not John Lethman. You were 'the doctor' Jassim was talking about when Hamid and I came to the gate . . . John Lethman certainly made a quick recovery from that one! But I was puzzled, because the Gab—the dogs liked him."

"The dogs?"

"Oh, nothing to matter. She sent a letter home in February, did you know? She said her dog 'couldn't abide the doctor.'"

"Oh yes, that was the wretched little brute that I—that died. . . . Yes, indeed, I was the 'resident physician.' That was part of the Stanhope legend, as you'll probably know; your great-aunt rather fancied having her own 'Dr. Meryon' in attendance." He looked not unamused. "It was a small price to pay. She was entitled to her own legend, even though I didn't quite see myself in the role of that unfortunate man ministering to that monstrous egoism day and night."

"Don't tell me that poor Aunt Harriet made you minister to her monstrous egoism day and night? Even if she had it, which seems likely, since she was a Mansel, she had a sense of humor too."

"Don't try and find motives for me. I told you I liked her." He gave a little twist of a smile. "Though I must admit that she was pushing it a bit the last year or two. On occasions the impersonation could get to be a little trying."

I glanced above the bed to where the stick and the rifle hung. "It'd be too much to hope that she really used them on Halide?"

He laughed, quite genuinely. "She did occasionally throw things at Jassim, but that's about as far as it went. And you mustn't be too hard on Halide. She's working very hard for what she wants."

"John Lethman? Or Dar Ibrahim? Both sacred, I assure you." I leaned forward to stub out my cigarette on the saucer. Then I regarded him for a moment. "You know, I think I do believe you about my great-aunt . . . I mean, I doubt if you meant her any harm. For one thing you don't seem worried about what she may have written in her letters . . . unless you censored all her letters, and I doubt if you did, since I gather she was free to speak to the village people and to the carriers who brought supplies across. You obviously never saw her last letter inviting Charles to visit her, or Humphrey Ford's letter, either."

I half expected him to ask what I was talking about, but he didn't. He was watching me steadily.

"And I'm inclined to pass John Lethman," I said, "but what about the servants? Are you quite sure that Halide didn't have a good reason for wanting the old lady out of the way?"

"No, no, that's nonsense. Your aunt used to be pretty fierce sometimes with the servants—they tend to do nothing at all unless one stands over them—but she liked the girl."

"That wasn't quite what I suggested."

"And Halide looked after her devotedly. I told you your aunt could be difficult, and the late-night sessions really were a fact. The girl was sometimes run off her feet." He waved a hand. "These rooms—they've only been neglected since her death, you must realize that. We cleared them a bit roughly of some of the worst clutter because we wanted to use them—they were naturally the best kept and most central rooms—but there simply wasn't time to clean them up properly before you saw them." A look. "We were glad of the darkness for more reasons than one. Oh, the place was always shabby, and she liked to live in a clutter, but the rooms were kept clean when she was alive . . . my God, they had to be! But to suggest that Halide hated your great-aunt enough to . . . No, Miss Mansel."

He broke off as Halide came in with the tray. She set it down near me on the table with no more than a bit of a rattle, then, without looking at either of us or speaking a word, went straight out of the room. She had taken me at my word and just brought coffee. It was a bit weak, but it was hot and fresh. I poured a cup, and drank some, and felt better.

"What's more," said Henry Grafton, "the same applies to John and Halide as applied to me. They had more reasons to wish the Lady Harriet alive than dead."

"Meaning that they're in your racket with you?"

"You could put it like that."

"Did my great-aunt leave a Will?" I asked bluntly.

He grinned. "She made them every week. Apart from crossword puzzles it was her favorite amusement."

"I knew that. We sometimes got copies. What happened to them all?"

"They'll be somewhere about." He sounded unconcerned. "She used to hide them away in odd corners. I'm afraid this isn't exactly an easy place to search, but you're welcome to try."

I must have looked surprised. "You mean you'll let me look around?"

"Naturally. In fact it's possible that the property now belongs to you—or more probably to your cousin."

"Or to John Lethman?"

He shot me a look. "As you say. She was very fond of him."

"Another of her eccentricities?"

"A very common one. But I'm afraid that there'll be little left of any value. There may be one or two personal souvenirs you may care to unearth from the general chaos, and as I say you're welcome to try."

"Such as the ring that Halide's wearing?"

He looked surprised. "The garnet? You would have liked that? It was certainly your aunt's favorite, she always wore it, but I understand she gave it to Halide . . . well, of course . . . probably Halide wouldn't mind . . ."

"Dr. Grafton, please don't think I'm standing with one foot in my aunt's grave, but the ring has what they call 'sentimental value,' and I'm pretty sure that the family will fight to get it back. Besides, she meant me to have it. If she did give it to Halide then she must really have been round the bend, and no court would allot it to her."

"Is it so very valuable?"

"I know nothing at all about the value of garnets," I said, momentarily truthful, "but you can take it from me it's not just a keepsake for the maid, however devoted. It belonged to my great-grandmother and I want it back."

"Then you must certainly have it. I'll speak to Halide."

"Tell her I'll get her something to take its place, or there may be something else left she'd like to have."

I put down my cup. There was a pause. Some big insect, a beetle, hurtled in through the bright doorway, blundered around the room for a moment or two, and went out. I felt suddenly very tired, as if the conversation were slipping away from me. I believed him . . . and if I believed him surely the rest didn't make any sense?

"All right," I said at length, "so we come to what's happened since her death. But before we go on, will you show me where she is?"

He got to his feet. "Of course. She's out here in the Prince's Garden, as she wished to be."

He led the way out into the little court, past the dry fountain, through diagonals of sun and shadow and between beds of baked earth where in early spring there would be irises and Persian tulips. Over the high outer wall fell a tangle of white jasmine, and beside it a cascade of yellow roses made a blinding curtain. The scent was wonderful. In the shade thrown by the flowers was a flat white stone, uncarved, and at its head stood the stone turban of the Moslem dead.

I looked at this in silence for a moment. "Is this her grave?"

"Yes."

"No name?"

"There hasn't been time."

"You must know as well as I do that this is a man's grave."

He made a sudden movement, quickly suppressed, but I felt a jerk of apprehension as my body tightened back into wariness. This was still the man who had savaged me in the car, who was playing some nasty game or other where he had a lot at stake. . . . Somewhere, not far below the surface—just under the sweating skin, behind the oil-black eyes—was something not as calm, as pleasant, as Dr. Henry Grafton would like me to believe.

But he said with what sounded like gentle amusement: "No, really, I can't have you suspecting me of anything else! You know—of course you do!—that she liked to dress as a man, and indeed behaved like one. I suppose it gave her a kind of freedom in Arab countries that a woman couldn't have normally. When she was younger the Arabs called her 'the Prince' because of the way she rode, and the horses and state she liked to keep. She had this planned"—a gesture to the gravestone—"some time before she died. It was surely part of the same conceit."

I stared in silence at the slender column with its carved turban. Somehow of all that I had seen this was the most alien, the most foreign symbol. I thought of the leaning lichened stones in the old churchyard at home, the big elms, the yews by the lych gate, the rooks blown past the tower in the evening winds. A shower of yellow petals drifted down on the blank hot stones, and a lizard flashed out, palpitated for an instant there, watching us, then vanished.

" 'I have purchased an excellent Tombstone locally.' "

"What?" asked Henry Grafton.

"I'm sorry, I didn't realize I'd spoken aloud. You're right, this is what she wanted. And at least she's with friends."

"Friends?"

"In the next garden. The dogs, I saw the graves."

I turned away. The tired feeling persisted. The heavy scented heat, the sound of bees, perhaps still the effects of the injection and the strain of the day, were weighing on me.

"Come back in out of the sun." His dark eyes were peering at me. They looked very intent. "Are you all right?"

"Perfectly. Floating, rather, but it's not unpleasant. Was that only pentothal?"

"That's all. You weren't out for long, and it's quite harmless. Come along."

The room seemed comparatively cool after the trapped heat of the garden. I sat down with relief in the lacquer chair and leaned back. The corners of the room were swimming in shadow. Henry Grafton picked up a glass from the table and poured water into it.

"Drink this. Better? Here, have another cigarette. It'll help you."

I took it automatically, and he lit it for me and then moved away to hitch his chair out of the shaft of sunlight which slanted low now from a window, and sat down again.

I flattened my hands on the carved lacquer of the chair arms. Somehow the little, practiced touch of solicitude had changed the tone of the interview; the doctor-patient gesture had put him back, subtly, on top. I made an effort, through the invading fatigue, to resume the cool accusing tone of attack.

"All right, Dr. Grafton. That's the first part of the inquisition over. For the time being I'll accept that my great-aunt's death was a natural one, and that you did all you could. Now we come to why you had to conceal it, what you called the 'mystery and the masquerade' . . . and what you've done to me. You've an awful lot of explaining still to do. Go on."

He regarded his hands for a minute, clasped in his lap. Then he looked up.

"When you rang up my house and were told I was gone, did they tell you anything about me?"

"Not exactly, but they played hell with the silences. I gather you're in trouble."

"True, I was in trouble, so I got out while the going was good. I can think of a lot of places I'd rather be in than a Lebanese prison."

"As bad as that?"

"Oh, quite. A little matter of getting and selling medical supplies illegally. You can get away with murder here more easily."

"You wouldn't just have been deported?"

"That would hardly have helped. As it happens, I'm a Turkish national, and the penalties there are even worse. Take it from me, I had to get out, and fast, before they caught up with me. But I had assets in the country, and I was damned if I left without realizing them. Naturally, I'd been afraid this might happen one day, so I'd made arrangements. Dar Ibrahim had been my center and—shall we call it storeroom?—for some time, and over the past few months I had managed to—" a flick of the brown eyelids and a tiny pause—"engage John's interest. So the actual getaway went smoothly enough. I was driven to the airport and checked in, then someone else took over my ticket and boarded the flight. If you know the airport here you'll know it can be done. John was waiting outside the airport and drove me up here by the back road—the way I brought you today— and I walked down to Dar Ibrahim. Your great-aunt expected me. Naturally I hadn't told her the truth; I spun her some story about an abortion and procuring drugs without charge for certain poorer class patients. Like the Stanhope woman, she had the highest disregard for the laws of this country, so she took me in and kept it secret. She was too delighted to have her doctor here as a permanency to ask many questions, and she talked too much herself to be over-curious about other people. As for the servants—Halide had her eye on John as a one-way ticket out of Sal'q, and her brother was employed by me already. Jassim's silence one hardly has to buy; it takes practice to understand more than one word in twelve, and in any case he's too stupid to know what's going on. So here I was, sitting pretty, with a good base to work from and John's help as outside agent to start cashing in on my assets. It went like a dream, no suspicions, winding up as smoothly as clockwork, cash due to come in, myself due to check out finally at the end of the summer . . ."

He paused. I leaned forward to flick ash into the saucer. It missed, and went on to the table to add to the patina of dust.

He went on: "Then just a fortnight ago came your great-aunt's death. My God, for you to think I'd killed her! I spent nine hours solid at her bedside—right there—fighting for her life like a mother tiger. . . ." He wiped his upper lip. "Well, there you are. She died—and her death could have thrown the doors wide open, and me to the lions. In the end we decided to play it cool—I believe that's the expression nowadays?—and keep her death quiet. We thought we might just get away with it for the couple of weeks that were needed to complete the current operation. I couldn't hope to keep it quiet much longer than that, and the risks were too big. We had to cut our losses and plan a complete get-out in a big hurry—but we did it. What we didn't reckon with was you. Nothing your great-aunt had ever said led us to think we'd have a devoted family hammering at the door within a day or two. But—and just at the wrong moment—you came."

The sun had almost gone, and its last light sloped in a low bright shaft across my feet. Dust motes swirled in it. I watched them half idly. Beyond their quick dazzle the man in the other chair seemed oddly remote.

"We thought at first you'd be easy to fob off," he said, "but you're a persistent young woman, and a tough one. You managed to put the wind up John, and we were afraid you were in a position, if you really got worried, to whistle up all sorts of help and come back armed with lawyers and writs of habeas corpus and God knows what else; so we thought we hadn't much to lose by trying the masquerade, and if it seemed to satisfy you you might keep quiet for the few days' grace we needed. It was a desperate sort of idea, but I thought I might get away with it for a few minutes in semi-darkness, especially with the male clothes she used. In fact it was that habit of hers that gave me the idea in the first place. If we'd refused to let you see your aunt at all, you'd have been convinced she was ill, or that John was keeping you out for his own ends, and if you'd got suspicious enough to bring the doctor or a lawyer from Beirut, we'd have been sunk. So we tried it, and it worked."

I nodded, thinking back over the interview; the hoarse whisper disguising the man's voice, the grotesque glimpses of the balding skull under the turban, the sunken mouth from which presumably he had removed his lower teeth, the alert black eyes. Halide's nervousness and John Lethman's watchful, edgy look had been for none of the reasons I had imagined.

"I get it now," I said. "All that chat of John Lethman's at supper—he was finding out all he could about the family so as to fill you in on things Aunt H didn't tell you. You knew I hadn't seen her since I was a kid, so you thought you'd probably fool me easily enough, but Charles had seen her recently, so naturally 'Great-Aunt Harriet' wouldn't receive him. Oh, yes, clever enough, Dr. Grafton." I blew a long cloud of smoke into the air between us. "And as a matter of fact you rather enjoyed it, didn't you? John Lethman tried to hurry me out, and heaven knows I'd have gone, but you wouldn't let me, you were enjoying yourself too much making a fool of me."

He was grinning. Grotesquely, it was Great-Aunt Harriet's face as I had thought of her, vaguely seen through the smoke and the dusty shaft of sunlight, remote as something glimpsed down the wrong end of a telescope.

I said: "Yes, all right, so it worked. You fooled me, and you fobbed Charles off quite successfully, and surely after I'd left the place you were in the clear, so why drag me back? I'd gone, hadn't I, quite satisfied? Why drag me back here like this?"

"Because we hadn't fobbed your cousin off, and you know it. Oh, don't give me that great big innocent look, it doesn't suit you. Shall I tell you what happened? The first time you left here it wasn't your driver who met you, it was your cousin, and between you you hatched the plan to let him in on Monday night. He came, and you explored the place together. Yes, my dear, that stare's a bit more genuine."

"How do you know all this?"

"Your precious cousin told me all about it himself."

I don't think I spoke. I just stared. I couldn't quite take in what he was saying. The room seemed to be swirling round me, smoke and dusty sunlight dazzling like fog.

"After you'd gone back to your room that evening, he was to have left by the back gate—the mountain gate, wasn't he?" Grafton's voice was smooth as cream. "Well, he didn't. John and I came across him in the passageway below here, trying to force one of the padlocked doors. It wasn't much use denying who he was—you're very like one another, aren't you? So we—er, we took him in. He's been safely locked away in the palace prison ever since. It won't surprise you to know the palace has its own gaol? Unhappily there was only one cell serviceable, so when we caught you as well, we had to use the storeroom for you."

"Here? Charles here? I don't believe you. He can't be!" My brain seemed to be groping, like someone feeling through a roomful of smoke, not sure of the direction of the door or the distance to the window. I think I had a hand to my forehead, "You're lying. You know you're lying. He wrote me a letter, and left it for me in Beirut. He went to Damascus to see Ben's father . . . no, to Aleppo. And we saw him—yes we saw him on the way. . . ."

"He certainly wrote you a letter. He suggested doing that himself. If he hadn't done it to ensure you kept away from Dar Ibrahim and didn't start hunting for him when he failed to turn up at the Phoenicia, we couldn't have let you go in the morning."

"Why did you?"

"Your driver," he said shortly, "and your hotel. Your cousin pointed out that it was easier to let you go than to risk someone starting to ask questions. Besides, as he told us, you thought you'd seen your great-aunt alive and well, and could help spread the belief that all was normal."

"So he wrote the letter—all those elaborate lies—he even pretended he'd seen her himself and recognized her . . . I've been wondering about that, I thought he must have seen you and made the same mistake as I did . . . You mean—that letter—it was all quite deliberate? Just to keep me out?"

"Exactly that."

I said nothing. The conversation no longer seemed to have much to do with me. He was still smiling, and as I stared at him, bemused, I saw the grin widen. The top teeth were his own; the incisors were yellowish and long. He was talking again, fragments of information drifting like torn paper to lie in a crazy pattern: John Lethman—no doubt the 'Englishman' seen in the distance by the faun—had driven the Porsche down to Beirut in the early morning, hidden it in someone's backyard, woken the someone whose name seemed to be Yusuf and given him the letter, then been driven back by Yusuf, who later got the letter delivered to the hotel, and went himself to ride herd on me . . .

"But you, my dear, didn't stay out of the line of fire. You made it fairly obvious that you were going to ask some damned awkward questions and make some damned awkward contacts. You even telephoned England. And from what our man heard of your telephone conversation with Damascus, we decided to remove you."

"The Arab in the red tarboosh. He was in the next booth." I said it to myself, not to him.

"Certainly. Well, since you'd made your plans public, and that damned driver was already there with you, and we didn't want any eyes turning to Dar Ibrahim, we decided to get you the wrong side of the frontier and then let you disappear. All very simple, no great harm done—your car stopped, yourselves robbed, your papers taken and the car wrecked . . . somewhere beyond the Antilebanon, we thought, or even off towards Qatana. Yusuf was confident he could immobilize you for long enough. So he got the Porsche out and drove it through to wait. It was the bait, of course. You'd have followed it—"

"Hamid! If you've harmed Hamid—!"

"Not if he's sensible. Most Arabs are, if you make it worth their while." He laughed. "I thought at first your being stopped at the frontier was going to bitch all our plans, but it worked out like a dream. You didn't see me, but I was there, and I saw what happened. My driver followed yours into the frontier buildings and heard the whole thing, so I sent him through to tell Yusuf to go on south and get rid of your cousin's car, but as luck would have it you'd seen it yourself from above the road, and came running down to tell your driver to go through after it. My own car came straight back, and reported he'd crossed yours at the frontier. Since neither your driver nor the Porsche came back, one gathers Yusuf made him listen to reason, or else simply carried out the original plan and left him somewhere to cool off till tomorrow. We can't afford to let him near a telephone, you must see that." A little grunt of amused satisfaction. "After that it was so easy it was hardly true. You told everyone within hearing that you were going to the Adonis Hotel to get a car for Beirut, so I simply went there first and waited for you to come. The manager's new, so there was no fear of his recognizing me, but I'm damned sure that by the time you turned up he was sure he'd known me all his life. You'd never have accepted a lift from someone picking you up on the road, but someone you met in the hotel, someone you were introduced to by name . . ." That smile again. "I hope you appreciated the touch about the Great Mosque? You remember telling your 'great-aunt' all about it?"

"Very clever. You're so very clever. Quite a litle empire you've got, haven't you, with all your spies and drivers and cars. Something's paying pretty well. Don't grin at me like that, you snag-toothed little viper. What have you done with Charles?"

"I told you. He's in the lock-up." The grin had vanished.

"Have you hurt him?"

"There was a bit of a rough-up last night."

"You tried to rough Charles up? No wonder John looks the worst for wear. I thought his face was hurting him yesterday, and now I come to think of it, he kept that side turned away. It's come up lovely now, hasn't it? Good old Charles! And oh, my poor auntie! Did he hurt you much?"

The smile had certainly vanished. He had flushed darkly, and I saw the vein in his temple begin to beat. "He didn't touch me. I had a gun. I admit John isn't much use, but then he drugs."

"Drugs?" I don't think I managed to speak the question, I only looked it. He had gone far away from me again. The room was all shadows now. I found myself straining forward, peering to see where he had gone. Dimly, I knew I should be frantic with worry about Charles, with fear for myself. But I couldn't tie my brain down. It wouldn't work for me. It spun high and light. It floated, lifting me with it out of the chair, up toward the high dim corners of the room.

He was suddenly close, gigantic. He was out of his chair and standing over me. His voice was vicious. "Yes, drugs, you silly spoiled little bitch. Drugs. I said 'medical supplies,' didn't I? There's a fortune in Indian hemp lying there in the cellars waiting for collection tonight, and another fortune growing in the fields above Laklouk if your great-aunt hadn't died, and I'd been able to hang on till harvest." He drew in his breath. "And not only hemp. They grow opium in Turkey and Iran, didn't you know? That's the real stuff. Opium, morphine, heroin—and I've a pipeline across Syria that's been working like a dream, and all it needs for the processing is a bit of time and the kind of privacy we get here at Dar Ibrahim . . ."

I'd been meaning to stub my cigarette out in the saucer, but the saucer was too far away, and the effort was too much. The stub fell through my fingers to the floor. It seemed to fall in slow motion, and I made no attempt to retrieve it, but just sat there, looking down at my own hand, which seemed a long way away and not attached to my body at all.

". . . And that's just what we had, till you came. The room next to the storeroom where we put you, that's our lab. We've been working like slaves putting the stuff through since the last lot came down. Oh, we'd have had to pack it in this year, no doubt of that, and move our base—those bastards at the Narcotics Division of the U.N. have been putting the screws on, and the National Assembly's promising to make it hotter than ever in this country next year . . . and of course since the old lady went Dar Ibrahim was due to shut down anyway. Phased withdrawal, don't they call it? The caravan comes through tonight . . ." His voice trailed off, and I heard him laugh again. He stooped and picked up the stub, and dropped it in the saucer. His face swam near mine. "Feeling a bit far away, are you? Not exactly fit to cope? That was a reefer you had in the car, and you've just smoked two more, my pretty, and now you're going back to your nice little room to sleep them off . . . till tonight's over."

I wished I could care. I ought to care. Fragments of pictures were there in smoky darkness, like dreams edged with light. John Lethman's slack body and defeated young face with the sunken gray eyes. The Arab girl watching him fiercely. The patch of hemp with the label of the racing dog. The crates in the cellar. But they dislimned and the light beat in a steady echoing rhythm that was somehow my own heart beating, and someone's voice was coming and going in the throbbing air like the pulse of a drum, and I was out of it all, safe and high and floating as scatheless and beautiful and powerful as an angel among the cobwebs on the ceiling, while down there below in the dimming room sat a girl in a red lacquer chair, her body slack and drowsy in its plain expensive frock, her face pale, the cheekbones highlighted with a film of damp, her mouth vaguely smiling. Her hair was dark and smooth and fashionably cut. Her arms were sunburned, the hands long and slender, one wrist weighted down with a gold bracelet that had cost all of eighty pounds. . . . A spoiled silly bitch, he had called her. She was blinking at him now. She had very big eyes, dark-fringed, made bigger by the make-up she affected, and now by the drug . . . Poor silly bitch, she was in danger, and I couldn't do a thing for her, not that I cared. And she didn't even look afraid . . .

Not even when John Lethman came quietly in, floating like another shadow in slow motion across the dim floor, to stand over her and ask of Henry Grafton, as if it hardly mattered:

"She's out, is she?"

"Two cigarettes. Well taken care of. And the boy?"

"Blocked. Cell blue with smoke and himself out cold. No trouble there."

Henry Grafton laughed. "No trouble anywhere. Safe under our hands till it's over. And you, young John, will stick to your ration and stay with it. You've just had your fix, by the look of you? Well, that's the last you'll get. Oh, you can smoke if you want to, but don't come asking me for more of the hard stuff because you won't get it till that cargo's safely through Beirut. D'you hear me? Right. Take her back."

The younger man stooped over the chair. The girl moved her head dreamily and smiled at him, eyes misty. She seemed to be trying to speak, but couldn't manage it. Her head lolled back.

"I must say," said John Lethman, "I like her better this way."

"Meaning she's too pretty to have a tongue like a wasp's backside? I agree. My God, what a family! She reminds me of the old lady on her bad days. Well, she's asked for all she's getting. Take her away. I'm afraid you'll have to carry her."

Lethman leaned over the lacquer chair. At his touch, some of the fumes of the drug must have lifted for a second. I came down from where I had been floating, into the body on the chair, as he pulled me forward to slide an arm round me and lift me. I managed to say slowly and with what I thought was immense dignity: "Can manage qui' well, thank you."

He said with impatience: "Of course you can't. Come along, I won't hurt you. Don't be afraid."

"Of you?" I said. "Don't make me laugh."

He bit his lip, yanked me out of the chair, and heaved me over his shoulder in the he-man lift. I'm ashamed to say I spoiled the heroic scene by laughing like an idiot upside down all the way back to my dungeon.

16

Truly we have been at cost, yet we are forbidden harvest.

—THE KORAN: *Sura* LVI

AN EMPIRE I had called it, and I hadn't been far wrong. Heaven knows the clues had been there if I had only had the knowledge to work from; and heaven knows I had all the pieces now.

It was hours later. My watch said eleven, within a minute or two. The time had gone like a dream, literally like a dream, passed like smoke from the cigarettes that had sent me floating. I felt firmly enough based now—too firmly. I was back on the bed in my prison, sitting on top of the tumbled blankets holding an aching head, no longer the slack-boned, don't-careish girl hopped up with bhang, but a young woman with a crashing hangover, still in reasonably full possession of her five wits, and every one of them scared, with all the evidence literally under her eyes.

They had left me a light this time. Up in its niche the three-branched lamp held up its buds of flame. Beside the bed was a jug of water and a glass. I drank, and my mouth felt a little less as if someone had been cleaning it out with an abrasive cleaner. I tried putting my legs down, and my feet to the floor. I could feel the floor, which was probably something. I didn't try anything violent, like standing up, but sat there, holding my head on to my body, and gently, as gently as possible, allowing my eyes to look here and there in the swimming light . . .

The room was far bigger than I had thought, stretching away back into the shadow. Behind the clutter of broken-down furniture and the piled rugs and harness that would be all one could see from the corridor, I now saw that the place was stacked, literally stacked, with wooden boxes and cardboard cartons and small tins. Some of them, I thought, would probably be 'blinds'—genuine consignments of whatever article (like the cooking oil) was used to disguise the drugs, but if even a fraction of these held hashish or the opium derivatives, the room would have bought up Aladdin's cave four times over. I thought of Hamid's sheeps' droppings, but somehow it wasn't funny anymore.

On the cartons nearest me the device of the running dog stood out clear and damning, with its misspelled warning carefully stenciled below: "Best quality, beware immitations." It shook the last piece into place, and Henry Grafton's sketchy story, with all its gaps and evasions, became, with this gloss added, very clear indeed. The hashish, grown copiously in the high hills; John Lethman crop-watching, or bargaining with the growers, or arranging for the piecemeal ferrying of the stuff down by the peasants—perhaps one of them the very man whom Charles and I had seen approaching the back gate of the palace. Dar Ibrahim must have been used as the center of the filthy trade for some time, might even have been so used long before the old lady moved in. It was the perfect clearing house, and also the perfect retreat for anyone in Henry Grafton's situation—the lonely hilltop fortress kept by the strong-minded old woman who refused to receive visitors, and who had (like her prototype Lady Hester) once or twice defied the law and would presumably defy it again on a friend's behalf. I couldn't believe that my great-aunt would have concealed Henry Grafton had she known what trade he was engaged in, but no doubt his story had been plausible enough, and equally plausible the account of whatever 'experiments' he and John Lethman were conducting in the underground storeroom. And John Lethman's own role in the business became pathetically clear. He had probably started innocently enough, being persuaded by the unscrupulous Grafton that the occasional 'smoke' would do him no harm; then quietly, inevitably, hooked on the hard drugs that would ensure his dependence and continued help. It was not my Great-Aunt Harriet who was the victim of this affair—for every reason I was now convinced that Grafton would never have wished her out of the way—but John Lethman.

And I was very much afraid that there were going to be two more victims. Henry Grafton might keep insisting that he meant me and my cousin no real harm, but people have been murdered for a lot less than a fortune in drugs and a possible death sentence (since Grafton was a Turkish national) if they went astray. He could hardly imagine that Charles or I would fail to report all we knew the moment we were able to, yet I— and probably my cousin as well—had been handed both information and evidence with a carelessness that terrified me. Whether he had got round to realizing it yet or not, he would have to kill us both if he wanted to save his skin.

The door must have been very thick. I had heard no movement out in the passageway, but the door swung open suddenly to reveal Halide standing there with—as ever—a tray in her hands. There was nobody with her, and she managed the tray one-handed while she opened the door, so I supposed that my captors knew the condition their drugs would reduce me to. She now stood propping the door open with one shoulder, and eyeing me with her usual contempt and hostility.

"So, you are awake. Here is your food. And do not think that you can push past me and get away, because the one way is only to the back gate, which is locked this time, and the key out of it, and Jassim is in the outer court, and the men are in the Lady's room."

I eyed her sourly. "If you knew how funny that sounds in English."

"Quoi?"

"Never mind." Confronted with her shimmering grace—it was the green silk again—I felt terrible. And I didn't think the bathroom gambit would work again. I made no attempt to get to my feet, but watched her as she came gracefully away from the door and set the tray down on a box with a rap which made the crockery rattle.

"Halide—"

"Yes?"

"I suppose you know what they—the men—are doing, why they have locked me up, me and my cousin?"

"Oh, yes, John—" she brought the name out with a kind of flourish—"tells me everything."

"You lucky girl. Did he tell you what the penalties were for running drugs in this neck of the woods?"

"Quoi?"

"Even in this dirty corner of the dirty world? Even in Beirut? Didn't John warn you what the police would do, to you and your brother as well, if they discovered what was happening here at Dar Ibrahim?"

"Oh, yes." She smiled. "Everybody knows this. Everybody does it, here in the Lebanon. For many years before the doctor came here, my brother used to bring the hashish down from the hills. It is only the brave men who are the carriers from the hills to the sea."

I supposed it was too much to hope that the primitive mind would see it as anything other than a sort of Robin Hood gesture of bravery. To the peasant, the hashish brought pleasure, and money. If an unreasonable government chose to forbid its growth for private purposes, why then the government must be fooled. It was as simple as that. It was the same mentality which, in more sophisticated societies, assumes that the tax and speed laws are made to be broken.

"You need not be so afraid," said Halide to me, with contempt, "I think they do not mean to kill you."

"I'm not afraid." I met her derisive look as steadily as I could. "But I think you had better be, Halide. No, listen, I don't think you quite realize what is happening here, and I'm not quite sure if John knows, either, just what he's got himself into. It isn't just a case of you and your friends having a quiet smoke now and then and your brother shooting it out with a few local police on his way to the sea. Not any more. It's big business, and the governments of every responsible country are wild keen to stop it. Are you hoping to clear out with your John when this lot's been shifted and he's got his share of the money? Where d'you think you can go? Not into Syria—they'd catch you up in no time. Not into Turkey—there's a death penalty there. The same applies to Iran, Egypt, where you like. Believe me, Halide, there's no future in this for you or for John. Don't think he can take you to England, either, because you'll be picked up there as soon as I or my cousin open our mouths."

"Perhaps you will not get out of here for a long time."

"That's silly talk," I said. "You know as well as I do that any minute now the Damascus police will start looking for us, and where would the trail lead them first if not to Dar Ibrahim? Dr. Grafton'll be lucky if he gets the stuff away at all."

"He will get it away. I think you do not realize what time it is, or what day? It is nearly midnight, Wednesday. The caravan is already on its way here. The palace will be empty by daylight."

"I . . . suppose it will," I said slowly. I had lost count of time. I put a hand to my forehead, pressing the heel of it against my temple as if that would clear my thoughts. At least the headache had gone. "Listen, Halide, listen to what I have to say. And take that look off your face, I'm not pleading for anything, I'm offering you something, you and John Lethman, because he's nothing much worse than weak and stupid, and you've had no chance to know better. My family—my cousin's family—we're wealthy, what you'd call important people. I obviously can't offer you the kind of money you'll get by helping Grafton with this operation, but I can offer you some help which believe me you're going to need, and badly. I don't know your laws, but if you let me and my cousin go now, and if you and your John were to give evidence against Dr. Grafton, and the police stopped the cargo of drugs, I think you'd find they wouldn't prosecute you or your brother, or even John Lethman."

I had been watching her as I spoke, but her face was turned away from the lamplight and I couldn't see if my words were having any effect. I hesitated. It would certainly be no use beginning to talk about rights and wrongs, or why I should have any interest not strictly personal in stopping the cargo from reaching the sea. I added, flatly: "I don't know whether or not your Government would give a reward for information, but in any case I'd see that my family gave you money."

"You!" The blazing contempt in her voice made it an expletive in its own right. "I do not listen to you! All this talk of police and governments and laws. You are only a stupid woman, too stupid to get a man! Who are you?" And she spat on the floor at my feet.

It was all it needed. My head cleared miraculously, as the adrenalin came coursing out of the booster pumps. I laughed. "As a matter of fact I have got a man, I've had one for twenty-two years, and he's the grandson of your Lady's eldest brother, and therefore probably at the moment owner or part owner of this palace and its contents. So for a start, my nasty little Arab maiden—because in spite of your efforts I wouldn't back John Lethman ever to have got past first base—you can hand over my great-aunt's ring. And I may warn you that your precious Dr. Grafton will make you give it up even if I can't. Hand it over, poppet."

It was obvious that Grafton had already spoken to her. Her face darkened, and for a moment I saw her hand clench and hide itself in a fold of her silk robe. Then with a gesture she drew the ring off.

"Take it. Only because I wish. It is nothing. Take it, daughter of a bitch."

And she threw it at me with the gesture of an empress flinging a groat to a beggar. It landed with an accuracy she could never voluntarily have achieved in a dozen years, slap in the bowl of soup.

"Well," I said cheerfully, "that should sterilize it. Or should it? I've never seen the kitchens here, but when I was a guest I had to take them on trust. Now I'm only a prisoner I don't need to eat what I don't fancy, do I?"

I leaned over and picked up the fork from the tray, fished Great-Aunt Harriet's ruby out of the soup, dunked it in the glass of water, and dried it on the napkin provided. Then I noticed the silence. I looked up.

When she spoke I knew something had put her out considerably. "You do not wish the meal?"

"Oh, I'm quite glad of something, and it's a wise jailbird that lets nothing slip. I'll eat the bread and cheese. Thanks for the ring." And I slipped it onto my finger.

"Not the soup? The ring was clean . . . it . . ."

"I'm sure it was. I wouldn't have been rude about it if you, my proud beauty, had not just called me the daughter of a bitch. Not that I mind, I like dogs, but Mummy might be a bit narked. No, Halide, not the soup."

She had obviously not followed anything except the first and last statements. "Then let me bring you more—please."

I looked at her in surprise, then the surprise slid into a stare. To begin with it had only seemed odd that she had offered to oblige me at all, but the last request had carried an urgent, almost pleading note.

"Of course I will bring more. It is no trouble. Any minute now they will come to start loading the boxes and you will be taken out of here and put with the man, so you must eat while you can. Please allow me!" There was an abject quality in the eagerness, the automatic bending of the shoulders and thrusting of the chin and opening of hands, palms up, that suddenly spoke more clearly than any documentary could have done, of generations of slavery and the whip.

"It's good of you, but there's not the slightest need." My own reaction, I noticed with sour self-contempt, was also predictable. While she was insolent I was angry and unpleasant; as soon as she crept into her place, I could afford a cold civility. I made an effort. "I don't want the soup, thank you. The bread and cheese will do very well."

"I will take it back, then, just in case—"

"No, no, don't bother. But I'd be glad if you'd go straight to Dr. Grafton—"

I never finished the sentence. We had both reached forward together, she to lift the bowl from the tray, and I to stop her, and for a moment, inches apart, our eyes met.

Then I shot out a hand and took hold of her wrist before she could take the bowl. Her expression, and the tiny intake of breath, told me that—incredibly—I had been right.

"What's in it?" I demanded.

"Let me go!"

"What's in it?"

"Nothing! It is good soup, I made it myself . . ."

"I'm dead sure you did. What did you put in it? More of your *cannabis indica* to keep me quiet, or something worse?"

"I don't know what you're talking about! I put nothing in it, I tell you! Chicken and herbs and vegetables and a little *zafaran* and—"

"And a drop or two of poison to top it up?"

She drew back sharply, and I let her go and stood up. We were much of a height, but I felt inches the taller of the two and ice-cold with contemptuous rage. There is something infuriating, rather than frightening, about this kind of attack. That one is there to react to it at all means that the attempt has failed and the danger is over, and I suppose one's very relief at that failure explodes in contempt for the poisoner and blazing anger at the filthy method used.

"Well?" I said, quite softly.

"No, it was not! No! How can you be so foolish as to think so? Poison? Where would I find poison?"

The words were bitten off with a gasp as Henry Grafton said from the doorway behind her:

"What's this? Who's talking about poison?"

She swung round to face him, hands out as if to ward him off, her body still curved in that lovely windblown bow that one sees in the carved ivory ladies of Japan. Her mouth opened, and her tongue licked across her lips, but she said nothing. His eyes went past her to me.

"I was," I said. "The sweet creature seems to have put something in my soup that she doesn't care to talk about. Would this by any chance be by your orders?"

"Don't be a fool."

I raised my eyebrows. "Dope, yes, but poison, never? You and your Hypocritic Oath . . . Perhaps she'll tell you what it is, and why? Or would you like to take it away and analyze it in your little lab next door?"

He stared at me only briefly, then his eyes went to the tray.

"Did you take any of the soup?" he asked eventually.

"No, or I've no doubt I'd be writhing on the floor."

"Then how do you know there's anything wrong with it?"

"I don't, it's an inspired guess. But she was too anxious by half for me to drink it, and she hasn't cared terribly for my welfare up till now. She threw the ring into it by mistake, and when I said I didn't want it after that she was upset. Then I knew. Don't ask me how, but I'd take a twenty to one bet on it now, and don't tell me you don't think the same. Look at her. And as for where she got it, hasn't she got a whole roomful at her disposal, all that stuff of Great-Aunt Harriet's? Ask her," I nodded at the silent girl, "ask little Miss Borgia here. Perhaps she'll admit it to you."

Long before I had finished speaking his attention had switched back to Halide, the black eyes bright and deadly as an oil-slick. I had a moment's sharp relief that under this night's various pressures he should take time to handle this so seriously; it must only mean that he intended no real harm to Charles or myself. But the expression in his eyes as he looked at her, and the girl's obvious terror, surprised me. Her hands were tightly clasped at the base of her throat, clutching the lovely silk of the robe together as if for warmth.

"Is this true?"

She shook her head, then found her voice. "It's all lies, lies. Why should I poison her? There is nothing in the soup—only the meat, and the herbs, and onions and *zafaran* . . ."

"Then," said Henry Grafton, "you wouldn't object to drinking it yourself?"

And before I knew what he was about, he had whipped the bowl up from the tray, and was advancing on the girl with it held up to the level of her mouth.

I think I gave a gasp, and then said weakly: "Oh, no!" It was somehow too much, so absurdly the stock situation from a thousand and one Arabian Nights, an Eastern melodrama come ludicrously to life. "For God's sake," I said, "why not just call in the dogs and try it on them? That's the form, isn't it? For pity's sake call the scene off, I withdraw the complaint!"

Then I stopped as I realized, not amused anymore, that the melodrama was taking Dr. Grafton away from the door of the room as the girl backed in front of him . . . and there was a gun on the wall above the Prince's bed, if I could grab it before they got me . . .

Neither of them took the slightest notice of me. She had retreated until she was backed right up against a stack of crates beyond the bed, and her hands came up in front of her to push the bowl away. He drew back quickly to prevent its being spilled.

"Well, why don't you? Am I to believe this nonsense is true?"

"No, no, of course it isn't true! She only says this because she hates me! I will swear it if you like on my father's head! Where would I get poison?"

"Considering my great-aunt's room is like remnant day at the chemist's," I said drily, "I'd have thought one could lay hands on almost anything."

He didn't look round when I spoke; all his attention was fixed on the girl, who stared back at him like a mesmerized rabbit which might at any minute burrow its way backward through the stacked boxes. I edged a bit nearer the doorway.

"Why don't you call her bluff?" I asked.

I didn't see a movement, but she must have sensed that he was planning to do just that, for she gave in suddenly. "All right, if you won't believe me! I did put something in it, and I did want her to drink it, but it is not poison, it is only a purge, to give her pains and make her sick. She's a bitch and the daughter of a bitch, and you have made me give back the ring when she is rich already, and of course I do not try to kill her, but I hate her and I put the oil in the soup only to make her suffer a little . . . just a little . . ." Her voice faltered and seemed to strangle itself for a moment, defeated somehow by the heavy musty silence of the dungeon.

"Charming, my God, charming!" I was within two jumps of the door now. "Then you lock me in with Charles and leave me to it?"

Neither of them took the slightest notice of me. She finished in a rush: "And if I must drink it I will, to prove to you that it is true . . . but tonight you will need me to help you, you and John, so we will give it to a dog, or to Jassim, or to someone who does not matter, so that you will see . . ."

Grafton's face was suffused, and that ugly vein was beating again. Neither of them was concerned with me anymore; whatever was between them shut me out completely, and I stood rooted there watching, afraid now to move and direct that raging concentration back to myself.

"Where did you get it?" He spoke quite evenly.

"I forget. From her room, perhaps . . . I've had it a long time . . . all those bottles . . ."

"There were no purges in her room, I know that. Don't give me that, you never got it from there. I saw to it that there was nothing harmful lying about, and after she'd had her sick turns I checked to see if she'd been dosing herself. Come on, what was it? Did you get it from the village, or was it some filthy brew you made yourself?"

"No . . . I tell you it was nothing. It was something John had. I took it from his room."

"From John? Why should he have that kind of thing? You said 'oil.' Do you mean castor oil?"

"No, no, no, I tell you I don't know what it was! It was a black bottle. Why don't you ask John? He will tell you it was harmless! He said it tasted strong, so I used to put in extra herbs, and pepper—"

"When did you use it first? The time I was away near Chiba?"

"Yes, yes, but why do you look like that? It was nothing, a drop or two, and then a little sickness—the pain was not bad—and afterward she was always so quiet and good . . ."

I wouldn't have moved now for worlds, open door or not. The bowl had begun to shake in his hands, and his voice had that stretched, even thinness of a wire about to snap, but the girl didn't seem to recognize the signals. She had ceased to look alarmed, and had dropped her hands to twist them in the skirt of her dress, glowering back at him, sullen and defiant. I don't know just at what point through the swift, unemphatic exchange I had realized that they were no longer talking about me, but about Great-Aunt Harriet.

"Quiet and good!" He repeated the words with no expression at all. "I see. My God, I wondered. Now I begin to see . . . Did this happen whenever I went away?"

"Not always. Sometimes when she'd been too difficult. Oh, why the fuss, it did her no harm! You know how well I nursed her! You know how I had worked and cared for her all those months, and how she would ring her bell night and day, and never must we be tired, always ready to run for this thing and that thing, and cook special food . . . But I wouldn't have harmed her, you know that! Only one or two drops I gave her, and then I would nurse her through it, and afterward there would be peace for a few days."

"And she would be grateful. Yes, of course. Clever girl, Halide. Is that when she gave you the ring? Yes? What else did she give you?"

"Many things! And she meant me to have them! She said so! She gave me these things herself because I had cared for her! You shall not take them from me . . . indeed you dare not, because I gave them to my father and brother who will keep them! And then when I become an English lady—"

He spoke between his teeth. "You killed the old woman. Do you not realize that even now, you stupid bitch?"

"I did not!" Her voice was shrill with rage. "How can you say this? It was only medicine, I tell you, and I took it from the chest that John keeps in his room—you know the old medicine box that the Lady's husband took on his expeditions—"

"That prehistoric collection? God knows what was in it! Do you mean to tell me John knew about this?"

"No, I tell you I took it! But I asked him what it was before I used it. I would not have used it unless I knew it was safe! It was not poison! He said it was a purge, made from the seed of some plant . . . yes, a spurge plant—I remember that because the words were the same, and—"

He had been sniffing at the bowl he held. Now he gave a great gasp as though he needed air. "So that's it! Spurge plant, my God! It's croton oil, and I doubt if even old Boyd used the stuff in the last fifty years except for the camels! 'One or two drops,' indeed! Twenty drops and you'd kill a healthy horse! And you gave that stuff to an old woman, a sick woman—"

"It did her no harm! You know it did her no harm! Three times I gave it to her, and she got better—"

"And the last time," said Henry Grafton very softly, with the wire in his voice beginning to shake, "she'd had a coronary just three weeks before. And so she died . . . and if you'd kept your stupid fingers out of the pie she'd be alive today and we wouldn't have these damned people round our necks, and the whole job done as smoothly as kiss your hand and away with one fortune and time to collect another at harvest. But you—you—"

And he dashed the soup, bowl and all, in her face in an excess of blinding rage.

The stuff was no longer hot, but it was greasy and it took her full across the eyes. And the bowl smashed. It must have been of fine china, because it didn't smash against the boxes behind her, but right across her cheekbone. There was a still second before she screamed, and the scream choked because some of the slimy stuff went into her mouth and throat and gagged her, then she doubled up, retching and choking, and the blood came welling in a slabby stream on her cheek and mixed with the greensick slime of the soup.

Grafton swung his arm as if to strike her. I gave a cry of protest and jumped forward and grabbed it.

"That'll do! For pity's sake!"

He wrenched away to disengage himelf. The movement was violent, and— thrust by his shoulder—I went reeling back, sent the tray flying, and almost fell against the door. His face was that curious dark red, and his breath snorted in his throat. I don't know if he would have hit her again, but there was a flash in her hand, and she came away from the wall of crates like a leaping cat, claws and knife, and went for his face.

He was quick on his feet as many shortish men are, and I think it was purely reflex, too quick even for his thought, which made him leap back clear of those raking claws and the knife she had whipped from somewhere, Damascus-bright. She was on him. The knife flashed. He had no weapon—who would need it against me?—and he snatched up from the clutter the first thing that came to hand. I think even then what he snatched for was the whip that lay on the pile of camel harness, but his hand missed it by centimeters, and what he lifted and lashed down with was not the flexible whip, but the heavy, cruel goad.

It caught the girl full across the temple. She seemed to slacken in the middle, as if a spring had broken. She still lurched forward, but the claws slid loose and harmless down the man's neck, and the stabbing knife missed his throat by inches as her body pitched against him and slithered, joint by joint, into a slack and thudding collapse at his feet. The knife fell just before the final drop of the body, with a little tinkling sound on the floor. Then the upper part of her body slumped, and the head hit the stone with a small, and quite final little crack.

In the silence, I heard the lamp fluttering again like a caught moth.

My knees felt as if they didn't belong. I was back in the smoke, helpless, floating. I remember that I had to push myself away from the door, to go to Halide.

I had forgotten he was a doctor. Before I had done more than decide I must move, he was down beside her on one knee.

I took a step. I croaked somehow: "Is she dead?"

What he was doing took no more than a moment, then he got to his feet. He didn't speak. He didn't need to. I'd never seen a dead body before, only people shamming dead on stage or screen, and I can tell you, no one could ever mistake death for anything but death, not once they'd seen it.

Whatever I was trying to say, choking on it through bile in my throat, never got said. Henry Grafton turned round on me now. He still had the goad in his hand.

Of course he had never meant to kill her. But she was dead, and I had seen it. And something else, I believe, got through to me—how, I don't know, except that just at that moment in the horrible little room reeking with soup and the oil lamp and something else that may have been death, all nerves were stripped raw and felt as if they were exposed like white roots all over the skin. He had never killed before, and maybe he didn't quite believe it even yet, or believe how simple it had been. Whatever soothing lies he had been telling himself about Charles and me, now he knew. Now the decision had made itself. He had taken the first step on a very easy slide . . . And behind those dilated black eyes, for all I knew, he could be smoked as high as an Assassin with the damned drug himself.

I shall never be sure if what I did then was the stupidest thing I could have done. Perhaps I should have stayed where I was and spoken calmly, till the dark-red look went from his face and the suffused eyes cleared.

But all I could see was that the doorway was clear, and that I was nearer to it than he was.

I didn't stop to argue. I turned and ran.

17

The Stars are setting and the Caravan
Starts for the Dawn of Nothing—Oh, make haste!

—E. FITZGERALD: *The Rubáiyát of
Omar Khayyám*

THE PASSAGE was well enough lighted; someone had put oil lamps in one or two of the old torch-brackets—probably in preparation for the night's work—and these showed me the stairway to the Prince's Divan.

It was the only way to go. There was no point in making for the Seraglio, since I couldn't hope to get down from the window alone; the postern was locked, and Jassim was guarding the main door. Besides, there was Charles. My only hope was the Prince's Divan and the rifle.

I was about a third of the way up the stairs when the arras at the top was swept aside and John Lethman came through like a pea from a catapult, shouting, "Grafton! Grafton!" and hurtled downstairs three at a time. Before I could stop myself, I had run straight into him.

He gave a grunt of surprise and held me fast. What must have surprised him even more was that I made no attempt to get away. I suppose if I had been in a fit condition to think I might have expected Halide's murder to put him on my side against Grafton, but I wasn't thinking, and it was only instinct that made me see him almost as a rescuer, as corruptible rather than yet corrupt, a man who could surely not stand aside and watch me killed.

"How did you get out?" he snapped. Then—"What's happened?"

I couldn't speak, but as I clung to him, pointing back at the storeroom door, Henry Grafton erupted into the corridor below us with the goad in his hand.

At the sight of us he stopped dead, and the goad slowly sank until its iron tip rested on the floor. There was a little pause, during which nobody said anything, then Lethman, gripping me by the arm, dragged me after him down the staircase and back toward the door.

I didn't look. I think I shut my eyes. Lethman didn't go in, he stopped just short of the doorway.

Henry Grafton cleared his throat and spoke. "It was an accident. She went for me." Then as no one said anything, suddenly savage, to me: "Tell him it was an accident, you little fool! Tell him what happened!"

I didn't look at either of them. "Oh, yes, it was an accident. He never meant to kill her, I'm sure of that. He threw the soup at her in a temper and she went for him and he grabbed for something—the whip, I think—and got hold of that thing. I don't suppose he noticed in the mad rush that it was made of iron." I added, in a tight voice that was unfamiliar even to me: "And as a matter of fact I can't even pretend I'm sorry. I gather from what they were saying that she killed Great-Aunt Harriet."

That brought him up sharply. He still kept his grip on my wrist, but he seemed to have forgotten about me. He swung on Grafton.

"She what? Halide killed the old lady? What's this?"

"It's true." Grafton was staring down at the thing in his hand as if he'd never seen it before. "She'd apparently been treating her off and on to doses of croton oil."

"Doses of—Good grief, so *that* was it? I remember her asking about the stuff." His hand went to his head. He looked sick and shaken. "But why? I don't get it. That stuff—good God—what could she hope to gain?"

"A dowry," said Grafton drily, "Oh, she didn't mean to kill her, that was ignorance. She was just clever enough to choose the times when I was away. I admit it never entered my head—it was one of those simple, stupid schemes one might expect from that mentality—she wanted the old lady periodically ill and helpless so that she could nurse her through it with the sort of devotion that sticks out a mile and gets its due reward. Which it did."

He was watching the younger man as he spoke. Lethman said nothing. You can always tell when someone is thinking back, remembering. He was biting his lip, his face still shocked and sick-looking. Behind the slack lines and pin-pupiled eyes of the addict I thought I could see the ghost of the pleasant-faced boy who had been pulled into Henry Grafton's orbit. And I thought I saw, too, the ghost—hastily suppressed with shame—of a boy relieved of a burden.

Grafton saw it too. "Oh, yes, there were rewards. You know how lavish the Lady could be at times. I gather that most of her pickings are being kept for her by her family in the village. As I said, a dowry."

"For heaven's sake," I broke in, "cover her face and let's get out of here before I'm sick."

Grafton gave me a look, and then obeyed me, stooping over the thing on the floor to pull a greasy, merciful fold of the pretty silk across. John Lethman turned abruptly away, dragging me with him toward the stairs. I went, only too willingly. As we reached the top and he pulled the arras back, Grafton came out of the storeroom below, shutting the door behind him, then as an afterthought pushed it open again, and flung the goad back inside. I heard it go clattering down on the floor, then the door slammed again, finally, on the dreadful little room.

The Prince's Divan was brilliantly lit tonight. The usual lamp stood on the covered fountain which served as a table in the middle of the lower room, other lamps burned in niches by the door, and from a bracket high in the wall a double cresset gave a smoky red light. As Grafton followed us through and the arras swung shut behind him, the cresset blew and guttered in the draft, sending grotesque shadows reeling up the walls.

"For Christ's sake hang on to the girl." His voice was harsh but controlled. It seemed he was back in charge. "If you let her go we'll both be in the can. God knows I'm sorry about what happened, John—it's perfectly true that Halide killed the old woman and landed us both in this, but do you seriously imagine I'd have hit her if she hadn't gone for me with a knife? The way I see it, we'd better get out of the jam we're in before we start calling the odds over this. So snap out of it, and let's get back on the job. One thing, I suppose you know what'll happen if Nasirulla gets wind of it? We'll have to shift the body now, and think up some way of stalling him off if he asks where she is. Christ!—" He sounded suddenly, viciously irritable—"Stop gawping at me! What's done's done, and you can't pretend you won't be damned grateful to me when you're free as air and with money to burn and no dusky charmer wound round your neck like a god-damned snake! And for a start, you can get that girl under lock and key—and hurry up, she looks as if she's going to pass out on us. Shove her in the lock-up with the boy, there isn't long to go."

It was quite true that I wasn't feeling too good. Still held by John Lethman, I had got as far as the red lacquer chair, but as soon as he let go of my arm I felt my knees give way, and collapsed into it, fighting back the feeling of icy nausea that splashed over me again and again, alternating with drenching heat. Through the waves of goose-pimpling sickness I was aware of a sharp and urgent exchange of words going on over my head. I didn't catch what John Lethman said, but Grafton's reaction was violent.

"*What?* What the devil do you mean?"

"I was coming to tell you. The boy's out."

"That's not possible!"

"It's true. He's out. Gone. No sign."

I surfaced for a moment. "Bully for Charles," I said.

"And," said John Lethman, "he'll be back here in an hour or two with every damned flic he can drum up."

"Back here?" Grafton took him up like lightning. "You mean *out*—he's right outside?"

"He must be. I found Jassim knocked out, and the main gate open. Of course he didn't know we had the girl here, or—"

"You bloody fool! And you've been wasting time!" This, it seemed, was how Halide's death could now be classed. "How long has he been gone?"

"Not long, I guess. He'd knocked over his water jug, and the footprints he'd left from treading in it were still wet when I came to find you."

"Get the dogs out," snapped Grafton. "Go on, get them now. He'll be making for the village, he won't have got far. They'll catch him easily enough, and you can tell Nasirulla it doesn't matter how they pull him down as long as they do it."

"They probably won't touch him. Don't you remember I told you—?"

"What the hell does that matter? Can't you see, the point is, kill two birds with one stone—get Nasirulla away from the place with the hounds, while we clear up down below. The dogs'll find the boy all right, and if Nasirulla takes a gun . . . He's to be stopped, do you hear me? I suppose Jassim's back on his feet again? Go on, man, hurry, leave this silly bitch, I'll deal with her. And get back here as fast as you can and help me with the job below stairs."

I made a grab at John Lethman's sleeve as he turned to go.

"Don't leave me with that little swine, for goodness' sake! Can't you see he's gone overboard? Halide, and now Charles . . . and you—can't you see you haven't a chance?" I gripped his arm, shaking it. It was like pleading with a zombie. "Look, I know you've only been doing as he made you! You'd nothing to do with Halide's death! If you let Charles go, and get me out of here, I swear I'll stand up for you and tell them—"

"Get," said Grafton, and John Lethman pulled himself free and went.

Grafton jerked his head at me. "Come on. Get going."

"Where to?"

"Back to your cage, my girl."

I gripped the arms of my chair until the lacquer scored my palms. "Not back in there with her?"

"By no means, we'll be busy there, didn't you hear? You can have the official dungeon this time, but don't think you'll get out of it, even if your cousin did."

I began to get slowly to my feet, helping myself by the chair arms. The swimming nausea had cleared and I was steady enough, but I still can't have looked much to reckon with, for he had obviously dismissed me from a mind leaping ahead to the next—and major—move.

"Come on, don't waste my time. Get moving."

I got moving. I shoved myself suddenly upright, and the heavy chair away from me with a jerk that sent it skating across the marble tiles between Grafton and myself. I ran the other way, toward the bed. Up the steps, across the dais, then I jumped onto the foot of the bed itself and yanked the rifle down from the wall.

I swung round, unsteady on the soft bed, bracing my shoulders against the wall, and had the thing leveled at his midriff before he had done more than take three strides after me.

I had no idea if the gun were loaded. I thought it probably wasn't, but Henry Grafton might not be sure. And you have to be very sure indeed to risk outfacing a gun. You only call a gun's bluff once.

He checked, as I had known he would. "Put the damned thing down, it isn't loaded."

"Are you sure?"

"Quite sure."

Outside, suddenly, the hounds bayed wildly from the court where Nasirulla was presumably loosing them in the fond hope that they would pull Charles down. I laughed in Henry Grafton's face.

"Then come and get me," I invited.

He didn't move. I laughed again, and keeping the rifle at the ready, put out a hand to the wall to steady myself as I stepped down from the bed.

And suddenly there it was again, the wave of heat, the choking nausea, the sweat and the stopped breathing. I groped for a fold of the arras and hung on, dimly aware of the rifle sinking forgotten to the trail, of Grafton hesitating momentarily before taking a step toward me, of the baying of the dogs wild and loud, of someone shouting.

I pulled myself upright. But it was too late. He was on me. He snatched the rifle from my slack hands, checked the empty magazine, kicked it under the bed, and with a vicious swing of the hand to the side of my head sent me sprawling across the bed just as the gray cat, spitting furiously, erupted from the blankets like a rocket on blastoff, and cleared me with a centimeter to spare and every hair on its body brushing my face.

I screamed. Grafton shouted something and I think he made a grab for me, but I had gone beyond fear or even thought of him. Caught up in my own private nightmare, fighting not the cat but my own terror, I struck out at him with feet and hands as I jack-knifed away toward the far side of the bed.

From the garden outside came a sudden volley of noise, a hoarse shout, a scrabble of racing paws, then the inhuman yell of a terrified cat, drowned in the wild exciting tumult of hounds sighting a kill. The cat shot back into the room, a hissing gray streak, and after it the salukis, full cry, with a broken leash trailing from one collar, and Nasirulla in loud pursuit.

The cat leaped for the bed hangings. The hounds saw it, and hurled themselves after it. The heavy chair went flying, crashed into the table, and toppled, smashing the lamp in a sprayed arc of oil. The flame ran along it like ball-lightning. Grafton yelled something, dragged a blanket from the bed, jumped clear down the dais steps, dodging the dogs, slipped in the burning oil and went down, striking his head hard on the stone edge of the table. Over my head the cat leaped like a silver bird for the high windowsill, and was gone.

It all seemed to happen in seconds. The flames ran, clawed out, rippled, caught the bed hangings, and went licking up them in great lapping gulps of flame. I rolled off the bed, fighting clear of the curtains, and hurled myself into the quiet dimness of the corridor beyond. The last thing I saw as the arras swung back behind me was the Arab bending to drag Grafton clear toward the other door.

The hounds came with me. Sofi, whining with fear, scrambled through the arras and went tumbling anyhow down the steps. The dog was at the foot of the staircase already. I slammed the door and raced down after them.

"Here!" I called breathlessly. "This way! Here!" And we ran on, down the curved corridor, past the room where poor Halide lay, through the still air already sharp with smoke—and there was the Prince's Door.

My hands were shaking, and twice the dogs, leaping in eager fear, shoved me aside before I could lift the heavy latch. Then I had it open, and we were through. It swung easily, massive and silent. It might make a lock on that dead air, and check the fire. I slammed it shut and drove the latch home. Then turned, to find that there was fire outside as well . . .

Or so I thought, for one heart-stopping moment, as I saw the outer passage lit and flickering before me. Then I saw why. This, too, had been illuminated for the night's work. The ancient brackets to either side of the Prince's Door held makeshift torches which flared sullenly, red and smoking. It must have been this smoke I had smelled in the corridor as I ran.

I hung there, irresolute, gasping, while the hounds whined and shivered and stayed close. The caravan was due soon, and presumably by the postern. But I had heard Halide say that the postern was locked, and the key out of it. It would have to be the main gate, and chance it.

I ran up the passage to my right, and had stumbled perhaps some twenty yards on the rough and ill-lit cobbles when Sofi whined again and I heard, clearly ahead of me, a turmoil of shouts from the main court. I stopped dead. Of course they would all be there: Grafton, Lethman, Nasirulla, Jassim—go that way, and I would run into them all. What was more, if they had any hopes of salvaging their precious cargo, this was the way they would come at any moment now. And even with the whole rotten place going up like tinder round them I wouldn't have betted a pin on any of them doing other than throw me straight back into the flames.

I ran back to the door for the Seraglio stairs.

It opened, and we tumbled through. Darkness dropped over us like a velvet drape, stifling, silent, terrifying. I shut the door behind me and took two hesitating steps forward, then stumbled over the bottom stair and fell, hurting my shin. One of the dogs whimpered, pressing close. Under the silky coat the hot skin shivered. On my other side a narrow head nudged me, and I felt for the beast's collar and got to my feet. With one hand on the collar, and the other groping for the handrail on the outer wall of the staircase, I began to fumble my way up the spiral.

"Show me the way, mates," I whispered.

The dogs thrust upward so eagerly that I realized they could see even here. I wondered if they smelled water. I could almost smell it myself. The thought of that great sheet of water lying above our heads was no longer terrifying; it was the bright, cool promise of safety. With the big hound pulling me, and my left hand groping past the invisible minarets, the cypresses, the singing birds, I stumbled and panted up the spiral stair. Then the bitch, leaping ahead, pushed open the painted doorway, and the three of us ran out into the night air, and the light.

But the night air smelled of smoke, and the light was red and gold and leaping. I ran with the dogs down the pavilion steps, and paused at the edge of the water.

Through all the buildings to the west of the lake, it seemed, ran the fire. The old rotten wood, crumbling dry, had caught like tinder in the night breeze, and as I stood there, afraid and dismayed, a stream of sparks like a comet's tail blew clear across the lake and scattered along the arcade to the east, near Charles's window, and began to burn.

18

But not against the flame shall they shade or help you.

—THE KORAN: *Sura* LXXVII

ONE THING the fire did; the place was as bright as day. There was still a chance I could get into the junk room under the eastern arcade, find the rope, and sling it down from the window before the flames took hold. As for the dogs—as far as I could afford to think about them at all—I certainly couldn't lower them from the window, rope or no rope, but they were in the safest place in the palace. They had only to take to the water.

I ran onto the bridge, the dogs pressing close to me—so close indeed that when we got to the broken span Sofi jumped first, and Star, pushing forward to follow, shoved against my legs and threw me off balance. I slipped, tried to recover, cried out as I trod on some stone not quite secure, and went into the water.

I suppose it was about four feet deep. I went right in, down under the lilies and the shiny lily pads and the floating weeds, before I struggled to the surface and stood again, ankle deep in mud and breast deep in water, with my hair streaming like weed across my face, and the hounds gazing at me, curious and excited, from the bridge.

Then Sofi, with a little yelp of excitement, plunged in beside me. Star, inevitably, followed. They swam round and round, with little whining barks, splashing and clawing, avid to be near me, and completely ignoring my distracted croaks of command as I tried to push them away among the creaking irises, and began myself to flap and struggle out through the clotted lily leaves.

But not to the arcade. The few minutes I had lost through my accident had cost me access to the junk room. Flakes of blazing stuff—straw or rags—had blown across the water and ignited the roof at several more points. Most of it was wooden shingles bleached dry for generations, and covered with creepers already brittle with coming summer heat. The honeysuckle went up like straw, and all along the arcade burning fragments fell or were blown like fire-arrows to start fresh buds of flame. A veil of smoke wavered across the junk-room door.

Even the garden was burning now. Here and there patches of the drier scrub smoldered, and at the tip of one young cypress, where some flying tinder had lodged, a brush of flame hovered like St. Elmo's fire. The smoke was aromatic with blazing herbs.

The northern arcade was still clear, but without the rope I knew the window was useless to me. Useless, too, the gate out into the buildings. There was only one thing for me to do, what the dogs had already made me do, take to the water. But I didn't think I needed to do it yet. The island was safe enough for the time being, most of its plants too moist with the abundant water to catch fire easily. And I, thanks to the dogs, was in the same case. I reached the built-up shore and clambered out. The hounds, dripping, scrambled after me. They shook themselves over me straight away, of course, and the water flew from them like showers of liquid fire, so fierce now was the light.

I pushed my way up through the tangle of cool green bushes, and reached the pavilion steps. Smoke swirled in a sudden eddy, making me cough, but then it fanned away and the air was clear. I ran up the last steps into the comparative shelter of the pavilion, then my legs gave way at last, and I sat down on the top step, with the dogs crouched close to me for comfort, and we had time to be afraid.

The hounds were really scared now, and huddled close, one on either side of me, shivering. I had an arm round each of them. Now and again some stream of sparks blew across the lake. The sky all around was ringed with fire, vivid tongues and spires and meteors of fire, so that the stars which swarmed thick and glittering overhead seemed cold and infinitely distant. Through the bright heart of the flames shot flashing pulses of blue and purple and green, and the noise they made was like the galloping of wild horses with the wind in their manes. There was very little smoke, and what there was streamed mercifully away in the light winds that fanned the blaze. The lake was a sheet of melted copper, so bright that it hurt the eye, with red and gold and silver flying through the stiff black spears of the irises, till the very water seemed alive, rippling and beating with flame like the sky.

I rubbed my stinging eyes to dispel the illusion. But when I looked again I saw that it was true. The water was moving, and not with the wind. This garden was a pocket of calm overleapt by the winds, but in it the water was moving, alive with spearhead ripples as the creatures of the garden, driven by the fire, came arrowing toward the island.

The peacocks came first. The two hens flew, clumsily and in panic, from stone to stone of the broken bridge, but the cock, weighted by the magnificence of his springtime tail, came noisily yelling across the open lake, half paddling, half flying, his great useless wings flailing the golden water, his streaming train bedraggled with mud and damp and laying a wake like a VC. 10; then the three big birds, oblivious of me and the hounds, raced with hunched and staring feathers up the rocky shore, and clucked to an uneasy roost near us on the marble steps.

The little rock partridges flew more easily. There were seven of them round my feet, fluffy with fear, their bright eyes winking like rubies as they stared at the flames that ringed the garden. In the flashing scarlet light their feathers shone like chased metal. One of them quivered warm against my ankle.

I didn't even see the squirrels till one slid up the steps beside me and sat bolt upright, chittering and bedraggled, within six inches of Star. Then I realized that the water was full of heads, little black arrow tips heading for the island. I suppose there were voles and shrews and housemice; I saw shadows galore, darting and squeaking under the evergreens. Rats I certainly saw, big beasts of every shade of gray and black and brown, who eyed us askance with bright intelligent eyes as they shimmied ashore and then streaked for the safety of the shadows. Lizards darted and weaved up the stones like something in an alcoholic's dream, and I saw two snakes within a handspan of my shoes; they lowered their beautiful deadly heads and went past like smoke, and the dogs never moved, and nor did I. I hadn't room for fear of them, or they of me; the ony thing that mattered was the fire. All of us, rats, birds, snakes, dogs and girl, had a right to that island until the danger was past. The hounds never even moved when one rat went clean across my feet and brushed its way through the silk of Sofi's tail.

A dove fell, out of the sky. The birds of the air were safe enough, they had been blown away on the first hot draft of air. But one gray dove fell, a wing damaged or slightly singed, almost into my hands. It came down like a badly made paper dart, sidelong and drifting, to flutter between my feet, and I leaned forward between the hounds and lifted it, then sat holding it gently. Below my feet I thought that even the water nearest the island boiled and bulged with fish, as the carp crowded away from the bright edges of the lake toward the quiet center. I could see them just under the surface, bright darts and gleams of gilt and silver and glowing firecoal red.

And above the noise of the galloping flames was the noise of the animals. The dogs whined, the peacocks vented their harsh, scared cry, the partridges crooned in panic, the rats and squirrels chittered and squealed, and I said at distressingly frequent intervals, as I hugged Sofi and Star close to me: "Oh, Charles . . . Oh, Charles . . . Oh, for heaven's sake, *Charles* . . ."

We hardly even noticed the heavy splash from the northeast corner of the lake, or saw the violent run and ripple of the melted-gold wake as the black head speared straight for the island. I sat and rocked and crooned comfort and held the gray dove and put my cheek down to Star's damp head and wondered how soon I would have to crawl down to the water's edge and plunge myself in again among the jostling fish.

The creature, whatever it was, had reached the island. It broke from the water, tossed a black lock of hair, and heaved itself ashore. Then it stood upright, and resolved itself into my cousin, dripping and plastered with weed, and dressed in the sodden drapes of what could only be a pair of baggy Arab cotton trousers girded up with a gilt belt, a pair of soggy Arab sandals, and nothing else at all.

He advanced to the bottom of the steps, and regarded me and the menagerie.

"Eve in the Garden of Eden. Hullo, love. But did you have to set the bloody place on fire to fetch me back?"

"Charles." It was all I could say. The dogs whined and wriggled and stayed close to me, and Sofi waved her wet tail. Half a dozen lizards whipped out of the way as he ran up the steps, and when he stopped in front of us a quail moved a couple of inches aside to get out of the drips. I looked up at him. "It wasn't me," I said rather waveringly, "the dogs did it. They knocked a lamp over. And I thought you'd gone, they said you'd escaped. They—they had me locked up . . . oh, Charles, darling . . ."

"Christy."

I don't remember his moving, but one moment he was there in front of me, with the firelight sliding in lovely slabs of rose and violet over his wet skin; the next he was down beside me on the marble floor, and Star was elbowed out of the way, and Charles's arms were round me and he was kissing me in an intense starving, furious way that somehow seemed part of the fire, as I suppose it was. They say that this is how fear and relief can take you. I know I went down to him like wax.

We were thrust apart by the wet jealous head of Star, and then Charles, with a laughing curse, rolled aside from Sofi's eager paws and tongue.

"Hey, pax, that's enough—hell's teeth, will you call your beastly dogs off? Why do you have to hole up with a zoo? Oh, dear heaven, and that peacock's filthy, and I've rolled all over its tail . . . Shove over, mate, will you? I've only known the girl twenty-two years, you might give me a chance. When did I last kiss you, Christabel?"

"You'd be about ten. You've changed."

"You must tell me some time . . ."

It was a lizard, dropping from the dome, that shook us apart this time. He swore, swiped at it as it shot away unhurt, and sat up.

"Christy, I love you, and I could spend the rest of my life making love to you and probably will, but if we're going, the sooner we go the better, *nicht war?*"

"What? What did you say?"

"I said we ought to go."

"Yes. I love you, too. Did I say?"

"You made it plain," he said. "Oh, Christy, love . . . *Christy!*"

"What?"

His grip on me changed, as it were, and it was no longer my lover, but my cousin Charles who took me by the shoulders and shook me. "Pull yourself together! Darling, are you doped, or what?"

"I'm all right."

"We've got to get out of here while there's still a chance!"

"Oh . . . Yes, let's." I sat up and blinked at the leaping flames. "But how? Unless you can fly? Oh, the sadist you are, you've nearly squashed my pigeon . . . No, there it goes, thank goodness, it must only have been doped with smoke." I started to get up. "Mind the squirrel, won't you?"

He laughed. "Is that what it is? Oh, and look at all the dear little rats. Come on!" He jumped up and pulled me to my feet and held me for a moment, steadying me. "Don't look so scared. We'd be safe enough here, probably, if we had to stay, but it might get a bit hot and uncomfortable before it dies down, so we'll have a bash at getting out straight away. There's only one possible way out, and we'd best be quick about it."

"What way? We'll never get down from the window now, because we'd never get at the rope, and I couldn't make it without one, I really couldn't—"

"It's all right, darling, I didn't mean the window. I meant the postern."

"But the corridor'll be going like a torch! The fire started in the Prince's room, you know."

"Even so, I doubt if it will. The shaft back there—"nodding at the painted door—"would act as a chimney if the underground passage really were going up, and it shows no sign of it. Come on let's look."

He pulled the door open cautiously. The smell of smoke was no stronger here than elsewhere, and the spiral shaft was pitch dark. Behind me, Sofi whined deep in her throat, and I made a comforting sound and touched her. "You'll come too. Don't worry."

My cousin turned his head. "Was the big door shut, the bronze one to the Prince's corridor?"

"Yes, I shut it. I came that way. I thought it would seal off the draft."

"You have your moments, don't you? And the air in there was so dead that it may only be burning slowly down from the Prince's room. We'll have to try it, anyway."

"But even if the passage is all right, we can't get to the main court—the fire's there too by now—you can see it! And it's no good trying the postern, Charles, it's locked, and the key's out, they said so. And even you surely can't pick locks in the dark?"

"Not to worry, I've got the key." He grinned at my look, fishing somewhere in the tatty off-white trousers, and producing a ring with keys that gleamed and rattled. "What do you bet it's one of these? I snitched it off poor old Jassim when I made a break for it. They were no use for getting back in with, because they bolt the gates as well here, but if one of these fits the postern we'll get out." He stopped short with his hand on the door. "Look, before we go down you'd better dip a hankie or something in the lake to hold over your mouth if the smoke's bad. Come on, it won't take a moment."

"Have you got something?"

"Half a trouser leg will do for me if I can tear the things."

We ran down the steps. "Where did you get that Carnaby Street rig anyway?" I asked.

"Oh, it's quite a saga, I'll tell you about it later. I suppose they're Jassim's, but never mind, they've had a dip now and only smell of weeds and water-mint and lovely mud. I only hope I can tear the beastly things, they're still damp and as tough as hell . . . There, that's it. What the well-dressed refugee is wearing. While you're about it I'd splash a bit more water over yourself, too . . ."

It was like kneeling by a lake of liquid fire, but the water was cool and sharply restorative. Its flickering refelction caught Charles's laughing face and brilliant eyes. I laughed back at him. It was impossible to be afraid. A light, almost wild exhilaration seemed to possess me, something sharp and positive and clear, the aftermath of a far more powerful drug than any Grafton had given me.

He jumped to his feet. "That's better, shall we go?" We ran up the steps. Most of the small animals and birds seemed to have dispersed into the cool shadows of the bushes, or among the wet growth at the water's edge. "This way, my lovely lady Christabel; give me your wet little hand. If anyone had told me when I had to share the bath with you twenty years ago . . ." A pause while we negotiated the threshold of the painted door. This was made no easier by the fact that he held me all the time, and I him . . . "Though as a matter of fact I don't think I had any doubt even then. It's just been a case of taking the air here and there for a few years till the true north pulled, and here we are. D'you feel like that?"

"Always did. When I saw you in Straight Street, the bells went off like a burglar alarm and I thought 'Well, really, here he is at last.'"

"As easy as that. Are you all right? There is a bit of smoke after all."

There was in fact a good deal. If it had been possible to feel fear anymore, I might have felt it then. As we crept down the spiral stair—slowly because we had no light and even a twisted ankle might have meant disaster—the heat grew palpable, and smoke met us, the real thing, acrid and heavy and scraping the lungs like a hot file. The dogs whined at our heels. Nothing else had followed us.

"Will they be all right—the animals?" I asked, coughing.

"Should be. There's always the water if things get desperate. Once the fire's out and the place is cool again, the birds will be able to get out into the valley, and I'm afraid I'm not just terribly concerned about the rats and mice. Hold it, here's the door. Let's see what's cooking outside."

He pulled it open cautiously. More smoke came wreathing in, and with it a red and sullen light, that flickered. He shut it quickly.

"Hell's delight! It looks as though we may have to try the window after all. We can—"

"Perhaps it's only the torches they lit for the fun and games tonight," I said quickly. "They frightened me to death when I came this way before. There's one just outside."

He inched the door open again and craned through, and I heard his grunt of relief. "You're right, praise be to Allah, that's all it is. Our luck's in. The smoke's seeping under the Prince's door like floodwater, but no fire." He pulled me through and let the door swing shut after the dogs. "Come on, darling, we'll run for it. Thank God to be able to see. Can you make it?"

"Of course. Let's just hope we don't run smack into the caravan."

"The camels are coming yoho, yoho . . . Don't worry about that, love, I tell you our luck's in—and it's going to hold."

And it did. Two minutes later, after a terrifying run along a passageway hot and choking and blind with smoke, we reached the postern, and while Charles fumbled with the lock I felt for and dragged back the heavy bolts. Then the key clicked sweetly in the oiled wards, and he pulled the door open.

The hounds brushed past us. Ahead was clear air, and the cool rustle of trees. My cousin's arm came round me and more or less scooped me up the rocky ramp and onto the clean rock under the trees. The postern door clanged to behind us, and shut us out of Dar Ibrahim.

19

        . . . A charm
For thee, my gentle-hearted Charles . . .

—S. T. COLERIDGE: *This Lime-Tree
Bower my Prison*

ONLY THEN did I notice the shouting. Not the noise from the direction of the *midan,* of which I had been vaguely conscious all the time, but a new uproar, as of an excited crowd, which came from beyond the west wall where the main gate stood.

With the hounds trotting, sober now, beside us, we picked our way through the dancing shadows of the trees and along under the rear wall. The shade it cast was inky black, the night sky above it fierce as a red dawn.

At the corner of the Seraglio, below Charles's window, we paused to reconnoiter. There seemed to be no one about. We ran across the path and into the belt of trees which overhung the Nahr el-Sal'q. High above us I could hear the cry of some wheeling birds, jackdaws, I think, flushed from the burning walls. Far down at the foot of the cliff I saw, through the stems of the trees, the red gleam of the river, this time dyed by the fire.

We paused in the darkness of the sycamore grove. There was smoke, thin and stinging, in the air, but it smelled fresh after the garden. Charles held me close.

"You're shivering. Are you cold?"

"Not a bit, not yet, there hasn't been time—and you must admit it was warm enough in there! Charles, the shouting. Ought we to go and help?"

"Not the slightest need," he said shortly. "Apart from the fact that I don't give a damn if Grafton and Lethman are both crisped to a cinder, half the village is there already by the sound of it, and with the place going up like a torch, any minute now they'll be running sight-seeing buses from Beirut. And there's the little fact that nobody came to look for you. Let them burn. But for heaven's sake, what were you doing back in there? You were supposed to be miles away and as innocent as the day. What happened?"

"They brought me back." As briefly as I could I told him my story, cutting through his shocked comments with a quick: "But you? What made you come back for me? How did you know I was there?"

"Darling, I heard you, screeching like a diesel train just before the place went up in smoke."

"You'd have screeched if you'd been me, let me tell you! But never mind that now—how did you get in? They said you'd escaped by the main gate."

"I had. They tried to dope me with their filthy pot, and I filled the place with smoke and pretended to be stoned, and poor old Jassim fell for it and I clobbered him and got out. The only trouble was that when they laid me out first and locked me up they took my clothes . . . I can't imagine why Lethman thought that would stop me from getting out if I could find a way, but it seems he did."

"He probably wanted them to wear. He went up to drive your car away, you know, and he'd want to look like you if anyone saw him."

"I suppose so. He might in that case have left me with something more than an old blanket for the duration. And I rather cared for that shirt, blast him. Well, I took Jassim's keys off him and hurtled out of my little pad in a state of nature, and grabbed a few dreary-looking garments that were lying about in the gatehouse. Don't you like them? I took what you might laughingly call the bare minimum, and ran for it. I knew if anyone followed me they'd go straight down by the ford, so I doubled round the back, this way, under the Seraglio windows. Big deal. There went our hero, stark naked, with his pants in his hand, and leaping like a grasshopper every time he trod on a thistle."

"My poor lamb. Still, you wouldn't be the first."

"What? Oh, storming the Seraglio. Sure . . . Well, I stopped under the trees to put the pants on. As a matter of fact there was a shirt and a kaffiyeh as well, if only I could find them . . . then I heard you scream. Did that so-and-so hurt you?"

"Not really. It was the cat I was screaming at, not him. Go on, I want to hear about you. How did you get back in?"

He had been casting about under the trees while we talked, and now pounced on something with a soft exclamation of satisfaction. "Here they are . . . I suppose I shall be thankful of this shirt, such as it is, before the night's out . . . Where was I? Oh, under the Seraglio windows—just about here, in fact—when I heard you scream. I tore into the pants and shoes and belted back to the main gate, but they'd barred it again. While I was trying it, all hell broke loose inside the palace, and then I smelled the smoke. I imagined that if the fire was bad they'd open the gate, but even so I didn't fancy our chances, so I ran round here again. I knew the postern had been bolted again after they caught me, so I didn't waste time trying it; I simply ran round to that window and climbed in. It's not a bad climb at all."

"Not bad!" It was the first time I had seen it from outside. I stared up at the sheer black wall. "It looks impossible!"

"Not for your big brave cousin. Anyway, I knew you were in the garden, because when I was halfway up I heard you swearing at the dogs, and as soon as I got in I saw the Noah's Ark act on the island. That's all . . . I wish Jassim's wardrobe ran to socks—there's nothing more disgusting than wet sandals. Look, why don't you put the headcloth round your shoulders? It's not too filthy, and at least it's dry. Let me tie it . . . What's this round your neck?"

"Oh, I forgot I'd put it on. It's a charm I got for you against the Evil Eye. You wanted one for your car, you said."

"For my love, I said. You'd better keep it, it seems to work . . . There. Now you're almost up to my standards."

"Flattery will get you nowhere."

"I'm not flattering, you look wonderful. There's some weed in your hair, and that frock looks as if it had been poured over you out of a dirty jug, and your eyes are as big as mill wheels and as black as outer space."

"I've been smoking their filthy pot, that's why."

"*Du vrai?*" he asked. "I thought as much. Nice?"

"Hellish. You think it's rather pleasant and you stop worrying about things, and then suddenly you find your bones have sort of rotted from inside and your brain's made from old rags and you can't even think. Oh, Charles, it was so awful, they're dealing in the stuff . . . they've been planning for months—"

"Darling, I know. Lethman told me quite a lot, probably more than he realized. Did you know he was a junkie?"

"Grafton told me. I ought to have guessed from the way he looks sometimes, but I never thought about it. Did he tell you Great-Aunt H was dead?"

"I knew that."

I stared. "You mean you knew it all along? Was that what you were making all the mystery about?"

"I'm afraid so."

"How did you find out?"

"Guessed, to begin with. Didn't you ever know that she had your cat phobia? Full blast and all the stops out?"

"Did she? I don't think I ever knew that. We never had a cat at home, of course, so when she stayed with us the subject wouldn't come up. Yes, I see now. I suppose as soon as I told you 'she' had a cat in her room you knew there must be something wrong. But Grafton would know, surely?"

"He can't have realized the cat was in the room that night. More likely he never even thought about it. They may have always had stableyard cats—must have, now that I think of the rat population of the Seraglio—but in Aunt H's day they'd never have invaded that room."

"Because of the dogs?"

"One imagines so. From the way these terrifying brutes behave with you and me—" he indicated Star and Sofi, who grinned amiably, feathering their tails— "they were probably treated as pets with the run of the place, and I know Samson always slept on her bed, and he was death on cats. If 'the doctor' was scared of the dogs and shut them up, then the inevitable would happen . . . Let's get somewhere where we can see, shall we?"

We began to pick our way along the stony cliff top through the thickest part of the grove.

"Yes, go on."

"Well, the cat business made me think there was something decidedly off-key somewhere, so I made up my mind to get in and look around and find out what, if anything, had happened to the real Aunt H. The fact that Lethman and Co. had let you wander around the place indicated that she wasn't hidden there. I thought she must be dead. Then when I got in and saw the way her things were left lying about derelict—the Koran and the Dogs of Fo—and that Samson had died and apparently not been buried properly with benefit of clergy along with the other dogs, I was sure of it. So after you'd gone off to bed that night I went snooping back, and you know what happened; I got caught and knocked out and locked up and that was that. Here we are, steady, hang on to those dogs and don't let anyone see you. My God!"

We had reached the corner now, and we could see.

The scene was like something from a colored film of epic proportions. The walls towered black and jagged against the leaping flames behind them, and one high roof, burning fiercely, was now nothing but a crumbling grid of beams. Windows pulsed with light. With every gust of the breeze great clouds of pale smoke, filled with sparks, rolled down and burst over the crowd which besieged the main gate, and the Arabs scattered, shouting and cursing and laughing with excitement, only to bunch again nearer the gate as the cloud dispersed. The gate was open; both the tall double leaves stood wide, and there was a coming and going of men through the general mêlée which indicated that some salvage work was going on—and also that Grafton would be lucky if he saw any of the salvaged goods again.

It was to be presumed that the remaining inmates of the palace were safe: the mules had certainly been got out; here and there among the crowd I saw the wicked heads tossing, the firelight bright on teeth and eyeballs, as the loot piled up on the glossy backs, and yelling Arabs fought for the head-ropes. Then I saw the chestnut horse, its coat as bright as fire, and someone who could only be John Lethman at its head.

He was dragging something—some cloth or blanket—from the beast's head. He must have had to muffle its eyes and nostrils to get it out of the burning stable. It was fighting him, jibbing and terrified, as he tried to pull it clear of the crowd.

I clutched Charles's arm. "Lethman's there! He's got the horse out. Charles, he's mounting! He'll get away!"

"Let him go. We can't do a thing. Grafton's the one—hello, look, they're stopping him."

Lethman, astride the chestnut, was fighting with knees, whip and head-rope to turn it for the corner where we stood hidden, and the track past the Seraglio wall to the open hillside and freedom. The animal, its ears laid flat back on its skull, whirled plunging in the dust, and the crowd scattered in front of it—all but one man, and he ran in under the vicious hooves and jumped for the head-rope and held it fast. He was shouting something at John Lethman. I saw the latter throw out an arm, pointing back to the blazing building, and he yelled something, his voice suddenly clear and powerful above the excited roar of the crowd. Faces turned to him like leaves when the wind blows through them. He brought his whip slashing down at the man below him, and drove the chestnut forward at full gallop toward the grove where we stood.

The Arab, struck by the beast's shoulder, was sent flying. As he rolled clean over, and came unhurt in one swift bunching movement to his feet, I saw that it was Nasirulla. Two or three other men had started, vainly, to run after John Lethman. One of them, yelling like a dervish, waved a shotgun. Nasirulla snatched it from him, whirled, leveled it, and shot.

But the chestnut was already out of range round the palace wall. It went by within a few feet of us. I never even saw John Lethman's face; he was just a crouching shadow against the bright mane, gone with a crash and sparkle of hooves and the horse's snorting terror.

Nor did I notice at what moment Star and Sofi left us. I thought I saw two shadows, swifter than the horse and far more silent, whip through the trees to vanish in its dust, and when I looked round the hounds had gone.

The shot harmlessly chipped the masonry at the corner of the palace. The men who were running our way hesitated, saw it was no use, and milled aimlessly about, shouting.

"I think that's our cue to go, my love," said Charles in my ear. "Any minute now and they'll all be coming to look for a way round the back."

"Wait . . . look!"

What happened next was almost too quick to understand, and certainly too quick to describe.

Nasirulla had hardly paused to see if his shot had gone home. While plaster still scaled from the bullet marks on the wall he turned and shoved his way back toward the gate. The others crowded back with him.

Then we saw Henry Grafton. The knock on the head had obviously not incapacitated him for long, and apparently he had been organizing the salvage operations. As the crowd by the gate eddied and momentarily thinned I saw him, just emerging past the gatehouse, his arms full.

One or two men ran forward, presumably to help him. Another tugged one of the mules nearer. Then Nasirulla yelled something, high and clear, and I saw the crowd check again, and men turning. There must have been women there; I heard one screaming something that sounded like invective. Grafton paused, staggering a little as the man who had taken half his load abandoned it suddenly and left him. Nasirulla ran forward, still yelling, and as Grafton turned to face him, flung the gun up at a range of perhaps ten yards, and fired again.

Grafton fell. As he dropped the load and went slowly, how slowly, forward over it, the Arab swung the gun butt uppermost, and ran forward, and the crowd with him.

Charles pulled me back under the trees.

"No. No. There's nothing you can do. He's dead, quite certainly. We'll get the hell out of here, Christy my girl, before that bunch of J. Arthur Rank extras really gets going."

I was shaking so much that for a moment I could only cling, and say through chattering teeth: "It was Nasirulla. I suppose—was it because of Halide?"

"Sure to be. Nasirulla may have tried to salvage the stockpile before Grafton could stop him, and found the body. Or he may simply have been asking Lethman if she'd got out, and what we just saw was Lethman passing the buck. Hold up, sweetheart, I think we can get down to the ford this way. Can you make it? Let's get the hell out, shall we? Arab mobs are not exactly my thing at the best of times, and I doubt if this lot found us here if they'd stop to listen to my elegant literary Arabic. It's all right for you, they'd only rape you, but I don't want to be castrated the day I get engaged."

"That's my big brave cousin." The little spurt of laughter I gave was more than half hysterical, but it steadied me. He took my hand, and together, by the light of the now dwindling fire, we made our way down the cliff path, across the river still running scarlet for Adonis, and gained the safe shadows of the far valley side.

20

My dog brought by Kings from Saluq.

—Ancient Arabian Poem

It was noon next day. The high hot sun poured into the village street. We sat on the low wall that bordered the graveyard, waiting for the car to take us to Beirut.

It was already difficult to remember clearly what had happened last night after we had left the scene of the fire. I had no recollection of the climb up the path to the village. I must have accomplished it on some emergency high-octane mixture of reaction, love, and residual hashish fumes. The only memory I retain to this day is some queer detached nightmare of staring eyes and neat hooves pattering like rain and the smell of goat, as (Charles tells me) we disturbed the sleeping flock, and from some invisible corner the faun tore himself from a fascinated grandstand view of the fire to offer his entirely practical help as escort up to the village.

It was he who piloted us at length through the deserted street to a house near the far end, set slightly apart behind a terrace of apple trees. No light showed, but a woman was awake and peering half fearfully out of the door at the fire which still spurted among the smoking ruins across the valley.

The boy shouted a greeting, and then a flood of what must have been explanation. I was too dazed by now and too tired to care what was said or what happened, just so that I could get out of my damp and filthy clothes, and lie down somewhere and sleep.

Charles's arms half lifted me up the steep rough steps of the terrace. He must have been as tired as I, because I seem to remember that he paused to collect himself before trying to speak to the woman in Arabic. Some minutes later, after an exchange helped out (from somewhere out of sight) by the faun, we were taken into the house; and there, behind the curtain which divided the single room, I undressed by the light of a small yellowish candle which spluttered as it burned, wrapped myself in some loose cotton garment which came from a box in the corner and which smelled clean, lay down on a bed of blankets which did not, and was almost immediately asleep. The last thing I remember was my cousin's voice, softly talking in his slow Arabic, and waiting—as I found out later—for the headman, the woman's husband, to come home from the fire.

So all the explanations had been made. Henry Grafton was dead—had died mercifully enough from the shot—and Lethman had vanished clear away into the High Lebanon. I never heard or cared overmuch what happened to him. He had gone, faceless and shadowy as the night hunter with his horse and his Gabriel Hounds, as much a victim as poor Halide of Grafton's single-minded greed. The girl's body had been recovered. Some freak of breeze and fire had left the underground corridor more or less undamaged, and with it the contents of the storeroom, which the police, arriving with the dawn light, found mysteriously depleted but still well worth impounding and investigating.

Our turn came next. We had answered the first round of questions this morning, and now the police were down on the plateau where the palace ruins stuck up on their crag like a blackened tooth, still idly smoking. From the height where we sat we could just see the gleam of the lake, calm and jewel-like, with its unburned frame of green. The plateau and the charred ruins scurried with movement, like a corpse full of maggots, where—presumably dodging the police with some ease—looters prodded about the wreckage.

At length I stirred. "I wonder if she'd have liked to know we were here?"

"From what I remember of the old dear," said Charles crisply, "she'd have been delighted to know she'd taken the whole place up with her—and laughed like a banshee to see you and me scurrying about in the lake with the rats and mice. Well, at least those hounds of hers put a nice flourish on the end of her legend. Talk about a funeral pyre. Nobody in the Lebanon will ever forget her now."

"It certainly looks as if most of the local households will have a souvenir or two," I said drily. "And your own 'Gabriel Hounds', Charles? If the storerooms didn't burn they may still be there."

"They'd hardly survive that." He nodded at the scene below us. "Anyway, I'm damned if I'll compete with those jackals and go raking among the ruins. Someday I'll find another pair, and buy them in memory of her. Ah, well . . ."

Some children, too small to be in the schoolroom or the looting party, came running by, kicking a tin, and stopped to play in the dirt under the graveyard wall. Two or three thin dogs skulked by, sniffing for scraps. A three-year-old boy threw a stone at the smallest of them, and it swerved automatically and dodged behind a rusty oil drum. A dirty white cockerel padded past, intent on a tattered brown hen.

"Love is everywhere," said Charles. "Which reminds me, Christy love—"

What it reminded him of I never knew, and have never asked him. With a gush of diesel smoke and a squeal of brakes, a tourist coach drew up not fifty yards from where we sat, and the driver turned in his seat to point across to the ruins of Dar Ibrahim before he killed the engine and dismounted to open the door. The passengers piled out, English, a party who knew one another and who talked and laughed as they trod forward in twos and threes to the edge of the valley and stared down at the smoking ruins. Cameras clicked. I could hear the driver telling someone a version of last night's story. The legend was on its way.

Charles and I sat still. The children, retreating from the strangers, backed till they stood right beside us. The small dog, its long hair filthy and tousled like a wilting chrysanthemum, crept out from behind the oil drum and watched with bright avid eyes a biscuit which one of the women was eating.

Her friend, a stout lady in a wide straw hat and sensible jersey suit, lowered her camera and looked about her.

"A pity it's not a more appetizing village." She had a splendidly carrying middle-class voice. "The mosque's quite pretty, though. I wonder if they'd mind if I took a photograph?"

"Offer them something."

"Oh, it's not worth it. You remember how horrible that man was in Baalbek, the old chap with the camel? *He* looks as if he could make himself quite unpleasant, too. Look at the way he's staring."

"Layabouts, the lot of them. It's a wonder she isn't slaving in the fields to keep the children. Look at them all, and hardly a year between them. Rather revolting. He'd be quite good looking, too, if he were clean."

It was only then, as I felt Charles quiver beside me, that I realized who they were talking about. Actually he was as clean as cold water and a gourd full of Omo could make him; but he hadn't shaved for two days, and he still only wore the grubby cotton trousers girdled with a cheap and cracking gilt belt, and a shirt which exposed more than it covered of his brown chest. My frock had dried remarkably filthy, and my bare legs were scratched and bruised and hadn't answered terribly well to the Omo. The dip in the lake had done my sandals no good at all. The red checked kaffiyeh Charles had given me last night covered what was left of my very Western hairdo, and Great-Aunt Harriet's ruby looked like Woolworth's last word on my hand.

I felt my mouth drop open, but Charles said under his breath, "Don't spoil it," and the women were already turning away.

"It's not worth it anyway," the thin one was saying, "there'll be better places. Oh, look, they're going. Well, what a stroke of luck seeing that! What did you say the place was called?"

She put the last of the biscuit into her mouth and wiped her fingers on a handkerchief. The children looked disappointed, and the small dog's ears sank, but she never noticed. The coach drove off. The children threw a few stones after it, then turned on the small dog again, till Charles clicked his fingers and said something to it in Arabic, and it came slinking to hide behind his legs.

"And they were dead right," I said indignantly. "Layabout's the word. Sitting there laughing! You might at least have *begged* or something! We could do with some cash! If the police don't give us a lift after all—"

"Then we'll walk, you trailing suitably in my wake with your children. Hullo, here's another car coming. More police, do you suppose? It can't be for us, it must be top brass, a car like that."

"It looks like a taxi. Do you suppose they'd take us on credit if we told them we were staying at the Phoenicia?"

"Not a chance. The way we look they wouldn't let us set foot in it."

"Oh, I don't know, you'd be quite good looking if you were clean."

"My God." Charles, who had been in the act of rising, sank back on the wall. At the far end of the village street the big glossy car had slid to a stop behind a gaggle of police vehicles. The driver dismounted to open the rear door, and a man got out, a tall man, unmistakably English as to tailoring, and unmistakably self-assured as to bearing.

"Father!" exclaimed Charles.

"Daddy!" I cried at the same moment.

"It's my father," said my cousin, "not yours. After I telephoned home from Damascus he must have decided—"

"It's not your father, it's mine. I telephoned from Beirut, and he must have caught last night's plane. D'you think I don't know my own father when I see him?"

"Want to bet? Hullo, Father!"

"Hullo, Daddy!"

The newcomer, for his part, had identified us even at that distance with unerring eye. He came our way, not hurrying.

"Give you twenty to one?" said Charles in my ear.

"N—no." Whichever it was, he had come. It was absurd and unadult to feel such a pleased rush of relief and pleasure.

He stopped in front of us, surveying us. If he felt the same way, he concealed it very well. "My poor children. Well, I'm very glad to see you. I won't say it's a relief to see how well you've brushed through what happened, because I have never seen you look worse, but I take it it's nothing that a bath won't put right? No?" His eyes went beyond us, to Dar Ibrahim across the valley. "So that's the place?" He watched the distant scene for perhaps a half a minute, without comment. Then he turned back to us. "All right, you can tell me the whole thing later on, but I'll get you back to Beirut now, and into those baths before I do anything else. I've squared the police, they say you can come, and they'll see you again later."

"I suppose you know what's happened?" said Charles.

"Roughly. Nobody's talking about anything else in Beirut. I gather you two young idiots got into some nasty doings up to your necks. What the devil were you about to let Christy in for that, Charles?"

"Unjust, unjust," said Charles, without heat. "The stupid girl got herself into a jam and I rescued her. Wait till her own father hears the story, I'm demanding a hero's welcome and his half of the kingdom. Incidentally, you might settle a bet for us, and tell her it's only you."

"It's a wise child." He smiled down at me, lifting an eyebrow. "Actually, I don't think I particularly want to lay claim to either of you at the moment."

My cousin uncurled from the wall. "You're going to have to lay claim to both. One of us wants your consent and the other your welcome or blessing or whatever, you can take your pick which."

"So? I'm very glad. Welcome, darling." He put an arm round me and hugged me to him, reaching the other hand to my cousin. "Congratulations, boy, we were beginning to think you'd never make it. Certainly far more than you deserve." And he kissed us both in turn.

My cousin grinned at me. "Well?"

"You win, of course. You always do. Oh, Uncle Chas, it's wonderful to see you!" I hugged him again. "Thank you for coming! Couldn't Daddy make it?"

"Afraid not. He sent me as deputy. You look a bit battered, child, are you sure you're all right?"

"Oh, yes, truly! And it's true Charles looked after me. Real hero stuff, too, wait till you hear!"

"This seems the right moment to tell you," said Charles, "that I lost the Porsche."

"So I gather. It's at the Phoenicia."

"Efficient devil you are," said his son admiringly. "How did you do that?"

"Christy's driver brought it back."

"Hamid!" I cried. "Oh, thank goodness! What happened to him?"

"The man who had stolen Charles's car was a bit too zealous with it, and ran it off the road at a bend. No, Charles, it's all right, a scratch or two, that's all; it simply went wide into the shale and bogged down. Hamid was right on its tail, and managed to lay the man out before he'd quite realized what had happened. You'll be able to thank him yourself—he's here, he drove me up."

"Is that his taxi?" I asked. "They all look alike, I didn't recognize it. Oh, that's marvelous! Do you think we could go now?"

"Why not?" He turned to look again, a longer look this time, at Dar Ibrahim. There was a pause. It was very quiet. The children had long since abandoned us to go and talk to Hamid, and now the little dog, perhaps encouraged by the silence, ventured out of hiding and crept across the space of dust to my uncle's feet. At length the latter turned. "Well . . . that's the end of a long story. When you're both rested you can tell me all about it, and Charles can come back with me when the excitement's died down a bit. For the moment, you two had certainly better try to forget it. Leave it to me." He stretched out a hand to me. "Come along, child, you look tired out . . . What in the world—?" As he turned to go, he had almost tripped over the little dog, tangled and shapeless as a dirty mop, crouching flat at his feet in the dust. Through the filthy hair an eye shone out eagerly. An apology for a tail wagged furiously. "Not yours, surely?"

"Good grief, no," said Charles. "It's one of these miserable village dogs."

"Then do you mind discouraging the poor little beast? I'm afraid we can't— what is it?" This as Charles, who had stooped obediently to pull the dog aside, let out an exclamation.

"Believe it or not, it's got a collar on—" I peered over my cousin's shoulder as he disentangled the collar from the dirty hair—"and a label. Thy life hath had some snatch of honor in it . . . Yes, there's something printed. If there's an address, then it's genuinely lost, poor little beast, and perhaps we can return it. Any dog in this country that achieves a collar must be one of the aristoc————"
He stopped dead.

"One of the what?"

Then I saw the name printed on the collar. SAMSON.

Charles looked up. "He knew our voices." His voice was so dry that I knew he felt, as I did, absurdly moved. "He recognized us, me and Father. Some snatch of honor, by heck. He must have run away after she died, or more likely that little swine threw him out to starve."

"Do you know the dog after all?" asked his father.

"Indeed, yes." Charles had swung the little creature up, and now tucked him under one arm. "And quarantine'll seem like the Phoenicia to him after this."

"Quarantine? You're surely never thinking of taking that living mophead home?"

"Mophead nothing," said my cousin. "Don't you remember Samson? This is Great-Aunt Harriet's wedding present to me, Father. My personal Gabriel Hound. We can hardly leave him here to fend for himself; he's one of the family."

Hamid, all smiles, was at the door of the car. I got into the back seat between the two men. Charles's arm held me close and my head went down on his shoulder.

The little dog and I were both fast asleep before the car had covered the first mile to Beirut.

This Rough Magic

For John Attenborough

AUTHOR'S NOTE

Among the many debts I have incurred while writing this book, two are outstanding. I should like to thank especially Mr. Micháel Halikiopoulos, Director of the Corfu Tourist Services, 5, Arseniou Street, Corfu, for all his kindness, and for the help he gave me. My other debt is to Mr. Antony Alpers, whose enchanting *Book of Dolphins* (John Murray, 1960) provided not only an inspiration, but also a great deal of information for this book.

M.S.

1

. . . a relation for a breakfast . . .

The Tempest, Act v, Scene 1

"AND IF it's a boy," said Phyllida cheerfully, "we'll call him Prospero."

I laughed. "Poor little chap, why on earth? Oh, of course . . . Has someone been telling you that Corfu was Shakespeare's magic island for *The Tempest*?"

"As a matter of fact, yes, the other day, but for goodness' sake don't ask me about it now. Whatever you may be used to, I draw the line at Shakespeare for breakfast." My sister yawned, stretched out a foot into the sunshine at the edge of the terrace, and admired the expensive beach sandal on it. "I didn't mean that, anyway, I only meant that we've already got a Miranda here, and a Spiro, which may not be short for Prospero, but sounds very like it."

"Oh? It sounds highly romantic. Who are they?"

"A local boy and girl: they're twins."

"Good heavens. Papa must be a literary gent?"

Phyllida smiled. "You could say so."

Something in her expression roused my curiosity, just as something else told me she had meant to; so I—who can be every bit as provoking as Phyllida when I try—said merely, "Well, in that case hadn't you better have a change? How about Caliban for your unborn young? It fits like a glove."

"Why?" she demanded indignantly.

" 'This blue-eyed hag was hither brought with child,' " I quoted. "Is there some more coffee?"

"Of course. Here. Oh, my goodness, it's nice to have you here, Lucy! I suppose I oughtn't to call it luck that you were free to come just now, but I'm awfully glad you could. This is heaven after Rome."

"And paradise after London. I feel different already. When I think where I was this time yesterday . . . and when I *think* about the rain . . ."

I shuddered, and drank my coffee, leaning back in my chair to gaze out across pine tops furry with gold toward the sparkling sea, and surrendering myself to the dreamlike feeling that marks the start of a holiday in a place like this when one is tired and has been transported overnight from the April chill of England to the sunlight of a magic island in the Ionian Sea.

Perhaps I should explain (for those who are not so lucky as I) that Corfu is an island off the west coast of Greece. It is long and sickle-shaped, and lies along the curve of the coast; at its nearest, in the north, it is barely two miles off the Albanian mainland, but from the town of Corfu, which is about halfway down the curve of the sickle, the coast of Greece is about seven or eight miles distant. At its northern end the island is broad and mountainous, tailing off through rich valleys and even decreasing hills into the long, flat scorpion's tail of the south from which some think that Corfu, or Kerkyra, gets its name.

My sister's house lies some twelve miles north of Corfu town, where the coast begins its curve toward the mainland, and where the foothills of Mount Pantokrator provide shelter for the rich little pocket of land which has been part of her husband's family property for a good many years.

My sister Phyllida is three years older than I, and when she was twenty she married a Roman banker, Leonardo Forli. His family had settled in Corfu during the Venetian occupation of that island, and had managed somehow to survive the various subsequent "occupations" with their small estate more or less intact, and had even, like the Vicar of Bray, contrived to prosper. It was under the British Protectorate that Leo's great-grandfather had built the pretentious and romantic Castello dei Fiori in the woods above the little bay where the estate runs down to the sea. He had planted vineyards, and orange orchards, including a small plantation (if that is the word) of the Japanese miniature oranges called *koùm koyàt* for which the Forli estate later became famous. He even cleared space in the woods for a garden, and built—beyond the southern arm of the bay and just out of sight of the Castello—a jetty and a vast boathouse, which (according to Phyllida) would almost have housed the Sixth Fleet, and had indeed housed the complicated flock of vessels in which his guests used to visit him. In his day, I gathered, the Castello had been the scene of one large and continuous house party: in summer they sailed and fished, and in the fall there were hunting parties, when thirty or so guests would invade the Greek and Albanian mainlands to harry the birds and ibexes.

But those days had vanished with the first war, and the family moved to Rome, though without selling the Castello, which remained, through the twenties and thirties, their summer home. The shifting fortunes of the Second World War almost destroyed the estate, but the Forlis emerged in postwar Rome with the family fortunes mysteriously repaired, and the then Forli Senior—Leo's father— turned his attention once more to the Corfu property. He had done something to restore the place, but after his death three years ago his son had decided that the Castello's rubbed and faded splendors were no longer for him, and had built a pair of smallish modern villas—in reality twin bungalows—on the two headlands enclosing the bay of which the Castello overlooked the center. He and Phyllida themselves used the Villa Forli, as they called the house on the northern headland; its twin, the Villa Rotha, stood to the south of the bay, above the creek where the boathouse was. The Villa Rotha had been rented by an Englishman, a Mr. Manning, who had been there since the previous autumn working on a book ("you know the kind," said my sister, "all photographs, with a thin trickle of text in large type, but they're *good*"). The three houses were connected with the road by the main drive to the Castello, and with one another by various paths through the woods and down into the bay.

This year the hot spring in Rome, with worse promised, had driven the Forlis early to Corfu. Phyllida, who was pregnant, had been feeling the heat badly, so had been persuaded to leave the two older children (whose school term was still running) with their grandmother, and Leo had brought her over a few days before I arrived, but had had to go back to his business in Rome, with the promise to fly over when he could at weekends, and to bring the children for Easter. So Phyllida, hearing that I was currently at a loose end, had written begging me to join her in Corfu and keep her company.

The invitation couldn't have been better timed. The play I was in had just folded after the merest face-saver of a run, and I was out of a job. That the job had been my first in London—my "big chance"—accounted partly for my present depression. There was nothing more on the cards: the agencies were polite, but evasive; and besides, we had had a dreadful winter and I was tired, dispirited, and seriously wondering, at twenty-five, if I had made a fool of myself in insisting against all advice on the stage as a career. But—as everyone knows who has anything to do with it—the stage is not a profession, but a virus, and I had it. So I had worked and scraped my way through the usual beginnings until last year, when I finally decided, after three years of juvenile leads in provincial rep., that it was time to try my luck in London. And luck had seemed at last to be with me. After ten months or so of television walk-ons and the odd commercial, I had landed a promising part, only to have the play fold under me like a dying camel, after a two-month run.

But at least I could count myself luckier than the other few thousand still fighting their way toward the bottom rung of the ladder: while they were sitting in the agents' stuffy offices, here was I on the terrace of the Villa Forli, with as many weeks in front of me as I cared to take in the dazzling sunshine of Corfu.

The terrace was a wide tiled platform perched at the end of the promontory where wooded cliffs fell steeply to the sea. Below the balustrade hung cloud on cloud of pines, already smelling warm and spicy in the morning sun. Behind the house and to either side sloped the cool woods where small birds flashed and twittered. The bay itself was hidden by trees, but the view ahead was glorious—a stretch of the calm, shimmering gulf that lies in the curved arm of Corfu. Away northward, across the dark blue strait, loomed, insubstantial as mist, the ghostly snows of Albania.

It was a scene of the most profound and enchanted peace. No sound but the birds; nothing in sight but trees and sky and sun-reflecting sea.

I sighed. "Well, if it isn't Prospero's magic island it ought to be. . . . Who are these romantic twins of yours, anyway?"

"Spiro and Miranda? Oh, they belong to the woman who works for us here, Maria. She has that cottage at the main Castello gate—you'd see it last night on your way in from the airport."

"I remember a light there . . . A tiny place, wasn't it? So they're Corfu people—what's the word? Corfusians?"

She laughed. "Idiot. Corfiotes. Yes, they're Corfiote peasants. The brother works for Godfrey Manning over at the Villa Rotha. Miranda helps her mother here."

"Peasants?" Mildly intrigued, I gave her the lead I thought she wanted. "It does seem a bit odd to find those names here. Who was this well-read father of theirs, then? Leo?"

"Leo," said his loving wife, "has to my certain knowledge read nothing but the Roman *Financial Times* for the last eight years. He'd think 'Prospero and

Miranda' was the name of an investment trust. No, it's even odder than you think, my love . . ." She gave her small cat-and-canary smile, the one I recognized as preceding the more farfetched flights of gossip that she calls "interesting facts that I feel you ought to know." . . . "Actually, Spiro's officially called after the island Saint—every second boy's called Spiridion in Corfu—but since our distinguished tenant at the Castello was responsible for the christening—and for the twins as well, one gathers—I'll bet he's down as Prospero in the parish register, or whatever they have here."

"Your 'distinguished tenant'?" This was obviously the *bonne bouche* she had been saving for me, but I looked at her in some surprise, remembering the vivid description she had once given me of the Castello dei Fiori: "tatty beyond words, sort of Wagnerian Gothic, like a set for a musical version of *Dracula*." I wondered who could have been persuaded to pay for these operatic splendors. "Someone's rented Valhalla, then? Aren't you lucky. Who?"

"Julian Gale."

"*Julian Gale*?" I sat up abruptly, staring at her. "You can't mean—*do* you mean Julian Gale? The actor?"

"As ever was." My sister looked pleased with the effect she had produced. I was wide awake now, as I had certainly not been during the long recital of our family affairs earlier. Sir Julian Gale was not only "an actor," he had been one of the more brilliant lights of the English theater for more years than I could well remember . . . And, more recently, one of its mysteries.

"Well!" I said. "So this is where he went."

"I thought you'd be interested," said Phyl, rather smugly.

"I'll say I am! Everyone's still wondering, on and off, why he packed it in like that two years ago. Of course I knew he'd been ill after that ghastly accident, but to give it up and then just quietly vanish . . . You should have heard the rumors."

"I can imagine. We've our own brand here. But don't go all shiny-eyed and imagine you'll get anywhere near him, my child. He's here for privacy, and I mean for privacy. He doesn't go out at all—socially, that is—except to the houses of a couple of friends, and they've got TRESPASSERS WILL BE SHOT plastered at intervals of one yard all over the grounds, and the gardener throws all callers over the cliff into the sea."

"I shan't worry him. I think too darned much of him for that. I suppose you must have met him. How is he?"

"Oh, I—he seems all right. Just doesn't get around, that's all. I've only met him a couple of times. Actually, it was he who told me that Corfu was supposed to be the setting of *The Tempest*." She glanced at me sideways. "I, er, I suppose you'd allow him to be 'a literary gent'?"

But this time I ignored the lead. "*The Tempest* was his swan song," I said. "I saw it at Stratford, the last performance, and cried my eyes out over the 'this rough magic I here abjure' bit. Is that what made him choose Corfu to retire to?"

She laughed. "I doubt it. Didn't you know he was practically a native? He was here during the war, and apparently stayed on for a bit after it was over, and then, I'm told, he used to bring his family back almost every year for holidays, when the children were young. They had a house near Ipsos, and kept it on till quite recently, but it was sold after his wife and daughter were killed. However, I suppose he still had . . . connections . . . here, so when he thought of retiring he remembered the Castello. We hadn't meant to let the place, it wasn't really fit, but he was so anxious to find somewhere quite isolated and quiet, and it really did seem a godsend that the Castello was empty, with Maria and her family just next door; so Leo let it go. Maria and the twins turned to and fixed up a few of the rooms, and there's a couple who live at the far side of the orange orchards; they look after the place, and their grandson does the Castello garden and helps around, so for anyone who really only wants peace and privacy I suppose it's a pretty fair bargain . . . Well, that's our little colony. I won't say it's just another Saint-Trop. in the height of the season, but there's plenty of what you want, if it's only peace and sunshine and bathing."

"Suits me," I said dreamily. "Oh, how it suits me."

"D'you want to go down this morning?"

"I'd love to. Where?"

"Well, the bay, of course. It's down that way." She pointed vaguely through the trees.

"I thought you said there were notices warning trespassers off."

"Oh, goodness, not literally, and not from the beach, anyway, only the grounds. We'd never let anyone else have the bay, that's what we come here for! Actually, it's quite nice straight down from here on the north side of the headland where our own little jetty is, but there's sand in the bay, and it's heaven for lying about, and quite private . . . Well, you do as you like. I might go down later, but if you want to swim this morning, I'll get Miranda to show you the way."

"She's here now?"

"Darling," said my sister, "you're in the lap of vulgar luxury now, remember? Did you think I made the coffee myself?"

"Get you, Contessa," I said crudely. "I can remember the day—"

I broke off as a girl came out on to the terrace with a tray, to clear away the breakfast things. She eyed me curiously, with that unabashed stare of the Greeks which one learns to get used to, as it is virtually impossible to stare it down in return, and smiled at me, the smile broadening into a grin as I tried a "Good morning" in Greek—a phrase which was, as yet, my whole vocabulary. She was short and stockily built, with a thick neck and round face, and heavy brows almost meeting over her nose. Her bright dark eyes and warm skin were attractive with the simple, animal attraction of youth and health. The dress of faded red suited her, giving her a sort of dark, gentle glow that was very different from the electric sparkle of the urban expatriate Greeks I had met. She looked about seventeen.

My attempt to greet her undammed a flood of delighted Greek which my sister, laughing, managed at length to stem.

"She doesn't understand, Miranda, she only knows two words. Speak English. Will you show her the way down to the beach when you've cleared away, please?"

"Of course! I shall be pleased!"

She looked more than pleased, she looked so delighted that I smiled to myself, presuming cynically that it was probably only pleasure at having an outing in the middle of a working morning. As it happened, I was wrong. Coming so recently from the gray depressions of London and the backstage bad tempers of failure, I wasn't able as yet to grasp the Greek's simple delight in doing anyone a service.

She began to pile the breakfast dishes on her tray with clattering vigor. "I shall not be long. A minute, only a minute . . ."

"And that means half an hour," said my sister placidly, as the girl bustled out. "Anyway, what's the hurry? You've all the time in the world."

"So I have," I said, in deep contentment.

The way to the beach was a shady path quilted with pine needles. It twisted through the trees, to lead out suddenly into a small clearing where a stream, trickling down to the sea, was trapped in a sunny pool under a bank of honeysuckle.

Here the path forked, one track going uphill, deeper into the woods, the other turning down steeply through pines and golden oaks toward the sea.

Miranda paused and pointed downhill. "That is the way you go. The other is to the Castello, and it is private. Nobody goes that way, it is only to the house, you understand?"

"Whereabouts is the other villa, Mr. Manning's?"

"On the other side of the bay, at the top of the cliff. You cannot see it from the beach because the trees are in the way, but there is a path going like this"—she sketched a steep zigzag—"from the boathouse up the cliff. My brother works there, my brother Spiro. It is a fine house, very beautiful, like the Signora's, though of course not so wonderful as the Castello. *That* is like a palace."

"So I believe. Does your father work on the estate, too?"

The query was no more than idle; I had completely forgotten Phyllida's nonsense, and hadn't believed it anyway, but to my intense embarrassment the girl hesitated, and I wondered for one horrified second if Phyllida had been right. I did not know, then, that the Greek takes the most intensely personal questions serenely for granted, just as he asks them himself, and I had begun to stammer something, but Miranda was already answering:

"Many years ago my father left us. He went over there."

"Over there" was at the moment a wall of trees laced with shrubs of myrtle, but I knew what lay beyond them: the grim, shut land of Communist Albania.

"You mean as a prisoner?" I asked, horrified.

She shook her head. "No. He was a Communist. We lived then in Argyrathes, in the south of Corfu, and in that part of the island there are many such." She hesitated. "I do not know why this is. It is different in the north, where my mother comes from." She spoke as if the island were four hundred miles long instead of nearly forty, but I believed her. Where two Greeks are gathered together, there will be at least three political parties represented, and possibly more.

"You've never heard from him?"

"Never. In the old days my mother still hoped, but now, of course, the frontiers are shut to all, and no one can pass in or out. If he is still alive, he must stay there. But we do not know this either."

"D'you mean that no one can travel to Albania?"

"No one." The black eyes suddenly glittered to life, as if something had sparked behind their placid orbs. "Except those who break the law."

"Not a law I'd care to break myself." Those alien snows had looked high and cold and cruel. I said awkwardly, "I'm sorry, Miranda. It must be an unhappy business for your mother."

She shrugged. "It is a long time ago. Fourteen years. I do not even know if I remember him. And we have Spiro to look after us." The sparkle again. "He works for Mr. Manning, I told you this—with the boat, and with the car, a wonderful car, very expensive!—and also with the photographs that Mr. Manning is taking for a book. He has said that when the book is finished—a real book that is sold in the shops—he will put Spiro's name in it, in print. Imagine! Oh, there is nothing that Spiro cannot do! He is my twin, you understand."

"Is he like you?"

She looked surprised. "Like me? Why, no, he is a man, and have I not just told you that he is clever? Me, I am not clever, but then I am a woman, and there is no need. With men it is different. Yes?"

"So the men say." I laughed. "Well, thanks very much for showing me the way. Will you tell my sister that I'll be back in good time for lunch?"

I turned down the steep path under the pines. As I reached the first bend something made me glance back toward the clearing.

Miranda had gone. But I thought I saw a whisk of faded scarlet, not from the direction of the Villa Forli, but higher up in the woods, on the forbidden path to the Castello.

2

Sir, I am vex'd . . .

Act IV, Scene 1

THE BAY was small and sheltered, a sickle of pure white sand holding back the aquamarine sea, and held in its turn by the towering backdrop of cliff and pine and golden-green trees. My path led me steeply down past a knot of young oaks, straight on to the sand. I changed quickly in a sheltered corner, and walked out into the white blaze of the sun.

The bay was deserted and very quiet. To either side of it the wooded promontories thrust out into the calm, glittering water. Beyond them the sea deepened through peacock shades to a rich, dark blue, where the mountains of Epirus floated in the clear distance, less substantial than a bank of mist. The far snows of Albania seemed to drift like cloud.

After the heat of the sand, the water felt cool and silky. I let myself down into the milky calm, and began to swim idly along parallel to the shore, toward the southern arm of the bay. There was the faintest breeze blowing off the land, its heady mixture of orange blossom and pine, sweet and sharp, coming in warm puffs through the salt smell of the sea. Soon I was nearing the promontory, where white rocks came down to the water, and a grove of pines hung out, shadowing a deep green pool. I stayed in the sun, turning lazily on my back to float, eyes shut against the brilliance of the sky.

The pines breathed and whispered; the tranquil water made no sound at all. . . .

A ripple rocked me, nearly turning me over. As I floundered, trying to right myself, another came, a wash like that of a small boat passing, rolling me in its wake. But I had heard neither oars nor engine; could hear nothing now except the slap of the exhausted ripples against the rock.

Treading water, I looked around me, puzzled and a little alarmed. Nothing. The sea shimmered, empty and calm, to the turquoise and blue of its horizon. I felt downward with my feet, to find that I had drifted a little farther out from shore, and could barely touch bottom with the tips of my toes. I turned back toward the shallows.

This time the wash lifted me clear off my feet, and as I plunged clumsily forward another followed it, tumbling me over, so that I struggled helplessly for a minute, swallowing water, before striking out, thoroughly alarmed now, for shore.

Beside me, suddenly, the water swirled and hissed. Something touched me—a cold, momentary graze along the thigh—as a body drove past me under water. . . .

I gave a gasp of sheer fright, and the only reason I didn't scream was because I gasped myself full of water, and went under. Fighting back, terrified, to the surface, I shook the salt out of my eyes and looked wildly round—to see the bay as empty as before, but with its surface marked now by the arrowing ripples of whatever sea creature had brushed by me. The arrow's point was moving fast away, its wake as clear as a vapor trail across the flat water of the bay. It tore on its way, straight for the open sea . . . then curved in a long arc, heading back. . . .

I didn't wait to see what it was. My ignorant mind, panic-stricken, screamed *"Sharks!"* and I struck out madly for the rocks of the promontory.

It was coming fast. Thirty yards off, the surface of the water bulged, swelled, and broke to the curved thrust of a huge, silver-black back. The water parted, and poured off its sides like liquid glass. There was a gasping puff of breath; I caught the glimpse of a dark bright eye, and a dorsal fin cusped like a crescent moon, then the creature submerged again, its wash lifting me a couple of yards forward toward my rock. I found a handhold, clung, and scrambled out, gasping, and thoroughly scared.

It surely wasn't a shark. Hundreds of adventure stories had told me that one knew a shark by the great triangular fin, and I had seen pictures of the terrible jaws and tiny, brutal eye. This creature had breathed air, and the eye had been big and dark, like a dog's—like a seal's, perhaps? But there were no seals in these warm waters, and besides, seals didn't have dorsal fins. A porpoise, then? Too big . . .

Then I had the answer, and with it a rush of relief and delight. This was the darling of the Aegean, "the lad who lives before the wind," Apollo's beloved, "desire of the sea," the dolphin . . . the lovely names went rippling by with him as I drew myself up on to the warm rock in the shade of the pines, clasped my knees, and settled down to watch.

Here he came again, in a great curve, smooth and glistening, dark-backed and light-bellied, and as graceful as a racing yacht. This time he came right out, to lie on the surface watching me.

He was large, as dolphins go, something over eight feet long. He lay rocking gently, with the powerful shoulders waiting curved for the plunge below, and the tail—crescent-shaped, and quite unlike a fish's upright rudder—hugging the water flatly, holding the big body level. The dark-ringed eye watched me steadily, with what I could have sworn was a friendly and interested light. The smooth muzzle was curved into the perpetual dolphin smile.

Excitement and pleasure made me light-headed. "Oh, you darling!" I said foolishly, and put out a hand, rather as one puts it out to the pigeons in Trafalgar Square.

The dolphin, naturally, ignored it, but lay there placidly smiling, rocking a little closer, and watching me, entirely unafraid.

So they were true, those stories . . . I knew of the legends, of course—ancient literature was studded with stories of dolphins who had befriended man; and while one couldn't quite accept all the miraculous dolphins of legend, there were also many more recent tales, sworn to with every kind of modern proof. There was the dolphin called Pelorus Jack, fifty years ago in New Zealand, who saw the ships through Cook Strait for twenty years; the Opononi dolphin of the fifties, who entertained the holiday-makers in the bay; the one more recently in Italy, who played with the children near the shore, attracting such large crowds that eventually a little group of businessmen from a nearby resort, whose custom was being drawn away, lay in wait for the dolphin and shot her dead as she came in to play. These, and others, gave the old legends rather more than the benefit of the doubt.

And here, indeed, was the living proof. Here was I, Lucy Waring, being asked into the water for a game. The dolphin couldn't have made it clearer if he'd been carrying a placard on that lovely moon's-horn fin of his. He rocked himself, watching me, then half turned, rolled, and came up again, nearer still. . . .

A stray breeze moved the pines, and I heard a bee go past my cheek, traveling like a bullet. The dolphin arched suddenly away in a deep dive. The sea sucked, swirled, and settled, rocking, back to emptiness.

So that was that. With a disappointment so sharp that it felt like a bereavement, I turned my head to watch for him moving out to sea, when suddenly, not far from my rock, the sea burst apart as if it had been shelled and the dolphin shot upward on a steep slant that took him out of the water in a yard-high leap and down again with a smack of the tail as loud as a cannon shot. He tore by like a torpedo, to fetch up all standing twenty yards out from my rock and fix me once again with that bright, humorous eye.

It was an enchanting piece of show-off, and it did the trick. "All right," I said softly, "I'll come in. But if you knock me over again, I'll drown you, my lad, see if I don't!"

I lowered my legs into the water, ready to slide down off the rock. Another bee shot past above me, seaward, with a curious high humming. Something—some small fish, I suppose—splashed a white jet of water just beyond the dolphin. Even as I wondered, vaguely, what it was, the humming came again, nearer . . . and then another white spurt of water, and a curious thin, curving whine, like singing wire.

I understood then. I'd heard that sound before. These were neither bees nor fish. They were bullets, presumably from a silenced rifle, and one of them had ricocheted off the surface of the sea. Someone was shooting at the dolphin from the woods above the bay.

That I was in some danger from the ricochets myself didn't at first enter my head. I was merely furious, and concerned to do something quickly. There lay the dolphin, smiling at me on the water, while some murderous "sportsman" was no doubt taking aim yet again. . . .

Presumably he hadn't yet seen me in the shadow of the pines. I shouted at the top of my voice, "Stop that shooting! Stop it at once!" and thrust myself forward into the water.

Nobody, surely, would fire at the beast when there was the chance of hitting me. I plunged straight out into the sunlight, clumsily breasting the water, hoping that my rough approach would scare the dolphin away from the danger.

It did. He allowed me to come within a few feet, but as I lunged farther, with a hand out as if to touch him, he rolled gently away from me, submerged, and vanished.

I stood breast-deep, watching the sea. Nothing. It stretched silent and empty toward the tranquil, floating hills of the mainland. The ripples ran back to the shore, and flattened, whispering. The dolphin had gone. And the magic had gone with him. This was only a small—and lonely—bathing place, above which waited an unpleasant and frustrated character with a gun.

I turned to look up at the enclosing cliffs.

The first thing I saw, high up above the bay's center, was what must be the upper stories of the Castello dei Fiori, rearing their incongruously embattled turrets against a background of holm oak and cedar and Mediterranean cypress. The house was set well back, so that I could not see the ground-floor windows, but a wide balcony, or terrace, edged with a stone balustrade, jutted forward right to the cliff's edge over the bay. From the beach directly below nothing of this would be visible through the tangle of flowering shrubs that curtained the steep, broken cliff, but from where I stood I could see the full length of the balustrade with its moss-grown statues at the corners, a stone jar or two full of flowers showing bright against the dark background of cypress, and, a little way back from the balustrade, a table and chairs set in the shadow of a stone pine.

And a man standing, half invisible in the shade of the pine, watching me.

A moment's study convinced me that it could not be Sir Julian Gale. This man was too dark, and even from this distance looked quite unfamiliar—too casual in his bearing, perhaps, and certainly too young. The gardener, probably; the one who threw the trespassers over the cliff. Well, if Sir Julian's gardener had the habit of amusing himself with a bit of shooting practice, it was high time he was stopped.

I was out of the water before even the dolphin could have dived twice, had snatched up shoes and wrap, and was making for a dilapidated flight of steps near the cliff which, I assumed, led up to the terrace.

From above I heard a shout, and looked up. He had come forward to the balustrade, and was leaning over. I could barely see him through the thick screen of hibiscus and bramble, but he didn't look like a Greek, and as I paused he shouted in English, "That way, please!" and his arm went out in a gesture toward the southern end of the bay.

I ignored it. Whoever he was—some guest of Julian Gale's, presumably—I was going to have this out with him here and now, while I was hot with temper; not wait until I had to meet him at some polite bun fight of Phyllida's. . . . "But you really mustn't shoot at dolphins, Mr. Whosit, they do no harm. . . ." The same old polite spiel, gone through a thousand times with stupid, trigger-happy men who shot or trapped badgers, otters, kestrels—harmless creatures, killed because some man wanted a walk out with his dog on a fine day. No, this time I was white-hot, and brave with it, and I was going to say my piece.

I went up those steps like a rocket leaving the launching pad.

They were steep and crooked, and wound up through the thickest of the wood. They skirted the roots of the cliff, flicked up and round thickets of myrtle and summer jasmine, and emerged into a sloping glade full of dappled sunlight.

He was there, looking annoyed, having apparently come down from the terrace to intercept me. I only realized when I stopped to face him how very much at a disadvantage I was. He had come down some fifty feet; I had hurtled up a hundred or so. He presumably had a right to be where he was; I had not. He was also minding his own business, which was emphatically none of mine. Moreover, he was fully dressed, and I was in swimming costume, with a wet wrap flying loose round me. I clutched it to me, and fought for breath, feeling angrier than ever, but now this didn't help at all, as I couldn't get a word out.

He said, not aggressively but not politely, "This is private ground, you know. Perhaps you'd be good enough to leave by the way you came? This only takes you up to the terrace, and then more or less through the house."

I got enough breath to speak, and wasted neither time nor words. "Why were you shooting at that dolphin?"

He looked as blank as if I had suddenly slapped his face. "Why was I what?"

"That was you just now, wasn't it, shooting at the dolphin down in the bay?"

"My dear g—" He checked himself, and said, like someone dealing with a lunatic, "Just what are you talking about?"

"Don't pretend you don't know! It must have been you! If you're such death on trespassers, who else would be there?" I was panting hard, and my hands were shaking as I clutched the wrap to me clumsily. "Someone took a couple of potshots at it, just a few minutes ago. I was down there, and I saw you on the terrace."

"I certainly saw a dolphin there. I didn't see you, until you shouted and came jumping out from under the trees. But you must be mistaken. There was no shooting. I'd have been bound to hear it if there was."

"It was silenced, of course," I said impatiently. "I tell you, I was down there when the shots came! D'you think I'd have come running up here for the fun of the thing? They were bullets all right! I know a ricochet when I hear it."

His brows snapped down at that, and he stared at me frowningly, as if seeing me for the first time as a person, and not just a nuisance to be thrown down the cliff as quickly as possible.

"Then why did you jump into the water near the dolphin?"

"Well, obviously! I wanted to drive it away before it got hurt!"

"But you might have been badly hurt yourself. Don't you know that a bullet ricochets off water the way it does off rock?"

"Of course I do! But I had to do something, hadn't I?"

"Brave girl." There was a dryness in his voice that brought my cooling temper fizzing to the boil again. I said hotly:

"You don't believe me, do you? I tell you it's true! They *were* shots, and *of course* I jumped in to stop you! I knew you'd have to stop if someone was there."

"You know," he said, "you can't have it both ways. Either I did the shooting or I don't believe there was any shooting. Not both. You can take your pick. If I were you, I'd choose the second; I mean, it's simply not credible, is it? Even supposing someone wanted to shoot a dolphin, why use a silencer?"

"I'm asking *you,"* I said.

For a moment I thought I had gone too far. His lips compressed, and his eyes looked angry. There was a short silence, while he stared at me frowningly and we measured each other.

I saw a strongly built man of about thirty, carelessly dressed in slacks and a sleeveless Sea Island shirt which exposed a chest and arms that might have belonged to any of the Greek navvies I was to see building the roads with their bare hands and very little more. Like theirs, too, his hair and eyes were very dark. But something at once sensual and sensitive about the mouth contradicted the impression of a purely physical personality; here, one felt, was a man of aggressive impulses, but one who paid for them in his own private coinage.

What impression he was getting of me I hated to think—damp hair, flushed face, half-embarrassed fury, and a damned wrap that kept slipping—but of one thing I could feel pretty sure: at this very moment he was having one of those aggressive impulses of his. Fortunately it wasn't physical . . . yet.

"Well," he said shortly, "I'm afraid you'll have to take my word for it. I did not shoot at the beast, with a rifle or a catapult or anything else. Will that do? And now if you'll excuse me, I'll be obliged if you would—"

"Get out by the way I came in? All right. I get the message. I'm sorry, perhaps I was wrong. But I certainly wasn't wrong about the shooting. I don't see any more than you do why anyone should do it, but the fact remains that they did." I hesitated, faltering now under his indifferent eye. "Look, I don't want to be any more of a nuisance, but I can't just leave it at that. . . . It might happen again. . . . Since it wasn't you, have you any idea who it could have been?"

"No."

"Not the gardener?"

"No."

"Or the tenant at the Villa Rotha?"

"Manning? On the contrary, if you want help in your protection campaign I suggest you go to the Villa Rotha straight away. Manning's been photographing that beast for weeks. It was he who tamed it in the first place, he and the Greek boy who works for him."

"Tamed it? Oh . . . I see. Well, then," I added lamely, "it wouldn't be him, obviously."

He said nothing, waiting, it seemed, with a kind of neutral patience for me to go. I bit my lip, hesitating miserably, feeling a fool. (Why did one always feel such a fool when it was a matter of kindness—what the more sophisticated saw as sentimentality?) I found that I was shivering. Anger and energy had drained out of me together. The glade was cool with shadows.

I said, "Well, I imagine I'll see Mr. Manning sometime soon, and if he can't help, I'm sure my brother-in-law will. I mean, if this is all private land, and the shore as well, then we ought to be able to stop that kind of trespasser, oughtn't we?"

He said quickly, "We?"

"The people who own the place. I'm Lucy Waring, Phyllida Forli's sister. I take it you're staying with Sir Julian?"

"I'm his son. So you're Miss Waring? I hadn't realized you were here already." He appeared to be hesitating on the brink of some apology, but asked instead, "Is Forli at home now?"

"No," I said shortly, and turned to go. There was a trail of bramble across my shoe, and I bent to disengage it.

"I'm sorry if I was a little abrupt." His voice had not noticeably softened, but that might have been due to awkwardness. "We've had rather a lot of bother with people coming around lately, and my father . . . he's been ill, and came here to convalesce, so you can imagine that he prefers to be left to himself."

"Did I look like an autograph hunter?"

For the first time there was a twitch of amusement. "Well, no. But your dolphin has been more of an attraction even than my father: the word got round somehow that it was being photographed hereabouts, and then of course the rumor started that a film was being made, so we got a few boatloads of sightseers coming round into the bay, not to mention stray parties in the woods. It's all been a bit trying. I wouldn't mind, personally, if people wanted to use the beach, if it weren't that they always come armed with transistor radios, and that I cannot stand. I'm a professional musician, and I'm here to work." He added dryly, "And if you're thinking that this gives me the best of reasons for wanting to get rid of the dolphin, I can only assure you again that it didn't occur to me."

"Well," I said, "it seems there's no more to be said, doesn't it? I'm sorry if I interrupted your work. I'll go now and let you get back to it. Good-bye, Mr. Gale."

My exit from the clearing was ruined by the fact that my wrap caught on the bramble and came clean off me. It took me some three horrible minutes to disentangle it and go.

But I needn't have worried about the threat to my dignity. He had already gone. From somewhere above, and alarmingly near, I heard voices, question and answer, so brief and idle as to be in themselves an insult. Then music, as a wireless or gramophone let loose a flood of weird atonal chords on the still air.

I could be sure I was already forgotten.

3

This gallant which thou seest
Was in the wreck; and, but he's something stain'd
With grief (that's beauty's canker) thou mightst call him
A goodly person.

Act I, Scene 2

BY THE time I had showered and dressed I felt calmer, and very ready to tell Phyllida all about it, and possibly to hear her barbed comments on the unaccommodating Mr. Gale. But when I looked on the terrace she was not to be seen, only the table half laid for lunch, with the silver thrown down, as if hastily, in the middle of the cloth. There was no sign of Miranda or her mother.

Then I heard the door from the kitchen premises swing open and shut, and the quick tap of my sister's steps crossing the hall, to enter the big living room she called the *salotto*.

"Lucy? Was that you I heard?"

"I'm out here." I made for the French windows as I spoke, but she had already hurried out to meet me, and one look at her face drove all thoughts of my morning's adventure from my head.

"Phyl! What's the matter? You look ghastly. Is it Caliban?"

She shook her hand. "Nothing so simple. There's been bad news, an awful thing. Poor Maria's boy's been drowned: Spiro, the boy I told you about at breakfast."

"*Phyl!* Oh, my dear, how frightful! But—how? When?"

"Last night. He was out with Godfrey in the boat—Godfrey Manning, that is—and there was an accident. Godfrey's just come over with the news, and I've been breaking it to Maria and Miranda. I—I've sent them home." She put a hand to her head. "Lucy, it was so awful! I simply can't tell you. If Maria had even *said* anything, but she didn't, not one single word. . . . Oh well, come on in. Godfrey's still here; you'd better come and meet him."

I drew back. "No, no, don't you bother about me: I'll go to my room, or something. Mr. Manning won't want to have to do the polite. Poor Phyl; I'm sorry. . . . Look, would you like me to take myself right away for the rest of the day? I'll go and get lunch somewhere, and then—"

"No, please, I'd rather you stayed." She dropped her voice for a moment. "He's taking it pretty hard, and quite honestly I think it might do him good to talk about it. Come on in. . . . God! I could do with a drink! Caliban'll have to lump it, for once." She smiled a bit thinly, and led the way in through the long window.

The *salotto* was a long, cool room, with three big windows opening on the terrace with its dazzling view. The sun was tempered by the wistaria that roofed the terrace, and the room was cool and airy, its duck-egg-blue walls and white paint setting off to perfection the gilt of the Italian mirrors and the pale gold polished wood of the floor. A calm room, with the kind of graceful simplicity that money and good taste can produce. Phyllida had always had excellent taste. It was a good thing, I sometimes reflected, that she, and not I, had married the rich man. My own taste—since I had outgrown the gingham-and-Chianti-bottle stage—had been heavily conditioned by the fact that I had lived for so long in a perpetual welter of junk-shop props picked up cheaply and licked into stageworthiness for the current show. At best, the effect was a kind of poor man's Cecil Beaton; at worst, a cross between sets designed by Emmett and Ronald Searle for a stage version of Samuel Beckett's *Watt*. That I enjoyed my kind of life didn't stop me from admiring my sister's undoubted talent for elegance.

There was a table at the far end of the room, laden with bottles. A man stood with his back to us, splashing soda into a glass. He turned as we came in.

My first quick impression was of a mask of rather chilly control held hard down over some strong emotion. Then the impression faded, and I saw that I was wrong: the control was not a mask; it was part of the man, and was created by the emotion itself, as a Westinghouse brake is slammed on automatically by the head of steam. Here was something very different from Mr. Gale. I looked at him with interest, and some compassion.

He was tall, and toughly built, with brown hair bleached by the sun, a narrow, clever face, and gray eyes which looked tired and dragged down at the corners, as if he had had no sleep. I put his age somewhere in the middle thirties.

Phyllida introduced us, and he acknowledged me civilly, but all his attention was on my sister. "You've told them? Was it very bad?"

"Worse than bad. Get me a drink, for heaven's sake, will you?" She sank into a chair. "What? . . . Oh, Scotch, please. What about you, Lucy?"

"If that's fruit juice in the jug, may I have that, please? Is there ice?"

"Of course." He handed the drinks. "Look, Phyl, ought I to go and talk to them now? There'll be things they'll want to ask."

She drank, sighed, and seemed to relax a little. "I'd leave it for now, if I were you. I told them they could go home, and they didn't say a word, just picked up their things. I suppose the police'll be there to see them. . . . Later on they'll want to hear every last detail from you, but just at the moment I doubt if Maria's fit to take anything in at all, except that he's dead. As a matter of fact, I don't think she even took *that* in, I don't think she believes it, yet." She looked up at him. "Godfrey, I suppose . . . I suppose there couldn't be any doubt?"

He hesitated, swirling the whisky in his glass, frowning down at it. The lines of fatigue were deep in his face, and made me wonder if he was older than I had thought.

"Well, yes. That's rather the hell of it, don't you see? That's why I didn't come over till now. . . . I've been phoning around all over the place, trying to find out if he could possibly have got ashore either here or on the mainland, or if he'd been . . . well, found. If his body had been washed ashore, that is." He looked up from the drink. "But I'm morally certain there's no chance. I mean, I saw him go."

"And how far out were you?"

He grimaced. "About dead-center."

"From here?"

"Farther north, out from Kouloura, right in the strait. But that's still a mile each way."

I said, "What happened?"

They both started as if they had forgotten my presence completely. Godfrey Manning straightened his shoulders, and smoothed back his hair in a gesture I was to know well.

"Do you know, I'm still hardly sure. Does that sound incredibly stupid? It's no more than the truth. I've been over it so many times in my mind since it happened that I'm beginning to wonder now how much I really do remember. And of course a night without sleep doesn't help." He crossed to the table to pour himself another drink, saying over his shoulder, "The worst of it is, I can't get rid of the feeling that there must have been something I could have done to prevent it."

Phyllida cried out at that, and I said quickly, "I'm sure that's not true! I'm sorry, I shouldn't have asked. You won't want to talk about it any more."

"It's all right." He came back to a chair, but didn't sit in it, just perched rather restlessly on the arm. "I've already been through it with the police, and given Phyl a sketch of a sort. You might say the worst part is over . . . except, God help me, that I'll have to talk to the boy's mother. She'll want to know rather more than the police were concerned with. . . . As a matter of fact, it would be quite a relief to talk it out." He took a pull at the whisky as if he needed it, and looked at me straight for the first time. "You hadn't met Spiro?"

"I only came last night."

His mouth turned down at the corners. "What a start to your visit. Well, he was Miranda's twin—I take it you'll have met her and her mother?—and he works, or rather worked, for me."

"Phyl told me."

"I was lucky to have him. He was a clever mechanic, and that's something not so easy to find in these parts. In most of the villages the only 'machines' are donkeys and mules, and there's no work for a mechanically minded boy. They move to the towns. But of course Spiro wanted work near home; his father's dead, and he wanted to live with his mother and sister. I came here last year, and he's worked for me all that time. What he didn't know about boats wasn't worth knowing, and when I tell you that I even let him loose in my car, you'll realize he was pretty good." He nodded toward the window, where a big portfolio lay on the table. "I don't know if Phyl told you, but I'm working on a book, mainly photographs, and even with that Spiro was invaluable. He not only picked up enough to help me technically—with the processing, and so on—but I actually got him to model for a few of them."

"They're marvellous, too," Phyllida told me warmly.

He smiled, a tight, meaningless little smile. "They are good, aren't they? Well, that was Spiro. Not a world-beater, whatever poor Miranda says about him. What brains he had were in his hands, and he was slow, and as stubborn as a blind mule—but he was tough, and you could trust him. And he had that one extra, priceless quality which was worth the earth to me—he photographed like a dream. He was a 'natural' for the camera—you simply couldn't miss." He swallowed the last of his whisky, and stooped to set the glass down. The click of glass on wood sounded oddly final, like the full stop after the valediction. "Which brings me to last night."

There was a little pause. The tired gray eyes came back to me.

"I've been doing some experiments in night photography—fishing boats at night, moonscapes, that kind of thing—and I wanted to try my hand at the sunrise over the mainland while there's still snow on the mountains. Spiro and I took my boat out last night. There was a stiffish breeze, but it was nothing to worry about. We went up the coast. You'll know, perhaps, that Mount Pantokrator lies north of here? Well, the coast curves right out, running almost due east under the shelter of the mountain. It's only when you come to the end of this and turn north through the open strait that you get the weather. We got there within half an hour or so of dawn, and turned up about opposite Kouloura—that's the narrowest bit between here and the mainland. The sea was choppy, but nothing a sailor would call rough, though the wind was still rising from the north. . . . Well, I was in the cabin, busy with my camera, and Spiro was aft, when the engine suddenly stopped. I called to ask what was wrong, and he shouted that he thought something was fouling the screw, and he'd have it clear in a minute. So I went on with my job, only then I found he'd let the boat's head fall away, and she'd turned across the wind and was rolling rather too much for comfort. So I went out to see what was going on."

He lifted one hand in a slight, but oddly final gesture. "Then it happened. I saw Spiro in the stern, leaning over. The boat was heeling pretty steeply, and I think—I can't be sure—that I yelled to him to take care. Then a gust or a wave or something got her on the beam, and she kicked over like a mule. He'd had hold of the toe rail, but it was slippery, and he lost it. I saw him grab again as he went over, but he missed. He just disappeared. By the time I got to the stern I couldn't even see him."

"He couldn't swim?"

"Oh, yes, but it was very dark, and the boat was drifting fast, with a fair sea on by that time. The wind must have got up more than I'd realized while I was working in the cabin and we must have been driven yards apart in as many seconds. Even if he'd stayed afloat it would have been hard to find him . . . and I don't think he can have done, or he'd have shouted, and I'd surely have heard something. I yelled myself hoarse, as it was, and there was no answer. . . ."

He got up again, restlessly, and prowled over to the window. "Well, that's all. I threw a life belt out, but we were being blown away at a fair speed, and by the time I'd got the engine started, and gone back to where I thought he'd gone overboard, there wasn't a sign. I must have been somewhere near the right place, because I found the life belt. I cruised about for a couple of hours—rather stupidly, I suppose, but then one can't somehow give up and go. A fishing boat came within hail, and helped, but it was no use."

There was a pause. He stood with his back to us, looking out.

Phyllida said drearily, "It's a horrible thing to happen. Horrible."

"And was the propeller fouled after all?" I asked.

He turned. "What? No, it wasn't. At least, I saw nothing there. It was a choked jet. It only took a few seconds to put right. If he'd looked there first . . ." He lifted his shoulders, letting the sentence hang.

"Well," said Phyl, with an attempt at briskness, "I honestly don't see why you should reproach yourself at all. What could you have done more?"

"Oh, it's not that I blame myself for what happened, I know that's absurd. It's my failure to find him that I find so hard to live with. Casting round for two hours in that black windy sea, and knowing all the time that at any minute it would be too late . . . Don't misunderstand me, but it would be a lot easier if I'd had to bring the boy's body home."

"Because his mother can't believe he's gone?"

He nodded. "As it is, she'll probably hope against hope and sit waiting for him to turn up. And then when—if—his body is washed ashore, this will all be to go through again."

Phyllida said, "Then all we can do is hope the body will turn up soon."

"I doubt if it will. The wind and tide were setting the other way. And if he went ashore on the Albanian coast, we may never hear about it. She may wait for years."

"The way she did for his father," I said.

He stared at me, as if for some seconds he hardly saw me. "His father? Oh, God, yes, I forgot that."

Phyllida stirred. "Then go on forgetting it, for heaven's sake, Godfrey! You're not to flay yourself over this any more! The situation's horrible enough without your trying to blame yourself for something you couldn't help and couldn't have prevented!"

"As long as his mother and sister understand that."

"Of course they will! Once the shock's over and you can talk to them, you'll have to tell them the whole story, just as you've told us. You'll find they'll accept it, without even thinking of praise or blame—just as they'd accept anything fate chose to hand out to them. These people do. They're as strong as their own rocks, and so's their faith."

He was looking at her in some surprise. People who only see the everyday side of Phyllida—the volatile, pretty-butterfly side—are always surprised when they come up against her core of solid maternal warmth. He also looked grateful, and relieved, as if she had somehow excused him from blame, and this mattered.

She smiled at him. "Your trouble is, you've not only had a rotten experience and a bad shock, but now you're dreading having to face Maria and stand a scene; and I don't blame you one bit." Her frankness was as comfortable as it was devastating. "But you needn't worry. There'll be no scenes, and it won't even occur to them to ask you questions."

"You don't quite understand. Spiro wasn't to have gone with me last night— he had a date of some sort in the town. I persuaded him to break it. His mother didn't even know till the last minute."

"So what? No doubt you were paying him overtime of a sort, the way you always did? . . . I thought as much. . . . Oh, yes, I knew all about it, Maria told me. Believe me, they were terribly grateful for the work you gave him, *and* for the way you paid, always so generous. Spiro thought the world of you, and so does Maria. Good heavens, *you* to worry what they'll say to you?"

"Could I offer them anything, do you think?"

"Money?" She knitted her brows. "I don't know. I'll have to think. I don't know quite what they'll do now . . . But don't let's worry about that yet. I'll ask a tactful question or two, and let you know, shall I? But I'll tell you one thing, you'd better take those pictures home with you when you go. I've not looked at them properly, but it'd be a pity if Maria saw them just now."

"Oh. Yes, of course. I'll take them."

He picked up the portfolio, and stood holding it irresolutely, as if he didn't quite know what to do next. One habit my profession has taught me is to watch faces and listen to voices; and if the people concerned are under some kind of stress, so much the better. As an actress I shall never be in the top class, but I am fairly good at reading people, and I felt here, in Godfrey Manning's hesitation and hunger for reassurance, something not quite in character: the contrast between the man as one felt he should be and what shock had made of him was obscurely disquieting, like watching an actor badly miscast. It made me say hastily, and not very tactfully—almost as if any diversion were better than none:

"Are those the photographs for your book?"

"Some of them, prints I brought the other day for Phyl to look at. Would you care to see them?"

He came quickly across the room, and laid the portfolio on a low table beside my chair. I wasn't sure that I wanted, at this moment, to look at the prints, among which were presumably some of the dead boy, but Phyl made no protest, and to Godfrey Manning, quite obviously, it was some kind of a relief. So I said nothing as he pulled the big prints from between the guard sheets and began to spread them out.

The first ones he showed me were mainly of scenery: bold pieces of cliff and brilliant sea, with the bright tangled flowers splashing down over sunlit rock and pictures of peasant women with their goats and donkeys passing between hedgerows of apple blossom and purple broom, or stooping over a stone cistern with their piles of colored washing. And the sea: this was in most of the pictures; sometimes just the corner of a pool laced with seaweed, or the inside of a curling wave, or the pattern of withdrawing foam over damp sand; and one marvelous one of a rocky inlet where, smiling and with bright intelligent eye, the dolphin lay watching the camera.

"Oh, look, the dolphin!" I cried, for the first time remembering my morning's adventure. Godfrey Manning looked curiously at me, but before I could say anything further Phyllida had lifted the print aside and I found myself staring down at a picture of the dead boy.

He was very like his sister: there were the round face and wide smile, the sunburned skin, the thick black hair as springy as heather. I saw at once what Godfrey had meant when he called the boy a "natural model": the sturdy body and thick neck which gave Miranda her heavy, peasant look were translated in the boy into a kind of classical strength, the familiar, deliberately thickened lines of sculpture. He fitted into the background of rock and sea as inevitably as the pillars of the temple at Sunium.

Just as I was wondering how to break the silence, my sister broke it quite easily.

"You know, Godfrey, I'm quite sure that later on, when things ease off a bit, Maria would love to have one of these. Why don't you do one for her?"

"If you think she would . . . It might be an idea. Yes, and I could frame it for her." He began to put the prints back into the portfolio. "Sometime, perhaps, you'd help me choose the one you think she'd like?"

"Oh, there's no question," said Phyllida, and pulled one out of the pile. "This. It's the best I've seen in years, and exactly like him."

He gave it a brief glance. "Oh, yes. It was a lucky one." His voice was quite colorless.

I said nothing, but stared and stared.

There was the dolphin, arching gently out of a turquoise sea, its back streaming silver drops. Standing thigh-deep beside the animal, laughing, with one hand stretched out to touch it, was the boy, bronzed and naked, his arrow-straight body cutting the arc made by the silver dolphin at the exact point known to painters as golden section. It was one of those miracles of photography—skill and chance combining to throw color, light, and mass into a flawless moment caught and held forever.

I said, "It's marvelous! There's no other word for it! It's a myth come true! If I hadn't seen the dolphin myself, I'd have thought it was faked!"

He had been looking down at the picture without expression. Now he smiled. "Oh, it's genuine enough. Spiro tamed the beast for me, and it would come right in to play when he went swimming. It was a most cooperative creature, with a lot of personal charm. Did you say you'd seen it?"

"Yes. I've just been down for a swim, and it came to take a look at me. What's more, I may tell you, you nearly lost your dolphin for good and all this morning."

"Lost the dolphin?" said Phyl. "What on earth d'you mean?"

"Someone was shooting at it," I said crisply. "I came panting up here to tell you about it, but then your news knocked it clean out of my head till now." I glanced up at Godfrey. "When I was down in the bay, there was somebody up in the woods above, with a rifle, taking potshots. If I hadn't been there and shooed the dolphin away, he'd probably have got it."

"But . . . this is incredible!" This, at least, had broken through his preoccupation with Spiro's death. He stared at me frowningly. "Someone up in these woods, shooting? Are you sure?"

"Quite sure. And, which makes it worse, the rifle was silenced—so it wasn't just some sportsman out after hares or something, amusing himself by sniping at the dolphin. It was a deliberate attempt to kill it. I was sitting up under the trees, and I suppose he hadn't seen me. But when I yelled and jumped in beside the dolphin, the shooting stopped."

"But, *Lucy!*" Phyllida was horrified. "You might have been hurt!"

"I didn't think," I confessed. "I was just so blazing-mad, I had to stop him somehow."

"You never do think! One of these days you *will* get hurt!" She turned, with a gesture half of exasperation, half of amusement, to Godfrey. "She's always been the same. It's the only thing I've ever seen her really fly off the handle about—animals. She even rescues drowning wasps, and spiders out of the bath, and worms that come out when it rains and get caught crossing the road. The funny thing is, they see her coming. She once put her hand down on an adder, and it didn't even bite her."

"It was probably knocked cold," I said curtly, as embarrassed under Godfrey's amused look as if I were being accused of some odd perversion. I added defiantly, "I can't stand seeing anything hurt, that's all. So from now on I'll keep my eye on it if I have to bathe there every day. That dolphin of yours has got itself a one girl guard, Mr. Manning."

"I'm delighted to hear it."

Phyl said, "I still can't believe it. Who in the world could it have been, up in those woods with a gun?"

I thought for a moment he was going to answer, but he turned back to his task of stowing away the photographs, shutting the portfolio on the last of them with a snap. "I can't imagine." Then, to me, "I suppose you didn't see anyone?"

"Oh, yes."

This produced a gratifying amount of sensation. Phyllida gave a little squeak, and clapped a hand to where, roughly, one imagined Caliban to be. Godfrey Manning said quickly, "You did? Where? I suppose you didn't get near enough to see who it was."

"I did indeed, in the wood below the Castello terrace, and he was utterly beastly!" I said warmly. "He said he was Julian Gale's son, and—"

"*Max Gale!*" This from Phyllida, incredulously. "Lucy, you're not trying to tell me that Max Gale was running round in the woods with a rifle, loosing it off at all and sundry? Don't be silly!"

"Well, he did say it wasn't him," I admitted, "and he'd got rid of the gun, so I couldn't prove it was, but I didn't believe him. He *looked* as if he'd be capable of anything, and anyway, he was quite foully rude, and it wasn't a bit necessary!"

"You were trespassing," said Godfrey dryly.

"Even so, it couldn't have been him!" said my sister positively.

"Probably not," said Godfrey.

She looked at him sharply. "What is it?"

"Nothing."

But she had obviously understood whatever it was he hadn't said. Her eyes widened. "But why in the world—" She caught her breath, and I thought she changed color. "Oh, my God, I suppose it could be . . . ! But, Godfrey, that's frightful! If *he* got his hands on a gun—"

"Quite. And if he did, naturally Gale would cover up."

"Well, but what can we do? I mean, if there's any danger—"

"There won't be now," he said calmly. "Look, Phyl, it'll be all right. If Max Gale didn't know before, he does now, and he'll have the sense to keep anything like that out of the old man's hands."

"How?" she demanded. "Just tell me how? Have you ever *been* in that ghastly museum of a place?"

"No. Why? Is there a gun room or something?"

"Gun room!" said Phyllida. "Give me strength! Gun room! The Castello walls are just about *papered* with the things! Guns, daggers, spears, assegais, the lot. I'll swear there's everything there from carbines to knuckle-dusters. There's even a cannon at the front door! Good heavens, Leo's grandfather *collected* the things! Nobody's going to know if a dozen rifles or so go missing!"

"Now isn't that nice?" said Godfrey.

"Look," I said forcibly, "one minute more of this, and I shall scream. What's all the mystery? Are you two talking about Julian Gale? Because if you are I never heard anything so silly in my life. Why in the world should *he* go round getting savage with a rifle? He might pick off a few theatre critics—I can think of one who's been asking for it for years—but not that dolphin! It's just not possible."

"D'you know him?" Godfrey Manning's tone was abrupt and surprised.

"I've never met him, he's way out of my star. But I've known stacks of people who've worked with him, and they all adored him. I tell you, it's not in character. And if you ask how I know that, let me tell you I've seen every play he's been in for the last ten years, and if there's one kind of person who can't hide what sort of man he is under everything he has to do and say, it's an actor. That's a paradox, I suppose, but it's true. And that Julian Gale could kill a living creature straight out of a Greek myth—no, it simply isn't *on*. Unless he was drunk, or went raving-mad—"

I stopped. The look that had flashed between them would have wrecked a geiger counter. There was a silence that could be felt.

"Well?" I said.

Godfrey cleared his throat awkwardly. He seemed uncertain of how to begin.

"Oh, for goodness' sake, if she's going to be here for a few weeks she'd better know," said my sister. "She's almost certain to meet him sooner or later. I know he only goes to the Karithis place, and to play chess with someone in Corfu, and they never leave him alone the rest of the time, but I met him myself at the Karithises', and she may come across him any day in the grounds."

"I suppose so."

She turned to me. "You said this morning that you wondered why he disappeared like that after he'd retired. You know about the car smash three or four years ago, when his wife and daughter were killed?"

"Oh, Lord, yes. It happened just the week before he opened in *Tiger, Tiger*. I saw it after it had been running about a month. Lucky for him it was a part to tear a cat in, so he was better than ever, if possible, but he'd lost a couple of stones' weight. I know he was ill after he left the cast, and rumors started going round then that he was planning to retire, but of course nobody really believed them, and he seemed quite all right for the Stratford season; then they suddenly announced *The Tempest* as his last appearance. What happened, then? Was he ill again after that came off?"

"In a way. He finished up in a nursing home with a nervous breakdown, and he was there over a year."

I stared at her, deeply shocked. "I never knew that."

"Nobody knew," said my sister. "It's not the sort of thing one advertises, especially if one's a public person like Julian Gale. I only knew myself because

Max Gale said something to Leo when they rented the house, and then a friend of mine told me the rest. He's supposed to be better, and he does go out sometimes to visit friends, but there's always someone with him."

I said flatly, "You mean he has to be watched? You're trying to tell me that Julian Gale is—" I paused. Why were all the words so awful? If they didn't conjure up grotesque images of Bedlam, they were even worse, genteel synonyms for the most tragic sickness of all. "—Unbalanced?" I finished.

"I don't know!" Phyllida looked distressed. "Heaven knows, one doesn't want to make too much of it, and the very fact that he was discharged—if that's the word—from the home must mean that he's all right, surely?"

"But he *must* be all right! Anyway, you said you'd met him. How did he seem then?"

"Perfectly normal. In fact, I fell for him like a ton of bricks. He's very charming." She looked worriedly across at Godfrey. "But I suppose these things can recur? I never thought . . . the idea wasn't even raised . . . but if I'd thought, with the children coming here for their holidays and everything—"

"Look," said Godfrey briskly, "you're making altogether too much of this, you know. The very mention of a gun seems to have blown everything up right out of proportion. The man's not a homicidal maniac or anything like it—and never has been, or he wouldn't be here at all."

"Yes, I suppose you're right. Silly of me to panic." She gave a sigh, and subsided in her chair. "In any case, Lucy probably dreamed it! If she never even *saw* a gun, and never heard it, either . . . ! Oh well, let's forget it, shall we?"

I didn't trouble to insist. It no longer mattered. What I had just learned was too fresh and too distressing. I said miserably, "I wish I'd been a bit nicer to Mr. Gale, that's all. He must have had a foul time. It's bad enough for other people, but for his son—"

"Oh, honey, don't look so stricken!" Phyl, her worry apparently gone, was back in the role of comforter. "We're all probably *quite* wrong, and there's nothing the matter at all, except that the old man needs a bit of peace and quiet to recuperate in, and Max is seeing he gets it! If it comes to that, I wouldn't be surprised if it's Max who insists on the quarantine for his own sake; he's writing the score for some film or other, so the story goes, and *he* never appears at all. Hence all the 'trespassers will be shot' stuff, and young Adonis playing bodyguard."

"Young *who?*"

"Adonis. The gardener."

"Good heavens! Can anyone get away with a name like that, even in Greece?"

She laughed. "Oh, he does, believe you me!"

She turned to Godfrey then, saying something about Adonis, who had apparently been a close friend of Spiro's. I caught Miranda's name again, and something about a dowry, and difficulties now that the brother was dead; but I wasn't really listening. I was still caught up unhappily in the news I had just heard. We do not take easily to the displacing of our idols. It was like making a long and difficult journey to see Michelangelo's David and finding nothing there but a broken pedestal.

I found I was reliving, as clearly as if it had been yesterday, that "last appearance" in *The Tempest*; the gentle, disciplined verses resigning Prospero's dark powers, and with them, if this story was true, so much more:

> *. . . This rough magic*
> *I here abjure, and, when I have requir'd*
> *Some heavenly music (which even now I do)*
> *To work mine end upon their senses that*
> *This airy charm is for, I'll break my staff,*
> *Bury it certain fathoms in the earth.*
> *And deeper than did ever plummet sound*
> *I'll drown my book.*

I stirred in my chair, pushed my own distress aside with an effort of will, and came back to the *salotto,* where Godfrey Manning was taking his leave.

"I'd better go. I meant to ask you, Phyl, when's Leo coming over?"

"He may manage this next weekend, I'm not sure. But definitely for Easter, with the children. D'you have to go? Stay to lunch if you like. Maria's done the vegetables, thank goodness—how I hate potatoes in the raw!—and the rest's cold. Won't you stay?"

"I'd like to, but I want to get back to the telephone. There may be news."

"Oh, yes, of course. You'll phone me straight away if you hear anything, won't you?"

"Certainly." He picked up the portfolio. "Let me know as soon as you think Maria would like to see me."

He said his good-byes, and went. We sat in silence till the engine of his car faded among the trees.

"Well," said my sister, "I suppose we'd better find something to eat. Poor Godfrey, he's taking it hard. A bit surprising, really, I never thought he'd be knocked endways quite like that. He must have been fonder of Spiro than he cares to admit."

"Phyl," I said abruptly.

"Mm?"

"Was that true, or was it just another of your stories, when you said Julian Gale was probably Miranda's father?"

She looked at me sideways. "Well . . . Oh, damn it, Lucy, you don't have to take everything quite so literally! Heaven knows—but there's *something* in it, only I don't know what. He christened the girl 'Miranda,' and can you imagine any Corfiote hatching up a name like that? And then Maria's husband deserted them. What's more, I'll swear Julian Gale's been supporting the family. Maria's never said a word, but Miranda's let things drop once or twice, and I'm sure he does. And why, tell me that? Not just because he happened to know the husband during the war!"

"Then if Miranda and Spiro are twins, he's Spiro's father, too?"

"The facts of life being what they are, you might even be right. Oh!" She went rigid in her chair, and turned large eyes on me. "You mean—you mean someone ought to go and break the news to *him?*" All at once she looked very uncertain and flustered. "But, Lucy, it's only a rumor, and one could hardly *assume* it, could one? I mean, think if one went over there, and—"

"I didn't mean that," I said. "In any case, it's not our job to tell him, Maria'll tell him herself. He'll hear soon enough. Forget it. Where's this lunch you were talking about? I'm starving."

As I followed her out to the kitchen, I was reflecting that Julian Gale had almost certainly had the news already. From my chair facing the *salotto* windows, I had seen Maria and her daughter leave the house together. And not by the drive that would take them back to their own cottage. They had taken the little path that Miranda had shown me that morning, the path that led only to the empty bay, or to the Castello dei Fiori.

4

He is drown'd
Whom thus we stray to find, and the sea mocks
Our frustrate search on land. Well, let him go.

Act III, Scene 3

DAYS WENT by; peaceful, lovely days. I kept my word, and went down daily to the bay. Sometimes the dolphin came, though never near enough for me to touch him, and, although I knew that for the animal's own sake I ought to try to frighten him and drive him away, his friendly presence delighted me so much that I couldn't bring myself to what would seem an act of betrayal.

I did keep a wary eye on the Castello terrace, but there was no further shooting incident, nor had there been any rumor that a local man might have been trespassing with a rifle. But I swam every day, and watched, and never left the bay until the dolphin had finally submerged and headed for the open sea.

There had been no news of Spiro. Maria and her daughter had come back to the Villa Forli the morning after the boy's death, and had gone stoically on with their work. Miranda had lost the plump brightness that characterized her; she looked as if she cried a lot, and her voice and movements were subdued. I saw little of Maria, who kept mostly to the kitchen, going silently about her work with the black headkerchief pulled across her face.

The weather was brilliant, and hot even in the shade. Phyllida was rather listless. Once or twice she went with me on my sightseeing trips, or into the town of Corfu, and one evening Godfrey Manning took us both to dine at the Corfu Palace Hotel, but on the whole the week slipped quietly by, while I bathed and sat on the terrace with Phyllida, or took the little car and drove myself out in the afternoons to explore.

Leo, Phyllida's husband, hadn't managed to get away for the weekend, and Palm Sunday came without a visit from him. Phyllida had advised me to go into the town that morning to watch the Palm Sunday procession, which is one of the four occasions in the year when the island Saint, Spiridion, is brought out of the church where he lies the year round in a dim shrine all smoky with taperlight, and is carried through the streets in his golden palanquin. It is not an image of the Saint, but his actual mummified body which is carried in the procession, and this, somehow, makes him a very personal and homely kind of patron saint to have: the islanders believe that he has Corfu and all its people in his personal and always benevolent care, and has nothing to do but concern himself deeply in all their affairs, however trivial—which may explain why, on the procession days, just about the whole population of the island crowds into the town to greet him.

"What's more," said my sister, "it's a *pretty* procession, not just a gaggle of top brass. And St. Spiro's golden chair is beautiful; you can see his face quite clearly through the glass. You'd think it would be creepy, but it's not, not a bit. He's so tiny, and so . . . well, he's a sort of *cozy* saint!" She laughed. "If you stay long in Corfu you'll begin to get the feeling you know him personally. He's pretty well in charge of the island, you know: looks after the fishing, raises the wind, watches the weather for the crops, brings your boys safe home from sea . . ." She stopped, then sighed. "Poor Maria. I wonder if she'll go today. She doesn't usually miss it."

"What about you?" I asked. "Are you sure you won't come with me?"

She shook her head. "I'll stay at home. You have to stand about for rather a long time while the procession goes past, and there'll be a bit of a crush. Caliban and I take up too much room. Home for lunch? . . . Good. Well, enjoy yourself."

The little town of Corfu was packed with a holiday crowd, and the air was loud with bells. Caught up in the river of people which flowed through the narrow streets, I wandered happily along under the sound of the bells, which competed with the subdued roar of voices and the occasional bursts of raucous brass from some upper window, where a village band was struggling with some last-minute practice. Shops were open, selling food and sweets and toys, their windows crammed with scarlet eggs ready for Easter, cockerels, dolls, baskets of tiny crystallized oranges, or enormous rabbits laden with Easter eggs. Someone tried to sell me a sponge the size of a football, and someone else to convince me that I must need a string of onions and a red plush donkey, but I managed to stay unburdened, and presently found my way to the Esplanade, which is Corfu's main square. Here the pavements were already packed, but when I tried to take my place at the back, the peasants—who must have come into town in the early morning and waited hours for their places—made way for me with insistent gestures, almost forcing me forward into the place of honor.

Presently, from somewhere, a big bell struck, and there came the distant sound of the bands starting up. The vast crowd fell almost silent, all eyes turned to watch the narrow mouth of Nikephoros Street, where the first banners glinted, slowly moving up into the sunlight of the square. The procession had begun.

I am not sure what I had expected—a spectacle at once quaint and interesting, because "foreign"—something to take photographs of, and then forget, till you got them out to look at, some evening at home. In fact, I found it very moving.

The bands—there were four of them, all gorgeously uniformed—played solemnly and rather badly, each a different tune. The village banners with their pious legends were crudely painted, enormous, and cruelly heavy, so that the men carrying them sweated and trembled under the weight, and the faces of the boys helping them wore expressions of fierce and dedicated gravity. There were variations in the uniforms of the schoolchildren that were distinctly unconventional, but the standard of personal beauty was so high that one hardly noticed the shabby coats of the boys, or the cheap shoes the girls wore; and the young servicemen in their reach-me-down uniforms, with their noticeable absence of pipe clay and their ragged timing, had still about them, visibly, the glamor of two Thermopylaes.

And there was never a moment's doubt that all this was done in honor of the

Saint. Crowded along the pavements in the heat, the people watched in silence, neither moving nor pushing. There were no police, as there would have had to be in Athens: this was their own Spiridion, their island's patron, come out into the sunlight to bless them.

And here he came. The Archbishop, a white-bearded ninety-two, walked ahead, followed by Church dignitaries, whose robes of saffron and white and rose shone splendidly in the sun, until, as they passed nearer, you saw the rubbed and faded patches, and the darns. Then came the forest of tall white candles, each with its gilt crown and wreath of flowers, and each one fluttering its long ribbons of white and lilac and scarlet. Then finally, flanked by the four great gilded lanterns, and shaded by its canopy, the gold palanquin approached, with the Saint himself inside it, sitting up for all to see; a tiny, withered mummy, his head sagging on to his left shoulder, the dead features flattened and formless, a pattern of shadows behind the gleaming glass.

All around me, the women crossed themselves, and their lips moved. The Saint and his party paused for prayer, and the music stopped. A gun boomed once in salute from the Old Fort, and as the echo died a flight of pigeons went over, their wings whistling in the silence.

I stood watching the colored ribbons glinting in the sun, the wreaths of flowers fading already, and hanging crookedly from the crowned candles; the old, upraised hand of the Archbishop, and the faces of the peasant women near me, rapt and shining under the snowy coifs. To my own surprise, I felt my throat tighten, as if with tears.

A woman sobbed, in sudden, uncontrollable distress. The sound was loud in the silence, and I had glanced round before I could prevent myself. Then I saw it was Miranda. She was standing some yards from me, back among the crowd, staring with fiercely intent eyes at the palanquin, her lips moving as she crossed herself repeatedly. There were passion and grief in her face, as if she were reproaching the Saint for his negligence. There was nothing irreverent in such a thought: the Greek's religion is based on such simplicities. I suppose the old Church knew how great an emotional satisfaction there is in being able to lay the blame squarely and personally where it belongs.

The procession had passed; the crowd was breaking up. I saw Miranda duck back through it, as if ashamed of her tears, and walk quickly away. The crowds began to filter back again down the narrow main streets of the town, and I drifted with the tide, back down Nikephoros Street, toward the open space near the harbor where I had left the car.

Halfway down, the street opens into a little square. It chanced that as I passed this I saw Miranda again. She was standing under a plane tree, with her back to me and her hands up to her face. I thought she was weeping.

I hesitated, but a man who had been hovering near, watching her, now walked across and spoke. She neither moved nor gave any sign that she had heard him, but stood still with her back turned to him and her head bowed. I couldn't see his face, but he was young, with a strong and graceful build that the cheap navy blue of his Sunday best suit could not disguise.

He moved up closer behind the girl, speaking softly and, it seemed, with a sort of urgent persuasion. It appeared to me from his gestures that he was pressing her to go with him up one of the side streets away from the crowd; but at this she shook her head, and I saw her reach quickly for the corner of her kerchief and pull it across to hide her face. Her attitude was one of shy, even shrinking, dejection.

I went quickly across to them.

"Miranda? It's Miss Lucy. I have the car here, and I'm going back now. Would you like me to take you home?"

She did turn then. Above the kerchief her eyes were swollen with tears. She nodded without speaking.

I hadn't looked at the youth, assuming that he would now give up his importunities and vanish into the crowd. But he, too, swung round, exclaiming as though in relief.

"Oh, thank you! That's very kind! She ought not to have come, of course—and now there's no bus for an hour! Of course she must go home!"

I found myself staring, not at his easy assumption of responsibility for the girl, or even at the near perfect English he spoke, but simply because of his looks.

In a country where beauty among the young is a commonplace, he was still striking. He had the fine Byzantine features, with the clear skin and huge, long-lashed eyes that one sees staring down from the walls of every church in Greece; the type which El Greco himself immortalized, and which still, recognizably, walks the streets. Not that this young man conformed in anything but the brilliant eyes and the hauntingly perfect structure of the face: there was nothing to be seen here of the melancholy and weakness which (understandably) tends to afflict the saintly persons who spend their days gazing down from the plaster on the church walls—the small-lipped mouths, the meekly slanted heads, the air of resignation and surprise with which the Byzantine saint properly faces the sinful world. This youth had, indeed, the air of one who had faced the sinful world for some years now, but had obviously liked it enormously, and had cheerfully sampled a good deal of what it had to offer. No church-plaster saint, this one. And not, I judged, a day over nineteen.

The beautiful eyes were taking me in with the frank appraisal of the Greek. "You must be Miss Waring?"

"Why, yes," I said, in surprise; then suddenly saw who, inevitably, this must be. "And you're—Adonis?"

I couldn't for the life of me help bringing out the name with the kind of embarrassment one would feel in labeling one's own compatriot "Venus" or "Cupid." That in Greece one could meet any day a Pericles, an Aspasia, an Electra, or even an Alcibiades, didn't help at all. It was the looks that did it.

He grinned. He had very white teeth, and eyelashes at least an inch long. "It's a bit much, isn't it? In Greek we say 'Àdoni.'" (He pronounced it *À-thoni*.) "Perhaps you'd find that easier to say? Not quite so sissy?"

"You know too much by half!" I said involuntarily and quite naturally, and he laughed, then sobered abruptly.

"Where is your car, Miss Waring?"

"It's down near the harbor." I looked dubiously at the crowded street, then at the girl's bent head. "It's not far, but there's a dreadful crowd."

"We can go by a back way." He indicated a narrow opening at the corner of the square, where steps led up into the shadow between two tall houses.

I glanced again at the silent girl, who waited passively. "She will come," said Adoni, and spoke to her in Greek, briefly, then turned to me and began to usher me across the square and up the steps. Miranda followed, keeping a pace or so behind us.

He said in my ear, "It was a mistake for her to come, but she is very religious. She should have waited. It is barely a week since he died."

"You knew him well, didn't you?"

"He was my friend." His face shut, as if everything had been said. As, I suppose, it had.

"I'm sorry," I said.

We walked for a while in silence. The alleys were deserted, save for the thin cats, and the singing birds in cages on the walls. Here and there, where a gap in the houses laid a blazing wedge of sunlight across the stones, dusty kittens baked themselves in patches of marigolds, or very old women peered from the black doorways. The smell of charcoal-cooking hung in the warm air. Our steps echoed up the walls, while from the main streets the sound of talk and laughter surged back to us, muted like the roar of a river in a distant gorge. Eventually our way opened into a broader lane, and a long flight of shallow steps, which dropped down past a church wall straight to the harbor square where I had left Phyl's little Fiat.

There were crowds here, too, but these were broken knots of people, moving purposefully in search of transport home, or the midday meal. Nobody paid any attention to us.

Adoni, who apparently knew the car, shouldered his way purposefully through the groups of people, and held out a hand to me for the keys.

Almost as meekly as Miranda (who hadn't yet spoken a word) I handed them over, and our escort unlocked the doors and ushered her into the back seat. She got in with bent head, and sat well back in a corner. I wondered, with some amusement, if this masterful young man intended to drive us both home—and whether Phyl would mind—but he made no such attempt. He shut the driver's door on me and then got in beside me.

"You are used to our traffic now?"

"Oh, yes." If he meant was I used to driving on the right-hand side, I was. As for traffic, there was none in Corfu worth mentioning: if I met one lorry and half a dozen donkeys on an average afternoon's excursion, it was the most I had had to contend with. But today there was the packed and teeming harbor boulevard, and possibly because of this, Adoni said nothing more as we weaved our way through the people and out on to the road north. We climbed a steep, badly cambered turn, and then the road was clear between high hedges of judas trees and asphodel. The surface was in places badly pitted by the winter's rain, so I had to drive slowly, and the third gear was noisy. Under cover of its noise I said quietly to Adoni:

"Will Miranda and her mother be able to keep themselves, now that Spiro has gone?"

"They will be cared for." It was said flatly, and with complete confidence.

I was surprised, and also curious. If Godfrey Manning had made an offer, he would surely have told Phyllida so; and besides, whatever he chose to give Maria now, he would hardly feel that he owed this kind of conscience money. But if it was Julian Gale who was providing for the family, as Phyllida had alleged, it might mean that her story of the twins' parentage was true. I would have been less than human if I hadn't madly wanted to know.

I put out a cautious feeler. "I'm glad to hear that. I didn't realize there was some other relative."

"Well," said Adoni, "there is Sir Gale, in a way, but I didn't mean him or Max. I meant that I would look after them myself."

"You?"

He nodded, and I saw him throw a half glance over his shoulder at Miranda. I could see her in the driving mirror; she was taking no notice of our soft conversation in English, which in any case may have been too rapid for her to follow, but was staring dully out of the window, obviously miles away. Adoni leaned forward and put a finger on the radio button, a gadget without which no Greek or Italian car ever seems to take the road. "You permit?"

"Of course."

Some pop singer from Athens Radio mooed from under the dash. Adoni said quietly, "I shall marry her. There is no dowry, but that's no matter, Spiro was my friend, and one has obligations. He had saved to provide for her, but now that he is dead her mother must keep it; I can't take it."

I knew that in the old Greek marriage contract, the girl brought goods and land, the boy nothing but his virility, and this was considered good exchange; but families with a crop of daughters to marry off had been beggared before now, and Miranda, circumstanced as she was, would hardly have had a hope of marriage. Now here was this handsome boy calmly offering her a contract which any family would have been glad to accept, and one in which, moreover, he was providing all the capital; of the virility there could certainly be no doubt, and besides, he had a good job in a country where jobs are scarce, and, if I was any judge of character, he would keep it. The handsome Adoni would have been a bargain at any reckoning. He knew this, of course, he'd have been a fool not to; but it seemed that he felt a duty to his dead friend, and from what I had seen of him, he would fulfill it completely, efficiently, and to everyone's satisfaction— not least Miranda's. And besides (I thought prosaically), Leo would probably come through with a handsome wedding present.

"Of course," added Adoni, "Sir Gale may give her a dowry, I don't know. But it would make no difference; I shall take her. I haven't told her so yet, but later, when it's more fitting, I shall tell Sir Gale, and he will arrange it."

"I— Yes, of course. I hope you'll both be very happy."

"Thank you."

I said, "Sir Julian is— He makes himself responsible for them, then?"

"He was godfather to the twins." He glanced at me. "I think you have this in England, don't you, but it is not quite the same? Here in Greece, the godfather, the *koumbàros,* is very important in the child's life, often as important as the real father, and it is he who arranges the marriage contract."

"I see." As simple as that. "I did know Sir Julian had known the family for years, and had christened the twins, but I don't know he—well, had a responsibility. The accident must have been a dreadful shock to him, too." I added awkwardly, "How is he?"

"He is well. Have you met him yet, Miss Waring?"

"No. I understood he didn't see anyone."

"He doesn't go out much, it's true, but since the summer he has had visitors. You've met Max, though, haven't you?"

"Yes." There had been nothing in Adoni's voice to show what he knew about that meeting, but since he called him "Max," without prefix, one might assume a relationship informal enough for Max to have told him just what had passed. Anyway, this was the faithful watchdog who threw the callers over the cliff. No doubt he had heard all about it—and might even have had orders regarding further encroachments by Miss Lucy Waring. . . .

I added woodenly, "I understood he didn't see anyone, either."

"Well, it depends," said Adoni cheerfully. He pulled a duster out from somewhere under the dashboard, and began to polish the inside of the screen. "Not that this helps much, it's all the insects that get squashed on the outside. We're nearly there, or you could stop and I'd do it for you."

"It doesn't matter, thanks."

So that was as far as I'd get. In any case, Miranda seemed to be coming back to life. The back seat creaked as she moved, and in the mirror I could see that she had put back her kerchief and was watching the back of Adoni's head. Something in her expression, still blurred though it was with tears, indicated that I had been right about the probable success of the marriage.

I said, in the brisk tone of one who changes the subject to neutral ground, "Do you ever go out shooting, Adoni?"

He laughed, undeceived. "Are you still looking for your criminal? I think you must have been mistaken—there's no Greek would shoot a dolphin. I am a sailor, too—all Corfiotes are sailors—and the dolphin is the beast of fair weather. We even call it 'dolphin weather'—the summertime, when the dolphins go with the boats. No, me, I only shoot people."

"People?"

"That was a joke," explained Adoni. "Here we are. Thank you very much for bringing us. I'll take Miranda to her mother now, then I've promised to go back to the Castello. Max wants to go out this afternoon. Perhaps I shall see you there soon?"

"Thank you, but I— No, I doubt if you will."

"That would be a pity. While you are here, you should see the orange orchards; they are something quite special. You have heard of the *koùm koyàts*—the miniature trees? They are very attractive." That quick, enchanting smile. "I should like to show them to you."

"Perhaps sometime."

"I hope so. Come, Miranda."

As I put the car into gear, I saw him usher the silent girl through her mother's door as if he already owned the place. Suppressing a sharp—and surely primitive—envy for a woman who could have her problems simply taken out of her hands and solved for her, willy-nilly, I put down my own independent and emancipated foot and sent the little Fiat bucketing over the ruts of the drive and down the turning to the Villa Forli.

At least, if Max Gale was to be out, I could have my afternoon swim in peace.

I went down after tea, when the heat was slackening off and the cliff cast a crescent of shade at the edge of the sand.

Afterward I dressed, picked up my towel, and began slowly to climb the path back to the villa.

When I reached the little clearing where the pool lay, I paused to get my breath. The trickle of the falling stream was cool and lovely, and light spangled down golden through the young oak leaves. A bird sang somewhere, but only one. The woods were silent, stretching away dim-shadowed in the heat of the late afternoon. Bee orchises swarmed by the water, over a bank of daisies. A blue tit flew across the clearing, obviously in a great hurry, its beak stuffed with insects for the waiting family.

A moment later the shriek came, a bird's cry of terror, then the rapid, machine-gun swearing of the parent tit. Some other small birds joined the clamor. The shrieks of terror jagged through the peaceful woods. I dropped my towel on the grass, and ran toward the noise.

The blue tits met me, the two parent birds, fluttering and shrieking, their wings almost brushing me as I ran up a twisting path and out into the open stretch of thin grass and irises where the tragedy was taking place.

This couldn't have been easier to locate. The first thing I saw as I burst from the bushes was a magnificent white Persian cat, crouched picturesquely to spring, tail jerking to and fro in the scanty grass. Two yards from his nose, crying wildly, and unable to move an inch, was the baby blue tit. The parents, with anguished cries, darted repeatedly and ineffectually at the cat, which took not the slightest notice.

I did the only possible thing. I dived on the cat in a flying tackle, took him gently by the body, and held him fast. The tits swept past me, their wings brushing my hands. The little one sat corpse-still now, not even squeaking.

I suppose I could have been badly scratched, but the white cat had strong nerves and excellent manners. He spat furiously, which was only to be expected, and wriggled to be free, but he neither scratched nor bit. I held him down, talking soothingly till he was quiet, then lifted him and turned away, while behind me the parent birds swooped down to chivvy their baby out of sight.

I hurried my captive out of the clearing before he got a chance to see where the birds were making for, and away at random through the bushes. Far from objecting to this, the cat seemed now rather pleased at the attention than otherwise; having had to surrender to *force majeure,* he managed—in the way of his species—to let me know that he did in fact prefer to be carried. . . . And when, presently, I found myself toiling up a ferny bank which grew steeper, and steeper yet, he even began to purr.

This was too much. I stopped.

"I'll tell you something," I said to him, "you weigh a ton. You can darned well walk, Butch, as from now! And I hope you know your way home from here, because I'm not letting you go back to those birds!"

I put him down. Still purring, he stropped himself against me a couple of times, then strolled ahead of me up the bank, tail high, to where at the top the bushes thinned to show bright sunlight. There he paused, glancing back and down at me, before stalking forward out of view.

He knew his way, no doubt of that. Hoping there was a path there that would take me back clear of the tangled bushes, I clambered up in his wake, to find myself in a big clearing, full of sunshine, the hum of bees, and a blaze of flowers that pulled me up short, gaping.

After the dappled dimness of the woods, it took some moments before one could do more than blink at the dazzle of color. Straight ahead of me an arras of wistaria hung fully fifteen feet, and below it there were roses. Somewhere to one side was a thicket of purple judas trees, and apple blossom glinting with the wings of working bees. Arum lilies grew in a damp corner, and some other lily with petals like gold parchment, transparent in the light. And everywhere, roses. Great bushes of them rampaged up the trees; a blue spruce was half smothered with sprays of vivid Persian pink, and one dense bush of frilled white roses must have been ten feet high. There were moss roses, musk roses, damask roses, roses pied and streaked, and one old pink rose straight from a medieval manuscript, hemispherical, as if a knife had sliced it across, its hundred petals as tightly whorled and packed as the layers of an onion. There must have been twenty or thirty varieties there, all in full bloom; old roses, planted years ago and left to run wild, as if in some secret garden whose key is lost. The place seemed hardly real.

I must have stood stock-still for some minutes, looking about me, dizzied with the scent and the sunlight. I had forgotten roses could smell like that. A spray of speckled carmine brushed my hand, and I broke it off and held it to my face. Deep among the leaves, in the gap I had made, I saw the edge of an old metal label, and reached gingerly for it among the thorns. It was thick with lichen, but the stamped name showed clearly: Belle de Crécy.

I knew where I was now. Roses: they had been another hobby of Leo's grandfather. Phyl had some of his books up at the Villa, and I had turned them over idly the other night, enjoying the plates and the old names which evoked, like poetry, the old gardens of France, of Persia, of Provence . . . Belle de Crécy, Belle Isis, Deuil du Roi de Rome, Rosamunde, Camaïeux, Ispahan . . .

The names were all there, hidden deep in the rampant leaves, where some predecessor of Adoni's had lovingly attached them a century ago. The white cat, posing in front of an elegant background of dark fern, watched benevolently as I hunted for them, my hands filling with plundered roses. The scent was heavy as a drug. The air zoomed with bees. The general effect was of having strayed out of the dark wood into some fairy tale. One almost expected the cat to speak.

When the voice did come, suddenly, from somewhere above, it nearly startled me out of my wits. It was a beautiful voice, and it enhanced, rather than broke, the spell. It spoke, moreover, in poetry, as deliberately elegant as the white cat:

> " 'Most sure, the goddess
> On whom these airs attend! Vouchsafe my prayer
> May know if you remain upon this Island . . .' "

I peered upward, at first seeing no one. Then a man's head appeared at the top of the wistaria—and only then did I realize that the curtain of blossom hung in fact down some kind of high retaining wall, which it had hidden. I saw, between the thick trusses of flowers, sections of the stone balustrading. The terrace of the Castello. The rose garden had been planted right up beside it.

I wanted to turn and run, but the voice held me. Needless to say, it was not Max Gale's; this was a voice I had heard many times before, spinning just such a toil of grace as this in the stuffy darkness of London theatres.

" 'My prime request,' " added Sir Julian Gale, " 'Which I do last pronounce,' and which in fact you may think impertinent, 'is, O you wonder! If you be maid, or no?' "

I suppose if I had met him normally, on our common ground of the theatre, I might have been too overawed to do more than stutter. But here at least the answer was laid down in the text, and had, besides, the advantage of being the truth. I narrowed my eyes against the sun, and smiled up at the head.

> " 'No wonder, sir,
> But certainly a maid.' "

"My language! Heavens!" The actor abruptly abandoned the Bard, and looked delighted. "I was right! You're Max's trespasser!"

I felt myself flushing. "I'm afraid I am, and I seem to be trespassing again. I'm terribly sorry, I didn't realize the terrace was quite so near. I wouldn't have dreamed of coming so far up, but I was rescuing a bird from Butch there."

"From whom?"

"The cat. Is he yours? I suppose he's called something terribly aristocratic, like Florizel, or Cosimo dei Fiori?"

"As a matter of fact," said Julian Gale, "I call him Nit. I'm sorry, but it's short for Nitwit, and when you get to know him, you'll see why. He's a gentleman, but he has very little brain. Now you're here, won't you come up?"

"Oh, no!" I spoke hastily, backing a little. "Thanks all the same, but I've got to get back."

"I can't believe there's all that hurry. Won't you please take pity on me and break the deadly Sabbath peace up a little? Ah!" He leaned farther over. "Not only trespass, I see, but theft as well! You've been stealing my roses!"

This statement, uttered in the voice whose least whisper was clearly audible in the back row of the gallery, had all the force of an accusation made before the High Praesidium. I started guiltily, glanced down at the forgotten blooms in my hands, and stammered:

"Well, yes, I—I have. Oh, murder . . . I never thought . . . I mean, I took it they were sort of wild. You know, planted ages ago and just left . . ." My voice faltered as I looked round me and saw what I hadn't noticed before, that the bushes, in spite of their riotous appearance, were well shaped, and that the edges of the mossed paths were tidily clipped. "I—I suppose this is your garden now, or something? I'm most terribly sorry!"

"'Or something'? By heaven, she picks an armful of my beloved Gallicas, and then thinks they come out of my garden 'or something'! That settles it, young woman! By all the rules you have to pay a forfeit. If Beauty strays into the Beast's garden, literally loaded with his roses, she's asking for trouble, isn't she? Come along, now, and no arguments! There are the steps, Nit'll bring you up. Nitwit! Show the lady the way!"

The white cat rose, blinked at me, then swarmed in an elaborately careless manner up the wistaria, straight into Julian Gale's arms. The latter straightened, smiling.

"Did I say he hadn't much brain? I traduced him. Do you think you could manage something similar?"

His charm, the charm that had made Phyllida fall for him "like a ton of bricks," was having its effect. I believe I had completely forgotten what else she had told me about him.

I laughed. "In my own plodding way, I might."

"Then come along."

The way up was a flight of shallow steps, half hidden by a bush of York and Lancaster. It curved round the base of some moss-green statue, and brought me out between two enormous cypresses, on to the terrace.

Julian Gale had set the cat down, and now advanced on me.

"Come in, Miss Lucy Waring. You see, I've heard all about you. And here's my son. But of course you've already met. . . ."

5

You do look, my son, in a mov'd sort,
As if you were dismay'd. Be cheerful, sir . . .

Act IV, Scene 1

MAX GALE was sitting there under the stone pine, at a big table covered with papers. As he got to his feet, I stopped in my tracks.

"But I thought you weren't here!" I hadn't thought I could have blurted out anything quite so naïve. I finished the performance by blushing furiously and adding, in confusion, "Adoni said . . . I thought . . . I'm sure he said you'd be out!"

"I was, but only till teatime. How do you do?" His eyes, indifferent rather than hostile, touched mine briefly, and dropped to the roses in my hands. It was possibly only to fill the sizzling pause of embarrassment that he asked, "Was Adoni down in the garden?"

I saw Sir Julian's glance flick from one to the other of us. "He was not, or he might have stopped her pillaging the place! She's made a good selection, hasn't she? I thought she should be made to pay a forfeit, *à la* Beauty and the Beast. We'll let her off the kiss on such short acquaintance, but she'll have to stay and have a drink with us, at least!"

I thought I saw the younger man hesitate, and his glance went down to the littered table as if looking there for a quick excuse. There wasn't far to look; the table was spread with scribbled manuscript scores, notebooks, and papers galore, and on a chair beside it stood a tape recorder with a long flex that trailed over the flags and in through an open French window.

I said quickly, "Thank you, but I really can't—"

"You're in no position to refuse, young lady!" Sir Julian's eyes held a gleam of amusement, whether at my reluctance or his son's it was impossible to guess. "Come now, half an hour spent entertaining a recluse is a small price to pay for your loot. Have we some sherry, Max?"

"Yes, of course." The colorlessness of his voice might after all only be in comparison with his father's. "I'm afraid we've no choice, Miss Waring. Do you like it dry?"

"Well . . ." I hesitated. I would have to stay now. I could hardly snub Sir Julian, who was after all my host, and besides, I had no wish to pass up the chance to talk to a man who was at the head of my own profession, and whom I had admired and loved for as long as I could remember. "Actually, if there is one, I'd love a long drink, long and cold . . . ? I've just been swimming, and I'm genuinely thirsty. Would there be any orange juice, or something like that?"

"You ask that here? Of course." Max Gale smiled at me suddenly, and with unexpected charm, and went into the house.

As at the Villa Forli, there were long windows opening from the terrace into some big room, all of them shuttered against the sun except the one through which Max Gale had vanished. Through this dark opening I thought I could make out the shapes of a grand piano, what looked like a huge gramophone, and a revolving bookcase. The tops of the two last were stacked with books and records.

"Sun or shade?" asked Sir Julian, pulling up a gaudy camp chair for me. I chose sun, and he settled himself beside me, the somber wall of cypresses beyond the balustrade making as effective a backcloth for him as the ferns had for the white cat. The latter, purring, jumped up on to the actor's knee, turned carefully round twice, and settled down, paws going.

The pair of them made a striking picture. Sir Julian was not—had never been—handsome, but he was a big man, of the physical type to which the years can add a sort of heavy splendor. (One remembered his Mark Antony, and how after it all other attempts at the part seemed to be variations of his; attempts, in fact, to play *him*.) He had the powerful breadth of chest and shoulder that runs to weight in middle age, and his head was what is commonly called leonine—thick gray hair, a brow and nose in the grand manner, and fine gray eyes—but with some hint of weakness about the jaw from which the charm of the wide mouth distracted you. His eyes looked pouchy and a little strained, and there were sagging lines in his face which naturally I had never seen across the footlights, lines which might be those of petulance or dissipation, or merely a result of his illness and consequent loss of weight. It was difficult to tell just where his undeniable attractiveness lay; it would, indeed, be hard to give any definite description of him: his face was too familiar for that, melting as one watched him into one character after another that he had made his own, as if the man existed only as one saw him on the stage—king, madman, insurance salesman, soldier, fop . . . as if in leaving that lighted frame, he ceased to exist. It was a disquieting idea when one remembered that he had, in fact, left his frame. If he could not be himself now, he was nothing.

He glanced up from the cat, caught me staring, and smiled. He must be very used to it. What he cannot have realized is that I was trying to find in his face and movements some evidence of nervous strain that might justify Phyllida's fears. But he seemed quite self-contained and relaxed, his hands (those betrayers) lying motionless and elegantly disposed—perhaps just a bit too elegantly disposed?—over the cat's fur.

"I'm sorry," I said, "was I staring? I've never been so close to you before. It's usually the upper circle."

"With me tastefully disguised behind several pounds of false beard, and robed and crowned at that? Well, here you see the man himself, poor, bare forked creature that he is. I won't ask you what you think of him, but you must at least give me your opinion of his setting. What do you think of our crumbling splendors?"

"The Castello? Well, since you ask . . . I'd have said it wasn't quite *you*. It would make a marvelous background for a Gothic thriller—*Frankenstein,* or *The Mysteries of Udolpho,* or something."

"It would, wouldn't it? One feels it ought to be permanently shrouded in mist, with vampires crawling down the walls—not surrounded by flowers, and the peace and sunshine of this enchanted island. However, I suppose it's highly appropriate for a decayed actor to retire to, and it's certainly a haven of peace, now that Max has clamped down on the sightseers."

"I heard you'd been ill. I'm sorry. We—we miss you terribly in London."

"Do you, my dear? That's nice of you. Ah, Max, here you are. Miss Waring thinks the house is a perfect setting for Frankenstein and his monster."

"I did not! I never said—I certainly didn't put it like that!"

Max Gale laughed. "I heard what you said. You could hardly insult this kind of crazy baroque anyway. Loco rococo. This is fresh orange, is that all right for you?"

"Lovely, thank you."

He had brought the same for himself, and for his father. I noticed that the latter's hand, as he put it out for the glass, shook badly, and his son quickly lifted a small iron table within reach, set the glass down on that, and poured the iced juice in. Sir Julian dropped his hands back into the cat's fur, where they once more lay statue-still. I had been right about the self-consciousness of that pose. But it hadn't been vanity, unless it is vanity that conceals a weakness of which one is ashamed.

As Max Gale poured my drink, I made to lay the roses on the table, but he set the jug down and put out a hand.

"Give them to me. I'll put them in water for you till you go."

"So I'm to be allowed to keep them, after I've paid the forfeit?"

"My dear child," said Sir Julian, "you're welcome to the lot! I hope you don't take my teasing seriously, it was only an excuse to make you come up. I'm only glad you liked them so much."

"I love them. They look like the roses in old pictures—you know, *real* roses in old storybooks. *The Secret Garden,* and Andrew Lang's *Sleeping Beauty,* and *The Arabian Nights.*"

"That's just what they are. That one was found growing on a pavilion in Persia, where Haroun-al-Raschid may have seen it. This is the one out of the *Romance of the Rose.* And this was found growing in Fair Rosamund's garden at Woodstock. And this, they say, is the oldest rose in the world." His hands were almost steady as he touched the flowers one by one. "You must come back for more when these die. I'd leave them in the music room, Max, it's reasonably cool. . . . Now, pay up, Miss Lucy Waring. I'm told you're in the business, and one of the reasons I lured you up here was to hear all you can give me of the latest gossip. The facts I can get from the periodicals, but the gossip is usually a great deal more entertaining—and quite often twice as true. Tell me . . ."

I forget now just what he asked me, or how much I was able to tell him, but though I moved in very different theatrical circles from him, I did know a good deal of what was going on in town; and I remember that in my turn I found it exciting to hear him using, casually and in passing, names which were as far above my touch as the clouds on Mount Pantokrator. He certainly gave me the impression that he found me good value as an entertainer, but how far this was due to his own charm I can't guess, even today. I know that when, finally, he turned the conversation to my affairs, you'd have thought this was the big moment toward which all the star-spangled conversation had been leading.

"And now tell me about yourself. What are you doing, and where? And why have we never met before?"

"Oh, heavens, I'm not anywhere near your league! I'd only just got to the West End as it was!"

I stopped. The last phrase had been a dead giveaway, not only of the facts, but of feelings which I had not discussed, even with Phyllida. I had my vanities, too.

"Play folded?" Where a layman's sympathy would have jarred, his matter-of-fact tone was marvelously comforting. "What was it?"

I told him, and he nodded.

"Yes, that was McAndrew's pet pigeon, wasn't it? Not a very wise venture on Mac's part, I thought. I read the play. Who were you? What's-her-name, the girl who has those unlikely hysterics all over Act Two?"

"Shirley. Yes. I was rotten."

"There was nothing there to get hold of. That sort of fantasy masquerading as working-class realism needs rigid selection and perfect timing—not merely uncontrolled verbal vomit, if you'll forgive the phrase. And he never can do women, haven't you noticed?"

"Maggie in *The Single End*?"

"Do you call her a woman?"

"Well . . . I suppose you're right."

"I'm right in telling you not to blame yourself over Shirley. What comes next?"

I hesitated.

"Like that, is it?" he said. "Well, it happens. How wise of you to cut and run for Corfu while you could! I remember . . ." And he turned neatly off into a couple of malicious and very funny stories involving a well-known agent of the thirties, and a brash young actor whom I had no difficulty in identifying as Sir Julian Gale himself. When he had finished, and we had done laughing, I found myself countering with some of my own experiences which I had certainly never expected to find funny—or even to tell anybody about. Now, for some reason, to talk about them was a kind of release, even a pleasure, while the crenellated shadow of the Castello advanced unheeded across the weedy flags, and Sir Julian Gale listened, and commented, and asked questions, as if he had "lured" me to his terrace for no other reason than to hear the life story of a mediocre young actress who would never play anything but seconds in her life.

A slight sound stopped me, and brought me sharply round. I had forgotten all about Max Gale. I hadn't heard him come out of the house again, but he was there, sitting on the balustrade, well within hearing. How long he had been there I had no idea.

It was only then that I realized how the light had faded. My forfeit was paid, and it was time to be gone, but I could hardly take my leave within seconds, as it were, of acknowledging Max Gale's presence. I had to make some motion of civility toward him first.

I looked across at him. "Did you go to watch the procession this morning, Mr. Gale?"

"I? Yes, I was there. I saw you in the town. Did you get a good place?"

"I was on the Esplanade, at the corner by the Palace."

"It's rather . . . appealing, don't you think?"

"Very." I smiled. "Being a musician, you'd appreciate the bands."

He laughed, and all at once I saw his father in him. "Very much. And when all four play at the same time, it really is something."

"The leitmotiv for your *Tempest*, Max," said his father, stroking the white cat. " 'The isle is full of noises.' "

Max grinned. "Perhaps. Though even I might fight shy of reproducing some of them."

Sir Julian turned to me. "My son is writing a score for a film version of *The Tempest*."

"Is that what it's to be? How exciting! I gather you've come to the right place to do it, too. Is that why you chose Corfu after you'd drowned your book at Stratford, Sir Julian?"

"Not really; the thing's fortuitous. I've known the island on and off for thirty years, and I've friends here. But it's a pleasant chance that brought this work to Max when we happened to be marooned here."

"Do you really think this is Prospero's island?"

"Why not?" asked Julian Gale, and Max said, "That's torn it," and laughed. I looked at him in surprise. "What have I said?"

"Nothing. Nothing at all. But if you will invite a man to explain a theory he's been brooding over for weeks, you must be prepared for a lecture, and by the gleam in my father's eye, nothing can save you now."

"But I'd love to hear it! Besides, your father could make the Telephone Directory sound like *War and Peace* if he tried, so his private theory about *The Tempest* ought to be *something!* Don't take any notice of him, Sir Julian! Why do you think this might be Prospero's island?"

"You are a delightful young lady," said Sir Julian, "and if you wish to dig my roses out by the roots and carry them away, I shall send Adoni to help you. No, on second thought, Max can do it. It would be good for him to do a little real work, instead of floating around in the lunatic fringe where musicians seem to live. . . . Who was it who said that the really wise man isn't the man who wants a thing proved before he'll believe in it, but the man who is prepared to believe anything until it's shown to be false?"

"I don't know, but it sounds to me like somebody's definition of a visionary or a genius."

"*All* the roses," said Sir Julian warmly. "Did you hear that, Max? My theories about *The Tempest* are those of a visionary and a genius."

"Oh, sure," said his son.

He was still sitting on the balustrade, leaning back against the stone urn that stood at the corner. I had been watching his face covertly for some resemblance to his father, but, except for his build and an occasional chance expression, could see none. His eyes were dark, and more deeply set, the mouth straighter, the whole face less mobile. I thought the hint of the neurotic was there, too, in the faint lines between the brows, and somewhere in the set of the mouth. The careful underemphasis in all he said and did might well be a deliberate attempt to control this, or merely to avoid profiting by his father's charm. Where Sir Julian seemed automatically, as it were, to make the most of his lines, Max threw his away. It seemed to me that he was even concerned not to be liked, where his father, consciously or not, had the actor's need to be loved.

"There is no evidence of any kind," Sir Julian was saying, "to connect this island with the island of the play, any more than we can prove it was the 'Scheria' of Odysseus and Nausicaä; but in both cases tradition is strong, and when traditions persist hard enough it seems only sensible to conclude that there may be something in them worth investigating."

"Schliemann and Troy," murmured Max.

"Exactly," said Sir Julian. He gave me that sudden smile that was so like his son's. "So, being like Schliemann a genius and a visionary, and being determined to believe that Corfu *is* Prospero's island, I've been looking for evidence to prove it."

"And is there any?"

"Perhaps not 'evidence.' That's a strong word. But once you start looking, you can find all sorts of fascinating parallels. Start with the easiest, the description of the natural details of the island, if you can remember them."

"I think I can, fairly well. There's rather more physical description of the setting than you usually find in Shakespeare, isn't there?"

"I'd say more than anywhere, except *Venus and Adonis*. And what description one gleans from the play fits this island well enough: the pines, tilled lands, the fertility (not so many of the Mediterranean islands are really fertile, you know), the beaches and coves, the lime groves outside Prospero's cave . . ." He lifted a hand to point where a group of trees stood golden green beside the pines on the southern promontory. "There are young limes growing all down the cliff beyond Manning's villa, and the whole coast is honeycombed with caves. You might say these things are found on any island, but one thing isn't—the brine pits that Caliban talks about, remember?"

"And there are some here?"

"Yes, down at Korissia, in the south. They've been there for centuries."

"What about the pignuts and filberts he promised to dig up? Do they grow here?"

"Filberts certainly, and pignuts, too, if he means the English sort. And if he means truffles—as I believe—yes, those too."

"And the marmosets?" I asked it diffidently, as one who puts a question in doubtful taste.

Sir Julian waved the marmosets aside. "A momentary confusion with the still vex'd Bermoothes. No doubt Ariel had been shooting a nice line in travel tales, and the poor monster was muddled."

Max said, "You can't argue with a man with an obsession. Humor him, Miss Waring."

"I'll do no such thing! If a theory's worth holding, it's worth fighting over! What about the *story*, then, Sir Julian? Take the start of it, the shipwreck. If the ship was on its way from Tunis to Naples, you'd think Corfu was just a little too far off course—"

"Ah, yes, you run up against the same thing in the Odysseus story, where they're supposed to have rowed—rowed, mark you—from Scheria to Euboea in a single night. But to my mind, that does nothing to discount Corfu's claim to be Scheria. It's poetic truth, the kind of telescoping that you find in the seven days of Creation—one assumes that the gods helped them. The same with the Neapolitan ship in *The Tempest*. The storm was a tremendous one, an historic tempest. The ship was blown right off her course, and could have driven blindly along for days before fetching up on these coastal rocks. Can't you see that what makes the story plausible is its very unlikelihood?"

"Have a heart," said his son. "Of course she can't."

"It's very simple. The fact that the ship did end up here, so fantastically off course, made it necessary later on to explain the storm as being magical, or somehow supernatural."

"Just a minute," I said quickly. " 'The fact'? Are you trying to say that the business of the shipwreck is *true*?"

"Only that like all legends it could be founded on the truth, just as there really was a Cretan labyrinth, and a Troy that burned. It's my guess—strictly as a visionary—that there was in fact some spectacular wreck here that became the basis of a legend."

"No more than a guess? You haven't found any actual Corfiote story, or any real record?"

"No."

"Then why here? Why Corfu? Your geographical details don't prove a thing. They might confirm, but they're hardly a start."

Sir Julian nodded, smoothing the cat's head with a gentle finger. "I started at the wrong end. I should have begun not with the 'facts,' but with the play—the play's kingpin, Prospero. To my mind, the conception of his character is the most remarkable thing about the play; his use as a sort of summing up of Shakespeare's essay on human power. Look at the way he's presented: a father figure, a magician in control of natural forces like the winds and the sea, a sort of benevolent and supernatural Machiavelli who controls the island and all who are in it."

He finished on a faint note of inquiry, and looked at me with raised eyebrows, waiting for my reply.

"Saint Spiridion?"

"Saint Spiridion. Exactly!" He glanced up at Max, as if showing off the cleverness of a favorite pupil. I saw Max smile faintly. "Even the name . . . you'll notice the similarity; and its abbreviation, 'Spiro,' makes it even closer." The shadow which touched his face was gone immediately. "Saint Spiridion—his body, that is—was brought here in 1489, and in no time at all he had the reputation for all sorts of magic, miracles if you like, especially weather magic. There was another saint, a female, brought with him. Her mummy is also in a church in the town, but she didn't catch the public imagination, so she doesn't get the outings. In fact, I can't even remember her name."

"I've never even heard she existed," I said.

He smiled. "It's a man's country. But she may well be the origin of the *idea* of Miranda, the magician's daughter. She would hardly survive into legend merely as a female companion, or even as a wife. Magicians don't have them, for reasons which I suppose it would be fascinating to explore, but which you might disagree with, Miss Lucy Waring."

"I know, Delilah and Co. All right, I don't resent it, it's a man's world. If it comes to that, witches don't have husbands, not the real old fairy-story witches, anyway."

"Fair enough." Sir Julian leaned back in his chair. "Well, there you have your starting point, the fabulously fertile island of Corfu, guarded by a Saint who is believed to control the weather. Now we postulate a tempest, some historic humdinger of a storm, when some important ship—perhaps even with a few Italian VIP's on board—was driven far off course and wrecked here, but with her passengers saved from drowning by some apparent miracle that would be imputed to the Saint. So a legend starts to grow. Later the Germanic elements of fairy tale are added to it—the 'magic,' the beautiful daughter, the fairy characters." He paused, with a mischievous gleam at me. "It would be nice if one could somehow equate the elementals with the facts of the island's history, wouldn't it? I've tried my hardest to see the 'foul witch Sycorax' from 'Argier,' as a sort of personification of the Moslem rulers who penned the heavenly power—Ariel—in a cloven pine till the Saint-magician released him . . . But I'm afraid I can't quite make that one stick."

"What a pity!" I said it quite without irony: I was enjoying myself vastly. "And Caliban? Paganism or something?"

"If you like. There's the brutality, the sexuality, and the superbly sensitive poetry. And he was certainly a Greek."

"How d'you work that out?" I asked, startled.

He chuckled. "He welcomed Prospero to the island with 'water with berries in it.' Haven't you come across the Greek custom of giving you berried jam in a glass of water?"

"No, I haven't. But really, you can't have that! It could even be coffee! What would that make him? French?"

"All right," he said amiably, "we'll leave poor Caliban as an 'infernal' seeking for grace. Well, that's all." Here the white cat stretched, flexed its claws, and yawned, very loudly. Sir Julian laughed. "You shouldn't have encouraged me. Nitwit has heard it all before, and so, I'm afraid, has poor Max."

"Well, I hadn't, and it's fascinating. One could have endless fun. I must read it again and look for all these things. I wish I thought my sister had a copy here."

"Take mine," he said immediately. "It should be somewhere on top of the bookcase, I think, Max. . . . Thanks very much." This as his son went to get it.

I said quickly, "But if you're working on it—"

"Working?" The word, lightly spoken as it was, sounded somehow out of tune. "You've just heard how seriously. In any case, I use a Penguin for working, one I can mark and cut up . . . Ah, thank you, Max; and here are your roses, too. That's my own copy; it's a bit ancient, and I'm afraid it's been scribbled in, but perhaps you can ignore that."

I had already seen the penciled notes. Holding the book as if it were the original Blackfriars prompt copy, with the author's jottings in the margin, I got to my feet. Sir Julian rose with me, and the white cat, displaced, jumped down and stalked with offended dignity off the terrace and down to the steps to the rose garden.

"I'll really have to go," I said. "Thank you for the book, I'll take great care of it. I—I know I've stayed far too long, but I've really loved it."

"My dear child, you've done us both a kindness. I've enjoyed your visit enormously, and I hope you'll come back soon. As you see, there's a limit to the amount of my conversation that Max and the cat will stand, and it's pleasant to have a good-mannered and captive audience again. Well, if you must . . ."

The woods were dark already with the quickly falling twilight. Mr. Gale, accompanying me politely to the edge of the rose garden, pointed out the path which led down to the clearing where the pool lay. The beautiful Nitwit was there, dreamily regarding a large moth which hovered near some honeysuckle. Max Gale picked him up, said good-bye to me, and went quickly back. A very few minutes later I heard the sound of the piano. He had lost no time in getting back to work. Then the woods closed in and I was out of hearing.

The woods were always quiet, but now, with the darkness muffling their boughs, they seemed to hold a hushed and heavy stillness that might be the herald of storm. The scent of flowers hung like musk on the air.

As I picked my way carefully down the path I was thinking of the recent interview; not of the "theory" with which Sir Julian had been beguiling his exile, but of Sir Julian himself, and what Phyl and Godfrey had said about him.

That there had been—still was—something badly wrong seemed obvious: not only was there the physical evidence that even I could see, there was also that attitude of watchful tension in the younger man. But against this could be set the recent conversation, not the normal—and even gay—tone of it, but the use of certain phrases that had struck me. Would a man who had recently emerged from a mental home talk so casually and cheerfully about the "lunatic fringe" inhabited by his son? A son had, after all, a big stake in his father's sanity. And would the son, in his turn, speak of his father's "obsession," and the need to "humor" him? Perhaps if the need was serious, this was Mr. Gale's way of passing off a potentially tricky situation? Perhaps that edgy, watchful air of his was on my behalf as much as his father's?

Here I gave up. But as for the idea of Sir Julian's roaming the countryside with a rifle to the danger of all and sundry, I could believe it no more than formerly. I would as soon suspect Phyllida, or Godfrey Manning himself.

And (I thought) I would suspect Max Gale a darned sight sooner than any.

I could hear the trickle of water now, and ahead of me was the break in the trees where the pool lay. At the same moment I became conscious of a strange noise, new to me, like nothing more or less than the clucking and chattering of a collection of hens. It seemed to come from the clearing.

Then I realized what it was: the evening chorus at the pool—the croaking of the innumerable frogs who must live there. I had stopped at the edge of the clearing to pick up my towel, and some of them must have seen me, for the croaking stopped, and then I heard the rhythmic plopping of small bodies diving into the water. Intrigued, I drew back behind the bushes, then made a silent way round the outer edge of the clearing toward the far side of the pool, where there was cover. Now I was above the bank. I gently pressed the branches aside, and peered down.

At first, in the dusk, I could see nothing but the dark gleam of the water where the sky's reflection struck it between the upper boughs, and the mat circles of the small lily leaves and some floating weed. Then I saw a frog, a big one, sitting on a lily pad, his throat distended and pulsing with his queer little song. His body was fat and freckled, like a laurel leaf by moonlight, and the light struck back from eyes bright as blackberry pips. Close by him sang another, and then another. . . .

Amused and interested, I stood very still. Growing every moment in volume, the chorus gobbled happily on.

Silence, as sudden as if a switch had been pressed. Then my frog dived. All around the lily pads the surface ringed and plopped as the whole choir took to the water. Someone was coming up the path from the bay.

For a moment I wondered if Phyllida had been down to the beach to find me; then I realized that the newcomer was a man. His steps were heavy, and his breathing, and then I heard him clear his throat softly and spit. It was a cautious sound, as if he were anxious not to make too much noise. The heavy steps were cautious, too, and the rough, hurried breathing, which he was obviously trying to control, sounded oddly disquieting in the now silent woods. I let the bushes slip back into place, and stood still where I was, to wait for him to pass.

The dimming light showed him as he emerged into the clearing; Greek, someone I hadn't seen before, a young man, thickset and broad-chested, in dark trousers and a high-necked fisherman's sweater. He carried an old jacket of some lighter color over one arm.

He paused at the other side of the pool, but only to reach into a pocket for a cigarette, which he put between his lips. But in the very act of striking the match, he checked himself, then shrugged, and put it away again, shoving the cigarette behind his ear. He could not have indicated his need for secrecy more plainly if he had spoken.

As he turned to go on his way, I saw his face fairly clearly. There was a furtive, sweating excitement there that was disturbing, so that when he glanced round as if he had heard some noise I found myself shrinking back behind my screen of leaves, conscious of my own quickened heartbeats.

He saw nothing. He drew the back of a hand over his forehead, shifted his coat to the other arm, and trod with the same hasty caution up the steep path toward the Castello.

Above me a sudden gust of wind ran through the treetops, and chilly air blew through the trunks with the fresh, sharp smell of coming rain.

But I kept quite still until the sound of the Greek's footsteps had died away and beside me the frog had climbed out again on to his lily pad and swelled his little throat for song.

6

Methinks he hath no drowning mark upon him . . .

Act I, Scene 1

FOR SOME reason that I never paused to examine, I didn't tell my sister about my visit to the Gales, not even when next morning she decided that for once she would go down to the bay with me, and, as we passed the pool, pointed out the path that led up to the Castello.

The clearing looked very different this morning with the high clear light pouring into it. There had been a sudden little snap of storm during the night, with a strong wind that died with the dawn, and this had cleared the air and freshened the woods. Down in the bay the sand was dazzling in the morning sun, and the wake of the wind had left a ripple at the sea's edge.

I spread a rug in the shade of the pines that overhung the sand, and dumped our things on it.

"You are coming in, aren't you?"

"Sure thing. Now I'm down here, nothing will stop me from wallowing in the shallow bit, even if I do look like a mother elephant expecting twins. That's a smashing swimsuit, Lucy, where'd you get it?"

"Marks and Spencers."

"Good heavens."

"Well, *I* didn't marry a rich man," I said cheerfully, pulling up the shoulder straps.

"And a fat lot of good it does me in my condition." She looked sadly down at her figure, sighed, and dropped her smart beach coat beside the hold-all containing all the sun lotions, magazines, Elizabeth Arden cosmetics, and other paraphernalia without which she would never dream of committing herself to the beach. "It isn't fair. Just look at me, and these things come from Fabiani."

"You poor thing," I said derisively. "Will they go in the water? And for Pete's sake, are you going to bathe with that Koh-i-noor thing on?"

"Heavens, *no!*" She slipped the enormous marquise diamond off her finger, dropped it into the plastic bag that held her cosmetics, and zipped the bag shut. "Well, let's go in. I only hope your friend doesn't mistake me for the dolphin and let fly. Much the same general shape, wouldn't you say?"

"You'll be all right. He doesn't wear yellow."

"Seriously, there *isn't* anyone watching, is there, Lucy? I'd just as soon not have an audience."

"If you keep near inshore they can't see you anyway, unless they come to the front of the terrace. I'll go and look."

The water in the shade of the pines was a deep, deep green, lighting to a dazzling pale blue where a bar of sand ran out into the bay. I walked out along this, thigh-deep, until I was about fifty yards from the shore, then turned and looked up toward the terrace of the Castello. There was no one visible, so I waved to Phyllida to follow me in. As we swam and splashed, I kept an eye open to seaward for the dolphin, but, though I thought once that I could see a gleaming wheel turning a long way out, the creature did not approach the bay. After a time we waded back to the beach, where we lay sunning ourselves and talking idly, until Phyl's remarks, which had been getting briefer and briefer, and more and more sleepy, ceased altogether.

I left her sleeping, and went back into the water.

Though I had kept a wary eye on the woods and the terrace every time I bathed, I had never seen anyone since the first day, so it was with a slight feeling of surprise that I now saw someone sitting there, at the table under the stone pine. Gray hair. Sir Julian Gale. He lifted a hand to me, and I waved back, feeling absurdly pleased that he should have bothered. He turned away immediately, his head bent over a book. I caught the flutter of its pages.

There was no one with him on the terrace, but as I turned to let myself down into the deep water beyond the bar, something else caught my eye.

In one of the upper windows, which stood open, something had flashed. And behind the flash I saw movement, as whoever stood watching there lifted the binoculars again to focus them on the bay. . . .

There is something particularly infuriating about being watched in this way. I should have dearly loved to return rudeness for rudeness by pulling a very nasty face straight at the Castello windows, but Sir Julian might have seen it and thought it was meant for him, so I merely splashed back to the sandbar, where I stood up, and, without another glance, stalked expressively (drama school exercise: Outraged Bather Driven from Water) toward the rocks at the southern edge of the bay. I would finish my swim from the rocks beyond the point, out of range of the Castello.

I hadn't reckoned on its being quite so difficult to stalk with dignity through three feet of water. By the time I reached the end of the sandbar and the deep pool near the rocks, I was furiously angry with Max Gale and wishing I had gone straight out on to the beach. But I was damned if I would be driven back now. I plunged across the deep water, and was soon scrambling out under the pines.

A path ran through the tumble of rocks at the cliff's foot, leading, I supposed, to Godfrey Manning's villa, but its surface looked stony, so I stayed on the rocks below. These, scoured white by the sea and seamed with rock pools, stretched out from the cliff in stacks and ridges, with their roots in the calm, creaming water.

I began to pick my way along between the pools. The rocks were hot, and smooth to the feet. There were crevices filled with flowering bushes, running right down to the water's edge, where the green swell lifted and sank, and here and there a jut of the living cliff thrust out into the water, with the path above it, and bushes at its rim hanging right out over the sea.

At the point I paused. Here the rocks were more broken, as if the tide was driven hard that way when there was a wind, and under the cliff was a pile of broken rock and sea wrack, some of which looked fresh enough to have come up in last night's squall. Farther round, beyond the next curve of the cliff, I could see where a cove or inlet ran in, deep and narrow and surrounded by thick trees which stretched right up the slopes of the cliff; there were pines and oaks and hollies, and among them the limes of which Sir Julian had spoken. Through the boughs of a young thicket at the cliff's foot I caught a glimpse of red tiling which must be the roof of Godfrey's boathouse.

There was nobody about. I decided to finish my bathe in the deep water off the point and then return by the path.

I made my way carefully through the piled rocks and the sea wrack. Here and there a shallow pool barred the way, and I paddled across with caution, wondering uneasily about sea urchins, which in these waters (I had read) can drive poisonous spines into your feet. "Like hedgehogs which Lie tumbling in my barefoot way and mount Their pricks at my footfall . . ." Poor Caliban. Was Julian Gale right? I wondered. I had read *The Tempest* late into the night, following up the fascinating game he had suggested, and I had even had a few ideas myself, things I must ask him when I went to the Castello again . . . if I ever went to the Castello again. . . . But of course I would have to return the Shakespeare . . . if I could find out from Miranda or Adoni or someone when Max Gale was likely to be out. . . .

I had come to the edge of a deep inlet, a miniature cove running back through the rocks. This would be as good a place as any. I paused, peering down into it, to see what the bottom was like.

The water was the color of Imperial jade. Tiny shrimplike creatures scudded here and there among the olive and scarlet bladders, and shoals of small fish darted and nibbled. The shadows cast by the sun looked blue-black, and were alive with the movements of crabs which shuffled through the brown weed that clothed the bottom. The weed itself moved all the time, faintly and continuously, like rags in the swell. A cuttlefish bone showed white and bare. "Of his bones are coral made. Those are pearls . . ."

The body was lying half in, half out, of the largest patch of shadow. The sun, shining straight into my eyes, had hidden it till now, the hump of flesh and clothes not holding any kind of human shape, just a lump of rags rolled over and over by the swell and dumped there, jammed somehow under an overhang at the base of the pool.

Even now, with the sun directly in my eyes, I could hardly be sure. Sick and shaken, I hesitated; but of course I would have to look. I sank to my knees at the edge of the pool, and shaded my eyes to peer downward. . . .

The rags moved in the faint swell like weed. Surely it was only weed . . . ?

But then I saw the head, the face, a shape blurred and bleached under dark hair. Some sea creatures had already been at it. The tiny fish flicked to and fro, busily, in the green water.

Spiro, I thought, *Spiro.* . . . And his mother would have to see this. Surely it would be better to say nothing, to let the tide carry it away again; let the busy sea creatures purge and clean it to its sea change, like the cuttlefish bone showing white beside the dark hair . . . ?

Then reason threw its ice water on my confusion. She would have to be told. It would be crueler not to tell her. And there was no tide here. Without another storm, the thing could be held down here for days, for anyone to find.

Some freak current thrust a tentacle of movement through the pool. The water swayed, and the dead man moved his head. With the movement, I knew him. It wasn't specifically the face that I recognized; that would have been impossible: but somehow everything came together in the same moment to enforce recognition—the shape of face and head, the colors, better seen now, of the sodden lumps of rag that had been navy trousers and sweater and light gray jacket. . . .

It wasn't Spiro after all; not, that is, unless it had been Spiro in the woods last night, still alive and making his way up toward the Castello.

There could be no doubt about it, no possible doubt. This was the man I had seen last night in the clearing. I found that I was sitting back on my heels, slumped to one side, with a hand out to the hot face of a boulder beside me. It was one thing to find a dead man; but to recognize him, and to know where he had been shortly before he had met his death . . .

I had my eyes shut as tightly as the fingers that gripped the hot stone. The sunlight boiled and fizzed against the closed lids. I bit my lips, and breathed slowly and hard, and concentrated on not being sick. Phyllida: the thought was as bracing as sal volatile: Phyllida mustn't see this, or even be allowed to suspect the horror that lay just round the point from her. I must steady myself decently, then go back to Phyllida, and somehow persuade her to leave the beach soon. Then get quietly to the telephone and get in touch with the police.

I opened my eyes with a silly hope that somehow I had been wrong and there was no dead man there in the water. But he still lay in his splash of inky shadow, grotesque and faintly moving and familiar. I got to my feet, held myself steady by the boulder for another full minute, then, without looking back, made my way through the tumble of rock toward the thicket that edged the cliff path. It was only when I had reached the bushes, and was wondering if I could pull myself up the eight feet or so to the path, that some sound, vaguely heard a few moments ago, and now repeated, made me pause and glance to my left, toward the boathouse. Someone had slammed a door. Something appeared to be wrong with the catch, because I heard, clearly now, an exclamation of irritation, and the slam was repeated. This time the door shut firmly, and a moment later I heard footsteps, and Godfrey Manning came briskly into view along the path.

I wasn't sure if he was coming my way, or if the path branched off above the trees somewhere for the Villa Rotha. I opened my mouth to call him, hoping that this wouldn't also bring Phyllida, but at the same moment Godfrey glanced up and saw me below him on the rocks. He lifted a hand in greeting, but before he could call out I put a finger to my lips, then beckoned urgently.

Not surprisingly, he looked startled, but his expression deepened sharply into concern as he approached and paused on the path above me.

"Lucy? Is something wrong? Are you feeling ill? The sun?" Then his voice changed. "It's not that damned lunatic again with the rifle?"

I shook my head. Infuriatingly, after I had so far controlled myself, I found I couldn't speak. I pointed.

He glanced over toward the pool, but at that distance nothing was visible. Then he swung himself lightly down through the bushes to where I stood, and his arm went round me, gently.

"You'd better sit down. . . . There. Better? . . . All right, don't try to talk any more. Something scared you, over there in the big pool? . . . Relax a minute now; I'll go and take a look, but don't you move. Just sit there quietly, and don't worry. I won't be long."

I sat with my hands jammed tightly together between my knees, and watched my feet. I heard Godfrey's steps, quick and confident, cross the rocks toward the pool. Then there was silence, prolonged. The sea murmured, and some cliff-building swallows twittered shrilly as they cut in and out above the path.

I looked up. He was standing stock-still where I had stood, staring down. He was in profile to me, and I could see that he looked considerably shaken. It was only then that it occurred to me that he, too, must in the first moment of shock have expected it to be Spiro. If I had been capable of reasoned thought or speech, I should have known this, and spared him.

I cleared my throat. "It's not . . . Spiro, is it?"

"No."

"Do you know who it is?"

I thought he hesitated, then he nodded. "His name's Yanni Zoulas."

"Oh? You *do* know him?" Somehow this shook me, too, though it was reasonable to assume that the man had been drowned locally. "Is he from near here, then?"

"Yes, from the village."

"What—what do you suppose happened?"

"God knows. Some accident at sea, that's obvious. He was a fisherman, and usually went out alone . . . You must have seen his boat; it was always plying to and fro along this bit of shore—the rather pretty blue boat, with the dark brown sail. But in last night's sea . . . I wouldn't have thought . . ."

His voice trailed away as he stared frowningly down at the pool. Then he turned and made his way back across the rock to where I sat.

"Two in a week?" I said. It came out as a query, asked quite as if Godfrey could supply the answer. I hadn't meant even to say it aloud, and could have bitten my tongue with vexation as soon as it was out.

"Two in a week?" He spoke so blankly that it was evident my meaning hadn't registered. "Oh, I see."

"I'm sorry. It was stupid of me. I was thinking aloud. I shouldn't have reminded you. It's just one of those ghastly coincidences."

"Normally," he said, "I'd have said I didn't believe in coincidence. In fact, if I hadn't seen with my own eyes what happened to Spiro, I'd certainly be starting to wonder what was going on around here." He paused, and his eyes went back to the pool. "As it is, all that has happened is that two young men from the same district have died this week by drowning, and in a community that lives largely by the sea that's hardly surprising. Only—" He stopped.

"Only what?"

He looked at me with troubled eyes. "One doesn't expect an epidemic of it in summer weather, that's all."

"Godfrey, what is it? You look as if you thought—" I, too, checked myself, biting my lip. He watched me bleakly, saying nothing. I finished, rather hoarsely, "Are you trying to tell me that this wasn't an accident?"

"Good God, no! Just that it poses problems. But none that you need worry about. In any case, they may never arise."

None that you need worry about. . . . Heaven knew what he'd have said if he had had even the slightest inkling of the problem it had set me. . . . Why I still said nothing about last night I am not quite sure. I think now that this last incident took its place in a context of violence, felt rather than apprehended, that made it unsurprising and that forced me, through some instinct of fear, to hold my tongue. It was as if the first shot from that silenced rifle had been the signal for danger and fear to crowd in; as if by my silence I could still detach myself from them and stay inside my own bubble of security, keep my own enchanted island free of invaders from the violent world I had come here to escape.

So I said instead, "Has he any people?"

"A wife. They live with his parents. You probably know the house, it's that pink one at the crossroads."

"Yes, I do. It's very pretty. I remember thinking that the folk in it must be well off."

"They were. They're going to miss him."

I looked at him, startled, not by the words, which were trite, but by the quite undue dryness of his tone.

"You *are* getting at something. You *know* something about this, don't you? Why won't you tell me?"

He hesitated, then smiled suddenly. "I don't really know why not. It hardly concerns me, and it certainly won't touch you. It's only that when the police move in on this, something might crop up that could be awkward."

"Such as?"

He lifted his shoulders. "No plain and simple fisherman lived as well as Yanni and his family. Rumor has it that he was a smuggler, with a regular 'milk run' into Albania, and that he made a good bit on the side."

"Well, but surely . . . I'd have imagined that an awful lot of men played around with that sort of thing hereabouts? And Corfu's very well placed, just next door to the Iron Curtain. I suppose any sort of 'luxury goods' would go well there? But how could anyone like Yanni Zoulas get supplies of things like that?"

"How do I know? He'd have his contacts: someone in Corfu town, perhaps, who has connections with Athens or Italy. . . . But I'm sure that Yanni Zoulas wouldn't be in it on his own account. He wasn't exactly a mastermind. He probably did it for a salary."

I licked my lips. "Even so . . . You wouldn't suggest that that there could be any connection—that he was *killed* because of this? Is that what you're getting at? That—that would make it murder, Godfrey."

"No, no. For goodness' sake, I wasn't suggesting anything like that! Good God, no! Don't upset yourself. Why, you're as white as a sheet! Look, the idea's pure nonsense. I doubt if poor Yanni would ever be important enough to get himself murdered! You can forget that. But it did occur to me to wonder if he could have run into trouble on the other side—coast guard trouble: I believe they're hot stuff over there, searchlights, machine guns, the lot. If he did, and was wounded, and then ran for home, that might account for an accident happening on a night that wasn't particularly rough. He might have fainted and gone overboard."

"I see. But even if the police do find out something about it, his family won't be in trouble, will they?"

"I doubt it. It isn't that."

"Then what's worrying *you?*"

"It might bring them closer to young Spiro than would be quite pleasant," said Godfrey frankly. "I've a strong suspicion that he'd been out with Yanni more than once. It didn't worry me, and I asked no questions; the boy had a mother and sister to keep, and how he did it was his own affair. But I don't want them to find out about it now. It would serve no purpose, and might distress his mother. According to her, Spiro was *sans peur et sans reproche,* and a good Christian into the bargain. I'm sure she'd label smuggling as immoral, however lightly you or I might regard it."

"I didn't say I regarded it lightly. I think that if you live under a country's protection you should obey its laws. I just wasn't surprised. But you know, even if the police do find out something discreditable about Spiro, I'm sure they'd never tell Maria. Police are human, when all's said and done, and the boy's dead."

"You're probably right. Ah well . . ." He stretched, and sighed. "Hell, what a wretched business. We'd better go and get it over. Do you feel as if you'd like to move now?"

"Oh, yes, I'm fine."

He took my arm, and helped me up the rough bank to the path.

"I'm going to take you up to my house now, to telephone," he said. "It's nearer, and there's no need to alarm your sister till you're feeling a bit more the thing yourself. The police will want to see you, and you can see them at my place if you like, then I'll take you home by road, in the car. . . . Now, did you have some clothes with you, or some sort of wrap and shoes? If you wait here a moment, I'll get them."

"They're back in the bay, but I'm afraid Phyl's there, too. I left her asleep on the beach. She's probably awake by now, and wondering where I am."

"Oh." He looked uncertain. "Well, that alters things, doesn't it? We'll have to tell her. I don't know much about these things, but will it—well, upset her, or anything?"

"I think she'll be okay as long as she doesn't see the body. She'll have to know soon enough. . . . Wait a minute, someone's coming. That'll be her."

A second later she appeared on the path, round the point of the cliff. She must have been awake for some time, for all traces of the sea had been removed; she was freshly made up, her hair was shining and immaculate, she had clipped a pretty beach skirt on over her bathing costume, and she wore her gay beach coat. As usual, the sight of her brought my own shortcomings immediately to mind. I was conscious for the first time of what I must look like, with the salt dried on my skin, my hair damp, and my face—I imagined—still sallow with shock.

She said gaily, "I thought I heard voices! Hullo, Godfrey! Were you on your way over to us, or did you just come down to swim?"

"Neither. I was down at the boathouse giving the boat a once-over, when I saw Lucy."

I said, "Are those my shoes you've brought? Thanks very much. How did you guess I'd be wanting them?"

"Well, dearie, knowing you," said Phyllida, "when I woke up and found you'd vanished, I knew you'd be straying along here, poking around in the rock pools, and heaven knew how far you'd get." She laughed up at Godfrey. "It wouldn't surprise me in the least to find her with a jam jar full of assorted shrimps and things to take home. I remember once—" She stopped. There was a pause, in which she looked from one to the other of us. Then her voice sharpened. "Lucy. Godfrey. Something's wrong. What is it?"

He hesitated just that second too long. "Your sister was feeling the heat a bit, and I offered to take her up to my house and give her a drink. She told me you were on the beach, so I was just coming across for you. I hope you'll come up, too?"

His tone was perfect, easy and natural, but my sister was never anybody's fool. She had seen all she needed to see in my face, and in the fact that Godfrey's hand still supported my arm.

She said, more sharply still, "Something *is* wrong. Lucy, you look awful . . . and it's not the heat, either; don't give me that; you never felt the heat in your life. What's happened? Have you hurt yourself, or something?"

"No, no. There's nothing the matter with me, honestly." I disengaged myself gently, and looked up at Godfrey. It struck me suddenly, irrelevantly, that he was better-looking than I had thought. The sunlight showed up the deep tan of his skin and the crisp hair bleached fair at the front. Against the tan his eyes looked a very clear gray.

I said, "You may as well tell her straight away."

"Very well. Phyl, I'm afraid a beastly thing's happened. One of the local fishermen's been drowned and washed ashore over there, and Lucy found the body."

"Oh, my God, how ghastly! Lucy, my dear . . . you poor kid! I suppose it looked—" Then her eyes widened and a hand went up to her face. "Did you *see?* Could you tell? I mean . . . after a week . . ."

"It's not Spiro." Godfrey spoke quickly, almost harshly.

"It's not?" The hand dropped, and she let out a long breath of relief. "Oh, I was so sure . . . But does that mean *two,* in just a few days? Have you any idea who it is?"

"It's a local man called Yanni Zoulas. I doubt if you know him. Look, we were just going up to telephone. Will you come with us? If I just go back now to the bay for the rest of—"

He stopped abruptly, and turned. A shadow fell across me where I sat pulling on my sandals. Max Gale's voice said, just behind me:

"Is anything the matter?"

I know I jumped as if he had hit me. The other two were caught gaping, as if in some guilty act. He must be stones heavier than Phyllida, but we had none of us heard a sound. I thought, He must move like a cat.

For seconds nobody replied. It was a queer, hair-prickling little pause, during which the men eyed each other like unfriendly dogs circling one another, and I sat with a sandal half on, watching them.

"The matter?" said Godfrey.

I knew then that he didn't want to tell Gale what had happened. The knowledge, somehow not surprising, came like a cold breath along my skin. Mr. Gale glanced from Godfrey to Phyl, then down at me, and I bent my head quickly, pulled the sandal on, and began to fasten the strap.

He said impatiently, "It's obvious there's something. I was watching the bay with glasses, and I thought I saw something odd—some debris or other floating, away out; I couldn't make it out. Then Miss Waring came this way, and I saw her on the rocks that run out from the point. She stopped and looked into one of the pools, and her reactions made it pretty obvious that there was something very wrong indeed. Then you went over and made it rather plainer. What is it? Or shall I go and see for myself?"

It was Phyllida who answered him. She must not have felt the overtones that had chilled me—but then she didn't know what I knew. She said, in a sort of rush, "It's a dead body. Drowned. In that pool, there. We were just going up to phone the police."

There was a moment in which I seemed to hear the cliff swallows, very loud and shrill, just overhead. Then Max Gale said, "Who is it? Do you know?"

Godfrey still said nothing. He had not taken his eyes off the other man's face. It was again Phyllida who answered.

"I forget the name. Godfrey says he's from the village. Yanni something."

"Yanni Zoulas," I said.

He looked down at me as if he were aware fully for the first time that I was there. But I got the strong impression that he wasn't seeing me even now. He didn't speak.

"Did you know him?" I asked.

The dark eyes focused on me for a moment, then he looked away again, over toward the pool. "Why, yes, slightly."

Godfrey said, "You say you were watching something floating, some debris. You couldn't say what sort of thing? Could it have been flotsam from a sunk boat?"

"Eh? Well, I told you I couldn't see at that distance, but it could have been . . . My God, yes, I suppose it could!" All of a sudden Gale was fully with us; his gaze sharpened, and he spoke abruptly. "I wonder what time he went out last night. I thought I heard a boat soon after midnight, bearing northeast." He looked at Godfrey. "Did you hear it?"

"No."

"Last night?" said Phyllida. "Did it happen as recently as that? Could you tell, Godfrey?"

"I'm not an expert. I don't know. I don't think he's been there long. However, it shouldn't be hard to find out when he was last seen."

I had been watching Max Gale's face. He was looking thoughtful now, grave—anything but the way I knew he ought to be looking. "It must have happened within the last forty-eight hours. I saw his boat myself on Saturday. It went past the bay at about three in the afternoon."

If I hadn't known what I did, I'd never have known that he was lying—or rather, implying a lie. For a moment I even wondered if perhaps Yanni had not been on his way to the Castello last night, then I remembered that Mr. Gale had, in the last few minutes, given me another reason for doubting his good faith. He looked down suddenly, and caught me watching him. I bent my head again, and fiddled with the second sandal.

"Well," said Godfrey, "it'll be easy enough to check with his family, and the sooner we let the experts get on the job, the better. Shall we go? One thing, nobody need stay with the body. There's no tide to shift it . . . Where are you going?"

Max Gale didn't trouble to answer; he was already swinging himself down to the rocks below us. Godfrey made a quick, involuntary movement as if to stop him, then he shrugged, said softly to us, "Do you mind? We won't be long," and slithered in his turn down through the bushes.

Gale was bending over the pool. Like Godfrey, he stood looking down at the body for some time in silence, then he did what neither Godfrey nor I had done: he lay flat at the edge of the rock, and reached down through the water as if to touch the dead man. I saw Godfrey make another of those sharp, involuntary movements, but he must have decided that what evidence there was could hardly be damaged further by a touch, for he said nothing, merely stooping down himself to watch with close attention.

"What in the world are they doing?" asked Phyl, rather petulantly.

I was clasping my knees, hugging myself together closely. In spite of the sun, I had begun to feel cold. "I don't know and I don't care. I hope they hurry, that's all. I want to get some clothes on and get the police over and done with."

"You poor lamb, are you cold? Here, have my coat." She took it off and dropped it over my shoulders, and I hugged it gratefully round me.

"Thanks a lot. That's marvelous." I laughed a little. "At least it puts me in competition again! I wish you didn't always look as if you'd just got back from Elizabeth Arden, when I feel like a bit of Mr. Gale's debris. It was probably me he saw floating. If, that is, he saw anything."

She looked quickly down at me. "What does that mean? It sounds loaded."

"Not really."

She sat down beside me. "You don't often make remarks for nothing. What *did* you mean?"

"I'm not happy about this affair, that's all."

"Well, heavens, who is? But is it an 'affair'?"

"I don't know. There's a feeling . . . a feeling that there's something going on. I can't put it better than that, and I'm probably wrong, but I think—I *think*—Godfrey feels it, too. Why don't he and Mr. Gale like each other?"

"I didn't know they didn't. They *were* a bit wary today, weren't they? I suppose Godfrey's more upset than he lets on . . . after all, it's rather soon after the Spiro business . . . and Max Gale doesn't just put himself out to be charming, does he?"

"He has things on his mind," I said.

The remark was intended merely as an evasion, to imply only that his personal worries—over his father—made him difficult to know or like, but she took it to refer specifically to what had just happened. She nodded.

"I thought so, too. Oh, nothing special, just that he seemed to be thinking about something else. But what did *you* mean?" She shot me another look. "Something's really worrying you, isn't it?"

I hesitated. "Did it strike you as odd, the way Mr. Gale took the news?"

"Well, no, it didn't. Perhaps because I know him better than you. He's never very forthcoming. What sort of 'odd' did you mean?"

I hesitated again, then decided not to specify. "As if he weren't surprised that a body should roll up here."

"I don't suppose he was. He'd be expecting it to be Spiro."

"Oh, of course," I said. "Look, they seem to be coming back."

Mr. Gale had finished whatever grisly examination he had been conducting, and had withdrawn his hand. He rinsed it in the salt water, then stood up, drying it on a handkerchief. As far as I could make out, the two men still hadn't spoken a word. Now Godfrey said something with a gesture toward Phyl and myself, and they turned together and started over to us.

"Thank goodness," I said.

"You'll feel better when you've had a drink, old dear," said my sister.

"Coffee," I said, "as hot as love and as sweet as hell."

"Godfrey might even run to that, you never know."

The men scrambled up to the path beside us.

"Well?" said Phyl and I, together.

They exchanged a glance, which might even be said to hold complicity. Then Gale said, "It should be interesting to hear what the doctor has to say. He seems to have been knocked about the head a bit. I was wondering if the neck was broken, but I don't think so."

Godfrey's eyes met mine. I stood up. "Well, when the boat's found, there may be something there to show how it happened."

"For all we know," said Godfrey, "that's been done and the hue and cry's on already. Let's go, shall we?"

"Thank goodness!" I said. "But I still want to get dressed. My things—"

"Good God, I was forgetting. Well, hang on another minute or two, I won't be long."

Max Gale said, in that abrupt, rather aggressive way of his, "You three start up the path. I'll go and pick your stuff up and bring it along."

He had so plainly not been invited to go with us, and just as plainly fully intended to hear all that was said to the police, that I thought Godfrey was going to demur. But Phyllida got eagerly to her feet.

"Yes, let's get away from here! It's giving me the grue. Mr. Gale, if you *would* be an angel . . . I've left some things, too; they're under the pine trees."

"I saw where they were. I won't be long. Don't wait for me; I'll catch you up."

He went quickly. Godfrey looked after him, the gray eyes curiously cold. Then he caught me watching him, and smiled. "Well, this way."

The path followed the cliff as far as the boathouse, then turned up a steep zigzag through the trees. We toiled up it, grateful for the shade. Godfrey walked between us, in a sort of awkwardly divided solicitude that might at any other time have been amusing; but just now all I could think of was a bit of solitude in his bathroom, then a comfortable chair, and—failing the coffee—a long, cool drink. I hoped Max Gale would hurry with the clothes. I thought he probably would: he wouldn't want to miss what was said to the police. It had surprised me that he had risked this by offering to go back.

Godfrey had paused to help Phyl negotiate a dry gully which the winter's rain had gouged across the path. I was a few paces ahead of them when I came to a corner where a sudden gap in the trees gave a view of the point below.

I might have known there would be a good reason for Max Gale's offer. He was back at the rock pool, lying flat as before, reaching down into the water. I could just see his head and shoulders. Just as I caught the glimpse of him he withdrew his arm and got quickly to his feet. As he turned, I drew back into the shade of the trees, and just in time, for he glanced up briefly before he vaulted up to the path and out of sight.

"Tired?" asked Godfrey, just behind me.

I started. "No, not a bit. Just getting my breath. But I'll be glad when it's all over."

"So shall we all. I seem to have spent the whole week with the police as it is."
He added, rather bitterly, "At least they know their way here, and most of the
questions to ask."

Phyllida touched his arm gently. "Poor Godfrey. But we're terribly grateful.
And at least this time it doesn't touch you . . . except as a rather ghastly sort of
coincidence."

His eyes met mine. They held the bleak expression I was beginning to know.
"I don't believe in coincidence," he said.

7

What have we here? A man or a fish? Dead or alive?

Act II, Scene 2

EITHER SHE had been more distressed than she had allowed us to see or else the
trip down to the beach in the heat, with the bathe and the climb to the Villa
Rotha, had been too much for Phyllida. Though we spent the rest of the day
quietly and she lay down after lunch for a couple of hours, by evening she was
tired, fidgety, and more than somewhat out of temper, and very ready to be
persuaded to go to bed early.

Maria and Miranda had gone as soon as dinner was over. By ten o'clock the
house was very quiet. Even the pines on the hill behind it were still, and once I
had shut the windows I could hear no sound from the sea.

I felt tired myself, but restless, with sleep still a long way off, so I went along
to the scrubbed and empty kitchen, made myself more coffee, then took it
through to the *salotto,* put my feet on a chair, some Mozart on the gramophone,
and settled myself for a quiet evening.

But things didn't quite work out that way. The calm, beautiful room, even the
music, did not manage to keep at bay the thoughts that had been knocking for
admission since that morning. In spite of myself, my mind went persistently back
to the morning's incidents: the discovery in the pool, the two men's raw
antagonism, and the long, wearying aftermath of interrogation, with the fresh
problems it had brought to light.

The police from Corfu had been civil, thorough, and kind. They had arrived
fairly soon after we had reached Godfrey's house, and had gone straight down
with the two men to see the body. Shortly after that a boat had arrived from
somewhere, and presently departed with its burden. Another came soon
afterward, and cruised off out to sea—searching, one assumed, for the "debris"
which Mr. Gale insisted that he had seen. From the terrace of the Villa Rotha,
Phyl and I had watched it tacking to and fro some way out from land, but with
what success it had been impossible—failing Mr. Gale's binoculars—to guess.

Then the men came back. The questions had been searching, but easy enough
for my part to answer, because of course nobody imagined that I had seen Yanni

before in my life, so the only questions I was asked were those touching on my finding of the body.

And when Max Gale reiterated to the police that he had not laid eyes on Yanni Zoulas since a possible glimpse of his boat on Saturday afternoon, I had not said a word.

It was this that bore on me now, heavily, as I sat there alone in the *salotto,* with darkness thickening outside the windows and moths thumping against the lighted glass. And if I was beginning to get too clear an idea why, I didn't want to face that, either. I pushed that line of thought to one side, and concentrated firmly on the facts.

These were, in their own way, comforting. Godfrey had rung up in the late afternoon to give us the latest reports. It appeared that Yanni's boat had been found drifting, and on the boom were traces of hairs and blood where, as the boat heeled in a sudden squall, it must have struck him and sent him overboard. An almost empty bottle of ouzo, which had rolled away behind a pile of rope and tackle, seemed to provide a clue to the young fisherman's carelessness. The doctor had given it as his opinion (said Godfrey) that Yanni had been dead when he went into the water. The police did not seem inclined to press the matter further. Of the debris reported by Mr. Gale no trace had been found.

Finally—Godfrey was a little cryptic over this part of the message, as the telephone was on a party line—finally, no mention had been made of any illegal activities of the dead man. Presumably his boat had been searched, and nothing had come to light, so the police (who preferred to turn a blind eye to small offenses unless action was forced on them) were satisfied that the fatal voyage had been a routine fishing trip, and that Yanni's death had been accidental. It was obvious that they had no intention of opening any further line of inquiry.

So much for Godfrey's anxiety. My own went a little further.

It had transpired, from police inquiries, that the last time Yanni's family had seen him alive was on Sunday: he had spent the day with them, they said, going with them to watch the procession and returning home in the late afternoon. Yes, he had seemed in good spirits. Yes, he had been drinking a fair amount. He had had a meal, and then had gone out. No, he had not said where he was going, why should he? They had assumed he was going fishing, as usual. He had gone down to the boat. Yes, alone; he usually went alone. That was the last time they had seen him.

It was the last time anyone had seen him, according to the police report. And I had said nothing to make them alter it. Where Godfrey had been worrying about the inquiry's leading back to Spiro, I was worrying about its involving Julian Gale. That Max Gale was somehow implicated seemed obvious, but I had my own theories about that, and they hardly justified turning the police searchlight on Yanni's activities, and so wrecking Sir Julian's precarious peace. With Yanni's death an accident—and I saw no reason to doubt this—it didn't matter if he had indeed paid a furtive visit to the Castello before going out last night. So if Max Gale chose to say nothing about it, then it was none of my business. I could stay in my enchanted bubble and keep quiet. It didn't matter one way or the other. . . .

But I knew quite well that it did, and it was this knowledge that kept me sleepless in my chair, while one record followed another, unheeded, and the clock crawled on toward midnight. For one thing, I had had information forced on me that I would rather not have owned. For another—

The record stopped. With its slow, deliberate series of robot clicks, the auto-changer dropped another on the turntable, moved a gentle arm down on it, and loosed Gervase de Peyer's clarinet into the room in a brilliant shower of gold.

I switched my own thoughts back into the groove of facts. One thing at a time. The best way of forgetting how you think you feel is to concentrate on what you know you know. . . .

Godfrey had been sure that Yanni was a smuggler, and that he must have some "contact" who was probably his boss. I was pretty sure now that the contact was Max Gale. It all tied up: it would explain that furtive visit just before Yanni's voyage, and Gale's silence on the subject. It would also account for the thing that had so much worried me this morning—Gale's reaction to the news of Yanni's death. He had not been surprised at the news that a body was on the rocks, and this was not, as Phyl had assumed, because he thought it was Spiro. To me it was obvious that Spiro had never entered his head. His first questions had been, "Who is it? Do you know?" though the obvious assumption would have been the one the rest of us had made, that this must be the body of the drowned boy.

If my guess about him was correct, then his actions were perfectly consistent. He had known Yanni was to make a trip the night before; he must have known there was some risk involved. He would obviously not have expected Yanni to meet his death, but, once faced with a drowned body, he had had no doubts as to who it would be. His story of floating debris was nonsense, of that I was sure: what had happened was that he had seen me, and then Godfrey, at the rock pool, had jumped to conclusions, and had made an excuse to come down to see for himself. There had been that sharp "Who is it?" and then the next, immediate, reaction—to examine the body as closely as he dared, presumably for any evidence of violence. No doubt if such evidence had been there, he would have had to come out with the truth, or part of it. As it was, he had held his tongue, and no doubt shared Godfrey's relief that the matter need not be brought into the open.

Yet, it all tied up, even Gale's surreptitious return to the pool, presumably to examine the body more closely than he had dared with Godfrey there, and to remove anything Yanni might have been carrying which might link him with his "contact." And it was Gale's luck that the boat had proved innocent: either poor Yanni had been on his way home when the accident happened or last night's trip had, in fact, merely been a routine one to the fishing grounds. Even the attack on the dolphin took its place with the rest. I was certain, now, that Gale had shot at the creature because he was afraid it would attract the tourist crowds and destroy his badly needed privacy. But the anger that this action had roused in me didn't give me the right, I decided, to open up a field of inquiry that would probably hurt Spiro's people, and would certainly hurt Yanni's. The two bereaved families had already quite enough to bear. No, I would hold my tongue, and be thankful that I had been allowed to stay inside my enchanted bubble with a quiet conscience. And as for Max Gale—

The Clarinet Concerto came to an end, the bright pomp ascending, jubilant, into a triumph of golden chords. The player switched itself off. In the silence that followed I heard sounds from Phyllida's room. She was up and busy.

I glanced at the clock. Twenty past twelve. She should have been asleep long ago. I went across the hallway to her door.

"Phyllida?"

"Oh, come in, come in!"

She sounded thoroughly edgy and upset. I went in, to find her out of bed and rummaging through a drawer, dragging the contents out anyhow and strewing them on the floor. She was looking enchantingly pretty in some voluminous affair of yellow nylon, with her hair down and her eyes wide and dark-shadowed. She also looked as if she were on the verge of tears.

"What's up? Are you looking for something?"

"Oh, God!" She jerked open another drawer and rummaged in it, and slammed it shut again. "Not that it'll be *there*. . . . I would do a damn-fool thing like that, wouldn't I?"

I looked at her in some alarm. Phyllida hardly ever swears. "Like what? Lost something?"

"My ring. The diamond. The goddamned Forli blasted diamond. When we were down at the bay. I've only just this moment remembered it, what with everything. I had it on, didn't I? *Didn't* I?"

"Oh, my heaven, yes, you did! But don't you remember, you took it off before we went in the water? Look, stop fussing, Phyl, it's not lost. You put it in your make-up bag, that little zip thing covered with roses. I saw you."

She was at the wardrobe now, feeling in the pockets of the beach coat. "Did I or did I not put it on again after I'd left the water?"

"I don't think so. I don't remember . . . No, I'm sure you didn't. I'd have noticed it on your hand. You didn't have it on when we were having coffee up at Godfrey's. But, honey, it'll be in the little bag. I know you put it there."

She shoved the coat back, and slammed the wardrobe shut. "That's the whole blasted point! The beastly bag's still down on the beach!"

"Oh, no!"

"It must be! I tell you, it's not here, I've looked everywhere." The bathroom was ajar, and on the floor her beach bag lay in a heap with slippers and towel. She picked up the bag for what was obviously the umpteenth time, turned it upside down, shook it, and let it fall. She kicked over the towel with her foot, then turned to face me, eyes tragic, hands spread like a mourning angel invoking a blessing. "You see? I bloody *left* the thing, on the bloody *beach!*"

"Yes, but listen a minute. . . ." I thought back rapidly. "Perhaps you did put it back on. After all, you used the zip bag when you did your face. Did you put the ring on then, and take it off again when you washed at Godfrey's? Perhaps you left it in his bathroom."

"I'm sure I didn't. I can't remember a thing about it, and I know that if I *had* the thing on when I washed at Godfrey's, I'd have known it. You can't help knowing," she said ingenuously, "when you're flashing a thing like that about on your hand. Oh, what a *fool* I am! I didn't mean to bring it here at all, but I forgot to put it in the bank, and it's safer on my hand than off it. . . . Or so I thought! Oh, hell, hell, *hell!*"

"Well, look," I said soothingly, "don't start to worry yet. If you didn't put it back on, it's still in the little bag. Where was that when you last saw it?"

"Just where we were sitting. It must have got pushed to one side under the trees or something, and when Max Gale went back for our things he just wouldn't see it. He'd just grab the things and chase after us."

"Probably. He'd be in a hurry."

"That's what I mean." She noticed nothing in my tone, but spoke quite simply, staring at me with those wide, scared eyes. "The wretched thing's just *sitting* there on the sand, and—"

"Well, for heaven's sake, don't look like that! It'll be as safe as a house! Nobody'll be there, and if they were, who'd pick up a scruffy plastic bag with make-up in?"

"It's not scruffy, and Leo gave it to me." She began to cry. "If it comes to that, he gave me the beastly ring, and it belongs to his beastly family, and if I lose it—"

"You haven't lost it."

"The tide'll wash it away."

"There's no tide."

"Your foul dolphin'll eat it. *Something*'ll happen to it, I know it will." She had cast reason to the winds now, and was crying quite hard. "Leo had no *business* to give me anything like that and expect me to watch it *all the time!* Diamonds are hell anyway—if they're not in the bank you feel as miserable as sin, and if they *are* in the bank you're all frustrated, so you simply can't *win;* they're not worth having, and that ring cost thousands and thousands, and it's worse in lire, *millions* of lire," wept Phyl unreasonably, "and there'll be his mother to face, not to mention that ghastly collection of aunts, and did I tell you his uncle's probably going to be a C-Cardinal—"

"Well, honey, this won't exactly wreck his chances, so take a pull at yourself, will you, and—Hey! Just what do you think you're doing?"

She had yanked the wardrobe door open again, and was pulling out a coat. "If you think I'll get a wink, a *single wink* of sleep while that ring's lying out there—"

"Oh, no, you don't!" I said with great firmness, taking the coat from her and putting it back. "Now, don't be a nit! Of course you're worried stiff—who wouldn't be?—but you're certainly not going down there tonight!"

"But I've got to!" Her voice thinned and rose, and she grabbed for the coat again. She was very near to real hysteria.

I said quickly, "You have not. I'll go myself."

"You can't! You can't go alone. It's after midnight!"

I laughed. "So what? It's a nice night, and I'd a darned sight rather take a walk out than see you work yourself into a fit of the screaming abdabs. I don't blame you, I'd be climbing the walls myself! Serves you right for flashing that kind of ice around, my girl!"

"But, Lucy—"

"I mean it. I'll go straight away and get the wretched thing, so for sweet pete's sake, dry your eyes or you'll be fretting yourself into a miscarriage or something, and then Leo *will* have something to say, not to mention his mother and the aunts."

"I'll come with you."

"You'll do no such thing. Don't argue. Get back into bed. Go on . . . I know exactly where we were sitting, and I'll take a torch. Now mop up, and I'll make you some Ovaltine or something, and then go. Hurry up now, get *in!"*

I don't often get tough with Phyllida, but she is surprisingly meek when I do. She got in, and smiled shakily.

"You're an angel, you really are. I feel so ashamed of myself, but it's no use, I shan't rest till I've got it. . . . Look, I've had an idea, couldn't we just ring Godfrey and ask him to go? Oh, no, he said he was going to be out late, didn't he? Well, what about Max Gale? It's his fault, in a way, for not seeing the thing. . . . We could ring him up to ask if he'd noticed it, and then he'd *have* to offer to go down—"

"I'm not asking favors of Max Gale."

This time she did notice my tone. I added hastily, "I'd rather go myself. I honestly don't mind."

"You won't be scared?"

"What's there to be scared of? I don't believe in ghosts. Anyway, it's not so dark as it looks from in here; the sky's thick with stars. I suppose you've got a torch?"

"There's one in the kitchen, on the shelf beside the door. Oh, Lucy, you *are* a saint! I shouldn't have slept a wink without that beastly thing safe in its box!"

I laughed at her. "You should be like me, and get your jewelry you-know-where. Then you could lose the lot down on the beach and not worry about Leo's beating you."

"If that was all I thought would happen," said Phyllida, with a spice of her usual self, "I'd probably enjoy it. But it's his mother."

"I know. And the aunts. And the Cardinal. Don't come that one over me, my girl, I know darned well they all spoil you to death. Now, stop worrying. I'll bring you the Ovaltine, and you shall have the Grand Cham's diamond safe under your pillow 'or ere your pulse twice beat.' See you."

The woods were still and silent, the clearing full of starlight. The frogs had dived at my approach; the only sound now from the pool was the lap and stir of the lily pads as the rings of water shimmered through them and set them rocking.

I paused for a moment. I had told Phyllida that I didn't believe in ghosts, and I knew I had no reason to be afraid, but for the life of me I couldn't help glancing toward the place where Yanni had appeared last night, while just for a moment I felt my skin prickle and rush up like a cat's fur.

Next moment, very faintly, I heard the piano. I tilted my head to listen to the thin, falling melodic line that crept down through the trees. I recognized phrases that I had heard last night. It was this, no doubt, that had unconsciously given me pause and called up poor Yanni for me.

The ghost had gone. The pathway to the beach was just a pathway. But I didn't follow it yet: slowly, rather as if I were breasting water instead of air, I climbed the path to the Castello.

I paused at the edge of the rose garden, hanging back in shadow. The roses smelled heavy and sweet. The music was clear now, but muted, so that I guessed it came from the house rather than the terrace. I recognized another passage, a simple, almost lyrical line that suddenly broke and stumbled in the middle, like a step missed in the dark. I found it disquieting. After a while the pianist stopped, started again, played for another half minute before he broke off to go back a few bars; then the same long phrase was played over several times before being allowed to flow on unchecked.

The next time he stopped I heard the murmur of voices. Julian Gale's tones carried beautifully; Max replied indistinguishably. Then the piano began again.

He was there, and working. They were both there. As if I had had something proved to me—whatever it was I had come for—I turned away and, with the help of the torch, followed the Castello's own path downhill, through the clearing where I had met Max Gale, and on down the broken steps to the bay.

After the heavy shade of the path, the open beach seemed as light as day. The white crescent of sand was firm and easy walking. As I left the woods I switched off the torch, and went rapidly across the bay to where we had been sitting that morning. The pines, overhanging, made a black pool of shadow, so black that for a moment it looked as if something were lying there. Another body.

But this time I didn't pause. I knew it for a trick of the shadows, no more; just another ghost to fur the skin with gooseflesh; an image painted on the memory, not of the living Yanni this time, but of the dead.

The music sounded faintly from above. I kept the torch switched off in case the flash attracted the Gales' attention, and approached the trees.

Something *was* lying there. Not shadows; it was solid, a long, dark bundle shape, like the thing in the rock pool. And it was real.

This time the shock really did hit me. I still remember the kick over the heart, the sharp, frightening pain that knocked all the blood in my body into hammering motion, the way a kick starts a motorcycle engine. The blood slammed in heavy, painful strokes in my head, my fingers, my throat. My hand tightened so convulsively on the torch that the switch went down and the light came on, pinpointing whatever it was that lay here under the pines.

It wasn't a body. It was a long, smoothly wrapped bundle of something, longer than a man. It was lying just where we had been sitting that morning.

I had my free hand clamped tightly against my ribs, under the left breast. It is a theatrical gesture, but, like all the theater's clichés, it is based soundly on truth. I believe I felt I must hold my terrified heart from battering its way out of the rib cage. I must have stood there for several minutes, rigid, unable either to move forward or to run away.

The thing didn't move. There was no sound other than the distant notes of the piano and the soft hushing of the sea.

My terror slowly faded. Body or no body, it obviously wasn't going to hurt me, and, I thought grimly, I'd be better facing a dozen bodies than going back to Phyllida without the Forli diamond.

I pointed the torchlight straight at the thing under the trees, and approached it bravely.

The bundle stirred. As my breath whistled sharply in, I saw, in the torchlight, the gleam of a living eye. But then in the split half second that prevented me from screaming, I saw what—not who—this was. It was the dolphin.

Apollo's child. Amphitrite's darling. The sea magician. High and dry.

The eye moved, watching me. The tail stirred again, as if trying to beat movement out of the hard earth as it would from water. It struck the edge of the crisping ripples with a slash that seemed to echo right up the rocks.

I tiptoed closer, under the blackness of the pines. "Darling?" I said softly. "What's the matter? Are you hurt?"

The creature lay still, unblinking, the eye liquid and watchful. It was silly to look, as I did, for recognition, but at least I could see no fear of me. I shone the torch carefully over the big body. There seemed to be no wound, or mark of any kind. I examined the sand round about. There was no blood, only a wide, dragged wake where the animal had been hauled or thrown out of the water. Near a pine root the torchlight caught the pale gleam of Phyllida's make-up bag. I snatched this up; I didn't even look inside, but rammed it into my pocket and then forgot it. Presumably the diamond was safe inside it, but more important now than any diamond was the dolphin, stranded and helpless, a prey for anyone who wanted to hurt him. And that someone did want to hurt him, I very well knew. . . . Moreover, unless he could be got back into the water, he would die as soon as the sun got up and dried his body out.

I straightened up, trying to force my thoughts into order, and to recall everything I had ever read or known about dolphins. It was little enough. I knew that, like whales, they sometimes stranded themselves for no obvious reason, but that if they were unhurt and could be refloated fairly soon, they would suffer no ill effects. I knew, too, that they must be kept wet, or the skin cracked and went septic; and that they breathed through an air hole on the top of the head, and that this must be kept clear.

I shone the torch again. Yes, there was the air hole, a crescent-shaped, glistening nostril on top of the head. It was open, but half clotted with sand thrown up as the creature had ploughed ashore. I fixed the torch as best I could in the crotch of a pine bough, dipped my hands in the sea, and gently wiped the sand from the hole.

The dolphin's breath was warm on my hands, and this was somehow surprising: the creature was all at once less alien, his friendliness and intelligence at the same time were less magical and more touching. It was unthinkable that I might have to watch him die.

I ran my hands over his skin, noticing with fear how rough this was; the breeze was drying it out. I tried to judge the distance I would have to drag him. Now and again a ripple, driven by that same breeze, washed right up to the dolphin's tail, but this was the thinnest film of water licking up from the shallows four yards away. Another few feet out, as I knew, the sand shelved sharply to deeper water beside the rocks. Once get him even half floating, and I should be able easily to manage his weight.

I switched off the torch, then put my arms round the dolphin as far as I could and tried to pull him. But I couldn't get hold of him; my hands slipped over the faultless streamlining of his body. Nor could I grasp the dorsal fin, and when I tried tugging at his flippers he fidgeted for the first time, and I thought he was going to struggle and work himself farther up the shore. Finally, kneeling, I got my shoulder right against his and tried to thrust him backward with all the strength I could muster. But he never moved an inch.

I stood back at length, panting, sweating, and almost in tears. "I can't do it. Sweetie, I can't even *budge* you!" The bright liquid eye watched me silently. Behind him, four yards away, the sea heaved and whispered under the tail of the wind. Four yards: life or death.

I reached the torch down from the tree. "I'll go and get a rope. If I tie it around you, I could *pull* you. Get a leverage round a tree—anything!" I stooped to caress his shoulder, whispering, "I'll hurry, love; I'll run all the way."

But the feel of the dolphin's skin, dry and roughening, made me hesitate. It might take some time to find a rope or get help. No good going for Godfrey: if he was still up, it would be time lost. And I couldn't go to the Castello. I would have to go all the way home. I had better throw some seawater over the animal's skin before I left him, to keep him safe while I was away.

I kicked off my sandals and ran into the shallows. But the spray I splashed up barely reached beyond his tail, and (so shallow was the water here) came up full of sand and grit that would dry on him even more disastrously than before.

Then I remembered the plastic bag, stupidly small, but better than nothing. I ran out of the water, dragged the bag from my pocket, shone the torch down, and tipped Phyllida's make-up out on the sand. The Forli diamond fell into the torchlight with a flash and a shimmer. I snatched it up and pushed it on my finger, and dropped the rest of the things back into my pocket, along with the torch. Then I ran back to the sea's edge and scooped up my pathetic pint of water to throw over the dolphin.

It seemed to take an age. Stooping, straightening, running, tipping, stooping, running, tipping . . . When I reached the beast's shoulders I put a hand over the air hole and poured the water carefully round it; unbelievably, dolphins could drown, and under the circumstances, one couldn't expect the right reflexes to be working. When I poured water over his face the first time he blinked, which startled me a little, but after that he watched me steadily, the nearer eye swivelling as I moved to and fro.

At last he seemed wet enough to be safe. I dropped the dripping bag, wiped my hands on my coat, which was probably already ruined beyond repair, pulled on my sandals, and petted the damp shoulder again.

"I'll be back, sweetie; don't worry. I'll be as quick as I can. Keep breathing. And let's pray no one comes."

This was the nearest I had got to admitting, even to myself, why I had been whispering, and why, as soon as I no longer needed the light, I had snapped the torch out.

I ran back across the sand. The piano had stopped, but I could still see the faint glow of light from the open terrace window. Nothing moved on the terrace itself. Then I was in the shadow of the woods, where the path to the Villa Forli went up steeply. Using the torch once more, I clambered breathlessly. The breeze, steady now, had filled the woods with a rustling that drowned my steps.

And now the starlit clearing. The frogs plopped into the pool. The stream glittered in the flying edge of my torchlight. I switched off as I emerged from the trees, and crossed the open space quietly, pausing at the far side of it to get my breath, landing up against a young oak that stood where the path tunnelled afresh into the black burrow of the woods.

As I came out from under the oak, something moved on the path.

I checked, fingers fumbling clumsily with the torch. It flashed on, catching the edge of a side-stepping figure. A man, only a yard or so away. I would have run straight into him.

The bushes rustled just beside me. Someone jumped. The torch was struck out of my hand. I whipped round, and I think I would have screamed to wake the dead, only he grabbed me, pulled me to him brutally, and his hand came down hard over my mouth.

8

*Pray you, tread softly, that the blind mole may not
Hear a foot fall; we now are near his cell.*

Act IV, Scene 1

HE WAS very strong. I struggled and fought, necessarily in silence, but I couldn't do a thing. I must have hurt him, though, in clawing at his hand, for he flinched, and I heard his breath go in sharply. He took the hand away with a hissed *"Keep quiet, will you?"* in English, and then made it certain by jamming my head hard into the front of his jacket, so that I was not only dumb, but blinded, too. His coat was damp, and smelled of the sea. I got the swift impression of other movement nearby, but heard nothing above my own and my assailant's breathing, and the thudding of my heart. The pressure of his hand on the back of my head was hurting me, and a button scored my cheek. My ribs, held in the hard embrace of his other arm, felt as if they were cracking.

I stopped fighting and went slack, and straight away the cruel grip eased, but he still held me pressed to him, both arms caught now and firmly pinioned. As his hold relaxed I pulled my head free. If I screamed, they would hear me from the Castello terrace . . . they could be down here in a few seconds. . . . Surely, even Max Gale—

"Where have you been?" demanded my captor.

I gaped at him. As soon as he saw I had no intention of screaming, he let me go. *"You?"* I said.

"Where have you been?"

I had my hands to my face, rubbing the sore cheeks. "What's that got to do with you?" I asked furiously. "You go a bit far, don't you, Mr. Gale?"

"Have you been up at the Castello?"

"I have not! And if I had—"

"Then you've been to the beach. Why?"

"Is there any reason—" I began, then stopped. Fright and fury, together, had let me forget for a moment what else had happened that day. Max Gale might have no business to demand an account of my movements, but he might well have the best of reasons for wanting to know them.

Nothing was to be gained by refusing to tell him. I said, rather sulkily. "I went down to get Phyl's ring. She left it on the beach this morning. You needn't look as if you don't believe me: it was in a little bag, and you missed it. There, see?" I flashed the diamond at him, then pushed the hand deep into my coat pocket, almost as if I expected him to grab it from me, and glared up at him. "And now perhaps you'll tell me what *you're* playing at? This game of yours is way beyond a joke, let me tell you! It'll be man-traps next, I suppose. You hurt me."

"I'm sorry. I didn't mean to. I thought you were going to scream."

"Good heavens, of course I was! But why should you have minded if I had?"

"Well, I—" He hesitated. "Anyone might have heard . . . My father . . . It might have startled him."

"Thoughtful of you!" I said tartly. "It didn't matter, did it, if you scared *me*

415

half out of my wits? What a model son you are, aren't you? I'm surprised you could bring yourself to go out so late and leave your father alone! If it comes to that, where've *you* been that you don't want anyone to know about?"

"Fishing."

"Oh?" The heavily ironic retort that jumped to my lips withered there and died. I said slowly, "But you were up there at the Castello half an hour ago."

"What do you mean? I thought you said you hadn't been near the Castello."

"The noise *you* make with that piano," I said nastily, "you could hear it from the mainland. I heard you from the beach."

"That's impossible." He spoke abruptly, but with a note of puzzlement.

"I tell you I did! You were playing the piano, and then talking to your father. I know your voices. It *was* you."

He was silent for a moment. Then he said slowly, "It sounds to me as if you heard a working session on tape being played through, comments and all. But I still don't see how that could be. My father isn't there. He's away, staying the night at a friend's house."

"How far away?"

"If it's anything to do with you, Corfu."

"You must think I've a scream like a steam whistle," I said dryly.

"What? Oh, I . . . ." He had the grace to stammer slightly. "I'm afraid I did rather say the first thing that came into my head. But it's true that he's not at home."

"And neither were you?" I said. "Well, whoever was playing the tape, it certainly made a wonderful alibi."

"Don't be silly." His laugh was excellently done. He must have some of his father's talent, after all. Possibly only someone as experienced with actors' voices as I could have told that the easy amusement was assumed over some urgent preoccupation. "Your imagination's working overtime, Miss Waring! Please don't go making a mystery out of this. All that'll have happened is that my father's decided for some reason to come home, and he was amusing himself with the tape recorder. As for myself, I've been out fishing with Adoni. . . . And if it's any satisfaction to you, *you* frightened *me* half out of my wits. I'm afraid my reactions were a bit rough. I'm sorry for that. But if someone suddenly breaks out of the dark and runs straight into you, you—well, you act according."

"According to what? Jungle law?" I was still smarting. "I wouldn't have said those reactions were exactly normal, unless you were expecting— Just what *were* you expecting, Mr. Gale?"

"I'm not sure." This, at any rate, sounded like the truth. "I thought I heard someone coming up from the beach, fast, and trying not to be heard, but the breeze was covering most of the sounds, and I couldn't be certain. Then the sounds stopped, as if whoever it was, was hiding and waiting. Naturally that made me begin to wonder what they might be up to, so I waited, too."

"I only stopped to get my breath. Your imagination's working overtime, Mr. Gale."

"Very probably." I wasn't sure if he had even noticed the gibe. His head was bent, and he seemed to be studying one of his hands, turning it this way and that. "Well, just as I decided I'd been mistaken, you erupted from the trees like a deer on the run. I grabbed you. Pure reflex."

"I see. And I suppose it was pure reflex that you knocked the torch out of my hand before I could see anything?"

"Of course," he said woodenly.

"And that even when you saw who it was you acted like a—a Gestapo?" No reply to that. I can only suppose that excitement and the moment's fright had pumped too much adrenalin into my bloodstream; I think I was a bit "high" with it. I remember feeling vaguely surprised that I was not in the least afraid of him. At some level, I suppose, I was reasoning that the man (in spite of his dubious bit of adventuring in what Godfrey had called the "milk run") was hardly a dangerous criminal, and that he obviously intended me no harm: on the conscious level I was damned if I went tamely home now without finding exactly what was going on around here. It had already touched me far too closely to be ignored. The enchanted bubble had never really existed. I was beginning to suspect that there was no such thing.

So I asked, as if it were a matter of purely academic interest, "I still want to know why it should have mattered to you where I'd been. Or that I might recognize you. Or was it the others I wasn't supposed to see?"

I thought for a moment that he wasn't going to answer. From somewhere farther up in the woods, an owl called breathily once, and then again. In the pool, a frog tried his voice tentatively for a moment, lost his nerve, and dived again. Max Gale said quietly, "Others?"

"The men who went past while you were holding me."

"You're mistaken."

"Oh, no, I'm not. There was somebody else there. I saw him beside the path, just as you jumped on me."

"Then you probably recognized him as well. That was Adoni, our gardener. You've met him, I believe?"

You wouldn't have thought he was admitting another lie, or even conceding a slight point. The tone was that of a cool social brush-off. I felt the adrenalin soaring dangerously again as he added calmly. "He usually comes with me when I go fishing. What's the matter? Don't you believe me?"

I managed to say, quite pleasantly, "I was just wondering why you didn't beach the boat in your own bay. This seems a funny way to come—if you've just been fishing."

"The wind was getting up, and it was easier to come in the other side of the point. And now, if you'll excuse me—"

"You mean," I said, "that you left your boat on *our* side of the point? Tied to our jetty, even? Now, isn't that too bad? I think you'd better go straight down again and move it, Mr. Gale. We don't like trespassers at the Villa Forli."

There was a short, sharp pause. Then, unexpectedly, he laughed. "All right. One to you. But not tonight. It's late, and I've got things to do."

"I suppose you ought to be helping Adoni to carry home the fish? Or would it be more correct to call it 'the catch'?"

That got through. You'd have thought I'd hit him. He made a sudden movement, not toward me, but I felt my muscles tighten, and I think I even backed a pace. I wondered why I had ever thought him a subdued edition of his father. And, quite suddenly, I was scared.

I spoke quickly. "You needn't worry. I don't mean to give you away! Why should I? It's nothing to me, but you must see it's awful to be in the middle of something and not know just what's going on! Oh, yes, I know about it, it was obvious enough. But I'll not say anything—I think too much of Miranda and her mother, and, if it comes to that, of your father, to drag the police back here with a lot more questions. Why should I care what you've got yourself into? But I *do* care about Adoni. . . . Did you know he's going to marry Miranda? Why did you have to involve him in this? Hasn't there been enough trouble?"

After that first, uncontrollable start, he had listened without movement or comment, but I could see his eyes on me, narrow and intent in the dim light. Now he said, very quietly, "Just what are you talking about?"

"You know quite well. I suppose poor Yanni never got the job done last night, so you've been across there tonight, to the Albanian coast, to do it yourself. Am I right?"

"Where did you get this . . . fantasy?"

"Fantasy, nothing," I said roundly. "Godfrey Manning told me this morning."

"What?" If I had got through before, this was straight between the joints of the harness. The word alone sent me back another pace, and this time he followed. I felt my back come up against a tree, and turned aside blindly—I think to run away—but his hand shot out and took my wrist, not hard, but in a grip I couldn't have broken without struggling, and probably not even then. "Manning? *He* told you?"

"Let me go!"

"No, wait a minute. I'm not going to hurt you, don't be scared . . . but you've got to tell me. What did Manning say to you?"

"Let me go, please!"

He dropped the wrist immediately. I rubbed it, though it was not in the least hurt. But I was shaking now. Something had happened that had changed the whole pitch of the scene; in place of the slightly pleasurable bitchiness of the previous exchange, there was now something urgent, hard, and yes, threatening. And it was Godfrey's name that had done it.

Gale repeated, "What did he tell you?"

"About Yanni? That he was a smuggler, and that he would probably have a 'contact,' or whatever you call it, who'd get his supplies for him, and that he hoped the police wouldn't tumble to it, because Spiro had been in it, too, and it would hurt Maria if it came out."

"That was all?"

"Yes."

"When did he tell you all this?"

"This morning, at the point, before you came down."

"Ah." I heard his breath go out. "Then you weren't up at Manning's house just now?"

"Of course I wasn't! Have you any idea what time it is?"

"I—of course. I'm sorry. I didn't think. I wasn't trying to be offensive. Did Manning tell you that I was Yanni's 'contact'?"

"No. I worked that out for myself."

"You did? How?"

I hesitated. The feeling of fear had gone, and common sense had come back to tell me that I was in no danger. Smuggler or not, he would hardly murder me for this. I said, "I saw Yanni coming up to the Castello last night."

"I . . . see." I could almost feel the amazement, the rapid reassessment of the situation. "But you said nothing to the police."

"No."

"Why not?"

I said carefully, "I'm not quite sure. To begin with, I kept quiet because I thought I might be mistaken, and Yanni possibly hadn't been going up to the Castello at all. If I'd thought you'd had anything to do with his death, I'd have told straight away. Then later I realized that there *was* some connection between you and Yanni, and that you'd known he was going out last night."

"How?"

"Because you weren't surprised when you heard he'd been drowned—"

"You noticed that, did you? My mistake. Go on."

"But you *were* shocked. I saw that."

"You see a darned sight too much." He sounded grim. "Was that what made you decide I hadn't killed him?"

"Good heavens, no! It wouldn't have occurred to me that you'd killed him! If I'd thought it was anything but an accident, I'd have told the whole thing straight away! It—it wasn't, was it?"

"Not that I'm aware of. Go on. What else did you see?"

"I saw you go back to the body and have another look at it."

"Did you, by God? From the path? Careless of me. I thought I was out of view. Who else saw that?"

"Nobody."

"You're sure of that?"

"Pretty well."

"And you said nothing about that, either? Well, well. So it was entirely your own idea that I was smuggling along with Yanni?"

"Yes."

"And now you've found out for certain. Do you still propose to say nothing?"

I said, without challenge, but out of simple curiosity, "How would you make sure of it?"

He said, equally simply, "My dear, I couldn't begin to try. I can only tell you that it's urgent that nobody should know I've been out tonight, nobody at all, and beg you to keep quiet."

"Then don't worry. I will."

There was a short pause. "As easy as that?" he said in an odd tone.

"I told you—for your father's sake," I said, perhaps a little too quickly, "and for Maria's. The only thing is—"

"Yes?"

"Things go in threes, they say, and if anything should happen to Adoni—"

He laughed. "Nothing shall, I promise you! I couldn't take the responsibility for damaging a work of art like Adoni! We-ell . . ." There was a whole world of relief in the long-drawn syllable. Then his voice changed; it was brisk, easy, normal. "I mustn't keep you any more. Heaven knows what the time is, and you must get home with that treasure trove of yours. I'm sorry I missed it this morning and gave your sister a bad half hour . . . And I'm sorry I frightened you just now. To say that I'm grateful is the understatement of the year. You'll let me see you home?"

"There's no need, really, thank you. In any case, hadn't you better get up there to help Adoni?"

"He's all right. Didn't you hear the signal?"

"Signal? But there hasn't been—" I stopped as I saw him smile. "Not the owls? No, really, how corny can you get! Was that really Adoni?"

He laughed. "It was. The robber's mate is home and dry, complete with 'catch.' So come along now, I'll take you home."

"No, really, I—"

"Please. After all, these woods are pretty dark and you were nervous, weren't you?"

"Nervous? No, of course not!"

He looked down in surprise. "Then what in the world were you racing back like that for?"

"Because I—" I stopped dead. The dolphin. I had forgotten the dolphin. The breeze, riffling the treetops, breathed gooseflesh along my skin. I thought of the dolphin, drying in it, back there on the beach. I said quickly, "It was so late, and Phyl was worrying. Don't bother, please, I'll go alone. Good night."

But as I reached the tunnel of trees, he caught me up. "I'd sooner see you safely home. Besides, you were quite right about shifting the boat; I'd rather have her nearer to hand in the morning. I'll take her across into the lee of the pines."

For the life of me, I couldn't suppress a jerk of apprehension. He felt it, and stopped.

"Just a minute."

His hand was on my arm. I turned. It was very dark under the trees.

He said, "You've found out more about me than is quite comfortable. It's time you were a little bit honest about yourself, I think. Did you meet anyone down in the bay?"

"No."

"See anyone?"

"N-no."

"Quite sure? This is important."

"Yes."

"Then why don't you want me to go down there?"

I said nothing. My throat was stiff and dry as cardboard. Tears of strain, fear, and exhaustion were not very far away.

"Look," he said urgently and not unkindly, "I have to know. Someday I'll tell you why. Damn it, I've got to trust you; what about your trusting me for a change? Something did happen down there to scare you, didn't it? It sent you running up here like a hare in front of a gun. Now, what was it? Either you tell me what it was or I go down and look for myself. Well?"

I threw in my cards. I said shakily, "It was the dolphin."

"It's in the bay."

There was a pause, then he said, with a sharpness that was part exasperation, part relief, "And am I supposed to be going down there to shoot it in the middle of the night? I told you before that I'd never touched the beast!" He added, more kindly, "Look, you've had a grim sort of day, and you're frightened and upset. Nobody's going to hurt your dolphin, so dry your eyes, and I'll take you back home now. He can look after himself, you know."

"He can't. He's on the beach."

"He's what?"

"He's stranded. He can't get away."

"Well, my God, you don't *still* think I'd do him any harm—" He stopped, and seemed for the first time to take in what I had been telling him. *"Stranded?* You mean the creature's actually beached?"

"Yes. High and dry. He'll die. I've been trying and trying to move him, and I can't. I was running just now to get a rope, that's why I was hurrying. If he's out of water too long, the wind'll dry him and he'll die. And all this time we've been wasting—"

"Where is he?"

"The other side, under the pines. What are you— Oh!" This was an involuntary cry as his hand tightened on my arm and swung me round. "What are you doing?"

"Don't worry, this isn't another assault. Now listen, there's a rope in my boat. I'll go down and get it, and I'll be with you as soon as I can. Get away back to your dolphin now, and wait for me. Can you keep him going another twenty minutes? . . . Good. We'll manage him between us, don't worry. But"—a slight pause—"be very quiet, do you mind?"

Before I could reply, he was gone, and I heard him making a swift but still stealthy course back the way he had come.

9

. . . To the elements
Be free, and fare thou well!

Act v, Scene 1

THERE WAS no time for doubt or questioning. That could come later. I obeyed him, flying down the path to the beach, back across the pale sand to where the big bulk still lay motionless.

The dark eye watched. He was alive. I whispered, "It's all right now, he's coming," and went straight back to my scooping and tipping of seawater. If I noticed that I hadn't bothered, even in my thoughts, to specify the "he," that was another question that could wait till later.

He came, sooner than I had expected. A small motorboat came nosing round the bay, without her engine, just with a dip and splash of oars as she was poled gently along. The breeze and the lapping of the sea on the rocks covered all sound until the boat was a rocking shadow within yards of me. I saw him stand up then, and lever it nearer the shore. Timber grated gently on rock, and he stepped out, making fast to a young pine, and then he was beside me on the sand, with a coil of rope over his arm.

"Good God! How did he get out here?"

"They do," I said. "I've read about it. Sometimes a storm blows them in, but sometimes they get their radar beams fogged up, or something, and they come in at a fast lick, and before they know where they are they're high and dry. We're lucky there's only a foot or so of tide, or the water might have been miles away from him by now. Can you move him, d'you think?"

"I can try." He stooped over the animal. "Trouble is, you can't really get a hold. Didn't you have a torch?"

"I dropped it when you savaged me up in the woods."

"So you did. There's one in the boat—no, perhaps not, we'll do without. Now, can you get to his other side?"

Together we fought to grasp and lift the dolphin, and with some success, for we did drag and shove him a foot or so downshore. But the dolphin himself defeated us; frightened, possibly, of the man's presence, or hurt by our tugging and by the friction of sand and pebbles, he began to struggle, spasmodically but violently; and at the end of the first strenuous minutes we had gained only a foot. I was exhausted, and Max Gale was breathing very hard.

"No good." He stood back. "He weighs a ton, and it's like trying to get hold of an outsize greased bomb. It'll have to be the rope. Won't it hurt him?"

"I don't know, but we'll have to try it. He'll die if he stays here."

"True enough. All right, help me get it round the narrow bit above the tail."

The dolphin lay like a log, his eye turning slowly back to watch us as we bent to tackle the tail rope. Without the torch it was impossible to tell, but I had begun to imagine that the eye wasn't so bright or watchful now. The tail felt heavy and cold, like something already dead. He never flickered a muscle as we fought to lift and put a loop round it.

"He's dying," I said, on a sort of gulp. "That fight must have finished him." I dashed the back of my hand over my eyes, and bent to the job. The rope was damp and horrible to handle, and the dolphin's tail was covered with coarse sand.

"You do tear yourself up rather, don't you?"

I looked up at him as he worked over the loop. His tone was not ungentle, but I got the impression from it that half his mind was elsewhere: he cared nothing for the dolphin, but wanted merely to get this over, and get back himself to whatever his own queer and shady night's work had been.

Well, fair enough. It was good of him to have come at all. But some old instinct of defensiveness made me say a little bitterly:

"It seems to me you can be awfully happy in this life if you stand aside and watch and mind your own business, and let other people do as they like about damaging themselves and one another. You go on kidding yourself that you're impartial and tolerant and all that, then all of a sudden you realize you're dead, and you've never been alive at all. Being alive hurts."

"So you have to break your heart over an animal who wouldn't even know you, and who doesn't even recognize you?"

"Someone has to bother," I said feebly. "Besides, he does recognize me, he knows me perfectly well."

He let that one pass, straightening up from the rope. "Well, there it is, that's the best we can do, and I'm hoping to heaven we can get it off again before he takes off at sixty knots or so. . . . Well, here goes. Ready?"

I dropped my coat on the sand, kicked off my sandals, and splashed into the shallows beside him. We took the strain of the rope together. It didn't even strike me as odd that we should be there, hands touching, working together as naturally as if we had done it every day of our lives. But I was very conscious of the touch of his hand against mine on the rope.

The dolphin moved an inch or two; another inch; slid smoothly for a foot; stuck fast. This way he seemed even heavier to haul, a dead weight on a rope that bit our hands and must surely be hurting him abominably, perhaps even cutting the skin. . . .

"Easy, now," said Max Gale in my ear.

We relaxed. I let go the rope, and splashed shorewards. "I'll go and take a look at him. I'm so afraid he's—"

"Blast!" This from Gale as the dolphin heaved forward suddenly, beating with his tail, slapping up water and sand. I heard the rope creak through Gale's hands, and another sharp curse from him as he plunged to keep his footing.

I ran back. "I'm sorry— Oh! What is it?" He had twisted the rope round his right hand and wrist, and I saw how he held his left arm up, taut, the fingers half clenched as if it had hurt him. I remembered how he had examined it, up in the glade. This must be why he had made such heavy weather of fixing the rope, and had been unable to shift the dolphin.

"Your hand?" I said sharply. "Is it hurt?"

"No. Sorry, but I nearly went in then. Well, at least the beast's still alive. Come on, we'll have another go before he really does take fright."

He laid hold once more, and we tried again. This time the dolphin lay still, dead weight again, moving slowly, slowly, till the lost ground was regained; but then he stuck once more, apparently immovable.

"There must be a ridge or something, he sticks every time." Gale paused to brush the sweat out of his eyes. I saw him drop his left hand from the rope and let it hang.

"Look," I said tentatively, "this'll take all night. Couldn't we possibly—I mean, could the *boat* tow him out . . . with the engine?"

He was silent for so long that I lost my nerve, and said hurriedly, "It's all right, I do understand. I—I just thought, if Adoni really had got safe in, it wouldn't matter. Forget it. It was marvelous of you to bother at all, with your hand and everything. Perhaps . . . if I just stay here all night and keep him damp and if you could . . . *do* you think you could ring Phyl for me and tell her? You could say you saw me from the terrace, and came down? And if you could come back in the morning, when it doesn't matter, with the boat, or with Adoni . . ." He had turned and was looking down at me. I couldn't see him except as a shadow against the stars. "If you wouldn't mind?" I finished.

"We'll use the boat now," he said abruptly. "What do we do—make the rope fast to the bows, and then back her out slowly?"

I nodded eagerly. "I'll stay beside him till he's floated. I'll probably have to hold him upright in the water till he recovers. If he rolls, he'll drown. The air hole gets covered, and they have to breathe terribly often."

"You'll be soaked."

"I'm soaked now."

"Well, you'd better have my knife. Here. If you have to cut the rope, cut it as near his tail as you can."

I stuck the knife in my belt, piratewise, then splashed back to where the dolphin lay. It wasn't my imagination, the lovely dark eye was duller, and the skin felt harsh and dry again. I put a hand on him, and bent down.

"Only a minute now, sweetheart. Don't be frightened. Only a minute."

"Okay?" called Max softly, from the boat, which was bobbing a few yards from shore. He had fixed the rope; it trailed through the water from the dolphin's tail to a ring on the bows.

"Okay," I said.

The engine started with a splutter and then a throbbing that seemed to fill the night. My hand was on the dolphin's body still. . . . Not even a tremor; boats' engines held no terrors for him. Then the motor steadied down to a mutter and the boat began to back quietly out from shore.

The rope lifted, vibrated, with the water flying from it in shining spray; then it tightened. The engine's note quickened; the rope stretched, the starlight running and dripping along it. The loop, fastened just where the great bow of the tail springs out horizontally from the spine, seemed to bite into the beast's flesh. It was very tight; the skin was straining; it must be hurting vilely.

The dolphin made a convulsive movement, and my hand clenched on the knife, but I kept still. My lip bled where I was biting on it, and I was sweating as if I were being hurt myself. The boat's engine beat gently, steadily; the starlight ran and dripped along the rope. . . .

The dolphin moved. Softly, smoothly, the huge body began to slide backwards down the sand toward the water. With my hand still on the loop of the tail rope, I went with it.

"It's working!" I said breathlessly. "Can you keep it very slow?"

"Right. That okay? Sing out as soon as he's afloat, and I'll cast off here."

The dolphin slithered slowly backwards, like a vessel beginning its run down the launching ramp. The grating of sand and broken shells under his body sounded as loud to me as the throbbing engine a few yards out to sea. Now, at last, he touched water . . . was drawn through the crisping ripples . . . was slowly, slowly, gaining the sea. I followed him as he slid deeper. The ripples washed over my feet, my ankles, my knees; the hand that I kept on the loop of rope was under water to the wrist.

And now we had reached the place where the bottom shelved more steeply. All in a moment I found myself standing nearly breast-deep, gasping as the water rose round me in the night chill. The dolphin, moving with me, rocked as the water began to take his weight. Another few seconds, and he would be afloat. He only moved once, a convulsive, flapping heave that twanged the rope like a bowstring and hurt my hand abominably, so that I cried out, and the engine shut to a murmur as Max said sharply:

"Are you hurt?"

"No. Go on. It held him."

"How far now?"

"Nearly deep enough. He's quiet now, I think he's— Oh, God, I think he's dead! Oh, Max „ . . ."

"Steady, my dear, I'll come. Hold him, we'll float him first. Say when."

"Nearly . . . *Right! Stop!*"

The engine shut off, as suddenly as if a soundproof door had slammed. The dolphin's body floated past me, bumping and wallowing. I braced myself to hold him. Max had paid out the rope, and was swiftly poling the boat back to her mooring under the pines. I heard the rattle of a chain as he made fast, and in another few moments he was beside me in the water, with the slack of the rope looped over his arm.

"How goes it? Is he dead?"

"I don't know. I don't know. I'll hold him up while you get the rope off."

"Turn his head to seaward first, just in case. . . . Come along, old chap, round you come. . . . There. Fine. Now hang on, my dear; I'll be as quick as I can."

The dolphin lay motionless in my arms, the air hole flaccid and wide open, just out of water, his body rolling heavily, like a leaky boat about to founder. "You're all right now," I told him in an agonized whisper that he certainly couldn't hear, "you're in the sea . . . the *sea*. You can't die now . . . you can't. . . ."

"Stop worrying." Max's voice came, cheerfully brisk, from the other end of the dolphin. "St. Spiridion looks after his own. He is a bit sub, poor beast, isn't he? However, heaven keep him so till I've got this damned rope off him. Are you cold?"

"Not very," I said, teeth chattering.

As he bent over the rope again, I thought I felt the dolphin stir against me. Next moment I was sure. The muscles flexed under the skin, a slow ripple of strength ran along the powerful back, a flipper stirred, feeling the water, using it, taking his weight. . . .

"He's moving!" I said excitedly. "He's all right! Oh, Max—quick—if he takes off now—"

"If he takes off now, we'll go with him. The rope's wet, I can't do a thing, I'll have to cut it. Knife, please."

As he slid the blade in under the rope and started to saw at it, the dolphin came to life. The huge muscles flexed smoothly once, twice, against me, then I saw the big shoulders ripple and bunch. The air hole closed.

I said urgently, "Quick! He's going!"

The dolphin pulled out of my arms. There was a sudden surge of cold water that soaked me to the breast as the great body went by in a splendid diving roll, heading straight out to sea. I heard Max swear sharply, and there was a nearer, secondary splash and swell as he disappeared in his turn, completely under the water. The double wash swept over me, so that I staggered, almost losing my footing, and for one ghastly moment I thought that Max, hanging grimly on to the rope, had been towed straight out to sea in the dolphin's wake, like a minnow on a line. But as I regained my own balance, staggering back toward shallower water, he surfaced beside me, waist-deep and dripping, with the cut loop in his hand, and the rope trailing.

I gripped his arm, almost crying with relief and excitement. "Oh, Max!" I staggered again, and his soaking arm came round me. I hardly noticed. I was watching the dark, starry sea where, far out, a trail of sea fire burned and burst in long, joyous leaps and curves, and vanished into the blackness. . . .

"Oh, Max . . . look, there he goes; d'you see the light? There . . . he's gone. He's gone. Oh, wasn't it *marvelous?*"

For the second time that night I felt myself gripped, and roughly silenced, but this time by his mouth. It was cold, and tasted of salt, and the kiss seemed to last forever. We were both soaked to the skin, and chilled, but where our bodies met and clung I could feel the quick heat of his skin and the blood beating warm against mine. We might as well have been naked.

He let me go, and we stood there staring at each other.

I pulled myself together with an effort. "What was that, the forfeit for the roses?"

"Hardly. Call it the climax of a hell of a night." He pushed the soaking hair back off his forehead, and I saw him grin. "The recreation of the warrior, Miss Waring. Do you mind?"

"You're welcome." *Take it lightly, I thought, take it lightly.* "You and Adoni must have had yourselves quite a time out fishing."

"Quite a time." He was not trying to take it any way at all; he merely sounded cheerful, and decidedly pleased with himself. "As a matter of fact, that was the pent-up feelings of a hell of a week. Didn't you see it coming? My father did."

"Your father? After that first meeting? I don't believe you. You looked as if you'd have liked to lynch me."

"My feelings," he said carefully, "could best be described as mixed. And damn it, if you will persist in being half naked every time you come near me—"

"Max Gale!"

He laughed at me. "Didn't they ever tell you that men were only human, Lucy Waring? And some a bit more human than others?"

"If you call it human. You flatter yourself."

"All right, darling, we'll call it the forfeit for the roses. You took a fair number, didn't you? Splendid. Come here."

"Max, you're impossible . . . Of all the complacent— This is ridiculous! What a time to *choose*. . . ."

"Well, my love, since you spark like a cat every time I come near you, what can I do but duck you first?"

"Shows what a lot you know about electricity."

"Uh-huh. No, keep still a minute. You pack a pretty lethal charge, don't you?"

"You could blow a few fuses yourself, if it comes to that. . . . For pity's sake, we must be mad." I pushed him away. "Come on out. I'd love to die with you and be buried in one grave, but not of pneumonia, it's not romantic. . . . *No*, Max! I admit I owe you anything you like, but let's reckon it up on dry land! Come on *out*, for goodness' sake."

He laughed, and let me go. "All right. Come on. Oh, God, I've dropped the rope . . . No, here it is. And that's to pay for, too, let me tell you; a brand-new sisal rope, sixty feet of it—"

"You're not the only one. This frock cost five guineas, and the sandals were three pounds ten, and I don't suppose they'll ever be quite be the same again."

"I'm perfectly willing to pay for them," said Max cheerfully, stopping in eighteen inches of water.

"I'm sure you are, but it's not your bill. Oh, darling, don't be *crazy*, come *out*!"

"Pity. Who do you suppose settles the dolphin's accounts? Apollo, or the Saint? I think I'd opt for Apollo if I were you. Of course, if you've lost your sister's diamond it'll step the bill up quite a lot."

"*Murder!* Oh, no, here it is." The great marquise flashed blue in the starlight. "Oh, Max, seriously, thank you most awfully—you were so wonderful . . . I've been such a fool! As if you could ever—"

His hand tightened warningly on my arm, and in the same moment I saw a light, a small dancing light, like that of an electric torch, coming round the point along the path from the Villa Rotha. It skipped along the rocks, paused on the moored boat, so that for the first time I saw her name, *Ariel*; then it glanced over the water and caught us, dripping and bedraggled, splashing out of the shallows. We were also, by the time it caught us, at least four feet apart.

"Great God in heaven!" said Godfrey's voice. "What goes on? Gale—

Lucy . . . you're soaked, both of you! Is this another accident, for heaven's sake?"

"No," said Max. "What brought you down?"

His tone was about as informative, and as welcoming, as a blank wall with broken glass on the top. But Godfrey seemed not to have noticed. He had already jumped lightly down from the rocks to the sand beneath the pines. I saw the torchlight pause again, then rake the place where the dolphin had lain, and the wide, gouged track where he had been dragged down to the sea. My coat lay there in a huddle, with the sandals kicked off anyhow.

"For pity's sake, what gives?" Godfrey sounded distinctly alarmed, and very curious. "Lucy, you haven't had trouble, have you? Did you get the diamond?"

"How did you know that?" I asked blankly.

"Good God, Phyl rang up, of course. She said you'd come down hours ago, and she was worried. I said I'd come and look for you. I'd only just got in." The torchlight fingered us both again, and rested on Max. "What happened?"

"Don't flash that thing in my face," said Max irritably. "Nothing's happened, at least not in the sense you mean. That dolphin of yours got itself stranded. Miss Waring was trying to heave it back into the water, and couldn't manage, so I brought the boat along and towed the beast out to sea. We got drenched in the process."

"You mean to tell me"—Godfrey sounded frankly incredulous—"that you brought your boat out at this time of night to rescue *a dolphin?*"

"Wasn't it good of him?" I put in eagerly.

"Very," said Godfrey. He hadn't taken his eyes off Max. "I could have sworn I heard you go out some time ago."

"I thought you were out yourself," said Max. "And had only just come in."

Here we were again, I thought, the stiff-backed dogs warily circling. But it might be that Max's tone was repressive only because he was talking through clenched teeth—owing to cold, rather than emotion—because he added, civilly enough, "I said 'along,' not 'out.' We went out, as it happened, sometime after ten. We got in a few minutes ago. Adoni had just gone up when Miss Waring came running. I was still in the boat."

Godfrey laughed. "I'm sorry, I didn't mean to belittle the good deed! What a piece of luck for Lucy and the dolphin!"

"Yes, wasn't it?" I said. "I was just wondering what on earth to do, when I heard Mr. Gale. I'd have come for you, but Phyl had said you wouldn't be there."

"I wasn't." I thought he was going to say something further, but he changed it to: "I went out about ten thirty, and I'd only just got into the house when the telephone rang. *Did* you find the ring?"

"Yes, thank you. Oh, it's been quite a saga, you've no idea!"

"I'm sorry I missed it," he said. "I'd have enjoyed the party."

"I enjoyed it myself," said Max. "Now, look, to hell with the civilities, you'll have to hear it all some other time. If we're not to die of pneumonia, we've got to go. Where are your shoes, Miss Waring? . . . Oh, thanks." This as Godfrey's torch picked them out and he handed them to me. "Get them on quickly, will you?"

"What's this?" Godfrey's voice altered sharply.

"My coat." I paid very little attention to his tone; I was shivering freely now, and engaged in the very unpleasant struggle to get my sandals on over wet and sandy feet. "Oh, and there's Phyl's bag. Mr. Gale, would you mind—"

"That's blood!" said Godfrey. He was holding the coat up, and his torch shone, powerful as a head lamp, on the sleeve. I looked up, startled.

It was indeed blood. One sleeve of the coat was streaked with it.

I felt, rather than saw, Max stiffen beside me. The torch beam started its swing toward him. I said sharply, *"Please* put the torch out, Godfrey! I don't feel decent in this sopping dress. Give me the coat, please. Yes, it's blood . . . The dolphin had a cut from a stone, or something; it bled all over me before I saw it. I'll be lucky if I ever get the stain out."

"Hurry up," said Max brusquely, "you're shivering. Put this round you. Come on, we'll have to go."

He slung the coat round my shoulders. My teeth were chattering now like a typewriter; the coat was no comfort at all over the soaked and clinging dress. "Y-yes," I said, "I'm coming. I'll tell you about it when I see you, Godfrey. Th-thanks for coming down."

"Good night," said Godfrey. "I'll come over tomorrow and see how you are."

He turned back into the shadow of the pines. I saw the torchlight move slowly over the ground where the dolphin had lain before it dodged once again up on to the rocks.

Max and I went briskly across the sand. The wind blew cold on our wet clothing.

"The coat cost nine pounds fifteen," I said, "and *that* bill's yours. That dolphin wasn't bleeding. What have you done to your hand?"

"Nothing that won't mend. Here, this way."

We were at the foot of the Castello steps and I would have gone past, but he put out a hand and checked me.

"You can't go all the way home in those things. Come on up."

"Oh, no, I think I'd better—"

"Don't be silly, why not? Manning'll telephone your sister. So can you, if it comes to that. And I'm not going to escort you all the way over there and then tramp back myself in these. What's more, these blasted boots are full of water."

"You might have drowned."

"So I might. And how much would that have been to Apollo's account?"

"You know how much," I said, not lightly at all, but not for him to hear.

10

He is drunk now. Where had he wine?

Act V, Scene 1

THE TERRACE was empty, but one of the long windows stood open, and Max led the way in through this.

The room was lit only by one small shaded lamp on a low table, and looked enormous and mysterious, a cave full of shadows. The piano showed its teeth vaguely near a darkened window, and the unlit stove and the huge gramophone loomed like sarcophagi in some dim museum.

Sir Julian sat in an armchair beside the lamp, which cast an almost melodramatic slant of light on the silver hair and emphatic brow. The white cat on his knee, and the elegant hand that stroked it, completed the picture. The effect was stagy in the extreme. Poe's "Raven," I thought appreciatively; all it needs is the purple drapes, and the croaking from the shadows over the door. . . .

In the same moment I became aware of other, even less comfortable stage effects than these. On the table at his elbow, under the lamp, stood a bottle of Turkish gin, two thirds empty, a jug of water, and two glasses. And Sir Julian was talking to himself. He was reciting from *The Tempest,* the speech where Prospero drowns his book; he was saying it softly, an old magician talking half to himself, half to the heavenly powers from whose kingdom he was abdicating. I had never heard him do it better. And if anyone had wanted to know how much sheer technique—as opposed to nightly sweat and blood in front of the lights—was worth, here was the answer. It was doubtful if Sir Julian Gale even knew what he was saying. He was very drunk indeed.

Max had stopped dead just inside the window, with me close behind him, and I heard him make some sort of sound under his breath. Then I saw that Sir Julian was not alone. Adoni detached himself from the thicker darkness beyond the lamp, and came forward. He was dressed, like Max, in a fisherman's sweater and boots, rough clothing which only served to emphasize his startling good looks. But his face was sharp with anxiety.

"Max—" he began, then stopped abruptly as he saw me and the state we were both in. "It was *you?* What's happened?"

"Nothing that matters," said Max shortly.

This wasn't the time to choose words, or, certainly, to resent them. So much was made more than ever obvious as he advanced into the light, and I saw him clearly for the first time that night. Whatever aggressive high spirits had prompted the little interlude there in the sea had vanished abruptly; he looked not only worried now, but angry and ashamed, and also very tired indeed. His left hand was thrust deep into his trouser pocket, and there was some rag—a handkerchief, perhaps—twisted round the wrist, and blotched with blood.

Sir Julian had turned his head at the same time.

"Ah, Max . . ." Then he, too, saw me, and the hand which had been stroking the cat lifted in a graceful, practiced gesture that looked as natural as breathing. " 'Most sure, the goddess, On whom'— No, we had that before, didn't we? But how delightful to see you again, Miss Lucy . . . Forgive me for not getting up; the cat, as you see . . ." His voice trailed away uncertainly. It seemed he was dimly realizing that there was need of more excuse than the cat would provide. A smile, loose enough to be disturbing, slackened his mouth. "I was having some music. If you'd care to listen . . ."

The hand moved, not very steadily, to the switch of the tape recorder which stood on a chair beside him, but Adoni stooped quickly and laid a hand over it, with a gentle phrase in Greek. Sir Julian gave up the attempt, and sank back in his chair, nodding and smiling. I saw with horrified compassion that the nod had changed to a tremor which it cost him an effort to check.

"Who's been here, Father?" asked Max.

The actor glanced up at him, then away, with a look that might, in a less distinguished face, have been called shifty. "Been here? Who should have been here?"

"Do you know, Adoni?"

The young man lifted his shoulders. "No. He was like this when I got in. I didn't know there was any in the house."

"There wasn't. I suppose he was alone when you got in? You'd hardly have given me the 'all clear' otherwise." He glanced down at his father, who was taking not the slightest notice of the conversation, but had retreated once more into some private world of his own, some gin-fumed distance apparently lit by strong ambers and swimming in a haze of poetry. "Why did he come back? I wonder. He hasn't told you that?"

"He said something about Michael Andiakis being taken ill, but I haven't had time to get anything more out of him. He's not been talking sense . . . he keeps trying to switch that thing on again. It was going when I got up to the house. I got a fright; I thought someone was here with him."

"Someone certainly has been." Max's voice was tight and grim. "He didn't say how he got back from town?"

Adoni shook his head. "I did think of telephoning Andiakis' house to ask, but at this time of night—"

"No, you can't do that." He bent over his father's chair and spoke gently and clearly. "Father. Who's been here?"

Sir Julian, starting out of his dreams, glanced up, focussed, and said, with dignity, "There were matters to discuss."

His enunciation was as faultless as ever; the only thing was, you could hear him working to keep it so. His hands lay motionless now on the cat's fur, and there, again, you could see the controls being switched on. The same with Max, who had himself well in hand now, but I could hear the effort that the patient tone was costing him. Watching them, I felt myself so shaken with compassion and love that it seemed it was that, and not my wet clothes, which made me shiver.

"Naturally," said Julian clearly, "I had to ask him in when he had driven me home. It was very good of him."

Max and Adoni exchanged glances. "Who had?"

No reply. Adoni said, "He won't answer anything straight. It's no use."

"It's got to be. We've got to know who this was and what he's told him."

"I doubt if he told him much. He wouldn't say anything to me, only tried to turn the tape on, and talked on and on about the story you are writing the music for, you know, the old story of the island that he was telling Miranda and Spiro."

Max pushed the damp hair off his brow with a gesture almost of desperation. "We've got to find out—now, before he passes out. He knew perfectly well where we were going. He agreed to stay out of the way. My God, I was sure he could be trusted now. I thought he'd be safe with Michael. Why the *hell* did he come home?"

"Home is where the heart is," said Sir Julian. "When my wife died, the house was empty as a lord's great kitchen without a fire in it. Lucy knows, don't you, my dear?"

"Yes," I said. "Shall I go, Max?"

"No, please . . . if you don't mind. If you'll please stay . . . Look, Father, it's all right now. There's only me and Adoni and Lucy. You can tell us about it. Why didn't you stay at Michael's?"

"Poor Michael was playing a very interesting game, Steinitz gambit, and I lost a rook in the first few minutes. Do you play chess, my dear?"

"I know the moves," I said.

"Five moves would have done it. White to play, and mate in five moves. A foregone conclusion. But then he had the attack."

"What sort of attack?" asked Max.

"I had no idea that his heart wasn't all it should be, for all he never drinks. I am quite aware that this is one reason why you like me to visit Michael, but a drink occasionally, for purely social reasons, never does the least harm. My heart is as strong as a bell. As strong as a bell. One's heart," added Sir Julian, with the air of one dismissing the subject, "is where the home is. Good night."

"Just a minute. You mean Michael Andiakis has died of a heart attack? I *see*. I'm sorry, Father. No wonder you felt you needed—"

"No, *no!* Who said he had died? Of course he didn't, I was there. They have no telephone, so it was a good thing, the doctor said so, a very good thing. But then if I hadn't been there, I doubt if Michael would have had the attack at all. He always did get too excitable over our little game. Poor Michael."

"You went to fetch the doctor?"

"I told you," said his father impatiently. "Why can't you listen? I think I'd like to go to bed."

"What happened when the doctor came?"

"He put Michael to bed, and I helped him." It was the first direct answer he had given, and he seemed to feel obscurely that something was wrong, for he gave that sidelong look at his son before going on. "It's as well that I'm as sound as a bell myself, though I have never understood why bells should be particularly—particularly sound. Sweet bells jangled, out of tune and harsh. Then I went to get the doctor." He paused. "I mean the daughter. Yes, the daughter."

Adoni said, "There's a married daughter who lives in Capodistrias Street. She has three children. If she had to bring them with her, there would be no room for Sir Gale to stay."

"I see. How did you get the lift back, Father?"

"Well, I went to Karamanlis' garage, of course." Sir Julian suddenly sounded sober, and very irritable. "Really, Max, I don't know why you talk as if I'm incapable of looking after myself! Please try to remember that I lived here before you were born! I thought Leander might oblige me, but he was away. There was only one boy on duty, but he offered to get his brother to take me. We had a very interesting chat, very interesting indeed. I knew his uncle, Manoulis was the name. I remember once, when I was at Avra—"

"Was it Manoulis who brought you home?"

Sir Julian focussed. "Home?"

"Back here?" amended Max quickly.

The older man hesitated. "The thing was, I had to ask him in. When he came in for petrol and saw me there, you might say he had to offer the lift, but all the same, one has to be civil. I'm sorry, Max."

"It's all right, I understand. Of course one must. He brought you home, and you felt you'd have to ask him in, so you bought the gin?"

"Gin?" Sir Julian was drifting again. I thought I could see something struggling in his face, some intelligence half drowned with gin and sleep, holding on by a gleam of cunning. "That's Turkish gin, too, terrible stuff. God knows what they put in it. It was what he said he liked. . . . We stopped at that taverna—Constantinos' it used to be, but I forget the name now—two miles out of Ipsos. I think he must have guessed there wouldn't be any in the house."

Max was silent. I couldn't see his face.

Adoni broke the pause. "Max, look." I had seen him stoop to pick something up, and now he held out a hand, with some small object on the palm: a cigarette stub. "It was down there, by the stove. It's not one of yours, is it?"

"No." Max picked the thing up, and held it closer to the light.

Adoni said, "It is, isn't it?"

"Obviously." Their eyes met again, over the old man's head. There was a silence, in which the cat suddenly purred. " 'Things to discuss' " Max quoted it softly, but with a new note in his voice that I found frightening. "What the sweet hell can *he* have wanted to discuss with my father?"

"This meeting," said Adoni, "could it be accidental?"

"It must have been. He was driving by, and picked my father up. Pure chance. Who could have foreseen that? Damn and damn and damn."

"And getting him . . . like this?"

"Letting him get like this. There's a difference. That can't have been deliberate. Nobody knew he was like this except us, and Michael and the Karithises."

Adoni said, "Maybe he's been talking this sort of nonsense all evening. Maybe *he* couldn't get any sense out of him, either."

"He couldn't get any sense out of me," said Sir Julian, with intense satisfaction.

"Oh, my God," said Max, "let's hope he's right." He flicked the cigarette butt toward the stove, and straightened his shoulders. "Well, I'll get him to bed. Be a good chap and look after Miss Lucy, will you? Show her the bathroom—the one my father uses is the least repulsive, I think. Find her a towel and show her a spare bedroom—the one Michael sleeps in. There's an electric fire there."

"All right, but what about your hand? Haven't you seen to it at all?"

"Not yet, but I will in a moment. Go on, man, don't fuss. Believe me, I'd fuss plenty if I thought it was serious; I'm a pianist of a sort, don't forget! Lucy, I'm sorry about this. Will you go with him now?"

"Of course."

"This way," said Adoni.

The massive door swung shut behind us, and our steps rattled across the checkerboard marble of the hall floor.

It would have taken Dali and Ronald Searle, working overtime on alternate jags of mescal and Benzedrine, to design the interior of the Castello dei Fiori. At one end of a hall was a massive curved staircase, with a wrought-iron banister and bare stone treads. The walls were paneled in the darkest possible oak, and what small rugs lay islanded on the marble sea were done (as far as I could judge in the gloom) in uniform shades of drab and olive green. A colossal open fireplace, built for roasting oxen whole, by men who had never roasted, and would never roast, an ox whole in their lives, half filled one wall. The hearth of this bristled with spits and dogs and tongs and cauldrons and a hundred other medieval kitchen gadgets whose functions I couldn't even guess at; they looked like—and probably were—instruments of torture. For the rest, the hall was cluttered like a bargain basement: the Gales must have thrown most of the furniture out of their big living room to clear the acoustics—or perhaps merely in the interests of sane living—and as a result the hall was crammed full of enormous overstuffed furniture in various shades of mud, with innumerable extras in the way of bamboo tables, Chinese screens, and whatnots in spindly and very shiny wood. I thought I glimpsed a harmonium, but might have been wrong, because there was a full-sized organ, pipes and all, in the darkness beyond a fretwork dresser and a coatrack made of stags' antlers. There was certainly a harp, and a small forest of pampas grass stuck in what I am sure was the severed foot of an elephant. These riches were lit with a merciful dimness by a single weak bulb in a torch held by a fully armed Javanese warrior who looked a bit like a gila monster in rut.

Adoni ran gracefully up the wide stairs in front of me. I followed more slowly, hampered by my icily clinging clothes, my sandals leaving horrible wet marks on the treads. He paused to wait for me, eyeing me curiously.

"What happened to you and Max?"

"The dolphin—Spiro's dolphin—was stranded on the beach, and he helped me to float it again. It pulled us both in."

"No, did it really?" He laughed. "I'd like to have seen that!"

"I'm sure you would." At least his spirits didn't seem to have been damped by the recent scene in the music room. I wondered if he was used to it.

"When you ran into Max, then you were coming for help? I see! But why were you out on the beach in the dark?"

"Now don't *you* start!" I said warmly. "I had plenty of that from Max! I was down there picking up a ring—this ring—that my sister had left this morning."

His eyes and mouth rounded at the sight of the diamond. *"Po po po!* That must be worth a few drachs, that one! No wonder you didn't mind making a journey in the dark!"

"Worth more than your journey?" I asked innocently.

The beautiful eyes danced. "I wouldn't say that."

"No?" I regarded him uneasily. What on earth—what in heaven—could they have been up to? Drugs? Surely not! Arms? Ridiculous! But then, what did I know about Max, after all? And his worry in case his father might have "talked" hadn't just been worry; it had been fear. As for Adoni—I had few illusions as to what my young Byzantine saint would be capable of. . . .

He asked, "When you first went out through the woods, you saw nobody?"

"Max asked me that. I heard Sir Julian playing the tape recorder, but I've no idea if his visitor was still there. I gather you know who it was?"

"I think so. It's a guess, but I think so. Sir Gale may tell Max when they are alone, I don't know."

"Max doesn't normally have drink in the house at all?"

"None that his—none that can be found."

"I see."

I did indeed see. I saw how the rumors had arisen, and just how false Phyl's picture of the situation had been. Except in so far as this sort of periodic "bender" was a symptom of mental strain, Sir Julian Gale was sane enough. And now that I thought even further back, there had been whispers in the theater world, possibly strong ones among those who knew him, but on my level the merest breath . . . rumors scotched once and for all by Sir Julian's faultless performances right up to the moment of retirement. Well, I had had a personal demonstration tonight of how it had been done.

"We thought he was better," said Adoni. "He has not done this for, oh, a long time. This will make Max very . . ." He searched for a word and came up with one that was, I felt, not quite adequate. ". . . unhappy."

"I'm sorry. But he does seem to have been pushed into it this time."

"Pushed in? Oh, yes, I understand. That is true. Well, Max will deal with it." He gave a little laugh. "Poor Max, he gets everything to deal with. Look, we had better hurry, or you will get cold, and then Max will deal with *me!*"

"Could he?"

"Easily. He pays my wages."

He paused, and pressed a switch in the paneling, invisible except to its intimates. Another dim light faltered into life, this time held aloft by a startling figure in flesh-pink marble, carved by some robust Victorian with a mind above fig leaves. A wide corridor now stretched ahead of us, lined on one side by massive iron-studded doors, and on the other by what would, in daylight, be stained-glass windows of a peculiarly repulsive design.

"This way."

He led the way quickly along the corridor. To either side the light glimmered yellow on the pathetic heads of deer and ibexes, and case after case where stuffed birds stood enthroned and moth-eaten. Every other available foot of wall space was filled with weapons—axes, swords, daggers, and ancient firearms which I (who had furnished a few period plays in my time) identified as flintlocks and muskets, probably dating from the Greek War of Independence. It was to be hoped that Sir Julian and his son were as blind to the murderous décor as Adoni appeared to be.

"Your bathroom is along there." He pointed ahead to a vast door, opposite which hung a tasteful design in crossed whips and spurs. "I'll just show you where everything is, then I must go and dress his wrist."

"How badly is he hurt? He wouldn't say."

"Not badly at all. I think it's only a graze, for all it bled a lot. Don't worry, Max is sensible, he'll take all the care he should."

"And you?" I said.

He looked surprised. "I?"

"Will you take care of yourself as well? Oh, I know it's nothing to do with me, Adoni, but . . . well, be careful. For Miranda's sake, if not for your own."

He laughed at me, and touched a thin silver chain at his neck which must have held a cross or some sort of medal. "Don't you worry about me, either, Miss Lucy. The Saint looks after his own." A vivid look. "Believe me, he does."

"I take it you did well tonight?" I said, a little dryly.

"I think so. Here we are." He shoved the door wide, and found another switch. I glimpsed the splendors of marble and mahogany beyond him. "The bedroom is the next one, through there. I'll find you a towel, and later I shall make you something hot to drink. You can find the way down?"

"Yes, thank you."

He rummaged in a cupboard the size of a small garage, and emerged with a couple of towels. "Here you are. You have everything now?"

"I think so. The only thing is—do I have to touch that thing?"

"That thing" was a fearsome contraption which, apparently, heated the water. It looked like a stranded mine, and sat on a panel of dials and switches that might have come straight off the flight deck of an airliner designed by Emmett.

"You are as bad as Sir Gale," said Adoni indulgently. "He calls it Lolita, and refuses to touch it. It's perfectly safe, Spiro made it."

"Oh."

"It did go on fire once, but it's all right now. We rewired it only last month, Spiro and I."

Another dazzling smile, and the door shut gently. I was alone with Lolita.

You had to climb three steps to the bath, which was about the size of a swimming pool, and fairly bristling with gadgets in blackened brass. But I forgave the Castello everything when I turned the tap marked C and the water rushed out in a boiling cloud of steam. I hoped poor Max wouldn't be long before he achieved a similar state of bliss—it was to be assumed there was another bathroom, and another Lolita as efficient as mine—but just at the moment I spared Max no more than the most passing of thoughts, and none whatever for the rest of the night's adventures. All I wanted was to be out of those dreadful, sodden clothes and into that glorious bath. . . .

By the time I was languidly drying a body broiled all over to a glowing pink, my underclothing, which was mostly nylon, was dry. The dress and coat were still wet, so I left them spread over the hot pipes, put on the dressing gown which hung behind the door, then padded through into the bedroom to attend to my face and hair.

I had what I had salvaged of Phyl's make-up, which included a comb, so I did the best I could with the inevitable dim light and a cheval-glass swinging between two mahogany pillars, which seemed designed to hang perpetually facing the carpet, until I found on the floor and replaced the wedge of newspaper that had held it in position since, apparently, July 20, 1917.

In the greenish glass my reflection swam like something that might well have startled the Lady of Shalott out of her few wits. The dressing gown was obviously one of Sir Julian's stagier efforts; it was long, of thick, dark red silk, and made one think of Coward comedies. With Phyl's lipstick, and my short, damply curling hair, and the enormous diamond on my hand, it made a pretty high camp effect.

Well, it was no odder than the other guises he had seen me in up to now. I wondered if this, too, would qualify as "half naked." Not that it mattered, just now he would have other things very much on his mind.

I grimaced briefly at the image in the glass, then went out, back along Murder Alley, and down the stairs.

11

The very instant that I saw you, did
My heart fly to your service; there resides,
To make me slave to it . . .

Act III, Scene 1

THE MUSIC-ROOM door was standing open, but, though the lamp still burned, there was no one there. The gin had vanished, too, and in its place was something that looked like the remains of a stiff Alka-Seltzer, and a cup that had probably contained coffee.

As I hesitated in the doorway, I heard a quick step, and the service door under the stairway opened with a swish of chilly air.

"Lucy? Ah, I thought I heard you. You're all right? Warm now?"

"Lovely, thank you." He himself looked a different person. I noticed that there was a fresh white bandage on his wrist, and that his dry clothes—another thick sweater and dark trousers—made him look as tough as before, but younger, rather nearer Adoni's league. So did the look in his face: he looked tired still, but with a tautness that now seemed to have some sort of affinity with Adoni's dark glow of excitement. A worthwhile trip, indeed. . . .

I said quickly, "Your clothes . . . You're surely not planning to go out again?"

"Only to drive you home, don't worry. Come along to the kitchen, will you? It's warm there, and there's coffee. Adoni and I have been having something to eat."

"I'd adore some coffee. But I don't know if I ought to stay—my sister really will have the wind up by now."

"I rang her up and told her what had happened . . . more or less." He grinned, a boy's grin. "Actually, Godfrey Manning had already called up and told her about the dolphin, and that her ring was safe, so she's quite happy, and says she'll expect you when she sees you. So come along."

I followed him through the service door and down a bare, echoing passage. It seemed that the Castello servants could not be allowed to share the glories which fell to their betters, for "below stairs" the Castello was unadorned by dead animals and lethal weapons. Personally I'd have traded the whole building, organ pipes and all, for the kitchen, a wonderful, huge cavern of a place, with a smaller cave for fireplace, where big logs burned merrily in their iron basket, adding their sweet, pungent smells to the smells of food and coffee, and lighting the big room with a living, beating glow. Hanging from the rafters, among the high, flickering shadows, bunches of dried herbs and strings of onions stirred and glimmered in the updraught of warm air.

In the center of the kitchen was about an acre of scrubbed wooden table, and in a corner of the room Adoni was frying something on an electric cooker which had probably been built, or at any rate wired, by himself and Spiro. There was a wonderful smell of bacon and coffee.

"You can eat some bacon and eggs, surely?" asked Max.

"She will have to," said Adoni briefly, over his shoulder. "I have done them already."

"Well . . ." I said, and Max pulled out a chair for me at the end of the table nearest to the fire, where a rather peculiar assortment of plates and cutlery were set in a space comprising about a fiftieth of the table's total area. Adoni put a plate down in front of me, and I realized that I was suddenly, marvelously hungry. "Have you had yours?" I asked.

"Adoni has, and I've just reached the coffee stage," said Max. "Shall I pour some for you straight away?"

"Yes, please." I wondered whether it would be tactful to ask after Sir Julian, and this made me remember my borrowed finery. "My things were still wet, so I borrowed your father's dressing gown. Will he mind, do you think? It's a terribly grand one."

"Present Laughter," said Max. "Of course he won't. He'll be delighted. Sugar?"

"Yes, please."

"There. If you can get outside that lot, I doubt if the pneumonia bugs will stand a chance. Adoni's a good cook, when pushed to it."

"It's marvelous," I said, with my mouth full, and Adoni gave me that heart-shaking smile of his, said, "It's a pleasure," and then, to Max, something that I recognized (from a week's painful study of a phrase book) as "Does she speak Greek?"

Max jerked his head in that curious gesture—like a refractory camel snorting—that the Greeks use for "No," and the boy plunged forthwith into a long and earnest speech of which I caught no intelligible word at all. It was, I guessed, urgent and excited rather than apprehensive. Max listened, frowning, and without comment, except that twice he interrupted with a Greek phrase—the same one each time—that checked the flow and sent Adoni back to speak more slowly and clearly. I ate placidly through my bacon and eggs, trying not to notice the deepening frown on Max's face or the steadily heightened excitement of Adoni's narrative.

At length the latter straightened up, glancing at my empty plate. "Would you like some more? Or cheese, perhaps?"

"Oh, no, thank you. That was wonderful."

"Some more coffee, then?"

"Is there some?"

"Of course." Max poured it, and pushed the sugar nearer. "Cigarette?"

"No, thanks."

He was returning the pack to his pocket when Adoni, who had been removing my plate, said something quickly and softly in Greek, and Max held the pack out to him. Adoni took three cigarettes, with the glimmer of a smile at me when he saw that I was watching, then he said something else in Greek to Max, added "Good night, Miss Lucy," and went out through a door I hadn't noticed before, in a far corner of the kitchen.

Max said easily, "Forgive the mystery. We've been putting my father to bed."

"Is he all right?"

"He will be." He threw me a look. "I suppose you knew about his—difficulty?"

"No, how could I? I'd no idea."

"But if you're in the business . . . I thought it must surely have got round."

"It didn't get to me," I said. "I suppose there must have been rumors, but all I ever knew was that he wasn't well. I thought it was heart or something. And honestly, nobody knew here—at least, Phyl didn't, and if there's been any talk you can bet she'd be the first to hear it. She just knew what you told Leo, that he'd been ill, and in a nursing home. Does it happen often?"

"If you'd asked me that yesterday," he said, a little bitterly, "I'd have said it probably wouldn't happen again."

"Did he talk when you took him upstairs?"

"A little."

"Tell you who it was?"

"Yes."

"And what they'd talked about?"

"Not really, no. He just kept repeating that he 'hadn't got anything out of him.' That, with variations. He seemed rather more pleased and amused than anything else. Then he went to sleep."

I said, "You know, I think you can stop worrying. I'd be willing to bet that your father's said nothing whatever."

He looked at me with surprise. I hadn't realized before how dark his eyes were. "What makes you so sure?"

"Well . . ." I hesitated. "You were a bit upset in there, but I had nothing to do but notice things. I'll tell you how it struck me. He was certainly drunk, but I think he was hanging on to something he knew . . . he'd forgotten *why*, but just knew he had to. He knew he hadn't to say anything about—about whatever you and Adoni were doing. He was so fuddled that he couldn't sort out who was safe and who wasn't, but he wasn't parting with anything: he even kept stalling you and Adoni because I was there, and even about things that didn't matter, like what happened at Mr. Andiakis'." I smiled. "And then the way he was reciting, and fiddling with the tape recorder . . . You can't tell me he normally gives private renderings of Shakespeare in his own drawing room. Actors don't. They may go on acting their heads off offstage, but they aren't usually bores. It struck me— Look, I'm sorry, am I speaking out of turn? Perhaps you'd rather I didn't—"

"God, no. Go on."

"It struck me that he was reciting because he knew that once he'd got himself—or the tape—safely switched into a groove, he could just go on and on without any danger of being jumped into saying the wrong thing. When I heard it, he was probably playing the tape to his visitor."

His mouth twitched in momentary amusement. "Serve him right. What's more, I'm certain that the meeting at the garage was an accident. If Adoni and I had been suspected, we'd have been watched, and perhaps followed . . . or intercepted on our way home."

"Well, there you are; and it stands to reason that if your father had told him anything, or even dropped a hint where you both were, there's been masses of time to have the police along, or . . . or anything."

"Of course." The look he gave me was not quite easy, for all that.

I hesitated. "Worrying about your father, though—that's a different thing. I don't know about these things. Do you think it may have, well, started him drinking again?"

"One can't tell. He's not an alcoholic, you know; it wasn't chronic, or approaching it. It's just that he started to go on these periodic drunks to get out of his jags of depression. We can only wait and see."

I said no more, but turned my chair away from the table to face the fire and drank my coffee. The logs purred and hissed, and the resin came bubbling out of one of them, in little opal globes that popped and swelled against the charring bark. The big airy room was filled with the companionable noises of the night: the bubbling of the resin, the spurt and flutter of flames, the creak of some ancient wooden floor settling for the night, the clang of the old hot-water system. As I stretched Sir Julian's bedroom slippers nearer the fire a cricket chirped, suddenly and clearly, about a yard away. I jumped, then, looking up, caught Max watching me, and we smiled at each other. Neither of us moved or spoke, but a kind of wordless conversation seemed to take place, and I was filled with a sudden, heart-swelling elation and happiness, as if the sun had come out on my birthday morning and I had been given the world.

Then he had turned away, and was looking into the fire again. He said, as if he were simply going on from where we had left off:

"It started just over four years ago. Father was rehearsing at the time for that rather spectacular thing that Hayward wrote for him, *Tiger, Tiger*. You'll remember it; it ran forever. Just eight days before the play was due to open, my mother and sister were both killed together in a motor accident. My sister was driving the car when it happened; it wasn't her fault, but that was no comfort. My mother was killed instantly; my sister regained consciousness and lived for a day—long enough to guess what had happened, though they tried to keep it from her. I was away at the time in the States, and, as bad luck would have it, was in hospital there with appendicitis, and couldn't go home. Well, I told you, it was only eight days before *Tiger, Tiger* was due to open, and it did open. I don't have to tell you what a situation like that would do to someone like my father. It would damage anybody, and it half killed him."

"I can imagine." I was also imagining Max himself, chained to his alien hospital bed, getting it all by telephone, by cable, through the mail. . . .

"That was when he started drinking. It was nearly two months before I got home, and a lot of the damage had been done. Of course, I had realized how it would hit him, but it took the shock of actually coming home to make me realize . . ." He paused. "You can imagine that, too; the house empty, and looking lost, almost as if it hadn't even been dusted for weeks, though that was silly, of course it had. But it felt deserted—echoing, almost. Sally—my sister— had always been a bit of a live wire. And there was Father, as thin as a telegraph post, with his hair three shades whiter, drifting about that damned great place like a dead leaf in a draughty barn. Not sleeping, of course, and drinking." He shifted in his chair. "What was that he said about the house being like a lord's kitchen without a fire?"

"It's from a play, Tourneur's *Revenger's Tragedy*. 'Hell would look like a lord's great kitchen without fire in't.'"

"'Hell'?" he quoted. "Yes, I see."

I said quickly, "It wasn't even relevant. It only occurred to him as a sort of image."

"Of emptiness?" He smiled suddenly. "Sweet of you, but don't worry, things pass." He paused. "That was the start. It got better, of course; shock wears off, and with me at home he didn't drink so much, but now and again, when he was

tired or overstrained, or just in one of those damned abysmal depressions that his
sort of person suffers—they're as real as the measles, I don't have to tell you
that—he would drink himself blind, 'just this once.' Unhappily, it takes
remarkably little to do it. Well, if you remember, the play ran for a long time, and
he stayed in it eighteen months. In all that time I only got him away for three
weeks, then back he'd go to London, and after a while the house would get him
down, and 'just this once' he'd go on another drunk."

"You couldn't get him to sell the house and move?"

"No. He'd been born there, and his father. It was something he wouldn't even
begin to think about. Well, a couple of years of that, and he was going downhill
like something on the Cresta Run. Then the 'breakdowns' started, still, thanks to
his friends, attributed publicly to strain and overwork. He had the sense to know
what was happening to him, and the integrity and pride to get out while he could
still do it with his legend intact. He did what he could . . . went into a 'home'
and was 'cured.' Then I got him to come away here, to make quite sure he was
all right, and to rest. Now he's breaking his heart to get back, but I know he
won't do it while there's any danger of its starting again." He gave a quick sigh.
"I thought he was through with it, but now I don't know. It isn't just a question of
willpower, you know. Don't despise him."

"I know that. And how could I despise him? I love him."

"Lucy Waring's specialty. Given away regardless and for no known reason.
No, I'm not laughing at you, heaven forbid. . . . Will you tell me something?"

"What?"

"Did you mean what you said down there on the beach?"

The abrupt, almost casual question threw me for a moment. "On the beach?
When? What did I say?"

"I realize I wasn't meant to hear it. We were just starting up the steps."

There was a pause. A log fell in with a soft crash and a jet of hissing light.
I said, with some difficulty, "You don't ask much, do you?"

"I'm sorry, that was stupid of me. Skip it. My God, I choose my moments, as
you say."

He leaned down, picked a poker up from the hearthstone, and busied himself
with rearranging the pieces of burning wood. I stared at his averted face, while a
straitjacket of shyness gripped me, and with a sort of anger at his obtuseness in
asking this. I couldn't have spoken if I'd tried.

A jet of flame, stirred by the poker, leaped up and caught the other log. It lit his
face, briefly highlighting the traces of the night's excitement and pain and
tension, the frowning brows so like his father's, the hard, exciting line of his
cheek; his mouth. And the same brief flash lit something else for me. I was the
one who was stupid. If one asks a question, it is because one wants to know the
answer. Why should he have to wait and wrap it up some other way when the
"moment" suited me?

I said it quite easily after all. "If you'd asked me a thing like that three hours
ago, I think I'd have said I didn't even like you, and I . . . I think I'd have
believed it . . . I think. . . . And now there you sit looking at me, and all
you do is look—like that—and my damned bones turn to water, and it isn't fair,
it's never happened to me before, and I'd do anything in the world for you, and
you know it, or if you don't you ought to— No, look, I—I didn't mean . . .
you *asked* me . . ."

It was a better kiss this time, no less breathless, but at least we were dry and warm, and had known each other nearly two hours longer. . . .

From somewhere in the shadows came a sharp click and a whirring sound. Instantly, we were a yard apart.

A small, fluting voice said, *"Cuckoo, cuckoo, cuckoo, cuckoo,"* and clicked back into silence.

"That damned clock!" said Max explosively, then began to laugh. "It always frightens me out of my wits. It sounds like someone sneaking in with a tommy gun. I'm sorry, did I drop you too hard?"

"Right down to earth," I said shakily. "Four o'clock, I'll have to go."

"Wait just a little longer, can't you? No, listen, there's something you've got to know. I'll try not to take too long, if you'll just sit down again . . . ? Don't take any notice of that clock, it's always fast." He cocked an eyebrow. "What are you looking at me like that for?"

"For a start," I said, "men don't usually jump sky-high when they hear a noise like a tommy gun. Unless they could be expecting one, that is. Were you?"

"Could be," he said cheerfully.

"Goodness me! Then I'll certainly stay to hear all about it!" I sat down, folding my silk skirts demurely about me. "Go on."

"A moment. I'll put another log on the fire. Are you warm enough?"

"Yes, thank you."

"You won't smoke? You never do? Wise girl. Well . . .."

He leaned his elbows on his knees, and stared once more at the fire.

". . . I'm not quite sure where to start, but I'll try to make it short. You can have the details later, those you can't fill in for yourself. I want to tell you what's happened tonight, and especially what's going to happen tomorrow—today, I mean—because I want you to help me, if you will. But to make it clear I'll have to go back to the start of the story. I suppose you could say that it starts with Yanni Zoulas; at any rate, that's where I'll begin."

"It was true, then? He was a smuggler?"

"Yes, indeed. Yanni carried stuff regularly—all kinds of goods in short supply—over to the Albanian coast. Your guess was right about the 'contacts': he had his 'contact' on the other side, a man called Milo, and he had people over here who supplied the stuff and paid him. But not me. Your guess was wrong there. Now, how much d'you know about Albania?"

"Hardly a thing. I did try to read it up before I came here, but there's so little to read. I know it's Communist, of course, and at daggers drawn with Tito's Yugoslavia, *and* with Greece on the other border. I gather that it's a poor country, without much workable land and no industries, just peasant villages perched on the edge of starvation, like some of the Greek ones. I don't know any of the towns except Durrës, on the coast, and Tirana, the capital. I gathered that they were still pretty Stone Age at the end of the war, but trying hard and looking round for help. That was when the U.S.S.R. stepped in, wasn't it?"

"Yes. She supplied Albania with tools and tractors and seeds, and so forth, all it needed to get its agriculture going again after the war. But it wasn't all plain sailing. I won't go into it now—in fact, I'm not at all sure that I've got it straight myself—but a few years ago Albania quarreled with Russia, and broke with the Cominform, but because it still badly needed help (and possible support against Russia) it applied to Communist China; and China, which was then at loggerheads with Russia, jumped happily in to play fairy godmother to Albania

as Russia had done before—and presumably to get one foot wedged in Europe's
back door. The situation's still roughly that, and now Albania's closed its
frontiers completely, except to China. You can't get in, and by heaven, you
certainly can't get out."

"Like Spiro's father?"

"I suspect he didn't want to. But you might say he brings us to the next point
in the story, which is Spiro. I suppose you've heard about our connection with
Maria and her family?"

"In a way. Adoni told me."

"My father was here in Corfu during the war, and he was working in with
Spiro's father for a time—a wild type, I gather, but rather picturesque and
appealing. He appealed to the romantic in my father, anyway." Max grinned.
"One gathers they had some pretty tearing times together. When the twins were
born, Father stood godfather to them. You won't know this, but over here it's a
relationship that's taken very seriously. The godfather really does take
responsibility—he has as much say in the kids' future as their father does,
sometimes more."

"I gathered that from Adoni. It was obvious he had a say in the christening,
anyway!"

He laughed. "It certainly was. The isle of Corfu went to his head even in those
days. Thank God I was born in London, or I've a feeling nothing could have
saved me from Ferdinand. Would you have minded?"

"Terribly. Ferdinand makes me think of a rather pansy kind of bull. What is
your name, anyway? Maximilian?"

"Praise heaven, no. Maxwell. It was my mother's name."

"I take it you had a godfather with no obsessions."

He grinned. "Too right. In the correct English manner, he gave me a silver
teaspoon, then vanished from my life. But you can't do that in Corfu. When
Spiro's own father did actually vanish, the godfather was almost literally left
holding the babies."

"He was still over here when that happened?"

"Yes. He was here for a bit after the European War was finished, and during
that time he felt himself more or less responsible for the family. He would have
been if he'd been a Greek, since Maria had no relatives and they were as poor as
mice, so he took the family on, and even after he'd gone home sent money to
them every month."

"Good heavens! But surely, with children of his own—"

"He managed." Max's voice was suddenly grave. "We're not rich, heaven
knows . . . and an actor's life's a darned uncertain one at best . . . but it's
rather frightening how little a Greek family can manage on quite cheerfully. He
kept them completely till Maria went out to work, and even after that he more or
less kept them until the children could work, too." He stretched out a foot and
shoved the log deeper on its bed of burning ash. "We came over here for
holidays most years; that's where I learned my Greek and the kids their English.
We had a whale of a time, and Father always loved it. I was thankful I had
somewhere like this to bring him when the crash came . . . it was like having
another family ready-made. It's helped him more than anything else could have
done. Being wanted does."

"Good heavens, the thousands that want him! But I know it's different. So he came back here for peace to recover in, and then Spiro was killed. It must have hit him terribly."

"The trouble was," said Max, "that Maria wouldn't believe the boy could be dead. She never stopped begging and praying my father to find out what really happened to him, and to bring him back. Apparently she'd made a special petition to St. Spiridion for him, so she simply wouldn't believe he could have drowned. She got some sort of idea that he'd gone after his father and must be brought home."

The second cigarette stub went after the first. It hit a bar of the fire, and fell back on the hearthstone. He got up, picked it up and dropped it on the fire, then stayed on his feet with a shoulder propped against the high mantel.

"I know it wasn't reasonable, not after Manning had told her what had happened, but mothers don't always listen to reason, and there was always the faint chance that the boy *had* survived. My father didn't feel equal to handling it, and I knew that neither he nor Maria would have any peace of mind till they found what had become of his body, so I took it on. I've been having inquiries made wherever I could, here and on the mainland, to find out in the first place if he'd been washed ashore, dead or alive. I've also had someone in Athens trying to get information from the Albanian side. Where Spiro went in, the current sets dead toward the Albanian coast. Well, I did manage to get through in the end, but with no results. He hadn't been seen, either on the Greek coast or the Albanian."

I said, "And I read you a lesson on helping other people. I'm sorry."

"You couldn't know it was any concern of mine."

"Well, no, it did rather seem to be Godfrey's."

"I suppose so, but the local Greeks at any rate assumed that it was my father's job—or mine—to do it. So the police kept in touch with us, and we knew we'd get any information that was going. And when Yanni Zoulas went across on his routine smuggling trip on Saturday night and did actually get some news of Spiro through his Albanian 'contact,' he came straight to us. Or rather, as straight as he could. You saw him on his way up to see us, on Sunday evening."

I was bolt-upright in my chair. *"News of Spiro?* Good news?"

I knew the answer before he spoke. The gleam in his eyes reminded me suddenly, vividly, of the way Adoni had looked at me on the staircase, glowing.

"Oh, yes. He came to tell us Spiro was alive."

"Max!"

"Yes, I know. You can guess how we felt. He'd been washed ashore on the Albanian side, with a broken leg, and in the last stages of exhaustion, but he'd survived. The people who found him were simple coast folk, shepherds, who didn't see any reason to report things to the People's Police, or whatever it's called over there. Most people know about the smuggling that goes on, and I gather that these folk assumed that Spiro was mixed up in something of the sort, so they kept quiet about him. What's more, they informed the local smuggler, who—naturally—knew Spiro, Yanni's 'contact,' who in turn passed the news along to Yanni on Saturday."

"Oh, Max, this is marvelous! It really is! Did Yanni actually see him?"

"No. It all came at rather third hand. Milo hasn't much Greek, so all that Yanni got from him was the bare facts, and an urgent message that Spiro somehow managed to convey that no one, no one at all—not even Maria—was to be told that he was still alive, except myself, my father, and Adoni . . . the people who'd presumably get him out somehow." He paused briefly. "Well, obviously we couldn't go to the police and get him out by normal channels, or the people who'd rescued him would be in trouble, not to mention Yanni and Milo. So Yanni fixed up a rendezvous to bring the boy off by night."

"And he went back last night after he'd seen you, and ran into the coastguards and got hurt?"

But he was shaking his head. "He couldn't have gone back alone; getting that boy off wasn't one man's job—don't forget he was strapped to a stretcher. No, when Yanni came up on Sunday night, he came to ask me to go across with him. The rendezvous was fixed for tonight; Milo and his friend were to have Spiro there, and Yanni and I were to take him off. So you see . . ."

I didn't hear what he was going to say. It had all come together at last, and I could only wonder at my slowness in not seeing it all before. My eyes flew to his bandaged wrist as the events of the night came rushing back: the secrecy of his journey through the woods, the impression I had had of more than one man passing me there, the owl's call, Adoni's vivid face . . .

I was on my feet. "The catch! Adoni and the catch! You took Adoni, and went over there yourself tonight! You mean it's *done?* You've actually *brought Spiro home?*"

His eyes were dancing. "We have indeed. He's here at this moment, a bit tired, but alive and well. I told you our night's work had been worthwhile."

I sat down again, rather heavily. "I can hardly take it in. This is . . . wonderful. Oh, Maria will be able to light herself a lovely candle this Easter! Think of it, Maria, Miranda, Sir Julian, Godfrey, Phyl . . . how happy everyone's going to be! I can hardly wait till daylight, to see the news go round!"

The glow faded abruptly from his face. It must have been only imagination, but the gay firelight seemed dimmer, too.

He said somberly, "I'm afraid it mustn't go round yet, not any further."

"But"—I stared, bewildered—"not to his mother or sister? Why on earth not, if he's safely home? Surely, once he's out of Albania he has nothing to fear. And Milo needn't be involved at all—no one need even know Spiro was ever on Albanian soil. We could invent some story—"

"I'd thought of that. The story will be that he was thrown ashore on one of the islands in the strait, the Peristeroi Islands, and that he managed to attract our attention when we were out fishing. It won't fool the Greek police, or the doctor, but it'll do for general release, as it were. But that's not the point."

"Then what is?"

He hesitated, then said slowly, "Spiro may still be in danger . . . not from the other side, but here. What touched him touched Yanni, too. And Yanni died."

Something in his face—his very reluctance to speak—frightened me. I found myself protesting violently, too violently, as if by protesting I could push the unwanted knowledge further away. "But we *know* what happened to Spiro! He went overboard from Godfrey's boat! How *can* he be in any danger now? And Yanni's death was an accident! You *said* so!"

I stopped. The silence was so intense that you could hear the crazy ticking of the cuckoo clock and the scrape of silk on flesh as my hands gripped together in my lap.

I said quietly, "Go on. Say it straight out, you may as well. You're insinuating that Godfrey Manning—"

"I'm insinuating nothing." His voice was curt, even to rudeness. "I'm telling you. Here it is. Godfrey Manning threw Spiro overboard, and left him to drown."

Silence again, a different kind of silence.

"Max, I—I can't accept that. I'm sorry, but it isn't possible."

"It's fact, no more nor less. Spiro says so. Yes, I thought you were forgetting that I've talked to him. He says so, and I believe him. He has no reason to lie."

Seconds were out with a vengeance. Now that he had decided he must tell me, he hurled his facts like stones. And they hit like stones.

"But—*why?*"

"I don't know. Neither does the boy, which, when you come to think about it, makes it the more likely that he's telling the truth. It's something he'd have no reason to invent. He's as stunned by it as you are." He added, more gently, "I'm sorry, Lucy, but I'm afraid it's true."

I sat in silence for a minute or two, not thinking, but looking down at my hands, twisting and turning the great diamond, and watching the firelight break and dazzle among its facets. Slowly the stunned feeling faded, and I began to think. . . .

"Did you suspect Godfrey before?"

"No," he said, "why should I? But when I got that message from Yanni, I did wonder why Godfrey hadn't to be told. After all, it seemed reasonable to keep the news from Spiro's mother and sister, because they'd be so elated that they might give everything away before Yanni had done the job; but Godfrey was a different matter. He would presumably be worrying about Spiro, and he has by far the best boat. What's more, he's an experienced seaman, and I'm not. I'd have expected him to be asked in on the rescue, rather than me and Adoni. It wasn't much, but it did make me wonder. Then when Yanni was found dead next day, on top of Spiro's odd warning, I wondered still more."

I said, "You're not suggesting now—you *can't* be suggesting that Godfrey killed Yanni Zoulas? Max—"

"What I've told you about Spiro is fact: what happened to Yanni is guesswork. But to my mind the one murder follows the other as the night the day."

Murder . . . I don't think I said it aloud, but he nodded as if I had.

"I'm pretty sure of it. Same method, too. He'd been hit hard on the head and thrown into the sea. The bottle of ouzo was a nice touch, I thought."

"He was hit by the boom. The police said there were hairs—"

"He could also have been hit *with* the boom. Anyone can crack an unconscious man's head on a handy chunk of wood like that, hard enough to kill him before you throw him overboard—and hard enough to hide the crack you knocked him out with. I'm not bringing this out as a theory; I'm only saying it could have been done."

"Why did you go back to the body after we'd left?"

"After Yanni left us on Sunday night I heard his boat go out, and I did wonder if he'd been stupid enough to go back on his own and had run into trouble with the coastguards. From all that we'd been able to see, he might have had a bullet hole in him somewhere, or some other evidence that would start a serious investigation. I was pretty anxious in case they started patrolling local waters before I'd got Spiro safely home."

"I see. And your own wrist—was that the coastguards?"

"Yes, a stray bullet, and a spent one at that. It's honestly only a graze; I'll get it looked at when I get Spiro's leg seen to. They must have heard something, and fired blind. We were just about out of range, and well beyond their lights."

I said, rather wearily, "I suppose you do know what you're saying, but it all seems so . . . so impossible to me. And I don't understand even the start of it."

"My God, who does? But I told you, it's all guesswork about Yanni, and there's no future in discussing that now. The first thing is to talk to Spiro again. I've only had time to get the barest statement from him, and I want to hear the rest before I decide what's best to do. He should be fit enough by now to tell us exactly what happened; and whether he knows it or not, he may have some clue as to why Manning tried to kill him. If he has, it may be a pointer to Yanni's death. And whatever it is that makes two murders necessary." He straightened abruptly, his shoulder coming away from the mantel. "Well, you can see that we have to get the boy safely into the hands of the authorities with his story before Godfrey Manning has even a suspicion that he's not as dead as Yanni. Will you come with me now and see him?"

I looked up in surprise. "Me? You want me to?"

"If you will. I told you I wanted you to help me, and—if you'll agree—you'd better know as much as we do about it."

"Of course, whatever I can."

"Darling. Come here. Now, stop looking like that, and stop worrying. It's all impossible, as you say, but then this sort of situation is bound to be when one gets mixed up in it oneself. All we can do is play for safety, and that means, for the moment, believing Spiro. All right?"

I nodded as best I could with my head comfortably against his shoulder.

"Then listen. What I've got to do, as I see it, is get the boy straight off to Athens in the morning, to the hospital, then to the police. Once he's told his story there, he'll be safe to come home." He loosed me. "Well, shall we go?"

"Where is he?"

He laughed. "Right below our feet, in a very Gothic but reasonably safe dungeon, with Adoni standing guard over him with the one efficient rifle in this damned great arsenal of Leo's. Come along, then. Straight under the cuckoo clock, and fork right for the dungeons!"

12

My cellar is a rock by th' seaside where my wine is hid.

Act II, Scene 2

A WIDE flight of stone steps led downward from just beyond the door. Max touched a switch, and a weak yellow light came on to show us the way. He shut the ponderous door, and I heard a key grate in the lock behind us.

"I'll go first, shall I?"

I followed him, curiously looking about me. The rest of the building had led me to expect goodness knew what horrors down here: it would hardly have come as a surprise to have found moldering skeletons dangling in chains from the walls. But the underground corridor into which the stairs led us was innocent of anything except racks for wine—largely empty—which lined the wide passageway. The floor was clean, and the walls surprisingly free of the dust and webs which would have accumulated in a similar place in England. The air smelled fresh, and slightly damp.

I said as much to Max, who nodded. "You'll see why in a minute. This is the official wine cellar, but it leads off into a natural cave farther along. I don't know where the opening is—it's probably no bigger than a chimney—but the air's always fresh, and you can smell the sea. There are more wine racks down there. In the last century, when one drank one's four bottles a day, rather a lot of room was needed. Anyway, it must have seemed a natural to use the caves in the cliff when they built the Castello."

"It's rather exciting. I suppose these are the caves your father was talking about."

"Yes. Most of the cliffs along this coast have caves in them, but as you can imagine, he'd love to think the Castello cave was the original Prospero's cell. When I point out that it doesn't look as if it had ever been open to the outside air, he says that doesn't matter. I gather it's more 'poetic truth,' like the marmosets."

"Well, it's a lovely romantic theory, and I'm all for it! After all, what are facts? We get those every day. . . . Whereabouts are we now in relation to 'outside'?"

"At present we're still moving along under the foundations of the house. The cave itself is in the southern headland, fairly deep down. We go down more steps in a moment, and then there's a natural passage through to the cave. Wait, here we are."

He had stopped two thirds of the way along the corridor, and put a hand up to the empty racks. I watched him, puzzled. He laid hold of what looked like part of the wall of racks, and pulled. Ponderously, and by no means silently, a narrow section swung out into the corridor. Beyond where it had been was a gap in the wall, opening on blackness.

"Goodness me!" I exclaimed, and Max laughed.

"Marvelous, isn't it? I tell you, the Castello's got everything! As a matter of fact, I have a suspicion that old Forli kept the better vintages down here, out of the butler's reach. . . . Careful, now, there's no light from here on. I've brought a torch—here, take it for a moment, will you, while I shut this behind us. Don't look so scared!"

"It won't stay shut and trap us here forever, till our bones bleach?"

"Not even till morning, I'm sorry to say. There. The torch, please. I'll go ahead."

The second flight sloped more steeply down, and, instead of being made of smooth slabs, seemed to be hacked out of solid rock. At the foot of the flight a rock-hewn passage curved away into darkness, still descending. Max went ahead, shining the beam for me. Here and there the walls showed a glint of damp, and the fresh smell was stronger, and perceptibly salty, while the hollow rock seemed—perhaps only in imagination—to hold a faint, echoing hum like the shushing of the sea through the curves of a shell. A moment I thought I heard it, then it was gone, and there was only the still, cold air, and the sound of our footsteps on the rock.

The yellow torchlight flung sharp lights and shadows on Max's face as he turned to guide me, sketching in, momentarily, the face of a stranger. His shadow moved distorted and huge on the rough walls.

"Is it much farther?" My voice sounded unfamiliar, like a whisper in an echo chamber.

"Round this corner," said Max, "and down five, no, six steps—and there's the watchdog."

A flash of the torch showed the pale blur of a face upturned, and a gun barrel gleaming blue.

"Adoni? It's Max, and I've brought Miss Lucy along. Is he all right?"

"He's fine now. He's awake."

Behind Adoni hung a rough curtain of some material like sacking, from beyond which came a dim, warm glow. Adoni drew the curtain aside for me and stood back. Max put the torch out and motioned me past him. I went into the cave.

This was large, with a great arched roof lost in shadows where stalactites hung like icicles; but the walls had been whitewashed to a height of six feet or so, and were lined with wine racks and crates and the comfortable, bulging shapes of barrels. On one of these, upturned to make a table, stood an old-fashioned lantern, a coach lamp of about 1830 vintage, probably borrowed from the museum upstairs, which dispensed a soft orange light and the cheerful twinkle of brass. The air was warmed by a paraffin stove which stood in the middle of the floor, with a pan of coffee on it. Somewhere in the shadows a drip of water fell regularly—some stalactite dripping fresh water into a pocket of rock; the sound was as homely as a dripping tap. The unexpected effect of coziness was enhanced by the smell of cigarettes and coffee and the faint fumes of the paraffin stove.

The injured boy lay at the far side of the cave, on a bed pushed up against a row of crates. The bed was a makeshift affair which nevertheless looked extremely comfortable—a couple of spring mattresses laid one above the other, with blankets galore, and feather pillows, and a vast eiderdown. Some sort of cage had been rigged up under the bedclothes to keep their weight off the injured leg.

Spiro, lying there in what looked like a pair of Sir Julian's pyjamas (pale blue silk with crimson piping), looked comfortable enough, and not at the moment particularly ill. He was propped up on his pillows, drinking coffee.

He looked up across the cup, a little startled at the sight of me, and threw a quick question at Max, who answered in English:

"It's Kyria Forli's sister. She's my friend, and yours. She's going to help us, and I want her to hear your story."

Spiro regarded me steadily, without noticeable welcome, the round dark eyes, so like his sister's, wary and appraising. I could recognize the boy in the photographs, but only just; there was the thick, springing hair and the stocky body, with obvious strength in the shoulders and thick neck; but the bloom of health and sunlight—and happiness—was gone. He looked pale, and—in the pyjamas—young and unprotected-looking.

Max pulled a box forward for me to sit on. "How do you feel?" he asked the boy. "Is it hurting?"

"No," said Spiro. That this was a lie was quite obvious, but it was not said with any sort of bravado. It was simply that one did not admit to weakness, and pain was weakness.

"He has slept," said Adoni.

"Good." Max perched himself half sitting against the cask which held the lantern. His shadow, thrown hugely up the walls, arched brooding and gigantic across the cave. He studied the younger boy for a minute or two, then said briskly:

"If you're feeling better, I want you to tell us exactly what happened to you. All the details this time, please."

"All the what?"

"Everything you can remember," said Max, and Adoni, from the head of the bed, added a soft gloss in Greek.

"All right." Spiro drained the coffee cup and handed it up, without looking, to Adoni. The latter took it, set it quietly aside, then crossed back to the bed and sat down, curling up gracefully, naturally, like a cat, near the head of the bed, away from the injured leg. He reached into a pocket for two of the cigarettes he had got from Max, stuck them in his mouth, lit them both, and handed one to Spiro. Spiro took it without word or glance, but there was no suggestion, as there had been with me, of anything withdrawn or unfriendly. It was obvious that these two young men knew each other almost too well to need words. They sat there side by side against the pillows, Adoni relaxed and graceful, Spiro square and watchful and smoking jerkily, with his hand cupped working-class fashion round the cigarette.

He sent one more wary glance at me, then took no more notice of me: all his attention was on Max, almost as if the latter were judging him—at once judge and savior and final court of appeal. Max listened without moving, the huge, curved shadow thrown right up the wall and over half the ceiling of the cave.

The boy spoke slowly, with the signs of fatigue deepening in his face. I have no recollection now of what language he spoke; whether his English was good, or whether Max and Adoni eked it out with translation: the latter, I suspect; but whatever the case, the story came over vividly and sharply in that darkened cellar cave, with the lantern light, and the smell of the cigarettes, and the two boys curled in the welter of bedclothes, and the faint tangy scent from the silk of Julian Gale's dressing gown.

I suppose that the strange, secret surroundings, the time of night, my own weariness and recent emotional encounter with Max, had edged the scene somehow; but it seemed real now only as a dream is real. In the dream I found I had already accepted Godfrey's guilt; I only waited now to hear how he had done it. Perhaps in the light of morning things would take a different dimension; but now it seemed as if any tale could be true, even the old man's romantic theory that this was Prospero's cave, and that here on this rough floor the Neapolitan lords had waited to hear the story from the long-drowned Duke, as I now waited to hear Spiro's.

There had been nothing, he said, that had struck him as unusual about the trip that night. The only thing that had surprised him was that the sky was none too clear, and from what the wireless had said, it might well be stormy at dawn. He had pointed this out to Godfrey, but Godfrey had said, a little abruptly, that it would clear. They had got the boat out, and gone shortly before midnight. As Spiro had anticipated, the night was black and thick, but he had said nothing more to Godfrey, who had stayed in the cabin, allegedly busying himself with his camera and equipment.

"He seemed much as usual?" asked Max.

Spiro frowned, considering this. "I cannot say," he replied at length. "He was quiet, and perhaps a bit sharp with me when I protested about the weather, but all day he had been the same. I thought he was still angry with me because I had gone into the boathouse that morning on my own to service the engine, so I said nothing, and thought nothing. He pays me, and that is that."

"All the same, that might be interesting," said Max slowly. "But go on now. You were out in the strait, and the night was black."

Spiro took a quick drag on the cigarette, and reached awkwardly, hampered by the leg, to tap the ash onto the floor. Adoni slipped the saucer from under the empty coffee cup, and slid it within his reach.

"I reckoned we were about halfway over," said Spiro, "in the strait between Kouloura and the mainland. We had gone close to the Peristeroi islands; there was enough of a sea running to see the white foam quite distinctly. I asked Mr. Manning if we should lie up a little in the lee of them and wait for the cloud to clear; there were gaps under the wind, where you could see stars; but he said no, we would go farther across. We went on for a time, till I reckoned we were about two miles out. He came out of the cabin then, and sent me in to make some coffee." The boy glanced up under his thick brows at Max. "The camera was there, on the table, but I did not think he could have been looking at it, because he had had no light on, only a storm lantern hardly lit. At the time I did not think of these things; while we took pictures at night, we always—naturally—ran without lights. But afterward, when I had all that time lying in bed, and nothing to do but think, and wonder . . . then I remembered all the things that seemed strange. It was strange that we were going at all on that dark night to take pictures, it was strange that he lied to me about the camera, and the next thing that happened was more strange still."

Adoni grinned. "I know, the engine failed. And what was so strange about that, when you'd been taking it to bits that morning, my little genius?"

Spiro smiled for the first time, and said something in Greek which nobody bothered to translate for me. "If that had happened," he added, with fine simplicity, "it would indeed have been strange. But it did not."

"But you told us before—"

"I told you the engine stopped. I did not say that it failed. There was nothing wrong with the engine."

Max stirred. "You're sure, naturally."

The boy nodded. "And it didn't need a genius with engines to know there was nothing wrong. Even you"—a glint at Adoni—"even you would have known, my pretty one." He ducked aside from Adoni's feint, and laughed. "Go on, hit me, no doubt you could do it now."

"I'll wait," said Adoni.

Spiro turned back to Max. "No, the engine was all right. Listen. I heard it stop, then Mr. Manning called me. I put my head out of the door and shouted that I would take a look—the engine hatch is under the cabin steps, you understand. But he said, 'I don't think it's there, Spiro, I think something's fouled the screw and stalled it. Can you take a look?' I went to the stern. He was standing there, at the tiller. He said, 'Steady as you go, boy, she's pitching a bit. Here, I'll hold the torch for you.' I gave him the torch, and then I leaned over to see if the shaft was fouled. The boat was pitching, and the toe rail was wet, but I was holding on tightly. I should have been quite safe."

He paused, and stirred in the bed, as if the leg were hurting him. Adoni slipped to the floor and padded across to where a bottle stood on a box beside two empty glasses. He slopped some of the wine—it looked like the dark, sweet stuff they called *demèstica*—into one of the glasses and took it to the other boy, then glanced inquiringly at Max, who shook his head. Adoni set the bottle down, and returned to his place on the bed, adjusting his body, catlike, to the new position of the injured boy.

"It all happened very fast. The boat gave a lurch, very sharp, as if Mr. Manning had turned her across the wind too quickly. I was thrown against the rail, but still safe enough, because I had a good grip, but then something hits me from behind, on the head. It does not stun me, but I think I try to turn and put an arm up, then the boat pitches again, and before I know what has happened, I am falling. I try to grip the rail, but it slips from me. Something hits me across the hand—here—and I let go. Then I am in the water. When I come up, the boat is still near, and I see Mr. Manning in the stern, peering out for me in the darkness. I shout—not loudly, you understand, because I am full of water and too cold, gasping for air. But he must have heard me."

He shot a look up at Max, all of a sudden vivid, alive with pure hatred.

"And if he did not hear me, then he saw me. He put the torch on, and shone it on me in the sea."

"Yes?" said Max. His voice was expressionless, but I got the impression of a cold wind stirring in the cellar. Adoni felt it, too. He glanced fleetingly up at Max before his eyes went back to Spiro.

"I was not afraid, you understand," said Spiro, "not of him. It did not occur to me that it was he who had hit me, I thought it had been some accident. No, I was not afraid. I am a good swimmer, and though he had no engine, the boat was drifting down toward me, and he could see me. In a moment he could pick me up again. I called out again and swam toward him. I saw he had the starting handle in his hand, but I still did not imagine what this was for. Then as I came within reach, he leaned down and hit me again. But the boat was pitching and he had to hold the rail, so he could not point the torch properly. The blow touched me, but this time I saw it coming, and I ducked away, and he hit my arm and not my head. I think he felt the blow, but did not see, because the torch went out and a big wave swept me away from the boat's stern and out of his sight. You can imagine that this time I let it take me. I saw the light go on again, but I made no sound, and let myself be carried away into the dark. Then I heard the engine start." He drained the glass, and looked up at Max. "He looked for me for a little while, but the current took me away fast and the waves hid me. Then he turned the boat away and left me there in the sea."

There was silence. Nobody moved. For me, the dreamlike feeling persisted. The cave seemed darker, echoing with the sounds of the sea, the mutter of the receding boat, the empty hissing of waves running under the night wind.

"But the Saint was with you," said Adoni, and the deep human satisfaction in his voice sent the shadows scurrying. The cave was warm again, and full of the soft light from the English Victorian lantern.

Spiro handed the empty glass to Adoni, pulled the bedclothes more comfortably round him, and nodded. "Yes, he was with me. Do you want the rest, Kyrie Max? You know what happened."

"I want Miss Lucy to hear it. Go on, but make it short. You're tired, and it's very late."

The rest of the story was pure classic, made predictable and credible by half a hundred stories from Odysseus to St. Paul.

It was the murderer's bad luck that the wind that night had set a fast current in to the Albanian coast. Spiro was a fair swimmer, and the Ionian Sea is very salt, but even so he would have been hard put to it to survive if he had not gone overboard into the stream of the current. Between that, the buoyancy of the water, and his stubborn efforts, he managed to keep afloat long enough for the sea race to throw him ashore sometime just before dawn.

By the time he neared the shore he was almost exhausted, all his energy taken by the mere effort of keeping afloat, and at the mercy of the tide. He was not even aware that he had come to shore, but when a driving swell flung him against the cruel coastal rocks, he found just enough strength to cling there, resisting the backward drag once, twice, three times, before he could pull himself clear of it and crawl farther up the slimy rock.

And here the luck turned. St. Spiridion, having seen him ashore, and out of his own territory, abandoned him abruptly. Spiro slipped, fell back across a jut of sharp rock with a broken leg twisted under him, and at last fainted.

He had no recollection of being found—by an old shepherd who had clambered down a section of cliff after a crag-fast ewe. When Spiro woke he was bedded down, roughly but dry and warm, in the shepherd's cottage, and it appeared that the shepherd had some rough surgical skill, for the leg had been set and strapped up. The old woman produced a drink that sent him to sleep again, and when he woke for the second time, the pain was a good deal easier, and he was able to remember, and think. . . .

"And the rest you know." He yawned suddenly, tremendously, like an animal, and lay back among the blankets.

"Yes, the rest we know." Max got to his feet, stretching. "Well, you'd better get some sleep. In the morning—my God, in about three hours!—I'm going to get you out of here; don't ask me how, but I'll do it somehow, with Mr. Manning none the wiser. I want to get that leg of yours properly seen to, and then you've got to tell your story to the right authorities."

The boy glanced up, weariness and puzzlement lending his face a sullen, heavy look. "Authorities? Police? You mean you are going to accuse Kyrios Manning of trying to drown me? On my word alone? They will laugh at you."

"It's not just a question of accusing Mr. Manning of throwing you overboard. What I want to know is why? There's something here that must be investigated, Spiro. You'll have to trust me. Now, just for a few minutes longer, I want you to think back. You must have thought about it a lot yourself while you were lying in bed. . . . Why do you think he did it? Have you any idea at all? You surely don't imagine it was because he was irritated with you for overhauling the engine without being told."

"Of course not."

"There was nothing else—nothing had happened at any other time?"

"No. I have thought. Of course I have thought. No."

"Then we come back to the morning of the trip. When one has nothing to go on, one looks for anything, however slight, that's out of pattern—out of the ordinary. Did you usually overhaul that boat by yourself?"

"No, but I have done so before." Spiro stirred as if his leg hurt him. "And I have been alone on it before."

"You have always asked him first?"

"Of course."

"But this time you didn't. Why did you go to work on the boat this time without asking him?"

"Because he had told me that he meant to go out and he wanted the engine serviced. I was to go that morning after breakfast, and work on it. But I had got up very early, to swim, and when I had done, I thought I would go straight along and start work. I knew where he kept the extra key, so I let myself in and made some coffee in the galley, then opened the big doors for the light and started work. It was a good morning, with the summer coming, and I felt good. I worked well. When Mr. Manning had finished his breakfast and came down, I was half finished already. I thought he would be pleased, but he was very angry and asked how I got in, and then I didn't like to tell him that I had seen where he hid the key, so I said the door was not locked properly, and he believed this, because the catch is stiff sometimes. But he was still very angry, and said he would have the lock changed, and then I was angry also, and asked if he thought I was a thief, and if he thought so he had better count the money in his wallet which he had left in the galley. As if I would touch it! I was very angry!" Spiro remembered this with some satisfaction. "I told him also that I would mend his lock for him myself, and that I would never come to his house again. After that he was pleasant, and said he was sorry, and it was all right."

Max was frowning. "It was then that he asked you to go out that night?"

"I think . . . Yes, it must have been. He had said before that he did not want me with him, but he changed his mind . . . I thought because he was sorry he had spoken to me like that." He added naïvely, "It was a way to give me extra money without offense."

"Then it looks as if that was when he decided to take you and get rid of you. You can see that it only makes sense if he thought you'd seen something you shouldn't have seen . . . And that means in the boat, or the boathouse. Now, think hard, Spiro. Was there anything unusual about the boat? Or the boathouse? Or about anything that Mr. Manning said, or did . . . or carried with him?"

"No." The boy repeated himself with a kind of weary emphasis. "I have thought. Nothing."

"The wallet. You say he'd left his wallet lying. Where did you find it?"

"Down beside the stove in the galley. It had slipped there and he had not noticed. I put it on the cabin table."

"Were there papers in it? Money?"

"How should I know?" Spiro ruffled up again, like a young turkey cock, then subsided under Max's look with a grin. "Well, I did take a look, a very small one. There was money, but I don't know how much, I only saw the corners. It wasn't Greek money, anyway, so what use did he think it would have been to me? But if it had been a million drachmas, I would not have taken it! You know that, Kyrie Max!"

"Of course I know it. Did he leave you alone in the boat after this?"

"No. When I had finished there, he asked me to go up to the house and help him with some photographs. I worked there all day. He telephoned to the Forli house to tell my mother that I was to go with him that night."

"In fact, he made sure that you saw nobody all that day. Did you ever have any suspicion that he did anything illegal on these expeditions?"

"No—and why should it matter? I would not have told the police." Spiro's eyes glinted up at him. "He would not be the only one."

Max declined the gambit, merely nodding. "All right, Spiro, I'll not bother you any more now. Adoni, I'm going to lock the pair of you in while I take Miss Lucy home. I'll be back within the half hour. You have the gun."

"Yes."

"And this." Spiro searched under his pillow and produced, with as much drama as if it had been a handkerchief, a commando knife sharpened to a murderous glitter.

"That's the stuff," said Max cheerfully. "Now, you go to sleep, and very soon I'll get you away." He stooped, and dropped a hand for a moment on the boy's shoulder. "All will be well, *Spiro mou.*"

Adoni followed us to the door.

"And Sir Gale?" he asked softly.

"I'll look in on him," promised Max. "He'll sleep soundly enough, you can be sure of that. He's in no danger, so stop worrying and get some sleep yourself. When I get back I'll spend the rest of the night in the kitchen. If you need me, you've only to come to the upper door and call me. Good night."

"Good night, Adoni," I said.

"Good night." Adoni gave me that smile again, perhaps a little frayed at the edges, then let the curtain fall into place across the cave entrance, lopping off the warm glow and shutting Max and me out into the darkness of the rocky passage.

He switched on the torch, and we started up the steps. The rough walls, the curving passageway, the hewn flight of stairs, swam past in a sort of dream of fatigue, but a corner of my brain still felt awake and restless, alert to what he was saying.

"You can see now why I'm hiding that boy away till I can smuggle him out to Athens? It's not so much that he's in actual danger still—though he may well be—as simply that we stand a far better chance of finding out what Manning's up to if he has no idea that we suspect him. It's something big—that seems obvious . . . And I'm pretty sure in my own mind where to start looking for it."

"The boat?"

"Either that or the boathouse. He's up to something involving that boat, and the damned good 'cover' that his photography gives him. If you accept Spiro's story, which I do, his little quarrel with Manning that morning provides the only faint clue . . . the only deviation from pattern that I can see . . . and could tie in with Yanni's death as well. I've been thinking about that. When Yanni brought Spiro's message here on Sunday night we discussed it pretty freely, and I let it be seen that I thought it very odd that Manning hadn't to be told. Yanni then said that he'd seen Manning's boat out at odd times and in odd places and that he'd thought for some time he was up to no good, and when I mentioned the photographs he just shrugged and looked cynical. Well, that's nothing to go by—a man like Yanni would think that photography was a pretty queer occupation for anyone; but he could have very well been suspicious and curious enough after our conversation to go down that night and snoop around the boathouse, or somewhere else he had no right to be, and so got himself murdered. It's my guess he was taken by surprise and knocked out from behind, then bundled into his own boat, with Manning's dinghy attached, taken out to sea, had his head smashed on the boom, and was dumped overboard. Manning then set the boom loose, emptied a bottle of ouzo around, turned the boat adrift, and rowed himself silently home. Oh, yes, it could have been done. He couldn't take him a great distance, since he'd have to row himself home, and then there was the squall which washed the body straight back—but it worked; he got away with it. An impulsive chap, our Godfrey . . . and with one hell of a lot at stake, that's for sure. Yes, I could bear to know just what it is."

I said, in quick apprehension, "You've got to promise me something."

"What's that?"

"You're not going there tonight. You wouldn't be so silly!"

He laughed. "You're dead-right I would not, my love! I've got to see Spiro safe where he belongs before I go arguing with anyone with Manning's peculiar ideas on life and death. He must have shot at the dolphin, you'd realized that?" He nodded at my exclamation. "Who else? There's only one plausible reason, the one you imputed to me, that the word had gone round, and people were beginning to come to this piece of coast to see the creature. When Manning first saw you there in the bay, he may have thought you were one of them—a stranger, getting too close to whatever he was trying to keep secret. As Spiro and Yanni did."

"But . . . those beautiful pictures! They really are beautiful, Max! He *couldn't* destroy it when he'd worked with it like that! He must have been fond of it!"

His smile was crooked. "And of Spiro, too?" I was silent. "Well, here we are. A moment while I push the racks back."

"What do you want me to do?"

"Something I know will be safe, and I hope will be easy. Cover my trip back from Athens with Spiro."

"Of course, if I can. How?"

"By keeping Manning away from Corfu harbor tomorrow at the time when I'm likely to be there. It would be quicker to go by plane, but I can't take the boy that way without the whole island knowing, so I'll have to take him in my car, hidden under a rug or something, across by the *Igoumenitsa.*"

"The what?"

"The ferry to the mainland. I'll drive to Jannina and get the Athens plane from there. It means we can't get there and back in the one day, but I'll try to get home tomorrow, and I'll ring up this evening to let you know which ferry we'll get. The late one doesn't get in till a quarter to eleven; it's pitch-dark then, and I doubt if he'd be around. But I'd like to get the earlier one if I can, and that gets in at five fifteen. So if you could bear to be having tea with him or something till after six, to give me time to drive home . . . ?"

"Just at the moment I feel it would choke me, but I'll do my best," I said.

We were back in the kitchen. Its light and warmth and comfortable food smells closed round us like memories from a real but distant world, something safe and bright beyond the tossing straits of the night's dream. He pulled the great door shut behind us, and I heard the key drive the lock shut with a grating snap.

"There. Now you must go home. Come upstairs and get your things, and I'll look along to see if my father's safely asleep."

"Let's hope Phyl is, too, or heaven knows what story I'll have to cook up! Anything but the truth, I suppose!" I stared up at him. "I can't believe it. You realize that, don't you? I know it's true, but I can't believe it. And in the morning, in daylight, it'll be quite impossible."

"I know. Don't think about it now. You've had yourself quite an evening, as they say; but you'll feel different when you've had some sleep."

"My watch has stopped. Oh, hell, I suppose I got water in it. What's the time, Max?"

He glanced at his wrist. "So has mine. Blast. That little sea bathe doesn't seem to have done either of us much good, does it?"

I laughed. "Things that might have been better expressed, Mr. Gale?"

He reached out, and pulled me to him. "Things that might have been better done," he said, and did them.

13

While you here do snoring lie,
Open-ey'd Conspiracy
His time doth take.

Act II, Scene 1

I SLEPT very late that day. The first thing I remember is the sound of shutters being folded back, and then the sudden hot blaze of sunlight striking across the pillow into my eyes.

Phyllida's voice said, "And high time, too, Rip Van Winkle!"

As I murmured something, dragging myself up out of the depths of sleep, she added, "Godfrey rang you up."

"Oh?" I blinked into the sunlight. "Rang *me* up? What did he want—did you say *Godfrey?*" The jerk of recollection brought me awake, and up off the pillow so sharply that I saw her look of surprise, and it helped me to pull myself together.

"I was dreaming," I said, rubbing my eyes. "What on earth's the time?"

"High noon, my child."

"Goodness! What was he ringing about?"

"To know if you'd got safely home with the ring, of course."

"Did he expect Mr. Gale to steal it en route?"

Too late, I heard the tartness in my voice, and my sister looked at me curiously, but all she said was, "I woke you up too suddenly. Never mind, I brought some coffee. Here."

"Angel . . .Thank you. Heavens, I must have slept like the dead. . . . Your ring's over there on the dressing table. Oh, you've got it."

"You bet your sweet life I have. I came in a couple of hours ago and took it, but I couldn't bear to wake you, you were flat out, you poor kid." She turned her hand in the sunlight, and the diamond flashed. "Thank heaven for that! Bless you, Lucy, I'm really terribly grateful! I'd have gone stark ravers if I'd had to sit there all night, wondering if someone had wandered by and picked it up. And I wouldn't have dared go down myself! What on earth time did you get in?"

"I hardly know," I said truthfully. "My watch stopped. I thought I'd got water in it, but I'd only forgotten to wind it up. Some ghastly hour of the morning." I laughed. "There were complications, actually. Didn't Godfrey tell you about them?"

"I didn't quite get that bit. Something about the dolphin being up on the beach and you and Max Gale wrestling about with it in the water. I must say it all sounded highly unlikely. What did happen?"

"More or less that." I gave her a rapid—and suitably expurgated—version of the dolphin's rescue, finishing with Godfrey's arrival on the beach. "And you'll find the wreck of your precious plastic bag in the bathroom, I'm afraid. I'm fearfully sorry, but I had to use something."

"Good heavens, that old thing! It couldn't matter less!"

"I'm relieved. The way you were talking last night, I thought it was practically a holy relic."

She shot me a look as she disappeared through the bathroom door. "I was not myself last night, and you know it."

"Well, no." I reached for the coffeepot which she had put down beside the bed, and poured myself more coffee.

She emerged from the bathroom, holding the bag between thumb and forefinger. "'Wreck' was the word, wasn't it? I suppose you don't even know what happened to my Lizzie Arden lipstick?"

"Lord, I suppose that was a holy relic, too?"

"Well, it was gold."

I drank coffee. "You'll find it in Sir Julian Gale's dressing-gown pocket. I forgot it. I'm sorry again. You might say I was not myself last night either."

"Julian Gale's dressing gown? This gets better and better! What happened?" She sat down on the edge of the bed. "I tried like mad to stay awake till you got in, but those beastly pills put me right out, once Godfrey'd phoned and I stopped worrying. Go on. I want to know what I've missed."

"Oh, nothing, really. We were both soaked, so I had to go up to the Castello to get dry, and they gave me coffee, and I had a bath. . . . Phyl, the bathroom! You'd hardly *believe* the ghastly— Oh, sorry; I forgot, it's the Forli ancestral palace. Well, then you'll know the bathroom."

"There are two," said Phyl. "Don't forget there are twenty bedrooms. One must have one's comforts. I'll say I know the bathrooms. Was it the one with the alabaster bath, or the porphyry?"

"You make it sound like the New Jerusalem. I don't know, I don't live at those levels. It was a rather nasty dark red with white spots, exactly like stale salami."

"Porphyry," said my sister. "Was the water hot?"

"Boiling."

"*Was* it? They must have done something, then. It never used to get more than warm, and in fact I seem to remember a tap for *sea*water, which was pumped up in some weird way from the caves. There are caves under the Castello."

"Are there?"

"They used to use them to keep the wine in."

"Really. How exciting."

"Only, shrimps and things kept coming in, which was discouraging, and once a baby squid."

"It must have been."

"So Leo stopped it. It was supposed to be terribly health-giving, but there are limits."

"I'm sure there are," I said. "Shrimps in the wine would be one of them."

"Shrimps in the *wine?* What on earth are you talking about?"

I put down my empty cup. "I'm not quite sure. I thought it was the wine cellars."

"The seawater baths, idiot! Leo stopped them. Oh, I see, you're laughing at me. Well, go on, anyway. You had a bath. But I still don't see how you got hot water; they *can't* have got the furnaces to work. They used to burn about a ton of coal a day, and it practically needed three slaves to stoke all round the clock."

"Adoni and Spiro invented a geyser."

"Dear God," said Phyl devoutly, "does it work?"

"Yes, I told you, the water was marvelous. What's more, there were hot pipes to dry my things on, *and* an electric fire in the bedroom next door. Well, while my things dried I wore Sir Julian's dressing gown—which is why I left all your make-up in the pockets—and had coffee and bacon and eggs in the kitchen. Then Max Gale brought me home with the diamond, and that's the end of the saga." I leaned back and grinned at her. "As a matter of fact, it was rather fun."

"It sounds it! Was Max Gale civil?"

"Oh, yes. Very."

"I must say I'm surprised he helped you. I thought he was supposed to be trying to get rid of the dolphin."

"It can't have been him after all. He helped me as soon as I asked him. And it wasn't his father, either, I'm certain of that. I think it must just have been some beastly local lad out for a bit of fun." I sat up and pushed back the coverlet. "I'd better get up."

My sister glanced at her wrist, and stood up with an exclamation. "Heavens, yes, I'll have to run if I'm to be ready."

"Where are you going?"

"To get my hair done, and I've got some shopping to do, so I thought I'd have lunch in town. I ought to have waked you before to ask if you'd like to come, but you looked so tired. . . . There's cold meat and a fruit flan if you stay home, but you're welcome to come if you like. Can you make it? I'll have to leave in about twenty minutes."

I hesitated. "Did Godfrey expect me to ring him back or anything?"

"Oh, heavens, yes, I'd forgotten. He's pining to hear all about last night at first hand, I gather. I told him I'd be out to lunch, or I'd have asked him over, but I think he was going to ask you to lunch with him." She paused, a hand on the door. "There's the phone now, that'll be him. What shall I tell him?"

I reached for my stockings, and sat down to pull them on. The action covered some rapid thinking.

Godfrey would obviously be very curious to know what had passed at the Castello last night—what Sir Julian had told us, and what Max's reactions had been. If I could put him off till tomorrow, I might use this curiosity to keep him out of Max's way.

I said, "Say I'm in the bathroom or something, and can't come to the phone now, and tell him I'm going out with you, and I don't know when I'll be in, but I'll ring him . . . No, he can ring me. Sometime tonight."

Phyl raised an eyebrow. "Hard to get, huh? All right. Then you are coming with me?"

"No, I'll never make it, thanks all the same. I'll laze around and go down to the beach later."

"Okay," said my sister amiably, and went to silence the telephone.

I had no intention of going down to the beach, as it happened, it being more than likely that Godfrey would see me there and come down. But I did want to go over to the Castello to find out if Max and Spiro had got safely away. I hesitated to use the party telephone, and in any case, I doubted if Sir Julian would want to talk to me this morning, but I had hopes of finding Adoni about in the garden, and of seeing him alone.

So I ate my cold luncheon early, and rather hurriedly, then, telling Miranda that I was going down to the beach for the afternoon, went to my room for my things.

But she was waiting for me in the hall as I came out, with a small package in her hand.

"For me?" I said. "What is it?"

"Adoni just brought it. It's some things you left there last night."

I took it from her. Through the paper I could feel the small hard shapes of Phyl's lipstick and powder box. "Oh, that's good of him. I was thinking I'd have to go across to collect them. Is he still here?"

"No, miss, he wouldn't stay. But I was to say to you that all was well."

There was just the faintest lift of curiosity in her voice. I noticed then how bright her eyes were, and that the flush was back in her cheeks, and for a moment I wondered if Adoni had given her some hint of the truth.

"I'm glad of that. Did he tell you about the adventure we had last night?"

"The dolphin? Yes, he told me. It must have been strange." The strangest thing to her Greek mind was, I could see, that anyone should have gone to that amount of trouble. "But your coat, Miss Lucy! I don't know if it will ever come right!"

I laughed. "It did get rather a beating, didn't it? I thought you'd be wondering what I'd been doing."

"I knew you must have fallen in the sea, because of your dress and coat . . . and the bathroom, *po po po*. I have washed the dress, but the coat must go to a proper cleaner."

"Oh, goodness, yes, you mustn't bother with it. Thanks very much for doing the dress, Miranda. Well, when you see Adoni, will you thank him for bringing these things? And for the message. That was all, that all was well?"

"Yes."

"That's fine," I said heartily. "I did wonder. Sir Julian wasn't feeling well last night, and I was worried."

She nodded. "He will be all right this morning."

I stared for a moment, then realized that she knew exactly what my careful meiosis meant, and was untroubled by it. The Greek mind again: if a man chose to get drunk now and again, what did it matter except to himself? His women would accept it as they accepted all else. Life here had its shining simplicities.

"I'm very glad," I said, and went out toward the pine woods.

As soon as I was out of sight of the house I left the path and climbed higher through the woods, where the trees thinned and a few scattered pines stood on top of the promontory. I spread my rug in the shade, and lay down. The ground was felted with pine needles, and here and there grew soft furry leaves of ground ivy, and the pretty, dull pink orchids, and lilac irises flecked with white. The Castello was hidden from view by its trees, but from this height I could just see, on the southern headland, the roof of the Villa Rotha. The Forli house was visible below me. In the distance, beyond the sparkling sea, lay the mountains of Epirus. Their snow had almost gone, but farther north the Albanian peaks still gleamed white. There, beneath them, would be the rocks where Spiro had gone ashore, and where Max had brought him off under the coastguards' guns. And there, a colored cluster under the violet hills of Epirus, was Igoumenitsa, where the ferry ran. . . .

I had brought a book, but couldn't read, and it was not long before I saw what I had been expecting: Godfrey, coming with an air of purpose along the path round the headland. He didn't descend into the bay; just stood there, as if looking for someone who might have been on the beach or in the sea. He waited a little while, and I thought at one point that he was going to cross the sand and climb to the Forli house, but he didn't. He hung around for a few minutes more, then turned and went back.

Some time later my eye was caught by a glimpse of moving white, a glint beyond the treetops that rimmed the sea; and presently a boat stole out under sail from beyond the farther headland, cutting a curved path of white through the glittering blue.

I lay, chin on hand, watching her.

She was not unlike a boat that Leo had owned some years back, and on which I had spent a holiday one summer, the year I had left school. She was a powered sloop, perhaps thirty feet overall, Bermuda-rigged, with—as far as I could make out—a mast that could be lowered. That this was so seemed probable, since from something Godfrey had said I assumed she was Dutch-built, so might presumably be adapted for canal cruising and negotiating low bridges. In any case, I had gathered last night that she was customarily moored not in the bay, but in the boathouse; and even if this was built on the same lavish scale as the Castello and designed to house several craft, it would have to be a vast place indeed to take the sloop's forty-odd-foot mast. Her hull was sea gray, with a white line at the bows. She was a lovely craft, and at any other time I would have lain dreamily admiring her sleek lines and the beauty of her canvas, but today I merely wondered about her speed—seven or eight knots, I supposed—and narrowed my eyes to watch the small black figure at the tiller, which was Godfrey.

The sea raced glittering along the gray hull (gray for camouflage?); the white wake creamed; she turned, beautiful, between me and the sun, and I could see no more of her except as a winged shape heading in a long tack out to sea, and then south, toward Corfu town.

"Lucy?" said the telephone.

"Yes. Hullo. You're very faint."

"Did you get the message from Adoni?"

"Yes. Just that all was well, so I assumed you'd got away safely. I hope it still is?"

"So far, a bit discouraging, but I'm still hoping. What about you?"

"I'm fine, thank you, and all's well here. Calm and normal, as far as I can see. Don't worry about this end."

"Ah." A slight pause. Though I knew there was no one else in the house, I found myself glancing quickly around me. Max's voice said, distant in my ear, "You know this libretto I came over here to discuss with that friend of mine?

We've been talking over the story all afternoon now, and he's not very keen on it. Says it's not plausible. I'm not sure if I'm going to be able to persuade him to do much about it."

"I get it," I said, "but look, this line's all right. My sister's out, and so is the other party on the line; I saw his boat go out, with him in it, quite a bit ago, and it's not back yet. I've been watching till now. You can say what you like."

"Well, I'm not sure how good their English is at the Corfu Exchange," said Max, "but you'll have gathered it's not very good news in any language. We've been with the police all afternoon, and they've listened civilly enough, but they're not inclined to take it all that seriously—certainly not to take action against our friend without some solid proof."

"If he were to be watched—"

"They're inclined to think it's not worth it. The general idea is that it's only another spot of illegal trading, and no one's prepared to take it seriously enough to spend money on investigating."

"Don't they believe the boy's story, then?"

He hesitated. "I can't quite make that out. I don't think they do. They think he may be mistaken, and they're favoring the idea of an accident."

"A nice, trouble-free verdict," I said dryly. "And was Y.'s death an accident, too?"

"They're inclined to stick to the first verdict there as well. The trouble is, you see, they're furious with me over last night's little effort, which I've had to tell them about, and which might have started some trouble. The Greek-Albanian frontier's always like a train of dynamite with a slow fuse crawling up to it. Oh, they did admit in the end that I could hardly have called the police in on a rendezvous with Milo and his pal, but I did also withhold evidence in the inquiry on Y.Z., after they'd been so helpful to Father and myself over Spiro. . . . I must say I rather see their point, but my name's mud for the moment, and they're simply not prepared to take action on my say-so, especially if it means coming in over the heads of the local coppers. You see, there's no possible motive."

"But if it was . . . 'illegal trading'?"

"That would hardly have led to murder. As we know, it's barely even taken seriously from this side of the border."

"I see."

"So they look like accepting accident on both counts. And of course, damn it, we can't prove a thing. I simply don't know what's going to happen."

"Can you bring him back—the boy?"

"I don't know that either. As far as the hospital's concerned, it's all right, but as to whether it's safe for him . . . If only one could find even some shred of an idea why it happened, let alone proof that it did . . . If I didn't know the boy so well, and if it weren't for Y.'s death, I'd take the same attitude as the police, I can tell you that. You were right last night when you said it was incredible. In the cold light of day the idea's fantastic—but still my bones tell me it's true. . . . Ah, well. I'm going to talk to them again later tonight, and there's still tomorrow. We may get something done yet."

"When will you come back?"

"Tomorrow. I'll try to manage the earlier time I gave you."

"All right. I'm fairly sure I can have that under control. You won't be met."

"Well, that's one load off my mind." I heard him laugh. "We managed fine on the way out, but the hospital's fitted a wonderful new cast that won't go in the boot, so it's the back seat and a rug—and a damned awkward situation if anyone is hanging about. Will it be hard to arrange?"

"Dead-easy—I think. I'm not sure which is the spider and which is the fly, but I don't think I'll even have to try."

"Well, for pity's sake, watch your step."

"Don't worry, he'll get nothing out of me. I may be a darned bad actress on the stage, but off it I'm terrific."

He laughed again. "Who's telling whom? But that's not what I meant."

"I know. It's all right, I'll be careful."

I heard him take a long breath. "I feel better now. I'll go and tackle this bunch of very nice but all too sensible policemen again. I must go. Bless you. Take care of yourself."

"And you," I said.

The receiver at the other end was cradled, and through the wire washed the crackling hiss of the miles of sea and air that lay between us. As I put my own receiver down gently, I found that I was staring out of the long glass pane of the door that led to the terrace. It framed an oblong of the empty evening sky, dusk, with one burning planet among a trail of dusty stars. I sat for a few minutes without moving, one hand still on the receiver, not thinking of anything, just watching that bright planet and feeling in me all tensions stilled at once, as if someone had laid a finger across a thrumming string.

When the telephone rang again, right under my hand, I hardly even jumped. I sat back in the chair and put the receiver to my ear.

"Yes?" I said. "Oh, hullo, Godfrey. Yes, it's Lucy. In Corfu, are you? No, I've been home a little while. I was wondering when you'd ring. . . ."

14

He's safe for these three hours.

Act III, Scene I

HE CALLED for me next day immediately after lunch. He had suggested that I lunch with him, and certainly he had sounded flatteringly anxious for my company, but since I didn't imagine he really wanted anything from me but information, and I had no idea how long I could hold him, I pleaded an engagement for lunch, but allowed myself to be suitably eager for a drive in the afternoon.

I even managed to suggest the route. Not that there was much choice in the matter: the road north was barely navigable by a car one cared about, so I could hardly suggest that Godfrey take it. We would have to go south on the road by which Max and Spiro would eventually be driving home, but there was, happily, a road leading off this to Palaiokastritsa, a famous beauty spot on the western coast which I could be legitimately anxious to visit. It was in fact true that I had looked the place up on the map, but had put off going there because the road seemed mountainous and I had been slightly nervous of tackling it in Phyl's little car. With me driving (I told Godfrey) it would be nerve-racking, and with Phyl driving it would be suicide. But if Godfrey would drive me, and if he had a car that would manage the gradients . . .

He had laughed, sounding pleased, and had professed himself delighted to brave any gradients I wished, and yes, he had a car that would manage it quite easily. . . .

He certainly had. It was a black XK 150, blunt-nosed, powerful, and about as accommodating on the narrow roads as a bull seal on his own bit of beach. It nosed its way impatiently along the drive, humming like a hive of killer bees, bucked on to the rutted sweep of the Castello's private road, and turned to swoop down to the gate where Maria's cottage stood.

Maria was outside, bending over a rusty tin with a stick, stirring what seemed to be hen food. When she heard the car she straightened up with the tin clutched to her breast and the hens clucking and chattering round her feet. Godfrey, slowing down for the turn into the main road, raised a hand and called out a greeting, to which she returned a look of pleasure mingled with respect, as warm a look as I had seen on her face in the last week or so. I had noticed the same look, shy but pleased, in Miranda's face as she had showed him into the *salotto* earlier, as if the two women were grateful to Spiro's employer for his continued kindness to them in their bereavement.

I stole a look at him as the car swerved—rather too fast, and with a blare of its twin horns that sent Maria's hens up in a squawking cloud—on to the main road. I don't know quite what I had expected to see this afternoon—some smooth-skinned monster, perhaps, with hoofs, horns, and tail all visible to the eye of knowledge—but he was just the same, an undeniably attractive man, who handled his exciting car with skill and obvious enjoyment.

And this man, I thought, was supposed to have brushed the boy—the beloved son and brother—off the stern of his boat as if he were a jellyfish, and then sailed on, leaving him to drown. . . .

He must have felt me watching him, for he flicked me a glance and smiled, and I found myself smiling back spontaneously, and quite without guile. In spite of myself, in spite of Max, and Spiro's story, I could not believe it. The thing was, as I had said to Max, impossible in daylight.

Which was just as well. If I was to spend the next few hours with him, I would have to shut my mind to all that I had learned, to blot out the scene in the cellar, drop Spiro out of existence as if he were indeed dead. And, harder than all, drop Max. There was a curiously strong and secret pleasure, I had found, in speaking of him as "Mr. Gale" in the offhand tones that Godfrey and Phyllida commonly used, as one might of a stranger to whom one is under an obligation, but whom one hardly considers enough to like or dislike. Once, as I had mentioned his name in passing, my eye, downcast, caught the faint mark of a bruise on my arm. The secret thrill of pleasure that ran up my spine startled me a little; I slipped my other hand over the mark to hide it, and found it cupping the flesh as if it were his, and not my own. I looked away, out of the car, and made some random remark about the scenery.

It was a very pretty road. To our left was the sea, blue and smooth, broken only by a tiny white crescent of sail thin as a nail paring and almost lost in the heat haze. On the right was a high hedge of apple blossom and judas trees, their

feet deep in a vivid pink of meadow flowers, yellow and purple and white. Two
little girls, in patched and faded dresses of scarlet, stood barefoot in the dust to
watch us go by, one of them holding a bough of oranges as an English child
might hold a stick of balloons, the fruit bulging and glowing among the green
leaves.

The road straightened, and the XK 150 surged forward with a smooth burst of
speed. My spirits lifted. This was going to be easy; in fact, there was no reason
why I shouldn't simply relax and enjoy it, too. I sat back and chatted on—I
hoped naturally—about nothings: the view, the people Phyl had met yesterday in
Corfu, the prospect of Leo's coming with the children for Easter. . . .

We flashed by a fork in the road.

I sat up sharply. "That was the turning, wasn't it? I'm sure the signpost said
Palaiokastritsa!"

"Oh, yes, it was. I'm sorry, I wasn't thinking; I meant to have told you, I'm
not taking you there today. It's a long way, and we've hardly time. We'll go
another day if you like, when we don't have to be back early."

"*Do* we have to be back early?"

The question slipped out before I thought, ingenuous in its dismay. I saw the
faint shadow of gratified surprise in his face, and reflected that after my evasions
over the telephone he had every right to find provocation in it.

"I'm afraid so. I'm going out tonight. I don't say we couldn't do it, but it's a
shame to go all the way for a short time; it's a lovely place, and there's a lot to
see. Besides which, it's a damned waste to go there and not have lunch; there's a
restaurant high on the beach where they keep crayfish alive in pots in the sea, and
you choose your own and they take them out fresh to cook." A sideways look at
me and a teasing smile. "I suppose you disapprove, but I can tell you, they're
wonderful. I'll take you there soon if you promise not to stand me up for lunch
next time."

"I didn't—that would be lovely."

We flicked through a tiny village, one narrow street of houses and a baked
white church with a red roof. The snarl of the engine echoed back in a quick blast
from the hot walls, and we were through, nose down through a scatter of goats,
children, a scraggy puppy, and a donkey trailing a frayed end of rope. The
children stared after us, admiring and unresentful.

"One thing," said Godfrey cheerfully, "one doesn't have to plan one's outing
here according to the weather. The sun's always on call in this blessed isle, and
one day's as good as another."

That's what you think, I said savagely to myself. My hands were tight together
in my lap now, as much because of his driving as in a panic-stricken attempt to
think of the map. How to get him off this road, head him away from Corfu?

I said aloud, "I'll hold you to that one day, *and* I'll eat the crayfish! I can't feel
strongly about fish, I'm afraid! Where are we going then, Pellekas?" For
Pellekas one turned off just at the north end of Corfu—the only other turning
before the town.

"No, the Achilleion."

"Oh? That's a wonderful idea!"

It was a bloody awful idea, as well I knew. To get there one went right through
Corfu—not quite to the harbor, but near enough—and of course the whole way
home we would be using the same road as Max. Well, I'd just have to see that we
didn't head for home around five thirty, and I could only hope there was plenty of

scope for sightseeing to the south of Corfu town. I reached for my handbag and fished in it for the guide I had brought, adding with great enthusiasm, "I'd planned to visit it one day, but there was the same objection—Phyl told me it was on top of a hill with the most ghastly zigzag going up to it! Yes, here it is: 'The villa of Achilleion, erected for the Empress Elizabeth of Austria. . . . The villa, which is in Italian Renaissance style, was purchased in 1907 by the German Emperor. The gardens are open to visitors (admission one drachma, applied to charitable purposes).'"

"What? What on earth's that?"

"An ancient Baedeker I found on Phyl's shelves. It was my grandfather's—date 1909. It's really rather sweet. Listen to the bit at the beginning about the history of the island. He says 'it came into the possession of' the Romans, then 'fell to the share of' the Venetians, then 'was occupied by' the French, then 'was under Turkish, then Russian sway,' but—notice the *but*—from 1815 to 1863 it 'came under the protection of' the British. Rule Britannia. Those were the days."

"They certainly were." He laughed. "Well, you can see the whole palace as well, today, and it will cost a damned sight more than a drachma, and I imagine the gate money'll go straight to the Greek Government. As usual, charity begins at home. . . . I wish there'd been some classical relics to take you to—Phyl told me you were interested—but I don't know any, apart from some temple or other inside the Mon Repos park, which is private. However, you might say Achilles is the patron saint of the Achilleion, so perhaps it'll do! There's some talk of turning it into a casino, so this may be the last chance of seeing it more or less in the original state. And the drive up there is very pretty, you'll enjoy it."

"You're very kind," I said. It was all I could do not to stare. He spoke so easily and charmingly, sitting there relaxed and handsome at the wheel, the sun throwing up fair highlights in his hair, and a dusting of freckles along the bare brown arms. He was wearing an open-necked shirt, with a yellow silk scarf tucked in at the neck—Top People summer uniform—which suited him very well. He looked calm and contented, and perfectly normal.

Well, why not? When a felon's not engaged in his employment, he has to look as ordinary as possible for his own skin's sake. I supposed it was perfectly possible for a man to drown two young men one week and enjoy a pleasant day out with a girl the next, take a lot of trouble to plan an outing for her and even enjoy the view himself. . . .

"And there's a marvelous view," he said. "The palace is set on a steep wooded hill over the sea. From the belvedere you can see practically the whole way from Vutrinto, in Albania, to Perdika, along the Greek coast. On a clear day the harbor at Igoumenitsa's quite plain."

"How splendid."

"And now supposing you tell me exactly what happened last night at the Castello?"

It took every scrap of discipline and technique I had not to jump like a shot rabbit. "What happened? Well . . . nothing much—what should? I got home with the diamond, you know that."

"Oh, to hell with the diamond, you know quite well what I mean." He sent me another sideways, amused look. "Did you see Julian Gale?"

"Oh. Yes, I did. Adoni was with him when we got up there."

"Ah, yes, the faithful watch-pup. He would be. How was Sir Julian?"

"He went to bed pretty soon," I said cautiously. I kept my eyes on the road, and in the windscreen I saw Godfrey glance at me again. "He was—tired," I said.

"Say what you mean," said Godfrey. "He was stoned."

"How do you know?" The question came out flatly and even accusingly, but since he himself had hit the ball into the open with the last phrase there was no reason why I shouldn't keep it there.

"Come off it, they knew who'd been with him, didn't they?"

"We-ll, it was mentioned." I leaned back in my seat and let a spice of mischievous amusement creep into my voice. It sounded so like Phyl as to be startling. "Mr. Gale wasn't awfully pleased with you, Godfrey."

"Damn it all, what's it got to do with me if he wants to get plastered? By the time I saw which way the land lay, he was halfway there. Do they imagine it was up to me to stop him?"

"I wouldn't know. But I'd watch out for Mr. Gale if I were you."

"So?" His mouth curved. "Pistols for two and coffee for one, or just a horsewhip? Well, maybe he does owe it me, after all."

I knew then. I'm not sure what it was, something in his voice, or the infinitesimal degree of satisfaction at the corners of his mouth; something at once cruel and gay and quite terrifying. All the daylight doubts fled, once forever. Of course he was a murderer. The man was a natural destroyer. "Evil, be thou my good. . . ." And the instinct that had allowed him to create those pictures wasn't even incongruous: no doubt it had given him much the same pleasure to destroy Spiro as it had to photograph him. Destroying Sir Julian would hardly have cost him a moment's thought.

I dragged my eyes and thoughts away from the evil sitting beside me in the car, and concentrated on the idyll of silver olive and black cypress through which the XK 150 slashed its way in a train of dust.

"What a lovely road."

"I wish they'd do something about these potholes, that's all. Don't sidetrack, Lucy. Was it really horsewhips?"

"I wouldn't be surprised. I mean, Mr. Gale had had a trying evening. I'd had hysterics all over him and dragged him out to help with the dolphin, and he fell slap in the sea, and then on top of it all when we got up to the house we found his father drunk . . . in front of me, too. You can't blame him if he's out for your blood."

"I suppose not." He didn't sound as if it worried him vastly. "Where is he today?"

"I believe he said he was going to Athens. It was just some remark to Adoni—I didn't take much notice. But you're probably safe for today."

He laughed. "I breathe again. Just look at the color of that girl's frock, the one picking up olives over there, that dusty red against the rather acid green."

"Don't *you* sidetrack. I want to know what happened."

He raised his brows. "Heavens, nothing, really. I saw the old man at the garage on the harbor, and he was looking for a lift, so I took him home. I was rather pleased to have the chance to talk to him, as it happened—you can never get near him alone, and it was too good a chance to miss."

"What on earth did you want to get him alone for? Don't tell me you're looking for a walk-on in the next Gale play!"

He grinned. "That'll be the day—always providing there is one. No, there were things I wanted to know, and I thought he'd be the softest touch. Max Gale and I aren't just the best of friends, and the watch-pup dislikes me, I can't think why."

"Godfrey! Are you telling me you got him drunk on purpose?"

"Good God, no. Why should I? I wasn't trying to get state secrets out of him. But by the time he'd had a couple there was no stopping him, and it wasn't my business to stop him, was it? I admit I didn't try." That fleeting smile again, gone in an instant; a flash of satisfaction, no more. "It was quite entertaining up to a point."

"What on earth *were* you wanting to get out of him?"

"Only what the police were up to."

"Police?"

He glanced at me with a lifted eyebrow. "Don't sound so startled. What have you been doing? No, it's only that on this island everything gets to the Gales' ears and to no one else's. I had a hell of a job finding anything out about the Spiro affair—nobody seemed to think it was my business, but I'm damned sure they tell the Gales everything that turns up."

"Well, I gather there's some sort of family connection."

"So I'm told. But I don't see why that gives them an 'exclusive' on a police inquiry that involved me as closely as Spiro's death did."

"I do so agree," I said sympathetically. "It must have been a terribly nerve-racking time for you."

"It still is." Certainly if I hadn't known what I knew, I'd have heard nothing in the grave rejoinder but what should properly be there. But, keyed as I was, the two brief syllables hid a whole world of secret amusement. I found that the hand in my lap was clenched tightly, and deliberately relaxed it.

"Did Sir Julian have any news? What has turned up about Spiro?"

"Search me. He wouldn't say a word. We had a couple of drinks at the taverna, and I thought his manner was a bit odd; I thought at first he was being cagey and there was something he didn't want to tell me, but after a bit I realized that he was merely feeling his corn and trying to hide it. It's my guess the poor old chap hasn't had anything stronger than half a mild sherry for a year." His mouth twitched. "Well, after that I'm afraid I did rather give the party a push along the right lines. . . . I wanted to lay in a few bottles for myself—I was out of ouzo, for one thing, and there was a new *koùm koyàt* liqueur I was wanting to try, so I bought them, but when I suggested we should go along to my place the old man wouldn't have it. He was mellowing a bit by that time, and insisted on taking me to the Castello and buying a bottle of gin to treat me to. It didn't take much of that stuff to get him good and lit, but I'm afraid it finished any hope I'd had of getting sense out of him. He'd got it fixed in his head that the only reason I'd gone to the Castello was to hear the recording of their blasted film music." He gave a short laugh where the exasperation still lingered. "Believe you me, I got the lot, words and all."

"Oh, I believe you! Hunks of *The Tempest?*"

"Did he do that for you, too?"

I laughed. "He was reciting when Mr. Gale and I got up to the house. As a matter of fact, I enjoyed it. He did it marvelously, gin or no gin."

"He's had plenty of practice."

The cruel words were lightly spoken, but I think it was at that moment that I began to hate Godfrey Manning. I remembered Max's face, strained and tired; Sir Julian's, blurred and drowning, holding on to heaven knew what straw of integrity; the two boys curled close together on the makeshift bed; Maria's grateful humility. Until this moment I had been content to think that I was helping Max: this had franked a piece of deception whose end I had not let myself explore. But now I explored it, and with relish. If Godfrey Manning was to be proved a murderer, then presumably he was going to be punished for it; and I was going to help with everything I had. Something settled in me, cold and hard. I sat down in the saddle and prepared to ride him down.

I felt him glance at me, and got my face into order.

"What actually happened when you got to the house?" he asked. "What did he tell them, Max and the model-boy?"

"Nothing, while I was there. No honestly, Godfrey!" I was pleased to hear how very honest I sounded. "They only guessed it was you who'd been with him because you'd thrown a Sobranie butt into the stove."

He gave a crack of laughter. "Detectives Unlimited! You did have an exciting night, didn't you? Did they let anything drop in front of you—about Spiro, I mean?"

"Not a thing."

"Or Yanni Zoulas?"

I turned wide, surprised eyes on him. "Yanni— Oh, the fisherman who was drowned. No, why?"

"I wondered. Pure curiosity."

I said nothing, letting the silence hang. Now we were getting some-where. . . . It was obvious that he was still uncertain whether the police really had accepted "accident" as the verdict on Spiro and Yanni; and I thought it was obvious, too, that he badly wanted to know. And since he wasn't the man to sweat about what he had done, it must be what he still had to do that was occupying him: he needed a clear field, and no watchers. His efforts with Sir Julian, and now with me, showed that he had no suspicion that he was being watched, just that he badly needed a green light, and soon.

Well, I thought cheerfully, leaning back in my seat, let him sweat a bit longer. He'd get no green light from me.

The road was climbing now, zigzagging steeply up a wooded hill clothed with vineyards and olive groves, and the fields of green corn with their shifting grape bloom shadows.

He said suddenly, "Didn't you see him go back to the body after we'd left it?"

"What? See who?"

"Gale, of course."

"Oh, yes . . . sorry, I was looking at the view. Yes, I did. Why?"

"Didn't you wonder why he did that?"

"I can't say I did. I supposed he just wanted another look." I gave a little shiver. "Better him than me. Why, did you think he saw something we didn't?"

He shrugged. "Nothing was said to you?"

"Nothing at all. Anyway, I hardly know the Gales; they wouldn't tell me things any more than you. You aren't beginning to think there was more in Yanni's death than met the eye?"

"Oh, no. Let's just say it's curiosity, and a little natural human resentment at having things taken out of my hands. The man was drowned on my doorstep—as Spiro was from my boat—and I think I should have been kept in the picture. That's all."

"Well," I said, "if anything had turned up about Spiro, Maria would know, and she'd tell my sister and me straight away. If there is anything, I'll let you know. I realize how you must be feeling."

"I'm sure you do. And here we are. Shall we see if they'll let us in for one drachma?"

The gates were open, rusting on their seedy pillars. Huge trees, heavy already with summer, hung over the walls. A sleepy janitor relieved us of twenty drachmas or so and nodded us through.

The house was very near the gate, set among thick trees. The doors were open. I had vaguely expected a museum of some kind, a carefully kept relic of the past, but this was merely an empty house, a summer residence from which the owners had moved out, leaving doors and windows unlocked, so that dead leaves and insects had drifted year by year into the deserted rooms, floorboards had rotted, paintwork had decayed, metal had rusted. . . . The place was a derelict, set in the derelict remains of formal gardens and terraces, and beyond the garden boundaries crowded the trees and bushes of a park run wild.

I remember very little now of my tour of the Achilleion. I am sure Godfrey was a good guide: I recollect that he talked charmingly and informatively all the time, and I must have made the right responses; but I was obsessed with my new hatred of him, which I felt must be bound to show as plainly as a stain; in consequence I was possibly even a little too charming back again. I know that as the afternoon went on his manner warmed perceptibly. It was a relief to escape at length from the dusty rooms on to the terrace.

Here at least the air was fresh, and it wasn't quite as hard to linger admiringly as it had been in the dusty rooms of the palace, with their unkempt and shabby grandeurs. The terrace was floored with horrible liver-colored tiles, and the crowding trees below it obscured any view there might have been, but I did my best with the hideous metal statues at the corners and the row of dim-looking marble "Muses" posing sadly along a loggia. I was a model sightseer. I stopped at every one. You'd have thought they were Michelangelos. Three fifteen . . . three twenty . . . Even at three minutes per Muse it would keep us there only till three forty-seven. . . .

There remained the garden. We went in detail round it; arum lilies deep in the weeds at the foot of palm trees; a few unhappy peonies struggling up in the dank shade; a dreadful statue of Achilles triumphant (six minutes) and a worse one of Achilles dying (four); some Teutonic warriors mercifully cutting one another's throats in a riot of brambles (one and a half). I would even have braved the thorny tangle of the wood to admire a statue of Heine sitting in a chair if the gate hadn't been secured with barbed wire, and if I hadn't been afraid that I would wear out even Godfrey's patience.

I needn't have worried. It was unassailable. He had to put the time in somehow, and I am certain that it never once crossed his mind that a day out with him could be anything but a thrill for me from first to last.

Which, to be fair, it certainly was. The thrill that I got, quite literally, when he took me by the elbow to lead me gently back toward the gate and the waiting Jaguar went through my bone marrow as if the bones had been electrically wired. It was only twenty past four. If we left for home now, and if Godfrey, as seemed likely, suggested tea in Corfu, we should just be in nice time to meet the ferry.

There was one more statue near the gate, a small one of a fisher boy sitting on the fragment of a boat, bare-legged, chubby, smiling down at something, and wearing a dreadful hat. It was on about the same level of genius as the Muses, but of course I stopped in front of it, rapt, with Baedeker at the ready and my eyes madly searching the tiny print to see if there were any other "sights" between here and Corfu which I could use to delay my blessedly complacent guide.

"Do you like it?" Godfrey's tone was amused and indulgent. He laid the back of a finger against the childish cheek. "Do you notice? If this had been done seven years ago instead of seventy it might have been Spiro. One wonders if the model wasn't a grandfather or something. It's very like, don't you think?"

"I never knew Spiro."

"Of course not, I forgot. Well, Miranda, then."

"Yes, perhaps I do see it. I was just thinking it was charming."

"The face is warm," said Godfrey, running a light hand down the line of the cheek. I turned away quickly, feeling my face too naked. Half past four.

He dropped his hand. "You keep looking at your watch. I suppose you're like Phyl, always gasping for tea at this time? Shall we go and look for some in Corfu?"

"What's the other way? The coast looked so lovely from the belvedere."

"Nothing much, the usual pretty road, and a fishing village called Benitses."

"There'll be a *kafenéion* there, surely? That would be more fun for a change. Wouldn't there be tea there?"

He laughed. "The usual wide choice, Nescafé or lemonade. There might even be some of those slices of bread, cut thick and dried in the oven. I've never yet discovered who eats them or even how. I can't even break them. Well, on your head be it. Jump in."

We got tea after all at Benitses, at a plain, clean little hotel set right on the sea. It couldn't have been better placed—for me, that is. There were tables outside, and I chose one right on the dusty shore, under a pepper tree, and sat down facing the sea. Just beside us a whole stable of colored boats dozed at their moorings, vermilion and turquoise and peacock, their masts swaying gently with the breathing of the sea; but beyond them I saw nothing but one red sail dancing alone on the empty and glittering acres.

Godfrey glanced over his shoulder. "What's going on there that's so interesting?"

"Nothing, really, but I could watch the sea by the hour, couldn't you? Those boats are so pretty. Your own is a real beauty."

"When did you see her?"

"Yesterday afternoon. I saw you go out."

"Oh? Where were you? I'd been looking for you down on the beach."

"What a pity! No, I didn't go down after all, I stayed up in the woods and slept." I laughed. "I rather needed the sleep."

"You'd certainly had a strenuous time. I wish I'd seen your rescue act with the dolphin. Some pictures by flash would have been interesting." He stirred the pale tea, squashing the lemon slice against the side of the cup. "I read somewhere—I think it was Norman Douglas—that while dolphins are dying they change color. I believe it can be a remarkable display. Fascinating if one could get that, don't you think?"

"Marvelous. Did you say you were going out tonight?"

"Yes."

"I suppose you couldn't do with a crew? I'd adore to come."

"Brave of you, under the circumstances. You'd not be afraid to crew for me?"

"Not in the least, I'd love it. You mean I may? What time are you going?"

If he had accepted the offer I'm not sure what I'd have done; broken an ankle at least, I expect. But he said:

"Of course you may, someday soon, but you've got me wrong, I didn't mean I was going out with the boat tonight. Actually, I'm going by car to visit friends."

"Oh, I'm sorry, I must have got hold of the wrong end of the stick. A pity, I was getting all excited."

He smiled. "I tell you what: I'll take you sailing soon—Friday, perhaps? Or Saturday? We'll go round to Lake Kalikiopoulos and look for the place—one of the places, I should say—where Odysseus is supposed to have stepped ashore into the arms of Nausicaä. Would that be classical enough for you?"

"It would be marvelous."

"Then I'll look forward to it. . . . Look, there's the ferry."

"Ferry?" It came out in a startled croak, and I cleared my throat. "What ferry?"

"The mainland boat. She crosses to Igoumenitsa and back. There, see? It's not easy to see her against the glitter. She'll be in in about twenty minutes." He looked at his watch, and pushed back his chair. "Hm, she's late. Well, shall we go?"

"I'd like to go upstairs, please, if they have one."

The owner of the hotel, who was at Godfrey's elbow with the check, interpreted this remark with no difficulty, and led me up an outside stair and along a scrubbed corridor to an enormous room which had been made into a bathroom. It was spotlessly clean, and furnished, apart from the usual offices, with a whole gallery of devotional pictures. Perhaps others before me had fled to this sanctuary to think. . . .

But it was Baedeker I had come to study. I whipped it open and ran a finger down the page. The print was hideously small, and danced under my eyes. "One drachma a day for the dragoman is ample . . . valets-de-place, 5 dr. per day, may be dispensed with. . . ."

Ah, here was something that might be expected to appeal to an avid classicist like myself. *"The Tomb of Menecrates, dating from the 6th or 7th century B.C. . . ."* And bang on the way home, at that. Now, if only I could persuade Godfrey that my day would be blighted if I didn't visit this tomb, whatever it was . . .

I could; and it was a winner, for the simple reason that nobody knew where it was. We asked everybody we met, and were directed in turn, with the utmost eagerness and goodwill, to a prison, a football ground, the site of a Venetian fort, and a pond; and I could have felt sorry for Godfrey if I hadn't seen quite clearly that he thought that I was trying desperately to spin out my afternoon with him. The man's armor was complete. In his vocabulary, God was short for Godfrey.

I was paid out when we did finally run Menecrates to earth in the garden of the police station, and the custodian, welcoming us as if the last tourist to visit it had been Herr Karl Baedeker himself in 1909, pressed on me a faded document to read, and thereafter solemnly walked me round the thing three times, while Godfrey sat on the wall and smoked, and the lovely dusk fell, and the hands of my watch slid imperceptibly round, and into the clear. . . .

"After six o'clock," said Godfrey, rising. "Well, I hope you've time to have a drink with me before I take you home. The Astir has a very nice terrace overlooking the harbor."

"That would be wonderful," I said.

15

I prithee now, lead the way without any more talking.

Act II, Scene 2

IT WAS quite dark when Godfrey finally drove me back to the Villa Forli. I said good-bye at the front door, waited till the car had vanished among the trees, then turned and hurried indoors.

A light from the kitchen showed that either Miranda or her mother was there; but the *salotto* was empty in its cool, gray dusk and no light showed from Phyl's bedroom door. In a moment I knew why: I had made straight for the telephone, and just before I lifted the receiver I saw the pale oblong of a note left on the table beside it. I switched on the table lamp, to find a note from Phyl.

> *Lucy dear,* [it ran] *got a wire this afternoon to say that Leo and the kids are coming on Saturday, and he can stay two whole weeks. Calloo, callay! Anyway, I've gone into Corfu to lay in a few things. Don't wait for me if you're hungry. There's plenty for G., too, if he wants to stay. Love, Phyl.*

As I finished reading this, Miranda came into the hall.

"Oh, it's you, Miss Lucy! I thought I heard a car. Did you see the letter from the Signora?"

"Yes, thank you. Look, Miranda, there's no need for you to stay. Mr. Manning's gone home and my sister may be late, so if there's something cold I can get—"

"I came to tell you. She telephoned just a few minutes ago. She has met friends in Corfu—Italian friends who are spending one night only—and is having dinner with them. She said if you wanted to go, to get a taxi and join them at the Corfu Palace, but"—a dimple showed—"none of them speaks any English, so she thinks you would rather stay here, yes?"

I laughed. "But definitely yes. Well, in that case, I'll have a bath, and then have supper as soon as you like. But I can easily look after myself, you know. If you'll tell me what there is, you can go home if you want to."

"No, no, I shall stay. There is cold lobster, and salad, but I am making soup." She gave her wide, flashing smile. "I make good soup, Miss Lucy. You will like it."

"I'm sure I shall. Thank you."

She didn't go, but lingered at the edge of the light thrown by the little lamp, her hands busily, almost nervously, pleating the skirt of the red dress. I realized then, suddenly, what my preoccupation hadn't let me notice till now: this was not the subdued and tear-bleached Miranda of the last week. Some of the gloss was back on her, and there was a sort of eagerness in her face, as if she were on the edge of speech.

But all she said was, "Of course I will stay. I had a day off this afternoon. A day off? Is that what the Signora calls it?"

"Yes, that's right. The afternoon off. What do you do when you get an afternoon off?"

She hesitated again, and I saw her skin darken and glow. "Sometimes also Adoni has the afternoon off."

"I see." I couldn't quite keep the uneasiness out of my voice. So she had spent the afternoon with Adoni. It might be that fact alone which had set her shining again, but I wondered if anyone as young as Adoni could possibly be trusted not to have told her about Spiro. Even for myself, the temptation to break the news to the girl and her mother had been very strong, while for the nineteen-year-old Adoni, longing, like anyone of his age, to boast of his own share in last night's exploits, the urge must have been overwhelming. I added, "No, don't go for a moment, Miranda; I want to make a phone call in rather a hurry, and I don't know how to ask for the number. The Castello, please; Mr. Max."

"But he is not there, he is away."

"I know, but he was to be back before six."

She shook her head. "He will not be here till late. Adoni told me so. Mr. Max rang up at five o'clock. He said he would be home tonight, but late, and not to expect him to dinner."

"Oh." I found that I had sat down rather heavily in the chair beside the telephone, as if the news was in actual physical fact a letdown. I did not think then of the effort that had been wasted, but simply of the empty spaces of the evening that stretched ahead, without news . . . and without him. "Did he say anything else?"

"Only that 'nothing had changed.'" She gave the words quotation marks, and there was something puzzled and inquiring in her look that told me what I had wanted to know. Adoni had after all kept his word: the girl had no idea that there was anything afoot.

Meanwhile I must make do with what crumbs I had. "Nothing had changed." We could presumably expect him on the late ferry, but if nothing had changed it didn't sound as if a police escort was likely, so he might not bring Spiro back with him, either. More I could not guess, but my part in the affair was decidedly over for the day: I couldn't have kept Godfrey any longer, and it didn't seem now as if it was going to matter.

"Where was Mr. Max speaking from?"

"I don't know. From Athens, I suppose."

"From *Athens?* At five o'clock? But if he was planning to come back tonight—"

"I forgot. It couldn't have been Athens, could it? Adoni didn't say, just that it was the mainland." She waved a hand largely. "Somewhere over there, that's all." And, her tone implied, it didn't matter much one way or the other; outside Corfu all places were the same, and not worth visiting anyway.

I laughed, and she laughed with me, the first spontaneous sound of pleasure that I had heard from her since the news of her brother's loss. I said, "What is it, Miranda? You seem excited tonight. Has something nice happened?"

She was opening her lips to answer, when some sound from the kitchen made her whisk round. "The soup! I must go! Excuse me!" And she vanished toward the kitchen door.

I went to have my bath, then made my way to the dining room, where Miranda was just setting the contents of a large tray out in lonely state at one end of the

table. She showed no desire to leave me, but hovered anxiously as I tasted the
soup, and glowed again at my praise. We talked cooking all through the soup,
and while I helped myself to the lobster salad. I asked no more questions, but ate,
and listened, and wondered again what magic the "afternoon off" with young
Adoni had done for her. (I should say here that Miranda's English, unlike
Adoni's, was not nearly as good as I have reported it; but it was rapid enough,
and perfectly understandable, so for the sake of clarity I have translated it fairly
freely.)

"This is a dressing from the Signora's book," she told me, handing a dish.
"She does not like the Greek dressing, so I have tried it from the French book. Is
it good? You had a nice day, Miss Lucy?"

"Lovely, thanks. We went to the Achilleion."

"I have been there once. It is very wonderful, is it not?"

"Very. Then we had tea at Benitses."

"Benitses? Why did you go there? There is nothing at Benitses! In Corfu it is
better."

"I wanted to see it, and to drive back along the sea. Besides, I was longing for
some tea, and Corfu was too far, and I wanted to look at some antiquities on the
way home."

She knitted her brows. "Antiquities? Oh, you mean statues, like the ones on
the Esplanade, the fine English ones."

"In a way, though those aren't old enough. It really means things many
hundreds of years old, like the things in the museum in Corfu."

"Are they valuable, these antiquities?"

"Very. I don't know if you could say what they were worth in terms of money,
but I'd say they're beyond price. Have you seen them?"

She shook her head. She said nothing, but that was because she was biting her
lips together as if forcibly to prevent speech. Her eyes were brilliant.

I stopped with my glass halfway to my mouth. "Miranda, what is it?
Something *has* happened—you can't pretend—you look as if you'd been given a
present. Can't you tell me?"

She took in her breath with something of a gulp. Her fingers were once again
pleating and unpleating a fold of her skirt. "It is something . . . something
Adoni has found."

I put down the glass. It clattered against the table. I waited.

A silence, then she said, with a rush, "Adoni and I, we found it together, this
afternoon. When I got the afternoon off I went over to the Castello." She sent me
a sideways glance. "Sometimes, you see, Adoni works in the garden while Sir
Gale sleeps, and then we talk. But today Mr. Karithis was visiting with Sir Gale,
and they told me Adoni had gone to swim. So I went down to the bay."

"Yes?" She had my attention now, every scrap of it.

"I could not find him, so after a bit I walked along the path, round the rocks
toward the Villa Rotha. Then I saw him. He was up the cliff, coming out of a
bush."

"Coming out of a *bush?*"

"It was really a cave," explained Miranda. "Everybody knows that there are
caves in the rock under the Castello, they used to use them for wine; and Adoni
told me that he had seen down through a crack, and heard water, so he knew that

there must be more caves below. This island is full of caves. Why, over near Ermones—"

"Adoni has found a new cave?"

She nodded. "He had not been on that part of the cliff before. I did not know he was interested in—I don't know the word—exploring? . . . Thank you. But today he said he wanted to find out where the water was that lay under the Castello, and he knew that Mr. Manning was away with you, so it was all right. I think"—here she dimpled—"that he was not very pleased to see me. I think he had heard me, and thought it was Mr. Manning come back. He looked quite frightened."

And well he might, I thought. My heart was bumping a bit. "Go on, what had he found?"

Her face went all at once solemn, and lighted. "He had found proof."

I jumped. *"Proof?"*

"That is what he said. Myself, I do not think that proof is needed, but that is what he said."

"Miranda!" I heard my voice rise sharply on the word, and controlled it. "Please explain. I have no idea what you're talking about. What proof had Adoni found?"

"Proof of St. Spiridion and his miracles."

I sat back in my chair. She stared at me solemnly, and as the silence drew out I felt my heartbeats slowing down to normal. I had a near-hysterical desire to laugh, but managed to stop myself. After a while I said gently, "Well, go on. Tell me— No, don't hover there, I've finished, thank you. Look, would you like to bring the coffee, and then sit down here and have some with me and tell me all about it?"

She hurried out, but when she came back with the coffee she refused to take any with me, or to sit down, but stood gripping a chair back, obviously bursting to get on with her story.

I poured coffee. "Go on. What's this about the Saint?"

"You were at the procession on Palm Sunday."

"Yes."

"Then perhaps you know about the Saint, the patron of this island?"

"Yes, I know about him. I read a lot about the island before I came here. He was Bishop of Cyprus, wasn't he, who was tortured by the Romans, and after he died his body was embalmed, and carried from place to place until it came to Corfu. We have a Saint like that in England, too, called Cuthbert. There are lots of stories about him, and about the miracles his body did."

"In England also?" It was plain that she had never credited that cold and misty land with anything as heart-warming as a real saint. "Then you understand that we of Corfu are taught all about our Saint as children, and many stories of the miracles and marvels. And they are true. I know this."

"Of course."

She swallowed. "But there are other stories—stories that Sir Gale has told me of the Saint, that I have never heard before. He—my *koumbàros*—told us many tales when we were children, Spiro and me. He is a very learned man, as learned as the *papàs*—the priest—and he knows very many stories about Greece, the stories of our history that we learn in school, Pericles and Alexander and Odysseus and Agamemnon, and also stories of our Saint, things that happened long, long ago, in this very place, things that the *papàs* never told us, and that I have not heard before."

She paused. I said, "Yes?" but I knew what was coming now.

"He has told us how the Saint lived here, in a cave, and had his daughter with him, a princess she was, very beautiful. He had angels and devils to do his bidding, and worked much magic, raising storms and stilling them, and saving the shipwrecked sailors."

She paused doubtfully. "I don't believe, me, about the daughter. The Saint was a bishop, and they do not have daughters. Perhaps she was a holy nun. . . . It is possible that Sir Gale has got the story a little bit wrong?"

"Very possible," I said. "Was the daughter called Miranda?"

"Yes! It was after this holy woman, a Corfiote, that I was called! Then you know this story, too?"

"In a way." I was wondering, in some apprehension, what rich and strange confusion Sir Julian's Shakespearean theories might have created. "In the English story we call him Prospero, and he was a magician—but he wasn't a bishop; he was a duke, and he came from Milan, in Italy. So you see, it's only a—"

"He lived in a cave behind the grove of lime trees along the cliff." She waved northward, and I recognized Sir Julian's cheerfully arbitrary placing of the scene of *The Tempest*. "And there he did all his magic, but when he became old he turned to God, and drowned his books and his magic staff."

"But, Miranda . . ." I began, then stopped. This wasn't the time to try to point out the discrepancies between this story and that of the Bishop of Cyprus, who (for one thing) had already been with God for some thousand years when his body arrived at the island. I hoped there was some way of explaining how legends grew round some central figure like alum crystals round a thread. "Yes?" I said again.

She leaned forward over the chair back. "Well, Adoni says that Mr. Max is making a play out of this story, like . . . like . . ." She searched her mind, and then, being a Greek, came up with the best there is. ". . . like *Oedipus* (that is a play of the old gods; they do it in Athens). I asked Sir Gale about this play, and when he told me the story I said that the priests should know of this, because I had not heard it, and the *papàs* in my village has not heard it either, and he must be told, so that he can ask the Bishop. Why do you smile, Miss Lucy?"

"Nothing." I was thinking that I need hardly have worried. The Greeks invented cynicism, after all; and every Greek is born with an inquiring mind, just as every foxhound is born with a nose. "Go on; what did Sir Julian say?"

"He laughed, and said that his story—of the magic and the books—is not true, or perhaps it is only a little true, and changed with time, and that the poet who wrote the story added things from other stories and from his own mind, to make it more beautiful." She looked earnestly at me. "This happens. My *koumbàros* said it was like the story of Odysseus—that is another story of this island that we have in our schools, but you will not know it."

"I do know the story."

She stared. "You know this, too? Are all English so learned, Miss Lucy?"

I laughed. "It's a very famous story. We have it in our schools, too."

She gaped. This was fame indeed.

"We learn all your Greek stories," I said. "Well, Sir Julian's story of the magician may have some tiny fragment of truth in it, like the legends about

Odysseus, but I honestly think not much more. I'm sure he didn't mean you to believe it word for word. The story he told you, that Mr. Max is making a film play out of, *is* just something that a poet invented, and probably has nothing to do with the real St. Spiridion at all. And you must see for yourself that the bit about the cave and the princess can't possibly be true—"

"But it is!"

"But look, Miranda, when the Saint was brought here in 1489, he was already—"

"Dead many years, I know that! But there is *something* that is true in Sir Gale's story, and the priests must be told of it. We can prove it, Adoni and I! I told you, we found the proof today!"

"Proof that *The Tempest* is true?" It was my turn to stare blankly. Somehow, after the mounting excitement of Miranda's narrative, this came as a climax of the most stunning irrelevance.

"I don't know about any tempest, but today we found them, in the cave behind the lime trees. There's a passage, and a cave, very deep in the cliff, with water, and that is where he drowned his books." She leaned forward over the chair back. "That is what Adoni found today, and he took me in and showed me. They are there in the water, plain to see, in the very same place where Sir Gale told us—the magic books of the Saint!"

Her voice rose to a dramatic stop that Edith Evans might have envied. Her face was shining, lighted, and full of awe. For a full half minute all I could do was sit there, gazing blankly back at her, framing kind little sentences which might explain and question without too cruel a disillusionment. Adoni had been with her, I thought impatiently; what in the world had Adoni been thinking about to allow this fantasy to go on breeding? Certainly he would not share her beliefs, and she would have accepted an explanation from him, whereas from me, now . . .

Adoni. The name stabbed through the haze in my mind like a spearpoint going through butter muslin. What Adoni did, he usually had a good reason for. I sat up, demanding sharply, "Adoni found these—things—in a cave in the cliff? Where's the entrance?"

"Round the point, halfway up the cliff, above the boathouse."

"Ah. Could it be seen from the bay—our bay?"

She shook her head. "You go halfway up the path to the Villa Rotha. Then it is above the path, in the rocks, behind bushes."

"I see." My heart was bumping again. "Now, when Adoni saw it was you, what did he say? Try to remember exactly."

"I told you, he was angry at first, and would have hurried me away, because we should not have been there. Then he stopped and thought, and said no, I must come into the cave and see what he had found. He took me in; it was a steep passage, and long, going right down, but he had a torch, and it was dry. At the bottom was a big cave, full of water, very deep, but clear. Under a ledge, hidden with pebbles, we saw the books."

"A moment. What made you think they were books?"

"They looked like books," said Miranda reasonably. "Old, old books, colored. The corners showed from under the pebbles. You could see the writing on them."

"Writing?"

She nodded. "Yes, in a foreign tongue, and pictures and magical signs."

"But, my dear girl, *books?* In seawater? They'd be pulp in a couple of hours!"
She said simply, "You forget. They are holy books. They would not perish.
I let that one pass. "Didn't Adoni try to get at them?"

"It was too deep, and very cold, and besides, there was an eel." She shivered.
"And he said they must not be disturbed; he would tell Sir Gale, he said, and Mr.
Max, and they would come. He said that I was his witness that he had found
them there, and that I was to tell nobody about them, except you, Miss Lucy."

I put my hands flat on the table and held them there, hard. I could feel the
blood pumping in the fingertips.

"He told you to tell me?"

"Yes."

"Miranda. You told me earlier that Adoni had said these books were 'proof.'
Did he say proof of what?"

She knitted her brows. "What could he have meant, but proof of the story?"

"I see," I said. "Well, that's marvelous, and thank you for telling me. I can
hardly wait to see them, but you won't tell anyone else, will you, anyone at all,
even your mother? If—if it turns out to be a mistake, it would be dreadful to have
raised people's hopes."

"I won't tell. I promised Adoni. It is our secret, his and mine."

"Of course. But I'd love to ask him about it. I think I'll go over to the Castello
now. D'you think you could get him on the phone for me?"

She glanced at the clock. "There will be nobody there now. Sir Gale was
going back to Corfu with Mr. Karithis for dinner, and Adoni went with them."

"But Max has the car. Adoni didn't have to drive them, surely?"

"No, Mr. Karithis brought his car. But Adoni wanted to go into Corfu, so he
went with them, and he said he would come back with Mr. Max later."

Of course he would. Whatever he had found in the cave by the Villa Rotha,
whatever "proof" he had now got, Adoni would get it to Max at the first possible
moment, and if he was right about his discovery—and I had no doubt he was—
then tonight the hounds would close in, and the end I had wanted this afternoon
to hasten would come.

I glanced at my watch. If the ferry docked at ten forty-five . . . give Max an
hour at most to hear Adoni's story and possibly collect police help in
Corfu . . . half an hour more for the drive . . . at the outside that made it a
quarter past midnight. Even if Godfrey had got back from his date, whatever it
was, he might be in bed by that time, not where he would hear or see explorers
probing the secrets of the cliff. . . .

My hands moved of their own accord to the edge of the table, and gripped it.
My thoughts, till now formlessly spinning, settled and stood.

Godfrey had said he was going out tonight, and there was the impression I had
had of urgent business to be done and a clear field needed to do it in. Was it not
conceivable that the objects so mysteriously hidden under his house were part of
this same night's business? That in fact by the time Max and the police were led
to the cave in the small hours the "proof" would have gone? And even with
Adoni's word and that of his witness there would be nothing to show what had
been there, or where it had gone? We would be back where we were, possibly
with Godfrey's business finished, and himself in the clear. . . .

Reluctantly, I worked it out. Reluctantly, I reached the obvious, the only
conclusion. I stood up.

"Will you show me this cave and the books? Now?"

She had started to stack the supper things back on the tray. She paused, startled. "Now, miss?"

"Yes, now. It may be important. I'd like to see them myself."

"But—it's so dark. You wouldn't want to go along there in the dark. In the morning, when Adoni's back—"

"Don't ask me to explain, Miranda, but I must go now, it might be important. If you'll just show me the cave, the entrance, that's all."

"Well, of course, miss." But the words dragged doubtfully. "What would happen if Mr. Manning came down?"

"He won't. He's out, away somewhere in his car, he told me so, so he's not likely to be using the cliff path. But we'll make sure he's out, we'll ring up the house . . . I can pretend I left something in the car. Will you get me the number, please?"

Somewhere in Godfrey's empty house the telephone bell shrilled on and on, while I waited and Miranda hung over me, uneasy, but obviously flattered by my interest in her story.

At length I put the receiver back. "That's that. He's out, so it's all right." I looked at her. "Will you, Miranda? Please? Just show me where the cave is, and you can come straight back."

"Well, of course, if you really want to. . . . If Kyrios Manning is away I don't mind at all. Shall I get the torch, Miss Lucy?"

"Yes, please. Give me five minutes to get a coat, and some other shoes," I said, "and have you got a coat here, or something extra to put on?" I didn't bother to ask if it was something dark; by the Saint's mercy the Corfiote peasants never wore anything else.

Three minutes later I was dressed in light rubber-soled shoes and a dark coat, and was rummaging through Leo's dressing-table drawer for the gun I knew he kept there.

16

This is the mouth o' th' cell. No noise, and enter . . .

Act IV, Scene 1

THE BAY was dark and silent: no sound, no point of light. It was easy enough to see our way across the pale sand without using the torch we had brought; and once we had scrambled up under the shadow of the pines where the dolphin had lain and gained the rocky path along the foot of the southern headland, we found that we could again make our way without a betraying light.

We turned off the track into the bushes some way before reaching the zigzag path that led up toward the Villa Rotha. Miranda led the way, plunging steeply uphill, apparently straight into the thickest tangle of bushes that masked the cliff. Above us the limes leaned out, densely black and silent. Not a leaf stirred. You could hardly hear the sea. Even after we had switched the torch on to help us, our stealthy progress through the bushes sounded like the charge of a couple of healthy buffaloes.

Fortunately it wasn't far. Miranda stopped where a clump of evergreens—junipers, by the scent—lay back, apparently right against the cliff.

"Here," she whispered, and pulled the bushes back. I shone the torchlight through.

It showed a narrow gap, scarcely more than a fissure, giving on a passage that sloped sharply downward for perhaps four yards, to be apparently blocked by a wall of rock. The floor of the passage looked smooth, and the walls were dry.

I hesitated. A puff of breeze brought a murmur from the trees, and the bushes rustled. I could feel the same breeze—or was it the same?—run cold along my skin.

"The passage goes to the left there"—Miranda's whisper betrayed nothing but pleased excitement—"and then down again, quite a long way, but it is easy. Will you go first, or shall I?"

I had originally intended merely to stay hidden where I could watch the cave's entrance until Adoni brought the men down, and to send Miranda home, out of harm's way. But now it occurred to me that if Godfrey did come to remove the "books" before Max arrived I, too, should need a witness. This was to put it at its highest. To put it at its lowest, I wanted company. And even if Godfrey found us (which seemed unlikely in this tangle of darkness), there was no risk of our meeting with Yanni's fate. I was prepared, and there was the gun—the gun, and the simple fact that two people were more than twice as hard to dispose of as one.

But still I hesitated. Now that we were here, in the quiet dark, with the sounds and gentle airs of the night so normal around us, I wanted nothing so much as to see for myself what it was Adoni had found. If Godfrey did come tonight to remove it, if I should be unable to get a look at it, or to follow him, then we were back at the post, and no better off than before. . . .

Three parts bravado, three parts revenge for these people I had come so quickly to love and admire, and three parts sheer blazing human curiosity—it was no very creditable mixture of emotions that made me say with a briskness that might pass for bravery in the dark, "Is there anywhere to hide once you get inside the cave?"

I saw the glint of her eyes, but she answered simply, "Yes, a lot of places, other caves, with fallen rocks, and passages—"

"Fair enough. Let's go. You lead the way."

Behind us the juniper rustled back into its place across the gap.

The passage led steadily downward, as sharply right-angled as a maze; I guessed that the mass of rock had weathered into great rectangular blocks, and that the passage led down the cracks between them. Here and there side cracks led off, but the main route was as unmistakable as a highway running through a labyrinth of country lanes.

Miranda led the way without faltering; left, then right, then straight on for thirty feet or so, then right again, and along . . . well into the heart of the promontory, I supposed. At the end of the last stretch it looked as if the floor of the passage dropped sheer away into black depths.

She paused, pointing. "The cave is down there. You can climb down quite easily, it is like steps."

A few moments later we were at the edge of the drop, with before us a sort of subterranean Giants' Staircase—a vast natural stairway of weathered rock leading down block by block on to a ledge that ran the length of a long, lozenge-shaped cave floored with black water, overhanging the smooth, scooped-out sides of the pool.

We clambered down the stairway, and I shone the light forward into the cave.

This was large, but not awesomely so. At the end where we stood the roof was not so very high—perhaps twenty feet; but as the torchlight traveled farther, it was lost in the shadows where the roof arched upward into darkness. There, I suppose, would be the funneled cracks or chimneys which carried the fresh air into the upper caves, and through which Adoni had first detected the existence of the one where we now stood. Farther along the ledge there were recesses and tunnels leading off the main cave, which promised a good choice of bolt hole should the need arise. The walls were of pale limestone, scoured and damp, so that I guessed that with the wind on shore the sea must find its way in through more of the cracks and crevices. Now the deep vat of seawater at our feet lay still and dead, and the place smelled of salt and wet stone.

Miranda gripped my arm. "Down there! Shine the light. Down there!"

I turned the torch downward. At first I could see nothing but the rich dazzle as the water threw back the beam, then the light seemed to soak down through the water like a stain through silk, and I saw the bottom, a jumble of smooth, round pebbles, their colors all drained by the torchlight to bone white and washed green and pearl. Something moved across them, a whip of shadow flicking out of sight into a crevice.

"See?" Miranda crouched, pointing. "In under the ledge, where the stones have been moved. There!"

I saw it then, a corner like the corner of a big book, or box, jutting out from among the pebbles. It looked as if the object, whatever it was, had been thrust well under the ledge where we stood and the stones piled roughly over it.

I kneeled beside Miranda, peering intently down. Some stray movement of the sea outside had communicated itself to the pool, and the water shifted, shadows and reflections breaking and coalescing through the rocking torch beam. The thing was colored, I thought, and smooth-surfaced; a simple mind conditioned by Sir Julian's stories might well have thought it was a book; myself, I took it for the corner of a box with some sort of a label. Vaguely, I could see what might be lettering.

"You see?" Miranda's whisper echoed in the cave.

"Yes, I see." Any thoughts I might have had of braving the eel and the icy water to get at the object died a natural and unregretted death. Even if I could have dived for the thing and lifted it, I couldn't have climbed the four smooth feet of overhang out of the pool without a rope.

"It is a book, yes?"

"It could be. But if it is, I don't think you'll find it's a very old one. The only way it could be kept down there is if it was wrapped in polythene or something, and that means—"

I broke off. Something had made a noise, some new noise that wasn't part of the cave's echo, or the faint whispers of the night that reached us through the invisible fissures in the cliff. I switched the light out, and the darkness came down like a candle-snuffer, thick as black wool. I put a hand on the girl's arm.

"Keep very still. I heard something. Listen."

Through the drip of water on limestone it came again: the sound of a careful footstep somewhere in the passage above.

Here he came. Dear God, here he came.

Miranda stirred. "Something coming. It must be Adoni back already. Perhaps—"

I stopped her with a touch, my lips at her ear. "That won't be Adoni. We mustn't be found here, we've got to hide. Quickly. . . ."

I took her arm, pulling her deeper into the cave. She came without question. We kept close to the wall, feeling our way inch by inch till we came to a corner, and rounded it safely.

"Wait." I dared a single brief flash of the torch, and breathed relief. We were in a deep recess or blocked tunnel, low-roofed, and filled with long-since-fallen debris that burrowed its way back into the cliff above the water level.

I put the light out. Slowly, carefully, and almost without a sound, we slithered our way into cover, deep into a crevice under a wedged block of limestone, flattening ourselves back into it like starfish hiding from the pronged hooks of the bait-fishers.

Not a moment too soon. Light spread, and warmed the cave. I was too deeply tucked back into the cleft to be able to see more than a curved section of the roof and far side of the main cave, but of course I could hear very clearly, as the cave and the water magnified every sound: the tread of boots on rock; the chink as the powerful torch was put down somewhere and the light steadied; the man's breathing. Then the splash of something—whether his body or something else I couldn't tell—that was let down into the pool.

A pause, while the water lapped and sucked, and the breathing sounded loud and urgent with some sort of effort. Then a different splashing noise, a sucking and slapping of water, as if something had been withdrawn from the pool. Another pause, filled now with the sounds of dripping, streaming water. Then at last the light moved, the slow footsteps retreated, and the sea sounds of the disturbed pool, slowly diminishing, held the cave.

I felt Miranda stir beside me.

"He has taken the book. *Could* it not be Adoni, Miss Lucy? Perhaps he has come back to get the book for Sir Gale? Who else would know? Shall I go—"

"No!" My whisper was as urgent as I could make it. "It's not Adoni, I'm sure of that. This is something else, Miranda. I can't tell you now, but trust me, please. Stay here. Don't move. I'm going to take a look."

I slid out of the cleft and switched on the torch, but kept a hand over the glass, so that the light came in dimmed slits between my fingers. I caught the gleam of her eyes watching me, but she neither moved again nor spoke. I inched my cautious way forward to the main cave, to pause at the corner of the ledge, switch off the torch, and listen yet again. There was no sound but the steady drip of water and the faint residual murmur from the pool.

Flashing the light full on, I knelt at the edge and looked down.

As I expected, the pile of stones had been rudely disturbed, and, as far as I could judge, had dwindled in height. But there must have been more than one of the rectangular objects there, for I could see another corner jutting from the cobbles at a different angle from the one that had been visible before. And there on the ledge, leaning against the wall as if waiting for him to come back, was an iron grapple, a long hooked shaft which dripped sluggishly on to the limestone.

I stood up, thinking furiously. So much for that. Adoni had been right: here was the key we were wanting, the clue to Godfrey's murderous business. And it was surely simple enough to see what I ought to do next. I had no means of telling what proportion of his cache Godfrey had taken, or if he would come back tonight for the rest; but in either case, nothing would be gained by taking the appalling risk of following him now. If he came back, we might meet in the passage. If he didn't—well, the rest of the "proof" would still be safely there for Max when he arrived at last.

And so, let's face it, would I . . .

I was hardly back in my niche before we heard him coming back, the light growing and brightening before him up the limestone walls. The performance was repeated almost exactly: the plunge of the grapple, the grating haul through the pebbles, the withdrawal, the pause while the water drained . . . then once more the light retreated, and we were left in blackness, with the hollow sucking of the troubled pool.

"Wait," I whispered again.

As soon as I got to the main cave I saw that the grapple was gone. I crouched once more on the streaming rock and peered down. As I expected, the pile of pebbles had settled lower, spreading level as what it had hidden had been dragged away. The pool was empty of its treasure.

No need, this time, to stop and think. The decision was, unhappily, as clear as before. I would have to follow him now. And I had better hurry.

In a matter of seconds I was back beside Miranda. "You can come out now. Quick!"

She materialized beside me. Her breathing was fast and shallow, and she was shivering. She was still taut and bright-eyed, but the quality of her excitement had changed. She looked scared.

"What is it, miss? What is it?"

I tried to sound calm and sure. "The 'books' have gone, and it was Mr. Manning who took them, I'm sure it was. I have to see where he puts them, but he mustn't see us. D'you understand, *he mustn't see us*. . . . I'll explain it all later, but we'll have to hurry now. Come on."

We heaved ourselves up the last of the Giants' Staircase, and crept from angle to angle of the passage, lighting the way warily and stopping at each corner to listen ahead. But nothing disturbed us, and soon we were at the mouth of the cleft, cautiously parting the junipers. The air smelled warm and sweet after the cave, full of flower scents and the tang of bruised herbs; and a breeze had got up and was moving the bushes, ready to mask what sounds we made.

We edged down, feeling our way, through the tangle of bushes and young trees. Although no moon was visible, the sky was alight with stars, and we went quickly enough. I dared not make for the path, but pushed a cautious way, bent double, above one arm of the zigzag from which I thought we should be able to see the boathouse, and at length we came to the end of the ridge where honeysuckle and (less happily) brambles made thick cover between the young limes.

We were just above the boathouse. Its roof was silhouetted like a black wedge against the paler sea beyond. I thought, but could not quite make out, that the landward door stood open.

Next moment it shut softly, but with the definite *chunk* of a spring-locking door. A shadow moved along the boathouse wall, and then he came quietly up the path. We lay mouse-still, hardly breathing. He rounded the corner below us, and came on up, with a quick, stealthy stride whose grace I recognized, and next moment, as he passed within feet of us, I saw him clearly. He had changed from the light clothes of the afternoon, and now wore dark trousers and a heavy dark jersey. He carried nothing in his hands. He went straight on past us, and his light tread was lost in the movements of the breeze.

In the heavy shadow where we lay I couldn't see Miranda, but I felt her turn to look at me, and presently she put out a hand and touched my arm. The hand was trembling.

"Miss—miss, what *is* it?"

I put a hand over hers, and held it, "You're quite right, it's not just a case of being caught trespassing, it's something much more serious, and it might be dangerous. I'm sorry you're in it, too, but I want your help."

She said nothing. I took a breath, and tightened my hand over hers.

"Listen. I can't tell you it all now, but there have been . . . things have been happening, and we think . . . Mr. Max and I . . . that they have something to do with your brother's accident. Adoni thinks so, too. We want to find out. Will you just trust me and do as I say?"

There was a pause. Still she didn't speak, but this time the air between us was so charged that I felt it vibrate like a bowstring after the shaft has gone.

"Yes."

"You saw who it was?"

"Of course. It was Mr. Manning."

"Good. You may be asked— What is it?"

"Look there." She had moved sharply, pointing past me up the cliff to where, above the black trees, a light had just flashed on. The Villa Rotha.

I felt my breath go out. "Then he's safe there for a bit, thank God. I wish I knew the time."

"We dare not shine the torch?"

"No. I should have looked before. Never mind. It looks as if he's put those things in the boathouse; I wish to heaven I dared go down and take a look at them . . . he did say he was going out tonight, and *not* with the boat, but he might only have been putting me off so that he'd be able to go to the cave. He may hang around here all night . . . or he may have been lying, and he'll come down again and take the boat, and that will be that." I stirred restlessly, watching that steady square of light with hatred. "In any case, the damned thing's locked. Even if—"

"I know where the key is."

I jerked round to peer at her. *"You do?"*

"Spiro told me. There was an extra key which was kept underneath the floor, where the house reaches the water. I know the place; he showed me."

I swallowed. "It's probably not there now, and in any case—"

I stopped abruptly. The light had gone out.

Minutes later we heard the car. That it was Godfrey's car there could be no manner of doubt: he switched on her lights, and they swept round in a wide curve, lancing through the trees and out into space, to move on and vanish in the blackness over the headland as the engine's note receded through the woods. There was a brief, distant stutter as he accelerated, then the sound died and there was darkness.

"He's gone," said Miranda unnecessarily.

I sat up. I was furious to find that my teeth were chattering, and clenched them hard, pushing a hand down into the pocket where Leo's gun hung heavy and awkward against my thigh. Two things were quite certain: I did not want to go anywhere near Godfrey Manning's boathouse; and if I didn't, I should despise myself for a coward as long as I lived. I had a gun. There was probably a key. I had at least to try it.

"Come on, then," I said, and pushed my way out of cover and dropped to the path, Miranda behind me. As we ran downhill I gasped out instructions. "You must get straight back to the house. Can you get into the Castello?"

"Yes."

"Then go there. That way, you'll see them as soon as they get home. But try to telephone Adoni first. Do you know where he might be?"

"Sometimes he eats at Chrisomalis', or the Corfu Bar."

"Then try them. If he's not there, some of his friends may know where he'll be. He may have gone down to the harbor to wait, or even to the police. . . . Try, anyway."

We had reached the boathouse. I stopped at the door, trying it . . . futilely, of course: it was fast locked. Miranda thrust past me, and I heard her fumbling in the shadows round the side of the building, then she was beside me, pushing the cold shape of a Yale key into my hand.

"Here. What shall I tell Adoni?"

"Don't tell him what's happened. Mr. Manning may get back to the house and pick the phone up, you never know. Just say he must come straight back here, it's urgent, Miss Lucy says so. He'll understand. If he doesn't, tell him anything you like—tell him I'm ill and you have to have help—anything to get him back here. He's not to tell Sir Julian. Then you wait for him. Don't leave the Castello, and don't open the door to anyone else except Max or the police . . . or me. If I'm not back by the time he comes, tell him everything that's happened, and that I'm down here. Okay?"

"Yes." She was an ally in a million. Confused and frightened though she must have been, she obeyed as unquestioningly as before. I heard her say, "The Saint be with you, miss," and then she was gone, running at a fair speed along the shore path to the Castello's bay.

With one more glance up at the lightless headland and a prayer on my own account, I prodded around the lock with a shamefully shaky key until at last I got it home.

The catch gave, stiffly, and I slipped inside.

17

No tongue! all eyes! Be silent.

Act IV, Scene 1

THE BOATHOUSE was a vast structure with a high roof lost in shadows, where the sea sounds echoed hollowly, as in a cave. Running round the three walls was a narrow platform of planks set above the water, and along the near side of this lay the sloop. The rapidly dimming light of my torch showed me the lovely, powerful lines, and the name painted along the bows: *Aleister.* It also showed me, propped against the wall by the door, the grapple from the cave.

There was no hiding place in the boathouse other than the boat itself. I clicked the lock shut behind me, then stepped in over the cockpit coaming to try the cabin door.

It was unlocked, but I didn't go straight in. There was a window in the back of the boathouse, facing the cliff, which showed a section of the path, then the black looming mass of cliff and tree, and—at the top—a paler section of sky where stars burned. With eyes now adjusted to the darkness, I could just make out the sharp angle of some part of the Villa Rotha's roof. So far, excellent. If Godfrey did come back too soon, I should have the warning of the car or house lights.

Inside the cabin, I let the torchlight move round once, twice. . . .

The layout was much as I remembered in Leo's boat. Big curtained windows to either side, under which were settee berths with cushions in bright chintz; between these a fixed drop-leaf table above which swung a lamp. A curtain was drawn over the doorway in the forward bulkhead, but no doubt beyond it I would find another berth, the w.c., and the usual sail bags, ropes, and spare anchor stowed in the bows. Immediately to my right, just inside the door, was the galley, and opposite this the quarter berth—a space-saving berth with half its length in the cabin and the other half burrowing, as it were, into the space beyond the after bulkhead, under the port cockpit seat. The quarter berth was heaped with blankets, and was separated from the settee berth by a small table with a cupboard underneath.

And everywhere, lockers and cupboards. . . .

I started, methodically, along the starboard side.

Nothing in the galley: the oven empty, the cupboards stocked with cooking equipment so compact as to leave no hiding place. In the lockers, crockery, photographic stuff, tins of food, cardboard boxes full of an innocent miscellany of gear. In the wardrobe cupboards, coats, oilskins, sweaters, and a shelf holding sea boots, and shoes neatly racked, all as well polished and slick as Godfrey himself.

It was the same everywhere: everything was open to the searcher, all the contents normal and innocent—clothing, spare blankets, photographic equipment, tools. The only place not open to the prying eye was the cupboard at the end of the quarter berth, which was locked. But—from its shallow shape and my memory of Leo's boat—I imagined that this was only because it held the liquor; there was none elsewhere, and it was hardly big enough to store the packages I was looking for. I left it, and went on, even prodding the mattresses and feeling under the piled blankets, but all that came to light was a paperback copy of

Tropic of Cancer, which I pushed back, rearranging the blankets as they had been before. Then I started on the floor.

Here there would be, I knew, a couple of "traps," or sections of the flooring which were made to lift out and give access to the bilges. Sure enough, under the table, and set in the boards, my eye caught the gleam of a sunken ring which, when pulled, lifted an eighteen-inch square of the planking, like a small trap door. But there was no treasure cave below, only the gleam of bilge water shifting between the frames with the boat's motion, and a faint smell of gas. And the same with the trap in the fo'c'sle.

The engine hatchway under the cabin steps was hardly a likely place for a cache; all the same, I looked there, and even lifted the inspection cover off the fresh-water tank, to see nothing but the ghostly reflection of the torchlight and my own shadow shivering on the surface of the full forty-gallon complement of water. Not here. . . .

I screwed the cover down with hands that sweated now, and shook, then I put the torch out and fled up the steps and on to the deck.

The window first. . . . No light showed outside, but I had to make sure. I ran aft, ducked under the boom, and climbed on the stern seat to peer anxiously out.

All was dark and still, I could—I must—allow myself a little longer.

I started over the cockpit, using the torch again, but keeping a wary eye on the boathouse window. Here, too, all seemed innocent. Under the starboard seat was the space occupied by the Calor gas cylinders, and nothing else. Under the stern seat was nothing but folded tarpaulins and skin-diving equipment. The port seat merely hid the end of the quarter berth. Nothing. Nor were there any strange objects fastened overside, or trailing under the *Aleister* in the sea; that bright idea was disposed of in a very few seconds. I straightened up finally from my inspection, and stood there, hovering, miserably undecided, and trying hard to think through the tension that gripped me.

He must have brought the packages here. He had not had time to take them up to his house, and he would hardly have cached them somewhere outside when he had the *Aleister* handy, and, moreover, no idea that he was even suspected. He might, of course, have handed them to some accomplice there and then, and merely have been returning the grapple to the boathouse, but the accomplice would have had to have some means of transport, which meant either a donkey or a boat; if a donkey, Miranda and I must surely have heard it; we might not have heard a rowing boat, but why should Godfrey use one when the *Aleister* and her dinghy lay ready to his own hand? No, it was obvious that there could be no innocent explanation of his use of the hidden cave.

But I had looked everywhere. They were not in the boat, or tied under the boat; they were not on the platform, or on the single shelf above it. Where in the world could he, in this scoured-out space, have hidden those bulky and dripping objects so quickly and effectively?

An answer came then—so obvious as to be insulting. In the water. He had moved them merely from the bottom of the cave to the bottom of the bay. They must be under the *Aleister*, right under, and if I could only see them there was the grapple ready to hand, with the water still dripping off it to make a pool on the boards.

I was actually up on the cockpit coaming, making for the grapple, when I saw the real answer, the obvious, easy answer which I should have seen straight away; which would have saved me all those precious minutes, and how much more besides; the trail of drops leading in through the boathouse door and along the platform; the trail left by the dripping packages, as obvious to the intelligent eye as footprints in fresh snow. I had no excuse, except fear and haste, and (I thought bitterly) Nemesis armed with a nice, heavy gun had no business to be afraid at all.

And the trail was already drying. I was calling myself names that I hadn't even known I knew, as I shone the yellow and flickering torchlight over the boards of the platform.

Yes, there they were, the footprints in the snow: the two faint, irregular trails, interweaving like the track of bicycle wheels, leading in through the door, along the platform, over the edge . . .

But not into the water after all. They went in over the side of the *Aleister* and across her deck and straight in through the cabin door.

I was in after them in a flash. Down the steps, to the table. . . .I had never even glanced at the bare tabletop, but now I saw on the formica surface the still damp square where he had laid the packages down.

And there the trail stopped. But this time there was only one answer. The trail had stopped simply because all Godfrey had had to do from there was to open the trap door under the table and lift the things straight down.

I had the trap open again in seconds. I laid it aside. The square hole gaped.

I ran back to the steps and peered up at the window. No light showed. I dropped on my knees beside the trap, clicked on the torch, and sent the small yellow eye which was all it had left skidding over the greasy water in the *Aleister*'s bilges.

Nothing. No sign. But now I knew they had to be there . . . and they were there. I had gone flat down on the floor, and was hanging half inside the trap door before I saw them, but they were there; not in the bottom, but tucked, as neatly as could be, right up under the floorboards, in what were obviously racks made specially to carry them. They were clear of the water, and well back from the edges of the hatch, so that you would have had—like me—to be half in the bilges yourself before you saw them.

I ducked back, checked on the window again, then dived once more into the bilges.

Two sweating minutes, and I had it, a big, heavy square package wrapped in polythene. I heaved it out on deck, spreading the skirts of my coat for it so that I in my turn would leave no trail, then turned the light on it.

The torch was shaking now in my hand. The yellow glow-worm crawled and prodded over the surface to the package, but the glossy wrapping almost defeated the miserable light, and all I got, in the three seconds' look I allowed myself, was the impression of a jumble of faint colors, something looking like a picture, a badge, even (Miranda had been right) a couple of words . . . LEKE, I read, and in front of this something that could be—but surely wasn't—NJEMIJE.

Somewhere something slammed, nearly frightening me out of what wits I still had. The torch dropped with a rattle, rolling in a wide semicircle that missed the trap by millimeters. I grabbed it back again, and whirled to look. There was nothing there. Only darkness.

Which was just as well, I thought, recovering my senses rather wryly. Even if I had reacted properly, and grabbed for the gun instead of the torch, I couldn't have got it. Prospero's damned book, or whatever the package was, was sitting right on top of it, on the skirts of my coat. I had a long way to go, I reflected bitterly, before I got into the James Bond class.

The wind must be rising fast. The big seaward doors shook again, as if someone were pulling at the padlock, and the other door bumped and rattled. The water ran hissing and lapping along the walls, and shadows, thrown by some faint reflection of starlight, shivered up into the rafters.

The window was still dark, but I had had my warning, and enough was enough. The trap door went snugly back into place, my torch dropped into my other pocket, and, clasping the package to me with both hands, I clambered carefully out of the *Aleister*.

At the same instant as I gained the platform, I saw the movement on the path outside the window. Only a shadow, but as before there was no mistaking the way he moved. No light, no nothing, but here he was, just above the boathouse, and coming fast.

And here was I, stuck with my arms full of his precious package, for which he had almost certainly tried to do double murder. And I couldn't get out of the place if I tried.

The first thing was to get rid of the package.

I crouched and let the thing slide down between the platform and the boat. The boat was moored close, and for a panic-stricken moment I thought there wasn't enough room there; the package was tangled in my coat, then it jammed in the gap, and I couldn't move it either way, and when I tried to grab it back I couldn't, it was slippery and I couldn't get a grip on it again. . . .

I flung myself down, got a shoulder to the *Aleister*, and shoved. She moved the inch or so I needed, and with a brief, sharp struggle I managed to ram the package through and down.

It vanished with a faint splash. And then, like an echo, came the fainter but quite final splash of Leo's gun slipping from the pocket of my coat, to vanish in its turn under the water.

For one wild, crazy moment of fear I thought of swinging myself down to follow gun and package and hide under the platform, but I couldn't get down here, and there was no time to run the length of the boat. In any case, he would have heard me. He was at the door. His key scraped the lock.

There was only one place big enough to hide, and that was right bang in the target area. The boat itself. It did cross my mind that I could stand still and try to bluff it out, but even had the *Aleister* been innocent and Godfrey found me here at this hour, inside a locked door, no bluff would have worked. With the boat literally loaded, I hadn't a hope. It was the cabin or nothing.

I was already over the side, and letting myself as quietly as a ghost into the cabin, as his key went home in the lock and turned with a click. I didn't hear the door open. I was already, like a hunted mouse, holed up in the covered end of the quarter berth, with the pile of blankets pulled up as best I could to hide me.

The blankets smelled of dust and carbolic soap. They covered me with a thick, stuffy darkness that at least felt a bit like security. The trouble was that they deprived me of my hearing, the only sense that was left to tell what Godfrey was up to. Strain as I might through the thudding of my own heartbeats, I could only get the vaguest impression of where he was and what he was doing. All I could do was lie still and pray he wouldn't come into the cabin.

The boat rocked sharply, and for a moment I thought he was already in her, but again it was only the wind. This seemed to be rising still, in sharper gusts which sent little waves slapping hard along the hull, and sucking up and down the piles on which the platform stood. I could feel the jerking motion as the *Aleister* tugged at her rope, then she bucked, sharply and unmistakably: Godfrey had jumped into her.

Minutes passed, filled with the muffled night noises, but I could feel, rather than hear, his weight moving about the boat, and strained my senses, trying to judge where he was and what he was doing. The boat was steadier now, swaying gently to the small ripples passing under her keel. A draught moved through the cabin, smelling freshly of the sea wind, so that I guessed he must have left the boathouse door open, and this might mean he didn't mean to stay long. . . .

The wind must be quite strong now. The boat swayed under me, and a hissing wave ran right along beside my head. The *Aleister* lifted to it with a creak of timber, and I heard the unmistakable sound of straining rope and the rattle of metal.

Then I knew what had happened. There was no mistaking it, rope and metal and timber active and moving—the boat was alive, and out in the living sea. He must have swung the big doors open without my hearing him, then poled her gently out, and now she was alive, under sail, slipping silently along shore, away from the bay.

I couldn't move. I simply lay there, shivering under my load of blankets, every muscle knotted and tense with the effort of keeping my head, and trying to think. . . .

Max would surely be back by now; and even if he was still in Corfu, Adoni was probably already on his way home . . . and he would have left Miranda's message for Max, so Max wouldn't linger in Corfu, but would come straight here, and probably bring the police. When they got down to the boathouse and found the boat gone, and me with it, they would guess what had happened. There wasn't—I knew this—much hope of their finding the *Aleister* in the darkness, but at least I might have a card or two I could play if Godfrey found me. Under the circumstances, he could hardly expect to get away with my disappearance as well.

Or so I hoped. I knew that if he discovered about the missing package he would probably search the sloop and find me. But since there was nothing I could do about that, my only course was to stay hidden here and pray for a choppy sea that would keep him on deck looking after the *Aleister*. Why, he might not even come below at all. . . .

Just three minutes later he opened the cabin door.

18

What shall I do? say what. What shall I do?

Act I, Scene 2

I HEARD the click, and felt the sudden swirl of fresh air, cut off as the door shut again.

There was the rasp of a match; the sharp tang of it pierced right up into my hidden corner, and with it the first smoke of a newly lighted cigarette. He must have come in out of the wind for this, and now he would go . . .

But he didn't. No movement followed. He must be very near me; I could feel, like an animal in the presence of danger, the hair brushing up along my skin. Now I was thankful for the chop and hiss of water, and for the hundred creaking, straining noises of the *Aleister* scudding on her way through the darkness. Without them, I thought he would have heard my heartbeats.

He can only have stood there for a few seconds, though for me it was a pause prolonged almost to screaming point. But it seemed he had only waited to get his cigarette properly alight: he struck another match, dropped it and the box after it on the table, and then went out and shut the door behind him.

Relief left me weak and sweating. The closed end of the berth seemed like an oven, so I pushed the blanket folds back a little, to let the air in, and cautiously peered over them, out into the cabin.

A weapon; that was the first thing. . . . I had the torch, but it was not a heavy one, and would hardly count as adequate armament against a murderer. Not that it was easy in the circumstances to think of anything (short of Leo's gun) that would have been "adequate," though I would have settled for a good, loaded bottle, if only the damned cupboard had been open. But bottles there were none. I cast my mind furiously back over the cabin's contents. . . . The galley? Surely the galley must be packed with implements? Pans were too clumsy; it must be something I could conceal. . . . A knife? I hadn't opened the shallow drawers during my search, but one of them was bound to hold a knife. Or there was the starting handle for the engine, if I could get the engine hatch opened silently, and then station myself on the galley side, behind the door, and wait for him. . . .

Cautiously, one eye on the door, I reached down to push the blanket aside, ready to slide out of the quarter berth.

Then froze, staring with horror at the foot of the berth.

Even in the almost-darkness I could see it, and Godfrey, in the matchlight, must have seen it quite clearly—my toe, clad in a light yellow canvas shoe, protruding from the huddle of blankets. I was about as well hidden as an ostrich beak deep in sand.

Now I knew what had happened. He had come in quickly out of the wind to light his cigarette, had seen what he thought was a foot, had struck another match to make sure—and, having made sure, had done what?

I was answered immediately. The boat had leveled and steadied, as if she were losing way. Now, seemingly just beside me, the engine fired with a jerk and a brief, coughing roar that nearly sent me straight through the bulkhead; then it was throttled quickly back to a murmur, the merest throb and quiver of the boards, as the *Aleister* moved sedately forward on an even keel. He had merely turned the boat head to wind without taking in the mainsail, and started the engine, so that she would hold herself steady without attention. I didn't have to guess why. His quick step was already at the cabin door.

I whisked off the berth, dropped my wet coat, and straightened my dress. There wasn't even time to dive across the cabin and open the knife drawer. As Godfrey opened the door I was heading for the table and the box of matches, apparently intent on nothing more deadly than lighting the lamp.

I threw a gay greeting at him over my shoulder.

"Hullo, there. I hope you don't mind a stowaway?"

The wick caught, and the light spread. I got the globe fitted back at the third try, but perhaps he hadn't noticed my shaking hands. He had moved to draw the curtains.

"Naturally I'm delighted. How did you know I'd decided to come out after all?"

"Oh, I didn't, but I was hoping!" I added, with what I'm sure was a ghastly archness, "You saw me, didn't you? You were coming in to unmask me. What's the penalty for stowing away in these seas?"

"We'll arrange that later," said Godfrey.

His voice and manner were pleasant as ever, but after that first bright glance I didn't dare let him see my eyes; not yet. There was a mirror set in a cupboard door. I turned to this and made the gestures of tidying my hair.

"What brought you down?" he asked.

"Well, I wanted a walk after supper, and— *Have* you a comb, Godfrey? I look like a mouse's nest!"

Without a word he took one from a pocket and handed it to me. I began, rather elaborately, to fuss with my hair.

"I went down to the beach; I had a sort of vague idea the dolphin might come back—they do, I believe. Anyway, I went to look, but it wasn't there. I walked along the path a bit, listening to the sea and wishing you *had* been going out. Then I heard you—I knew it must be you—over at the boathouse, so I hurried. You know, just hoping."

He had moved so that he was directly behind me. He stood very close, watching my face in the glass. I smiled at him, but got no response; the light eyes were like stones.

"You heard me at the boathouse?"

"Yes. I heard the door."

"When was this?"

"Oh, goodness knows, half an hour ago? Less? I'm no good over times. I'd have called out, but you seemed to be in a hurry, so—"

"You saw me?"

His breath on the back of my neck brought panic, just a flash of it, like a heart spasm. I turned away quickly, handed him his comb, and sat down on the settee berth, curling my legs up under me with an assumption of ease.

"I did. You were just coming out of the boathouse, and you went rushing off up the path to the house."

I saw the slightest relaxation as he registered that I hadn't seen him coming down from the cave with the packages. He drew on his cigarette, blowing out a long jet of gray smoke into a haze round the lamp. "And then?"

I smiled up at him—I hoped provocatively. "Oh, I was going to call after you, but then I saw you had a sweater and things on, so you probably *were* going out after all. I thought if I just stuck around you'd be back and I could ask you."

"Why didn't you?"

"Why didn't I what?"

"Ask me."

I looked embarrassed and fidgeted with a bit of blanket. "Well, I'm sorry, I know I should have, but you were quite a time, and I got bored and tried the door, and it was open, so—"

"The door was open?"

"Yes."

"That's not possible. I locked it."

I nodded. "I know. I heard you. But it hadn't quite caught, or something, you know how those spring locks are. I'd only tried it for something to do—you know how one fidgets about—and when it opened I was quite surprised."

There was no way of knowing whether he believed me or not, but according to Spiro, the catch had been stiff, and Godfrey had no idea I could have known that. I didn't think he could have changed the lock as he had threatened, for I had heard him myself wrestling with it on Monday; but that was a chance I had to take.

He tapped ash into a bowl on the liquor cupboard, and waited. He looked very tall; the slightly swaying lamp was on a level with his eyes. I toyed with the idea of giving it a sudden shove that would knock his head in, but doubted if I could get there quickly enough. Later, perhaps. Now I smiled at him instead, letting a touch of uncertainty, even of distress, appear.

"I—I'm sorry. I suppose it was awful of me, and I should have waited, but I was *sure* you wouldn't mind my looking at the boat—"

"Then why did you hide when I came down?"

"I don't know!" The note of exasperated honesty came out exactly right. "I honestly don't know! But I was *in* the boat, you see, in here, actually, poking about in the cupboards and the ga—kitchen and everything—"

"What for?"

"What *for?*" Every bit of technique I'd ever had went into it. "Well, what does a woman usually poke around in other people's houses for? And a boat's so much more fun than a house; I wanted to see how it was fitted, and the cooking arrangements, and—well, everything!" I laughed, wooing him back to good temper with all I had, playing the ignorant: it might be as well not to let him know how much I knew about the sloop's layout. "And it really is smashing, Godfrey! I'd no idea!" I faltered then, biting my lip. "You're annoyed with me. You *do* mind. I—I suppose it *was* the hell of a nerve. In fact, I *knew* it was, and I suppose that's why I hid when I heard you at the door. . . . I suddenly thought how it must look, and you might be furious, so I got in a panic and hid. I had a vague idea that if you weren't going sailing after all I could slip out after you had gone. That's all."

I sat back, wondering if tears at this point would be too much, and deciding that they probably would. Instead, I looked at him meltingly through my lashes—at least, that's what I tried to do, but I shall never believe the romantic novelists again; it's a physical impossibility. Godfrey, at any rate, remained unmelted, so I abandoned the attempt and made do with a quivering little smile, and a hand, genuinely none too steady, brushing my eyes. "I'm sorry," I said, "I truly am. Please don't be angry."

"I'm not angry." For the first time he took his eyes off me. He mounted a step to pull the door open, and looked out into the blackness. What he saw appeared to satisfy him, but when he turned back he didn't shut the door.

"Well, now you are here you might as well enjoy it. I can't leave the tiller much longer, so come along out. That's not a very thick coat, is it? Try this." And he pulled the cupboard and produced a heavy navy duffel coat, which he held for me.

"Don't bother, mine will do." I stood up and reached for my own coat, with the torch in the pocket, then remembered how wet it was. For the life of me I couldn't think offhand of any reason for the soaked skirt where I had knelt in the puddles of water. I dropped the coat back on the bunk. "Well, thanks awfully, yours'll be warmer, I suppose. It sounds like quite a windy night now."

As he held it for me to put on, I smiled up at him over my shoulder. "Have you forgiven me? It was a silly thing to do, and you've a right to be furious."

"I wasn't furious," said Godfrey, and smiled. Then he turned me round and kissed me.

Well, I had asked for it, and now I was getting it. I shut my eyes. If I pretended it was Max . . . No, that wasn't possible. Well, then, someone who didn't matter—for instance, that rather nice boy I'd once had an abortive affair with but hadn't cared about when it came to the push . . . But that wouldn't work either. Whatever Godfrey was or wasn't, he didn't kiss like a rather nice boy. . . .

I opened my eyes and watched, over his shoulder, the lovely heavy lamp swinging about a foot away from his head. If I could maneuver him into its orbit . . . I supposed there were circumstances in which it was correct, even praiseworthy, for a girl to bash a man's head in with a lamp while he was kissing her. . . .

The *Aleister* gave a sudden lurch, and yawed sharply. Godfrey dropped me as if I had bitten him.

"Put the lamp out, will you?"

"Of course."

He ran up the steps. I blew the lamp out, and had the glass back in a matter of seconds, but already the *Aleister* was steady again, and Godfrey paused in the doorway without leaving the cabin, and turned back to hold a hand down to me.

"Come out and see the stars."

"Just a moment."

His voice sharpened a fraction. He wasn't as calm as he made out. "What is it?"

"My hankie. It's in my own coat pocket." I was fumbling in the dimness of the quarter berth among the folds of coat and blanket. The torch dropped sweetly into the pocket of the duffel coat; I snatched the handkerchief, then ran up the steps and put a hand into his.

Outside was a lovely windswept night, stars and spray, and black sea glinting as it rushed up to burst in great fans of spindrift. Dimly on our left I could see the coast outlined black against the sky, a mass of high land blocking out the stars. Low down there were lights, small and few, and seemingly not too far away.

"Where are we?"

"About half a mile out from Glyfa."

"Where's that?"

"You know how the coast curves eastward here along the foot of Mount Pantokrator, toward the mainland? We're about halfway along the curve . . ."

"So we're running east?"

"For the moment. Off Kouloura we turn up into the strait."

("I reckoned we were about halfway over," Spiro had said, "in the strait between Kouloura and the mainland.")

"You'll feel the wind a bit more when we get out of the lee of Pantokrator," said Godfrey. "It's rising quite strongly now." He slipped an arm round me, friendly, inexorable. "Come and sit by me. She won't look after herself forever. Do you know anything about sailing?"

"Not a thing." As he urged me toward the stern seat, my eyes were busily searching the dimly seen cockpit. Only too well did I know there was no handy weapon lying about, even if that loverlike arm would have allowed me to reach for it. But I looked all the same. It had occurred to me that he probably carried a gun, and I had already found out that there was nothing in the pocket nearest me, the left; if he got amorous again it might be possible to find out if it was in the other pocket. . . . As he drew me down beside him on the stern seat I pulled the duffel coat round me for protection against his hands, at the same time relaxing right into the curve of his shoulder. I was thinking that if he wore a shoulder holster he would hardly have cuddled me so blithely to his left side, and I was right. There was no gun there. I leaned cozily back, and set myself to show him how little I knew about sailing. "How fast will it go?"

"About eight knots."

"Oh?" I let it be heard that I had no idea what a knot was, but didn't want to expose my ignorance. He didn't enlighten me. He settled the arm round me, threw his cigarette overside, and added:

"Under sail, that is. Six or seven under power."

"Oh?" I had another shot at the same intonation, and was apparently successful, because he laughed indulgently as he turned to kiss me again.

The *Aleister* tilted and swung up to a cross-sea, and the boom came over above us with the mainsail cracking like a rifle shot. It supplied me with an excuse for the instinctive recoil I gave as his mouth fastened on mine, but next moment I had hold of myself, and responded with a sort of guarded enthusiasm while my open eyes watched the boom's pendulum movements above our heads and I tried to detach my mind from Godfrey and think.

What he was doing was obvious enough: not being sure yet of my innocence, he hadn't wanted to risk leaving me unguarded while he got the mainsail in and took the *Aleister* along under power. All he could do was hold her as she was, head to the wind, the engine ticking over, the idle mainsail weathercocking her along, until he had decided what to do with me. It was just my luck, I thought sourly, stroking his cheek with a caressing hand, that the wind was more or less in the direction he wanted. If he was aiming (as I supposed he was) for the same place as on the night he had tried to drown Spiro, then he must still be pretty well on course.

A sudden gust on the beam sent the *Aleister*'s bows rearing up at an angle that brought the boom back again overhead with a creak and a thud, and Godfrey released me abruptly, his right hand going to the tiller. And as he moved, leaning forward momentarily, I saw my weapon.

Just beyond him, hanging on its hooks behind the stern cockpit seat, was the sloop's life belt, and attached to this by a length of rope was the smoke flare . . . a metal tube about a foot long, with a drum-shaped float of hollow metal about two thirds of the way up its length. It was heavy enough, and deadly enough in shape, to make a formidable weapon if I could only manage to reach it down from the hook where it hung a foot to my side of the life belt. The rope attaching it was coiled lightly over the hook, and would be some ten or fifteen feet long—ample play for such a weapon. It only remained to get hold of it. I could hardly reach past him for it, and would certainly get no chance to use it if I did. If I could only get him to his feet for a moment, away from me . . .

"Why do you leave the sail up?" I asked. "I'd have thought it ought to come down if the engine was going."

"Not necessarily. I'll want to take her in under sail soon, and in the meantime she'll take care of herself this way."

"I see." It was all I could do, this time, to sound as if I didn't. I saw, all right. He would take her in under sail for the same reason that he had taken her out: for silence. And it was pretty obvious where we were heading. We were making for the Albanian coast with our cargo; and "in the meantime" I, no doubt, would be shed as Spiro had been shed. After I had gone he could spare both hands for the *Aleister*.

I took a deep breath of the salt air, and leaned my head confidingly against his shoulder. "Heavenly, isn't it? I'm so glad I stowed away, and that you're not really angry with me about it. Look at those stars . . . that's a thing one misses terribly in London now: no night sky; only that horrible dirty glare from five million sodium lamps. Oughtn't you to have a light, Godfrey?"

"I ought, but I don't. As long as I don't meet anyone else breaking the law, *we see them,* so there's no harm done."

"Breaking the law?"

I thought he was smiling. "Running without lights."

"Oh. You're taking photographs, then? Of the dawn?" I giggled. "What'll Phyl say *this* time, I wonder, when I land home with the milk?"

"Where is she tonight? Did she know you'd come out?"

"She's out with friends at the Corfu Palace. I got a note from her when I got in, and it was too late to join them, so I just stayed home. I . . . felt kind of blue. We'd had such a lovely day, you and I, I just couldn't stay in the house, somehow."

"Poor Lucy. And then I was foul to you, I'm so sorry. Anybody know where you are?"

The question was casual, almost caressing, and it went off like a fire alarm. I hesitated perhaps a second too long. "Miranda was in the house. I told her I was coming out."

"To the boathouse?"

"Well, no. I didn't know that myself, did I?"

He did not reply. I had no way of knowing whether my wretched bluff had worked. The cool uncommitted tone—pleasant enough—and the cold sensuality of his love-making, gave no clue at all to what he felt, or planned to do. It was a personality from which normal human guesses simply glanced off. But whether or not he had accepted my innocence, I had reckoned that nothing I could say would make any difference to my fate. The only weapon I held so far against him was the knowledge I possessed: that Spiro was alive, that Godfrey might be accused of Yanni's murder, that Adoni and Miranda had seen the packages, and that Miranda had watched him carrying them to the boathouse, and must know where I was now. And finally, that Godfrey on his return would certainly be met by Max, Adoni, and (by now) the police, who this time would not be prepared to accept easily any story he might dream up. In plain words, whether he killed me or not, his game was up.

The trouble was, it worked both ways. If it made no difference what he did with me, then obviously his best course would be to kill me, and make his getaway (surely already planned for) without going back at all into the waiting hands of Max and the Greek police.

So silence was the only course. It was faintly possible, that, if he believed me innocent, he might abandon his mission and take me home, or that I might be able to persuade him to relax his watch on me for long enough to let me get hold of the more tangible weapon that hung beyond his right shoulder.

I said quickly, "Listen. What's the matter with the engine? Did you hear that?"

He turned his head. "What? It sounds all right to me."

"I don't know . . . I thought it made a queer noise, a sort of knocking."

He listened for a moment, while the engine purred smoothly on, then shook his head. "You must be hearing that other boat—there's one over there, see, northeast of us, out from Kentroma. You can hear it in the gusts of the wind." His arm tightened as I twisted to look, pulling away as if to get to my feet. "It's nothing. Some clapped-out old scow from Kentroma with a prewar engine. Sit still."

I strained my eyes over the black and tossing water to where the light, dim and rocking, appeared and disappeared with the heaving sea. Upwind of us, I was thinking: they'd never hear anything; and if they did, they'd never catch the *Aleister* with her lovely lines and silken engine.

Suddenly, only a short way from us, a flash caught my eye, a curve and splash of light where some big fish cut a phosphorescent track like a line of green fire.

"Godfrey! Look!"

He glanced across sharply. "What?"

I was half out of my seat. "Light, lovely green light, just there in the sea! Honestly, it was just *there* . . ."

"A school of fish or some such thing." His tone was barely patient, and I realized with a jerk of fear that his mind was moving toward some goal of its own. "You often see phosphorescence at night hereabouts."

"There it is again! Could it be photographed? Oh, look! Let me go a moment, Godfrey, please, I—"

"No. Stay here." The arm was like an iron bar. "I want to ask you something."

"What?"

"I've had the answer to one question alredy. But that leaves me with another. Why did you come?"

"I told you—"

"I know what you told me. Do you expect me to believe you?"

"I don't understand what you—"

"I've kissed women before. Don't ask me to believe you came along because you wanted to be with me."

"Well," I said, "I admit I wasn't expecting it to be quite like that."

"Like what?"

"You know quite well."

"I believe I do. But if you follow a man round and hide in his bed and play Cleopatra wrapped in a rug you can hardly expect him to say it with lace-edged Valentines."

It was like acid spilling over a polished surface, to show the stripped wood, coarse and ugly. There had been splashes of the same corrosive this afternoon. If there had been light enough to see by, he would have caught me staring.

"Do you have to be so offensive? I know you were annoyed, but I thought you'd got over that, and if you want the truth I can't see why you should mind so damned much if someone *does* have a look at your boat. I've told you exactly what happened, and if you don't believe me, or if you think I should fall straight into bed with you here and now, you can just think again. It's not a habit of mine."

"Then why did you behave as if it were?"

"Now, look!" I broke off, and then laughed. At all costs I mustn't let him force a showdown on me yet. I would have to let anger go, and try a bit more sweet apology. "Look, Godfrey, forget it! I'm sorry, it's silly to blame you, I did ask for it . . . and I *was* putting on a bit of an act in the cabin, I admit it. That was silly, too. But when a woman gets in a jam, and finds herself faced with an angry male, it's an instinct to use her sex to get her out of it. I haven't shown up a bit well tonight, have I? But I never thought you would be quite so furious, or quite so . . . well, quick off the mark."

"Sexually? How little you know."

"Well, you've had your revenge. I haven't felt so idiotic and miserable since I remember. And you needn't worry that I'll follow you around again . . . I'll never face you by daylight again as long as I live!"

He did not answer, but to my stretching senses it was as if he had laughed aloud. I could feel the irony of my words ring and bite in the windy air. A little way to starboard the trail of green fire curved and flashed again, and was gone. I said, "Well, after that, I suppose I must ask you to ruin your trip finally and completely, and take me home."

"No use, my dear." The words were brisk, the tone quite different. I felt a quiver run through me. "Here you are, and here you stay. You're coming the whole way."

"But you can't want me—"

"I don't. You came because you wanted to—or so you say—and now you'll stay because I say you have to. I've no time to take you back, even if I wished to. You've wasted too much of my time as it is. I'm on an urgent trip tonight and I'm running to schedule—"

"Godfrey—"

"—Taking a load of forged currency across to the Albanian coast. It's under the cabin floor. Seven hundred thousand leks, slightly used, in small denominations; and damned good ones, too. If I'm caught, I'll be shot. Get it?"

"I . . . don't believe you, you're ribbing me."

"Far from it. Want to see them?"

"No. No. I'll believe you if you like, but I don't understand. Why? What would you do a thing like that for?"

Kentroma was abeam of us now, about the same distance away. I thought I saw the faint outline of ghostly foam very near, and the loom of land, and my heart leaped; but it vanished. A small rocky islet at most, lightless, and scoured by the wind. As we ran clear of it I felt the sudden freshening kick of the wind, no longer steady from the east but veering and gusting as the mountains to either side of the strait caught and volleyed the currents of air.

And there, not so far off now, were the lights of Kouloura, where the land ended and the strait began. . . .

I dragged my mind back to what he was saying.

". . . And at the moment the situation in Albania is that anything could happen, and it's to certain interests—I'm sure you follow me?—to see that it does. The Balkan pot can always be made to boil, if you apply heat in the right place. You've got Yugoslavia, and Greece, and Bulgaria, all at daggers drawn, all sitting round on the Albanian frontier, prepared for trouble, but none of them daring to make it."

"Or wanting to," I said sharply. "Don't give me that! The last thing Greece wants is any sort of frontier trouble that she can be blamed for . . . Oh!''

"Yes. I thought you might see it. Dead-easy, isn't it? A lovely setup. Communist China sitting pretty in Albania, with a nice little base in Europe, the sort of foothold that Big Brother over there'd give his eye teeth to have. And if the present pro-Chinese government fell, and the fall was attributed to Greece, there'd be a nice almighty Balkan blowup, and the Chinese would be out and the Russians in. And maybe into Greece as well. Get it now?"

"Oh, God, yes. It's an old dodge. Hitler tried it in the last war. Flood a country with forged currency and down goes the government like a house of cards. How long has this been going on?"

"Ferrying the currency? For some time now. This is the last load. D day is Good Friday; it's to filter as from then, and believe you me, after that the bang comes in a matter of days." He laughed. "They'll see the mushroom cloud right from Washington."

"And you? Where will you see it from?"

"Oh, I'll have a ringside seat, don't worry—but it won't be the Villa Rotha. 'G. Manning, Esquire,' will be vanishing almost immediately. You wouldn't have got your trip out with me on Saturday after all, my dear. A pity, I thought so at the time. I enjoyed our day out; we've a lot in common."

"Do you have to be so insulting?"

It didn't even register. He was staring into the darkness to the north. "The thing I really regret is that I'll never be able to use the photographs. Poor Spiro won't even get that memorial. We'll soon be reaching the place where I threw him in."

There had been no change of tone. He was still holding me, his arm about as personal as a steel fetter; which was just as well; the touch of his body jammed against mine was making my skin crawl. The cracking of the sail as the boom moved overhead made me jump as if he had laid a whip to me.

"Nervy, aren't you?" said Godfrey, and laughed.

"Who's paying you?"

"Shall we just leave it that it isn't Greece?"

"I hardly supposed that it was. Who is it?"

"What would you say if I told you I was being paid twice?"

"I'd say it was a pity you couldn't be shot twice."

"Sweet girl." The smooth voice mocked. "That's the least of what the Greeks would do to me if they caught me!"

"Where's the currency made? I can't believe anyone in Corfu—"

"Oh, God, no. There's a clever little chap who lives out near Ciampino . . . I've been getting my photographic supplies from him for a long time now. He used to work in the local branch of Leo's bank. It was through him I was brought in on this . . . and, of course, because I knew Leo."

I must have gone white: I felt the blood leave my face, and the skin round my mouth was cold and rigid. *"Leo?* I will not believe that Leo even *begins to know* about this!"

He hesitated fractionally. I could almost feel the cruel impulse to lie; then he must have decided it would be more amusing after all to keep the credit. "No, no. Pure as the driven snow, our Leo. I only meant because I had an 'in' with him to get the house, a perfect situation for this job, and of course with that boathouse, which is ideal. And then there's my own cover, being next door to the Forlis themselves. If anything had gone wrong and inquiries had been made, where do you suppose the official eye would have gone first? Where but the Villa Forli, where the director of the bank lived? And by the time they got round to the Villa Rotha, it would be empty of evidence, and possibly—if things were really bad—of me."

"And when the 'mushroom cloud' goes up? I take it that part of the plan is to have the currency traceable to Greece?"

"Of course. Eventually, as far back as Corfu, but with luck, no farther."

"I see. I suppose Spiro had found out?"

He lifted his shoulders. "I doubt it. But there was a chance he'd seen a sample I was carrying in my wallet."

"So you murdered him on the off chance." I drew in my breath. "And you don't even care, do you? It's almost funny to think what fuss I made about the dolphin . . . you must have shot at him for sheer jolly fun, since you were leaving in a few days anyway." I peered at him in the darkness. "How do people *get* like you? You simply don't care who or what you wreck, do you? You're a traitor to your own country, and the one you're a guest in, and not only that, you wreck God knows how many people into the bargain. I don't only mean Spiro, I mean Phyl and Leo and the children. You know what it will do to them."

"Don't be sentimental. There's no room for that sort of talk in a man's world."

"Funny, isn't it, how often that so-called 'man's world' works out as a sort of juvenile deliquents' playground? Bombs and lies and cloak-and-dagger nonsense and uniforms and loud voices. All right, have it your own way, but remember I'm an actress, and I'm interested in how people work, even sawn-off morons like you. Just tell me *why?"*

I felt it at last, the movement of anger through his body. His arm had slackened.

"Do you do it for the money?" My voice nagged sharply at him. "But surely you've got money. And you've got a talent of a sort with a camera, so it can't be frustration—unless that turn-of-the-century technique of yours can't get you any sex that's willing. And you can't be committed politically, since you bragged you were working for two sides. Why, then? I'd love to know, just for the record, what makes a horro-comic like you tick over."

"You've got a poisonous tongue, haven't you?"

"It's the company I keep. Well? Just a wrecker, is that it? You do it for kicks?"

I heard his breath go in, then he laughed, an ugly little sound. I suppose he could afford to. He must have found, back there in the cabin, that I had no weapon on me, and he knew I couldn't escape him now. His hold was loose on me, but he could still have grabbed me if I had moved. I sat still.

"Just exactly that," he said.

"I thought as much. It measures up. Is that why you called your boat *Aleister?*"

"What a well-read little girl it is, to be sure! Of course. His motto was the same as mine, *'Fais ce que veult.'*"

" 'Do what thou wilt'?" I said. "Well, Rabelais had it first. I doubt if you'll ever be anything but thirdhand, Godfrey. Throwing people overboard hardly gets you into the master class."

He made no reply. The lights of Kouloura were coming abeam of us. The wind backed in a sudden squall, leaping the black waves from the north. His hand moved on the tiller, and the *Aleister* bucked and rose to meet it. The stars swung behind the mast, tilted. The wind sang in the ropes. The deck heeled steeply as the starboard rail lifted against the rush of stars. The boom crashed over.

"Is that what you're going to do with me?" I asked. "Throw me overboard?"

The *Aleister* came back head to wind, and steadied sweetly. Godfrey's hand left the tiller.

"By the time I do, by God," he said, "you'll be glad to go."

Then he was out of his seat, and swinging round on me, his hands reaching for my throat.

I flinched back as far as I could from the brutal hands, dragging the torch from my pocket as I went. My back came up hard against the port coaming. Then he was on me. The boat lurched; the boom thudded to starboard with the sail cracking like a whip; a glistening fan of water burst over the rail so that his foot slipped and the wet hands slithered, missing their grip on my throat.

The *Aleister* was turning into the seas; the boom was coming back. His hands had found their hold, the thumbs digging in. I braced my back against the coaming, wrenched my left hand free, and smashed a blow with the torch at his face.

It wasn't much of a blow. He didn't let go, but he jerked back from it instinctively, straightening his body, dragging me with him. . . .

I kicked upward with my right foot past his body, jammed the foot against the tiller with all my strength, and shoved it hard over.

The *Aleister*, already starting the swing, came round like a boomerang, heeling so steeply into the starboard tack that the rail went under.

And the boom slammed over with the force of a ramjet, straight at Godfrey's head.

19

*Swam ashore, man, like a duck. I can
swim like a duck, I'll be sworn.*

Act II, Scene 2

IF I had been able to take him completely by surprise, it would have ended the business then and there. But he had felt my foot go lashing past his body, and the sudden heeling of the *Aleister* gave him a split second's warning of what must happen. His yachtsman's instinct did the rest.

He ducked forward over me, one arm flying up to protect his head—but I was in his way, hitting at his face, struggling to thrust him back and up into the path of the boom as it came over with a whistle and a crash that could have felled a bull.

It struck him with appalling force, but a glancing blow, the upflung arm taking the force of the smash. He was flung sprawling right across me, a dead weight bearing me back helplessly against the seat.

I had no idea if he was still conscious, or even alive. The seat was wet and slippery; my hands scrabbled for a hold to drag myself free, but before I could do this the *Aleister*, caught now with the wind on her beam, swung hard into the other tack. Godfrey's body was flung back off mine. He went to the deck all anyhow, and I with him, helplessly tangled in the loose folds of the duffel coat. The two of us slithered together across the streaming boards, to fetch up hard against the starboard side of the cockpit.

The *Aleister* kicked her way upward, shuddered, hung posed for the next perilous swing. I tore myself free of the tangling coat and managed somehow to claw my way to my feet, bent double to avoid the murderous boom, staggering and sprawling as the deck went up like a lift, and the boom came back again to port with a force that threatened to take the whole mast overside. I threw myself at the wildly swinging tiller, grabbed it somehow and clung there, fighting to steady the sloop and trying, through the bursting fans of spray, to see.

At first I thought he was dead. His body sprawled in a slack heap where it had been thrown back to the port side by the last violent tack. His head rolled, and I could see the blur of his face, not the pale oval that had been visible before, but half an oval . . . half his face must be black with blood. Then the *Aleister* shipped another wave, and the cold salt must have brought him sharply to his senses, for the head moved, lifting this time from the deck, and a hand went with terrifying precision to the edge of the cockpit seat, groping for a hold to pull his body up.

I thrust the tiller hard to starboard again and laid the sloop right over. His hand slipped, and he was thrown violently back across the deck. It was now or never. I let go the tiller and tore the smoke flare down from its hook behind me. I could only pray that its rope was long enough to let me reach Godfrey where he lay against the side, his left hand now strongly grasping the seat, his right dragging at something in his pocket.

I lifted the metal flare and lurched forward.

Too late: the gun was in his hand. He was shouting something: words that were lost in the noise of wind and cracking spars and the hammering of the boom. But the message was unmistakable. I dropped the smoke flare, and leaped back for the stern seat.

The pale half face turned with me. The gun's eye lifted.

I yanked wildly at the life belt hanging there on its hooks. It came free suddenly, and I went staggering against the side with it clutched to me like a shield. As I gripped the coaming and hauled myself up, the engine controls were just beside my feet. I kicked the throttle full open, and jumped for the rail.

The *Aleister* surged forward with a roar. I saw Godfrey let go his hold, dash the blood from his eyes with his free hand, jerk the muzzle of the gun after me, and fire.

I heard no shot. I saw the tiny jet of smoke spurt and vanish in the wind. I put a hand to my stomach, doubled up and pitched headlong into the sea.

I was coughing, swallowing salt water, gasping with lungs that hurt vilely, fighting the black weight of the sea with a wild instinct that brought me at last to the surface. My eyes opened wide, stinging, on pitch blackness. My arms flailed the water; my legs kicked like those of a hanging man; then I went out of control, lurching forward again and down, down. . . .

The cold water closing over me for the second time struck me back to full consciousness. Godfrey. The shot which—fired at a dim target on a wildly bucking boat—had missed me completely. The life belt which had been torn from me as I fell, its rope pulled tight on the hooks by my own hasty action with the smoke flare. The *Aleister*, which I had sent swerving away fast at full throttle from the place where I went in, but whose master would have her under control again, searching for me to make sure. . . .

I fought my panic down, as I had fought the sea. I surfaced easily enough, and this time the thick blackness was reassuring. I felt a shoe go, and even this little load lightened me. I trod water, retching and gasping, and tried to look about me.

Darkness. Nothing but darkness, and the noises of wind and sea. Then I heard the engine, I couldn't judge how far from me, but in the pauses of the wind it seemed to be coming nearer. He would come back to look for me; of course he would. I hoped he would think I had been hit and couldn't possibly survive, but he could hardly take the risk. He would stay here, beating the sea between me and the land, until he found me.

A mounting hill of a wave caught and lifted me. As I reached its crest I saw him; he had a light on, and the *Aleister*, now bare of canvas, was slipping along at half throttle, searching the waves. She was still a good way off, and moving away from me at a slant, but she would be back.

What was more, she was between me and the land. I saw this now, dimly, a black mass studded with faint points of light. It seemed a lot farther away than it had from the deck of the *Aleister*.

Half a mile, he had said. I could never swim half a mile; not in this sea. The water was very buoyant, and I was lightly clad, but I wasn't in Spiro's class as a swimmer, and could hardly hope for his luck. I dared do no other than swim straight toward the nearest land, and if Godfrey hunted about long enough he would be bound to see me.

He had turned, and was beating back on a long tack, still between me and the shore. All around me the crests of the seas were creaming and blowing. I was carried up climbing slopes of glass, their tops streaming off against the black sky till the whole night seemed a windy race of wet stars. Foam blew into my eyes, my mouth. My body was no longer mine, but a thing of unfamiliar action, cold and buoyant. I could do little more than stay afloat, try to swim in the right direction, and let the seas take me.

As I swam up the next mounting wave I caught, clearly, the reek of petrol in the wind, and saw a light not two hundred yards away. The engine was throttled back to the merest throb, and the boat circled slowly round the beam, which was directed downward into the water. I even thought I saw him stooping over the side, reaching for something—my shoe, perhaps, kept floating by its rubber sole. He might take it as evidence that I was drowned; on the other hand, he might beat in widening circles round the place until he found me. . . .

Then not far away I saw another light, dimmer than the *Aleister*'s and riding high. The *Aleister*'s light went out. I heard the beat of another engine, and the second light bobbed closer. Faintly, a hail sounded. The clapped-out old scow from Kentroma was coming to take a look at the odd light on her fishing pitch. . . .

The *Aleister*'s throttle opened with a roar, and I heard it dwindling away until the wind took all sound.

Then I shouted.

The sound came out as little more than a gasping cry, a feeble yell that was picked up by the wind and thrown away like the cry of a gull. The Kentroma boat may have attempted to go in the track of the *Aleister*, I do not know, but I had lost sight of her yellow light, and the sound of her engine, long before I gave up from sheer exhaustion, and concentrated on swimming rather than merely keeping afloat.

It was then that I realized that the sea was dropping. I was well into the lee of the great curve of Corfu, where Pantokrator broke the winds and held the gulf quiet. And the lights of Kouloura were a long way to my right. I had been drifting westward, far faster than I could have swum.

The discovery was like a shot of Benzedrine. My brain cleared. Of course. We had been still some distance from the eastbound current that had carried Spiro to the Albanian coast. And tonight it was an east wind. Where I had gone in the drift must be strongly to the southwest. He had thrown Yanni's body in the gulf, and Yanni's body had fetched up at the Villa Rotha. I doubted if St. Spiridion would take me quite so neatly home, but at least, if I could stay afloat and make some progress, I might hope to stay alive.

So I swam and prayed, and if St. Spiridion got muddled up in my wordless prayers with Poseidon and Prospero, and even Max, no doubt it would come to the right ears in the end.

Twenty minutes later, in a sea that was little more than choppy, and with the roar of the rocky shore barely a hundred yards ahead, I knew I couldn't make it. What had been chance for Spiro was none at all for me. Under the lee of the cliff some freak current was setting hard off shore, probably only the backwash of the main stream that had brought me here, striking the coast at an angle and being volleyed back to the open water; but where I had till now been able to keep afloat and even angle my course slightly north across the current, I no longer had strength to fight any sea that wasn't going my way: my arms felt like cotton wool, my body like lead; I gulped and floundered as the cross-waves met me, and every little slapping crest threatened to submerge me.

Eventually one did. I swallowed more water, and in my panic began to struggle again. I burst free of the water, my eyes wide and sore, arms flapping feebly now, failing to drive me on or even to keep me above water. The roar of the breakers came to me oddly muffled, as if they were far away, or as if their noise came only through the water that was filling my ears. . . . I was being carried back, down, down, like a sackful of lead, like a body already drowned, to be tumbled with the other sea wrack on the rocks in the bright morning. . . .

It was bright morning now. It was silly to struggle and fight my way up into darkness when I could just let myself drift down like this, when in a moment or two if I put my feet down I would find sand, golden sand, and sweet air, sweet airs that give delight and hurt not . . . no, that was music, and this was a dream . . . how silly of me to panic so about a dream . . . I had had a thousand dreams like this, floating and flying away in darkness. In a few moments I would wake, and the sun would be out, and Max would be here. . . .

He was here now. He was lifting me. He thrust and shoved at me, up, up, out of the nightmare of choking blackness, into the air.

I could breathe. I was at the surface, thrown there by a strength I hadn't believed a man could command outside his own element. As I floundered forward, spewing the sea from burning lungs, his body turned beside me in a rolling dive that half lifted, half threw me across the current; then before the sea could lay hold on me again to whirl me back and away, I was struck and batted forward, brutally, right into the white surge and confusion of the breakers, rolling over slack and jointless as a rag in the wind.

A huge wave lifted me forward, tumbled me over helpless in its breaking foam, then dropped me hard in its wake. I went down like a stone, hit something, and went flat on the bottom . . . pancaked on the sand of a sloping beach, with the sea recoiling past me, my hands already driven into the land, like hooks to hold me there against the drag and suck of the retreating wave. The sea tore and pulled and streamed back past me. Sobbing and retching, I crawled and humped myself up the slope, while wave after wave, diminishing, broke over me and then drew back, combing the sand where I clung. And then I was crawling through the creaming shallows, on to the firm dry beach.

I have a half memory, just as I collapsed, of looking back for my rescuer and of seeing him rear up from the waves as if to see me safe home, his body gleaming black through the phosphorescence, the witches' oils of his track burning green and white on the water. The starlight caught the cusp of the dorsal fin, glittered there briefly, then he was gone, with a triumphant smack of the tail that echoed right up the rocks.

Then I went out flat on the sand, barely a foot above the edge of the sea.

20

Though the seas threaten, they are merciful,
' I have curs'd them without cause.

Act v, Scene 1

THERE WAS a light, hanging seemingly in the sky far above me.

When this resolved itself into a lamp set in a cottage window, high up near the head of the cliffs, it still seemed as remote as the moon. I cannot even remember now what it cost me to drag myself in my dripping, icy clothes up the path that clung to the rock face, but I suppose I was lucky that there was a path at all. Eventually I made it, stopping to lean—collapse—against the trunk of an ancient olive that stood where a stream cut through the path to fall sharply seaward under a rough bridge.

Here a shallow valley ran back through a gap in the cliff. Dimly I could see the stretches of smoothed ground between the olive trees, painfully cultivated with beans and corn. Here and there among the trees were the scattered lights of the cottages, each with its own grove and its grazing for goats and sheep. The groves were old; the immense heads of the trees stirred and whispered even in that sheltered spot, and the small hard fruit pattered to the ground like rain. The twisted boughs stood out black against the light from the nearest window.

I forced my shivering, lead-weight limbs to move. Under my feet the rubbery olives rolled and squashed. The stems of camomile caught between my bare toes, and I stubbed my foot on a stone and cried out. Immediately there was a volley of barking, and a dog—one of the vicious, half-wild dogs that are a hazard of the Greek countryside—hurled itself toward me through the trees. I took no notice of it, except to speak as I limped forward, and the dog, every hair on end, circled behind me, growling. I felt the touch of his nose, cold on the cold flesh of my leg, but he didn't snap. Next moment the cottage door opened, loosing a shaft of light across the grass. A man, in thickset silhouette, peered out.

I stumbled into the light. "Please," I said breathlessly, in English, "please . . . can you help me?"

There was a startled moment of silence while he stared at me, coming ghostlike out of the night, soaked and filthy with sand and dust, with the dog circling at my heels. Then he shouted something at the dog which sent it swerving away, and fired some sharp question at me. I didn't know what it was; didn't even recognize the language, but in any case I doubt if I could have spoken again. I just went forward blindly toward the light and the human warmth of the house, my hand stretched out like those of the traditional suppliant, and came heavily to my knees over the threshold, right at his feet.

The blackout cannot have lasted more than a couple of seconds. I heard him call out, then there came a woman's voice, questioning shrilly, and hands were on me, half lifting, half dragging me in to the light and warmth of a room where the embers of a wood fire still burned red. The man said something rough and urgent to his wife, and then went quickly out, slamming the door. For a dazed, frightened moment I wondered where he had gone, then as the woman, chattering in some undistinguishable gutturals, began to fumble with my soaked

506

and clinging clothes, I realized that her husband had merely left the cottage's single room while I undressed.

I struggled out of the sopping clothes. I suppose the old woman was asking questions, but I couldn't understand, and in fact hardly heard. My brain was as numb as my body with the dreadful cold and shivering of exhaustion and shock. But presently I was stripped and dried—on a fine linen towel so stiff and yellowed that I imagined it must have been part of the woman's dowry, never used till now, and then a rough blanket was wrapped round me, I was pushed gently into a wooden chair near the fire, logs were thrown on, a pot shoved down into the leaping flames, and only when my discarded clothes were carefully hung up above the fireplace—with much interested fingering of the nylon—did the old woman go to the door and call her man back.

He came in, an elderly, villainous-looking peasant, with a ferocious moustache, and a dirty homemade cigarette drooping from his lips. He was followed, inevitably, by two others, shortish, tough-bodied men out of the same mould, with dark, fierce faces. They came into the light, staring at me. My host asked a question.

I shook my head, but the thing that mattered most to me at that moment was easy enough. I put an arm out of my blanket to make a gesture embracing my surroundings. "Kerkyra?" I asked. "This—Kerkyra?"

The storm of nods and assenting "*ne's*" that this provoked broke over me with a physical sense of relief. To open human communications, to know where one was on the map . . . of such is sanity. Heaven knows what I had expected the answer to be: I suppose that shreds of nightmare still clung to me, and it needed the spoken assurance to bring me finally out of the bad dream—the isolated near death of the sea, the prison of the *Aleister* with Godfrey, the unknown black cliff I had been climbing. This was Corfu, and these were Greeks. I was safe.

I said, "I'm English. Do you speak English?"

This time the heads were shaken, but I heard the word go round, "Anglìtha," so they had understood.

I tried again. "Villa Forli? Castello dei Fiori?"

Again they understood. Another fire of talk where I caught a word I knew, "*thàlassa,*" which means the sea.

I nodded, with another gesture. "Me," I said, indicating my swaddled person, "*thàlassa* . . . boat . . ." A pantomime, rather hampered by the blanket. "Swim . . . drown."

Exclamations, while the woman thrust a bowl into my hands, with words of invitation and sympathy. It was soup of some kind—beans, I think—and rather thick and tasteless, but it was hot and filling, and under the circumstances, delicious. The men looked the other way politely while I ate, talking in quick-fire undertones among themselves.

As I finished, and gave the bowl back to the woman, one of them—not my host—came forward a pace, clearing his throat. He spoke in very bad German.

"You are from the Castello dei Fiori?"

"*Ja.*" My German was very little better than his, but even a smattering might see us through. I said slowly, picking the words, "To go to Castello, how far?"

More muttering. "Ten." He held up his fingers. "*Ja,* ten."

"Ten kilometers?"

"*Ja.*"

"Is—a road?"

"*Ja, ja.*"

"Is—a car?"

'No.' He was too polite to say so, but the impression that the single syllable gave was that of course there was no car. There never had been a car. What would they want with a car? They had the donkeys and the women.

I swallowed. So I wasn't yet free of the nightmare; I still had the long frustrations of the impossible journey ahead of me. I tried, not very coherently, to think what Godfrey would do.

He was bound to discover at his rendezvous that the package was missing, and would know that I must have taken it, and where I must have hidden it. But I hoped he would decide that as yet no one else could have reason to suspect him: he might well reckon that if there had been any suspicion of him his journey would have been intercepted. No, it was to be hoped that he would think I had made a chance discovery—possibly that I had seen him carrying the packages, had hunted for them out of curiosity, and having seen them, had realized that something big was afoot, and had been frightened into hiding and carrying out the elaborate pantomime of innocence on the *Aleister* to save my skin. I was sure that he wouldn't even give Miranda a thought.

Well, he had got rid of me. My disappearance would provoke a hue and cry which he might well find embarrassing after what had happened to Spiro and Yanni, and this might decide him to cut his losses here and now, but the sudden absence of "G. Manning, Esquire," would naturally focus official attention on his house, and the boathouse, so (since it was unlikely that any official alarm had been raised for me yet) I felt sure that he would have to risk going back tonight to find and remove the last package of forged currency.

And this was where I had to come in. Even if Max were there to receive him, it would take evidence to hold him—hard evidence, not just the hearsay of Adoni and Miranda, or even Spiro, which I was sure Godfrey could cut his way through without much trouble. Once they had taken their hands off him for five minutes, "G. Manning, Esquire," with his prepared getaway, could vanish without trace, for good and all.

I looked up at the ring of men.

"Is—a telephone?" I asked it without much hope, but they all brightened. Yes, of course there was a telephone, up in the village, farther up the hill, where the road started. (This came in Greek from everybody at once, with gestures, and was surprisingly easy to understand.) Did I want the telephone now? They would take me there.

I nodded and smiled and thanked them, and then, indicating my clothes, turned an inquiring look on the woman. In a moment the men had melted from the room, and she began to take my things off the line. The nylon was dry, but the cotton dress was still damp and unpleasant. I threw the blanket off thankfully—it smelled of what I tried charitably to imagine was goat—and began to dress. But when I tried to put on my frock the old woman restrained me.

"No, no, no, *this* . . . it is an honor for me. You are welcome. . . ." The words couldn't have been plainer if she had said them in English. "*This*" was a blouse of white lawn, beautifully embroidered in scarlet and green and gold, and with it a full black skirt, gay with the same colors at the hem—the Corfiote national dress, worn for high days and holidays. Either this also had been part of her trousseau as a young bride, or else it was her daughter's. I put it on. It fitted, too. The skirt was of thick, hand-woven stuff, and there was a warm jacket to go over the blouse. She hovered round me, delighted, stroking and praising, and then called the men in to see.

They were all waiting outside, not three now, but—I counted—sixteen. On an impulse I stooped and kissed the wrinkled cheek of the old woman, and she caught my hand in both of hers. There were tears in her eyes.

"You are welcome," she said. "English. You are welcome."

Then I was outside, swept up by the band of men and escorted royally up the stony track through the groves to the tiny village, to rouse the sleeping owner of the shop where stood the telephone.

No reply from the Castello. I hesitated, then tried the Villa Forli.

The bell had hardly sounded before Phyl was on the line, alert and anxious.

"*Lucy*. Where in the world—"

"It's all right, Phyl, don't worry. I'm sorry I couldn't ring you up before, but I'm quite okay."

"Where *are* you? I tried Godfrey, but—"

"When?"

"An hour ago—three quarters, perhaps. He wasn't in, so I thought you might be out with him. Are you?"

"No. Listen, Phyl, will you do something for me?"

"What? What *is* all this?"

"I'll tell you when I see you, but there's no time now. Just don't ask any questions, but will you ring up Godfrey's house again now? If he answers, tell him I'm not home yet, and ask if I'm still with him—just as you would if you hadn't heard from me and were worried. It's terribly important not to let him know I rang up. Will you do that? It's *terribly* important, Phyl."

"Yes, but—"

"Then please do it, there's an angel. I promise you I'll be home soon and tell you all about it. But I must know if he's got home. As soon as you've rung him, ring me back here." I gave her the number.

"How in the world did you get *there*? Did you go out with him again? I know you were in to supper, because it wasn't washed up; Miranda seems to have just walked out and left everything."

"That was my fault. I sent her on a message."

"You did? Look, just what *is* going on? What with all the supper things just left lying, and you halfway up Pantokrator in the middle of the night—"

"You might say Godfrey ditched me. You know, the long walk home."

"*Lucy!* You mean he tried something on?"

"You might say so," I said. "I don't like your Godfrey, Phyl, but just in case he's home by now, I'll ring off and wait to hear from you. But please do just as I say, it's important."

"My God, I will. Let him worry," said Phyl viciously. "Okay, sweetie, hang on, I'll ring you back. D'you want me to come for you?"

"I might at that."

"Stinking twerp," said my sister, but presumably not to me, and rang off.

* * *

There were twenty-three men now in the village shop, and something had happened. There were smiles all round. As I put down the receiver, my German-speaking friend was at my elbow.

"*Fräulein*, come and see." He gestured proudly to the door of the shop. "For you, at your service."

Outside in the starlight stood a motorcycle, a magnificent, almost new two-stroke affair, straddled proudly but shyly by a youth of about twenty. Round this now crowded the men, delighted that they had been able to help.

"He comes from Spartylas," said my friend, pointing behind the shop up the towering side of Pantokrator, where, a few miles away, I could see a couple of vague lights which must mark another village. "He has been visiting in Kouloura, at the house of his uncle, and we heard him coming, and stopped him. See? It is a very good machine, as good as a car. You cannot stay here, this village is not good enough for a foreigner. But he will take you home."

I felt the tears of emotion, brought on by anxiety and sheer exhaustion, sting my eyes. "You are too good. You are too good. Thank you, thank you all."

It was all I could say, and it seemed to be all they could desire. The kindness and goodwill that surrounded me were as palpable as light and fire; they warmed the night.

Someone was bringing a cushion; it looked like the best one his house could offer. Someone else strapped it on. A third man thrust the bundle containing my damp frock into a carrier behind the saddle. The youth stood smiling, eyeing me sideways, curiously.

The telephone rang once, briefly, and I ran back.

"Yes?"

"Lucy. I got the Villa Rotha, but he's not there."

"No reply?"

"Well, of course not. Look, can't you tell me what all this is about?"

"Darling, I can't, not just now . . . I'll be home soon. Don't worry. But don't tell anyone I rang you up. *Anyone*. Not even Max."

"Not *even* Max? Since when did—"

"And don't bother to come for me, I've got transport. Be seeing you."

The shopkeeper refused to take money for the telephone. It was a pleasure, I gathered, a pleasure to be roused from his bed in the middle of the night by a half-drowned, incoherent stranger. And the men who had helped me would not even take my thanks; it was a privilege to help me, indeed it was. They sat me on the pillion, showed me where to put my feet and how to hang on to the young man's waist, wished me Godspeed, and stood back as my new friend kicked the engine into an unsilenced roar that slashed through the village like Pandemonium itself. It must have woken every sleeper within miles. No doubt they would count this, also, as a privilege. . . .

We roared off with a jerk and a cloud of smoke. The road was rutted, surfaced with loose gravel, and twisted like a snake through the olive groves that skirted the steep cliffs, some three hundred feet above the sea. Not a fast road, one would have said—but we took it fast, heeling over on the bends as the *Aleister* had heeled to the seas, with gravel spurting out under our front wheel like a bow wave, and behind us a wake of dust half a mile long. I didn't care. The feel of the wind in my hair and the bouncing, roaring speed between my thighs were at once exciting and satisfying after the terrors and frustrations of the night. And I couldn't be afraid. This was—quite liberally—the "god in the machine" who had come to the rescue, and he couldn't fail me. I clung grimly to his leather-clad back as we roared along, the shadowy groves flicking past us in a blur of speed, and down—way down—on our left the hollow darkness of the sea.

The god turned his curly head and shouted something cheerfully. We shot round a bend, through a small stream, up something remarkably like a rough flight of steps, and met the blessed smooth camber of a metalled road.

Not that this was really an improvement: it swooped clean down the side of Pantokrator in a series of tight-packed hairpin bends which I suppose were steep and dangerous, but which we took at a speed that carried us each time to the very verge, where a tuft or so of daisies or a small stone would catch us and cannon us back on to the metal. The tires screeched, the god shouted gaily, the smell of burning rubber filled the night, and down we went, in a series of birdlike swoops which carried us at last to the foot of the mountain and the level of the sea.

The road straightened. I saw the god's hand move hopefully to the throttle.

"Okay?" he yelled over his shoulder.

"Okay!" I screamed, clinging like a monkey in a hurricane.

The hand moved. The night, the flying trees, the hedgerows ghostly with apple blossom, accelerated past us into a streaming blur. . . .

All at once we were running through a village I knew, and he was slowing down. We ran gently between walls of black cypress, past the cottage in the lemon grove, past the little tea garden with its deserted tables, under the pine, and up to the Castello gate, to stop almost between the pillars.

The youth put his feet down and turned inquiringly, jerking a thumb toward the drive, but I shook my head. It was a long walk up through the grounds of the Castello, but until I knew what was going on I certainly wasn't going to advertise my homecoming by roaring right up to the front door.

So I loosed my limpet catch from the leather jacket, and got rather stiffly off my perch, shaking out the pretty embroidered skirt and pulling my own bedraggled cotton dress from the carrier.

When I tried to thank my rescuer, he smiled and shook his head, wheeling the machine back to face the way we had come and shouting something, which, of course, must mean, "It was a pleasure."

As his hand moved on the controls I put mine out quickly to touch it.

"Your name?" I knew the Greek for that. "Your name, please?"

I saw him grin and bob his head. "Spiridion," he said. "God with you."

Next second he was nothing but a receding roar in the darkness and a cloud of dust swirling to settle in the road.

21

Thou does here usurp
The name thou ow'st not; and hast put thyself
Upon this island, as a spy . . .

Act I, Scene 2

THERE WAS no light in the Castello. The house loomed huge in the starlight, turreted and embattled and almost as romantic-looking as its builder had intended. I walked round it to the terrace, treading softly on the mossed tiles. No light there either, no movement, nothing. The long windows were blank and curtained, and—when I tried them—locked.

Keeping to the deepest shadows, I skirted the terrace till I reached the balustrade overhanging the cliff and the bay. The invisible sea whispered, and all round me was the dark, peppery smell of the cypresses. I could smell the roses, too, and there were bats about, cutting the silence with their thin, knife-edge cries. A movement caught my eye and made me turn quickly—a small slither of pale color vanishing like ectoplasm through the stone balustrade and drifting downhill. The white cat, out on his wild lone.

Then I caught a glimpse of light. This came from somewhere beyond the trees to the right where the Villa Rotha must lie. As softly as the white cat, and almost as silently as the ghost from the sea that I was, I crept off the terrace and padded down through the woods toward the light.

I nearly fell over the XK 150, parked among the trees. He must simply have driven her away from the house, so that a chance caller would assume he was out with the car and look no farther.

A few minutes later I was edging my way through the thicket of myrtle that overhung the bungalow.

This was, as I have said before, the twin of the Forli house. The main door, facing the woods, had a cleared sweep of driveway in front of it, and from this a paved path led round the house to the wide terrace overlooking the sea. A light burned over the door. I parted the leaves and peered through.

Two cars stood on the sweep, Max's big, shabby black Buick and a small car I didn't know.

So he was back, and it was battle stations. I wondered if the other car was the police.

My borrowed rope soles made no sound as I crept round toward the terrace, hugging the house wall.

The terrace, too, was the twin of Phyllida's, except that the pergola was covered with a vine instead of wistaria and there was no dining table, only a couple of large chairs and a low table which held a tray with bottles and glasses. I bypassed these quietly, making for the French windows.

All three were shut and curtained, but the center one showed a gap between the curtains some three inches wide through which I could see the room; and as I reached it I realized that I would be able to hear as well. . . . In the glass beside the window catch gaped a big, starred hole where someone had smashed a way in. . . .

The first person I saw was Godfrey, near the window and to one side of it, sitting very much at his ease in a chair beside the big elmwood desk, with a glass of whisky in his hand. He was still dressed in the jersey and dark trousers, and over the back of his chair hung the navy duffel coat which I had torn free of before I went into the sea. I was delighted to see that one side of his face bore a really classic bruise, smeared liberally with dried blood, and that the good-looking mouth appeared to hurt him when he drank. He was dabbing at a swollen lip with his handkerchief.

The room had seemed at that first glance full of people, but the crowd now resolved itself into a fairly simple pattern. A couple of yards from Godfrey, in the middle of the floor and half turned away from me, stood Max. I couldn't see his face. Adoni was over beside the door, facing toward the windows, but with his attention also riveted on Godfrey. Near me and just to one side of my window was Spiro, sitting rather on the edge of a low chair, with the injured leg in its new white cast thrust out awkwardly in front of him, and Miranda crouched on the floor beside his chair, hugging its arm against her breast as (it seemed) she would have liked to hug Spiro's. The two faces were amazingly alike, even allowing for the difference of male from female; and at the moment the likeness was made more striking still by the expression that both faces shared: a pure, uncomplicated hatred, directed unwinkingly at Godfrey. On the floor beside the boy's chair lay a rifle, and from the way his hand hung near it, twitching from time to time, I guessed that only a forcible order from the police had made him lay it down.

For the police were here. Across the width of the room from Godfrey, and near the door, sat a man I recognized as the Inspector (I didn't know the Greek equivalent) from Corfu who had been in charge of the inquiry into Yanni's death. This was a stoutish, gray-haired man with a thick moustache and black, intelligent eyes. His clothes were untidy, and had obviously been hastily put on, and in spite of the deadpan face and calm, steady stare I sensed that he was not quite sure of his ground, even ill at ease.

Godfrey was speaking in that light, cool voice that I knew so well, so very well.

"As you wish, Mr. Papadopoulos. But I warn you that I'm not prepared to overlook what happened down in my boathouse, or the fact that these two men have apparently broken into my house. As for the girl, I'm not quite sure what it is that I'm supposed to have done with her, but I have given you a complete account of our movements this afternoon, and I'm sure you can find any number of people who will bear me out."

"It's your movements tonight that we're interested in." Max's voice was rough, and only precariously controlled. "For a start, what happened to your face?"

"An accident with the main boom," said Godfrey shortly.

"Another? Rather too common, these accidents, wouldn't you say? How did it happen?"

"Are you a yachtsman?"

"No."

"Then don't ask stupid questions." Godfrey gave him a brief, cold look. "You've had your turn, damn you. Back down. You've no more right to question

me than you had to manhandle me or break in here to ransack the place. If you
hadn't telephoned for the police, you can be very sure I'd have done so myself.
We'll talk about your methods later."

Papadopoulos said heavily, "If you please, Max. Now, Mr. Manning, you
have told us that you have not seen Miss Lucy Waring since shortly after seven
this last evening, when you took her home?"

"That is so." To the Inspector his tone was one of tired but patient courtesy.
He was playing his part to perfection. All his dislike of Max was there, patent
through tonight's more immediate outrage, with weariness and puzzlement and a
nice touch of worry about me. "I took her home before dinner. I myself had to go
out again."

"And you have not seen her since?"

"How often must I—I'm sorry, Inspector, I'm a little tired. No, I have not seen
her since."

"You have given us an account of your movements after you took Miss
Waring home. Now, when you finally went down to take out your boat you found
the boathouse still locked, and as far as you are aware, there was nobody there?"

"That is so."

"There was nothing to indicate that anyone—Miss Waring or anyone else—
had been there, and gone again?"

I thought Godfrey hesitated, but it was barely perceptible. He must be very
sure that he had sunk me without trace. "No."

"You heard what this girl had to say?"

"Miranda?" Godfrey's tone was not even contemptuous, merely lightly
dismissive. "She'd say anything. She's got some bee in her bonnet over her
brother, and she'd invent any tale to see me in trouble. Heaven knows why, or
where the boy's got this incredible idea of his from. I've never been happier
about anything in my life than I was to see him here tonight."

Spiro said something in Greek, one short, vicious-sounding phrase whose
import there was no mistaking, and which drew a shocked glance from his sister.
He made it clear. "I spit," he said, and did so.

"Spiro," said Max sharply, and Godfrey raised an eyebrow—a very civilized
eyebrow—at the Inspector, and laughed.

"Satan rebuking sin? Always an amusing sight, don't you think?"

"I'm sorry," said Papadopoulos. "You will control yourself, Spiro, or you
will go. Let us go back, Mr. Manning. You must excuse me, my English is not so
very good; I do not follow this about Satan, and bees, was it? Bees in the
bonnet?" He glanced up at Max, who hesitated, and Adoni snapped out some
phrase in Greek. "I see." The stout man sat back. "You were saying?" This to
Godfrey.

"I was saying that whatever Miranda accuses me of, the fact remains that she
did not see Lucy Waring enter my boathouse or go near my boat. There is
nothing to show that she did either."

"No. Well, Mr. Manning, we'll leave that for the moment. . . . Yes, Max, I
know, but there is nothing more we can do until Petros gets up here from the
boathouse and reports on his search there. He will be here before long.
Meanwhile, Mr. Manning, with your permission, there are a few other questions
I want to ask you."

"Well?"

"Forgetting about Miss Waring's movements for the moment, I should like to hear about yours . . . after you went down to your boathouse. When Mr. Gale met you on your return, and accused you—"

"Attacked me, you mean."

"As you wish. When he asked you where you had been, you told him this was a 'normal trip.' What do you mean by a 'normal trip,' Mr. Manning? Fishing, perhaps?"

Adoni said, without expression, "His cameras were in the cabin."

"So you were out taking photographs, Mr. Manning? May one know where?"

There was a short silence. Godfrey took a sip of whisky, then sat for a moment staring down at the glass, swirling the spirit round gently. Then he looked up, meeting the policeman's eyes, and gave a faint smile that had the effect of a shrug.

"I can see that I'll have to make a clean breast of it. I never thought you'd get on to me. If it hadn't been for this misunderstanding about the girl, I doubt if you would have. Or were you tipped off?"

There was no change in the Inspector's expression, but I saw Max stiffen, and Adoni was staring. Capitulation, when they hadn't even brought up a gun?

"If you please," said Papadopoulos courteously, "I do not understand. If you would use simpler English—"

"More idioms," said Adoni. "He means that he knows you've been told about him, so he's going to confess."

"I meant no such thing. Keep your pretty mouth shut, if you can. This is between men." Godfrey flung it at him without even a glance, indifferently, as one might swat a midge. Adoni's eyes went back to him, and his expression did not change, but I thought, with a queer jump of the heart, Your mistake, Godfrey. . . .

"Please," said Papadopoulos. "Let us not waste time. Well, Mr. Manning?"

Godfrey leaned back in his chair, regarding him coolly. You'd have thought there was nobody else in the room. "With your man down there searching my boat it's not much use pretending I have been taking photographs, is it? You have only to look at the cameras . . . No, as a matter of cold truth, I had business over the other side."

If the room had been still before, it was stiller now. I thought dazedly, He can't just confess like that. . . . Why? Why? Then I saw. Miranda had told the police what she knew, and Godfrey realized now that she had been with me on the shore. I did not think that the cave or the packages had been mentioned yet in front of him, but he could guess that she had seen as much as I, and must have told the police about the packages. Moreover, a police constable was now searching the *Aleister*, and if he was even half good at his job he would find the cache under the cabin floor. I guessed that Godfrey was intent on getting some relatively harmless explanation in before the inevitable discovery was made.

"Whereabouts on the other side?" asked Papadopoulos.

"Albania."

"And the business?"

"Shall we call it 'importing'?"

"What you call it does not matter. This I understand perfectly." The Greek regarded him for a moment in silence. "So you admit this?"

Godfrey moved impatiently. "I have admitted it. Surely you aren't going to pretend you didn't know that this went on? I know you've shut your eyes to the way Yanni Zoulas was killed, but between ourselves—"

"Yanni Zoulas?" I saw Papadopoulos flash a glance at Max. Godfrey was taking the wind out of this sail, too, before it had even been hoisted.

"Ah," said Godfrey, "I see you understand me. I thought you would."

"You know something about Zoulas' death that you didn't tell the police?"

"Not a thing. I'm only guessing, from my own experiences with the coast guard system the other side. It's quite remarkably efficient."

"So you think he ran into trouble there?"

"I think nothing. I was only guessing. But guesses aren't evidence, are they?" The gray eyes touched Max's briefly. "I only mean that if one runs the gauntlet of those coasts often enough, it's not surprising if one gets hurt. What was surprising was that the police made so little of it. You must have known what he was doing."

"What was Zoulas' connection with you?"

"With me? None at all. I didn't know the man."

"Then how do you know this about him?"

Godfrey smiled. "In the trade, word goes round."

"He was not connected with you?"

"I've answered that. Not in any way."

Papadopoulos said, "It has been suggested that Spiro here, and after him Yanni Zoulas, discovered something about your business . . ."

I missed the rest. From somewhere behind me, below the terrace, came the moving flicker of a torch and the sound of footsteps. This would be the constable coming up from his search of the boathouse. I drew away from the lighted window, wondering if I should approach him now and tell him about the package I had sunk in the boathouse; then I remembered that he probably spoke no English. He passed below the end of the terrace, and trod gently round the house.

I tiptoed back to the window. It was just possible that the man had found the package, and if so, I might as well wait a little longer and hear what Godfrey's defense would be before I went in to blow it apart.

He had changed his ground, and was now giving a fine rendering of an angry man who has got himself in hand, but only just. He said, with controlled violence, "And perhaps you will tell me what in hell's name I could be doing that would drive me to wholesale murder?"

"I cannot," said Papadopoulos regretfully. "From what you are telling me of the type of goods you 'trade in,' I cannot. Radio parts, tobacco, antibiotics? And so on, and so on. The usual list, Mr. Manning. One wonders merely why it should have paid you. . . . The rent of this house, your boat, the trouble to make the contacts, the risks . . . You are not a poor man. Why do you do it?"

"Is it so hard to understand?" said Godfrey. "I was stuck here working on my damned book, and I was bored. Of course I don't need the money. But I was bored, and there was the boat, and the promise of a bit of fun with her . . ." He broke off, turning up a hand. "But do you really want all that tonight? Say I do it for kicks, and leave it at that. Apollo will translate."

Adoni said gently, "He means that he likes risks and violence for their own sakes. It is a phrase that irresponsible criminals use, and adolescents."

Max laughed. Godfrey's hand whitened on his glass. "Why, you little—"

"Markos!" Max broke across it, swinging round on the Greek. I saw his face for the first time. "None of this matters just now! I'm sorry, I realize that if this man's smuggling across the border it's very much your affair, but all that really matters here and now is the girl. If he insists that—"

"A moment," said Papadopoulos, and turned his head. Adoni put a hand to the door beside him and pulled it open, and the constable came into the room.

He had obviously not found the package, and apparently nothing else either, for when his superior barked a question at him he spread empty hands and shrugged, answering with a swift spate of Greek. Max asked another question in Greek, and the man turned to him, speaking volubly and with many gestures. But I no longer paid him any heed. As I had craned forward to see if the package was in his hands, I must have made some movement that caught Adoni's attention. I found myself meeting his eyes, clear across the room.

Nobody was looking at him; all eyes were for the newcomer, except Spiro's, whose flick-knife gaze never left Godfrey. Nobody seemed to notice as Adoni slipped quietly out through the open door, pulling it shut behind him.

I backed quickly away from the window, out of the fringe of light, and soft-footed my way back round the corner of the house.

A light step beside me in the darkness, and a whisper:

"*Miss Lucy!* Miss Lucy! I thought—I could not be sure—in those clothes. . . . But it is you! We thought you must be dead!" Somehow his arms were round me, quite unselfconsciously hugging me to him. It was amazingly comforting. "Oh, Miss Lucy, we thought you had gone with that devil in his boat and been killed!"

I found myself clinging to him. "I did. I did go with him . . . and he did try to kill me, but I got away. I went overboard, like Spiro, and he left me to drown, but—*Adoni!* You mustn't say things like that! Where *did* you learn them? . . . No, hush, they'll hear you. . . ."

"We've got to get him now. We've got to make sure of him."

"We will, I promise you we will. I know all about it now, Adoni. It's not just Spiro and Yanni and me—he's a traitor and a paid spy, and I can prove it."

"So?" He let me go. "Come in now, Miss Lucy, there's no need to be afraid of him. Come in straight away. Max is half crazy, I thought he would kill him."

"Not for a minute. . . . No, wait, I *must* know what's happened. Can you tell me, very quickly? Those are the Corfu police, aren't they? Didn't anyone come from Athens?"

"No. The Athens people said that Max must bring Spiro home and go to the Corfu police in the morning. They said they would look into it, but I don't think they were much interested—they had their hands full after that Communist demonstration on Tuesday, and this is the affair of the Corfu people anyway. So Max and Spiro came back alone, and I met the ferry. I told Max about the cave and the boxes that were hidden there, and he was afraid to waste more time by going to the police then—it was eleven o'clock, and only the night man was on duty—so he decided to drive home quickly and go to the cave himself."

"Then you hadn't had my message from Miranda?"

"No. She telephoned the Corfu Bar, but I hadn't been in there. I'd gone to Dionysios' house, a friend of mine, and had supper there, and then we went to the Mimosa on the harbor, to wait for the ferry. They sent a boy running to look for me from the Corfu Bar, but he didn't find me. When we got to the Castello, Miranda was waiting for us, and after a time she remembered, and told us about you."

"'After a time?'"

I heard the smile even through the whisper. "There was Spiro."

"Oh, Lord, yes, of course! She'd forget everything else. Well, I don't blame her. . . . Go on. She told you about me."

"Yes. I have never seen Max like that before. We ran down to the boathouse, he and I, but the boat was gone, and you. We searched there, and along the shore, and then went up to the Villa Rotha. It was locked, so Max broke the window, and we looked for you, but found nothing. So he got to the telephone, and got Mr. Papadopoulos at his home, and told him everything very quickly, and told him to bring Spiro and Miranda from the Castello as he came. Then Max and I went back to the boathouse to wait for Mr. Manning."

"Yes?"

"We waited for some time. Then we saw him coming, no engine, just the sail, very quiet. We stood in the shadow, just inside the doors, waiting. He did not come in through the doors, but just to the end of the jetty, and he berthed the boat facing the sea, then got out very quietly and tied her up, so we knew he meant to leave again soon. Then he came back along the jetty and into the boathouse." He stirred. "We took him, Max and I. He fought, but we had him. Then Max sent me to look in the boat for you, and when I got back Mr. Manning was pretending to be surprised and very angry, but Max just said, 'Where is she? Where's my girl?' and had him by the throat, and I thought he was going to kill him, and when Mr. Manning said he knew nothing Max said to me, 'Hurry up, Adoni, before the police get here. They won't like it.'"

"Won't like what?"

"What we would have done to make him talk," said Adoni simply. "But the police came then. Mr. Manning was very angry, and complained, and one could see that Mr. Papadopoulos was uncomfortable. We had to come up to the house. The other man stayed to search the boat. You saw him come back just now? He hasn't found anything, only the place under the deck where Mr. Manning had hidden the boxes. But you heard all that, didn't you?"

"Guessed it. It was in Greek."

"Of course. I forget. Well, that was all. Wait a moment." He vanished round the house wall, and in a few seconds materialized again beside me. A glass was pushed into my hand. "Drink this. There was some whisky on the terrace. You're cold?"

"No. Excited. But thanks all the same." I drank the spirit, and handed back the glass. I saw him stoop to put it down somewhere, then he straightened, and his hand closed over my arm. "What now, Miss Lucy? You said we could get him. Is this true?"

"Quite true. There's not time enough to tell you it all now, but I must tell you some of it—enough—just in case anything happens to me. . . . Listen." In a few brief sentences I gave him the gist of what Godfrey had told me. "So that's it. Athens can follow up his contacts, I suppose, and it should be possible to work out roughly where he'd go ashore, in the time it took him. They'll have to get on to Tirana straight away and find some way of stopping the stuff circulating. But that's not our concern. What we have to do now is to get the police to hold him, and hold him good and hard."

"What's your proof you said you had? Enough to make them listen?"

"Yes. I've got one of the boxes of currency. Yes, really. I dumped it off the platform in the boathouse, about halfway along the left side. I want you to go down and get it."

"Of course. But I'll go in with you first."

"There's no need. I'd rather you got the box safe. He knows I took it—he must know—and he'll have a good idea where I hid it. He's a dangerous man, Adoni, and if this should go wrong . . . I don't want to run any risks at all of his getting down there somehow and getting away, or of his having another shot at killing me if he thinks I'm the only one who knows where the box is. So we'd better not both be exposed to him at once. You must go and get it straight away."

"All right. Be careful of yourself."

"I'll do that. The swine had a gun. I suppose you took it?"

"Yes. And the police took it from us."

"Well, here we go." I took a shaky little breath. "Oh, Adoni . . ."

"You are afraid?"

"Afraid?" I said. "It'll be the entrance of my life. Come on."

The scene was unchanged except that the constable now stood in Adoni's place by the door. Godfrey had lit a cigarette, and looked once more at his ease, but still ruffled and irritated, like a man who has been caught out in some misdemeanor for which he will now have to pay a stiff fine. They had apparently got to the cave and the packages, which were, according to Godfrey, radio sets. He was explaining, wearily yet civilly, how the "sets" had been packed and stored.

I put a cautious hand in through the broken pane, and began to ease the window catch open. It moved stiffly, but without noise.

" . . . But surely this can wait till morning? I've admitted to an offense, and I'm perfectly willing to tell you more, but not now—and certainly not in front of a bunch of amateurs and children who seem to be trying to pin a mass murder on me." He paused, adding in a reasonable voice, "Look, Inspector, if you insist, I'll come in to Corfu with you now, but if Miss Waring is genuinely missing, I really do think you should concentrate on her and leave my small sins till morning."

The Inspector and Max started to speak together, the former stolidly, the latter with passion and anger, but Miranda cried out suddenly for the first time, on a piercing note that drowned them both.

"He knows where she is! He has killed her! Do not listen to him! He has killed her! I know she went to the boat! He took her and killed her, as he tried to kill Spiro, my brother!"

"It is true," said Spiro violently. "As God watches me now, it is true."

"Oh, for God's sake," said Godfrey. He got abruptly to his feet, a man whose patience has suddenly given way. "I think this has gone on long enough. I've answered your questions civilly, Papadopoulos, but it's time this scene came to an end! This is my house, and I'll put up with you and your man if I have to, but I'm damned if I sit here any longer being yapped at by the local peasants. I suggest you clear them out of here, now, please, this minute, and Gale with them."

The catch was off. As the window yielded softly to my hand, I heard Max say, in a voice I hardly knew was his:

"Markos, I beg of you. The girl . . . there's no time. Give me five minutes alone with him. Just five minutes. You'll not regret it."

Papadopoulos' reply was cut off by a crash as Godfrey slammed the flat of his hand down on the desk and exploded.

"This is beyond anything! It's more, it's a criminal conspiracy! By God, Inspector, you'll have to answer for this! What the hell are you trying to do, the lot of you? Papadopoulos, you'll clear these people out of my house immediately, do you hear me? I've told you all I'm going to tell you tonight, and as for Lucy Waring, how often do I have to repeat that I took the damned girl home at seven and I haven't seen her since? That's the truth, I swear to God!"

No actress ever had a better cue. I pulled the window open, and went in.

22

Let us not burthen our remembrances with
A heaviness that's gone.

Act V, Scene I

FOR A moment no one moved. I was watching Godfrey, and Godfrey alone, so I was conscious only of that moment's desperate stillness, then of exclamations and confused movement as Max started forward and Papadopoulos jerked out a restraining hand and gripped his sleeve.

I said, "I suppose you weren't expecting me, Godfrey?"

He didn't speak. His face had drained, visibly, of color, and he took a step backward, his hand seeking the edge of the desk. Down beside me I caught the flutter of a hand as Miranda crossed herself.

"Lucy," said Max hoarsely. "Lucy—my dear . . ."

The Inspector had recovered from his surprise. He sat back. "It is Miss Waring, is not? I did not know you for the moment. We have been wondering where you were." I noticed suddenly that Petros, the constable, had a gun in his hand.

I said, "I know. I'm afraid I've been listening, but I wanted to hear what Mr. Manning had to say; and I wanted to know what had happened since I left him an hour or so ago."

"By God," said Max, "we were right. Markos—"

"An hour ago, Miss Waring? He was out in his boat an hour ago."

"Oh, yes. I was with him. I must have gone overboard some way to the east of Kouloura, beyond the island."

"Ah . . ." said Spiro, his face blazing with excitement and satisfaction. There were exclamations, and I saw Petros move forward from the door, gun in hand. Godfrey hadn't spoken or moved. He was leaning on the desk now as if for support. He was very pale, and the bruised side of his face stood out blacker as the blood ebbed from the rest.

"Are we to understand—" began Papadopoulos.

Max said, "Look at his face. He tried to kill you?"

I nodded.

"Max!" cried Papadopoulas warningly. "Petros? Ah . . . Now, Miss Waring, your story, please, and quickly."

"Yes, of course, but there's something—something urgent—that I've got to tell you first."

"Well?" demanded the Inspector.

I opened my mouth to answer, but what I had to say was drowned by the sudden, strident ringing of the telephone. The sound seemed to rip the quiet room. I know I jumped, and I suppose everyone's attention flicked to the instrument for a split second. The constable, who held the gun, made an automatic move toward it as if to answer it.

It was enough. I hardly even saw Godfrey move, but in one lightning movement the hand that leaned on the edge of the desk had flashed an inch lower, flicked open a drawer, jerked a gun up, and fired, all in one movement as swift and fluid as the rake of a cat's paw. Like an echo, Petros' gun answered, but fractionally too late. His bullet smacked into the wall behind the desk, and then his gun spun smoking to the floor and skidded, scoring the polish, out of sight under the desk. Petros made some sound, clapped a hand to his right arm, and reeled back a pace, right into Max's path as the latter jumped forward.

Simultaneously with the crack of the gun Godfrey had leaped for the open window where I stood, two paces from him. I felt my arm seized and twisted up behind my back in a brutal grip as he dragged my body back against him as a shield. And a hostage. The gun was digging into my side.

"Keep back!"

Max, who was halfway across the room, stopped dead. Papadopoulos froze in the act of rising, his hands clamped to the arms of his chair. The constable leaned against the wall where Max's thrust had sent him, blood oozing between his fingers. The twins never moved, but I heard a little sobbing moan from Miranda.

I felt myself sway as my knees loosened, and the gun jabbed cruelly. "Keep on your feet, bitch-eyes," said Godfrey, "or I'll shoot you here and now. The rest of you listen. I'm going now, and the girl with me. If I'm followed, I don't have to tell you what'll happen to her. You've shown me how little I've got to lose . . . Oh, no, I'm not taking her with me . . . She's a damned uncomfortable companion on a boat. You can come down for her as soon as you hear me leave—not before. Understand? Do it before, and . . ." A movement with the gun completed the sentence, so that I cried out, and Max moved uncontrollably. "Keep your distance!" snapped Godfrey.

He had been slowly pulling me backward toward the window as he spoke. I didn't dare fight, but I tried to hang against him like a dead weight.

Max said hoarsely, "He won't leave her alive, Markos. He'll kill her."

"It won't help him." I managed to gasp it somehow. "I told . . . everything . . . to Adoni. Adoni knows—"

"Shut your goddamned mouth," said Godfrey.

"You heard that?" said Max. "Let her go, blast your soul. You don't imagine you can get away with this, do you? Let her go!"

Papadopoulos said quickly, "If you do not hurt the girl, perhaps we will—"

"It will give me great pleasure," said Godfrey, "to hurt her very much." He jerked hard on my arm, and took a step toward the window. "Come along, you. Where's the pretty boy, eh? Where did he go?"

He stopped. We were full in the window. For a moment I felt his body grow still and rigid against mine, then he pulled me out of the shaft of light, backing up sharply against the window frame, with me swung round to cover him, and the gun thrust forward now beside my waist and nosing round in a half circle. Behind us, out on the dark terrace, something had moved.

Adoni . . . It was Adoni with the package, delivering it and himself neatly into the muzzle of Godfrey's gun.

The next second I knew I was wrong. There was the tinkle of glass, the splashing of liquid, and the sound of someone humming a tune, " 'Come where the booze is cheaper,' " sang Sir Julian happily, helping himself to Godfrey's whisky. Then he saw us. The slurred and beautiful voice said cheerfully, "Hullo, Manning. Hope you don't mind my coming over? Saw the light . . . thought Max might be here. Why, Lucy, m'dear . . ."

I think I must have been half fainting. I have only the haziest recollection of the next minute or so. Sir Julian came forward, blinking amiably, with a slopping glass in one hand and the bottle still grasped in the other. His face had the gentle, foolish smile of someone already very drunk, and he waved the bottle at Godfrey.

"Helped myself, my dear Manning. Hope you don't mind?"

"You're welcome," said Godfrey shortly, and jerked his head. "Into the room."

Sir Julian seemed to have noticed nothing amiss. I tried to speak, and couldn't. Dimly I wondered why Max had made no sound. Then his father saw him. "Why, Max . . ." He paused as if a vague sense of something wrong was filtering through the fog of alcohol. His eyes came uncertainly back to Godfrey, peering through the shaft of light thrown by the window. "There's the telephone. Someone's ringing up." He frowned. "Can't be me. I thought of it, but came instead."

"Inside, you drunken old fool," said Godfrey, and dragged at my arm to pull me out past him.

Sir Julian merely smiled stupidly, raised the bottle in a wavering salute, and then hurled it straight at the light.

It missed, but only just. It caught the flex, and the light careened wildly up to the ceiling and swung down again, sending wild shadows lurching and flying up the walls, so that the ensuing maelstrom of action seemed like something from an old film, flickering drunkenly, and far too fast. . . .

Something white scraped along the floor . . . Spiro's cast, thrust hard against Godfrey's legs. Godfrey staggered, recovered as his shoulder met the window frame, and with an obscene little grunt in my ear, fired down at the boy. I felt the jerk of the gun against my waist and smelled the acrid tang of singeing cloth. He may have been aiming at Spiro, but the light still reeled as if in an earthquake, and off balance as I was, I spoiled his aim. The bullet hit the cast, which shattered. It must have been like a blow right across the broken leg. The boy screamed, rolling aside, with Miranda shrieking something as she threw herself down beside him.

I don't know whether I tore myself away, or whether Godfrey flung me aside, but suddenly I was free, my arm dropping, half broken, to my side. As I fell he fired again, and then something hit me, hurling me down and to the floor. Max, going past me in a silent, murderous dive for Godfrey's gun hand.

I went down heavily into the wreckage of the plaster cast. The place stank of whisky and cordite. The telephone still screeched. I was deafened, blinded, sobbing with pain. The two men hurtled backward out on to the terrace, locked together in a struggle of grunting breaths and stamping feet. One of them trod on my hand as he passed. Papadopoulos thudded past and out, and Petros was on his knees nearby, cursing and groping under the desk for his gun.

Then someone's arms came round me, and held me tightly. Sir Julian reeked of whisky, but his voice was quite sober. "Are you all right, dear child?"

I nodded. I couldn't speak. I clung to him, flinching and shaking as the sound of the fight crashed round the terrace. It was impossible, in that diffused and rocking light, to see which man was which. I saw Papadopoulos standing near me, legs apart, the gun in his hand moving irresolutely as the locked bodies stamped and wrestled past him. Godfrey's gun spat again, and the metal table whanged. Papadopoulos yelled something, and the injured constable lurched to his feet and ran to the windows, dragging the curtains wide, so that the light poured out.

But already they were beyond the reach of it, hurtling back against the balustrade that edged the steep and tree-hung cliff. I saw them, dimly silhouetted against the sky. One of them had the other rammed back across the stone. There was a crack, a sound of pain. Sir Julian's breath whistled in my ear and he said *"Lord Almighty,"* and I saw that the man over the stone was Max.

Beside us was a scraping sound and a harshly drawn breath. Spiro's voice said urgently, *"Koumbàre . . ."* and a hand thrust Sir Julian aside. The boy had dragged himself through the welter of broken plaster to the window, and lay on his belly, with the leveled rifle hugged to his cheek. I cried out, and Sir Julian shot a hand down and thrust the barrel lower. *"No! Wait!"*

From the locked and straining bodies over the balustrade came a curse, a sudden flurry of movement, a grunt. Max kicked up savagely, twisted with surprising force, and tore sideways and free. He lost his grip of Godfrey's gun hand, but before the latter could collect himself to use it Max smashed a blow at the bad side of his face, a cruel blow which sent Godfrey spinning back, to lose his balance and fall in his turn violently against the stone.

For two long seconds the men were feet apart. Beside me, Spiro jerked the rifle up and fired. I heard the bullet chip stone. Max, flinching back, checked for a vital instant, and in that instant Godfrey had rolled over the wide stone parapet in a sideways, kicking vault, and had dropped down into the bushes out of sight.

By all the laws he should have broken his back, or at least a leg, but he must have been unhurt. There was a series of slithering crashes as he hurled himself downhill, and then a thud as he jumped to the track.

I don't even remember moving, but I beat Papadopoulos and Miranda to Max's side as he hung, gasping, over the parapet.

"Are you hurt?"

"No." It was hardly a word. He had already thrust himself upright and was making for the shallow steps that led down from the terrace to the zigzag path.

Godfrey was visible below, a shadow racing from patch to patch of starlight downhill between the trees. Papadopoulos leveled his pistol across the parapet, then put it up again with an exclamation. For a moment I couldn't see why, then I realized that Adoni was on the branch of the zigzag path below Godfrey, and more or less in line with him. Godfrey hadn't seen him for the bushes in between.

But the boy must have heard the shots and the fracas up above, and now the thudding of Godfrey's racing steps must have warned him what was happening. He stopped. One moment he was there in the path, standing rigid, head up, listening, then the next he had melted into the shadow of the trees. Godfrey, unaware or uncaring, ran on and down.

Beside me, Miranda caught her breath. Papadopoulos was craning to see. Max had stopped dead at the head of the steps.

Godfrey turned the corner and ran down past the place where Adoni stood waiting.

Ran down . . . and past . . . and was lost to sight beyond the lower thicket of lime trees.

Miranda cried out shrilly, and Papadopoulos said incredulously, "He let him go."

I said quickly, "He has the evidence I sent him for. He had to keep it safely."

"He is a coward!" cried Miranda passionately, and ran for the steps.

Next moment Adoni emerged from the trees. I couldn't see if he had the package, but he was coming fast uphill. Max had started down the steps in what was now obviously a futile attempt to catch the fugitive, but Miranda flew past him, shrieking, and met Adoni head on, her fists beating furiously against his chest.

"Coward! Coward! Coward! To be afraid of that Bulgar swine! After what he did to your brother, to let him go? Coward! Woman! I spit on you, I spit! If I were a man I would eat his heart out!"

She tried with the last words to tear away and past him, but he caught and held her with one arm, whirling her aside with an almost absent-minded ease as he stepped full into Max's way and thrust the other arm across his chest, barring his path. As I ran down the steps and came up to them I heard, through Miranda's breathless and sobbing abuse, Adoni saying quick and low, "No. No, Max. Wait. Wait and see."

Where there had been pandemonium before, now quite suddenly there was stillness. Max, at the boy's words, had stopped dead. The three of them looked like some group of statuary, the two men still, staring into each other's eyes, Adoni full in Max's path, looking in the starlight like Michael barring the gates of Paradise: the girl collapsed now and weeping against his side. At some time the telephone must have stopped ringing. Papadopoulos had run back to it and could be heard shouting urgently into it. Sir Julian must have gone to Spiro. The constable was starting down the steps, but slowly, because of his wound, and because it was so obviously too late. . . .

The last of the wind had died, and the air was still with the hush before dawn. We heard it all quite clearly, the slam of the boathouse door and the quick thud of running feet along the wooden platform. The pause as he reached the *Aleister* and tore her loose from her rope. He would be thrusting her hard away from the jetty. . . .

The sudden stutter of her motor was as loud as gunfire. There was a brief, racing crescendo as the *Aleister* leaped toward the open sea and freedom.

Then the sound was swallowed, shattered, blanked out in the great sheeted roar of flame as the sloop exploded. The blast hit us where we stood. The flames licked and flared over the water, and were gone. The echo of the blast ran up the cliff and beat from rock to rock, humming, before it died into the rustle of the trees.

Sir Julian was saying, "What happened? What happened?" and I heard a flood of breathless Greek from Spiro.

Papadopoulos had dropped the telephone and ran forward above us to the parapet.

"Max? What in hell's name happened?"

Max tore his eyes from Adoni. He cleared his throat, hesitating. I said shakenly, "I think I know. When I was on board I smelled gas. It's a terribly easy thing to do . . . leave a gas tap on by mistake in the galley, and then the gas leaks down and builds up under the deck boards. You don't notice it, but as soon as the engine fires, up she goes. I—I once saw it happen on the Norfolk Broads."

"Spiro was saying something about gas." He mopped his face. "My God, what a night. My God. I suppose it must have been . . . Had he been using the galley?"

"Not on the way out. It stands to reason, anyway, he'd have noticed the smell when he took the boxes out from under the deck if it had been really bad. No, he must have used it on the way home. When I took a box out myself the smell was pretty faint. Did you get the box, Adoni?"

"Yes."

"You got a box?" The Inspector's attention sharpened, diverted for a moment. "This is what you were going to tell us, eh? Is it a radio set?"

"It is not. It's a batch of forged currency, Inspector Papadopoulos, part of a cargo of seven hundred thousand Albanian leks that he took across tonight. I managed to steal one package and hide it in the boathouse before he—he took me. That's where Adoni's been. I sent him to collect it." I added, "I think that you may find that this—accident—has saved everybody a lot of trouble. I mean, if the Greeks had had to shoot him . . ."

I let the sentence hang. Beside me, Max and Adoni stood very still. The Inspector surveyed us for a moment, then he nodded.

"You may be right. Well, Miss Waring, I'll be with you again in a minute or two, and I'll be very glad to listen to you then. You have the box safe, young Adoni? . . . Good. Bring it up, will you? Now we'd better get down there and see if there's anything to pick up. Are you still on your feet, Petros?"

The two police vanished down the track. There was another silence. Everyone turned, as if impelled, and looked at Adoni. He met our eyes levelly, and smiled. He looked very beautiful. Miranda said, on a long, whispered note, "It was you. It was you," and sank down to the ground beside him, with his hand to her cheek and a face of shining worship lifted to his.

He looked down at her, and said something in Greek, a sentence spoken very tenderly. I heard Max take in a sharp little breath, and then he came to me and took me in his arms and kissed me.

Sir Julian was waiting for us on the terrace. We need not have been afraid that he would comment on what had just passed between his son and me. He was basking in a warm bath of self-congratulation.

"The performance of my life," he said complacently.

"It certainly was. It fooled me. Did you know he wasn't drunk?" I asked Max.

"Yes, I wasn't quite sure what he'd try on, but I thought it might break the situation our way. Which it did—but only just. You're a lousy shot, Father."

"It was the waste of good whisky. It put me off my stroke," said his father. "However, there was enough left in the glass to put Spiro under; I've got the poor child strapped up again, and flat out on the sofa in there. That'll be another trip to hospital as soon as it's light, I'm afraid. Oh, and I telephoned your sister, Lucy. I reassured her quite successfully. It's been quite a night, as they say."

"And not over yet by a damned long way," said Max, a little grimly. "I shan't get any rest till I've heard Lucy's story . . . No, it's all right, darling, we'll leave it till Markos gets back. You won't want to go through it all again for him. You must be exhausted."

"I think I've gone beyond that. I feel more or less all right . . . floating a bit, that's all." I went slowly to the parapet, and leaned there, gazing out over the dark sea. The dawn was coming: the faintest glimmer touched the far Albanian snows. "Do you suppose there'll be—anything—for them to find?"

"I'm sure there won't." He came to my side and slipped an arm round me. "Forget it. Don't let it haunt you. It was better this way."

"I know."

Sir Julian, at my other side, quoted: " 'Let us not burthen our remembrances with the heaviness that's gone.' And I may say, Max, that I have come to the conclusion that Prospero is not for me. A waste of talent. I shall set my sights at Trinculo for this film of ours. I shall write and tell Sandy so today."

"Then you're coming back to us?" I said.

"I shall hate it," said Sir Julian, "but I shall do it. Who wants to leave an enchanted island for the icy, damp, roaring, garish, glorious lights of London?"

Max said nothing, but I felt his arm tighten. Adoni and Miranda came softly up the terrace steps, heads bent, whispering, and vanished in through the French windows.

"Beatrice and Benedick," said Sir Julian softly. "I never thought to hear that magnificently Shakespearean outburst actually in the flesh, as it were. 'O God, that I were a man! I would eat his heart in the market-place.' Did you catch it, Lucy?"

"I didn't understand the Greek. Was that it? What did she actually say?" When he told me, I asked, "And Adoni? What was it he said when she was kissing his hand?"

"I didn't hear that."

Max glanced down at me, hesitated, and then quoted, rather dryly:

" 'You wanted to eat his heart, little sister. I have cooked it for you.' "

"Dear heaven," I said.

Sir Julian smiled. "You've seen the other face of the enchanted isle tonight, haven't you, my poor child? It's a rough sort of magic for such as we are—a mere musician, and a couple of players."

"Much as I adore being bracketed with you," I said, "it's putting me too high."

"Then could you bear to be bracketed with me instead?" asked Max.

"Well, that is rather going to the other end of the scale," said his father, "but I'd be delighted if she'd give the matter some thought. Do you think, my dear, that you could ever consider dwindling as far as a musician's wife?"

I laughed. "I'm not at all sure who this proposal's coming from," I said, "but to either, or to both of you, yes."

Far out in the bay a curve of blue fire melted, rolled in a silver wheel, and was lost under the light of day.

My Brother Michael

for KIM
In Loving Memory

AUTHOR'S NOTE

The quotations from Professor Gilbert Murray's translation of the *Electra* of Euripides appear by kind permission of Messrs. Allen & Unwin. I am also indebted to the editors of the Penguin Classics for permission to use extracts from Sophocles and Euripides in translations by E. F. Watling and Philip Vellacott; to Messrs. Faber and Faber for their leave to use the lines from Dudley Fitts' translation of *The Frogs* of Aristophanes; and to the Clarenden Press, Oxford, for the lines from Ingram Bywater's translation of Aristotle *On the Art of Poetry.*

If it were possible to do so adequately, I should like here to thank my friends in Greece—especially Electra and her family— for their very great kindness to me during my visits to their country; and I must add a particular note of thanks to those people in Delphi itself who helped me to gather information for this book: Mr. George Vouzas, of the Apollon Hotel; Mario, who showed me round; "Pete" Gerousis, who patiently answered all my questions; and the caretaker of the studio, who assured me that "things like that could never happen in Delphi." I believe him. At any rate, they never did.

M.S.

If you do not love the Greeks, you cannot love anything.

REX WARNER

1

Why, woman,
What are you waiting for?

SOPHOCLES: *Electra*
(tr. E. F. Watling)

"NOTHING EVER happens to me."

I wrote the words slowly, looked at them for a moment with a little sigh, then put my ballpoint pen down on the café table and rummaged in my handbag for a cigarette.

As I breathed the smoke in I looked about me. It occurred to me, thinking of that last depressed sentence in my letter to Elizabeth, that enough was happening at the moment to satisfy all but the most adventure-hungry. That is the impression that Athens gives you. Everyone is moving, talking, gesticulating—but particularly talking. The sound one remembers in Athens is not the clamor of the impatiently congested traffic, or the perpetual hammer of pneumatic drills, or even the age-old sound of chisels chipping away at the Pentelic marble which is still the cheapest stone for building . . . what one remembers about Athens is the roar of talking. Up to your high hotel window, above the smell of dust and the blare of traffic it comes, surging like the sea below the temple at Sunium—the sound of Athenian voices arguing, laughing, talk-talk-talking, as once they talked the world into shape in the busy colonnades of the Agora, not so very far from where I sat.

It was a popular and crowded café. I had found a table at the back of the room near the bar. All along the outer wall big glass doors gave on to the pavement, standing open to the dust and din of Omonia Square, which is, in effect, the commercial center of Athens. It is certainly the center of all the noise and bustle of the city. The traffic crawled or surged past in a ceaseless confusion. Crowds—as jammed as the traffic—eddied on the wide pavements. Knots of men, most of them impeccably dressed in dark city clothes, discussed whatever men do discuss at mid-morning in Athens; their faces were lively and intent, their hands fidgeting unceasingly with the little loops of amber "nervous beads" that the men of the Eastern Mediterranean carry. Women, some fashionably dressed, others with the wide black skirt and black head-covering of the peasant, went about their shopping. A donkey, so laden with massed flowers that it looked like a moving garden, passed slowly by, its owner shouting his wares in vain against the hurly-burly of the hot morning streets.

I pushed my coffee cup aside, drew again at my cigarette, and picked up my letter. I began to read over what I had written.

"You'll have had my other letters by now, about Mykonos and Delos, and the one I wrote a couple of days ago from Crete. It's difficult to know just how to write—I want so much to tell you what a wonderful country this is, and yet I feel I mustn't pile it on too thick or you'll find that wretched broken leg that prevented your coming even more of a tragedy than before! Well, I won't go on about *that*, either. . . . I'm sitting in a café on Omonia Square—it's about the busiest place in this eternally busy city—and calculating what to do next. I've just come off the boat from Crete. I can't believe that there's any place on earth more beautiful than the Greek islands, and Crete's in a class by itself, magnificent and exciting and a bit grim as well—but I told you about it in my last letter. Now there's Delphi still to come, and everyone, solo and chorus, has assured me that it'll be the crown of the trip. I hope they're right; some of the places, like Eleusis and Argos and even Corinth, are a bit disappointing . . . one leaves oneself open to the ghosts, as it were, but the myths and magic are all gone. However, I'm told that Delphi really is *something*. So I've left it till last. The only trouble is, I'm getting a bit worried about the cash. I suppose I'm a bit of a fool where money is concerned. Philip ran all that, and how right he was. . . ."

Here a passing customer, pushing his way between the tables toward the bar-counter, jogged my chair, and I looked up, jerked momentarily out of my thoughts.

A crowd of customers—all male—seemed to be gathering at the bar for what looked like a very substantial mid-morning snack. It appeared that the Athenian businessman had to bridge the gap between breakfast and luncheon with something rather more sustaining than coffee. I saw one plate piled high with Russian salad and thick dressing, another full of savory meatballs and green beans swimming in oil, and innumerable smaller dishes heaped with fried potatoes and small onions and fish and pimentos and half a dozen things I didn't recognize. Behind the counter was a row of earthenware jars, and in the shadow of their narrow necks I saw olives, fresh from the cool farm-sheds in Aegina and Salamis. The winebottles on the shelf above bore names like Samos and Nemea and Chios and Mavrodaphne.

I smiled, and looked down again at the page.

". . . but in a way I'm finding it wonderful to be here alone. Don't misunderstand me, I don't mean *you!* I wish like anything you were here, for your own sake as well as mine. But you know what I do mean, don't you? This is the first time for years I've been away on my own—I was almost going to say 'off the leash'—and I'm really enjoying myself in a way I hadn't thought possible before. You know, I don't suppose he'd ever have come here at all; I just can't see Philip prowling round Mycenae or Cnossos or Delos, can you? Or letting me prowl either? He'd have been all set to dash off to Istanbul or Beirut or even Cyprus—anywhere, in short, where things are *happening,* not centuries ago in the past, but *now*—and even if they weren't happening, he'd make them.

"Fun—yes, it was always fun, but—oh, I'm not going to write about that either, Elizabeth, but I was right, absolutely right. I'm sure of it now. It wouldn't have worked, not in a million years. This trip on my own has shown me that, more clearly than ever. There's no regret, only relief that perhaps, now, I'll have time to be myself. There, now I've admitted it, and we'll drop the subject. Even if I am quite shatteringly incompetent when I am being myself, it's fun, and I muddle along somehow. But I do admit . . .''

I turned the page, reaching forward absently with my left hand to tap ash from my cigarette. There was a paler circle showing still against the tan at the base of the third finger, where Philip's ring had been. In ten days of Aegean sunshine, it had begun to fade . . . six long years fading now without regret, leaving behind them a store of gay memories that would fade too, and a sneaking curiosity to know if the beggar maid had been really happy once she was married to King Cophetua. . . .

"But I do admit there's another side to this Great Emancipation. Things do seem a trifle dull occasionally, after so many years spent being swept along in Philip's—you must admit—magnificent wake! I feel just a little bit high and dry. You'd have thought that something—some sniff of an adventure—would have happened to a young woman (is one still young at twenty-five?) marooned on her own in the wilds of Hellas, but no! I go tamely from temple to temple, guidebook in hand, and spend the rather long evenings writing up notes for that wonderful book I was always going to write, and persuading myself I'm enjoying the peace and quiet. . . . I suppose it's the other side of the picture, and I'll adjust myself in time. And if something exciting did happen, I wonder just what sort of a showing I'd make—surely I've got *some* talent for living, even if it looked feeble beside *his* overplus? But life never does seem to deliver itself into the hands of females, does it? I'll just finish up as usual in the hotel bedroom, making notes for that book that'll never get written. Nothing ever happens to me.''

I put down the cigarette, and picked up my pen again. I had better finish the letter, and on a slightly different note, or Elizabeth was going to wonder if I wasn't, after all, regretting the so-called emancipation of that broken engagement.

I wrote cheerfully, "On the whole, I'm doing fine. The language wasn't a difficulty after all. Most people seem to speak a bit of French or English, and I have managed to acquire about six words of Greek—though there have been difficult moments! I haven't managed the money quite so well. I won't pretend I'm exactly broke yet, but I rather let myself go in Crete—it was worth it, ye gods, but if it means passing up Delphi I shall regret it. Not that I *can* miss Delphi. That's unthinkable. I must get there somehow, but I'm afraid I may have to scamp it in a one-day tour, which is all I can afford. There's a tour bus on Thursday, and I think I'll have to be content with that. If only I could afford a car! Do you suppose that if I prayed to all the gods at once—?''

Someone cleared his throat just above me. A shadow crept half-apologetically across the page.

I looked up.

It wasn't the waiter, trying to winkle me out of my corner table. It was a little dark man with patched and shabby dungarees, a greasy blue shirt, and a hesitant smirk behind the inevitable moustache. His trousers were held up with string, which it appeared he didn't trust, because he held on to them firmly with one grimy hand.

I must have looked at him with a chilly surprise, because the apologetic look deepened, but instead of going away he spoke in very bad French.

He said, "It is about the car for Delphi."

I said stupidly, looking down at the letter under my hand, "The car for Delphi?"

"You wanted a car for Delphi, *non?*"

The sun had probed even into this corner of the café. I peered at him against it. "Why, yes, I did. But I really don't see how—"

"I bring it." One grimy hand—the one that wasn't holding up his trousers—waved toward the blazing doorway.

My eyes followed the gesture, bemusedly. There was indeed a car, a large shabby-looking black affair, parked at the pavement's edge.

"Look here," I said, "I don't understand—"

"Voilà!" With a grin, he fished what was patently a car key from his pocket, and dangled it above the table. "This is it. It is a matter of life and death, I understand that—oh, perfectly. So I come as quick as I can—"

I said with some exasperation, "I haven't the remotest idea what you're talking about."

The grin vanished, to be replaced by a look of vivid anxiety. "I am late. This I know. I am sorry. Mademoiselle will forgive me? She will be in time. The car—she does not look much but she is good, oh, a very good car. If mademoiselle—"

"Look," I said patiently, "I don't want a car. I'm sorry if I misled you, but I can't hire one. You see—"

"But mademoiselle said she desired a car."

"I know I did. I'm sorry. But the fact is—"

"And mademoiselle said it was a matter of life and death."

"Madem—I didn't. You said that. I'm afraid I don't want your car, monsieur. I regret. But I don't want it."

"But mademoiselle—"

I said flatly, "I can't afford it."

His face lighted at once with a very white-toothed and singularly attractive grin. "Money!" The word was contemptuous. "We do not speak of money! Besides," he added with great simplicity, "the deposit is already paid."

I said blankly, "Deposit? Paid?"

"But yes. Mademoiselle paid it earlier."

I drew a breath that was three parts relief. It wasn't witchcraft after all, nor was it an intervention of the ironic gods of Greece. It was a simple case of mistaken identity.

I said firmly, "I'm sorry. There has been a mistake. That is not my car. I didn't hire it at all."

The dangling key stilled for a moment, then swung in front of me with unimpaired vigor. "It is not the car mademoiselle saw, no, but that one was bad, bad. It had a—how do you say?—a crack in it that the water came out."

"A leak. But—"

"A leak. That is why I am late, you see, but we get this car, oh so good, since mademoiselle say it is so urgent a matter that Monsieur Simon have the car at Delphi straightaway. You leave straightaway you are in Delphi in three hours—four hours"—his look lingered on me momentarily, summing me up—"five hours maybe? And then perhaps all is well with Monsieur Simon and this matter of life and—"

"Death," I said. "Yes, I know. But the fact remains, monsieur, that I don't know what you're talking about! There is some mistake, and I'm sorry. It was not I who asked for the car, I gather that this, er, Monsieur Simon's girl was to have been in this café waiting for the car? . . . Well, I can't see anybody here at present who might fill the bill. . . ."

He spoke quickly, so quickly that I realized afterward that he must have followed my rapid French only sketchily, and was pouncing on a phrase that made sense—the sense he wanted to hear. The key still swung on his fingertip as if it were hot and he wanted to drop it. He said, "That is it. This café. A young lady sitting alone. Half past ten. But I am late. You are Simon's girl, yes?"

He looked, with that bright brown uncomprehending gaze, so like an anxious monkey that my near-exasperation vanished, and I smiled at him, shaking my head, and summoned up one of my six hard-learned words of Greek. *"Ne,"* I said, as forcefully as I could. *"Ne, ne, ne."* I laughed and held out my cigarette case. "I'm sorry there's been a muddle. Have a cigarette."

The cigarette seemed to be an amazing cure-all for worry. The lines vanished magically from his face. The vivid smile flashed. The key dropped with a jingle in front of me while the hand that wasn't holding up his pants reached for my cigarette case. "Thank you, mademoiselle. It is a good car, mademoiselle. Have a good journey."

I was feeling in my bag for matches, and not until I raised my head did I really take in what he'd said. And by then it was too late. He had gone. I caught a glimpse of him sliding through the crowd at the café door like a whippet let off a string, then he vanished. Three of my cigarettes had gone too. But the car key lay on the table in front of me, and the black car still stood outside in the violent sunlight.

It was only then, as I sat gaping like an idiot at the key, the car, and the sunlight on the cloth where a moment ago the little man had cast a shadow, that I realized that my momentary piece of showing-off was likely to cost me pretty dear. I remembered a little sickly that in Greek, *"ne"* means "yes."

Of course I ran after him. But the crowd surged and swayed on the pavement, regardless, and there was no sign in any direction of the shabby messenger of the gods. My waiter followed me anxiously onto the pavement, ready to grab, I suppose, if I showed signs of taking off without paying him for my coffee. I ignored him and peered earnestly in all directions. But when he showed signs of retreating to bring up reinforcements to escort me personally back to my table and the bill, I judged it time to give up the search. I went back to my corner, picked up the key, threw a quick, worried smile at the still-pursuing waiter, who didn't speak English, and pushed my way toward the bar-counter to seek out the proprietor, who did.

I elbowed my way through the crowd of men, with a nervously reiterated *"Parakalo,"* which, apparently, was the right word for "Please." At any rate the men gave way, and I leaned anxiously over the counter.'

"Parakalo, kyrie—"

The proprietor threw me a harassed sweating glance over a pile of fried potatoes, and placed me unerringly. "Miss?"

"Kyrie, I am in difficulty. A queer thing has just happened. A man has brought that car over there—you see it, beyond the blue tables—to deliver it to someone in the café. By a mistake he appears to think I'm the person who hired it. He

thinks I'm driving it up to Delphi for someone. But I know nothing about it, *kyrie;* it's all a mistake, and I don't know what to do!"

He threw a dollop of dressing over some tomatoes, pushed them toward a large man perched on a small stool at the counter, and wiped a hand over his brow. "Do you wish me to explain to him? Where is he?"

"That's the trouble, *kyrie.* He's gone. He just left me the key—here it is—and then went. I tried to catch him but he's vanished. I wondered if you knew who was supposed to be here to collect the car?"

"No. I know nothing." He picked up a large ladle, stirred something under the counter, and threw another look at the car outside. "Nothing. Who was the car for?"

"Monsieur, I told you, I don't know who—"

"You said it was to be driven somehwere—to Delphi, was it? Did this man not say who it was for?"

"Oh, Yes. A—a Mr. Simon."

He spooned some of the mixture—it seemed to be a sort of bouillabaisse—into a plate, handed it to a hovering waiter, and then said, with a shrug, "At Delphi? I have not heard of such a one. It is possible somebody here saw the man, or knows the car. If you wait a moment I will ask."

He said something then, in Greek, to the men at the counter, and became on the instant the center of an animated, even passionate discussion which lasted some four or five minutes and involved in the end every male customer in the café, and which eventually produced, with all the goodwill in the world, the information that nobody had noticed the little man with the key, nobody knew the car, nobody had ever heard of a Monsieur Simon at Delphi (this though one of the men was a native of Crissa, only a few kilometers distant from Delphi), nobody thought it in the least likely that anyone from Delphi would hire a car in Athens, and (finally) nobody in their senses would drive it up there anyway.

"Though," said the man from Crissa, who was talking with his mouth full, "it is possible that this Simon is an English tourist staying at Delphi. That would explain everything." He didn't say why, merely smiling with great kindness and charm through a mouthful of prawns, but I got his meaning.

I said apologetically, "I know it seems mad, *kyrie,* but I can't help feeling one ought to do something about it. The man who brought the key said it was"—I hesitated—"well, a matter of life and death."

The Greek raised his eyebrows; then he shrugged. I got the impression that matters of life and death were everyday affairs in Athens. He said, with another charming smile, "Quite an adventure, mademoiselle," and turned back to his plate.

I looked at him thoughtfully for a moment. "Yes," I said slowly, "yes." I turned back to the proprietor, who was struggling to scoop olives out of one of the beautiful jars. It was apparent that the rush hour and the heat were beginning to overset even his Athenian good manners and patience so I merely smiled at him and said, "Thank you for your goodness, *kyrie.* I'm sorry to have troubled you. It seems to me that if the matter really is urgent, then the person who wants the car will certainly come and get it as arranged."

"You wish to leave the key with me? I will take it, and then you need have no more worry. No, it will be a pleasure, I assure you."

"I won't trouble you yet, thanks. I must confess"—I laughed—"to a little curiosity. I'll wait here for a bit, and if this girl comes, I'll give her the key myself."

And to the poor man's relief, I wriggled back out of the press and returned to my table. I sat down and ordered another coffee, then lit another cigarette, and settled down to a pretence of finishing my letter, but in reality to keep one watchful eye on the door, and the other on the shabby black car that should— surely—by now have been hurtling along the Delphi road on that matter of life and death. . . .

I waited an hour. The waiter had begun to look askance again, so I pushed aside my untouched letter and gave an order, then sat playing with a plateful of beans and some small pink fish while I watched, in an expectancy that gradually gave way to uneasiness, the constant coming-and-going at the café door.

My motive in waiting hadn't been quite as straightforward as I had suggested to the proprietor of the café. It had occurred to me that, since I had become involved in the affair through no fault of my own, I might be able to turn it to advantage. When "Simon's girl" arrived to claim the car, it might surely be possible to suggest—or even ask outright—that I might be her passenger as far as Delphi. And the possibility of getting a lift up to Delphi was not the only one which had occurred to me. . . .

So the minutes dragged by, and still no one came, and somehow, the longer I waited, the less possible it seemed to walk out of the café and leave everything to settle itself without me, and the more insidiously did that other possibility begin to present itself. Dry-mouthed, I pushed it aside, but there it was, a challenge, a gift, a dare from the gods. . . .

At twelve o'clock, when nobody had appeared to claim the car, I thrust my plate aside, and set myself to consider that other possibility as coolly as I could.

It was, simply, to drive the car up to Delphi myself.

It was apparent that, for whatever reason, the girl wasn't coming. Something must have prevented her, for otherwise she would simply have telephoned the garage to cancel the order. But the car—the urgently wanted car—was still there, already an hour and a half late in starting. I, on the other hand, wanted very badly to go to Delphi, and could start straightaway. I had come straight up from Piraeus off the Crete steamer, and had everything with me that I needed for a short stay in Delphi. I could go up today, deliver the car, have two days there with the money saved on the bus fare, and come back with the tourist bus on Thursday. The thing was simple, obvious, and a direct intervention of providence.

I picked up the key with fingers that felt as if they didn't belong to me, and reached slowly for my only luggage—the big brightly colored hold-all of Mykonos weaving—that hung on the back of a chair.

I hesitated with my hand touching it. Then I let the hand drop, and sat, twisting the key over and over, watching with unseeing eyes the way the sun glinted on it as it turned.

It couldn't be done. It was just one of those things that couldn't be done. I must have been mad even to consider doing it. All that had happened was that Simon's girl had forgotten to cancel the order for the car and claim the deposit. It was nothing to do with me. No one would thank me for intervening in an affair that, in spite of my silly mistake, had nothing whatever to do with me. That phrase "a matter of life and death," so glib a chorus, so persuasive an excuse to interfere— it was only a phrase, after all, a phrase from which I had built up this feeling of urgency which gave me (I pretended) the excuse to act. *In any case, it had nothing to do with me.* The obvious—the only—thing to do was to leave the car standing there, hand over the key, and go away.

The decision brought with it a sense of relief so vivid, so physical almost, that it startled me. On the wave of it I stood up, picked up the car key, and swung my hold-all up to my shoulder. The unfinished letter to Elizabeth lay on the table. I reached for it, and as I folded it over to thrust it into my bag, the sentence caught my eye again. "Nothing ever happens to me."

The paper crackled suddenly as my fingers tightened. I suppose moments of self-knowledge come at all sorts of odd times. I have often wondered if they are ever pleasant. I had one such moment now.

It didn't last long. I didn't let it. It was with a sort of resigned surprise that I found myself once more at the counter, handing a slip of paper across it to the proprietor.

"My name and address," I said rather breathlessly, "just in case someone does come for the car later on. Miss Camilla Haven, the Olympias Hotel, Rue Marnis. . . . Tell them I—I'll take care of the car. Tell them I did it for the best."

I was out in the street and getting into the car before it occurred to me that my last words had sounded uncommonly like an epitaph.

2

It's a long way to Delphi.

EURIPIDES: *Ion*
(tr. Philip Vellacott)

EVEN IF it wasn't Hermes himself who had brought me the key, the hand of every god in Hellas must have been over me that day, because I got out of Athens alive. More, unscathed.

There were some sticky moments. There was the shoeblack who was so urgent to clean my shoes that he followed me to the car and clung to the side and would certainly have been hurt when I started off, if only I'd remembered to put the car into gear. There was the moment when I turned—at a cautious ten miles per hour and hugging the left-hand pavement—out of Omonia Square into St. Constantine Street, and met a taxi almost head-on on what I thought was his wrong side, till the volume and fervor of his abuse shocked me back onto my own right. Then there was the encounter in the narrow alley with two furious pedestrians who stepped off the pavement without a single glance in my direction. How was I to know it was a one-way street? I was lucky with my brakes that time. I wasn't so lucky with the flower-donkey, but it was only the flowers I touched, and the driver was charming about it. He refused the note I hastily held out to him and he actually gave me the flowers I'd knocked out of the donkey's pannier.

All things considered, people were very forgiving. The only really unpleasant person was the man who spat on the hood as I came hesitatingly out from behind a stationary bus. There was no need for such a display of temper. I'd hardly touched him.

By the time I got to the main road that leads out of Athens along the Sacred Way I'd found out two things. One was that a few weeks spent in punting around the English country roads in Elizabeth's old Hillman (Philip, understandably, had never let me touch his car) was not really an adequate preparation for driving through Athens in a strange car with a left-hand drive. The other was that the shabby black car had an unexpectedly powerful engine. If it had been less shabby and ancient-looking—if it had been one of the sleek winged transatlantic monsters commonly used as taxis in Athens—I should never have dared myself to drive it, but its shabby façade had reassured me. Almost it could have been the old Hillman I'd learned on. Almost. I hadn't been in it three minutes before I discovered that it had an acceleration like the kick of a jet, and by the time I'd assessed its possibilities as a lethal weapon—which were limitless—it was too late. I was out in the traffic and it seemed safer to stay there. So I hung on grimly to the wheel, changing hands now and again as I remembered that the gear levers were on the right, and prayed to the whole Olympian hierarchy as we jerked and nudged our terrified and apologetic way out through the city suburbs, turning at length into the great double road that runs along the coast toward Eleusis and Corinth.

After the packed and flashing streets, the road seemed open and comparatively empty. This was the Sacred Way; down this wide sea-bordered road the ancient pilgrims had gone with songs and torches to celebrate the Mysteries at Eleusis. This lake now lying to the right was the holy lake of Demeter. Across that bay on the left, the island of Salamis lay like a drowned dragon, and there—*there*—Themistocles had smashed the Persian fleet. . . .

But I looked neither to right nor left as I drove. I had been this way before, and had got the first sharp disillusion over. There was no need, here, to leave oneself open to the ghosts; they had long since gone. Now, the Sacred Way ran straight and wide (the tar sweating a little in the sun) between the cement factories and the ironworks; the holy lake was silted up with weeds and slag; in the bay of Salamis lay the rusty hulks of tankers, and the wine-dark water reflected the aluminum towers of the refinery. At the other side of the bay belched the chimneys of Megara, and above them a trio of Vampire jets wheeled, screaming, against the ineffable Greek sky. And this was Eleusis itself, this dirty village almost hidden in the choking clouds of ocherous smoke from the cement works.

I kept my eyes on the road, my attention on the car, and drove as fast as I dared. Soon the industrial country was behind us, and the road, narrower now and whitening with dust under the pitiless September sun, lifted itself away from the shore and wound up between fields of red earth set with olives, where small box-like houses squatted, haphazardly it seemed, among the trees. Children, ragged and brown and thin, stood in the dust to stare as I went by. A woman, black-clad, and veiled like a Moslem, bent to lift bread from the white beehive oven that stood under an olive tree. Scrawny hens scratched about, and a dog hurled itself yelling after the car. Donkeys plodded along in the deep dust at the road's edge, half hidden under their top-heavy loads of brushwood. A high cart swayed along a track toward the road; it was piled with grapes, gleaming waxily, cloudy green. The flanks of the mule were glossy, and bloomy as dark grapes. The air smelt of heat and dung and dust and the lees of the grape harvest.

The sun beat down. Wherever the trees stood near the road the shade fell like a blessing. It was not long past noon, and the heat was terrific. The only relief was the breeze of the car's movement, and the cloudy heads of the great olives sailing between the road and the great brazen bowl of the sky.

There was very little traffic out in the heat of the day, and I was determined to take full advantage of the afternoon lull, so I drove on through the hot bright minutes, feeling confident now, and even secure. I had got the feel of the car, and I was still steadfastly refusing to think about what I had done. I had taken a "dare" from the gods, and the results would wait till I got—if I got—to Delphi.

If I got to Delphi.

My confidence in myself had been steadily growing as I drove on through an empty landscape, through country that grew wilder and more beautiful as the road shook itself clear of the olive groves and climbed the hills that lie to the north of Attica. It even survived the series of frightening hairpin bends that sink from the summit of these hills toward the flat fields of the Boeotian plain. But it didn't survive the bus.

This was the service bus from Athens and I caught up with it halfway along the dead-straight road that bisects the plain. It was small, evil-looking, and smelly. It also seemed to be packed to the doors with people, boxes, and various livestock, including hens and at least one small goat. It was roaring along in a fifty-yard trail of dust. I drew carefully out to the left, and pressed forward to pass.

The bus, which was already in the middle of the road, swung over promptly to the left and accelerated slightly. I moved back, swallowing dust. The bus went back to the crown of the road and settled back to its rackety thirty miles an hour.

I waited half a minute, and tried again. I crept cautiously up to its rear wheel and hoped the driver would see me.

He did. Accelerating madly, he surged once again into my path, got me well and truly behind him, then settled back complacently into the center of the road. I went back once more into the choking dust-train. I was trying not to mind, to tell myself that when he had had his joke, he would let me safely by, but I could feel my hands beginning to tighten on the wheel, and a nerve was jumping somewhere in my throat. If Philip had been driving . . . but then I told myself, if Philip had been driving, it wouldn't have happened. Women drivers are fair game on the roads of Greece.

Here we passed a board which said, in Greek and English letters: THEBES 4 km.; DELPHI 77 km. If I had to stay behind the bus all the way to Delphi. . . .

I tried again. This time as I pulled out to approach him I sounded the horn decisively. To my surprise and gratitude, he drew over promptly to the right, and slowed down. I made for the gap. There was just room, no more, between the bus and the verge, which was of deep, crumbling dry soil. Taut with nervous concentration, I pressed forward and accelerated.

I wasn't getting past. The bus rocked and roared alongside, traveling faster, keeping pace with me. My car had the speed of it, but the gap was narrowing and I wasn't sure enough of my judgment to force the big car past. The driver of the bus closed in more sharply. I don't know if he would actually have forced me off the road, but as the swaying dirty-green enamel rocked nearer, I lost my nerve, as he had known I would. I stood on the brakes. The bus roared on. I was left once more in the dust.

Ahead of us I could see the first scattered houses of Thebes, the legendary city that, I knew, was gone even more irrecoverably than Eleusis. Where Antigone led the blind Oedipus out into exile, the old men of Thebes sit on the concrete pavements in the sun, beside the gas pumps. The game of *tric-trac* that they sit over, hour after hour, is probably the oldest thing in Thebes. There is a fountain somewhere, beloved of the nymphs. That's all. But I had no time then to mourn the passing of the legends. I wasn't thinking about Oedipus or Antigone, or even about Philip or Simon or my own miserable prelude to adventure. I just drove on toward Thebes with my eyes fixed in hatred ahead of me. There was nothing left in life at that moment but the desire to pass that filthy bus.

Presently the chance came. A knot of women, waiting by the roadside, signaled him to stop, and he slowed down. I closed up behind, my eyes on the strip to the left of him, my hands slippery on the wheel, and that nerve beginning to jump again.

He stopped, right in the center of the road. There was no possible space to pass. I stopped behind him and waited, then, as he drew away from me again, and I let in the clutch, I stalled the engine. My hand shook on the ignition. The engine wouldn't start. At the edge of my vision I caught sight of a face at the rear window of the withdrawing bus, a dark young face, split in a wide grin. As I started the car and followed I saw the youth turn as if to nudge someone on the back seat beside him. Another face turned to stare and grin. And another.

Then, close behind me—so close that it nearly sent me into the ditch with fright—I heard a horn. As I swerved automatically to the right a jeep, driven fast on its wrong side, roared up from behind, overtook me rather too wide, with the nearside wheels churning dust, and charged straight, at the same headlong pace, for the rear of the bus, with its horn still blasting like a siren. I caught a fleeting glimpse of a girl driving, a young, dark face, with lashes drooping over her eyes and a bored, sulky mouth. She was lounging back in her seat, handling the jeep with casual, almost insolent, expertise. And, woman driver or no, the bus made way for her, whipping smartly over to the right and staying there respectfully while she tore by. I didn't consciously decide to follow her; in fact I'm not sure yet whether I trod on the accelerator deliberately, or whether I was feeling for the brake, but something hit me in the small of the back, and the big black car shot forward, missed the bus by inches, and stormed past in the wake of the jeep, with two wheels on the crown of the road and the other two churning up enough dust to have guided the children of Israel straight into Thebes. Where the bus had its offside wheels I neither knew nor cared. I didn't even look in the mirror.

I swept into Thebes and dived smartly down the wrong side of the dual carriageway which is the road through to Levadia and Delphi.

The hand of Hermes, god of wayfarers, was over me still. There was a horse fair at Levadia, which, with its accompanying trappings of fiesta, jammed the streets; but after that I met nothing, except slow little caravans of country people on their way by mule and donkey-back to the fair; and once a train of gypsies—real Egyptians—on the move with mules and ponies covered in bright blankets.

Soon after I had passed Levadia the country began to change. The grim banalities of Attica, the heavy Technicolor prosperity of the plains, sank back and were forgotten as the hills crowded in. The road reared and twisted between great ribs of brown hill that thrust the landscape up into folded ranges. At the foot of the steep waterless valleys dead streams curled white along their single beds, like the sloughed skins of snakes. The sides of the valley were dry with the yellowish growth of burned grass, and drifts of stones and crumbling soil.

Bigger and bigger grew the circling hills, barer the land, drawn in with great sweeps of color that ran from red to ocher, from ocher to burnt umber to lion-tawny, with, above all, the burning, the limitless, the lovely light. And beyond all, at length, a gray ghost of a mountain massif; not purple, not faintly blue with distance like the mountains of a softer country, but specter-white, magnificent, a lion silvered. Parnassus, home of the ghosts of the old gods.

I stopped only once to rest, some way beyond Levadia. The road, which wound high along the hillside, was in shadow, and the air, at that height, was cool. I sat for about fifteen minutes on the parapet that edged the road. Below me, deep in a forked valley, was a place where three tracks met; the ghost of an ancient crossroads where once a young man, coming from Delphi to Thebes, struck an old man down out of his chariot, and killed him. . . .

But no ghosts moved today. No sound, no breath, not even the shadow of a hanging hawk. Only the bare lion-colored hills, and the illimitable, merciless light.

I got back into the car. As I started the engine I reflected that the god of wayfarers, who had done very well by me so far, had only some twenty miles' more duty to do, and then he could abandon me to my fate.

In fact, he abandoned me just ten kilometers short of Delphi, in the middle of the village of Arachova.

3

But if I don't get out from under pretty damned soon, there'll be a disaster in the rear.

ARISTOPHANES: *The Frogs*
(tr. Dudley Fitts)

ARACHOVA IS a showplace. It is not self-consciously so, but its setting is picturesque in the extreme, and the Greek style of building does the rest.

The village is perched on a precipitous hillside, and the houses are built in tiers, one up behind the other, the floor of one level with the roof of the next. The whole village looks as if it were just about to slide into the depths of the valley below. The walls are white and the roofs are rose-red, and over every wall hang flowering plants, and vines rich with grapes, and great dollops of wool dyed the colors of amber and hyacinth and blood. Along the short main street are places selling rugs which hang out in the sunlight, brilliant against the blinding white walls. The street itself has some corners, and is about eight feet wide. On one of these corners I ran into a truck.

Not quite literally. I managed to stop with the hood of my car about nine inches away from his, and there I stayed, paralyzed, unable even to think. The two vehicles stood headlamp to headlamp, like a pair of cats staring one another out, one of them preserving a mysterious silence. I had, of course, stalled the engine. . . .

It became apparent all too soon that it was I, and not the truck driver, who would have to back. The whole village—the male portion of it—turned out to tell me so, with gestures. They were charming and delightful and terribly helpful. They did everything except reverse the car for me. And they obviously couldn't understand why anyone who was in charge of such a car shouldn't be able to reverse it just like *that*.

Eventually I reversed it into somebody's shop doorway.

The whole village helped to pick up the trestle table, rehang the rugs, and assure me that it didn't matter a scrap.

I straightened up the car and reversed again, into a donkey. The whole village assured me that the donkey wasn't hurt and it would stop in a kilometer or so and come home.

I straightened up the car. This time I churned out a reasonably straight course for ten yards while the village held its breath. Then came a bend in the road. I stopped. I definitely was not prepared to chance reversing over the two-foot parapet into somebody's garden twenty feet down the hillside. I sat there breathing hard, smiling ferociously back at the villagers, and wishing I had never been born and that Simon hadn't either. My bolt was shot.

I had stopped in a patch of sunlight and the glare from the white walls was blinding. The men crowded closer, grinning delightedly and making gallant and—no doubt fortunately—incomprehensible remarks. The truck driver, also grinning, hung out of his cab with the air of a man prepared to spend the whole afternoon enjoying the show.

In desperation, I leaned over the door of the car and addressed the most forward of my helpers, a stout, florid-looking man with small twinkling eyes, who was obviously vastly delighted with the whole business. He spoke a fluent if decidedly odd mixture of French and English.

"Monsieur," I said, "I do not think I can manage this. You see, it's not my car; it belongs to a Monsieur Simon, of Delphi, who requires it urgently, for business. I—I'm not very used to it yet, and since it's not mine I don't like to take risks. . . . I wonder, could you or one of these gentlemen back it for me? Or perhaps the driver of the truck would help, if you would ask him? You see, it's not my car. . . ."

Some rag of pride led me to insist on this, until I saw he wasn't listening. The smile had gone from the cheerful sweating face. He said, "Who did you say the car was for?"

"A Monsieur Simon, of Delphi. He hired it from Athens, urgently." I regarded him hopefully. "Do you know him?"

"No," he said, and shook his head. But he spoke a little too quickly, and as he spoke his eyes flickered away from mine. The man at his elbow looked at me sharply, and then asked a question in rapid Greek, where I thought I caught the word "Simon." My friend nodded once, with that swift flicker of a sidelong look back at me, and said something under his breath. The men near him stared, and muttered, and I thought I saw a new kind of curiosity, furtive, and perhaps even avid, replacing the naïve amusement of a moment ago.

But this was only the most fleeting of impressions. Before I could decide whether to pursue the inquiry or not, I realized that none of the men were looking at me anymore. There was some more of that swift and semi-furtive muttering;

the last of the cheery grins had disappeared, and the men who had been crowding most closely round the car were moving away, unobtrusively yet swiftly, bunching as sheep bunch at the approach of the dog. One and all, they were looking in the same direction.

At my elbow came the fluttering click of "nervous beads," and the stout man's voice said softly, "He will help you."

I said "Who?" before I realized he was no longer beside me.

I turned my head and looked where they all were looking.

A man was coming slowly down a steep-stepped alley that led uphill between the houses on my right.

He was about thirty years old, dark-haired and tanned like all the others in the group near the car, but his clothes, no less than his air and bearing, made him look unmistakably English.

He was not tall, an inch or two under six feet, perhaps, but he was broad in the shoulder, and held himself well, with a sort of easy, well-knit movement that spoke of training and perfect physical fitness. I thought him good-looking; a thinnish sun-browned face, black brows, straight nose, and a hard mouth; but just at the moment his expression was what Jane Austen would have called repulsive—meaning that, whatever thoughts held him in that slightly frowning abstraction, it was obvious that he didn't intend them to be disturbed.

He seemed to be hardly aware of where he was, or what he was doing. A child scampered up the steps and pushed by him, apparently unnoticed. A couple of hens flapped across under his feet without making him pause. A hanging plant splashed petals in a scarlet shower over the white sleeve of his shirt, but he made no move to brush them away.

When he reached the foot of the alleyway, he paused. He seemed to come abruptly out of his preoccupation, whatever it was, and stood there, hands thrust into the pockets of his flannels, surveying the scene in the street. His eyes went straight to the group of men. I saw the slight frown disappear, and the brown face became a mask, remote, cold, reflecting oddly the wariness that I had seen in the villagers. Then he looked straight at me, and it was with something of a shock that I met his eyes. They weren't dark, as I had expected. They were gray, very clear and light, and violently alive.

He came down the last step and crossed to the door of the car. The group melted away from us. He took no more notice of them than he had of the hens, or the falling geranium petals.

He looked down at me. "You seem to be in trouble. Is there anything I can do?"

"I'd be terribly grateful if you *could* help me," I said. "I—I've been trying to back the car."

"I see." I thought I heard amusement behind the pleasant voice, but his face still expressed nothing. I said bleakly, "I was trying to get it to go *there*." "There" was a space beyond the curve of the road which, about fifty yards back, looked as remote as the moon.

"And she won't go?"

"No," I said shortly.

"Is there something wrong with her?"

"Just," I said, "that I can't drive."

"Oh." It was amusement. I said quickly, "It's not my car."

Here the truck driver leaned out of his cabin and shouted something in Greek, and the Englishman laughed. The laugh transformed his face. The mask of rather careful indifference broke up, and he looked all at once younger and quite approachable, even attractive. He shouted something back in what sounded to me like excellent Greek. At any rate the driver understood, because he nodded and withdrew into his cab, and I heard the truck's engine begin to roar.

The newcomer laid a hand on the door.

"If you'll allow me, perhaps I can persuade her to go."

"I shouldn't be surprised," I said bitterly, as I moved over. "I was told this was a man's country. It's true. Go ahead."

He got into the car. I found myself hoping that he would miss the gears, forget to start the engine, leave the handbrake on—do even a single one of the damned silly things I'd been doing all day, but he didn't. To my fury the car moved quietly backward, slid into the cobbled space beyond the corner, paused about two inches away from a house wall, and waited there politely for the truck to pass.

It approached with an appalling noise and a cloud of black smoke. As it drew level, its driver, leaning out of his cab, yelled something at my companion and sent a grinning black-eyed salutation to me that somehow, without a word being intelligible, made me understand that, though incompetent, I was female and therefore delightful, and that was just how it should be.

The truck roared on its way. I saw its driver glance back and lift a hand to the men who still stood in a little group near the café door. One or two of them responded, but most were still watching, not the car, but my companion.

I glanced at him. I knew then that I was right. He was aware of it too. His eyes, narrowed against the sun, showed none of that vivid aliveness that I had surprised in them. He sent the group a look, slow, appraising, utterly without expression. I thought he hesitated. A hand went to the car door, as if he were going to get out, then it dropped back onto the wheel, and he turned to me in inquiry.

I answered his look before he spoke. "Don't give a thought to my *amour-propre*, will you? Of course I should love you to drive the beastly thing through the village for me. I haven't a rag of pride left, and as long as I get this car to Delphi in one piece, my self-respect can be salvaged later. Believe me, I'm terribly grateful."

He smiled. "You must be tired, and it's dreadfully hot. Have you come far?"

"From Athens."

His brows shot up, but he said nothing. The car was moving with the minimum of noise and fuss through the narrow street. The little group of men had disappeared, melting chin-on-shoulder into the café as the car approached them. He didn't glance aside after them.

I said defiantly, "Yes, all the way. And not a scratch."

"Congratulations. . . . And here we are. Clear of the houses and all set for Delphi. You did say Delphi?"

"I did." I regarded him thoughtfully. "I suppose you wouldn't by any chance be going that way yourself?"

"As it happens, yes."

"Would you—?" I hesitated, then took the plunge. "Would you like a lift? In a manner of speaking, that is?"

"I should be delighted. And if the manner of speaking means will I drive—with pleasure, ma'am."

"That's wonderful." I relaxed with a little sigh. The car purred round the last corner and gathered speed up a long curling hill. "I've really quite enjoyed myself, but you know, I've missed half the scenery."

"Never mind. You brought some of it with you."

"What d'you mean?"

He said coolly, "The feathers on the hood. Very original they look, and quite striking."

"The—oh!" My hand flew to my mouth. *"Feathers?* Honestly?"

"Indeed yes. Lots of them."

I said guiltily, "That must be the hen just outside Levadia. At least, it was a cockerel. White ones?"

"Yes."

"Well, it was asking for it. I even hooted the horn, and if you'd heard this horn you'd know that cockerel was bent on death. I didn't kill him, though, really I didn't. I saw him come out the other side and dash away. It *is* only feathers, truly it is."

He laughed. He, too, seemed in some indefinable way to have relaxed. It was as if he had left his preoccupations behind him in Arachova, and with them that impression he had given of a rather formidable reserve. He might have been any pleasant, casually met stranger on holiday.

"No hen'll look at that chap till he's grown a new tail," he said cheerfully, "and you don't have to make excuses to me. It wasn't my cockerel."

"No," I said, "but I've a feeling this is your—" I stopped.

"This is what?"

"Oh, nothing. Merciful heavens, what a view!"

We were running along a high white road that hugged the side of Parnassus. Below us to the left the steep hillside fell away to the valley of the Pleistus, the river that winds down between Parnassus' great flanks and the rounded ridges of Mount Cirphis, toward the plain of Crissa and the sea. All along the Pleistus—at this season a dry white serpent of shingle beds that glittered in the sun—all along its course, filling the valley bottom with the tumbling, whispering green-silver of water, flowed the olive woods; themselves a river, a green-and-silver flood of plumy branches as soft as sea spray, over which the ever-present breezes slid, not as they do over corn, in flying shadows, but in whitening breaths, little gasps that lift and toss the olive crests for all the world like breaking spray. Long pale ripples followed one another down the valley. Where, at the valley's end, Parnassus thrust a sudden buttress of gaunt rock into the flood, the sea of gray trees seemed to break round it, flowing on, flooding out to fill the flat plain beyond, still rippling, still moving with the ceaseless sheen and shadow of flowing water, till in the west the motion was stilled against the flanks of the distant hills, and to the south against the sudden sharp bright gleam of the sea.

I said, after a while, "Are you staying in Delphi?"

"Yes. I've been there a few days. Have you come for long?"

I laughed. "Till the money gives out, and I'm afraid that won't be long enough. I only hope there'll be a room for me somewhere. I came up unexpectedly and haven't booked. Someone told me the Apollon was good."

"It's very nice. Delphi's fairly full just now, but you'll get a room somewhere, I'm sure. Perhaps we can persuade the Apollon to throw someone out for you." A pause. "Hadn't we better introduce ourselves? My name's Lester."

"I'm Camilla Haven." I hesitated. Could I possibly be right in my guess about him? I thought over it again: the villagers' reaction to the name Simon in Arachova; their demeanor when this man appeared; the voice at my elbow murmuring, "He will help you. . . ." Together, they seemed to add up to the solution of my problem. I said slowly, watching him, "I've got a sort of alias today, though. You might say I'm . . . 'Simon's girl.'"

The dark brows shot up. One of those quick, light, electrifying glances, then he was watching the road again. He said evenly, "How very gratifying. But why? Because I rescued you in Arachova?"

I felt the blood coming into my cheeks. I hadn't thought of that one. I said quickly, "No. I only meant I'd been deputizing for her—the other girl—since Athens. With the car."

"The car?" he said blankly.

"Yes." I swallowed and shot a glance at him. This was going to sound even sillier than I had imagined. "This is—oh, dear, I've begun at the wrong end but . . . well, this is your car. The one from Athens."

I could see nothing in his glance this time except puzzlement, with possibly a dash of doubt about my sanity.

"I'm afraid I don't follow. My car? From Athens? And what 'other girl'? Forgive me, but—just what are you talking about?"

"I'm sorry. I shouldn't have jumped it on you like that. I'd better begin at the beginning. I—I've done a rather silly thing, and I hope you're not going to be too angry with me, Mr. Lester. I'll explain exactly how it happened in a moment, if you'll let me, but the important thing is that this is the car you're expecting. The girl you sent to hire it didn't turn up to claim it, and I was handed the key by mistake, so—well, I brought it up here for you. I—I hope it's all right. It was the most marvelous luck to find you—"

"Just a moment. Forgive me for interrupting, but—well, I still haven't the remotest idea what you're talking about. You say someone hired this car in Athens and you were given the key, and drove it up here?"

"Yes." This time it was my voice that sounded flat and blank. "It wasn't—it wasn't you?"

"Decidedly not. I know nothing about a car from Athens or anywhere else."

"But back there in Arachova—" I hesitated, feeling more than ever confused and foolish.

"Yes?" The car slowed, dipped onto a little bridge set at an angle over a narrow gorge, then accelerated up the curling hill beyond. His tone was casual, but somehow I got the impression of sharp interest. "Just what made you think I ought to know about it?"

I said quickly, "Was I wrong? I thought . . . look, you *are* called Simon, aren't you?"

"That is my name. They told you in Arachova? Those men?"

"No. That is, yes, in a way. But . . . never mind that now. You did say you were staying in Delphi?"

"Yes."

I said flatly, stupidly, "Then it *must* be you! It must be!"

"I do assure you it isn't." The quick appraising glance he gave me must have shown him the distress in my face, because he smiled then, and said gently, "But I'm afraid I still don't quite see where the mystery comes in. Surely the garage also gave you the hirer's name and address? Have you lost it, or forgotten to write it down, or something?"

I said in a very small voice, "That's just it. I never knew it."

He looked startled, and then, I thought, amused. "I see. You never knew it. Except, I take it, that his name was Simon?"

"Yes. I told you I'd done something silly. It seemed all right at the time, and I thought in Arachova that it had turned out beautifully, like a story, but now . . ." My voice trailed away. I looked away from him across the blue depths of the valley, and spoke my thoughts with artless and quite unguarded emphasis. "Oh dear, and it would have been so *wonderful* if it *had* been you!"

The words were hardly out before I realized what they sounded like. For the second time in a few minutes I felt the heat wash scarlet into my cheeks. I opened my lips to say something, anything, but before I could speak he said pleasantly, "I wish it had. But look, don't worry so about it. It can't be as bad as you think, and perhaps, if you'll let me, I can help you. Would you care to tell me just what's happened?"

I told him. I kept to a bare recital of the facts, from the moment when the little man approached me with the key, to the fateful second of decision which had landed me—so neatly, as I had thought—at Simon Lester's feet in Arachova. Only the facts: nothing of the miserable tangle of motive; the fear and self-questioning and uneasy bravado . . . but somehow, as I finished the story, I had a feeling that I had told him rather more than I intended. Oddly, I didn't mind. I had told him. He had said he would help. It was over to him. It was a familiar feeling, and yet not quite familiar. . . .

I sat back, relaxed and at ease for the first time since eleven that morning, while below us the breeze ran with white feet over the billowing olives, and beside us, along the high hot road, the sun beat the smell of dust out of the red earth, and the rock glowed and sent the heat back like a blast.

He had made no comment on the silly story as I told it. Now he merely said, "I see. So it really only amounts to this: that you've brought up an unknown car for an unknown man who wants it for something unspecified, and you don't know where to find him."

"That's not a very kind way of putting it, but—yes. I told you it was silly."

"Maybe. But in your place I'd have done exactly the same."

"Would you?"

He laughed. "Of course. What right-minded person could resist a challenge like that?"

"Honestly?"

"Honestly."

I let out a long breath. "You've no idea how much better you've made me feel! But at least you'd have managed the adventure properly! It seems to me that it's not enough to be bold; one has to be competent as well. *You'd* never have got stuck in Arachova—and if you had, you'd have been able to back the car!"

"Ah, yes," he said, "Arachova." The shutters were up once more. He added, half under his breath, "Simon, of Delphi. . . ."

I said quickly, "It does seem odd, doesn't it? That there should be two? I told you that the man from Crissa didn't know anyone of that name hereabouts. Delphi's small, isn't it?"

"Lord, yes."

"Then he'd know, wouldn't he? That was why I was so sure it must be you."

He didn't answer. There was that look again, smooth, blank; the unclimbable wall with spikes at the top. I gave him a doubtful glance he didn't see, and said, tentatively, "Could there have been some kind of mistake? I mean, suppose it *is* you; suppose someone got a message wrong, and the whole thing is just a mix-up? Do you know anyone in Athens, perhaps, who might have—?"

"No." The syllable was definite to the point of curtness. "It's quite impossible. I've had no communication with Athens during the last week at all, so it's hard to see how any message can have gone astray. And you say it was a girl who did the hiring. I've no idea who that could be. No, I'm afraid it's nothing whatever to do with me." A pause, then he added in a different voice, as if he felt he had been too abrupt, "But please don't worry about it any more. We'll soon get it straightened out, and then you can settle down and enjoy Delphi. I think you'll vote it's been worth it."

"It'll have to be pretty good."

"It is." He nodded, almost idly, ahead of the car. "You can't see the village from here, but the ruins are this side of the bluff, in the curve of the mountain under those high cliffs. There—that's Apollo's temple, below the cliffs they call the Shining Ones. You see?"

I saw. Ahead of us the mountain thrust that great buttress out into the valley, the river of olive trees swirling round it as the water swirls round the prow of a ship, to spread out beyond into a great flat lake that filled the plain. High up, in the angle where the bluff joined the mountain, I saw it, Apollo's temple, six columns of apricot stone, glowing against the climbing darkness of the trees behind. Above them soared the sunburned cliffs; below was a tumble, as yet unrecognizable, of what must be monument and treasury and shrine. From where we were the pillars seemed hardly real; not stone that had ever felt hand or chisel, but insubstantial, the music-built columns of legend: Olympian building, left floating—warm from the god's hand—between sky and earth. Above, the indescribable sky of Hellas; below, the silver tide of the olives everlastingly rippling down to the sea. No house, no man, no beast. As it was in the beginning.

I realized then that Simon Lester had stopped the car. We must have stood there for some minutes, at the edge of the road, in the shadow of a stone pine. He didn't speak, and neither did I.

But I noticed that it wasn't Apollo's shining columns that held him. His gaze was on something nearer at hand, away up the side of Parnassus above the road. I followed his look, but could see nothing; only the bare rock shifting and flowing upward with the liquid shimmer of the heat.

After a bit I said merely, "And the village is just the other side of the bluff?"

"Yes. The road runs through those trees below the ruins and then round that shoulder into Delphi. Beyond the village it drops rather steeply to the plain. Crissa—where your friend in the café comes from—is about halfway down. At the bottom the road forks for Amphissa and Itea."

"Itea? That's the fishing port, isn't it? Where the pilgrims used to land in the old days when they were making for the shrine?"

"Yes. You can just see the houses away over there at the edge of the sea." He turned the subject abruptly, but so smoothly that I realized that he was following his own thoughts, and that these had not been about the view, or the road to Itea. "I'm still rather curious to know how you knew my name. I understand it was from those men in Arachova. Was . . . something said?"

"Not really. I'd been trying to explain to the men why I really didn't dare try and reverse the car there—I'd never reversed it before, of course, and it *is* such a length. I told them it wasn't mine, but that it was for someone called Simon, at Delphi. I thought they looked as if that meant something. . . . Then one of them said something to the others, and they all turned and stared at you. It was just the way they looked, somehow. I don't know if you noticed?"

"I noticed."

"Well, that was all. I suppose, when you arrived, they assumed that you were the person to deal with the car. Then, when you told me you came from Delphi, I guessed you might be Simon—my 'Simon.' They . . ."—I hesitated—"they seemed to assume you were the right one, too."

There was an infinitesimal pause before his hand went to the ignition. "Ah, well," he said smoothly, "the sooner we get to Delphi and find your man, the better, don't you think?"

"I do indeed." I laughed. "After all this, we'll probably find him watching beside the road and dancing with impatience; that is, if the little man was right and it really is a matter—" I stopped. Until I repeated the words, half-automatically, I'd forgotten them myself.

"It is what?"

I said slowly, looking at him, "A matter of life and death. . . ."

We were moving again, quickly now. Below us the sea of olives flowed and rippled like smoke. Above, the pitiless sun beat down on the rock with a heat like the clang of brass.

He said, "Is that all he told you?"

"Yes. But he repeated it."

"'A matter of life and death'?"

"Just that. Only of course we were speaking in French. The phrase was *'il y va de la vie.'* "

"And you got the impression he meant it seriously?"

I said slowly, "Yes. I believe I did. I don't know if I took it in really urgently at the time, but you know, I think that's really why I did this silly thing with the car."

"You took the car, and the risks with it, because of some subconscious feeling of urgency about the affair?"

I said, "That makes it sound more definite than it was, and there were—other reasons. . . . But yes. Yes."

The car roared up a long incline, swept round and down a curling hill. I leaned back against the hot leather, folded my hands in my lap, and said, not looking at him, "If the little man was right, it's just as well you're not 'Simon,' isn't it?"

He said, quite without expression, "Just as well. And here we are. What comes first? Simon, or the hotel?"

"Both. I imagine the hotel people are as likely to know of him as anyone, and at least I expect they speak English. My six words of Greek won't get me very far alone."

"On the other hand," said Simon gravely, "they might get you a good deal further than you intended."

4

"And thou camest to Crissa under snow-clad Parnassus, to its foot that faces west, and rocks overhang the spot, and a hollow, stony, wood-clad vale stretches beneath it."

Homeric *Hymn to Apollo*

To MY relief the hotel had a room to offer.

"But only for tonight, I'm afraid," said the proprietor, who spoke, after all, excellent English. "I deeply regret, but I cannot be certain about tomorrow. I have had a—what do you call it? A provisional booking. Perhaps I can take you, perhaps not. If not, there is the Kastalia further along the street, or the Tourist Pavilion at the other end of Delphi. It has a magnificent view, but," he smiled charmingly, "it is very expensive."

"It couldn't have a better view than this," I said.

This was true. The village consists only of two or three rows of flat-topped houses, washed ocher and pink and dazzling white, set in their tiers along the steep side of the hill. At the beginning of the village the road divides into a Y that makes the two main streets, and at the junction stands the Apollon Hotel, facing over the valley toward the distant gleam of the Corinthian Gulf.

Outside the hotel, on the edge of the road which was used as a terrace, two big plane trees made a deep island of shade for some wooden tables and chairs. Simon Lester had parked the car just beyond these, and was waiting there. When I had completed the formalities of booking I went out to speak to him.

"It's all right. They can take me for tonight, and just at the moment that's all I care about." I held out my hand. "I have to thank you very much, Mr. Lester. I don't quite know where I'd have been without your help. I've a feeling it might have been somewhere at the bottom of the valley, with the eagles of Zeus picking my bones!"

"It was a pleasure." He was looking down at me, measuringly. "And now what are you planning to do? Rest and have some tea first, or is that"—a gesture indicated the car—"worrying you too much?"

I said uncertainly, "It is, rather. I think I'd better go right ahead and do what I can."

"Look," he said, "if you'll forgive my saying so, you look as if you'd better have that rest. Won't you please leave this to me, at any rate for the time being? Why don't you go and lie down, and have tea brought to your room—they make excellent tea here, by the way—while I make a few inquiries for you?"

"Why, I—you mustn't—I mean, it's absurd that you should be landed with my difficulties," I said, a little confusedly, and conscious only of a strong desire that he should, in fact, be landed with them all. I finished feebly, "I couldn't let you."

"Why not? It would be too cruel if you turned on me now and told me to mind my own business."

"I didn't mean it like that. You know I didn't. It's only—"

"That it's your affair and you want to see it through? Of course. But I must confess I'm seething with curiosity myself by now, and after all it's partly my affair too, since my alter ego has managed to involve me. I really would be very grateful if you'd let me help. Besides," he added, "wouldn't you honestly much rather go and have a rest and some tea now, while I do the detecting for you in my fluent but no doubt peculiar Greek?"

"I—" I hesitated again, then said truthfully, "I should adore to."

"Then that's settled." He glanced at his wrist. "It's about twenty past four now. Shall we say an hour? I'll report back at five-thirty. Right?"

"Right." I looked at him a little helplessly. "But if you do find him, and he's angry—"

"Well?"

"I don't want you made responsible for what's happened. It wouldn't be fair, and I'd much rather face my own music."

"You'd be surprised," he said cryptically, "how responsible I feel already. All right, then. See you later."

With a quick wave of the hand he was gone down the steps to the lower road.

My room overlooked the valley, and had a long window with a balcony. The shutters were closed against the sun, but even so the room seemed full of light, globed in light, incandescent with it. As the door shut behind the maid who had shown me upstairs, I went across to the window and pulled back the shutters. Like a blast the heat met me. The sun was wheeling over now toward the west, full across the valley from my window, and valley and plain were heavy with sleepy heat. The tide of olives had stilled itself, and even the illusion of coolness created by those rippling gray leaves was gone. In the distance the wedge of shining water that showed at the edge of the plain struck at the eyes like the flash from a burning-glass.

I closed my eyes against it, pulling the shutters to again. Then I slipped off my dress, and had a long, cool wash. I sat on the edge of the bed for some minutes after that, brushing my hair, till I heard the maid coming back with the tea. I had my tea—Simon Lester had been right about its excellence—propped against pillows, and with my feet up on the bed. I don't think I thought any more about Simon—either of the Simons—or about the car, or about anything except the shadowed quiet of the little white room.

Presently I put the tray off my knees onto the table by the bed, and lay back to relax. Before I knew it was even near, sleep had overtaken me. . . .

I woke to a feeling of freshness and the incongruous sound of rain. But the light still drove white against the shutters, and when I opened them a crack I saw that the sun still blazed, deeper now and lower, but at full power. Half my window was in shadow now, where the plane trees put a bough or two between it and the falling sun. The sound of rain, I realized, was the sound of their leaves, pattering and rustling in the breeze that had got up to cool the evening.

I glanced down at the terrace below the balcony. He was there, sitting under one of the plane trees, smoking. His chair was pulled up to the railing that edged the terrace, and one arm lay along this. He sat there, relaxed, looking at nothing, completely at ease. The car was standing where he had parked it before. If—as appeared to be the case—he had not located another "Simon" to deliver it to, the fact didn't appear to worry him unduly.

I reflected, as I looked down at him thoughtfully, that it would probably take a good deal to worry Simon Lester. That quiet manner, that air of being casually and good-temperedly on terms with life . . . with it all went something that is particularly hard to describe. To say that he knew what he wanted and took it, would be to give the wrong impression; it was rather that whatever decisions he had to make, were made, and then dismissed—this with an ease that argued an almost frightening brand of self-confidence.

I don't know how much of this I saw in him on that first day; it may be that I simply recognized straightaway the presence of qualities I myself so conspicuously lacked; but I do remember the immediate and vivid impression I got of a self-sufficiency harder and more complete than anything conveyed in years of Philip's *grand-seigneur* gasconading, and at the same time quite different in quality. I didn't see yet where the difference lay. I only know that I felt obscurely grateful to Simon for not having made me feel too much of a fool, and, less obscurely, for having so calmly undertaken to help me in the matter of the "other Simon. . . ."

I wondered, as I closed the shutters again, if he had even bothered to make the gesture of looking for him.

On the whole, I imagined not.

In this, it seemed, I had done him less than justice.

When I went downstairs I found him, hands thrust deep in trouser pockets, in earnest contemplation of the car, together with a Greek to whose bright blue shirt was pinned the insignia of a guide.

Simon looked up and smiled at me. "Rested?"

"Perfectly, thank you. And the tea *was* good."

"I'm glad to hear it. Perhaps you're strong enough, then, to bear the blow?" He jerked his head toward the car.

"I thought as much. You've not found him?"

"Not a sign. I've been to the other hotels, but there's no visitor of that name. Then I went along to the Museum to meet George here. He tells me that he doesn't know anyone called Simon in Delphi, either."

The Greek said, "Only yourself, *Kyrie* Lester."

"Only myself," agreed Simon.

I said, rather helplessly, "What shall we do?"

"*Kyrie* Lester," said the Greek, watching him rather curiously, "could it not be, perhaps, that there *is* no other Simon? And that it is not a mistake? That someone is—how do you put it?—using your name?"

"Taking my name in vain?" Simon laughed, but I knew that this had already occurred to him. It had occurred to me, too. "It doesn't seem likely. For one thing, who would? And for another, if they did, and it was urgent, they'd surely have appeared by now to claim the damned thing."

"That is probably true."

"You can bet it's true. But I'm going to get to the bottom of this very odd little affair—and not only for the sake of Miss Haven here, who's worried about it. Look, George, you are sure about it? No Simons at all, however unlikely? A grandfather with a wooden leg, or a mule-boy aged seven and a half, or one of the men working up on the excavations?"

"About the last I do not know, of course, though assuredly you are right and they would have come to look for it. In Delphi, nobody. Nobody at all."

"Then the places nearby? You're a native, aren't you? You'll know a fair number of people all round here. Crissa, for instance. It might be Crissa . . . that's only a few kilometers away. What about that?"

George shook his head. "No. I am sure. I would have remembered. And in Arachova . . ."

Simon ran a finger along the wing of the car, then contemplated the tip of it for a moment. "Yes?"

George said, regretfully, "No, I do not remember anyone in Arachova, either."

Simon took out a handkerchief and wiped his fingertip clean again. "In any case I can find out. I'm going back there tonight."

The Greek gave him a quick bright glance that held, I thought, curiosity. But he only said, "Ah. Well, I regret, but that is all I can tell you, except—oh, but that is not the same; it is of no use to you."

"We'll have it, though, please. You've thought of someone?"

George said slowly, "There is a Simonides at Itea. I do not think this is the man, but he is the only one I know of. But perhaps, *kyrie,* you would like to ask someone else? I do not know everybody, me. Elias Sarantopoulou, my cousin, he is also in the Tourist Police. He is at the office now, or perhaps he is at the café . . . if you like to come with me I will show you the place; it is opposite the Post Office."

"I know it," said Simon. "Thanks, but I really doubt if your cousin will know any more than you. This is an irritating little problem, isn't it? It'll probably solve itself very soon, but meanwhile I suppose we must do something. We'll try your Simonides at Itea. Who is Simonides, what is he?"

George, of course, took him literally. "He has a little baker's shop near the cinema in the middle of the main street, facing the sea. Giannakis Simonides." He glanced at his wrist. "The bus goes in ten minutes. The shop is not far from the place where the bus stops."

Simon said, "We have a car," then grinned as he caught my eye. My answering smile was a rather brittle one. The car stood there like a mockery. I hated the sight of it.

Simon nodded to George, said something in Greek, then pulled open the car door for me.

I said doubtfully, "Ought we to?"

"Why not? This is a quite legitimate attempt at delivery. Come along, the sooner we get down to Itea the better. It'll be dark in an hour. Are you tired?"

"Not now. But—you'll drive, won't you, Mr. Lester?"

"You bet I will. You haven't seen the Itea road. And please call me Simon. It's more euphonious than 'Mr. Lester,' and besides . . ." his grin, as he slid into his seat beside me, was malicious ". . . it'll give you an illusion of comfort."

I didn't answer that one, except with a look, but as we drove off I said suddenly, and almost to my own surprise, "I'm beginning to feel frightened."

The glance he gave me held surprise but, oddly enough, no amusement. "That's a strong word."

"I suppose so. Perhaps it isn't, either, from me. I'm the world's most complete coward. I—I wish I'd had the sense to let well enough alone. The beastly thing should still be standing there in Omonia Square, and—"

"And you'd still be wishing madly you were in Delphi?"

"There is that," I acknowledged. "But you do see, don't you?"

"Of course I do."

The car had crept carefully through Delphi's narrow upper street, topped the rise opposite the presbytery, and then dived down to meet the lower road out of the village.

I said abruptly, "Do you suppose for a moment that this Simonides is the man we're looking for?"

"It doesn't seem very probable." Perhaps he felt this to be a little brusque, for he added, "We might as well try it, all the same."

"Something to make me feel progress is being made?" No answer to this. I said, "You know, it really would be carrying coincidence a bit too far to suppose there are two Simons in Delphi."

"It's not," he said evenly, "a very common name."

I waited, but he didn't speak again. We had left the village behind, dropping in a gradual descent between dykes of red earth and stones where the road had been recently widened. The ditches and mounds showed raw as wounds in the sunburnt earth. The rich rays of the now-setting sun flooded it with strong amber light against which the dry thistles that grew everywhere stood up delicate and sharp, like intricate filigree of copper wire. Above the road the new hotel, the Tourist Pavilion, showed as raw and new and wounding as the torn ditches alongside us. The curved windows flashed as we passed beneath and wheeled into the first hairpin of the descent to the plain of olives.

I said casually, "Are you just holidaying here in Delphi?"

I had meant it as a non sequitur, a conversational make-weight, the normal casual query with which you might greet anyone you met in such a place; but even as I said it I could hear how it pointed back to my last remark. I started to say something else, but he was already answering without any indication that he saw my question as other than innocent.

"In a way. I'm a schoolmaster. I have a house at Wintringham. Classics is my subject."

Whatever I had expected it wasn't this; this seal and parchment of respectability. I said feebly, "Then of course you're interested in the classical sites. Like me."

"Don't tell me you're a colleague? Another beggarly usher?"

"Afraid so."

"Classics?"

"Yes. Only in a girls' school that just means Latin, to my sorrow and shame."

"You don't know Ancient Greek?"

"A little. A very little. Enough sometimes to catch a word and follow what's being said. Enough to know my alphabet and make a wild guess at what some of the notices mean, and to have had a queer feeling at the pit of the stomach when I went to see *Antigone* in the Herodes Atticus Theatre in Athens and heard the chorus calling on Zeus against that deep black sky that had heard the same call for three thousand years." I added, feeling slightly ashamed of what I'd let him see, "What a ghastly road."

The car heeled yet again round a hairpin curve and plunged on down the great shoulder of Parnassus that sticks out into the Crissa Plain. Below us was a village, and below it again the flood of olives, flowing mile-wide now down to the sea.

Simon said cheerfully, "The buses all have icons stuck up in front of the driver, *and* with a little red light in front, run off the battery. On this road the icon swings madly from side to side at the bends and everybody crosses themselves."

I laughed. "Including the driver?"

"This is true. Yes, including the driver. I have a feeling that sometimes," said Simon, "he also shuts his eyes." He pulled the big car round an even sharper bend, missed an upcoming truck by inches, and added, "You can open yours now. This is Crissa."

I felt the color come into my cheeks. "I'm sorry. I must be losing my nerve."

"You're still tired, that's all. We'll have something to drink in Itea before we seek out this Simonides."

"No, please," I protested, almost too quickly.

He eyed me for a moment. "You really are scared, aren't you?"

"I—yes, I am."

"I shouldn't worry; I really shouldn't. It can't matter, or it'd have been settled long before this."

"I know. I know it's nonsense. It's silly and it's trivial and it doesn't mean a thing, but I told you I'm the world's worst coward. It's true. I've been persuading myself for years that I'd be as competent and self-sufficient as anyone else, given the chance, but now I know. . . . Why, I can't even bear *scenes,* so why I ever thought I could get away with this sort of mayhem I have no idea." I stopped. It occurred to me with a queer little shock that I would never have said anything like that to Philip, not in a hundred years.

Simon was saying calmly, "Never mind. I'm here, aren't I? Whatever we get into, I'll talk you out of it, so sit back and relax."

"If," I said, "we find Simon."

"If," said Simon, "we do."

I was glad enough, when we got to Itea, to leave everything to him.

Itea is the port which in ancient times saw the landing of the pilgrims bound for the shrine of Apollo at Delphi. The shrine was a religious center for the whole ancient world for many hundreds of years, and to us nowadays, used to modern transport, it is astonishing to contemplate the distances that men traveled on foot and on horseback or in small ships, to worship the God of light and peace and healing, or to ask the advice of the famous Oracle enshrined below the temple. The easy way was by Itea. The sea journey, for all its hazards, was less exhausting and dangerous than the journey by road through the mountains, and here into the little port of Itea the pilgrims crowded, to see from the harbor the winding river valley of the Pleistus and, beyond the shoulder of Parnassus where modern Delphi stands, the bright cliffs of the Shining Ones that guard the holy spring.

Today Itea is a grubby little fishing village, with one long street of shops and *tavernas* facing the sea and separated from it by the road and then perhaps fifty yards of dusty boulevard where pepper trees give shade and the men of the village gather for the usual drinks and ices and sticky honey-cakes.

Simon stopped the car under the trees and led me to a rickety iron table which seemed to have fewer attendant wasps than the others. I would have liked tea again, but felt so ashamed of this insular craving—and so doubtful of getting anything approaching what I wanted—that I asked for fresh lemonade, and got it, delicious and cold and tangy with the real fruit, and with it a *pasta* something like shredded wheat, but frantically oversweet with honey and chopped nuts. It was wonderful. The wasps loved it too. When we had finished it, I defiantly asked for another, and stayed to eat it while Simon went off to look for the baker's shop of Simonides.

I watched him go, thoughtfully beating off an extra-large and persistent wasp. Somehow I didn't think Giannakis Simonides was our man. "Monsieur Simon, at Delphi . . ." And there was only one Monsieur Simon at Delphi.

There was that queer reserve, too, in Simon's manner; there was Arachova; and the way he had shelved my question as to what he was doing in Delphi. The thing had ceased to be a slightly awkward puzzle. It was fast becoming a mystery, with Simon Lester at its center. And Simon's girl . . .

I finished my cake now and got up. Simon had paid the waiter before he had left me. I could see him standing in a doorway some distance up the street. The place was apparently a restaurant, for outside it stood the big charcoal stove, and over this a whole lamb revolved slowly on the spit, which was being turned by a stout woman in a blue apron. Simon appeared to be questioning her; she was nodding vigorously, and then, with a wave of her free hand, seemed to be directing him further up the street.

He looked back, saw me standing under the pepper trees, and raised a hand in salute. Then he made a vague gesture toward the other end of the street, and set off that way, walking fast.

Taking his gesture to mean that he had some information, but that he didn't expect me to follow him, I stayed where I was and watched him. He went perhaps a hundred yards, hesitated, then glanced up at a billboard and plunged into the darkness of a deserted cinema. As he vanished, I turned in the opposite direction and began to walk along the boulevard. I was only too thankful to leave the enquiry to him. If he really was in the center of the mystery, he could keep it to himself, and welcome. . . .

Meanwhile I would do what I had come to Delphi for. Since chance had brought me down to Itea, the start of the ancient pilgrimage, I would try and see the shrine as the old pilgrims had seen it on their first landing from the Corinthian Gulf.

I walked quickly along the harbor's edge. On my right the sea paled toward sunset, and across the opal shimmer of the bay came a fishing boat, turquoise and white, with her prow raked in a proud pure curve above its liquid image. Under a sail of that same scarlet had the worshipers come into harbor when the God was still at Delphi.

I left the sea's edge and walked rapidly across the street. I wanted to get behind the ugly row of houses, back into the old olive woods, where I could look straight up toward the Pleistus valley with nothing but immemorial rock and tree and sky between me and the shrine.

Behind the main street were a few sorry alleys of concrete, with houses, as usual, scattered seemingly at random in the dust patches between the trees. I passed the last house, skirted a building that looked like a ruined warehouse, and followed a cracked stretch of concrete which appeared to lead straight into the outskirts of the forest of olives. The concrete was criss-crossed with cracks, like crazy paving, and thistles grew in the fissures. I startled a browsing donkey, and it plunged off under the trees in a smother of dust, to be lost in the shadows. Soon the concrete came to an end, and I found myself walking through soft earth in the deeper twilight of the trees. The breeze had strengthened with the approach of evening, and overhead the olives had resumed their liquid rippling.

I hurried on toward a space ahead where stronger light promised a clearing. I was lucky. There was a slight rise in the ground, and to the north of it the great olives thinned. From the top of the little ridge, across the ruffling crests of the trees, I could see the old Pilgrims' Way, unscarred by my own century. I stood for a few minutes, gazing up toward the shrine in the now rapidly fading light.

The temple columns were invisible behind the curve of the Crissa bluff, but there was the black cleft of Castalia, and above it the great cliffs whose names are Flamboyant and Roseate, the Shining Ones. . . . The dying sun ran up the Flamboyant cliff like fire.

This was, I thought, the way to come to Delphi . . . not straight up into the ruins in the wake of a guide, but to land from a small boat in a bay of pearl, and see it as they would have seen it, flaming in the distance like a beacon, the journey's end.

Something like a fleck of darkness went by my cheek. A bat. It was deep twilight now, the swift-falling Aegean dusk. I turned to see lights pricking out in the houses behind me. I could just see the streetlamps, faint and far between, along the sea front. They looked a long way away. Where I stood the shadow of a huge olive brooded like a cloud. I turned to go back to the village.

Instead of returning the way I had come, I took what I judged to be the direction of the car, and, plunging down from the ridge into the depths of the wood, I set off quickly through the twisted and shadowy trunks.

I had gone perhaps a hundred yards before the trees began to thin. Some way off to my left I saw the lights of the first house, an outpost of the village, and was hurrying toward it through the soft dust when a sudden flash of light quite near me, and to my right, brought me up short, startled. It was the flash of an electric torch, deep in the trees. Perhaps my adventures of the day had worked on my imagination rather too well, or perhaps it was the ancient mystery that I had been attempting to call up, but the fact remains that I felt suddenly frightened, and stood very still, with the trunk of an enormous olive between me and the torchlight.

Then I realized what it was. There was a house set by itself deep in the grove, the usual two-windowed box of a place with its woodpile and its lean-to shed and its scrawny chickens gone to roost in the vine. The flash I had seen showed me a man bending over a motor vehicle of some sort which was parked close to the side of the house. It looked like a jeep. As I watched he jerked the hood open, shone the light into the engine, and leaned over it. I saw his face highlighted by the queerly refracted light, a very Greek face, dark, with hair crisping down the wide cheekbones in the manner of the heroes, and a roundish head covered with close curls like a statue's.

Then somebody in the cottage must have kindled the lamp, for a soft oblong of light slanted out of one of the windows, showing the dusty clutter outside—a woodman's block with the axe still sunk in it and gleaming as the light caught it, a couple of old gasoline cans, and a chipped enamel bowl for the hens' food. My causeless fear vanished and I turned quickly to go.

The man by the jeep must have seen the movement of my skirt in the darkness, because he looked up. I caught a glimpse of his face before the torch went out. He was smiling. I turned and hurried away. As I went, I thought the torchbeam flicked out to touch me momentarily, but the Greek made no move to follow.

Simon was sitting in the car, smoking. He got out when he saw me and came round to open my door. He answered my look with a shake of the head.

"No go. I've asked all the questions I could and it's a dead end." He got into the driver's seat and started the engine. "I really think we'll have to call it a day—go back to Delphi and have dinner and leave it to sort itself out in its own good time."

"But will it?"

He turned the car and started back toward Delphi. "I think so."

Bearing in mind what I had been thinking before about the "mystery," I didn't argue. I said simply, "Then we'll leave it. As you wish."

I saw him glance at me sideways, but he made no comment. The lights of the village were behind us, and we gathered speed up the narrow road. He dropped something into my lap, a leafy twig that smelt delicious when my fingers touched it.

"What is it?"

"Basil. The herb of kings."

I brushed it to and fro across my lips. The smell was sweet and minty, pungent above the smell of dust. "The pot of basil? Was it under this stuff that poor Isabella buried Lorenzo's head?"

"That's it."

There was a pause. We passed a crossroads where our lights showed a sign, AMPHISSA 9. We turned right for Crissa.

"Did you go to look for the Pilgrims' Way back there in Itea?" asked Simon.

"Yes. I got a wonderful view just before the light went. The Shining Ones were terrific."

"You found the ridge, then?"

I must have sounded surprised. "You know it? You've been here before?"

"I was down here yesterday."

"In Itea?"

"Yes." The road was climbing now. After a short silence he said, with no perceptible change of expression, "You know, I really don't know any more about it than you do."

The basil leaves were cool and still against my mouth. At length I said, "I'm sorry. Did I make it so obvious? But what was I to think?"

"Probably just what you did think. The thing's slightly crazy anyway, and I doubt if it'll prove to matter at all." I saw him smile. "Thank you for not pretending you didn't know what I meant."

"But I did. I'd been thinking about very little else myself."

"I know that. But nine women out of ten would have said *'What d'you mean?'* and there we'd have been, submerged in a lovely welter of personalities and explanations."

"There wasn't any need of either."

Simon said, "'O rare for Antony.'"

I said involuntarily, "What d'you mean?"

He laughed then. "Skip it. Will you have dinner with me tonight?"

"Why, thank you, Mr. Lester—"

"Simon."

"Simon, then, but perhaps I should—I mean—"

"That's wonderful then. At your hotel?"

"Look, I didn't say—"

"You owe it to me," said Simon coolly.

"I owe it to you? I do not! How d'you work that out?"

"As reparation for suspecting me of—whatever you did suspect me of." We were climbing through the twisting street of Crissa, and as we passed a lighted shop he glanced at his wrist. "It's nearly seven now. Could you bear to dine in half an hour's time—say at half past seven?"

I gave up. "Whenever it suits you. But isn't that fearfully early for Greece? Are you so very hungry?"

"Reasonably. But it's not that. I—well, I've things to do and I want to get them done tonight."

"I see. Well, it won't be too early for me. I only had a snack for lunch, and I was too frightened to enjoy that. So thank you. I'd like that. At the Apollon, you said? You're not staying there yourself?"

"No. When I got here the place was full up so I got permission to sleep in the studio up the hill. You won't have seen it yet. It's a big ugly square building a couple of hundred feet up behind the village."

"A studio? An artist's studio, do you mean?"

"Yes. I don't know what it was used for originally, but now it has a caretaker, and is let out to visiting artists and bona fide students who can't afford to pay for a hotel. I suppose I'm up there under slightly false pretenses, but I wanted to be in Delphi for some days and I couldn't find a room. Now that I'm settled into the studio I find it'll do me admirably. There's only one other tenant at present, an English boy, who's a genuine artist . . . and good, too, though he won't let you say so."

"But surely you've a perfectly good claim on the studio, too?" I said. "After all, you count as a student. And as a classicist you've a bona fide claim on any concession. It's not a question of 'false pretenses' at all."

He sent me a sideways look that I couldn't read in the darkness. He said rather shortly, "I'm not here to pursue my classical studies."

"Oh." It sounded lame, and I hoped it hadn't sounded like a question. But the syllable hung there between us like a dominant awaiting resolution.

Simon said suddenly, into the darkness straight ahead, "My brother Michael was here during the war."

Crissa was below us now. Far down to our left as we climbed along the face of the bluff the lights of Itea were strung along like beads under the thin moon.

He said, still in that expressionless way, "He was in the Peloponnese for some time, as B.L.O.—that's British Liaison Officer—between our chaps and the *andartes,* the Greek guerrillas under Zervas. Later he moved over into the Pindus region with ELAS, the main resistance group. He was in this part of the country in nineteen forty-four. He stayed with some people in Arachova; a shepherd called Stephanos and his son Nikolaos. Nikolaos is dead, but Stephanos still lives in Arachova. I went over to try and see him today, but he's away in Levadia, and not expected back till this evening—so the woman of his house told me."

"The woman of his house?"

He laughed. "His wife. You'll find everyone has to belong, hereabouts. Every man belongs to a place, and I'm afraid that every woman belongs to a man."

"I believe you," I said, without rancor. "I suppose it gives meaning to her life, poor thing?"

"But of course. . . . Anyway I'm going down to Arachova again tonight to see Stephanos."

"I see. Then this is a—a sort of pilgrimage for you? A genuine pilgrimage to Delphi?"

"You could call it that. I've come to appease his shade."

I caught my breath. "Oh. How stupid of me. I'm sorry. I didn't realize."

"That he died? Yes."

"Here?"

"Yes, in nineteen forty-four. Somewhere on Parnassus."

We had wheeled up onto the last stretch of the road before Delphi. To our left blazed the lighted windows of the luxurious Tourist Pavilion. Far down now on the right the thin moon was already dying out in a welter of stars. The sea was faintly luminous beneath them, like a black satin ribbon.

Something made me say suddenly, into the dark, "Simon."

"Yes?"

"Why did you say 'appease'?"

A little silence. Then he spoke quite lightly. "I'll tell you about that, if I may. But not just at this moment. Here's Delphi. I'll leave you and the car at your hotel, and I'll meet you on the terrace here in half an hour. Right?"

"Right." The car drew up where it had stood before. He came round and opened my door for me. I got out, and when I would have turned to repeat some words of thanks for his help in my afternoon's quest he shook his head, laughed, raised a hand in farewell and vanished up the steep lane beside the hotel.

With a feeling that things were moving altogether too fast for me, I turned and went indoors.

5

"But enough of tales—I have wept for these
things once already."

EURIPIDES: *Helen*
(tr. Philip Vellacott)

ANY FEARS I might have had that Simon's melancholy pilgrimage would be allowed to cloud my first visit to Delphi were dispelled when I came down at length to dinner, and walked out to the hotel terrace to find a table.

Seven-thirty was certainly an outrageously early hour for dining in Greece, and only one other of the tables under the plane trees was occupied, and that, too, by English people. Simon Lester wasn't there yet, so I sat down under one of the trees from whose dark boughs hung lights, which swung gently in the warm evening air. I saw Simon then below the terrace railing, making one of an extremely gay and noisy group of Greeks which surrounded a fair boy in the garb of a hiker, and a very small donkey almost hidden under its awkwardly loaded panniers.

The fair young man looked very much as if he had just completed some arduous trek in the wilds. His face, hands, and clothes were filthy; he had a generous stubble on his chin, and his eyes—I could see it even from where I sat—were bloodshot with fatigue. The donkey was in rather better case, and stood smugly beside him, under its load of what appeared to be the paraphernalia of an artist—boxes, roughly wrapped canvases, and a small collapsible easel, as well as a sleeping bag and the rather unappetizing end of a large black loaf.

Half the youth of Delphi seemed to have rallied to the stranger's welcome, like the wasps to my honey-cake. There was a great deal of loud laughter, atrocious English, and back-slapping—the last an attention which the stranger could well have done without. He was reeling with tiredness, but a white grin split the dirty bearded face as he responded to the welcome. Simon was laughing too, pulling the donkey's ears and exchanging what appeared to be the most uproarious of jokes with the young Greeks. Frequent cries of "Avanti! Avanti!" puzzled me, till I realized that they coincided with the jolly slaps under which the donkey, too, was reeling. At each slap a cloud of dust rose from Avanti's fur.

Eventually Simon looked up and saw me. He said something to the fair boy, exchanged some laughing password with the Greeks, and came swiftly up to the terrace.

"I'm sorry, have you been waiting long?"

"No, I've just come down. What's going on down there? A modern Stevenson?"

"Just that. He's a Dutch painter who's been making his way through the mountains with a donkey, and sleeping rough. He's done pretty well. He's just here from Jannina now, and that's a long way through rough country."

"He certainly got a welcome," I said, laughing. "It looked as if all Delphi had turned out."

"Even the tourist traffic hasn't quite spoiled the Greek *philoxenia*—the 'welcome' that literally means 'love of a stranger,'" said Simon, "though goodness knows Delphi ought to be getting a bit blasé by now. At least he'll get the traditional night's lodging free."

"Up at the studio?"

"Yes. This is the end of his trek. Tomorrow, he says, he'll sell Modestine—the donkey Avanti—and get the bus for Athens."

I said, "I thought when I saw the easel and what-not that he must be your English painter friend from the studio."

"Nigel? No. I doubt if a venture like that would ever occur to Nigel. He hasn't the self-confidence."

"You said he was a good painter, though?"

"I think he's good," said Simon, picking up the menu and absently handing it to me. It was in Greek, so I handed it back again. "But he's convinced himself— or else some fool has told him—that his own particular style is no good any more. I admit it's not the fashion, but the boy can draw like an angel when he likes, and I should have thought that was a gift rare enough to command attention even among some of today's more strident talents." He handed me the menu. "He doesn't use color much—what will you have to start with?—but the drawing's very sure and delicate, and exciting at the same time."

I gave the menu back to him. He scrutinized the scrawled columns. "Hm. Yes. Well, some fool's told Nigel that his style's *vieux jeu,* or something. 'Emasculate' was one of the words, I believe. It's got him on the raw, so he's hard at work trying to form a style that he thinks will 'take,' but I'm terribly afraid it won't work. Oh, he's clever, and it's arresting enough, and it may catch on and find him a market of a sort—but it's not his own, and that never works fully. Another pity is that he's been here in Delphi a bit too long and got tied up with a girl who wasn't very good for him. She's gone, but the melancholy remains." He smiled. "As you see, it's with me, rather. I'm all the company Nigel's had up at the studio for the last three days, and I've been playing confidant."

"Or housemaster?"

He laughed. "If you like. He's very young in many ways, and habit dies hard. One takes it for granted one is there to help, though I'm not just sure how much anyone can do for an artist at the best of times. And at the worst they go into a kind of wilderness of the spirit where the best-intentioned listener can't even follow them."

"As bad as that?"

"I think so. I told you he was good. I believe the agony is in proportion to the talent. . . . Look, what are you going to eat? Why don't you choose something?" He handed me the menu.

I gave it patiently back. "I shall die of hunger in a minute," I told him. Have you *looked* at this dashed menu? The only things I recognize are *patates, tomates,* and *melon,* and I refuse to be a vegetarian in a land which produces those heavenly little chunks of lamb on sticks with mushrooms between."

"I'm sorry," said Simon penitently, "Here they are, see? *Souvlaka.* Well, so be it." He ordered the meal, then finally cocked an eyebrow at me. "What shall we drink? How's the palate coming on?"

"If that means can I swallow retsina yet," I said, "the answer is yes, though what it has to do with a palate I cannot see." Retsina is a mild wine strongly flavoured with resin. It can be pleasant; it can also be rough enough to fur the tongue with a sort of antiseptic gooseflesh. It comes in beautiful little copper tankards, and smells like turpentine. To acquire—or to pretend to acquire—a taste for retsina is the right thing to do when in Greece. As a tourist, I'm as much of a snob as anyone. "Retsina, certainly," I said. "What else, with *souvlaka?*"

I thought I saw the faintest shade of irony in Simon's eye. "Well, if you'd rather have wine—"

I said firmly, "They say that once you've got used to retsina it's the finest drink in the world and you won't ever take anything else. Burgundies and clarets and— well, other drinks, lose their flavor. Don't interrupt the process. The palate is faint yet pursuing and I expect I'll like it soon. Unless, of course, *you'd* like a nice sweet Samian wine?"

"Heaven forfend," said Simon basely, and, to the waiter, "Retsina, please."

When it came, it was good, as retsina goes—and the dinner along with it was excellent. I'm not a person whom the sight of olive oil repels, and I love Greek cooking. We had onion soup with grated cheese on top; then the *souvlaka,* which comes spiced with lemon and herbs, and flanked with chips and green beans in oil and a big dish of tomato salad. Then cheese, and *halvas,* which is a sort of loaf made of grated nuts and honey, and is delicious. And finally the wonderful grapes of Greece, bloomed over like misted agates and cooled with water from the spring above the temple of Apollo.

Simon talked entertainingly through the meal without once mentioning Michael Lester or his purpose in visiting Delphi, and I myself forgot completely the cloud that was still hanging over my day, and only recollected it when a truck, chugging up past the terrace, slowed down to pass the car which stood parked at the edge of the narrow road.

Simon followed my look. He set down his little cup of Greek coffee, and then looked across the table at me.

"Conscience still active?"

"Not so active as it was. There's not so much room. That was a heavenly meal, and thank you very much."

"I wondered—" said Simon thoughtfully, and then stopped.

I said just as thoughtfully, "It's a long walk to Arachova. Is that it?"

He grinned. "That's it. Well? It's your car."

I said fervently, "It's not, you know. I never want to touch it again. I—I've renounced it."

"That's a pity, because—with your permission which I take it I have—I'm going to drive down to Arachova in a few minutes' time, and I was rather hoping you'd come too."

I said, in very real amazement, "Me? But you don't want me!"

"Please," said Simon.

For some reason I felt the color coming hot into my cheeks. "But you don't. It's your own—your private affair, and you can't possibly want a stranger tagging along with you. This may be Greece, but that's carrying *philoxenia* a bit too far! After all—"

"I promise not to let anything upset you." He smiled. "It's a long time ago, and it's not a present tragedy anymore. It's just—well, you can call it curiosity, if you like."

"I wasn't worrying about its upsetting me. I was thinking only that—well, dash it, you hardly know me, and it *is* a private matter. You said it could be called a 'pilgrimage,' remember?"

He said slowly, "If I said what I really want to say you'd think I was crazy. But let me say this—and it's true—I'd be terribly grateful if you'd give me your company this evening."

There was a little pause. The group of Greeks had long since dispersed. Both artist and donkey had vanished. The other English diners had finished and gone into the hotel. Away over the invisible sea the thin moon hung, apricot now among the white scatter of stars. Above us the breeze in the plane trees sounded like rain.

I said, "Of course I'll come," and got to my feet. As he stubbed out his cigarette and rose I smiled at him with a touch of malice. "After all, you did tell me I owed you something."

He said quickly, "Look, I never meant—" and he caught my look and grinned. "All right, ma'am, you win. I won't try and bully you again." And he opened the car door for me.

"Michael was ten years older than me," said Simon. "There were just the two of us, and our mother died when I was fifteen. My father thought the sun rose and set in Michael—and so did I, I suppose. I remember how dead the house seemed when he was drafted off to the Med. . . . and Father just sat every day with the papers and the radio, trying to learn what he could." A little smile touched his lips. "It wasn't easy. I told you Michael came over here with the S.A.S.—the Special Air Service—when Germany occupied Greece. He was doing undercover work with the resistance in the mountains for eighteen months before he was killed, and of course news came very thinly and not always accurately. Occasionally men managed to get letters out. . . . If you knew someone was going to be picked up at night and taken off you did your damnedest to get a letter to him in the hope that he in his turn would get through, and the letter might eventually be mailed home from Cairo . . . but it was chancy, and no one in those days carried any more papers on him than he could help. So news was sparse and not very satisfactory. We only ever got three letters from Michael in all that time. All he told us in the first two was that he was well, and things were going according to plan—and all the usual formulae that you don't believe, but that just tell you he was alive when he wrote the letter four months before you got it."

He paused while he negotiated a sharp bend made more hair-raising than ever by the dark.

"We did eventually find out a certain amount about his work in Greece from chaps who'd been with him here in Force One Thirty-three, and had been in touch with him off and on through the fighting. I told you he was a B.L.O. attached to guerrillas. Perhaps I'd better tell you the setup in Greece after the German invasion—or do you know all about it?"

"Not a great deal. Only that ELAS was the main guerrilla organization, and was more concerned in feathering its own Commie nest than in fighting Germans."

"So you do know that? You'd be surprised how many people never grasped it, even in nineteen forty-four when the Germans got out of Greece and ELAS turned on its own country—tried to stage a Communist *coup d'état*—and started murdering Greeks with the arms and cash we'd smuggled to them, and which they'd hidden safely away in the mountains till they could use them for the Party."

"But there were other guerrillas who did an honest job, surely?"

"Oh, yes. To begin with there were quite a few groups, and it was Michael's job among other things to try and bring them together in a more or less coherent plan of campaign. But it broke his heart as it broke the heart of every B.L.O. in Greece. ELAS set to work and smashed every other guerrilla organization it could get its filthy hands on."

"You mean actually fought its own people *during* the German occupation?"

"Indeed, yes. Smashed some groups and assimilated others until eventually there was only one other important resistance group, EDES, under a leader called Zervas, an honest man and a fine soldier."

"I remember. You said he was in the Peloponnese."

"That's it. ELAS tried hard to liquidate him too, of course. Don't mistake me, there were some brave and good men with ELAS too, and they did some damned good work, but there was rather a load of . . ." he paused fractionally, "infamy . . . to counteract the better things. It doesn't make good reading, the story of the resistance in Greece. Village after village, raped and burned by the Germans, was thereafter raped and burned by ELAS—their own people—for whatever pathetic supplies they could produce. And the final abomination was the famous battle of Mount Tzoumerka where Zervas with EDES was facing the

Germans, and ELAS under Ares—of all the damned arrogant pseudonyms for
one of the most filthy sadistic devils that ever walked—ELAS waited till Zervas
was heavily engaged, and then attacked him on the flank."

"Attacked *Zervas?* While he was fighting the Germans?"

"Yes. Zervas fought a double-sided battle for several hours, and managed to
beat off the Germans, but he still lost some of his valuable supplies to ELAS,
who stashed them away, no doubt, against the end of the German war and the day
of the New Dawn."

There was a silence, underlined by the humming of the engine. I could smell
dust, and dead verbena. The autumn stars were milky-white and as large as
asters. Against their mild radiance the young cypresses stood like spears.

"And that brings me to the reason for my visit to Delphi," said Simon.

I said, "Michael's third letter?

"You're quick, aren't you? Yes, indeed, Michael's third letter."

He changed gear, and the car slowed and turned carefully onto a narrow bridge
set at right angles to the road. He went on in his pleasant, unemotional voice, "It
came after we had had news of his death. I didn't read it then. In fact, I never
knew Father had had it. I suppose he thought it would bring the thing alive again
for me, when I'd just got over the worst. I was seventeen. And later, Father never
talked about Michael. I didn't know of the letter's existence till six months ago,
when Father died, and I, as his executor, had to go through his papers. The
letter . . ."

He paused again, and I felt a curious little thrill go through me—the inevitable
response (conditioned by tales told through how many centuries?) to the age-old
device of fable: the dead man . . . the mysterious paper . . . the frayed and
faded clue leading through the hills of a strange land. . . .

"The letter didn't say much," said Simon. "But it was—I don't know quite
how to describe it—it was excited. Even the writing. I knew Michael pretty well,
for all the difference in our ages, and I tell you he was as excited as all-get-out
when he wrote that letter. And I think it was something he'd found, somewhere
on Parnassus."

Again that queer little thrill. The night swooped by, full of stars. On our left
the mountain loomed like the lost world of the gods. All of a sudden it didn't
seem possible that I was here, and that this—this ground where our tires
whispered through the dust—was Parnassus. The name was a shiver up the
spine.

I said, "Yes?" in a very queer voice.

"You must understand," he said, "that when I read that letter in the end, I
read it against a background of information picked up after the war. We'd found
out, my father and I, just where and how Michael had been working, and we'd
talked to some of the fellows he'd met here. We were told that he'd been sent up
into this area in the spring of nineteen forty-three and for over a year before he
was killed he was working with one of the ELAS bands whose leader was a man
called Angelos Dragoumis. I couldn't learn very much about this Angelos—that
was the name he was generally known by, and I gather that it was desperately
inappropriate; only one of the other Force One Thirty-three chaps had actually
met him, and the few enquiries I've made here in the last day or so have been
quietly stone-walled. The Greeks aren't proud of men like Angelos. I don't mean
that his group didn't do one or two brilliant things: they were with Ares and

Zervas when the Gorgopotamos viaduct was destroyed in the teeth of the Germans, and there was the affair of the bridge at Lidorikion, where they—oh, well, that doesn't matter just now. The thing is that this man Angelos seems to have rather modeled himself on the ELAS Commander, Ares, and he made himself felt in the country hereabouts just as Ares did."

"You mean he plundered his own side?"

"That and worse. The usual beastly record of burning and rape and torture and smashed houses, and people—where they weren't murdered—left to starve. The extra unpleasant touch is that Angelos came from this district himself . . . yes, I know. It's hard to take, isn't it? He's dead, anyway . . . at least, that's the assumption. He vanished across the Yugoslav border when the Communist *putsch* failed in December, nineteen forty-four and he hasn't been heard of since."

"I imagine that in any case he'd not dare reappear in these parts," I said.

"True enough. Well, anyway, that was the man Michael was working with, and, as I say, they did get some pretty good results in the military line—but then the Germans arrived here in force, and Angelos' band scattered and went into hiding in the hills. Michael, I gather, was on his own. He evaded capture for some weeks, hiding somewhere up here on Parnassus. Then one day a patrol spotted him. He got away, but one of their bullets hit him—not a bad wound, but enough to disable him, and with no attention it might have proved serious. One of his contacts was Stephanos, the shepherd from Arachova that we're going to see tonight. Stephanos took Michael in, and he and his wife nursed and hid him and would, I think, have got him out of the country if the Germans hadn't descended on Arachova while Michael was still here."

Along the road the young cypresses stood like swords. They had come along this very road. I said, "And they found him."

"No. But they'd been told he was here, and so they took Stephanos' son Nikolaos out and shot him, because his parents wouldn't give Michael away."

"Simon!"

He said gently, "It was a commonplace. You don't know these people yet. They stood and let their families be murdered in front of them rather than betray an ally who'd eaten their salt."

"The other side of the picture," I said, thinking of ELAS, and Angelos.

"As you say. And when you think harshly of ELAS, remember two things. One is that the Greek is born a fighting animal. Doesn't their magnificent and pathetic history show you that? If a Greek can't find anyone else to fight, he'll fight his neighbor. The other is the poverty of Greece, and to the very poor, any creed that brings promise has a quick way to the heart."

I said, "I'll remember."

"Perhaps we've forgotten," he said, "what poverty means. When one sees . . . ah, well, never mind now. But I think that most things can be forgiven to the poor."

I was silent. I was remembering Philip again, and a beggar under the ramparts at Carcassonne; Philip saying "Good God!" in a shocked voice, dropping five hundred francs into the scrofulous hand, and then forgetting it. And now here was this quiet, easy voice, talking in the dark of past infamies, expressing as a matter of course the sort of enormous and tolerant compassion that I had never met—in the flesh—before. . . .

"Poor naked wretches, wheresoe'er you are,
That bide the pelting of this pitiless storm,
How shall your houseless heads and unfed sides,
Your looped and windowed raggedness, defend you . . .?"

It came to me with a shock like an arrow out of the dark that—mystery or no mystery—I liked Simon Lester very much indeed.

He said, "What is it?"

"Nothing. Go on. The Germans shot Nikolaos and Michael left."

"Yes. Apparently he moved out again into the mountains. After this point I know very little about what happened. So far I've pieced together the bare facts from what we were told after the war by one of the other B.L.O.'s who was over here, and from the priest at Delphi, who wrote to my father some time back, when he was making his first enquiries."

"Didn't Stephanos write?"

"Stephanos can't write," said Simon. "What happened next we can only guess at. Michael went off back into the hills after the tragedy of Nikolaos' death. His shoulder wasn't fully healed, but he was all right. Stephanos and his wife wanted him to stay, but Nikolaos had left a small son and a daughter, and . . . well, Michael said he wasn't risking any more lives. He went. And that's all we know. He went up there"—a gesture toward the shadow-haunted mountain—"and he was caught and killed there, somewhere on Parnassus."

I said after a minute or two, "And you want to talk to Stephanos and find out where he is?"

"I know where he is. He's buried at Delphi, in a little graveyard not far from the studio, above the shrine of Apollo. I've been to the grave already. No, that's not what I want from Stephanos. I want to know just where Michael died on Parnassus."

"Stephanos knows?"

"He found the body. It was he who sent Michael's last letter off, together with the other things he found on the body. He got them smuggled somehow to this other B.L.O. and we got them eventually. We didn't know who'd sent them until later we were officially told that Michael was buried at Delphi. We wrote to the *papa*—the priest. He told us the simple facts, so of course my father wrote to Stephanos, and got a reply through the priest again, and—well, that seemed to be that."

"Until you saw Michael's letter."

"Until I saw Michael's letter."

We had rounded a shadowy bluff and there ahead, pouring down the mountainside like a cascade, were the steep lights of Arachova.

The car drew gently in to the side of the road and stopped. Simon switched the engine off and reached into an inner pocket for a wallet. From this he took a piece of paper and handed it to me.

"Wait a moment till I get my lighter to work. Would you like a cigarette?"

"Thank you."

After we had lighted our cigarettes he held the little flame for me while I unfolded the flimsy paper. It was a scrawl on a single sheet of cheap paper, smudged as if with rain, a bit dirty, torn here and there along the old folds, and dog-eared from being read and re-read. I opened it gently. I had the queerest feeling that I shouldn't have been touching it.

It was fairly short. "Dear Daddy," it began . . . why should there be something so very endearing about the thought of Michael Lester, a tough twenty-seven, using the childhood's diminutive? . . .

"Dear Daddy, God knows when you'll get this, as I see no chance of its getting taken off in the near future, but I've got to write. We've been having a bit of a party, but that's over now and I'm quite all right, so don't worry. I wonder, do you find this code of army-slang clichés as bloodily maddening as I do? At the best of times I suppose it has its uses, but just now—tonight—there is something I really want to say to you; to record, somehow, on paper—nothing to do with the war or my job here or anything like that, but still impossible to commit to paper and how *the hell* can I get it across to you? You know as well as I do that anything might happen before I see anyone I can send a private message by. If my memory were a little better—and if I'd paid a bit more attention to those classical studies (oh God, a world ago!) I might send you to the right bit in Callimachus. I think it's Callimachus. But I've forgotten where it comes. I'll have to leave it at that. However, I'm seeing a man I can trust tomorrow, and I'll tell him, come what may. And all being well, this'll be over some day soon, and we'll come back here together to the bright citadel, and I can show you then—and little brother Simon too. How is he? Give him my love. Till the day—and what a day it'll be!

"YOUR LOVING SON,
"MICHAEL."

The signature was a scrawl, running down almost off the page. I folded the paper carefully, and gave it back to Simon. He snapped the lighter out, and put the letter carefully away. He said, "You see what I mean?"

"Well, I don't know your brother, but I take it that wasn't his usual style."

"Far from it. This reads very oddly to me. Queer, rapid, allusive; almost—if I didn't know Michael so well—hysterical. A feminine type of letter."

"I see what you mean."

He laughed, and started the engine. "Sorry. But it's my guess he really was under some strong emotion when he wrote that letter."

"I think I'd agree. Of course he was in a tough spot, and—"

"He'd been in dozens before. And then all that about a private message, and 'getting it across.' He really had something to say."

"Yes. I take it you've had a look through your Callimachus, whoever he may be?"

"I have. He wrote a deuce of a lot. No, there's no clue there."

"And the 'bright citadel'?"

"That's a translation of a phrase the Delphic Oracle once used to Julian the Apostate. I think that must be the one he means. It refers to Apollo's shrine at Delphi."

"I see. That doesn't get us much further."

We were moving again toward the lights of Arachova. I said, "You used the word 'clue.' Just what are you hoping to find, Simon?"

"What Michael found."

After a little pause I said slowly, "Yes, I see. You mean the bit about 'we'll come back here together to the bright citadel and I'll show you'?"

"Yes. He'd found something and he was excited about it and he wanted to 'record' it—he uses that word, too, remember?"

"Yes. But don't you think that perhaps—?" I stopped.

"Well?"

I said, with some difficulty, "Might you not be seeing something that isn't there? I do agree it's an odd letter, but there's another way of reading it, isn't there? A quite simple way. It's the way that I'd have taken it myself . . . except of course that I didn't know your brother Michael."

"And that way?"

"Well, say it *was* excitement, or rather emotion, of a sort, wouldn't there be a reason for it? Might he not quite naturally have things he wanted to say to your father and to you? I mean . . ." I stopped again, embarrassed.

He said simply, "You mean it was plain and simple affection? That Michael may have had a premonition he'd not get out of the jam he was in, and wanted to say something to my father . . . a sort of farewell? No . . . no, Camilla, not Michael. If he felt very deeply about people he kept it to himself. Nor do I think he'd dabble in 'premonitions.' He knew the risks and he didn't fuss. Besides he does say he wants to 'show' Father something, and me . . . here, in Greece."

"Perhaps the country itself. Heaven knows it's exciting enough. Would your father have been interested?"

Simon laughed. "He was a classicist too. He'd been here half a score of times before."

"Oh. Oh, I see. Yes, that does make a difference."

"I think so. No, I'm right. He'd found something, Camilla." A tiny pause, and that electric thrill again, which quivered to nothing as Simon added flatly, "I'm pretty certain I know what it was, too, but I could bear to make sure. And for a start, I'd like to know just where Michael died, and how. . . ."

Another pause. He must have been thinking back to my remarks about the letter, for he said thoughtfully, "No, all things taken together, I know I'm right. Though it does seem a little odd. . . . You may be right about the 'emotion'— though it wouldn't be like Mick. He was the most casual-seeming devil to talk to that you ever knew. It took quite some time before you guessed that he was probably the toughest too, and the most self-sufficient."

Like little brother Simon. . . . The thought came so pat and so clearly that for one terrible moment I was afraid I had said it aloud. And I had an uncomfortable feeling that he knew just what I was thinking.

I said quickly and idiotically, "Here's Arachova."

It was one of the rather less necessary remarks. Already we were hemmed in by the crowding walls, and the colored rugs—still hanging outside the vividly lit shops—almost brushed the sides of the car. There were two or three donkeys, freed from rope and saddle, wandering loose in the street. I saw a goat on someone's garden wall. It gave us an evil, gleaming glance before it leaped away into shadow and vanished. There was the familiar smell of dust and dung and gasoline fumes and the lees of wine.

Simon parked the car in the place where it had been that afternoon. He stopped the engine and we got out. We walked back toward the steep alleyway, where I had first seen him. Opposite the foot of it was one of the village cafés, a dozen tables in a whitewashed room open to the road. Most of the tables were full. The men watched us . . . or rather, they didn't look at me. They all watched Simon.

He paused at the foot of the alley and put a hand under my elbow. I saw that light, wary look touch the groups of dark-faced men, linger, leave them. He smiled down at me.

"Up here," he said, "and watch where you go. The steps are tricky and the donkeys have provided a few extra natural hazards. Stephanos, naturally, lives at the very top."

I looked up. The alley was about four feet wide and had a gradient of one in three. The steps were just too far apart and were made of sharp chunks of Parnassus with the minimum of dressing. The donkeys—a herd of healthy donkeys—had been that way many times. There was one dim light halfway up.

For some reason it occurred to me at that moment to wonder just what I had got myelf into. ELAS, Stephanos, a man called Michael dying on Parnassus and lying bleaching to earth again above Delphi . . . all this, out of nowhere, and now a steep dark little alley and the pressure of Simon's hand on my arm. I wondered sharply just what we were going to learn from Stephanos.

And suddenly, I knew that I didn't want to hear it.

"Avanti," said Simon beside me, sounding amused.

I pushed the coward impulse aside, and started up the alleyway.

6

. . . Seek
Thy brother with a tale that must be heard
Howe'er it sicken.

EURIPIDES: *Electra*
(tr. Gilbert Murray)

STEPHANOS' HOUSE was a small two-storied building, set at the top of the stairway. Its bottom storey opened straight on the alley, and housed the beasts—a donkey and two goats and a gaggle of skinny hens—while stone stairs led up the outer wall of the house to the top storey where the family lived. At the head of the steps a wide concrete platform served as porch and garden in one. Its low parapet was crowded with pots full of greenery, and roofed with a trellis of rough branches which formed a pergola for the vine. I saw Simon stoop to avoid a loaded bough, and a hanging bunch of grapes brushed my cheek with a cold gentle touch. The top half of the door was open, and the light streamed out to gild the vine tendrils. There was a hot oily smell from the family's supper, mixed with goat, and donkey, and the furry musk-smell of geraniums where I had brushed a hand against one of the flowerpots.

We had been heard coming up the steps. As we crossed the platform the lower half of the door opened, and an old man stood there, large against the weak light from within.

I paused. Simon was behind me, still in shadow. I moved aside to let him pass me, and he came forward, hand outstretched, with some greeting in Greek. I saw the old man stiffen as he peered out. His mouth opened as if to make some involuntary exclamation, then he seemed to draw back a little. He said formally, "Brother of Michael, you are welcome. The woman of the house said you would come tonight."

Simon withdrew the hand which the old man hadn't appeared to notice, and said, with equal formality, "My name is Simon. I'm glad to meet you, *Kyrie* Stephanos. This is *Kyria* Haven, a friend who has brought me down in her car."

The old man's look touched me, no more. He inclined his head, saying slowly, "You are both welcome. Be pleased to come in."

He turned, then, and went into the room.

I should perhaps make it clear here that this and most of the subsequent conversation was in Greek, and that therefore I didn't understand it. But afterwards Simon gave me as exact a translation as he could, and at the time I was able to follow what I may perhaps call the emotional movements of the conversation. So I shall set the interview down as it occurred.

It seemed apparent to me, from the first short exchange on the balcony, that our welcome wasn't exactly a glowing one, and this surprised me. I had seen during my stay in Greece so much of the miracle of Greek hospitality, that I was both disconcerted and repelled. It didn't worry me that Stephanos hadn't spoken to me—I was only a woman, after all, and as such had pretty low social rating—but his rejection of Simon's outstretched hand had been quite deliberate, and his gesture now, as he invited us to follow him in, was heavy and (it seemed) reluctant.

I hesitated, glancing at Simon doubtfully.

He didn't appear to be in the least put out. He merely lifted an eyebrow at me, and waited for me to precede him into the house.

The single living and sleeping room of the house was high and square. The floor was of scrubbed boards, the walls whitewashed and hung with vivid holy pictures in appalling colors. Light came from a single naked electric bulb. In one corner stood an old-fashioned oil stove, and above it shelves for pans and a blue curtain that no doubt concealed food and crockery. Against one wall was an immense bed, covered now with a brown blanket and obviously used during the day as a sofa. Above the bed hung a small icon of the Virgin and Child, with a red electric bulb glowing in front of it. A Victorian-looking cupboard, a scrubbed table, a couple of kitchen chairs and a bench covered with cheap oil cloth made up the rest of the furniture. A note of vivid color was supplied by the one rug on the boarded floor. It was locally woven, in brilliant scarlet and parrot green. The room had the air of great poverty and an almost fierce cleanliness.

There was an old woman sitting over near the stove on one of the hard chairs. I took her to be Stephanos' wife—the woman of the house. She was dressed in black, and even in the house wore the Moslem-looking headscarf, which veils mouth and chin, and which gives the field workers of Greece such an Eastern look. It was pulled down now below her chin, and I could see her face. She looked very old, as the peasant women of the hot countries do. Her face had lovely bones, fine and regular, but the skin had dried into a thousand wrinkles, and her teeth had decayed. She smiled at me and made a gesture of shy welcome, to which I responded with a sort of bow and an embarrassed "Good evening" in Greek, as I took the chair she indicated. She made no further move to greet us, and I noticed that her look in reply to Simon's greeting was uneasy, almost scared. Her gnarled hands moved in her lap, and then she dropped her eyes to them and kept them there.

Simon had taken the other chair near the door, and the old man sat down on the bench. I found myself staring up at him. So much a part of the land of myth was he that he might have come straight out of Homer. His face was brown, wrinkled like the woman's, and in expression patriarchal and benevolent. The white hair and beard were curled like those of the great Zeus in the Athens Museum. He was dressed in a sort of long tunic of faded blue, buttoned close down the front and reaching to his thighs; beneath it he wore what looked like white cotton jodhpurs bound at the knee with black bands. On his head was a small soft black cap. The knotted, powerful hands looked as if they were uneasy without a crook to grasp.

He looked at Simon under thick white brows, ignoring me. The look was grave and—I thought—measuring. In the corner beside me, the old woman sat silent. I could hear the animals moving about below us, and the quick tread of someone coming up the alley from the street.

Stephanos had just opened his mouth to speak, when there was an interruption. The quick steps outside mounted the stone stairs at a run. A youth came across the balcony with a rush and paused in the doorway, one hand on the jamb of the door, the other thrust into his waistband. It was a very dramatic pose, and he was a very dramatic young man. He was about eighteen, lean and brown and beautiful, with thick black curls and a vivid, excited face. He wore ancient striped flannels, and the loudest and most awful shirt I have ever seen.

He said, "Grandfather? He's come?"

Then he saw Simon. He didn't appear to notice me at all, but I was getting used to that, and merely sat quiet, like the woman of the house. The boy flashed a delighted smile at Simon, and a flood of rapid Greek, which was interrupted by his grandfather's saying repressively, "Who told you to come, Niko?"

Niko whirled back to him. All his movements were swift like those of a graceful but restless young cat. "They told me at Lefteris' that he had come again. I wanted to see him."

"And now you see him. Sit down and be silent, Niko. We have much to say."

I saw Niko throw a quick appraising glance at Simon. "Have you told him?"

"I have told him nothing. Sit down and be silent."

Niko turned to obey, but his look lingered on Simon. The dark eyes glinted with something that could have been excitement mixed with amusement—or even malice. Simon met it with that masked indifferent look that I was beginning to know. He had taken out his cigarette case and now he glanced at me. I shook my head. "Niko?" The boy put out a hand, then stopped, drew it back, and sent Simon another of his vivid smiles. "No, thank you, *kyrie*." A glance at his grandfather, then he crossed to the big bed and threw himself on it. Simon found his lighter, lit a cigarette with a certain deliberation, then put his lighter carefully back in his pocket before he turned to Stephanos.

The latter was sitting motionless. He still didn't speak. The silence came back, heavy, charged, and the boy stirred restlessly on the bed. His eyes never left Simon's face. Beside me the woman hadn't moved, but as I glanced at her I saw her eyes slide sideways to meet mine, only to drop swiftly to the hands in her lap as if in an ecstasy of shyness. I realized then that she had been covertly studying my frock, and the knowledge came to me suddenly, warmingly, that Stephanos, too, was shy.

Perhaps Simon had divined this too, for he didn't wait for Stephanos, but spoke easily, bridging the moment.

"*Kyrie* Stephanos, I'm very glad to meet you at last, and the woman of your house. My father and I wrote to you to thank you for what you did for my brother, but—well, letters can't say it all. My father is dead now, but I'm speaking for him too when I say thank you again. You'll understand it isn't always possible to put into words all that one feels—all one would like to say, but I think you will understand what I feel, and what my father felt." He turned his head to smile at the woman. She didn't smile back. I thought she made a little sound as if of pain, and she moved in her chair. Her narrow lips worked in and out, and her fingers gripped each other painfully.

Stephanos said, almost roughly, "There is nothing for you to say, *kyrie*. We did no more than we should."

"It was a very great deal," said Simon gently. "You couldn't have done more if he, too, had been your son." A quick glance at the old woman. "I shan't say much about that, *kyria,* because there are memories that you won't want to revive; and I shall try not to ask any questions that might distress you. But I had to come and thank you, for my father, and for myself . . . and to see the house where my brother Michael found friends in the last days of his life."

He paused, and looked round him slowly. There was silence again. Below us the animals shuffled and one of them sneezed. There was nothing in Simon's face to read, but I saw the boy's speculative glance on him again before it turned as if in impatience to his grandfather. But Stephanos said nothing.

At length Simon said, "So it was here."

"It was here, *kyrie*. Below, behind the manger, there is a gap in the wall. He hid there. The dirty Germans did not think to look behind the sacks of straw, and the dung. Would you like me to show you?"

Simon shook his head. "No. I told you I don't want to remind you of that day. And I don't think I need ask you anything much about it, as you told us most of it in the letter that the *papa* wrote for you. You told me how Michael had been wounded in the shoulder and had come here for shelter, and how, after . . . later on, he went back into the mountains."

"It was just before dawn," said the old man, "on the second of October. We begged him to stay with us, because he was not yet well, and the wet weather comes early in the mountains. But he would not. He helped us to bury my son Nikolaos, and then he went." He nodded toward the intent youth on the bed. "There was that one, you understand, and his sister Maria, who is since married to Georgios who has a shop in the village. When the Germans came the children were out in the fields with their mother, or who knows? They too might have been killed. *Kyrie* Michael"—he pronounced it as a trisyllable, Mi-ha-eel—"would not stay, because of them. He went up into the mountains."

"Yes. A few days later he was killed. You found his body somewhere over between here and Delphi, and you took it down to be buried."

"That is so. What I found on his body I gave after three weeks to Perikles Grivas, and he took it to an Englishman who was going by night from Galaxeidion. But this you know."

"This I know. I want you to show me where he was killed, Stephanos."

There was a short silence. The boy Niko watched Simon unwinkingly. I noticed that he had taken out a cigarette of his own and was smoking it.

The old man said heavily, "I will do that, of course. Tomorrow?"

"If it's convenient."

"For you, it is convenient."

"You're very good."

"You are the brother of Michael."

Simon said gently, "He was here a long time, wasn't he?"

Beside me the woman moved suddenly and said in a clear soft voice, "He was my son." I saw with a wrench of discomfort that there were tears on her cheeks. "He should have stayed," she said, and then repeated it almost desperately, "He should have stayed."

Simon said, "But he had to go. How could he stay and put you and your family in that danger again? When the Germans came back—"

"They didn't come back." It was Niko who spoke, clearly, from the bed.

"No." Simon turned his head. "Because they caught Michael in the mountains. But if they hadn't caught him—if he had still been hiding here—they might have come back to the village, and then—"

"They did not catch him," said the old man.

Simon turned back sharply. Stephanos was sitting still on the bench, knees apart, hands clasped between them, his heavy body bent slightly forward. His eyes looked fathoms dark under the white brows. The two men stared at one another. I found myself stirring on my hard chair. It was as if the scene were taking place in slow motion, silent and incomprehensible, yet powered with emotions that plucked uncomfortably at the nerves.

Simon said slowly, "What are you trying to tell me?"

"Only," said Stephanos, "that Michael was not killed by the Germans. He was killed by a Greek."

"By a Greek?" Simon echoed it almost blankly.

The old man made a gesture that might have come straight from *Oedipus Rex*. To me, still not understanding anything except that the men's talk had an overtone of tragedy, it conveyed a curiously powerful impression of resignation and shame.

"By a man from Arachova," he said.

It was at this moment that the light chose to go out.

The Greeks were obviously accustomed to the whims of the electric system. With scarcely a moment's delay the old woman had found and lit an oil lamp, and placed it on the table in the middle of the room. It was a frightful-looking lamp of some cheap bright metal, but it burned with a soft apricot light and the sweet smell of olive oil. With the heavy shadows cast on his face, Stephanos looked more than ever like a tragic actor. Niko had rolled over on his stomach and was watching the two other men bright-eyed, as if it were indeed a play. I supposed that, for him, his father's death and Michael's seemed so remote that this talk of them was no more than a breath from an exciting past.

Simon was saying, "I . . . see. That makes a lot of things a lot plainer. And of course you don't know who it was."

"Indeed we do."

Simon's brows shot up. The old man smiled sourly. "You are wondering why we have not killed him, *kyrie,* when we called Michael our son?"

From the bed Niko said in a smooth voice that was certainly malicious, "That is not the way the English work, grandfather."

Simon flicked him a look but said, mildly, to Stephanos, "Not exactly. I was wondering what had happened to him. I gather he's alive."

"I'll explain. I should tell you first of all that the man's name was Dragoumis. Angelos Dragoumis."

"*Angelos?*"

The old man nodded. "Yes. You know of him, of course. I told you in the letter the *papa* wrote for me that Michael had worked with him. But I should never have told you this of Angelos, if you had not come. Now that you are here, these things cannot be hidden. It is your right to know."

Simon was carefully extinguishing his cigarette in the lid of a matchbox. His face was still and shuttered, his eyes hidden. I saw the boy Niko roll over again on the bed and grin to himself.

"You know that Angelos was the leader of the ELAS troop that Michael was working with," said Stephanos. "When Michael left here he went up, I think, with the intention of rejoining them. They had scattered when the big German search operation started in the hills, and most of them had moved north, Angelos with them. What brought Angelos back in this direction I don't know, but certain it is that he fetched up against Michael over on Parnassus and murdered him there."

"Why?"

"I do not know. Except that such murders were not rare in those days. It may be that Michael and Angelos had had some quarrel over the action of Angelos' troops. Perhaps Michael was putting too much pressure on him; we know now that Angelos was anxious to save his men and his supplies for a different battle later—after the Germans had gone."

I saw Simon look up sharply, those light-gray eyes vividly intent. "Angelos was one of them? Are you sure?"

"Certain. He played for high stakes, did Angelos Dragoumis. He was in Athens soon after the Germans had left Greece, and we knew he was active in the massacre at Kalamai. Oh yes, you may be sure that he was betraying the Allies all the time."

He smiled thinly. "I do not think that Michael can have known. No, this was some other quarrel. It may simply have been that two such men could never come together, and agree. Angelos was bad, bad from the heart, and Michael . . . he did not like having to work with such a one. They had quarreled before. He told me so. Angelos was an arrogant man, and a bully, and Michael—well, Michael could not be driven either."

"True enough." Simon was selecting another cigarette. "But you said he was 'murdered.' If two men quarrel and there's a fight, that isn't murder, Stephanos."

"It was murder. It was a fight, but not a fair one. Michael had been wounded, remember."

"Even so—"

"He was struck from behind first, with a stone or with the butt of a gun. There was a great mark there, and the skin was broken. It is a miracle that the blow didn't kill him, or stun him, at least. But he must have heard Angelos behind him, and turned, because in spite of the traitor's blow from behind, and Michael's wounded shoulder, there was a fight. Michael was—a good deal marked."

"I see." Simon was lighting his cigarette. "How did Angelos kill him? I take it he wasn't using a gun. A knife?"

"His neck was broken."

The match paused, an inch from Simon's cigarette. The gray eyes lifted to the old man's. I couldn't see their expression from where I sat, but I saw Stephanos nod, once, as Zeus might have nodded. Niko's eyes narrowed suddenly and glinted between their long lashes. The match made contact. "It must have been quite a scrap," said Simon.

"He wouldn't be easy to kill," said the old man. "But with the wounded shoulder, and the blow on the head . . ."

His voice trailed off. He wasn't looking at Simon now; he seemed to be seeing something beyond the lamplit walls of the room, something remote in place and time.

There was a pause. Then Simon blew out a long cloud of tobacco smoke. "Yes," he said. "Well. And the man Angelos . . . what happened to him?"

"That I can't tell you. He has not been back to Arachova, naturally. It was said that he went with many of his kind into Yugoslavia, when their bid for power failed. In fourteen years, nobody has heard of him, and it is probable that he is dead. He had only one relative, a cousin, Dimitrios Dragoumis, who has had no news of him."

"A cousin? Here?"

"Dragoumis lives now at Itea. He also fought in Angelos' troop, but he was not a leader, and—well, some things are best forgotten." The old man's voice roughened. "But the things that Angelos did to his own people, these are not forgotten. He was at Kalamai; it is said he was also at Pyrgos, where many hundred Greeks died, and among them my own cousin Panos, an old man." The gnarled hands moved convulsively on his knees. "No matter of that. . . . But I do not speak merely of his politics, *Kyrie* Simon, or even of what such as he do in war. He was evil, *kyrie,* he was a man who delighted in evil. He liked the sight of pain. He liked best to hurt children and old women, and he boasted like Ares of how many he himself had killed. He would put a man's eyes out—or a woman's—and smile while he did it. Always that smile. He was an evil man, and he betrayed Michael and murdered him."

"And if he has not been seen here since my brother died, how can you be sure he murdered him?"

"I saw him," said the old man simply.

"You saw him?"

"Yes. It was he beyond doubt. When I came on them he turned and ran. But I couldn't follow him." He paused again, one of those heavy terrible little pauses. "You see, Michael was still alive."

I saw Simon's eyes jerk up again to meet his. The old man nodded. "Yes. He lived only a minute or so. But it was enough to hold me there beside him and let Angelos get away."

"Angelos made no attempt to attack you?"

"None. He, too, had been badly mauled." There was satisfaction in the old shepherd's eyes. "Michael died hard, even with that traitor's bash on the back of the head. Angelos might have shot at me, but later I found his revolver lying under a boulder, as if it had been flung there in the struggle. The countryside was full of Germans, you see, and he must have counted on killing Michael quietly, after he'd stunned him, but he wasn't quick or clever enough, and Michael managed to turn on him. When I came to the head of the cliff and saw them below me, Angelos was just getting to his feet. He turned to look for his gun then, but my dog attacked him, and it was all he could do to get clear away. Without his gun, he could have done nothing." He wiped his mouth with the back of a knotted brown hand. "I took Michael down to Delphi. It was the nearest. That's all."

"He didn't speak?"

Stephanos hesitated, and Simon's glance sharpened. Stephanos shook his head. "It was nothing, *kyrie*. If there had been anything I would have put it in the letter."

"But he did speak?"

"Two words. He said, 'The Charioteer.' "

The words were *"O Eniochos,"* and they were classical, not modern, Greek. They were also familiar to me, as to many visitors to Delphi, because they refer to the famous bronze statue that stands in the Delphi Museum. It is the statue of a youth, the Charioteer, robed in a stiffly pleated robe, still holding in his hands the reins of his vanished horses. I glanced at Simon, wondering where, in an exchange bristling with the names "Angelos," and "Michael," the Charioteer could have a place.

Simon was looking as puzzled as I. ''The Charioteer'? Are you sure?"

"I am not quite sure. I had run hard down the path to the foot of the cliff, and I was out of breath and much distressed. He lived only a matter of seconds after I got to him. But he knew me, and I thought that was what he said. It is a classical word, but of course it is familiar because it is used of the statue in the Delphi Museum. But why Michael should have tried to tell me about that, I do not know. If indeed that was what he whispered." He straightened his back a little. "I repeat, I would have told you if I had been sure, or if it had meant anything."

"Why did you not tell us about Angelos?"

"It was over then, and he had gone, and it was better to let Michael's father think he had died in battle and not at the hands of a traitor. Besides," said Stephanos simply, "we were ashamed."

"It was so much over," said Simon, "that when Michael's brother comes to Arachova to find out just how his brother died, the men in Arachova avoid him, and his host won't shake his hand."

The old man smiled. "Very well, then. It is not over. The shame remains."

"The shame isn't yours."

"It is that of Greece."

"My country's done a thing or two lately to balance it, Stephanos."

"Politics!" The old man made a gesture highly expressive of what he would wish to see done to all politicians, and Simon laughed. As if at a signal, the old woman got to her feet, pulled back the blue curtain, and brought out a big stone jar. She put glasses on the table and began to pour out the dark sweet wine. Stephanos said, "You will drink with us, then?"

"With the greatest of pleasure," said Simon. The old woman handed him a glass, then Stephanos, Niko, and finally me. She didn't take one herself, but remained standing, watching me with a sort of shy pleasure. I sipped the wine. It was as dark as mavrodaphne and tasted of cherries. I smiled at her over the glass and said tentatively, in Greek, "It's very good."

Her face split into a wide smile. She bobbed her head and repeated delightedly,

"Very good, very good," and Niko turned over on the bed and said in American-accented English, "You speak Greek, miss?"

"No. Only a few words."

He turned to Simon. "How come you speak such good Greek, eh?"

"My brother Michael taught me when I was younger than you. I went on learning and reading it afterward. I knew I would come here one day."

"Why you not come before?"

"It costs too much, Niko."

"And now you are rich, eh?"

"I get by."

"*Oriste?*"

"I mean, I have enough."

"I see." The dark eyes widened in a limpid look. "And now you have come. You know about Angelos and your brother. What would you say if I told you something else, *kyrie?*"

"What?"

"That Angelos is still alive?"

Simon said slowly, "Are you telling me that, Niko?"

"He has been seen near Delphi, on the mountain."

"What? Recently?" said Simon sharply.

"Oh, yes." Niko flashed that beautiful mischievous smile up at him. "But perhaps it is only a ghost. There are ghosts on Parnassus, *kyrie,* lights that move and voices that carry across the rocks. There are those who see these things. Myself, no. It is the old gods, not?"

"Possibly," said Simon. "Is this the truth, Niko? That Angelos was seen?"

Niko shrugged. "How can I tell? It was Janis who saw him, and Janis is—" he made a significant gesture toward his forehead. "Angelos killed his mother when the *andartes* burned his father's farm, and ever since then Janis has been queer in the head, and has 'seen' Angelos—oh, many times. If ghosts are true, then he still walks on Parnassus. But Dimitrios Dragoumis—that is true enough. He has asked many questions about your coming. All the men here in Arachova know that you are coming, and they talk about it and wonder—but Dragoumis, he has been to Delphi and to Arachova and has asked questions—oh, many questions."

"What is he like?"

"He is a little like his cousin. Not in the face, but in the—what do you say?— the build. But not in the spirit either." His look was innocent. "It may be that you will meet Dragoumis. But do not be afraid of him. And do not worry yourself about Angelos, *Kyrie* Simon."

Simon grinned. "Do I look as if I was worrying?"

"No," said Niko frankly, "but then, he is dead."

"And if Janis is right, and he is not dead?"

"I think," said Niko almost insolently, "that you are only an Englishman, *Kyrie* Simon. Not?"

"So what?"

Niko gave a charming little crack of laughter and rolled over on the bed. Stephanos said suddenly and angrily, in Greek, "Niko, behave yourself. What does he say, *Kyrie* Simon?"

"He thinks I couldn't deal with Angelos," said Simon idly. "Here, Niko, catch." He threw the boy a cigarette. Niko fielded it with a graceful clawed gesture. He was still laughing. Simon turned to Stephanos. "Do you think it's true that Angelos has been seen hereabouts?"

The old shepherd slanted a fierce look at his grandson under his white brows. "So he has told you that tale, has he? Some rumor started by an idiot who has seen Angelos at least a dozen times since the end of the war. Aye, and Germans too, a score of times. Don't pay any attention to *that* moonshine."

Simon laughed. "Or to the lights and voices on Parnassus?"

Stephanos said, "If a man goes up into Parnassus after sunset, why should he not see strange things? The gods still walk there, and a man who would not go carefully in the country of the gods is a fool." Another of those glowering looks at his grandson. "You, Niko, have learned a lot of folly in Athens. And that is a terrible shirt."

Niko sat up straight. "It is not!" he protested, stung. "It is American!"

Stephanos snorted and Simon grinned. "Aid to Greece?"

The old man gave a gruff bark of laughter. "He is not a bad boy, *kyrie,* even if Athens has spoiled him. But now he comes home to work, and I will make a man of him. Give *Kyrie* Simon some more wine." This to his wife, who hurried to refill Simon's glass.

"Thank you." Simon added, in a different tone, "Is it true that this man Dragoumis has been asking questions about me?"

"Quite true. After it was known that you were coming, he asked many questions—when you came, for how long, what you meant to do, and all that." He smiled sourly. "I don't speak much to that one, me."

"But why? Why should he be interested? Do you suppose he had anything to do with Michael's death?"

"He had nothing to do with it. That much we found out after the war, before he came back here. Otherwise he would not," said Stephanos simply, "have dared come back. No, he knew nothing about it. Once before, a year—more—eighteen months ago—he spoke to me and asked me what had happened, and where it was that Michael was killed. He showed a decent shame and he spoke well of Michael; but I do not talk of my sons to every man. I refused to speak of it. And no one else knew the whole truth except the priest at Delphi who is since dead, and my own brother Alkis who was killed in the war."

"And now me."

"And now you. I will take you there tomorrow and show you the place. It is your right."

He looked up under the white brows at Simon for another considering moment. Then he said slowly, irrelevantly, "I think, *Kyrie* Simon, that you are very like Michael. And Niko—Niko is even more of a fool than I had thought. . . ."

7

The Oracles are dumm,
No voice or hideous humm
   Runs through the arched roof in words deceiving
Apollo from his shrine
Can no more divine . . .

MILTON: *Nativity Hymn*

SIMON DIDN'T speak on the way back to Delphi, so I sat quietly beside him, wondering what had been said in that somber and somehow very foreign-seeming interview. Nothing that Stephanos—exotically Homeric—had said could have been ordinary, while about Niko's racy intelligent beauty there was something essentially Greek—a quicksilver quality that is as evident today under the cheaply Americanized trappings of his kind as it was in the black and red of the classical vase paintings.

When at length, as we neared Delphi, trees crowded in above the road blocking out the starlight, Simon slowed the car, drove into a wide bay, and stopped. He switched the engine off. Immediately the sound of running water filled the air. He turned out the lights, and the dark trees crowded closer. I could smell the pines, cool and pungent. They loomed thick in the starlight, rank on rank of scented stone pines crowding up toward the cleft where the water sprang. Beyond the trees reared the immense darkness of rock, the Shining Ones no longer shining, but pinnacles and towers of imminent blackness.

Simon took out cigarettes and offered one to me. "How much of that did you understand?"

"Nothing whatever, except that you were talking about Michael and the ELAS leader Angelos." I smiled. "I see now why you didn't mind my sitting in on your private affairs."

He said abruptly, "They've taken a very queer turn."

I waited.

"I'd like to tell you, if I may."

"Of course."

So we sat there in the car and smoked, while he told me, fully and accurately, what had passed in the shepherd's cottage. So vivid were my own visual impressions of the recent scene that I was able without difficulty to impose my picture, so to speak, over his, and see where movement and gesture had fitted in with the words.

When he had finished I didn't speak, for the sufficient reason that I could find nothing to say. The instinct that had halted me at the foot of the alley steps had been a true one: these waters were too deep for me. If I had felt myself inadequate before—I, who had been afraid of a mild skirmish over a hired car—what was I to feel now? Who was I, to offer comfort or even comment on a brother's murder? The murder might be fourteen years old, but there's a kind of shock in the very word, let alone the knowledge of the deed, however many years lie between it and the discovery. I didn't know Simon well enough to say the right thing, so I said nothing.

He himself made no comment, beyond telling me the story of the interview in that give-nothing-away voice of his that I was beginning to know. I did wonder fleetingly if he would say anything more about Michael's letter, or about the "find" which he, Simon, had said he knew of. . . . But he said nothing. He threw his finished cigarette over the side of the car into the dust, and it appeared that he threw the story with it, because he said, with a complete change of tone and subject:

"Shall we walk up through the ruins? You haven't seen them yet, and starlight's not a bad start. Unless, of course, you'd rather wait and see them for the first time alone?"

"No. I'd like to go."

We went up the steep path through the pines. Now that my eyes were used to the darkness it was just possible to see the way. We crossed the narrow rush of water and were on a track soft with pine needles.

After a while we came out from under the trees into an open space where fallen blocks made treacherous walking, and dimly in the starlight I could see the shape of ruined walls.

"The Roman market place," said Simon. "Those were shops and so on over there. By Delphi's standards this is modern stuff, so we by-pass it quickly. . . . Here we are. This is the gate of the temple precinct. The step's steep, but there's a wide smooth way up through the buildings to the temple itself. Can you see?"

"Fairly well. It's rather . . . stupendous by starlight, isn't it?"

Dimly I could make out the paved road that zigzagged up between the ruined walls of treasuries and shrines. The precinct seemed in this light enormous. Everywhere ahead of us, along the hillside, below among the pines that edged the road, above as far as the eye could reach in the starlight, loomed the broken walls, the spectral pillars, the steps and pedestals and altars of the ancient sanctuary. We walked slowly up the Sacred Way. I could make out the little Doric building that once housed the Athenian treasure, the grim stone where the Sybil sat to foretell the Trojan War, the slender pillars of the Portico of the Athenians, the shape of a great altar . . . then we had reached the temple itself, a naked and broken floor, half up the mountainside, held there in space by its massive retaining walls, and bordered with the six great columns that even in the darkness stood emphatic against the star-crowded sky.

I took a little breath.

Beside me, Simon quoted softly, " 'The gods still walk there, and a man who would not go carefully in the country of the gods is a fool.' "

"They *are* still here," I said. "Is it silly of me? But they are."

"Three thousand years," he said. "Wars, treachery, earthquake, slavery, oblivion. And men still recognize them here. No, it's not silly of you. It happens to everyone with intelligence and imagination. This is Delphi . . . and, well, we're not the first to hear the chariot wheels. Not by a long way."

"It's the only place in Greece I've really heard them. I've tried to imagine things—oh, you know how one does. But no, nothing, really, even on Delos. There are ghosts at Mycenae, but it's not the same. . . ."

"Poor human ghosts," he said. "But here . . . I suppose that if a place was, like Delphi, a center of worship for—how many?—about two thousand years, something remains. Something inheres in stone, I'll swear, and here it's in the very air. The effect's helped by the landscape; I suppose it must be one of the most magnificent in the world. And of course this is just the setting for the holy place. Come up into the temple."

A ramp led up to the temple floor, which was paved with great stone blocks, some broken and dangerous. We picked our way carefully across this until we stood at the edge of the floor, between the columns. Below us was the sheer drop of the retaining wall; below that the steep mountainside and the ghosts of the scattered shrines. The far valley was an immensity of darkness, filled with the small movements of the night wind, and the sound of pine and olive.

Simon's cigarette beside me glowed and faded. I saw that he had turned his back on the spaces of the starlit valley. He was leaning against a column, gazing up the hill behind the temple. I could see nothing there but the thick shadows of trees, and against them more pale shapes of stone.

"What's up there?"

"That's where they found the Charioteer."

The word brought me back to the present with the tingle of a small electric shock. I had forgotten, in the overpowering discovery of Delphi, that Simon would have other preoccupations.

I hesitated; it was he, after all, who had sheered away from the story onto the neutral ground of Delphi. I said a little awkwardly, "Do you suppose Stephanos was right? Does it make any kind of sense to you?"

"None at all," he said cheerfully. His shoulder came away from the pillar. "Why don't you come up to the studio now, and meet Nigel, and have some coffee or a drink?"

"I'd like to, of course, but isn't it awfully late?"

"Not for this country. As far as I can make out nobody goes to bed at all, except in the afternoons. When in Greece, you know. . . . Are you tired?"

"Not a bit. I keep feeling I ought to be, but I'm not."

He laughed. "It's the air, or the light, or the simple intoxication of being alive in Hellas. It lasts, too. Then you will come?"

"I should love to."

As I picked my way across the temple floor with his hand under my arm I had time to feel surprise at myself, and a sort of resignation. Here I went again, I reflected. . . . Just in this way I had drifted along at Philip's bidding, in Philip's wake. But this was different. Just what the difference was I didn't stop to analyze.

I said, "Aren't we going down to the road? Why this way?"

"We don't need to go down. The studio's away up above the temple, just over the mountain's shoulder toward Delphi. It's easier to go up through the rest of the shrine."

"But the car?"

"I'll go and get it later when I've seen you down to your hotel. It's no distance from there by the road. This way, and watch your step. It's easier here. . . . These steps lead up toward the little theatre. That thing on the right was put up by Alexander the Great after a narrow escape in a lion hunt. . . . Here's the theatre. It's tiny compared with Athens or Epidaurus, but isn't it a gem?"

In the starlight the broken floor looked smooth. The semi-circular tiers of seats rose, seemingly new and unbroken, toward their backdrop of holly and cypress; it lay, a little broken marble cup of a theatre, silent except for the tiny scuffling of a dry twig that the breeze was patting idly along the empty flags.

I said on an impulse, "I suppose you wouldn't—no, I'm sorry. Of course not."

"What do you suppose I wouldn't do?"

"Nothing. It was silly, under the circumstances."

"The circumstances? Oh, that. Don't let that worry you. I suppose you want to hear something recited here in Greek, even if it's only *thalassa! thalassa!* Is that it? . . . What's the matter?"

"Nothing. Only that if you go on reading my thoughts like that you're going to be a very uncomfortable companion."

"You ought to practice too."

"I haven't the talent."

"Perhaps that's just as well."

"What d'you mean?"

He laughed. "Never mind. Was I right?"

"Yes. And not just *thalassa,* please. Some lines of verse, if you can think of anything. I heard someone reciting in the theatre at Epidaurus and it was like a miracle. Even a whisper carried right up to the topmost tier."

"It does the same here," he said, "only it's not so stupendous. All right, if you'd like it." He was feeling in his pockets as he spoke. "Half a minute; I'll have to find my lighter. . . . If you want to get your voice properly carried you have to locate the center of the stage . . . it's marked by a cross on the flagstones. . . ."

As he pulled the lighter from his pocket I heard the small musical chink of metal on stone. I stooped quickly after the sound. "Something fell; some money, I think. Here . . . not far away, anyway. Shine the light down, will you?"

The lighter flicked into flame and he bent with it near the ground. Almost immediately I saw the sharp gleam of a coin. I picked it up and held it toward him. The orange-colored flame slid alive and sparkling across the little disc in my palm. I said, "That's surely—*gold?*"

"Yes. Thank you." He took it and dropped it into his pocket. He might have been discussing a lost halfpenny, or at most a threepenny stamp. "That was one of the souvenirs that Stephanos sent us. I told you he sent what was on Michael's body when he died. There were three of these gold sovereigns." He moved away from me, holding the lighter low over the flags, searching for the central mark. You'd have thought there was nothing in his mind except the pleasant task of showing a girl over the Delphic ruins.

"Simon . . ."

"Here it is." He straightened up, the lighter still burning in his hand. He must have seen my look, because he smiled at me, that sudden, very attractive smile. "You know, I did tell you it was no longer a present tragedy, didn't I? I told you not to worry. Now, come here to the center, and hear how your voice is picked up and carried high over those tiers of seats."

I moved forward to the spot. "I know you did. But when you told me that, you didn't know that your brother Michael had been murdered. Doesn't that make a difference?"

"Perhaps. There, do you hear the echo?"

"Glory, yes. It's weird, isn't it? As if the sound were coming back at you from those crags up there, and swirling all round you. It's like something tangible; like—yes, like sound made solid. . . . Are you really going to recite something, or would you rather not?"

I thought he misunderstood me deliberately. "With this lack of audience, I think I might. What'll you have?"

"You're the classicist. I leave it to you. But wait a moment. I'm going up into the back stalls."

I climbed the narrow aisle and found a seat two thirds of the way up the amphitheatre. The shaped marble of the seat was surprisingly comfortable, and the stone was still warm from the day's sun. The circular stage looked small below me. I could just make out its shape. Simon was nothing but a bodiless shadow. Then his voice came up out of the well of darkness, and the great rolling Greek lines rose and broke and echoed, rounding like a wind among the high crags. A phrase, a name, swam up from the flood of sound, giving directions to the music, like flights to an arrow. "Hades, Persephone, Hermes. . . ." I shut my eyes and listened.

He stopped. There was a pause. The echo went up the cliff, hung like the murmur of a gong, and died. Then his voice came clearly and softly, speaking in English; music translating music.

". . . Hades, Persephone,
Hermes, steward of death,
Eternal Wrath and Furies,
Children of gods,
Who see all murderers
And all adulterous thieves, come soon!
Be near me, and avenge
My father's death, and bring
My brother home!"

He had stopped speaking again. The words died into silence high above me, and in the wake of the echo, it seemed, the night wind moved. I heard the hollies rustle behind me, and then, further up the hill, a scatter of dust and pebbles under the foot of some wandering beast, a goat, perhaps, or a donkey; I thought I heard the clink of metal. Then the night was still again. I got up and started down the steep aisle.

Simon's voice came, pitched quietly and perfectly clear. "That do?"

"Beautifully." I reached the bottom and crossed the stage. "Thank you very much; but—I thought you said the tragedy was over?"

For the first time since I had known him (some seven hours? Could it possibly be only half a day?) he sounded disconcerted. "What d'you mean?" He left the center of the stage and came to meet me.

"That speech was a bit—immediate, wasn't it?"

"You recognized it?"

"Yes. It's from Sophocles' *Electra*, isn't it?"

"Yes." There was a pause. He had a hand in his pocket, and now as he withdrew it I heard the chink of coins. He jingled them absently up and down. Then he said, "I was wrong, then. It's not over . . . at least not until Stephanos shows us the place tomorrow, and—"

He stopped. I reflected that Simon Lester seemed to have a remarkably royal habit of using the first person plural. I should have liked to say " 'Show *us?* ' " but didn't. I said merely, "And?"

He said abruptly, "And I find what Michael found—what he was killed for. The gold."

"The gold?"

"Yes. I told you I'd an idea what it was that Michael might have found. I thought that, as soon as I read his letters, and remembered the sovereigns he was carrying. And after what Stephanos told us, I'm sure. It was gold he found, Angelos' little hoard of British gold, stashed away against the day of the Red Dawn."

"Yes, but Simon . . ." I began, then stopped. He knew Michael better than I did, after all.

The sovereigns clinked together as he thrust them back into his pocket. He turned away toward the side of the amphitheatre.

"This is the way up to the path. I'd better go first, perhaps; the steps are badly broken in places."

He reached a hand back to me, and together we mounted the steep flight. At the top he paused and seemed to reach up into the darkness. I heard the rustle of leaves. He turned back to me and put something round and polished and cool into my hand. "There you are. It's pomegranate. There's a little tree growing behind the topmost seats, and I've been longing for an excuse to pick one. Eat it soon, Persephone; then you'll have to stay in Delphi."

The path led us out at last above the trees, where we could see our way more clearly. It was wide enough now to walk side by side. Simon went on, speaking softly, "I think I'm right, Camilla; I think that's what Michael found. I'd suspected it before, but now I know he was murdered by this man Angelos, I'd bet on it for a certainty."

I said rather stupidly, still following my own thoughts, "But Stephanos said he was killed in a quarrel. Angelos and he—"

"If Michael had been quarrelling with a type like that he wouldn't be very likely to turn his back on him," said Simon. "I'm surprised Stephanos didn't think that one out for himself."

"But if it was an old quarrel, and Michael thought it was forgotten, but Angelos—"

"The same applies. I just don't see Michael trustfully turning his back on a man who'd once had—or thought he had—the sort of grudge that leads to murder."

"I suppose not."

"But take all the bits of the picture and put them together," said Simon, "and what d'you get? I told you that we—the British—were flying in arms and gold during the Occupation, for the use of the *andartes*. Angelos, as we now learn from Stephanos, was working for the Communist *putsch* at the end of the German Occupation of Greece; therefore, we can assume that he had an interest in holding back arms and supplies for later use. That's an assumption; but what facts have we? Angelos, when his men scatter northwards to avoid the Germans, comes south—alone. He meets Michael and kills him. He is interrupted before he can search the body, and on Michael are found gold sovereigns, and a hastily scribbled letter indicating that he has found something."

"Yes," I said, "but—"

"If Angelos had such a cache of guns and gold, and Michael, the B.L.O., had found it, would it not be the complete motive for Michael's murder?"

"Yes, of course it would. You mean that Michael, when he met him, tackled him about it and—oh, no, that won't do, will it? There's the same objection—that Angelos wouldn't have had the chance to hit him over the head."

"I can't help thinking," said Simon softly, "that Angelos saw something that told him Michael had found the cache. It's probably in some cave or other—Parnassus is honey-combed with them; and supposing that Michael, after he left Stephanos' house, had taken shelter in the one where the stuff was hidden? He'd stay there a few days till the Germans left the area, and then Angelos, doubling back to his treasure chest, would see the British officer coming out of the cave, his cave. . . . It could be, you know. And if Michael didn't see Angelos, as seems obvious, the Greek waited and took his chance and tried to wipe him out then and there. Which means—"

"Which means that, if you're right, the cache was very near the place where Michael was murdered," I said.

"Exactly. Well, we shall see."

"If there was anything, it'll have been taken long since."

"Probably."

"Angelos would come back and take it. If not immediately, then later."

"If he lived to come back. Three months after Mick's death he was out of the country for good."

I said, as casually as I could, "Was he? And what if Niko was possibly—just possibly—right? If he *were* still alive? Now, I mean?"

Simon laughed. "It's on the lap of the gods, isn't it?" One of the coins spun in his hand as he tossed it and caught it. "What do you say? Shall we offer gold to Apollo if he'll bring Angelos back to Delphi now?"

"Aegisthus to Orestes' knife?" I tried to speak equally lightly, but in spite of myself the words sounded harsh and hollow.

"Why not?" The coin dropped into his hand again and his fingers closed on it. He was a shadow in the starlight, watching me. "You know, I told you the truth when I said the tragedy was over. I don't feel chewed up or dramatic about Mick's death, even after what I've learned tonight. But, damn it all, he was murdered, in a filthy way, and—if I'm right—for the filthiest of motives. And the murderer got away with it, and possibly with a fortune into the bargain. I've no particular desire to find the fortune, but I want to know, Camilla. That's all."

"Yes, I see."

"I came here to talk to Stephanos and see Michael's grave, and to leave it at that. But I can't leave it now, not till it's really over, and I know why it happened. I don't suppose there'll be anything left to tell me, after all this time, but I have to look. And as for Orestes"—I heard the smile in his voice—"I've no particular ambition for revenge, either, but if I did meet the murderer . . . don't you see that I'd quite like a word with him?" He laughed again. "Or do you share Niko's opinion of my abilities?"

"No. No, of course not. But this man Angelos . . . well, he's—" I floundered and stopped.

"Dangerous? So you don't think that—if I do meet him—I ought to have it out with him?"

"An eye for an eye?" I said. "I thought we didn't believe in that anymore."

"Don't you believe it. We do. But in England there's a fine, impersonal, and expensive machinery to get your eye for you, and no personal guilt except your signature on a cheque to the Inland Revenue. Here, it's different. Nobody's going to do the dirty work for you. You do it yourself and nobody knows but the vultures. And Apollo."

"Simon, it's immoral."

"So is all natural law. Morals are social phenomena. Didn't you know?"

"I don't agree."

"No? You stick to that, Camilla. This is the loveliest country in the world, and the hardest. Much of it, and you're apt to find yourself thinking in its terms instead of your own. There are times, I'd say, when you have to. . . . But you stand by your guns." He laughed down at me. "And for a start, don't believe a word I say. I'm a normal law-abiding citizen, and a most upright and solemn schoolmaster. . . . Now, enough of this Orestean tragedy. Michael's dead these fourteen years, and Delphi's been here three thousand, so we'll let Delphi bury its dead. It does it just here, incidentally; that's the graveyard just beside the path, under the trees. And now, if you're to get any sleep at all tonight, what about chasing up that drink? That's the studio there."

Without another glance in the direction of the graveyard, he led the way at a quickened pace over level ground toward the lights of the studio.

8

Whom the gods love . . .

Menander
(tr. Lord Byron)

THE STUDIO was a big rectangular building situated on top of the bluff behind the village of Delphi. Later, in daylight, I was to see it as a big ugly box of a place, set down on a flat plateau quarried out of the living rock, so that, while its front windows commanded a magnificent view of the valley, its back looked out onto a wall of rock as high as its second storey. On this, the north side, were the big "front" doors, impressive affairs of plate glass which were never used. The tenants got in and out by a small door in the east end, which gave on the corridor running the length of the ground floor.

Inside, the place was as bare and functional as possible. Corridors and stairs were of marble, and spotlessly clean. On the lower floor, and to the left of the corridor, were the artists' bedrooms, facing south over the valley. These were simple in the extreme, each bedroom holding nothing but an iron bedstead with blankets and pillows, a washbasin with h. and c. both perpetually c., a small and inevitably unsteady table, and hooks for hanging clothes. Opening off each bedroom was a marble-floored shower stall—also, presumably, c. Opposite the bedrooms were other doors which I never saw opened, but which I imagined might be some sort of kitchen premises, or rooms for the caretaker. The resident artists worked on the upper floor where the light was better; here a row of rooms on the north side of the corridor served as studios and storerooms for their work.

But all this I was to discover later. Tonight the building was merely an ugly oblong box of a place planted down in a small quarry, with the light from a bare electric bulb showing us the door.

We had hardly got into the echoing corridor, when a door a short way along it opened, and a young man came out like a bullet from a gun. He caught at the jamb of the door as he catapulted out and hung on, almost as if he felt the need of the door's support. He said in a high excited voice, "Oh, Simon, I was just—" Then he saw me and stopped, disconcerted, still theatrically posed in the stream of light that came from the door.

There was something about this method of appearance that was very like Niko's, but there the resemblance ended. The young man—who I supposed was Nigel—had none of Niko's beauty or promise of strength, and very little, in consequence, of Niko's assurance. There was no conscious drama in his actions, and indeed now he was looking miserably embarrassed, almost as if he would have liked to retreat into his room and lock the door. He was tallish, and thin, and fair. His skin had taken the sun badly, and his eyes, which were that puckered blue that you see in sailors and airmen and men who habitually gaze into the distances, looked as if they had had too much sun. He had a straggling little beard that made him look young and rather vulnerable, and his hair was bleached to the color and texture of dry hay. He had a weakly sensual mouth and the strong ugly hands of the artist.

Simon said, "Hullo, Nigel. This is Camilla Haven, who's staying at the Apollon. I've brought her up for a drink, and she wants to see your drawings. Do you mind?"

"Oh. No. Not at all. Delighted," said Nigel, stammering a little. "C-come into my room, then. We'll have a drink here." As he stood aside for me to pass him, slightly more flushed than before, I found myself wondering if he had been drinking alone in his room. There was that queer look about his eyes, a sort of sense that he was clutching at himself as really, as physically, as he had clutched at the door jamb, and in the same effort to control.

His room, basically as bare as the rest of the building, was frantically but rather pleasantly untidy. It was as if the artist's personality, far richer than it appeared from the look of him, had spilled over without his knowing it into the monastic-looking little cell. At the foot of the bed a rucksack stood on the floor, its contents bursting out in confusion. I saw two shirts, as brightly but rather more respectably colored than Niko's, a tangle of rope, some dirty handkerchiefs which had obviously been pressed into use as paint rags, three oranges, and a copy of the *Collected Poems of Dylan Thomas*. The towel which was flung over the edge of the washbasin was as brightly yellow as a dandelion. Nigel's pajamas, in a huddle on the bed, were striped in wine and turquoise. And everywhere on the cracked white walls there were sketches, drawing-pinned haphazardly; they were in a variety of styles, so that, looking from the bold to the delicate, from the pencil sketches to the watercolors curling up at the edges as they dried, I remembered what Simon had told me.

But I had no time to do more than glance, because our host had dived past me, and was dragging forward the room's best chair, a canvas affair of grubby orange.

"W-won't you sit down, Miss—Er? It's the best there is. It's quite clean really."

I thanked him and sat down. Simon had wandered over to the window, and hitched himself up onto the wide sill, where he sat, one leg swinging. Nigel, still with that air of disconcerted fussiness, was rummaging rather wildly among bottles on the floor of the shower stall. In a moment he emerged clutching two tumblers and a large bottle of ouzo.

"Do you like this stuff?" he asked me anxiously. "It's all there is."

There was something about Nigel that disarmed me into a deliberate lie. "I love it," I said, and waited resignedly while he poured a generous dollop into one of the tumblers, and handed it to me. "Would you like water with it?"

Now, ouzo is the Greek absinthe. It is made from aniseed, and tastes fairly mild and (to my mind) incredibly unpleasant. I find it quite undrinkable neat. On the other hand, if you add sufficient water to make it swallowable, there is a lot more to swallow.

I said bravely, "Yes, please."

Nigel grabbed a carafe from above the washbasin. Again it struck me sharply that his movements were a parody of Niko's. They were swift and abrupt and angular, but where Niko's had the grace of a striking cat, Nigel's were clumsy and almost uncoordinated. It was odd for an artist to be clumsy, I thought, then as I watched Nigel pour water into my glass, I saw that his hand was shaking. That was still odder.

The liquid misted, clouded, and went entirely beastly like quinine. I said, "When. Thanks," and smiled at Nigel, who was watching me with an anxious-puppy expression that made him look younger than ever. He was, I judged, about twenty-three, but the beard made him look nineteen. I smiled bravely and lifted the glass.

"*Gia sou, Kyrie* Nigel," I said. "I'm sorry, but I don't know your other name."

"Make it Nigel," he said unhelpfully, but with apparent pleasure.

As I drank carefully, I caught Simon's eye, to see that he knew quite well what I felt about ouzo. I scowled at him and took another drink, reflecting yet again that *Kyrie* Simon Lester saw a damned sight too much. I controlled the shudder that shook me as the liquor went down, and then watched fascinated as Nigel filled Simon's tumbler two thirds full, grabbed a glass for himself and filled that, and then raised it to his lips, said "*Gia sou*" quickly, and drank half of it at one fell gulp, neat.

"Cheers, comrade," said Simon. "Have you had a good day?"

Nigel, choking a little over the liquor, managed to say, "Yes. Oh, yes, thanks. Very."

"Where did you go?"

The young man waved a vague hand, which almost knocked the ouzo bottle off the table, but unfortunately didn't quite. "Up there."

"You mean up in the precinct?"

"No. Up the hill."

"Onto Parnassus again? Did you go up over the old track to hunt up some shepherds after all?" He turned to me. "Nigel's got a contract for a series of drawings of 'Hellenic types'—heads of peasants and old women and shepherd boys and so forth. He's done some quite striking ones in a sort of heavy ink line-and-wash."

Nigel said suddenly, "It's exciting. You can't know how exciting. You see a grubby little boy watching the goats, and when you really start to draw him you realize you've seen him a dozen times already in the museums. And I found a girl last week in Amphissa who was pure Minoan, crimped hair and all. It makes it difficult, too, of course, because try as you will, it looks as if you're copying the original Grecian Urn."

I laughed. "I know. I've met one Zeus and one rather wicked Eros and a couple of dozen assorted satyrs today already."

"Stephanos and Niko?" said Simon.

I nodded. "Nigel ought to meet them."

Nigel said, "Who are they?"

"Stephanos is a shepherd from Arachova and he's straight out of Homer. Niko's his grandson and he's—well, simply a beauty, American-Greek style. But if it's only the head you want, you could hardly do better." I reflected, as I spoke, that Simon had apparently told Nigel nothing about Michael or his mission that evening.

Nor did he tell him now. He said, "You may meet them yet. Stephanos is usually somewhere up between Delphi and Arachova—near that track I took you over yesterday. Is that the way you went again today? How far?"

"Quite a long way." Nigel looked round him vaguely, as if embarrassment had descended on him again, and added quickly, "I was sick of sitting about in the precinct and the valley. I wanted a walk. I got up above the Shining Ones and onto the track and then—well, I just went on walking. It was hot, but up there, there was a breeze."

"No work today?"

Simon's question was no more than idle, but a flush had crept up under Nigel's raw sunburn. It made him look cagey, but I guessed it was only shyness. He said, "No," very shortly, and buried his nose in his glass.

I said, "No shepherds playing pan-pipes to their flocks? On Parnassus? You shake me, Nigel."

He grinned at that. "No, more's the pity."

"And no gods?" I said, thinking of the starlit temple.

But his shyness asserted itself here completely. He said, almost snappily, "No! I tell you I did hardly anything! I was just walking. Anyway those heads are a bore. They're only bread and butter. You wouldn't like them."

"I'd love to see some of your work, though, if you could be bothered to show it. Simon's been telling me how awfully good your drawings are—"

He interrupted in a voice so quick and hoarse that it gave the effect of a small outburst of temper. "Good? Simon's talking bilge. They're not good. They please me, but that's all."

"Some of them are, very good," said Simon quietly.

Nigel sneered at him. "The niminy-piminy ones. The sweet little Ruskin-and-water ones. Can't you just hear the Sunday-paper critics turned loose over them? They're useless and you know it."

"They're first class and *you* know it. If you could—"

"Oh God, if, if, if," said Nigel rudely. He set his glass down on the table with a sharp click. "You know damn well they're useless."

"But they're what you want to do, and they show the way you want to go, and that's the point, isn't it? They are 'Nigel Barlow,' and what's more, they're uncommon."

"*They're useless.*" The repetition was emphatic.

"If you mean they're not easy to make a living out of here and now, I agree. But I still think—"

"'To thine own self be true'?" said Nigel, on a high-edged note that might have been excitement but sounded like bitterness. "Oh God, don't be a prosy old bore! And anyway it doesn't matter a damn. Not a damn, do you hear me?"

Simon smiled at him. I think it was then that I first really saw what lay behind that good-tempered and apparently unruffled self-command of Simon's; what made it so very different from the more flamboyant self-confidence I had envied. Simon cared. He really did care what happened to this casually-met, troubled, and not very attractive boy who was being so wretchedly rude. And that was why he had come back after fourteen years to find out what had happened to Michael. It was not a present tragedy, and he was not, after all, an Orestes. But he cared— for his father's sake, for Stephanos', for the woman's. "Any man's death diminishes me, because I am involved in Mankind." That was it. He was involved in mankind, and, just at this moment, that meant Nigel. "One takes it for granted," he had said, "that one is there to help." I suppose one gets to know men quickest by the things they take for granted.

He had set his glass down and now laced his fingers round one knee. "All right. Exit Polonius. Well, d'you want us to find you a selling line, Nigel?"

Nigel said, not rudely now, but still with a touch of that hot and slightly sulky impatience, "You mean a gimmick to make people come and look at them? A bloody little quick-sales trick to crowd a one-man show somewhere in the wilds of Sheffield or something? Two pretty drawings sold and my name in the local press? Is that what you mean?"

Simon said mildly, "One has to start somewhere. Couldn't you count it as part of the fight? And at least it might mean you hadn't to fall back on the ultimate degradation."

"What's that?" I asked.

He grinned. "Teaching."

"Oh. Well, I do see what you mean," I said.

"I thought you would."

Nigel said sulkily, "It's all very well to laugh, but I wouldn't be any good at it and I should loathe it, and that would be dreadful."

"The final hell," agreed Simon cheerfully. "Well, we must find you a gimmick, Nigel. Make them come to mock and remain to pay. You must make your pictures out of sequins, or do all your painting under water, or get yourself into the popular press as the Man who Always Paints to the Strains of Mozart."

Nigel gave him a reluctant and slightly shamefaced grin. "Count Basie, more likely. All right, what shall it be? *Art trouvé,* or bits of rusty iron twisted any old way and called 'Woman in Love,' or 'Dog eat Dog,' or something?"

"You could always," I said, "travel through Greece with a donkey, and then write a book, illustrated."

Nigel turned to me at that, but with the look of someone who has hardly been listening. I wondered again if he had been drinking too much. "What? A donkey?"

"Yes. There was a Dutch boy in Delphi this evening who'd just got in from Jannina. He'd been walking over the hills like Stevenson, with a donkey, and painting on the way. I gathered that he'd done a lot of sketching in the villages and more or less paid his way with them."

"Oh, that chap. Yes, I've met him. He's here now."

"Of course, I forgot. Simon told me he'd come up here to sleep tonight. Did you see his work?"

"No. He was too tired to bother. He went to bed at about nine, and I think it'd take an atom bomb to wake him." His look lingered on me as if he were with difficulty bringing me into focus and himself back into the conversation. He said slowly, "Being true to oneself . . . knowing that one can do a thing if only the world will give one the chance . . . but having to fight for it every step of the way. . . ." The blurred blue gaze sharpened and fixed itself on Simon. "Simon . . ."

"Yes?"

"You say a gimmick would be 'part of the fight,' because, in the first place, it would make people stop and look? If my stuff's not really good, no gimmick will get it anywhere beyond the first hurdle. You know that. But if it *is* good, then once people have stopped and paid attention, the *work itself* is what'll count. That's true, isn't it?"

"It could be. In your case I imagine a lot might depend on the gimmick." Simon smiled. "I have a feeling that quite a few good artists have been driven along a path they never intended in the first place as anything but an odd deviation—a wallop in the public's eye. Naming no names, but you know who."

Nigel didn't smile. He seemed still hardly to be listening, but very busy following his own thoughts. He hesitated, then said suddenly, "Well, and that's being true to oneself, isn't it? And don't you think *that* means, come what may, one should take what one wants and needs? Go straight ahead the way you know you have to go, and the devil take the hindmost? Artists—great artists—work that way, don't they? And doesn't the end justify them?" As Simon seemed to hesitate, he whipped round on me. "What do *you* think?"

I said, "I don't know specially about great artists, but I've always imagined that the secret of personality—I won't say 'success'—was one-track-mindedness. Great men *do* know where they're going, and they never turn aside. Socrates and the 'beautiful and good.' Alexander and the Hellenizing of the world. On a different level, if I may—Christ."

Nigel looked at Simon. "Well?" His voice was sharp, like a challenge. *"Well?"*

I thought, There *is* something going on here that I don't understand. And I don't think Simon understands it either, and it worries him.

Simon said slowly, those cool eyes vividly alive now, watching the younger man, "You're partly right. The great men know where they're going; yes, and they get there, but surely it's a case of driving themselves without pause, rather than juggernauting over all the opposition? You think Polonius was a prosy old bore—you brought him in, remember, not me. I don't agree with him, but do him the justice of looking at the end of the quotation. 'To thine own self be true, . . . Thou canst not then be false to any man.' If being true to oneself means ignoring the claims of other people then it simply doesn't work, does it? No, your really great man—your Socrates—doesn't drive along a straight path of his own cutting. He knows what the end is, yes, and he doesn't turn aside from it, but all the way there he's reckoning with whatever—and whoever—else is in his way. He sees the whole thing as a pattern, and his own place in it."

I quoted, thinking back, " 'I am involved in Mankind'?"

"Exactly."

"What's that?" said Nigel.

"A quotation from John Donne, a poet who became Dean of St. Paul's. This comes in one of his Devotions . . . 'No man is an island, entire of itself.' He's right. In the end it's our place in the pattern that matters."

"Yes, but the artist?" said Nigel almost fiercely. "He's different, you know he is. He's driven by some compulsion: if he can't do what he knows he *has* to do with his life he might as well be dead. He's got to break through the world's indifference, or else break himself against it. He can't help it. Wouldn't he be justified in doing almost anything to fulfill himself, if his art were worth it in the end?"

"The end justifying the means? As a working principle, never," said Simon. "Never, never, never."

Nigel sat forward in his chair. "Look, I don't mean anything dreadful like— like murder or crime or something! But if there was no other way—"

I said, "What are you planning to do, for goodness' sake? Steal the donkey?"

He swung round on me so sharply that I thought he was going to fall off his chair. Then he gave a sudden laugh that sounded very much to me like the edge of hysteria. "Me? Walk to Jannina and write a book about it? Me? Never! I'd be scared of the wolves!"

"There aren't any wolves," Simon's voice was light, but he was watching Nigel rather closely, and I saw the shadow of trouble in his face.

"The tortoises then!" He grabbed the bottle again and turned back to me. "Have some more ouzo? No? Simon? Here, hold your glass. Did you know, Miss Camilla I've-forgotten-your-other-name, that there were tortoises running about on the hills here? Wild ones? Imagine meeting one of those when you were all alone and miles from anywhere."

"I'd run a mile," I said.

"What *is* it, Nigel?" asked Simon from the windowsill.

For a moment I wondered just what was going to happen. Nigel stopped in mid-movement, with the bottle in one hand. He was rigid. His face went redder, then white, under the peeling sunburn. His ugly spatulate fingers clenched round the bottle as if he were going to throw it. His eyes looked suffused. Then they fell away from Simon's, and he turned to set the bottle down. He said in a curiously muffled voice, "I'm sorry. I'm behaving badly. I was a bit high before you came in, that's all."

Then he turned back to me with one of his quick angular movements that were like those of an awkward small boy. "I don't know what you must think of me. You must think I'm a pretty good heel, but things were getting me down a bit. I—I'm temperamental, that's what it is. Great artists are." He grinned shamefacedly at me, and I smiled back.

"It's all right," I said. "And all great artists have had a horrid struggle for recognition. As long as it doesn't come after you're dead, it's all the sweeter when you get it, and I'm sure you will."

He was down on his knees, lugging a battered portfolio from under the bed. "Here," he said, "I'll show you my drawings. You can tell me if you think they're worth anything. You can tell me." He was dragging a sheaf of papers out of the portfolio.

I said feebly, "But my opinion's no use. I really don't know anything about it."

"Here." He thrust a drawing into my hand. "That's one of the ones Simon talks about. And this." He sat back on his heels on the floor, and sent Simon a look that might almost have been hatred. "I'll be true to myself, Polonius. You can be bloody sure I will. Even if it means being true to nobody else. I'm not involved with mankind, as your old parson friend puts it. I'm myself. Nigel Barlow. And someday you'll know it, you and all the rest. Do you hear?"

"I hear," said Simon peaceably. "Let's see what you've done, shall we?"

Nigel pushed a drawing toward him, and then a handful at me. "This. And this. And this and this and this. They may never set the Thames on fire, but given a push and a bit of luck they're good enough to make me. . . . Aren't they?"

As I looked down at the drawings on my knee I was conscious of Nigel's fixed stare. For all the wild and whirling words the vulnerable look was there again, and on that final question the overemphatic voice had broken into naïve and anxious query. I found myself hoping with ridiculous fervor that the drawings might be good.

They were. His touch was sure and strong, yet delicate. Each line was clean and definite and almost frighteningly effective; he had managed to suggest not only shape, but bulk and texture, by pure drawing with the minimum of fuss. Somehow the technique suggested the faded elegance of a French flower-print combined with the sharp, delicate, and yet virile impact of a Dürer drawing. Some were mere sketches, but over others he had taken greater pains. There were rapid studies of the ruined buildings—part of a broken arch with the sharp exclamatory cypresses behind it; Apollo's columns standing very clear and clean; a delightful drawing of three pomegranates on a twig with shiny drooping leaves. There were several of olive trees, lovely twisted shapes with heads of blown silver cloud. In the plant and flower studies he used color, in faint washes of an almost Chinese subtlety.

I looked up to see him watching me with that anxious-puppy stare from which all trace of belligerence had gone. "But Nigel, they're wonderful! I told you I didn't know much about it, but I haven't seen anything I liked as much in years!"

I got up from my chair and sat down on the bed, spreading the drawings round me, studying them. I picked one of them up; it was the drawing of a clump of cyclamen springing from a small cleft in a bare rock. The textural differences of petal, leaf and stone were beautifully indicated. Below the flowers, in the same cleft, grew the remains of some rock plant that I remember having seen everywhere in Greece; it was dead and dry-dusty, crumbling away against the rock. Above it the cyclamen's winged flowers looked pure and delicate and strong.

Over my shoulder Simon said, "Nigel, that's terrific. I haven't seen it before."

"Of course you haven't. I only did it today," said Nigel rudely, making a quick movement as if to snatch it back. Then he appeared to remember, as I had, that he'd told Simon he had done no work that day, for he dropped his hand and sat back down on his heels, looking uncomfortable.

As usual, Simon took no notice. He lifted the drawing and studied it. "Did you mean to use color in it? What made you change your mind?"

"Simply that there wasn't any water handy." And Nigel took the paper from him and put it back in the portfolio on the floor.

I said, rather quickly, "May I see the portraits?"

"Of course. Here they are—my bread-and-butter drawings." There was a curious note in his voice, and I saw Simon glance again at him, sharply.

There was a whole sheaf of portraits, done in an entirely different style. This was effective in its way, the beautiful economy of his drawing telling even in the thick, dramatic, and overemphatic line. His brilliance of execution had here become a slickness, the clever blending of a few stock statements into a formula. In a way, too, the originals of the portraits might have come from stock. What Nigel had been doing was, of course, to find "types" and to set these down; but, while some of these were discernibly living people, others could have been abstractions of well-known "Hellenic types" taken from statues or vase paintings or even from the imagination. There was one fine-looking head that might have been Stephanos, but it had a formal and over-typed air like an illustration to a set of Greek myths. A girl's face, all eyes, and deep shadows thrown by a veil, could have been captioned, "Greece: the Gate to the East." Another portrait—more familiar in type to me and so possibly more alive—was that of a young woman with the Juliette Gréco face, large lost eyes and a sulky mouth. Beneath it was the drawing of a man's head that, again, seemed purely formal, but was oddly arresting. The head was round, set on a powerful neck, and covered with close curls that grew low on the brow, like a bull's. The hair grew down thickly past the ears, almost to the jawline, as one sees it in the heroic vase paintings, and these sidepieces were drawn in formally, like the hard curls on a sculptured cheek. The upper lip was short, the lips thick, and drawn tightly up at the corners in the fixed half-moon smile that shows always on the statues of the archaic gods of Greece.

I said, "Simon, look at that. That's the real 'archaic smile.' When you see it on crumbly old statues of Hermes and Apollo you think it's unreal and crude. But I've actually seen it on men's faces here and there in Greece."

"Is that new too?" asked Simon.

"Which? Oh, that. Yes." Nigel gave him a quick upward glance, hesitated, then appeared to abandon his pretenses, whatever they were. "I did it today." He took the drawing from me and studied it for a moment. "Perhaps you're right; it's too formal. I did it half from memory, and it's gone a bit too much like a vase painting. However."

"It's the Phormis head to the life," said Simon.

Nigel looked up. "Yes, so it is! That's it. I wondered what he reminded me of. I suppose I drew it in. Still, it makes a 'type' for the collection, and as Camilla says, it does exist. She's seen that queer fixed grin here and there, and so've I. Interesting, I thought."

"What's the Phormis head?" I asked.

Simon said, "It's a head found, as far as I remember, at Olympia, and is supposed to be that of Phormis, who was a playwright. That head is bearded, and this isn't, but it's got the same heavy wide cheeks and tight curls, and that typical smile."

I laughed. "Oh dear, and it's still walking these mountains. It makes me feel raw and new and very, very Western. That face, now—"

My hand was hovering over the Juliette Gréco girl.

Simon laughed. "That's real enough, and very Western indeed," he said. "That's our one and only Danielle, isn't it, Nigel? You're surely not going to put her in among the 'Hellenic types'?"

"Danielle?" I said. "Oh, she *is* French, then? Somehow I thought she looked it."

Nigel had taken the drawing from Simon, and was stuffing that, too, away. He said in a muffled voice, "She was here as secretary to a chap attached to the French School."

"French School?"

"Of archaeology," said Simon. "It's the French School which has the 'right' or whatever they call it to excavate here at Delphi. They've been working here again recently on the site—there was some talk of a hunt for a lost treasury fairly high up the hill. You'll see a lot of exploratory pits dug on both sides of the road, too, but all they found there was Roman."

"Ah, yes. Modern stuff."

He grinned. "That's it. Well, they've had to pack up, because I believe funds gave out. Some of their workmen are still here tidying up—there are trucks and tools and what-have-you to be removed. But the archaeologists have gone, more's the pity."

I saw Nigel throw him a sidelong glance, and remembered suddenly something that Simon had said to me earlier. "He's been here in Delphi too long, and got tied up with a girl who wasn't very good for him."

I said, "Yes. I'd rather have liked to watch them at it. And think of the excitement if anything did turn up!"

He laughed. *"That* sort of excitement, I believe, is the rarest kind! Most of the long years are spent shifting tons of earth a couple of yards, and then putting them back again. But I agree. It would be terrific. And what a country! Did you see that glorious thing of the Negro and the horse that the workmen dug up when they were mending the drains in Omonia Square a few years ago? Imagine wondering what you might find every time you set out to dig your garden or put a plough to the hillside! After all, even the Charioteer—" He stopped, and turned his cigarette over in his fingers as if he were admiring the twist of blue smoke that curled and frothed from it.

Nigel looked up. "The Charioteer?" He was still kneeling on the floor, shuffling the drawings in the folder into some sort of order. "The Charioteer?" he repeated mechanically, as if his mind was on something else.

Simon drew on the cigarette. "Uh-huh. He wasn't dug up till eighteen ninety-six, long after the main shrines and treasuries had been excavated. Not long ago I read Murray's *History of Greek Sculpture,* and wondered why the author was so sketchy about Delphi, till I realized that, when he wrote his book in eighteen ninety, the half was not told him. Who knows what else is still up there in the odd corners under the trees?"

Nigel had sat back on his heels, his hands moving vaguely and clumsily among the drawings. If they were indeed his bread and butter he was, it occurred to me, remarkably careless of them.

He looked up now, the drawings spilling again from his hands.

"Simon." It was that strung-up voice again.

"Well?"

"I think I—" Then he stopped abruptly and turned his head. The studio's outer door had opened and shut with a bang. Rapid footsteps approached along the corridor.

To my surprise Nigel went as white as a sheet. He swung round toward me, swept the rest of the drawings off the bed into an unceremonious heap, then hastily gathered them all together to shove back into the folder on the floor.

As unceremoniously, the door burst open.

A girl stood there, surveying the untidy and crowded little room with an expression of weary distaste. It was the girl of the portrait, Gréco-look and all. It was also, I thought with a lightly quickened interest, the girl whose jeep, outside Thebes, had bullied the bus into submission in such a masterly way. She looked as she had then, completely in control of the situation, and rather bored with it.

She drawled, without removing the cigarette from the corner of her mouth, "Hullo, Simon, my love. Hullo, Nigel. On your knees praying over my picture? Well, the prayer's answered. I've come back."

9

A girl—
No virgin either, I should guess—a baggage
Thrust on me like a cargo on a ship
To wreck my peace of mind!

SOPHOCLES: *Women of Trachis*
(tr. E. P. Watling)

DANIELLE WAS slightly built, of medium height, and had made the most (or the worst, according to the point of view) of her figure by encasing it in drainpipe jeans and a very tight sweater of thin wool, which left nothing to wonder at except how in the world did she get her breasts that shape and into that position. They were very high and very pointed and the first thing that one noticed about her. The second was her expression, which was very much the weary-waif look of Nigel's picture. Her face was oval, and palely sallow. Her eyes were very big and very black, carefully shadowed with a blend of brown and green that made them look huge and tired. She had long curling lashes that caught the smoke wisping up blue from the cigarette that appeared fixed to her lower lip. She wore pale lipstick, which looked odd and striking with the sallow face and huge dark eyes. Her hair was black and straight and deliberately untidy, cut in that madly smart way that looks as if it had been hacked off in the dark with a pair of curved nail-scissors. Her expression was one of world-weary disdain. Her age might have been anything from seventeen to twenty-five. She looked as if she hoped you would put it at something over thirty.

I should perhaps say here that her eyelashes were very long, quite real, and quite beautiful. This is in case it should be thought that my description of Danielle smacks of prejudice. The only reason that I had then for prejudice was the expression on Nigel's face, stuck there on his knees on the floor with his ungainly hands full of the delicate drawings, turning to face the door, and saying *"Danielle!"* in a cracked young voice that gave him away immediately and very cruelly.

He shoved the drawings clumsily into the folder and got to his feet.

After that first greeting she had ignored him. Nor, after one cool glance, had she looked at me. Her eyes were all over Simon.

She said again, "Hullo." I don't quite know how she made the simple dissyllable sound sexy, but she did.

"Hullo," said Simon, not sounding sexy at all. He was looking ever so slightly amused, and also wary, which annoyed me. Why it should, I'm not prepared to say, and didn't try at the time.

Nigel said hoarsely, "What are you doing here? I thought you'd left Delphi."

"I had. But I came back. Aren't you going to ask me in, Nigel dear?"

"Of course. Come in. It's wonderful—I mean I didn't expect you back. Come in. Sit down." He darted forward and dragged out the best chair—the one I had vacated—for her. But she walked past it toward Simon, who was standing by the window. She went very close to him. "I'm sleeping in the studio, Simon. I got tired of the Tourist Hotel, and anyway I can't afford it now. You don't mind me coming here, do you . . . Simon?"

"Not in the very least." He looked across her at me. "You'd better be introduced. Camilla, this, as you'll have guessed, is Danielle. Camilla Haven; Danielle Lascaux. I told you that Danielle was here for some time with the French School. She was Hervé Clément's secretary. You probably know the name. He wrote *Later Discoveries at Delphi*."

"I read it not long before I came here. How d'you do?" I said to Danielle.

She gave me a brief stare, and a barely civil nod. Then she turned, and with what looked like very conscious grace, sat down at the opposite end of the bed from me, curled her slim legs up under her, and leaned back against the bed-head. She tilted her head and sent Simon a long look between narrowed lids. "So you've been talking about me?"

Nigel said eagerly, "It was your portrait—the one I did of you." With one of his ungraceful gestures he indicated the untidily stuffed portfolio lying on the bed beside me.

"Oh, that."

"It's very good, don't you think?" I said. "I recognized you as soon as you came in."

"Uh-huh. Nigel's quite a clever boy, we know that." She sent him a smile that was a shadow of the one she'd given Simon, then reached out an idle hand and pulled two or three sheets out of the folder. I saw Nigel make a small sharp movement, as if of involuntary protest, then he sat down in the orange canvas chair, his hands dangling between his bony knees.

"Yes, I suppose it's a good enough portrait. Are my eyes really as big as that, Nigel?" She was leafing through the drawings: her own portrait; the one we had called the "Phormis head," with the close curls and tight smile; the cyclamen; and a drawing I hadn't yet seen, of a man's head and shoulders. "Flowers?" said Danielle. "Are they *paying* you to do things like that, Nigel? . . . *Who's this?*"

Her voice had changed on the query, so abruptly that I was startled. I saw Simon turn his head, and Nigel almost jumped. "Who? Oh, that. That's a chap I saw today on Parnassus. We were just saying before you came in that he was like—"

"No, no!" She had been holding the Phormis head and another drawing. She dropped the former abruptly, and thrust the other forward. "Not that one. This."

Something in her voice suggested an effort for self-command, and to my surprise her hand was unsteady. But when I said, "May I?" and leaned forward to take the drawing gently from her, she let it go without protest. I looked at it with interest, and then more sharply. It showed the head and bared throat of a young man. The face was beautiful, but not with Niko's vital and very Greek beauty; this was remote, stern, perhaps a little sad. He was not, I thought, a "Hellenic type" at all, though something about him was oddly familiar. But it appeared that he was not intended to form part of Nigel's gallery. This was the only portrait I had seen where Nigel had used what I might call his "flower technique." It was in his own style; the work was delicate, sure and arrestingly beautiful.

"Why, *Nigel* . . ." I said. "Simon, look at this!" Danielle let the others fall to the coverlet. She appeared abruptly to have lost interest, only asking, "Did you do these today?"

"Yes." And Nigel, before Simon had time to do more than glance at the drawing, had finally and this time effectively swept every drawing back into the folder and shoved it under the bed. He looked flustered, and every bit as resentful as he had earlier. But Danielle didn't pursue the subject. She leaned back again and said in her usual slightly bored tone, "For God's sake, Nigel, *are* you going to offer me a drink?"

"Of course." Nigel dived for the bottle of ouzo, put it down again so that it rocked and nearly spilt, then dashed to rinse a tumbler out in the basin.

I put my own glass down and made as if to get to my feet. But at that moment I caught Simon's eye, and I thought he shook his head very slightly. I sat back.

He looked down at the girl. "I thought you'd gone, Danielle. Hasn't the 'dig' packed up?"

"Oh, that. Yes. We got to Athens last night, and really I thought it would be rather a *thing* to be back in civilization again, but I had the most dreary scene with Hervé, and then I thought to myself I really might as well be back in Delphi with . . ." she smiled suddenly, showing very white teeth . . . "back in Delphi. So here I am."

Nigel said, "You mean you've got the sack?"

"You could call it that." She watched him for a moment through the cigarette smoke, then she turned to me. "Simon told you the polite fiction," she said. "Actually, of course, I was Hervé Clément's mistress."

"Danielle!"

"For God's sake, Nigel!" She hunched an impatient shoulder. "Don't pretend you didn't know." Then to me, "But he was getting to be a bit of a bore."

"Really?" I said politely.

I thought her look was calculating under the long lashes. "Yes, really. They all do, sooner or later, don't you think? Do you find men bore you, Camilla Haven?"

"Occasionally," I said. "But then so—occasionally—do women."

That one went straight past her. "I hate women anyway," she said simply. "But Hervé, he was honestly getting to be the utter *end*. Even if he hadn't quit the 'dig' here and gone back to Athens, I'd have had to leave him." She blew out a long cloud of smoke, and turned her head to look up at Simon. "So back I came. But I'll have to sleep here, at the studio. I'm on my own now, so I haven't got the cash for the Tourist Pavilion, or anywhere else for that matter. . . ." She smiled slowly, still looking at Simon. "So I'll have to sleep rough."

What it was in her intonation I do not know, but somehow she managed to say the last simple sentence as if it meant sharing a bed with a sadist, and that meant Simon. I felt another spasm of intense irritation. I knew I should have wanted to feel sorry for Danielle, or even amused, but somehow it wasn't possible. I was beginning to suspect that she was not trying to ape a pathetic maturity; the *weltschmerz* wasn't a pose, it was real, and rather dreadful. So was the weariness in the big lost eyes. But the pity I should have owed her I felt for Nigel, now feverishly drying the tumbler and saying rapidly:

"It's wonderful to have you back. You know that. And of course you must stay in the studio. We'd love to have you, and you'll be quite all right here. There's only me and Simon and a Dutch painter—"

"A Dutch painter?"

Simon said smoothly, "A boy of about twenty who has walked from Jannina and is very, very tired."

She shot him a look up under the fabulous lashes. "Oh." She threw the half-smoked cigarette into the washbasin where it lay smoldering. "Give me another cigarette, Simon."

He obeyed. "Camilla?"

"Thank you," I said.

Nigel pushed past me with a tumbler three parts full of neat ouzo. "Here's your drink, Danielle." His face was anxious, concentrated. He might have been carrying the Holy Grail. She took it from him and gave him a brilliant smile. I saw him blink, and the flush on the burnt cheek-bones deepened. She lifted the glass toward him.

"*Gia sou*, Nigel darling. I'm glad I came back. . . . But you're not drinking with me."

It should have been corny, but it wasn't. The expression on the boy's face was naked. He turned and grabbed the bottle and poured an inch or two of liquor into his empty glass. But even as he turned back, the girl yawned, stretched, tilted her head back on its long neck, and put out a hand toward Simon. Her fingernails were very long and very red. Her fingers ran caressingly down his sleeve. "Actually," she said, still in that bored, velvet voice, "actually, you know, I'm Simon's girl. Aren't I, Simon?"

I must have jumped about a foot. Simon looked down through the smoke of his cigarette, and said lazily, "Are you? Delighted, of course. But perhaps in that case you'll tell me why you hired a car for me in Athens this morning?"

The hand froze, then withdrew quickly. The thin body twisted on the bed in the first movement she had made unconsciously since she came in. It wasn't sexy in the least. It was plain startled. "What are you talking about?"

"The car you hired in my name this morning. The car you were to have picked up at the Alexandros restaurant."

The black eyes held his for a moment, then dropped. "Oh, that." Her voice was calm and husky as usual. "How did you find out?"

"My dear Danielle, you hired it for me, didn't you? And you failed to pick it up. Naturally the people at the Alexandros got in touch with me."

"But that's impossible! How did they know?" She was scowling up at him now.

"Never mind how. Tell me why."

She shrugged and drank ouzo. "I wanted to come back to Delphi. I told you that I hired a car. They never take any notice in Greece of a woman, so I gave your name."

"And said it was a matter of life and death?"

"What? Don't be silly. Of course I never said that." She laughed. "You're very dramatic, Simon."

"Perhaps. A dramatic place, this. It gets into the blood. But you did hire the car."

"Yes."

"And came without it."

"Yes."

"Why?"

I thought unhappily, Because a fool of a girl called Camilla Haven had already taken it. Why couldn't Simon let well enough alone? Somehow I didn't particularly want to tangle with Danielle Lascaux. And she had every right to be mad with me if she had hired the beastly car—in whatever name—and had then presumably had to hunt up other transport for herself when she found it gone. All the same, she would have to be told sooner or later. . . .

"Why?" asked Simon.

She said sulkily, "Because I got the offer of the jeep from Hervé. It was more convenient."

I said, "I was right, then. I thought I recognized you. You were the girl in the jeep that overtook me just before Thebes. I remember you particularly. You were driving on the wrong side of the road."

She yawned, showing her tongue between her teeth. She didn't even look at me. "Probably. I find it more exciting that way."

Simon said, "Then you got up here well before Camilla did. Where've you been?"

She said, almost bad-temperedly, "What's it matter? Around."

I said, "In Itea?"

Danielle shot upright on the bed. Some ouzo spilled. "What are you talking about?" I saw a look of surprise touch Simon's face, then the familiar expressionless mask shut down. With the faintest quickening of the blood, I thought, He's interested. This means something.

I said, "I saw the jeep in Itea this evening. It was parked beside a house that stands right away from the village in the olive woods. I hadn't realized till this minute that it was the same one, but now I remember. It had a little tinsel doll hanging in the windscreen—where they usually have the icons. I remember noticing that when you passed me near Thebes."

She wasn't drinking. The smoke from that eternal cigarette crept up in a veil hiding the expression of her eyes. "This evening? How can you be so sure? Wasn't it dark?"

"Oh, yes. But there was a man with a torch tinkering with the engine, and the light caught the tinsel. Then the lights went on in the house."

"Oh." She drank a gulp of neat ouzo. It didn't appear to affect her. "Well, I expect it was the same jeep. I was down there, with . . . someone I know." Again that intonation, that glance up toward Simon. Nigel was watching her like a lost dog. I thought it was some—surprising—impulse of mercy that made her add, "I always go down to Itea in the afternoons. I've done it for weeks. I go to swim. Nigel knows that."

Nigel responded instantly, almost as if the last sentence had been a plea of proof. "Of course I know. But—did you really go there today before you even came up here?"

"Uh-huh." She gave him a narrow, glinting smile. "You were out, weren't you?"

"Yes."

"I thought you might be. And I'd brought Elena a present from Athens, so—"

"Elena?" said Nigel quickly.

"My friend in Itea. She often bathes from the same place as me, so I went back to her house with her."

"Oh!" said Nigel.

I thought she watched him for a second before she turned back to me. "And you, Camilla Haven? *You* went down to Itea first, before you came up here?"

"I only came up here an hour ago. I'm only visiting. I'm staying at the Apollon."

"But you went straight to Itea." The words were sharp, almost, and sounded so much like an accusation that I said quickly, "I called at the hotel first." Then I added, "I went down to Itea to find the hirer of the car."

There was a little silence. "The . . . hirer of the car?" repeated Danielle.

"Yes. I—it was I who brought the car up from the Alexandros in Omonia Square. I—I was looking for the 'Monsieur Simon' who was alleged to be wanting it."

She blew out a small cloud of smoke and leaned back against the head of the bed, regarding me through it. "I . . . see. You brought my car up here? You?"

"Yes," I said unhappily. "I was in the Alexandros restaurant when the man from the garage came, and he mistook me for you. He gave me the keys and told me it was urgent, and that 'Monsieur Simon' wanted the car at Delphi as soon as possible. I—we got in a muddle of cross-purposes, and he vanished, leaving me with the key, and no idea of the address of the garage. I didn't know what to do, but I wanted to come here myself, and—well, he'd been so insistent that it was a 'matter of life and death' that—"

"That stuff again," said Danielle.

"That stuff again." I added, "I'm glad I don't seem to have inconvenienced you after all. You must have got here well before me. I told you you passed me before Thebes."

She said quite sharply, "And why did you have to go to Itea to find Simon?"

"Oh, I didn't. I—well, he found me quite easily. But of course as he didn't know anything about the car, that didn't help. We went to look for another 'Simon,' actually a Simonides who keeps a baker's shop near the cinema."

"That's not," said Danielle, "in the olive woods."

"No. I went to see the Pilgrims' Way."

"The Pilgrims' Way?" she said blankly.

Simon said, "Yes. You ought to know all about that, Danielle."

She said quickly, "Why?"

"My dear girl. Because you've worked here as an archaeologist's secretary."

"Mistress," said Danielle automatically.

Nigel said suddenly from behind me, "I wish you wouldn't talk like that."

She opened her mouth as if to say something blistering, but shut it again, and gave him one of her slow smiles. I didn't look at him. I said quickly, "Look, Danielle, I really am terribly sorry about this car. I suppose I—yes, I did think I might be doing the right thing, but it seems I was a bit hasty. I do hope it isn't going to cause any inconvenience *now,* because—"

"You brought it up here." She turned her head to give me a narrow look through the curling smoke. "You keep it."

I looked at her for a moment. Then I said slowly, "I suppose that is fair enough."

"You weren't asked to bring it here. I don't want it. You're stuck with it, and I hope you can afford to pay for it." She turned away to flick ash toward the washbasin. It missed and fell to the floor.

There was a short silence. I said carefully, "Whom do I pay?"

Her head came quickly back to me. "What d'you mean?"

"What I said."

"Well, me, of course. Didn't they tell you the deposit had been paid?"

"Oh, yes, they told me that."

"So what?" said Danielle.

I stood up and picked up my handbag. "Only that it surprises me a bit that you didn't call in on the garage after you'd got the jeep, and cancel the car. If you're as short of money as you've been telling us, I'd have imagined the deposit would have come in very handy. In fact, I can't see why you should have hired a car at all. The bus is cheaper. Perhaps you'll let me have the receipt, with the address of the garage?"

She sounded sulky. "Tomorrow. I have it somewhere."

"Very well." I turned to smile at Nigel. "I really must go, Nigel, or it'll be dawn before I get to bed. Thank you very much for the drink, and for letting me see the drawings. I think they're wonderful—I honestly do; and that last one is . . . well, a masterpiece. That isn't trite; it's true. Good night."

Simon was on his feet. As I turned to go, he made as if to move forward, but Danielle came off the bed in one quick wriggle. It brought her very close to him.

"Simon"—the claws were on his arm again—"my room's the one at the end, and the shower's stuck, or something. The damned thing drips and I'll never get to sleep. D'you suppose you could fix it for me?"

"I doubt if I'd be much good with it. In any case I'm seeing Camilla home now, and then I—"

I said stiffly, "There's not the slightest need to see me home. I can find my way quite easily."

"—and then I've got to go back and pick the car up. We left it below the shrine."

Nigel had opened the door for me. I looked back at Simon, with Danielle clinging to his arm. "You really needn't trouble. The car is my responsibility . . . as Danielle has pointed out."

His eyes, amused, met mine. I bit my lip, and said, "All right. I—it's very kind of you."

"Not at all. After all, if the car was hired in my name I've a sort of responsibility myself, wouldn't you say, Danielle?"

She flashed me one look of pure venom, under her lashes, then lifted them again to him. Her voice was all honey. "Not really. But if that's how you feel. . . . You'll come and fix that shower later, won't you? It really is a bore."

"Not tonight," said Simon. "Good night. Good night, Nigel, and thanks a lot. See you later."

On the way down to the hotel—which took about twelve minutes and was very steep and rough—we concentrated on not breaking our ankles and on not talking about Danielle. For me, the first was the easier task of the two.

At the hotel Simon said, "Camilla."

"Yes?"

"Come off it."

I laughed. "Very well."

"I grant you every right to the highest horse, or deepest dudgeon, or whatever it is, in Christendom. All right?"

"Perfectly."

"Don't worry about the damned car. I didn't pursue it in front of—well, back there, but I'll be very glad of it myself now that it's here, so don't give it another thought."

"I will not," I said clearly, "allow you to pay for my—my folly."

"We will not," said Simon calmly, "argue about it now. You should be in bed. You've had a long day, and tomorrow will probably be longer."

"I shall probably have to go tomorrow."

"Tomorrow? My God, the dudgeon isn't as deep as that, is it?"

"Dudgeons are high. No, it's not that. But there may not be a room at the hotel."

"Oh, I forgot. Well, look here, why not come up to the studio? You've seen it. It's plain, but clean, and very convenient. And now it seems"—the gray eyes crinkled at the corners—"that you'll be chaperoned."

"I'll think about it," I said, without much enthusiasm.

He hesitated, then said, "I hope you will. I—please don't go tomorrow. I was hoping you'd come with me."

I stared at him. "But—I thought you were going up Parnassus with Stephanos?"

"I am. I want you to come. Will you?"

"But Simon—"

"Will you?"

I said huskily, "This is absurd."

"I know. But there it is."

"It's your own very private business. Just because I—I bulldozed you into my affairs it doesn't mean you have to ask me to tag along in yours."

The amusement was there again. "No. Will you?"

"Yes. Of course."

"It'll be a long trek. An all-day job. If the hotel say they can't keep you you'll let me ring up Athens for you and get you into the studio?"

"Ring up Athens?"

"It's the property of the University Fine Arts Department, and you're not an accredited artist any more than I am. You'll have to come in as a student."

"Oh, of course. And Danielle?"

He grinned. "Maybe archaeologists count. If she gives my name to hire a car, she may give Hervé's when she wants a room in the studio."

"I suppose so. Well, please ring up Athens for me and I'll move in tomorrow night. What time do we start?"

"I'll call for you at half past eight." He gave me his sudden smile. "Good night, Camilla. And thank you."

"Good night."

As he turned to go, I said, before I could prevent myself, "Don't forget to go and fix the taps, will you?"

"Taps," said Simon gently, "bore me. Good night."

10

What a personage says or does reveals a certain moral purpose; and a good element of character, if the purpose so revealed is good. Such goodness is possible in every type of personage, even in a woman.

ARISTOTLE: *The Art of Poetry*
(tr. Ingram Bywater)

NEXT MORNING I awoke early, so early that, when I found I couldn't easily go to sleep again, I decided to get up and see the ruins on my own before the day's adventures started. The thought made me, with a wry little smile, remember that I hadn't yet posted my letter to Elizabeth. When I was ready to leave my room I fished it out of my bag, opened it, and added a hasty postscript.

> "Did I say nothing ever happened to me? It's started as from yesterday. If I live I'll write and let you know what you're missing.

"LOVE, CAMILLA."

The sun was already hot and bright, though it was only just a little past seven o'clock. I walked along the village street to post my letter, then turned into the steep way that climbs between terraced streets to the mountainside above.

This was a flight of wide steps, bounded by whitewashed walls from which the sun beat back. The already blinding white was muted everywhere by greenery; from every wall and roof spilled vines and hanging ferns, the vivid pinks and scarlets of geraniums, and brilliant cascades of marigolds and black-eyed Susans. At my feet hens pecked and scratched about. Now and then I stood aside as a donkey or a mule picked its dainty accurate way down the steps, while a black-veiled peasant woman, following it, smiled and gave me a soft "Good morning."

The steps took me eventually clear of the village, on to the hillside where piles of rubble and curbstones indicated that a new road was being built. I made my way carefully along this, watched by the friendly and curious stares of the workmen, and, before I was aware that I had come so far, found myself clear of the last house, and out on the open hillside above the studio.

The climb had been steep, and the sun was hot. The path led along the foot of a low cliff-wall, which cast, at this early hour, a narrow shade. I found a flat rock in a recess of shadow, and sat down to recover from the climb.

The path that I was on seemed to be a continuation of the one that Simon and I had taken last night. It passed above the studio, then slanted down into the knot of pines that I remembered, and vanished thence more steeply toward the ruined temple precincts. Not far from where I sat, below me now and to the right of the path, I could see the studio, dumped down raw and square and ugly in its quarried plateau. Beyond it the valley of the olives swam and shimmered in the immense liquid distance of light, and beyond that again mountain after mountain, and the sea.

Then my attention was taken by a movement near the studio.

Someone was as early abroad as I. I heard the scuffle of footsteps mounting the rough path that led up from the plateau. Then I saw him, a thin, fair-haired figure carrying a rucksack, and clambering at a fair speed but with very little noise toward the path where I sat in the shadow. He hadn't looked in my direction; he was making for the knot of pines above the shrine, and moving away from me rapidly.

He reached the path. He was about seventy yards away from me, near the fence that marked the graveyard. He stopped, and turned, as if to pause for breath and survey the view.

I was just about to get to my feet and hail him, when something about the way he was acting caught my attention, and I stayed still. He had taken a couple of quick steps back and sideways, into the shadow of a pine tree. The dappled shade netted and hid him, maculate, invisible. He stayed there, stock-still, and he wasn't looking at any view; his head was bent as if he studied the ground at his feet, but I knew, suddenly, that he was listening. He didn't move. There was no sound in the lovely bright morning but the chime of a goat bell from the other side of the valley, and the crowing of a cock down in the village. No sound from the studio; no movement.

Nigel lifted his head, and was looking about him, still with those wary, abruptly stealthy movements. It was quite obvious that, wherever he was going, he didn't want to be followed and, remembering Danielle, I thought I saw his point. And I wouldn't interrupt his getaway either. Smiling to myself, I stayed where I was. I didn't think he would see me unless I moved, nor did he. He turned suddenly, and, leaving the path, plunged uphill through the pines toward the higher levels where the ancient stadium stood, and, beyond it, the track that led above the Shining Ones and away into the upper reaches of Parnassus.

I gave him a minute or two, and then I got up and went on. Soon I, too, was under the shadow of the pines, and to my right was the tumbledown fence, and the thicket of dried weeds that edged the graveyard.

I don't quite know what made me do it, except that somehow, already, Michael Lester's affair was my own. I pushed open the creaking gate and went in among the stones. When I found it I had to spell it out very slowly to be sure it was the one.

ΜΙΧΑΕΛ ΛΗΣΤΗΡ

This alien cross, an alien epitaph . . . and in my ear Simon's voice, claiming him still. " 'My brother Michael.' " And behind that again I could hear the ghosts of other voices, other claims: " 'The woman of my house, the cousin of Angelos, the brother of Michael' " . . . " 'No man is an Island, entire of itself.' "

I stood there in the hot early-morning silence and thought about Simon. Today, I was committed to Simon's quest. I, too, had answered a claim. He was going to see the place where Michael had died, and he had wanted me to go too.

And I? Why had I said that I would go? I had said last night that it was absurd, and so it was. . . . But I had a queer feeling that, quite apart from Simon's need of me, I had a need of my own. I, too, had something to find.

A bird, small and bright as a blown leaf, flew across the hot stillness. I turned away and made my way between the dusty mounds toward the gate.

I was thinking now, not of Simon, but of myself. Not of the self, the identity I had felt it so necessary to assert when I had sent back Phil's ring, but of the identity I had assumed so lightly yesterday and which, it seemed, I could not yet put off. Not Camilla Haven, but just "Simon's girl."

I let myself quickly through the gate and hurried down the path till it brought me out above the ruins of the great shrine.

I've already written enough of Delphi, and indeed it's not easy to write about. The place takes the heart and the senses and wrings them dry. Eyes and ears and the instinct of worship are all that is needed there.

I walked slowly downhill in the sunlight. Here was the little pomegranate tree, clinging to a cleft in the marble of the theatre. Its leaves hung now without a rustle, dark green and still. The fruit was flame-colored and as glossy as witchballs. Here were the breakneck steps . . . and here the stage of the theatre, where Simon had spoken last night; I could see the mark at the center, where one's voice was taken and flung high up the mountainside. And now the steps to the precinct . . . that must be the monument of Alexander . . . and this the temple floor of Apollo.

The six great columns stood up like fire against the immense depths of the valley.

No one was about. I crossed the temple floor and sat down at the edge with my back to one of the columns. The stone was hot. Above my head the crumbling capitals were alive with the wings of martins. Far below me the olives shimmered along the valley. In the distance Helicon was blue, was silver, was gray as Aphrodite's doves. Everywhere were the voices of songbirds, because Delphi is sanctuary. Somewhere in the morning distance sheep bells were ringing. . . .

It was still only eight o'clock when I left my seat and walked down the Sacred Way from the temple to the edge of the precinct, where a thick rank of pines keeps it from the road below. I went along the path under the pines, then down to the museum which sits in a curve of the road. I already seemed to have been up and about for so long that it was a surprise to find the doors still shut. There was a man in guide's uniform sitting under the trees on the other side of the road, so I crossed over to speak to him.

"The Museum?" he said in answer to my query. "I am afraid it doesn't open till half past nine. But would you like a guide now for the ruins, no?"

"Not this morning, thank you," I said. "I've just been up there. But possibly tomorrow, if I'm still in Delphi. . . . Will you be about here?"

"Always, at this time." He had a dark square face, and, surprisingly, blue eyes. His look was sophisticated, and he spoke very good English.

I said, "I wanted to see the Charioteer."

"Of course." He grinned, showing very white teeth. "But there are other things too, here in Delphi."

"Oh, yes, I know, but isn't he the first thing everyone looks for in the Museum?"

"Of course," he said again. "If you come with me tomorrow I will take you also round the Museum myself."

"I should like that very much." I hesitated. "Do you—I wonder if you know the young English artist who is staying up at the studio? Thin and fair, with a little beard?''

"Yes. I know him. He has been here in Delphi for quite a time, no?"

"I believe so. Does he—has he been to the Museum much?"

"Indeed, yes. He comes very often to draw. Have you seen any of his drawings, *kyria?* They are very good, very good indeed."

"He showed me some of them last night, but not, I think, any of the statues and antiquities. I imagine he would do those well. Did he do any of the Charioteer?"

"Of course. Did you not say yourself that he is the first thing one looks for? And certainly in our small Museum he is the *pièce de résistance.*"

"Was he—did you notice if the artist was here yesterday?"

The guide didn't seem to be at all surprised at the odd catechism. His experience of tourists must have bred in him a vast tolerance. He shook his head. "I do not think so. I was here all day, but he may have been down here while I was up in the ruins. The tour takes nearly an hour. If you wish to see him, he sleeps up at the studio above the site, where they are building the new road."

"Perhaps I'll see him later." I judged it time to drop that particular catechism. "What new road are they making away up there above the village? Where can it possibly go?"

"To the stadium. Have you seen that yet?"

"Not yet."

"It is high above the shrine. Many tourists who come to Delphi never see it at all, because the climb is too steep. It is very beautiful—just the old oval race-track with the tiers of seats, exactly as it was in ancient times, and with the view . . . always that view of the olives and the valley and the sea. So now they make a road to let the cars and buses take the tourists up."

I stifled a pang at the thought of yet another wild and lovely sanctuary invaded by cars and buses, and said, "Ah, yes. I suppose anything that will bring money into Greece is a good thing. You are a native of Delphi, *kyrie?*"

"No. I am a man of Tinos."

"Oh. Then . . . I suppose you weren't here during the war?"

He smiled. "No. I was busy—very busy—on my island."

My island. There it was again. *A man of Tinos.*

Then he would not remember Michael Lester. It was possible that he had never heard of him. In any case—I caught at myself—I must not let myself go beyond even Simon's claim on my interest. I said merely, "Of course."

He was rolling a cigarette with neat, quick movements.

"There was certainly no need *then* for guides in Delphi, *kyria.* No one was troubling then about the shrine and the sanctuary and the Charioteer! We may say, if you like, that it is a pity—if men had had the time to come, as they came here in the days of the Oracle, when Delphi was the center of the world, no doubt they would have found their quarrels healed." That quick sophisticated look, and the sudden grin again. "That, you understand, is what I always say when I show my tourists round. It is a very effective bit of patter. The Amphictyonic League of Delphi. The League of Nations. The U.N. Very effective."

"I'm sure it is. Do you add the bits about the fights between Delphi and her neighbors, and the laying waste of Crissa, and the monuments for Athenian victories over the Spartans, and Spartan victories over the Athenians, and the

Argive monument stuck down just where it would annoy the Spartans most, and—"

"Sometimes." He was laughing. "I shall have to—what do you say?—watch my step when I show you round tomorrow, shall I not?"

"Not really. I read up an awful lot specially before I came. It makes it more exciting to *know* what happened here. I looked at a lot of photographs too." I hesitated again. "The Charioteer . . ." I said slowly.

"What of him?"

I was carrying a guidebook in my hand; *A Concise Guide of Delphi,* it was called, and on the cover there was a photographic reproduction of the head of the famous statue. I held it out. "This. I've heard so much about him, but I can't help wondering if I'll really like him. Those eyes; they're inlaid with onyx and white enamel, aren't they? And there are long metal eyelashes? They do look alive, I admit, but—look, you see what I mean?" I indicated the print. "That narrow forehead and the heavy jaw; it's not strictly a beautiful face, is it? And yet everyone says he's so wonderful."

"And so will you. No picture gives the true impression. It's the same with the great Hermes at Olympia. In photographs he is effeminate, the marble too smooth, and shining like soap. But the statue itself takes away the breath."

"I know. I've seen it."

"Then prepare yourself to see the Charioteer. It is one of the great statues of Greece. Do you know the thing that comes to me first whenever I see him again—which is every day?"

"What?"

"He is so very young. All that gravity, that grace, and so young with it. It used to be thought that he was the owner of the team—the winner of the race—but now they say that he was probably the driver for some lord who owned the chariot."

I said hesitantly, "There's a bit in Pausanias' account of Delphi, isn't there, about a chariot of bronze with a naked 'lord of the car' who might have had a driver, a youth of good family?"

"I believe there is, yes. But it could hardly apply to our Charioteer, *kyria;* the evidence is that he was probably buried in a great landslip during an earthquake in three seventy-three B.C., and, without being uncovered again, was built into the—what do you call it?—the supporting wall—the 'earth-holder' is the Greek word—that was erected to stop the rocks and earth from engulfing the temple again."

"Retaining wall," I said.

"Ah, thank you. The retaining wall. Well, you see, our Charioteer had vanished a few centuries before Pausanias came to Delphi."

"I see. I didn't know that."

He had finished rolling the cigarette. He put it between his lips and lit it with a spluttering of loose tobacco.

He said, "They say now that the Charioteer was part of a victory group erected by one Gelon, the winner of a chariot race, but anything may be true. So much was lost or destroyed or stolen over the centuries that the truth about our discoveries is only guesswork. And Delphi suffered much, because she was so rich. I think it is reckoned that there were six thousand monuments here—at any rate that is the number of inscriptions that have been uncovered." He smiled.

"The landslide that broke and hid the Charioteer was an act of the gods, because it kept him out of the hands of the robbers. The Phocians laid the sanctuary waste barely twenty years after he was buried, and of course in later times countless treasures were destroyed or stolen."

"I know. Sulla and Nero and the rest. How many bronzes do they reckon Nero took to Rome?"

"Five hundred." He laughed again. "I *shall* have to watch my patter tomorrow, I can see!"

"I told you I only read it up just before I came. And there's so much—"

A sudden clatter and a volley of shouts from somewhere behind the Museum startled me, and I stopped and glanced over my shoulder. "What on earth's that?"

"Nothing. A little disagreement among the workmen."

"A little disagreement? It sounds like a major war!"

"We are always a fighting race, I am afraid. There is trouble today among the workmen. There are still men here from the 'dig' of the French archaeologists— the 'dig' is finished, but workmen have remained to clear up, and to remove the rails that the trucks ran on, and things of that kind. A mule strayed during the night, and now they have discovered that some tools are missing, and they are accusing the men who work on the stadium road of theft, and so—well, you hear that there is a little disagreement."

"Some tools and a mule?" I listened to the uproar for a moment or two. It sounded like the battle of El Alamein in stereophonic sound. I said drily, "Perhaps they haven't heard of the Amphictyonic League and the peace of Delphi."

He smiled. "Perhaps not."

"And now I really must go. I'll let you know if I can come with you tomorrow. You say you'll be here at this time?"

"Always."

I had a sharp inner vision of a life where one would be—always—serenely on the Delphi road in the early morning sun. "I'll try and be here by eight if I'm coming. If I can't—"

"It does not matter. If you come, I will take you with the greatest of pleasure. If not, it does not matter. Are you staying at the Apollon?"

"Yes."

"It is very nice, yes?"

"Delightful." I lingered for a moment, looking at the closed door of the Museum. He was watching me through the smoke of his cigarette with that shrewd, incurious blue gaze. I said, *"Kyrie . . .* you weren't here during the war, of course, but you'll know what happened to the statues and things from the Museum? The Charioteer, for instance? Where was he? Hidden?"

"Only in a manner of speaking. He was in Athens."

"Oh. Yes. I see."

Behind me a shabby black car slid to a halt. Simon grinned at me over the door and said, "Good morning."

"Oh, Simon! Am I late? Have you had to hunt for me?"

"The answer to both those is no. I was early and they told me you'd come down here. Have you had breakfast?"

"Hours ago."

"Why people should adopt that disgustingly self-righteous tone whenever they manage to achieve breakfast before eight o'clock I do not know," said Simon. He leaned across the car and opened the door for me. "Come along, then, let's go. Unless of course you'd like to drive?"

I didn't bother to answer that one, but slipped quickly into the passenger's seat beside him.

As the car turned the corner and gathered speed along the straight stretch below the temple I said, without preliminary, "The Charioteer was in Athens during the war. Presumably in hiding."

He gave me a quick glance. "Oh. Yes, it would be, wouldn't it?" I saw him smile.

I said, almost defensively, "Well, you did get me into it, after all."

"I did, didn't I?" A little pause. "Did you come down through the temple this morning?"

"Yes."

"I thought you might do that. I've been up there myself most mornings by about six."

"Not today?"

He smiled. "No. I thought you'd like it to yourself."

"You've very—" I began, and stopped. He didn't ask me what I'd been going to say. I said, not quite irrelevantly, "Do you ever lose your temper, Simon?"

"What in the world makes you ask that?"

"Oh, come, I thought you were a thought-reader!"

"Oh. Well, let me see. . . . Last night?"

"That didn't take much guessing. Yes, of course. Nigel was abominably rude to you. Didn't you mind?"

"Mind? No."

"Why not?"

"I don't think I'd have minded from Nigel anyway, because he's not very happy. Life isn't easy for him, and on top of everything he has to fall for that girl, and she's led him the hell of a dance. But last night—" He paused, and I saw again that pucker of worry round his eyes. "Last night there was something wrong. Really wrong, I mean; not just Nigel's too-usual brand of nerves and temperament and frustrated talent, and that little she-witch playing him on a very barbed hook. There was something more."

"Are you sure he wasn't just a bit drunk? He said he was."

"Possibly. But that's part of the trouble—he doesn't drink much as a rule, and last night he was fairly putting it away, though he's like you—he doesn't like ouzo. No, there was definitely something very wrong, and I'd give quite a lot to know what it was."

"I take it he didn't tell you anything after you got back to the studio? I got the impression he was going to come out with something just as Danielle interrupted."

"Yes, so did I. But I didn't see him again. His room was empty when I went back. I waited a bit, but eventually went to bed. I didn't hear him come in."

"Perhaps," I said a little drily, "he was fixing the taps."

"That did occur to me. But no. Danielle's door was standing open. She wasn't there either. I think they'd gone for a walk, or down to the village for another drink, or something. And Nigel had gone when I got up this morning."

I said, "He went up the mountain. I saw him."

"You saw him?"

"Yes, at about seven o'clock. He went up past the graveyard through those pines, as if he were going farther up the hill."

"Alone?"

"Yes. In fact, he looked rather as if he wanted to be left very much alone. I didn't speak to him, and I don't think he saw me."

Simon said, "Well, let's hope he does some work today, and draws it out of himself, whatever it is. I expect I'll see him tonight." He glanced at me, smiling. "Did you make any more discoveries this morning?"

"Only one," I said, before I thought.

"And that?"

I found myself telling him, quite simply. "It was just my own discovery. We talked about it last night, with Nigel. It's something we're taught from childhood, but I'd never really had it brought home to me till now."

"What is it?"

"That saying of 'your parson friend,' as Nigel called him."

"Ah, yes, that." He was silent for a moment, then he quoted it softly, as if half to himself, " 'No man is an Island, entire of itself; every man is a piece of the Continent, a part of the main; if a Clod be washed away by the Sea, Europe is the less, as well as if a Promontory were, as well as if a Manor of thy friends or of thine own were; any man's death diminishes me, because I am involved in Mankind; And therefore never send to know for whom the bell tolls; It tolls for thee.' . . . Terrific piece of writing, isn't it? One should remember it more often."

The car slowed down and drew out to pass a little group of three donkeys pattering along in the dust at the edge of the road. On the foremost an old woman sat sideways; she had a distaff in her left hand, the spindle in her right, and as she rode she spun the white wool ceaselessly, without looking at it. She ducked a smiling salute to us as we went by.

Simon said, "What brought that home to you this morning?"

I hesitated, then said flatly, "Michael's grave."

"I see." And I thought he did.

I said, "It's this confounded country. It does things to one—mentally and physically and, I suppose morally. The past is so living and the present so intense and the future so blooming imminent. The light seems to burn life into you twice as intensely as anywhere else I've known. I suppose that's why the Greeks did what they did so miraculously, and why they could stay themselves through twenty generations of slavery that would have crushed any other race on earth. You come here thinking you're going to look at a lot of myth-haunted ruins and picturesque peasants and you find that . . . ." I stopped.

"That what?"

"No. I'm talking piffle."

"It's good piffle. Go on. What do you find?"

"You find that the grave of Michael Lester is as moving and as important as the 'tomb of Agamemnon' at Mycenae, or Byron or Venizelos or Alexander. He, and the men like him, are a part of the same picture." I stopped, and then said helplessly, "Greece. Damn it, what is that it does to one?"

He was silent a moment, then he said, "I think the secret is that it belongs to all of us—to us of the West. We've learned to think in its terms, and to live in its laws. It's given us almost everything that our world has that is worth while. Truth, straight thinking, freedom, beauty. It's our second language, our second line of thought, our second country. We all have our own country—and Greece."

We sailed round a bend of the road and ahead of us the deep valley opened to show a great rounded beauty of a mountain, silver-green, blue-veined, cloud-gray.

"Why, damn it all," said Simon. "That hill in front of us. That's Helicon. *Helicon*. And then you wonder why this country gets you in the wind?"

"Not any more," I said.

And we didn't speak again till we came to Arachova and found Stephanos and Niko waiting for us in the café on the corner.

"Do you like my socks?" asked Niko.

"They're wonderful," I said truthfully. They were, indeed, in that landscape, something to be wondered at. They were luminous, and of a startling shade of shocking pink. They shone among the bleached hot stones of the mountain track like neon signs against a clear sky.

"They light up," explained Niko.

"I can see that. Where did you get them?"

"In Athens. They are the latest thing from New York."

"Do you go to Athens often?"

"No. I went to work there when I was fourteen. I was a page boy at the Acropole Palace Hotel."

"I see. Is that where you learned your English?"

"Some of it. I also learn it here in the school. Is good, huh?"

"Very good. Why didn't you stay in Athens?"

"Is better here." Niko looked back along the track we were climbing. Away below us Arachova had dwindled to a toy waterfall of colored roofs. Niko turned back to me almost as if he were puzzled. "Here there is nothing. Is no money. But is better here. Arachova is my village." Again that look. "You think I am crazy? *You* come from London where there is plenty money. All Greeks are a little crazy, huh? But you think I am stupid to leave Athens?"

"There is a sort of divine madness about all the Greeks I've met," I said, laughing. "But you're not crazy, Niko. It's better here, certainly, money or no money. Don't ever live in a town unless you have to! And I don't live in London. I live miles away from it, in a country village, just like you."

"Like Arachova?" He was vastly surprised. I had long since discovered that to all Greeks England meant London and nothing else. London, the huge, the golden-pavemented, the jacinth-gated.

"Not quite like Arachova."

"And that is your village, as Arachova is mine."

I said, "Not quite, Niko. We've lost that way of feeling, I'm afraid. How far is this place that we're making for?"

"Making? *Oriste?*"

"Going to. The place where Michael died." I said it softly, with my eye on Simon's back where he walked with Stephanos a few yards ahead of us.

"About an hour from here. More, perhaps. It is nearer to Delphi than Arachova. It is in a . . . I do not know the word: a hollow place, a—" he stopped and made a scooping gesture.

"A corrie? Like this?"

"Yes. That is it. A corrie, where the rocks have fallen near the foot of a cliff. My grandfather know the way. He tell me it looks to the northwest—that is, away from Delphi and Arachova, toward Amphissa. This track goes along the face of the mountains and then we leave it and climb up toward these cliffs where the corrie is. I think that many, many years ago there was a road for beasts, but not now. I do not know how far. I have never been, me. My grandfather, he know the way. You are tired?"

"No. It's rather hot, but I'm not tired."

"In Greece," said Niko reflectively, eyeing me, "the women are very strong."

I thought of the village cafés, with their day-long complement of cheerfully idle men. "I imagine they have to be," I said.

"Oh, yes." Niko misunderstood me, probably deliberately. "In Greece the men are tough. Oh, very tough."

Somehow, at that moment, Niko's racy beauty managed to look very tough indeed. His swagger, and the look he gave me, were the plainest possible invitation to the kind of suggestive verbal sparring that the Mediterranean men seem to love. But two could play at the game of misunderstanding. I said cheerfully, "Then if we do meet the shade of Angelos on the hill, I shall feel quite, quite safe with you, Niko."

"How?" He was momentarily thrown off his stride. "Oh, yes! But of course you will be safe with me! I should kill him, you understand. He helped to kill my great-grandfather's brother's son Panos, so of course I should kill him. And"—the swagger gave way again to Niko's own brand of youthful and artless high spirits—"it would be easy, because he is old and I am young."

"I suppose he's all of forty," I agreed. "And just how old are you, Niko?"

"I am seventeen."

I said mendaciously, "Really? I'd have thought you were much older than that."

He flashed me his delighted smile. "Would you? Would you really? And how old are you, beautiful miss?"

"Niko! Don't you know the rules better than that? I'm twenty-five."

"So old? But you do not look like twenty-five," he said generously. "It is a good age to be, not? See, this bit is rough. Take my hand, miss."

I laughed. "I'm not as old as all that, Niko. And I'm truly not a bit tired. Just hot."

It was indeed very hot. As we climbed steadily northwest, the sun beat down on the right, throwing shadows sharp and hard as graphite along the white rock. The track where we walked was only by courtesy a track. It was not steep, cutting at a slant along the great flank of the mountain, but it was very rough, and some of the stones were sharp. We had long since left any trees behind, and the mountainside, unpunctuated now by pine or cypress, stretched one great wing of burning white from the high hard blue sky down to the dry watercourse deep on our left. Beyond the tortured path of this dead stream, the rock rose again, this time violently blocked in with cobalt shadow. High above, so that to glance at them hurt the eyes, three birds hung, circling slowly and with moveless wings, like some mobile toy on invisible threads. I thought I could hear their faint, sweet mewing. Nothing else broke the silence except the scrape and clink of our feet, and the sound of our breathing.

The track ran straight up to what looked like a wall of fallen rocks and rubble, and there stopped, obliterated. Stephanos, in front, had halted, and turned to speak to Simon, who was just behind him. He said something, gesturing toward the barricade of rock.

It looked like a landslip, a great torrent of red and ocherous earth frozen even as it poured down the steep wing of the mountain. It was spiked with broken rock and great white slabs of fallen limestone. Further down the mountainside it fanned out like the delta of a red river. Enormous blocks of stone had hurtled down with it, flung carelessly, as by the hand of an angry god, to dam the narrow gash of the watercourse.

Stephanos had turned aside to climb rather painfully up the steep hill-face beside the landslide.

"Is this where we leave the track?" I asked.

Simon turned. "No. That's still with us. This stuff's just lying across it. If we follow Stephanos up a little there's a place where it's safer to cross."

"It must have been quite a storm," I said, surveying the torrent of rocks in front, and the gigantic flung boulders far below us.

"Not storm. Earthquake," said Simon, then laughed at my expression. "Yes, one forgets, doesn't one? I told you this was a savage country. And this, I believe, is a baddish area. They've had quite a history of tremors hereabouts. The miracle is that any of the shrines and temples have a single pillar left standing. Can you manage?"

"Yes, thanks. Don't help me, Simon. I've got to keep my end up with Niko."

"Of course—and mine too, I think . . . That's it. We cross here. It seems stable enough, but watch yourself."

We made our way slowly across the detritus of the earthquake. From higher up I could see where a whole slice of the mountain cliff above us had been torn away and thrown down. It had splintered into great white spearheads, against which the smaller fragments were piled in the drift of dark-red earth. We scrambled down this uncomfortable ramp toward the path which had shaken itself clear of the debris.

"I suppose the Earth-Shaker turned over in his sleep," I said, "and not so very long ago, either, by the look of it. The cracks look fairly fresh, don't they?"

Stephanos must have understood the drift of what I was saying. He had turned to wait for us on the track, and now spoke to Simon. "What does he say?" I asked.

"He says that there were two or three small shocks—this, by the way, is a small shock—about twelve years ago. A little further on, the mountain has been shifted about much more drastically. He says that only someone who was out on this part of Parnassus almost daily would still know his way about, once he had left the track. He also says that the place we are making for is almost completely changed since he found Michael there. It was just an open space at the foot of a low cliff, and now it's closed in by fallen rock into a kind of corrie, or hollow."

Stephanos nodded as he finished. He gave me a look from under his magnificent white brows. He asked Simon a question.

"Are you tired?" asked Simon.

"No, thanks."

Simon smiled. "Don't exhaust yourself keeping Britain's end up, will you?"

"I'm not. It's only the heat."

There was a flash of shocking-pink socks beside me as Niko dropped off the rubble to land as neatly as a goat. He dragged a water bottle out of a large pocket and unscrewed the top. "Have a drink, miss."

I drank thankfully. The bottle smelt ammoniac, like a nice donkey, but the water was good and still reasonably cool.

"Greek peasant women," said Niko, watching me with that limpid look of his, "can go for hours over the roughest country without food or drink."

"So," I said, stoppering the bottle and handing it back to him, "can camels. Thank you, Niko, that was wonderful."

"It was a pleasure, beautiful miss." Niko turned to Simon and held out the bottle. His look and gesture expressed, somehow, the most tender solicitude.

Simon, smiling, shook his head.

"Good," said Stephanos, and turned to go on. He and Simon forged ahead once more, and Niko and I took up our positions in the rear.

It must have been getting on for noon when we neared the corrie.

We left the track some way beyond the fall of rock and turned, in Stephanos' unfaltering wake, up into a markless desert of rock and dry earth. Sometimes we trudged upward through sienna-colored dust strewn cruelly with small boulders, and sometimes we walked more easily across great serrated flanges of the white and living rock. The sun was at its height and the heat was intense. The air wavered with it till the whole vast sweep of rock seemed to pulsate. If it hadn't been for the cool breeze that blew steadily at that height, it would have been insupportable.

By the time we were two-thirds of the way to the corrie, and had done most of the climbing, I had got my second wind, and was walking fairly easily. I was, I felt, upholding British Womanhood not too badly.

"The Greek peasant women," said Niko, beside me, "used to carry great loads of wood and grapes and things across here. Regularly."

"If you tell me one more thing about Greek peasant women," I said, "I shall scream and lie down and refuse to move another step. Besides, I don't believe you."

He grinned. "It is not true," he conceded. "I think that you are very wonderful."

"Why, Niko, that's nice of you!"

"And very beautiful too," said Niko. "Would you like an apple?"

And he fished an apple out of his pocket and handed it to me with very much the air of a Paris presenting the prize to Aphrodite. His look of intense and dazzled admiration was, one felt, one that had been tried before and found to work.

It still worked. My morale soared. I laughed and took the apple and thanked him, and then a diversion was created because neither he nor Stephanos would allow me to eat it without peeling it, and Niko wanted to peel it for me and Stephanos had the knife, so, being Greeks, they plunged into a passionate discussion about this while Simon peeled the apple and then handed it to me.

"For the fairest," he said.

"There's not," I said, "a lot of competition. But thank you all the same."

Soon after that we reached our destination.

11

That ground will take no footprint. All of it
Is bitter stone. . . .

EURIPIDES: *Electra*
(tr. Gilbert Murray)

THE CORRIE did not lie at any great height. Arachova itself is almost three thousand feet above sea level, and we had climbed no more than eight or nine hundred feet in all since we had left the village. We were still only in the foothills of the vast highland of Parnassus, but we might have been lost, a million miles from anywhere. Since the village had dwindled out of sight we had seen no living creature except the lizards, and the vultures that circled and cried so sweetly, high in the dazzling air.

The place wasn't, properly speaking, a corrie. It was a hollow scooped out of a line of low cliffs that topped a steep, mile-long ridge like the crest along a horse's neck. From a distance the cliff looked fairly uniform, but on approach it could be seen that it had been split and torn into ragged bays and promontories where half a hundred winter torrents had gouged their headlong way down the mountainside.

Here and there lay evidence of a swifter and more wholesale violence. Earthquakes had wrested great chunks from the crag, quarrying back into the limestone face, throwing the enormous debris down, so that for hundreds of feet below the jagged cliffs, a loose and sometimes dangerous scree valanced the sloping hillside.

As we neared the edge of this, Stephanos turned aside, into a short steep detour that took us out above the level of the cliff top, and we approached the line of crags at a long slant that brought us eventually to the edge.

The old man stopped then, leaning on his crook, and waited for us to come up with him.

Simon stood beside him, looking down.

"This is the place?"

"This is the place."

It could have been a quarry hacked out of the cliff face during countless patient years. It had probably taken five seconds of earthquake for the Earth-Shaker to tear that semi-circular scar back into the cliff and fling the wreckage down before it in still formidable walls of jagged rock. The result of the earthquake's action was to make a roughly circular hollow, a sort of irregular crater some seventy yards across, which was walled to the north by the living cliff on which we stood, and shut in almost completely for the rest of its diameter by the vast sections of tumbled rock.

The center of the crater floor was clear, but the encircling walls were piled in the now familiar way with red dust and rock debris. In spring, I thought, it would probably be beautiful, for it was sheltered, and I could see the dead remains of some scrubby plants and bushes where the melting snows and then the rain must have fed some alpine vegetation. Below us clung the lovely green of a little

622

juniper, and just beside my feet the rock held two thick bushes that looked like holly, but which bore, incongruously, acorns with enormous cups as prickly as sea urchins.

To the right, on the west side of the corrie, was what appeared to be the only way out. This was a break in the wall of rock, toward which the smooth crater floor lifted in a rocky ramp. From the height where we stood I thought I could see, beyond and below this "gate," the ghost of an old track, leading westward to vanish round a spur of the mountain.

Stephanos caught the direction of my glance. "That is the way he went."

He spoke in Greek, of course, and Simon translated for me, at the time in snatches, and more fully later; but once again I shall put the old man's words down directly, as they came.

"That is the way he went, down the old track toward Amphissa. It comes out above a disused quarry near the Amphissa road, behind the olive groves." He fell silent for a moment or two, looking down at the hollow beneath our feet. No one spoke. The sun beat on the back of our necks, and I felt, suddenly, very tired.

Then the old man spoke again, slowly, reminiscently. "I came to the head of the cliff just at this point. It was different then, you understand . . . here, where we stand, there was a pinnacle of rock, like a cat's tooth. It disappeared in the earthquake, but then it was a landmark that even an Athenian could not have missed. And below the cliff, then, there was no hollow, as you see it now, walled and gated like a fortress. There was only the cliff, and below us some big rocks lying, and a space of clean stone. It was there that I saw them, Michael and Angelos. And the place is not covered. I marked it, and I know. It was there." The crook pointed. Almost in the center of the dazzling floor of smooth stone, a little pile of stones, a cairn, threw a small triangular shadow. "I put those there later," said Stephanos, "after the earthquake had moved the cliff and the place was altered beyond recognition." There was another pause of silence, then he glanced sideways at me. "We will go down now. . . . Will you tell the lady to be very careful, *Kyrie* Simon? The path is steep, and made only for goats, but it is the quickest way."

As Simon transmitted the warning, I saw that there was indeed a path down into the corrie. It left the cliff top just beside us, between the two bushes of holly oak, and wound steeply down past more mats of holly and the dusty ghosts of thistles, into the bottom of the hollow. It was down this way that the dog must have raced to attack Angelos, and then Stephanos himself, to run to Michael's side as he lay dying in the sun. . . .

The sun was so high that almost the whole of the corrie bottom was shadowless. But where the cliff path debouched onto the level, a wing of rock cast a comforting angle of blue shade. I stopped there, and sat down with my back against the warm stone. Stephanos moved forward without pausing, and Simon followed him. Niko flung himself down beside me on the dusty ground. I hoped he wouldn't speak, and he didn't. He broke off a piece of dead thistle and began scratching patterns in the dust. He wasn't paying much attention to his drawing; his intent gaze never left the other men.

Stephanos led Simon across the floor of the corrie, and stopped beside the little cairn. He was pointing down at it and talking, rapidly now. His hand moved and gestured, then came back to the same spot. Almost I could see the dying man lying there in the baking sun, the shepherd coming to the cliff top where a fang of rock stuck up like a cat's tooth, the dog dashing down that snaking path, the murderer turning to bolt out of the "gate" and down the track toward Amphissa and the sea. . . .

Then Stephanos turned heavily and trudged back to where we sat. He lowered himself down beside me with a sigh, then said something short to Niko, who got out a battered packet of cigarettes and handed him one. He gave his grandfather a light, then turned, with his brilliant smile, to offer a cigarette to me. We lit up in silence.

Simon was still standing in the center of the corrie, but he wasn't looking down at the cairn where his brother had died. He had turned, and that cool appraising stare of his was slowly raking the sides of the corrie . . . the tumbled wall of rock that hemmed us in . . . the great sections that had fallen outward from the crag, and now made the two side wings of the corrie, piled high in vast slabs and wedges against the old solid rock of the cliff . . . the hollow curve of a shallow cave exposed in the scooped segment of broken crag, a cave that had been deep before the front of the cliff had fallen away and left its recesses naked to the air. . . .

My cigarette was mild and loosely packed and tasted slightly of goat; there was something about the beautiful Niko, I reflected, that harked back fairly consistently to the lower animals. I had half-smoked it, and Niko's was gone entirely, when Simon's shadow fell beside us.

"What about lunch?" he asked.

The slight tension—of Stephanos' making, not Simon's—was broken, and we chatted over lunch as if it had been a normal picnic. My tiredness was rapidly dissolving, with the rest in the pleasant shade, and the solid excellence of the food we had bought in Arachova. We had rolls—a little dry after their progress in Niko's rucksack—with generous pieces of cold lamb sandwiched in; cheese in thick juicy slices; a paper full of olives that felt as if they were warm from the tree but were really warm from Niko; a hard-boiled egg; a very solid and very sweet chunk of some sort of cake made with fresh cherries; and a large handful of grapes, also warm and slightly tired-looking, but tasting ambrosially of the sun.

I noticed that Simon, as he ate, still looked about him, his eyes returning time after time, thoughtfully, to the recently torn cliff behind us. "This was done in the earthquake you spoke of, soon after the war?"

Stephanos said, through a mouthful of cake, "That is so. There were three or four shocks that year. It was nineteen forty-six. The villages were not affected, but a lot of rock was moved up here." He jerked his head toward the cliff. "This is not the only place of its kind. All along this ridge there are places where the tremors, and then the weather, have taken bites out of the hill. What the earthquake starts, the ice and snow don't take many winters to finish. There are three, four, five hollows, much like this one, where very little trace of the original cliff face remains. Only the goat track that we came down on . . . see? . . . there the cliff itself has not been moved, but you see the rocks piled against it as high as a ruined church. Oh, yes, I told you, *Kyrie* Simon, that a man who was not always out on the hill would soon miss his landmarks."

"The pinnacle, for instance, that used to stand above the cliff?"

"I told you about that? Yes, I did, I remember. It was not so very high, but it served as a landmark for kilometers around. It was what guided me to Michael on that day. He knew of a cave here, he said, near the Cat's Tooth, and he meant to lie up in it until the German drive was over. I came up bringing him food, and to try and make him come back to Arachova where his wound might be cared for. But this I have spoken of already."

Simon's eyes were on the shallow apse of the exposed cave. They were narrowed slightly, as if against the sun, and his face gave nothing away. "A cave? That one? It would be deep enough before half of it fell in."

Stephanos lifted his heavy shoulders. "I do not know if that was the one or not. Possibly. But you must understand that the cliff is full of caves . . . some parts of Parnassus are a honeycomb of such places where an army could hide in safety."

Simon had taken out cigarettes. "Camilla? I think I'd like to take a quick look around, all the same. Cigarette? Catch, Niko. . . ." He got slowly to his feet, and stood looking down at the old man sitting heavily in the shade. "And you carried Michael from here to Delphi?"

Stephanos smiled. "It was fourteen years ago, and I was younger. And the way to Delphi is much shorter than the way we came . . . but steep, you understand, because Arachova lies nearly four hundred meters higher than Delphi. That is a big start on a climb like this, so we came by Arachova today."

"I still think it was . . . well, quite a feat. And now I'm going to poke around for a bit. I want a good look at that cave. It looks as if there's another small opening at the back of it. Will you come, or are you resting?"

"I will come."

"Niko?"

One swift graceful wriggle, and Niko was on his feet and brushing dust from his trousers. "I come. I have very good eyesight, me. If there is anything to be seen, I will see it. I can see in the dark, as well as any cat, so if there is an inner cave, I shall guide you, *Kyrie* Simon."

"We'll follow your socks," said Simon drily, and Niko grinned. The socks flashed across the corrie at a run, and were dimmed in the shadow of the cave's recess. Stephanos was getting slowly to his feet. Simon looked down at me and raised his eyebrows.

I shook my head, so he and Stephanos left me, and went more slowly in the wake of the luminous socks. A buttress of shadow swallowed them.

I finished the cigarette and stubbed it out, then sat relaxed and still, enjoying the shade and the silence and the bright dazzle of heat beyond my shadowed corner. The men were out of sight, either in the cave or somewhere beyond the piles of massive debris that buttressed the far side of the corrie. I couldn't hear them now. The silence was intense, thick as the heat. I was part of it, sitting as still as a lizard on my stone.

Some movement, real or imagined, at the head of the cliff path, caught my eye, and I turned to look, wondering half idly if Niko had found some way back to the cliff's head while I had been sitting there half-asleep. But there was nothing there, only the sun hammering on the white rock. The shadows, purple and anthracite and red, seemed themselves to flicker with movement. Against the violent patterns of light and shade, the green of the holly oaks and the cool curve of the juniper arching out from the face of the cliff were as refreshing as the sound of a spring. I remembered, suddenly, that as I had clambered down past them, there had been other green things below us, hardly noticed in the hazards of that steep exhausted scramble down the cliff.

Where there was green, there must certainly, in September, be water
. . . cold water, not Niko's tepid bottle that smelled of goat. The thought
brought me eagerly to my feet. A shadow at the cliff top flickered again, but I
hardly noticed. My eyes were on the corner below the slim bow of the juniper,
where, like a mirage, showed a glimpse of vivid emerald. . . .

I got up, skirting the corrie's edge, picking my way between the enormous
fallen blocks. I slid between two rough rocks that caught at my clothes, bent my
head to pass under a wing of limestone that shored up the cliff like a flying
buttress—and there was the grass. The color was so startling, and so beautiful
after the dazzling changes rung by sun and stone that I must have stood quite
still, gazing at it, for a full minute. It flowed in a deep and vivid ribbon of green
between two boulders streaked liberally with the red of water-borne iron. But
there was no water now. There might be some spring, I thought, that was
dependent on intermittent showers high on the peaks; perhaps, like snow on the
desert's face, the grass sprang up in the wake of a shower and faded with the next
day's sunset. . . . It lay there, itself like a small pool of cool water, a green
thought in a green shade, moist to the touch, and lending the corner of the corrie
a freshness that the shadowed rock had not had.

I sat gratefully down, with my hands spread on the ground and the soft grass
springing up between my fingers. Among the green were tiny flowers, bells of
pale blue, like pygmy harebells. Some of these grew on the face of the cliff itself,
and their seeds had, in the last decade, flown and rooted everywhere in the fallen
debris of earthquake. Only here in this moist corner were they still in flower, but I
could see fading clumps of seeding stems on all sides among the boulders. Other
alpines had grown here too; there was something with a pale furry leaf and a thin
dry flower-stem left sticking out like a hummingbird's tongue; a tuft of tendrils
dried into hexagonal shapes till they looked like bunches of brown chicken-wire;
a tiny plant of the acorned holly, rooting purposefully in a thin crack. Then with
another shock of pleasure I saw one more flower that had not yet died of drought.
In a cleft just above eye level there was a plant of cyclamen. The leaves, blue-
green and veined palely, were held out in stiff formal curves on their red stems.
The flowers were soft rose-pink, a dozen of them, and clung like a flight of moths
to the dry cliff. Below the flowers, in the same cleft, grew the remains of another
rock plant, dead, fraying away to dust in the drought. Above it the cyclamen's
flowers looked pure and delicate and strong. . . .

Something was fretting at the edge of my mind. I stared at the cyclamen, and
found I was thinking of the Dutch painter and his donkey surrounded by the
laughing village lads, and I wondered, without knowing why, what Nigel was
doing now.

We went back by the shorter route.

It appeared that the search of the cave had yielded nothing, and apparently
Simon didn't want to delay Stephanos and Niko by making a more prolonged
investigation. We left the corrie by the gap in the west side, and scrambled down
the steep slope below the scree.

We had nearly reached the bottom of the dry valley that lay below the ridge,
when we came on the barely visible track that I had glimpsed from the top of the
crags. Even this was appallingly rough going. We made our careful way along it
for some hundred yards or so, and then it forked. The right branch fell steeply

away, curling out of sight almost at once round a spur of cliff. The left-hand branch turned downhill for Delphi. We took this, and in just over half the time the outward journey had taken, we saw ahead of us the edge of the high land and, beyond it, the gap where the Pleistus valley cuts its way down to the sea.

Stephanos paused and spoke to Simon. The latter turned to me.

"Stephanos has come back this way because he thinks you may be tired. This path will lead you straight down to Delphi. It comes out above the temple, and you can get down behind the Shining Ones, and then through the stadium. The drop down to the cliff top is steep, but there's no danger if you take care. I'll come down with you if you like, but you can't possibly miss the way."

I must have looked slightly surprised, because he added, "The car's at Arachova—remember? I thought I'd go back along the top with Stephanos now, and collect it. But there's no need to drag you the whole way."

I said gratefully, "Oh, Simon—that car! I'd forgotten all about it. I don't really see why you should have to shoulder all the responsibility for my bit of nonsense, but I must confess I'll be awfully glad if you will! Don't tell Niko, but I really am beginning to feel I'd like to be home."

"Well, it won't take you long from here, and it's all downhill. No—look, dash it, I'll come with you."

"I wouldn't dream of letting you, if it means your trailing back later on to Arachova for the car. I can't possibly get lost between here and Delphi, and I promise to be careful on the cliff path." I turned to hold out a hand to Stephanos and thank him, then did the same to Niko. It was like Stephanos, I thought, virtually to ignore me all the time, and yet to lead the whole party some hour or so out of its way to show me the quick way home. The old man nodded gravely over my hand and turned away. Niko took it with a melting look from those beautiful eyes and said, "I will see you again, miss? You come to Arachova often?"

"I hope so."

"And you will come to see the rugs in my sister's shop? Is very good rugs, all colors. Local. Is also brooches and pots of the very best Greek style. For you they are cheap. I tell my sister you are my friend, yes?"

I laughed. "If I buy any rugs and pots I'll come to your sister's shop, Niko. That's a promise. And now good-bye, and thank you."

"Good-bye, miss. Thank you, beautiful miss."

The luminous socks plunged away along the path after Stephanos.

Simon grinned. "His grandfather'd have the hide off him if he could understand half he says. Is there such a thing as innocent depravity? Niko's it if there is. A little of Athens superimposed on Arachova. It's a fascinating mixture, isn't it?"

"When it's as beautiful as Niko, yes. . . . Simon, was it true that you didn't find anything in the cave? Or was there something that you didn't want to talk about in front of the others? You didn't see anything at all?"

"Nothing. There was a small inner cave, but it was as blank as a scoured pot. . . . I'll tell you about it later on; I'd better be off after them now. I'll be in to the Apollon for dinner and I'll see you then. Afterwards we'll get you installed at the studio. You'll dine with me, of course?"

"Why, thank you. I—"

"Take care of yourself, then. See you at dinner." And with a lift of the hand he was gone in the wake of the shocking pink socks.

I stared after him for a few seconds, but he didn't look back.

It occurred to me, with a slight sense of surprise, that this time yesterday I hadn't even met him.

I turned and began to make my careful way down toward Delphi.

12

Seize her! Throw her from Parnassus, send her bounding down the cliff-ledges, let the crags comb out her dainty hair!

EURIPIDES: *Ion*
(tr. Philip Vellacott)

IT WAS late afternoon, and the sun was straight ahead of me when at length I came out on top of one of the great cliffs that stand above the Shrine at Delphi. Far below me and to the right lay the temple precinct, its monuments and porticos and its Sacred Way looking small and very clean-cut in the sun, like the plaster models that you see in museums. The pillars of Apollo were foreshortened, and tiny as toys. Directly beneath me was the cleft of the Castalian Spring. The tangle of trees filled it like a dark waterfall. Already, beyond the tree-filled cleft, the Flamboyant cliff was taking the late-afternoon sun like flame.

I moved back a few feet from the edge, and sat down on a stone. To one side of me grew a thicket of tallish juniper. Beyond and all around this was the usual dusty expanse of hot stone. The path to the stadium led off to the right past the bushes, but I was tired, and here at the cliff top a cool breeze from the sea allayed the still-hot blaze of afternoon.

I sat quietly, chin on hand, looking down at the dreaming marbles of the shrine below, at the blue-and-silver depths of the valley where hawks circled below eye level, at the great cliff beside me burning in the sun. . . . No, I thought, I could not leave Delphi yet. Even if it meant sleeping in the studio near the intolerable Danielle, in order to save what I must owe on the car, I couldn't leave. There must be tomorrow—and the day after, and the day after . . . how long a succession of days would it take before I had begun to learn and see and taste what Delphi had to show? I must stay. And my decision (I told myself quickly) had nothing to do with Simon Lester and his affairs. Nothing. Nothing whatever. On the thought I found myself wondering just what Simon would have decided that we should do tomorrow. . . .

"What are you doing up here?"

The question came from close behind me. I turned sharply. Danielle had come out from behind the thicket of juniper. Today she had on a wide bell of scarlet skirt and a turquoise-colored blouse that was open at the neck. Very open. The inevitable cigarette clung to her bottom lip. Her mouth was rouged a pale pink against her sallow skin. Today her fingernails were pale pink too. On the thin brown hands it looked odd and slightly improper.

"Why, hullo," I said pleasantly. If I was to be the girl's neighbor tonight in the studio, it didn't do to let last night's irritation with her bad manners reappear.

But Danielle had no such scruples. It was quite obvious that manners, bad or good, had no place in her scheme of things. She simply was, and if others didn't like it, they had to endure it. She repeated in that sharp voice that sounded as if she really wanted to know, "What are you doing up here?"

I said, letting a note of mild surprise creep in, "Sitting looking at the view. And you?"

She came toward me. She moved like a model, hips thrown forward and knees close. She stood between me and the edge of the cliff in one of the attitudes you see in fashion drawings—one hip out, toes at twenty past seven, one thin hand gesturing with the cigarette. Any minute now she would open her mouth and let the tip of her tongue appear.

She said, "It's a long climb from the shrine on a hot afternoon."

"Isn't it? Has it tired you very much, or did you just come round the top from the studio?"

She gave me a glittering glance. I couldn't see for the life of me why she should care what I was doing up here, but she obviously did. And I certainly wasn't going to tell her where we had been. That was Simon's pilgrimage, and no one else's. If he chose to take me along, well, that was his affair. But I wasn't going to tell Danielle.

She said, "Where's Simon?"

"I don't know," I said truthfully. "Were you looking for him?"

"Oh, not really." To my surprise she came forward and sat down not two yards from my feet. She swore once, viciously, in French, as her hip met a thistle, then she settled herself gracefully on the dusty ground and smiled at me. "A cigarette?"

"Why, thanks very much," I said, before I thought.

She regarded me for a while in silence, while I smoked and tried not to feel annoyed that now I could hardly get up and leave her, which I very much wanted to do. Really, I reflected, when faced with this sort of person why do we hold madly on to our own tabus; why could my careful manners not allow me to get up—as Danielle certainly would have done in my place—say, "I'm bored and you are a mannerless little trollop and I don't like you," and then walk away down the hill? But there I sat and looked pleasantly noncommittal and smoked her cigarette. I must admit that it was a good one, and—after Niko's—nectar and ambrosia. I wondered why she had offered the olive branch, and eyed her warily. "I fear the Greeks, even when bringing gifts. . . ."

"You weren't in to lunch at the Apollon."

"No," I agreed. "Were you?"

"Where did you have lunch?"

"I had a picnic. Out."

"With Simon?"

I raised my eyebrows and tried to register cold surprise at the inquisition. It had no effect whatever. "With Simon?" she repeated.

"Yes."

"I saw him go out in the car."

"Did you?"

"He picked you up somewhere?"

"Yes."

"Where did you go?"

"South."

This set her back for half a minute. Then she said, "Why don't you want to tell me where you went and what you've been doing?"

I looked at her rather helplessly. "Why should I?"

"Why shouldn't you?"

"Because," I said, "I don't like being catechized."

She digested this. "Oh?" She turned those big tired eyes up to me, and asked, "Why? Have you and Simon been up to something?"

Said by Danielle, the harmless question could only mean one thing. I said explosively, "My God!" Then I began to laugh. I said, "No, Danielle. We have not. We took the car down to Arachova and left it there, then we walked back over the hill toward Delphi. We had a picnic at a place where there is a lovely view of Parnassus.Then I came on toward home and Simon went back for the car. If you sit here long enough you'll see him drive past below you. In case you don't know it by sight, the car you hired is a big black one. I don't know the make. I know very little about cars. Will that do? And thank you for the cigarette. I must be going." And I stubbed out the two-thirds-smoked cigarette and got to my feet.

She made a little movement without getting up, a sinuous little wriggle in the dust, like a snake. She smiled up at me. The cigarette had dropped from her lip and was smoldering on the ground beside her. She made no attempt to retrieve it. She was smiling and showing pretty white teeth with her tongue between them. The tongue was pale like her lips and nails. "You're annoyed with me," she said.

I felt suddenly very old with all the adult weight of my twenty-five years. "My dear girl," I said, "what could possibly lead you to imagine that?"

"You see, it's only," said Danielle from the dust, "that I'm jealous about Simon."

I wanted passionately to turn and run, but this gambit hardly provided me with a good exit line. I merely shed most of those adult years at one go and said feebly and childlishly, "Oh?"

"Men," said the voice of the dust snake, "are all the same, mostly. But there really is something about Simon. I expect even you feel it, don't you? On the whole my lovers bore me, but I want Simon. I genuinely do."

"Really."

"Yes. Really." The flat little voice held no inflection. "And I can tell you just what it is about Simon. It's—"

I said sharply, "No, really, Danielle!"

She shot me a look. "You're in love with him yourself, aren't you?"

"Don't be absurd!" To my horror I sounded almost too emphatic. "I hardly know him! And besides, this is not the—"

"What difference does that make? It takes me two seconds to know whether I want a man or not."

I turned away. "Look," I said, "I must go. I expect I'll be seeing you later. Good-bye."

"Are you seeing him again tomorrow?"

The question was said idly, in that same flat voice; but it was not quite idle. Something made me pause and turn back to her.

She didn't meet my look. She was tracing a line in the dust with a pink-tipped forefinger. "What's he doing tomorrow?"

Definitely not quite idle. I said, "How do I know?" as coldly as I could, before it occurred to me that I did know, quite well. He would certainly go straight back to the corrie, to look for Michael's hypothetical cave. And he just as certainly wouldn't want Danielle tagging after him. The whole of this embarrassing interview seemed to indicate that she was prepared to do just that.

I said, in the tone of one conceding a point to a stubborn adversary, "All right. I'll tell you. I am seeing him. We're going to Levadia for the day. There's a horse fair, and gipsies, and he wants to take photographs."

"Oh." She was looking away over the valley with eyes narrowed against the sun. Then she sent another of those glinting looks up at me. "But what a bloody waste," she said.

Though I was used to her by now, I didn't quite manage to control the little flicker of anger that ran through me. I said, "So he didn't come to repair the taps last night?"

The beautiful eyelashes fluttered, and her eyes narrowed over a look of the most intense venom. "You're very outspoken, aren't you?" said Danielle.

"My bad manners," I said. "I'm sorry. And now I must go if I'm to get a bath before dinner. See you later. Did you know I was to come and stay at the studio from tonight?"

Her eyes opened wide. The dislike was still there, and now annoyance, and then both were suddenly, curiously, overlaid by what looked like calculation. "That'll be convenient, won't it?" said Danielle, meaning what only Danielle could mean. Then I saw her look change again. It slid over my shoulder and I saw surprise in her face, and something else.

I turned quickly.

A man had come out from behind the clump of juniper. He was obviously a Greek, dark, broad-cheekboned, with crisp curled hair that showed a hint of gray, and a smudge of a moustache over a mouth at once thin-lipped and sensual. He was of medium height, and stockily built. I guessed his age to be around forty. He was dressed in a gray striped suit, rather shabby, and a dark crimson shirt with a vermilion tie that would have clashed if the colors had not been harmlessly faded.

He spoke in French. "Why, hullo, Danielle."

It was as if he had told her quite plainly, *"It's all right."* I could see the look of surprise fade. She relaxed. "Hullo. How did you know I was here?"

I thought, Because you've just been together behind the juniper bushes and I interrupted you. Then I shook the thought away with the wry reflection that this was what contact with Danielle did. Five minutes with her, and a full half-pound of civet would hardly sweeten the imagination.

Danielle said idly—too idly—from the dust, "This is Camilla Haven. She's been out with Simon this afternoon and she's sleeping at the studio tonight." Then to me, "Dimitrios is a guide."

The man bowed and sent me a smile. *"Enchanté."*

"He doesn't speak English," said Danielle. "Do you know French?"

"Yes," I said, and murmured something polite.

Dimitrios said, "Mademoiselle has been to see the shrine this afternoon?"

"No. I went this morning early."

"Ah. And now you come up to the top of the Shining Ones to see the last of the sun."

I said, "It'll be some time still till dark, surely?"

"Perhaps not so long," said Dimitrios. I saw Danielle turn her head to look at him. Her head was on a level with my thigh, and I couldn't see her eyes for the curtaining lashes. Something crept along my spine like a cold-footed insect. The man, no less than the girl, gave me the creeps.

I gave myself another of those hearty mental shakes. "I must be going. If I'm to have a bath before dinner and arrange about—"

"These rocks," said Dimitrios, "are called the Phaedriades, the Shining Ones. Always I tell my tourists the story of the Shining Ones. Between them flows the Castalian Spring, whose water is the best in Greece. Have you tried the water of the spring, mademoiselle?"

"No, not yet. I—"

He came a step nearer. I was between him and the edge of the cliff. "They stand over the shrine like guardians, do they not? Because that is what they are. They were not only the protectors of the holy place, but they were themselves the place of execution. There were people executed on these cliffs—for sacrilege, mademoiselle. Did you know that?"

"No. But—"

Another step. He was smiling, a smile of great charm. He had a pleasant voice. Beside me in the dust I saw Danielle lift her head. I saw that her eyes now watched me, not the man. She was smiling at me with the utmost friendliness, her eyes for once bright, not tired at all. I moved back from him a step or two. It brought me within four feet of the edge.

Dimitrios said suddenly, "Be careful." I jumped and his hand came out to my arm. It was gentle on the flesh. "You are not here for execution as a traitor to the god, mademoiselle." He laughed, and Danielle smiled, and I thought suddenly, wildly, Why the hell can't I just pull my arm away and run? I hate the pair of them and they frighten me, and here I stand because it isn't polite to go while the damned man's talking.

"I always tell my tourists," he was saying, "one particular story. There was a certain traitor who was brought up here for execution. Two of them came with him to the edge . . . just there . . . to throw him over. He looked over . . . yes, mademoiselle, it is a long way down, is it not? . . . and then he said to them, Please will you not send me over face first, please will you let me fall with my back to the drop? One understands how he felt, mademoiselle, does one not?"

His hand was still on my arm. I pulled back against it. It slid gently up the flesh to the inside of my elbow. I noticed that his nails were bitten to the quick and that his thumb was badly cut and crusted with dried blood. I started to turn from him and to pull my arm away, but his fingers tightened. His voice quickened a little in my ear, "So they threw him over, mademoiselle, and as he fell, he—"

I said breathlessly, "Let me go. I don't like heights. Let me go, please."

He smiled. "Why, mademoiselle—"

Danielle's voice said, dry and thin, "Are these your tourists, Dimitrios?"

He gave an exclamation under his breath. His hand dropped from my arm. He turned sharply.

Three people, a man and two women, were coming slowly along the path from the direction of Arachova. The women were plain, dumpy, middle-aged; the man was stoutish, and wore khaki shorts and had an enormous camera slung over one perspiring shoulder. They looked at us with incurious red faces as they plodded past like beef cattle in a row, like angels of heaven.

I shot away from the brink of the cliff the way a cork leaves the very best champagne. I didn't bother to say anything polite to Dimitrios, and I didn't even fling a good-bye at Danielle.

I hurried down the path in the wake of the three tourists. Neither the Greek nor the girl made any move to follow me, and after a while I slackened my pace and walked more slowly, trying to control my thoughts. If Danielle and her damned lover—for that the Greek was her lover I had no doubt at all—had tried for some silly reason to frighten me, they had succeeded. I had felt both frightened, and a fool, and it was a beastly mixture. But there had surely been nothing more than that . . . a spiteful trick and a distorted sense of humor? It was absurd to imagine anything more. I had only done so because I had spent an exacting and physically tiring day. I disliked Danielle and I had shown it, and she had wanted to frighten and humiliate me because I had interrupted her sordid meeting with the Greek behind the junipers. And even, perhaps, because of Simon. . . .

I had reached the stadium. The flat racetrack lay empty and silent in the sun, cupped in its tiers of marble seats. I almost ran across the bare dust, hurried between the columns of the starting gate, and down into the path that led to the shrine. I found that my heart was still hammering in my breast, and my throat was tight. The path dipped, dropped, twisted past a well where water trickled, and came precipitously down onto the smooth track above the theatre. There were my three tourists, still comfortably trudging along, talking something incomprehensible that might have been Dutch. There were people, too, in the theatre just below me, people on the steps, people everywhere on the floor of Apollo's temple. It was quite safe to stand here under the trees and wait for my heart to slow down. Quite safe. . . .

The slanting sun was golden on the quiet stones, was apricot, was amber, was a lovely liquid wash of light and peace. A bee went past my cheek.

Beside me was the pomegranate tree. The fruit glowed in the rich light. I remembered the cool feel of it in my hand last night, and Simon's voice saying: "Eat it soon, Persephone, then you'll have to stay in Delphi. . . ."

Well, I was going to stay. I was still going to stay.

My breathing was back to normal. Apollo the healer had done his work.

I went composedly down the steps, across the sunbaked circle of the theatre, down through the scented pines that rim the shrine, and along the main road to the hotel.

Even when, washing for dinner, I saw on my bare arm a streak of dried blood—Dimitrios' blood from that cut thumb—I felt only a brief moment of disgust. I had been stupid and imaginative and had had a fright; that was all.

But I felt a curious reluctance to go down to dinner before Simon appeared, and I wished with a quite startling fervor that I was not committed to sleeping in the studio that night.

13

. . . With hollow shriek the steep of *Delphos* leaving.

MILTON: *Nativity Hymn*

IT MUST have been close on three o'clock in the morning when something woke me. My room was second from the end of the long corridor, next to Danielle's, and at the opposite end from the outer door, near which were the rooms of the two men. The Dutch painter had gone that day, so we four were the only occupants of the studio.

For some time I lay in that heavy state between sleep and waking where it is hard to disentangle reality from the trailing clouds of dream. Something had woken me, but whether I had heard a noise, or whether it was the dream itself that had startled me awake, I couldn't tell. There was no sound outside. The quiet air of Delphi wrapped us round. I moved my cheek against the hard pillow— pillows in Greece are always made like bricks—and prepared to drift back into sleep again.

From the next room came the sound of a movement, and then the creak of the bed—two sounds so completely normal and expected that they should never have roused me further. But with them came a third sound that brought my eyes wide open in the dark and my cheek up off the pillow, and made nonsense of the normality of the night. Someone was talking, very softly: a man.

My first thought was embarrassment of having heard, my next irritation succeeded by disgust. If Danielle had to have her lover in her room I didn't want to be pilloried, sleepless, on the other side of a too-thin partition. I turned over with as much fuss of bedclothes and creak of bedsprings as I could, to let them know how thin the wall was, then I pulled the sheet—it was too hot for blankets—over my head, and tried to stop my ears to the sounds that succeeded the whispering.

Sleep had gone for good. I lay rigid under the sheet with my eyes wide open in the darkness and my hands as hard as I could bear to hold them over my ears. It wasn't that I'm particularly a prude; but being forced to listen in on anyone's more private moments isn't pleasant, and I didn't want any part or parcel or hint of the more private moments of Danielle. Her public moments were quite embarrassing enough.

I wondered how the unpleasant Dimitrios had got into the place. Even though he was only here to visit Danielle, I didn't one bit like the idea of his being free to come and go. I supposed that he might have climbed in by her window, and if so, sooner or later he would go out the same way. I would no doubt hear him scramble out and drop the twelve feet or so to the floor of the rocky platform where the studio was built. I waited, furious with Danielle for subjecting me to this, furious with myself for minding, furious with Dimitrios for pandering to her monstrous egotism. It was a beastly experience.

How long it was before there was quiet from the next room I don't know. It seemed an age. But after a while all was silent, except for the whispering again, and then I heard someone moving furtively across the floor. I waited for the sounds of the window, and the cat-foot drop to the ground outside. But they didn't come. I heard the door to the corridor open, and steps went stealthily past my door.

That brought me upright in bed with a quick nervous jerk of the heart. If Danielle wanted to let a man in and out of her room, very well. But she had no damned right to let a man like Dimitrios loose inside the place. Had she—*had she?*—given him a key?

Then, out of the dark, came another thought that kicked through those nerves again.

Perhaps it wasn't Dimitrios at all.

Perhaps it was Nigel.

I was out of bed and had thrust my feet into my slippers, and was shrugging my way into the light summer coat that also served me for a dressing gown, before I quite realized myself what I was going to do. Then I had fled across the little room and had, very softly, opened my door and was peering out into the corridor.

I suppose this bit isn't pretty. It wasn't any business of mine if Nigel had gone to Danielle's room and got what had been so patently his heart's desire. But when I had thought of him I had had a memory, sudden and bright and clean, of the young eagerness of Nigel's face; the vulnerable eyes and the weak mouth and the silly boy's beard. And I had seen his drawings, the visions of tree and flower and stone that he had translated with such impeccable and yet impassioned skill. If this, too, was Nigel . . . I had to know. Call it sheer, vulgar, woman's curiosity if you like, but I had to know if the impossible Danielle could really annex him like that—if she was really prepared to make Nigel, whom she despised, squander himself in worship at her shoddy little shrine.

I believe I was thinking, incoherently, that something must be done to stop her ruining Nigel, and then, even more incoherently, of Simon. Simon must be told tomorrow. Simon would know what to do. . . .

I slipped softly out of my room. The outer door at the end of the corridor had its upper half of glass, and outside it the dark was slackening off into dawn. The pane was gray. Against it I saw him.

He was almost at the end of the corridor, standing outside a door—Nigel's door—as if he had paused there waiting for something. I shrank against the wall, but even if he had looked back he could not have seen me against the darkness at my end of the passage. I stayed still, pressed against the cold marble, and felt humiliated and angry and ashamed all at once, wishing I hadn't known, wishing I was still fathoms deep in sleep, wishing I could remember Nigel by his work and not, as now, through the smudgy little whispers of Danielle. . . . "Men are all the same anyway . . . it bores me . . . I want Simon . . . I genuinely do. . . ."

The silhouette at the corridor's end moved at last. He took a step forward and put his hand to the knob of the door. Then he paused again, momentarily, with his head bent, as if listening.

I thought I must have made some sound and that he had heard me, because I could see, now, that it wasn't the Greek: it was too tall. It wasn't Nigel either. It was Simon.

* * *

If I had been in a condition to think, the swift and complete rebellion of every nerve and muscle in my body, and of every drop of blood in my brain, would have told me finally about myself and Simon. But I had hardly realized what I had seen, when the night broke open rather more really, and very much more noisily.

Simon pushed open Nigel's door. I saw him reach up as if for the light switch, but even as he moved the beam of a powerful torch speared out of the darkness of the room to catch him full on the face and chest. I saw his fractional check and recoil, as if the light were a physical blow in the eyes, but the pause was less than momentary, no more than the tensing before the spring. Before he had even blinked once he had launched himself forward along the beam of light, with the speed of a bullet. I heard an impact, a curse, the swift stamp and flurry of feet on the stone floor, and then all hell seemed to break loose inside the room.

I ran down the corridor and paused in the doorway. The little room seemed to be a pandemonium of violently struggling bodies. In the weaving, flashing beam of the torch the two men looked enormous, and their shadows towered and waved grotesquely over ceiling and walls. Simon was the taller, and seemed to have a momentary advantage. He had the other's wrist in one hand and seemed to be struggling to twist the man's arm so that the torch would light his features. The beam swung wildly, erratically, as the other fought to resist him, the light sweeping in violent, broken arcs through the darkness. It caught me, standing in the doorway, and raked a brilliant curve across my feet and the skirt of the nightdress below my coat. Someone snarled something incomprehensible in Greek, and then the man had wrenched his arm free from Simon's grip and, with a grunt of effort, brought the heavy torch down in a vicious blow aimed for Simon's head. Even as the blow whistled down, Simon jerked aside, so that the torch came down with a sickening sound on the side of his neck. It must have struck a muscle, for his grip seemed to loosen, and the Greek tore free.

It must, after all, have been Dimitrios. I saw the stocky body and broad shoulders in the erratic light before Simon was on him again, and the torch flew wide, to strike the wall beside me and fall to roll somewhere near the foot of the bed. Darkness stamped down. I had no time to wonder about Dimitrios—why he had come to Nigel's room, why Simon had followed him, or even—strangest of all—why Nigel himself didn't appear to be here, when the two men, at grips again, hurtled past me to come violently up against the door of the shower stall. There was a crack as a wooden panel gave way; somewhere on the floor was the sharp explosion of breaking glass; one of the flimsy chairs went over with a splintering sound; then the bedsprings crashed and whined as the two bodies went down on the bed together.

I flung myself to my knees not two feet from the heaving bed, groping wildly for the torch. Somewhere here I had heard it roll . . . not far, surely? . . . these things rolled in semicircles . . . ah! . . . there is was. I clutched it, groping at the metal to find the catch, wondering if the fall had broken the bulb. . . .

It was a heavy torch and the catch was stiff. The bed, rocking like a ship in a storm, shot away a foot from the wall on screaming castors, hurtled back again with a crash that should have brought the plaster off the walls. The springs creaked, strained, gave again with an appalling noise as the men slithered to the edge and then fell to the floor.

A moment of gasping stillness, and then they were on their feet again. A pause, filled with the sound of heavy breathing. I jumped to my feet, still wrestling with the torch, and suddenly the thing flashed on in my hand. For the second time that night it caught Simon full in the eyes. And this time the Greek, seizing the advantage like lightning, charged down the beam, out of the blinding light. Simon went down with a crash that shook the room. I saw him catch the edge of the bed with his shoulder as he fell. The blow must have momentarily crippled him, but, surprisingly, the Greek didn't follow it up. Nor did he turn to deal with me. He had his back to me, and the light waveringly pinned for a moment the heavy bull-like shoulders, the dark curled hair. . . . He didn't even look round. I heard a gasping snarl in French, *"Put the bloody thing out, will you?"*

I hit him as hard as I could over the head.

I missed him. Just as the blow fell, something warned him. He didn't turn into the light. He lashed backwards with a crooked elbow that caught the torch, knocking it flying, then swept on to strike me full across the breast in a heavy blow that sent me staggering to fall at the foot of the bed. The torch hurtled wide a second time and went out for good. As I went down I saw, in one swift flash of the flying light, the Greek turn and leap for the doorway, with Simon after him in a lunge. And in the doorway stood Danielle, fully dressed, with wide brilliant eyes and parted lips.

She whipped back to let the man past. Then, with a languid-seeming movement that was nevertheless as swift as a snake's, she stepped into the path of Simon's rush. I heard the other man running up the corridor toward her room and the open window, as Simon came violently up against her body. I heard her gasp as his weight jammed her hard against the doorpost. He stopped short.

I couldn't see more than the dim outlines of movement against the gray light of the corridor, but she must have been clinging to him, for he said, harsh and breathless, *"Let me go!"* and she laughed in her throat. Along the corridor a door slammed. Simon moved sharply and I heard him say, very softly, "Do you hear me? Take your hands away, or you'll get hurt."

I hadn't heard him even sound ruffled before; now I realized with something like a sharp little shock that he was angry. Danielle must not have set much store by it, for I heard her murmur, with the breath hurrying through the husky voice, "Go on doing that. I like it. . . ."

There was a second of frozen silence, then in the near-darkness the group by the door exploded into movement. The girl was flung aside against the other door jamb with a violence that sent the breath out of her in a sharp cry that held more surprise than anything else. Before she could recover herself Simon was back in the room, hurling himself across it toward the window, tearing at the catch.

The casement was rusty, and it must have been stiff. As it screeched wider I heard, like an echo at the other end of the building, the shriek of rusty hinges, and the thud as a heavy body dropped to the ground. Steps clattered and slithered away into the darkness.

Simon was up on the sill, a dark bulk against the graying sky. But before he could swing himself out and after the quarry Danielle flew after him like an arrow and clung to his arm.

"Simon . . . Simon, let him go, Simon dear, what a fuss. . . ." In spite of his recent violence she clung to him still, pleading in that voice which under its overtones of sexiness might have held a touch of fear. "Simon, no! He was with me. Don't you understand? *With me.*"

I saw his hand fall from the window catch. He turned. "What? What d'you mean?"

"What I say. He was in my room. He only came to see me."

I said from the floor beside the bed where I was still sitting, "It's true. I heard them."

I heard her laugh again, but the sound didn't hold its usual assurance. Simon shook her off as if she didn't exist and dropped lightly back into the room. "I— see. He's gone, anyway . . . Camilla? Are you all right?"

"Perfectly. Is there any light?"

"I think the bulb's out. Half a minute." He seemed to be feeling in his pockets. "What are you doing down there? Did that brute hit you?"

"Yes, but I'm all right. I was just—I was keeping out of the way." I got up a bit unsteadily and sat on the bed, just as Simon found matches and struck one. He surveyed me by its light. I smiled rather waveringly up at him. I saw then that he was dressed only in a pair of gray flannels. In the light of the match I could see the gleam of sweat on his chest and a shining dark trickle of blood from a cut at the base of the neck, where a deep V of sunburn showed. He was breathing a little faster than usual—not much, but perceptibly a bit faster—and his eyes for once didn't look cool and amused at all. But the match burned steadily in a tremorless hand. I asked anxiously, "What about you?"

"Don't give it a thought. Honors were about even . . . more's the pity."

Danielle said petulantly, "What did you have to fight for?"

He said crisply, "My dear girl, he attacked me. What would you expect me to do?" He had lit another match and was looking round the room for the light bulb.

I said, "That was Dimitrios, wasn't it?"

Simon gave me a fleeting look of surprise as he picked the light bulb up from the washbasin. Danielle turned her head as if startled, then smiled that cat-and-cream smile of hers. "You recognized him? Of course."

Simon had dragged one of the wooden chairs forward, and now mounted it to fit the light bulb into its socket. The light flashed on, harsh on the disorder of the bare little room. He got off the chair, looking at me.

"Are you sure you're all right?"

"Quite. But, Simon—where's Nigel?"

"I've no idea. He hasn't been to bed; that much is apparent." In spite of the tossed state of the bed, the sheet still lay tucked flatly in. No one had slept there. Simon hesitated, then turned to Danielle. She was standing near the door, leaning against the wall in a pose of lazy grace. Her eyes looked long and sleepy again under the thick lashes. She had taken a cigarette out of a pocket and was lighting it. She dropped the burnt-out match on the floor. All through the operation the narrow glinting gaze had been on Simon . . . all over him.

He said flatly, "You say that man was with you? How did he get in?"

"I let him in."

"By the door?"

"No. By my window."

"Come off it, Danielle. Your window's twelve feet from the ground. Don't tell me you plaited sheets or let down your hair for him. Did you unlock the door for him, or has he got a key?"

She said sulkily, under the coldness of his voice, "I don't see what the hell it's got to do with you, but yes, I did unlock it."

"It's got everything to do with me that your visitor was apparently prowling round where he's no damned right to be. And there's the little detail that he went for me with apparent intent to do damage, if not worse. What was he doing in Nigel's room?"

"How do I know?"

"He jumped out of your window in the end. He could have gone that way in the first place. Why didn't he?"

"It was easier to get out through the door, and quieter. The key's in the lock."

"Then why did he come in here?"

She shrugged. "He must have heard you moving and dodged in so that you wouldn't see him. I don't know."

"He couldn't have known there was no one in the room."

"I'd told him they were nearly all empty. I expect he took a chance. And now I'm tired of this, and tired of the inquisition, and I'm going to bed." She straightened, yawning deliberately and daintily, like a cat, showing all her pretty teeth and that pale pink tongue. Then she turned her head and let the big sleepy eyes move insolently over me. Simon had found the end of a battered pack of cigarettes in his trouser pocket and had given me one. He bent over me to light it. His breathing was quite even again now. If it hadn't been for the cut where the torch had hit him, and that thin glaze of sweat drying on his skin, you would never have guessed that a few minutes ago he had been fighting for his life in the dark.

Danielle said, sounding suddenly waspish, "What are you doing here anyway, Camilla?"

"I heard a noise and I came along."

She smiled. "And got knocked down. Did he hurt you?"

"I hope not as much as I hurt him."

She looked momentarily startled, and this gave me a quite absurd prick of satisfaction. "You hurt him? How?"

"I hit him over the back of the neck with the torch. Hard."

She stared at me for a moment longer, a very queer look.

"You hit him?" Her voice sounded quite shaken. "I can't see—you have no business. . . . He is my lover, and if I wish to let him come here—"

I said sharply, "He was doing his best to kill Simon. And besides, I owed him something."

She looked at me almost stupidly. "You—owed him something?"

"Yes. And don't play the innocent, Danielle. You didn't look so innocent on the Shining Ones this afternoon."

"I . . . see."

She let out a breath. Simon said sharply, "What are you talking about? What happened?"

"Nothing. It was Camilla's imagination. She thinks Dimitrios—oh, it's so silly that I won't speak of it. It was a joke. And now I'm sick of this. I'm going." She dropped the half-smoked cigarette on the floor and turned quickly. I got to my feet.

"Just a minute," said Simon pleasantly. "No, please don't go yet, Camilla. We're forgetting Nigel. Danielle, have you any idea where he might be? Did he say anything last night to—?"

She said viciously, "Why should I know where the fool went? I don't know and I don't care. He could be dead as far as I'm concerned."

I said, "I think I know where he went."

Simon was dabbing at his cut neck with a handkerchief. I saw his brows shoot up. "You seem to know an awful lot tonight."

"Doesn't she?" Danielle had stopped in the doorway, and turned her head sharply. Her voice was not, like his, amused. "All right, you tell us."

I said, "It's only a guess. But . . . well, Simon, d'you remember our talk in here the other night, about Nigel and his work, and needing a gimmick, and the Dutch boy walking from Jannina and all that?"

"Yes. You're not suggesting that Nigel has taken a leaf out of that boy's book, are you?"

I said, "There's been a mule stolen from the excavations above the shrine. I know because the guide told me this morning . . . yesterday morning, I suppose I should say. And I saw Nigel early the same morning, and he was trying not to be seen—"

"Where?" asked Danielle.

"Just outside the studio here."

"Which way was he going?"

"I didn't see. He seemed to be making farther up Parnassus—toward the stadium."

"Ah well," said Simon, "you may be right. I suppose what Nigel does is very much his own affair, and he was certainly feeling thoroughly unsettled. He may easily have cut loose for a few days." He turned to rinse his bloodstained handkerchief out under the tap. "I think we'd better just tidy his room up and get out of it. There's blood on the washbasin here, and I'm afraid the floor isn't all it should be. We'd better have a look at the damage and do what we can."

I said, "Leave that. I'll clean the basin up. But let me have a look at that cut, will you? Danielle, perhaps you'll be good enough to clear the floor and pick up that broken glass?"

She sent me one of those looks of glittering dislike, which was, this time, quite justified. "It won't take you long. I'm tired. You forget, I haven't been to sleep yet tonight, and oh, how I need that sleep. . . ." She yawned, sent another narrow-eyed look at me, and went out rather quickly, shutting the door behind her.

Seconds later, from the other end of the corridor, came like an echo the slam of her bedroom door.

14

Courage is a thing
All men admire. Think what it will mean
For your good name and mine, if you do this.

SOPHOCLES: *Ajax*
(tr. E. F. Watling)

IN NIGEL'S room there was the sort of silence that is usually called pregnant. But at least, I reflected, there was no longer any need to suppress the urge to discuss Danielle. . . .

My eyes met Simon's in the mirror. "You wanted to get rid of her, didn't you?"

"You're coming on with that thought-reading, aren't you? I did indeed."

"Why?" I added, carefully, "Apart, that is, from the obvious reasons."

The brief amusement in his eyes vanished as he turned and looked down at me. His look was grave, somber even. "Because I don't like the feel of this thing, Camilla."

"The feel of it?"

"Yes. Too much is happening. Some of it may be irrelevant, or it may matter the hell of a lot. Danielle and this man, for instance. . . . And Danielle and Nigel. I've begun to wonder."

"Then I was right. Turn round toward the light and let me have a look at that cut . . . you didn't want me to go on talking about Nigel in front of her?"

"No."

"It's not deep, but you're going to have a bruise and a stiff shoulder, I think. Have you any antiseptic in your room? You don't think he's gone off with a Modestine into the mountains?"

"Yes. No, I mean. No, I don't believe he's off on a trip, but yes, I have some antiseptic."

"Then don't forget to put it on. The wound's quite clean and it's stopped bleeding." I stood back and looked at him inquiringly. "Then what have Danielle and Nigel and this Greek of hers got to do with us—with you, I mean?"

He said slowly, "This Greek—this lover of Danielle's . . . you said his name was Dimitrios?"

"Yes. I met him yesterday on the way back from the corrie. He was with her above the Shining Ones."

"Ah, yes. The Shining Ones. What happened there, incidentally? What did you 'owe' Dimitrios?"

"Oh, it was nothing, really. He was unpleasant in a greasy sort of way, and talked a lot about people being thrown off the cliff and so on. We were awfully near the edge and he could see I didn't like it, and it amused him . . . and Danielle too. It was just a nasty little trick to make me look a fool—which I did, I may say. I bolted."

There was a frown between his eyes. "I see. Camilla, has nothing occurred to you about this—Dimitrios?"

"Occurred to me? What sort of thing? I don't like him, and I think—" I stopped short. I said, on a long breath, *"Dimitrios!"*

"Exactly. You remember? Angelos had a cousin called Dimitrios Dragoumis, who had gone to live at Itea. At Itea, mark you."

"And I saw the jeep down at Itea . . . Danielle had driven it straight down there when she got in from Athens! If it's the same Dimitrios . . . then Dimitrios Dragoumis is Danielle's lover, and that was his house I saw. She wasn't visiting any friend called 'Elena,' she was visiting him, and I'll bet, if the jeep's anything to go by, that she was there when I passed the house!"

"You're certain it was the same jeep?"

"Quite. I told you I recognized the doll hanging in the windscreen. There was someone tinkering with the engine, and that wasn't Dimitrios, but all the same, I've a feeling we're right. It's the same Dimitrios. That would explain why Danielle's so darned interested in you." I added, "Or partly."

He passed that one.

"Well, then, say we're right, and let's look at what we have . . . Dimitrios Dragoumis is Danielle's lover. Whether there actually is anyone called Elena or not, it's quite true that Danielle has been in the habit of spending her afternoons down near Itea, swimming. She told me once she'd found a secluded little cove where the water was clean (it's filthy in Itea itself) but she wouldn't tell me where it was. My guess is that she met, not 'Elena,' but Dimitrios, on these swimming expeditions, and took up with him. He may have been there to fish—he's a fisherman, did I tell you, and owns a caique?"

"He told me he was a guide."

"There's no guide in Delphi of that name, that I do know; and if he took the trouble to lie . . ." He didn't finish the sentence. He was frowning down at his cigarette. "Well, let's go on. Dimitrios, the cousin of Angelos, sends Danielle into Athens to hire him a car—on a matter of life and death. In other words, in a hell of a hurry."

"Well?"

His eyes lifted. "An expensive need. And he's a sailor. Why would he want a car?"

I sat down again on the bed. "I don't know. Go on."

Absently, he flicked a gout of ash into the washbasin.

"Danielle hired a car for him, but then got the better offer of a jeep from her French friend Hervé Clément, and came up in that. She didn't revisit the garage to let them know . . . and she hadn't given them Dragoumis' name—hence all the nonsense about 'Monsieur Simon,' and the interfering but well-meant efforts of Miss Camilla Haven. But Danielle's actions do spell something, don't they?"

"Urgency," I said slowly, "yes. And secrecy?"

"Exactly. And I could bear to know what's urgent and secret about Danielle, and Dimitrios the cousin of Angelos," said Simon.

A pause. A beetle blundered in through the open casement, hit the wall with a crack like a pistol shot, and zoomed out again into the dark.

"But—the car?" I said, seizing on what was still my own piece of the mystery. "Why the car? You said Dimitrios Dragoumis was a fisherman. What would he need a car for, from Athens, with all that hush-hush nonsense about it?"

"That's just it," said Simon. "He is a fisherman, and he owns a boat. And now he has a jeep . . . got from Athens and kept very quiet locally. To me, that adds up to one thing. Transport."

I said, in a voice that sounded queer, "Urgent, secret transport . . ." Then, sitting up briskly, "But—*no*, Simon. It's absurd."

"Why?"

"I can see what you're getting at . . . the reason why Angelos' cousin might need this urgent and secret transport. You mean that you think Dimitrios has found Angelos' cache—whatever it was that Michael found on Parnassus? And the jeep and the caique are to carry—oh!"

"Well?"

"*The mule!* Simon—the mule!"

He nodded. "You can't take a jeep up Parnassus, can you? The mule was stolen the night I saw Stephanos. Danielle brought the jeep up the same day. I'll bet you anything you like that Dimitrios' caique will shortly be lying carefully invisible in one of the tiny inlets beyond Amphissa."

I said, "Look, hold on, Simon. You're only guessing. It *could* have been Nigel who took the mule. He's gone off somewhere, and we were talking about the Dutch boy to him, and—"

"And it would have been very much simpler for Nigel to have bought the donkey—which went dirt cheap—off the Dutch boy," said Simon, "than to have stolen a mule from the excavations. He wasn't all that hard up, and there really wasn't all that need of secrecy for *him*. In fact, if he was off on a trek of that sort, you'd even have thought publicity was necessary."

"Yes, I suppose so. All the same, he looked pretty secretive when I saw him sloping off yesterday morning."

"Oh? But I still don't think he took the mule. It vanished on Monday night, and that night Nigel was up here. Of course he did go out later for a walk with Danielle, but I hardly think—"

I said tautly, "You're right. It wasn't Nigel. I've just remembered something. When we were in the theatre, and you were reciting, I was up near the top row of seats, and I heard something moving up the hillside above me. You know how you hear something without really taking it in consciously, until, later, something reminds you? Well, it was like that. I thought nothing of it—if I heard it at all, I thought it was just the breeze, or a stray goat or donkey or something. But I remember now that I heard metal—a small chinking of metal, like a shod hoof, or the nails of a boot."

Simon smiled slightly. "The beasts here aren't shod. Hadn't you noticed? And the locals wear rope-soled espadrilles on the hill. If you heard movement and the chink of metal, Camilla, then you heard a beast's bridle. It sounds to me as if you really might have heard the mule being stolen. Friend Dimitrios, taking the mule off up the hill. Well, well."

I said sharply, "Simon, if he was above the theatre when you were reciting, he'd hear us, wouldn't he?"

"Almost certainly." He laughed. "Though I'm afraid he'd hardly appreciate *Electra*. He's not likely to know any classical Greek."

"Not only that," I said uneasily, trying to remember. "We talked about Michael, and—"

"In English, though. It's very probable he doesn't understand that well enough, either. Let's hope not."

I cried, "He doesn't! Danielle told me so yesterday—and there'd be no reason for her to lie to me then. . . . But look, Simon, you can't be right; about the reason for all this, I mean. It really is absurd. Maybe Dimitrios is up to no good, and maybe Danielle is in it, and maybe they did steal the mule and hire the car to transport something, but it can't, it just can't, be Michael's 'treasure'!"

"Why not?"

"Because it's too much to swallow that Dimitrios should have spent fourteen years or so looking for the stuff, and just have found it now. Oh, I grant you he could have searched a thousand years and never found it, especially if he didn't have precise information from Angelos—and he probably didn't, because you can be sure Angelos meant to come back when things had simmered down enough for him to leave Yugoslavia and come home. He may not have told Dimitrios at all. Dimitrios may merely have guessed that Angelos had hidden something, and not have known where to start looking. But what I can't swallow is the assumption that he should have found Angelos' cache *now,* this week, the very week you're in Delphi. That's too much of a coincidence, and I don't believe it."

"But is it?"

"How d'you mean?"

He said slowly, "You've got it the wrong way round. Supposing those two things *have* happened at the same time: I am here in Delphi, and Dimitrios finds Angelos' cache on Parnassus. You call it coincidence. I call it cause and effect."

"You mean—?"

"That the two incidents are certainly related, but not by chance. Dimitrios found the hiding place, not just while I happen to be here—but simply *because* I'm here."

I stared up at him. I passed my tongue over my lips. "You mean—that he followed us up to the corrie yesterday?"

"Precisely that. He could have found out when we were going and he could have come to spy."

I said hoarsely, "He did. When I was sitting there in the corrie and you were in the cave with the other two men, I thought I saw something move at the top of the cliff. It could have been someone watching."

His gaze sharpened. "Are you sure of that?"

"Not really. But I thought there was movement, and looked up, but couldn't see anything. The sun was in my eyes."

"I see. Well, it might have been Dimitrios. And then he followed us down, intending to meet Danielle on top of the Shining Ones. Could be."

I said, "I did her an injustice. I thought they'd been together, and I'd interrupted them."

"He'd hardly have had time to get down there before you. Most of the way it's pretty open, and we might have seen him." He thought for a few moments. "Well, let's look at the sequence of events, shall we? Dimitrios, you'll remember, did try to find out from Stephanos—the only man who knew anything definite about the place where Michael died—anything he could about Michael's death. He didn't get anything out of Stephanos. Perhaps he did try to find the place himself. Perhaps he did gather a slender clue or two from his cousin before he left the country. But even with definite instructions from Angelos he still could have been raking the mountain all this time and found nothing. All the marks, like the Cat's Tooth pinnacle, have gone, and anything could lie buried under that earthquake rubble for fourteen years—or fourteen hundred—undiscovered. Angelos himself, if he were still alive, and if he came back to look, would be in exactly the same case."

I said, rather breathlessly, "Niko said there were ghosts on the hill . . . lights . . . d'you remember?"

"Niko talked a lot of rubbish, but he may well have told the truth there. Dimitrios may have been seen searching. But, to go on with the story— supposing he *had* searched all that time, and had had no luck in locating the cache, then, after years, he heard that I, Michael Lester's brother, was coming to Delphi. This might prove to be his chance. What is more likely than that Stephanos would show me, Michael's brother, the place? When I arrived, Stephanos was away in Levadia, but Dimitrios could easily find out when he was coming back. It's quite some time since I planned this visit; Dimitrios could have known, and taken time over his preparations. Supposing we were right, and he had noticed Danielle driving down almost daily to Itea with the jeep to bathe? Here was transport of the kind he would need. He wouldn't dare buy or hire transport locally; he's well known, and people would ask questions. But it would be easy enough to scrape acquaintance with Danielle, and buy her silence—and her help—with a promise to cut her in on the final haul. It would only remain to collect a mule or a donkey, and there again Danielle was the answer. I'll bet you she took the mule; she'd worked with the archaeologists for weeks, and she knew just where everything was kept and how to get at it. . . . What is it?"

"I've just remembered. It wasn't only a mule. I remember. The guide said 'some tools and a mule.' "

"*Did* he?" His voice was still quiet, but the light-gray eyes blazed in his brown face. "Well, well, well. . . . Does it make sense, or not? Or am I jumping ahead too fast?"

"Pretty fast. They're rather scrappy bricks, and made with awfully little straw, but they could be solid. Go on."

"Where was I? Yes: Dimitrios has everything lined up for the day when Simon Lester should arrive and lead him straight to the spot where Michael died. But then he—Dimitrios—has a stroke of bad luck."

"Danielle's boss leaves Delphi, and she has to go too—with the jeep?"

"Exactly. She went on Sunday, perforce. She must have gone straight to the garage in Athens and arranged to pick up a car next day, as soon as she could get free of Monsieur Clément." He grinned. "We know what happened next. Her error. But luck came in again, as she persuaded Hervé to let her have the jeep. And she came back. She took the jeep down to Itea. Whether she brought Dimitrios up that night with her we can't know, but she probably did. She—or he—took the mule and a crowbar or so from the workmen's sheds above the shrine, *et voilà.*"

I said, "And then all Dimitrios had to do was to wait and follow us. Too easy."

"Much too easy. I should have thought of it after what Stephanos told me, but I admit it never seriously occurred to me—till I saw the earthquake damage up there—that anything that Mick found might still be hidden. However. There it is. You can bet your boots he was up there yesterday, and now all he has to do is to hunt that fairly small stretch of cliff, and then he and Danielle are made for life." He smiled down at me. "I admit it *is* a lot of bricks to make with very little straw, but where else is the straw to go? We have certain facts, and we must fit them in somewhere with the knowledge that friend Dimitrios is up to no sort of good."

"And he is the cousin of Angelos. . . . Yes, I see what you mean. But why did he come here tonight? Just to see Danielle again?"

He said soberly, "Ah, that . . . that's what I meant when I said I didn't like the feel of this affair. What we've discovered—or guessed, if you like—so far, is straightforward enough, but Nigel . . ." He paused, then turned to pitch the stub of his cigarette out of the open window. "Nigel. He's in this somewhere and I want to know where."

"You mean that Dimitrios came to see *him?*"

"No. Dimitrios came here looking for something. And I could bear to know what." He glanced round the room. "And I could also bear to know where Nigel is."

I said, "The drawings have gone."

"What? Oh, the ones on the wall. So they have. Well, the sooner we find out what else is gone the better. . . ." He began to move round the bare untidy little room as he spoke. "We'll soon see if he intended—no, don't you bother, Camilla. Sit still. There's not much searching to be done in a place this size, even if a couple of gorillas have turned everything upside down first. . . ."

"Dimitrios didn't take anything with him, anyway," I said.

"No, he didn't, did he? One might say he hardly had time. That's one satisfactory thing about tonight's affair."

"Perhaps Danielle was telling the truth. Perhaps he did only come in here to hide from you when he heard you move."

"Not on your life." He had opened the shower stall and was rummaging inside. "He didn't have time, after he'd heard me move, to take that light bulb out. He did that as soon as he got into the room, and to me that means he had some business in here that was going to take a minute or two, and he didn't want to risk being surprised and recognized. I must have heard him almost straightaway—I'd been lying awake wondering where the blazes Nigel was, and as soon as I heard the movements I got up. It didn't take me long to roll off the bed and grab my flannels and get into them, and then to get to the door. He hadn't quite shut the door—for quietness' sake, I suppose—and when I saw torchlight moving beyond it I knew it wasn't Nigel, and I went carefully. As I shoved the door open, I saw the light swinging round the room as if it was looking for something. That was all, because of course he turned on me."

I laughed. "Yes, and you told Danielle he attacked you—which, sir, was a lie. I was watching, and you went bald-headed for the poor chap before he even had time to say 'Good evening!'"

He grinned. "And for a very good reason. He whipped round when he heard me at the door, and he pulled a knife. I thought it best not to give him time to think about using it."

I drew a long breath. "I—see. You were right about the feel of this thing, weren't you? All I can say is, that for a member of our staid and slightly stuffy profession, your reactions are—well, fairly rapid, not to say decisive."

He was still smiling. "Two strenuous years' conscription in the tough end of the Artists' Rifles . . . besides what Michael taught me all unofficial-like. It bears fruit—besides, I'm rather afraid I enjoyed it. I like a good and dirty fight. . . . I say, Camilla."

"Yes?"

"His things *are* all gone."

"Everything? Not just his painting things?"

"Everything, I think. The rucksack—see, he used to hang it on this peg. I suppose he didn't carry a razor, but the towel's gone too, and the soap, and what clothes he had. And unlike me he was conventional even in this climate and wore pajamas. Are they tucked down there under the sheet?"

"I don't think so. No, they're not."

He said, sounding at once puzzled and relieved, "Then he meant to go anyway. Damn the boy, he might have told me, and saved me a couple of sleepless hours. Well, at least he isn't sitting up on Parnassus somewhere with a sprained ankle, whatever else he's got himself into. I'll just make sure there's nothing down here. . . . ah, there's the Greek's knife. I thought I heard it fly under the bed. And that hellish clanging noise we made was Nigel's apology for a wastepaper basket. . . . Lord, what a mess! Orange peel and pencil shavings and all the dud drawings he's thrown away. I really think we'll have to bribe our way out of this, Camilla my girl."

"For goodness' sake, let me help." I slipped from the bed to the floor and gathered up a handful of papers. I dropped them into the biscuit tin that served Nigel for a wastebasket. "I'll clear this stuff up. You see if that chair'll mend, and straighten the table. There's no damage except the broken glass, and we better leave that till morning and see if we can find a brush and—*Simon!*"

He was busy straightening the furniture. He swung round. "What is it?"

"These papers . . . they're not 'dud drawings' at all. They're—they're the finished things, his Hellenic types!" I shuffled them through my hands. "Yes, look, here they are! There's that head that's a bit like Stephanos, and the smiling one that looked like a statue, and that must be the Minoan girl he told us about—and here's a shepherd boy. And more . . . look." I began to leaf through them rapidly. My hand wasn't quite steady. I said, "I know he was doing them under protest, and he *was* feeling at odds with life, but surely, Simon, he can't afford to throw them away? What in the world—?" I stopped short.

Simon said sharply from above me, "What is it?"

I said shakily, "This one. This is the head, that lovely, lovely head. The young man with the strange face. And look, he's torn it up. Not the others, but this. It's torn right across." I looked down at the fragments on my lap and said sadly, "He needn't have torn it up. It was beautiful."

He stooped to take the pieces from me, and studied them for a few moments in silence.

At length he said, "What else is there? Not the flower studies, surely?"

"No. No. They're all the 'types,' except that lovely head."

I heard him take a breath, as if of relief, and when he spoke I knew he had had the same fleeting stab of fear as I myself. "Then—whatever made him go—I don't think we need worry overmuch. That fit of the blues hasn't made him plan anything foolish after all; he's taken the good stuff with him. Except this . . ." He opened his fingers, and let the fragments drift down onto my lap. The action was like a shrug; a sigh. "Ah, well, we can't guess what's biting the boy. But I'll be thankful when I know—"

I said abruptly, *"The cyclamen."*

He said, suddenly sounding very weary, "Is that there as well, after all?"

"No. It's not here. That's not what I meant. But I've remembered something, Simon, and I think it's important. Yesterday, when we were up in the corrie—Michael's corrie—I saw a plant of cyclamen growing in the rock. I didn't realize it at the time—at least I think I must have subconsciously, because I know I was thinking about Nigel as I looked at it—but it was the same plant that was in the drawing. I tell you, I didn't connect it then; but now, when we were talking about his drawings, I somehow saw it again. And it was the same. I'm sure of it. And that means that Nigel's been up in that corrie too!'' I drew a deep breath. "And perhaps, if *Nigel* had found Angelos' cave, that would explain some of the things he said on Monday night. Simon, Nigel was in that corrie, and, if you ask me, Nigel found the cave! And Angelos' hoard was still there!''

Simon said, hard and sharp, "Then if Nigel found anything in that corrie, he found it on Monday. He did that drawing on Monday.''

"Yes, and he told you he'd done no work, till we found that he'd slipped up over the Phormis head and the cyclamen!''

He said slowly, "It could be. I went up some of the way over the track with him on Sunday. He might have gone back on his own and stumbled on the place. One of those weird freaks of chance, but they do happen. Oh, my God, suppose he did?''

We stared at each other. I said, "And yesterday morning I saw him setting off again . . . and looking secretive about it. Simon, perhaps it was *Nigel* who took the mule. Perhaps we're wrong about Danielle. Perhaps Nigel's trying to move the stuff, whatever it is, himself.''

Simon said, in a harsh voice that was anything but casual, "And if he is? If he's got across that damned Greek in the process? Don't forget he's somewhere in this too.''

"Perhaps he's working with that damned Greek,'' I said.

"Perhaps.''

I said, "Simon, don't worry so. One thing's obvious; he did mean to go. He's cleared up here, and he's scrapped the stuff he didn't want. Whatever he's up to, and even if his affairs *have* tangled with Dimitrios', he's gone deliberately. He may have got himself into something illegal, or at most immoral, but he meant to, and—well, you can't really be his keeper to that extent, can you?''

He hesitated, then suddenly smiled. "I suppose not. At least, not till it's daylight.''

I said, making a statement of it, "You're going up there, of course.''

"Of course. I intended to anyway, and now it seems I shall have to.''

"When do we start?''

He looked down at me for a moment. That unreadable mask had shut down again over his face. I don't know what I expected him to say. I know what nine men out of ten would have said—and Philip would have said it twice.

Simon didn't say it at all. He said merely, "I'll come and call you. And now you'd better go and sleep. We'll have to make an early start.''

I got to my feet. "Will you take Stephanos and Niko?''

"No. For one thing it would take too long, and for another, if there's anything to be found that Nigel and/or Dimitrios haven't already found and moved, I don't want witnesses till I know where Nigel comes in, and whose property it is. If it is arms and gold, the ownership might be a rather delicate political question under present circumstances.''

"Heavens, yes. I hadn't thought of that.''

"And now let me see you back to your room. . . . By the way I haven't thanked you yet for bashing friend Dimitrios over the head for me.''

"I'd never have got near him,'' I said truthfully, "if he hadn't thought I was Danielle. And I missed him anyway.''

"All the same it was a stout effort."

He opened the door, and I went past him into the chilly corridor.

"They taught us a lot," I said sedately, "in the tough end of St. Trinian's."

15

"Tell the Emperor that the bright citadel is fallen to the ground; Apollo has no longer any shelter, or oracular laurel tree, or speaking fountain. Even the vocal stream has ceased to flow."

The Delphic Oracle to the Emperor Julian

IT CAN'T have been much after six when Simon woke me. I had sleepily answered. "Come in" to his knock before I remembered that I was no longer in the hotel, and this was not likely to be a chambermaid with a cup of tea. As I turned my head, looking, still sleepy-eyed, toward the door, it opened. Simon didn't come in, but I heard his voice.

"Camilla."

"Mmm? Oh—Simon. Yes?"

"Could you bear to get up now, d'you suppose? I think we ought to move. I've got coffee on a Primus if you would like to come along and get it when you're dressed."

"All right."

"Good." The door shut. I shot, fully awake now, out of bed, and began to dress quickly. From my window I could see the morning sunlight sliding like apricot bloom over the rounded top of Mount Cirphis.

In my room it was still cool, for which I was grateful. I wasn't so grateful about the icy gush of water from the taps—both taps—but in any case washing at Delphi is a penance; the water is as hard as pumice stone, and just about as good for the skin . . . but it woke me up fully and finally, and it was with a tingling sense of new adventure that at length I went quickly along to Simon's door and tapped.

"Come in."

I noticed that he was making no attempt to keep his voice low this morning, and he must have seen a query in my face as I entered, because he looked up from the Primus he was tending and said briefly, "Danielle checked out an hour ago."

"Oh?"

"I followed her down as far as the upper road. I didn't see where she went in the village, but I did see a jeep drive off north."

"That means she's either making for Itea or further along toward Amphissa?"

"Yes. Coffee?"

"Lovely. Simon, this smells like heaven. Rolls too? You're very efficient."

"I went along to the baker's after I'd seen Danielle off the premises. Here's the sugar."

"Thank you. Where do you think she's gone?"

"God knows, and there's not much point in guessing. Probably to pick Dimitrios up in Itea—though if the jeep was in Delphi it seems odd he didn't take it last night when he got out of the studio. How d'you feel today?"

"I'm fine, thanks. And you? How's the shoulder? You're sure that was all the damage?"

"Certain. And it's really hardly stiff at all. I feel ready for anything."

He was sitting on the edge of his bed, a cup of coffee in one hand and a roll in the other, looking, as ever, completely relaxed and at ease. "And you?" he said. "Ready for your adventure?"

I laughed. "I can hardly believe that two days ago I was writing to my friend that nothing ever happened to me. Is it Goethe who says somewhere that we ought to beware what we ask the gods for, because they might grant it? I asked for adventure, and it seems I got it."

He didn't smile. He appeared to consider what I'd been saying for a minute or two, then he said, quite seriously, "I ought not to let you come, you know."

I didn't ask why. I drank coffee and watched the sunlight wheel a fraction to touch the edge of the windowframe. A butterfly hovered, then winnowed down to cling to the strip of sunlit stone. Its wings fanned gently, black velvet shot with gold.

Simon said, "Don't mistake me. I don't think we—you, are in any danger; but it'll be a hard day, especially following after yesterday and last night. The only possible danger is running unexpectedly into Dimitrios, who'll certainly be up there, but if we're reasonably careful, that can be avoided. I don't think he'll be expecting us. He probably thinks that, now I've seen the place, that closes the account for me."

"In any case I told Danielle we were going to the fair at Levadia."

"*Did* you? Good for you. Was she showing interest, then?"

I smiled. "Yes, she showed interest. She asked me flat out where you were going today. I—well, I'm afraid I just mistrusted her on principle, and told her a lie." I set down my coffee cup. "It seems it's just as well. Dimitrios certainly won't be looking out for us."

"Excellent," said Simon. "Of course, there's no reason anyway why he should have expected me to go up there again, is there? He doesn't know I know of the existence of any 'treasure.' If Michael had sent any information home, Dimitrios might well imagine I'd have come long ago. Cigarette?"

"Thank you."

He leaned forward to hold his lighter for me. "No," he said, "I think Dimitrios will see it as a pilgrimage for me; and that's over. All the better. But we'll be very careful, just the same. With any luck we'll see what's going on, and where Nigel comes in—and then we can think about possible reinforcements." He sent me a grin as he got up off the bed and reached for his haversack. "In any case, don't worry. All things being equal, I can deal with friend Dimitrios. And I refuse to be afraid of Nigel. Even if he has got himself mixed up in anything for the sake of the cash, he'd never in a million years do violence for gain. Or so I think."

"I agree."

"Apart from those two there's Danielle." That swift grin again. "Well, I wouldn't like to swear that I could precisely 'deal with' Danielle, but let's say I'm not afraid of her."

"We might be wrong about them," I said. "There may be nobody up there at all, except Nigel."

"It's possible"—he was packing the haversack as he talked: more of the fresh rolls, some fruit, chocolate, water: Spartan fare, but nonetheless appropriate for that—"it's quite possible that we are wrong about Dimitrios and Danielle, but in any case I'm not concerned at the moment with Michael's 'find' except as it touches Nigel." A look. "You're convinced about those flowers in the drawing, aren't you?"

"Absolutely."

"Well, that's one thing we're sure of in a maze of guess work. We don't really know a damned thing about Dimitrios and Danielle, but we do know Nigel has been in that corrie, and we do know he was wildly excited about something that same night. And Dimitrios came here, for some purpose, to visit Nigel's room. We'll freeze on to those facts, and let the rest develop as it will. . . . Are you ready to start?"

"Yes."

"Then let's go."

Already the morning sun was warm overhead, but the rocks were still cool from the night. The path past the graveyard was wide enough for us to walk side by side.

Simon said, "All I'm hoping today is that—if you're right—we run across Nigel and see what he's up to, and knock some sense into his silly young head before he gets himself involved in something he can't get out of. And incidentally—this is the path off to the stadium—and incidentally, find the cave."

He had stopped where the narrow path left our track, and waited for me to precede him. I paused, and looked at him straightly. "Tell me one thing. Why *are* you letting me come?"

For the second time since I had known him, he seemed oddly at a loss. He hesitated, as if looking for the right words.

I said, "Granted that you don't want Stephanos and Niko along. But you'd get along much faster and do much better alone, *Kyrie* Lester, and you know it. You also know quite well that if we *do* run into Dimitrios it might develop into quite a sticky party. Why don't you leave me at home to get on with my knitting?"

A pine branch cast a bar of shade across his face, but I thought I saw a smile behind the light-gray eyes. "You know the reasons quite well, *Kyria* Haven."

"Reasons?"

"Yes."

"Well, I know the first. I wished a little too hard for an adventure, so I can darned well take what comes, and four eyes are better than two if we want to find Nigel and the cave?"

"Not quite. I had the idea that you were looking rather hard for something on your own account."

I turned abruptly and led the way up the narrow path between the pines. I said, after a bit, "Perhaps I was." Then, later still, "You—do see rather a lot, don't you?"

"And you know the second reason."

It was shady under the pines, but my cheeks felt hot. I said, "Oh?" and then felt furious with myself because the syllable seemed to be inviting an answer. I added hastily, "I can show you where the cyclamen is, of course."

"Of course," said Simon agreeably.

We had reached the stadium. We crossed the slanting shadows of the starting gate and left the trees. Behind us in the holly oaks and cypresses the birds flashed and sang. The singing echoed and rang up the limestone cliffs.

We crossed the stadium floor in silence and took the steep path that led to the rocky reaches of Parnassus.

We saw no one on our way to the corrie.

Most of the way from Delphi the track was easy to follow, and, apart from one open stretch soon after we had left the top of the Shining Ones, it wound along rocky valleys which would have offered plenty of cover in case of alarm. But the hot desert of broken rocks seemed as empty as yesterday. We traveled in short bursts, going fairly fast, but with frequent pauses in the shade to get our breath and to scan the surrounding country for signs of movement.

At length, as we made our way up a steep dry watercourse, I looked upward to the right and saw the line of cliffs that held the corrie. Simon, who was ahead of me, stopped and turned.

"We'll wait here, I think, and eat. Look, here's a good place, in the shade between these two boulders. We can't be seen, and we can keep an eye on the valley and on those cliffs. I'd like to be quite sure no one else is about before we make our way up."

I sat down thankfully in the place he indicated, and he produced food from the haversack. The rolls didn't taste quite as good as they had in the cool of the morning, but as I ate I began to feel better. The tepid water was a benison, and the fruit was ambrosia itself. . . .

I let Simon do the watching. After I had eaten I relaxed against the rock with eyes half-shut against the light, and he lit a cigarette for me. He showed no sign of hurry or impatience, or even curiosity. We smoked in silence, and I saw his eyes move almost idly across the landscape, up to the corrie, along the cliff, down the scree, back to the corrie.

At the very edge of my vision there was a movement.

I turned my head sharply, eyes fully open now. I could see nothing. But there had been a movement; of that I was sure. I was just about to touch Simon's arm when I saw it again; it was as if one of the rocks of the scree had moved . . . a goat. It was only a goat. As it walked forward, taking shape against the void of tumbled rock, I saw others with it, two, three of them, moving purposefully along some age-old track of their own. I was wondering half-idly if there was a goatherd with them, and if perhaps they had strayed from the troop, when I thought I heard, far away over the cliff top, the sound of a pipe. Even as I heard it and strained my ears to catch the notes, it faded, and I dismissed it as fancy. The thin, broken stave had been purely pastoral, something from a myth of Arcady, nymphs and shepherds and pan-pipes and green valleys. But this was Parnassus, home of more terrible gods.

I relaxed again and watched the smoke from my cigarette wind up in the sunlight. I remember that I didn't think at all about the business of the day. I thought about Parnassus, and the gods who lived there, and Simon. . . .

I stole a look at him. He was looking almost dreamily up toward the cliffs. He looked about as tense and vigilant as in the fifth hour of the House Cricket

Match. He caught my look and smiled, and moved his hand lazily to knock ash from his cigarette. I said, "A penny for them?"

"I was wondering if there was anyone with those goats. I don't think so."

"I thought I heard a pipe being played, away over there," I said, "but I expect I imagined it. Did you hear anything?"

"No. But it's possible. I don't think those three would be up here on their own. You must have very good hearing. I never heard a sound."

He crushed out his cigarette and got up, reaching a hand down to me. "Shall we go up now? I think we're unobserved, but I don't want to cross that big open stretch toward the corrie 'gateway.' If we skirt it, and go up that gully there, I think we can get round without the risk of being seen, and it'll bring us out above the cliff where we were yesterday. It'll be a bit of a stiff pull, I'm afraid. Are you tired?"

"Not a bit."

He laughed. "One up to British womanhood. Come along. And keep down. This is where the real stalk starts."

Simon lay flat at the corrie's lip, looking downward. I crouched behind him, a little way back from the cliff edge. I waited, watching him for a signal.

It seemed an age before he moved. Then he turned his head and lifted a hand, with a slow cautious movement that carried its own warning.

In spite of myself, I could feel tension pull my nerves taut, like cold wires touching the skin. I inched forward until I lay beside Simon. I was screened by one of the low holly oaks. I lifted my head slowly till my eyes were above the level of the edge. I looked down into the corrie. There was no one there.

As I looked at him, with surprise in my face and a question, he put his lips to my ear. "Dimitrios is here."

Again that coward jerk of the heart. Every vein in my body was contracting, little thrilling wires tightening till my muscles wouldn't obey me. I found I had ducked my head down again behind the holly oak, and my cheek was on my hand in the hot dust. The hand was cold.

Simon breathed, just beside my ear, "He's just vanished somewhere underneath us. I saw him duck under that piece in the corner." He jerked his head slightly toward it. "Is that where you went exploring yesterday?"

I nodded. I swallowed, and managed to say quite evenly, "What was he doing?"

"I don't know. He just seemed to be hanging about. Waiting for someone or something. Nigel, perhaps, or—"

He broke off and seemed to go lower into the ground. I shrank down beside him. The holly oak hid me, and I peered down.

Then I saw Dimitrios. He came out from somewhere below us, ducking his head as he passed under the flying buttress that seemed to shore up the cliff. He was smoking, and his eyes were frowning and narrowed against the high blaze of the sun. He walked carefully over the rocky floor of the corrie toward the northern gap in the wall. Every now and again he stopped, and slanted his head as if to listen.

He reached the corrie entrance, and stopped there, looking down toward Amphissa. Once he turned his head and looked the other way, the way we had come, from Delphi. Then he came back into the corrie. He flung down the butt of his cigarette and lit another. I noticed sweat on his dark face and dust yellowish-white on his clothes. He wasn't in the dark suit today; he was wearing dungarees in dull faded blue, and a khaki shirt with a red kerchief knotted at the neck.

The cigarette was lit now. He dropped the match, then looked round him for a few moments as if undecided. He took a few steps into the corrie and I thought he was going back toward the corner where the cyclamen was, but he stopped suddenly, as if impatient of waiting, turned sharply on his heel, and walked, rapidly now, as if his mind was at last made up, out of the corrie.

Simon said in my ear, "Gone to meet Nigel, or Danielle, do you suppose? Give him a minute or two."

We gave him five. They seemed very long minutes. There was no other sound in the hot morning but our own breathing. The sun beat down on us as we lay on the bare earth. I was thankful when Simon moved at last.

We got quickly to our feet, and went down the twisting little path like a couple of mountain goats. We almost ran across the corrie floor and ducked under the fallen rock into the corner.

There it was, the patch of brilliant green, and the drifts of tiny blue bells, the lovely traces of the mountain rain. But today it was different.

Simon had checked. "Is this the place?"

"Yes, but—" I caught my breath and pushed past him, to stand staring at the cliff.

The cyclamen had gone. Where it had clung to its crack in the rock there was now a black fissure. The crack had widened, split, and gaped open, as pressure had been exerted on the weather-rotted rock. I could see the raw white marks where the crowbars had gained their leverage.

A slab, similarly marked, lay at our feet, newly fallen, and crushing the fresh grass. Yesterday it had been leaning against the rock face, masking what lay behind from my casual glance. Today there was a split in the face of the rock, some seven feet high by a foot and a half wide—a narrow fissure which angled sharply up to a point at the top. It opened onto darkness. The cave. Michael's cave.

My mouth was dry. I said hoarsely, "Yesterday that slab was leaning up against the cliff, at an angle. There was a crack behind it, very narrow. I remember now. It didn't look like an entrance to anything, but that must have been it."

He nodded, but he wasn't looking at me, or at the mouth of the cave. He looked past me, up at the cliff top, the corrie walls, all round us.

No movement; no sound.

There was a pile of mule droppings on the grass, that hadn't been there yesterday. I pointed to them silently, and Simon nodded. He said softly, "We were right, then. . . . We'll go in. You wait here a moment. And keep those ears of yours open. I won't be long."

He disappeared into the darkness of the cleft. I waited. Once again, far away, I thought I heard that little thread of music, the ghostly echo of the pan-pipes. Heard now, in this hot cruel corrie, the sound spoke no longer of Arcadia, and the kindly god of flocks and herds. It was a panic prickle along the flesh.

It had gone. I had imagined it again. I stood with my hands tightly clasped together in front of me, and made myself wait without moving.

Simon showed in the darkness of the cleft, like a beckoning ghost. I almost ran toward him into the cool darkness of the cave.

After the glare of day the place was dead-dark. It was like running against a black velvet curtain. I stopped, blinded. I felt Simon's arm come round me, guiding me in out of the light, then he switched on a torch. The light seemed feeble and probing after the blaze of day, but we could see.

We were in a widish passage which sloped gently downward for some five or six yards and then turned abruptly to the left. The original entrance must have been wide, but it had been blocked by successive falls of stone to leave only the narrow cleft through which we had come. The passage itself was clear enough, and smelt fresh and cool.

Simon said, "The slope gets steeper. There's another twist down to the right, and then the cave itself . . . Here. Quite a place, isn't it?"

It was indeed. The main cave was huge, a great natural cavern the size of a young cathedral, with a high curved ceiling that vanished into darkness, and clefts and recesses that swallowed the feebly-probing torch-light. Stalactites and stalagmites made strangely shaped, enormous pillars. Fallen rock lay here as well. In some of the dimly seen apses there were boulders and masses of rough stone showing, in the elusive light, like the massive tombs that lie between the columns of a cathedral. Somewhere I could hear the faint drip of water. The place was impressive, magnificent even, but it was a ruin. Dust and rubble lay everywhere, some of it recent-looking, some of it apparently undisturbed for centuries.

The torch-light moved, swept, checked. . . .

Simon said, "There."

He said it softly, almost idly, but I knew him now. My heart gave that painful little jerk of excitement. The light was holding something in its dim circle, a circle which seemed to have brightened, sharpened, focussed. . . . There was a pile of rubble by a column to the left of the cavern mouth. It looked at first like any of the other heaps of fallen debris, then I saw that among the shapes of the broken rock, more regular shapes showed . . . a cubed corner . . . the dusty outline of a box . . . And beside them in the rubble the dull gleam of metal: a crowbar and a shovel.

The torch-light swept further. "See that? They've shifted some of it already. See where it's been dragged through the dust?" He sent the light skating quickly round the rest of the great cavern. Nothing. Another time I would have exclaimed over the ghostly icicles of rock, the arches, the chambered darknesses that the corners held, but now my whole interest, like the torch-light, was centered on that pile of rock debris and what it contained.

Simon paused for a moment, cocking his head. No sound except the drip of water somewhere, very faintly. He moved forward with me beside him, and bent over the exposed corner of the box.

He didn't disturb it. The torch worked for him. "There's the government stamp. This isn't gold, Camilla. It's guns."

"Guns?"

"Uh-huh. Small and useful Sten guns." He straightened up and switched the light out for a moment. In the thick darkness his voice was soft and grim. "There's an excellent market for this sort of thing at several points in the Med just now. Well, well."

I said, "I don't believe that Nigel would do that."

The torch flashed on again. "Come to think of it, neither do I. I wonder . . ." He moved off round the pile, exploring deeper into the darkness behind the big stalagmite.

"Simon," I said, "d'you mean these were flown in here during the war?"

"Yes. I told you. Gold and arms galore."

"But that was nineteen forty-two, wasn't it? They wouldn't keep, surely?"

I heard him laugh. "You talk as if they were fish. Of course they'll 'keep.' They're packed in grease. They'll come out as good as new. . . . Ah. . . ."

"What is it?" In spite of myself my voice sharpened.

"Ammo. Stacks of it. My God, this'd take a couple of days to shift, this stuff. No wonder . . ." His voice trailed away.

"Simon? What is it?"

He said without a trace of inflection, "The gold."

I moved forward so fast that I tripped over a root of the stalagmite and almost fell. *"Where?"*

"Steady there. So this is what treasure trove does to you. Here." The torchlight was steady on the pile of broken rock. Among the dust and splintered fragments the corners of two small boxes showed. They were of metal, but the corner of one had been smashed open, and under the dusty gaping metal was the living gleam of gold.

Simon was saying, "That's Michael's little find, Camilla. That's why Mick was murdered. But I still don't quite see. . . ." He paused, and I saw his brows draw together, but after a while he went on in his even voice, "Well, we were right, as far as it went. Two boxes, at least, and there may be more under the rubble."

"They're very small, aren't they?"

"One of them would be one man's work, all the same. Did you know that gold was almost twice as heavy as lead? They'll have quite a job shifting what they've got here."

I said, "They?"

He answered my look. "I'm afraid you were right about Nigel. I think he *was* on his way up here yesterday morning, and it's Nigel who's been working here while Dimitrios was in Delphi."

I said apprehensively, "But we still don't know they're working together. If Dimitrios came up last night, or early today, and found Nigel here, and set about him the way he did with you—"

He shook his head. "No. Think it out. There must be two of them in it. Look at this stuff again; look how it's buried. Angelos probably did throw a bit of rubble and small stones over it to hide it, but he never put this pile of rock over it. This has come down in an earth tremor—probably the one that shut the cave and broke the cliff above us. Shifting this kind of thing is sheer hard work, and Dimitrios just hasn't had time to do everything alone."

"You mean—?"

"Work it out. There must be two men on the job, Camilla. If Nigel found the cave, it still hadn't been opened up yesterday, enough to let those boxes be carried out. Whether Nigel showed it to Dimitrios, or whether Dimitrios found it himself as soon as we left the corrie yesterday, the man simply hasn't had time single-handed to do all this. Remember he followed us almost straight down to Delphi; he wouldn't have had time to get his tools from where they were hidden, and shift that slab. And even if he came back to do that later, he was down in Delphi again in the middle of the night."

"What about Danielle?"

"She couldn't have got up here and then back again between the time you saw her on the Shining Ones, and the time she went to bed last night. What's more she couldn't physically, do this sort of job."

He paused for a moment, as if listening, and then went on. "And look at the situation just now. We know Danielle went north with the jeep. She won't have had time to get up here from the Amphissa road. Dimitrios is waiting for someone, but it's not Danielle. The mule's been here, hasn't it, and gone? At a guess, Dimitrios is waiting for whoever has taken the mule over, loaded, to meet the jeep. Nigel."

The torch flashed again, momentarily, over the gold. He said, "You remember Stephanos saying that the old track leads to a disused quarry near the Amphissa road? It sounds the sort of place where they might park the jeep out of sight while they ferry the stuff across the hill with the mule. They seem to have made a start on the guns. I imagine they'll stack the loot somewhere down near the road till they can get it all away together; and if they've any sense they'll leave the gold safely here till the last minute. . . . Did you hear anything?"

We stood very still with the light out. "No," I said. Then, slowly, "You know, I—I don't trust Dimitrios."

I heard the ghost of a laugh in the dark. "Today's great thought, Camilla, my darling? You surprise me."

He had surprised me too, but I hoped my voice didn't show it. I said, "I was thinking of Nigel. Even if they are working together now, it's only because Nigel found the stuff first, and Dimitrios wants help to shift it. Once the work's done—" I stopped, and licked dry lips.

"I know." No trace of amusement now. "Well, we're here now, so that should be taken care of."

"Yes. But Simon"—even to me the whisper sounded thin and miserably uncertain—"Simon, what are we going to do?"

"Wait. What else can we do? We don't know the score yet, but no doubt we soon will."

He switched on again, and the light flicked round the cavern. "There's plenty of cover here, and we'll hear them in good time—or at least you will. If Nigel comes up alone, all the better, but if it should be Dimitrios coming back . . ."

He grinned down at me, but some quality in the grin brought the reverse of comfort. I said suddenly, accusingly, "You *want* him to come back."

"And if I do?" The smile deepened at the expression on my face. "By God, Camilla, don't you see? I pray he does come back. There's your score to settle as well as mine, and now there's that idiotic boy to straighten out. . . . It would be better if Dimitrios came. Don't you see?"

"Oh, yes, I see."

His hand came out, momentarily, to touch my cheek, a moth-light touch. "Don't be scared, my dear. I'm not going to get myself killed and leave you alone with the wolves." He gave a little laugh. "I've not the slightest intention of fighting fair . . . and two can play at the game of attacking down a torch-beam."

I said, I hoped steadily, "He may be armed."

"I'm pretty sure he's not. There wasn't room for a gun in those dungarees."

"He's probably got himself another knife."

"Probably. And I've got his. Two can play at that game too."

"Simon!"

I heard him laugh again as he moved away. "Poor Camilla. . . . Now, half a minute. Stay where you are. I'll be back."

He slid, with wary flashes of the torch, out of the cave, and the small light dwindled and vanished into the curve of the passageway. He was gone perhaps two minutes. I stayed just where I was, with the gold at my feet, and one hand in my pocket nervously fingering the bulk of the Greek's torch, which I had picked up in Nigel's room last night, and found to be still serviceable. Then the will-o'-the-wisp light danced back along the passage wall, and Simon was beside me.

"Not a sign of either of them, so we'll have a closer look at this stuff, I think."

"Do you want any help?"

"No, thanks. Scout around and find a bolt hole to make for when he comes." He was already busy, crouching beside the pile of rubble, his hands moving gently over the dusty surfaces.

I left him to his task, his hands moving among the dust just as Michael's hands must have moved fourteen years ago when he made the same discovery. I flashed my torch back momentarily as I moved away. It showed his crouching body, the quiet intent face, the hands. . . . Michael Lester finding evidence of treachery to the Allies. For some reason I gave a little shiver. They said ghosts walked, didn't they? And the ghost of Angelos, who smiled as he killed? "If ghosts are true," Niko had said, "then he still walks on Parnassus. . . ."

The cave was even bigger than I had thought. I passed between pillars of stalagmites as massive as Apollo's columns at Delphi, and into an anteroom as deep as a private chapel. There was ample cover. Simon and I could lie hidden almost anywhere, when Dimitrios came. . . .

The light was uncertain in my hand. Its beam touched the walls, the fallen masses that blocked the antechamber, and diffused itself into nothingness among the dark recesses. But even as I turned back, the edge of the light shimmered momentarily with a sliding, liquid gleam. I paused. There was the drip of water again, more clearly now. I went forward, the torch exploring ahead of me. The floor lifted a little, and there was a streak of damp on it that caught the light. I could feel the freshness in the air, above the dead dust-smells of the cave, and there was the drip of water, closer now and clearer; there must be some spring in the cave—perhaps the same spring whose overflow fed the grass and flowers outside. I went forward quickly now, the light flicking over the rock in eager search. There was the now-familiar pile of broken rock against the rear wall of the cave; there the wall itself, streaked with damp and seamed with black fissures; there a wrecked stalagmite leaning drunkenly against a slab that lay at an angle to the wall. . . .

There was something very familiar about the slab. It only took me a couple of seconds to realize why. It was the same shape, and leaned in the same way, as the slab that yesterday had barred the cave mouth, and today lay tumbled in the grass outside.

I approached it slowly, knowing what I would find. As I paused beside it I could hear the drip of water plainly. Then I felt the skin prickle cold again along my arms and back.

With the drip of water came another sound, a sound that I had heard already twice that day and disbelieved, as I disbelieved it now. The sound of a pipe. Pan's pipe . . . it played a delicate little fall of notes; another; again. Silence, and the drip of water.

And the sound had come from behind the leaning slab.

With the hair lifting along my arms I bent to peer behind it. I was right. There was a gap, narrow, perhaps eight inches wide, but still a gap. And it didn't, like the other cave mouth, give onto darkness. Beyond it, the darkness slackened.

I think I had forgotten Dimitrios. I said softly, and even to me the echoes of my voice sounded queer, "There's a way through here. I'm going to see."

I don't know if Simon answered. I was squeezing through the narrow gap. The rock scraped me, caught at my clothes, then let me through. I was in a widish passage which led upward in a gentle curve. The floor was smooth. Round me the darkness slackened further, and more clearly through the torch-light the walls of the gallery took shape. Ahead of me it curved more sharply to the right, and beyond the curve I could see that the light grew clearer. The drip of the water was clear and loud.

Then it came again, the sound I had been listening for above the trickle of water; a little stave of music, hauntingly off-key. . . .

I rounded the corner. Ahead was the light, the arch of the gallery framing a blaze muted by moving green. I caught a glimpse of grass, and the hanging boughs of some slender tree dappling the sunlight at the mouth of the tunnel.

I almost ran the rest of the way. I ducked under the arch and came suddenly, blindingly, into a little dell.

It wasn't a way out. It was a small enclosure, like a light-well. Centuries ago this had been a circular cave into which the gallery had run, but the roof had fallen in and let in the sun and the seeds of grass and wild vines, and the spring had fed them, so that now, in the heart of the mountain, was this little well of vivid light roofed with the moving green of some delicate tree.

The music had stopped. The only sound was the drip of the spring and the rustle of leaves.

But I had no thought to spare for Pan and his music. Apollo himself was here. He was standing not ten feet from me as I came out of the tunnel. He was naked, and in his hand was a bow. He stood looking over my head as he had stood for two thousand years.

I heard Simon coming along the tunnel behind me. I moved aside. He came quickly out of the dark archway into the dappled light. He was saying, "Camilla, I—" then he stopped as if he'd been struck in the throat. I heard him say, "Oh, God," under his breath. He stopped just behind me.

Some draft moved the curtain of leaves. Light flickered and burned from the bow, and shifted along the bronze of the throat and face. A broken arrow of gold lay in the grass at the statue's feet.

After a lifetime or so I heard myself saying shakily, "This . . . *this* is what Nigel found. He was here. Look."

I stooped and picked up the little water pot from where it lay in the damp moss at my feet.

16

Apollo shows himself not to everyone, but only to him who is good.
He who sees him is great; he who sees him is not a small man. We will
see thee, O far-striker, and we will never become small!

CALLIMACHUS: 2.9

"YES." SIMON turned the pot over in his hand. "That's out of Nigel's sketching-
box. He may have heard the water when he was drawing the cyclamen outside,
and that led him into the cave and then through here . . . to this." His eyes,
like mine, were fixed on the statue. The face was god-like; remote, wise, serene,
but young, and with a kind of eagerness behind the level brows.

I said breathlessly, "It's the face in the drawing, isn't it?—the lovely drawing
he tore up. . . . I said it looked like a statue. D'you remember how he snatched
it back from us?"

Simon said slowly, "That was when Danielle was there. But before that—
d'you remember my saying that he seemed to be on the verge of telling me
something, and then when Danielle came in he stopped short and shut up?"

"Of course. Then she *can't* have recognized it, can she? He'd only found the
cave that day, and it's obvious he wasn't going to tell her about it!"

"And by God he was right," said Simon. "Guns and gold is one thing; in a
way that kind of treasure trove is legitimate prey for greasy thugs like Dimitrios,
and if the boy thought he could get something out of a spot of gun-running, well,
that's his affair. But *this* . . ." he went down on one knee in the grass. Very
gently he lifted the golden arrow. Where it had lain the whitened grass roots
showed a clear print. He put it down again. "As I thought. Nothing's been
touched. You can't tell me friend Dimitrios could have kept his paws off a bit of
loose gold." He got to his feet with a breath of relief. "No, the boy's kept his
mouth shut, and there's quite enough in the outer cave to fix Dimitrios' interest
there. Thank God for the artist's conscience. But I think the sooner I get hold of
Nigel the better."

"You—you don't think Dimitrios'll come exploring, like I did, and find it?"

He laughed under his breath. "I'd bet on it that he won't; he's far too busy, for
one thing, and for another, now that I come to think of it, even if he was dying of
thirst he'd never squeeze through the gap."

"I suppose not. But how in the world did *he* get in here? And why?" I put a
hand to my head. "I—I can't seem to think straight about anything just at the
moment. I feel knocked kind of sideways."

"I'm not surprised. No wonder Nigel was 'high' that night. He must have
been half out of his mind with excitement. And no wonder Mick—well, never
mind that now. I doubt if we'll ever know just how and why the Apollo got here,
but we can make a pretty good guess, I think. You know that the sanctuary at
Delphi, after it ceased to be able to protect itself and its vast wealth, was
plundered again and again. We don't know where a fraction of the stolen statues
went. It was the metal ones that were taken; gold went first, of course; and then
bronze, to be melted down for weapons. . . . From the look of this one, with
that gold on it, it would be one of the most precious, and it's certainly one of the

660

most beautiful. Why shouldn't some priest, or some small band of devotees, have decided to save it; cart it out of Delphi and find sanctuary for it till the troubled times were over?"

"But—why here? And *how?*"

"There used to be a track this way—the natives refer to it as 'the old track,' and, in these parts, God knows how old it might be. We came along it part of the way. Even so, it must have been quite a trek. Myself, I'd have brought the thing up in a mule litter. I suppose the plan was to retrieve the statue later when things were safe, or even, if this happened at a very desperate time, to set up a sort of small secret sanctuary high on the mountain. If they'd just wanted to hide the statue, after all, they could have buried it, but they've *placed* it, haven't they? And with the Greek instinct for drama, they've put it at the end of a dark tunnel, in the blazing light, and all its trappings round it. . . . Did anything strike you about the cave, Camilla?"

"You mean that it was a bit like a cathedral—or a temple?"

He nodded. "It's a common enough quality in big vaulted places with stalactites and so on, but nonetheless impressive. The priests who were so fanatical to save this statue must have known of the cave for long enough. Not only that . . . there was this inner shrine, full of light, the perfect 'bright citadel' for the god—so here he is. Look at that vine, Camilla, and that tree."

I looked at him stupidly. "The vine? It's a wild vine, isn't it? And the tree—is that a sort of laurel?"

"A bay. Apollo's laurel," said Simon softly.

"But Simon, after two thousand years—"

"Trees live a long time, and when they die they leave seedlings. And vines run wild. Those were planted, Camilla. You notice how the Apollo is just under the lip of the overhang, and the vines and that spindly tree make a screen? I don't know if you *can* get to the top of this light-well and look down, but you'd see nothing. . . . And there is the spring. Yes, I think this was a sacred cave, with a sacred spring, and what more natural than that the priest who was so eager to save his god should house him here? And I'll bet that if we look closely we'll find that the entrances to both inner and outer caves were artificially blocked up—"

"They were. I noticed that. The slab that Dimitrios had moved was the same as the one that was across this inner tunnel."

"And then, after God knows how many years, the earthquakes opened the doors again . . . for Angelos. And Michael."

"Michael!" I looked at him almost guiltily. I had forgotten Michael. "Of course. The letter. The bright citadel. Oh, Simon."

He gave a little smile, and quoted softly: " 'Tell the Emperor that the bright citadel is fallen to the ground; Apollo has no longer any shelter, or oracular laurel tree, or speaking fountain. Even the vocal stream has ceased to flow.' Yes, Mick proved the Delphic Oracle wrong. That's what the letter meant."

I said, "You know, I didn't say anything, but I thought your brother wouldn't have written quite the way he did about a cache of arms, or even gold. All he'd have had to do, surely, was to divert them back to their proper uses?"

"I know. That's what got me too. But I never thought of anything like *this.*" His voice didn't change, but suddenly I got the sharp impression of intense excitement. "My God," said Simon, "who could have imagined this?"

We stood side by side staring at the statue. I think it was the loveliest thing I have ever seen. The shadows played over the bloomed bronze of the body; the eyes dwelt on some remote distance beyond and above our heads, as the eyes of lions do. They were curiously alive, carefully inlaid with enamel and some black stone, so that the dark pupils seemed to flicker and glow with the movement of light and shade. I only knew of one other statue that had eyes like that.

Simon echoed my thoughts, softly, "The Charioteer."

I said, "You think so? You think he's by the same hand?"

"I don't know a darned thing about it, but that's what he makes me think of."

"That's what he made Michael think of," I said.

He nodded. "And Nigel too, if you remember. . . . It was when we were talking about the Charioteer that Nigel seemed suddenly to make up his mind to tell me about this. It may only have been because we were talking in general about discovering statues, but I don't think so. I seem to recollect some tension when the Charioteer was mentioned."

"It's not only the eyes," I said, "but the whole impression of strength going along with grace . . . a sort of liquid quality—no, that's the wrong word, it sounds too weak, whereas this is—well, terrific. Simon, why shouldn't he be not only by the same hand, but part of the same group? It's only so much guesswork, isn't it, that the Charioteer was part of a victory statue for some potentate or other? Heavens above, if there were six thousand statues there, you'd think there might have been a chariot statue of Apollo somewhere in Apollo's own sanctuary? And why shouldn't the Charioteer be the driver, and this—the god himself—the Lord of the Car?"

"Why not indeed?" said Simon.

"What are you smiling at? I can't help getting excited, can I? And why shouldn't I have a theory? It seems to me—"

"No reason at all. And it seems to me that one theory's as good as another. Yours at any rate is the most exciting one that comes to hand. . . . No, I was smiling at something quite different. Dimitrios."

"Oh!" It was like being jerked out of the sunlight into cold water. "I—I'd forgotten all about him."

"I should like to . . . now," said Simon. He had never taken his eyes off the statue. "But I'm afraid we must deal with that little matter before we come back to this."

"What do we do about it?" I asked, rather blankly.

He gave it one long look before he turned away. "We leave it here in its bright citadel, and we get back to the land of shadows, my dear. We know now what Michael found, and we also know what Michael was murdered for. That chapter's closed, I think, with the death of Angelos. But the one that's still open is what we've got to deal with now. Nigel found the bright citadel too, and I admit to feeling rather strongly that Dimitrios and Danielle shouldn't really be let in on . . . this."

I said almost violently, "They'll not touch it if I can stop them."

"Then we'd better get back into the cave and play watchdog. Camilla . . ."

"Yes?"

He stood for a moment looking down at me. The guarded look was there again, with some expression behind the cool eyes that made me wonder what was coming. But he only said, rather lamely, "I shouldn't have let you come."

I didn't answer.

He said, "You're frightened, aren't you?"

Still I said nothing. I wasn't looking at him. I wondered fleetingly why I didn't mind his knowing. All at once he was very close to me, and his hand came under my chin, gently lifting my face to meet his gaze. "You know why I brought you, don't you?"

"Yes."

"And I was right."

"Yes. I know."

"You underrate yourself so shockingly, Camilla. You're not to play second fiddle any more. Understand?"

"Yes."

He hesitated, and then said rather abruptly, "You made a discovery yesterday; remember? 'No man is an Island.' It's true in more ways than one. Don't go on hating yourself because there are some things you can't do and can't face on your own. None of us can. You seem to think you ought to be able to deal with anything that comes along, much as I might, or someone like me. That's absurd; and it's time you stopped despising yourself for not being something you were never meant to be. You'll do as you are, Camilla; believe me, you will."

I didn't quite trust myself to answer. After a second or so I said, lightly, "All I ask the gods is that one day I'll see you, too, shaken right out of that—that more-than-sufficient calmness of yours, onto the plane of mortals like me! The day that happens, I'll sacrifice to Apollo myself!"

He grinned. "I might have to hold you to that. But meanwhile you can be sure that it won't be friend Dimitrios that'll do it. I'm going back now to see if he's around—or Nigel. Would you rather stay here?"

"No. I'll come with you. I—I'd like to know what's going on."

His hand touched my cheek as it had once before, a moth's touch. "Then don't be scared, please. I'll not let Dimitrios get near you."

"All right. What do I do?"

"Nothing yet. Just keep out of sight, and do as you're told before you're told to do it."

"What could be simpler? Very well."

"And now we'll go back."

The Apollo looked serenely over our heads as we turned and left the sunlight.

The cave was still empty. We waited in the shelter of the cleft, listening, and then Simon squeezed his way through without using the torch. After a minute or two I heard his voice softly in the dark. "It's all right. You can come through."

I slid through the narrow opening. The beam of Simon's torch lit the way for me, and then played over the tilted slab. "See? Those are chisel marks. You were right. The slab was hacked to fit across the opening. And that crack above . . . that'll be where the rock shifted in the tremor that opened up the cave again for you and me . . . and Michael."

I ran a slightly unsteady finger along one of the marks. "Two thousand years. . . . Oh, Simon, I wish we could know—" I stopped abruptly.

"Mmm?" The torch was still moving over the old tool marks. He seemed absorbed.

I managed to whisper calmly enough, "He's coming back. I can hear him."

The torch snapped out. A moment's unbreathing silence. "Yes. You get back through the cleft and wait till we see what he's up to. I hope to God it's Nigel."

As the breathed sentence ended I felt his hand on my arm. I obeyed him, slipping back through the narrow opening to wait, heart beating jerkily again, against the rock on the other side of the slab. I felt him beside me, pressed close to the edge of the cleft.

The steps came closer, hesitated at the door of the cave, and then came in. The sounds were at once dulled by the dust and made hollower by the cave's echoes. They were succeeded by other sounds: the dull thud of a spade hacking at the pile of rubble; the chink as it struck stone, and then metal; the sounds of breathing and effort; a soft expletive in Greek and then the splintering of wood and a thud; a dragging sound. . . . He had uncovered a box and was dragging it nearer the mouth of the cave in readiness for transportation.

I felt Simon's body, close to mine, tense like a runner's at the starting tape. His arm was across me, holding me still against him. It was like a steel bar. I wondered if he would attack Dimitrios now, out of the dark. . . .

But he didn't move, except to shift his shoulders and head slightly so that I thought he could see round the edge of the slab. He stayed like that for what seemed an age, rock-still. I could feel the pulse beating in the hollow of his elbow; it was unhurried. Mine, under it, was tumbling along anyhow, like a faulty engine.

The arm relaxed. I felt him turn his head, and his breath was on my temple. I heard the barest thread of a whisper, "He's gone out again. Did you hear a mule?"

"I don't think so."

"Stay here. I'll come back."

A swift, compelling pressure of the arm round me, then it lifted. A movement beside me, the scrape of cloth on stone, and he was gone. The cleft felt cold and damp. I shifted my shoulders with the sudden chill and hunched my arms close to my sides and waited, listening. The echo of my coward pulses seemed to fill the cave. . . .

I heard his steps in the dust just before he reached the cleft again and slid through. It was warmer with him there. He bent his head and said softly, "He's left the box just inside the entrance and gone out again. He seems uneasy; I think he's wondering if anything's happened to whoever's coming with the mule. I think I'd better go after him."

He wasn't touching me, so he didn't feel the jerk of my heart. He just heard me say, "Yes?" quite calmly.

"It's just on the cards something has happened to delay Nigel, and I'd like to know what. And I want to know the way they're taking. That track peters out very soon. I'll follow Dimitrios down till I see where he's bound, and then if a chance occurs I'll . . . well, deal with him."

"You mean you'll *kill* him?"

"Good God, no. But I'd like him put safely out of action while we get time to work this thing out our own way. . . . And now I must go, or I'll lose the blighter."

I hadn't realized that my hand had gone up to the breast of his shirt. His came up to cover it, warm and steadying. I said, and I couldn't quite keep the shake out of my voice, "Simon, take care."

"Be sure of that. Now, don't worry, my—don't worry. I'll be all right, and so will you. Stay here, under cover. You'll be as safe as a house in this part of the cave, and anyway I promise you I won't let Dimitrios out of my sight. Right?"

"R-right."

His other arm came round my shoulders, and momentarily he pulled me against him. It was a gesture of comfort and reassurance, no more. . . . But I thought his lips brushed my hair.

For the second time the arm dropped from my shoulders and he turned away as swiftly and lightly as a ghost. This time he switched on his torch, and I saw his shadow leap back, gigantic, along the wall of the cleft as he slipped through. I pressed forward till I could see into the cave. The little circle of light danced away through the faintly echoing spaces of darkness; the pillars and buttresses and masses of rock sent towering shadows reeling up the walls to stretch and lose themselves into the blackness of the vaulted roof. Simon, moving swiftly, himself like a shadow, dwindled across the empty darkness and was gone like a wraith into the outer tunnel. A shadow flickered back momentarily over the rock, then darkness swallowed it.

My hands were spread flat against the inner side of the slab. My eyes ached with the darkness. It was cold again. I had to exert all my self-control to stop myself running out and across the cave after him into the blessed sunlight.

At length I turned and made my way rather drearily back to the bright solitude of Apollo's sanctuary.

How long I waited there I don't know. At first I sat quietly enough in a corner where the sun fell unmasked by leaves, gazing at the statue of the god and trying to empty my mind of all worry about what was going on outside.

But after a while the very beauty and stillness of the place began to oppress me. I found I could sit still no longer, and, getting to my feet, I picked up Nigel's waterpot and carried it over to the spring. Under the thin trickle I rinsed it carefully, and drank. I rummaged in Simon's haversack and found what remained of our food, half of which I ate. After that I got myself another drink. Then I fidgeted about the little glade, examining the statue more closely, looking—but without touching them—at the broken pieces of gold in the grass, fingering the leaves and ferns. . . .

When I found myself stooping for a third time to drink at the spring, I realized that fear had given place to a sort of impatient irritation. Sunlight and peace had done their work too well: I was now thoroughly on the fidget. I found myself glancing almost second by second at the watch on my wrist—an automatic act which irritated my nerves still further, as I hadn't the remotest idea what time it had been when Simon left me. I hovered near the mouth of the tunnel, fingering my torch. . . .

After all, I told myself, I was perfectly safe. Simon was with Dimitrios, and I wasn't in the least afraid of Nigel. I wanted something to do; I wanted to know what was going on; I wanted Simon's presence. . . .

I went cautiously along the tunnel, back into darkness, hesitated in the shelter of the slab, then let myself through into the main cave.

I, too, used my torch this time. A last absurd jump of the nerves made me send the light skating once round the vaulted darkness, almost as if I expected to find that, after all, Dimitrios had not gone. But the place was empty. There really was nothing to be afraid of; if he came back I would hear him, and would have ample time to take sanctuary again. Moreover, Simon was on his tail, and if Dimitrios returned I could depend on Simon to come with him.

The torch-beam was steady now. I went softly across to the arch of the outer tunnel, and then turned off the light. I felt my way carefully along the wall of the curving passage, until, as I rounded the first bend, the darkness slackened, and I could see my way.

There was no box standing beside the entrance. Dimitrios must have set off carrying it. So much the better, I thought, vaguely. It meant he did intend to go right down to the jeep; and it would slow him down and make it easier for Simon to follow him.

I edged forward until I could see out into the corrie.

Here, too, that faint sense of surprise assailed me to see it unchanged; dazzlingly hot, still, deserted. . . .

The glare hit at the eyes. I could smell the dust and the mule dung and some dried aromatic plant that crumbled to powder under the hand I put up to the rock beside me. There was no sound at all. Nothing moved; even the hot air hung still.

I hesitated. The temptation to get out of the cave was strong, to climb the cliff path above me, and take refuge somewhere higher up the mountain where I could at once be free and yet hidden, and, more important, see any movement that there might chance to be near the corrie. But Simon must know where to find me, and he had told me to stay here. I must stay.

I went back into the cave.

I remember that I stood there for some minutes, looking round me almost idly. I was trying to picture the place before the earthquake that had first shaken down some of the stuff that blocked the aisles and recesses between the pillars. It was very possible that this had been a sacred cave. Here the Apollo had been carried by hasty, reverent hands; here, perhaps, sacrifices and other acts of worship had been made before the holy place had been finally sealed and hidden and left to its two thousand years of silence.

The beam of my torch suddenly dimmed, then brightened again. But the warning spurred me into movement. With only one brief glance back at the entrance, and a couple of seconds' pause to listen for sounds of Dimitrios' approach, I set myself to a careful exploration of the cave.

I don't quite know what I was looking for. I certainly wasn't consciously hoping to find further "treasure"—either of the kind of Angelos' hoard, or relics of Apollo's worship. But it wasn't very long before I did in fact come on evidence of another cache. In a deep bay between two pillars, at the edge of the cave not far from the stack of boxes, a pile of rubble—a shallow barrow of the stuff heaped away in a bay of rock—looked as if it had been recently disturbed.

I approached it and bent over, sending the now perceptibly dimming beam probing among the broken fragments.

I could see nothing that suggested boxes or articles concealed there, but, quite clear in the dust at my feet, was the print of a rope-soled shoe, and the marks beside it as of something being dragged.

I went closer and stooped to peer. The beam slid over the pile, caught on something, and halted. It jerked in my hand once, then fixed, still, and far too bright now, on what lay behind the pile of rock and dirt.

The murderer hadn't bothered to bury Nigel. His body had been dragged and then flung into this meager hiding, and now lay, stiff and horrible and indescribably grotesque, between the heaped rubble and the wall of the cave.

In the paralyzed moment before I dropped the torch from a numbed hand, and let the merciful darkness loose again, I saw what had happened to Nigel. You can see an awful lot in a split second's acute terror and shock; the picture your brain registers then is complete, the stuff of a million lingering nightmares still to come. Nothing is missed; every bestial detail is there for the mind to come back to, turn over, re-picture without ceasing.

He had been tied. The rope had gone now—no doubt the murderer had need of it—but the boy's wrists were scored raw where he had struggled. He had been tied, and tortured. In that one glance I had seen the shabby green shirt ripped down off one thin shoulder, and, on the upper arm, shocking against the peeling skin, a series of marks whose sickening regularity could mean only one thing. He had been burned four or five times, deliberately. Other things I saw that, at the time, meant nothing, but which, in nightmare recapitulations of that second's horror, I have since seen and recognized a score of times. I don't intend to describe them. Let it remain that Nigel had died, in pain. His eyes were open. I remember how they gleamed in the light of the torch. And his teeth clenched, grinning, on some fragment that might have been skin . . . Dimitrios' bitten thumb . . . the filthy murderous hand that had slid down my arm yesterday at the Roseate Cliff.

It was on that flash of realization that the torch dropped and the dark stamped down. I don't know what happened then. I remember, one moment, the picture in the torch-light, vivid, terrible, complete, then the next moment it was dark, and the rock was cold; it was crushing me, tearing my clothes, tripping my running footsteps; it was soft to my falling, whimpering body. . . .

I was lying at Apollo's feet on the damp moss. My hair was wet, and my hands, and the breast of my frock. Something was hurting my right hand where it pressed deeply into the grass. It was the broken end of the gold arrow. I sat looking at it for a very long time before I even saw it.

Dimitrios, I was thinking stupidly, confusedly; Dimitrios . . . he had murdered Nigel yesterday. While we had been here in the corrie, in the bright sunlight, Nigel had been in the cave with his murderer, tied and hurt and—no, that wouldn't do; he hadn't been gagged, and we'd have heard him. He was dead before we got up here, and then Dimitrios had come down to Delphi to search his room. . . .

I stared down at the beautifully worked fragment of gold in my hand, and tried to think. . . . But all that would come to me was that Nigel, poor muddled, eager young Nigel, who was a good artist, had been murdered by Dimitrios. . . .

Dimitrios! This time the thought came anything but confusedly; it whipped into my brain with a point as sharp as the one that pricked my palm. I was on my feet, and the gold arrow spun, glittering, forgotten, to the grass. Dimitrios, whom Simon and I had casually dismissed as someone who could easily be "dealt with"—Dimitrios was out there on the hillside, and Simon was tailing him, waiting for a chance to attack him, unconscious of the fact that the Greek was a murderer as vile and ruthless as ever his cousin Angelos had been. . . .

Momentarily I had forgotten poor Nigel. I ran back into the tunnel with never a thought of what lay there in the cave.

The darkness came up against me like a tangling net. As I rounded the first bend in the tunned I had to stop short, then feel my way forward slowly, my hands shaking and slipping on the cool rock.

I reached the slab. I pressed my body into the narrow cleft, craning to peer forward into the cave. But I couldn't see at all; the darkness boiled still against my wide-open eyes with shapes and spangles of a million fizzing colors. Without my torch, and blinded like this with my swift dive back out of the light, I would be helpless to cross the cave. I shut my eyes and waited there for the swarming dark to clear. The slab felt cold and damp under my flat-spread hands.

Then I heard him.

I thought at first it was the surge of the knocking pulses that nailed me to the rock, but then I knew it was the soft tread of rope-soled shoes in the dust.

I stayed where I was, frozen to the rock, and opened my eyes.

I could see now. Light was moving in the cave, a powerful light. Not Simon— Simon's torch, like mine, had begun to fail . . . and in any case, the steps had not been Simon's. But at least where Dimitrios was, Simon would be. And from the way the Greek came forward into the cave with unhurried confidence, he still didn't know of Simon's presence.

Even as the thought came, I heard a tiny sound outside the cave. My eyes flew in apprehension to the Greek. He was behind the light and I couldn't see him, but the moving beam never faltered. He hadn't heard. The sound came again, and now I knew it for what it was; the chink of metal was a bit jangled. Dimitrios had brought the mule.

The Greek passed out of my small range of vision. I waited till I heard the familiar scrape and shift of a box and the clatter of settling stones, and the grunts and short breathing of effort. Then I inched my way nearer the edge of the slab and peered round it, a centimeter at a time.

He had put the torch down in a little niche above him, so that the beam was directed onto the rock pile. His thick powerful body was stooping over this. His back was toward me; he had laid his jacket down beside him, and under the blue shirt I could see the bulge and play of his muscles as he heaved at one of the half-buried boxes. Then he dragged it out into his arms, and straightened up, holding it. I hadn't before realized how immensely strong he must be. He carried the box slowly over to the cave mouth and went out of sight with it up into the tunnel. I heard him dump it there. I heard him coming back. Still with that unhurried soft tread he came out of the tunnel mouth, into the steady beam that illumined the cave.

For the second time in those few minutes, I felt the kick of shock over the heart.

It wasn't Dimitrios. It wasn't anyone I had seen before.

But hard on the moment of shock and confusion, I knew that I was wrong. I had seen him before, and more than once. Now, faced in the queerly lit darkness with that heavy head, the thick dark curls tight like a bull's and crisping down the swarthy cheekbones toward the smiling thick-lipped mouth, I knew him. This was the Phormis head of Nigel's drawing: this was the face like an archaic statue's, with the wide fleshy cheekbones and the up-cornered, tight-lipped smile. More—this was the face I had seen, unnoticing and unremembering, bending over the engine of the jeep outside Dimitrios' cottage. And it must have been *this* face, not the Apollo (which it was certain she had never seen), that Danielle had recognized among Nigel's drawings. . . .

But before I could follow this further, two other memories flashed, sparks into the dry tinder of fear . . . Nigel saying to Danielle, "That's a chap I saw today on Parnassus," and Simon's voice in the dark, translating for me something Stephanos had told him, "He'd kill, and smile while he did it. Always that smile. . . ."

Angelos. Angelos himself. And Dimitrios was God knows where. And Simon was with him.

Angelos turned back to the pile of rubble. The torch-light slid over the thick skin, shiny with sweat. The smile never altered. No doubt he had smiled as he and Dimitrios killed Nigel between them. No doubt he would smile when Simon, having disposed of Dimitrios, came openly up to the cave to find me. . . .

Angelos straightened his thick body and stood still, as if listening. He turned his head. There were sounds outside, not metal-shod this time, but the sounds of someone hurrying toward the cave.

I remember thinking, with a kind of numbed calmness, that if I screamed, it would warn Simon—but it would warn Angelos too. He was expecting Dimitrios, and he could have no idea that Simon and I were here. He had made no move to douse the torch. But on the other hand, if Simon had dealt with Dimitrios, Simon too would be off his guard. . . .

The steps came closer; were in the tunnel. Angelos' hand went to his pocket. I took in my breath.

With a stumbling rush and a flurry of breathing, Danielle hurried into the cave.

17

Ah there is Justice in heaven,
And fire in the hand of God,
The reckoning must be made in the end.

SOPHOCLES: *Electra*
(tr. E. F. Watling)

THE MAN relaxed, but his voice, pitched low, was angry. "What the hell are you doing here?"

She had stopped at the edge of the torch-light. She looked at once younger and much prettier than I had seen her. She had on the turquoise blouse and scarlet cotton skirt, and her haste had flushed her face and hurried her breathing, making her seem more normal and less cynically in control of herself. She hadn't looked at Angelos. Her eyes were riveted on what remained of the cache of boxes.

"So that's it!" Like him, she spoke in French.

"That's it." He regarded her sourly. "I told you last night we'd located it, didn't I? So why the devil didn't you do as you were told and stay out of sight till I came for you?"

She walked forward slowly while he was speaking, her eyes still on the stuff at his feet. Now she looked up under her lashes with that provocative gamine grin. "I wanted to see for myself what was going on. Don't be angry . . . nobody saw me come."

"Did you see Dimitrios on your way up?"

She shook her head. She was stooping over the pile, prodding with a toe at the broken box that showed the gleam of gold. I saw her breasts rise and fall quickly, as if with excitement. He said sharply, "No sign of him?"

"No."

He swore and struck the spade almost savagely into the stones. "Then where the hell is he? I came by the high way—it's shorter if you know your road . . . and if you didn't see him either—"

"I came by the high way too." Again that smiling look up through the lovely lashes. "How did you think I found my way here? I waited where I thought you'd come, and then I followed you."

He grunted. "Clever, eh? Then that means he's gone down the other way to look for me. Blast the man; he's as jumpy as a bean on a griddle, and about as much use. And you—you should have stayed away till I came for you. I told you I didn't want you up here."

She laughed. "Maybe I didn't trust you, Angelos. Maybe you wouldn't have come for me."

He gave a short laugh. "Maybe."

"Well, I wanted to see *this*," she said, almost childishly, "and besides, I didn't want to hang about down there all day. That damned jeep's dynamite anyway."

"Why? The stuff's not in it."

"No, but—"

"Did you park it where I told you?"

"Of course I did. Angelos, why d'you have to do this in daylight? You're crazy."

"I know what I'm doing. There's next to no moon just now, and this country's murder with a mule on a black night, and I daren't use a light. There'll be nobody about between here and the place where I'm stacking the stuff, and we can ferry the whole lot from there to the jeep in a couple of hours after dusk." He added, with a sort of heavy irony, "Always providing, of course, that you do as you're told, and that my cool-headed cousin gets back in time to give me a bit of help with the hard work!"

She laughed. She had recovered her breath now, and with it her own particular brand of throaty charm. She straightened up and gave him one of her long-lidded glinting looks. "Well, I can help instead, can't I? You won't send me back now? Don't you think, Angelos *mou*, that you might pretend to be a little bit pleased to see me?"

She moved up close to him as she spoke, and he pulled her to him and kissed her in a way that managed to be perfunctory and yet lustful. I saw her press her thin body against him, and her hands crept up to move among the thick curls on the back of his head.

I drew back a little in my crevice, shutting my eyes momentarily as if against this new discovery. *Angelos* her lover. *Angelos*. Through the whirl of fear and confusion the facts twisted and readjusted themselves into a different pattern.

It had been Angelos, not Dimitrios, who had scraped acquaintance with Danielle on those long afternoons at Itea; this deliberately, not only to while away the boredom of inaction, but because she had the use of the jeep, whereas to buy or hire other transport would involve inquiries later, and provoke the very gossip the cousins had to avoid.

And by the same token it had been Angelos, not Dimitrios, who had broken into the studio last night. I remembered now, quite clearly, that the hand which had reached back for the torch had not had a torn thumb. And I remembered Danielle's little smile when I had so swiftly identified her lover as Dimitrios. . . .

Angelos pushed her away, not too gently. "You know damned well you should have stayed away. There's no room in the games I play for anyone with baby-nerves."

She was lighting a cigarette. She said, almost snappishly, "It wasn't nerves; it was curiosity, and I've a right to know what's going on. Baby-nerves, indeed, after what I've done for you! You'd never have got the jeep but for me, and I got you the tools and the mule on Monday night, didn't I? And I've played spy on the Englishman and that wretched girl he's taken in tow—and all you do is walk in last night out of the blue, stay with me half an hour, and tell me damn all except that today's the day, and I'm to get the jeep to the quarry, and you expect that to be that! You might have landed me in a hell of a jam last night, but you never said a word to me!"

"What d'you mean?" He was working again, levering at a solid lump of rock that was wedging down a couple of boxes. The dislodged dirt and small stones hissed down to the floor. He seemed hardly to be listening to her.

She said sharply, "You know quite well what I mean. When you came to my room last night, you said you hadn't seen Nigel, and—"

"Nigel?"

"The English artist. I told you. He was throwing out hints on Monday night about getting rich and famous, and he was drunk. After the others had left I gave him another couple of ouzos and took him for a walk. . . . Did I tell you that?" She was watching the man through the wisping smoke of her cigarette, and her tone was provocative. He neither looked up nor took the slightest notice.

She tapped ash off with a sharply pettish movement. "Well? It was obvious he'd found something up here on the hill. You said you were going to wait for him yesterday and find out what it was, and where—"

"So what? We didn't need to, did we? Your English friends came and showed us the way."

"They showed you the cave too?"

He laughed shortly. "Hardly. If they'd found the cave yesterday we'd not have been able to get near it now for troops three deep round the door!"

She moved impatiently. "I didn't mean that way. Of course they didn't find it, or they wouldn't be trailing harmlessly off to Levadia today. But you *did* find it pretty quickly, didn't you? Dimitrios told me at the Shining Ones that you'd found the place, and that you were working on it then while he came down to do some final clearing-up."

He had laid aside the crowbar, and was using the spade to shift some of the smaller debris. The thud of digging echoed dully. He didn't look up. He said, "When Stephanos showed them the spot where I broke Michael's neck I knew where the cave lay. Everything was changed, but I knew the crack must open on the cave. I couldn't get through it the way it was, but after I'd sent Dimitrios down I got to work and opened it up."

"I know. You told me this last night." She wasn't, as usual, letting the cigarette hang from her lips as she talked. She was smoking in jerky movements that spoke of tightly strung nerves. She said, making it sound like an accusation, *"But you never mentioned Nigel."*

He straightened up from his work, eyeing her, his head thrust forward like a bull's, and his look at once formidable and wary. The fixed half-moon smile on the thick mouth was in its own way terrifying. He said roughly, "Come on. What is all this? Why the hell should I mention Nigel?"

She blew a long plume of smoke, then said flatly, "When you left me last night, you went to Nigel's room. Why?"

"That's simple enough, isn't it? You'd told me he'd done a drawing of me as like as a photograph. I wanted to destroy it."

"But he'd cleared out—packed up and gone. You knew that. I'd told you that. I'd been in myself that evening to try and find the drawing, and all his stuff was gone. He'd taken it with him."

"Oh, no," said Angelos, "he hadn't."

"What d'you mean? You never saw him. How d'you know what he had on him?"

She stopped. I saw her eyes widen as they met his look. Her lips parted so that the cigarette fell to the ground and lay there smoldering. She ignored it. She was staring at him. He was standing very still, leaning on the spade, watching her. I could see sweat on the heavy face and on his hairy forearms.

He said again, softly, "Well?"

Her voice was shaken clear of any of its carefully affected overtones. It came clear and thin, like a little girl's. "You did see him? Yesterday? He *did* tell you where the cave was?"

"Yes, we saw him. But he didn't tell us anything. I told you the truth about that."

"Then—then—why did you lie about seeing him?"

The smile deepened as the thick lips parted. "You know why. Don't you?"

There was a long pause. I saw the pink tongue come out to lick once, quick as a lizard's, across her rouged lips. "You—killed him? Nigel?"

No reply. He didn't stir. I saw her throat muscles move as she swallowed. There was no horror or regret or fear in her face; it was blank of expression, with parted lips, and wide eyes fixed on the man. But her breathing hurried. "I . . . see. You didn't tell me."

His voice was soft, almost amused. "No, I didn't tell you. I didn't want to scare you away."

"But—I still don't understand. Didn't he know about the cave? Wasn't I right?"

"He knew; you can be sure of that. But he didn't tell us. We tried, but he wouldn't come through with anything that made sense."

She swallowed again. She hadn't taken her eyes off him. She might have been a waxwork but for the eyes, and the convulsive muscles of the throat. "Did you—have to kill him?"

He shrugged his heavy shoulders. "We didn't, in a manner of speaking. The bloody little pansy died on us. A pity." His head sank lower. The smile seemed to thicken. "Well? Scared? Going to scream and run?"

She moved then. She came close to him again, and her hands came up to the breast of his shirt. "Do I look as if I wanted to run, Angelos *mou?* Would I be the sort you'd want along with you if I was that kind of baby-nerve?" The hands slid up his shoulders and over them to the back of his neck. She pressed closer. "I know all about you, Angelos Dragoumis. . . . Don't think that I don't. They still tell quite a few stories about you, here in Delphi. . . ."

A laugh shook him. "You surprise me."

She pulled his head down, and said, against his mouth, "Do I? Does it surprise you to know that that's why I'm here? That that's why I like you?"

He kissed her, lingeringly this time, then thrust her away from him with his free hand. "No. Why should it? I've met women like you before." He still held the spade in his other hand, and now he turned back to his task. Danielle said, eyeing the broad back a little sulkily, "Where is he?"

"Near enough."

I saw her eyes show white for a moment as she gave a quick over-the-shoulder look into the shadowed corners. Then she shrugged and reached in her pocket for another cigarette. "You may as well tell me what happened."

"All right. Only stand back out of the way. That's better. Well. . . . We waited beside the Delphi track for the boy, but he didn't come that way. He must have started early and gone some other way round, because the first we saw of him was when he was away beyond us and almost up to these cliffs. We got up as close as we could without his seeing us, but when we'd worked our way up that gully that lies east of here, he'd vanished. We got up above the line of cliff, and separated; then waited. After a bit we saw him, just appearing walking out of the corrie here, as cool as you please. So we came down the cliff and got hold of him."

"Why did you have to do that? The English couple were coming. Once you saw the place where Michael died—"

"A bird in the hand," said Angelos, and I saw the thick grin deepen again. "For all I knew, Stephanos wouldn't remember the exact spot, and it was certain that your artist friend had just come out of some hiding place. Besides, he'd done that drawing of me. He'd seen me."

She was lighting another cigarette. The flame of the match wasn't quite steady. Her eyes looked wide and brilliant above it. "What did you do?"

He sounded indifferent. "We tried to scare him into talking at first, but he wouldn't come through. To tell you the truth I began to think you were wrong and he hadn't found a thing, only then he began to babble something about a cave and 'something beyond price' and he was damned if he'd let us touch it. Then we really got going. . . ." He straightened up and got out a cigarette. He thrust it between his lips, and leaned forward to get a light from hers.

I thought, I shall see that smile in my dreams. . . .

"But he still wouldn't say anything that made sense," said Angelos. "Babbled about water, and some flowers. . . ." The contempt in the thick French made the words sound obscene. "My English is fair enough, but I couldn't get all the words. In the end there was something about gold, I'm pretty sure, but just as we were getting to that, he died on us. God knows we'd hardly started. It looked to me as if he had a groggy heart."

"What happened then?"

"We'd hardly finished with him when we saw Stephanos and the boy from Arachova bringing the English couple along. We threw the body behind some rocks and waited and watched till the old man took them to the corrie and showed them the place. It's altered completely; I might have looked for a thousand years, let alone the last two. As soon as they'd gone, I got down into the corrie and started looking round. It was dead easy. Your Nigel helped us after all with his crazy blathering; there was only one place where grass grew, and flowers, and it was much where I expected the cave to lie, if Stephanos had been accurate. We soon saw where the entrance was. Getting into it was another matter, but of course with the boy dead on our hands we had to be sure there'd be no inquiries until we'd got clear off and no traces left. So I got on with the job alone while I sent Dimitrios down to see you as arranged. I told him not to tell you about Nigel, but to get quietly into the studio and clear the stuff out of his room as if he'd packed up and gone. He did that. You'll find all the boy's stuff in the back of the jeep under the sacking. Dimitrios brought a big folder of drawings, but like a fool he was in too much of a hurry to check them, and he never saw that the picture of me wasn't there. . . . It mightn't have mattered, but that's the sort of detail that can sometimes matter the hell of a lot. I thought it worth attending to, anyway. I'm officially dead, and by God I'm staying that way, and no rumors!"

"Did you find it?"

"No. I didn't have time. There was a lot of paper with the rubbish in a tin on the floor of his room. That fool Dimitrios hadn't thought it worth bothering about. But in fact if that's where the drawings are, nobody's going to take any notice of them. They'll just think he's tidied up and left."

"They do. The English couple think he's gone on a trek over the hills—with the mule."

"Do they?" He sounded amused. "Then that's that, isn't it?"

He had cleared the boxes now of their covering of stones. He stooped to work one of them clear of the pile. She watched the play of the great muscles for a few moments in silence. Then she said again, "Where is he?"

"Who?"

"My God, Nigel of course! Did you just leave him out there for the vultures?"

"Not likely. They'd have given us away more quickly than anything else. He's here."

For the first time I saw some strong feeling move her. It was like a spring tensing. *"Here?"*

He jerked his head sideways. "Over there." He jerked the box free at last, straightened up, and carried it out of the cave. The torch still shone strongly enough from its niche on the pillar. Danielle stood still for a moment, staring toward the dark corner where Nigel's body lay, then, as if with an effort, she walked forward, took the torch down from its niche, and went over to the pile of rubble that hid the pathetic body. The light shone down on what lay, mercifully, beyond my range of vision.

It was at that moment that I remembered my own torch, dropped near Nigel's body. If she saw it . . . if the light from her torch picked up its glint in the dust. . . .

Angelos was coming back. He said irritably, "Still no sign. He seems to have taken one of the small boxes down himself by the lower track. Or else we'd have seen him." Then he looked across and saw where she was. She still had her back to him. The heavy face watching her didn't change its expression, but something in the look of the eyes made my blood thicken. "Well?"

She turned abruptly, "Are you going to leave him here?"

"Where else? Take him in the jeep to the bay at Galaxeidion?"

She ignored the irony. "Aren't you going to bury him?"

"My God, girl, there's no time. I've got enough to do shoveling half Parnassus off this stuff. You can throw some dirt down over him if you like, but it hardly matters. Something for you to do while I load up."

She came quickly back into the middle of the cave. "I'm not staying here."

He laughed. "As you wish. I thought you weren't squeamish, *ma poule?*"

"I'm not," she said pettishly, "but can't you see it won't do to leave him here, even if we do cover him? It's obvious already there's been someone at work here, and if anyone does come up they're bound to see—"

"Why should anyone come?"

She hesitated, eyeing him. "The Englishman, Simon—"

"What of him? You told me yourself he'd gone off to Levadia."

"I know, but—well, I was still thinking about what happened in the theatre, on Monday night."

In the theatre, on Monday night . . . I leaned back against the rock, trying, through the mists of tension and fear, to remember . . . the sounds I had heard as I sat there: the tiny jingling . . . it had after all been Danielle, taking the stolen mule off to meet the men. And Simon and I had talked, down there in the theatre. . . . It wasn't only the speech from *Electra* that those wonderful acoustics had sent up to Danielle, above us in the dark. And Danielle understood English . . . What had we said? *What, in heaven's name, had we said?*

It appeared that, whatever it was, she had reported it to him before. He laughed. "Oh, that. It's no news. Of course he knows Michael was murdered. D'you think Stephanos wouldn't tell him that? What difference does it make? Nobody knows *why.*"

"But if he suspected you were still alive—"

"Him?" The thick voice held nothing but amused contempt. "In any case, how should he? Nigel's dead, and no one's going to recognize that picture now."

"There was the gold," said Danielle.

The dark was boiling round me. As clearly as if he were just beside me, I heard Simon's voice again. *"It's not over . . . till I find what Michael found . . . the gold."*

"Gold, gold, gold—you see it everywhere, don't you, *ma poule?*" He laughed again. For some reason his spirits seemed to be rising. "You didn't *see* it was gold, now, did you? She picked something up and you saw it glitter, and your imagination did the rest."

"I tell you it was gold. I saw her staring at it."

The dark slowly cleared. Against it I saw a picture—not the one they were speaking of, but later; Simon, coming away from the center-mark just before he spoke. . . . She hadn't heard. By the mercy of the gods of the place, she hadn't heard.

Angelos had turned away and was lugging another box clear of the pile. "There. That's as much as the poor bloody mule can take on one trip. . . . Now, forget that nonsense for five minutes, and you can give me a hand loading up. He found no gold yesterday, and that's a fact. He's got no reason to come back here. He's been, and seen all he can. Why should he come again? To bring a posy for Michael?" He laughed again, unpleasantly. "By God, I almost wish he would! . . . I owe him something, after all."

She said, with a sort of spite, "And her. She hit you."

"She did, didn't she?" he said cheerfully. "I think we'll wait till Dimitrios comes. He can't be much longer." He paused, looking round the cave. "It's queer to be back . . . and it looks just the same. Just the same. These pillars, and that bit of rock like a lion's head, and the drip of water somewhere. I never found the spring. . . . Can you hear it?"

She said impatiently, "But Nigel. You must do something about the body. Can't you see—?"

"You may be right." His voice was almost absent. It was clear that Nigel had long since ceased to matter at all. "In fact he may do us a better turn dead than he did alive. . . . *He* can go over the cliff with the jeep. Yes, there's the water. I thought so. It's over here somewhere. . . ."

Danielle's voice stopped him as he moved. There was a note in it that I hadn't heard before. "The jeep? Over the cliff? I didn't know you planned to do that."

"You don't know all I plan to do, my fair lady," he said. He turned back to her as he spoke, and I couldn't see his face. I saw hers. It looked suddenly thinner, and sharp, like a frightened urchin's. He said, "What is it now? We've got to get rid of the jeep somehow, haven't we? If the boy's found in the sea with it, that accounts for him as well."

She said, almost in a whisper, "It's mine. Everybody knows I brought it up from Athens."

"So what? Everybody'll assume you were in it too, and that will be that."

Still she didn't move, but stared up at him. She looked very childish in the turquoise top, and scarlet bell of skirt. He went toward her till she had to tilt back her head to look him in the eyes. He said on a note of impatience, and something else, "What is it now? Scared?"

"No. No. But I was wondering—"

"What?"

She spoke still in that hurried whisper. "What you were going to do with the jeep if you . . . if you hadn't had Nigel's body to send over the cliffs with it?"

He said slowly, "The same, of course. They'd have thought you were in it and had been—"

He stopped abruptly. Then I heard him laugh. His big hand went slowly out and ran down her bare arm. It looked very dark against her pale olive flesh. There were black hairs on the back of it. "Well, well, well . . . My poor little pretty, did you really think I'd do a thing like that to you?"

She didn't move. The thin arm hung slack by her side. Her head was tilted back, the big eyes searching on his face. She said in that flat little voice, "You said *'He* can go over the cliff in the jeep. . . .' as if you'd planned it for someone else. As if—"

He had an arm round her now, and had pulled her close to him. She went to him unresisting. His voice thickened. "And you thought I meant you? *You?* My little Danielle . . ."

"Then who?"

He didn't answer, but I saw her eyes narrow and then flare wide again. She whispered, *"Dimitrios?"*

His hand came quickly over her mouth and his body shook as if with a laugh. "Quietly, little fool, quietly! In Greece, the mountains have ears."

"But, Angelos *mou*—"

"Well? I thought you said you knew me, my girl? Don't you see? I had to have his help, and his boat, but when did *he* earn the half share of a fortune? The stuff's mine, and I've waited fourteen years for it, and now I've got it. D'you think I'm going to share it—with anyone?"

"And—what about me?"

He pulled her unresisting body closer to him. He laughed again, deep in his throat. "That's not sharing. You and I, *ma poule,* we count as one. . . ." His free hand slid up her throat, under her chin, and then forced her head up so that her mouth met his. "And I still need *you*. Do I still have to convince you of that?" His mouth closed on hers then, avidly, and I saw her stiffen for just a moment as if she was going to resist, then she relaxed against him and her arms went up to his neck. I heard him laugh against her lips, and then he said hoarsely, "Over there. Hurry."

I shut my eyes. I turned my head away so that my cheek, like my hands, pressed against the cool rock. It smelt fresh, like rain. I remember that under my left hand there was a little knob of stone the shape of a limpet shell. . . .

I don't want to write about what happened next, but in justice to myself I think I must. As I shut my eyes the man was kissing her, and I saw his hand beginning to fumble with her clothes. She was clinging to him, her body melting toward his, her hands pulling his head down fiercely to meet her kisses. Then when I couldn't see any more I heard him talking, little breathless sentences I couldn't catch—didn't try to catch—in a mixture of Greek and his thick fluent French. I heard him kick a stone out of the way as he pulled her down onto the dusty floor of the cave near the rubble pile . . . near Nigel's body. . . .

I only heard one sound from her, and it was a little half-sigh, half-whimper of pleasure. I'll swear it was of pleasure.

I was shaking, and covered with sweat, and hot as though the chilly cleft were an oven. Under the fingers of my left hand the stone limpet had broken away. I was holding a fragment of it in my curled fingers, and it was embedded in the flesh, hurting me.

I don't know how long it was before I realized that the cave was quiet, except for the heavy breathing.

Then I heard him getting to his feet. His breathing was deep and even. He didn't say anything, and I didn't hear him move away. There was no sound from Danielle.

I opened my eyes again, and the dimming torch-light met them. He was standing beside the pile of rubble, smiling down at Danielle. She lay there, still looking up at him. I could see the glint of her eyes. The sweat on his face made the wide fleshy cheeks gleam like soapstone. He stood quite still, smiling down at the girl who lay at his feet staring back at him, her bright skirt all tossed-looking in the dust.

I thought, with crazy inconsequence, How uncomfortable she looks. Then, suddenly, She looks dead.

Presently Angelos stooped, took her body by the shoulders, and dragged it across the cave to pitch it down in the rubble beside Nigel.

And that is how Danielle Lascaux was murdered within twenty yards of me, and I never lifted a finger to help her.

18

Go while the going's good,
Is my advice. . . .

SOPHOCLES: *Philoctetes*
(tr. E. F. Watling)

BY THE mercy of providence I didn't faint, or I'd have pitched straight out into the torch-light. But the narrow cleft held my body up, and my mind (numbed, I suppose, by the repetition of shock), seemed only very slowly to take in what had happened.

It was as if some sort of mental censor had dropped a curtain of gauze between me and the scene in the cave, so that it took on a kind of long-distance quality, the murderer moving about his dreadful business at a far remove from me, as a creature of fiction moves on a lighted stage. I was invisible, inaudible, powerless, the dreamer of the dream. With light would come sanity, and the nightmare vanish.

I watched him, still in that queer dead trance of calm. I think if he had turned in my direction I would hardly have had the wit to draw back, but he didn't. He dropped Danielle's body down in the dust beside Nigel's, and stood for a moment looking down at them, lightly dusting his hands together. I wondered for a moment if he was, after all, going to shovel the dirt over the bodies, then it occurred to me that Danielle's useless spark of instinct had been right; his plan for disposing of Nigel in the jeep had come a little too pat. It was Danielle who had brought the jeep; it was Danielle who was to be found with the wreck of it. . . . That had been his plan all along. I saw it now clearly. I didn't believe for a moment that he intended to kill his cousin Dimitrios—but even if that were true, he had certainly never intended to share anything with Danielle. What she had to offer was only too easily found elsewhere. What was equally certain was that he hadn't wanted to kill her here. He must have intended to save himself the transport of her body by killing her when the job was over, but her half-frightened queries had aimed just a little too near the mark for comfort. Better kill her now, and risk the extra load to be ferried down after dusk.

He had turned back now to the pillar where the torch was lodged. I watched him, still as if he were an actor in a play—a bad actor; there was no expression on his face, no horror or anxiety, or even interest. He reached up a hand, picked up the torch, and switched it off. The darkness came down like a lid on a stifling box. He seemed to be listening. I could hear his untroubled breathing, and the tiny rustle of settling dust under the girl's body. There was no sound from outside.

He switched on the light again and went out of the cave. A bridle jingled as the mule moved, but it appeared that he hadn't untied it. I heard him move off, his soft footsteps unaccompanied by the sharper ones of the beast. He must have decided to reconnoiter the corrie before daring to lead out the mule. . . .

The footsteps dwindled steadily. I couldn't hear them anymore. I waited, straining my ears. Nothing but the soft movement of dust in the cave, and the restless shifting of the mule's hoofs in its corner. He must have left the corrie—perhaps to look for Dimitrios' approach.

One thing was certain: Angelos had no idea that Simon had any reason for further curiosity about the corrie. He felt as safe from discovery in this remote stretch of Parnassus as he would on the mountains of the moon.

And Simon? Simon, too. . . .

I was out of the cleft and flying across the dark cave. There was no light, but I don't remember that I needed it. My body was acting of itself, like a sleepwalker's, and like a sleepwalker's it must have dodged every obstacle by instinct. My brain, too . . . I had no conscious plan, not even any coherent thought, but at some queer submerged level I knew I had to get out of that cave, to Simon. . . . There was something about Dimitrios coming back, and Simon . . . something about warning Simon that here was not one shifty little crook to deal with, but two men who were murderers . . . something important to tell Simon . . . and more important than anything, I had to get out of the darkness, out of that stifling cage of rock, into the blessed light . . .

The sun struck down at me like a bright axe. I put a hand to my eyes, flinching as if at an actual blow. I was blinded, swimming in a sea of light. My other hand, groping out before me, touched something warm and soft, that moved. I jerked away with a little gasp of terror and in the same moment I realized that it was the mule, tethered in the narrow corner outside the cave. Its muzzle was deep in the grass, and it hardly paused to roll a white eye back at me before it resumed its eager cropping. The warm ammoniac smell of its coat brought a momentary, comfortless, memory of Niko. I thrust past it, ducked heedlessly under the buttress, and ran out into the corrie.

There was no sign of Angelos. I turned and ran for the foot of the cliff path.

The heat in the bottom of the corrie was palpable. I felt the sweat start out on my body as soon as I left the shade. The air weighed on me as I ran. My lungs labored to drag it in, and dust was burning and rough in my throat. The corrie was a well of heat, in which nothing moved except me, and I thrust through it blindly, with the whip of panic on me. . . .

I reached the foot of the cliff. I believe I realized that if Angelos had gone to meet his cousin, he would have gone by the gateway, and not up the cliff. But this again was not a conscious thought. I only knew that I had to get up, out of the hot enclosing walls of rock, out onto the high open stretches above the cliff.

The afternoon sun shone full on the cliff where the path lay. The brightness of the white limestone splintered against the eyes. As I plunged up the steep, twisting little goat-track I felt the rock burn the soles of my shoes like hot metal. When I put a hand to the face of the cliff it seemed to scorch the flesh.

I climbed as fast as I dared, trying to make no sound. The dust hissed like sand under my feet. A pebble rolled and fell to the foot of the cliff with a crack like a pistol shot. My breathing was as loud in the still air as sobbing.

I was a little less than halfway up when I heard him coming back.

I stopped dead, pilloried against the naked rock, clamped to it, like a lizard on the bare stone. The rock burned through my thin dress. As soon as he got to the gateway he would see me. I couldn't possibly get to the top in time. If there were somewhere to hide. . . .

There was nowhere to hide. A bare zigzag of goat track; a couple of steep steps of natural rock open to the sun; a ledge holding a low tangle of brown scrub. . . .

Regardless now of noise I scrambled anyhow over the rocky steps, pulled myself off the path onto the ledge, and flung myself down behind the meager shelter of the dead bushes.

There was one small holly oak, shining green, among a mass of foot-high tufted stuff like a tangle of rusty wire netting. This was prickly to the touch, but as I dragged myself nearer its shelter, pressing against it, it crumbled under my desperate hands. I remember that it seemed quite a natural part of the nightmare, that the barrier between me and murder should crumble as I touched it.

I drew back from the dead bushes and pressed myself deep into the dust of the ledge, as if like a mole I could dig myself into the ground for safety. I put my cheek to the hot dust and lay still. Above me an overhang dealt a narrow shade, but where I lay the ledge was exposed to the sun. I could feel its cruel weight on my back and hand, but I hardly heeded it. Through the wiry scrub I was watching the corrie below me.

Angelos came up into the gateway and then walked quickly down the ramp and across the corrie. He didn't look up, but made straight for the cave, disappearing from my view in the corner.

I waited, pressed down in the burning dust. . . .

I was just getting ready to move, when I saw him again. He came out into the sunlight, moving very quietly now, and looking about him. He had brought his jacket out of the cave, and held it carefully over one arm. In the other hand he held something that shone in the sunlight. It was the torch I had dropped by Nigel's body. Angelos' own torch.

The black arched brows were drawn frowning over his eyes. The smile pulled the thick lips. He stopped in the center of the corrie, turning the torch over in his hand.

I lay still. Invisible, the mule moved restlessly, and metal clinked.

Angelos raised his head and sent one long look round the corrie. It raked the cliff, touched me, passed me by. Then the massive shoulders lifted in a tiny shrug, and he thrust the torch into a pocket of the jacket. I saw him slide his hand into the other pocket and bring out a gun. He weighed this for a moment in his hand, thoughtfully, and then turned back toward the cave.

My hands braced themselves in the dust. He would have recognized the torch, no doubt of that. He was going back into the cave to search for whoever had dropped it. And this time I didn't propose to linger till he came out again. I wasn't going to wait here, to be brushed off the cliff by that gun like a lizard off a wall.

I felt the muscles tighten up like vibrating wires. He was moving deliberately across the corrie floor. Soon he would be out of sight.

Something fell onto my hand with a sharp little rap of pain that nearly made me cry out. A pebble. Then a shower of dust and small stones, dislodged from somewhere above me, rattled down the cliff like a charge of small shot.

Angelos stopped dead, turned, and stared upward straight at me.

I didn't move. I didn't think he could see me at that angle. But my mind stampeded with another, and worse panic, as I heard the sounds approaching the top of the cliff. Dimitrios, as yet scatheless, with Simon behind him? Or Simon, coming cheerfully to tell me that justice had been done on "last night's marauder"? Any hope I had had that Dimitrios might have been forced into telling Simon himself about Angelos, vanished now as I listened to that incautious approach.

I saw Angelos stiffen, then he whipped out of sight behind a jut of rock.

The sounds came nearer. I turned my head till, by twisting my eyes in their sockets, I could see the cliff top. If it was Simon I must shout . . . my mouth opened ready for the cry, and I licked the dust off my dry lips. Then something moved suddenly against the sky at the brim of the cliff, and I saw what it was.

A goat. Another. Three big black goats, yellow-eyed, flop-eared, peacefully intent on the dry scrub at the cliff's head. . . . They turned aside at the brink of the cliff and moved slowly across above me, outlined against the deep blue of that translucent sky. As they went I thought I heard again the sweet faraway stave of the goat-herd's pipe. The coolly pastoral sound fell through the heat like the trickle of Apollo's spring.

The relief was dizzying. The rock swam in the dazzling light. I shut my eyes and put my head down beside the dusty scrub. Something smelt sweet and aromatic—some memory, wisping out of the dust, of potpourri and English gardens and bees among the thyme. . . .

I don't know how long it was before I realized that the afternoon held no sound at all.

When I looked again, Angelos had come out of concealment, and was standing where he had been before, in the center of the corrie floor. He was standing very still, staring up, not at me, but at the edge of the cliff above me where the goats had been. Slowly I followed his gaze. I could feel the breath of the hot stone on my cheek.

The goats were still there. They, too, were standing stock-still, side by side, at the brink of the cliff. They were looking down, with ears forward and eyes intent and curious . . . six yellow satyrs' eyes, staring fixedly down at me, some forty feet below them.

Angelos dropped his coat onto a boulder beside him, and started for the foot of the cliff.

At his movement I heard the flurry of dust and pebbles as the goats fled. It echoed the quick jump and kick of my own heart. But I didn't move. Whether some instinct kept me clamped still like a hiding animal, or whether the flood of fear that washed and ebbed through my blood actually drained the power of movement from me, I can't tell. At any rate I lay flat for the few decisive moments during which the Greek crossed the corrie and plunged up the goat path toward me. And then it seemed that he was almost on me, and it was too late to escape. I remembered the gun and lay there, unbreathing, pressed flat to the hot earth.

I had a shelter of a sort from below, and from above the overhang might partly hide me. The path sloped sharply past the end of the ledge where I lay. It was possible—it was surely possible?—that he might hurry past it and never look back to see me lying there behind the crumbling scrub? My dress was of pale-colored cotton, now sufficiently streaked with dust. Against the glaring rock and the red pebble-strewn dust he might miss me. He might yet—surely?—miss me.

He was just below me now. He stopped. His head was a few feet below the level of my ledge. I couldn't—daren't—look, but I heard the climbing steps stilled, and then his breathing close beneath me. He was looking up. My own breath hardly stirred the dust under my mouth.

He paused where he was for a few seconds, and then I heard the soft steps moving on. But they didn't come on up the track. They moved carefully away to the left, below my ledge.

Through the pathetic barrier of dead plants I could just see the top of his head. It was turned away now, and I knew that he must have left the track. I could hear loose pebbles slither and spatter down the rock, and the rustle of the dry plants he trod over. He went very carefully, with pauses almost between each step.

I had to know what he was doing. I moved my head slightly, and saw him better.

There was a ledge below mine, with a few sparse plants and a tumble of loose fragments of stone. I had noticed it in that second's wild glance round for shelter. It wouldn't have hidden anyone larger than a child. But he searched it, gun in hand, quartering it methodically, like a dog.

Then he left it, and came back carefully onto the track. He paused there briefly once again, so that for a silly moment I wondered if he was satisfied, and would go down again into the corrie, thinking perhaps that the goats had been watching a snake. . . . But he turned without further hesitation and started up the steep section that would bring him up to me.

I don't even think I was frightened; not now. It was as if fear had been raised to such a pitch that it killed itself, like a light that goes vividly bright just before it goes out. I was back in that dim-lit, remote theatre of unreality. This wasn't happening to me.

I suppose that nobody, in their heart of hearts, ever believes that they themselves will die. Volumes of philosophies have been written out of this belief alone. And I'm sure that nobody ever believes that a foul thing like murder can overtake them. Something will stop it. It can't happen. To others, but not to them. Not to *me*.

I lay, almost relaxed, abandoned to fate and chance, in the hot dust, and Angelos swiftly climbed the path toward me. In a moment now he would reach the end of my ledge. He might see me straightaway, or he might turn aside and beat the scrub till he flushed me, scared and filthy with dust, from my hiding place. He was there now. He couldn't miss me. . . .

I have read somewhere that when a man is hunted for his life, one of the chief dangers he undergoes is the desperate urge to give himself up, and have done. I had never believed it. I had thought that fear would drive him till he dropped, like a hunted hare. But it's true. It may have been that something forbade me to let the man find me crouching, dirty and frightened, at his feet; it may simply have been the terrible blind instinct of the hunted. But the impulsion came and I didn't attempt to resist it.

I stood up and began to brush the dirt off my frock.

I didn't look at him. He had stopped dead when I moved. He was standing just where my ledge left the track. To get off it I would have to pass him.

I walked forward through the scrub and stones as if I were walking in my sleep. I didn't meet his eyes, but watched my feet on the rough going. He moved a little to one side and I passed him. I went slowly down the path again to the bottom of the corrie. He came just behind me.

When I got to the level ground I stumbled and nearly fell. His hand took hold of my arm from behind, and my flesh seemed to wince and shrink from the touch. I stopped.

The hand tightened, then with a jerk he pulled me round to face him. I think if he had gone on touching me I would have screamed then and there, but he let me go, so I kept silent. I knew that if I tried to scream I would be killed out of hand. But I backed away from him a step or so till a boulder touched the back of my legs. Without meaning to, I sat down; I couldn't have stood. I put both hands flat on the hot surface of the stone as if I could draw strength from it, and looked at Angelos.

He was standing perhaps five feet from me, his legs a little apart, one hand thrust negligently into the belt of his trousers, the other arm hanging loose at his side with the gun dangling. His head was forward slightly, like a bull's when it is deciding to charge. The heavy face was terrifying with its tight, curved smile, the perfect arch of the black brows and the cruel eyes that seemed to be solid, opaque black, without pupils, and without light from within. The thick nostrils were flared and he was breathing fast. The bulls' curls along his forehead were damp and tight with sweat.

He had recognized me, of course. I saw that as his slow stare raked me. He must have seen me distinctly last night in the light of the torch.

He said, "So it's my little friend of the studio, is it?" He was speaking in the quick guttural French he had used with Danielle.

I tried to say something, but no sound came. As I cleared my throat I saw the smile deepen. My voice came back. "I hope I hurt you," I said.

"That score," said Angelos, very pleasantly, "will soon be quite even." My hands pressed hard on the warm stone. I said nothing. He said abruptly, "Where's the Englishman?"

"I don't know."

He made a small movement toward me and I shrank back against the boulder. His expression didn't change but his voice did. "Don't be a fool. You didn't come up here alone. Where is he?"

I said hoarsely, "I—we were sitting up there on the cliff and we saw a man hanging about . . . that chap Dimitrios. He's a guide . . . I don't know if you know him. Simon . . . my friend . . . went off to speak to him. He—he thought it was him last night at the studio and I think—I think he wanted to find out what he'd been after."

It was so near the truth that I hoped he might be satisfied as far as Simon was concerned. But it wouldn't help me. Nothing would.

"And you've been up on the cliff all this time?"

"I—why, no. I went over the hill a little way, and then I thought Simon might have come back, so I—"

"And you haven't been in the cave?"

"Cave?" I said.

"That's what I said. The cave."

The sun was cold. The rock was cold. I suppose even till this I had been hoping against silly hope, but now I knew for certain. Of course I was going to die. Whatever I had seen or not seen—the mule, the cave, the treasure, Nigel, Danielle—it wouldn't help me in the least to play the innocent. None of these things mattered beside the one fact that now I had seen Angelos.

He had taken two paces away to where his coat lay over a boulder. He slipped a hand in the pocket and brought out the torch. "You left this, didn't you?"

"Yes."

A gleam of surprise in the black eyes showed that he had expected me to deny it. I said flatly, "I dropped it when I saw Nigel's body. And I was in the cave just now when you killed Danielle."

The metal of the torch flashed as he made a sudden little movement. At least I had startled him into interest. If I could keep him talking . . . if I could keep alive for just a few more minutes . . . perhaps the miracle would happen, and I wouldn't die. Murderers were conceited, weren't they? They talked about their murders? But then Angelos took murder so for granted that it had hardly seemed to interest him to commit, let alone to discuss. . . . But he was a sadist, too; perhaps he would enjoy talking to frighten me before he killed me. . . .

I said hoarsely, gripping the stone, "Why did you torture Nigel? Did you really mean to kill Danielle?"

It wasn't going to work. He dropped the torch back on top of the coat, and gave a quick glance round the encircling cliffs. Then he put the gun down gently beside the torch, and turned to me.

I did manage to move then, but the thrust of my hands that took me off the warm stone sent me a pace toward him. As I whirled to run he caught me from behind and pulled me back as easily as if I had been a rag doll. I suppose I fought him; I don't remember anything except the blind panic and the feel of his hands and the acrid smell of his sweat, and the appalling iron strength that held me as effortlessly as a man's hand holds a caught moth. One hand came hard over my mouth, crushing my lips against my teeth, but the palm was slimy with sweat; it slipped, and I wrenched my head away and managed at the same moment to kick him hard on the shinbone. I paid dearly for the moment of advantage, for as I twisted my body in a vain attempt to break away, he half-lunged forward to drag me close again and silence me, trod on a loose stone that rolled under his foot, and we fell together.

If I had fallen undermost I should probably have been badly hurt, if not stunned, for he was a heavy man; but he went down onto his side in a stumbling fall, dragging me with him. Even then the brutal grip never loosened, and as we hit the ground he moved like lightning, flinging himself over my body with a quick heave, and holding me down on the ground underneath him.

Then his grip shifted. I was on my back, my left arm twisted up under me, so that our double weight held it there, almost breaking. My right wrist was in his grip, clamped down against the rock beside me. His free hand flashed up to my throat. The heavy body held me down; I couldn't move, but frantic now with terror I screamed and twisted uselessly under him and jerked my head from side to side, trying to avoid the hand that slipped and groped on my throat for the hold he wanted. I screamed again. He cursed in Greek and hit me hard across the mouth and then as my head went back against the rock the hand gripped my throat at last, moved a little, tightened. . . .

I was still alive. It was years later and the boiling agonized black had cleared, and I was still alive. I was still lying on my back in the hot dust, and above me the sky arched in a great flashing, pulsating dome of blue. Angelos' weight was still on me. I could feel the heave of his heavy breathing; the smell of his sweat was rank; his hand was wet and sour and foul across my mouth; the other hand was still on my throat, but it lay loosely there, and now it lifted.

He didn't move away. He lay there quite still, with rigid muscles, looking up and away from me toward the entrance to the corrie. Then his hand slid from my face and went down onto the dusty rock beside my head, ready to thrust him to his feet. I remember that the hand was on my spread hair, and the tug as he put his weight on it hurt me. The tiny pain was like a spur. It pricked me back to consciousness. I stopped blinking up into the vibrating blue of the sky, and managed to move my head a fraction, to look where Angelos was looking.

He was staring straight into the sun. At first I could see nothing in the dazzle at the mouth of the corrie. Then I saw him.

I knew who it was straightaway, though he was only a shadow against the glare. But even so I felt the sharp cold thrill run up the marrow of my spine as I felt Angelos' heart jerk, once, in his body, and heard him say, thickly, "Michael?"

19

I am come,
Fresh from the cleansing of Apollo . . .
. . . To pay the bloody twain their debt
Of blood.

EURIPIDES: *Electra*
(tr. Gilbert Murray)

REALIZATION, SHOCK, recognition—it must only have taken a few seconds, but it seemed an age.

One moment Simon was silhouetted in fractional pause against the glare of the gateway, the next, Angelos had swung himself off my body and onto his feet as lightly as a dancer. He must have forgotten that his gun had been laid aside, for I remember that his hand flashed, as if automatically, to his hip just as Simon, coming down the ramp with the speed of a ski-jumper, brought up not five yards from him in a flurry of dust and shale.

Angelos was standing right over me, hand still at hip, watching him.

Simon had stopped dead where he was. I couldn't see his expression, but I could see Angelos', and fear seeped back into my blood as agonizingly as warmth after frostbite. I stirred in the dust and tried to say something, to tell Simon who and what he was, but my throat was swollen and sore, and the brilliant light swam round me sickeningly as I moved, and I couldn't make a sound. Angelos must have felt me move at his feet, but he took no notice. Simon hadn't glanced at me either. The two men watched one another, as wary and slow as two dogs circling before a fight.

I waited for Simon to rush him as he had done last night. I didn't notice then how hard he was breathing, fighting to get heart and lungs under control after his rush up the steep track toward my terrified screaming. Nor did I realize that he still thought the Greek might be armed . . . and I was lying where knife or gun could reach me, seconds before Simon could make contact. . . . None of this was I in any state to realize. I only knew that Simon didn't move, and I remember wondering, with a sick cold little feeling, if he was afraid. Then he took two paces forward, very slowly, and now that he was no longer between me and the sun, I saw his face. The cold feeling went, and I wasn't afraid any more. With the fear, the tenseness went out of my body, and I felt myself relax and begin to tremble. The bruises the Greek had inflicted began to hurt. I turned on my side and tried to pull myself a little further away from him. I couldn't have got up, but I dragged myself a foot or so away to crouch, shaking and still gasping for breath, against the base of the boulder where I had sat before.

He took no notice of me. He had dealt with me, and thrown me aside, and now he was going to deal with Simon. I could be finished after that.

Simon said pleasantly, "I take it you are Angelos?" His breathing was still over-fast, but his voice was level.

"The same. And you are Michael's little brother."

"The same."

The Greek said, on a note between satisfaction and contempt, "You are welcome."

Simon's lips thinned. "I doubt that. I believe, Angelos, that you and I have met before."

"Last night."

"Yes." Simon looked at him for a few seconds in silence. His voice went flat and uninflected. Knowing him now, I felt my heart tighten and begin to race. He added, "I wish I had known—last night."

I turned my head painfully and managed to say, "He killed Nigel . . . and Danielle." It was some seconds before I realized that I had made no sound at all.

"You murdered my brother Michael." Simon hadn't even glanced at me. He was breathing evenly now, his face wiped clean of all expression but that light, watchful look. I recognized it for what it was. Just so must Michael have looked when he faced Angelos here all those years ago. Just so must this blazing sky have looked down, those indifferent rocks throwing back its blinding heat. Time had run back. Angelos faced Michael again, and this time the odds were on Michael.

It seemed that Angelos didn't think so. He laughed. "Yes, I killed Michael. And I shall kill you, little brother. In your country they do not teach men to be men. It is different here."

Simon was moving now, very slowly, forward a pace; another.

"How did you kill my brother, Angelos?"

"I broke his neck." I noticed with surprise that the Greek was giving ground. He had lowered his head in that characteristic way he had. I could see the contraction of the flat black eyes against the light. I saw him blink rapidly once or twice, and he moved his head as a bull does whose horns pain him. Then he took a slow step backward, sidling a little. . . .

I thought for a moment that he was trying to get Simon out of line with him and the sun, and wondered fleetingly at the same time why he should have let the other play for time like this, when suddenly, like a flash out of a black night, I knew what he was doing. I remembered the gun, lying hidden from Simon in the tumble of Angelos' dropped coat.

Somehow I moved. It was like lifting a mattress stuffed with clay to lift my body from the scuffled dust, but I rolled over, kicked myself along the ground with one convulsive jack-knifing motion, like a fish, and grabbed at the dangling sleeve of the coat just as Angelos took a sudden, swift step aside, and stooped for the gun.

I had the sleeve. I yanked at it with all my strength. It caught at a bit of the rock, tore, and came with a jerk. The torch flashed over like a rocket and crashed on a stone by my head. The gun flew high and wide, hit a pile of stones three yards away, and slithered out of sight. It actually struck the Greek's hand as he reached to grab it. He whirled with a curse and kicked me and then went down sickeningly across the boulder as Simon hit him like a steam hammer.

Simon came in with the blow. The Greek's forearm, even as he went down over the rock, just managed to block the side-handed chop at the throat that followed it, and counter in the same movement with a wicked elbow punch that took Simon in the lower part of the stomach. I saw pain explode through him like a bursting shell, and as he recoiled the Greek, using the rock as a springboard, came away from it in a lunge with all his weight behind it. Simon's mouth disappeared in a smear of blood. His head snapped back in front of another blow that looked as if it had broken his neck, and he went down, but as he went he hooked one leg round Angelos' knee and, using the man's own momentum, brought him crashing down over him. Before the Greek hit the ground Simon had rolled aside and was above him. I saw the Greek lash out with a foot, miss, and aim a short chopping blow with the edge of a hand at Simon's neck; Simon hit him in the throat and then the two were locked, heaving and rolling in the dust that mushroomed up round them.

I couldn't see . . . couldn't make out . . . Angelos was on his back, and Simon seemed to be across him, trying to fix the man's arm in a lock, to drag it under him as Angelos had dragged mine; the Greek smashed again and again at his face; the shortened punches hadn't much force behind them but the blood was running from Simon's mouth. Then suddenly the flailing fist opened, clawed, came down onto Simon's cheekbone and slithered across it, the big spatulate thumb digging, digging, for his eye. . . .

I had dragged myself to my feet, holding on to the boulder beside me. He couldn't do it after all; he couldn't be expected to do it . . . he was the younger, and he knew how to fight, but Angelos had the weight, and all those desperate years behind him. . . . If I could help . . . if I could only help. . . .

I stooped giddily, and reached for a lump of rough rock, lifting it in hands that shook like leaves. I could hit him as I had last night . . . if I could find a weapon—perhaps the torch—

The gun.

I dropped the knob of rock and flung myself, with sobbing little breaths, at the pile of stones where the gun had gone. Here, surely, it had struck and slid out of sight? No sign. Then here? No. Here . . . oh, dear God, *here.* . . .

There, white on the limestone, a scratch had marked its passage . . . I drove a shaking hand down between the jammed rocks. They scraped the skin and it hurt me but I hardly noticed. I thrust my arm down as far as I could. My fingers, stretching, touched something cold and smooth . . . metal. I couldn't reach it; the tips of my fingers slipped over it, no more. I could feel my lips trembling as the tears spilt salt onto them. I lay down hard against the stones and thrust my arm further into the narrowing crack. The cruel stone rasped at the skin and I felt blood running down my wrist. My fingers slid further, curled, gripped. I had the gun. I tried to withdraw it. But with my hand now curved round the butt I couldn't pull it back between the stones. I dragged at it, hopelessly, stupidly, and my hand hurt till I cried out with the pain, but I couldn't drag the gun out. . . .

Simon had twisted back from that gouging thumb. The Greek lunged violently
to one side as the other's hold slackened, and then, somehow, was free. With a
movement incredibly quick for a man of his build he had rolled aside and was
bunching to jump to his feet. As he went I saw his hand close, like mine, on a
cruelly jagged chunk of rock. But Simon was as quick. The same movement that
threw him back and away from the clawing hand had brought him to his feet. He
saw the Greek clutch the rock. Even as the fist closed on it and the arm muscles
tightened Simon jumped. His foot stamped down on the man's hand. The rock
was undermost, and I heard the man make a dreadful sound as his hand was
smashed down onto it. But he whipped over and brought his foot up with what
looked like appalling force into Simon's groin. Simon saw it coming, and tried to
sidestep. The foot grazed the inside of his thigh. Simon's hand came up under the
lashing ankle; I saw a heave and a twist, and the Greek crashed back onto his side
like a felled ox, and Simon plummeted down onto him again in the smother of
dust. Another blow, a sick sound of flesh and bone smacking together, and then
Angelos was uppermost, his fist smashing down like a hammer. . . .

I opened my hand and let the gun go. I dropped to the base of the pile of
stones, and began to claw at them with those useless, shaking fingers, trying to
pull the heavy stuff aside. From behind me came the thud and slither of their
bodies on the ground, the torn dreadful breathing, and, again, the sudden sharp
sound of pain. I thought it came from Simon.

The stone under my hands gave way, and I threw it down and tore at the next.
And the next. And then a pile of dry earth and small jagged pebbles.

Then I saw the blue-dark gleam of the gun.

I thrust the last lump of rock aside and pushed my hand through. The muzzle
was toward me. I grabbed it and dragged the thing out. I didn't even think once
of the danger of holding it like that. I just dragged it out between the rough stones
and turned, holding it in my aspen hands. I remember thinking with surprise how
heavy it was. . . .

I'd never touched a gun before in my life. But of course it was quite easy. You
simply pointed it and pressed the trigger: I knew that. Provided I got close
enough . . . and if the men would only break apart for a moment and let me see
through that stifling dust. . . . One simply pointed the thing and pulled the
trigger, and Angelos would be dead, blasted out of life in a fraction of time. It
didn't occur to me that this was in any way a wrong or a momentous thing to do. I
took a couple of faltering steps in the direction of the struggling bodies on the
ground. . . .

It was funny, but it was difficult to walk. The ground was unsteady and the
dust dragged at my feet and the gun was too heavy and the sky was far too bright
but still I couldn't see properly. . . .

The locked bodies on the ground moved as the man underneath made a
seemingly titanic effort. Both men were covered with dust: I couldn't see who it
was lying prone with one arm twisted into that cruel lock behind his
back . . . or who it was who lay astride him, shifting his grip now, straining in
some final agonizing effort. If only they would break apart . . . if only I could
see which was Angelos. . . .

The man uppermost lay clamped over the other, one hand hard round the wrist
of the locked arm, his own free arm flung round the prone man's neck in a tight
embrace. As I watched, the embrace tightened still further. . . .

The prostrate man's head came painfully back. The red dust was thick in the black curls. The broad cruel face was smeared red with it too, an archaic mask carved grimacing in red sandstone. It was Angelos who lay there in the dust, breath sobbing through the grinning lips, trying with weaker and weaker movements to throw Simon off his body.

I stood there, the gun drooping in my hand, the driving purpose snapped in me, staring like someone in a dream at the two bodies that heaved, breathing as one, on the ground at my feet.

A muscle bunched in Simon's shoulder. The Greek's head moved back another fraction. The grin was a rictus, fixed, horrible. His body gave one last desperate heave to rid itself of its killer, threshing sideways across the dusty rock. But Simon's grip didn't shift. Even as the two bodies, still locked, slithered a yard or so across the dusty rock to fetch up hard against the cairn where Michael had been murdered, I saw Simon's arm tense, and jerk tightly back, and heard Angelos' breath tear out of his throat in a sort of whistling gasp that broke off short. . . .

I knew then that Simon didn't need me or the gun. I turned aside and sat down on the boulder. I leaned back very wearily against the hot rock and shut my eyes.

After a while there was silence.

Angelos lay still, sprawled face downward against the little cairn. Simon got very slowly to his feet. He stood for a moment looking down. His face was filthy with dust and blood, and lined with fatigue. I could see how his muscles slumped with weariness as he stood there. He put up the back of his hand to wipe the blood from his face. His hands were bloody too.

Then he turned away and for the first time looked at me. He made as if to speak, and then I saw his tongue come out to wet the dust-caked lips. I answered his look quickly.

"I'm quite all right, Simon. He—he didn't hurt me." My voice had come back, hoarse and not too steady. But there was nothing to say. I whispered, "There's a rope on the mule. It's down by the cave."

"Rope?" His voice wasn't his own either. He was coming slowly toward me. "What for?"

"Him, of course. If he came round—"

"My dear Camilla," said Simon. And then, as he saw the look in my face, in a kind of anger, "What else did you expect me to do?"

"I don't know. Of course you had to kill him. It's just—of course you did."

His mouth twisted. It wasn't quite a smile, but nothing about him seemed, just at that moment, to be like himself. It was a stranger who stood in front of me in the blazing sunlight, with a stranger's voice, and something gone from his face that I remembered there. He stood there in silence, looking down at his hands. I still remember the blood on them.

The nausea had gone, and the world steadied. I said quickly, almost desperately, out of a rush of shame, "Simon. Forgive me. I—I guess I can't think straight yet. Of course you had to. It was only . . . coming so close to it. But you were right. There comes a time when one has to . . . accept . . . things like this. It was damnable of me."

He did smile then, a trace of genuine amusement showing through the weariness. "Not really. You were right too. But—just exactly what were you planning to do with that?"

"With what?" Following his look, I stared stupidly down at the gun in my hand.

He leaned forward and took it from me gently. The blood-stained fingers avoided mine. They were shaking a little. He laid the gun carefully to one side. "I think perhaps it's safer there."

Silence. He stood over me, looking down still with that stranger's look. "Camilla."

I met it then.

"If you hadn't got rid of that thing," he said, "I should be dead."

"And so should I. But you came."

"My dear, of course. But if he'd got to that gun . . ." A tiny pause, so slight it didn't seem that what he said could be important. "Would you have shot him, Camilla?"

Quite suddenly, I was shaking uncontrollably. I said, with a sort of violence, "Yes. Yes, I would. I was just going to, but then you . . . you killed him yourself. . . ."

I began to cry then, helplessly. I reached out blindly with both hands, and took his between them, blood and all.

He was sitting beside me on the boulder, with his arm round me. I don't remember what he said; I think part of the time he was swearing under his breath, and this seemed so unlike him that I had to fight harder to control the little spurts of laughter that shook me through the sobbing.

I managed to say, "I'm sorry. I'm all right. I'm not hysterical. It's—it's reaction or something."

He said with violence, the more shocking because it was the first time I had heard it from him, "I'll not forgive myself in a hurry for dragging you into this, by God! If I'd had any idea—"

"You didn't drag me in. I asked to be in, so I had to take what came, didn't I? It wasn't your fault it turned out as it did. A man does what he has to do, and since you *did* feel like that about Michael, after all, you did it. That's all."

"About Michael?"

"Yes. You said the tragedy was over, but of course once you knew Angelos was still alive—"

"My dear girl," said Simon, "you didn't imagine that I really killed him for Mick, did you?"

I looked up at him rather numbly. "No? But you told Angelos—"

"I was talking the language he'd understand. This is still Orestes' country, after all." He looked down at the scuffled dust between his feet. "Oh, I admit it was partly Mick—once I found myself here, and facing him. I felt murderous enough about him when I knew he was still alive, even before Dimitrios told me the rest."

"Dimitrios? Of course. He told you?"

"He was persuaded to, quite quickly. Niko turned up and helped me." A pause. "He told me what the two of them had done to Nigel."

"Then you know. . . ." The breath I drew was three parts relief. I remembered that look in Simon's eyes, and the smooth single-mindedness with which he had killed Angelos. I shivered a little. "I see."

"And then," he said, "there was you."

I said nothing. My eyes were on two—no, three specks in the bright air, circling slowly, high above the corrie. Simon sat beside me without moving, looking at the trampled dust. He looked all at once unutterably weary. If it hadn't been for the evidence sprawled across the stones one might almost have thought that he, not Angelos, had been beaten. "Any man's death diminishes me, . . ." I thought of Nigel, tumbled grotesquely behind the pile of dirt, and understood.

The silence drew out. Away somewhere on the mountain I thought I heard something, the clatter of stones, a breathless call. Simon didn't move. I said, "Tell me about Angelos. How did he get into it? Why did he wait till now to come back?"

"He's been before. We were right in our guesses about the search for the gold—the lights and voices, and Dimitrios' questions—but we were wrong about the name of the seeker. It wasn't Dimitrios himself. He knew nothing about the cache originally. When Angelos left Greece for Yugoslavia at the end of nineteen forty-four, he intended to come back as soon as he could. But he committed murder—political murder this time—in his adopted country, and was put away for 'life.' He was released two years ago, and came secretly back to look up his cousin. He let him into the secret, since he had to have somewhere to hide, and an agent to help him. They looked for the stuff—just as we guessed—but failed to find it. Dimitrios did his best to pump Stephanos, and the two of them must have searched desperately over the earthquake area at intervals through the spring and summer, then they gave up for the time being, and Angelos went back to live in Italy. I imagine he intended to come back again in the spring of this year, as soon as the snows had melted, but by then I had written to Stephanos, and the rumors were going about that I was coming to Delphi. He decided to wait and let us show him the place. That's all."

He glanced down at me. "And now, what happened to you? Why on earth did you come out of the cave? Surely he never found you in there, in sanctuary?"

"No." I told him then all that had happened since he had left me to follow Dimitrios. I found that I could tell it all quite calmly now, with that queer detachment I had felt in the cave, as if it were a play; as if these things had happened, not to me, but in some story I had read. But I remember being glad of the feel of Simon's arm round my shoulders, and of the heat of the sun.

He listened in silence, and when I had finished he still didn't speak for some minutes. Then he said, "I seem to have rather more to forgive myself for than just bringing you in on—that." For the first time his eyes went back to the cairn where the body lay. They were as I first remembered them, vivid and hard and cool. "Quite a score," he said. "Mick, Nigel, poor silly little Danielle. And then, of course, you. . . . It would almost take an Orestes, wouldn't it?" He took in his breath. "No, I doubt if the Furies, the Kindly Ones, will haunt me for this day's work, Camilla."

"No, I don't think they will."

There was a shout from the gateway behind us. With a clatter of stones, Niko hurled himself into the corrie and raced down toward us.

"Beautiful miss!" he yelled. *"Kyrie* Simon! It's all right! I'm here!"

He slithered to a halt in front of us. His startled gaze took us both in—my torn and filthy dress, the bruises, my scraped wrists and hands, and Simon covered with blood and dust and marks of battle. "Mother of God, then he *was* here? Angelos was here? He got away? He—"

He stopped abruptly as he caught sight of the body lying against the cairn. He gulped, and flashed a look at Simon. He looked at me as if he were going to speak, but he just shut his mouth again, tightly, and then went—it seemed reluctantly—across to where Angelos lay. There was the sound of slower footsteps from the gateway of the corrie, and Stephanos came into sight. He paused there for a moment, just as Simon had done, then came deliberately down the ramp toward us. Simon got stiffly to his feet. The old man stopped at my elbow. His eyes, too, were on Angelos. Then he looked at Simon. He didn't speak, but he nodded, slowly. Then he smiled. I think he would have spoken to me then, but Niko had straightened up and now came running back. A flood of Greek was poured out at Simon, who answered, and presently seemed to be telling his story. I caught the name "Michael" several times, and then "the Englishman," and "the French girl," and the word *"speleos,"* which I took to mean "a cave." But I was suddenly too tired to pay any attention. I leaned back into a bar of shadow and waited, while the three of them talked across me. Presently, with a word from Simon, he and Stephanos left me and went toward the cave.

Niko lingered for a moment. "You are not well, beautiful miss?" he asked anxiously. "That one—that Bulgar—he hurt you?"

To call anyone a Bulgarian is the worst term of abuse a Greek can think up; and they have quite a range. "Not really, Niko," I said. "I'm a bit shaken, that's all." I smiled at him. "You should have been here."

"I wish I had been!" Niko's sidelong glance at the cairn was perhaps not as enthusiastic as his voice, but apparently it took more than murder really to dim his lights. He turned his look of dazzled admiration on me. "I should have dealt with him, me, and not on account of my grandfather's cousin Panos, but for *you,* beautiful miss. Though *Kyrie* Simon," he added generously, "did very well, not?"

"For an Englishman," I said deprecatingly.

"Indeed, for an Englishman." He caught my look and grinned, unabashed. "Of course," he added, "I help him with Dimitrios Dragoumis. I, Niko."

"He told me so. What did you do with him?"

The black eyes opened wide. He looked shocked. "I could not tell you *that.* You are a lady, and—oh, I *see.*" The devastating smile flashed out. "Afterwards, you mean? I take him down to the road, but not to Delphi, because I want to get back and help *Kyrie* Simon, you understand. There is a truck, and I explain to the men, and they take him to Delphi to the police. The police will come. I shall go presently to meet them and guide them here. And so."

"And so." I said it very wearily. It seemed as good a period to the day as anything.

Beyond my bar of shadow the sun seemed white-hot. Niko had on a shirt of vivid electric blue, patterned with scarlet lozenges. The effect was blinding. He seemed to shimmer at the edges.

I heard him say cheerfully, "You are tired. You do not want to talk. And the other men will be needing me, not? I go."

As I shut my eyes and leaned back, I heard him crossing the corrie at his usual impetuous gallop.

It seemed a long time before the three of them came out of the cave again into the sunlight.

Niko came first, leading the mule. He seemed subdued now, and a little pale.

He didn't come over to me again, but swung himself onto the mule's back, kicked it into reluctant motion, and, with a wave to me, clattered out of the corrie.

Stephanos and Simon stood talking for a few minutes longer. Stephanos looked somber. I saw him nod to something Simon said, then he gestured upward toward the blazing arch of sky where those black specks still hung and circled. Then he turned and trudged slowly across to a patch of shade near the body. He sat down there, and settled himself, as if to wait, leaning forward with his head against the hands clasped on his staff. He shut his eyes. He looked suddenly very old—with that Homeric head and the shut eyes as old as time itself.

It was a picture I was never to forget, that quiet tailpiece to tragedy. There was the blue arch of the brilliant sky; there the body that the Kindly Ones had hunted down and killed on the very spot where he himself had shed blood; there the old man, bearded like Zeus himself, nodding in the shade. At the head of the cliffs stood the black goats, staring.

From somewhere, not too far distant now, came the little stave of music; the goat-herd's pipe whose sound, drifting down through the light-well, had led me to the Apollo of the holy spring. At the sound the goats lifted their heads and, turning, moved off, black against the sky, an Attic frieze in slow procession.

Simon's shadow fell across me.

"Niko's gone to guide the police here. He wanted to escort you to Delphi, but I told him you wouldn't be fit for the trek quite yet. You and I have something still to do, haven't we?"

I hardly heard the question. I said, apprehensively, "The police?"

"Don't worry. There'll be no trouble for me. Apart from everything else, and God knows he's done plenty, he was trying to kill you." He smiled. "And now, are you coming? Stephanos is asleep, by the looks of it, so he won't wonder where we've gone."

"You didn't tell him and Niko about the shrine?"

"No. The question of what to do about the guns and gold is out of our hands now, thank heaven, but the other question's our own to answer. Do you know the answer?"

I looked at him inquiringly; perhaps a little doubtfully.

Then he nodded, and I said, slowly, "I suppose so."

He smiled and put down a hand to me.

We went into the cave in silence. Simon's torch was almost dead, but it showed the way. It was not strong enough to probe too far into the shadows. He paused just inside the entrance, and I saw him step aside and stoop over something that lay near the pile of rubble where the boxes had been. He straightened up with one of Angelos' crowbars in his hand. I didn't look further, but followed the mercifully dimming light through the pillared vaults until the slab barred the way.

The light paused on the old marks of tooling in the stone. "There," said Simon softly. "It should slide back easily enough. Even another three or four inches should block the entrance. . . . I'll leave this here for the moment."

He laid the crowbar down and we went through the cleft for the last time, and up the curving tunnel that led to the bright citadel.

* * *

He had stood there without move or change for more than two thousand years; now, it seemed a miracle that in the last hour he had remained untouched, unaltered. The sun had slid further toward the west and the light fell more slantingly through the leaves; that was all.

We knelt at his feet and drank. I cupped my hands under the spring and splashed the water over my face and neck, then held my wrists under the icy runnel. It stung on the bruises and the scraped flesh of my wrists, a sharp remedial stinging that seemed to signal my body's return from whatever numb borderlands of shock I had been straying in. I sat back, flicking the cool drops off my hands.

I noticed then that the mark had gone from the third finger of my left hand. There was no sign at all of the pale circle where Philip's ring had been.

I sat looking at my hands.

Simon was leaning forward, putting something on the stone plinth at the statue's feet. There was the gleam of gold.

He caught my look and smiled, a little wryly. "Gold for Apollo. I asked him to bring Angelos back, and he did it, even though it was done in that damned two-edged Delphic way that one always forgets to bargain for. However, there it is. It was a vow. Remember?"

"I remember."

"It comes to me that you made a vow too, in this very shrine."

"So I did. I'll have to share your coin, Simon. I've nothing here to give."

"Then we'll share," he said. That was all, in that casual easy voice with no change in it; but I turned quickly to look up at him. The vivid gray eyes held mine for a moment, then I turned from him almost at random and picked up Nigel's little water pot. "We'll leave this here too, shall we?"

Something glinted, deep in the grass, down beside the edge of the stone plinth. I smoothed the long stems aside and picked it up. It was another gold coin.

"Simon, look at this!"

"What is it? A talent? Don't tell me Apollo's provided a ram in the thicket for—" He stopped short as I held my hand out toward him.

I said, "It's a sovereign. That means Nigel did find the gold as well as the statue. He must have left this here."

"Must he?"

"Well, who else—?" Then I saw his face and stopped.

He nodded. "Yes. Of course. Michael made an offering, too."

He took it from me gently and laid it beside the water pot, at the feet of the god.